THE BOND

Dear Reader,

This fictional story includes sensitive topics such as sexual and familial violence, suicidal behaviour, self-harm, abortion, childbirth, death, explicit sex scenes, and discrimination based on gender and religion.

For more information, contact:

Candice Lochmanetz
www.thevendicchronicles.com

ISBN: 978-1-0697632-0-4

THE BOND

Book One of The Vendic Chronicles

Candice Lochmanetz

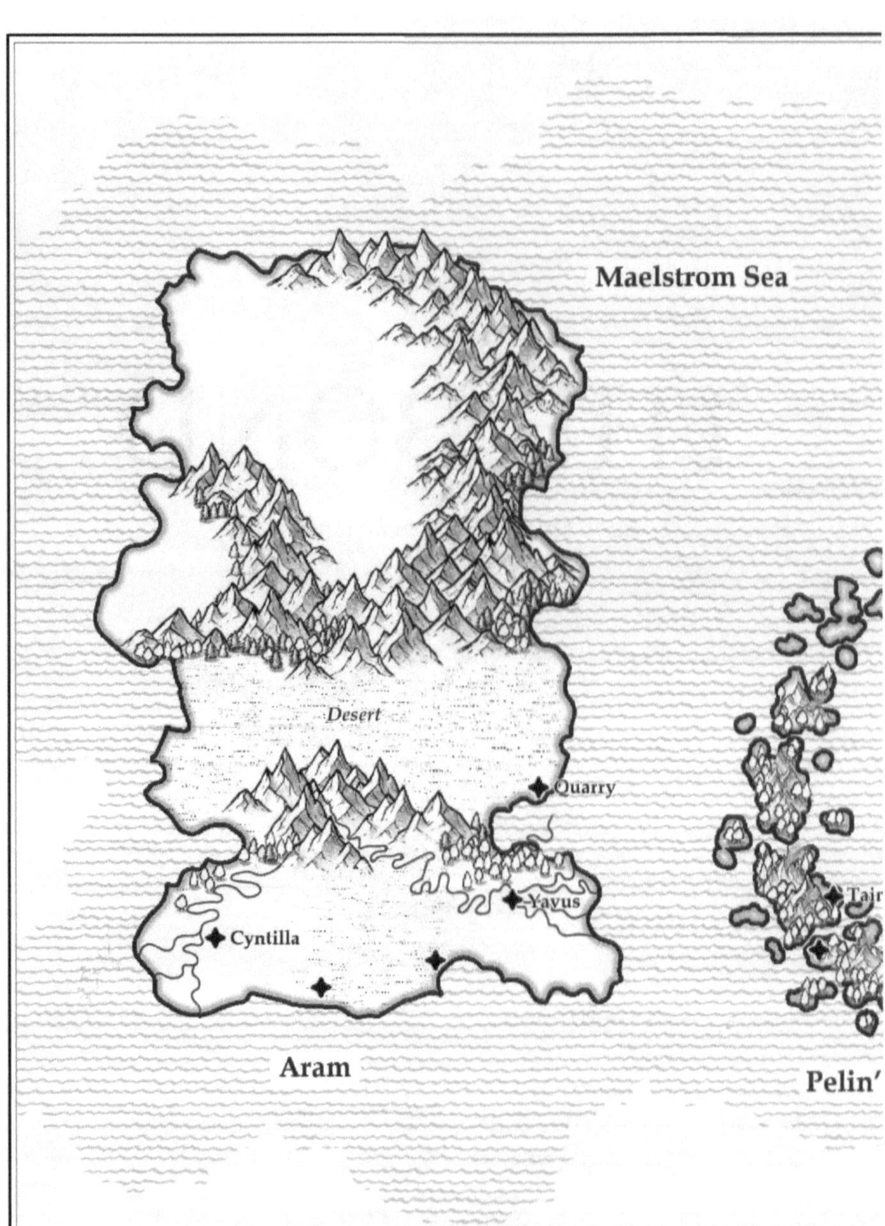

Maelstrom Sea
Desert
Quarry
Yavus
Cyntilla
Aram
Tair
Pelin'

Lanthia
Aerie
Hoil
Burnt
Lands
Kara
Merida
Du' Lanay
Heli
Dun

N

DEDICATION

A note from the Author

My story begins with two people, Bodan, and Iris. This book is dedicated to the memory of Bodan, gone twenty years, but not forgotten. My father always had good advice, he would say 'learn from your mistakes and don't repeat them.' I have tried, but some lessons in life need to be repeated before they are learned.

My mother, Iris, who has faith in my writing of this book. So, I made her a Goddess, every girl must have a role model to look up to. She read this book in its infancy, the first to do so, I could at least gift her a position of honour. She was the one that gave me the thirst for books, and a love for the imagination.

I hope I do them proud.

INTRODUCTION

Meera

Some people say I died that day, but for me, this was the day I began to live. It did not register in my mind as I leapt back, there was nothing there, just vaporous air from the tepid waterfall I was standing on. As my only thought was to save myself from the sting of the sword arcing towards my face, I instinctively felt my body surge back and what felt like a lengthy moment in time, but was in fact just mere moments, I began to plummet back.

For me, falling felt like I was floating, graceful, poised in time, in a mist which suspiciously looked very pink, like the pink of wild roses which flourished in the glades up the mountain ranges behind the Aerie. As I stretched my arms out to grasp droplets and gazing up at the diminishing edge of the cliff, through the mist, I imagined I saw a face staring down at me. Probably Vandrin, with the sword dangling by his side, edge trickling with my blood, wait... My blood!

This was when I comprehended, it was my blood making the mist of the falls pink, and I sensed a fiery, stinging pain on the left side of my face. My left eye saw nothing but a murky blur, and then as the mist began to solidify into droplets of substance, I heard a voice inside my head say,

"This is going to hurt,"

and then the world I was in, went dark.

CHAPTER 1

Meera

When there is naught but shadow

I sensed waves of pain ebb and flow, what I felt of my body, from my toes to the hair on my head, hurt. Not really awake but not unconscious either. Suspended between the spirit worlds, I ached everywhere. My head felt split open, my left arm felt like knives were stabbing it everywhere, and something kept hitting my right heel. I was not sure why I could not open my eyes, something heavy was pressing down on my torso and arms, and why did I smell rotten meat? I felt cold, as if a breeze were flowing, wet, but then warm fluid was running down certain parts of my body. Then I felt nothing as for a second time I fell into darkness, not knowing my right cheek had smacked a tree root protruding out of the ground, knocking me senseless.

"Meera, Meera,"

A voice whispered, trying to drag me away from my nothingness, or was it crooning, calling me to fall again? Sounding like a musical baritone, where had I heard this voice before? I felt detached.

"Hey girl, come back to the land of the living,"

That recognizable voice did not sound as if it was in my head but came from directly above me. I desired nothing but to drift on the currents of my thoughts, and then I felt an icy damp cloth being held against my forehead close to the flaming pain coming from the left side of my face. The sting shook me out of my thoughts and into being, I struggled to rise, yet nothing seemed to function from my brain to my muscles. Muscular male arms restrained me; I did not resist very hard as every movement generated waves of pain. Everywhere! It seemed one spot began to throb, then another took its place. As those male arms cradled my back, a stench of unwashed sweat and wood bark entered my nostrils, and I struggled to open my right eye, as the left felt weight pressing down upon it.

It took me more than a moment to focus on the owner of the voice. The figures before me finally merged into one.

"Uncle Kiem,"

I croaked out, voice gravelly from dryness.

"How…?"

Kiem was a Woodsman, a Ranger in the Ravenwood Mountains and beyond. Middle-aged, a free spirit, or man of no lands. His hair was of an indescribable colour as it was always dirty with something. Taller than the average person of the Aerie, and they were tall. Northmen were large strapping men, dark of hair, fair skin where the sun did not meet it, bronzed brown where it did. Even the women were for the most part, tall, and some were broad-shouldered themselves; they could qualify for men. Well, maybe their silhouettes could.

Kiem had soulful green eyes, quite unlike the blue of Northerners. I could get lost in them! They reminded one of green fields in the summer, before the harvest. People would recoil until they knew him, sometimes giving the demon sign, which he ignored. I had eyes like his, green, maybe a bit more yellow, I do not remember, it was not important to me.

He held me up, his face was close to mine as I tried to organize my mind, still groggy with muddled thoughts. Now where was I? Oh, yah…probably in the mountains, if I was with Kiem.

Ravenwood Mountain range ran east to west in the Northern part of the Du'Lanay continent. To the South of the Aerie were half rolling hills, as far as the eye could see. Grasslands, a smattering of broadleaf trees, winding streams, and creeks in the valleys. The odd homestead visible in the day, and a few town-ships evident by night. A great deal of fodder was produced in those hills, and everyone helped to harvest, before the snows came. It eased us through, as the winters were severe. A partially stone paved road was sporadically seen on its way, winding and tucked into the vales. These led eventually to the Capital, the seat of power for some, I had never been.

If one were to ascend the high tower of the Aerie, one glimpsed the shimmer of the Western Sea on the horizon. If one scanned to the east and to the North, they would see mountain after mountain, awash with trees, of the Darkest blue. Hence the Ravenwood name, dark blue bark, and a blackened wood much the colour of ravens and crows. The leaves in spring, a beautiful silver-green, deepening to blue green in full bloom. Before they gathered their last strength to fall from their perch in the fall, they dried and darkened to blue black. The wood of the tree was the hardest and most durable and dwellings were constructed from this resource.

Bows were crafted from saplings, as it was flexible for a season as a juvenile tree. The famed longbow turned a good coin in the South; however, no Northerner parted with his bow during his lifetime, and no other man had strength to draw it. Every man, as a young boy and into maturity, would create their own bow, until they had one which would sustain a pull, and aim true. The sound of his voice shook me from my wandering thoughts.

"Shush, child, you have plummeted from the God's Neck and survived. Nejan carried you here to me. You have been sleeping like you had no spirit for two days."

"Nejan?"

My voice echoed in my aching head, sounding deeper than I normally did, I had no time to ponder this.

"Yes, Childing, that would be I."

A feminine sounding voice reverberated within my head, and I snapped my head to the door. Which was not the correct thing to do, because stabs of pain coursed down my left side. I could not comprehend where it began and where it ended. It gave me pause.

"Ohhh, owwww!"

From the bed I was resting on against the far wall of the small cabin, I observed through the eye I had open, a shifting shadow beyond the door opening, growing larger indicating something substantial was approaching. It had the strangest shape, not human for sure. I gripped tightly onto Uncle's arm which was supporting me vertically and squeezed it with my right hand. I continued to turn my head slowly as to not experience additional pain, staring at him with apprehension and disbelief.

"Did you hear that?"

He gazed down at me, not puzzled at all by my question.

"Hear what?"

"I just heard a voice inside my head; it called me a childling."

"Ah, so it has happened…"

"What has happened? Why am I here? Are we in your cabin? What in blazes happened to me? I remember Vandrin seizing the sword from my hand and giving chase to the God's Basin…"

The God's River, had its origins on the crest of a plateau, emerging as an eternal warm spring from the rock face. The Temple to the Gods was erected surrounding it centuries ago, the water channeled down to the basin. A free formed natural indentation in the surface, rumoured to once be a bathing basin for Dragons, with waters which flowed over the rock face. The Temple itself erected from stone mined in the quarry far below, walls and pillars smooth faced. The beams above, black wood with the roof also of black wood especially cut into shingles. It was existing for centuries, erected to stand the test of time. In winter, the outer shell of water on the basin would freeze, water still flowing under it over the falls, until it froze halfway down, creating the most bizarre shapes in the heart of winter.

Surrounding the Temple were natural gardens, with hardy plants which grew every year. Trees transported from the steppes below which managed to survive. There were areas for contemplation, stone benches and stairs, engraved into the rock face, all aesthetically pleasing to the eye. Designs of the North, etched into the woods and stone, drew the eye to soften.

In spring this water was diverted from the basin, into special constructed soffits and channels to each level of the city to cleanse away filth in a special two-day event. Water still flowed into the city, during the other months to fountains built in all levels of the city. Levels built over time, in the age of Dragons. There were special conduits for fresh water and similar conduits for drainage water. Flow of water to the various areas was well managed. On every level were sections for gardens, herbs and edible plants grew as much as the weather permitted.

I came back to my mind as Kiem spoke quietly.

"Hush, Meera, you have had a huge shock to your spirit, and you are about to get a few more…"

The shadow in the doorway became visible and the blurry edges materialized into a giant cat, a feline known as a NightStalker, as told in tales around fires. Named as such, no one living had seen anything of them but in the dead of night. Yet this animal before me could not be one of the stories? This was the largest one, I had ever seen! Wait! I have never seen one in my entire life of eighteen winters! The golden ember of its eyes smouldered against the blackest of fur shimmering blue where the now setting sun in the west illuminated its head which barely had room to squeeze into the narrow cabin doorway!

Stories told of NightStalkers the size of a mountain pony or farmer's cart oxen. They were accurate, she was enormous, barely fitting into the doorway. None were seen in years, but Rangers and Woodsmen would return with tales of sightings, or evidence they roamed the back mountains. Many Woodsmen disappeared on their ranges, and it was always accredited to a NightStalker.

My panic accelerated the thumping in my heart; however, it soon dissipated as I felt no aggression from its presence.

"I thought NightStalkers were stories to scare us into behaving? Sssstt… Owwww… Now I see before me something out of a tale."

I groaned my question through clenched teeth as wave after wave of pain coursed through my body. I lay back, sweat breaking out on my forehead, and my vision threatening to close in on me. Kiem helped me slowly lie down on my right-side propping something behind my head which did not smell particularly good. I am unsure why my nose was so sharp of all days when nothing else seemed to function.

"Is this what you have been told?"

The voice was soft and comforting, feminine in nature and I heard the humour in the vibrating sound. The feline looked at me with its beautiful luminescent eyes as the rest of the body came in, circled around in the open space in front of the door and laid down. The vibration of her movements reaching me laying on the bed. I comprehended the spot was vacant for this very purpose.

"Is Nejan speaking with you?" Uncle Kiem asked.

"Wha, how?"

He looked away for a moment, silence reigning until he turned back to my prone body.

"Well, legends I read, and you may not believe, however, you will see in the course of time, there are a few people chosen who have the ability to hear certain animals and communicate directly inside their heads. It is a bond the Namanists and those with no understanding tried over the years or so they thought, to eradicate completely!"

"Is this why they are so fervent with their sermons? I always thought … ssst… it was about the herders who tended their flocks. They always talk to their fold."

Kiem laughed at my vision.

"No, not them, but they tend to watch the herders more often. They are looking for potential DragonRiders. When Dragons roamed these lands, they and their

Riders communicated in such a manner and they were leaders of men, Godlike to some. Nejan is such an animal, and only you and I, that I know of, have this gift. You will get more comfortable as time passes however, keep this to yourself as people will be afraid. Afraid people lash out against what they do not understand."

"You just said Dragons."

"Yes, I did."

"Dragons are nothing but m…"

Uncle Kiem picked himself up off the floor where he was kneeling beside me. A knee crackled loudly in the silence, as he walked over to the now resting feline taking up a fair bit of space in front of the door, scratching her behind the ears and sides of her now drying fur. I felt the darkness pulling me back down as I understood they were communicating, as the silence in the room was deafening and blackness overtook me again.

As I lay there in my darkness, hovering over the pain which ebbed and flowed with my steady pulse, Kiem checked my bandages which were bloody again, replacing them for newer, if not the cleanest cloth. When I woke up, I would look around and take stock of my surroundings, I noticed the smallest of details.

I would find they were stored for quite some time in the only other piece of furniture, if you can call a homemade box made of roughhewn wood, with a not so fitted lid, a piece of furniture. The bed was off the floor by four blocks and was a frame of logs fitted together with strips of leather and covered by a mix of furs from various animals Kiem had hunted. It lay against the furthest wall, away from the draft coming through the door.

At the other end of the room was a makeshift firepit rimmed with river rock on the packed dirt floor, which had a hollow log built into the wood wall to vent smoke outside, and upon venturing outside, one saw how the hollow logs were situated to dissipate smoke so no one would be able to see the visible indicators from the lower valley hidden from view. I would not be able to see this for a time, being unconscious for the moment and unable to move. The only telltale clue someone dwelled there was the fragrance of the smoke if the wind was gusting in the right direction. Over the firepit was an ingenious hook and arm an iron pot hung from, currently containing a mixture of edible things.

The only illumination was from the fire and daylight entering the doorway, which could be hidden with a curtain of moss. There was a wooden door, but Kiem liked to keep it open during daylight hours. The roofline was also obscured with a carpet of greenery growing haphazardly against the walls. It was a true Ranger's hovel, and at some point, animals had used it, their signs still visible to the trained eye. The roughhewn walls of Ravenwood were fitted quite well, not too many cracks between and were stuffed with various things, but the bulk of spaces had over the years been permeated with mosses. Heat generated inside drew them in and gave a natural barrier to winds when they were dancing outside.

The NightStalker stretched her front legs out in front and verbalized to Kiem,

"The Little One is not damaged much? I tried to be gentle, but my teeth may not have been,"

Her voice reverberated inside Kiem's head, and he responded,

"She will be on her back for a while and her shoulder will heal, however, I am worried for her eye. Although it looks like the blade missed it, the tissue damage around it does concerns me. It may take a few blessings from the Gods to heal. Was there much evidence at the river where you found her? I noticed she is missing some of her head fur and most of her leg coverings."

Nejan stretched out further with her front paws, clawed the floorboards and proceeded to lick one of them as she tucked the other under her massive body.

"I chewed off some of her head fur and shook it on the side of a broadleaf bush, trampled around, and tore her leg covers off leaving them in a pool of her blood. I left footprints in the soft ground; I even sprayed a couple of bushes with my mating scent to make the little canines go crazy if they were to venture down the cliff to look. It smells like the rains will be here soon, so that may not last long. I hunted quickly on the way down to the river taking my meal there and leaving enough blood and tissue to confuse any man who may not know what to look for. I walked softly through various paths, but I am worried her blood may be evident to the eye further from the river, which is where I sprayed to muddy any nose. I was in a rush to get her to you and was not cautious enough, I am afraid, I did not want her spirit to leave, as she is our gift."

Nejan exchanged paws and began cleaning the other. Her large tongue flicking in-between her toe pads, the odd chewing sound emanated from deep within her throat.

"Thank you, Great Mader, you thought well. Hopefully, they will be satisfied with the evidence presented and think not of her after this. It will be better for her if they do not. I will go look in a day or so, just to make certain there is no trail to pursue, as it would lead here."

Kiem rose from his current position on the box, walking over to the fire and using a piece of wood to stir the contents in the metal pot which hung on a hook over the stoked coals. The smell of whatever he had cooking in there set me to groaning in my pain of unconsciousness.

The expression of worry which traversed his face, was well founded. If ever any were known to speak to animals or have an affinity for them, they were marked by Naman. Ever since inception, the men of the Namanist Faith seized those who spoke to voices, conversed with animals, had eyes with a hint of unnatural colour…any of those with a 'hint' of magic were 'chastised.' One point in history a whole village were 'chastised,' and was emptied. It was a whole century before it was 'blessed' and inhabited again.

The stories of torture, the Church inflicted upon any who were branded a 'demon' or 'unclean' were very, very accurate. A few Northmen were taken to the Capital, never to return. Not just men, most of the people taken were females. There was an underlining hatred for women, especially those of red hair, or from the Islands. The land of the North did not adore the Church as well as the Empire would like. Their women were precious to them, some worked along side with their men, in the fields, the smithies, in the quarries. The North bowed and scraped and paid lip service, and they kept their secrets close to their hearts.

It would be the rest of the day and through the night to the next morning, before I was conscious enough to request water, then ask for assistance to use a pot or go outside to relieve myself. Which became an urgency I did not have the time or thought to be uncomfortable with help from a man I only saw once or twice a year throughout my lifetime. To me, he was family, as the honorific title of Uncle indicated. He had, over my childhood, attended more to me than my blood relatives. As Kiem helped me, he explained to me, my injuries.

"You dislocated your left shoulder, from what I speculate it was the point of impact of hitting water at the base of the falls. It took most of the damage, and I reset it while you were not in this world of men and will carry bruising for quite some time before you feel right using it. The bruising on your legs and arms are unfortunately from the way Nejan carried you back. It was not the most practical as she was worried for your spirit life. My primary concern is the slash on your face, which looks like it was executed from a very sharp knife or sword…"

"That would be a sword as Vandrin was chasing me and trying to cut me down with it…"

I said sarcastically, recalling myself dodging lingering people in the halls on my way outside and the panic to escape the pissed-off man I had misfortune to be related to. My Uncle assisted me to the cabin entrance and down the one step to the packed earth.

"Care to elaborate?"

"SSSSSsss, ohhhh."

I hissed under my breath, remembering the pain was still there. Kiem aiding me with my trouser rope belt, pulling down what remained of my trousers. He helped me to sit on a stump hollowed out in a particular fashion, meant for the exact purpose I was using it for, judging from the smell the slightly damp stump emitted.

"I may have found the Sword of Purity…."

I muttered under my breath, he was holding me upright, so I did not topple over from exhaustion and pain. He was breathing in my face, his close enough I could smell his breath.

Stories secretly told around fires in the Great Hall of the Aerie when I was a child, spellbound me with the six gems of clarity. Bound to Riders and their Dragons in six items of antiquity, each gem shone when the true wielder used it in battle or ceremony. The Sword of Purity had a clear gem, a large diamond at the end of the hilt and the sword I held in my hand matched the stories of old.

"You what!!!"

He was so startled, he practically yelled in my ear, and I felt a spray of spit land on my nose.

"I am finished, Uncle."

He helped me, drawing my shortened pants back up over my buttocks tying my belt. I was too wracked with pain to ponder at the intimacy of the action.

"You are sure, you found Noster's sword? It has been lost for centuries! Where on this earth did you see it?"

He stood up in front of me grabbing me around my waist on my right side, and we walked to the cabin slowly.

"Well…I did not know that was what it was, until I…ohhh… unwrapped the hilt and saw the crystal. You… know as a child I was shunned and left to my own devices. I spent an enormous amount of time… exploring the catacombs while I was trying to hide from whoever was my minder. I remember… passing by this pile of rags…ughh…tucked into a corner. I forgot about it when I went to study herbology… with Healer Nena, it was not until this past month I remembered…ooogh… where it was."

Here I had to stop and take in a breath. Walking and talking, I should do one or the other, not both at the same time. Kiem held me while I tried to calm.

"Well, Vandrin was in the Throne room and the Stable Master was recounting the stories of old… The six gems of Valor, the one sword of Purity, how it glowed with the light of the one who wielded it…. How it was lost in the time of the Great War of Dragons. I remembered the pile of rags I had passed by, tucked away in a corner of a vault behind the monolith of some dead bloke…oooff… The shape of the pile triggered my memory."

Kiem helped me up the one step into the shack and gently lowered me to sit on the edge of the bed, the motion alone took away my breath.

"Let us look at this eye of yours while you catch your breath, you can keep up on your story after. I'm not sure you should be talking so much anyway."

He unwrapped my face and as the air hit the fresh wound on my face I gasped. "Ooohh…"

"Well doesn't look too bad, my stitching has held up, but we should wash it with some river water, it's a little bit red over here,"

He poked a finger on the bone of my brow, and I gasped.

"Hey, that hurts."

"So, it should. Looks like the tip of the sword cut you from the bottom up, went through your cheek, glanced off your cheek bone, and just caught your brow. You will mend nicely but will have a beautiful scar to show for it. Your eye is inflamed, I cannot see any visible damage, but there is some residual blood in it. I am going to have to rinse it out with your help now that you are awake to help me. We will keep a bandage on it for a while to help with healing."

He rinsed it off as best as we could manage and rewrapped my face with different bandages tying them off, just snug enough not to hurt too much. I would have to find a root of the Red Stoat to make into a poultice to bolster the healing when I could. Maybe some Numbweed, that couldn't hurt, not anymore than it already did.

"So, keep on with your story, I would like to hear how you decided to jump off the God's Neck!"

"I did not jump!"

I exclaimed trying not to take a deep breath, as the motion of doing so elicited pain to my torso. Kiem rose and strode over to the firepit in the corner. He began to transfer dried things off the one shelf on the wall and hanging from the ceiling. He proceeded to crumple them up placing them in the pot over the fire. I tried to lay down against the wall, but it ended up more a fumble with my good arm. As I ungracefully slanted toward the wall, Kiem rushed over blocking my decent with his arms and cursing,

"Bloody 'ell!"

Once I was set in place as comfortable as he could make me, he returned to throwing random items, which once looked alive into the pot.

"What will happen now? Do you think Vandrin will look for me? He has the sword."

Pouring in a ration of water from a leather skin bag, I took notice what Kiem was handling. The leather bag looked well oiled and worn. Those were the best kind, supple enough to withstand any flex in carrying, without leaking too much water. It looked as though it did not leak at all. Who ever crafted it knew what they were about. Aunt Nena taught me in the few years I spent with her, all manner of storing goods, from drying to tonics, and the skinning of animals and curing of hides.

"He may, or he may not. If he thinks you died, over the falls and by a Nightstalker, it may suffice. I am going back to the river, see if the clues Nejan left are sufficient, and if they are satisfied that you are deceased. Hopefully, they will think so. Right now, I will brew you some broth which will keep you for a couple of days until I return. Nejan will watch over you and keep you safe, you and she can speak and get used to communication as such. When I return, I have my story to tell and we plan our next course of action. I will collect more water in a stream nearby for you."

He stood up from feeding the fire glancing towards me, I detected a small amount of deadfall and branches in the corner behind the firepit.

"I will not head out until you walk unassisted to the stump and back. Do not wish any accidents!"

He lifted the skins hanging from hooks walking outside and was gone for a time, I was nodding off, when I heard his step and opened my eyes. Kiem pulled the wood box with the wobbly lid over and sat on it facing me, then he rose and walked to the shelf.

"All right, let us hear the rest!"

He grabbed a small wooden cup off the shelf pouring a cup of cool water he had collected from the stream I had yet to find, handing it to me, I drank it all in one go.

"Well, I walked into the room and slid through people standing around chatting and hid behind the blacksmith Cureb. Listening to the story, I did not realize Byrik was watching me, he must have seen my face light up with remembrance and sneak off to the side door of the back passageways. He surely told Vandrin, they followed me down and laid in wait for me.

I emerged from the bowels of the castle, stood in the light passing through the stained-glass windows and unwrapped the dirty rags from the hilt. When I saw the jewel, I knew what I held in my hands. I began polishing the gem, imagining I saw a glow, or perhaps it was a reflection from the sun, I was not sure, however, it was then Vandrin and Byrik set upon me from one of the alcoves."

Here I had to take another sip of water before I continued, Kiem refilled it without me noticing.

"Vandrin seized the hilt from my hand and gasped with glee, then in rage, so he gave chase through the hallways, the Great Hall, and through the gardens up to the Temple and the God's Basin. He was screaming obscenities, I am sure, yet it was hard to hear what he was saying. I did not stick 'round, until I had no choice, I halted at the edge of the basin, turning to face him."

The drop from the basin was so long to the bottom of the chasm in the valley below, it was given the name of the God's Neck. It remained the God's River, the Namanists had never renamed it, and if they did, the Northerners still called it the name given by the old Vendic religion, which was secretly revered.

"I turned to face him, succeeding in deflecting blows with my knife. All the while he was slowly forcing me to retreat. He came into the water after me, slowly inching me back. When I saw the blow coming, I heard a voice in my head, I thought it might be Paders, yet it was deeper in tone, and it spoke, *"Just let yourself fall back, it will be all right."*

"So, you heard a male voice?"

Kiem leaned towards me, and I gazed at him puzzled. He seated himself down on the box and dragged it closer to in front of me. As he got nearer to my face, he spoke.

"Look towards the door."

I glanced over at the door very slowly as I felt my muscles not cooperating very well. He held my face gently with his right hand and peered closely into my right eye.

"It was a male voice? Not female like Nejan's?"

"Definitely male. Like I said, I thought it was Paders. Why? Uncle?"

"Hmmmm, I see a bit of fleck there… no… it cannot be…hmmm."

"You are scaring me, what are you looking for?"

I tried to wrench my head away from his hand, but was unable to move comfortably without creating pain, it was futile. I stared at him mere inches from my face, noticing some scars above his eyes. He slowly sat back removing his hand.

"Well, how to say this gently... You know the stories as stories, but there is truth to them. They are forbidden here, because the Namanists faith does not want us to remember how it was. Centuries ago, there were Dragons…there were Riders. Each Rider had a Dragon they cleaved to, as one would in a marriage. Not in the physical sense but in a relationship which was binding and only cleaved to one another. Some say they spoke through the minds, and this I do believe, for we, you and I can communicate with Nejan through our minds. The Riders had talents; each had their own. Some could do the same things, as in knowing when one was lying… seeing the future… moving things. There are other traits, not well known were the Riders' eyes reflected that of their Dragon. An opalescence which saw through lies and deceit. This is what placed them above other men. I believe you may have already bonded, though I know not of any Dragon. Your eyes may have the beginnings of a Rider."

"You're mad! These are just stories; there are no Dragons!"

I could not comprehend what he was saying! Those were stories told, secretly around fires late at night. Dragons were a thing of myth; none had been seen in hundreds of years and the stories were forbidden openly for the fear of death or worse. Only the bravest dare tells, and usually with liquid courage to boost the telling. The soldiers of the Namarch were like hounds on the scent if they heard anyone openly telling tales. I was still trying to process the height my body had survived from.

"Says who? Perhaps there is."

The last minstrel to travel to the Aerie openly told the story of the last battle. The last Rider Noster was betrayed and murdered by his closest companions and that night; the minstrel found himself accidently falling down the rampart walls into the valley below. It was said he indulged himself with too much honey mead and tripped. When his body was found the next day, wild animals had eaten most of the carcass. People never spoke of it after, but fear was there. The Namanist faith ruled with fear, and a strong arm to those who did not listen and told the forbidden tales. The why of it, I never questioned until now.

"There would be proof!"

The Aerie, or Ravenwood castle, or locals called it the Raven's Roost, from where I fell, was an impregnable stone fortress high on the headlands of the mountains. Built on top of a quarry mined for iron and metals, built slowly, layer by layer, one on top of the other. Expanded to encompass the cliffsides flanking it as it became mined and inhabited.

Over the course of centuries, each layer brought a different function of living, until it finally crested the top of the plateau and further than the cliffs around it. The Temple to the Gods was built around the living well. The spring flowing, perhaps not so naturally into the formed basin in the surface of the rock. Careening over the tallest edge into a chasm, the river meandered through the cliffs widening into the lowlands and eventually to the sea, or so I was told.

"The basin is partial proof. It was used in the days of Dragons."

The lower layers of the city became vacant, some used for storage, blacksmiths used the most central of cavernous areas for their craft, which in winter, helped to heat the above layers through channels and soffits. These were the channels used in the spring for cleaning with flowing water. In the deep winter months, animals were brought into the caverns for housing during harsh temperatures. I became familiar with the catacombs as a child, out of necessity and later from curiosity. This castle city housed the bulk of the Northmen in the winter, some winters were so cold and the snows so heavy, those who lived in the furthest reaches came and sheltered if only to save their livestock.

"There must be more than this. It was natural formed."

"Was it? Ever wonder what those dais's in the Temple are for?"

"Religious ceremony. The cleansing of the spirit… Pader Reudin uses them all the time."

"That is what he was told to use them for. They are a little big, are they not?"

"What else could they be for?"

"Hmmm, a statue, perhaps… A stone Dragon…"

I gasped. The dais in the temple we were discussing took up a fair amount of space on the floor. The temple itself was huge. It housed several of these daises, and the spring emerged from the center into a small pool and funneled outside via channels. The hot spring created mist inside, which acolytes spent most of their day scrubbing mosses and green slime off the stone walls.

"You forget, I am from the Islands. The Rulers there have opalescent eyes, and they rule without Dragons, yet their religion is of the Gods, although they do not advocate talk of Dragons. There are effigies in Temples there. They are on their own dais's, each Temple harkens to one God and if my memory serves me, only the Temple on the Mount has effigies of all the Dragons... It may have changed in the years I have been gone."

I had many questions forming. I had not a clue what a Dragon may resemble. There were no pictures, hardly any literature around, what there was, belonged to the Naman Pader. There were no known statues, in any of the city. Ones which could alleviate my growing curiosity. I knew they were an animal, larger than the great horses used in the valleys below, I listened to the stories told. Many different tales had everyone confused to the countenance of a Dragon, but the common ground was they flew.

"Next time you gaze at your reflection in the water, you will see the change in your eye. You need to tell me more about this 'other' voice you heard, but for now, let us get you on your feet and moving so I can see what is happening at the river."

Kiem pushed himself up and reached out his left hand, I hung onto his arm with my good hand and slowly lifted myself upright. It was a struggle, after three attempts I managed to rise and not fall back. After wobbling and tottering for a minute, my stomach rumbled so loud it startled me and Kiem belly laughed.

"Alright, food first, then some walking!"

He gently lowered me back down. After eating some of Kiem's mysterious stew, which was surprisingly very hearty and delicious, I stumbled on my own to the stump without falling and relieved myself.

"All right, you will do just fine. Make sure you go to the stream around the back and wash your wounds every day, I may be gone more than a few days, Nejan will know if anything happens to me, but I have not been seen yet by the Raven'sGuard. If I do not return, you must leave, for they will know and come looking for you. Head North into the mountains, then east to the rolling lands, Nejan knows the way. Find the nomads who travel through there and you will find your path. Meet with the leader, his name is Lon'an, he knows what you are to do. 'Tis all I will say for the moment, I will tell all when I return."

Kiem strode over, picked up his blackwood bow and quiver of arrows from the back corner, and glanced quickly at the knife tucked into his belt. He lifted a loose leather satchel, hiked it over his broad shoulder, and began walking out the door.

"With any luck I will bring home more dinner for my wonderful stew!"

As he disappeared down the hill and into the woods, I rose slowly following him outside. I lost my vision in the bright overhead sun, my legs giving out from under me, and I whooshed ungracefully to the ground. Nejan came bounding out from behind the cabin, water dripping from her jaws, she had been at the stream, cleaning herself.

"You are losing spirit, Little One?"

"No Great Mader, I was blinded by the brightness of the sun and light of spirit, I will be fine,"

I slowly rolled to my good side trying to duck from her tongue; however, it caught me on my poor shoulder which sported a very green, blue, and purple bruise.

"Ow! Careful, Mader!"

I cried out a bit loud for my own ears.

"You will need to practice speaking in your mind, I can be your teacher. If what Little Uncle and I believe you to be, men will hunt you. You must be able, not only to fend for yourself but speak quietly in your mind, so no one is the wiser. Once it is known, you will never be safe until you find your Dragon, or he finds you, even after this you may still be hunted."

"How does one speak in their mind? I hear you but I am not sure about … speaking."

"You must figure out how on your own, I cannot say how to, I just do it."

Nejan's voice echoed in my head, and I sat up crossing my legs very slowly, as the bruises on them were as sore and decorative as the ones on my shoulder and arms. Thankfully we were in the middle of the summer months, the sun was still warm on the skin, but the breeze coming in from the North had a bite. The season would be changing soon.

The notion of a Dragon had me in disbelief. I imagined a great beast, wings larger than any bird. In my mind, it was larger than the stature of the Temple. We had geese, and to hear tales, they had necks of fowl, wings with arm claws. Much like fowl feet claws, I imagined. I was unsure what scales looked like, fowl had feathers, which we used for many items. One storyteller said the scales looked like the shingles we used for roofs of homes.

"So, tell me of these Dragons, or what you know of them, if you have knowledge… Better yet please explain about yourself, are there more like you? Where do you come from? Why are you with Uncle? Why have we not seen you before?"

"One question at a time, Little Cub."

Nejan laughed in my head, however, it sounded like a purreow to my ears.

"Once there were many of us, but when the Dragon's disappeared many moons ago, men hunted us. With the disappearance of the great beasts our ability to replenish also expired. We walked side by side with the Dragons of old, we were their caretakers of many things. They protected us, we cared for them, a mutually beneficial relationship. We were not walkers of the night as men call us, we walked in the light, we are the Li'on-sa! We hid ourselves from men who hunted us for sport and to rid us of our fur and relocated into the mountain passes men were unable to traverse and there we remain. The few of us that are left, wait

for one such as you, to bring forth the Dragons, so we may once again, replenish and serve as we once did."

"This is a lot to be putting on one very beat up and sore wisp of a girl, I do not know how I can be the one of whom you speak. Dragons are beasts of legends. I am still trying to believe I am here talking to you! I am a woman, who lost her Mader at an early age, and shunned by people for being strange and having red hair. Which was the reason for a lot of the torment. Which I happen to be missing a lot of!"

I raised myself. Most in the castle proper, other than my siblings treated me with indifference, but not with malice. The persecution came from my younger sister, she had a mean streak, and I learned to avoid her. I tugged at the remnants of what used to be red tresses but now was matted, tangled and somewhat brown…. I picked out a few twigs, and a Jupa bug, dead, but squished enough to know his remains were in my hair!

"OOOgh, a wash is in order now! Let us go to the stream, I must wash this offal out! Ugh!"

I rose slowly. Very slowly, my body ached, and moving made me aware of its hurts. I followed Nejan through a path amongst the trees of the Ravenwood. The tall majestic blue barked trees, showing blue green leaves darkening with the advent of the weather changes in due course.

They graced the mountains with their magnificence; I felt small weaving among their bases, aged bark, showing black, Nena taught me many uses of just the bark alone. Their canopy overhead shadowing the mosses underfoot, muffling the sound of our passage. I followed the great black cat through a slight path, around greenery clinging to the rock faces, noticing the fading flowers of the Gooseweed moss, its properties best not used after bloom.

"Please do not get to far ahead of me. Is this stream far?"

The wood alone of these majestic trees were in every fiber of our lives. We ate, breathed, lived with this wood. So much so, I had not taken notice until now. The peace of walking through the forest had me contemplating the life from which I escaped. Many talented carpenters made every item of use in our busy lives, tables and chairs, bowls and vessels, cutlery, with only prominent persons of note using objects made of metal. Trees were cut in the fall, brought into the bowels of the city, and used during the long winter days and nights. Carvers would sit around the fires, telling tales, singing ballads. Lost loves, fallen comrades, and some of the lost Gods.

"No, Little Cub, not far."

The iron and other ores were mined from the mountains, and to hear the stories told, the lower caverns would ring with the songs of the smiths hard at work. Since most of the men departed to the lowlands to fight in the Emperor's war against the Infidels of Aram, smiths of some middling talent were hard to come by. The inner city was sometimes a single tempo. Not much in the way of household goods was produced the past few years, only weapons. The Aramites were slowly gaining lands in the ten years or so since they first came from overseas.

Men of all ages left the North for the war effort, only the young, weak, or infirm were left.

There was a smattering of green leaf trees, Oak, Birch and giant Cedar, and Pine needle trees down in the Southlands, however, Ravenwood trees dominated the landscape on the western shores. I saw the hint of sky through the canopy overhead, the odd ray of sun showing me the velvet greenery I was trodding on.

We emerged from the woods to a small bend in the stream trickling through the rocks of the mountainside. The bend creating a natural pool in which I could wade into without stumbling. Various mosses and ferns creating the immediate landscape the opening in the trees allowed, I saw the evidence of Nejan's entrance to the waters, I smelled the headiness of the mosses and detected the hint of wild garlic.

I walked in, clothes and all, washing each piece as I took it off, muttering on how little I had left, and once I had divested myself of all my clothing, I laid myself back on the sand bank and began on my hair.

"Ahhh, nice."

Quite the ordeal to wash one's hair with only use of one hand, as my left arm did not feel comfortable going too high over my head. Using the sand on the bank of the stream, I scrubbed and scrubbed until the water surrounding me was no longer muddled with bits of leaves and twigs and the odd shell, which I really did not care to know what kind of bug it may have belonged to. One side of my hair was shortened quite a bit; I would have to fix this later. I saw the portion of hair I could bring into view was gleaming red, the darkening rinse I was using, gone. When had it been this red?

Nejan left quietly when I entered the stream but now returned. I heard her paws padding on the moss before I saw her. I was still studying the lock of hair in my hand, not looking up at the cat.

"Your ears will get better with practice. In fact, all your senses will be heightened as your connection with your Dragon grows. It is truth of the DragonRiders of old, they could determine right from wrong by looking at someone. But sadly, some used their talents for their own gain and this helped fashion their fate."

"These Dragons you speak of. You have seen them?"

"Yes, I have. I was born and raised in the time of the end. My Mader had the foresight to travel into the mountains, our relationship with the last Riders deteriorated so much that we left, slowly so as to not alarm. As it was, many were killed after the end. She met her end saving me from a group of men, I will forever mourn her."

"I am sorry for your loss. Have you met others, like yourself?"

"No, I have seen signs, but we live solitary lives. We do not encroach on others hunting grounds, we do not live close to man, it has proven to be the end of those that would. I was living far to the North when I was told to come South."

Nejan padded over to the clearing, laying herself down on the mossy banks and began the odious task of cleaning herself. I had more questions and was itching to know more about her history, but she distracted me from my thoughts.

"Your wounds do not look as bad, how is the sight in your eye?"

As Nejan spoke inside my head, I finished washing my face as gently as I could, ducking my head in the stream and washing it with my eyes open. I rose up and I saw out of both and stood still and let the water eddy and ripple around me. I gazed down into the water, looking for the hint of sparkle, but most likely it was the sunlight filtering through the treetops above.

"I can see, there seems to be no damage. I am lucky I did not remain still for that last blow."

I was amazed I had survived the fall, not to mention the sword tip which arced towards my face. I had no formal training; I watched men train in the yard. My attempts to block the sword Vandrin was trying to kill me with, was borne from fear. Fear of dying. I had no thought, other than the voice who said it would be all right, than to leap backwards. The thought of dying from the fall never entered my mind. There were a few accounts in the past, of those who fell, found at the bottom, deceased. I was nothing short of a miracle, it seemed. None in my lifetime had walked away from a fall of those heights. I returned to the present.

I had only seen my reflection once or twice in a mirror. Precious items only the richest of nobles could afford, being made in the Capital. Most did not survive the journey North. My Mader had one in her room, but with her death and my Pader departing South to fight in the war, I spent more time in the city warren than in the castle on high.

I was an errant child and ran amuck, not in the least interested in staying in rooms which had no meaning to me over the course of time. I was what I believed to be an anomaly. I had red hair, and green eyes, and the fair skin which fit into the collective of the North, but the colour of my hair had me tormented by all. I kept it lackluster by a walnut rinse which shielded me from the Namanist view so far. It was no longer evident by my perusal. It was the colour of flame!

In remembering, I felt a wave of homesickness. Oh, how I missed Danyc, the only girl in the castle who spoke to me on occasion. This seemed like a lifetime ago, my apprenticeship with Healer Nena took me away more often than naught. These last three years, I was learning the ways of the woods, healing plants and plants which could kill.

I gazed into the treetops; a gentle breeze was swaying the branches. I was mesmerized by the dance, and as I let my mind wander, I realized I saw the swallows in their habitat and even the bugs which flew haphazardly out of their path of hunger! My eyesight had sharpened considerably! How is this possible?

"Because you are becoming who you are meant to be,"

Nejan's voice came into my thoughts.

"Try to think again to me,"

"Like a song sung in my head,"

I tried to project my thoughts and was surprised when she answered.

"Yes, if 'tis what helps you to think to me, let us use this."

She rose and padded over to me still standing in the tepid water. The water came from a hot spring higher up in the mountain, and by the time it reached the pool where I was, it was a warm, if slightly cool temperature. The mountains were shrouded in dense fogs most of the year, in winter, it lay heavy in the air. In fact, most of the natural springs which fed the rivers and came up inside the Temple were all naturally hot. It made for some interesting specimens of fungi and mosses, but more on that later. She stood there majestically, a legend but oh so real!

"You can find your path home? I will find a small meal and then I will make certain no one is exploring the area; I will see you this evening."

She padded quietly off, and I soon lost sight as she crested the hill above. I picked up my sopping wet clothes, twisted what water I could out of them, and slowly walked back, naked. I was amazed at how I felt, my body not as sore as a couple of days ago. My face felt tight, the stitches pulled, and I would have to remove them soon. I would have a vicious scar down the left side of my face, but that was the least of my worries.

I did not notice my looks, having been ridiculed all my life, I felt very plain and ordinary, except for my red locks. Red hair was not common in the North. Black, brown and the occasional blonde from across the sea, with red a phenomenon which had one persecuted and under intense scrutiny from the Namanists. Lucky for me, I had people who looked out for me, Kiem being one of them. In thinking about it now, I was realizing how much he looked after my well being. In every memory of note, he was not far from them.

I hope Uncle is not gone too long; I am very curious what he wishes to tell me. This past while has been nothing short of a dream.

I stumbled over roots and had to catch my breath a few times, but I managed to get back. Still naked but at least dry, perhaps I would do well to concentrate on walking and not past dreaming. I was not embarrassed by my body; it was what the Gods gave me, I was an average height, slim with muscles, my legs had some definition.

I had small but adequate breasts, and no reason to compare with any other female, so my breast size was what it was. My skin was fair, mind you, my face was tanned, and my arms were gradual tan from my shoulders to my hands, depending on what tunic I wore. I wore my full tunic when I went into the castle from Aunt Nena's cabin to sell her wares in the summers. Which is why I was at the Aerie in the first place.

When I arrived back at the cabin, I entered, grabbing the shirt and pants I saw hanging on the back wall. While I did not mind nakedness, a breeze had picked up and the sun was cresting the mountains.

I should really get the fire going again and warm up what is in the pot,

As soon as I thought this my tummy growled. So, I pulled the shirt over my head, the smell of it, making me wish I had taken it to the stream.

Oh well, it will be mine until my own clothes are dry and mended,

I busied myself with stoking the exhausted fire getting it roaring again. I poured more water into the pot which had a dried skim of what I hoped was fat and then hung my wet clothes on the hooks I grabbed the other clothing from.

I ate once the stew had bubbled for a while, tidying up the room and sweeping some branch bits and dirt clumps outside with a makeshift broom I found leaning in a corner. At least that is what I used it for, assuming it was an actual broom.

Then I swung the pot back against the wall where it could cool down for the following day. I ate a wooden bowl full and washed it by licking it clean and then with a spot of water, found a needle and some thread and proceeded to mend my somewhat dry clothes.

I tried to process the few days events which were more unreal than any story I had heard. I found a sword, long forgotten by time. In the finding of, I was chased by my half-brother who grabbed it from me to the top of the Temple. I dodged his well-aimed thrusts shot with anger, and what I suspect was hatred, only to fall off the highest waterfall, survive, and carried to safety by a beast of legend. Then, to top off that, she communicated in my mind, and my Uncle could also speak to her. This was remarkable, if found out could mean my death. Nena mentioned it in tales, but I brushed it off as fancy… Now I knew better.

I hurt from all my wounds, but not as bad I thought. Then Kiem said I was a DragonRider of the old legends, which made me think he was losing his mind. A DragonRider! In a world with no Dragons! This was much to fathom; my head hurt with all the remembrance; it was too surreal.

The old legends, rarely spoken, at least not in the presence of Pader Reudin. It meant extra time spent in the Temple, under his watchful gaze. I learned more from Healer Nena in three years, than I had the whole of my life. She told me about the old Gods, and what each was. No one spoke aloud of these Gods, Na-man was harsh in punishments if one was known to be speaking to others or celebrating old traditions.

As I waited for Nejan to return, I became conscious how drained I was. I do not remember laying down and did not hear when she padded through the doorway, laid on the floor with her face looking out, her nostrils constantly assessing the breeze.

"Rest, Little Cub, I will watch over you."

CHAPTER 2

Rowan

A Glimmer in the Sand

Marriage, I should be excited.

Rowan thought to herself, and she was, after all, it was a distraction from her boring life. Nothing but parties, afternoon teas, listening to musicians, endless dress fittings, and living as the perfect embodiment of the Dader of the Emperor of Du'Lanay. Rowan walked around her garden reminiscing of the place she resided and thought about her life.

Taught by people handpicked by her Mader, Rowan was a spokesperson for the elite. Not that she went out in public, if anything, she did not. This was a title given to her, by her Mader. She was to lead the others by example; be the perfect woman and biddable. So… Rowan did. She held her afternoon teas, only the highest titled ladies attended, many twice her age and then some. Rowan knew they reported back to her Mader… so, she perfected the role of host. She was perfection.

Sometimes her handmaid would tell of the outside world below in the lower city. Rowan would beg for more stories, but Tannah's experience was only to the market level below the compound in which Rowan resided.

"Tell me again of the stalls. What was the old man selling this time?"

"Well, last week it was spices from the eastern shores, and this week he had beeswax candles and a few small leather goods. There were your favorite lavender soaps, I picked up a few more bars."

"Thank you, you know me so well."

"He says he has some candles specially made for you, but I told him I would inquire first."

"Oh please, do! We used all the others. I love the scent; it makes me dream of far-off places. Go tomorrow and purchase all. We must support our favorite venders."

"He knows exactly what you like, Princess. There was a new clothier. An Aram, husband, and wife, she was hiding behind him, I believe she was there for the female customers. There were vivid colours! Many blues and greens."

"I have all I need, yet it would be nice to have a few more blues. Nada Du'Tan has darker blues and did not have many when I was picking out my trousseau."

"Do you want any? It will probably be the last time; the Aram was insisting he would be gone soon."

"If he is there, buy enough of their blue for a gown, and perhaps another colour. Surprise me. Perhaps there is one that Nada Du'Tan does not have."

"We may not have time to create a gown before the wedding."

"We will take it with us then; there will be plenty of time after. Tell me more on the other venders, was the basket seller with one arm there...?"

It always fascinated Rowan. Rowan felt like she had visited, after she made her maid retell everything. She dared not ask any of the other noble ladies about life outside, they would see it as a mark on her character. Rowan pretended she knew all about the city, the country, and its inhabitants.

The Palace of the Emperor and Empress was placed on the highest hill dominating the rest of the smaller Palaces surrounding it, overlooking a panoramic view of the Southern Ocean, and the hills surrounding the North. One could not see the rivers on either side for the Palaces, but they were there, providing a natural break from the rest of the world. There were huge stone bridges crossing the naturally formed canyons cutting through the high stone cliffs. There were several on either side of the Palaces. These bridges connecting the nobility to the rest of the world were always monitored. Not that any one person had ever threatened the idyllic world she existed in.

Rowan was restricted by protocols, not permitted to leave on her own accord. A prisoner of sorts, she was informed the Palace she lived in was her haven from the squalor of the lower city. She was to do remarkable things, marry and beget an heir to the Empire. She just had to do such from her small piece of paradise.

I cannot wait for children!

She had an older brother who married but he died in the war. For the five years he was married, he never sired any children off his wife. When he was announced dead, his wife was pensioned off to live on a family villa. It was not even half a year before she disappeared from all talk. As Rowan was the next in line, the future of her house rested on her... The future of the Empire... Not exactly a small task, as she was constantly reminded. For all the telling, Rowan did not have a swelled head. She was a quiet girl and did not feel arrogant or self important.

Rowan lived one level below the Grand Emperor's Palace. She had to inquire through five officials to see her own Mader and had siblings she used to play with, but when she began to bleed her monthly cycle this all changed. Her sister, younger by three years had cried something horrible when Rowan left the children's apartment. She often wondered how they were if they missed her. She missed them terribly the first year, until she was too busy with studies and sewing to reflect on their absence from her life.

She was relocated into her own apartments, her Mader handpicked her attendants, and was told there were big plans for her. Rowan was to be groomed to be a bride for the Emperor's favorite family, the eldest son of the Commander of the Army. She was so excited at first. This was a status change for her, and she embraced the concept with great enthusiasm. She wanted nothing more than to please her Pader and Mader and had no reason to believe that her spirit was not grace. There was an engagement ceremony, which when she thought about it, was the last time she was out in public.

Hhhhmmmm, strange, had it been that long?

This was when she met her betrothed, however, now she could not remember what he looked like, or what he was like. She probably would not know who he was if she were to observe him again in a crowded room.

She was to be the perfect wife and knew she would excel. Rowan was 5'2", round with some substance to her, which for nobility was a symbol of prosperity, had beautiful long brown hair, free flowing as per her status in life. Her eyes were a paler version of green than most, not unlike petals in the spring before they unfolded their beauty. Or so her attendants had told her plenty of times, when she lamented her eyes were not the right shade.

She was well-educated in music and composition, well read of all the tomes of known poetry, and had knowledge of running a large household. The best of tutors in the nation were procured, and she was careful not to anger any of them. Her Mader said Rowan's duty was to learn, her education would cater to a new era of ruler, and she must ensure her children were as duly brought into knowledge as herself.

Cannot better perfection, but why does it have to be sooo… boring?

She did not like waiting for anything. Her tutors had left some time ago and now was almost finished the embroidery she was creating for her joining ceremony. It was coming up soon yet could not arrive fast enough.

She lay on her velvet chaise of the deepest red, sipping a cold citrus infused tea, with petals of nasturtium flowers. The petals decorated the tray and ground around her, and she began to notice the scent. The soft flower fragrance had always been one of her favorites. What began as a slight scent on the air, hit her hard like a slap of water on her face. It became overpowering in an instant, she reached over to the side table to ring the bell for Tannah, and her headache exploded into shots of pain. Grasping her head with her hands, she screamed for her maid, then her Mader. It was like shards of glass, inside her head.

"Oh, my head. Ahhhh! It hurts so bad…Ahhhh!"

Servants appeared from all corners of the adjoining rooms, as she kept screaming, struggling to rise but collapsing to her knees in a faint, as Tannah ran into the room.

"Princess, what is wrong? Quick, you, find the physician, and you, go inform the Empress. This could be profoundly serious; I do not know what triggered this."

Tannah rattled off directions like a general, to the other servants milling around. The two she directed moved off like a rattlesnake had bitten them. Picking up Rowan with the help of two other servant girls, they half carried, half dragged their mistress to her bedchamber, placing her on an enormous feather filled mattress, draped in silk cloths. She tied back the sheer gold netting at the blonde wood bedposts, while she anticipated the physician's arrival.

Her mistress had not roused when the doctor strode in, his shadow of an apprentice trailing with hands crammed full of bags and books, threatening to fall out of his grasp. Had Rowan been awake to notice, she would have wondered at the gilt embroidery on his robe. It was so heavily done; one could only think he may topple over from the excess. In contrast, his apprentice was plainly robed in dark red. Its plainness was accentuated by the fading at the elbows and seams.

"What is wrong now, with the little Princess?"

"I do not know; I was in the room with her. She began screaming about her head and fainted, I could not catch her in time. We placed her on the bed in anticipation of your arrival, sir."

The physician attended the Princess as far back as Rowan remembered. His stature would be higher than Rowan if he walked upright, but he was stooped from advanced years. He was there when she was born and only served the children of the Empire. Her Mader and Pader had their own personal doctors.

"Was she partaking of any food?"

"No, Great Sir, she was laying on her chaise, sipping her favorite tea."

"Bring it to me."

"Right away."

"This doesn't smell different… tastes like her tea. No other food or drink?"

"No, Sir. She had her usual meal this morning. I tasted everything. I also tasted this tea. As you can see, I am still standing."

"Well, as a precaution, let us have another taster. I am sure her Majesty will agree with my synopsis. Lian."

His apprentice, a skinny stick of a man, located a table and positioned a worn leather roll of tools and knives on the surface, and the largest book, opening the book to a blank page above it. The dirty-blonde haired apprentice also placed a jar of squirming black creatures down. As the ancient physician reached the bed, Rowan groaned opening her eyes, struggling to rise.

"Remain still, Princess, this will not take long."

Rowan settled back against a bolster Tannah placed behind her head and shoulders, closed her eyes, and waited.

"Hand me the extractors, Lian."

Rowan opened her mouth to protest as she opened her eyes to see the physician reach into the opened jar with the long-handled tweezers.

"Lay still Princess… Lian, tilt it this way, just a little. This will bleed the ill humours out of you, Princess, you will feel better after tomorrow."

Rowan tried to protest, but as she started to speak, she realized how futile it was. They would tie her down and it would take longer to convince them nothing was wrong. So, she lay there letting them attach the leeches, as they finished taking the last one off, her Mader strode in, a ferocious expression on her countenance.

"This better be worth it, I had a particularly important tea with the groom's Mader. I had to explain your hysterical maids rambling, so I told her it was nothing but a mild disagreement among servants."

Rowan lay there with eyes closed as Tannah explained to the Empress what transpired.

Mader was always cross with anything I do or say, She could not recall if she ever saw her Mader smile.

"Well, no more tea. She can rest for a couple of days out of the heat and sun. See to it she listens, or I will dismiss you myself."

Rowan sat up to protest, but her Mader had exited the room, the doctor right behind jabbering to her back constantly bowing, his apprentice barely scrambling to grab the book and tools scooting behind him.

How does he manage to walk at all?

Rowan speculated as she rolled herself up sitting on the edge of the bed. Mustering her strength to stand, she felt a bit woozy from the loss of blood.

"Princess, not so quickly, you should lay down and rest."

"I have been laying down; it was just a headache."

"I know you had them before, but you have never lost spirit, I will be right back. Do not move, I will get you a drink."

Tannah left the room bringing back a glass of citrus juice which past practice, had servants trained to keep on the ready for such an occasion. The application of leeches was the physicians cure for everything; Rowan had several past experiences to know exactly what transpired.

This was the first splitting headache Rowan had experienced with such a result and hoped it was the last. She did not like the fact she fainted at all. Sitting there and feeling the breeze caressing her skin, as it came off the ocean, Rowan smelled the salt. Not that she had even been near the ocean, hopefully someday she and her husband would travel.

The Capital of Du'Lanay, Merida was set in the South of the continent. The Palaces of the Emperor and Namarch were high on a hill surrounded on two sides by rivers, the ocean to the South and rolling hills to the North. The whole of the Capital was well fortified by huge stone walls. The hills to the farther North, farmed and dotted with citrus groves, olive groves, and crops of hay, alfalfa, and potatoes, on the larger slopes, grew grapes white and red.

While the South flank was cliff face the city proper was protected by huge stone walls on the other three sides. The out lying hills dotted with personal villas with all forms of vegetation grown for consumption. If one were to climb the highest tower of the Namarch's Palace, and look to the hills to the North, there were townships and a blue haze which was the Southern mountain range that divided the South of the continent from the middle land of rolling hills and swamplands.

"Princess, you have not had a headache in a while, I thought perhaps we were rid of them. Do you still suffer one?"

Tannah announced like it was an introduction to the assembly. The young maid was only five years older than Rowan but often acted as if she were double in age, with a madering Rowan appreciated. She had black hair and blue eyes, which had Rowan thinking she was of the Northern peoples, but Tannah told her once when asked, her Mader was born and raised in the Capital.

"No, it has gone, but for a moment, the smell of nasturtium was very overpowering."

"The physician called for another tester. I will get Yana to assist."

"Is this even necessary? I trust you, Tannah."

"I know you do yet others are not, best to do what is required, you will manage your own house soon enough."

"Oh, how right you are! I can hardly wait!"

"Your citrus drink, Princess."

"Thank you. (sniff). This has more orange in it today… Mmm, I like it."

She began to notice other smells… her body odour, Tannah's, dirty feet smells, different plants, the crushed grass beneath someone's foot. She drank her glass of citrus juice, placing the hand-blown gold glass on the table beside her bed.

"Please instruct the lower staff to bathe more, I do not like their smell."

As Rowan lay down again, Tannah was sniffing the other girls to see if she smelled body odors, directing the girls to clean up the petals outside and then to bathe.

"Make sure you put on new robes,"

Tannah called after the girls as they headed outside. Rowan slept for the rest of the day, waking up as servants brought in the evening meal. She lay there, the dream still vivid in her mind.

That was odd, I was walking in a forest, barefoot and the trees and shrubs were bending towards me. Even the grasses were swaying as I walked through them. Every time I touched a bud it would bloom! How wonderous it would be if this transpired, as though I had the ability of The Lord God above, Narman. May he be Blessed. That would be the most wonderous gift, the gift of life! I hope in my new home I grow many plants; I have such a love of flowers.

She sat up, then rose to her feet, feeling much better and clearer in the mind. Walking bare foot on the glossy white marble floors into the next chamber, she sat herself at the Blackwood dining table. Gobbling down her dinner, she discovered herself quite ravenous, as she ate, Rowan found wonder in singling out specific spices the cooks used in her dinner. When she raised her glass of punch to her lips and drew a sip, she picked out every fruit which had gone into the creation, from the orange and lemon to the pineapple and grapes. Sipping slowly, she was amazed at the insight into her observations. Rowan dipped her fingers into the water bowl, dabbed her hands on the napkin, and brought it up to her mouth to wipe her lips, and noticed the sharp citrus of lemon used.

'Tis diverting. Why can I smell everything? As the earth after the rains, the sharp tang of the fruits, I can pick them all out.

Rowan rose from the dining room table, sauntered through her bedroom to the dressing room, and through this room to the one beyond. As she walked, she undressed, dropping each piece on the floor, discarding layers as a snake shed its skin. By the time she reached the bathing pool, she walked into the pool naked as the day she was born. The bathing pool sunk into the floor by three steps, and was fed by a system of pipes, which Rowan did not care to know how it functioned. Water was piped in, and it was piped out, there was a natural flow to it, and was constantly replenished, and while it was not hot, it was not cold either. One of her servant girls proceeded to wash her long locks, another came into the water and began to bathe her with scented soaps.

"Find some unscented soap, this scent is beginning to hurt my head."

"Yes, Princess, right away."

Rowan found the scent of lavender too overpowering and did not wish another episode like the one she just endured… the lavender was threatening to initiate another headache.

She finished bathing, rose out of the water and her servants dried her with towels of the softest linen. She walked into her dressing room, picking out a dress of yellow and orange silk which her attendants outfitted her in as well as matching necklace and rings. One girl dried her hair and tidied it into a simple braid which lay flat behind her. As she was finishing, her maid Tannah came into the room, admonishing her that she should be laying down.

"Nonsense, I feel right as rain. I will walk outside for a while and then take up my embroidery. The fresh air will help clear out any cobwebs in my head; it is bracing."

"Yes, Princess, I only have your well being foremost in my thoughts."

"While I appreciate the soaps, have others brought. Place the lavender away for now, I will use unscented. The smell was vexing to me."

"Yes, I will send one of the girls tomorrow to purchase some."

"Just go yourself, you are so much faster, the other girls will not bargain well."

"As you wish."

Rowan walked barefoot past her maid onto the outdoor marble patio. The marble floor from the inside continued to the outdoor slab, only separated by huge, shuttered doors of blonde wood. She stood there in the setting of the sun watching the colours of the sky change in the clear night. She inhaled deeply a couple of times, wondering why the smells were not as pronounced as earlier in the day.

That is strange, 'tis like I cannot smell at all. I hope I am not getting an illness. Not good, right before my joining. I will watch my intake, maybe I should not partake of any seafoods.

She smelled the scent of grass, the flowers which graced her gardens, the dirt, and other smells on the light breeze flowing through, but she did not want to know what those scents would be, as she was scared concentrating would set her off again. The air was cooler than during the heaviness of the day. She felt a shiver on her neck, then it left.

She walked down the granite steps, into her own personal garden, and curled her toes into shortly trimmed grass. Walking softly, she fingered blossoms, leaning forward to sniff some of the blooms, only sniffing gently. As she stood still Rowan felt with wonder the vibration of the earth against her toes. It began as a murmur, she noticed it, then as she concentrated, she felt it more. She felt a pulse, slow and steady, and comfortable.

Why have I never noticed this before? I find it quite soothing... a warm hug against another's breast. Ahhh, I could stay out here forever, but must not upset the girls, I see the newest one observing me with concern.

She paused for a minute, absorbing the feeling, it helped her to feel more at ease, relaxing her shoulders lowering in calmness. Rowan curled her toes deeper into the grass and closed her eyes, the vibration ran through her feet and up into her limbs, she had never experienced such a sensation and revelled in it.

All the while, Tannah and several other attendants followed behind her, chatting amongst themselves. Rowan noticed her hearing become sharp and could pick out their conversation which was about her, but she kept this to herself.

"The Princess is acting odd. Should we tell her Mader?"

"Odd? In what way? She is getting nerves for her upcoming joining. All women act odd."

Tannah brushed off the other girl's comments with a tired whisper.

"She seems agitated, and mutters."

"She is trying to remember everything. You are new here, Yana. I have known Rowan for many years; she always speaks under her breath. When she had tutors and was trying to remember all told, she would spend days, talking to herself. Its normal for her, 'tis how she learns. I believe she is memorizing her vows."

"Oh, I suppose… She is very entitled. Always dropping her clothes on the floor. She could at least throw them on the bedding."

"Oh Yana. You are so overworked. Does it hurt your back to bend over? Maybe you would be suited to another job in the Palace. I hear the vegetable cleaners in the kitchens do not have to bend over. Shall I put in a word for you?"

"No. Tannah. I misspoke. I like it here. I do not want to go back to the kitchens, I will not say anymore on the subject."

"See that you do not. Princess is not an entitled mistress. You have it very lax here. I hear her Mader is more demanding if you need a challenge."

"No. I mean no disrespect. Do you have any orders for me?"

"Go and prepare the bedding. Her Highness will finish her walk soon and may wish to retire for the night. Remember, you have it quite easy here, Rowan is not demanding, I will hear no more from you, or I will replace you. You have a great honour being here and being one of her attendants in the joining ceremony. Many other servants in this Palace would gladly take your place. Now go, I am tired and wish some peace from lazy girls."

"Yes, Tannah, thank you."

Rowan smiled to herself as she bent down to the rose, she singled out to sniff. She never heard her main maid speak ill of her, and to hear her speak up for her mistress made Rowan feel appreciative of Tannah.

Gazing back at the Palace, she could not imagine leaving this one day but leave she must.

I am a little uncertain of sharing my life with a man. Will I have to share a bed? Will he snore? Is that what a marriage is? No one has told me, what a marriage consists of. Will we eat together? Should I find a common topic to discuss? His Pader is Lord Commander of the Army. Should I be reading books on war? Will he be interested in gardening? I think not. What man is concerned with growing things? I should count myself rich if he even chooses to talk to me. Will he let me have a garden, I wonder.

Her personal gardens were enclosed in one section of the Palace. The walls of adjacent buildings provided some of the enclosure, with high stone walls of golden granite, fitted such one had to look hard for the joins. She had never attempted to leave; and had no desire, this was her own private paradise. Other than the boredom she was experiencing lately, she was content.

Will I have my own gardens to grow? I cannot imagine not having them, with all my children running through with an attendant or two to mind them,

She imagined a dream husband, them sitting together, holding hands watching their children play in the garden. The visions behind her eyes flickered through her mind, always the same, happy thoughts of a happy couple. Many children laughing and playing with their parents. She smiled to herself. She knew love would not come at first and would make every effort to find out what made her husband happy and strive to address his every need. She wanted nothing but a happy life.

She had over the five years, planted flowers of her choosing, watching as her servants would do the work. Rowan organized a small herb garden and read tomes on the uses of herbs and the making of tonics, she always had an interest in plants and having them thrive. It brought her a sense of fulfilment. She used a lot of her lotions on herself, and she also dabbled in a few perfume scents, of her own making. Of course, any mess she created, would be cleaned up by her servants.

After a long walk through her gardens, Rowan returned to the patios which embraced the back of her Palace surroundings and in the torchlight, she picked up her needlepoint, sat herself on her chaise, and began working on her veil for her joining dress. She worked on it for about three to four hours, before having a light repast and went back to bed.

The next few weeks blended into each other, walking around the gardens, finishing the lacework on her veil, dress fittings, listening to musicians, all the while she was bored. She likened her Palace to a cage and remembered the little songbirds she used to have. Several were unique, native to their lands, but one was a Purple Sennet from Aram.

When she first received the Sennet from her Mader, it was for her thirteenth name day. Soon after, the little purple bird became listless, it would hang its head and feathers would drop. Rowan remembered opening the cage and gently grasping the small bird in her hand. She cuddled and lay on her chaise with the bird on her breast. She stroked its' back and sang lullabies. It rested on her breast the first night and when she placed it back, it had perked up a little. She tended to this bird and gave it a name of Rue. Every night for a month she sang softly, tucking it into her robe and lay down and caressed the feathers.

She noticed behind its eye on one side was one blue feather, one could only see it when others were moved. She marvelled at such a perfect bird could have a flaw, but it did not take away from its beauty. It was her bird, yet she thought about how she felt when she nursed it to when she let it free.

Less than five months ago, she was laying on her lounger, drinking a hot tea, with her birds surrounding her, when she began to listen to them more, all were voicing themselves and she grew irritated with the noise. The more she focused, the louder their clamour! She called Tannah.

"Tannah, open their doors."

"But Princess, they will fly away."

"I am aware of this, open the doors."

"'Tis winter, are you certain?"

"Yes, I am. They were never meant to be caged. 'Tis not for me to keep them thus. They are kept here against their will."

"I am fairly sure they have not the spirit we do, we keep them fed, while out there they may starve. What about the special one your Mader gave you? 'Tis exceedingly rare, no one else has one like it."

"I will explain to the Empress if I need to."

"Yes, your Highness. Girls, you heard your Princess, open the doors. Let the birds out."

"Remove the cages and all the rest. I will walk outside while you do so."

"'Tis raining hard, you will get very wet, are you sure?"

"A little rain never hurt anyone, Tannah. Now if you can get this all done…" She smiled at the memory; she had let all her captives go. It had felt good inside, to not keep a caged animal against its' will. She had gotten very wet, but inside she felt like it cleansing her, she raised her face to the downpour, closed her eyes, and felt it clean her energy. She had gotten terribly ill; a sore throat and stuffed head had her laid up for a week.

Her Mader was very cross with the escape of her gift, The Purple Sennet cost many coins, it was the only one in Du'Lanay, apparently. She saw it several days in a row, then not for a few months. She hoped it would find its way, or a mate.

Rowan made her apologies, which her Mader ignored, after which the Empress did not return for several months. When she did, it was to discuss the progression of the gown, nothing more. Rowan often wondered about her Mader's lack of caring. Being used to no affection, her Mader's indifference was expected, but Rowan hoped for something akin to companionship.

I wonder what a person of the lower city has in the way of family? Tannah has told me of the caring of her Mader. I hear the longing and sadness in her voice, and what she tells me of her, I hear the love for her Mader. I feel nothing for mine. Am I wrong to do so? Why do I feel like I am not content? Every book I have read on husbandry says a woman must care and nurture her husbands needs, care for her children by her husband. I know I shall do so. I have no reason not to. Is my Mader's lack of caring because she is Empress?

She knew deep in her heart, she was destined to do more than this, but she would suffice with walking barefoot at night more often than naught. Feeling at peace after a couple of turns around the garden, Rowan muttering to herself, about the extreme boring life she had. At one point, Tannah, her most constant companion, heard her mutterings and commented once she was joined, her life would probably not be as boring. How right Tannah was, but Rowan did not know then how precise her maid was…

Watching her maid one day, Rowan could not fathom how life would be for her,

"Tannah, are you happy?"

"In what way are you meaning, Princess?"

"In life. What you do, day after day. Does it make you content?"

"My life as it is, is fulfilling. Keeping the body busy keeps the mind and spirit satisfied. When my spirit is reborn, it will choose to help another. In helping others, doing honorable deeds, the spirit will seek out enlightenment, by the grace of our God. He is all that is good."

"May he be Blessed."

Rowan studied religion but could not be bothered to take a devout stance, not if one had to deal with the current Namarch. He was old and well, sly looking! He had an energy surrounding him which set hers on edge. Rowan did not want to be around him any more than she had to. Her tutor on Naman had thankfully been a younger man, a most devout follower, who did not look upon her face, while he was in her presence. Religion for Rowan was not a priority, she was left alone, if she observed the correct days. It was as routine as sleeping and eating.

One warm and breezeless day, she was muttering to herself that she wished she were free from this boring life, when she heard a voice saying back to her, a whisper in her ear.

"Well, you could have my life and have a chain around your ankle,"

She replied without thinking.

"A chain?"

She was facing the doorway to the outside patio and did not realize her maid Tannah had entered the room behind her.

"Who are you speaking to?"

Tannah had a nuance of question in her voice.

"You mentioned a chain."

Rowan turned around abruptly, her silken gown flowing around her legs with the movement.

"Why you, did you not just tell me….?"

Then she realized Tannah had entered the room as she was carrying Rowan's lunch on a tray towards the table.

Tannah gave her an odd look.

"Never mind, I am talking to myself again."

Rowan heard about punishments given to people hearing voices and she casually brushed it off as talking to herself. She should be given no more mind and hopefully was imagining she heard a voice. Spirit help her if it was a voice!

"Do not forget you have your final dress fitting today, The Empress will be here in two days. We have the girls finish anything needed to satisfy and placate your Mader, while you complete the veil."

"I have only two last leaves to complete, then I am done. Have the girls double check all the seams and edges. I thought for a moment, one was not completed."

"Yes, Your Highness. I will."

The dress as per her royal status, was red silk and resplendent in gold embroidered threads depicting a design of her own she had spent the last five years stitching, with her favorite flower the Blood Rose. There was extensive gold embroidery on the bodice, sleeves and on the lower hem of the dress. While she did all the embroidery herself, she had seamstresses who did all the manual sewing.

If she were to take on all of it by herself, she would not be getting joined for another ten years! The dress itself was a long affair; it took ten paces behind her of just the skirt. The bodice clung to her ample bosom and then let out slowly above her waist and gave the illusion of a full and robust silhouette, Rowan was immensely proud of.

The veil was a mirror image of the dress. Gold lace with red flowers, all complimentary to the bride. The stitching of a wedding dress by any highborn was done by the bride herself. Rowan began when she moved into the suite when she was ten. She was enormously proud of her accomplishments, it was no small feat, but as the joining day was looming closer, she conceded to get assistance on the skirt. She knew it would not reflect badly on herself. It was something which kept her busy for the most part and she used the time to reflect upon her life and discussions with her maids when they were in attendance.

"I have never seen a more beautiful gown, Princess."

"Do you think so, Tannah? This has been a most fulfilling endeavor. Do you think the embroidery is not too much? The Empress was most fervent I create this design. It has her blessing; do you think the Namarch will say 'tis too extravagant?"

"I am sure your Mader, the blessed Empress smoothed the way. 'Tis not showing any skin, so he cannot say 'tis provocative, if anything, it covers you most well. I am sure the nobility will love the embroidery. 'Tis your design, and many young brides will wish to mimic this, or create their own."

"How do you know? He may create a sermon from just my dress."

"I heard your Mader's main maid tell another the Empress expressly told the Namarch you would be suited to embroider your gown."

"When was this? You never told me."

"Forgive me, this was many years ago. When you were meeting the Nada Du'Tan for the purchase of the fabrics. You remember your Mader was with you, that day? I listened to the women servants when we were waiting for your decision."

"I remember. I also remember it was not my decision on fabric or colour."

"You are Royal. Your colours are red and gold. You are the only royal bride who has the right to wear these colours."

"I am not sure I like red, I wish I could have picked my own colours."

"You can, with other gowns and fabrics. Everyday use."

Rowan sighed. Her maid meant well, but she did not get the point, Rowan wished to wear a colour of her choosing.

"Yes, but a bride should have her own choice."

"Princess. No one else can wear a red wedding gown. 'Tis law."

"'Tis a silly law. I would have liked to wear green, a light green, like the silver green of new Ravenwood leaves in the spring."

"That colour would compliment your eyes, Princess, however, not for your joining. Your husband's colours are green and black. You would be able to wear his colours once you are joined."

"His green is too dark, as the colour of olives. Not that I do not like such, but I prefer a softer green."

"Perhaps 'tis where his family colours came from. I hear they grow a vast amount of olives in the hills to the North."

Rowan sighed again. Her boredom with her gown, was almost too much to bear. It was almost complete. Just trivial things here and there which needed to be completed. Thankfully, Tannah was organized, the young woman would make lists and keep Rowan on schedule with every little thing needing completion... She remembered when she was told she was engaged to the young man. Rowan had Tannah get her every book on the genealogy of his house.

"Grapes as well. His family is second richest in our land. It must be why my Mader wanted this joining."

"Most assuredly, Princess. The joining of the two largest houses, will mean a huge boon to the Emperor."

"Yes. I remember Mader insisted it be announced with great ceremony. Was not the Namarch vexed for a time?"

"You remember? He was livid. Somehow the Empress had him see her way. I am not sure how she convinced him. You know it means the shift of power will favor your Pader?"

"How so? Am I just a pawn, then? To be used for political means?"

"You know 'tis so. That is what royal joinings are, with marrying you to the Army, it gives the Emperor the backing he needs."

"To do what?"

"You know our history, Princess. You have read books and were taught what a shift would do."

"Yes… yes Tannah. It would mean Pader could wage war against the Namarch and win. Therefor becoming ruler over Naman. It seems so ludicrous men would fight for the top of the heap."

"That is what men do. They fight, like male dogs. Only the strongest alpha wins."

"While we are just ornaments, to be worn on an arm."

"You will be the prettiest, Princess. Now we should remember to get the edge seam complete on the right sleeve. I will check over everything, a couple times, to make sure I have not forgotten anything. If you see anything amiss, let me address it before you present to your Mader."

The next few days were busy with the dress fitting; her seamstresses were working long days and into the night to finish what seams and embroidery required their help on.

Rowan found time to work in her gardens, trimming flowers, removing dead buds, and preparing seeds to take to her new home. She especially wanted to bring the Blood Rose and wanted all the herbs and various plants used in salves and lotions, so she prepared those as well. Or more to the point, her attendants did as she instructed.

All the while she roamed barefoot, it calmed the raging boredom she otherwise felt. Her new home? She was not sure what to expect of her groom. She had only met him once formally. Rowan knew his villa was across the Capital, on one of the lesser hills to the North. His family also owned a Palace located in the Capital for state business.

At least his level of living is not much different from my own. Mader must have my comfort in mind, I should thank her for the joining contract. We will be able to live in the Palace when it is winter. Live on his villa during growing season. It will be ideal.

Provided she could take some of her servants with her, she felt confident that she would be able to run a smaller home than what she was used to. They were packing all she ordered them to, into wooden chests, which were specially built by craftsmen for her own personal use. These would be taken to her new home, the day of the joining while the ceremony was held.

Will he like me?

If she thought about it hard enough, Rowan could not remember what the man looked like, he had dark hair and was not bad to look at. It was a long time since the formal engagement, she remembered he smiled at her and asked many questions, to which she answered him, but only looked at him once. He never inquired about her after. She thought of the proceedings as normal business, she was after all, a Princess of the Empire.

Will I like him? Will I like him well enough to live the rest of my life with him?

The weather was still holding if there were no breeze the heat was stifling. High summer was too warm for a joining, so she desired to have it towards the fall, as the summer days still held but the nights were cooling. Fall would see the harvests coming in and so far South on the continent meant winter would be full of rains. Only the North had the white stuff called snow in the winter. Frozen rain, she had never seen anything like it. It was only described to her. She hoped with marriage she and her husband, would travel the continent. She often wondered about the rest of the Empire, Rowan read a few books describing the highest mountains of the North, some never lost the white caps of snow. She would love to see snow for herself.

The day came for her final dress fitting and for her to present it in front of her Mader and GrandMader. GrandMader had not seen Rowan in an exceptionally long time as she was unwell and had to be carried on a special chair. Her GrandMader lived in another section of the Palace and had her own servants to attend to her. Rowan had to ask permission to step outside her own Palace. It sometimes took several days for the communication, and most times the answer was no, so she gave up. She would have liked to visit her GrandMader, but as her Gran's illness had the older woman sequestered these last three years, some of Rowan's attempts were turned away, she stopped trying.

I will not ask permission anymore, I can go where my husband lets me, we can go places together and I will see some of this land. I sure wish he wishes to travel also.

So, from the time she woke in the morning, on this late summer day, bathed, had her morning breakfast, she was busy. Midmorning they made their way to the reception hall in her Palace where her Mader, GrandMader and their respective attendants were waiting. Rowan was undressed in front of everyone, all except her loincloth and bodice, all of silk, on a raised platform in the center of the Hall so her audience saw all. The dressing attendants helped her with the dress and arranged the veil on her head after Tannah and her maids had fixed her hair.

Rowan's GrandMader looked older than the last time, she saw her. Her hair was completely white and she was inattentive; her maid was constantly wiping her chin with a linen. Rowan saw her mind and spirit were wandering and it saddened her. The Empress looked annoyed her own Mader was not all attentive. The Empress was a regal figure, she had Rowan's brown hair, delicately coiffed with multiple braids holding her long locks in place, a delicate lace snood held it hostage. Rowan could not wait to contain her hair. It was annoying sometimes when the wind blew it into her face. The Empress had hazel eyes which were always criticizing her Dader it seemed.

If her eyes could be any harsher. What is she angry about? The embroidery was her idea from the very beginning; I have done what she wished me to do. Why is it that I cannot do anything right?

For the duration of the dress fitting, Rowan heard nothing positive from her Mader. Starting from the design of the pattern and muttering very loudly parts of the dress did not fit right. The veil was not long enough, and her hair should not be done up but left long and flowing. She dare not say anything to her Mader as she did not wish to be reprimanded.

Just keep thinking to yourself within the month you will have your own home, and your Mader will be much further away.

"Empress, will I have my own servants to take with me?"

She turned to face her Mader and GrandMader.

"It would help greatly with the transition to my new home."

"As your husband has his own staff, I only see you taking a few of your best servants. You need not burden him with all, I suggest you take two or three. Those you do not need you send back."

Her Mader nodded to the girls as one held the veil, Tannah undid their handiwork and finger brushed Rowan's silky hair down her back, then placed the veil back on her head.

"Yes, that will do much better, a young bride must always have her hair down, not until you have children can you hide it under braids and a hood."

Her Mader had all the customary advice which she now bestowed upon Rowan, more to placate her GrandMader than to be maderly. Rowan wondered what she had done to earn her Mader's displeasure. She barely saw her these last five years. Even before she had her own place, her Mader was distant. Rowan could not remember ever being held or hugged by her Mader, there had always been a maderly servant or two who would soothe Rowan in her times of distress, never her Mader. She swore to herself when she had children, she would hold them always and be the direct opposite from what she lacked in her childhood.

"You must always obey your husband; he will know what is best for you and you will never say or do anything to embarrass him. This would reflect badly onto your Pader and ultimately, me. You need to always maintain dignity; you are a representative of the Royal House. Action of any kind, be it small and in your own home, is always under scrutiny and will be commented upon. You will bear him a son right away. He needs an heir, and your Pader will announce the heir to the Empire if 'tis a boy! You will keep his needs always. You have none."

Her Mader's speech broke her out of her musings, and she took a moment to process what the Empress had said.

Do I not already obey all the protocols? Do I not already know how to conduct myself? I am not stupid. I had this continually drummed into my head since I came into my own apartments. Errgg! She talks to me like I know nothing.

Here Rowan began to say something, but the look on her Mader's face stopped her. It was a look she had never seen before, and it gave her pause. She had a sneaking feeling her Mader was not telling her something.

She is hiding something from me. There is a hidden message there, but what?

The Empress motioned to have Rowan's GrandMader taken back to her Palace as her GrandMader was beginning to nod off. The Empress rose to her feet, all the while avoiding her Daders' eyes, and Rowan knew the audience was over. Rowan gave her the customary small bow, even though she was her Mader, she was first her Empress. Rowan was well disciplined with the protocols all nobility had to practice.

She knows something, of which she does not wish to tell, and if I am reading her correctly it does not sit well. What could be so horrible at such a glorious moment in my life. Does it mean she will miss me? I think not. It must be something else, yet I know not what. I just hope that the joining will take place. I do not think I can bear another year here.

The remainder of the month passed all too quickly with preparations for the joining. Rowan had no time to mull over the feeling something was not right. Only when she had a few spare moments to herself and her needlework she remembered the look on her Mader's face.

Very often she could read her Mader's face but that one time she could not.

CHAPTER 3

Solina

When the Advent of Fire

Would the voices ever shut up?

Solina thought to herself. The clamour inside her head was deafening. So many cries of pain, it more often than naught gave her a headache.

"Can you please be quieter? My head is splitting!"

"Aghhh! Pain! Free. Damned humans. Nooooo!"

She tried reasoning with them internally; however, some would not listen, just elevating their volume. Solina wished sometimes to be deaf or hit on the head, it was so painful.

They were the severest precisely before the festivals of Rites and Passage. The celebrations leading up to the Rites were a full weeklong. Among the city dwellers, there were many devotions in the Temples for each of the Gods, and the chosen initiate. The potential honorary Riders were given elixir to cull the weak from those who would rule.

Elixir of the Dragons. It was a special drink. None but the chosen could partake, none knew what it was. Only taken in the Rite. There were discussions among the girls, but Solina paid no attention, it was not a topic that interested her. She was sure it was a wine blend. There were many crops of grapes on the hillsides which yielded different vintages, the Pader would seasonally receive a few amphorae. She had snuck a look this time last year. Each year she had to endure the clamor inside her head, it would rise and rise, in volume until the night before, then silence. She felt a loss sometimes; she was so used to the constant hum of voices. When she did not hear them, she always had to ask them if they were still there.

The candidates for the Ritual were selected by the Rulers, which she had never watched just heard of. Listening in the streets, she placed the pieces together. Many times, she would sit and listen to the older sisters, some liked to gossip. They were outside and watched the processions up the mountain. Only a couple of them and the Pader witnessed the actual ceremony, not one would speak on it. Some of the candidates paid their way in, and others were just chosen out of the few houses which ruled the Islands. Only one out of twenty candidates would show an indication of potential, the rest would become sicker than ever, and often, they would die.

Someone could give me poison; it would be better than what I must endure day in day out.

Some days the voices would drive her mad and she wanted to wrench her hair out by the roots. Other days it was not so bad, and they left her alone. Sometimes she would sit and talk to all her voices all day and forget to eat when they were calmer.

Solina sat in the garden of the Church in the lower city trying to think of when she first heard her voices. Absently placing her single braid of bright red hair behind her back. In her garden, she would go without her cowl. In the heat of summer, the cowl was heavy and she hated the sweat it would cause. In her garden, she was mostly alone, Yona present when she was mobile.

Solina thought back to when she was a child… seven maybe eight years old. She was happily minding her own business, playing in the kitchen of the rectory behind the Church. Hands in dough, helping the sisters bake bread for the needy, when she had the biggest pain in her head. Voices! All at once! Clamoring at her! At each other! She grabbed at her head, flour flying everywhere, and then she blacked out.

When she came to, she was laying in a strange bed, hair wet, wearing a clean wool robe, and the sister Yona, oldest but no less wise, gazing down at her with a wet cloth in her hand. Yona started when Solina opened her eyes, Solina would find out later her eyes, hazel in colour transformed into opalescent gold orbs. This startled the old sister, having seen a lot of things, but this being a first. The eyes of the Riders only changed from the ritual itself. In adults.

"Hush, Lina. You fainted."

"Where…am I?"

"You are in my room; I carried you here."

"Oh. Ow, my head hurts."

"You fell and hit your head on the edge of the table. You will have a bruise for a while."

Only the Rulers of Pelin'Dun had opalescent eyes, men, and a few women of the ruling class, not anyone from the dregs of the lower streets. Solina was told by the Pader of the Church she was allowed to live by the graces of the Rulers, however she had to keep herself hidden by a robe and a veil to protect her life, when she went out in public. She could be shunned or worse, and Solina grew a backbone by the teasing and intimidation inside the nunnery where she grew up. Solina was brought to the orphanage as a baby, left on the back step of the Church during a rainstorm, crying wretchedly for an hour before someone heard the cries above the thunder.

The Church was her home, the members her family of sorts. She was at peace here; they catered to the less favorable. Not that there were any, most Islanders had a place, food, and a trade. Only the most infirm or aged would grace their door. Some of the baser needs would come by, and the odd Aramite or Layanese. Most foreigners graced the lower city markets, beyond the gates and other townships along the coastline.

Pelin'Dun was the string of Islands in the middle of the ocean separating the continent of the land of Aram in the west and the continent kingdom of Du'Lanay in the east. The Islands themselves were formed from active volcanoes but only the main Island was still smoking, the others lay dormant. A few sported lakes in their craters, but since there were no inhabitants in the water, they did not gain visitors. Over time, vegetation grew on the largest four. The Islands to the far North were ravaged by storms and the tidal ocean. Only seals and birds inhabited the barren shoals. Many little Islands speckled the ocean around the main ones, resembling grain thrown to chickens, some were inhabited, some were not.

The main Island was the Southern most one, it boasted the Capital on the eastern side of the smoking mountain and a few settlements dotted the Northern sides. The Islands travelling North were also dotted with inhabitants and smaller towns, but everyone did their trading at the marketplace below the lower city. There were Pelinese, Aramites and people from Du'Lanay, Lanayese, but by law, the peoples from the continents were not permitted to enter the other areas of the city without permission and most times, not at all. Oil and water do not mix very well, was what everyone said to that.

Not that the oil and water did not attempt to get stirred together. Over the last few centuries, there were ventures to gain a foothold on the Islands. Physically with war and several infiltrations by covert men. Negotiations by Ambassadors never amounted to much. The Rulers always came back with a reason or two why the other religion was not welcome. Once or twice war was brought to the Islands, but the Rulers worked some sort of magics, or negotiated peace, depending on the terms. It was a good hundred years since the last attempt by the Namanists and longer than this by Aram, they were warring with each other lately.

Yona left quickly and just as quickly returned. She murmured to Solina the Pader would be here shortly. Solina was still trying to sort through the voices, some were cries of pain and rage,

"Shut the blazes up!"

Some of the noise diminished. Yona smacked her in the face with her hand,

"'Tis not proper to tell an elder to shut up."

"I have voices in my head, many at once and it hurts! Very much!"

Solina could make out one of the voices which was coherent and asked what and who it was.

"We are the eldest of all, and we are imprisoned, chained, they drink our essence for the need of many, we are drained, unable to move, some of us will leave our spirit soon. You must set us free."

As she was listening to this voice above the others moaning in pain, she repeated the words. "Essence, spirit, free."

Speaking these words aloud, the Pader walked in and heard, he motioned to Yona to leave the room with him, and they hovered outside listening to Solina's ravings.

"Pader, her eyes have changed to that of a DragonRider, and she is certainly mad. Solina says she has voices in her head... Many... They will surely kill her if they find out."

They, referring to the Rulers of Pelin'Dun, an elitist group, calling themselves DragonRiders, even though Dragons were of legend and long gone. The last Dragon flew away when Noster, the last of the Riders, was brutally murdered by one of his own men. These were tales told, romantic stories. The lives of the Islanders were built on the belief system of the Vendar religion, a religion of which the foundation was love of all, man, plant, and animal. There were plenty of tapestries depicting Dragons, in the homes of the upper classes, but strangely enough, not written word.

"Well, she is but a child, if we can prove she is harmless, then maybe she will be safe. I will inform the Magistrates, they will wish to see her for themselves, as word will surely reach them, if we tell them or not."

"But what if they wish her dead?"

Yona was an advocate on her side; she cared for the girl ever since that stormy night.

"I am confident they will not, you will see, however, they will restrict her to be sure. We will contain her away from the markets and crowds, even our own people for a while until we are given instructions from the Magistrates. You stay here with her; I will send a message right away."

Walking down the stone steps to the rooms behind the great hall, he dispatched one of his interns to run a message to the Palace.

Yona returned to a drooling and spitting Solina as the girl tried to make sense of the many voices which were clamoring inside her head. Holding Solina in her arms she crooned softly to the muttering girl.

"Hush, Lina. It will be fine, just fine. Hush, there, there."

Solina sat in the gardens, reliving those memories, remembering her childhood, recalling those first years were the toughest. As years passed, the voices who spoke to her, would always get frenzied before the festival. In those first years, Yona would sequester her, as she would begin ranting and it was not a pretty sight. She would harm herself, as she did not know how to stop the torture in her head the voices were causing. One time, or was it twice, Yona had to tie her down on the bed, she was thrashing so hard and beating her head with her fists. It diminished every year, or was she simply better able to manage it, now? Gradually some would drop away, like petals of the rose like the one she was staring at, across from her on the pathway. Now, she could lay count to maybe a handful, she could identify each by the timber or resonance of their volume, and she recollected more of what happened those first few years.

She stayed with Yona for a fortnight in a room at the top of the only tower of the centuries old Church. The old woman meticulously catered to her in her delirium, in her absence Solina would gaze out of the solitary window. When she did, the voices would lessen to some degree. The open sky was mesmerizing and spoke to her. One defining moment, as she gazed outside at the slow drifting clouds, she imagined what it would feel like to fly. She was close to leaving the sill when Yona caught her robe holding her back, as she was chanting,

"I want to fly and be free."

This was the last day she was in the tower. After this episode, both were relocated to a room at the back of the rectory, opening directly into the gardens. She was required to wear a hood and netting. Yona explained, showing Solina her reflection in the Pader's mirror her eyes had changed. The golden hue amplified by an opalescent edge to the pupil. She would be shunned by her companions, ridiculed as fear of reprisal or worse would dictate their actions.

"'Tis for your protection, lass. You must not bring attention to yourself; you must be humble always. We do not question the why of something, our Gods choose us for doing their works. You would be shunned outside these walls, and even inside. Always walk a soft path."

"Why am I so different? Why me?"

"You are granted a gift, even if you do not think it as such. No other child has ever been given the eyes of a DragonRider. You may have a purpose in the great wheel of life. You will study, and become knowledgeable in our history, learn about the plants you tend, learn all you can, and someday your purpose may be revealed. Always be humble, the Gods do not like a proud person."

It was the day after she heard the voices, the Magistrates came to the rectory to see and give their judgement. She was bathed and dressed in a clean dark green robe, her red hair brushed and braided back off her face. Being a ward of the Church, no adornments were permitted, and she went barefoot, the robe's cowl over her head and in front of her face, with her head bowed. No one could see it was her as she walked through the vestibule into the antechamber where the six Riders were seated awaiting her arrival.

She went in muttering under her breath, her voices were still murmuring to her. Solina was trying to sift through them and make sense of their ramblings. She must have passed some sort of test; the people sitting asked her questions and she answered with incoherent responses. One woman approached her, lifted her head by the chin, and peered at her face closely. She remembered seeing moisture begin in the older woman's eyes. The older woman dropped her hand from Solina's face. Solina could not recall the questions, they were fired at her so quickly. After some deliberation, they dismissed her out of hand, telling Pader and Yona she could live as long as she was chaperoned out on the streets and kept sequestered on the Church grounds.

Thus, her childhood was regulated to the Church and the gardens. She sometimes would accompany Yona to assist with purchases in the market, but only if she behaved and was covered up. Solina learned the hard way to listen as one day she wandered off into the market and was punished for two seasons. After that, Solina stuck to Yona like glue in the market when her sentence was rescinded.

She thought more about it, as the years passed and she grew, the voices dropped off. It was almost one voice a year. She would converse with them, sometimes aloud in the beginning, but when she began her womanly courses, she discovered she could converse to them in her thoughts and one or two would answer her. Yona became concerned when she observed Solina sitting for hours staring blankly. One time she sat for so long she wet herself. Luckily, it was a garden bench outside, 'By the Pader!' Did she get a beating for this!

Other things began to happen. Occurrences she did not tell Yona. As time progressed Yona began to slow down and Solina became her constant companion. Solina would assist her with all her daily duties. Help her walk and carry things for her.

One day a year prior, as she was labouring in her garden, she knew the time of the Rituals for the Rites of Passage was nigh. The volume of the voices amplified in scale and continuity. Solina tried to remain calm and not have a seizure. She was in her garden, as she always was, when the cries of pain in her head burst out.

"Ahhhh,"

She dropped to her knees in the sand. Solina grabbed a handful in each hand in a struggle to remain calm. She closed her fists in agony and waited for the fit to pass. It was with great surprise when she opened her fists to see a sparkling lump in each. She clung to the sand so hard she created an odd shaped yellowish diamond in each hand. She dropped them as if they were scorching hot but picked them up just as quickly before anyone could possibly see. Wandering over to the well in the corner, dropping them into the water, Solina knew she could not explain what happened anymore than she could explain where they came from.

Another time, further back in her memories, she found she could think objects to move through the air. Occasionally she would play pranks on some of the girls. Especially the ones who would pick on her. As she did this, it would tone down, or muffle the voices, so she could function. It was satisfying in a sense, but she did not attempt many as it left her tired for a few days.

Solina could also make small little tornadoes in the air with the sand. In the fall when leaves fell, and they lay dry on the ground she would have them turn in the air. She felt pleased with her ability to make cute little winds but soon became bored with this talent. Solina worked her garden, growing what they needed to eat and harvesting herbs for the healer women in the market. For her it was not a chore, as some of the other girls would complain, Solina enjoyed every moment spent outside, she found solace in the methodical tending.

Solina would not know until much later, her practicing magic was draining the other end of the voices, it was part of the cause of some disappearing forever. For now, she gloried in her newfound gift. She did not extend herself often, it was a natural occurrence which she accepted as it was.

She was careful not to bring attention to herself, blending into the crowd, covered from head to toe, when she was in public. A heavy veil covered her eyes, Yona was not satisfied until she could not see Solina's eyes, then she let the girl go on her own. This was the garb for women of Aram to be wearing; no one took any notice. She loved to roam the markets, outside of the lower city. The peoples were so diverse, she would see all sorts of goods. One time, she bought a book stand for Yona, made of black Ravenwood, delicately hand carved. It took almost all her savings, but the look on Yona's face was well worth it for Solina.

She learned fast at everything she placed her mind to task. Attended classes to learn language, reading and writing, she found she excelled. So, Yona and other sisters taught her other languages, Lanayese, and the Aramese. Solina would absorb the content of each book given to her. She learned about the countries which flanked their Islands to either side and read about their topography. She loved to look at maps, at least the few the Church had. She learned about their seasons, especially about the phenomenon of snow! Having never seen it herself, the Islands were too warm for such weather.

The continent of Aram was barren except the Southern most part, and even then, just the river valleys were inhabited, the land was mostly sand. The North half of Aram was active and dormant volcanos, and a few quarries for marbles and granites close to the shores. No maps showed anything in the center of the land, it had never been traversed, from what she could see of the maps they had.

She learned the history of the Islands, the six rulers, honorific title of Dragon Riders. Throughout the centuries, their skills which saw lies and ruled by the laws they gave. The Vendar religion was still actively worshipped, the six Gods had effigies and statues throughout the city and the other Islands. Everyone lived in harmony, as it was taught as their main course of life.

The Islands had shipbuilders, and salt flats. These two trades alone were the backbone of their economy. Solina learned this by studying and by the evidence presented in the markets. Black salt was on the Island North of the capital, and the Northern most Island was where the plants for production of the sails, and ropes were grown. Each township had a use, and it was brought together in the shipyards in the North of Peli.

Solina absorbed books on horticulture. She loved new species of plants and their properties. She would roam the markets when she was allowed out by herself. Lately Yona was bedridden, her mobility ebbing and flowing with the seasons. Solina would go to Yona's favorite vendors gathering whatever her mentor wanted. Once it was for a portion of lace, delicate work by a woman whose Mader was an Aramite, but Pader was an Islander. The lacemaker and Yona had a special friendship, and almost always there was a little extra something in the parcel.

Solina sold her own harvests in the markets. She grew some flowers which needed meticulous care, and dried them carefully, for they were used to dye fabrics of silk, linens and wool, a delicious colour of orange. More vibrant than the fruit harvested from the tree. She made an exceptionally good profit off this one plant alone. She created tonics and teas, lotions and perfumes, and a couple of other plants she grew for their dye properties. Other girls would take care of other gardens the Church had in their possession. Solina had the rear of the Church and rectory. Other gardens to the side were used mostly for vegetables. Solina's garden was primarily herbs and flowers. Oft-times, they would ask if they could utilize her supply, and over time, as the demand for such dictated, she would grow more volume. Soon she had her time taken up by just her gardens and the time would fly by, she was so occupied.

She also learned politics and law, math and even some ancient tomes written by unknown authors. She read those in secret. She found a secret room, by the dust layered inside it was vacant for some time. As she read and replaced each book or scroll, she would order the dust back to cover her tracks and the disturbance she created. She knew these to be property from a past leader of the Church.

The current Pader was not concerned overly much with past events. He catered to the needy and was always off, trying to wedge his way into one of the Halls up on the hill. He would come back sometimes with funds to put towards one or two of their charities. She would listen to conversations, not intentionally, but some of the sisters liked to gossip about the happenings of everyone else.

Solina was sitting in her garden chatting in her head to one of her voices when a conversation on the other side of the stone wall separating her section from the side garden caught her attention. The voices were female, and they were trying hard to whisper, which may have been how it caught her ears.

"Did you see what the Pader came back with, Roma?"

"No, I was in the kitchens. What was it since you are busting at the seams to tell?"

"He walked in with a Dragon effigy; you know the one which now sits on the floor by the altar? The one in gold leaf. He was sweating, trying to stay upright from carrying it."

"Why do you even bother? You are so nosy, and what good can come of it? Sua, it can bring you no peace, why do the Pader's doings interest you so?"

"I have nothing else to occupy myself with, I have been here the longest, next to Yona and Aister, and I have seen a lot. I was even here before the Pader came. He always seems to bring something back before the Rituals. Have you ever wondered why?"

"No, I have not, however, I am sure you have a thought in your head and are about to enlighten me as to what that is."

Solina could hear the sarcasm in Roma's voice, even in the whisper.

"I think Pader has a connection to one of the Magistrates. He is either getting payment or something else in return for keeping silent."

Here Solina heard a loud inhale.

"What are you saying? The Pader is holding information for money? Over someone's head? 'Tis dangerous thoughts to be saying aloud, especially if not true. You could get expelled, or worse, you could disappear. You know the Rulers do not like dissention, if they were to hear your ideas…"

"'Tis why I am telling you, out here in secret. If I was to disappear, then this would live on. But here is where it gets interesting, I have noticed it has only been since the finding of Solina on the doorstep, these occurrences have been happening."

Here was another loud intake of breath, and Solina made sure she did not move, or make any noise to give herself away.

"The Pader knows something or is getting paid by someone to keep Solina here. 'Tis only obvious! I mean, look at her eyes. She is being hidden for a reason. She is not one of us. I think…"

"I think… you should not think. Sua, you will get yourself in trouble for sure! Who really cares why Solina is here? She is a good child, respectful and does what is required of her. She takes care of Yona, saving us from catering to her. I would wish Solina takes care of me when 'tis time. You will hear nothing more on the matter from me. Oh look, here comes Vida, shush no more on this, I will certainly keep my own council on the matter… Oh, good evening, Vida… Yes, we can, we were just admiring the number of shoots coming up for the blue beans, we should be getting a huge harvest this year, if we can keep the Caro bugs away. We should try more…"

The conversation left, and Solina knew the sisters were most likely walking inside the rectory. Interesting, she was a topic for conversation. These older sisters were not unkind to her, Roma was nicer, but Solina had no quarrel with any of the older sisters. If anything, it was some of the newer girls and ones her age who seemed to dislike her. She found keeping to herself in the gardens and tending to her plants much more rewarding as the other girls would leave her alone more often than naught.

"Solina, 'tis a little late, Yona sent me to fetch you to evening prayers. Are you fine?"

"Yes, why do you ask?"

"Well, I have watched you while I walked towards you. You have been standing in front of that stem for a few minutes. You have trimmed it down a fair bit. You seem… lost in thought."

"No more than I usually am. I am just wondering about this world we live in."

"Oh, this seems a bit of a heavy subject. What brought this on?"

"Not sure, Sheyna. I am feeling a bit… lonely, I guess."

"Well, I am here. Are we not friends?"

"Yes. I did not mean it in that sense, my voices are quiet, as of late. I guess I miss them when they are not here, yet they drive me mad when they are. I do not know…"

Solina confided in Sheyna about her voices in the past year. The two women became close, as much as the older sisters would let them.

"Do you think they are tied into the Rituals up on the hill?"

"Oh, I know they are, every year, I hear them, clamouring and yelling in my head, then silence. I do not know what is worse... The noise or the silence. Both hurt."

"I am sorry you are hurting. I wish I could help you."

Solina stood up from her pruning and looked at her friend.

"You do, just by being here. I feel like this ritual is going to be different. I have a feeling, I cannot shake."

"Well, if we hurry, we can sneak into prayers, and you can shake all you want in the back row. We should go. If we are not there, you know Dejan will tattle."

"You are right. I am glad you are watching out for me."

"'Tis what friends are for Lina. I am with you."

The women hurried off into the back of the rectory, Solina dropping her shears by the archway on a wooden crate, she would return after prayers. These flowers needed to be pruned in the coolness of the night air. The sense of solitude carried with her through prayers and back into the garden while she trimmed and pruned plants. She let her mind drift on the quiet currents of the late evening.

She often wondered why her parents did not want her and was left as a baby. Yona tried several times to suggest her parents may have died. Being here was an option, better than being raised in other areas, like the houses of ill repute, or working in the lower markets. While Peli was not a poor Island, there were still areas and people who catered to baser needs. Yona said not all people could choose where spirit took them, but they could choose where they took themselves.

"We are given a choice, stay where we are in life, or strive to make a better one. We are all given the same tools, hands, and feet to be used in the worship of the Gods, and a mind, to wield for good or for evil. It is up to the user, what he or she does. We have given you the means to better yourself, taught you to read and write, in our language and others. You take this and learn what you can and then apply it for good or for not good. It is always your choice. I feel you will use your talents for good; nothing comes of doing evil. Evil has a way of making it around the five-pointed circle, passing judgement through the six Gods, and coming back to harm the doer. Make sure you think about what ramifications your deeds and words will do before you make the choice to use them."

Solina always listened to Yona.

"I will remain here with you, Yona. Tending my flowers and herbs. Weaving you a crown of flowers."

"I thank you, Lina. You are a good girl. But you may have another path to follow. The Universe and Vendar may have you tending other flowers."

"What are you talking about? Another path? I am quite content here with you."

"I am happy here with you also, but I will not always be here. I can see the twilight of my life approaching. Nay, lass. Do not mourn me yet. It will come. My spirit is tired and I look forward to being reborn again. We have but a moment on this earth, in one life. Then we do it all again. We can only do great deeds while we can. To be reborn into a stronger spirit. That is what makes us who we are."

"And who am I?"

"Well, right now you are a good lass who wishes to get her mentor her supper."

"Oh, I am sorry, Yona. I will fetch it right away. Do you want gravy on your mash? I can smell the roast bird from here."

"Of course I do, you know how I like it."

"Yes. A volcano it is! I will be right back."

More often as the older woman was losing her mobility, Yona's lessons were making more sense to her now. She never listened to Yona when she was younger. It was kind of boring until she began her learning and opened a whole new world to her. She remembered the secret room and the books she would borrow. It took her a couple of years, but she read all the books in this room, and it made her wish to consume more.

These books were most informative and interesting. They were records of when lands were ruled by Riders and their Dragons! As she read these, she felt the presence of one or maybe two of her voices and she found comfort in it. They seemed to be learning with her, and she felt a nostalgic feeling emanating from the strongest one.

How to dress a deer, elk, or other four-legged creature…hmmmm…have the Dragon lift…this is interesting… the Dragon lifts the creature to facilitate drainage. I know nothing of this! Hmmmm, once blood has been collected… what did they do with the blood? Oh, here… they used it for…oh, let the Dragons drink it…well, this makes sense. This one is on cutting it up. Well, this tome is on dressing and cutting and various recipes.

This other one is on oils. When to oil? What are they oiling? When the youngling is molting? Growth cycles. Various growth cycles? As in children? When wing membranes begin to grow, one must oil constantly as to help wings to stretch… what fowl needs to be oiled? This is confusing…

She drew comfort from her strongest voice. She would discuss her learnings with it, and as she could converse in her head, Solina no longer drew glances from the other girls in the nunnery where she was constantly minding Yona. Her voices would sometimes correct points she would read. Another book was poetry. She loved reading the flowing words, and realised it was a sad love story.

"His eyes were brighter than the seas, they mesmerized and soothed me…"

"Where did you hear this?"

"Oh, I read a passage from… a vender had an old book, of poetry in the markets. I only read a few lines. He was sure I would purchase it."

"Oh. 'Tis a passage from the last known poem from the writer Lyana. I used to have a copy when I was younger, I am not sure what I did with it."

"Who is this, Lyana? Is she still alive?"

"Oh no, lass. Her life story was very tragic. She lived a few hundred years ago. At the height of Naman. She was brutally murdered by Naman as an example to all."

"Oh? This sounds sad and interesting. How about I get you a tea and I will be right back. Will you tell me this tragic story."

"Yes, I certainly will. I would like a drop of honey; I know you will want some tea as well. If there is any fresh baking…"

Solina laughed, there was always some fresh baking, it continued all day. She returned ten minutes later to Yona's bedchamber and set the tray beside the bed and served her mentor, a small cup of tea and a slice of freshly baked tart. Yona smiled at her charge.

"Have a seat, get yourself comfortable. This is a sad story but also uplifting."

"How can it be sad and happy?"

"Lyana was an example to all women of what can be done in the face of adversity. She did not let the rule of men, rule her, but let me start from the beginning.

"Lyana was born several hundred years ago, in the city of Kara, over on the shores of Southern Du'Lanay. You know by looking at maps where it is?"

"Yes. 'Tis the second largest city in the Southern half of the continent."

"Well, then. She was born into one of the ruling families and educated. Back then women of noble houses were educated and assisted their husbands when needed. A dutiful woman could keep books for her husband, read, and write. After her death, was when more laws were created. They would no longer be taught. They followed Aram's ideals, to the letter."

Here Yona giggled. She was finding herself humorous, and she took a bite, chewed then sipped her tea.

"She was a beautiful woman, and as she grew into her beauty, she had many suitors. However, she was very outspoken and turned many away with her boldness, and truthfulness."

"How is this daunting? Oh right, this is Du'Lanay."

"She was joined to another, an older man, it was a political joining, to cement two leading families together. The reigning ruler was trying to overthrow the Namarch. Much like the marriage due to take place now."

"How do you know all this?"

"We have our ways. This may come to be a repeat of history. The Princess Rowan is still quite young, and the man she is set to marry…"

"Do not all political matches end in tragedy?"

"Not all. But I digress. Lyana was beautiful. She had many suitors before her joining and after. She was invited to every dinner, every joining and birth. She had a way about her that had all loving her. Her husband became over time, very jealous. He petitioned the Halls for new laws, much against women. They took his petitions but did not implement any. Not until tragedy struck."

"She took a lover?"

"Not quite. She tried many times to fend other men off. She succeeded until one day her husband came to her and asked her to do one thing for him. She was to bed the Namarch. She refused. You see, she had fallen in love with the younger brother of another friend of the family, but not just any friend, the younger brother of the Emperor. He was a man of great learning. This is the muse for most of her writings and poems. She fell hard and ran away to get away from her husband, but also to meet him in secret. But that is later."

"Why would her husband ask her to have relations with the Namarch? Are they not men who give up relations with women? For their God?"

"Yes. They do. Narman's rule started this 'solitary' aspect of 'men of God.' She was to bed him, hopefully get herself with child so they could diminish his standing and stage a 'coup.' She refused to be a tool, and her husband beat her very badly. Had she said yes, it would have upset the rule of Naman. She recovered in the country; her husband sent her away. Which perhaps he should not have done."

"Let me guess, she ran away. Like you said."

"No, she was hidden, but not at his estate. The young man heard of the plot, from his brother and took him several years to find her. Her husband had hidden her well. He found her and they spent an idyllic summer together. She wrote most of her works from that summer alone. When he was found out, the Emperor was incensed."

"Why? Was she not allowed to have a lover, after all, she was married."

"Women did have affairs, but most were secrets. If found out, they could be whipped, beaten, and sometimes killed without repercussions. Lyana learned the way of a warrior when she was with her minders. She learned from them, the Vendar way, and she embraced it. Her writings reflect on this. You can see the shift if one were to have the whole collection. She started out with a view, the one she was born with, and when she was beaten, something inside her snapped."

"She learned how to fight?"

"Why yes. She became a fierce fighter."

"Did her husband not know?"

"Well, she ran away from her prison and hid from her family. Yet her beauty soon gave her away, she tried so hard to hide. It was many years before her lover found her. Once he did, another gave them away. She was good with a bow and even better with a sword. She swore she would not return. Her husband could fight her on the field. One account says she fought with Aram. Another says she killed her husband in his sleep."

"What about her lover? The brother of the Emperor?"

"He was secreted away by treachery. He left his wife for Lyana, and he was told to return. It was his son who became Emperor after his Uncle. He refused, was kidnapped, and returned to his wife. One account said his wife poisoned him, or knifed him, but he was said to have jumped off the newly built tower, the highest one of the Palace."

"That sounds tragic. What about Lyana?"

"She had a child, her lover and she had been joined, in secret. She bore the child and sent it off in secret. Our current ruler just found this out, from the Amman of Lanthia. They had an exchange of letters. She gave the Amman something, and he gave her this news. He likes his history, and some of Lyana's story may have taken place in Lanthia."

"How do you know this?"

"Pader gave us this piece of information. He was quite enthralled. Everyone has read Lyana's works. She was very forward-thinking for her background. You remember she became a Vendar. The Supreme Magistrate may have the collection as a whole. Lyana became Vendar, but when she heard the news her love was dead, she vowed to not back down to the Empire. She is said to have joined with Aram after this. Aram was trying to gain lands on Du'Lanay, for quite some time. They were smart to hire natives to the land. Can you get me some more tea, dear?"

"Yes, I can. I will be right back."

Solina left returning with another helping of tart, and more hot tea. Yona smiled up at her minder. Yona looked vibrant with her story, but Solina saw a tiredness in her eyes.

"Thank you, Lina. You are enjoying this tale?

"Oh, Yes! this is history, unlike I have ever heard. She seems fierce, and independent."

"Yes, but this is what spurred Naman to lay down the laws towards women. You remember I told you of the jealous husband?"

"Yes. Did she not kill him?"

"Yes. She did. On the field, she cleaved him with the sword. He was to have said to be weeping like a babe. Of course, Naman have another version, I am sure."

"So, he died?"

"Yes, he did. However, his petitions did not."

"So, Lyana bore a child, sent it away, her lover was spirited back to his wife, was killed, or killed himself. She killed her husband in battle, what happened to her?"

"She was wounded. It became infected and Aram left her, to die. The Emperors army found her, in the meantime, the old Namarch had passed, another took his place. A younger and smarter man…very fervent. He made a pact with the Emperor since they had common enemies. Such as Aram. The Emperor brought Lyana back to Merida, and to the dungeons. They brought her back to health just to torture her and subsequently kill her."

"Let me guess, publicly."

"Oh, did they ever. As they did so, all the petitions her husband had asked for were granted. Posthumously."

"So, women were treated somewhat better before then?"

"They had more rights, it was less… rigorous. The laws when they happened, happened overnight. Many women were burned at the stake. The town she had last been housed in, the one where she trained, was 'cleansed' by the Namanists. They had a revival of their ways. So many deaths."

"So how is this uplifting? I see it as it is, a tragedy."

"Well. Look at it from a Vendar point of view. She loved; it was her heart. Her spirit had always been Vendar. Through all her life, short as it was, she never swayed. It just shows the conviction of one woman and her drive to love and be loved. She did not let her husband rule her. She did not let the Namans rule her. She learned to fend for herself. It shows by the reaction of Naman how much they feared her."

"What of her child? What happened to it?"

"Well… not that we can confirm it, but the Amman may have dug up some genealogy of his own. He has alluded to the ruling house of the Northern reaches to be a descendant of hers. But this is not confirmed. One would have to have access to the archives of the ruling houses."

"Where? Oh, most likely on Du'Lanay, am I right?"

"The Supreme Magistrate may have some tomes. If ever you have access, you would have to ask her."

"I do not see how I could ever…"

"Dear child. Do not discount the future. The Universe may place you on your path. You are the first child with Dragon eyes. Your path has not happened yet. I foresee wonderful things for you. You must believe in yourself."

"Thank you for your belief. I am very intrigued now by this tale. It is very romantic but tragic. It is sad Naman and Aram do not treat women very well."

"Yes, but we look at it differently. Du'Lanay and Aram have beaten down women, yet we have not. We have Vendar, our Gods who we serve. We have love in our hearts and spirits. They supress it. Why?"

"I do not know, why?"

"Think about it Lina. The tale of Lyana. She lived not so long ago. She represented an independent woman. They feared her."

"How? They ended up killing her."

"They made her an example. Publicly. She was a strong willed, outspoken woman who did not bend or break. One account of her execution had her spitting in the face of Naman. Another said she recounted the five sermons of Vendar. She did not fear her death. She was a figure they could not break, even as they broke her body. She was filled with love, the spirit of Vendar was with her until the end."

"Then it is not so much a tragedy than a martyr."

"The Amman has said in his missive, when she died, the witnesses saw her spirit rise. No, one unless worthy has their spirit rise from their body. Many saw it. Several wrote about it, but Naman tracked them down and destroyed all the accounts they could find. The Amman found or acquired his copy, somehow. It was a lesser poet. He was later killed and his works were destroyed also. Naman has tried and succeeded in destroying all who would not reflect their views."

"So, Naman fears women?"

"It historically looks this way. But perhaps, it is time for change."

"Change cannot happen overnight."

"Mayhap it can, but I am now tired and would like to fall asleep. Would you sing one of your many songs for me?"

"Yes, I can. It is only a fair exchange, for the wonderful tale you told me. I thank you for enlightening me. It is something to ponder over."

"Yes, in the telling of history, is a lesson of life."

Solina spent the next ten minutes singing softly to her mentor, one of the many songs sung in the Temples. When worship was convened, the songs of praise filled the many halls, it filled Solina with a sense of fulfillment. She loved to sing and had quite a strong voice, but she sang softly for the older woman, who fell asleep quickly.

Solina rose quietly and left with the tray of cups in her hands.

Then the moment she had been dreading finally arrived. Yona was bedridden for a couple of months and her health declined rapidly. One stormy night, the thunder, lightening, and rain had Yona saying it was not unlike the day they found Solina. She was murmuring in and out of consciousness and as Solina catered to her, she beckoned the young woman closer.

"I remember the day we found you on the step. You were so mad, screaming at the rain drenching you, I feared you would be taken ill by the amount of water, you were soaked through and through. But you prevailed. You are such a sweet child. Always helping, and I love you like you were mine."

"And I love you, like you were a Mader. You have always been good to me."

"Do not let them tell you different."

"Tell me what? What do you mean?"

"Do not let them…"

"Do not let them, what, Yona? You are not making sense."

"Do not let anyone know what you can do, as they will use you to their own gain. Do not think I have not seen you, but you must be careful, as others may have also seen, and you may not be safe. Do the Rites of Passage. I am sure you will be called. This will determine your path. Free your voices, this is your destiny, I know what you are… You are a DragonRider!"

"A what? You are now definitely not making sense. Yona? Yona? Please answer me, do not go! Yona!"

At that, Yona lay back down on the bed, it sapped the last of her strength. She quietly passed away at the age of 101 years. Solina lay the older woman's hands on her lap and placed them together, tears streaming down the young woman's face. Solina cried hard, all her emotions came up and let themselves known. Yona was the only Mader she had known, and the Church the only home she knew for the last eighteen years.

"Oh, Yona! I will miss you. Dear heart, may your spirit rise and be reborn. May you be Blessed."

Yona's last words had her puzzled. The Riders had to partake of the Ritual to become a Ruler. She had not, yet Yona may have seen her doing some of her things. Solina was sure she was alone. Now her mind was travelling fast on what Yona said. How could she be a DragonRider if she had not had the elixir? Yet, somehow, she had strange talents. Ones she hid from her companions, and she had her voices. What did this make her?

How can I be a DragonRider? There are no Dragons. Yet there was, in the ancient books, it could not be false information. Where did they go? They are not present in our teachings now…

Their religion was rooted in Dragon lore, it was based on the affinity of the six Gods, a life etched in harmony with each other and even forgiveness for those of different religions. The Church and grounds she grew up in was dedicated to the Goddess Viana, the Aunt deity, grounded in nature and agriculture, wine and the harvest. Each Temple or place of worship had robes for their acolytes, based on the God it was dedicated to in corresponding colours. Viana was green.

When I first heard my voices, they told me they were in prison. Prison where? Over the years they have not repeated themselves but seem to be waiting for something. What if they are Dragons? Am I to set them free? Should I be looking at the statues? What if those are the Dragons? Maybe some strange magic changed them to stone. Hmmmm, I must begin looking. This is a definite mystery to unravel.

Pelin'Dun had Churches for all the Gods, the Temple on the mountain was devoted to the Pader of all, Vendar. Their robes were white. The God of governing law, order and justice, wisdom and honour, and the measure of time. He ruled the heavens, and the bodies in it, the sun, and stars. The moon belonged to Ilyan, the sister Goddess. Many times, over the years the members of all Churches would gather during solstice and other religious observations, and Solina had traveled to the other Churches, and marvelled at the architecture of the structures that housed the effigies of the six Gods which were the basis of their beliefs. One thing Solina observed over the years was the common denominator of a Dragon statue in each worship hall.

I should make plans, then. I will find an excuse to visit every one of the Temples. I will investigate these stone statues. The detail is exquisite. This must be what they are. How could it not? But how can I, change them back? Free them from their prison. I will have to ask the Gods for help. Hmmm.

The Dragons of old were monumental, the largess of the marble statue in the Hall of the Mader Iris was floor to ceiling! It was so wonderous, Solina had stood for a half span of the sundial staring at it. She felt recognition, and peace when she looked at it.

How was it only two seasons ago I saw this for the first time? I should find reasons to travel around the city again. Maybe I could take around my harvested herbs and dried flowers. I am sure several of the elder sisters would like to have some of my Joy Root tea. I would like to see that glorious statue again. It gave me a sense of purpose, and calm when I gazed upon it. I wonder how they lived. Why do we not have them anymore? Why are there no teachings on the Dragons? Just our Gods. Our way of life. Why would our Rulers be given the title of DragonRider if there is no evidence of Dragons? Where did they go? Especially the Great One. It was told he flew away. Away to where?

Thinking about the Dragons had her drying her tears, her voices were strangely silent for once. It must be time for the Rituals again. She wondered if there was some correlation between her voices and the Dragons of old, but there were no Dragons. She felt so confused sometimes. They clamored insistently then nothing. Was she losing her mind?

Am I cursed?

CHAPTER 4

Atin

Sweeps Across the Land

I really don't like people,
Atin reflected to herself as she wandered through the marketplace on the main
Island of Pelin'Dun. She tucked an errant piece of blonde hair under her hat. The
heat of the sun was directly overhead, making her sweat uncontrollably.

*It's too busy here, I could never get used to this craziness. It's too hectic, way
too many bodies, and the smell! This summer has been so hot. I want to go back
and go pearling, least I can stay cool in the warm water. Ugh.*

She lived on one of the many Islands with her family. It was North of the
Island she was now on. The famed Riders ruled them. Not that she had ever seen
any in the lower markets, one had to go to them in their Hall of Laws or the
Palace, high on the hill. One could only see the Palace, the Halls, and the Temple
of the Pader, when they were sailing in. There were dark lines dissecting the
mountain, which looked to be dark scrub brush.

In the lower city, the view was much different. A multitude of wooden structures, mainly the houses, markets and piers which contained the mixed races of
all the nations. It was a mixing pot of poor and rich. The rich only coming out of
the upper city to buy and trade. The lower city walls were tall, thick, dark stone,
and the upper city was hidden from view from the piers and marketplace. They
had been standing forever.

"Get your habberfish and eels here!"

"Silk from Aram, linen from Du'Lanay!"

She imagined the market she was wandering through was busier than the small
fish trying to escape the maw of a whale. The smell! Rotten fish, the smell of
sweaty unwashed people, and another odor, she could not put a name to, she really
did not care to know. The market was just above the docks, and below the lower
city gates. It was well built, and clean except for the smells, but one could only
do so much. Canvas sails covered the walkway to help cut the heat of the sun, but
it also caused the heat to be trapped.

*Ugh, the smell of sweaty men. My nose is assaulted. Even the smell of fish,
added to this. I should just go to the herbalist and stay there. I do not mind the
smells of herbs and tonics.*

Further North of the lower market were the shipyards, and it stretched into the
next township. The coastline of the main Island was covered with housing,

resembling seaweed brought in by winter storms. She had only sailed around the Island once with her brothers. The other side of the Island was a sharp contrast. The smoking mountain fell straight into the seas on the South side of the Island. There was no area habitable, it was sheer rock. The Palace grounds were the whole east end, and it was patrolled and kept by guards. Zohan pointed out all to her.

"This is easily defensible, except for that one spot, it has been the place for dares among men."

Atin looked puzzled, and Zohan laughed at her expression.

"Many men have tried to scale the smaller peak, right there. However, one has to time it exactly right. There are guards patrolling constantly now. This side of the Island is all Palace grounds."

"There is nothing here, I just see trees. What's the point? If you are not growing a crop. It looks like wild vegetation."

"The enemy could land here. 'Tis lower on the other side… here, the enemy could land, climb up, and sneak in the back door, so to speak. Many have tried. The Rulers have a small cohort here all the time."

"Oh, that makes sense. How do you know all this."

"Well, let me say… some of us tried…"

"You did not?"

"This is between you and I, Atin…"

"Oh, no worries, Zoh…I will keep your secret… for a price."

Atin remembered their conversation led into a tickling contest which she had won. She smiled in the remembrance, walking through the markets, wondering when they could leave. She could not wait for her Da's business to be finished. Then she could go home! Back to exploring the deep, colourful reefs where she felt most at ease. Atin felt the press of people on her spirit. She enjoyed more the company of her family and the solitude of the beaches at their home.

I hope Da and Zohan finish soon, I feel agitated. It seems crowded today. Too many people for me. and I can see dark clouds in the distance. Hope we get a storm. I love storms.

Storms made Atin feel at peace. It was irony the stronger the storm, the more she relaxed. Summer storms did not last as long as winter ones. Prevailing winds would drive them in and out just as fast. Some winter storms lasted days. She loved to sit in them, feeling the energy of the lightning and thunder when she could. Her Mader did not like them and often bade Atin to not cause her worry. Atin would listen to her Mader, she was more short-tempered of late.

All races of peoples gathered on the main island of Peli, every summer equinox, to trade, drink, fight, get married, to talk about rumours about the Rulers and their families, and any other gossip. And of course, the war. As long as she could remember, there was always talk of the war. Far off in Du'Lanay, of interest to those who wanted to know. She had never been anywhere but her home. Looking around she began to notice the people. She saw Aramites, the women covered up with long robes, with only their eyes visible, and Lanayese, these people were noticeable, by their arrogance, regardless of their hair colouring or gender.

At least the war has nothing to do with me. I just gather pearls for Pader to sell to acquire nets and supplies we need to live by. I wish they were done; I really wish to leave.

Atin strode down to the end of the market, adjusting the Strawweed hat on her damp blonde head. Her Pader and older brother were by the piers, busy bartering with a colourfully clad stranger, probably from Aram, they liked colour! While her Pader and brother were wearing simple tunics and leggings, the stranger had an array of dress, a robe over his tunic which was longer, one could just barely see the leggings underneath. The robe was a beautiful colour of blue, darker than the depths to which she would sometimes dive. His headdress was a lighter shade and she wondered at the colours.

Then she took another look, something caught her interest.

How can he be cool in so many layers of clothing? I am sweating in this heat, and I am in simple tunic and leggings. He better offer a decent price for that one. Da better not take less than double the value of those smaller ones. I am thinking the Aramite knows its value.

The stranger had a focused gaze on the largest pink pearl. It was the largest she had ever found. He was trying to barter the price down with his gestures and had sufficient speech to know his money. Finally, Atin's Pader threw his arms in the air and agreed to the price the strange man was repeatedly insisting was all he would pay.

As she sat down on a piling behind her Pader and brother, she happened to glance at the man, and he looked at her briefly. Their eyes connected for an instant, and Atin felt a stillness of time. She could feel nervous energy, and something else emanating from the stranger. She focused her eyes on the Aramite.

What the...? What is this? Am I seeing things now?

She was always nervous around people she did not know. Briefly the air around him began to change colour and she blinked her blue eyes shut a couple times to clear her vision. It seemed to her the moment their eyes met, she felt a strong connection to this man from another land.

You are interesting. To be sure. Oh yah, do not think I cannot see your bartering. Oh, you know, I know. Just you wait. Next time, I know the value of what I find. I will make you pay their value, dear sir. Just you wait.

She was intrigued, attracted by him and what she saw, she saw he recognized his efforts to barter down the price was found out. He seemed to read her thoughts, or perhaps he was good at reading faces. Hers was an open book at the moment. Regarding the pearls, she knew next time, she would take matters into her own hands, this was her hard work being purchased.

She began to speak to her Pader as the two of them broke eye contact, but her Pader was busy cursing the stranger as he strode off. She had another look at the Aramite, but he ducked away and she caught a glimpse of his blue attire before he was lost in the crowd. When she looked back, her Da and her brother Zohan were already packing up the remainder of their goods into the boat behind her. She helped them, and they set off for the half day of sailing to their Island home off in the distance.

After an hour of brisk sailing, Atin ventured the question to her Pader.

"Why are you angry? Was the price not good enough for the pearl?"

She tried not to be so direct, but at this point her curiosity became too much. Her Pader still looked angry, his silence at the tiller of the boat was absolute, so Zohan filled her in,

"Da's not upset over the pearl, Atin. Although the Aramite was not willing to budge, Da just gave in, cause he's more upset over something else. The Emperor in the East lands want sons, and taxes, not necessarily in this order. To keep the Empire from invading us, Pelin'Dun sends sons and money. So, I and my brothers are to be sent off, in the next season, which means less income from our catches."

She tried to understand this, as most of the family income came from the pearls, she, and her siblings, mostly her, would risk the depths for. Not the fish catches. Most of what they caught was preserved for their own use. The pink pearl the stranger was haggling for, was the largest anyone had seen, in a long time. She hoped her Da had gotten a decent sum for it.

"Why do we have to send our men? We are not fighting either one."

"'Tis what is decreed by the Rulers. They know best."

"Well, this means more time out in the lesser Islands, which I have no problem with, I can not wait to get back out there. I hate the markets; they smell and too many people for me."

Atin was quite happy, it just meant she could sail off for more than a few days. She always seemed to get the best ones and had no problem staying under water, longer than most of her siblings could. One time she was gone down for so long everyone began diving and looking for her. She remembered because their frantic splashing scared away the stingray she was swimming with.

"I agree, but 'tis high summer, give it another month. The crowds will lessen and be more locals over others."

"When do you have to go? Wait, all of you? What will Da do?"

"I am not sure. He may try to keep me back."

"I hope so, it will be quiet without all of you around."

"Yes, I am sure it will, but then you can always move back into the hut with Ma and Da."

"Or not… I like quiet… I like my peace. 'Tis too busy in the markets, and the beaches are my happy places."

"Same."

She took off the hat required as a head covering in town and shook out her bleached blonde hair in the face of the wind, finger combed and braided it into a simple single braid down her back. Her clothing was unadorned gray cotton cloth, a tunic and short breeches, and her undergarments were a simple loin cloth and a bodice to cover her small breasts, this is what she swam in, when she was with her brothers and sisters. When she was alone, she dove bare as a babe, clothing was too restricting and then it was dry when she was finished.

"It means you and our little brothers and sisters will have to do all the chores and help Da with the fishing."

Zohan spoke to her, while their Pader sat at the stern of their boat with his hand on the tiller. Zohan handed her the main sail line,

"You might as well get used to the shifting winds."

"I forgot... Da will have to teach Tarik and Selim, but he likes his craft, and the boys have been pestering him lately."

"We have begun taking them out, Arno is much like Da, he has patience. I do not, but I will teach you. You listen."

"What?"

"Very funny. Ha ha."

Atin spent the rest of the trip fighting with the ropes, learning from her brother, and getting good blisters on her already weathered palms, relearning tacking into the wind while her Da remained quiet all the way home. While the dark clouds seemed to bypass them in the east, the winds had picked up. Her brother explaining everything again, although she knew it, and she was grateful for the time they were spending together.

"Remember an ebb in the winds, especially in spring and fall, does not mean they are gone. Always be prepared for them to catch in another direction. Like... right about now. Here. Good thing I was prepared. You read the winds."

"How did you know, Zohan?"

"Read the signs, I was watching the gull up there."

He pointed up.

"Birds coast on the winds, and he tacked to his left, which meant we would be getting a breeze from the direction we left. Summer breezes come from the South. You should know this. What direction do the winter breezes come from?"

"The North."

"Wrong. They come from the east. Maybe they originate in the North, but from the North of Du'Lanay. They travel around the mainland, and east to the Islands, then towards Aram. Only do we get currents from the east and west when the seasons are changing. In the summer, we get currents from the South, this brings us the bounty of habberfish, the eels, and the many other species we sell in the markets."

"Why are there never currents from the North?"

"The Maelstrom Sea is a violent place, 'tis death to any trying to cross through it, none have returned. The Sea itself is shrouded in mystery; magic some call it. It does not travel down. It will catch one unawares, and draw them in, if they were to sail too close. Once you see the dark horizon, and the dark gets bigger, you would be well to sail away. Many curious sailors have found themselves not able to turn around. Once the magic winds catch your sails, you are doomed."

"Have you ever seen this darkness?"

"Yes, Da took us boys there once. To show us what to look for, it took all of us five hours to row out of there, we could not use the sails. Da was worried for a couple of hours, we would be pulled in, leaving you and the girls bereft. I dare not go there again. Promise me, you will not go looking."

"I will not. It does not hold any interest for me. I enjoy my diving way too much. Too much to see under the water."

"I think you are part fish yourself, little sister."

They arrived home in their quiet cove, docking the boat on the wharf her Pader built when he had first set out to create a home for Zohan's Mader. She died in childbirth and Atin's Mader was contracted, for the sole use of taking care of his brood of five. There were a few years between Atin and her next oldest sibling Zohan, a couple of babies died young, her Mader had a rough time of it. Atin's Da had half a year of living alone with his children before finding himself another wife.

Her Mader birthed a child every year of Atin's life. Not all had lived, life was lean, and payment for midwives was dear especially when they were not readily accessible. What pearls they found, sustained most of the provisions for the year. As she began to find them in her early years, she was encouraged to continue and sometimes, the whole family would spend a day or two gleaning what they needed before a trip to the main Island.

As she helped unload baskets of goods taking them into the hut her Mader did the cooking in, she wondered if this meant more for the rest of them if the four oldest boys were to go, and how this was going to change for the rest of the children.

"Stop mind gazing,"

Her Mader took the basket from her, as she was standing still for more than a moment.

"Help get the rest. There is some melting pot stew on the fire for you, your brother and Da."

The cooking hut was built on the ground, from materials gleaned from the Islands. Raw cut timbers, thatched with straw from the lowland hills of their Island. It had taken a joint effort of all inhabitants. After hard hitting storms, if one had damage from such that took more than one or two men, they would help the others living on the Island, so no one would be without. It was part of their culture, and they gave thanks to the Gods for their lives and lifestyle.

"I had a visit from Parin today, she is near her time. I will be assisting her with her birth. She may need you to watch her others. We can go together when needed."

"Can not Medea go?"

"She will be assisting me with Parin. She needs to know about childbirth, for when she has children of her own."

"She has helped you. We all have."

"'Tis different with another woman, Atin. I am her Mader, and 'tis different. She needs to help another woman. It will be good for you also. 'Tis our way of life, we help them, they help us."

"Parin is always here, Ma. She is here, more than her own home."

"She had a hard upbringing, Atin. She is lonely and appreciative of my assistance. Her Ma passed when she was first married. I am only helping her to take care of her small family. You should not disparage another. 'Tis not healthy for the spirit."

"I am sorry, Ma. I am just upset, Da did not get the value for the large pearl I found. The Aram was too insistent, and Da let him have it."

"What do you mean? Here, take this and put it up high, I will talk with your Da later, when he's calmed down."

Perishables and foods were stored on shelves high enough predators on the Island could not access them. Sleeping quarters were built up on stilts, on another level around the outer edge, providing extra support for the outer walls and for more protection from the afore mentioned predators. The height enabled the sleeping quarters to keep cool in the hot summers. These were mostly for her Da, Ma and the littles. The older children had a hut of their own, one for females and one for the males, her brothers.

All the buildings were far enough away from the beach to protect them from high waves during seasonal storms. All were connected to each other by way of walkways, built with timbers brought over the years from the main Island. Her Da built his home by hand, and it showed his craftsmanship.

Atin finished with the baskets, one last trip back from the boat as most of her siblings had brought the rest. Later that evening, her Pader was talking to her Mader on the beach in the setting of the sun. Their silhouettes would be a memory she would never forget for the rest of her life. It would be one of the last pleasant things she remembered from the innocence of her childhood. Zohan came up beside her and enveloped Atin into a hug, his arm clutching her tight against him. She leaned into his ribs as her arm went around his waist.

"Da is telling Ma about what to expect. He is upset. I know you cannot tell…"

"I know Da well enough, he has been quiet. Do not think I cannot read him."

"You were always the intuitive one, Atin. Try not to worry too much. We will fight, and we will come home."

"Yes, but at what cost?"

"We will be men. Hardened by war, I am thinking. You will be a woman, next time I see you. Medea will have many children, and perhaps you will too. Our siblings will be grown, mayhap, I will not recognize them. Who can say. We can only pray to the Gods to end the war, but then the Magistrates will have to devise another way to keep the Namanists and the Aramites off the Islands. There is a cost for everything. I can only pray that you and our parents are safe. Safe from harms. It will keep me in fine spirit to know you are safe."

"I love you, Zohan. You know me best."

"And I love you, little sister. You will do wonderful things, I know it."

The next two months were busy with fishing and pickling their catch, preparing for the lean winter months ahead. Boats were brought onto shore and resealed. Every wall was patched, roofs rethatched, decks secured, clothing made, and shelves stocked. They made another trip down to Peli just to get more supplies for the winter. Atin sold pearls she found on a few trips to 'her Island,' she called it, to help with the purchases.

Pearling was year-round, but most of the harvesting was when the winter tides and storms happened. The warmer weather brought changing tides at the smaller Islands and this suited Atin to a tee. She could leave and be gone a week.

Sometimes she would have to take her older sister and two of the younger ones, but lately her oldest sister, Medea was more interested in learning craft from their Mader. She had an interest in one of the boys from the mainland, and the Paders engaged in the marriage proposal agreement, which was a process.

Medea had always excelled in homecraft, she was gleaning and weaving sea silk from the ocean shores and begun a dress when she was but a child. The dress was almost finished and was an art form in itself. Medea was almost finished the fine delicate embroidery, of blue silk threads. It was her creation, and their Ma said it was the finest she had ever seen.

One night, her Pader called them all together and said the time had come for some of them to leave. Medea would be escorted to the mainland to become a bride and her brothers would accompany them. Zohan, Arno, Timur and Orkun would sail east with a small contingent to the land of Du'Lanay to begin life in the Army of the Emperor. The Emperor could not get all his sons, so four would have to suffice. While Medea and Arno looked excited to go, Zohan was quiet and Atin asked him softly what bothered him.

"Da is not getting any younger and 'tis going to be more difficult to get all he needs. You are next oldest, you will have to forget leaving for days and make sure you help him fish now, the little boys will not be able to manage the sails in fierce winds. They will have to do the pearling, and do not forget to go up the mountain and get the eggs for Mader."

He was referring to the eggs of the large birds which had nests high on the top of the dormant volcanoes, now covered by vegetation and trees. Getting those eggs was an adventure, someone could easily break a limb or two climbing the trees these birds nested in.

"I do not understand why we must send men to fight. We deal with both lands in the marketplace, and yet we are fighting one against the other on the continent. Why is that?"

"You would not understand. Here I will try to explain it to you."

Zohan was always the most patient with her questions, which is what she loved about him.

"We have always worshiped the six Gods. It has always been this way for us. Yet the continents only believe in one God, each have a different version of their religion. To keep their religion from taking root in our lands, our Rulers have succeeded in creating terms to keep us safe from invasion by both lands. It could cripple us, if we were to give them our foods and timbers, so they send men and coin. Somehow it has worked, and our current Rulers have managed to keep it working. We offer ourselves to the cause, to keep you and our families safe. I am proud to serve and know I will gladly give my life to keep you and my sisters safe."

She glanced at her Da who heard the last of Zohan's speech to her, and she saw he looked immensely proud of his son. Zohan was a younger version of her Da. He learned with his brothers how to build and maintain their boats and huts. She knew without having to say anything it was going to be vastly different without her older siblings to help around the Island. Her other brothers were older and had differing opinions about the war. Timur loved a good disagreement and did not hesitate to have one. Atin's Da and him would have 'discussions' well into the night.

Arno and Orkun were softer spoken, Ma said they took after their Mader in temperament. Timur was hardheaded like his Da. But lately, his opinions seemed to reflect more controversial subjects, with their religion being one of them. This subject alone had Atin disturbed. She believed in the Gods. They quietly worshiped the six Gods rooted in their everyday life. Atin felt herself in each of the Gods, her Ma said she was well rounded in her beliefs.

Atin looked over to her Mader, who was having difficulty deciding whether to be happy for her Dader or sad for her boys leaving. Even though they were not hers by blood, she raised them, and she was the kind of woman to give all her heart. To Atin's Mader, they were her children. Sad won out and the tears slipped silently down her cheeks as she cried and hugged her children, who were trying all to be grown up and failing.

The day to leave arrived, Medea's trousseau was meager, she had her dress for the ceremony, and a few other items. Delicate shell necklaces, interwoven with tiny white pearls, that Atin gave her. She would wear both on her joining day. Atin had snuck off for her last solo trip and managed to bring back an exceptionally large volume of pearls, her gift for her older sister. A storm churned up a shoal full of shells. Atin had a tough time leaving the area, but she knew she had to go with everyone, to help her Da on the trip back.

She found deep blue pearls, so rare it fetched a dear price. Purple pearls and a huge black opal one, which she would have liked to keep for herself, but she knew there would always be more. She hoped the trip to the mainland did not take too long so she could return to her coves in hopes of finding more. Swimming in the shallows was where Atin found her peace, however, Medea needed help with her bride price. So, the pearls Atin found helped to cushion this.

The boys managed to get all the goods on board the small skiff and they set off in the light of the rising sun. Atin's Mader and the small ones stood on the shore waving, and she knew her Mader was openly crying now. There was no room for the whole family to attend. Their Ma had come to terms with not attending, the little girls would be a distraction and with the boys leaving, Atin knew it would be harder for her Mader to not show her emotions in the city. Her Mader managed to refrain as they were saying goodbye.

"You make sure you have the time to prepare; they cannot take this away from you. Let them wait until you are ready. Atin, you make sure your sister is beautiful for her man. You take it all in, so you can retell all to me when you return. Now, give me a hug, you will do fine, Medea. You know all you can about woman craft, and be respectful of your new Mader and Pader, 'tis important you have their care. Your Pader and sister will give me updates as they happen, I am sure of it. By Iris, safe path and May you be Blessed."

The trip did not seem to take as long as it used to, maybe because there was too much going on, or the weight in the boat helped it to travel faster. The boys and Medea were in high spirits. Soon the coastline of the main Island was in sight and the port where they docked seemed to be more busy than usual. They moored the boat and her Pader got out and began to do his business. Zohan and her brothers unloading, and she and Medea organized her goods waiting for their Da. Soon the three of them set off for the groom's home, Zohan and her brothers staying behind with the boat.

Poorer folk like themselves did not deal with pomp and ceremony when it came to transactions. Atin's Da and the groom's Da had made the arrangements in the last two months. Now it was just to get the joining registered and the exchange of goods.

While Medea and Atin waited with the groom's Mader and family in their home in the city, the men set off to the great Hall of Law to pay the joining dues and have it written into the books.

She helped Medea wash and dress in her bridal gown and fixed her hair with one of the shell necklaces which framed her beaming face.

"You look gorgeous, Medea. You are a beautiful bride and I wish you all the joy. Hess is a lucky man."

"Oh, Atin. I am so happy. Hess and I wish to start a family right away, and I am to help his family with a bit of the business. I can only wish the same for you."

"I think I am happy enough going off on my own. I cannot imagine leaving Da and Ma right now. Too many changes, with all you older ones gone, I am next oldest. I must help Da more now."

"I am sorry about this, too many changes to be sure. All our brothers going off at once was not planned, Da is crazy to send them all. He should have at least kept Zohan back for a year, however, 'tis required of us. I heard Da say for each boy held back it would cost them in coin, which we all know Da does not have."

"Well, enough sad talk, let us finish, and we can go out to your new family. They are nice enough."

"I think they are too. They are giving us a suite of rooms at the back of this house for our own use until we can get a home of our own. I can not wait; I am so excited!"

"I am excited seeing you excited. May the Gods bless you with all you desire. May the Mader bless you with lots of children and may the Sister bless you with one like me!"

Laughing, they finished prepping the beaming bride and entered the parlour to join the groom's family. The dress of sea silk was admired and well received. The Mader by law was fingering the silky sleeves and the smile on her face was an indication to Atin Medea was welcome. The groom's family consisted of the parents and immediate members, Atin wished her brothers wished to attend, but Arno said Medea would not miss them, they needed to think about their new career in the Army. The girls were served a light meal and Atin could not help but feel uncomfortable in such opulent surroundings. Even though the family was by no means rich, they were better off than the fisher folk.

Atin wondered how things would change, now she was the eldest of the children left to help her Da and Ma. Medea was the eldest, but with her gone, and her four older brothers, Atin was now the eldest. She was left to do as she wished, going off on her own and pearling, she never had to go fishing. Her older brothers would take one of their boats to help fish with their Da, but with the boys going off to war, her Pader decided to sell the small boat, his reasoning was he could not manage to sail both at once, and the family could use the extra coin to get them through the lean months. Her Pader was a wise man and knew best.

She knew now she would place aside her solo trips, and it weighed her down. Atin felt like her childhood was ending and hoped she could make her Da proud and not fail him. Breaking herself out of her thoughts she returned to the moment at hand and smiled as a plate of food was given to her by the GrandMader, thanking her for the gesture. She listened to the conversations surrounding her.

Atin could not help but feel from what was not outright spoken, if it were not for the bounty her pearl diving produced, they would not even considered a marriage. Luckily for Medea, she and her betrothed met a few times, and they were both smitten with each other. Atin was sure Medea would be fine in her new home. Medea had a calming demeanor, she was an expert at diffusing situations, had plenty of practice with all the siblings and skilled in all things in the home.

The men returned, goods were exchanged, and a small ceremony with them, Medea and her husband exchanging vows which had the groom's Mader shedding a tear. The pearls were the most appreciated when they saw the glorious colours. Medea looked incredibly happy and when it came time to leave, she and Atin did not even cry when they hugged and parted.

Atin followed her Da back to the boat and her brothers. A mooring fee was paid to protect the boat and their goods on it, a guard was sent to watch the boat, and the six of them headed off to the barracks of the army. They had a fair hike up the hill from the port and around the base of one of the mountains. It was a good day out for the walk; she was glad her legs were in good condition from her swimming in the shallows.

Atin had never been this far away from the docks and was quite enthralled by the sights and smells. The lower market housed all sorts of wares, from the far away lands, all sorts of denizens, and she told herself next time, she would explore more. As they climbed, they crossed into the lower city, through a huge set of gates, and her Da had to prove to the guards they were citizens. Only natives to the Islands were allowed inside, the continent peoples were prohibited unless they had special authorization. They were granted permission to enter, and they continued.

"Zohan, I wonder when we will sail?"

"I would not know. At least with us from the Islands, we are all good sailors."

"Yes, thanks to Pader. Atin, you have several boots to fill."

Arno turned back to Atin, then back to his brothers and they kept on with their questions and imaginings.

"Will they teach us sword craft?"

"It will just be like gutting a tuna, Timur. Remember the one with the brown on its fin..."

Orkun told the story, he was teasing Timur, about the time when they caught a small tuna and Timur jumped when the supposedly dead tuna, "woke" and knocked the boy over with its brown fin. The boys laughed and chatted as they walked behind their Da. Atin, smiled at the telling, she had seen her brother jump from down the shore, and the boys continued to tease the other for two months after the incident. Now they had brought it up, she knew it would be a while before they tired of it.

She looked at their backs; they were all a similar height and carried themselves with pride. She felt she was memorizing their looks for her Mader, perhaps for herself as well. Very few men made it home. Atin's face fell with the thought and looked around to take her away from that sad thought.

The landscape itself, the wide paved walk paths with flat stone, the walls of cut stone and brick, the houses of brick. Blonde, and red woods. The finer houses, some with doors of Blackwood, all were things she had never seen before. She found all to be very fascinating and had to rush to keep up when she lingered behind, from a distraction or two.

One inner mountain on the main Island was still smoking. The occasional earth shakes, and spew of smoke kept people in fear of a huge event. None had been felt in her lifetime, but people kept the fear alive by talking about the next 'big one'! She saw if she looked directly up the slope before her, the small but visible plume of smoke leaking from the top.

After passing the three larger Islands which had these mountains on them, the Island they inhabited, had only a couple scalable mountains. Atin had been to the top of the smaller of the two and saw the larger Islands in the distance when she looked South. When she skirted the top and looked North, the Islands were smaller, just hills of rock, no mountains. These Islands were where she did all her searching. It was a haven for seals and many birds. Sometimes when she raided their nests, she would come across trinkets and the odd piece of metal.

Once she found a bracelet and gave it to her Da. The next trip to the main Island for trade, he found the bracelets owner through the Hall of Law and was handsomely rewarded. Her Da was strict but a caring man, and because of the largess of the reward he gave her and her sisters a purchase of new clothing material and her Mader gladly sewed new outfits for them.

Most times Atin would get Medea's cast offs, and consequently the younger girls would get hers, until eventually the remnants would be woven together into baskets. Nothing was ever wasted. Her Mader had the gift of making something out of nothing, fisher folk lived leanly but also could survive off little to nothing. Ma was passing this talent onto her offspring. Atin was currently wearing a cast off, and she reminded herself to stop lollygagging and to set her mind back into the present.

They finally came to a stop at a large iron hinged gate of Blonde wood, and she concluded this was the entrance to the Barracks. Atin and her brothers waited outside the gate while their Pader went inside and spoke to the Commanding Officer. Coming out with the man, Da did not say much, but gave each boy a handshake and a quick hug. Atin followed suit trying hard not to tear up.

It was not until she got to the last, which was Zohan that she openly started crying.

"Please, stay alive and come back to us. Take care of the others, you know how rash Timur is, do not let him get you into trouble."

"Do not worry, sis. I will. Arno can help, we will watch over each other, it is what family does. You just make sure you help Da now, more than ever, he will be a little lost. You teach the others, as much as you can. Selim and Tarik will have to grow up fast. You just make sure they help Da too. Tarik is capable, Selim, well… he will have to stop with his games."

"You come back, that is all I will pray to the Uncle for. Just come back. Ohh, I will miss you all."

"I will miss you too. Now they are waiting patiently for us, we must go. I love you, Atin."

"I love you too, all of you."

He gave her an extra squeeze reassuring her he would watch out for the boys and bring them all home safely. She knew there would be a huge chance she would not see them for many years if at all. Folks did not call it the Long War for no reason. This war had been going on for longer than she could remember, and it did not seem to be ending soon. She still did not understand the reason their men went off to fight, with an enemy who hated them, or their faith in the Gods, against another enemy who hated their faith as well. The dynamics of such hurt her head.

Her Da had already left and was walking back down the hill so she gave Zohan a quick hug again scurrying off after him. As she appeared beside him, she knew he was upset, so she placed her small hand in his, holding it while they walked back to the boat. The walk back was quiet. She did not speak to her Da, by the way he carried himself, he was internally distressed.

Arriving back at the moored boat, she saw a small crowd of men standing nearby. Her Da strode up, chatted with them and then the crowd dispersed.

"Grab the line, lass. We will have pearls next time. Untie it and give us a shove."

"Yes, Da. I will get busy right away when we get home."

"Maybe, I may need you on fishing trips. Hauling nets, we will take out one boy at a time."

"Yes, Da. I cannot leave pearling too long."

"You may have to, but if there is a storm, you can go out after. Perhaps take one of the boys, or Soya."

"She is easily distracted, Da. More of a hinderance, really. She is better minding her sisters with Ma."

"Well, perhaps we all go fishing, then we all go pearling."

"Da, I can go by myself."

"We will see how the Universe plays it out for us. Grab the line, the wind is going to snap."

"Offph!

She knew the next while would be terribly busy, but secretly she hoped she could go off by herself to harvest.

This was a huge test for her, and her arms felt like they were ripped off by the time they arrived home. The seas were very choppy, and she struggled to keep the sails from ripping out of her hands. They drifted off course halfway back, her Da did not say anything to her, as he wanted her to recognize and correct her own error. As they arrived at their wharf, her little brothers were waiting to help tie the boat. Atin was grateful for this. Walking into the hut, her Mader silently handed her a bowl of soup which she almost drank, she was so hungry. Her Pader came in motioning for her to sit down, so he could discuss their plan for the winter.

"Here is what we will do…you are going to take your siblings, one each trip and teach them the ways of pearling and harvesting on the rocky shores. No more heading off by yourself, as one day you will leave us, and we pass on our knowledge to others. Your little sisters will help your Mader in food preparations, and I will take your brothers out on the sea and teach them. I will need the extra hands to control the boat. I may need you when the seas are the roughest, they will not be able to manage the sails or tiller. We will have to adjust ourselves, like flowing with the seasonal tides."

"Yes, Da. I know. May I go to my hut? I am very tired; my arms feel like they were ripped off."

"Yes, dear child. Why do you not have a sleep in, you did well out there. The chop was getting high. Now come here."

He smiled and she rose giving him a great big hug. He was not much for affection; she saw his heart was hurting from the absence of her brothers. All his first-born children from the other Mader were gone, his helping hands diminished by half. She yawned, leaving to stumble back to the now empty hut, she was the only occupant. She barely stayed on the path, her eyes were heavy,

Perhaps I should move back with Ma and Da. 'Tis a little too empty, but not tonight, I am bushed.

Tomorrow would be a day to repair nets, gather their tools, and repair what needed to be done. She headed inside to her sleeping bunk and just flopped into it, asleep before she hit the cushion.

The next day had her not sleeping in late. Perhaps it was the imbalance of voices, more little ones than older ones which had her forgetting for just one moment, the events of the previous day. She rose up from her mat going outside to the privy where she relieved herself. Wondering as she went to the main hut, what her day was going to be like.

It seems very strange and quiet now. I miss my brothers. Now they are gone, I feel empty inside. I wish they had not all gone at once. This is so quiet, I even miss Timur's opinions.

She sat outside on a lip of the walkway watching her Pader, already working on the side of the skiff. They managed to winch it up onto the track of rock from one of the small streams pouring into the ocean from a waterfall and freshwater spring high up one of the two mountains. He devised a winch and pulley system, with grooved lumber set under the heel of the boat, to help it from breaking upon any rock. It would travel the groove as it was pulled out of the water, the water providing the lubrication needed to help with its removal from the ocean. He managed with her little brothers help to get the skiff out of the water, at the edge of the low tide.

"Da, you could have woken me, I could have helped you!"

She was more than upset with him. Atin saw a haze forming around him, brown and green, not the best way to be beginning the morning, and set the tone for the rest of the day.

"I did not want to wake you dear girl, the boys managed to help with the boat, and we are going to pitch it as much as we can before the tide comes in. If you want to go grab a bucket and rag, it will help get done faster."

Helping her Pader and the boys, they pitched the boat in less time than she thought it would take. She found her Da straggling behind after a while. Atin tried to encourage him to take his time, but only once did he have a rest. She suspected Zohan had known something was troubling their Da, in his cryptic message when he advised her to help more.

Atin sat for a lunch break taking a good look at her Da, she was not sure how old he was, but lately he looked more worn. He was fair haired like herself. Arno and Medea had red hair. Their Mader had been a red head, and the other boys had fair hair. The littlest ones all had fair hair, as her Mader was. Her Da's face and upper body was very tanned, and her brothers were as well, any chance they got, they worked without shirts and had bronzed upper bodies. Atin was fair under her clothing, but doing more pearling by herself had her falling asleep with no clothes on and her body was changing colour as she aged. More like it changed with her being able to go out by herself more.

After the skiff was finished, it lay in the sun until the tide turned and with the high tide, it helped them to push the boat back into the water without too much effort. Her Da knew his calling and she was happy with her family life. Atin hated her brothers had to go off to a war, so far away it seemed not even theirs to worry about. Yet they all served their Rulers, who were fair in the ruling. She sat there watching her Da. He was instructing her brothers on knot tying.

What is this colour I am seeing? A haze of brown with a green tinge. It looks sickly. When I look at the boys, I see yellow, and reds. When I look at my sisters, I see pink, and blue. Da's colour looked putrid. What does this mean? Why do I see colours? Is it the air? Am I odd? Is this what happens when I become a woman? I will have to ask Mader about this.

Her Mader hardly ever left the Island, often saying she was happy to be in solitude, away from the crazy politics and sometimes other women could be cruel. Atin tried to ask her Ma to explain, but her Ma said 'that' life for her was over, she was glad to just be with Atin's Da, he was kind to her, and they seemed to be well suited. From what Atin could see, they never argued, and often saw them being affectionate.

She hoped if she were ever to become attached to a man, she would have the caring she saw from her parents, Medea had seemed genuinely happy to be a bride. Atin was not hoping it was anytime soon for her; she was thinking way into the future. There were many things to do, helping her family survive with less hands to help was a beginning.

She fell asleep that night determined she was going to get many more pearls the next time she was out. Atin wanted to see how long she could stay under water; she was her own worst competitor. She knew there might be a day that this would all be gone, so she better get moving.

Pearls waited for no woman!

CHAPTER 5

Andic

Through Dust and Ash

Andic sat on the top of the high yellow rock wall, her dirty bare feet tucked under her bum, covertly watching the rich Aramite family inside their villa.

The family were sitting on their velvet and silk floor cushions, which covered a beautiful mosaic tile floor, eating their evening repast. The Patriarch conversing with the boys. The Matriarch and the girls remained quiet, while nibbling on fruits, vegetables, and other dishes. The breeze coming in from the coast below the hill behind her was cooling and set the sheer silk curtains flowing in the rooms behind the family, the candles in their cages flickering.

The Darkness of the clear night, the enclosed shrubbery and coconut trees hid her from view of the pacing soldiers the family used for security. Their bootsteps echoing on the concrete rock paving stones warning her when they were close to her hiding spot. She had exceptionally sharp hearing, which to her, was getting better every day. She could hear the family speaking clear as Day, as if they were right beside her, but were a fair bit away, across a garden, with a fountain in between them.

She glanced around her; fearful someone was watching her. This fear had saved her from some sticky situations more than once. Andic turned back to watch,

Looks like there is still a shortage of Pelinese spice, and the lack of ships in the harbour corroborate this. This Oban always has the cream of the stores. I can see his kitchen staff have tried to and failed to cook a satisfying meal.

The FirPader's emissaries did not let a lot of ships in since the war had begun.

Thing is, they were not the only ones suffering. The homeless and poor were dying by the dozens every day. The burning pits to the South of the city occasionally would send a smell of rotten sick. It would set her stomach to rolling. Other times it would smell so good and make her so hungry she would focus on getting into a storehouse at all costs. In this heat, the burn pits were lit every night.

This family was her favorite to come watch, out of force of habit. They were of nobility. The Patriarch was one of the FirPader's Obans, a treasurer. Some of the chests she saw coming and going periodically, contained gold coins, with the influx of boats and trading ships docked in the now closed off port. The Oban had his secret storerooms, but Andic knew of them, and she would glean slightly from his coffers. Not enough to raise any alarm, just a few he would not miss. She was sure he gleaned his own skim before the chests went into the Royal Treasury. This was the way of the world she lived in; everyone took a cut.

This Oban was one of the kinder ones she watched, which was probably why she favoured him with more observations. The other men she watched in their just as opulent homes, were not. A few did not let their women eat with them, they had their own suites. She did not understand the dynamics of marriage. She hoped she never had to. She was her own person and could not imagine taking orders from a man. Not if she could help it, this was not in her future!

Their villa was like all the others on the hill. Made of locally sourced granites and marbles from the Quarries to the North, shipped down the coast on barges close to shore and constructed for the rich. Only the Palace and the odd overly rich Obans had dome structures in their buildings. Most other villas were flat topped roofs, made of blonde timbers utilized from upriver, and some of the western coastal towns. Not that Andic could verify this information, it was what she learned growing up in the streets.

Andic shifted herself onto the pads of her bare feet, quietly and fluidly, in anticipation of leaving to go about her rounds, if one were to call them that. It was still early hours of the evening. The sun set a while ago, and the temperatures were finally lowering with breezes off the water. She still had a lot to do.

Time to get moving, my boys are waiting. I hope this is a quiet night.

Those who did not know her, mistook her for a child, not the fourteen plus years she may be, she did not know her age or cared. Her small stature was lean and muscular, be it from lack of diet or from running from guards or predators. She also dressed and acted like a male; it worked to her advantage in her dealings with others like her. She lived on the streets but holed up in various areas. The Houses of Delights were her favorite spots, one in particular was a home, of sorts. More like a home base.

She looked like every other person who was a native of the land, black hair, which she liked to shave off when it got long enough to get into her eyes, brown eyes, and medium brown skin. Maybe she was a shade Darker from dirt, but this suited her simply fine. Andic's coarse linen tunic caught on the well-worn leather belt her knife was strapped to, and which held up her equally coarse linen legging pants. She scratched her ankle by the other leather strap which hid another smaller knife. She had several on her person. One had to find them; her leggings and tunic had hidden pockets and cavities which she took time to create herself.

Ox balls, this heat makes my skin so itchy. I cannot imagine being awake during the day. Ugh!

As she shifted positions a shimmer caught the corner of her vision and glanced up into the Dark sky to see a star in the east that sparkled quite spectacularly, as if it winked. She watched it for a period of time thinking it was quite remarkable.

Shrugging it off, she thought,

Maybe I should ask Zenzol next time I see him to find out what this bright star is.

Andic had a few friends, more acquaintances really, who she saw occasionally, for information or food. The rest of her associates were her network of thugs, street rats, beggars, prostitutes, and a couple of mean ones who she used for the dirty jobs of disappearing people. She had some in every district and treated everyone fairly. One trapped more flies with honey than vinegar, Delma told her, and she applied this to her dealings.

Most of her work was done at night the days saved for sleeping. The sun burned extremely hot in the Southlands of Aram, regardless of what season it may be. For her there were only two. Rainy or no rain. Andic thought about her life. What she remembered as a child.

How far back can I remember? Oh, yes. I ran errands. It all started when I outran the guards, stealing bread. I was hmmm, five, six?

She fell into her role gradually, first a couple of them joined forces. Being a runner, she learned a lot of secrets and thought to organize a few more of them. After a few years and more than a few people later, the organization began in earnest. It was not until she managed to best the top boys, they began to defer to her. Of course, there was her reputation at getting out of sticky situations. Some of those situations were planned and some were not. She beat all odds.

Most of her network came alive during the night, as it was cooler and more comfortable. The night hid so many things the bright sun would reveal. She could not cover the whole of the city and all districts, so others, she called deputies controlled other neighbourhoods. They met in varying spots weekly or nightly to discuss news they thought others should know. She dealt in secrets, information, and death. Tonight was one of those meetings.

Many times over, leadership would change overnight, due to power struggles, accidental or deliberate deaths, yet no one wanted her district. It was too heavily guarded and everyone else always got caught. She managed to… knock on rock, remain hidden. It also held the most coin and Andic managed to keep the business running by her light fingers. No one else managed to do what she did, many tried and she let them, however, all were caught some put to death. So, she kept the district that kept her busy, and she kept it well. It was hers.

She attributed her abilities at remaining hidden to many things. Most of all, due to her exceptional hearing. Andic was beginning to focus on specific sounds, narrow her focus, tunnel in on sounds. Her night vision, which over time had increased substantially, was to the point where she could enter a pitch-black warehouse and move around as if in daylight. Still, she always felt she was being watched and never attributed her abilities to anything else, but her own skill set.

She was proud of her skills; she alone honed them as a matter of preservation of her life. She was an incredibly light sleeper, and her lieutenants never knew where she would hole up for sleeping. She preferred to be fluid, never static. Andic was caught off guard a few times, however her abilities and being downwind, saved her. These abilities and a knack for deflection, had her earning the names The Black Shadow, the Child Killer, the Little Dragon. She was not sure what a Dragon was, maybe a dog? Dogs were smart, at least here they were. They ran fast and fought hard. So being compared to such an animal suited her fine.

Its been me, Laza, Hayk and Zabi for the last five years. We have seen many come and go. I was loath to see Kiet leave, but he has Cyntilla in order. We seem to have here working just fine.

The city which she lived in… survived in… was Yavuz, the Capital of the land of Aram which covered the Southern half of the great continent. The North of the continent was uninhabited. A vast scape of active and dormant volcanoes, sheer rock faces, granite, and limestone quarries. No green thing grew there, and no legged animal thrived there.

Homes in the lower city were built of mud brick. Those high up in the hills, the homes of the rich nobility were usually granite or stone. The Palace the Fir-Pader lived in was marble, and granite. The Palace for his Harem was no less grand. His Palace, a few lesser ones and the Grand Gates to the city were decorated with blue glazed brick, a bright blue which competed with the colour of the sea. There were quarries and trade areas to the North, where prisoners were kept. She heard it was a den of unwanted peoples, slaves and rougher than the city she lived in.

But she oft heard other fanciful things if she listened at the right moments and right places. Certain minerals and ores could be mined, in cites to the west. In the places to the North, inland towards a range of active volcanoes, there were caves where one could hide. One so vast it had been said to once house Dragons. Again, she was not sure what kind of animal could survive off nothing, but these were just spectacular stories, secretly told behind closed doors. She listened to it all.

The South land of Aram was sand, lots of it, steppes to the west and North of rock and the odd area of vegetation in the river valleys close to the shores. The valley in which Yavuz thrived was green after seasonal flooding of the Vuz River, the 'Ya' of Yavuz meaning "of the river." Canals were constantly being built further up the river valley as a way of housing and feeding the continually expanding population. It was green year-round on either side of the river, and closer to the mouth, many tributaries, which helped to keep the ever-growing population fed. Upriver there were two other large cities which traded with Yavuz.

Every year the soldiers of war would bring back people they defeated as slaves. Which meant more food and more deaths, a never-ending cycle. The ports at the mouth of the river, contained the slave markets, the homeless, the ragged. The South side of the river was home to traders, farmers, businesses which kept economy thriving.

North of the river, the fertile land, were wealthy villas, and on the highest hill overlooking the river, was the Palace of the FirPader, his royal family, and immediate subjects of distinction. It was heavily guarded, but this was no deterrent to Andic. Traveling upriver on both sides, one found vineyards, groves of olive trees, fields of grains, fig groves, and other fruits and vegetables. Silk farms were everywhere, this was their main trade, and a major export to even the land they were at war with, Aram sold to everyone. The Yanaberry leaf was grown on slightly higher slopes so the seasonal floods did not destroy the plant, susceptible to rot and needed to be well drained. The silkworm was their pride and was well protected. Strangers to their land were well chaperoned and ships leaving the harbour were well inspected before being allowed to leave.

One could also find predators, not the two-legged kind she dealt with, but the animal kind. Long scaled beasts which lurked in the marsh grasses of the river, with long snouts filled with sharp teeth that could snatch a man out of one of the low reed boats they used for fishing. Men fished together to fend off these predators with long spears. She had eaten the meat. For some reason, it was called a delicacy, to her it was just food. The skin or leather of such an animal was in all the markets and made interesting items come to life. In the ranges beyond the city proper, were animals akin to dogs, and strange humped animals men used for riding. They lasted days without water, used for travel between the cities and prized for their function.

Andic shook herself out of her musings, pushing off her reconnoitring, to begin her way to the port, keeping her muscles warm by racing through the alleyways and unoccupied rooftops. She stopped by the few houses of ill repute, in the lower North side of the river, to gather information girls gleaned from their clients who unintentionally let slip. There were other houses catering to other delights of the flesh, but she did not enter them often. Most times those clients were under the influence of substances leaving them incapable of moving or speaking. It was not the most invigorating of places, a last stop for the most depraved and inebriated. She hardly gleaned information from those.

She would be meeting her deputies by the docks tonight, in an empty storehouse usually full, be it human or edible stores. She sauntered over one of the many stone bridges spanning the river, engineered by a civilization long past, of no interest to this busy young woman.

She greeted a few soldiers by name. On occasion she paid them coin to look the other way, nothing in this city transpired without payment of some sort. Andic had all kinds of deals with all sorts of citizens of this city. She would skim her coins from shipments coming in, sometimes on their way out. She had her methods, and her deputies had theirs, hers were more covert.

As she neared the docks she took primarily to the rooftops, jumping spans and climbing walls where needed, stopping on the edge of one warehouse to gather her breath and scan the area. Most of the buildings were two stories high, with awnings stretched across the alleyways which caught breezes when they came off the water.

She saw Zabi and Laza walking in brazenly with their lieutenants. Hayk and Manna coming in the opposite direction with a group of children, homeless ones who would do anything for food and protection. She saw others coming from all sides and a few lingering in shadows as guards and lookouts. As another precaution, the meetings were rotated amongst several areas to not draw unnecessary attention to themselves. When they contracted a job which demanded a death or kill, they systematically lay low until someone "solved' the crime or until something else happened to distract.

Andic jumped across the span of flat roofs and let herself into the upper room through a staircase which led down to the upper level. Flat roofs were used as a means for sleeping in the hot nights of summer, she had to be careful when using them for traveling, she did not traverse ones that were occupied. Maybe not so much in the warehouse district, but in housing areas, she would scan her way before crossing. She managed to evade the guard on the upper level who was busy looking down on the growing group. She quietly slipped down the next set of stairs and blended into the crowd, the cowl of her ragged cape hid her features, her shortness hid her until she was almost to the center of the small group.

She listened to one of her deputies, Laza, a tall and lanky young man, with piercing black eyes and a sparce beard on the end of his chin. He quietly told the group what his patrols had done, who was taken to the burning pits, and information on the war from one very drunk, pissed off sailor who waited a whole week to dock in port, only to have all their goods confiscated by port officials as 'tax.'

"More ships will be coming home from the 'infidels' lands, as their winter will soon be here, which means more soldiers, more pockets to pick, more contracts and also more information."

Laza smiled as he spotted Andic's feet from behind one of his lieutenants,

"What news from high and mighty land, eh, Andic?"

Andic emerged from behind Zabi grinning. She and her deputies had this little game, of them trying to find her in the crowd when it came meeting time. It honed their skills and kept them sharp. Only once had she really stumped them as to where she was, and since she was not one to give up secrets, she never did tell where her hiding spot was.

"Oh, nothing of extreme value. The FirPader's favorite poisoned a minor concubine, they caught it in time, the poor girl lives, however, has breathing difficulties now. The favorite was placed in the dungeons… she will be out in a month or two, you will see!"

She could say she knew more about what happened inside the FirPader's Harem than he did. Andic had several attendants feeding her information from inside the Palace on regular intervals and would acquire items for them from the outside. Most often it was poison of some kind. She knew where to get them and who did what to whom. It was the only drama she had, and she fed off it. Entertainment in an otherwise dull life.

"I also heard with returning soldiers there would be more slaves and concubines, Yasemin thinned down the herd quite a bit this past year. Word is, she has gotten quite full of herself as she birthed two heirs for FirPader Anuban."

"She may not have much competition; I heard most slaves are captured men. Only if they capture another city over in Du'Lanay will they bring females here."

"Well, we will pray to the FirPader for more women, Delma is getting low, as well."

Andic crouched down balancing on the balls of her feet. "What word from the Great Halls and Guilds?"

She turned her head to the side indicating Hayk's area of residence. Many did not know of his double life, he worked as a scroll maker's apprentice during the day and only came to meetings if it really warranted it.

Hayk spoke very quietly; the sound of shock reflecting in his speech.

"One of the young Masters had his eyes burned and thrown out of the Great Hall, today. A small man, I believe you may know of him… Andic … Jeral."

She hissed inward and shot to her feet. "Yes. I do. What did he do so terrible warranting such punishment? He is a quiet, resolute young man, eager to please. Shite, his Mader must be upset."

Hayk continued, "I do not know, whispers in the crowd say he destroyed a scroll or two of ancient tomes, yet others say he had his way with the Oban's Dader… not sure which is truth. They left him in the lower quarter with nothing but his robe of duty."

"Guess I need to find out for myself, as this is not a usual punishment. I will see you later."

Andic nodded to Laza and left through the dispersing crowd. These meetings did not last long as sometimes they were betrayed, and it was only to communicate information across neighbourhoods. Andic took great care in establishing her kingdom. The early years met with some resistance, but over time, when it proved its value, all others came on board and had run smoothly the last few years.

None of her deputies made any comment on her gender, if they knew it, there was no comment. Aram women were chattel… owned and treated like slaves. They could not be in the streets without being fully covered, had no rights, could own nothing, were not taught to read or write and relied solely on their men to take care of them. However, among the poorest of poor, it was every person for themselves. None took offense at her running the show, she would stick up for her people, proving herself as she had gotten a few out of some harrowing situations, earning their respect and trust.

She had gotten herself out of some scrapes from jealous boys wanting her position, and those setting her up. She proved nothing, and no one could keep her down for long, and those who thought they could, disappeared. She made examples out of the prominent contenders and dealt with them accordingly. She did the more delicate of jobs they contracted, the ones needing finesse, or ones no one else wanted. She did not like to do them, and made sure nothing traced back to her.

When the ships returned in the next few months with soldiers and slaves, they would meet less as they became busier with jobs.

Andic ran through the Dark streets, across the bridge and through the lower district until she came to the gate which led up the hill to the great Halls of Learning and Law. The Obans of State had offices, and the Great Mosques of Holiness also occupied this portion of the hill. The Temple of the FirPader was the dominant one, he would address his people from the Temple mount, the courtyard alone would hold several villas. She never attended; it was the best time to glean from some of the places she frequented.

She stopped and motioned to one of the guards on duty. The tall, Dark haired, very good-looking young man smiled when he saw his friend. The two grew up together, even if they travelled in different circles at present. Poor is poor.

"Tell me, Brecu, do you know where the scribe Jeral was taken? Do you know what his crime was?"

She had guards on her payroll also. She either bribed or work out favours in trade. Very lucrative she was, for being so young.

Brecu motioned to come in closer and whispered as she covertly slipped him a few coins.

"You never heard it from me, but talk is, he saw something he was not supposed to. He was always in areas forbidden to the younger Masters; guess this time it was more serious. They took him to the river, burned his eyes, and left him. Good luck finding him, though, he is probably dead and thrown in the pits."

Brecu turned and returned to his post at the gate, ignoring her as a good guard would be seen to do. She went down the hill taking a different path and crossed over the lower city bridge, it was of stone construction, but this one was frequented by horses and carts drawn by men, mostly in the transport of dead bodies on their way to the burning pits.

People were dying so fast from hunger and the summer heat; a decree was set, bodies would be burned, it took too long to bury them. This would also alleviate the mitigation of disease. Three winters ago, a horrific disease ravaged the land, a third of the population succumbed and there was no choice but to burn the dead. This decree was never lifted and still practiced to Date, more so in the summer months. The FirPader gave his blessings to those burned. His word was law. New prayers were added; the deceased spirit was still blessed.

The result to the decrease in population, was those who were Masters of their trade began charging more, and with this came the spending of more. The inhabitants of the lower district were reaping benefits as well… more coin to burn on the baser desires, created more supply to the demand. It benefited all, and the FirPader was worshipped by all his peoples.

Andic arrived at the gate separating the burning pits from the city, nodding to the guard, continuing down to the hut where the overseer had his 'office' if one were to call it thus. More like a shoddy lean to, reducing the burning heat of the sun. She ran up to the overseer, a man of huge stature with dirty yellow hair and markings on his skin. He grinned when he saw her and poured her a small cup of what passed for wine.

"What brings you here, little Dader?"

Aras grinned a somewhat toothless grin at Andic, she saved his life a few years back. His job, busy now, was not always so and had a few perks.

"Looking for the scribe…"

Andic did not see him in the immediate area so she peered up at the giant man.

"Hoping he is not dead yet, curious about what he did." She never needed to explain herself to Aras, for the most part, he never wished to know.

"One of his cronies took him to the river, I am sure he will be back soon though, he was in rough shape, no one would say what he did, so it must have been bad."

Andic drank down the swill, thanked him, and set off to the river and the bridge. Instead of crossing it, she descended the stairs to the side and set off through the makeshift huts and lean-tos along the river. Dodging lodgers sitting at firepits, she heard moaning over sounds of river folk. Andic kept on until she saw a crowd of a few men in white robes surrounding a man laying on the ground. One was tending to his head and placing wet rags over the man's eyes, he tried to turn his head as he heard her approach and was held still by the man at his side.

Andic knelt on the ground beside Jeral as the other rose to his feet, taking his hand, she whispered. "It is I, Andic, are you fine?"

Jeral rasped out, "Do I look fine to you?"

His rasp turned to coughing, raising his torso up off the ground which led to moans, and he laid back down. She squeezed his hand in a plea to comfort and knew then what she needed to do. It hurt her heart for a quick moment, then she shut it away.

"Listen up girl, I do not have long of spirit, get everyone away and I will tell you."

His voice was rasping and quiet and held the resignation of what he knew would be his end. It was a harsh life for the poor and lower caste citizens.

She motioned to the men surrounding Jeral, whispering among themselves, "Go fetch a cart, please. Jeral will be with the spirits soon."

Most knew what this meant, one would not let a friend suffer and give a mercy death. Reserved as a blessing, no one let suffering continue, it Damaged the spirit. They set off towards the bridge, and she leaned in close.

"A few of them, they feel bad, (cough, cough). They Dared me to enter the catacombs for some ancient tome which foretold a Prophecy about the star with a tail, it being called the Dragon's Breath. You have seen it?"

He took a deep rasping breath, and Andic realizing he could not see her nodding, quickly replied. "Yes."

"Well, there is a Prophecy, I read the first part before the great Master caught me. It tells of the Dragon's rebirth and the Riders who will be reborn. There are six, each for a God from the old religion, and six Dragon's and they will once more rule the earth. The star in the sky will begin the new age. I could not finish the scroll as I was caught. As I was being dragged out, I saw a jeweled Dagger, with a Dark purple almost black gem. For a moment I thought I saw a shimmer in the gem. It was on a Dais surrounded by other antiquities of old, it caught my eye. I was foolish enough to mention it, and 'tis why they took my eyes, however, you must tell no one or they might kill you.

This Dagger is of some importance, I do not know what, you must find out. Learn the Prophecy, why it is secret? Why it is against our sacred teachings? Find the owner of the Dagger. Promise me…."

He began to cough and as Andic heard the men returning with the cart, she gathered him into her embrace and whispered, "Rest easy my friend. Watch over me from the Otherlife."

She plunged her short-handled knife into his back where his heart was and gave it a quick twist to finish the job. Andic laid him gently back down as the men came into sight, standing up, she quietly tucked her knife back into her waist, telling them he was gone.

One of the men asked if he said anything to which she replied,

"No, he was sorry he was fooled by a prank, and I should tell his Mader. I will pay his death dues to his Mader. Hopefully no more pranks will be played for a while."

Andic sternly looked at the men to which a few hung their heads down but were quickly reminded they should take the body to the burn pit and return to their homes. The oldest of the men, continued to look at Andic with questions in his eyes. She just shrugged, heading to the bridge, crossing it to the North side of the Yavuz River. Taking a round about way to one of the houses of ill repute, Andic was lost in her thoughts.

What did the scribe mean by his ramblings? A jewelled Dagger? This will fetch a fair price to the right buyer or it could be broken into pieces if 'tis rare or Damaged. I am curious now! We need to pad our coffers. I have not seen anything good come in the harbours in a while. I will worry about this later, I am spent.

She had a nest in the attic where sometimes she lay her head. Andic chatted with a few of the girls, waiting for the Matron of the House, currently in the front chatting with clientele, or some of the girls. Andic had just taken a bite of cheese with bread, when she heard a shout coming from the back. She shot up off the seat she was lazily leaning on.

"You bitch! This blue will not come out! I told you to stay away from my outfits!"

The sounds of flesh on flesh met her ears and then sounds of a scuffle. A body or something heavy hit the wall several doors down. Andic and the few she was eating with leapt down the hall. Delma disapproved of fighting during 'business' hours. If there were disputes, the girls had to wait until after clients left. She would tear these girls a new arsehole, Andic and the others needed to have this sorted before Delma came back there. The screaming began anew.

"Ow, that hurt! I will have a bruise for weeks. I will kill you for that."

"You just ruined my best gown; you owe me five Vuza. That blue will not come out."

"How was I to know he was newly inked? Not like I saw under his uniform. The summer celebrations had been past for a good week. I needed a gown, mine had blood stains. I was going to wear this and place it back."

"Well, regardless, pay for it!"

Andic and the other girls crowded the doorway. One girl had the other on the floor, straddling her and most of the prone girl's hair in her grasp and ready to punch the one on the floor. Andic spoke quietly.

"If Delma finds you like this, she will punish you both. Mallias, did you borrow the gown from Noor's wardrobe?"

The girl on the floor tried to nod. "Yes." It was reluctantly spoken.

"Then you need to move, either pay Noor its worth, or get under a man and get the funds. You are new here. You earn your clothes. Only borrow if you have permission. You cannot go into anyone's wardrobe and pick what you want. Noor worked hard for that cloth and was to wear it tonight, with the intent on securing the Obans attention, Delma needed Noor to look her best. Now, best you get off her, Noor. I am sure Delma heard you screaming and everyone felt the walls shake."

The mad girl got off the one on the floor and looked at Andic still upset.

"How am I to look good for the Oban? He will be here in less than an hour. Now I must redo my hair as well. If it was not for this…'Pornai'… I would be ready."

Andic watched the bruised girl getting slowly up onto her knees and then feet.

"Mallias will assist you… Oh yes you will, you will take what you have earned and pay another girl to lend their dress, call it renting. Hurry up now, I hear a heavy tread, probably Delma."

Mallias left, a scowl on her face. Andic heard footfalls stop, murmuring and then the heavy steps arrived and sure enough Delma came into Noor's room.

"What was all that about? I heard a screech and then one felt the walls shake. Was there issue with the new girl Mallias?"

"Oh, not much. Andic has Mallias finding me a new dress, since she destroyed my new green one. I have not much time to prepare. She knows now not to 'borrow' what is not hers. She wore it for some soldier who had a new stigma. It was all over the front of my dress. 'Tis ruined!"

"Let me see this first, before you call it ruined. Where is the dress?"

Noor stooped and found the puddle of green silk. Holding it up, one saw the blue ink stains on the front, as if someone smeared blue dye in a random pattern. Delma looked it over, handling it with care.

"We will dye this Dark blue, and hope it covers. We could try the blue of the ink, the places where 'tis already blue will Darken. I will take it to the laundry tomorrow and Mallias will pay the redyeing out of her pocket. If I hear your voice raised that high again, Noor, I will have you punished. I can tell it was you, no one else can reach those notes. Do not shake your head at me, I know it was you."

Just then, Mallias returned with a pink gown, and threw it at Noor, who barely caught it. Delma moved fast and grabbed the blonde girl by the hair, twisting it until the girls head tilted down.

"As for you, if I hear of you helping yourself to what is not yours, I will have you under the roughest men for a week. You will not be able to walk upright and will be nothing more than a 'Pornai' here. Is this what you want?"

"Ow, no Matron, no. I will…ow…that hurts. I am sorry, Noor. I did not think…"

"I do not want you to think. Just smile at the men and spread your legs. That's all the men who come here want. They do not want you for your brain or your voice, only to hear, yes Master, no Master, you are so big…oh, oh, oh! Now get cleaned up…you will serve the lower men tonight. I will give you a few to warm you up and after tonight you will listen to the others when they give you advice."

Delma let go of the girl's hair and pushed her out the door and looked back at the two in the room. "Andic, after you are done with Noor, I wish to see you in my office."

"Yes, Delma. I will not be long." Andic glanced at the red-haired girl, who was almost crying fingering the pink silk.

"Everyone knows a redhead does not look good in pink. She did this deliberately. What am I going to do?"

"You are a beautiful red-haired girl who will look very ravishing in this pink dress. That is Verema's gown. It has a very plunging neckline; and will show your best assets. Mallias just saw the colour, Verema picked it for you, for its attributes. Why do you not try it on first, before you discount it, Verema has been here a while, Noor. You should take note when she gives you something."

The tall redhead, tore off her robe and put the pink silk on her body, not caring Andic was there with her. Andic helped her with the clasps and saw the smile begin on Noor's face when she saw the silk hug her body in all the right places.

"The Oban will love this! It does give my breasts some love, thank you! Andic, you better run along."

"Right, thank Verema later, perhaps a thank you to Mallias, if your night is successful."

"Oh, I will!"

Andic left the redhead, humming and searching for a ribbon for her hair to match the dress. She closed the door and walked down the now empty hall to the office around the corner, walked in and shut the door when Delma motioned for her to do so.

"Lass. That was some quick thinking. How is Noor?"

"She was upset about the pink silk, but Verema gave her a gown which will have the Oban creaming in his robe, before Noor can walk past him. I did not tell her he likes pink."

"How do you know this? I was only just informed the other night he likes his redheads."

"He has a few other tastes as well, anything from the Islands… or 'forbidden.'"

"Thank you, child. You know very well, our clients. Now, if I had known that soldier was stained…"

"Did he not say? Was it his coming-of-age stigma?"

"No. He is past the age of his first. That's why I did not think of it. His mark was one of…an Oban he serves. He did a service, I saw the pattern, after the dress was ruined. I did not think when I saw it, it was Noor's, she was right to be upset. She saved up for that silk. Hopefully, the laundress can fix it, a Dark blue will go well with her hair."

"Noor has settled in now? She was a mess when she first came here."

"The older girls listen to you, you know. Noor has come to terms with her lot in life and knows she has hair which will attract a lot of clients, she must join with the right ones. The ones who will have her and no other."

"She knows this... I am sure the Oban will pay. Did Verema teach her any tricks?"

"I believe so, however, we will find out… You missed a good celebration. Many received their stigmas. I think your friend, the soldier may have received another one."

"I was busy, you know I must work it. The best Vuza coins Dangle in the best pockets. I gleaned much; you know this serves me and you well."

"Yes, I thank you for the extra. If it was not for your help…"

"Are you not getting enough clients? I thought business was good."

"Yes, but I have rent, soldiers to pay, and sometimes 'tis not enough."

"Well, I will try to acquire more, however, do not tell."

"I do not. Somehow, he knew where to look and took my extra last time he came to collect rent."

"Hide it somewhere else. Outside. Under a rock."

Delma looked tiredly at her protégé, her underling. The girl she raised from a babe. Andic looked much like a small boy, who was sitting with her legs splayed out like many a boy would.

"You look and act like a boy. What happens when you cannot?"

"I am not worrying about this, not until I must. Do you have anything you wish me to do, while I have time."

"No, child. I see tiredness in your eyes, why do you not go off for a rest. There is nothing here I need you to do, I thank you for the asking, you are a good child."

"Thanks, Delma, I am off then." Andic picked herself up off the chair and left walking back to the kitchen to grab another bite. Only a heel of bread was left. She grabbed it, anyway, walking quietly up to her little corner in the rafters. She sat down with a broken heel of bread and portion of goat cheese, trying to digest what transpired this night.

Taking the man's life did not weigh her down, it was a kind deed she did not let him suffer. This was no place for a man with no eyes, and if his face became infected, someone else would end the young man's life. She was more concerned about the why. His eyes were taken because he saw something he should not have. Either the Dagger or the Prophecy. She would learn more about the sayings of other countries. She never had need before. Why did life have to have more complications? Was not trying to find food enough?

A Prophecy is written word. A future happening. Of this I know… Yet one about Dragons? What is a Dragon? I heard more on these supposed creatures in the last month, enough to make me curious, and this star is connected to these Dragons. I hate not knowing things. I need find out what I can… how? I will sleep on it, cover all the possibilities. First, I wish to see this star.

On a hunch, she opened the roof access panel turning until she faced the eastern sky to see the traveling star. It was still there. The more she focused on it; it became all she could see. It did indeed have a tail.

More like a tongue than breath, will this land here? How would any know of this many years ago? Would our God already know? Of course he would, he is our saviour. Would it lessen his power?

She left it propped open for the slight breeze, laying down to catch a bit of sleep and knew she would have some business in the daylight hours.

She had plenty of things to do now, a quest of her very own, and she felt finally her life may have a purpose.

CHAPTER 6

Damara

Arises New Life

Damara had a fairly good life; she had to admit. She ran her hands into her graying black hair and massaged her scalp before letting them drop to her lap.

After twenty-two years of marriage, she still loved her husband, maybe more than when she first was contracted to him. He loved her, she believed. They both were affectionate to each other; he would cater to her whims, helping when her business was busy during the winter season.

Winter was when most of the clothing orders she contracted were completed. She had one shop full of girls in the Capital, Merida and one in the city of Kara, with several warehouses where she and her husband lived. This joining in the late summer was sure to reap just as many orders. If any of the nobility had the sense to begin a new fashion, it would spread like a fire, she looked forward to the challenge.

With her family name, but of late her hard work and product, she built her clothier business into a large enough enterprise. With Ramis's assistance, of course, his family supplied the finances. Ramis was second son to the current Vezyr of Finance. His eldest brother was heir to the title and position. Her husband retired from his career in the Army due to an injury in his right leg. He was left with a slight limp, yet still able to help with the delivery of orders to both cities. She did not know what she would do without him. It was his name attached to her business which helped it remain fluid and functional.

Damara lounged in her garden on her chaise, watching the setting sun. Admiring the magnificent colours a clear summer day would never fail to present. Their villa overlooked the Southern Ocean. The sky shining all colours of orange, pink and red, reflected by the sea. It lit up her emotions, where sometimes she missed Ramis so much she burst out crying, just from longing. They had excellent conversations, she missed his companionship, he never failed to make her laugh and smile.

I wonder what Ramis is doing right now, I wonder if he misses me. He loves the sunset almost as much as I do, he is missing a beautiful one, full of colours.

She would say out of all the colours, pink was her favorite. Never had there been such a feminine colour which looked good on every woman. The sky was ever changing and lit up some of the city from her vantage point. She drew a sip from her smokey glass, the flavours tart on her tongue.

The city of Kara was situated on the Southeastern part of the continent. The topography was much the same as the Capital. Both cities opened upon the Southern Ocean. The cliffs of white creating a natural barrier against winter storms. Their villa was on a hill overlooking the ocean. It was fine as any other of their station, created from white marble, mined from quarries in the Northern interior mountain range.

She established orchards of olive, citrus, and gardens of herbs and flowers, that she took the pains to begin at the advent of their life together. The city was well kept, Ramis and Damara contributed to the upkeep of roads and paths, and it was a city where no homeless were left wanting. The city did outstanding trade in fishing and seafoods. Her clothing warehouses were along shores where there was access to docks and ships. Amongst other things, Kara had an extensive trade of goats, milk, cheeses, and meats, with an abundance of honey, bees, and waxes. A couple of candlemakers had the monopoly on candles with a friendly competition between them since they married themselves into each others' families.

In the early years of her business, after the children were well situated with their studies and tutors, Damara travelled the breadth of this continent, most times with her husband, Ramis. She dealt with local women of each area for dyes. She had one warehouse in the city for dying of white cloth to get the hues which helped make her in demand. Over the course of her business career, she had a fleet of ships which travelled the Western Ocean to the lands of Pelin'Dun and as far as Aram, which was famous for its silks and bold colours of blues and greens only they could perfect.

She tried for years to bargain for their dyes, but they would not deal with her once they found out she was a woman. She never returned and had a few Captains she trusted to deal for her, and they bartered for her. They dealt with Aram and never failed to purchase what she needed. One Captain on his last trip brought her a beautiful necklace of the palest pink pearls, which she loved to wear constantly.

Her drink of iced lemonade with hibiscus was also a shade of pink which made her feel blissful. She drank it slowly savoring the flavour, watching the ever-changing colours. There were a few clouds to reflect more saturation. Damara thought in colour, perhaps a little too much, if she was honest with herself.

Her husband was in Merida to attend the joining of the century. The Dader of the Emperor was contracted to the son of one of his best friends, the Commander of the Army. Damara had not gone with him as the day they were to leave, she suddenly fell sick with an illness which took her two weeks to finally feel she did not need twenty hours of sleep. She woke up that day, prepared to leave, and began vomiting so hard she fainted. Upon waking she began vomiting again. Damara told Ramis to go without her, it most likely was something she ate, and hopefully she would follow when able.

"You go dear. I will not be missed as much as you and am sure Berrin will be pleased to see you. I feel so weak, I am sure I can not travel far without my stomach revolting and would not have you miss this joyous occasion for looking after me. I have all the servants caring for me and will want for nothing."

"As long as you get better, Mara. I do not know what I would do without you. I will make your excuses to Berrin and his wife. You will be missed in my heart and will make note of any designs you may miss."

"Oh, dear Ramis, you will not! I am sure you will have someone do that for you! However, I will appreciate the effort, you know me all too well."

Ramis was willing to stay with her. She knew he was worried yet told him his lack of attendance would be noticed and if she could, she would try to make it.

"You represent our house; it would be a slight to the Emperor if you did not attend. We cannot afford to be under the notice of the Empire and the Church again. I am but a minor member of the royal family. I will convalesce and try to attend, but you must go."

"You promise to recuperate, try to rest, Mara. I could not imagine this life without you. You hold my heart in your hands."

"And you hold my heart in yours. I will miss you while you are gone. I do not know how this came about. My stomach is so sore, my throat is raw, and burns. I am so sorry this happened."

"'Tis not your fault. Keep the physician here, until you are on the mend, I will instruct him to do so."

"Thank you, this sounds reassuring. I am certain he will have the cure. You go now; I will be fine, dear husband."

Ramis kissed her and went to order the servants and the physician he detained while Damara was in the onset of illness. He reluctantly set off with his entourage. He always travelled with many attendants, Ramis had his personal assistant, a taster, and soldiers for protection. They both did. This entourage grew over the years as they learned to protect her goods and their clothier's name grew.

Her family was related to the royal family, her GrandMader and the current Mader of the Emperor were cousins. Important enough, however, not in the line of succession, so no one sent assassins their way. Her Pader married her Mader, his favorite concubine in an unsanctioned marriage, not waiting for royal permission. It took his lifetime to recoup his disgrace by winning lands in the Great War many years ago. The family name of Du'Landan was not one to be taken lightly, her Pader had many conquests to his credit. He had a prestigious, lengthy career in the army, and retired with many honours. The city was proud of their prominent patron.

It also helped her Pader being relocated to Kara for most of his career. It kept him and his growing family out of the Emperor's eye, and exploits on the field of battle kept him in favour. Damara's Mader had loved to dress in the finest clothes and passed her love onto her only Dader. Most of Damara's business in the Capital was with the current Empress and she also catered to the nobility in both cities.

With her name and the money Ramis brought into the marriage, it laid the foundation to begin her passion for colour and fabrics. She reveled in creating colours, travelling near and far. Bringing back the means to produce her own dyes when she could. She introduced and managed to maintain her business contacts with silk and linen production. She had a smattering of wools, but as the climate in the South did not warrant much need of wools, she just Dabbled with them.

It grew substantially in the last five years, she hired a few women her age to run the dye pots, and the seamstresses. She had the means to hire soldiers, her empire of clothing alone warranted plenty of security detail. This was done with permission of course, Ramis was her means to operate. Everything was done under his scrutiny; however he let her run the Daily operations. His presence in the warehouses and shipyards was just ornamental, Damara had full command of how it was managed. Women were not allowed to 'officially' own a business. By law.

I hope I feel better, so I can return, I do not want Tovah to think I have abandoned her. I do hope nothing is amiss. This is the longest I have been away, even when I was not feeling the energy earlier. 'Sigh' even the Darker colours with the disappearing sun are gorgeous. Very mysterious and slightly sensual. Hmmm... I miss Ramis...

As the sun set and disappeared, her servants kept busy lighting torches in the gardens and the villa. She reflected her second most favorite colour was orange, yellow, no, perhaps red. All warm colours really or was it just the colours of the sunset. She gazed at the changing sky still lost in her musings, thinking back over all the good and some not so good moments. Her musings were interrupted by her main maid, Peylin coming outside to her seat, handing her a sealed note.

"This came here by messenger. Nada, 'tis from Tovah."

Damara opened it and read the missive.

"I am to attend the shop tomorrow; she says there are items which need my attention but does not say what they may be. Peylin, wake me up early tomorrow. Have the cook prepare me something not too taxing for my stomach. I will head down in the carriage; I do not believe I have energy to deal with a horse."

"Do you think you should be going? Mayhap Tovah could attend you here?"

"She would if it were not something she needed me to see there. She knows I have been ill; I wish to get out. Maybe 'tis what I need to get me on my feet and active again. Thank you for thinking of me, though, it means a great deal you have my best interests at heart. I thank our God for you."

Peylin had been with her for a while now, even thought her maid was the same age as Damara's Dader, she sometimes treated her mistress as if Damara were the child. Damara smiled up at the young woman, her blonde hair neatly under a half cap.

"As long as you do not over do it, you do not want a relapse, it might take longer to recover."

Peylin removed her mistress's drink and walked inside the villa disappearing for a time, Damara knew she would be waiting inside her chamber to help prepare for sleeping.

She was woken up by the sun lighting up the room, Peylin craftily placed the shutters open for the evening breeze and let the sunlight wake her mistress naturally. Damara rose and dressed in serviceable attire, long leggings and a longer tunic, split up both sides for ease of movement. She introduced the long tunic, for women in the home, which served a functional purpose. It took one visit from another noblewoman to get this fashion into the other homes. Mayhap she hand-picked the most talkative of wives to help. Covertly of course.

Damara was careful not to draw too much attention to her house. She grew up in a house constantly beneath the Emperors eye and was cautious in her business dealings which may be the uppermost reason, she was still in business. Or her connections, she was after all, related to the Royal House. Or perhaps, it was because she knew how to clothe women in her class.

Clothing on women was to be demure, no excess of skin to be shown. In public, Damara wore a snood over her hair, some women of lower castes would wear full hoods over their hair. It was dictated by the Church women were to not be provocative in their dress, at least not the upper nobility. The snood was her preferred choice when she worked, it helped keep her long black hair contained. Some restrictions did work in a woman's favor.

She chose plainly in case she had to work and was looking forward to doing something today and hoped she did not overexert herself. She enlisted Peylin to make sure if she thought Damara was going to faint, she had full authority to boss her around.

After a breakfast of fresh bread and jelly from some of their own fruit, she felt she could set off. The ride down in the closed carriage was uneventful and saw the trees in full foliage when she opted for a peek out of the carriage window. With the sun making itself known, she placed the curtain back and rested back on the cushions. The fabric done in a red she dyed herself. She had her fingers in all their assets. Damara smiled and closed her eyes for the rest of the trip. Peylin wisely kept her thoughts to herself, she saw silence was what her mistress desired.

Soon enough the carriage came to a full stop outside her shop, in the inner courtyard. Damara alighted with Peylin following right behind, the carriage pulled ahead into the stable, getting the horses out of the sun. The coachman would keep them hooked up, as she did not think she would be very long, so he gave them water and a bit of fodder. She went into the shop attached to the warehouse where she would find Tovah, her deputy for the city of Kara.

Tovah, a middle-aged woman like herself, was bent over one of the tables holding papers with all orders for clothing and fabrics they created. It was piled high today and Tovah, her mahogany brown hair, usually neatly done was in a haphazard mess.

A little too early in the morning to be messy, I wonder what is going on.

For some of her clients, she created the fabric and colours, the Empress and Namarch being her best clientele. The Empress had her own seamstresses, and Damara was commissioned to keep her in fabrics. Mostly silks, she would routinely send one of each colour, and once a year they would have a meeting with the Empress's main staff, to either return what was not used or bring extra. This kept her business running smoothly and the Empress set a tone, which had Damara dying fabrics for her other clients.

Tovah glanced up as she heard Damara's footsteps on the floorboards, her expression of worry catching Damara's eyes.

"Nada. Thank the God you are here. There is an issue you should be aware of."

Tovah looked very tired, Damara thought but did not verbalize it.

"What is this matter you brought me here for?"

"I am fretting at what to do with this last shipment we received from Aram. It is silk but does not seem to be the best of quality. Here look at this sample."

Tovah had a bundle on the table next to her, she grabbed an armful and proceeded to show Damara the imperfections in the weave which seemed excessive even to her standards.

"You are astute, and you are right. We will bring this up to the Captain, to return what we cannot use. How many bolts are affected?"

Damara turned to the storage side of the warehouse to see bolts in disarray, and everything untidy.

"All."

That was all Tovah said, Damara had to sit in the one chair by the table. Her legs felt the rest of her was heavy and wobbled to the chair.

"All of them?"

She did not want to believe it. This was a vast number of orders which could not be fulfilled. She was thankful the Empress's order for the joining was sent last month. She looked gratefully at Peylin who entered the office returning with a cup of water. She took the cup and drank it down.

"I began looking at the orders yesterday, thinking to begin the silks for dying. I opened several bolts having a good look, only to see they were not the quality we usually get. I kept going… I spent all night going through every bolt we have here. Only the shipment from Aram is affected, this last Captain was not our usual supplier. Everything from other Captains is fine. We can only use the portion from that corner…"

Here she pointed with her finger moving it along,

"…to over there, for the more pressing orders. I have organized the orders, from oldest to newest, however, if any one client has priority, I can redo the list."

Here Tovah tried to stifle a yawn, her words sinking in.

"You will have a rest, before you collapse. Go into the office and have a lay down, I will try to figure this dilemma out. We will have these bolts rerolled and stacked and send them back to Aram on the next ship. Captain Olent will take care of this; he has contacts and will know how to deal with this error. As for silks, we will send a ship to Lanthia, buy what they have. 'Tis not the best silk, but even their lesser silk is better than this."

Damara turned to Tovah,

"I will put the word out, and we will find this solitary Aramite. He will not be allowed to trade, in Du'Lanay ever again after I am done with him. You go rest, and I will have the girls clean up this area. Thank you, Tovah, I do not know what I would do without your diligence. This will get sorted; it will work out in the end."

In the end, it worked out better than what she expected. She had her main Captain, sail up the coast with a massive amount of coin to purchase all he could from the province state of Lanthia. He brought back even better than what they usually acquired, and for a fraction of what she assumed it would cost. She instructed him to give a percentage over, if it would cement a contract to keep them supplied. He reported it would not be necessary; however, the supply would only transpire once a year as it was not an instant crop for the people in the North. He was not able to tell her why this was, and she told him it was better than not at all.

"Maybe we can change this for them. If we let them know we are willing to pay for the export of silks, they will provide us with more. Let us work on this. You have your people up there, let us begin a dialogue. You can accomplish this?"

"Yes. Certainly. Next time we travel there, I will relay your message."

With her deputy's aid they spent the next few days after her Captain returned fulfilling orders. For Damara, keeping busy kept her mind occupied and she forgot about the wedding of the century or the fact she was missing it. They managed to get most of the orders dyed.

"Captain Olent."

"Yes, Nada?"

"Relay the word on this Aramite. Find him and deal with him. He is not welcome in Kara. If he sets foot or docks here again, Ramis will have him arrested and the Empire will not deal kindly with him."

"Yes, Nada. We will find him; I have my contacts abroad."

"How Dare he give us inferior goods. 'Tis bad enough we rely on Aram for their silks. Mayhap I should travel to Lanthia and treat with them. If we have them as our major supplier it would lessen the lag in time. Not only is it closer, but also not someone we are at war with."

"You are wise, Nada. I will set sail soon."

The more she thought about it, the better the idea sounded. She finally took a pause from the shop, and stayed home, to have herself another night on her terrace. Now that she was not occupied with her business, she lay down on her favorite chaise and reflecting on her life and marriage to Ramis, she missed his cuddles and smooth words. She drank a light white wine from their own vineyard. Damara merely sipped at it, lingering on the fruity notes. She thought about her husband smiling to herself.

Many times, she and Ramis made love to the sunset and this made her feel like the world was hers. How she loved him so much, he was so supportive, never failing to tell her, always flattering her, and bringing her presents. She was willing to overlook the trivial things, to keep the good things they had together, their children being a big part of the good.

It was difficult in the early years, his career in the Army kept him away for extended periods of time. They had two sons and a Dader, and her servants assisted with the rearing of her children. Like all noble families, they kept maidservants and manservants in the traditions of their house. She was left alone to rear their children, Ramis absent most of the year, returning home periodically, if only to keep procreating. Damara was kept highly active with this since his injury, she helped restore him to health, deepening their emotional bond. Then his subsequent discharge from the Army, his devotion to her and assistance in the running of her ever-expanding clothier business, reinforced her devotion to him.

Their two sons joined the Army recently, and while it was hard to see them go, it was their duty to uphold their Pader's name and bring honour upon their house. Her Dader delivered their first grandchild, a girl, which they named after her, and she was a precocious child. Must take after her, indeed!

This mysterious illness knocked her off her feet for a time, the first week saw her completely bedridden, with no appetite. She dropped almost a quarter of her weight in the two weeks of being sequestered in her villa. Thankfully, she had her two deputies to take over the running of her business and there was no interruption to fulfilling orders until Tovah sent the message. Her husband had taken all orders to the Capital which were completed. He had competent employees to help him with that end of things when he arrived in Merida.

It gave her time to contemplate and reflect on her life up to now. She did not have as much to do now as she did in the early years. Things quieted once the children had their own lives, so she pondered on her many years of marriage. Thinking back to the very beginning of marriage, how she and Ramis almost parted ways.

She had delivered their second son and was convalescing after the birth, in the Capital. Rumours reached her of a possible mistress of her husband. It took her quite by surprise, she believed he was devoted to her and their family. She employed a man, through a female friend with connections, to find the legitimacy to the allegations. What the hired man discovered was never confirmed by her husband, he refuted it all, and she resolved to believe him. She had much to lose, and he was convincing in affirmation of devotion for her.

It rendered their bond greater than ever, and he made her feel she was the only one. She had no other hindrances after, never heard anything else to make her question his love, and she never had him followed again. If anything, he was always with her, was very attentive and helped make the business grow, he did most of the travel to the Capital. After a few years of going with him, she let him do the bulk of travel to the Capital, only on special occasions did she make the trip.

Like the last one, five months ago, she went to take a special number of silks to the Empress and her Dader for her trousseau. The trip left her unfulfilled, as though something was not right… missing. A feeling in her gut, had her doubting herself making her question decisions, second-guessing every choice made, to the point where she had to place down the dyes, and walk away for a time. This had her leaving work to her deputies and staying increasingly at home. She had very proficient deputies, Damara trained them herself; they began by coming with her on client visits, then showed their worth by going on their own. She had one in Merida and one here in Kara, and both worked well with Ramis, getting all orders done, and done well.

Damara was attended by physicians at the onset of her illness, but they could not find anything wrong. They conferred with each other the possibility of food poisoning an explanation of her illness. She tried to think what it was she may have eaten but could not think of anything unusual. Her diet consisted of the same throughout the years. Maybe it was the anxiety and stress she gave herself which set her stomach off; she did get herself worked up enough to warrant it.

Have I brought this illness onto myself? Have I worried myself sick? Why have I felt something is not quite right, even my dyes cannot get me from this mood.

Once she recovered enough to feel good about walking in her gardens, she sent a message to Ramis she still tired easily and thought attending the wedding would be too much for her. The trip alone would send her back to bed. As it was, she rose for an hour then spent most of the day, lounging and napping. The one trip she took to deal with the second-rate silk had her sleeping the next day almost right through. She wrote to him hoping he could smoothly make her excuses to the Commanders family to not make offence. Not like the Matriarch would miss her presence. The two wives had their own dynamics, which rendered them polite. But that was all.

He would be in the city for a couple of weeks after the wedding, so she would make the best of it and build up her strength.

She could not shake the feeling. Mayhap if she distracted herself with her Dader and GrandDader, she would not think about it. Damara went over to her Dader's house, however, the noise of her GrandDader had her begging off early. The girl was teething, and no amount of coddling would get the baby to settle. Damara suggested a piece of Ravenwood soaked in hard alcohol. It worked for her, so very long ago. Damara's Dader took offense at the suggestion.

"I am not going to get my baby drunk!"

Damara made excuses and left. Once it became quiet again, back at home, the sensation returned. As though a fuse ready to be lit.

She began to fidget with her clothing, and it was not until she had a calming tea, an herbal infusion which helped her to fall asleep, she felt her cares melt away. Pretty soon that was all she would drink, hot and then cold, as a variation to get through the day. She was reassured it was not an addictive tea and took comfort in the drinking of it. When Tovah reached out to her, she was consuming this tea for a good week, so it boosted her energy for the week she was up and about, and was also careful to rest when she could, Peylin was adamant she did not overexert herself.

For another distraction, she had her girls at her shop, prepare a dress. It was a red silk, the Empress and her Dader rejected. The colour was a Darker red than the colours of the royal house, so she added a hint of pink so it had undertones of a Dark fuchsia. Damara thought not to waste it and to commission an outfit for her own use. The day came when it was delivered, she gloried in it as soon as she tried it on.

She looked at herself in the full-length mirror which decorated the wall of her dressing chamber. She was one of the few matrons who could boast such a mirror, it was crafted by an artisan in the Capital. Only the Empress and the royal household boasted anything of its size. It nearly did not make the trip overland, but she had it transported in its own cart wrapped in multiple layers, upon layers upon layers of cloth.

She examined her reflection observing gray hairs had increased on her head, mostly above her temples, and sporadically throughout her black hair. She looked tired, Dark circles now seemed permanent below her brown eyes, and the rest of her skin seemed to have paled against the bruised look of illness. Her skin sagged in certain areas, under her arms, when she raised them, she had little flaps which jiggled, and her breasts looked diminished and wrinkled on top. Her waist had looser skin, dropping the weight too fast had the skin not recovering as quick.

She took time to look closer at her face and saw wrinkles at the outer corner of her eyes when she smiled to the reflection. Some slight puffiness under her eyes, depending on if she drank wine, but even now if she did not drink any vintages, she still had puffy eyes. Loose skin around her jowls, sometimes her jaw itched something fierce. She would scratch and raised white bumps would appear.

When did I age? Do I look like this to Ramis? Does he even find me attractive anymore?

She noticed he was losing hair on his head, the back had thinned, and he had a few silver strands running through. The last time she saw him with no clothes, she noticed he had hair on his back, not a lot, but in his youth, he had none. His body had changed some, over the years. He still had strength in his legs, but his middle section had softened somewhat. Ramis used to have a strong stomach and muscles, but she noticed he was sporting a paunch, not that she cared, since he always pleased her in the bedroom. Physical prowess in the bedroom overruled physical appearance to her.

The dress still looked good, even if the person wearing it had changed. She tried a newer addition to the sleeves, a longer flowing sleeve from the opening at the elbow, and if she twirled, slashes in the skirt showed a lighter red and complimentary glimpses of pink and orange were visible. She twirled and twirled for a good half hour, until she felt quite dizzy from the action. Then reluctantly Damara took the dress off, handing it to Peylin, who stood by patiently adding her appreciation to the innovative design.

All my favorite colours,

She would wear this dress for her benefit, and she would wear it on a special night for Ramis.

"I see an older woman in the mirror, Peylin. When did I get old?"

"'Tis this illness, it has set you back. You sit out in the sun and eat right, and you will regain your energy."

Peylin was very maderly when she wished to be.

"I have no problem with this, however, I feel somewhat restless lately, as though I have unfinished orders or something, as though I should be down at the shop."

"'Tis why you have Tovah, Nada. She has proven to be very competent, her observation of the shipment of silk and her dedication to look at all, proves her worth. You have a devoted woman in that worker."

"You are very right in this regard. She has proven herself, and she loves colours as much as I do. That is why I chose her. I thank the God she has taken over while I recover from my illness. I also thank the God for your care, Peylin. You have been right here beside me, and I do not know what I would have done without you."

"You are very gracious, Nada. I have never wanted for anything in serving you and I will follow you to the ends of the earth."

Peylin did not know her words spoken would have her speaking the truth on that matter.

Thinking about Ramis and their sparks in the bedroom had Damara feeling much better. She removed the dress and decided to have a nice long soak in the bathing house in the center of her wing of rooms. She hoped Ramis was home soon, she felt like she needed some physical affection.

I must be feeling better if that is all I can think of.

She ran her hands over her breasts under the water and down to her mound. She brushed her button between her lips and felt it harden to her touch. She opened her eyes to see if Peylin was there, she was not, and Damara heard sounds of her maid in the next room, so she very quietly and gently stroked herself with her fingers, quickly bringing herself to a climax.

That did not take long, but I do wish Ramis was here instead. He would know exactly how to make me feel complete. I should not have to please myself. Well, at least I know I can.

She rose out of her bath drying herself off and dressing herself in an evening gown and robe prepared for sleep.

She went to bed and for the first time in a month had a very restful sleep.

CHAPTER 7

Saliene

A Time Long Forgotten

Good, the red-haired bitch is dead,

Saliene thought to herself, as she saw Vandrin swing a sword catching Meera in the face before her sister fell backwards over the falls. From her place at one of the stone benches surrounding the water basin, she strode over to Vandrin as he was peering over the edge into the mist,

"Where did you get this sword?"

She was itching to touch it. The sword looked like a Master handcrafted it. It was a two-hand sword, hilt encased in black leather with a beautifully wrought iron cage encasing a gem. Clear with a bit of a glow, the mist in the air made it difficult to tell if it was shining or if the stray sunbeam was glancing off. She was fascinated by the thought beginning to form in her mind. Vandrin confirmed what she was thinking.

"The little bitch was hiding it in the tunnels, Byrik told me she was hiding something, but I did not know what until we caught her carrying it. This is mine by right."

He brought the sword up between them, hilt first, as he turned around to face his youngest sister, or half sister really. As he brought it up to peer at the crystal in the hilt, there was a loud concussion from the gorge. A vibration in the air, water spray came up in the falling water and rose above by thirty feet, spraying all those in the immediate area with mist. Meera had hit the bottom pool. The gem in the hilt crackled loudly then burst apart into tiny facets. Catching both in the face and torsos, the ones against their fronts bounced off the leather of jerkins they wore, as both dressed in the finery of their house. A few shards caught both in the chin, cheeks, and upper arms staying embedded. Both siblings yelped and jumped at the impact and Vandrin yelled for a healer woman,

"Get these out now!"

Vandrin started to shake his jerkin and brush bits off his sleeves.

"Fucking unbelievable! These little beasts hurt like hell. Healer! Where the fuck is that healer woman?"

Both strode over to sit down at the closest bench beside the basin and waited. Vandrin in his impatience picking at the ones he could feel for. The healer of the castle hurried up to them and methodically picked out the pieces of gem from their bodies. Dabbing the injuries with a salve to stop the welling of blood, she finished Saliene first, working on Vandrin next. Each piece left small indents and cuts once healed would leave tiny scars.

"At least you have a beard you can grow to cover your face; I will have to do with holes in mine."

"Like you care,"

"No, I do not. Did not feel a thing."

Saliene stood up, picking up the sword Vandrin dropped in his haste to sit down. She grabbed the hilt, looking at the now empty cage, a few dull shards falling out, bouncing on the smooth rock face of the garden ground floor. She swung it around, and a frown etched her young face.

"The balance is all wrong with this now, the blade is top heavy. Here you see what you think."

Saliene walked over to him, as the healer finished his face, handing Vandrin the sword, hilt first. He stood up and attempted a few swipes.

"Yah, this is no good, now. Useless, really. Maybe it can be reforged. Cannot be the legendary sword of Noster, then. It should not have shattered. Here, you have it, its nothing but a piece of shite."

He thrust it back at Saliene walking away, cursing while his entourage hurried after him. He had truly little patience for things or people if matters did not go his way. It left him with an expression of bitterness, which became his countenance and did nothing for his good looks. Her brother and she had the look of the Northmen, and the build. Saliene and her friend, Merise were sitting in the Temple garden talking about men of the guard, when Meera raced through with Vandrin chasing her brandishing the sword.

"I do not think this will do at all, it feels all wrong, unbalanced. Think I will take it down to the smithy."

She practiced a few swipes, which had her friend Merise yelping and jumping back.

"That is not nice, fine, go and practice. I am going back home then."

Merise strode off in the same direction Vandrin had and Saliene watched her friend leave. She knew eventually her brother and her only friend would find their way into one or the other's bed. As if she didn't know! This was the only reason Merise hung out with her. Sometimes Saliene wished her friend would just go away.

She walked down several levels to the training yard and found Mattias training with his wooden staff, going through several exercises the Master of War at the Aerie set for Daily routine.

She had gotten him to stop blushing when he saw her by finally getting him to make her a woman. He was eager enough, and she found out it was not as fine as the men around her made it out to be, but maybe with another partner it would be.

She was fourteen and had no patience to wait until her Pader found her a husband. She would find out on her own, what the men talked about in the training yards. She spent more time in the yard than she did anywhere else. She would train at arms, make herself known as a fighting woman, not a woman to stay home and bear children. There were a few women of the North who fought side by side with men, and to the east across the continent on the other shores were an army of women who fought.

She went to visit the healer to get the necessaries to ensure she did not bear any children out of wedlock, which was not in her plan. She did not see Meera there, her sister was in the woods that day, and frankly Saliene did not care if she knew Saliene's business.

She strode over to Mattias and threw the sword hilt first into a corner of the yard. She was almost of the same height as he, tall and Dark-haired, they could almost pass as siblings as most folk of the North were Dark haired.

"You want to go through the ten movements?"

"Sure. It makes a good warm up, then let us spar."

"As you command."

Not red haired and cursed, like the little bitch she never saw as she grew up. Saliene was adamant they were not related. She always dreamed her Mader was someone like the Housekeeper or the wife of the Gamekeeper or Metalsmith. Not the dead woman who died before she learned how to walk, the Mader to both. She was glad she did not have to be with the little runt who ran wild. Saliene picked up a wooden sword and began the warmup exercises she was taught.

Saliene was tall for her age, she obviously took after her Pader, she was already 5'9", Dark hair, eyes a bright shade of blue, and fair of skin. She dressed like a Northerner, leather pants dyed black, wool spun shirt dyed the house Dark blue, a black leather vest decorated with silver embroidery. She lived in her outfit, many times the housekeeper suggested she wear a skirt, but once Saliene found out they would bow to her wishes, she wore pants. No one could convince her otherwise. She was an avid rider and hunter, lately Saliene began to train with the men at arms, with staff and wooden swords.

Pader was off at war. He was gone so long this last time she did not remember what he looked like, not that it bothered her, she had her own agenda. Vandrin was itching to go, but as eldest son and heir, he had no choice but to stay and rule in his Pader's stead. Until such time he joined and begot his own heirs, he was stuck here much like her. It had irked him to no end, and he would often go hunting for his enjoyment.

A few options were presented to him, but such a marriage had to have political advantages, the consent of his Pader and the Emperor had to agree. There were a few candidates in the Aerie, a few in the lowlands, and even some in the Capital. It was pretty much who they told him he had to marry. It did not stop him from sampling where he could, and Saliene was sure he may have a few bastards wandering about. There was no bias on unwed Maders, the North did not care. Every child born was a boon to the North, if they had no Pader, they were raised by everyone and were loved in that fashion.

It was hard to erase some of the deeply rooted beliefs of the Vendar religion, especially in a people who did not want them to disappear. The larger effigies were destroyed many centuries ago, however, households still had smaller idols and likenesses of the Vendar Gods. The worship and songs were very much the same. The Namanists had cunningly changed the wording to conform to their beliefs, which helped ease part of the transition.

Down in the Southlands, in the Capital and regions, children born out of wedlock were given over to the Church, men were given full license to propagate as they wished. Women were raised to be pious and virtuous, not spread their legs to any man. They were punished very publicly if found out. It was not an equal life. In the North, women were treated a little better. They had children and kept to themselves, some contracting marriages if suitable. These last ten years of war, women were in vast supply, most men going South never came back. Children were highly valued.

Hopefully, this was not her future. Saliene had no wish to be burdened with a child or a husband. She would not wait for such a time, Saliene wanted nothing but to please her Pader, little she saw him. She would hone her skills in the meantime and was beginning to like her practices, a little too much. The adrenaline rush during her combat was heady and found she needed an outlet after her bouts. Saliene finished her warmup and put the wooden sword down, then looked at the young man. He finished his, putting his down on the rack against the stone wall.

"You ready for me to whip your ass, little boy?"

"What makes you think I will let you?"

"Hmmm, you are welcome to try. Then after I beat you here…I beat you later."

"You are welcome to try, little bird. I have an advantage of a larger…staff."

"You think so? Show me."

She grabbed a staff and motioned to Mattias and the two of them spent the better part of a half hour trying to score a hit on the other. Both were glowing with a sheen of sweat. Saliene liked a good sweat, but hated losing, she never liked to give up either until she scored a hit or beat her opponent.

"Not bad, can you handle a sword?"

"Better than you can."

"I like a challenge. Let us see what you have."

She motioned to Mattias to grab a sword. Saliene grabbed another wooden sword and broke into a stance. Mattias swung his wooden sword and managed to tap her on the side,

"Elk balls, Mattias. I was not ready."

"You think the enemy will wait for you to be ready? Think, Sal. What does the Master tell us. Always be ready."

As she stood there cursing, the Training Master came in.

"Your stance is all wrong for a two-handed sword, if the sword on the ground is what you plan on using someday."

"The sword is useless, Graic. There was a gem in the hilt, but it shattered."

"I heard that Vandrin killed your sister with it."

"Sure. Who cares. She slipped and fell. Not Vandrin's fault. He was trying to save her; she just leaped off the neck. Ask anyone. I was there; I saw it all. The gem, though. It would have fetched a fair price. It gave me these holes in my face.

The sword is yours if you want it. I was going to send it to the Hole, maybe Kayam can reforge it."

Graic strode behind the battling duo picking up the discarded sword. He hefted it in his hand, looked at the hilt and blade closely, then leaned it up against the stone wall.

"I will take it down to the smithy later, its balance is all wrong, 'tis of no use as is. Nice edge on the blade though, master craftsmanship this looks. Maybe Kayam does not have to do too much to this."

He swung his arms to warm up, then grabbed another wooden sword. The black wood of Ravenwood was as hard and hurt as bad as the wooden staffs they used. He did warm up exercises and stood in front of the two sweating trainees.

"Let us start with footwork and then with arms and positioning."

He had no issue with women fighting. Saliene was training for a couple of years now after she persistently bothered Graic for a year straight. She had proven herself an avid learner, this did not stop her receiving bruises from the men who were her mentors. She gave back just as much. It was something she was beginning to crave, hitting, and being hit. She sometimes would not back down and would be sore, black, and blue for days.

"You watch and gauge your opponent. Saliene, if you are not yourself, you can be excused. Losing a family member is a moment of remembrance. Everyone will understand."

"I am fine, Graic. It was just Meera. No one cares. I can keep going. Try to get me on the Raven's Dance. I still need work on the five end movements."

"Fine, child, however, you will be shaking by the time you master that one."

"Good."

So, for the next month, Saliene trained every day, arms and legs burning by the end of each day. She completely forgot about the discarded sword as it did her no service. As the weather began to change, she knew she had to go and see the healer woman before winter set in, she felt a need to get under Mattias, so to be provident, she had better ride up the pass to the healer's house before the snows came.

Or maybe she would find another to slide against the sheets with, she would keep her options open.

CHAPTER 8

Meera

Fraught with Pain and Strife

The next morning arrived sooner than I expected, it felt like I just laid down, when I heard Nejan quietly from beyond the door.

"Wake up Childling, we have training to do and stories to tell."

"MMmm, let me wake up first, great Mader."

Rolling onto my side, I propped myself up and gave my left arm a bit of a flex and stretch. While it ached a bit, the bruises stung worse. I knew from what the healer taught me, hastening activities before an injury had time to heal would in the end, make things worse. For whatever reason, I did not feel as pain ridden as I fully expected. Flexing muscles in my arm, I ran my other hand on my skin, poking when I came to a bruise. I knew the muscles were still tender, but I could not feel anything more than that. I was looking for anything indicating a tear which would impede my healing, but I could not feel such.

"I feel better, not as many aches as I thought. Should I not be more sore? It hurts worse when I poke at my coloured skin than my shoulder itself."

"You are healing fast, then. You have a connection with the Great One. The Earth Mader has the healing power of the earth once she has a Dragon connection. Or it would be as the Great One ordains. The last Rider could heal with a touch, she drew from the earth very rarely, as to give healing, drawing from the earth would rob it of its life. It was learned by accident. There are areas of death in this land. Nothing grows and they have become desolate places."

"That is interesting. How do you know all this?"

"Well, once, just before the end, I was there. The Great One will explain all to you, I can only tell you what I know. I was young and only saw what was before me."

"I understand. I am going to wash and collect more water."

So, after my morning routine was complete, I walked to the stream with the two skins which were hanging up. I filled them both with water using one of them just to rinse the stump off. It helped but the odour was still very pungent. Nejan laughed if a cat could laugh.

"The woodsman would move the piece of tree around and cover the feces with earth, then dig another hole."

"Well, I will let him, then, I do not think I could dig anything right now."

I hung them both back on their hooks.

"So, let us practice joining minds as we go through our day, I will explain all we Li'on-sa are and you can learn about what we did for the great Dragons."

Nejan stretched her hind legs before laying her great body down on the mossy grass and proceeded to clean herself.

The day flew by quicker than I expected. Listening to the great cat tell how the felines hunted their prey, and the Dragons would transport the kills back to the basins.

"There are caves, holes in the mountains the Dragons used as their lairs, we would cohabitate with them as needed. The Riders would live near in the boxes they built. Others were servants tending to wounds, or food preparation, and it was a peaceful existence. All that served lived in harmony... Until harmony was no longer."

"You say caves are secluded? Are there areas still in these hills?"

"Yes, more to the North beyond this range of mountains. There is one that smokes, and beyond this mountain it is unhabitable to humans. The outside weather is too harsh, and growing season too short. We would use this area for breeding, raising young, hunting for our meat, and use the warmth of the mountain caves. Other parts of this vast land have other caves, but I have never left here for many years. There are other lairs on the other large land Dragons lived on, but I do not know if any of my kind are there. Li'on-sa have only lived in this land of the North. I will have to search one day for a mate; I have not the urge to do so yet."

"The urge?"

"Yes, with the return of the Dragons, the ability to procreate will return for our kind. It is much like your bond. Li'on-sa have instincts, which serve us and the Dragons well. I will need to find a mate to bond myself with. We have kept to ourselves for without the need to bond, the only thing left is the need to survive. I do not want to perish just yet. I have found a purpose in finding you, and will help you to find your path, Little Cub."

I went to sleep that night; my head filled with too much knowledge. Nejan opened my eyes to a unique way of life I was trying hard to imagine. It still felt like what she was telling me was for someone else. I was learning a different history I had never heard before. The fact I was learning from a beast of legends still astounded my mind. It took me a while to fall asleep, thoughts of the past week churning around in my mind.

How was this our history? I need to know more. Why would Naman try to erase all? Well, that is easy. If under Dragon rule was kindness and love, like Nejan says, then Naman is the complete opposite. I have not the slightest idea how I can be this one they have been waiting for. I would have to go back to claim the sword, Vandrin would not willingly give it up. This I know.

As time passed during the next morning, I became comfortable with mind speech, it was effortless when I did not overthink it. The day was peaceful; the tranquility of the woods surrounded us, a sense of calm, in the rising of the sun. There was less fog in the summer months, the air was close to the same temperature of the water from the warm springs. In the fall and winter, one could not see for the dense moisture hanging in the air. I listened, lulled by the tranquility I felt. I could hear birds in their song, and other life sources travel through the bush, my senses honing themselves.

"How, may I ask, is it you know things? Me.. for instance... How do you know of me? How am I different?"

"The Great One made himself known to me, I do not know if he speaks to others, other than you. We communicated with Dragons of old. More like pictures in our minds, and most of it was for our living purposes. We did not discuss elaborate matters unless we had a human counterpart. My species live in the now, and I was content to be with Little Uncle, who I was directed towards. I did not know of you, or your role to play until the Great One told me. I live to serve you until I cannot. One day I hope to live for another of my kind, but until then, I am yours."

"So, the Great One? Is he around here?"

"I do not know; I have never seen him in this time. He has only been in my thoughts. He directed me to be here. 'Tis all I can tell you, Little Uncle will tell you what you need to know, he is well versed in his knowledge."

At the point when the sun was directly overhead in the sky, I collected every piece of material I could find and walked to the stream. Nejan followed and then kept climbing, I knew without mind speech the cat was hungry and would hunt for her meal. She continued to converse with me.

"You are different from the others. The Great One told me I needed to find you and protect you until you no longer needed me. You would be different in such you would think about your actions before you responded. You have a mind not tainted by hatred, lust, greed or self worth. Little Uncle was upset when I brought you to him, he feared for your spirit. I also sensed his happiness. He has watched over you from afar. His knowledge of the Great One is different than mine, he has not heard the voice, but he learned knowledge of the written word. We both live to serve."

"You have seen the Great One? Before the end? What is his countenance?"

"He is the Flying Death."

"Oh."

Her simple description had me ponder, he sounded imposing and stern. I was sceptical of my bond with him.

Would I be able to live up to his expectations?

I was wondering how I could accomplish this quest I knew truly little about.

I washed myself and every piece of fabric, a lot of which had my blood on them. I searched around the area, looking for the few herbs and weeds I knew grew among damp areas along the banks. Finding a few which would help in healing and picking a handful. I would return with a basket if I found such in the cabin. Healer Nena instructed me my first summer in the construction of reed baskets, and I was certain if I could not find one, making one would be the course of action.

Satisfied the clothes and linens were as clean as they would get, I headed back to the cabin, hanging them on surrounding branches and shrubs to dry, and tidied inside as best I could. Assessing my left arm, I stretched and swung it around, rotated it slowly and was amazed it did not ache as much as this morning. I was sure it would be tender for weeks, recalling how the Master of Horse, Feil had dislocated his shoulder from an incredibly young and boisterous colt named Blaze. The horse yanked his lead when startled from the clatter of weapons falling close. Feil nursed his arm for weeks.... now that I recalled the memory, it was probably the attention he got from Saragh, the undercook which prompted his reluctance to heal.

Our internal conversation ceased while I sensed Nejan had seized her prey and was busy consuming it. I felt satisfaction coming from her, smiling at the thought.

I set a pot of stew on, grabbing the dried herbs, smelling each one beforehand, amazed Uncle Kiem knew what ones to use. Using the bones of the coney Nejan caught the night before, wild onions and wild garlic I found by the stream near where I bathed.

As I busied myself with various tasks, I lost myself in thought, imagining what others were doing back home. Danyc would be baking breads and rolls in the kitchens, Nena would be collecting herbs, she had several plots where she cultivated healing plants. A disturbance in the woods caught my attention, Nejan erupted out of the woods at an alarming speed, the remains of her meal dangling in her dripping jaws. The cat dropped it by the doorway and spoke rather loudly in my head,

"The woodsman is coming, quickly."

She sprinted down the hill in the direction Kiem would be coming from. I flopped down on the one step of the cabin; there would be no running for me yet. I waited about ten minutes, which seemed an eternity leaning against the jamb. I was beginning to drift off, when I saw the two in the distance, heading up the hill in the long wild grasses. I stood up slowly. It was getting easier; I did not have time to reflect on how effortless it was before Kiem was standing before me.

"Greetings childling, By the Mader! You are healing rather fast, quicker than I thought."

He checked me over with a glance, looking intently at my face.

"The eye looks good. The scar is healing nicely. We should get those stitches out so it can finish. No chance it will break apart, maybe if you talk too much it might."

I was trying not to groan with the effort of rising. He seemed to be in a joyful mood, so I remained quiet while he talked on.

"You seem to be proving yourself to be the one we are needing. Especially if this rapid healing is a sign. Nejan mentioned it as we walked back up, but I can see for myself. Good. This will serve us well."

"How so?"

"We will have to work on fighting skills as we travel, I am afraid. While Vandrin's men did come down to look, they found the clues left by Nejan and were satisfied with them. I overheard one of the guards saying one of the older Woodsmen would be coming down the cliff banks when he arrived from the lowlands.

Vandrin would be sending him to check a wider footprint and verify their find-ings.

They were quite startled at the size of the paw prints, as a few had never seen prints this big. I saw them gather the remnants of your clothing and wisps of hair then leave. The rain washed away some of the blood, but evidence was still col-lected in pools. I took my time, trying to diminish signs Nejan could not erase in her haste to return here. If it is who I am thinking, Volan, the oldest Woodsman still alive, he will know what he is looking at and will know where to find us. He knows this place and will know my involvement also."

He stood facing me with all his gear still on. I had risen slowly, so I did not crane my neck up at him, managing it all by myself with no difficulty. I was also amazed at my healing ability. Never had I seen rapid healing. The mere mention of Vandrin brought me back to the conversation.

"Why would Vandrin care so much if I were still alive? He never paid any attention to me when he was at the castle. If anything, he stayed away. Always hanging with his cronies, drinking, getting maids pregnant. The girls would be coming to the healer for potions to get rid of the child. I saw this in the last two years I spent training with the healer. I am surprised he even knew I existed."

I asked questions, while I moved easily over to the bed, then decided to sit on the box next to it. Kiem unpacked what he carried over his shoulder, placing his bow and arrows back in their corner. He puttered around the fire, placing herbs on the hooks to dry, and all the while chatted with me.

"He may have seen the gem light up when you were cleaning it off. If he has a brain, he will piece it together. He heard the stories, everyone has, and he may think you are a threat. I am sure Secondary Reudin will confirm his fears. The faith has a different spin to it, those two are two peas in a pod when it comes to their ambitions. They walk a parallel path, and there can be no wrinkle in the fabric of their future plans…Your survival is paramount. We will leave soon."

"We are leaving? Where to? Why do I need to hide?"

"I will explain all when I come back from the stream. We are not leaving right now, Meera. After I wash, we can sit. I will fill this skin with fresh water. We can have some of your stew, it smells good."

Kiem finished at the fire, excusing himself to go wash at the stream before dark. I sat there trying to remember the time I first grabbed the sword to when Vandrin grabbed it out of my hands.

Now I thought about it, finding it in the dark corner, I suddenly remembered the exact moment my hand touched the hilt. I felt a slight vibration course through my body the moment my hand connected even through the rags covering it. I did not think anything of it then. Slight tremors and vibrations running through the bedrock from the mining done in other parts of the cliffs happened all the time. The catacombs below the city, a rabbit warren if ever there was one, were con-nected to the mining. Maze after maze, tunnel upon tunnel, only the miners and the poor folk, who had no place to sleep inhabited them. I knew them intimately from necessity of hiding from my minders and later from men who had groping hands.

The more I thought on it, the more I was sure there was a connection of sorts. I mentioned it to Kiem when he emerged from the bushes, hair wet and clothes clinging.

"You know, I recall the moment I touched the hilt, I felt a vibration. I had thought it was the movement of the earth; I was deep underground."

"See, you do have a connection. It may mean you will be coming back to the Aerie to collect it. But you must travel first. Best you learn what the Universe wants of you, what is thrown in your path."

Smiling he walked past me to check the stew over the fire.

"I see you have been busy, mmmm, tastes good. Washed everything have you?"

"Yes, some items had a bit of a… not so nice smell to them."

He stirred the contents with a wooden spoon. Just to be clear, this was a new batch. I had given the remainder to Nejan, that morning and had started a new stew with bones from the coney Nejan caught the day last.

"Let us eat and I will tell you my story, what I know, and then we must prepare to leave. Neither one of us is safe while you are here, not 'tis your fault, but I did promise your Mader I would protect you and keep you safe."

"You knew my Mader?"

No one, while I was growing up would willingly recall anything about my Mader. It was like she never existed. My Pader was in the throws of grief as he loved her deeply. I was about four when my Mader passed, shortly after the birth of my sister. I remember their joy, and then the sorrow. I remember the anger at not being able to find my Mader. Then the Emperor called for war, and my Pader was the first to leave with his men.

My Pader was none other than the Lord Commander of the Aerie Fortress. Vandrin was his natural son from a woman long dead, so my half-brother. We looked nothing alike. When my Mader died soon after childbirth, and my Pader left, I had only the Mistress of the house and the maids to look after me. I quickly learned how to disappear, and they left me to my own devices when my red hair became increasingly evident.

I always enjoyed Uncle Kiem's visits growing up. He would stop by every spring and fall. He always made sure I had clothing, as each visit, I would have outgrown the last set I was given. He was my steadfast.

I could only recollect ever seeing my Pader two other times, as he would re-turn during lulls in the fighting. The Long War people called it. Each time he saw me he would turn away with grief in his eyes. Vandrin on the other hand, grew up into the perfect likeness to his Pader, and began training at the age of nine. He was five years my senior with a wicked gleam in his eye. I learned how to stay out of his sight. My sister also had her Da's black hair, but the servants kept us apart. Honestly, I had other things to think about, mostly self preservation.

I learned how to run from my brother, and his cohorts. No one seemed to care what I did if it did not bother anyone. I explored the whole underground city, knew every hiding spot, knew areas where I heard secrets, and view them. I was content enough in my freedom, no one bothered me, I had no real friends, and I knew of no real enemies.

Until the day I became aware of Vandrin's men at arms looking intently at me when at this point, I was ill at ease being around any of them. It was a summer night, they had returned from a hunt and celebrating, one speared a boar. Clean kill, I heard them say. Enough to warrant a round, or two, or three of some of the best of the castle's liquor spirits. I happened on the Great Hall in the middle of one of the many toasts, it quite bored me. Vandrin's celebrations would sometimes last until daybreak. I slipped out of the dining hall, determined to see Blaze the now beautiful stallion. The stallion and I had an unspoken bond; he became calmer in my presence. I did not know I was being followed.

This very inebriated young man followed me down the halls and passageways leading to the stabling area. He snuck up behind me, pulling me into a doorway of an unused room. The yank on my hair was enough to startle me, his hand on my mouth was more than enough to alarm me. I may have had a look inside the room, but it was empty, so of no interest. It looked like it was for storage, having bare shelves and a bare wood table in the center of it.

"MMMMfftt!"

I tried to fight my way out of his grip, but he held firm, smacking me in the chest a few times which took my breath for an instant. He reaffirmed his hold on my hair which hurt like hell. He had his hand over my mouth threatening me,

"If you yell, I will tell everyone you are a whore like your Mader, and you seduced me, you red-haired bitch."

His hand left my mouth but the one in my hair remained fast as he pulled my head and neck into a twisted position. I oddly wondered if this was part of a Northman's combat training.

"MMM, you look like you need some training. Oh, yah, look at that. Your honey pot needs a stir. I am the man who is going to do it."

He pulled up the skirt of the ragged dress I was outgrowing and began undoing the ties at the front of his leggings. Pushing me back into the table, he leaned over me to the point I could not stand up. This is where my mind began to blur. My sense of foreboding sent my mind into a panic. I experienced heat in my stomach, not unlike nausea but more like a fiery burning sensation. It amplified with my fear, as his fumbling increased. I felt the abrasiveness of his trousers against my inner thighs.

"No, please do not. I swear I will not tell anyone. Please!"

"You will scream for me once I give you a stir. You will want my stick by the time I am done."

He slammed his lower body into mine. My back protested the angle it was placed at, and I had pain shoot up into my neck. I felt his manhood slap my inner thigh. I saw a few cocks in my growing up, accidental viewings, during pissing matches and they did not look then to be very threatening. This I knew was different.

"You will be screaming my name in a while. I have seen the way you look at us. You want all the others too. Just like you want what Cotts has for you. You wait, little whore, you are going to like this… Cotts will fill you up…"

I felt warm, hard flesh poking at my opening where I knew babies came out and I knew something monumental was going to happen. One of his hands had mine over my head with my hair. I forgot to struggle; he outweighed me by double my weight. I knew it was futile to even try. That is when I felt the heat travel up my throat, and I remember it was the first time I heard the voice, reverberating inside my head,

"NOOOOOO!"

It was so loud, I passed out.

I remember slowly coming back to my spirit. I smelled something akin to burnt meat, which made my stomach growl and twist. I found myself becoming aware, I was leaning against a wall in the passageway, my skirt still crookedly up around my waist, and I pulled it down. The smell triggered my stomach to empty its contents into a drain hole in the corner, and I staggered off to the stables, snuggling in with the stallion who greeted me with a wicker. I had a burn mark on my chest which hurt like crazy, and some weird grot in my hair, I thought to make sure I took care of it when I came to some water or a fountain.

I recollect the next day, wandering into the kitchen. People were whispering, some were crying and hugging. I groggily questioned Danyc what happened when I saw the girl in the laundry house. My head was pounding, and the light of day made me squint my eyes. My stomach felt sore and tender, and she told me something happened to Cotts. They found him in the cellars with his face melted and he had suffocated. The rumours went around that a troll was wandering the deep, or he upset a Blacksmith, or he was cursed.

"Venda coin for your thoughts,"

Kiem's voice interrupted my reverie, I told him what I was reflecting on, and it may have been the first time I heard the voice.

I saw him thinking on what I told him.

"I remember the cook retelling the story to me when I came in from my summer hunting. I kept my views to myself, but I vowed to get you out of there before more men took notice of you and tried the same. Only one man happened to remark about Cotts' pants being open and his worm being out as fish bait. It was at this time I suggested you would be better use as a healer. Training with Healer Nena was a skill you could flourish on, and you needed to have an occupation. The Head Chamberlain agreed with my proposal. As soon as I knew you were safer with her out in her section of forest, I returned to the cabin to prepare for winter."

He sat facing me.

"Back to your Mader. Yes, I knew her well. We travelled here from Pelin'Dun and were shipwrecked here together. We met when we were young and foolish and ran off to be together. Your Pader's men found us on the beach after a horrific storm and he fell in love at first sight. I chose to explore once I healed as I could not bear seeing him and later her in love. The last time I spoke with your Mader, she found out she was going to bear another child and she made me swear to always look out for you. I have, in my fashion. It was not until the young man lost his face; I took closer attention to who you might be."

He got up ladling stew into two wooden bowls and handed one to me. What he just told me, set my mouth to open. I was speechless, he knew my Mader before she was with my Pader…I felt there was more to come… Sitting back down, he looked at me thoughtfully. After a few spoonsful of stew, he proceeded with his story.

"We did not mean to fall in love with each other. It was forbidden where we were from. She was from a noble ruling family, and I was nothing but a scribe. Lowest of the apprentices, but I knew enough of love to know what I felt was real. I know she felt it too, at least at first. We decided to run away together and stole aboard a ship bound for the farthest reaches of our earth. We found out where we were headed as we emerged looking for food. The Captain let us stay, the crew was all for throwing us overboard, until they found out who she was. No one throws the Dader of one of the Magistrates of Pelin'Dun over to the eaters of the sea. No, the Captain put us to work to earn our keep. I learned about rigging and sails and she helped to keep us fed. No one could have predicted the storm that hit us, but it was nothing compared to the storm which brewed between us. The life of toil she was not suited to, and it took its toll on her, she began to resent me, and I did not deal with it well."

As Kiem spoke, I had this feeling in my gut. I sat there absorbing the information he was sharing. This had an ending. I did not know for sure what, but it was not until the next revelation that I knew exactly what he was saying…

"You see, young lass, I did not know at the time of the storm she was with child. The timing of your birth, her determination to marry the great Lord, it was all a part of her plan to raise you among what she knew. We had a falling out when I confronted her with it. I went into the deep forest wilderness to find peace and answers and she married to keep you safe. I think she may have told the great Lord, but I cannot know that for sure.

No one else survived the storm, and it was feared if word returned to the homeland, they would come searching for her. She was from a line of nobility Riders were culled from if they showed the gift. Both she and her twin sister were expected to attend these rituals. Their Mader was adamant they would succeed. Miiele found something secret and didn't want anything to do with these practices, she called them barbaric. I just loved her."

He hung his head for a moment then looked at me, a single tear making its way down his cheek. I was not prepared for the next portion of his story. I was still reeling over the facts he was presenting…

"I have every reason to believe you are my Dader and not Lord Bodan's. You have a particular birthmark; I and my brother have. Miiele asked me to not tell you until it was time. She feared conflict between the Lord and me. I loved her so much, I agreed. I knew you would have a Pader in his Lordship. I could not predict that he would not be here, for you. I could not step forward while he was gone. I am sorry I have not been around to keep you safe from harm. I did not want to draw any attention for those who would question. I left so there would be no conflict, and I was away when your Mader passed. For this I am terribly sorry, I would have liked to say goodbye before her spirit left, and I did not know until I returned from my ranging. I was told she called out to me in her pain before her last breath. For that alone I grieve, I could not be there with her."

Tears crept down his cheeks as Kiem recounted his pain.

I sat there in shock, not believing what I just heard. I had a real Pader! Hearing it spoken aloud had me frozen. I had tears welling in my eyes and they spilled down my cheeks. My left cheek began to sting, and I looked at the man in front of me. I had a Pader! I had the answer for all the questions I had ever wanted to ask! Especially now with everything happening to me. I belonged to someone, finally. Not abandoned by the one who was never there, but here, sitting right in front of me! My hands were shaking as I reached forward grabbing his hand so hard he looked up quickly.

"You are my Pader?"

There was a question within a question. He nodded and squeezed back.

"I hope you can forgive me, but what is done is done. I cannot take away your pain of growing up. I have watched over you since your birth, in my fashion. I could only give what I was able, I did not want to draw any more attention to you than warranted, Naman are fervent in their hunt for Redheads. Now I know what you are, and are free to make your own choices, I can prepare you for what may come. Life is short and fleeting, and I may not always walk beside you. I will do my best to fill in any gaps. Tell you of where you came from. Tell you of what I know of the legends, and what I know of Dragons. That I can do…. Dader."

He rose to his feet, and I rose with him. We embraced, awkwardly at first, but then it became a tight bear hug as if to make up for lost time. I began to down right sob, he held me while my pain was released. I shook as I heaved with gulps of air. My crying releasing all my pent-up emotions which had stayed with me, my fears, and my loneliness.

"Shhh, lass. 'Tis all right. Shhh."

"Oh…oh…"

I began to calm down and I squeezed him hard. We parted and he gazed down at me.

"I am proud of the young woman you have become. You look just like her, you know. She had the most beautiful red curls and was very feisty and resilient. I loved her the first moment I saw her, I will always love her, in memory. You are much a part of her as you are of me. I will hope in time, we have a true relationship…"

"Why would we not? You have always been there. Every memory of note, you have a place. I remember you tucking me under the cooks robes when the new Secondary came, and you asked her to rinse my hair, with… what was it? Bark juice, you called it?"

Kiem laughed at my recollection. "Yes, you were a very active five-year-old."

"Active? Is this what you call it? I hid from everyone. I was not nice, if my memory serves me."

"Yes, I saw you were angry at the world, for taking your Mader. I convinced the housekeeper and cook to cover your red curls. I told them his Lordship would not want a child of his love to be given over to the Namanists. They listened to me, finally, we argued for two days. When his Lordship returned, he told the cook her smart thinking eased his heart. They did not need to be reminded after this."

"Then I have you to thank for that odious and smelly ordeal. Thanks…, Pader."

I began to cry again, Kiem enfolded me in his arms. I was still vibrating with the shock of this confession.

"Hush, Meera. I am with you. I deeply regret the events of the past, but I look forward to the future. I am glad you finally know, it eases my heart greatly."

I sniffed into his chest. It felt right in his embrace. His arms tightened again, as if he were unwilling to detach.

"You do not mind if I call you Pader? I would like to call you such. It feels raw on my tongue."

"You can call me whichever you feel the most comfortable with. If my given name comes out, I will not mind. It is how you have known me."

"Pader. I have always wanted to have one. Last time, my…his Lordship came back, I only saw him for a moment. He was busy with his men. I remember he looked at me and then turned away. I never felt like he was pleased to see me."

"It was most like he saw Miiele in your manner, he loved her greatly. He would have moved the mountains for her. When she passed, he was greatly grieved, I do not grudge him his sorrow. I grieved for your Mader, in the first year. Your birth gave me hope, and I promised Miiele to not address your paternity. When she made me promise to watch over you, I had an inkling she was not well. I should have known…"

"How could you have known? What did she die from?"

"I have a feeling it was from homesickness. It festered in her breast, until she became physically sick. On the Islands, there were medical journals, I had the opportunity to research. In one it said the mind or spirit, if left unchecked could manifest illness to the physical realm. I should have stayed in the Aerie, instead of hunting, but the need to feed the city was great. There was a large group of us who left to forage and hunt. I missed her passing by a week. It grieves me still."

"Her spirit will rest now that we are together. She will know if what Nena tells me of our guardian spirits who watch over us."

"There are many traditions and lore even I do not know. We can learn them together."

We parted from each others' arms and sat down facing each other. I looked at this man before me, and I saw he was as emotional as I was. I saw it in his eyes, and the smile lines around his mouth, the creases in his face which I was now memorizing. He smiled back at me.

"Your hair will lose the staining; I see the redness poking through. Your Mader had glorious locks, I loved her hair. It was her pride and she was stubborn enough to show it off. The old Secondary must have said something to the Namarch in the Capital; however, she was untouchable, his Lordship has some standing in this land. I am surprised word did not reach the Islands and her family. Lord Bodan must have had a hand in that. We will never know. In Pelin'Dun everyone has red hair, so you would be normal and not be an oddity. The Northerners here are very superstitious and not trusting, some never see the rest of the world. Never be ashamed of who you are. I am also thinking you are a bit stubborn like me, if some of the stories I have heard are true."

We talked the rest of the day and into the evening, Kiem telling me about my Mader's family, what little he knew from his experiences back then. He told me how her twin sister would cover their tracks when they were trying to hide their love. He told me about my GrandMader. A mean bitch if ever there was one. She had only one purpose for her children, which was to have them follow in her footsteps. I asked question after question about his childhood. It was by far, quite different from my own.

"I studied everything I could get my hands on. My brother liked to do things with his hands, so he would fish with our Pader. My Mader had a hand in getting me into the learning centers. She convinced my Pader to let us follow our vocations. I was sent to the Capital when I was old enough, I was to become an understudy for the Hall of Learning, and I was well on my way, when I met your Mader. I was not interested in much after I fell in love. I do not recall much of what I read during this time. When she told me we should leave, I eagerly followed her. I would have moved Avanya and earth for her."

"I am sure she loved you."

"I am sure she did also, but she was not ready for the harsh reality we sailed into. It was a shock to her and would not entertain a lesser future. It was the wedge driven between us."

"The Universe knows what is best for us. You did not part enemies. She kept you close to her, in the form of me. You have your memories which are dear to your heart and now you and I are together. I know now you are my Pader and it makes me happy, incredibly happy."

"I am gladdened you know. I have wanted to tell you for some time, and I was prepared to do so before winter, but this happened."

"See? The Universe made it easier for you."

"Easier? If anything, it made me wish I had done it sooner. I feared for your life, for a moment. It brought back the fear I had during the storm and immediately after. When I woke up on the beach, for ten minutes I could not find Miiele. It was the worst ten minutes of my life. Seeing you injured and out of spirit brought all back. I am relieved in my spirit you pulled through and having you one of the chosen, well, 'tis like having a piece of cook's Ravenberry pie."

"Oh, yes! My favorite!"

"It was your Mader's also. She loved her pie's. The cooks were always trying to impress her. Miiele was exceedingly kind to the servants, they loved her."

He described my Mader to such detail I knew he still loved her deep in his heart. He described to me; the first time he saw her. He knew it was destined to be, and he unashamedly pursued her. I hoped he could love me, maybe in not the same capacity but the same intensity he had for my Mader. He reassured me he had always looked forward to the day when he would reveal himself to me but said he had wished I had not been hurt so badly.

"In all my years here in the North, you are the first person I know who has survived the fall. By the Gods! I give thanks to Vendar! You have healed rapidly as well; this must be a sign you are chosen. I can help you on your path, the rest will be on your shoulders. I can do my part, that which is shown to me, but from what I know, 'tis getting late."

He glanced up to the setting sun and stood up to gather the bowls we placed on the bed. He swirled a little water in the bowls, emptying them into a greater bowl Nejan eagerly lapped up.

"Let us get some sleep and then we can plan and prepare tomorrow. We will get what needs to be done before the weather begins changing. We must get started before the leaves change colour which will not be too long now. Nejan will watch down below for any signs of activity. If she sees any we will have to go in the moment. I will go sleep with the stars; you will have your chance to get used to this soon enough."

He left and I laid myself on the bed, drifting off to sleep dreaming of my new Pader and an imaginary life ahead.

CHAPTER 9

Rowan

From the Heavens Descend

The morning of the wedding soon arrived.

Rowan was woken up earlier than usual as the ceremony was to be performed at high sun and they had a lot of things to do in preparation.

"Princess, Rowan. Time to rise. We have prepared your bath, and your morning meal. Today is your special day."

"Mmmmnmmm, is it morning? Oh! Yes."

Rowan jumped out of bed nearly hitting Tannah in the back, which had the maid looking back,

"I will call the other girls to bathe you, while I get the meal placed. Watch your step, do not rush. We do not want you falling and getting bruised."

Before she was even allowed to have her morning repast she had to bathe. Then the Namarch would grace her with his presence and give her his blessing. Privately, as her Pader would give his blessing publicly. She did not like the Namarch, he was very affectionate with his hands, she did not like the look in his eyes, however, she had to serve the traditions which were part of the wedding process.

Thankfully she had only to kiss his hand, she heard the maids whispering about other parts of wedding ceremonies, forbidden now by law, of a first night bedding ceremony past Namarch's had gleefully partaken of. It was forbidden for over a hundred years, but this Namarch looked like he would gladly partake of it. To her, his look or countenance was one that she did not trust. This was her first thought, to others who were more worldly it was one of barely contained lust. She shuddered inside at the thought. Not that she knew what a first night was. She surmised from the level of disgust she could hear in the maid's voice; it was something men did which was revolting to women. She never worked up the courage to ask Tannah, Rowan felt it was beneath her to ask a servant about the machinations of men. It did not hold a priority in her life at this moment.

"Hurry up, Lena. No… not there. Put it here. Is the Princess's bath ready? Yana? Go check on her breakfast, Dejan. Now, please. Princess? This way…"

Her Palace was like a buzzing beehive, her servants, her Mader's servants, and the groom's servants who were there as observers of protocols and specific traditions, in the celebration of marriage. She would find out later they were there to make sure she did not flee. Had she known then what was soon to be found out by the end of the day, she would have scurried as fast as she could. For the now, she was ignorant in her bliss of every woman's dream joining. She smiled at the busyness at hand, it was the day her life would be forever changed!

Rowan bathed and came out of the bathing room to see Tannah holding a robe. Her robe for the day was a gift from her Mader, a red silk with golden embroidery of leaves and small flowers, she fingered the pattern as she sat down at her dining table. Tannah had set several of her favorite dishes down.

"This seems excessive, Tannah."

"There will be no opportunity for you to eat until the evening meal. I was directed to give you all your favorites, 'tis after all your special day."

"Thank you. Who am I to refuse such delights."

Rowan tucked in, eating until she was pleasantly full. Then it was all hands, as she was ceremoniously dressed, bejeweled and her hair brushed with one hundred strokes before the veil could be placed on. She looked at her reflection in the floor length mirror and smiled. She could not stop smiling at how detailed her dress was and how it made her feel.

She looked radiant, she felt radiant. The dress was the pinnacle of her achievements.

"Does it not look exquisite?"

"Princess, it will be the pillar to which all future gowns will be measured against. 'Tis gorgeous, as are you."

"Thank you, I feel gorgeous. This gown, though. Now, that 'tis complete…"

"You may have begun something, your Highness. Once this is seen, I will hazard a guess some of the noble Nomas and Nadas will want embroidery on their gowns. Perhaps not just evening wear."

"Do you think so? I heard the Namarch disapproves of every display on a woman. At least I heard from you and the others. I have no inkling of what is fashionable or not. I rely on you to assist me when I am to host dinners. I would not bring shame to my husband."

"I will assist you on this. You will be a grand hostess for sure; I will not fail you. This length of gown will be discussed for certain."

"The Empress wanted it this length. She said it would create an impression."

It fanned out behind her and into the full length which trailed onto the floor. The gold threading and delicate beading sparkled when it caught the sunlight filtering in through the open windows. She was immensely proud of her work. She was sure her dress would be the topic of discussion for many years. Rowan twisted to look at the train behind her and smiled again at the thought.

She had a moment of doubt, not of the actual ceremony itself but whether her husband would like her.

"Do you think he will like me? Maybe he will not like the way I look. What if we do not get along?"

She spoke to her maid, Tannah as the girl was brushing her hair. As head maid she was given the honour of brushing the Princess's hair and inserting the comb which held the veil secure.

"He will like you well enough, your Highness. How could he not?"

Rowan gave her maid a look in the mirror. Tannah had a few hair pins in her mouth and one in her hand. She had a look of concentration to her face. Rowan heard something different in her tone of voice. It sent her hair on the back of her neck to stand up. She shuddered and shook it off.

"I hope he does. We have not seen each other in years, and he has not asked to see me since. I hope we get on and have lots of children. I look forward to being a Mader. Oh, Tannah, I guess I should have asked you first, but would you like to come with me and serve at my new home? I am sorry this is late in the asking, but I did not want to command you if you did not want to come with me."

Rowan looked up at her maid, Tannah looking back at her in the mirror, her face breaking into a smile.

"Of course, your Highness, why would I not? I have always served you since the day I entered the Palace, and I will serve you still. I appreciate your thought to ask, but you could have commanded me also. I live to serve."

Tannah bowed her head behind her mistress, to her reflection in the mirror.

"I understand I have the authority to command, but I thought it appropriate in this moment to ask. You are my best maid and I want you to be happy in your service. You may choose who you want to accompany us to our new home. I am to be thrifty so only two others. You choose your best helpers; I trust your decision. Now this looks just grand, you will place the small veil over my head once we get to the Palace, for now it can trail behind."

Tannah placed the veil on Rowan's head, scooping her hair to lay flat on Rowan's back. Rowan rose from her chair when Dejan entered to tell them the Empress was walking down the hall to her room.

Her Mader the Empress came in amid much pomp. She had her butler announce her entrance to her Dader's chambers, entering with a retinue of servants carrying gifts to present to her Dader,

"You are presentable? Let us see your hair. Yes, that is what is acceptable for a young bride. Here, this ring was my Maders before me, and I present it to you. One day, you will present it to your Dader on her joining day."

"Oh, 'tis beautiful. 'Tis a topaz, and huge!"

"It sat on my ring finger, but it seems to only fit your baby finger. That will do."

"Thank you, your Majesty."

"It has been passed down through the centuries to the Daders of the family. Keep it safe. 'Tis a sentimental piece of antiquity. 'Tis a symbol of our bloodline. It would be wise to place it away and only wear it for special occasions."

The Empress did not say once her Dader looked beautiful, just she would do. Rowan tried not to be disappointed, she lived without praise from her parents. She thought if her Mader said anything of the sort sounding like praise it would be out of character for her, and Rowan would think her Mader ill.

The Namarch came in while her Mader was there and gave Rowan his blessing, stretching out his blessing until she could not help but fidget.

"We should begin the procession. I will leave you now, Rowan. May you be blessed on this auspicious day."

"Thank you, Empress. I thank you, and May you be Blessed."

"Namarch, after you."

Rowan's Mader was abrupt in her manner to the old Namarch. He stopped his blessing, with the customary, 'May you be Blessed' and left, followed by the Empress. Rowan was distracted by the butterflies beginning in her stomach and clutched Tannah's hand.

"Oh, here I go."

"Yes, Princess, here you go. It will be well."

Tannah directed the other girls to gather parts of the dress and veil and held out her arm for Rowan to hang onto. The girls began to walk forward.

Freedom, at last! Freedom awaits me at the end of this walk; I cannot wait for this day to end. I will be my own mistress. I will have my own household to run, gardens to tend, and children. Oh, May this Day be Blessed.

She thought of nothing but the happiness she would find outside of these Palace walls.

As a member of Royalty and especially being her Pader's Dader, she was not permitted to walk, it was her right to be carried. A palanquin of the blondest wood and decorated in gold filigree, gold linens and sheerest cloths of red, with the softest red silk cushions, was waiting for her at the garden gate which led to the main walkway to the Palace. The Namarch disappeared on his own and she knew he would be making his way to the Palace to stand behind her Pader and Mader.

"Grab the train. Lena, the end. Dejan, match the height of Yana. Just like we practiced. Yes, that looks better. Remember girls, everyone is watching today. Act accordingly."

Tannah had Rowan's other three bridal attendants directed to grab the train of her dress to not drag on the ground, there were several substrates to walk on to get outside to the palanquin. All her girls were dressed in simple white embroidered dresses, to not compete with but to compliment the bride, with red sashes. The dresses alone were plain and simple but in layman's terms, they cost more than a seamstress earned in a year of wages. Rowan was not skimping on anything; she had her position to live up to.

"Oh, the chair, it is exquisite."

"The Empress had it especially commissioned for this day. We will help you get situated and follow behind. You enjoy this, Princess. Smile and wave."

The Empress was not taking chances and hired extra brawny men to carry the chair. They were suited up in red and gold uniforms to match the chair they were carrying. It was set off the ground on a wooden box with stairs leading to it for ease of entry. Amongst cheers from attendants and servants, she entered the palanquin leaving the sheers tied back so everyone saw her on her way to the Palace. She entered and settled down into it, Tannah and the girls setting her train beside her so it would be the first thing they grabbed when it was time. She saw the Empress entered her own palanquin and set off first.

The men waited for about five minutes before picking up the chair, Rowan noticed the day, the sky was not too bright with the sun continually hiding behind white fluffy clouds. They set off through the main gardens accessing the pathway leading to the Palace. As they set off, Rowan looked out towards the gardens she would be leaving behind. Her gaze found a sight she had not seen for a while.

Oh, you are still here, Rue. Have you not left? Found your way back? You stayed for me? I wish you to find your kind, your way back to your homeland. Or if you wish, come with me. I will watch out for you.

Rowan smiled at the sight of the Purple Sennet. It was sitting high in the branches of the tall trees gracing the Palace gardens. She was sure no one else saw it, she was surprised she noticed it, hiding amongst the branches, full foliage. Rowan smiled, thinking it a good omen.

As they arrived at the main pathway, she observed crowds of people milling around behind the rows of soldiers lining the street, with attendants holding large palm fronds beside them, resembling a living arch as she was carried underneath. The roadway was set stone, worn over the years, and meticulously maintained by written decree. Anything higher beyond the Gold Gate, the Palace proper, was maintained by servants. Rowan smiled and waved periodically listening to the cheers of the witnesses to her happiness.

"Naman bless you."

"Princess."

"May you be Blessed."

"Bless the Emperor"

Reaching the main Palace, the Great Reception Hall doors were flung open, and she noticed many people inside. Inside was expansive to one who had never been there before. As a child it was very imposing, now it held little interest, with her focus getting to the Thrones at the far side.

It was a long narrow building, many rows of wooden seating, polished to a high gleam. The ceiling of the main hall reached into the skies, it was stone, with many arches, niches, and stained glass embedded in various niches gave a coloured view on the spectators below. The pictures were of men in battle and other pursuits of a religious nature. *The colours I see from here, 'tis like the God himself has blessed this day with a beautiful vista, I feel so blessed to be here. Oh... just breathe, just breathe. Oh, I hope I do not lose spirit walking down the long aisle.*

The long aisle in the middle covered in a red carpet, freshly woven with a gold embroidered edge. It had taken as long as her dress to make. Five years. There were very few carpet weavers in Merida who could boast this achievement. She glanced down at the leading edge flowing out of the Grand Entrance to the place where her palanquin stopped.

To the side of the great doors there was a place she could disembark from her carrier. Her attendants side shuffled the chair and placed the palanquin on an awaiting dais. She stepped out of her carriage onto the steps provided, with assistance from one of the guards beside. He lent her his arm, to cheers from the crowd, to which she answered with a few waves.

There had not been a Royal joining in ten years, so the crowds were excited and merry because there would be feasting in excess, compliments of the crown. Endless amounts of food and drink would be provided, and feasting would last for days, maybe even weeks. In the following nine months there would be many births marking this day of celebration.

Her five attendants arrived soon after her and held the fabric in the palanquin so Rowan could disembark without mishap. Then arranging her gown and veil, so she could make the long walk up the aisle to her groom, who waited for her at the other end. Tannah had a smile pasted on her face, she was happy for her mistress, and she, with the other girls pulled the veil over Rowans face covering her from the eyes inside.

"Just breathe, Princess, you will be fine. Just walk slow, enjoy your moment."

Tannah whispered to her as she lifted and settled the veil. Her words had Rowan coming back to the present. Rowan stared into the hall, her Pader would officiate the ceremonies, the Namarch was present standing behind them. As she gazed down the long aisle the veil giving her a golden view, she saw the Emperor and Empress sitting on their thrones raised up by four steps. A uniformed man stood to the side.

Her parents were awash in gold fabric. It was decree only those of Royal Blood were permitted to wear this colour. Each family of distinction had two colours they predominantly wore. This made it easy to see out on the battlefield she surmised once when she was learning about the great houses. The immediate royal family of which she was, their colours were gold and red. Her husbands were green and black. Once joined she would adopt his colours and leave hers behind, although being a member of the Emperor's direct line, she could keep her colours, as her Mader had.

My legs are shaking. Breathe... Rowan, just breathe. (inhale), (exhale), I will remember this day, forever. I hope.

She saw the outline of her groom, soon to be husband, and for the smallest moment, forgot his name. Tannah caught her eye and nodded for Rowan to proceed. She set out in a slow pace so everyone could have a good look. She barely heard the musicians by the main doors, as she moved closer and closer to the Thrones, she heard them clearly.

Almost there, left foot, right foot, left...

She stopped at the base of the Thrones, giving the customary bow to the Emperor and Empress, then turned to the groom and gave him one as well. The rest of the ceremony was a blur. They spoke the traditional words of the joining celebration. She practiced so many times she knew them by heart.

As part of the custom, the bride and groom were to hold hands and the officiate bound their clasped hands with a multicoloured scarf, the individual colours all meaning various aspects of marriage, or more like different levels of bondage, which she did not think of until much later. She felt his hands were cold, but it was a good thing since hers were warm. Before the scarf was wound around their hands and wrists, she could not help but notice how nicely manicured his hands were. As per custom a bride did not gaze upon her husband until her veil was raised over her head, so she kept her head lowered and her gaze on her hands.

His hands are gorgeous. Exceptionally clean and meticulous.

The next thing she knew the ceremony was over and the cheering crowds broke her out of her reverie. The Emperor taking hold of their clasped hands, raised them and the crowd cheered louder. She raised her head, looking at her husband out of the corner of her eye and saw a very handsome man. Older than her, with a sprinkle of gray hairs on his temples, a strong jaw, and a curved nose like that of a hawk. His lips looked thin, like he pursed them in thought. Other than his expression which she thought could have been boredom or more like a tough bowel movement one could not pass, he was a striking man.

He must be getting groomed to succeed his Pader in the army, he looks official and handsome in ceremonial attire.

They both smiled, waving to the crowds as they walked to the exceptionally large doors and led to a horse drawn open carriage. Thankfully, there were stairs in place to facilitate an easy ascent.

The next tradition the Emperor and Empress began when they were joined, was the bride and groom would travel to the poor quarters on a specific route, throwing bread and coins to crowds as homage to the people. After which they would return to the Palace for the celebration of the couple among their peers before setting off to their new home. The whole round trip he did not speak to her other than to tell her what to do. She was still in awe of the whole ceremony and what her Mader told her she did as she was told and did not venture to speak up. This was the last day she remembered being happy. Ignorance was definitely bliss.

The feast and celebration were extensive, round after round of toasts, she lost count. The amount of food consumed was more than she had ever seen. They had no chance to talk to each other, it seemed one or the other was commandeered by someone wishing their attention or congratulations. She did manage to sit for a while and eat some of the meal, she was hungry but also a little nervous of the bedding ceremony. She had no idea what it involved, and her new husband's friends were jokingly toasting to them as they consumed more drink and became more congenial. Her face became sore from the amount of smiling, and she consumed more wine than she usually did, if just to relax the muscles in her jaw.

She was completely exhausted when they arrived at their new villa, later that evening. For her it was new, however, her husband lived there for a few years. When they arrived, he exited the carriage and strode away. The estate was tucked away outside the gates to the city, in its own valley surrounded by groves of olives and grapes. The villa itself was built of stone local to the area, and it was spread out surrounded by a high stone wall.

She was left dumbfounded; he had not spoken a word to her, not at the dining hall, not during the ride to the villa and did not seem interested in conversation. She wondered what was going on in his head, she tried asking him questions on the ride, however, he gazed at her in silence. One of the carriage drivers offered his hand, and she took it, trying to gather her dress up in the other... as she stumbled out, Tannah ran out of the doorway.

"I am so sorry, my lady, I only arrived, and I am the only attendant he is allowing you to keep."

She spoke hurriedly as she took Rowan's gathered dress from her arms and ushered her in.

"You are to go to the end of the hall, where your room is, and I am to help you undress for the night ceremony."

"Ugh, there is more? I am so tired right now and I need to use a pot."

She was barely keeping her eyes open, and if she could take notice, which she would not until later that week, there were no visible neighbours. By the end of the week, she would know the reason…

They walked to the end of the hall, around a corner and down another hall barely lit by tapers, entering a small room with only a bed, small wardrobe, and small tables. There were no adornments on the walls apart from candle taper holders and a small tapestry depicting a hunting scene.

"Are you sure this is the room? It seems a bit sparse."

"This is it, Noda. This is what I was directed."

"I forgot. I am Noda now. For a minute there, I was not sure who you were addressing."

"If you care to sit, please."

She looked around at the room, too tired to care now. Rowan sat down on the bed which to her seemed a bit harder than what she was used to. Tannah began helping her take her slippers off. Rowan felt the coarseness of the rug beneath her feet, she stood, Tannah removed her veil and unhooked her gown. As she was almost finishing her new husband walked into the room and motioned with his hand for Tannah to leave. Rowan turned to face her husband.

"Greetings, Kavus."

"……"

"Do you talk at all?"

He strode up, slapping her in the face, "Do not say a word, unless I give you leave to do so."

When she began to speak again, he raised his hand. She held her face in her hand while the sting left. She was held speechless by the shock of his slap, from a simple question? Rowan was not used to being questioned herself. She was in shock at what he did next.

He then grabbed her dress by the open bodice and ripped the remainder off her body.

"Oh!"

She stood there trembling not knowing what to do. She was in silent disbelief, no one had ever laid a hand on her person like this, not even her tutors when she was sassy and naughty.

"Oh, my dress! That took me years to make."

"I said do not speak."

He slapped her again. She stared at him in shock, unsure of what to do. He threw the gown against the wall grabbing her upper arms throwing her backwards onto the bed, which confirmed her fears it was harder than the one she left in the Palace. She tried to lift herself, but he lifted his hand and with one finger motioned her not to. He ripped off her silk undergarments. They tore easily, and she was still unable to move, more in disbelief and now a little bit of fear. She watched him, the fear of the unknown settling in.

He undressed himself and if she was to be impressed at all, he had the body of a God, lightly muscled and lean. She did not notice the one part which would be her undoing, as it was in shadow from the low light in the room. He moved on top of her, not looking at her as he opened her legs with his and did the thing not one person told her to expect.

"No, unnngg. What are ynnnn…"

She began to protest his cock gaining entry to her core, and he swung his fist to her chest knocking the wind out of her. That is when he gained entry, and she felt a ripping pain. She woke up to Tannah shaking her awake.

"Princess, Noda, are you alright?"

Tannah's face was awash with tears, she had a wet cloth with her, and after Rowan nodded her consent, Tannah began to wash her lower regions with a cool damp cloth, which felt good but also reminded her of what happened.

"Nodan says to get you cleaned up. You are to expect him every night until it is confirmed you are with child; there are no exceptions. You may not have visitors and may not leave the villa for any reason. He will bring you what you need from Merida if he wills it. I am under the instruction of his Housekeeper who also runs the villa he has in the city. We only go there if it is an official stay by decree of the Emperor or his Pader, The Commander of the Army. I cannot bring you anything unless he wills it. I am sorry!"

Tannah burst out crying and Rowan began to console her, realizing her bottom lip was very swollen from the first punch he had given her.

"Mmmnnannah, my nody iissh thore. Issh you thine. You thine?"

"I am not allowed to say anything or tell anyone what goes on here or he will take me to the canyon and leave me for the wolves to eat, after his men have had their way with me. I am so scared, Mistress. I will stay with you, but for now I must change these linens."

Tannah tore the blood-stained sheets from the bed, hurrying out of the room, Rowan hobbled over to the one chair in the room closest to the bed gingerly sitting down on the edge.

Why had no one warned me of this? Is this normal between husband and wife?

She had no one to ask and compare notes with, growing up in the Palace, she was not allowed friends or companions. She felt violated, not just physically but mentally and emotionally, by omission of education. Her Mader had not told her about relations between man and woman, and there were no books she could have read. The only one available was Tannah, but she was not appropriate as she was a servant. Rowan felt it all strip away as she cried.

So much for my dreams of a happy marriage, I cannot think this is a very good beginning.

Tannah came back a few minutes later in a rush, not saying too much as she hurriedly made the bed again. Rowan rose stiffly, walking over to the bed rolling into the covers and cried herself to sleep.

The next morning, she was woken by her husband, climbing into bed and rolling himself on top of her. When she came fully awake and began to scream because it startled her, he clubbed her in the head with a closed fist. He held her hair in one fist as he guided his penis with the other hand into her center. He did not look at her, and this was to be how it was. He gained inside and ramming into her, not caring if she was ready or not, and kept at it until he was done his business. He took what was his by right of marriage, getting off as she groggily tried to recover from the blow. She laid back asking him, crying.

"Why did you marry me? Do I deserve this treatment?"

His answer was to come back to bed, and she did not remember anything after the second blow. He first punched her in the stomach and as she bent over from that, he hit her again on the head, then she blacked out.

She woke to see Tannah hovering over the bed. Tannah was crying and her cheek was also red from a blow, with blood coming from the corner of her mouth.

"I was told very distinctly not to protest too much."

Tannah touched her own cheek very gently.

"I suggest you do the same."

"isssh this 'appen to you? Ow, ssttts 'urtsss."

Tannah grabbed a wet cloth and began to clean up her mistress again, which this time hurt like hell.

"I can only bring you what I am told you are to eat, all foods to help you to bear children," Tannah motioned to the tray she brought, which had one orange, a bowl of now cooled grits and one piece of meat.

"If you do not eat this, you will get nothing else. You are not allowed outside until your face heals, no one is to see the bruises on your body, or he will hurt you again. If you do not listen and wander out, he will beat you again and beat me. I have a duty to instruct you in what is required and if you do not listen to me, then it is like you did not listen to the Master. I was told to tell you this."

"'id he beat you? I am ssho sorry, 'annah. Ish 'id not know Kavus was a mean man. I 'id not know at all."

"I heard rumours, but I was told not to tell you. Now you know the why of it. I am to bear your pain as well, as mine own."

"Will you shtay with me, 'e my comfort."

"Alas, I cannot."

Tannah left her mistress after explaining her duties were not solely taking care of Rowan, she was to clean the villa with the other girls there. Rowan could not believe her parents would knowingly allow her, their Dader, to be married to such a mean man.

What have I done? Was this always an act of violence? Did it require violence to be completed?

She was left with a sense of incredulous disbelief, as she gently touched the bruises and cuts inflicted on her while blacked out. What she saw when she looked gently down was redness, purple and blue, all colours. Rowan did not have a mirror, but she could only imagine what her face looked like. It hurt immensely, and one of her eyes was swollen shut. Her jaw was so sore, she could not formulate words. The whole side of her face was swollen and tender to the touch. If she had seen herself in a mirror, she would not have recognized herself. Other parts of her body were swollen, and everything hurt. She wondered if this was what she deserved for wishing so badly to escape the Palace. She hoped not.

Am I to bear this? This life is not fair, am I now a prisoner? I am required by law and duty to cleave to my husband. Will he always hurt me? Even though I have not done anything to warrant this. What have I done to deserve this?

The beginnings of self-doubt were planted, it would germinate with every day he raped her, because she did not want him to invade her body. She began to think she was deliberately kept ignorant of sexual relations. She was stubborn enough had she known he was a violent man; she would have refused the marriage. Rowan was sure if she wished a divorce, she might be able to obtain one, but few were given to women. Her uncertainty began with the first night and would grow as her husband fertilized it with his words. He taunted her with words, which she did not want to listen… they began to take root.

Kavus. That is his name. Why would he tell me I was all he could get? I am his to do what he wants when he wants. That if I do not, he will beat me worse.

Rowan wondered if her Mader knew about the man she was now joined with for life. Rowan knew without thinking too much about it, she was helpless to do anything. She would have to bear this, until she bore him a child, or died from the beatings. *Would he beat me more? Every night?*

She hoped not, she would have to find out what would make him stop. Other than letting him have his rights to her body, which hurt inside. She looked down at where it was throbbing and felt with her hand raising it to see the moisture between her legs was blood. She wiped it on the robe of coarse linen she was given to wear, rising slowly, and stumbled to the bed. Rowan eased herself onto the bed slowly, lying down as she continued to cry.

She would send a note to her Mader as soon as she figured out how.

CHAPTER 10

Solina

The Six-Pointed Star

Life as Solina knew it was about to change, slowly and then too rapidly to reflect on. After Yona passed her spirit, and her Celebration of Spirit was observed, Solina returned to her garden and the plants in it to gather some peace.

Oh, the air is a bit crisp this morning. Soon, I will begin harvesting. This is a sure sign the weather is changing. Hmmm, perhaps, I will just begin by removing the dead blooms. Maybe I will get more Pana flowers. Will not hurt to try, they are always last to bloom.

Not too many days after, Solina's presence was requested in the solar by one of the initiates. She quickly braided her hair into a semblance of neatness, dusted her pollen covered hands onto her robe and walked quickly into the solar followed by the older brother.

Inside was the Pader and one of the Magistrates, an older woman with red hair and shots of silver intertwined among the headpiece of gems and gold. She sat on a bench while the Pader sat opposite on a smaller iron chair looking uncomfortable. Solina gazed through her lashes at the Magistrate as she respectfully gazed at the floor before the Ruler's feet. She observed the woman could pass as an older version of herself other than the crooked nose. The woman watched Solina scrutinising her and smiled a crooked smile.

"You are not shy, are you?"

The older woman had a husky voice and a directness to it. The Pader began to admonish Solina, but the woman raised her hand and the Head of the Church sat back.

"Do you know why I am here?"

She asked Solina directly, to which Solina raised her eyes, seeing the gold opalescence reflected back at her, like a faded version of her own. She saw the curiosity in them and held the gaze.

"No, Magistrate."

At that moment, she felt the silence of her voices waiting on the next part of the conversation.

"Your eyes are very bright for one who has not partaken in the Rituals. We will have you join the next celebration, to see if you have what it takes to join the Rulers. If chosen, you will move in with the initiates. Learn the ways of the Rulers, protocols, and laws. Move your way up into positions, in which you will serve the people depending on your skill set. I have been told you hear voices; do you hear them still?"

She leaned toward Solina, who could hear in this question, a warning, a murmur inside to be incredibly careful on how she answered.

"Think of what you say before you say it."

"This is a test."

"She is baiting you."

"I do hear voices, Dame, all the time. Sometimes its gibberish like another language. Sometimes it hums, I have tried to distinguish a pattern, strange tunes, like I have never heard before. One likes to discuss plants; I sometimes must yell at it to be quiet. I find if I read, they will reduce their volume, so I read or garden a lot to ease my suffering. If I focus on a task, I can reduce the voices, but I am afraid I am mad for they do not leave me alone. I do not know what is wrong with me."

As Solina spoke, she lowered her eyes and bowed her head. She did not see the Magistrate look over at the Pader or see the look passing between them.

"Well, you must minimize speaking aloud to them when you come into the lower Palace, if chosen. You would be looked at differently and ostracized for sure. Once the ceremonies are over, you will live amongst the others on the same chosen path, you would be wise to hold your own council. There will be others fighting for the same positions, and it can be cutthroat. Do you have any other talents of which I should know? Any that would give you an advantage over the others?"

Solina knew the Magistrate was feeling her out. She had after all, read some of the secret tomes finding through them the talents Dragons and Riders bonded together created, so she felt confident enough to reply.

"I see clearly in the dark without a candle to guide me."

She also knew she could not lie to a Magistrate. They knew who was lying. She was sure this Magistrate had talents of her own. Solina had watched a few debates in the Great Hall of Law. This must have satisfied the older woman. The Magistrate waved Solina away. Solina backed out with her head down, as she left the room, her voices started jabbering inside her head.

"That woman is trouble; you need to be careful around her. She is of your blood, you are of her line, and she knows it. Your energies are coordinated, and we are not sure if you were convincing enough, but you will find out."

She gasped aloud as she passed into the gardens returning to her task of pruning the roses. Not knowing or caring she was being watched by the Pader and his guest through the solar windows. Her blood! The woman looked too old to be her Mader, and Solina wondered how they might be related. The voices kept on,

"The Ritual of passage. You are made to drink an elixir to determine if you have Rider blood in your veins. If you get sick or die you are not deemed suitable, however, you must drink it. As you are already bonded to us, it will not work for you. You may be cast off. You must free us! We are the last of us, and we are chained! They drug us with something placed in our food, which keeps us barely alive. I do not know how it is made, perhaps in your search you can find out. This

keeps us from our strength, we are weakened. They drain our spirit and collect it in vessels, then they leave us to leak out our essence. We need to be FREE! You MUST!"

"I will try. I must attend the Ritual like I am instructed; you may have to wait a while longer."

"We will wait forever for you; you are chosen... do not forget us."

"I will not. I promise."

There are Dragons! Somehow, somewhere. Where might they be? Does anyone else know? Will I be able to go through with it? 'Tis a mystery regarding the ceremony. Will I see a Dragon? There is no talk though, so maybe not?

The rituals were four days hence, Solina was required to move to the chambers of the initiates, bathe and read tomes of instruction, receive blessings from the Pader of Paders, reflect quietly, and be directed, she knew by the Magistrate who came to see her. Solina was apprehensive to leave all she knew, but also knew she was destined to do something else. If anything, she would find her voices and free them. No creature deserved to be kept in captivity, nor bled out. She shuddered.

Am I ready for this? This is monumental, will it create chaos?

The appointed day came soon enough. The amount of whispering in the dining hall diminished when she entered for her morning breakfast, Solina knew they were discussing her. She spooned gruel into the wooden bowl, taking an apple from the wicker basket and found a spot at one of the tables across from a couple of younger girls who plagued her with questions.

"Why was Dame Metina asking for you? Why is she getting tested?"

"Well, 'tis obvious, dummy, look at her eyes, she is one of them."

The girls chattered on to themselves and were satisfied with their own council. Solina nodded in the breaks of their conversation as most times her mouth was busy with the chewing of her meal.

"You will partake of the ceremonies?"

"Will you die?"

"She will not. She is already one."

"Will you come back here and visit?"

"She will be too busy. She will forget us down here. Have you ever seen the initiates down in the lower markets?"

"I hear you get ten different dishes each meal."

"Where did you hear this? Ten dishes, 'tis extravagant."

"Well, that is what I heard. Runa's sister by marriage works up the hill. She told Runa the Palace eats very well."

"Well, they do not have our bread, can you pass me another slice, while you talk about the dishes, and a slice of cheese. Thank you."

Finished eating, she left the conversation excusing herself, the girls nodded but kept talking. Solina walked out of the dining hall, through the kitchen and washed her bowl and spoon in the bucket of water. She laid them on the table to dry with all the other dishes there. It was each of their responsibility to wash what they used, not to make extra work for someone else.

As she entered the main hall, the Pader was striding down the stone passage towards her motioning for her to follow him into his study. Passing through the doorway, he asked her to close the door.

This must really be private,

Solina did as she was instructed, he motioned her to the chair in front of his desk and she sat on the edge of the seat, not sure what he may say. The Pader spoke, as he sat in an ornately decorated wooden chair behind a similarly decorated desk. The rest of the room was stark stone, but one wall had an elaborate tapestry, with a scene of flying Dragons, Solina was itching to look at it further but she sat down at his command.

"Dame Metina asks you make your way to the initiates gate this morning. After tomorrow we will know your fate, should you pass the ceremony, you will become one of the elite in time. Should you fail, you will die. That is the fate of the Riders. Few have passed through the Dragon Gate, you have already shown the Dame some promise, or she would not have asked for you. You must keep the voices in your head muffled; others may kill you if they think you are possessed."

"Yes, Pader. I can do this. 'Tis more manageable now."

He gave her a very direct look, which Solina returned, feeling a sense of purpose, not of foreboding.

"You must remember us here if you continue. We have sheltered you for many years, Yona thought of you as one of her own Daders. Did she ever tell you, her story?"

She shook her head in a negative and the Pader proceeded to tell her over the next half hour how Yona came to the Church; her own family killed in front of her eyes in a blood feud. He finished his tale, standing up so she also rose. As he came around the front of the desk, standing in front of her.

"You are not required to bring anything of a personal nature, as you will shed who you were before, and become anew. You may say your goodbyes and pick a companion to accompany you to the gate. I will bid you farewell and May the Pader of all speed you in the next portion of your journey. Many blessings, child."

He kissed his fingertips, pressing them onto Solina's forehead.

"Thank you, Pader."

She bowed her head, turned, and left the room, making her way back to her chamber.

The ritual. I feel that this will change everything for me. Should I be scared? No one has explained what it curtails. Why is it so secret?

Crossing the courtyard to the back rooms, she saw some girls lingering close by. Turning the corner of the hallway, she saw several by her door and they parted to let her into the room. Several of the older girls were inside, they had been through Solina's meager things, which were few as they were not permitted to own anything of a personal nature.

The eldest one she had played several tricks on, harrumphed, and striding out, saying very loudly,

"Good riddance, you were never one of us."

Her followers left with her, leaving a couple of girls remaining who were much kinder.

"Pader says one of you can accompany me to the lower gate, Sheyna, would you like to come?"

Solina asked the smallest of the two girls, who was tiny but the eldest by two years, just of a tinier countenance. Sheyna agreed, Solina gazed around the room. Kip, the other girl, began to cry as Solina gave her a hug.

"I will not forget you and your kindness to me."

Giving a quick look around Solina headed out the doorway with Sheyna following behind her on the right. She grabbed her cloak with veiled hood and put it on. Solina was taking no chances outside the Church walls. She did not know what others would say to her glowing eyes. Sheyna had never been afraid of her, but outside of the walls, Solina was unsure what form of reaction she would elicit.

"Please tend to the herbs. The lavender and mint make excellent teas you can sell in the market. The Kiran flowers, need particular care. They bring a lot of coin in the markets for their dye properties. You must watch them every day, to make sure they do not get those pesty bugs on their leaves or they will perish."

"Do you take them to the lower market? The Teas?"

"No. You can sell the teas in the upper city market. The Kiran flowers, there is a shop, a clothier on the east side, closer to the shipyards. They buy the bulk of the dyes, that the Kiran and Chamomile root yield. Try to get them to buy as much as you possibly can. They are good for it."

"You sound like its finite. You leaving to the Temple."

"Part of me is scared, Shey. I do not know what to expect. So many do not return."

"You will do fine. We will see each other again. I am sure."

"I wish I had your confidence."

"What are we told? The Universe will provide us with our path. You chose how to walk it. You will be given a choice, in the Ritual. How you choose to proceed, is how you progress."

"Well, I will have to drink what they give me, this I know. I am scared this will be my end, so many perish."

"No, Lina. This is but your beginning, you are chosen. Your eyes have been like this from your childhood, 'tis the Universe's gift. I feel you will do wonderful things."

"You have so much faith. I should have half your faith; I would do well. I am nervous."

"Lina. Think about what comes next, if you worry yourself too much, you will become ill. Just concern yourself with positive energies."

"Thank you, Shey. You have eased my angst."

Solina rambled on about what was in her garden to Sheyna as they passed through the main gates of the Churchyard and onto the main roadway leading up to the lower Palace.

"I feel a change in the air, soon you need to begin harvesting. Finish removing the dead blooms first, I only was able to get half the flowers done. You will see where I left off… in fact, I think I left my shears on the ground."

"I will take excellent care of your flowers, and…the shears."

"Only harvest the Kiran flowers in the coolness of evening or night. The heat will wilt them too fast and then you will end up with an orange, well not an orange. It will be more like the brown of vomit."

"Ewww! Disgusting. I take it you have done this before."

"Yes, I did not listen to Yona and I was in a hurry. They need to dry in the cool air. Then the flowers will not brown but keep their orange colouring. In powdering, make sure there is no brown petals. Even one small spot will ruin the whole batch… One small spot."

"I hear you. They sound like they need a lot of care."

"Yes, but the yield is great. You will get a huge compensation in the markets. We almost have the monopoly on this dye. Only another has figured out the method of harvesting. Keep it to yourself, or not. The Pader will let you have time to harvest. One time it took me all night. You can get out of morning prayers if you speak to him first. He likes the profit from those flowers, so he will accede to your wish."

"I heard him in passing, he says the Church needs a bit of brick work. The gardens for vegetables, the fence needs shoring up."

"Well, then. I believe you will be busy. The air is becoming cooler, so you will be able to begin soon. Hold a minute."

The Church itself was not elaborate; it was a bridge between the poor and the citizens of the inner city. It was not as elaborately decorated as the upper city Temples and Churches bound to the worship of the Gods. From the outside, it was as plain as the surrounding structures. Solina had one last look at her childhood home before turning the corner and losing it to the sights of another street.

She would see many things on her walk. Solina and Sheyna forgot for a moment their purpose and stopped at many shop fronts, laughing, and talking about the things they were viewing. The bakery shops had Solina's mouth watering, she loved the smell of fresh bread. Solina looked down at her hands, they were in incredibly good shape from the many loaves she helped knead. She laughed suddenly,

"What is so funny?"

"Do you remember the orange striped cat? The one with the crooked tail?"

"Yes, was that not the one the Pader could not catch? The cat tormented him in the halls; Pader finally gave up. Why? What makes you laugh?"

"Oh, just a memory, I believe it was before you arrived. I was in the kitchens, helping the sisters with the bread, and the darn cat, Pader was trying to catch it… he bounded onto the table, slid through the flour, and jumped onto the shelf, you know the one on the back wall? Well, it went behind the canisters and the large one with spices in it… the cat moved behind and the jar tipped and fell. It hit the edge of the table and broke apart. Scared the spirit out of Yona. She screamed so loud.

This made the cat jump onto the window ledge, and he scattered the dried lavender all over the place. Well, some of the spices landed on the rising loaves, with the lavender. Yona dare not touch the loaves; she did not like to waste food. We cooked the loaves, and this became our flower bread."

"That is how those loaves were created? I always thought it was a creation of Yona's. Those are my favorite."

"Yes, all because of an errant orange cat. Yona was so upset when he passed, she buried him in the back corner and planted lavender on his grave. She loved the cat in the end, even if he was not the friendliest."

"I will remember this always; the lavender bush always has the best yield. Thank you for this story, I will cherish it, as I cherish our friendship."

"Thank you, Shey. I will cherish you. If there is a chance I can visit, I will take it."

Friendships were highly discouraged yet most women had one person they connected with. As most of the novices distanced themselves from her, she had no regrets in leaving. Apart from Sheyna, the women became closer this last year. She would miss tending to her garden as well, Solina tried not to linger thoughts on what she was leaving behind.

Soon enough, they arrived at the lower gate to the main Palace. At first the guards beckoned her to move on, but once she raised the veil covering her face to let them see her eyes, they begged her pardon letting her pass.

"Bye, Shey, remember me in your prayers. I will need it."

"Lina, you will do fine. Remember, positive thoughts. We will meet again. Good Path."

"Good Path. Bye."

She gave Sheyna a quick hug and never looked back as she passed into the lower Palace.

As she entered a courtyard, many guards were milling around. Some were training at combat arms, she walked quietly to one sitting on a bench, sweating and drinking from a skin.

"Umm, pardon me. where do the initiates go?"

"Harrumph. There."

He pointed down a corridor. Walking down the passageway she was met half-way by a running, out of breath, page who bade her stop so he could catch his breath.

"So sorry miss…, we were told… you were arriving later…, please follow me to your chamber… and the Master of House will attend you there."

He led the way through various corridors so many, there would be no way of finding a way out if she were to attempt it. The smoothness of the inner granite walls had her running hands along them, admiring the colour and sheen, to the point her guide stopped and waited for her to catch up.

"I am sorry, the walls are so beautiful," Solina spoke, admiration in her voice.

"No one has ever said that before,"

Her guide who introduced himself as Kem, warmed up to her offering his name, his status was Herald and Assistant to the Second Attendant to the Master of the House.

"The lower Palace was added to house the various assistants to the members of the reigning authority when they were in the Capital. Initiates are housed separately, I will take you there, where you will wait further instruction."

There were six Rulers, each had an area of expertise, law, finance, education, exports and imports, war, and one designated to oversee the whole. No one questioned their rule, they had special abilities making them a higher caliber of person than the nobility class these Rulers came from. No one discussed the lack of Dragons, it was not taught in the learning centers, Religious studies pushed off any discussion as myth and were no longer viable. There were no rebellions against this system, they ruled with a firm hand. It seemed to work from an outside point of view.

"The lower Palace is also the place to screen the initiates before the Ritual of Rebirth and Death. Too many go out the east door, every quarter, to get cremated. Apparently, this is where the best vineyards are grown. The best soil conditions."

Kem was matter of fact in his monologue. Solina put two and two together in her head but kept silent.

She let him finish his speech before they arrived at a large wooden double door made of the darkest wood she had ever seen. Solina of course had to touch it to see if it was, in fact, wood. He opened the left side, bowing to her,

"Here are your chambers. There are maids to attend you. You are to bathe and redress in the appropriate clothing we provide all initiates for the ceremonies to follow."

"Thank you, Kem."

He let her pass through closing the door behind her. She entered an airy chamber with huge doorways to the outside. Flowing curtains of the sheerest cloth, hung limply in the heat of the day. It was simply the largest, most elaborate room she had ever been in, to date.

This room alone is bigger than the whole of the Church where worship was attended,

This was just for her.

Several girls in plain tunics were milling about and talking, they looked up, but no one approached her until she raised her veil, placing it over her head. She heard gasps and all the girls came up to her bowing their heads, the tallest one speaking.

"I am sorry miss, you must be in the wrong part of the Palace, the novices are placed in the upper Palace." She bowed her head; the others following suit.

"I am afraid I come from the lower city, from Nashta Church, I have not partaken of the Ceremony yet." She spoke softly to the tall girl, the girl looking sharply.

"But your eyes denote otherwise?"

"I have always had these but cover them to not draw attention to myself. The Magistrates gave me their blessing years ago. I am to participate in the Ceremony to advance further if the Gods ordain it."

This seemed to satisfy the girls in the room, and they ushered Solina to the next chamber which served as a bathing room with benches and a sunken chamber.

"This is your bathing chamber. We have directions to assist you in bathing, and after the Head Chamberlain will instruct you in the evening's schedule. We have scented soaps and your attire has been chosen for you. If you would allow me…"

To her delight it was filled with very warm aromatic water. She was well washed, towel dried by way too many hands. An incredibly soft red robe was belted around her waist, and an old, distinguished man dressed in a plain, but decent quality dark navy robe entered the chamber. He started at the sight of her eyes but recovering quickly, spoke to her.

"You will spend the evening repast in quiet contemplation with the other initiates, in the Great Dining Hall, then you will rest. The Vendic Chronicles are available for your contemplation. Tomorrow after you break your fast, you will be given instruction on the upcoming ceremony. At high sun you will be led to the High Temple on the side of the mountain to partake of the elixir which will either wake the Dragon, or you will die."

He then bowed to her and left the room.

"Miss, this is your attire for the evening, if we could dress you."

"Umm, yes. Certainly. Ohh, this is exceptionally fine. 'Tis silk is it not?"

Solina put on the leggings which felt unbelievably soft, like butter. An attendant helped her to secure the clasps on either side of her waist. Then the under tunic which was a pale golden yellow with a red overtunic. Patterns of leaves and flowers delicately embroidered in golden threads embellished the lapels and cuffs.

"Yes. 'Tis silk from Aram. We have our own dyes here; the red is from the Pana flower. We dye the red here in the Palace."

"'Tis beautiful. I love the pattern of the embroidery. This seems a bit opulent for me, I would be fine in something plainer."

"This is what we are instructed to dress you in, Miss. Each initiate will have their own robes especially made for the ceremony. These are yours."

"Thank you. 'Tis extremely comfortable."

The tall girl who seemed to oversee all the others, led her down the hall to a Great Dining Room, placing her at a table by herself. There were only six others, each at their own table. No one glanced up from their meals. She sat down as the girl went off, bringing back a simple fare of bread, cheese, and fruit. To Solina, it was the richest meal she had to date, and she ate it all. As she ate, she glanced at the others, all male, red haired and young like her. Only one dared to look up and smiled back when he saw her observation. Solina tried not to stare at anything too long. She was frowned at once.

This dining room is easy twice the size of the bed chamber and very empty. Look at the beautiful stained glass in the windows. These must have been made in Tain, to the North. The craftsmen there are world renowned.

After her meal, she was ushered back to the chamber she came from. Another chamber across from the bathing side, held the largest bed she had ever seen. Solina lay across the side and was the last thing she remembered until early morning arrived with the sounds of a bird she never heard before.

She kept her eyes closed, listening to the whispers of girls preparing. Solina was guessing another bath and clothes, from the sounds coming outside the chamber. Surprisingly she was not hearing her voices, they were quiet, and she was a little alarmed. She knew this day was going to be terribly busy and their absence, even as she noted it, was a blessing.

She had much to focus on. She had to concentrate on what was before her and hoped she did not fail. She hated not being able to do something and when all her voices were yammering at her, she found it difficult to think.

I am going to partake of this ceremony. What if I fail? Although my voices say I will not. Where will I find them? Will they be there? What is that bird making that weird sound?

Finally opening her eyes to the busyness of moving girls she pushed herself from the pillowy softness of the bed. She rose, ignoring the girls trying to whisk her off to the bath and walked over to an outside balcony, stopping at the stone railing to gaze upon the most beautiful, manicured garden with the strangest birds with the most beautiful tail feathers, some fanned out behind them. The garden she gazed on was one of many in the Palace. She saw this, surrounding walls higher up with the odd greenery on upper balconies.

"Ohh! Look at those! What are they?"

"They are called peacocks, Mistress, these are the pretty ones. There are others of pure white, sacred to the Temple of the Pader."

"They are beautiful! I love the greens and blues, and the eye in the tailfeathers!"

"The colourful ones are the males; they fan their feathers to attract the females. See, the plain ones are the females."

"The females are still gorgeous. They just do not need to be as opulent."

"Please, if you have seen enough? We need to prepare you for the ceremony ahead."

"Do you know what the ceremony curtails?"

"No, Mistress, we do not. We have never left the Palace; our place is here to see to your needs. If you would come inside, now."

"What is your name, may I ask?"

"Tamran, mistress."

"Thank, you Tamran. I will do as you bid."

Returning, Solina had yet another bath, and given a long red tunic with gold-coloured leggings. The red overcoat was another soft silk with gold threading woven into a pattern of leaves and birds, similar to the one she discarded, but more elaborate in the stitching. This one had a red leather belt, type sash which was worn around her waist and sandals of red leather which felt so good on her bare feet.

The girls finished brushing her hair, keeping it off her face in a simple braid. The older man came in and beckoned her over to him. She approached him and he explained the days events.

"You may not speak. To do so would be disrespectful of the Gods. We live to serve… In silence. To break the silence is to disrupt the solemnity of the Ceremony at hand. We will proceed after a private blessing, single file up the mountain. You will be placed last, you are the youngest, and new to the fold. The others have prepared long ago for this Blessing. Inside the grounds each of the Chosen will find their place around the Gods basin. There prayers will be offered and you will be given a chalice. You will drink the contents down, all of it. What happens next is up to the Gods to give or take."

"The ceremony is in Vendar's Temple? The one high on the hilltop?"

"Yes. Only those worthy may enter. You are Chosen. You will observe in silence. Vendar watches and he will choose from among those present, who is worthy of his gift."

"Thank you."

From what she heard of gossip in the streets growing up, maybe one or two from the Ritual would survive. During the course of their apprenticeship, some would become ill and die, others murdered in their sleep, a few disappeared and only the most motivated would ever make it to Magistrate. Solina hoped she made it this far. She was looking forward to learning more.

I wonder what area I will be in. Will it be Law, or Finance? Although war does intrigue me. We are not at war, I wonder why? It seems to be very secretive. I hope the ceremony indicates where I am placed.

The last she heard two of the eldest Magistrates were not healthy and were seeking replacements. No one remembered their age; they were around forever. This Ritual was to replace one who passed away quite suddenly. She was thought to have been murdered in her bed. She was young and only raised recently to her position. Solina heard gossip it was jealousy that caused her demise.

I hope this does not happen to me, I sleep soundly, I would not know if any came right to my sleeping mat.

She was subjected a few times to pranks, some of the older novices played, most involved icy water. She still slept through some of the loudest storms.

The woman who came to see her the second time at Church she thought to be about the age of sixty. Solina knew the woman was the Supreme Magistrate. The older woman looked extremely healthy, and the other rulers Solina had not seen recently. All these thoughts churning through her head she kept to herself, as the man beckoned for her to follow him outside. He led her down the hall back to the Great Dining Hall where this time, they all sat at the same table with attendants standing behind them as they were served the morning meal. They all looked at each other as they ate, the boys glancing several times at her eyes, listening to instruction from the Headmaster,

"After your meal, we will proceed to the Great Worship Hall. You will remain quiet. To speak is to disrespect Vendar. 'Tis a solemn and dignified initiate who may proceed. We contemplate our inner spirit, giving all over to the Universe. It will decide your fate. You will accept what the Universe and Vendar gives you with honour and grace. Loudness and vulgarity will not be accepted. You come from the noble houses, and you will remain dignified to the end... of the ceremonies. You would bring shame on your House if you do not."

No one spoke, it was so quiet, Solina heard them all chewing their food.

Noble houses? All but myself. The Magistrate picked me herself, is this a break from normal protocols? I wonder if they are running out of candidates...

After the morning repast, they were ushered up several hallways into the Great Worship Hall. It was gloriously decorated in gilt, stained glass windows depicting scenes. She would have to return and view another time to bask in their glory, it was the most beautiful room she had been in yet. Most if not all windows depicted scenes of Dragons, in all colours! It was casting glorious colours into the room! Solina tried not to stare, but it was all too much to view! Her neck was getting sore from staring up, and a lad hissed at her.

"Miss, you need to stop. The Headmaster is frowning at you. We are being watched."

"Thanks."

She put her head back to center and followed the back in front of her.

Beautiful. This must be a master's work. They must be incredibly old. This place and the Temples have always been here. I wonder what other creations? Will I get to see them all?

There was a solemn old man, the Pader of Paders, standing on a dais. They lined up and proceeded forward one by one, down the middle aisle between rows of black wooden benches. She was ushered into last place by one of the attendants and had a feeling she was not on the receiving end of any favoritism; many initiates bought their way in or bribed for a first spot on the Ceremonies. There was a moment when one young man looked at her, looking at her robe and whispered something to another, which had her wondering if she was dressed appropriately. She absently fingered the silk of the outer robe, it was the finest she had ever worn, the significance of house colours, never crossed her mind.

I wonder what he is speaking to the other one about. He looked at my robe. There are two more wearing red and gold, then I see red and black, and red and brown. Only one wearing blue, the other green. Why is what I am wearing so interesting? Have they never seen a woman in this ceremony? That is probably it. Given there is only one female Ruler. I think the one who is being replaced was female. Hmmm, not too many women go through this ritual. I wonder why?

She watched each of the young men, walk up to the Pader with head bowed and kneel before him as the old man would murmur, touching each candidate on the forehead with his blessing. Each person rose and moved to the side. Then it was her turn. She walked up slowly to the Pader, knelt with her head bowed, ready to receive his blessing. As he turned to the side table to dip his fingertips into a bowl of scented oil beside him, his robe moved with the movement and revealed his sandals, which contrasted with his ornate robes, very plain and worn.

"Oooh." She must have gasped aloud, he began to speak, and she looked up. He was not expecting her gaze and as he peered down, seeing her eyes, he squinted, bent down, grasping her chin with his hand. Examining her, he spoke softly so only she heard him.

"I know who you are, many blessings to you on this auspicious day. Remember who your friends are if the Dragons favour you."

He smiled gently, turning away leaving through a curtain at the back. Solina rose to her feet, following the others who were ushered out a side door. They moved into line, proceeding out the door through a garden to a side gate and were told their fates would be determined at the Dragon's bowl on the top of the hill.

I wonder what he meant by this. Who I am? Who am I, then? Especially if he knows. Even the brother at the Church seemed to allude to the same. So, who am I?

As they passed through the gate, onto the street path, there were crowds of people on either side. Cheers rose as each candidate passed through, some sobs as family members, mostly Maders, realized this could be the last time they saw their son. As she passed through, some cheers began but slowly diminished into shushed murmurs when she raised her head, and her eyes became visible. A whisper began, and volleyed around, bouncing off the stone walls surrounding the path.

"Can you see her eyes? She is already a Rider."

"She is so young. Barely a woman."

"She looks like…"

"Shhhh, she can hear, she is turning this way."

"May you be Blessed."

Not that she heard much, she was too busy gazing up at the top of the hill they were walking to. Walking what seemed like a good half hour, some of the young men had female admirers darting out to bestow kisses and flowers. Solina walked in silence. Some of the older women, as they saw her, touched their foreheads with their forefingers, and she saw recognition in their expressions. She ignored this as the procession neared the top. There were too many distractions of the location type, and Solina saw the heads of stone Dragons.

Reaching the top, they strode through the Dragon Gate into the Temple grounds, the bulk of the crowd left behind. The Temple sat on top of a hill before the smoking mountain, with pathways leading up around both sides of the behemoth. She wondered where those led to. The grounds were immaculately manicured with effigies of the Gods scattered around, and huge statues of Dragons! She hoped she could take a closer look at those later, the sight of them had her intrigued.

They were ushered forward past the statues to the center of the Temple garden where a large stone basin was set into the ground. It was the size of her bedchamber, larger than the Church dining hall! There were other people inside the

Temple, elegantly dressed. The ones working there, were plainly dressed in una-dorned white robes, but still better dressed than the Church she grew up in.

Each young man was ushered to stand at one of the seven points around the edge of the basin and as she was last, she was at the farthest point. She turned facing the archway they entered through, noticing each had an attendant behind them. Solina heard shallow breaths behind her. Excitement maybe?

She watched, looking around with her eyes to see lots of nobility following them in, lingering around the edges of the garden. All murmuring until the Pader who gave them the blessing inside strode to a dais behind her. She knew it was him from the sound of his sandals. She noticed and focused on his exit from the Worship Hall. It was the same sound. She felt justified when he began to speak to the observing crowd, blessing the day and the initiates seeking the Dragon's gift.

"We gather here today to welcome all to the gift of the Dragon. Only the Cho-sen will rise to begin anew as a Rider. By the grace of the Gods, the gift of spirit is not to be taken lightly. It gives new life or takes it. Only the purest will receive the Dragon's spirit and soar into a new life. Vendar blesses all who are gathered, and we honour him with reverence and love. May all who witness be Blessed, let us proceed."

As he finished, she saw the first young man's attendant given a chalice from another helper behind him. He was the one who smiled at her. He was handed the chalice by his attendant, after the servant held the chalice up high. The Bishop stated his name, blessed his family, and bade him drink the chalice.

"Blessed are you to be given the Dragon's gift, may it give you what you need, if you are to become a Dragon. May you be Blessed."

The young man brought the chalice up to his face, the way he wrinkled his nose, she knew it did not smell good. The lad brought it to his face, took a deep breath, tipped the cup forward and began to drink. He managed to get through the whole contents but some spilled down the sides of his chin, one could tell it was red. As she was contemplating whether it was wine or blood, he finished drinking.

The chalice fell from his grasp and rolled down into the shallow natural stone bowl. The silence in the crowd just highlighted the chalice tumbling into the ba-sin, the sound of it rocking slowly to a stop as it finally came to rest at the bottom. It was all they heard. He looked as if he had not taken a breath since. He struggled for a breath, falling to his knees, his hands and arms began shaking uncontrollably and he proceeded to vomit the contents of what he had partaken. Then collapsed into the bowl headfirst. The crowd gasped and there were a few sobs. She realized his family was watching, each candidate had some family members attending the ceremony judging by the dress. No one moved to help him, she saw his hands and feet moving sporadically then stop. He died; from whatever was in the chalice.

Oh great, we ARE drinking poison.

The next candidate did not look like he wanted to drink it at all. With some encouragement from the crowd behind him, he placed the cup against his lips drinking it down. He did not get sick, although his expression said it was not palatable. He sank to his knees, bowed his head, and remained there.

The next lad drank his down and had the same result as the first one. When it got to the fourth young man, he refused adamantly and was ushered away to a side gate. She was guessing he did not survive this either, no one ever refused. He would end up disappearing.

The fifth lad drank half of his down, the rest kind of soaked the front of his robe. He wobbled on his legs and abruptly sat on the ground. He did not vomit but ended up laying down on his back and closing his eyes.

As the ceremony made its way closer to Solina, she felt herself getting more anxious. The thoughts were speeding through her mind, and she felt hot then cold. The last lad drank down his chalice, promptly vomited and ended up rolling down into the bowl beside the others, spasming then lay still.

Then it was her turn, she took the chalice from the attendant who came up beside her. Listening absentmindedly to the blessing the Pader was giving behind her, she was too busy looking at the contents of the cup. She brought it up to her nose and took a sniff. Solina smelled certain herbs, one of which she could not place, all she could think was she hoped she did not vomit. She swirled the contents around and to her it looked like wine, but as she kept swirling it, she saw a clot and knew it was blood.

It certainly did not smell like blood that she knew… it looked thicker? She soon realized there was silence and the Pader behind her had stopped talking. Raising the chalice to her lips she drank down the contents. As she drank, she looked over the rim of the cup and saw the older Magistrate woman who came to visit her as a child. She was intently watching Solina and so as Solina drank it she caught the old woman's gaze and held it. She held her gaze until the rim of the chalice covered the woman from Solina's view. A feeling of calm came over her with their eye connection and all the thoughts which were jumbling around her head, disappeared.

Slowly she drank, and tasted herbs from her garden she knew would not be injurious, and the one she could not place. She felt sensations happening in her body, and like the world was closing in. Something was pulsing, and she felt more than her heart beating. Hers was pelting fast but she heard others, slow… and methodical. Solina doubled over, bending over at the waist, her eyes closed, as the high sun began hurting her eyes.

"Miss... Miss... Can you hear me?"

Her main voice inside her head reassured her whatever happened next would not harm her.

"Just let it happen. You are bound to us; you are a Dragon. Let our essence flow into your veins. It will give you an enhanced experience and will dictate to all who you are. We are one."

She stayed bent over for a few moments and her attendant must have called her name, several times to which she did not respond. Then he touched her shoulder, Solina felt a shock and her nerves jumped in response. What she did next, she could not explain, since she did not realize she was doing it.

In a voice not her own, she yelled, **"DO NOT TOUCH ME!"**

Solina straightened in a single fluid moment, turning while speaking and flame, yellow fire, shot out of her mouth and burned the poor attendant alive. He flailed around on fire falling over, screaming until at last he was quiet. The crowd gasped. Each and everyone of them apart from the Rulers fell to their knees.

In all Pelin'Dun's Dragon-less history not one of the Rulers was ever able to shoot flames. She would learn considerably later, when she entered what she called Dragon state (this would happen again), her eyes brightened considerably, changing from human golden orbs with a round iris to slitted irises, like that of a reptile. They whirled and glowed with a brightness to all who witnessed the ritual saw. To them she looked like she became a Dragon!

What just happened? Did I do that? My stomach hurts terribly. Why do I feel lightheaded? Am I losing my spirit?

"This is but one of your gifts. You have our blood in your body. It enhances your talents but for a while. The Chosen do not need to partake of our essence, however, you have need to show your people who you are. The effect will wear away in a couple moon passes. You are the Chosen, find us and set us free."

"I will, when I have the opportunity, right now I feel very disorientated."

"It will pass."

"Your blood? That was your blood…ohhh, my head. 'Tis so bright out here. My legs feel like they are not there. Why is the air yellow?"

Standing there shaking on her wobbly legs, she watched as the older Magistrate, the Rulers and their family members came around the side of the bowl. No one stopped her, people parted to the side. The Magistrate called out to the assembly, loud enough the people outside heard.

"This is my GrandDader, Solina. She is now the High Dragon. She is the greatest of all the Dragons. We hid her all these years to protect her. The D'un family are now the Supreme Magistrates of Pelin'Dun. We will bring the land into the new Dragon Age! Accolades to the High Dragon!"

"High Dragon! High Dragon!"

While she was speaking and walking over, the attendants were cleaning up the deceased bodies, carting off the one man who lived. He would succumb two days later. The cheering ebbed and disappeared and Solina slowly sank to her knees as her GrandMader waved to an attendant to retrieve a chair for Solina to sit in. Many people rushed to do the Dame's bidding. Closing her eyes, Solina lost consciousness until she came to in a chamber larger than the worship assembly room.

Coming to her senses, her main voice, sounded a bit clearer,

"Keep your eyes closed for a moment. In partaking of our essence you have awoken more talents, you have but to find. The eldest of us has closed her mind and her spirit awaits rebirth. There is not much more we can bestow upon you; you must find a way to release us. We are weakened, if we do not survive, you will not survive. We need fresh air and meat. We lie in our filth, and it eats into our flesh. We are chained and we cannot move, more of us will surely lose our spirit soon."

"So, you are not the stone Dragons in the garden?"

"Some of us are now stone, but we who remain have not seen the light for many years."

"So, you are somewhere where there is not light. I will find you, give me time to get to you."

She opened her eyes to behold a room full of attendants, her GrandMader sitting beside her, hovering and other members of her new family, nearby. She was sitting, propped up in a well-padded chair, and she saw from the darkness behind closed windows the afternoon had passed, it was now night. She began speak, but after a couple attempts, motioned with her hand, to which a very scared attendant handed her a glass. She looked down to find it was just water. She drank the cool substance down and motioned for more.

"How… long have I been out?" She asked her GrandMader.

CHAPTER 11

Atin

From Darkness comes the Light

Atin grew muscles she never knew she had and grew another inch higher that winter. She could manage the sails by herself or the tiller, while her Da would instruct whichever brother of hers that came with them, how to read the waves and the winds. She also developed a knack for bartering, when she went to the main Island with her Da and brothers to sell pearls, she helped teach her brothers to reap. She did not like how the same colourful stranger would continually harass her Da, so one day she jumped into the conversation and took over the haggling. Her Da looked annoyed, but she smiled sweetly back at him taking over. Men did most of the business, Daders were to know their place. She saw he tended to just agree with what was presented to him and people annoyed him when they were discussing prices.

She did not like the way her Da looked lately, more tired and worn out. She knew he worried about his family's well being and she vowed she would do her best to help. Their family was close; everyone pulled their weight, they laughed and enjoyed each other's company as they worked and played together.

She saw her brothers' absences weighed heavily on him and not because of the absence of helping hands. He genuinely missed their presence. She missed them too. Especially Zohan as he was closest to her age and her only friend.

"You like the pink one sir?"

'Yes, I would like that one and the smaller ones which match."

"I will sell them together, if you desire."

"I will offer you, fifty Venda coins."

"Oh, I am sorry sir. Last month's prices barely paid for our food. This bundle I can sell for one hundred Venda coins. No less. We must eat."

The stranger looked just as annoyed. Atin felt him taken aback by her forwardness. Thus began her adventure at business haggling, as she bartered, she began to see a haze of moisture begin to surround the man, a coloured aura which began as brown.

"That is too much. My employer has only given me so much for these pearls."

"I am sorry. If you are not willing to pay, then step aside for the next man, he will surely pay what I ask."

They kept at it, haggling, one excuse after another, and she kept on with her responses. As she kept insisting she would not accept his offer, the haze lightened up and changed colour to a pale pink with shots and swirls of purple. The strange man finally gave up and accepted her price. She saw his shoulders relax, with defeat and handed her Da the coins, and Atin handed the Aramite the pearls in a cloth bag they made from scraps of fabric.

As Atin handed the stranger the pearls, her hand brushed the top of his palm. A shock ran from her fingers to her head! It made her gasp quietly yet was loud enough the stranger heard her. They both glanced up and their eyes met again. Time stood still for Atin! She saw attraction in his eyes, the corners of his eyes, smiling with the movement of his mouth, still holding their gaze, she smiled back. They looked at each other, not saying anything, and the moment was lost when the stranger was jostled by another, trying to take his place. It broke her out of her revery, and she collected herself. The stranger, flushing moved away.

Atin had no time to ponder what just transpired, the next man approached, and the bartering began anew. She saw auras around people who stood nearby, and she began to figure out colours according to who was honestly trying to give a fair price and those who were buying her pearls for dirt-cheap. She kept this to herself, as every time she glanced back at her Da, she saw a sickly brown-green colour around him.

Soon she saw auras around all people and the colours astounded her. The auras gave her a feeling of awe; she saw coloured air around people! Atin knew if she said anything to her Da, he may believe her touched with madness. She finished with the last pearls and there were still a few men remaining.

"'Tis all I have for today. I promise I will have more the next trip back here."

One ventured to ask her hesitantly when that would be, as men did not talk openly to unmarried women, but since her Da was right beside her, he assumed it was fine. The fact she looked as though she could hold her own, her biceps were tight on her tunic, and he looked like a stiff breeze would blow him over.

"If you could wait, sir. We will return in two weeks time; I will bring you what I can."

"Yes, if you could I would be most generous. I have an incredibly special woman, my Mader. I would like to commission a necklace for her day of birth celebration which is arriving soon."

"Do you have a preference in colour, sir?"

"Why do you not surprise me. You are finding some unique colours."

She smiled at him, and he blushed, backing away, somehow embarrassed for them both. Her younger brothers helped without being told, placing the remaining baskets on the boat. They ventured into the market together and had their first foray at bargaining for items they needed. Her Da arranged it with people he dealt with. They needed to learn, as eleven-year-old Tarik, was the next man of the family.

"I did very well, at the smithy. I bartered Master Meradon down to ten Venda coins for this knife."

Atin smiled gently at her little brother and remembered back when she was this young, Zohan had been her minder in the markets. Her Da spoke to Tarik, his tone deepened in his seriousness.

"Just remember, if you had gone further in your negotiations, it would have been a slight to his work. I told you beforehand what its worth was. You may not always have me with you to bargain. If you had offered nine, he would have been affronted. Listen and remember key words for each craft you deal with. His has always been to say, 'I forged,' if he had spoken his apprentice's name or another smith, then you could buy it for less. His, is the work of a Master."

"What of other's? Do they all barter like the Smith?"

"No, the Herbalist does not barter. She has set prices. The tanner and leather goods, you can barter, and most times you will receive a few extra's… If they like you. Depends on if they had a good day, oft times, barter with them after midday or end of Day. Midday if you need something in particular, they will most like have it, and end of day if you need more strapping. 'Tis never sells. We need strapping in some of our nets, so you often will get what is left, but it suffices our needs."

"How will I remember all this?"

"I will be with you most times, until you can barter without me. I will let you lead the conversation next time. Now, come over here and grab the till. Can you feel the tension? Yes… then turn it to port. Feel the difference in the currents? When the sail snaps with wind, you will be hard pressed to hold on, if you flounder it will set you off course. You use stars at night, but for daytime, we use land on our port side. Keep a set sight of land in your eye."

This kept Tarik busy the rest of the way home, so she began to teach ten-year-old Selim the intricacy of sails, how to tack into the wind, and the differences between winter winds and summer winds. This kept them all occupied, the young lads did not have the strength to hold their own, and Atin hoped they grew fast as her arms and back really hurt after these boat trips to the main Island.

It was a couple of nights later, the evening meal was finished and Atin was helping her Mader clean, when Selim ran inside, telling them all to come outside to look at the sky.

"Atin, Ma, sisters, come outside! The stars are flying!"

The remaining women of the household ran onto the beach gazing up to see stars racing across the sky. It was a sight to be seen. Atin did not hesitate to lay down in the dry sand and watch for a while. It was so comforting she fell asleep right there and did not wake when her Da picked her up to take her to the sleeping cot in the building behind her.

The younger children watched a little longer. Selim told Atin the next morning there were a few huge ones.

"One sped across the sky, then a flash and lots of tails sped off in different directions. It lit up the sky, Atin! It was like the star was falling into the seas! They are flashing by."

"Well, I see they still are. Ma, what do you think?"

"Well… this could mean something… there is a Prophecy of old. I remember a sign from the Gods would herald a new age. It may spark a revival. We should pray and give thanks to Vendar tonight before our meal. It does good to acknowledge the Gods and the Universe. This is a sign, but I am not sure what… perhaps, Soren will know."

This meteor show went on during the days and for several nights. Each night, Atin would lay down falling asleep to the moving stars. She was exhausted by the amount of work she was helping her Da with. If she were not fishing with her Da and brothers, she would beg to escape up Island to pearl. She took two of her siblings with her. Taking them to her spots, she occupied them in the shallow areas while she risked the deeper reefs.

The boys quickly learned not to panic if she was underwater longer than them. The shells she brought up in her net, were just as heavy but she found she could raise more. She taught them how to extract the pearls without harming the animal inside and throw it back in the ocean to begin the cycle over.

"Gently with the point of the knife, catch it…in the seam, nearest to the longest edge, here. See the wrinkle in the seam, fit the tip in there, move it sideways… like this…and give a quick twist. See it opens. Dip it into the water, moisten the insides, not too much, or it will be much too slippery. Now with one hand holding it open, I insert my fingers here, it will try to close, which is why we give it some water…now, with my other hand, use one finger, some shells are too small and require us to open it further."

"Do we not eat those ones?"

"Yes, I have not had much success with the smaller shells. I still offer a prayer to the Gods, for the bounty we collect. Pearls or seafood flesh. As I extract…you see the outline, here? Tarik, look…those lumps are pearls, we gently massage the flesh, there will be some resistance, but if you pray to Ilyan, or Iris, I find humming does help, it will release its bounty into the shell."

"Humming? That sounds a bit…silly."

"Well, if humming is silly, think of a prayer. Mayhap one to Vendar, or one to Vandric. We are not here to kill every shell inhabitant. We thank them for their bounty. Then we place them back to begin the entire process again. If we do not kill the inhabitant, then they will create another pearl."

"How do you know they will do this again?"

"I do not, yet I respect all life in the seas. I sometimes make mistakes; I will press too hard with my knife… It will slip… I press too hard with a finger, detach the flesh from the shell."

"Then we have melting pot stew for days… did I do this one right, Atin?"

"Yes, now gently, help the shell to close. I find dunking it into the water helps. When we gather the shells, pressing into the flesh removes the water. The water is its natural habitat, having it up in the air, is not. As the air is our natural habitat, they breath under water."

"Just like you, you stay under much longer than us."

"I have had more time to practice, Selim. You lads will get better."

She had a few pools of water, small coves she would transport the ones she caught elsewhere, then place those empty of pearls in these coves. This is where she 'farmed' many of the smaller ones. This area was safer for the littles to practice their pearling while she escaped to the deep of the wider ocean. She had the thought when she was gone, it was in place for her family to reap the benefits.

The reefs where they dove were colourful with diverse types of coral, and they were careful to not touch these as it took many years for them to grow back. After violent storms, pieces would litter the beaches, the children would pick up pieces and grind them in a laborious task. They would use the ground coral in around their home, it had several uses.

There were countless varieties of fishes, beautiful colours and some not so nice. Jellyfish which glowed when they were attracting prey. She stayed away from those and never bothered any of the fish she swam with.

On one of her longer forays into the deep, she found a large plot of shells and was struggling to lift her catch when she thought it would be so helpful to have one of her fishy friends assist her to shore. She did not think anything was different about her, however, now she could stay underwater for ten minutes. She was not scared when larger fish came to observe her. They never came too close, yet she had a repeat friend. A group of turtles congregated every year around the same time. Atin would see the same large turtle and she knew it was him from a slice in his front fin.

As she thought of the turtle, it came up to her, bumping her in the back. She felt her lungs begin to strain as she grabbed on to his shell behind his neck while he rose straight up. She did not believe this was wrong or different and genuinely thought she had a relationship with the wild animals she spent time with. Her parents repeatedly told her and her siblings, people and animals had a symbiotic relationship, to respect their habitat and live in harmony with them.

They broke the surface of the cove, and she saw where the sand was shallow enough to stand. The turtle kept swimming and she held on until she could stand up. Letting go of his shell she ducked under the water as he prepared to swim away. She mentally thanked him, and he turned back to look at her. She got a mental image of his mutual love of fish, and she smiled at the thought. She stood up to see her brothers running pell mell down the beach toward her and she dragged the net full of shells to the shore, her brothers running into the water to help her all the while, jabbering about the turtle they saw her hanging onto.

"Please do not say anything to Da and Ma,"

She asked Selim and Tarik when they kept on about the turtle.

"They would not understand."

Atin tried to make light of it,

"I helped this turtle two seasons ago, he was returning the favour. We are all creatures of Vendar, living in harmony and assisting each other when in need. This turtle I removed a hook from of one of his fins. He saw me struggling with my load and air, he swam close and I took the assistance he offered. Our paths are to be travelled together, we walk side by side, sometimes our paths will cross, then separate."

"We know, Atin. Pader tells us countless times. Never harm another, never kill unless for food. We know, you do not have to explain this to us."

"Well. I am telling you how I was helped."

"But how can you speak underwater? Blow bubbles at it?"

"Never mind, let us get these pearls out. Now, gently use your finger to ease it out of the flesh…"

She had them explain and demonstrate pearl extraction back to her and by the time they finished, they stopped talking about the turtle.

This was a job well done; disaster avoided. The boys will have forgotten by the time they return home.

Working on the last of the shells, she found the hugest pearl she had ever seen. She was getting lots of purple blue pearls. The most beautiful colour mixture! Atin immediately thought of the young stick of a man who requested pearls.

Her finger caught on a huge lump of flesh inside and she asked her brothers' assistance to hold the shell still, to avoid damaging the animal inside. They each held a side while she gently extracted the hugest pearl. It was as large as her thumb, she thanked the shell, and her brothers helped to gently close it.

"We better get these back in the water on the other side in our cove. These pearls will fetch a dear price next week when we return to market."

thers carefully placed the shells on the flat, to keep the moisture inside, she was also careful to dip the basket back in the water until it was time to transport them across. She remembered where each basket load was placed, she began on one side and worked her way around. She would be able to harvest fresh pearls soon. Atin was carefully monitoring her cove and the shallows were the perfect habitat for her 'babies.' It also worked better for her siblings as none of them could go as far or stay down as long as she could.

They headed home in the little boat they used to navigate around the rocky coastlines of the shoals. It took an hour to travel from her island to home and the boys helped to carry the boat up to the cave overhang she used to protect it from elements. They collected their bags of treasure and walked for a while before they walked up to the hut. The boys were chattering to their Mader, and it was not until there was complete silence Atin realized the boys spilled about the turtle.

"Atin?" Her Mader was staring at her with mouth open.

"Is what they say truth? A turtle helped you?"

Atin very gently dumped her bag of pearls on the table, and everyone gasped at the colour and the size of the large one.

"Yes, Ma, I was deeper than I thought and struggling with the net. He swam by, and I grabbed his shell, you are always telling us to live in harmony and re-spect. I thanked him generously. Look at what we caught, this will fetch a really decent price, I am thinking of the young man and his gift for his Mader."

Her Mader shook her head as Atin and her brothers scooped up the pearls heading outside. They washed them in a bag with some of the finely ground coral and sea water, then washing them clean with tepid water from the stream in wooden buckets outside the hut. They would dry them off and she would grade them accordingly to size, shape, and level of glossiness.

As they were finishing, their Pader arrived with a decent haul of fish. This would keep them busy the next day, preparing for storing. He glanced at the catch in her bucket, reaching in, taking the large pearl out.

"By the Gods, this is amazing! This will fetch some good coin. I think with your new skills in the market we will not have to return for a while. Let us head out the day after tomorrow. When we return, we will have a rest and take a day or so off. You have worked extremely hard, Atin, I am immensely proud of the young woman you are becoming. You will make someone an exceptionally good wife. I am afraid you will have to spend more time with your Ma to learn from her more preparing skills to round out your pearling ones."

He dropped the pearl back in the bucket walking into the hut to speak to her Mader. He did not see the expression on her face at the mention of marriage, but Selim did and asked her what was wrong.

"I have never thought of joining, I do not want to leave here, this is my home. The thought of leaving makes me want to vomit."

Selim shrugged, to him it was a fact, he would grow up and follow either in his Paders footsteps or go to war like his older brothers. What she stated, he could not fathom, being a man and all. Her Pader emerged; his mouth open slightly.

"Atin, Ma told me something astonishing."

Atin sighed, she was still rinsing the pearls. She dropped them onto the sieve of rushes, it was used for many things, Atin learned to create baskets and lids out of the grasses grown for linens. Beyond their home, there were fields of special grasses, used in the making of the sails. She gently shook the large woven sieve as the water dripped out.

"Da, the turtle saw I was struggling, he came close enough so I could grab onto his shell. I saw he recognized me; it was the old one I helped with the large hook. You know the one I told you about. He was returning the favour. You told me to respect all creatures, it seems they have respect for us as well."

"Well, it seems very unlikely…You have quite the haul here. This cluster is for that young man?"

"Yes, Da. This should be a good set for his Mader present. I will bag these according to colour, instead of size. There is enough for several sets, then I will combine the small ones together."

"You are finding a vast amount. We seem to be having continued luck gathering these, when is your cove ready?"

"Next season, the boys can begin in the shallows and see if they are large enough to harvest. If not, then we will leave it for another term, I am checking the same shell periodically. They do not grow fast."

"Well, small ones sell just as fast, we can not get as much, but more people can afford the little ones. Excellent work harvesting and instructing your brothers."

"Thanks, Da. They should be able to gather them without my help, I hope they have been listening to me. I am going inside. I need to find the bags I have made."

They sailed out early two days later after spending the previous day mending nets and carving planks of wood. It was smooth sailing on calm seas which was very appreciated. Docking, they paid to have their boat watched, she thought to take the pearls, as she did not completely trust anyone. It was a good thing, because when they came back the guards were not around.

Atin and her Da only brought Selim, her brother needed to learn how his Da conducted business. Soren was teaching both together and each separately. First, they headed into the lower city to visit with Medea, who was more than surprised to see them. She marvelled at the size of the pearl, as it was bigger than her bride price one.

"Here you go, Medea. I have some for you. I know that you have your own finances, but mayhap you could use these to buy any extras you may need."

"Oh, thank you Atin. This is unexpected but very appreciated. It has come at the right time."

"What do you mean by the right time?"

"Well… I believe you can tell Mader, I am expecting a child now!"

"Oh, by the Mader! This is wonderful news! Mader will be overjoyed."

"Dear Medea. I am so happy for you and Hess! Thank you for the wonderful news. I will bring your Mader when the time is near if you would have her."

"Yes, Pader, I would. I do miss her, but having my own household to deal with is quite rewarding. Hess is building our home, now we will need the extra rooms."

It was one-time Atin saw her Paders face light up in joy. He left them to walk up to the barracks for any news, Atin and Selim waited with Medea for him to return. Atin knew it was highly unlikely there would be any news as her brothers were only gone less than two months. From listening to talk at the docks, it took under a month or so to get there by ship.

"The Rituals were last week. There is a newly christened Rider, Atin! She is different."

"Different, how?"

"She is more powerful, than the High Magistrate! She breathed fire!"

"Oh, breathed? Oh, 'tis amazing!"

"She is your age, Atin! She breathed fire and her eyes changed!"

"Changed? Is she the one I heard has eyes like the Riders since a child? I heard someone tell Da, but I was only half listening. How did they change?"

"Her eyes changed to resemble those of lizards, like the green Scarfnecks."

"Oh, so slitted iris?"

"Yes, there has never been any like her. The High Magistrate proclaims the new Rider as her GrandDader. Apparently, she was raised in one of the many Church orphanages to hide her identity, to protect her. We all know the tragedy of the High Magistrates Daders. She is called High Dragon, at least this is what I was told. Hess went to the Barracks to deliver goods and was told from some of the guards who saw it for themselves. There is talk of a new Dragon Age, Hess says times will be changing."

"Well, I hope it changes soon and for the good, then our brothers can come home."

"I asked Hess. He says not to get our hopes up. Our men sent to the mainland…please do not repeat this to Da… are as good as dead."

"Oh, Medea! How can you say this? 'Tis mean."

"Atin, think on it… I am sorry, but this is life. Grow up. If times change in our favour, because we have always believed in the old Gods, then Du'Lanay will use our men in the front lines. 'Tis war."

"Not our war. Not our war. I understand, 'tis to keep our life and our people safe. I wish they all did not have to go at once, 'tis not fair. Da is lost since they left. He is not well."

"What do you mean, not well? Oh, I thought something was off, he looks more tired. Him and Ma are not off?"

"No, they seem to be closer than ever. He looks tired and has no energy. Well, less energy. He takes both boys out fishing, and I have to go with them many times. My arms ache…everything aches, Medea."

"You look very fit, Atin. I see a maturity about you. I am sorry you seem to be working harder. You are certainly harvesting pearls, every time I see you, you have a larger volume. Hess says some of the older men believe you have a secret place. You should take caution."

"I do, but 'tis not ready yet… So, people talk about me?"

"Yes, you seem to have cornered the market, none reap your volume."

"Da does not get their value, I watch his negotiations, we could get more."

"Well, take care in your dealings, you do not want to create tensions and take care of your harvesting."

"Thank you, for telling me. I will."

Their Da soon returned, confirming Atin's belief of news being too early. They gave Medea their regards and many hugs, heading off to market.

The three of them walked a haphazard route so Selim could go to places their Da did business and be introduced to merchants. Atin could not help but feel a strange sense of foreboding. She closed her eyes for a moment.

I do not wish to see the haze or aura today, not around Da.

When she opened her eyes, nothing changed, except the men had moved away and she hurried through the crowd to catch up.

They reached their boat only to find it surrounded by merchants and no guards. One merchant took the liberty to be aboard, to which her Da took exception to and nearly threw him off with a punch to his face. The skinny stick of a man held Soren's arm back and said they all watched,

"He did not explore your boat. He was scaring off the pelicans. They seem to want to explore that basket there."

"Thank you."

Atin spoke to the gathered crowd. Her Da was securing the basket, which had dried fillets in it and was the focus of the hungry vultures. Pelicans would cart off anything not tied down.

"I have a special pearl this young man, Master Keyan will bid on first. If you care to gather around. I will show it to you all."

She reached into her bag at her waist, bringing out the large purplish-blue pearl with a handful of smaller ones. The crowd moved towards her, so she jumped up on a box, showing the crowd pearls while her Da and the now present guards held some of the men back.

"Now this is the largest one I have ever found, and while I am willing to let this young man offer first as he is most considerate of our possessions, I am willing to entertain the most sum if anyone were to offer it."

She gazed down at the young man, and he smiled at her.

"I had a feeling you would not disappoint; you are harvesting some of the most unique pearls ever seen and this is what I would like to offer you."

He proceeded to offer a sum of money, her Da automatically accepted without haggling, as it was triple what they ever made from the whole of one of their catches. The crowd moaned, and she spoke up.

"I have more, great sirs, if you will bear with me a moment."

Turning around, she reached into her bodice bringing out a few more bags. Her thought to bag them according to colour turned out to be a very good decision. Addressing the crowd, she proceeded to sell a bag of white, blue, baby blue and pink. Also, several bags of assorted small ones. After the auction, which her Da said worked out well, he told her their business was almost done and they would head home after he took Selim to buy goods to take back.

"Get the boat prepared, lass. We will be back shortly. Selim needs to bargain with the herbalist for his Ma. 'Tis a good opportunity for him. We should be back by the time you are done. The guard will stay until we return."

She untied a few ropes, placing their things on the deck. Packing the baskets tightly into the cubbies edging the outer hull and securing them, with ropes and tying them off. Coming over her was a feeling of being watched, she straightened to see the colourful man lingering. She studied him and saw the beginnings of an aura of yellow, green and it changed colours as she looked. She did not get a sense of unease. She greeted him but moved closer to the guard. Her Da paid for their services and they would be dismissed once the boat left.

"Can I help you, sir?"

She then bowed her head, because women were not encouraged to have direct eye contact, especially young, unmarried women. Atin recalled the way she felt when their eyes had met and she felt her heart beat a little faster. She felt uneasy but not in a bad way and had to remind herself this was not her Pader or brother she was addressing. Climbing back onto the pier she stood beside the guard.

"Yes, young miss. I would like you to supply me with a constant variation of pearls at regular intervals. I will pay handsomely for any uniqueness if you were lucky enough to find. I would have paid you double what the young man paid for the purple ones. I have a very wealthy benefactor, who likes uniqueness in his decoration."

She loved the timber of his voice! It seemed to caress her skin and she felt her heart skip faster and her body begin to heat up, glancing up to see if he was mocking her, she saw her Da and brother returning, their arms laden with baskets and goods. Putting her head down she responded,

"I will try my best, but I cannot promise. Pearling is contrary according to the weather."

"I am sure you will not disappoint. The more colourful, and unique in shape would be what I would pay you for. Sir…"

The stranger repeated his offer to her Da and they introduced each to the other. She heard him say that his name was Kaisan, and he hailed from Aram. He would stay for the winter months and sail back to the main continent in the spring, taking any pearls, she and her brothers would care to sell to him.

"One thing, Da, we cannot supply him and him alone, our other customers would be angry."

Kaisan heard her query and addressed her Da saying,

"If you would allow me the first look, I could be more selective and pay you handsomely for the opportunity. I realize I will not be able to get anything past your Dader and will not try to haggle down the price. This would guarantee my placement?"

Her Da agreed as they shook hands. On a whim, she strode forward offering the man her hand, which her Pader looked a little annoyed, but the man laughed, took her hand, and shook it,

"Now it is double binding, I look forward to seeing you again."

His palm was warm and his grip firm, she did not get chills from his grasp, and she gazed at him, smiling.

"You must give me a month to catch some, how about we meet again after winter solstice, which is about three and a bit weeks from now."

She looked at her Da and he agreed,

"It would be more appropriate, then, to do our business under cover of a roof and not out in the open."

"This sounds like an excellent idea."

"Perhaps we meet in the inn adjacent to the Dockmasters office as it is heavily trafficked by guards and honest businessmen."

"Yes, then we take our time, and I view pearls without the added distraction of contenders."

"Until then, Sir."

"Good Path, Sir, until then… Miss."

They parted ways, her Da and her brother jumping aboard after her and set off for a brisk ride home as the winds picked up and were dark clouds to the west.

"This looks like the advent of winter. Mayhap the storming season comes early this year. We should return before it hits and talk about how we are going to proceed with your pearling. You are finding plenty of bigger ones; you may have competition one day.

That young Aramite looked rather taken aback at your forwardness. Until you get to know people in the lower market, you would be wise to not be so forward. Some men will take offense by it. Especially those not of our religion, you know the continents are controlled by men?"

Her Da yelled his conversation at her as she was trying to hold the sails with her brother, it took all her strength. After nodding back at her Da, they concentrated on keeping the boat skimming across the water, the wind made it fly. Atin noticed the white caps increasing on the heaving waters, the dark skies followed them home.

They made it home before the wind got brisker. Her Da on checking the skyline, grabbed the ropes and began to winch the boat onto dry sand, she stayed behind to help. Selim took the first load and brought everyone else back with him, even their Mader. All assisted to pull the boat on land, her Da had a sixth sense about storms. They retrieved the goods and secured them in the hut as the rains hit.

As they waited, eating their meal, her Pader kept speaking as though they did not have a half daybreak in their conversation. He spoke louder than normal, over the beating staccato of the rain.

"You know Aram and Du'Lanay do not treat their women as proper citizens? Ever since conception of the Naman religion, women are degraded and subjected to horrors from their male counterparts. Here in Pelin'Dun we still respect women, for without them, we would have no compassion, no children, no caring. Women carry the family name, and 'tis through them we prosper. 'Tis as though men of the continents, fear women. This is how they keep them subservient. 'Tis a shame, women should be revered, and held in the highest esteem, here on the Islands, we have always had an equal relationship, it has always been. Never try to fix something not broken, maybe this is their undoing, you will see, times will change, mark my words!"

Her Pader had incredibly good advice sometimes, she often wondered if he was a bit of an oracle. He knew which storms would leave damage, and which ones you could still go out in.

The storm was a hard hitting one. They worried for a bit the hut would not bear up. Her Da was more worried about the boat, and they dragged it up the beach quite far, so Atin hoped it was serviceable when this was over. She loved storms. She was not afraid of the fierceness of the rain or the lightning which sometimes accompanied it. If her Mader did not worry so, she would be outside getting soaked to the skin.

Once she was caught out on one of her pearling trips, alone. Not watching the skies and had to wait one out for an entire day. She just lay there on the rocks, thinking it the most glorious thing. That day she found out the storms would churn up the water and shallows bringing shells up for easy pickings. She was so busy collecting pearls she lost track of time and her older brother Zohan came to find her. Their parents were angry at her until they saw how many pearls she brought from that one trip alone.

She had a feeling this storm would reap her many pearls. Atin and her family sat and discussed how everyone but her Mader and the three smallest would go pearling tomorrow.

"You may have competition one day. We will all attend to pearling tomorrow, that young Aramite was very eager to buy all. If we can bring more each time, then we will not have to worry about going to Peli often. Once a month would work out and it would give us more time to fish and harvest our catches."

Atin leaned against her Da, falling asleep with the winds and rain raging outside.

CHAPTER 12

Andic

And Love Comes From War

Andic only managed five hours of sleep before the sounds of daytime woke her. She would always sleep in the busy areas when she knew she had business during the day, so she could easily wake from all the noise and bustle surrounding the buildings. When she was daft tired, she would hole up at a noble's estate where she knew the discovery of being found was less. She had a few areas mapped out and would never use one twice in a row.

Her empire needed her more often than naught and now she had a quest of her own to puzzle out.

First thing on my agenda is to learn to read. Not an easy task and it will not happen overnight. I can pick out a few sounds from images, but I need to find a teacher, discreetly. Who would instruct a woman? Who to ask? Who will not give me away?

She lay another moment, before heading quietly downstairs to not wake the girls who were exhausted from the night's activities. She headed to the privy house to relieve herself. A splash on her face from the fountain in the private back yard, refreshed her.

The Great FirPader believed in running water for all. There were aqueducts and fountains in all sections of the city, less in the poorer section and less opulent, but everyone had access to water. In a land where water was a precious commodity, the dryness of the terrain, and the sole conduit of the river, he made it his gift to his people. This was a prior wish of his Pader, and the current one completed the fountains and inner machinations. This act alone had him the love of his people. The worship of him as their God was absolute. No one rebelled against him and when he asked for men to fight in the war, many men and young boys volunteered.

The aqueducts helped with sanitation. Since the great purge from disease, streets were cleaned and washed periodically using slaves and prisoners. Only during the summer did this cease, as there were always one or two sandstorms which raged in, polishing the streets clean.

Andic took a heel of bread from the kitchen and headed back upstairs to think.

Who, out of all the people I know, would have the time to teach me, a street rat, also a girl, how to read? They would have to be blind and dumb.

Maybe I should go ask Zenzol, like I planned. He knows everyone here. He would know a solution to my dilemma. Plus, he would keep it private. No one needs to know the 'Little Dragon's' business. He would know who might teach me and mayhap he would know something about the star. It seems to be brighter.

Curious, she stood up gazing out the roof hatch and damn, if it was not visible during the day! She did not know the Hall of Learning had a special glass they looked through to see the heavens, but to the naked eye it was but a small dot and not visible to anyone directly looking up. It would not be visible for a time. She had her skill, as she called it, to focus in on an object and view like it was close. Andic would not know why this was for a time. For the moment she assumed it was her skills at survival she honed.

Having decided this was what she should do, she stopped by one of the girls' rooms and borrowed a head covering and gown. It was a neutral colour used to walk the streets during the Day and not be noticed. Head coverings were mandatory for women, but she did not see the need for one during the night as she passed for a boy. During the Day, she needed to be as unnoticed as possible, it covered all of her, up to her eyes.

Satisfied with her disguise, she made her way out of the alley joining the many people on the Path of Delights. Few travelled around in the morning. Most were walking back to wherever they had come from. In the coolness of the morning, Andic walked to the Great Hall District, stopping when she arrived at the Scribe's Hall. Here, people paid to have their letter written or read for a fee. She wandered around until she found the man she sought. She waited for a half hour on a bench until called over.

Andic walked up to an older man, sporting a white beard, and turban headdress of white and tan covering his head. His robe was tan and an undertunic of white, and leather sandals on his feet. The fingers on his right hand stained with black ink. He did not look up as she sat down on the small stool in front of the bench table. He had papyrus and ink well on the surface beside the roll he was pinning down.

"What can I write for you on this auspicious day?"

He asked as he dipped the quill into the well and tapped on the edge.

"I was hoping to ask you a few questions, dear Zenzol, as I have a curiosity about a few things."

Zenzol started and spilled a drop of ink onto the paper, so she placed down a coin telling him to write a list of things he liked about her or something else un-important.

"I would like to know of a way I can learn to read and write, and if you know anything about the star in the sky with a tail and what it means. I have a need to know these things. Can you assist me?"

He leaned down into the bench and softly spoke. "How are you able to see the star? Only the great Masters have seen it through a great glass they have pointed at the sky. 'Tis a rumour being circulated quietly, if known to be heard 'tis death. There is a Prophecy written by the Vendar religion of old and forbidden to be read or spoken. The advent of the Dragon's Breath is the rebirth of Dragons and their Riders. That is all I know…'tis heresy, I could be overheard, we will speak no more about this.

As for learning to read, women are forbidden, so to teach you would also be a death sentence. However, I do know of an old scribe, half blind and not well, you might be able to fool him for a time. He lives upriver about a day and a half, at the Mosque of Remembrance. The Mosque is red, and you would have to adhere to his rules and quirks. His name, if you should go, is Kadir. Good luck Little Dragon."

He finished writing on the papyrus, rolled it up and gave it to her. She bowed and thanked him. He motioned for the next person in line as she left. Zenzol was an asset to her network. She would visit him occasionally outside of his working environment to glean information he would acquire. She paid him handsomely. It was unusual for Andic to visit him in his 'office' so his surprise to see her was genuine. She hoped it did not have negative repercussions and her disguise was complete. She was lost in her thoughts as she wandered through markets, beginning to come alive with vendors, business done before the heat of the day. Sounds of shouting brought her back to the now.

"You whore. How can you calmly say you are leaving? You have no right to leave."

The sounds of flesh on flesh met her as she rounded a corner to witness an older robed man, his arm had completed its path. The woman on the ground holding her face in her hands, her head covering askew showing the graying hair underneath. She stared up at the man above her, no tears. Andic leaned against the side of the building, this was nothing new to her. Men would beat their woman publicly. Some would happen privately, but Andic saw more in the markets than she saw in homes.

It is like they need an audience to perform. No different than the sex acts back home. Here I notice they get more congratulated by other men. The harder they hit, the more accolades they get.

Sure enough, it was happening as she thought it. The man was downright beating his wife. Other men encouraging him. She turned around and walked back around the corner to screams from the woman. There was nothing she could do. Any person for that matter who attempted to interfere with a man beating his wife would get the same. As she turned a few more corners, the screams abruptly stopped.

Well, she is dead.

Andic felt nothing. This was the world she lived in, men ruled women. Andic fit in where she could, no one really cared what or who you were in the lower city, many just survived. In the brothel she resided in, some of the girls used their talents to manipulate men, to acquire things they desired, but it was for the moment of pleasure they gave. Few could use their wiles beyond the pleasure houses. Some had tried, and they had died.

There must be more to this life… More than death… More than fighting for food. Fighting to have more. What is our purpose here? I am embarking on a journey. One to learn what is forbidden to women. And why is this? Why are women held in such low esteem? Men cannot have children, yet they tell it like they are the bringers of life. How would they fare if no women could bear children? If women could choose their mate? How would this work out?

Once I can decipher the written word, I will know what it is, men fear. Why? Do they think we can overpower them? We are weaker, physically. So that cannot be the reason, it must be of the mind. They fear our minds. So, it must be they fear what we may do with our thoughts. Hmmmm, I have never thought about this before, now I am to learn, it does make me wonder. What will I find?

Walking back to the brothel she vacated earlier she met with the owner as she was beginning her morning meal.

"I will be absent for a while, Delma. My deputies will be around should you need assistance. I will be back when my task is complete."

The older woman did not ask, as it was always better to not know more than needed. Andic thought at least one person should know where she was, in case of any pressing need.

"You are going upriver?"

Delma did not always ask her questions; she was the only woman Andic knew who never hit or beat her. Some of the newer girls would partake of hitting her until such time they needed a favor, then they changed their tune. Her first memories were with Delma. The older woman raised her as best she could. Wherever Andic got herself off to, she would always come back to Delma. It was an unwritten code which suited both just fine.

"Yes. I have a monumental task to do; you could say I seek illumination."

She smiled at the older woman. Delma used her girls for information and she was able to keep her status as Matron, by sheer will, bribes, and blackmail. A healthy dose of each. She brooked no disrespect from any of her clients or girls. Her house was well known for clean girls, which also catered to the more 'private' of clients. It was well guarded and set back behind high walls and at the end of the path.

"Well, you should probably tell one of your boys. Just in case, they need you. I cannot help them in their business ventures; I have my hands full with some of these girls who think they are too good for their clients. What am I going to do when I need certain things?"

"I will let Laza or Hayk know to expect you to ask for help. They will assist you, for a small fee of course. I hope I am not gone long, but it depends on me, I have a task to do and cannot return until I have completed it. You can oversee the girls with the same strong arm you used on me; I am sure?"

Andic smiled at Delma, the older woman grabbing her to give her a much needed and not often utilized hug.

"Do not you worry girl, I will set these lasses to rights. You do what you need to do and come back to me, so I do not worry myself to my grave."

They parted arms and Delma left the room returning with a package from the kitchen which she handed over to Andic.

"This should keep you for a bit. You need some more meat on those bones of yours. Soon you will grow. Grow into a girl, lass."

"Ugh. I can wait for this. Most think I am a boy. So do not wish this on me yet."

Andic was still a small person for her age, whatever this was, and her breasts had not formed yet, so she took advantage of resembling a boy and was not looking forward to the day she had to shed this part of her guise. She looked the part of the perfect street waif. The maderly woman had packed a small amount of food in a piece of cloth Andic could carry. She went back upstairs to nap before she saw her men and left them.

The sounds of music, laughter and pleasure woke her from her second sleep. Gathering her things she set off for the lower district where she could find at least one of her boys lingering around. She managed to find Laza in his hovel as he was waking up, startling him so much as to fist his blade at her.

"Gods, girl, do not do this, one of these days I will be faster and gut yah."

"Not bloody likely!"

"What brings you here? I did not know there was a meeting."

He stood up undoing the front ties on his pants. Andic raised her eyebrow watching as he strode to the corner of his room to piss in a small pot. No missing and shook it off, tucking it back before turning around, lacing up. Andic was impressed, but said nothing, she was not wanting to be in his sights, she was not interested in games under the sheets.

"There is not. I am heading upriver for a time, seeking answers, and will spend time there. So, for now things are yours. Before you ask, no, I do not know when I will be back... When the job is done."

"Care to explain?"

"No, less you know..."

"Of course, people will ask. The Little Dragon does not up and leave."

"Then tell them I died. I will not be back until I finish what needs to be done. If I do not come back, then 'tis yours anyway. If you can watch out for the girls..."

"Most certainly. I will miss your addition to the coffers though, I cannot see anyone stepping into your district. We will have to make up for it if we can. Thank you, now I need to get going, have some issues with a few fishermen to take care of."

Laza gave her an arm shake, grabbed his overtunic pulling it on. They both headed outside and parted ways. She headed North over a couple bridges, finding the main gate. Passing under it a feeling came to her, as though she entered a new adventure! She walked forward thinking about her life. She always watched out for herself but lived most of her early life in the House of Delights where she had one of her nests. As she grew, she began as a runner for messages. Everyday life gave her the skills she believed she earned and honed. She was an expert at hiding in the shadows and could outrun and out hide soldiers. Andic became the reputation she earned, by sheer determination and hard work.

It was not all easy. It may not be easy to learn to read and write. Yet one does not learn and learn well if it was always so. Keeping myself away from clients groping hands...now this was difficult. Until I learned where to hurt them, and not in the physical regions, finding secrets...now that is where I learned to hurt.

The Oban who liked little boys...his chief guard who liked to beat girls and then rape them. Now, there was a death I do not regret giving. Placing him where all saw, with his cock stuffed in his mouth... This message gave pause to those that like to hurt which began the reputation, I earned. Am I leaving such behind me?

She took the road North of the river. Their Ruler also believed in maintaining the roads as it manifested better business. Only a few parts were showing wear, so, the first part of her trek passed uneventful. She walked through fields of grain, a few small hamlets, and farms serving the fields to the river. Andic saw lights on the hills which boasted vineyards and groves of whatever trees were on them. She had never been out of the city before and wondered at the new vistas. In the gentle light of the full moon, she saw such beauty. There were a few men about, guards she surmised for a few crops.

As long as I stay on the path, I will not be mistaken for a scoundrel. This must be the fields of Yanaberry. Brecu told me the pay for guards out here, is less and very uneventful. He likes excitement. I wonder if I should have said anything to him...but why? He does not report to me...I hope he does not look for me. He might not like the fact I left. What is the longest we have not seen or chatted? Hmmm... two months? Perhaps longer... He will have to bear it. I will see him first when I get back.

The landscape she walked through was new to her, but it had been there for centuries. She was used to being surrounded by walls and buildings. Here there were none of those. She walked into higher elevations and saw a panoramic view of the river valley. The Vuz stretched out below her a silver stripe weaving in and out, tributaries branching off. Canals built to spread the elixir of water to the fields. The fields a darker shade than the hills on the other side of the river valley dotted with the lights of settlements. She saw all this and marvelled at the expanse of the Empire. She lived in a mere spot in all of it and wondered what the rest looked like. Andic thought after she finished her quest mayhap, she would continue on. Keep going. See more.

Why do I feel as though I am a bird who escaped its cage? The valley that feeds us is a huge area, yet this is just a portion of the world. I wonder what the other lands are like. Are they like this? All sand? Hmmm, perhaps I need to see for myself. But first I must learn to read, and maybe to write. Then learn about this heresy, the Prophecy from another land. 'Tis a writing another land believes. Does this make it wrong? Is there more to life than here?

She saw cliffs of layered rock. Reds, browns, white, silt the river had over time, brought down into the valley. The farther away she walked from the bosom of the river, the sparser the vegetation became. Less and less scrub, the trees thinned out until after a time, there was no more plant life. It was a stark and barren vista. The rock cliffs, looking like huge boulders with cuts in them as though a knife chopped away at a loaf of bread. It was into one of these she ventured, after a land marker of red rock indicated a path was the one she wanted. At least she hoped this was what it meant. She looked upriver and saw the signs of another city.

The scratches she knew was writing, meant nothing to her for the moment. Andic would take the path and hope she had not erred. Walking further from the city, she saw a flashing light from the corner of her eye. Stopping to look behind her she saw flashing stars over head. Enough for her to stop, sit down on a large rock and just look up to watch.

I wonder if this is a portent to something. I wonder if I will find anything of interest. Flying stars? This is amazing. What would happen if one should land?

Never seeing a meteor shower before, she enjoyed the site for a time, not until a terrific display hit the upper atmosphere, shattering apart into many sparks shooting off in different directions did she set off again.

I guess that is what would happen. It hits a barrier up there and sparks. Hmmm, interesting. Sparks from the sharpening of swords against stone wheels.

It seemed to follow her all night, after a while she stopped seeing them. Andic walked all night. It was the following day she came across the community surrounding the red mosque. Climbing up a hill into the cliffs, passing over a small stream, she hung back off the beaten track. Finding a small indent in the outcropping rock, she wanted to catch up on sleep before the heat of the day. Meanwhile the stars continued to flash overhead, the odd one hitting the atmosphere and sparking.

After viewing this all night, the novelty wore off. She napped for a time, then rose to observe the area. Andic noted which avenues might provide escape, watching movements and gauging her next step. She walked all around the area, noting the natural landscape kept it hidden and protected, from natural and unnatural predators. She walked up the path to the entry gate just before sunset asking the monk guard for entry after explaining her reason for being there.

"Hello, my name is Odan, I am here to attend to a Kadir. I am instructed to ease his end of life comfortably. Is this the right place?"

Andic tried to make it sound as official as she could.

"Yes, we have such a man here. I was not told of any attendants, but it would not be the first time. If you care to wait here, please, I will inquire."

She waited a mere few minutes before the guard came back and motioned for her to enter.

"You go into the main hall. You will find the man you seek in there. If not, he may be in one of the rooms or at prayers. In which case you will wait until he is finished. Someone inside will direct you."

"Thank you."

The guard pointed to the main building and the doors at the front. Out here the natural landscape was an interesting shade of red, which she understood the reasoning behind the name for the cluster of buildings she observed quietly on her own. The buildings were plain, made of the red mud bricks. It served mainly as a simple means of shelter, not a show of wealth. The wood of the doors and beams were also red. The trees used were native to the land, closer to the river. The only show of excessive decoration was the patterns on the ground. A natural mosaic using different stones, with spirals and the odd floral. Some waves and edging bands, with yellows, whites and the more common red, it was held together by red sand dust, which looked hardened by traffic of footsteps. All this she observed as she made her way across the courtyard.

After gaining entry, she was directed by a novice to the main room and an alcove where the man she was seeking, was sitting. Inside, the building was as plain as outside. The candle holders were of wood, the same red as the construction of the buildings. The floors were a continuation of the richly embossed mosaics. These looked a bit more polished than the paths outside. One thing she noticed before entering the alcove, which had her interest peaked, was the presence of a glass in the wall. In which one could see the outside, not fully transparent but enough it let the light of the moon in. She would find out what it was. Her curiosity was such she could not leave without knowing the how and why of it was created.

She found whom she was seeking, sitting by himself, surrounded by a few candelabras, reading from a book. He was an old man, hunched over, the few hairs on his chin were pure white and very sparce. He looked up and greeted her.

"Hello. You are…?"

"I am Odan. Zenzol sent me."

"Yes. I received a letter this morning. He said you were seeking instruction, in exchange for myself receiving some care in the twilight of my life. You are prepared to do so?"

"Yes, Master. I would very much like to learn from you."

"Well, I see from the look of you, you live a life of hardship. Nothing is free, you will be expected to do other chores, unless I have need of you."

"Whatever you require, I will do."

"I am sure you will… you will." He chuckled at his remark.

"You are expected to help me rise, and bring my fast, in the morning. Then I will instruct you for a time, at which you are expected to then bring my mid day meal. Then you will wash the few items I have, while I rest. There is late worship then the evening meal. Prayers are given in the evening for our Great God, I will need help to retire. Not every day is the same."

"I am prepared to do whatever you need me to do."

"If you are a fast learner, there are other chores and instruction from other Masters. They expect complete respect. I will teach you some easy learning tricks, which are unconventional but you seem like you would excel. I have a feeling you have an exceptional memory. Do you?"

"I do. I know the rotations of some of the guards at the Great Halls. There is a six-day rotation, then they have another six days but night duties. This is true for a cohort of the lower Halls. The Great Halls have a four-day rotation, the men will travel to all Halls, then after the full of the moon are back to start all over again."

"Well, it seems this has not changed in the years I was serving the Hall of Learning. You have this memorized; I see. What about the Hall of Finance?"

"It is on a five-day schedule, but the Oban uses the same guards. He trusts only the same thirty, they rotate between day and night. He pays them well, and only five I know of are honest. The rest skim where they can."

"You definitely know your schedules and guards."

"This is what I do. It makes it easier to know who can be bought."

"I am sure. Zenzol says you are clever. You should learn quickly. I am hoping you enjoy your time here, but watch out for the monks with swords, they are guards who will look through you, should you catch their eye. Some have … unique tastes … best you do not draw attention to yourself."

"I understand, I know the type you describe. I know how to blend into my surroundings."

"I am sure you are adept at this."

They chatted some more, and he peered at her, saying it was time for him to retire. She stood up helping him to rise.

She shook his hand, his grip soft and weak, Andic made to not grip it too tight, afraid he might break. He told her where to go to rest; he would find another of the order to tell her which one would be his to use for the duration of his stay. She did not correct the older man, she was after all, a male for the time she was there. His smile at her thanks, had her wondering if she in fact fooled him, it was more a smirk than a smile.

So then, began her journey into a new and magical world.

CHAPTER 13

Damara

From Old comes the New

Damara woke up from a lengthy sleep feeling more refreshed than she had in a very long time remembering Ramis would return soon from the Capital. She looked forward to their reunion. They always made love when he returned from his trips, be he gone a day or a week. This time he had been gone three weeks! She was getting lightheaded remembering the passion they shared, even though the frequency of their shared unions had diminished, the intenseness had not.

She rose with the intention of getting dressed and taking a trip into the city to visit a few of her favorite vendors. The apothecary, the lace makers, who supplied her with most of her lace adornments, and the local honey and bake shops.

She rose and immediately sat right back down. Her vision narrowed and a red haze coloured the room. Damara gazed around in amazement. Closing her eyes for a moment, she opened them to see the sun breaching the tops of the trees on the edge of their villa gardens and streaming in her rooms full force. There was no sign of redness anywhere.

By the God, what was this?

She thought she may be losing spirit, but from what she was told, was this not when vision turned dark?

I definitely can not say anything to anyone until I know what this is.

She rose to her feet and felt normal, however, the expression on her face when her maidservant walked in, had the girl asking if everything was all right.

"Yes, it is, I thought of what I am going to do today. I will be taking a carriage down into the city, time to collect a few things before winter sets in."

Damara kept herself busy buying things from all her favorite shops. When she finally arrived home in late afternoon, she realized how hungry she was. After the last few weeks of little appetite, she ordered her maid to have the cook prepare a fulfilling meal.

"Peylin, have the cook prepare a quail, I am craving such. I do hope this is a sign I am recovering."

"As long as the physician believes you can manage such."

"He says I am to begin small and build up from there. I know the cook loves his sauces, have him prepare it with minimal seasonings."

"Yes, this sounds like it may stay in your stomach, a sprinkle of Pelinese salt, should bring out the flavour."

"A light green salad with an olive vinaigrette. No cheese. Perhaps a few tomatoes. I would like to drink one of our wines, perhaps in a few days. I will begin with a delicious meal. I am tired of the plain fair the physician regimented; I feel a light meal would settle. Let us see how I do tonight and bring back gentle meals gradually."

"Yes, Nada. I will direct the cook. Would you like reading material?"

"Yes. Is the tome on Apple trees of the continent where I left it?"

"I will find it for you, Nada and place it on your chaise."

"Thank you."

She had a satisfying meal and lay down for her evening rest and another restful sleep. She kept busy the next day in her gardens. She went to check her shops and warehouses and was reassured all was exactly as she liked. Damara told Peylin she wanted to stop by a book shop.

"Will you be let in this time? Remember what happened last time?"

"Yes, but since then, the shop keeper has passed on and his son now resides in the back. His sister works for my Dader. I am sure it will be no issue. I can always say loudly I am catering to Ramis. Women do their husbands shopping all the time."

"It is getting harder for even myself to get into particular shops."

"It should not be like this. Our world still needs to operate. I do not see these new laws being effective. I think in my great, great GrandPaders day it was extremely strict. It only lasted ten or so years before the people had enough. I am sure we will be able to live through this."

"As you say. Should we walk?"

"I will have the carriage take us. It shows patronage, the carriage can wait while I venture inside. You will come with me, and we take the extra guard as well as I am doing my husband's bidding."

The two women rode in the carriage to the book seller and alighted with Damara making the carriage wait. The carriages they owned were made locally, showed their family crest and was a sure way to announce who they were. Damara much preferred to ride. Less vocal in her pursuits. But when pomp and ceremony were required of them, who was she to deny the townspeople their patron.

"If you must, make a loop, I will wait. If there is room for others to go around, stay here. Give the elders some gossip, I cannot see myself being too long."

"Yes, Nada. As you wish."

The two women opened the door entering. There were a few older men in there and gave her not too friendly looks. The store owner came to the front and bowed when he saw her.

"How can I assist you, Nada Du'Tan."

"I am here for my husband Ramis. He instructed me to purchase some interesting tomes, and whatnot. Would I be able to peruse the shelves?"

At the mention of Ramis the older men bowed in her direction, she nodded to the men. They knew the name and paid her deference, or Ramis, she knew it was his name they respected. She turned to the young man who gave consent.

"You have changed it around in here since you took possession. It looks better organized."

"I thank you. Yes, it was cluttered. Many unnecessary tomes, many are un-sanctioned and forbidden by law. I placed them aside and brought in some of the new readings of the Church and those of learning. They are here if you would like to have a look."

"Oh, may I? I thank you."

Damara wandered around the store front and the elders left after making purchases. She took a book of sermons and opened it while the men walked past. After they left, she turned to the young man who was made his way forward.

"I do not suppose I could have a look at these 'forbidden' tomes? If you still have them. I am wishing something a bit… controversial."

"I would be imprisoned if found out. Alas. I cannot."

"I am sure if you were to do so, a particular copy of a certain…caliber of war manual, may find its way into your hands. Merely to borrow, mind. I know your Pader loved his war tomes. Have you, his curiosity?"

The tome she was referring to was none other than her Paders writings when he served in the Great War of his time. Her Pader's writings were sought by this young man's Pader. He was an avid reader on teachings about war tactics. Damara's Pader kept an incredibly detailed journal; it was not widely known she still had his journals. She liked to keep it this way.

"Oh, yes! He always spoke about getting his hands on it! I would be happy to assist you, for just the opportunity to see it! Well... I cannot allow your maid to remain in the front, she will have to remain outside, when you enter the back. It would not be seemly."

"Have you a rear entrance? Enough for a carriage to wait by?"

"Yes, but 'tis a tight fit. Few travel back there, just small carts."

"I can have Peylin here wait for me back there, if you feel this would assist you."

"Yes. However, there are those who sit outside at the fountain and saw you enter. They would talk if you do not exit from the front."

"Here is what we will do. I will have Peylin, take the carriage to the back. If I find something, I will hand it to her, exit from the front while they come around to pick me up. Then, it will be just like the coachman had to move, so as to not be in the way. This way, I am not seen handling anything controversial, and you are not under suspicion. How does this work? I can have Peylin bring you what you desire, when I have her come to the markets."

"If you would follow me, to the back."

"Peylin, have the coachman drive around back. To the door with the sign…you will know which one. Tell him 'tis to give room for others. Have the other guard stay where he is at the door out front. Those are Ramis's orders."

"Yes, Nada."

Peylin left and Damara saw her speaking to the guard already by the door. They hired a few more men, Damara was not sure she needed them, but she was not about to argue this point with her husband. She would just have to find ways to distract while having more minders. She turned and followed the young man to the back of the store, into a few doorways and soon she could see the clutter of tomes and the disarray which was a true bookstore. He led her to a dark corner and moved a few stacks aside to reveal a shelf at the bottom with a few worn leather-bound books.

"I unfortunately had to destroy a few; mice chewed quite thoroughly. Pader was not the best at keeping the mice out. I have a few cats in here, which help, but a few were beyond repair. These are the forbidden tomes which would cost me my life. What were you looking for?"

"Something light to read. Easy."

"I have three tomes of Lyana's works. Her first, second and last. The last issue is badly eaten, but if you can stand crumbling pages… I do not need to have it back."

"Oh, I am certainly interested in this one. She was to have lured a man to leave his wife."

"Yes, she is most controversial, yet this is the most eloquent of works. I read this tome and cried, I am not ashamed to say. I shall wrap it up in linen for you… Here you go."

"Thank you. Have one of the copies of the newest sermons ready for me. I must give the illusion to have purchased for Ramis. I will take this outside and be right back out front."

Damara took the tome from the young man and went out the back door which he held open. He looked outside and motioned for her to exit. Damara handed the tome to her maid and told the coachman to meet her at the front door. He agreed and cracked his whip against the floorboards. Damara returned and met the owner at the front. He held this one open as well, and they waited for the carriage to arrive. She saw various persons sitting and talking by the fountain in the square. When the carriage arrived, she alighted and the man handed her the book.

"I hope your husband enjoys the book, Nada."

"I am sure Ramis will love to reflect on the sermons of the Namarch. We thank you for the excellent service and having such up-to-date versions. I will send Peylin down with your payment."

"Thank you, Nada, for your patronage."

"You are most welcome. We love our citizens. To home, please."

Damara addressed her driver as the young man bowed to her as they set off. She handed the uncovered book to her maid.

"Ugh, more sermons. We have a whole shelf of these."

Damara spoke quietly as they drove past people lounging around the fountain. Several bowed their heads and she nodded back through the window opening. Then leaned back against the cushions and closed her eyes.

"I have the other one here."

"'Tis fine, Peylin, take both in and leave the fragile one, by my bed."

"I will leave it under the cushion on the bed, and will prepare your bed tonight, there is less chance of it being found."

"Thank you, Peylin. You have my best interests at your heart."

One trip back from the city a few days later, had her stopped at the front entry by the Head Housekeeper handing her a sealed scroll. Damara saw it was her husbands seal and broke it open smiling as she walked inside.

'My exquisite Darling, holder of my heart. The wedding celebrations were the most extravagant and elaborate affair anyone has seen since the Prince's nuptials so many years ago. How my heart aches you were not here by my side. Many of our set asked about you and I made excuses on your behalf. Noma Kavena was most distraught, and you may receive a missive to this effect from her. I have some exciting drawings being created for your attention, you will be pleasantly surprised at some of the newest attempts of fabrics, and potential designs. One was not well received by his Holiness. I have included a rendition of such, so you have awareness of what was not liked by the Church. I will be delayed by a few days; however, I am longing to look upon you and embrace you in my arms. How I have longed for your touch, my Dear Heart. I know you would want every detail, and some orders have come in, so I will not delay any more than I must. This will be my gift to you, to gaze upon your face, when you see what I have brought. Rest well, My Love, I will be home soon, Ramis.'

She had no reason to not believe his delay as this happened quite often after a few ceremonies or small weddings. Someone always would have a fashion, maybe from the North, the rolling hills, or the Northeastern province of Lanthian, a land of women warriors. She was a little disappointed they would not be together for another while; she was missing his touch.

Later that evening, she reclined on her chaise watching the setting sun. Reading scripts about the wedding, scribes copied from attendees, given to her for her patience did not extend to wait for Ramis returning to hear gossip. She noticed the edges of her vision narrowing and a red haze around the edges. She placed the scroll down closing her eyes. This time when she opened them, the red haze was still there. She did not feel any different, so she stood and, on a hunch, walked to the mirror to have a look at her reflection. What she saw shocked her, the outer edges of her irises were rimmed with red. Not blood, but ruby, and had a shimmer to them.

Could it be a reflection from the candles?

As she peered closer, the glow diminished and disappeared, and a sense of unease which plagued her for the first two weeks of her illness, returned.

Am I dying?

She wondered, still studying her reflection in the mirror to see if it came back. If this feeling continued to plague her tomorrow, she would consult one of her many physicians. Mayhap a visit with the herb woman to acquire more tea for consumption and some answers. Almost as soon as she thought this the feeling disappeared.

Now I am to think, I am losing my mind?

Damara was not sure if she should say anything to anyone, they would certainly think that, and she did not wish Ramis to divorce her.

Men could divorce just by voicing it, for many reasons… Infidelity, lack of an heir, lack of any child, madness (this line was blurred, reasons of madness were liberally applied to anything, mostly because he did not want her anymore), all he needed was one witness, and to repeat the phrase, "I divorce you," three times. The most incredulous reason Ramis laughingly told her, was a man divorced a woman because she kept burning his dinners. She responded back to him it was a good thing she did not cook. After a man spoke the litany for the three times required, any legalities were taken care of by the man, in the Hall of Law at his leisure.

Damara only witnessed a divorce once. It was at one of Ramis's friends house parties and it shocked her into silence. She never wanted to go through what her friend went through. It left Lana devastated; they had children. The husband did take care of them until both her children grew up and began their own homes. However, after that, Lana disappeared. The divorcing husband took the home she raised the children in, giving her a smaller one, Lana had to depend on herself for a living. A couple of years ago, Ramis told her there was a rumour circulating, her friend, was "entertaining" men in her small home. Damara was not to visit and break their friendship, small as it was.

It would not do to associate with a fallen woman, especially with her family connections. So, to please her husband, and to not place a stain on his name or the business she dropped any contact. Not that she kept up after Lana's divorce, that is when business had really taken off and she was busy.

The thought of her once friend, made her a little depressed. She opted to have one of their vintages of red wine imported from one of their satisfied customers. She lay on her chaise enjoying the evening's sunset and went to bed a little tipsy, missing her husband falling immediately asleep.

She woke up the next morning with a slight headache, the sun directly overhead. As she nursed her head, drinking an herbal concoction, to ease her ache, she soaked in her bathing pool.

"Nada, a messenger arrived, Ramis is shortly behind him."

"Thank you, Peylin. Have you readied my new gown?"

"I did not, but I will do so. I placed the green one out."

"Yes, I will have my new one, please. I need to feel better. Perhaps the red will encourage me to greet Ramis with a smile."

"Your head is still foggy?"

"Yes, can you hand me the towel, dear?"

"Here you go, I will place the red out and get you another tonic, and a restorative tea. You will begin feeling better in a while."

"Oh, I hope so. I do not seem to hold my wine anymore. Can you do a simple braid?"

"Certainly. Rami, fetch Nada some of the mint, chamomile tea and the tonic, the deep brown bottle. Cook knows the one. Nada, how is this?"

Peylin finished with her hair, braiding a single braid to frame Damara's face, brushing the remainder to lay down her back. Damara drank half her tea and closed her eyes. Then opened them to gaze at her maid in the reflection of the mirror.

"Perfect. Oh, I hear horses."

She heard noise coming from the courtyard indicating his arrival. Damara hurried, not as fast as she liked, to arrive at the front entrance as Ramis was dismounting. He handed the reins to a groom enfolding Damara into his embrace. As he hugged her, he sniffed her hair,

"Smells like the red from Aram, were you indulging?"

He backed out of the hug to peer down at her. She looked up sheepishly.

"Just a little jug, I was missing you."

"Well, if you do not feel too bad later, we will have more with dinner and I will recount everything about the wedding, I have a few more orders to take to the warehouse to be filled, but right now I would very much love to wash this dirt off and then let us sit and chat."

Kissing her on the forehead he strode off to his wing of rooms. She walked down the hall to the kitchens to chat with the servants about dinner.

That night was wonderful; they had a beautifully prepared goose with chestnuts. Greens with feta, and a balsamic dressing, with some of the last raspberries of the season. The weather had begun to change; fall would bring winds and rain with winter monsoons. Damara hoped this winter would bring her boys home for a respite. Her headache had subsided, so she drank a small glass of another red, this time from their own backyard.

"The Princess's dress was elaborate; she created the embroidery. I am thinking, others will follow this trend. It was red silk, and the leaves and flowers on it were gold."

"Yes. I remember the yards we had to dye for the dress. She was working on the dress for five years. They had to let it out in the last year. The silk for the veil came directly from Aram, they will not share with me any of their secrets, of the gold thread."

"Well, Kavena was wearing her dark green you made for her last year, and some of the young were, trying out new sleeves. One young girl left crying when the Namarch made a snide remark very loudly to her Pader. The Patriarch was not pleased and rebuked his Dader before the assembly. She left before the ceremony of marriage even begun. The Grand Hall was draped in red cloth, and the Carpet down the procession hall was elaborate. You have never seen anything like it. The great Master outdid himself again. Berrin says the Master was given a villa in payment. A villa!"

"He took almost five years to create this. I heard he bought all the dyes in red I could have used. I am just fortunate I have other means to find dyes. I was prepared for his usage… He deserves a villa. I am surprised he did not ask for joining placements for his sons."

"Well…"

"No! Hah! I am right!"

"Yes, I heard after, during the feasting, his eldest has a placement in the army and a bride. You know everything, do you not?"

"I have my sources, Ramis. Our set does talk. We like to listen to what is going on."

"Well, more on the feasting. This is where more colours abounded. The young girl came back with a short cape over her shoulders. It was well received."

"Oh, a cape. I have toyed with this notion for a while. I am going down to the shop tomorrow. I have my drawings down there. Now would be the time to implement them. Tovah knows of it. However, I will worry about this in the morrow."

"You have your appetite back, dinner was excellent, Dear Heart."

"Thank you, I have several days to find my appetite. I have begun to partake of wine, but I do not consume as much as before. Tell me again about some more fashions. Were there any unusual colours?"

"Not I could see, most were ours…"

Damara always tried to stay on top of fashions and create her own ideas. After dinner they lay on the chaise together, and she made him recount the festivities again. He spoke on the elegance of the young Princess's dress and the over abundance of food and the merriness of the whole Capital.

"You have never seen a whole city, come out and celebrate. The Princess looked so joyous, she was beaming ear to ear with a smile, which reminded me so much of our own Dader's nuptials. How I wish you could have been there with me; you would have loved the colours!"

They snuggled and drank their wine. In the next half hour as she was trying not to close her eyes, a spectacular event happened. Stars began shooting across the sky. She accidentally elbowed Ramis which startled him out of his dozing.

"Ramis, oh by the God, look at the night sky!"

"Wha, wha… oh, by the name of Narman! It looks like stars are falling!"

They exclaimed aloud as a few hit the atmosphere and sparks shot in all different directions. A few of their servants came out to watch between duties. It was a show which kept going. After the initial first hour, Damara found herself and Ramis having a rest in the chair together for half the night.

The next day, during their breakfast, Ramis told her he would be going to the warehouse to process new orders.

"After I have Tovah begin on this new batch I am going fishing, I long for the quiet solitude of the seas."

"Shall I come with you?"

Damara thought of a few excursions they had taken out on the seas, Ramis was an excellent sailor, and they made turbulent love, in an effort to have time to themselves. She was wishing to recreate a few of those memories. She gazed at Ramis, watching her with concern.

"You still look like you need rest, the motion of a boat may not sit well with your stomach. I have only your well being in mind."

She beamed and knew this was his way of saying he was tired and needed idle time. Fishing was a way for him to relax. They both had their way of relaxing, hers was to hunt for new dyes or travel for new silks. His was to go fishing.

"Perhaps I will venture down there later, I want to find my drawings and use some of my readied silks. There is a navy I have an excess of…"

She had been once to Pelin'Dun, about five years ago and found a gorgeous orange. She never went as far as Aram. Not after her failed attempt but sent one of her Captains to get her a deep green and a cobalt blue, and Ramis had gone to the Northlands and purchased deep navy. The Northmen would not part with their secret, all she knew it had something to do with the bark of the Ravenwood tree. She had him bring back bark, and she tried in her shop, but could not figure out the secret.

Once she travelled to the city province of Lanthia. They had bright yellow, from a root plant, which they sold in their markets. She brought home not only the root itself, which she planted, but also silk, which helped supplement her fabrics, when Aram could not supply her.

She had the thought mayhap she should begin her own silk production. She had enough orders lately to warrant the endeavor. She thought of this it once before, in the beginning years, but Ramis said business was not enough at the time, to be cost effective. She wondered if the time would be now.

"You rest, Mara. There is plenty of time to work, I will have Tovah organized for you, she knows your business. You have trained her well. She is an excellent worker, very enthusiastic and very energetic."

"Yes, she is. A great asset."

A couple of hours later, she remembered he had new orders commissioned so decided she would go to the main shop and see if she could match these new orders with her new fabric. She opted to ride her horse, as it was a faster mode of travel. Damara was an excellent horsewoman, and the day was not burning hot. The breeze had changed. Fall breezes came in from the ocean, cooler and she was feeling well enough to attempt the ride.

"I will ride down to the shops; I would like to see these orders Ramis brought in. You do not need to come with me; I will not be long. I will take a guard with me."

"Yes, Nada, I will have your bath ready for your return."

"Thank you, I should be only a few hours."

Damara rode down the hill to the shore where her warehouse and office was. Adjoining the docks, there was a permanent stable and servants available. There was as well a small villa and courtyard for guests and the occasional sleepover when it was extremely busy. They had their own dock for their ships, as they had amassed their own fleet. It made things so much easier overall.

She dismounted, a stable boy taking the reins, and went into her office where workers were pouring over one of the tables, covered in fabrics and order books. Resting at her desk she had a glass of water while catching her breath. It had not taxed her as much as she thought it would, but it never did any harm to err in the realm of caution. She helped the girls for a while and then remembered about Ramis.

"Did Ramis drop off the new orders?"

She asked her deputy in charge, Tovah motioned to the other table in the room.

"Yes, he dropped them off and left."

Which was nothing new. Ramis did not help pick colours or designs. He was more delivery muscle and production expert. She scanned over the paperwork giving her deputy her input on styles, colours, and fabrics,

"Ooooh, Ramis must have had Raqia draw out the styles, or else she may have watched from afar. What do you think of these sleeves? Too frothy? What if we take this piece of fabric here and move it, say to about there. What do you think?"

Damara was always reinventing something. The pictures drawn, made the outfit a little too much, so she liked to minimize what others did. Most times it went off better than the original. As she aged, she liked to try new things, but if someone created something which did not look right, she would improvise. It almost always looked better. She catered more to the older women in her life's tastes and knew her clientele.

"I like that, but it still looks off, something… like this? Less fabric, appears more flattering."

"Yes, this does suit better. You are learning. Good eye… It must always flatter the wearer, regardless of being a fresh style. The original must have been a young girl trying something out. Yes, it probably looked good on her. The young of today can get away with so much more than I ever could when I was their age. Every woman wants a flattering figure, regardless of age, size, or colour for that matter. Not every woman can wear the same colour, there are some their complexion will wash out in the wrong shade or tone."

"Yes, Nada, I had an order from the Mader of the Magistrate of Learning here in the city. She wished so much to wear a light pink, with the summer light shoulder dress style from last year. I convinced her the darker shade of wine in a style covering her shoulders and a mid arm length would flatter her better. It was not until I demonstrated with the samples I brought with me she understood. I knew she would be tempted by a more youthful silhouette but with our flaws as we age, it is more complimentary to cover than to expose."

"How right you are, Tovah, I am glad you have this outlook. You are of the same mind as I am. It reassures me you are more than capable to run my business here in Kara, should I decide to step back at any time. I really appreciate your relentless efforts. You are making my life so worry-free right now when I need it."

"Oh, thank you, Nada, for your gratitude. I enjoy working with all fabrics and colours. I never thought I would be doing this, not in a thousand years. It was by the grace of our God we ran into each other at the bakery that day. I was wondering what to do with myself with the youngest newly married off. Your proposal took me by surprise. What decided it for me was your enthusiasm for your business. Your joy. I began to hear your name when I visited my friends, and I was intrigued by the styles they saw on their Mistress's. We had a group which met occasionally to discuss the latest fashion trends, I heard your name often. It has been wonderful to be a part of this enterprise. I absolutely love what I do! Many thanks to you for seeing my potential. You have given me a new life to aspire to. It has many benefits."

Tovah blushed with the attention. She was genuinely a shyer woman, but with her many years of working with Damara at her shop and lately with clients, she was coming out of her shell and becoming more confident. When she was talking about colour, she blossomed, in fact she looked beautiful to some. Her husband was on the receiving end of her joy, Tovah told her in confidence. Tovah's husband, was just as lost as his wife when their children began their own homes. He ran a small leathermaking goods store, making smaller items, like belts and small satchels. His scroll work which embellished his goods, was exquisite. Ramis had a few of his works, Damara gifted him over the years. With Tovah working so much, Damara wondered if it was not the coin Tovah brought home he enjoyed more, but Tovah was not one to lie to her.

"Tovah, Ramis told me of an incident with a young girl who showed too much skin. She was publicly rebuked and Ramis said she returned with a cape over her shoulders. He had Raqia draw it out. Have you seen it?"

"Yes… I think…here it is. I thought to find your rendition. Look at the differences. Yours is more… simple yet elegant. She most like improvised from a scarf. Yours is more permanent and if it is clasped at the back, there is no threat of it falling. If you were too drop a few more inches in the front, it will be well received. The Namarch would not find fault."

Tovah had drawn on Damara's drawing, making the cowl, or cape more suitable to what Ramis said were new protocols for women. Or more stringent ones. Damara adapted as much as she could. This was perfect!

"Tovah. You are amazing. Yes! I love this! We have a surplus of fabrics. This would take no time to make. Have the seamstresses begin on this. Once I show this off, I am sure others will want them. Especially in this heat. This is perfect!"

"Yes, I fully agree! What an effective way to use up all our stock. It is sitting in storage, and there were sightings of rats. Do not worry, I have found more cats. They are busy. If we do not have the fabrics sitting, then all the better."

"Very good. You have a good grasp on this. I will leave this in your hands. In fact, I will let it be known you created this. It will serve you well, to get your name on designs."

"Oh, Nada. Thank you! For your support, and the design, 'tis originally yours, are you certain?"

"Tovah, I will eventually leave you more work. I would have you establish yourself; this is the perfect way to begin."

"Thank you. I am incredibly grateful. What do you think of these new orders…?"

After pouring over more orders, Tovah had a good grasp of what needed to be done the soonest, Damara decided it was a good day to go to the market by the waterfront to pick up some fresh caught seafood for dinner. Sometimes Ramis's fishing trips could take into the night.

She was oblivious to the boats in the marina until after she paid for the catch she was buying. She happened to glance up after mounting her horse and saw their boat, the one Ramis used for fishing still moored at the pilings they owned.

That is strange, Ramis went fishing without his boat. Mayhap, he went with one of his cronies.

She sent the guard with her for the day, back to the villa with the dinner she bought. It was still warm out.

"I will be right after you, I wish to have a drink of water at the fountain. Take the fish up to the cook, he will want it as fresh as possible."

She mounted her horse as her manservant disappeared from sight and started off after her sip. She rode to the city gate on the main thoroughfare and a street urchin, fell out of a doorway spooking her horse. The horse stepping sideways, nearly threw her from the saddle. Her mount bolted through the streets; she was busy trying to rein him in and catch her seat. Several hands tried to catch the reins, spooking him further.

"Whoa, boy, whoa!"

It took her some time, as her arm strength was not quite up to full strength and the gelding had his ire up not listening. As she got a hold of him, forcing him to stop, she looked around, realizing she was in a poorer section of town and started heading back to the gate and the main road.

"Where have you taken me? Well, let us get back to the main path. My arms are quite tired now, thank you very much."

As she turned down the last alley, she looked over towards a cluster of houses and noticed a couple of very nicely decked out horses. They were tethered to a post outside one of the houses, the last in the cluster. She would not have taken anymore notice had not a man stood outside, smoking a cigar. She saw the inhale in the lessening light, the end of the cigar glowing, as the sun was low on the horizon. Certain parts of the city, the ones with taller buildings closer together, darkened sooner than outside city limits.

There were only a couple of men she knew who smoked those, one was her husband, and the other was his manservant. Only in private settings, for the manservant, it was a luxury he only received through Ramis. The man was too short for Ramis, by a bit, so it must be his man. He turned away from her direction to gaze up into the doorway, stubbing out his cigar on the hitching post, in response to the door opening. She saw this all in the few seconds it took for her horse to walk the opening in the alley.

The man walking out of the house was her husband.

CHAPTER 14

Meera

The Six Shall Rise Again

The next fortnight passed by very quickly with preparations for the upcoming adventure. The drying of food items and fighting skills I needed to know according to my Pader. I returned to the stream to collect the healing herbs, and wild onions and garlic I found earlier. There was also bark of a lesser shrub when dried and powdered added a subtle taste to any meal when sprinkled.

"Have the tubers dried enough, Meera?"

"Yes…I am going to grind them up more and lay them out while we have the sun."

"Good thought. We should practice some more bow skills."

"I can barely pull the bow. I cannot get it to go far."

"But you can. You must believe you can."

"'Tis as tall as I am! It gets caught up on the ground."

"Then turn it a bit."

I tried to cock it a bit, and it worked better. Pulling the bow string back my arms began to shake. The arrow flew a little longer than before, but it wobbled towards the end. The next arrow flew longer, and the third went off to the left. I notched another and took a deep breath.

"Just focus, Meera. Pull back with confidence. Narrow in on your target. Say that rock… the one I placed up there."

Kiem pointed to the top of the rock cliff slightly higher than his head. He placed a small stone on the lip. I pulled back and focused on the stone, drawing a bit further than before. It seemed easier… I released… The arrow flew through the air and hit the moss on the side of the stone, ricocheted off and into the woods behind.

"See. You are getting better."

"That is enough. My arms feel like butter."

"You did well, for one not used to the bow. It took me several years to master the pull. I never hit a target very well. When you have a chance, you practice. The Blackbow is an art. You are part of the North. Even if you are Pelinese by your birth."

"This is difficult. My arms hurt! How does one do this all the time?"

"This is what makes the North so strong and essential. The army of the Namarch is only as strong as the weakest link. It is not the North. His Lordship has trained with and all his men are a solid unit. 'Tis what makes him so valuable to the war going on right now. He may have not wanted to go, but he was told to go. His men have turned the tide of the war so many times. If they had not, then we would be Aram right now. The fact Aram is gaining lands in Du'Lanay speaks volumes."

"How so? Why would Aram even want to be here?"

"It has been Aram's mission from their inception. To conquer every land and bring them under their heel. Aram believes only their God, the FirPader is the almighty. He says all should worship him."

"But is he not a man? Like the Namarch?"

"Yes, but therein is their arrogance. They believe in themselves. Not everyone in their position is strong in spirit. Those who are weak are often killed, upheaved, one Namarch was beheaded. However, what I was getting at, is Aram has a plan. You notice, or have you paid attention, Aram is moving North."

"I did not know. Wait, I remember listening to Vandrin. He would complain his Pader should have done this, should have known. Now you have told me of Aram, have I placed the pieces together. You are saying Aram wants the North?"

"If they conquer the North, Aram thinks the Capital will fall. The North is strong. Aram is going for the strongest first. Once they conquer the North, they will flow South and sweep through the Capital."

"You know this?"

"I studied war. There were many discussions among the scholars on war tactics, past and present."

"Perhaps, you can enlighten me on war. I feel I should know something."

"I will tell you on our travels. 'Tis always good to know more on something than less. This is what knowledge gives us, the ability to choose our actions based on what we know. If you learn something, it is harder to claim ignorance."

"I am afraid I am quite ignorant, Pader. You will have to tell me all."

"You are not ignorant, child. You were not receptive to knowledge as you grew up. However, you had other ideas you were learning. How to survive. Using your instincts. Being able to decide when to run, when to hide. These are all tools to be used in living. Knowledge is not always learned through books and tomes. Experience is a great teacher."

"I would have you and Nejan as my teachers. You have already begun."

Soon the day chosen to leave and travel through the mountains came to pass. Not only did my bruises fade but the scar on my face healed up quite nicely and just a white raised line remained. Taking the stitches out hurt like a bugger, and a portion was angry and swollen after for a few days. This soon eased and I continued to train with my Pader. Nejan also instructed me in the art of tracking observing nature and oddities to watch out for during our traveling. I was ecstatic I had a Pader in the flesh. I asked him more than enough questions and found myself watching him and grinning. He would look up and catch me.

"You are happy, Meera?"

"Oh, yes! I cannot believe you are my Pader. I always thought I had one who did not care, he left so long ago."

"I do not think the Lord did not care for you. He was ordered by the Emperor to fight in the war. He has a great responsibility to his people. Not just the ones in the Aerie, but in the lower hills, and a duty to help protect the realm from invaders. He lost his wife, so for him, leaving was a way to cope with this. I understand all too well.

I do believe he loved her deeply like I did. She was a force to be reckoned with, for sure. I remember once, when we were hiding from her Mader's attendants, she could not stop laughing at their attempts to find us. She was such an independent thinker and a fast learner. Your Mader had her own ideas how things should be done. I think this may have been one of the reasons she did not have a good relationship with her Mader. They were too alike.

I would hope you have the same determination as her. You have a great destiny to fulfill and if you decide you cannot go on because the way is too hard, then all is lost. I will try my hardest to prepare you physically and mentally from what I know of life. If you have half the determination Miiele had and all my stubbornness, then you should have half a chance at succeeding."

His face changed when he talked about my Mader, it was radiant from the memories he shared with her. I hoped he could find solace someday in another love, he was not an old man. I was simply happy to be in the presence of him in the moment. He smiled at me, and I saw he had always been there for me, as much as he conceivably could. I did not hold his absence from me in the past years against him. I knew he did the best he could for the reasons he gave me.

"Do you think you would ever go back? To the homeland?"

"I do not know. If it was necessary, of course, but I have no desire to. My brother may still be around; he was a fisherman. If his big mouth has not seen his demise, the weather could have. He was always getting into trouble, if you can believe it, I was the quiet one."

"You were close?"

"As close as two brothers of opposite temperaments could be. We looked similar, but he was hot headed and got into a lot of scrapes when we were young. He never thought about what he was going to say before he said it. I liked to read and learn and calculate the outcome before speaking. Your Mader and I had exceptionally good debates and discussions. She never had an argument about harvesting before she met me. Oh, those were some good days."

His face crumpled a bit when he remembered the love of his life was gone. I walked over to the man who sired and for the most part raised me, giving him a hug, which startled him. He wrapped his arms around me and gave it right back, dropping the piece of wood he was shaving for the fire.

"I am sure that if I am half as stubborn as my Pader, we will be arguing about something sooner than later."

I smiled into his chest, which I am sure he felt, as he laughed into my hair.

"Oh, I am sure! I remember hearing from the Housekeeper how every time she put you in a skirt, you would sneak off to find a pair of leggings. She finally gave up. I do not think I remember ever seeing you in a skirt. Oh, you are just like me, lass. To be sure."

Him reminding me about wearing a skirt had me thinking about that young man. I had not worn a skirt since, and he felt my smile disappear.

"You must learn from the past. Meera."

He pulled out of our embrace holding my shoulders in his hands looking down at me.

"We learn the lessons the Universe sets for us. Sometimes they are lessons that teach us a little, or they are lessons that humble us. Sometimes they are extremely hard lessons. We must always see what it is we need to grow from or to. You would not know who you are if that young man had not done what he did, and from what you say, it did not happen… What I am trying to say, is you may be in a situation where something like this may happen again. Men will try to take what is not theirs by force, and if they physically can, they will. You, of course can not let them, but if it did happen, it is not something you will let diminish your spirit source. It would not reflect on your spirit; it would reflect on theirs. Do you understand what I am trying to say?"

"I think so, our choices we make, reflect on our spirit and how we feel about ourselves."

"You will be tried. Of this, I am sure. I want to make sure you think about the way others feel, about choices you make, in the things you say or do. Not everything will be a smooth path. You will have mountains to climb. Speaking of which, we will be doing this soon enough. Now young lady, if you would get us some water, this would be a choice with which I could live!"

He let go of my shoulders to ruffle his hand in my hair, messing up my semi neat mop. I let him trim it to make the sides even. There was still a portion which would be short for a time and I was able to braid and wear it in this fashion. I protested but not by much as I turned to go inside the cabin to collect the skins hanging on their hooks. The learning did not cease, there were lessons in everything we did, and he talked while we occupied ourselves with preparations.

"Body language, unspoken but if you read what the body is telling you, then you are prepared for the next move. Leaning forward means you are engaged. Leaning back is a form of defense, as is crossing the arms, when in conversation. It signals protection, for the heart and physically for the stomach, if one were to get a physical touch… a punch, like this."

Kiem demonstrated with a quick poke to my belly.

"Oooff! Are we sparring now?"

"No, just demonstrating to you, if you were reading my body language you would have been ready for me poking you. Read the eyes… Shifting eyes, people look towards what they will do next. If I were to look to your shoulder, like this, you would see I was thinking of poking you there next. See, you are catching on. Read the position of the body, then look to the eyes. You practice with people we meet with. You can practice with me as well, but our attention will be taken with travel, so I will be concentrating on that."

His conversation then led to visual signs during our travelling. I learned a bit from Aunt Nena but learning from Kiem and from an actual animal on the methods of tracking and signs was very enlightening. We busily hunted, gathered berries, edible plants and dried as much as we could. Furs were cleaned and rolled up, and our packs Kiem fashioned grew every day. Of course, his was bigger by far as his 6'5" frame could carry more weight than my 5'5" could. The weather was changing every day as well. One day it was sunny, and we dried what we could, the next it would rain. Then the following day the sun was back out as though it was there all along. Once the Redbushes' leaves began to turn yellow, this was the next season introducing itself. Kiem took a day trip down to the God's River to see if anyone had been there. When he returned, he reported even though most of the signs all but disappeared, it did not mean a Woodsman could not find them.

"We better head out anyway. There was a smell of smoke in the air. Not sure what was burning, and I would rather not find out. This trek will take us a couple of months and I would like to traverse the peaks before the heart of winter makes it impossible. I have only travelled the passes two times before and this is the only time of year which makes traversing the passes safe. Winter has too much snow, spring has too many avalanches, summer the river is too high. Fall is best, dry and plenty of game. We best be on our way! Let us finish packing up the rest of the gear and head out tomorrow at first light."

"I am of the mind if Vandrin thought of me as alive, he would have sent someone here to check."

"You could be right. We will make sure there is no sign of you left. It would be expected I would leave signs. The privy, we need to cover. You should use the stream to relieve yourself. Not that another Ranger could see a difference. I know of no other Ranger with a Li'on-sa. Nejan can smell the difference."

"She can?"

"Yes, Little Cub, I can. Female has a different scent to its urine. It alerts males to when females are in their breeding cycle."

"Ummm, is this not for your kind? Is there a noticeable odor to human feces?"

"Yes, and I expect you can not tell. Another of my kind could and if there is feral Li'on-sa out there, you would be stalked, you are weaker than the male of your species."

I told Kiem.

"This makes sense. We will cover it well; I should bring some new grass to take root. It may be some time before another comes this way and help disguise the area."

"Good idea, but not from too far. It would have a different colour and give it away. Best to not be too obvious in our attempts to hide. It gives the finder an excuse to 'dig' further. Hide in plain sight. Tomorrow is as good as any day, let us finish our tasks today. The fall rains will help cover up tracks."

Good as his word, the three of us rose before the cresting of the sun, we hoisted our packs and headed up the mountain. Passing the stream, stopping to fill our waterskins, then proceeded to the top of the mountain behind the cabin. We left the cabin as is, for the next Woodsman to stay. There was no need to destroy anything, Kiem stated. It would only raise questions… leave it for the next inhabitants.

Nejan headed our small group, her body leaping over boulders we sometimes traversed around or as a team. We skirted the sides of a mountain range, the grasses green and the trees sparse. The sun was on our right and it was not difficult, but not easy either. Kiem explained to go North, we would go around the valley, not through.

"There are many predators in this valley. It is the most hunted, the elk and caribou have not caught on to the fact and feeds the Aerie. The soft ground by the river would announce our passage. Up here is less travelled."

"That makes sense. We are going around to which passage?"

"That one, over in the distance… The high one. It leads to another valley which runs North to South. Beyond this is another. We have several valleys to traverse before we find the rolling hills."

"You have done this before?"

"Several times. I spend time with the Wanderers, during some winter periods. The first time was after your Mader passed. It shook me, and I regret I did not remember my vow, until I was reminded by a young Mader who gave birth. I came back during the summer, it was difficult, but I made it with Nejan's help. I have not erred since."

"Well, now you and I will have an adventure together! It will be easy to fulfil your vow, do you not think?"

"Until I cannot. The Universe may not always be on our side. I will go as far as I can, if I cannot, Nejan will be with you."

"Do you know something I do not? You speak as if we will be parted."

"I am preparing you if such an event does part us. Best to have awareness, always be prepared. Think about the future and several outcomes of what, where and when you are going. It will save you in the end, less worry."

"What else can you, oh wise one, impart on me?"

"Do not be mouthy, lass. I could vanish in the fog beginning to form and leave you here."

"Pity. You just told me where we were going."

"Maybe I was wrong in the telling."

"Hah, nice try!" I looked at my Pader and turned in a circle. I pointed to my left.

"North is that way."

"Good. How did you know this? Given you have never been here."

"Well. The sun is on our right side all the time, it rose in front of us and sets behind us."

"That is too easy. What if we have continuous cloud cover? How would you find your path forward?"

"Moss grows in less light, so the North side would be covered heavier than the South, on a tree."

"Better, but if there were no trees?"

"Moss on the rocks?"

"Yes but look at other vegetation. Leaves open to the sun, close when its dark, some plants travel with the path of the sun. Be aware of your surroundings, plants and animals do not lie."

We walked all day and rose in elevation by end of the day. We stopped beside a trickling stream in a basin and found an outcropping of rocks to lean our packs beside.

"We will stop and fill our skins, but we should keep going for a few more hours to protect our backs. There are many wild animals here, even with Nejan, they would still regard us as nourishment."

Kiem hoisted his pack handing me mine.

"It might take your legs a few days to get used to the hours of walking, and we have not even started real climbing yet!"

We climbed up the side of yet another mountain behind where we came from. There were a few more trees farther away from the Aerie once we left the Ravenwood forests. Others Kiem told me the names of, I knew a few, but some vastly different. He would periodically pick a stem or leaf of something and gave me lessons in botany. I learned to identify by sight and he told the various uses.

Finding a hollow too shallow to be called a cave with some dirt, fur and a few small bones littering the floor, Nejan sniffed around the immediate area of the depression. She must have given her endorsement to Kiem, as he stood for a moment waiting, then slung his pack off and leaned it against the far wall.

"All good, there has not been anything here since spring so let us collect some branches, start a small fire, and have sustenance. We may not always be able to have a fire, hence why we dried so much. We may only stop once a day to eat and sometimes not. So, we chew dried as we go, and hunt when we can when we need."

He walked down the hill and began looking for deadfall. I dropped my pack, stretched my back starting after him, Nejan lay down at the mouth of the cavity gazing up over the valley, scanning, and sniffing the air. Her majestic countenance still awed me.

I caught myself a few times in our preparations for travelling, looking, and admiring her profile. She sensed my energies, come over and rub her head against my hip or back. Several times she knocked me over. We would gaze at each other and I would smile. I imagined her smiling back.

"You are happy, childling? I can feel it."

"Oh, yes. I love animals. You are…more. I love your fur, and your eyes…"

"Well, I think you could love my fur…right below my eye. Yes, right there. Perhaps a bit lower…ahhhh. Yes."

I busied myself with scratching the great feline, and I felt then heard her satisfaction. To me, being so close, her purring at the attention I was giving her, was loud. She head butted me when I eased her itch.

"I thank you, Little One for your care. Now we need to help Little Uncle. He is looking at us."

"Hmmm, I think you are right."

"I am."

We collected enough wood, dropping it to one side when we returned. Kiem busied himself with getting a fire started. I rummaged through my pack bringing out a package we had put together. Taking the small pot from Kiem's pack, I dumped in the package and poured water from a skin. In a little while we had a stew going which made Nejan turn to Kiem, then saunter off.

"She went to hunt, soon we may have to share all."

Kiem sat back on his furs after he finished his portion, licked his bowl, and repacked his pack. The sun set while we ate, and I saw him thinking of our next day, by his facial expression. In his next sentence, he proved me right.

"We should repack before we sleep, in case of hasty retreat, always best to be prepared for anything. Out here in the wilderness, nature has its own agenda, best we abide by it."

He unrolled only one fur, and I followed his lead, sitting down across the fire facing him.

"Well, where to begin. How about where we are going. In case we are separated, or something happens, you should know where you are heading."

He told me what portion of the path I needed to take.

"I was going to ask you, but I have this feeling I cannot shake, as though I should be heading North anyway. Ever since being attacked, and increasingly since I heard the voice in my head, something is pulling me North."

I leaned forward raking the coals with my stick and grabbed another branch, to place on the fire, then leaned back into my fur.

"So, your senses are in tune to the North. Hah, you had me fooled. But if you had no idea, best to use nature to assist."

"No. I appreciate your knowledge. You know so much, and I have much to learn."

"I have always wished to teach you. It was hard to stay away and not tell you... Extremely hard. Now we are together, and you are also the Chosen, I am more than happy to tell you all I know. It can only benefit you; you have a monumental task ahead. You will listen to many voices in your journey, mine can be the first."

"What exactly is this other voice? It is not Pader's... I mean Lord Bodan's, is it?"

I stumbled over my words still trying to wrap my thoughts around the fact I was sitting here in this moment, with my true Pader of flesh and blood.

"I believe it may be your Dragon bond. If Dragons exist, it may be he, reaching out to you from wherever he is. This may be what is drawing you North. We will travel as far as we can. I will tell you what I know, what I have read, what I have been told. I am not sure all of what a bond entails, just 'tis unique to the pair. I read as much as I could of manuscripts in my homeland, as information was somewhat available to those who knew where to look.

If 'tis anything like speaking to Nejan, then you should continue to practice together. Then maybe when your bond reaches out, you connect and speak together. You are our gift. We will give of ourselves so you can be what you are destined. A DragonRider. There is a Prophecy, six shall be born to bring back the

Dragon's, rule the lands, bring peace and prosperity and the open worship of the six Gods. I found this in hidden scrolls, tucked away in the Hall of Learning."

He took a turn stoking the fire, as he continued.

"We are headed North for a time, Vandrin cannot send anyone after us, even by the time he decides to, it will be too late in the season. No other Woodsman has the advantage of a NightStalker like we do. Nejan will warn us of any hidden dangers. You will learn to see other signs from our teaching. It will be at least another full year of seasons before any will brave the peaks. However, we must expect he might, but if he thinks you no longer walk this earth, then all the better. He walks parallel with the Namanists. They will want to keep control of the people. They will not want to give up control or what they took by deceit."

"How will he know if I am dead or alive? Why should he care?"

"As long as you live, no one else can wield the Sword of Purity, and rule. I mean, he can use it to cut, but there is more than this. To wield it proper, with the Stone of Purity, is to rule. The last being Noster, the last of the DragonRiders, who was ultimately deceived by a brother. Not just any companion, but a hidden brother of the faith, their power grown so much by the time Noster was felled, they stepped into his position. They wielded their power to suit them and not the people. There have been so many centuries under their rule that all who remember the good years have long been gone. We have only stories and in rare cases tomes of the before times, but only if they have been hidden well.

No one would ever admit to having such items, as it is death to own any. They have been lost to all over the years. But remember well, there are six gems in all. Six gods, six Dragons and six Riders. So, there are others like you, fighting to stay alive, stay hidden, and trying to find their bonds. Which means the Age of Dragons is nigh to be upon us. We again shall see the advent and rise of good over evil, and you, my dearest one, shall be the one to lead us."

He became very reverent as he spoke the last sentence bowing his head.

I shook my head in disbelief, "How can I, be worthy of such a task? And have a Dragon to boot?" Tears welled up in my eyes and trickled down my face.

"YOU ARE MY BOND. YOU ARE WORTHY,"

The voice reverberated in my head so loud I blacked out for a moment, and when I came too, Kiem was holding me upright.

"Are you not well? For a second your eyes glowed then went dark."

"I think my voice was a little upset with me, give me a moment,"

Gathering myself, I closed my eyes, sending out my thoughts,

"That was loud, no need to shout,"

I received no answer back. I opened my eyes and Kiem had already moved back across the fire.

"I am not sure this worked, so I will hone my skills with Nejan."

I sat back, the cool stone behind my back.

"So, there are others like me, all possible DragonRiders, and all wielders of gems. How will I know who is who? How will I find them? Especially if I am to work on my own quest, whatever 'tis."

"I am sure everything will disclose itself at the proper moment. You cannot change what the Universe has fixed in place for you. Everything and everyone have a purpose in spirit. We take what is offered and shown, every decision we make is ordained to support us on our path. That is the way of our people. The Universe will reveal all in time, to each of you, and it may mean some of you will travel forward, and some will travel back. If spirit wills it, you may someday make the journey back to the Maderland. Sometimes the only way forward, is to go back."

Kiem stirred the coals, laid down using his pack as a pillow.

"Now, let us get rest, we have long days ahead."

I followed his lead; it took several tries to get comfortable and was a challenge with my limited means. I finally closed my eyes, partially leaning upright against my pack. Morning came too soon.

It was still dark and I felt I just closed my eyes, when Kiem kicked my legs which splayed over a bulge in the hard rock floor.

"Time to get moving, I am going around the left of the boulder to relieve my-self. I suggest covering your feces where possible, it will mask some of the scent. You must even cover urine traces; there are animals out here who will stalk us. Nejan will mask it with her own, but she may not always do so."

He gathered his pack leaving it on top of a small boulder at the mouth of the cave. I followed his lead, going to the right, but there was no dirt available, I found a crack in the rock and let my waste fall inside.

Let them try to find that,

We collected our packs, hoisting them on our backs turning to the right as Nejan crested a high boulder. She looked at us, and I heard a soft, *"This way."*

We set off in her direction. It was tough going, climbing around the heights, lots of rocks, sometimes descending before we climbed more. Kiem kept a quick pace, I had to catch my breath more than once.

"A couple of days of this and we will have a vantage point to view where we have come from. For now, we keep going at this pace, we do not want to be in this valley for much longer, as the weather changes. We need to get through a couple more passes before the snows come."

"Snow?" I spoke in disbelief.

"Do we not need the leaves drop first, and all the rains?"

I leaned against a rock face, to retie one of my boot laces.

"Take a look at your surroundings, do you see tree leaves? In the mountains there are only two seasons, winter and not winter. Snows come to the mountains months before the valleys men live in. We are higher and must travel when there is no or little snow fall. As it is, we will probably see more than we want to before we exit this range. It happened to me both times I came through here."

We walked beside a lazy river, through tall grasses and into forests. The valley was long and narrow, with rocky crags to either side as we approached more mountains. Soon we were climbing up embankments, and through majestic trees. I had a time of it, my head watching my footing, not realizing with the path light-ening, the canopy overhead was diminishing.

We continued up the partial cliff. I looked around at my environment, realizing we left trees a while back. We had two more days of climbing, and now traversed over rock faces, and in the areas of shadow were vestiges of ice which never thawed. We stopped at night to unpack a dried meal, drink direct from our skins and sat on rocks to sleep while Nejan kept guard with her eyes and ears. One night I woke abruptly because I swore, I heard a yell echo through the canyon we were in. Startling me awake, I must have jerked my foot and kicked Kiem beside me, because he spoke softly,

"What is it?"

"I thought I heard something like a yell or a howl." I whispered.

Nejan spoke to me, *"Good ears, Little Dader, that was a wolf cub trying out its voice on the mountain range across from us. Too far away to be a danger to us, but we must be careful. I am not the only Li'on-sa in this region and some are not used to humans. They would not hesitate to make you a tasty meal."*

She must have relayed the same message to Kiem, as there was silence for a minute, then Kiem spoke.

"We may as well begin, 'tis only a couple of hours until daybreak, and we can stop earlier tonight, have a fire and a hot meal. We should be at a plateau where we can look back at the Tynos mountains. We have made incredibly good time thus far, but we still have much to cover."

He turned to retrieve his pack, and I noticed I saw his profile somewhat in the Darkness.

"I see your profile, Pader. Much like 'tis daylight."

"Well, you may lead our pack for a while, if you are gaining night vision like the Li'on-sa."

"These attributes I am gaining, is it because of my link with Nejan, or my Dragon? Do you have these abilities also?"

We conversed while we climbed when I could speak from not being out of breath.

"It could be from both. I have better hearing and eyesight since my link with Nejan, but I cannot see in the dark like you are able. I also have better sense of smell. She has helped me to spot signs in the wild on our adventures over the years. She is the most patient of teachers."

"How is it you two came to meet?"

I was more than intrigued. The stories told in the castle had these great beasts, half-starved, mad for blood with a thirst for death.

"We met on one of the mountains in the ranges behind the Aerie. I was a new Ranger and did not know the fury of a harsh winter. I was half frozen and had a hungry pack of wolves on my scent. They were waiting for me to give up, and then they would attack. Nejan conveyed she was told by her spirit to come to the spot where I was and saved me. She fought the alpha and his mate before the rest decided I was not worth the effort. She outweighed them all by three times. This may have been a deterrent.

She did not explain more than that, she was directed by the Great One, and she saved my sorry arse. We have been together ever since, it has been many years, and we need no other. Other than you, of course. She says you were the reason she sought me out. Eventually the one to lead us would reveal themselves and she was to help guide. It was not until your voice spoke to you the first time; she knew her path was true. She waited patiently, and when you fell off the Neck and heard your bond again, she was certain. You know the rest."

"Your sire has the right of it. I have waited many years for you. The six have come full circle and we will again be ruled by justice and love instead of all the wrongness and hate. It has been foretold."

Nejan heard some of Kiem's speech to me. Sounds carried in the mountains. So, I asked her some questions while we walked and climbed.

"So, who's voice did you hear?"

"I do not know, it happened in my head, not unlike our speech. It was foretold many years ago, and I have waited to hear the call."

"Ummm, may I ask exactly how many years old you are?"

"Too many, I have lost count. When I have helped you on your way, I must return to find one of my own to replenish. I was there when it ended, and I am here when it will begin anew. This should tell you something of how many years I am."

"I am not sure of how long we have had no Dragons, as I am not learned of the history. I have only heard stories secretly told by the fire. Maybe Kiem knows."

I asked my Pader if he knew how long the Dragons had been gone.

"The only ones who know for sure are the Magistrates, I am sure there are written words on the genealogy of the Rulers. It was not widely taught, and I hate to admit, I did not think to learn... Or ask... It cannot be too many hundreds of years, but enough to have us forget. Having a fervent religion like Naman to help eradicate and erase any signs of the past has helped to speed this along.

I do remember seeing part of the Prophecy written but cannot recall any bit of it now. Miiele found it and we read in secret, but were almost caught, so in the excitement, I cast it out of my mind. All I remember is there will be very visible signs, I am unsure, however, it will be irrefutable. We must make sure you are ready when the time is nigh. After we traverse these mountains, you will have legs of hardened muscle to be sure."

"I remember stories the last Dragon flew off. Could this be the voice I heard. It was male."

"That is fact, Noster was the leader, he rode the male. The others, the females are lost to history. There is no tale of them, other than the tale they were banished. There is no location of their banishment. There is no location of the Great One. Perhaps it will be revealed to you. However, you learn what you can, while you can."

"So, I heard a male voice in my head, I hear a great cat, I touched the sword of Noster, felt a vibration when I touched it. It may have glowed. May have. I fell off a great waterfall and survived. I healed fast, faster than I have ever seen. So, it would seem I am bonded with the Great One. I am to be the leader of the New Dragon Age. Not a small task. It seems still unbelievable."

He grinned back at me.

"You will come to a point in the future, where you will believe it. Believing in yourself will only strengthen your belief in what you will do. It is natural to be in awe of what is about to transpire. Talking about it, brings acknowledgement. Acceptance, once you accept your role, comes easier the more you follow your path. You are the leader of the Dragon Age, Dader."

"I am the leader of the Dragon Age. This is still not real to me."

"Perhaps when you meet your bond, it will be more real, keep telling yourself. Time will tell you when to believe. For now, only I know who you are, as you travel others will believe and then soon the entire world. You prepare for this."

"Vandrin will be terribly upset. You should have seen his face. He was sure he was the owner of the sword. He may not want to give it up."

"You worry about that when you go back to retrieve it. It will not cleave to him. So, he may place it to the side. I cannot imagine he will display it if it does not glow with his touch. 'Tis not Vandrin. He is proud and arrogant. His Mader was a member of the Royal family. I cannot remember which branch. The cook did tell me she was beautiful. Beauty did not make her kind. She did not love his Lordship and was not kind to him."

"You sound like you know of a story behind her life."

"The cook told me her story. She was brought to the North to bind the North; it was a political joining. His Lordship was not very Naman at the time. This was a marriage she also did not want. They were two vastly different people in a situation they had to be in for the good of the Realm. She bore him a son. It was what she was told to do. She died when Vandrin was almost five. Four months before we washed up onto the shores. The Namarch almost sent another bride up to his Lordship. He married Miiele out of love and out of necessity."

Listening to my Pader recount history I had never known, was remarkably interesting, he made travelling time pass more quickly. Some of the mountain slope was easily traversed.

"How did she die? Natural causes?"

"Of course not. She was unbelievably beautiful, but very mean. She did not let his Lordship have his joining rites, so he began to look elsewhere. Every time he thought to look at a female, his wife would have her disappear. His Lordship caught on and managed to keep one secret. Until she was not. His wife was jealous, even though she did not let him touch her. The girl was from Hoil, his Lordship would visit frequently, but not enough to cause suspicion. The girl became pregnant and thought to come to the Aerie to tell his Lordship. Circumstances had the Lord hunting this day. His wife thought to take the girl to the tower on pretext this was where his Lordship was."

"She threw the girl off the tower?"

"No. This girl was not stupid and knew what this Lady of the Realm was about. She knew as soon as she was told about the tower it was a hoax. She confronted his Lordships wife, and there were words, shouting and fighting. It was his Lordships wife who fell that day from the gardens. But she took the girl with her. His Lordship mourned only one death, when he returned from his hunt."

"So then four months later, you two showed up."

"Yes. Miiele and I already had a few arguments on the ship when the storm hit, she did not tell me until she was joined to Lord Bodan she was carrying you. She was honest with me and knew I would figure it out. I was upset, yet she reassured me you would have a home, I was to tell you when you were old enough to decide on your own, which path you wished."

"How did you hide from Naman? And Pelin'Dun? Did they not look for her? If she was related to the Rulers."

"Miiele, had the protection of his Lordship. Miiele used bark juice to hide her hair. I left mine dirty. Plus, I was never much around, only long enough to see you. His Lordship let it be known none survived the storm. We were the only two to survive, and we hid ourselves from Ambassadors. Your GrandMader sent them twice, she did not believe the first one she sent."

I smiled at his reference to the walnut rinse I had to use to hide my locks.

"I remember holding you for the first time. Miiele let me, she said I would be not satisfied until I did, she was right. Until I held you in my arms, I was anxious and almost confronted Lord Bodan. You soothed me. When I held you, all my angst left and I agreed to have his Lordship raise you as his."

"But he did not. He left right after Mader passed. I remember not being able to find either of them. It left me hollow and fueled my hate. It took until Aunt Nena helped me, to work past it."

"Nena knew my story. I spent a few months with her, she knew we were different. She is very clever. I am glad she helped you; it would be harder to bear if you still hated his Lordship. When I held you, this was the best day of my life, telling you who you are is the second. All the in between is what the Universe directed. Holding hate inside is not the Vendar way."

"I do not hate anymore, Aunt Nena told me more on the Gods. She taught me to forgive. I forgive his Lordship, just like I forgive you… and Mader. It does one no good to dwell over events which cannot be taken back. It has happened. It has shaped me to be this…"

We travelled longer than Kiem thought as a stream washed out a section of the cliff we were trying to climb, and we had to back track to another vantage point. When we came to a plateau, we released our packs and Kiem spoke,

"Now turn around and enjoy the view."

Turning around to look I gasped, we were extremely high up. I saw a mountain range in the distance with a long narrow valley, various waterfalls and rivers contained in the vista. There were next to no trees this high up. Further away, the blueness of the trees was a gentle dark blue compared to the sky.

"The mountains straight to the left is where we have come through. We skirted the edge of the valley along that ridge line. Anything lower subjects you to carnivorous animals who do not like climbing and easy prey. Only travel by water if you can help it in the valley. Do not ever stop! If 'tis flowing and not blocked it takes about a day and a half in the opposite direction we have come. Do not ask how I know this."

He turned with a grimace, and I saw sadness etched in his eyes.

"Let us find a boulder to shelter us from the wind. We can start a fire and have a hot meal. It will be our last for a while. Next trek will be tough going, we may need to replenish our stocks with something fresh and save our dried for the last leg of the journey."

"We are going higher?"

"Yes, we need to cross two more ranges, and they are higher than this. We will not be sharing words as the air will make it harder for breathing. Not only the cold but it hurts the lungs. 'Tis best we speak now."

"Thank you for sharing with me what must be sad for you. Hearing you talk of Mader brings her to life for me."

"It has brought me joy to tell you. I will not love another like I loved her. Having you here… being here with you now is a blessing and a joy. I wish you to know the history of who you are. Your Mader, I can recount who she was when she was with me. When you meet others of your family, you learn from them, who she was. When you see his Lordship, he has another version of your Mader, his."

"He knows I am not his?"

"This I do not know. Miiele could have told him, but I am not certain. You have his name, his protection, to keep you safe. Until you do not need or want it. The choice is yours."

"Well, I will not worry about it, then. Perhaps when I next see him, it will be different. It makes no matter now. I am not living at the Aerie and his Lordship is probably still fighting in the South."

"Can you hand me the pot in my pack? Why do we not worry about our dinner?"

"This sounds just fine, Pader."

We busied ourselves with meal preparation, repacking after we finished. Nejan made herself scarce but came back shortly after the sun left its last touch on the tops of the mountains. She spoke with Kiem for a bit, then left into the woods behind us, Kiem turned to me and spoke.

"Not to alarm you there is some fresh spoor, which means there is another Li'on-sa here. Feral most likely, not too many are lovers of men. We need to be diligent and aware, Nejan can only protect us so much, and if 'tis a male, it will be stronger, larger, and hungrier. We will work together and leave no trace of our passing, eliminate in water to dissipate our scent where possible. Our footwear will leave marks on softer ground, but we cannot help this. Do you still have your knife? Good, you will need it. Here, let me show you some defensive moves."

Kiem then demonstrated to me some crucial areas of the body which would be fatal if poked.

"Think of it as cutting through a raw side of a hog. There will be a modicum of resistance, prepare for the shock of the thrust and if possible, give a twist of the knife before retracting it. Thrust with the blade up and down, like this not sideways, Nejan's ribs are that way, human ribs are this way."

He showed me and I felt my own ribs hoping I remembered this key point.

"Try to aim for the neck, but if its huge head is in the way, if possible, come at it from the side. Other areas you can inflict damage are the large muscles on the legs. It may not do any damage unless you think to slice here."

He showed me in his groin where the large artery was which fed the leg and I tried to imagine where it might be on an exceptionally large cat.

"Nejan will alert us if there is danger. I suggest you get some sleep; it may be our last night of it."

He lay down propping himself against his pack. Closing his eyes, he was asleep instantly. I followed suit.

It was our last night of restful sleep, strangely enough, I was not as sore as I used to be. I woke up seconds before Kiem stirred; I had no issues now getting off to sleep as the amount of exercise had me worn out. As soon as I made myself comfortable as I could, I shut my eyes and slept. We rose, did our necessary morning rituals, and consumed some dried foods. There would be no time to cook a morning meal, as we prepared to leave. Nejan padded over and gazed at Kiem, and he then looked at me.

"We need to get moving, there are signs we are spotted. 'Tis only because Nejan is with us, marking with her scent we have not been bothered. The feline following us is persistent, he may be starving, and a hungry predator will stop at nothing.

I am afraid curiosity will forgo caution in time, we will keep to the high ground as much as possible, 'tis the only advantage we may have."

CHAPTER 15

Rowan

Beated Wings Adrift

"You are a worthless whore. No better than breeding stock."

This violence became Rowan's routine every day, she could barely hobble over to the commode chair and from what parts of her body she saw, almost every piece of skin had darkened from bruising. It hurt to lift an arm; it hurt to walk. It hurt to sit; this was her life; she was in a world of hurt.

Her husband left her face alone after the first bruises healed, and he proved very attentive to the body parts which could be covered. Her scalp throbbed from his snatching and forcing her head into awkward positions, he liked to seize her hair in his grip, and she was thankful it was grabbed in whole; she was shedding hair from sheer fear or worry. She lamented the length of her tresses but was bound to keep the length by law. It became slick with oils and dirt, from confinement, it distressed her she was soiled and unwashed.

She tried to fight back once with her fists, but only once… he hit body parts she did not think would hurt but hurt they did. He said one day since she could not bruise any more than she had already, he would begin damaging her maid. She stopped trying then, she did not wish the same pain to be inflicted on another because of her.

He began to tell her she was not worthy, and her maid was worth more than her. The barrage of negative things about her began to take root. The unseen violence undermined her very mind, and it manifested a little each day. He planted the seeds, and they began to take root.

"Your parents sold you to the highest bidder."

"Your Mader did not even want you."

"You are just fat and lazy."

"You are not even worthy to have my name."

"You are just here to bear my child."

"You are nothing without me."

"You have no one but me now."

"If you lay there emptyheaded, I will take it out on her."

"No one asks about you. They do not care about you."

Every day was something new, and she began to believe him. Little by little, she felt her life had no purpose, his missives began to bloom. She began to retreat into her mind; it did not tell her untruths. Rowan some days would go the whole

189

of the Daylight hours, not uttering a sound. She would take his barrage of violence in silence, but he would beat her until she uttered moans and cries. It seemed to excite him, and he would finish faster.

She knew eventually she would be having visitors; her Mader sent word; she would be coming soon to see if Rowan was bearing yet.

How nice, she thought to herself, *I am just a brood mare, and she does not care to see if I am fine.*

If she just lay there, she would get smacked, if she tried to ask anything, she would get smacked. Kavus wanted a minimum of protest, if she closed her fists at him, he would hit her harder. His excitement grew if she slapped at him. She hated nightfall, and she lost her appetite in the evenings, anticipating the violence from which she could not hide. But the physical was nothing compared to the violence he was raping her mind with.

He toyed with her mind, telling her things one day and retracting it the next. He would tell her she was imagining the things he told her and make her believe he did not.

"'Tis all nonsense, you are a liar."

"I did not say that."

The constant inconsistent word play toyed with her sense of being. Eventually, she did not know what she was about. Not sleeping at night, hearing things in her room, and becoming skittish at the slightest sounds. She could not see it, but she was losing weight as her diet was not appetizing. Sometimes, Rowan could not finish her stew or broth. Tannah would finish her remainders, as she was not receiving ample nourishment either.

One morning in her grogginess, she heard a voice softly speaking to her as she gradually woke.

"The chains you wear are made from the laws you serve."

She murmured back, not quite fully awake.

"What do you mean?"

Rowan did not realize her husband was on his way out of the room. He finished his business with her slightly awake and she was not caring anymore. She could do nothing to stop it. He turned at the doorway and spoke.

"What did you say? I did not speak to you. I did not give you leave to speak. How dare you even consider it."

This inflamed him, he strode back and let fly with his fists managing to hit every part of her body he could find as she tried to curl up and shield herself. Sobbing and screaming because now she did not care who heard her or not.

"No, please. Stop. You are hurting me! Stop! I hate you!"

"Ungrateful whore! I will teach you to speak back."

Her shrieking enraged his mood and he hit her intensely and relentlessly. Then she blacked out.

She was swimming in a sea of pain; it ebbed and flowed like the seas. Her pulse vibrated to its own tune, her body stung and the pain of it woke her up. There were strangers in her room, she was cleaned up and covered in a cloth robe, the man who was a doctor by his clothing, had dressed the worst of her wounds with leeches. This managed to take down the swelling but left her very light-headed. This was possibly the one time she would appreciate their use. She murmured softly and Tannah came over to the bed.

"How are you mistress?"

Tannah was sporting a black eye and a bruise on her arm. Rowan tried to smile but could barely crack her lips. Tannah wet a cloth and dabbed her mistress's lips to which she was grateful for the moisture.

"Oh, please tell me this nightmare of a life is over. I cannot bear this any longer. How much more can this body take? I hurt."

"The doctor has taken down most of the swelling and while he was here, he did another check and confirmed you may be with child. I asked him to check."

She leaned in close to Rowan.

"I think the doctor will tell him to leave you alone now, as 'tis best for the child. Hopefully, you will get a reprieve."

Tannah left the room, following behind the others.

I am finally bearing a child; will this pain stop now? I cannot bear much more of this. How I wish I could go back in time, back to when I was happy in my innocence. How I hate this man, I wish he would go out to the battlefield and die a horrible death. Then I could be free. But then, I would just be married off again. I am nothing more than a brood mare. There must be more to this life.

"There is, be patient, Little Mader. You will have to bear this a while longer."

The whisper in her head, was gentle and soothing, she was alone in her room, where else would a disembodied voice come from? She was beaten down; any sympathy was welcomed. She thought back to it and was surprised when it answered her again.

"I do not want to. I am tired of this pain."

"Not even for the life you now have inside you?"

"Well...I will hold fast for now."

"You must hold fast, Earth Mader, let the sound of my pulse sooth you in your need. You are not alone."

"Thank you, I do not want to be alone."

The sound of low humming gently soothed her back to sleep.

Rowan could not comprehend what her next few months would be, but at least she would heal from her bruises for a while. She had a reprieve from the physical act he inflicted upon her, but his verbal barrage continued. When she failed to respond, Tannah would have more bruises. After a while, Kavus would not even seek her out. She was so grateful for his neglect.

Her husband would not visit her bed until after the child was born and for this alone, she was grateful. He would not dare hit her while she was carrying the potential heir to not just his family name but the Empire. Maybe he would stop taunting her as well. She was able to walk after a week of bedrest, the bruises on her body had faded somewhat to beautiful yellows and greens on her pale skin and she began to get curious about her home. Or jail, whatever you wished to call it.

She left her room with Tannah's help wandering down the hall, passing by other rooms which looked sparse and unused. They would only go when the rest of the villa was sleeping.

"I will show you around Noda, this end of the villa. I dare not take you further. If we were to be caught, I would be beaten."

"I know, however, show me around a little bit. I will go when all are sleeping. You know I cannot sleep sometimes. I wake up panicking and cannot settle down."

"We will not speak when we are out of the room. Wait until we get back to your room and I will tell you all. This way no one hears us."

"I agree. Sounds may carry when the halls are empty."

Around a few more corners she found a center courtyard, it was a beautiful garden area and she had to sit down on a stone bench for a time. This was to become her area of refuge from her mind. She had many unpleasant thoughts lately. She wanted to sneak down the hall and hit her husband while he slept. Payback, but she knew the outcome. He would beat her in response, regardless of carrying his child.

I cannot bear this cruelty anymore, how I wish the earth would open and swallow me whole. I do not wish to live.

"But you will live, Little One. You carry a life inside you, 'tis innocent of all you are receiving. Its spirit once born should be given the chance to make its own decisions. To take a spirit's chances away from it, is not our way."

"I hear you, voice. I am not as cruel as that."

"I know, Little One, that is why you have been Chosen."

"Chosen? For what?"

"To do wonderful things, Little One, wonderful things. Rest easy for the gift of spirit takes its toll on Maders. Get your rest."

While she was sitting in her solitude, the Chief of House came to her, she realized during the day, she would be found out.

"While you are my Mistress, the Master stated you are not to be outside for lengthy periods."

"Fresh air is for the health of the heir to the Empire. 'Tis for him I sit here."

She murmured back to him in a small act of defiance. He left her alone. She would have a servant with her always and was constantly watched night and day.

One evening, being restless, she ventured to the garden after her evening meal, watching the shadows play on the trees and shrubs, the sun setting in the sky beyond the confines of her prison. She sat in solitude with her disturbed thoughts hoping… no praying something, someone would rescue her. She laid back upon the bench she was resting on. Rowan noticed first her watching attendant was not with her, and it was silent, except for the sounds of birds and creatures beyond the walls of the villa. She could pick up the odd sound of voices coming from the direction of the kitchen and servant areas. As she was thinking about the sounds she heard from her spot on the bench, she gazed up at the heavens and was pleasantly surprised to see stars shooting across her plane of vision. First a couple, then a multitude, and she gloried in such an event.

Should I take this as a sign my prayers are heard, perhaps there is a glimmer of hope for me yet.

After a while, she grew tired and silently walked back to her room and fell asleep, in her one moment of happiness as she now knew it.

A week or so later… time travelled slow sometimes, fast other times… Rowan did not keep track in her misery. One could only tell the passing of time by the condition of the plants and their lifeline to the soil. As she was sitting in the garden, with her hands on her belly, which was firmer to the touch, her husband came into the garden.

"Get up. Follow me."

She obeyed, following him. He walked out of her hall to another, and turning many corners to a room she had not seen before. They entered it and Rowan saw assorted colours of clothing draped over the furniture. He picked out a few items.

"Make yourself presentable, the Empress is coming to see us."

He never called the Empress Rowan's Mader, his disassociation she would analyze later to be his way of controlling her, his methods to feel superior over her blood and name.

"You have an hour. Be ready."

He chose a green threaded cloth, with black and gold embroidery which integrated his house colours subtly with the Royal House colours. Tannah followed them into the room and her husband gave the maid the cloth,

"Wash her, and dress her hair according to her station, and dress her in what I have chosen. Have her presentable within the hour or I will beat you."

"Yes, Nodan, right away. Come, Noda."

The two women exited the parlor after Kavus gave them permission, Tannah's arms full of cloth. They did not speak to each other until they were around a couple corners in the hall.

"I did not know there was a bathhouse,"

"Yes, it has always been here. Now that you know, you could perhaps quietly use it when all are asleep. I know you roam more now in the middle of the night; I hear you. Do not worry, I will not say anything, I understand completely."

She had not been able or allowed to physically move outside her room for the last two months. Until she was with child, she had not the strength to move far. Just the garden, which she craved the sense of purpose it seemed to emit to her spirit.

"There is a whole section of the villa you have not seen, Noda,"

She leaned in close and whispered this to her,

"Your room is at the end of one of the wings and his rooms are in the main section of the villa. Now that it is daytime, you will have a better sense of where it is. Seeing the halls at night is confusing. You will see this when we greet your Mader. Those rooms are strictly for entertaining. We should hurry; we need to have you clean and presentable for your guest."

They went to the bathhouse, in another wing, across the garden courthouse, Tannah helped bathe and washed her hair. The water was colder than she was used to, but she did not care, she was finally clean. They went to an adjoining room where she sat down on a beautifully embroidered chair, Tannah helping her to dry her hair, brushed it out and created a simple braid which wrapped around her head and left her hair long. This was traditionally the only adornment she could do with her hair until after giving birth and only then she would be allowed to place her hair up, or contain it inside a snood, which was a hairnet matrons wore.

She was assisted with her dress, which conveniently covered from neck to foot and bore long flowing sleeves with only her fingertips exposed.

He planned that well,

Then Tannah provided her with a tray of jewels her husband was permitting her to wear. She picked up all the rubies. The only other ring was the Topaz her Mader gave her, which she realized was taken away when she first arrived. She made sure to put that one on, it seemed looser, so she placed it on her third finger. The rubies were her act of defiance; she was still a member of the Royal House. She thought to remind him of that.

Tannah dusted her face with a little powder which seemed to help hide a faded bruise hiding it quite well. She managed to get a quick glimpse of herself in a small mirror and did not recognize the face staring back at her. Devoid of all animated expression, she looked like a shadow of her former happy self. There was no life in the face staring back. The hour went by very quickly. She stole this glance as she walked out of the room down a long hall to another very well-lit room she saw was a receiving parlor.

Her husband was already there, and he motioned for her to sit on a chair beside him. "Sit."

She sat gingerly down seeing he wore his regimental formal dress, which to an outside eye, made him look smart, but to her, all she saw was his mental ugliness. He glanced at her, frowning, so she let her face 'go numb,' as she liked to call it. Her face she practiced in front of the mirror many times in her Palace. It seemed a lifetime ago. This seemed to placate him. He stood up as the Empress and her maidservant entered the room.

"Your Majesty, you honour us with your presence, please be seated."

He motioned to the settee across from them. Rowan stood up slowly bowing to the Empress, to which they were motioned to sit.

"I understand congratulations are in order. You will be having the heir in high summer. We will plan accordingly. Ruta, here."

The Empress signalled for her maidservant to bring forward an ornate box, which was placed on a low table between them and opened. The box lined with a gold silk and contained several different pieces of handblown glass of beautiful red and gold colours with greens and blacks portraying the colours of both their families.

"You are so generous, your Majesty, we humbly accept your beautiful gift. Do you not think this exquisite?"

Her husband graciously thanked her Majesty, meanwhile Rowan remained silent. He motioned with his hand back at her and so she thanked the Empress for her gift, her voice devoid of any expression. "Thank you very much."

The Empress gazed at Rowan with a quizzical eye while making idle observations and Rowan returned her gaze blankly making the required appropriate responses. The Empress spoke about the upcoming baby. When the baby was born, there would be a great celebration to welcome the newest member of the royal family. Depending on whether it was a boy or girl, would determine if it were heir to the throne.

At the mention of the line of succession, her husband's chest seemed to expand even more, and he smiled at the Empress, thanking her graciously.

"We are taking great care of the heir; Rowan is basking in her gardens every day."

As it was obvious, this was all her Mader had come for, the Empress stood up announcing she was leaving. Rowan's husband stood up and she stood slowly, bowing as the Empress turned to leave.

"You may return to your garden, my Dear."

"Thank you, may I make a request?"

Knowing her Mader was still in earshot; Rowan pressed her case forward. They followed behind seeing their guest to the front entrance of the villa. To the awaiting carriage, a full cohort of decorated guards surrounded the gilded conveyance. None could mistake the royal designation of the traveler; these men were armed to the teeth. History had dictated, the more men, the better.

"Yes, certainly. What is it you desire?"

He also knew their guest was still present, and he could not refuse her publicly. She hoped after her Mader was gone that he did not renege.

"May I have a few changes to my diet, it seems the baby is requiring more, and if I could have a variety of greens, I seem to crave cucumbers and dill."

"Yes, yes of course. We must take care of the heir. You may have all you desire. Now if 'tis all, I must make plans for my Pader. I will inform the cook."

"Thank you, dear husband."

Their guest alighted her carriage and they waited until it disappeared before each went their separate paths. Everything she asked for was always for the baby. This was the way she knew she could get things in one form or another. A couple of days later she asked for some more fruit.

"The child has more of an appetite, and I fear it will not develop properly if it is starved of necessary nutrition."

Later in the week Rowan requested to bathe once a week as good hygiene was better for the soon to be child. Oh, she was well aware after the child arrived, things may go back to the way they were before, but she was going to enjoy her freedom and requests as much as possible. If you could call her section of the villa freedom.

One day, Tannah came into her room waking her up as her sleep was still interrupted during the night so she slept as long as she could. She whispered into her Mistress's ear,

"The Master is leaving for the city for a fortnight. You are not permitted to leave the premises, but he is taking most of his men, and its just the Headmaster of the household, Cook and maidservants and a dozen soldiers left here. When he is gone, I can show you the rest of the villa as when I am not busy with you, I am busy cleaning the other rooms and now know the layout."

She helped her mistress, dressing her in one of the new robes the Master insisted she wear, in case of unexpected visitors. Rowan knew her Mader's visit was planned. Given there had been not other guests, she knew Kavus refused all others. However, she was not concerned about the lack of interest, she did not want to converse falsely. It somehow did not feel right, especially the display of happiness he showed to her Mader, she wanted no part of it. So, the lack of visitors sat fine with her.

She was brought a breakfast which changed with her request, and it had a little more substance and variety. As she was finishing what was on her plate, her husband strode in barking at her.

"I have business in the city. I will be gone for a fortnight. You will not leave. You will not send out missives, and you will not receive guests. If you were to do any of these, I will know. I will beat the soles of your feet and those of your maid. You will obey me in this. Do I have your obedience?"

"Yes, Nodan. I will obey you, as you command."

She was to rest and not cause any harm or stress to the soon to be heir to the throne. She responded in such a neutral tone, he regarded her closely, and she was sure his servants would be reporting her every move to him when he returned.

She stayed in the garden until she heard his retinue leave, sensing the tension abandon her shoulders which had not decreased for the four months she was joined. She occupied the next few Days exploring the villa which was her prison, first with Tannah and her escort of another maid. This girl soon disappeared, probably put to work. She walked down the halls finding the wing which was exclusively her husbands. It was ultimate luxury compared to the room she was assigned. He had an extensive dressing room with a bathing room adjoining, not dissimilar to the one she had at the Palace. On a smaller scale, but luxurious, none the less.

She found another beautifully decorated bedroom across the hall and as she was peering in, Tannah came by, her arms laden with linens.

"That is your receiving room once the baby is born, Noda."

"'Tis definitely different than where I am now."

Rowan made the observation with no bitterness or spite reflected in her tone. She spent the rest of the day wandering and later after the midday meal, she wandered down to the cooking hall. There she found the bulk of the servants. They rose up when they saw her, but she asked them to sit and pay her no mind. She got several sympathetic looks from the female servants, but condescending ones from the males. Several would not look at her at all. She left them, wandering into a rear courtyard where she saw several stables and outbuildings, Tannah came out rushing behind her, begging her to come inside.

"The Cook is your husband's man to the core, please come inside before he has cause to report to him."

"I just wanted to see my confinement as a whole. There seems to be an area of unuse..."

Following her servant back as she was tired from exploring. She would take afternoon naps which she found worked to her benefit. Rowan began to nap in the afternoons and into the dinner hour, waking up to find her dinner cold on the table where Tannah would leave it. She ate and Tannah would take the tray back on her way to retiring. Once she discovered where the servants' wings were, she made sure to avoid their area. She would busy herself with her embroidery on baby items she was creating, listening for the outside sounds to come indoors and diminish.

Then she would take to roaming the halls, find out where the sentries were. Her eyesight sharpened in the dark, and her hearing also, she would hear footsteps in the hall ahead of her and would duck into an open doorway, waiting for the footsteps to pass. She began to play a game the next day… listen to each person's personal sounds, steps and soon breathing patterns, memorizing everything she could. She found books in her husband's library, mostly on war, she had not seen before. Being inquisitive, she read them and always made sure she returned them exactly as found.

Her two weeks of freedom soon ended. She was sitting in her garden one cloudy day when she heard her husbands party returning through the canyon leading to the city. She was surprised when it took longer than she thought to enter the villa courtyard.

I didn't realize my hearing was that good

She was quite surprised when she heard the voice in her head answer.

"All your senses will sharpen in time; you still have a lot to learn."

"Who are you?" She asked the question in her thoughts and was again surprised when she received another answer.

"We are those who you will seek in another land, but first you will know great loss, and will seek us out of your own desire,"

She must have answered aloud, in her shock because she responded with, "What do you mean?" Right as her husband entered the garden. He looked annoyed and frowned asking who she was talking with, to cover her tracks, she just shrugged saying,

"I always talk to myself, 'tis comforting."

"You will not be seen doing this in public or here at home, I do not want it rumoured I married an unsound woman. If you do, I will wait until the child is born and I will beat it out of you, do I make myself clear?"

She readily agreed to adhere to his wishes, as she was already a recipient many times to his wrath.

"If you persist, I will beat the soles of your feet and you will not be able to walk without assistance. If you cannot stop, I will beat your maid. She is expendable, just stop this nonsense. I do not need this in my life right now. You carry my child, the heir to the Empire. He will not have a crazy Mader. I am stuck with you until you bear me a couple of sons. After that time, if you continue with this senseless chattering to yourself, I will hand you over to the Church myself, am I clear?"

He left, annoyed and frowning. Later that evening as Tannah brought her evening meal, sporting a swollen cheekbone with a redness which almost broke through the skin, she told her Mistress,

"I am not sure what upset him, but the Master is packing and leaving in the morning. Back to the Capital for another two weeks."

"Probably my talking to myself, he thinks I am crazy, and warned me to stop, or he will beat me and you, I am sorry I have brought this upon you. I cannot stop him beating you, and it pains me to no end."

"This is my fate, it is linked to yours, and I appreciate your kindness in thought. Now as spring approaches, perhaps you focus on something to keep your mind busy. You could always offer to tend to a garden. You used to love tending flowers and such. This would help your mind and function as an outlet for any negative energy you may carry. My Mader used to be a wonder with anything green, and she used to always encourage others to follow a positive energetic path."

"Do you remember your Mader much?"

Tannah was young when she began tending Rowan in the Palace, Rowan could not remember being without her attendant.

"Yes, when I was a child, she was loving and would always tell us stories to take our mind off troubles. She was happy for me to be chosen to serve in the Palace. Not just for the status, she genuinely was happy for the opportunity it provided to have a better life than hers. How she would roll over in her grave if she only knew."

This was the only time Rowan heard Tannah speak negatively about her current situation, and she did not pursue the conversation. She ate everything presented to her, finding an appetite for her meals which had her requesting more sustenance, and finding her requests granted. She opted not to explore this night, however in the early hours of the morning, she woke with a start. Using the commode as her bladder seemed to have shrunk some, she had to empty it more often.

As she was now awake, she thought to venture out. Casting her senses out, listening for the sounds which came with the night. First, she stood in the doorway, head leaning against the door jamb, gazing down the hallway, she heard sounds of snoring. So, she focused on the sound, following it back to the source. This was her husband, sleeping on his back no less. Rowan moved past his rooms and heard the sentry outside the main doorway, snorting quietly and spitting onto the dirt. She kept going, amazed she could distinguish these sounds. Sensing what the cook was doing, rising, pissing in a pot, scratching his ass crack, and stretching out his back, by the sounds of bones popping. Then she focused even more and heard his shuffling feet slip into his soft soled shoes moving towards the kitchen and ovens.

She was amazed she heard all this! Her focus dropped, and she gripped the door jam she was leaning on.

How is this possible?

Rowan knew from the voice in her head telling her, her senses would develop, but this was beyond imagining.

She returned to bed falling back to sleep, dreaming of better days. The next morning, she woke early as her husband came in and roughly shook her awake.

"I am heading back to the Capital. You will behave yourself; I do not wish to hear anything of the contrary. I will be gone for a couple more weeks preparing for the spring campaigns."

He turned to walk out the doorway of her bedroom and she spoke out.

"May I help with tending to a garden? It would ease my mental well being, keeping me occupied. It would engage my mind and I do love to garden, please?"

She presented her words carefully, knowing he held her happiness in his very voice and words.

"If you think it will stop you from talking to yourself, by all means, however no strenuous activities, you will not cause harm to yourself or the baby you carry. Others will do any heavy lifting."

He left. She knew he was not saying he cared about her. The child she carried inside her, was his way up in the world. If it was a boy, then the entire world could be his, if it was a girl, then he would try again.

Tannah entered the room shortly after, handing her a robe. Rowan dressed, then went with her maidservant to the bath, where she washed her hair thoroughly as though she was washing her husband away. Feeling much better, her spirit lighter, she dressed in leggings and a tunic Tannah provided. Walking down the hall to the kitchen she asked the Cook for any seeds he may have and the spot he recommended for a garden.

"The Master already told me you plan on growing herbs and vegetables, but the soil here is a bit stubborn and will not yield much. You will have to water it well, very well, and as you are not to be lifting buckets, I believe, Tannah, you will be terribly busy. You are welcome to try if 'tis what the Master ordered. Come with me and I will show you where we have the garden plot."

He grabbed a small urn off the top of the shelves heading outside, without looking to see if Rowan was following. He walked around the stables and at the farthest corner of the villa grounds was ground, just beginning to be tilled.

"May I have help in the tilling of the soil, as it looks as if you have started to prepare? I have brought seeds from the Palace I collected, but as most are flowers, I may plant them in the center garden to enhance it."

The cook reluctantly agreed to have her borrow a few of the groundsmen as everyone had other jobs to do. She was content with this. He left the urn of seeds on the ground for her to investigate.

The next week was busy. A few men helped in the morning, and Rowan used a hoe until her lower back ached. She would haul half empty buckets of horse manure. This was all she was willing to carry as she did not wish to overdo her efforts in the beginning. By the end of the week, double the men came to help and she had most of the ground allotted tilled and manure blended in. As the spring weather was approaching, she knew she could plant certain items which took longer to germinate. Rowan had help in tilling rows and she gleefully dropped seeds in. Blessing each one as it dropped from her hand into the row, using her bare foot to cover. She gloried in the feel of earth between her toes and felt a slight vibration as she walked and seeded.

She was sleeping soundly through the night; the fresh air was invigorating, and her task driven self was exhausted by nightfall. She did not hear any voices inside her head and did not seek them out. She had various servants helping her by carrying water. Rowan was pleased with the result when some of the plants began to emerge, but then her husband returned. The time seemed to have flown by.

When he returned, she sequestered herself in her wing, staying to herself in the center garden planting her flowers there. As she planted her favourite one, the Blood rose, a crazy thought came to her, which would have knocked her down on her knees if she were not already on them.

I will not be here to see them flower... Now why would I have thought this? She sat, pondering, and did not hear her husband enter the garden and stand there watching her.

"I hear you are busy."

He strode towards her, and his voice startled her out of her contemplation. Rowan rolled forward using her hands to support rising to stand in front of his advancing person, head bowed.

"Yes, with help, of course, we prepared the soil and planted a few things. We will plant more each week. It is exhausting but extremely rewarding, I am sleeping very well from the light exercise."

She kept her head bowed, and saw his booted feet stop in front of her.

"You may continue with your gardening, but as you get closer to laydown, the servants will take over. You may direct them, but you will not carry anything, I will not have any harm come to my child. The air has done you well, I heard no ill of you, from my servants."

He finished speaking and went his own way. She let out the breath she was holding, giving thanks she did not have to spend anymore time than she had to with him. If all she had to do was get pregnant, watch herself during the time he spent with her, then it was bearable. The break from his mental barrage had her thinking well about herself again. Still, it dented her self-confidence some. The silence she now received was better than the attention. With his absence her hatred of him lessened.

He is such a mean man. I am glad he chooses not to grace me with his presence and tell me such lies.

But back to her thought, or was it her thought? Why would she think this? Oh yes, she would know great loss, what could this be, maybe lose her child before she ended her term? She better watch it then, no lifting anymore. She did not want to lose her child before she bore it.

She looked forward to the day she held the child in her arms. Rowan remembered a few of her younger siblings. As a young child she would hold them in her arms and sooth them to sleep. She knew more about life now and to hold something she help create, this would be different than holding her brother or sister. The thought of her child had her absentmindedly rubbing her belly. There was a slight bulge, firm to her touch, like a meal undigested, or a belly full of air which had to be passed. At this moment she felt what she thought were bubbles, and she smiled gently at her midsection.

With those thoughts to keep her going, she did not miss her husband when he was there and did not miss him when he was not. Another week rolled around and a day past when he returned to the Capital before she realized he left. He never talked to her about anything unless it benefited him. The neglect, while five months ago bothered her, now she did not care if he spoke to her at all. She saw a glimpse into his soul, he was self motivated, there was no room for her and the baby. He was a dark, troubled man. His glorious, good looks did not deceive her anymore. He only cared about his pleasure. Hurting her or her maid, was his pleasure to inflict pain.

She knew one day; the Universe would come full circle and he would pay the tax on this.

CHAPTER 16

Solina

Thus Ends the One Man

Solina's life changed in the most unimaginable way from the day she drank the elixir.

Her GrandMader did not leave her side, except for her to rest. She picked out Solina's clothing, hovered around her meals, and eventually left her alone to bathe. It was all too much sometimes. She was dressed in the finest silks, bathed every Day, had the most delicious foods prepared every day. Her head spun with the busyness of it all.

She sat in the bath two-weeks later thinking about what happened after she woke up in the Throne Room. Her GrandMader cleared out almost everyone. The only attendees were the Rulers, her immediate family, and servants to both. She asked for water, looked to her GrandMader and Dame Metina took charge right from the get-go.

"You are the High Dragon now. I am currently the Grand Magistrate, but once you are instructed and trained in all we, the Rulers are, you may step in. It will be a relief to have a young mind, this is your Uncle, Tailer. He is the Magistrate of Law. Your other Uncle, this is Landrin, he is the Magistrate of War. By your leave, he must return to the barracks, those are his offices while we deal with Du'Lanay. Landrin, you may leave."

"So, your family have three positions? What of the others? These are my Uncles?"

"Our family, my dear child. You will have the position of overseeing it all. However, I will spend the next while instructing you in what a Magistrate does. These are indeed my sons, your Uncles. The other two here, are Education and Economy. They have assistance in their departments; they have been infirm for a time. The newly appointed Finance Rider was murdered; it was to be your position. I have taken over until I can find a replacement. You may leave."

Dame Metina motioned to the four other rulers to go and after they left, she turned to her GrandDader. Solina sipped at her water, trying to ingest all what this older woman was telling her. She had family.

"Tell me of my Mader, please."

Solina asked softly, she knew it was not a public subject, and she saw the older woman's facial expressions tense. There was a tone of resignation in her voice.

"Your Mader was a twin, both girls were close and looked the same. She was in her eighteenth year when she had you and passed her spirit. Her name was Shayatin. Miiele was my other Dader. Miiele left here when she was seventeen and died in a shipwreck on the shores of Du'Lanay with her lover. It was a tough time for me."

"I am sorry, but if it grieves you to tell me, I will wait for a more appropriate time."

"No. I knew this time would arrive; I was not prepared for the events as they unfolded today. I held onto the hope you would come and join the family. You have proven yourself worthy of a Rider. It makes me a proud Matriarch.

Your Mader was gentle, where Miiele was more…vigorous in her ideals. Shayatin loved to sing, she had the most glorious voice and was often requested to sing in the Great Halls during solstice celebrations. Miiele had a larger voice, the two girls when they sang together had such a… tremendous power over all who listened. They would bring all who listened to tears. Oh, how I miss them!"

Dame Metina shed a few tears, losing herself into her memories.

"'Tis good to hear in the remembrance they are not forgotten."

"They are not forgotten; however, I have not spoken of them for a very long time. I took you myself to the Church, I had to keep you hidden, for your safety. The Namarch heard of my girls, there were several attempts on their lives growing up. I could not take the chance with you. When you received your eyes as a child, I knew your life would have greater meaning. What happened today has never happened in our history."

Solina wanted to hear more on her Mader. She did not want to remember the man she killed. She finished her water.

"May I have a small repast and more water? My throat is very sore and I would like you to tell me more on my Mader if you care to share."

"Why yes. Headmaster, here. Please get the High Dragon some bread and cheese, nothing too elaborate, her stomach needs to settle. I will have my tea, and we will have it here."

"Yes, Dame, right away. High Dragon."

The older man bowed his way out of the Grand Hall and Solina gazed around. Her head was clearer and her voices were quiet. She knew they were listening also.

"Shayatin and Miiele were similar in looks, but quite different in spirit. Until they became women, I could not tell them apart. It was always Miiele who would get Shay to follow her lead. Several times I would have mistaken them for the other. They always played this on us, when they were not wishing to do some official event, it was irritating, but I do miss their antics, now they are no longer with spirit. I would have reports back on your developments, from the Church, and Yona."

"Yona. I will miss her; she was my mentor."

"I picked her for you. She was your Mader's minder when they were small. She was a gentle woman, I knew you would be well cared for. I trusted her with you."

"Oh, the Pader told me a story of her family."

"This part was truth, Du'Lanay was not kind. It was not a family thing, well yes it was… Her Mader was from Du'Lanay, it caused unrest and Yona suffered for it. When she came to our home, she was but a young woman. After she raised my girls and your two Uncles, she asked to go into the Church. It was her solace to worship the Gods and live the rest of her life in peace. It was the least I could do for her. She raised you well, I understand you have a thirst for knowledge?"

"Yes. I have written in all languages and can converse in all. I have read everything in the Church, and perhaps some not well known."

"Oh?"

"I found a hidden library. There were tomes on Dragons."

"Oh, I thought we had all of them. You may access my personal library, dear child. I have a copy of everything. Every poet, every map maker, everything on Dragons. Everything Du'Lanay would have burned. They are itching to get their hands on my collection. 'Tis not widely known the extent of my library… but more on the girls. I was not an…attentive Mader. I had a country to rule and I neglected them. They had their own minds and when it came time for me to prepare them for the Rituals, they had their own ideas. Miiele was extremely interested in what they were, and she investigated on her own and found something out and outright refused to participate. I had no idea she had a lover until I could not find her.

When your Mader told me Miiele was gone, I may have overreacted. Shayatin ran away, and when I finally found her, she was bearing you. I kept her and her lover hidden. I was furious. A pregnant woman could not partake of the Ritual, and there are laws even I have to follow. I sent men to all ends of the lands, to Aram, to Du'Lanay to find Miiele. I made the mistake of telling Shay the result and this sent her into depression, which sent her into early labour and she passed giving birth to you. I am sorry child; it was my fault your Mader passed."

"Oh, do not give yourself the fault. If anything, Yona told me, is everything has a reason for happening. I am saddened you lost both of your Daders, but the Universe has a path in place."

"How right you are. Ah, here is a small repast for you dear. If your stomach rebels, have the water. They brought you a tea also. This blend is my favorite."

"Oh, I have tried this, mmm, this is Joy Root."

"Oh, you know your teas. That is my girl, you are definitely one of mine."

"So, my two Uncles are Rulers?"

"Yes. after the girls… I had no choice but to offer up my boys. I was fearful they would not pass the Ritual, but they did. The D'un family have the majority of positions. This pleased me long ago, but now, I am of a different mind. I am glad to finally acknowledge your existence, but now you will have to guard yourself against assassins. It will be Du'Lanay's response."

"Will they do this? Send men to kill me?"

"Yes, they do not like change. You represent change. I feel you will bring forth a great transformation; it hangs in the air. I feel it, like the calm before the storm."

"Well, will I meet other members of our family?"

"Yes, I would have you know them all. Your Uncles will have told them by now. There are a few cousins, and several littles. We will host dinners; you can meet them all. If you are feeling better, you should rest. Tomorrow will come fast enough, I have organized your time for you, and the next few weeks will be tiring. There are many things you need to begin learning."

Solina was not hungry anymore and with a full belly the tiredness hit her hard. She felt drained of emotion, impatient, and spoke before she thought about it.

"But where are the Dragons?"

"There are no Dragons, my dear, what ever gave you this thought?"

"Hmmm, let me see. The elixir, made from grape juice, I am guessing."

Solina's sarcasm came out verbally and it astonished even herself. Her GrandMader looked at Solina in astonishment, it reflected back at the girl in the elders face. Dame Metina had not had someone speak back at her for a very long time.

"My voices tell me they are somewhere dark. I am thinking 'tis not here in the Palace, so let us try this again. Where are they?"

Dame Metina changed her demeanor so fast, Solina did not have time to reflect, a softer version of the Ruler was presented. She took one of Solina's hands in her own and squeezed it gently, Solina looked at her, tiredness etched on her face.

"My dear, you have been through a lot today and must be exhausted. Why do we not take this up tomorrow when you have rested. I can remember my first day, and the weeks after. I had no idea what time of year it was for a while. I know you are disorientated. A good rest will help you think clearer, let us get you to your new rooms and you can rest, dear GrandDader?"

Her GrandMader made sense. By the Gods! Solina looked at her in silence and made to rise. A manservant hesitantly moved towards her, perhaps he heard of the man she fried outside in the basin. Her GrandMader saw her pale complexion,

"Take my arm, dear girl. 'Tis right, let us get you to your chamber. You get a good sleep; it was a taxing day. When you have rested, we can continue with our conversation. There is so much more to tell you. It was good to tell you of your Mader. My spirit is lighter for the memories."

Solina was only too glad to oblige.

I cannot think, why did I say that? She has only been too accommodating in the telling of my Mader. Mader was a twin...

Thinking of rest had her momentarily forgetting her path of thought about the Dragons. She would rest and take up her cause tomorrow.

As she walked down the halls following the servants, she spoke in her mind,

"Do you know where you are kept?"

She heard a faint murmur.

"No, we know we are underground, in a warm cavern. It could be one of the homes of old. We are worn out from this Ritual, two of us have left spirit. They

leave the dead right where they lay. I feel my brothers spirit searching for a way out. You must set us free. There is no time left; you have the power of us. Use it."

"I understand, but I am exhausted right now, I promise I will get you out, just let me adjust to this new life I have. I will find you. I promise you."

"Right here, miss, I mean Ma'am. Umm what address are we to give to you, oh great Ruler?"

The Head Mistress had stopped at a door and was addressing Solina. Trying hard not to look into her eyes, which still glowed gold.

"You will accord my GrandDader the highest of names, High DragonRider, or Supreme Magistrate. She commands complete respect, to disobey her is death."

Her GrandMader let go of Solina's arm reluctantly, Solina was wondering to herself if Dame Metina was going to sleep in her room as well.

"I will be close by, my dear. This is a large adjustment for you, given your upbringing. I always kept an eye on you. You will be safe here; I will place extra guards at your disposal. Anything you need or want to know; it will be provided for you."

She must have read Solina's expression, Solina thought she better try to keep a neutral expression and practice it.

"Thank you, GrandMader. I am feeling very tired and cannot think right. I need a rest first, 'tis been a busy day."

Solina bowed to her GrandMader, more out of respect and habit, as this was what she was taught. Her GrandMader bowed back and went to a room across the hall. Solina walked through the door the maidservant opened finding several girls waiting for her, visibly scared at the sight of her.

The maidservant gave them instructions. They were to serve her Majesty the Supreme Magistrate in all things, and she introduced them to the very tired young woman.

"I am sorry, you will have to tell me your names again tomorrow. Right now, I feel like I am going to fall. Which way to a bed?"

Solina moved towards a huge opening in the far wall seeing the largest bed on a dais. It was larger than the room she grew up in. Walking up into it, Solina promptly half fell, rolling into it and closed her eyes.

Tomorrow turned into many, and her voices remained quiet. She forgot for a time, her promise to get them out. Solina had many adjustments to make. Her GrandMader seemed to make every effort to distract her from her Dragons.

Solina's days were full of instructions in the mornings. She was shown the gardens and this seemed to occupy her most afternoons. She intently looked for the one herb she smelled in the chalice she drank from but could not seem to find it. It illuded her, yet she smelled it in the air. The evenings were spent with dinners with family members and met them all. The extended family was large; she started to forget who was who. She especially liked when the littles were allowed to be there. They were not scared of her eyes; she liked their candor and straight-forward questions.

One evening, some time after her inauguration, the night sky lit up with shooting stars and flashes of light. Some would hit the atmosphere, lighting up and it brought everyone outside. She watched most of it, but after awhile became tired and excused herself to retire. The next few days, as the stars passed overhead, everywhere she went, she received looks, until finally she asked the Head of the Household, what had everyone scared?

"There is a Prophecy, High Magistrate. It heralds the advent of the rebirth of Dragons."

He reverently bowed his head as he spoke and then slowly backed away. She was beginning to get used to the reverence.

This declaration had her start, and she swore. She forgot, her GrandMader had proven herself amazingly effective at manipulating and distracting her. This would end or start today.

She thanked him, turning away and strode to the Throne Room where she knew her GrandMader would be,

"There can be no rebirth, without death. We are near death. You must!"

Solina's voices, diminished, regained some of their strength.

"Yes, I am sorry, I will get this done. I feel like it is now or never."

As she entered the Throne room, she saw her GrandMader sitting in the chair given over to her. She rose when Solina entered, reseating herself in the one to the right and down a step. Solina strode up to the chair, turned and spoke to the few there.

"I am going to Temple today. I must give thanks for the gift given to me. I feel remiss in my error of not thanking the Gods. With the advent of these shooting stars, it seems rebirth has more than one meaning. I would love for all who wish to join, come with me, and celebrate this new life."

Solina sat herself down and waited for her GrandMader to protest.

"This is an excellent idea, my dear. We were waiting for you to regain your strength as you will need to walk up the hill. Make it public spectacle, to reaffirm your place. Put substance to these rumours which began about the advent of the Dragons. Show them it is you who are the Dragon!"

Dame Metina busied herself with ordering the Palace servants to make the preparations so they could set off in a bit. She then spent the next couple of hours, boring Solina with daily and future events to come.

Soon they set off, Solina walking beside one of her Uncles, the younger of the two, Solina asked him about their family. He was only too happy to talk about her Mader and his other sister. Alas it was only about their childhood, as this was all he remembered of them. He was but a young adult when they disappeared.

"Your Mader, Shayatin was the quieter of the two. Miiele was the one who always began any trouble, and Shay would end up finishing it or taking the blame.

When they were younger, they were inseparable, but as they became young women, they had different ideas. I do not remember them much around this time, I never saw them much before… I am sorry, I heard about them much later, your Mader was reported to have died and you with her in childbirth. I am quite happy you are in fact alive. I see a quietness around you which reminds me of her. You have the same smile, and while I cannot tell if you have her eyes, I will say you have your very own look about you. Time will tell if you are as stubborn as…"

When she tried to ask about the circumstances which led to their disappearance, he glanced back at her GrandMader, then changed the subject. He talked about the duties one needed to know for each department of lawmaking.

She remembered this walk as vastly different than the one she took less than a month ago. Less people for one thing. Although by the time she arrived at the Temple there were quite a few loitering, and when they saw her, a chant began,

"DragonRider, DragonRider…."

She waved to a few, entering the Temple grounds through the same arch she had before.

I am glad I do not have to go through the same thing again. That took the stuffing out of me. I believe I smell the herb; 'tis on the wind.

Solina wandered around looking at plants and flowers. Observing the beautiful white feather birds also wandering around the green garden. The others mingled, watching her as she wandered. She knew they were not sure of what would happen next. Her GrandMader followed a discreet distance behind her, Solina was not sure why.

Is she protecting me or not letting the others approach?

It had this effect of what she saw from the corner of her vision. The Pader came out of the Temple walking up, taking her hand and kissing the back of it.

"How are you, DragonRider of all DragonRiders?"

He covered up her pulling her hand away with a laugh.

"You have fared well? You remember what I said to you?"

His last question was said very quietly, as Solina's GrandMader was hovering close to them. She observed there must be a dynamic between them. The Pader feared her GrandMader, but for what reason?

"Yes, I am doing fine, dear Pader. Have you fared well?"

"The word has gone out. With the star event in the sky above us, it has sent a ripple out into the world. You have brought new life into our Islands and the Vendar religion, bless you child."

"Thank you, Pader. Please do not tire the newest Dragon out. She came up here to give thanks to the Gods for her gift. The Blessing of the Dragons."

Solina's GrandMader moved up close behind them. For the slightest moment, Solina felt a hint of anger at being interrupted.

She turned to look at her GrandMader, who took one look and backed away slowly with her head bowed. Solina's eyes began to glow with her Dragon slitted eyes. The old woman instinctively knew she had better not cross her newly named GrandDader.

"I would like to see the Dragons please?"

Solina turned, looking at him in the eye, she saw recognition in them before he abruptly denied it.

"I am afraid there are no more. You are the Dragon now."

This she knew was well rehearsed. She began to get more vexed, feeling an anger build inside. She stared at him… not saying anything... For a while, until he saw she was still waiting for his answer. Silent, he dropped to his knees. He knew she saw the lie in his eyes. The air around her began to shimmer.

"I am tired of everyone lying to me. I know there are Dragons, you can stop postering! They are here, and they speak to me. This will stop, no more lies."

Her voice began to rise with her ire.

Solina's eyes glowed brighter, she turned slowly in a circle. Those closest to her, including her GrandMader, backing away slowly, it was baked on their minds the last events.

"Show me where they are. *NOW,*"

This last sentence had the air in front of her turning yellow. It shimmered and flickered to mimic flames but was enough for everyone inside the Temple grounds to fall to their knees. She had her hands out in front of her with her palms up. Solina was not sure of what was happening, and frankly she was getting beyond caring.

Her GrandMader began to protest.

"NO. NOW IS NOT THE TIME. WE WILL SEE THE LIGHT OF DAY. NO LONGER WILL WE BE CHAINED."

The voice which came out of her changed its timber. She unwittingly projected her bond into her voice; it spoke through her. This is the same thing which happened during the ceremony which started it all. This was not her voice and all who heard, bowed their heads.

Solina pointed at her GrandMader who backed down into her kneel. She could not see what they saw. The young woman in front of them, terribly angry, eyes blazing yellow with slitted irises. Whirling around the air in front of her, shimmering yellow, and pulsing to her heartbeat. It surrounded and palpitated with her anger, moving her red hair in currents the others could not feel. She was Air!

It was a wonder none ever witnessed before. All bowed and knelt before her. The air around her, swirling and pulsing. It lent substance to the rumours flying around the Dragon Age began anew. No one answered her, be it from fear or wonder.

"I will find them myself then." She had not expected anyone to answer her, but it would have been nice. She was not going to fry them all… however they did not know this.

Solina stood there with her eyes closed projecting out with her hands. The yellow air shimmering as it left, swirling around and up away from the Temple. She moved with it, turning around as if moved by an invisible string. Solina felt a heartbeat, vibrating through the air, moving closer as she faced the smoking mountain to the Northwest.

She opened her eyes, turning back to face the crowd still on their knees.

"I will have a horse please. And I will take a dozen guards, no more. You can stay here. This is my order."

Looking directly at her GrandMader, knowing Dame Metina had her own agenda all along. Her eyes had not stopped their craziness, and her GrandMader looked a bit frightened. Solina thought it might do her GrandMader some good to be put in her place. Solina was not sure exactly what that place was. Solina was new to life higher up in the Palace. It was more opulent than where she grew up in the Church in the lower city, but in some ways, it was the same. Solina's mind was whirling with her eyes, she spoke out before she could forget.

"GrandMader, if you can send down to Nashta Church for a woman named Sheyna, I would like her to be one of my attendants. Have her placed in her own room and see she is fed and bathed at her consent. If I need her, I will send for her. Please do this right away, and all will remain here in the Temple until I come back."

"Yes… High Dragon. It will be as you wish."

For the first time since being in the Palace, she felt like she had control of her life. Not she did not before, but with her drinking the elixir, being pulled one way or the other, Solina found stepping up and voicing her decision had everyone listening. She knew her purpose was her Dragons. Yona told her it was so, however, being here in the moment, made it all real. It was a heady experience, and she swore to herself she would not misuse her rise to power. That is not what she wished. If anything, she wanted companionship, friends who would listen, voicing their own opinions and listening to hers.

Solina mounted the horse brought to her and motioned for the guards to mount up.

"Captain, you lead the way. I will assume you know the path?"

"Yes, High Dragon. If you will follow me. Kallen, you, behind the High Dragon, the rest follow behind. Look sharp men! Hie, hie!"

It was a worn path, bare rock in some areas, but a path, none the less. The path wide in some areas, others it was single file. She saw more from the back of the horse and wondered why she had not come up here before. The view from up here was beautiful. Solina saw the lower city, the edge of the sea and part of the next township on the North end of the Island, and all the busyness between.

After some time, they arrived at an indentation close to the rock face, mid way up the mountain. They turned into a flat area which dipped toward the mountain and lost the view she was watching of the coast. She watched to where the Captain stopped in front of her. Set into the face of the mountain before her were two exceptionally large doors. Made of a black wood, strapped in black metal, some areas showing signs of rust. The frame was seamless rock, looking as though it was natural formed, and the hinges looked bolted tight.

She dismounted; the rest of the men followed suit.

"DragonRider. This is it. Let me take your mount. Kallen, have the men fan out. Watch the path."

She walked up to the door, noting it was sealed shut. There was no lock, no handle, nothing to indicate it was meant to open. She placed her hands upon the door, feeling the door pulse with a heartbeat. For a small moment she wondered how the Temple workers entered and realized there must be a smaller door they used. These doors looked as though they would vanish into the side of the mountain left unattended. Well… That would not do anymore. The young Captain followed behind her and watched her every move.

"Stand back."

"Men, you heard her. Stand back! High Dragon?"

Solina walked away from the door, then turning to face it. Lifting her hands in front of her, she closed her eyes and tried mentally to move them against the doors. The air which coloured her thoughts was there, and it moved pushing against the doors. It was not working, she felt resistance, as she tried to push forward. The horses began to get restless; they felt the energy swirling around.

"Further back, please. Hold on to the horses."

"Yes, High Dragon. Men, further back. High Dragon, the doors look solid. Almost as if formed this way."

"This is Blackwood is it not?"

"Yes, Ravenwood to be exact. 'Tis the hardest wood in our world. It is used for its obvious capabilities. 'Tis what makes it desirable to most shipbuilders, it withstands the very tempests. Our redwoods are almost as strong; our ships can hold their own against the seas and high winds."

Nothing. She tried again. Solina heard and registered the last few words of the Captains sentence.

"You better stand further back, Captain."

Feeling her anger rise, she thought of pushing the doors down, bringing the might of a strong wind against the solid entrance. Still keeping her eyes closed, she drew in her breath and reached up into the sky, using her arms and hands. She pulled in with her arms, as though pulling down a branch of a tree, and drawing in the winds swirling around her, she threw it at the doors with all her thoughts. Solina blasted the doors with a whirlwind of such strength the men could not hold onto the screaming, scared horses. They pulled their heads up, snatching the reins out of the hands of their minders. Taking off down the path, pushing each other, and galloping as fast as they could. Some of the men ran after them, once the Captain made a motion for them to do so.

The doors exploded inward, then outward and shattering into splinters. The pieces landed around her flying and puncturing the ground. The men closest behind her backed away, as some of the pieces landed right in front of them. Even with the doors being hundreds of years old, Ravenwood still held its strength, it was impenetrable. Her winds shattered the wood to splinters, broken down to the very life rings and one barely saw those in the darkness of the wood. Such was her anger, or determination in this circumstance.

At the shattering of the doors, the air visible to the eye, began to billow out, mid height of her person. Solina stepped back as it rushed at her person! The air was so foul coming out of the hole the doors covered, one saw the Dark haze of putridness, billowing out the top of the opening into the night air. It leaked out and dissipated into the sky. Casting out on the wind currents not unlike the smoke coming out of the top of the mountain above them.

She stood there on shaky legs, trying not to fall. It had taken a bit of her energy and her anger was diminished. Curiosity now crept in. Solina stood there, looking into the gaping maw of Darkness, searching with her mind and eyes.

She focused her gaze inward into the blackness until she saw the low glow of two gold orbs reflecting back at her.

CHAPTER 17

Atin

Let Fire Cleanse the Spirit

The next morning came all too soon, Atin slept solidly through another storm again. Once Atin stepped outside, she knew her Pader was not going pearling with her. The storm raged all night, and wreaked havoc on the flora and fauna outside. Broken branches off the largest trees lay everywhere.

"The boat needs repairs, and it is my number one priority."

As this was their only way off the Island they lived on, she valued his logic.

"I will take Tarik with me, I do not need all the helpers, you need them more. We will be all Day and if we find many, which I believe we will, we may stay overnight and return tomorrow."

Her Pader nodded his assent, already heading to the boat which had numerous branches covering it. Selim jumped on the bow and was handing them to the younger children to take to the burn piles. Atin watched her Da walk away from her, she saw the sickly brown aura surrounding him, and shuddered. She knew he was ill. He could not hide it as well as he used to. Even without her ability to see his aura, one knew by his listlessness and the tired look around his eyes, he was feeling something.

I wish I could do something. Perhaps I will need to take the boys to Peli for medicine. If the three of us can manage the skiff... We may have to, hopefully not for a few weeks yet. I still need to gather more pearls. Should I stay and help here? Hmmm, I will get Tarik and get those pearls. There should be plenty from last nights storm.

They would sail in three weeks or so, and as she walked into the hut to find her little brother, she resolved to gather the most she could, so she could buy her Da the best of care.

"Come on little brother, let us get moving. The seas are churned up enough, let us not let them settle before we attack. If we find many today and fill our baskets, then we come back and help with the mess here. Let us make haste. I am sure the storm surfaced a lot; we must get there and reap the benefits."

She ruffled his head of hair as he tried to duck. "Must you do that?"

His words of protest were spoken with a smile, so she knew he did not mind his sister bugging him.

"Until you grow taller, or can run faster, yes! Grab another basket, we may need it."

They set off to the North shore where there were caves. In one she regularly hid her canoe. The small boat looked like it shifted inside the cave and was wet. It must have been covered by crashing waves. She may have to find another spot to lay it in, higher up to protect it more. Atin had a few other caves in her mind she would have to check out again. They retrieved the canoe, looking it over, a habit her Da instilled in her. The boat was essential to their survival on the Islands. They both got in, setting off for her favorite place on the Islands. The third Island up was small, but the coves seemed to reap the biggest and best pearls. This was the Island where she fed her own private spot. Not that she owned it, but she knew every nook and cranny and felt a kinship for the place where she could let her guard down.

Atin was diving for half the day, surfacing with another haul, when Tarik rushed down to the shore. His last trip to her cove, he sent another batch of empty shells into the shoals, their inhabitants ruffled but intact. He did not wait for her to emerge and waded into the shallows.

"Atin, Atin, there is a boat approaching your cove. I hid, I do not think they saw me and I do not know who they are. I hurried here as fast as I could."

He was wheezing, trying to catch his breath.

"What did it look like, how many men?"

Atin dropped her net down into the water between two rocks, hopefully the tidal current did not pull it back out before she could return. There were a couple large shells of an odd shape and colour, she knew there would be something special in there to retrieve.

"Two, and she was a single sail."

She left the shore and they ran through the sparce brush separating the two shores, careful to not disturb the odd nest birds made. She memorized the path between, and as she got closer, ducked to not be seen from the water. Tarik followed closely behind her, almost stepping on her heels at one point.

Ducking down behind the last line of rocks lining the shore, she peered around to see a small single-sail boat with two men. One was undressed for diving and had a net in his hand. They were going to pearl in her cove! No! This was not going to happen! She stepped out and waved at them, her brother trying to hold her back by the arm.

"Do not sister. Can't you see they are armed?"

"Let me go. No, they cannot farm my spot."

She yelled out at them to stop; this was her cove. They laughed back at her and yelled back.

"Try and stop us, girl."

By this time, she was waist deep and ready to dive. Her fury was up! She did not know, but Tarik saw. Her eyes began to shine, her irises glowing with a sea blue glimmer. He backed off from trying to stop her, leaving the shallows to stand on the shore. One man dove into the shallows and the other began mocking her.

"This is my cove; you have no business here. Your haul is mine by rights."

"Like hell it is, you do not own this place. We will take what we find, go away little girl."

"How did you find this?"

"Everyone knows you have a special place, looks like we found it, by Vandric."

"Get out of here, or I will…"

"Or you will what?"

Atin was getting angry, not thinking about what she would do when she got to the boat. She knew they would not leave here with any of her pearls. She worked for years to meticulously transfer the larger shells she caught on the other side over to this side. It was getting time to search and harvest soon.

They would not reap the benefits of all my hard work. Not if I can help it.

She was preparing to dive and swim out to the boat when her brother yelled to look to the water.

"Look Atin, you do not want to go in there, look man-eaters."

There was a group of fins homing in on the boat. The man saw Tarik's pointing and turned to see fins. There were at least twenty, not a sight one saw on any average day. He began to haul on the rope his companion descended with, but to no avail, the fins disappeared and then churning around the boat and the water turned red.

The man frantically brought up the end of the rope. It was chewed through at the end. He hastily began opening his sail. The fins resurfaced on her side of the boat heading towards her. She stood there, hands trailing in the water. Tarik was yelling at her, but she did not hear. The fins came closer until she saw the gaping maws of the sharks. They circled around her, one or two butt their sides against her, but not one took a chomp. The man stopped his rigging to look back, his mouth agape, before he renewed opening his sail.

She dipped down into the water on her knees and placed her head under the murky water, the sharks swimming in the shallows, churning up silt. She thought a big thank you to the great beasts, asking they escort the man all the way back to the wharf, not letting him stray. They swam off flanking the boat on both sides, as the wind picked up in the man's sail. He cleared the protectiveness of the cove and sped off.

She stood up wading out of the shallows, Tarik was shaking, fear or adrenaline, and could not contain himself.

"What did you do? Why are your eyes glowing? Those sharks did not touch you. Did you command them? Like the turtle?"

He asked her so many questions on the way back, she shook her head so hard her neck was beginning to hurt.

"I do not know, little brother, I asked them to follow the boat back. I was so mad at my cove being discovered, I believe they thought I wanted the other dead. Are my eyes really glowing?"

"Not anymore. By the Gods! Wait until I tell Mader and Pader, they are going to think this is sooo amazing!"

"Please do not. Oh wait, you will tell anyway. Let us get some more pearling done. I do not wish to return empty handed. We may need all we find."

They arrived back at the other side and she dove in to look for her net, which was taken out aways by the tide. The next couple of hours were spent diving and divesting shells of their treasures. So many assorted colours and a large quantity. She was glad she thought to bring extra baskets. The past storm churned up a lot of shells and the team of siblings made fast work. The odd shaped shells she found in the first net full, yielded some unusual, shaped pearls, and a unique colour. Atin knew those would be bought by the stranger from Aram. Tarik hounded her all afternoon with questions, until she finally asked him to desist, she did not know exactly what she had done.

"Please stop, your questions are hurting my head. Let us get home, we have more than enough today. I am worried about Da, he looked tired today."

"He almost capsized the skiff the other day. He let go of the tiller. I was hard pressed to grab it. He said he felt faint. What is wrong with Da?"

"I am not sure. He does look very tired. Has he given you any other reason to suspect he is not feeling well?"

"Just his strength is lacking. He cannot haul up the nets fast. I must slow the pace down and we have lost many a fish for it."

"I was wondering about the amount. It seems to be…less of late. Let us get this last netful done, then return. I admit, I am worried. I do not wish to stay the night."

"I agree."

The sun was heading to the horizon when she stopped for the day, both had filled four baskets full of pearls. The motherload! Never has she found so many in such a brief period of time. She never wondered why she always found them. Atin would hear others at the market complain about having days where they were lucky to find a handful. She always found some! She instinctively knew which ones to take when she was under the deep.

They paddled back to the North shore of their Island and stashed the boat, having a slow trek back to their home. The baskets proving to be heavy. They had not placed them down when her Mader emerged from the hut, her facial expression of worry. Atin's hair on the back of her neck stood up.

"What is wrong, Mader?"

"Your Da is not feeling well. He was working on his boat, coming back to the hut this afternoon, he collapsed." Crying, her eyes red from previous crying, she was wringing her hands, both not good signs.

"I was waiting for you to return. I am not sure if you should attempt a trip to the mainland for medicine. He has not been complaining, but I know something is bothering him for some time."

Her Mader looked so worried, both Atin and her brother dropped their baskets at the doorway rushing in.

Her Da was on his back, sleeping on the bed mat. His expression looked so peaceful, but his skin had pallor. Atin watched and an aura began to form around him, sickly green and brown. Her Mader was asking a question and touched Atin's arm. It shook her out of her reverie.

"What is wrong with you? I asked you how your day was."

Tarik jumped right in, telling his Mader everything about their day. His excited voice kept rising their Pader woke up to hear the bulk of his narrative. She kept looking at her Pader, and he at her. When Tarik finished, he asked in a quiet voice, wavering.

"Is what Tarik saying truth?"

"I did not mean for the man to die; I did not ask this of them. They seem to listen to my thoughts, like the turtle. As long as I am in water, I seem to be able to communicate somehow."

"You should have seen her eyes, Pader, they glowed blue!"

Atin forgot that part.

"It was so wonderous! They glowed and the sharks did her bidding, but she did not speak to them. They swam around her and bumped into her. You should see their teeth! I saw from where I was! They are huge!"

Tarik had obviously gotten over any fear he entertained about his older sister.

"Da, you are not feeling well? You fell?"

Any attempt to divert attention, she took it.

"I lost my spirit there for a moment and fell. I am not feeling too energetic these last two months."

He closed his eyes for a moment. Atin looked at her Da and then at her Mader.

"Then I guess I should not tell you I see an aura around you, I knew a couple of months ago something was wrong. I was afraid to mention it."

Her Mader gasped, looking thoughtful for a moment.

"You speak to water animals, you see auras, you stay underwater longer than the rest of us. There is a new DragonRider in the Capital of Pelin'Dun, She spouts fire, and her eyes glow! What do you think Soren, our Dader's eyes glow, think you we have a DragonRider as well?"

She gazed down at her husband, who opened his eyes and pursed his lips.

"It would certainly explain a few things,"

Here he began coughing so hard he sat up. Atin saw red at the corner of his mouth.

"Da! Quick, bring some water."

Atin reached him first bringing the wooden cup her Ma brought to his lips, and he gratefully sipped at the nourishment.

"I was worried you would think I was not right in the head, but I see you entertaining these wild thoughts, and mayhap you are not right! How is it you think these things have anything to do with being a DragonRider?"

She stood to face her Ma.

"You know the stories we told you. They used to be common knowledge, now stories to be told. Word from the city, saying a young woman, has partaken of the ceremony and has some qualities you have shown. She is but one of six Riders. Six, Atin! Think about it. You have water abilities, she may be one of air, or of purity. Others speak the Age of Dragons are upon us. We may live secluded, but it does not mean we do not keep up on the news which travels around."

Her Ma knelt at her Da's bedside. He tried to move himself up but could not and began to cough again. She gave him more water, Atin saw the water was a pink in the cup, as he lay down and closed his eyes.

"Well, I think you both are not thinking straight, in the wake of Da's sickness. Let us get him better first."

Atin and her siblings brought in the baskets which all exclaimed over. She sent the younger ones to wash and sort them while she helped her Ma with cooking chores and chatted to her about her Da. They had their evening meal, talking about the upcoming trip to the main Island,

"I will take the boys, the three of us might be able to manage her. If Da does not rise, I will take them. For now, I will sleep in here with all of you, if the boys could help me…"

Atin and her brothers walked to the hut she was using, and they helped her to carry her things back. It was done quickly and quietly, all thinking about their Da, who coughed, while not waking. She sat for a while, watching him, the aura looking more putrid and swirling around his body. She thought about what she was seeing.

'Tis like a cloud, and hovers around him. It seems to be part of him, 'tis attached to his skin…like fog… moisture. It seems to be centered around his chest. Hmmm, what does this mean? I may have to leave for Peli sooner if it changes colour. Does the colour mean something? To me it looks bad, I know he is sick, so this colour must correspond. I see the colours around my family and it brings me joy. Their colours are beautiful. So, it must have something to do with our spirit. Is Da's spirit ill?

Atin told her Ma, who was tucking in the little girls into their mats, she may have to leave on the morrow if Da did not get better.

"I will inquire and get some medicine for Da. Do not worry, Mader, mayhap all he needs is a good rest."

"That is appreciated, Atin. The herbalist will give you some tonics, perhaps some other items. You would have to relay Soren's symptoms to her."

"The pearls can pay for it. We can afford to get Da better."

The more she tried to reassure her Mader, the more she knew it was not something a good rest would disappear. Just common sense, not her aura sight telling her, Da was sick with something serious.

In the dark early morning hours, they were all woken by her Da's coughing, which sounded worse. Atin was having an underwater dream in which the turtle was trying to communicate something to her. The turtle kept hiding behind her, from an octopus who kept trying to envelope them in a cloud of ink. It was the same colour as the aura around her Da. Octopus ink was darker in the waters. She was puzzled, and the turtle kept bumping into her. Atin kept turning around to see what the turtle was doing. She woke with a gasp to hear, her Da's attempt to gather a breath. Atin's legs were tangled up in her blankets, and it took a moment to free them. Atin did not like what she heard. It sounded raspy and shallow. Her Da was struggling with his breaths. She bounced up, her Mader was already tending to him.

"Ma, I have an idea. Crazy one, but can we pick Da up and get him in the ocean."

Her Ma looked up at her, seeing her Dader's eyes in the dark glowing blue. This alone convinced her to listen.

"Atin… Tarik, Selim, grab your Da's legs. One each. Do as your sister instructs. Atin, what would you have us do?"

"I am not certain. Let us get him into the shallows."

Atin, her Mader and the two oldest boy's half carried, half dragged her semi-conscious Da to the shore and then into the shallows. The moon was full, a clear night so they saw what they were about. He was half floating and Atin took him by the shoulders, walking him out a little further. His breathing was still shallow and he lapsed into unconsciousness.

"Just hold onto your spirit, Da. Let me try something."

Atin whispered into her Da's ears as she guided him by the shoulders into the calm surf. It was calm, hardly a ripple against the beach sands. She closed her eyes, thinking about the water, the flow of it, how their bodies were full of it. She remembered her dream. Atin did not notice the glow of the water around her and her Da. Her Ma and brothers moved closer to the shore and were observing her work her miracle. The waters glowed blue all around the duo in a wide circle. Atin thought to pray. It was all she could think of doing.

Ilyan, I humbly ask for your guidance. My Pader is ill, I know not what, but I would like him not to perish. He is sad, sad my brothers left to go off to war. It has festered until he has gotten ill. If you could guide my hand, I would very much appreciate trying to rid him of the energies surrounding him. Like a stream flows downhill, taking with it silt, the octopus letting go of ink, I imagine this sickness flowing out of my Pader. If you will it.

Then the spectators saw a brown staining around Soren. He was leaking stain as if an octopus, it flowed out and hovered around the two, the waters soon invaded, thinning it with its ebb and flow. It soon dissipated around the semi-conscious man. Atin opened her eyes to see the disappearing ink stain in the fading blue glow of the water around them. She watched it fade into a murky mess eventually becoming clearer. Her Da opened his eyes, gazing up, he saw the glow in her eyes diminish.

"Oh, child. Soren, my heart! Oh, my."

Atin's Ma could not contain herself; her tears changed from sorrow and fear to joy. Her Mader waded into the shallows, embracing her Da as he stood up. Soren looked at his wife and kissed her, wiping her tears away. They stared at Atin in awe and asked her what she did.

"I prayed to the Goddess Ilyan, I asked the sickness to leave you as though ink leaving the octopus, water flowing from a stream."

He moved forward slowly, embracing her in a tight hug. She hugged him back, and she felt the strength in his embrace.

"Oh, child, many blessings to you. I thought my spirit would be taking one last swim, I feel weak but so much lighter for it. You must entertain the thought of being a DragonRider. For now, keep this to yourself, people would learn of this, and the Namanists or Aramites would try to kill you. You must try to see the new DragonRider."

The three walked out of the water and into the hut together. The little ones still tired from the early interruption. Those who were wet changed out of their soggy clothing. Her Ma made hot tea. Those who did not fall asleep right away partook, then Atin lay down her head and fell into a dreamless sleep.

The next day she woke to her family bustling about, realizing it was mid morning. Her Da was sitting at the table talking to her Ma, stopping when she rose from her bed.

"Do not let me stop you from talking about me." She spoke with a huge yawn, "Why did you let me sleep so late?"

"Well, as a matter of fact, we tried to wake you, but you were sleeping like you had no spirit."

Her Da was alert, his smile tired looking but the pallor in his skin had left.

"We were speaking about the huge haul of pearls you collected. Not everything is always about you."

Her Da teased her and Atin knew he was feeling better.

"I think we should have a few days of minimal chores. A few days of enjoyment. You and your brother have reaped enough pearls; people will think we stole them. What troubles you, Atin? You look like you swallowed a sour peach."

"I forgot about our visitor. I let him go. We will not go unpunished for this."

"We will deal with this when we must. We have a little more than a few days before we head back to the main Island. Lots of preparations to make. There will be more storms, it will be winter soon, but in case they come to us, let us enjoy our family time, eh, girl? I will tell you again, I am eternally grateful for healing me."

"Da, I am not sure I did anything. I prayed to the Gods for your spirit. They answered me."

"They may well have, but your Mader tells me, the waters glowed blue and my skin leaked the illness."

"Yes. Atin's eyes glowed from the time she awoke, to the time you rose from the waters. She closed her eyes, and your skin looked as though an octopus, trapped in one of your nets."

"I saw the remnants when I looked into my Atin's eyes. I thought I was going to be given over to the fishes, lass. You are one of these Riders, you must see the Rulers. When we go, I will find a way to get you to the Palace. I am not sure how to approach; they have not taken kindly to 'rogue' Dragons. Others have claimed to be and have never been seen again. I would hate to lose you, so soon after my lads."

"Soren, this will not happen. Atin is one of these Dragons. She will have a huge task ahead of her. It will work out; the Universe will provide."

"You are always right, dear wife. Let us have a day to enjoy ourselves, why do we not have a fun day digging up clams? Show the girls how to find them, let them get dirty. They will have fun, and then they will have exceptionally good sleeps. We can feast on the rewards."

"Oh, you! Turning clamming into fun. Let us. I will require your assistance with the youngest. She is quite a handful."

"Give her a stick and she can get dirty as well, and if she eats sand, oh well. Let her, it will only come out the other end. I will deal with this. You can have an afternoon nap, and mayhap, I will rub your shoulders for you later in the evening."

"Oh, no you will not, Soren. Your back rubs always end up with a baby nine months later; I will take the nap though." Atin tried not to blush at her Mader's remarks, but she grinned, happy to see her parents laughing again. It was almost a tragedy, yet Atin wondered what exactly she did. *Thinking or praying? I can think thoughts to the denizens of the seas. Can I heal? Am I one of these Dragon-Riders, of history? What task will I have? Will it take me away from my family? I should enjoy today, there may not be many of these playful times again.* They had a pleasant day, the littles playing games.

"Come play, Atin."

"Yes… Kami, do not eat that… Let Ma cook it first."

"Atin, the only way Kami will learn if she eats it. Then she will not like what it does to her stomach.'

"But Da…'tis raw. She will be sick."

"Atin, we let you find out for yourself. Kami is much like you; you were sick for no more than a full day. See, Kami has popped it in her mouth, sand, and all."

"Oh, Ma. How long?"

"Oh, I will think it will probably take about an hour. First, she will throw it up and then it will come out the other end. You tore off all your clothes and ran around naked. You were quite happy to do so, every time you had to go, you just ran into the surf and washed off your bottom. I just sat and watched."

"You did?"

"Yes. I had Medea to help me. I do miss her; she will be happy in her new home? She seemed happy?"

"Oh, yes, Ma. You know she loves Hess and he loves her. It was the perfect match."

"Oh, where are the men headed? Your Da, he cannot let the opportunity pass by."

"What, Ma?"

"I am sure one of your brothers asked a question. Now your Pader will talk on and turn it into a lesson."

"Well, let him. He must instruct the boys. 'Tis not like Zohan is here. I miss him."

"So do I, Atin. Your Da does most of all. He is saddened by all the lads heading off. That is why he became ill; he let it fester; he did not tell me until it had taken hold. We have spoken about it, at length now. He has come to terms with it. So, I agree, let him talk. Now I am going inside, can you watch the girls?"

"Yes, Ma." Atin sat and watched the girls, sure enough Kami started to let go of the raw clam she had eaten. Both ends. Atin consoled her in between. She listened to her Da, instructing the boys, they crawled all over the boat. Atin smiled as she knew exactly what her Da was saying, she had once learned the same. Once

Kami was feeling a bit better and washed herself in the shallows, Atin wrapped her in a linen and carried her into the hut. She snuggled her sister while her Mader went to gather the other girls.

Soon the little girls were resting and Atin went to help her Mader with the meal. Atin learned a few things from her Ma, and when the conversation led to marriage, Atin could not hold back.

"Mader, I do not want a joining. I am happy with things as they are. If Da were to lose spirit, who would look after you and the littles?"

Her Mader gave her a hug,

"Your Da and I already discussed this before you cured him, we are good to have you a few more years until your brothers are old enough to take over. You will hear no more on this subject from us. However, if you are a DragonRider, you may get visitors and not friendly ones, so we must prepare for the day you may leave. Your Da is worried for you. The man you let leave may have told others. Guaranteed he has! This may bode ill for us. We must move in the way the Universe presents itself. Everything which happens, happens for a reason, and we cannot change our path."

The next two days passed by quickly, nets were mended, pearls were polished and bagged according to size and colour. Soren deciding both boys and Atin would go to the main Island, as they needed more bodies for the large haul they would be selling. The day arrived and they set sail in a choppy sea, clouds swirling dark on the horizon. Atin's Mader knew there was a possibility they may have to turn back if the storm headed towards them. She and the littles were as prepared as they could be. Halfway there, Atin placed her hand in the water, for a time. Soon her Da and brothers saw they had an escort for the remainder of the voyage. A pod of whales. Atin just smiled at her Da.

"No chance we will drink the deep today."

"Ah girl, no showing off, now!"

"Da, look, there is a great Gray! Atin, you called them?"

"I asked, Tarik… not called. One does not tell. One asks, 'tis how we live with other creatures. We cannot live by demanding."

The whales veered off at the mouth of the port, and the boys docked the boat at the wharf they usually docked at. Her Da got out and her brothers made fast the boat while Soren went to chat with the Dock Master. He returned with a few guards, telling Atin and her brothers they would go to the inn where they were to meet the Aramite.

Carrying their pearls with them, Atin was glad her Da thought to hire one of the heftier guards to escort and watch over them. He knew the value of what they had. Atin made sure to keep her straw hat low on her head, no point in drawing attention to herself. They settled into a darker corner of the inn and Soren sent a message boy to run to the Aramite's residence to invite him to the inn.

A half hour passed before Kaisan came, sitting down across from Atin and her Da,

"I have heard interesting things these past few days, about your Dader,"

Kaisan did not bother to greet them, just stated this fact.

"She can command sea animals! He claimed he had an escort of the same man eaters which killed his brother."

"Are you sure he was not drunk on sea water? Everyone knows what it can do to the brain if drunk, maybe this is what killed his brother."

Soren stated this nonchalantly, Kaisan took a long look at her and her Da. Atin lifted her head and gazed back at this man who was not treating them differently. She was not sure what she expected. Certainly not the feeling she was drowning, while looking into the man's eyes! She wished nothing more than to get to know this man. Even if he was from another land. His voice broke her out of her musings.

"You are probably right, eh. Let us see what treasures you brought me."

Atin quietly asked, "In what colour were you looking?"

He smiled at her, and she smiled back. She felt like she was floating on the ocean, weightless.

"We have a few oddities I thought you may be interested in. I thought first of you when I saw them."

She brought out a bag of oval shaped pearls. They were odd enough they seemed to absorb the colour of whatever light was presented. Inside the inn they were a darker hue of colour but reflected the gold of the candlelight.

"These are precious, and interesting enough."

Thus, she and the stranger began their haggling game while her Da and brothers sat back, enjoying the meal and conversation. Her Da let her handle this transaction. He thoroughly enjoyed listening to his Dader conduct her business with a hard-to-bargain with stranger. It made him smile to see she would not back down to anything the man from Aram said to throw her off. After a while, Kaisan sat back saying he met his match and would not bargain any more, he would pay what she wanted.

"I give in, your Dader, Atin is particularly good at getting her price. She has also the largest and most satisfying collections I have ever seen. My benefactor has demanded more, so this benefits both of us. I look forward to the next selection you come back with. I thank you both for this interlude and wish you well."

Kaisan bought half of their goods. As they were about to part, her Da spoke to the Aramite. "Would it not be better if you were to meet at our family home?"

At this Atin looked closely at her Da. One did not simply invite a stranger to one's home, but if this was better for business, so be it. "If that is what you are desiring, it can be arranged. Does once a month sound plausible?"

"Yes, we reside on the fourth Island which is our home. We need not worry about hiring guards or unnecessary gossip."

"Am I also to assume you would like reports of any news from the city?"

"That would be an extra bonus, if you were to provide such."

"I could certainly sail there until I leave for the homeland."

Atin knew it was to keep from exposing her to the ridiculous gossip Kaisan mentioned was floating around. The Aramite excused himself, the family rose and headed back to the boat. Atin felt a loss after her conversation with Kaisan, it was the most conversation she had ever with a man. Not related to her.

As they approached the skiff, a crowd had gathered. Parting to let the family pass, she heard the rumblings.

"There she is,"

"Blonde witch"

"DragonRider"

Her Pader turned to the crowd, "Are you wanting the pearls? If so, we have many distinct colours."

"You had best be wary."

"They are coming to get you."

"We know what you did, lass."

"What colours do you have?"

Knowing things could change instantly, her Da drew everyone's attention back to the pearls, taking over the selling, while she quietly sat behind her brothers, head bent and hat on her head.

He finished selling the last bag, and their coins filling a basket, when a commotion up the street drew everyone's attention. Sure enough, a regiment of Palace guards were marching in their direction. Atin peeked up knowing life was about to change again. Standing up and holding onto her Da's arm.

"You knew this would happen, did you not? If I do not come back, you head home. Do not let Mader worry."

Moving in front of her Da, they waited until the guards drew near and stopped. The crowd parted standing out of the way. A few of the more boisterous ones were loudly calling for justice. The Captain looked at her and her Da,

"Are you Soren? Is this woman your Dader?"

"Yes. I am Soren. This is my Dader, Atin."

"I am to escort her to the Palace. She is wanted for questioning."

A calmness overcame Atin, letting her breath out slowly, she lifted her head. The guards and the crowd who lingered gasped. Her eyes glowed, like the Dragon in the Palace above! Except hers were blue like the ocean. The crowd murmured. As she turned giving her Pader and brothers a quick hug, her eyes bright with tears.

"Do not forget what I said, Da. Leave! You have a wealth now that should not be stolen. Get what you need and set off. Do not wait for me, I will be fine."

"I am proud of you, Atin, remember that." Her Da had tears in his eyes. He was losing another of his brood. He fully expected not to see her again.

"I love you, Da."

She maneuvered herself into the center of the guards. They began walking up the street to the city gates and beyond. They marched up and up, through another and another gate, always up. Soon they reached a closed gate. It opened as they reached the base of the ridiculously huge door.

As she walked, Atin marvelled at the splendor of the structures. She felt boxed in, having lived her life out in the open wilderness as one would call it. Walking through the streets, she knew she would not be happy being so close to a neighbour. This was a different path than the one they took to the Barracks, but almost as long a walk. Walking through the last gate into what was the Palace of the highest order, she entered a very green garden. It was open and lush with a variety of flowers and shrubberies. She felt like this could be liveable. The Captain and five soldiers remained with her. The others stopped at the gate and the Captain motioned for her to follow him. They went into a large building; she would later learn was the reception room.

Atin went through two very grandiose doors, made of the blackest wood. She could not resist putting her hand out to touch them. She did not see the smile on the face of the person she was to meet. The same person who had done the very same thing several months ago. The Captain cleared his throat, bringing her back to the present. She kept walking, then was distracted by the stained glass on the windows. They were casting prisms of light with many colours on the walls and floors of the hall she was walking in.

Not paying attention to where she was walking, she came to a stop, only because she ran into the back of the Captain she was following.

Hearing a stifled laugh, she looked up at the sound and came face to face with glowing yellow eyes attached to a young woman's face not unlike her own.

CHAPTER 18

Andic

And Reverence Begin Anew

Andic dove into her new life with enthusiasm and some trepidation, not knowing life in a community setting full of men. Adjusting her fear to be less acute, she became more comfortable.

She catered to Kadir, the old man, in the confines of his room, carrying his things when he travelled the halls. She retrieved his meals and was responsible for laundering his robes. This she learned from the novices and initiates who made up the monastery. No one questioned her gender, she shaved her head like all the others, bathing by herself in the confines of her room with a pail and cloth, as per custom. She had a few days of uncertainty she would be found out, but no one questioned her. She observed asking questions when she did not understand something. Speaking slowly in a low voice, and it worked.

She spent her mornings learning a couple letters a day until she could manage rudimentary words progressing a little bit each day. She did not worry or wonder about time passing. Winter solstice came and went; the winter floods came and went. Being high in the desert mountains, one did not see these things. The only indicator she had was an outburst of desert flowers, with the advent of higher water volume.

On one of her trips to the kitchen to retrieve the midday meal, she saw a hive of activity in one of the courtyards. She asked one of the boys her age what was happening.

"This monastery has its own spring fed lake. It is behind us around the cliff, where the land flattens out. I will take you some time, but not until after harvest or we will be put to work and then our Master's would not see us for Days. The lake is quite shallow and the reeds which grow are harvested and brought here. They are peeled for the fibres inside, used to make papyrus, you can learn how we make our own for our scrolls. In good harvest years we take the excess to the city to sell. Our Master says since we are rewriting quite a few scrolls which are damaged, we will be using this year's bounty on our own writings. 'Tis quite the process, watch and learn what you can, next year they will expect you to be part of this whole thing."

She retrieved Kadir's lunch and her own. Chomping on her apple while she watched the stripping and soaking processes, with the addition of a few liquids. She would learn the ingredients later. As she finished her apple looking down for a spot to place it, she saw the lunch she forgot to deliver. She hurried back to his room, apologizing for being so late.

"They are harvesting the reeds, I take it."

"Yes, Master, I have never seen it done. I have only seen the result. It looks very time consuming."

"It is, do not linger out there too long, or I will have to get my own lunch, tee hee." Kadir was always laughing at his own humour; she did not know half of what he was talking about.

With his patient instruction she learned to read rudimentary sentences, the more she accomplished, her Master set her more tasks and the better she read. Soon she would read over his shoulder, as the scrolls her master was reading were becoming harder for him to focus. His eyes could not fashion the script closeup. One day she had an epiphany.

"Master, you have taught me our language, yet we speak Collective Speech."

"Ah, you see the difference. The Collective Speech, is the language spoken by all."

"But not all learn it."

"You are correct. It is mostly spoken by those who travel. Dignitaries, Ambassadors, and Rulers. We were once all Collective Speech. It is still spoken in Peli, the Islands."

"What happened?"

"We broke away. Our FirPader, when he became God, decreed we would have our own language. It was to facilitate a way to communicate with his Greatness. We have similar words with the Collective Speech, but many are different."

"The word for all the ruling bodies in all lands are the same."

"Yes. Our language is used when one does not want another of a different land to understand, such as secrets."

"So, tomes are understood by all?"

"For the most part. Our history is written in our language, much like Du'Lanay. All understand Pelin'Dun's speech and written language."

"That makes it easy for some, harder for others."

"You learn all you can. The only languages we have little knowledge of are those of Lanthia and the Wanderers have a guttural version of Layanese. We have some written Lanthian works, which have stumped many. It is not widely spoken. I can certainly teach you what I know. The Wanderers language is not a written one, so I have nothing to teach you. I have never heard it myself."

"So, learning all languages is essential to finding differences and creating balance."

"Oh, you are wise now. How would you go about doing so?"

"Well, if Pelinese was the original language, would it not be optimal to have this spoken by all?"

"Well, you are welcome to convince the FirPader, next time you visit him."

"I might just do that."

Andic smiled at her mentor. He was her kind of sarcastic, and they worked well together. Kadir sometimes would give her a task to do for him, which had her silently questioning why she was there. It was like he dared her to fail. Or get caught. She mastered the mannerism of the perfect student. Andic was fearful she would be found out. Kadir finally told her she had passed the test.

"What test?"

"You have been humbled, have you not? You came here to learn, and by humbling yourself, others are more willing to teach."

"Is this what I am doing?"

"You give your audience what they are looking for. You read what it is others need and then you give them such. One way is to repeat the last three words of the conversation given to you as to make them converse more and to make you seem engaged."

"To make me seem engaged?"

"Precisely. Ahhh, you catch on quick."

"I catch on quick? How so?"

"Run along, find my dinner, and get my robes cleaned."

"Yes, Master Kadir. Would you like a second scone tonight?"

"Why certainly. How did you know?"

"I have my methods."

Andic would sometimes get an extra portion. She would find herself ravenous, the meals here were different, but meager. In stating Kadir wished extra, which he did not, she could satisfy her belly. Kadir sometimes would not finish his dinners, and Andic was not proud. She let the others think Kadir regained his appetite. It served both well. He did not like others to know the real state of his health. He told her, well, she noticed it and he knew she was a master at knowing without it being spoken.

His health was declining, she had to clean up his body wastes which she could not complain about too much, as she was sure any day someone would find out, she was a girl. His mobility decreased and he spent more time in his rooms or his favorite spot in the garden, which was either in the early morning or late evening. Mid Day was still too hot to do much of anything.

Still, Andic absorbed everything she was given to read, asking questions of Kadir as her nerve boosted her resolve. She was permitted to ask other older mentors, while being careful to observe subservience, keeping her voice low and head bowed. The older men were extremely happy to hear their own voices and be of value to the younger novices. Oft times her questions would turn into sermons or discussions which would last. Once, one lasted three days of debate. Her learning what they knew about prior, had her views as fresh and sometimes controversial, but it made for some interesting discussions.

"The FirPader Akun, he was a younger son? Did he not kill his older brothers?"

"Yes, but he was also ordained by his Pader, to rule."

"You mean he was the favorite?"

"He was ordained…by the living God. He had to ensure his rule was not in jeopardy."

"No. He was the strongest of all the God's offspring. It was his Paders will Akun rule."

"He saved the God's life, which is what happened."

The Masters would argue points, and Andic would listen to their pattering, all the while thinking, the son Akun was the favorite. She would ask them, and would sit back and respectfully listen, as an acolyte would. All the while thinking they knew not of the world outside their Mosque. Only Kadir would have a better insight to some of her more interesting questions. He spent most of his life in Vuz, he left to the Mosque, because to stay would have meant his death.

"Why did you have to leave?"

"I had different ideals. I asked too many questions of my mentors and caused some unrest. I was told to come here or stay and find a knife in my back."

"You had enemies? I find this hard to believe."

"Here, I am no one. There is no hierarchy here. I am but a disciple to the written word. We create the papyrus that all our history is written on. Our history is not complete if it is not remembered. This Mosque alone has tomes from the beginning. 'Tis kept here because temperatures are constant. There are caves in the hill where all secrets are kept."

"Would I be able to see these 'secrets'?"

"You could try, but they are heavily guarded. To be caught means you would be killed. They do not ask questions of why, 'tis forbidden. I cannot even go inside."

"Well, now you have intrigued me. What is so secret, none can enter?"

"You must ask yourself, is it worth your life to try? If you are caught, not only your life but mine also would be forfeit. I ask you to think about not just yourself but others. Even Zenzol may be affected."

"Is it that much of a secret?"

"The FirPader does not rule with a weak hand. He has secrets to keep."

"Was not all this… here before him? The history tomes? Then it was passed on? Makes you wonder what it contains."

"I was told it was valuable to the FirPader. It is not for the lower castes to know. It may be information, or just historical accounts."

"That could be just to throw people off."

"You think it over. While you do so, my dinner would be appreciated."

"Yes, Master, right away. I will be back shortly."

Soon the hint of spring had come. Time for her had flown by, she was kept busy. Andic not only learned to read, write, and speak proper in the tongue of Aram, but had a knack for the Eastern land languages. There were similarities in both, and she took to learning, becoming fluent in all presented to her. Her mentor presented old scrolls he had her rewrite, as some were beginning to deteriorate. She learned about horticulture, laws, wars, history of Aram, history of Pelin'Dun, which she could not get enough of, and a small knowledge of Du'Lanay.

"You are doing very well; I am amazed at how quickly you learn. Sometimes teaching a fresh mind unspoiled by other languages is better than an older one set in their ways. Zenzol did say you had an inquisitive nature and an eye for detail,

I see he was right. Now finish that scroll and you fetch my evening fast. You may then retire."

This monastery studied science as they knew it. Mixing and drying of herbs. The crown jewel of the Pader was an object which had pieces of glass set inside a tube. With it they could see the stars. That spring, every novice was whispering about an object in the sky they could only see with the use of this device. Soon it was an object of dares, to sneak a peek while the monk brothers were not looking. She managed to look several times, as she was a master of sneaking, and saw very clearly the star she observed several months ago. Andic kept this all to herself.

The Red Mosque was not as big as some of the villas of the Obans, but as she moved around, for sometimes at night when she could not sleep, she found there were areas she never knew existed. A few halls opened into caverns into the rock which housed stores and was cooler by far in the heat of the day. She tried to explore, but these areas always had someone present. These areas had their own secrets. Regardless of the time of day, there were guards present. She opted to give up; it was not worth anyone's death to venture inside. Her curiosity abated. She knew the layout of the Mosque within the first month, in her wanderings, it kept her senses honed to her surroundings.

Only the main rooms had elaborate mosaics on the floor. The main worship room was embellished with murals on the walls one of the past brothers spent his lifetime painting. It depicted scenes like no other, very lifelike in detail. She saw veins on some of the leaves of the trees, and the shadows made some of the characters lifelike. She spent a lot of her spare time gazing at it. It was so beautiful.

"Oh, here you are Odan. Master Kin was looking for you. If you have a moment, he would like your assistance on the Book of Prayers for the master copy. He was upset when I left, a page came out while he was handling it and it fragmented into pieces."

"Oh, that is not good. I can certainly come help."

"He was on his knees picking up pieces when I left him."

"He probably wants me to rewrite it then, let's go."

Andic became indispensable to the head documenter, as she had an uncanny memory and could recite tomes she had rewritten. Soon Andic was spending more time organizing the library as it was being rewritten. She managed to get help with old Kadir, as she spent almost all her time sorting, rewriting, and absorbing everything which came across her path. She introduced a method of labelling the scrolls. Through her guidance, in the four months she was there, Andic had reorganized the entire library.

"Master Kin, this tome is fragile. And it has a certain smell. (sniff, sniff) like the smell...of...(sniff), it is of... Safran. Do we have Safran?"

"You have a good nose, Odan. The Safran is kept in the caves. It is valuable and we sell it in the cities. We keep it in the caves, for safeguarding. Once spring arrives, you will be assisting in collecting the blooms."

"Oh, yes, Master. I am almost done rewriting. Is there more to copy?"

"Yes, but you will swear on the Book of Prayers to not speak of what you read or write. It will mean death if you tell others."

"I swear on the FirPader, or the Book of Prayers. This tome speaks of nothing but trade agreements from two hundred years back. Not overly exciting."

"Again, you will not speak aloud what you see in the tomes. 'Tis not for the lesser castes to be knowing."

"Yes, Master."

Not one tome on Dragons or DragonRiders, though. For all her looking, she dare not ask.

I will hazard a guess this is what is inside the caverns. Why else would it be guarded? Is it worth getting caught though? I will have to bide my time. Depending on how long I am here.

She excelled at herbology. Most of what she knew was by visual and her sense of smell, but now she could name the plants and where to find them. She learned about lotions and salves, tonics, and poisons, fresh versus dried, and preserved and pickled. Sometimes she wondered, besides the brothels and the Harem, where she could use all this knowledge.

"Master Kadir. I have been busy copying some of the tomes from the caves. What is so secret about trade agreements, how much silk was sold, and the price of oxen?"

"You must keep this secret; you should not be speaking to me of this. But I will tell you. Look at the whole picture. A country has a good economy, no war. Poor economy, more war. Less men to harvest. Look at the years of the tomes, then cross reference to when we had wars. Who were we fighting with? Silk sales down…war with Du'lanay? The Islands? It is what you read that may not give you the answers, but what is not spoken."

"Why is this such a secret?"

"It gives one time to think of possible ways to change history. Our present FirPader knows this war could cripple his lands. He does not want to be overthrown. It was tried many hundreds of years ago. That is what is in the caves. Our history. He will protect it until his passing."

"What of his heir? Will he care?"

"Akishen will want war. That is what he knows. As for the history, that will be his decision. What he values, is war. The glory of battle, not history tomes. Yet we will persevere, it is our direction, we will protect our FirPader."

"You were sent here by the FirPader? Were you not? He did not like your outspokenness?"

"You are very astute. Yes, I was his son's tutor, I was sent here because I had different opinions than our God, I may have influenced our next one. It was this or embrace death."

"Well, I do not see the value in these tomes of secrets, however, I will not speak my thoughts, I will do as the Masters bid."

"You do well to keep your thoughts to yourself. There may be no value in the present. Perhaps as you travel down your path it will become clear. Knowledge is the key to all life, knowing when to use it, well…that is your choice."

"Thank you, Kadir. I must address writing for the afternoon, I will see you at evening prayers with your dinner."

"Thank you, Odan."

Andic rewrote many scrolls, books, and tomes. She read all and placed it into her memories to be assessed at another time. She did not see the value, but as Kadir said, one day it may make sense. She did see patterns arise, when there were wars, the cost of goods went up. She had to rewrite many scrolls on the expenses of the Harem and some of the Obans, all this information she tucked away.

How is a Harem's silk order even considered a secret? This is a boring account. Silk for all the girls, even... wait! This has been underlined, Orange silk. What is so special about orange silk? Well, I am sure I will find out some day. Now, oh, some herbals. So even poisons are official. These four are toxic plants. Seems one of the past... this is four generations back...wives were deeply knowledgeable. Guess some of this is not so boring.

"Novice Odan, are you finished with that?"

"Oh, yes. Let the ink dry. I am finishing for the day, I will wash out my brush, and when I return, you can have the dry sheets."

"You go and wash, I will gather these pages, I think Kadir was looking for you."

"Right away, Master Kin, I will go."

She copied many lists and books, and catered to Kadir, his mobility was slowing down. He gripped her arm so tight, she was getting bruises, but she said nothing. Andic began to feel her time was getting nigh, time to move along. The feeling persisted and sat in her belly.

Then, one day after rising, she was washing her body bits from the bucket she retrieved the evening prior. Andic noticed her breasts were sore to the touch, and her nipples looked swollen.

I will start wearing a bodice and lace it up tight if these decide to grow. Hopefully, the rest will hold off, my time here is ending.

She began to feel achy by the end of day and overnight she began her courses. Being a monastery full of men, she was not sure how she could hide something like this for long. She snuck out down to the laundry to find herself a linen cloth she could use and returned to bed. Andic woke up like clockwork but feeling not herself.

The next morning, after she cleaned herself up, fashioning a rag of sorts to wear, she went to see her mentor after breakfast taking him his. He was sitting up in bed and she sat by his side. Her mentor had slowly been going blind but could still see shapes and knew it was her.

"Ahh, my young protégé, so glad you are here. You will be leaving us soon. So much to tell you first."

He grinned a silly grin, weaving back and forth in his bed. Andic was not sure she heard him right.

"You are sending me away Master?"

"Well, once they find out who you really are, they will not let you stay."

He grinned even wider and rocked a little bit, side to side. A dribble of drool edged out the corner of his mouth, she reached over with a linen piece to wipe it off.

"And what am I?"

She fully expected him to catch her out, as even she could smell the scent of blood. She started thinking about her escape plan,

"Why, girl, you are a DragonRider! Do you think I did not know? Listen closely, I have not long of spirit left and there are things you need to know and do."

She gasped as he chuckled at his own findings. Laughing aloud he stated,

"I knew you were a girl the first time we met. I thought it would be a good lark, to teach you under everyone's nose. 'Tis not my fault the rest can not see what is before them. Your ability to learn quick, apply what you know, and to see the star everyone is sneaking a peek at through the glass. You spoke of it long before you took your own glance. I do not know what your future is, however, you must follow your path set out before you by divine will. It will guide you, and you must find others who walk with you.

You must go back to go forward! In the great Hall of Knowledge, under the library are catacombs filled with treasure forbidden by Law and State. Great tomes, ancient artifacts of a forgotten age. They speak of Dragons, their Riders, their history, long lost magics. Also, of egos and the problems which went with them. These are best to be forgotten, but if you must, find these tomes, read what you can, before they are destroyed, if they are not already.

There is only one true God. That is what we are taught, but maybe in your lifetime, you will come across diverse faith. Remember, keep your mind open and clear. There is not one kind of right in this world, many good peoples believe in different things. Some of the most faithless are ones to profess loudest. There may be a place in this discord for harmony.

The advent of the star is the Dawn of the Dragons! This much I read. You may be able to find the Prophecy as a whole, but do not expect to. Read, gain knowledge. You already know knowledge is the key to life. Your actions, deeds, what you speak in this lifetime, echoes and reverberates in spirit, as ripples in a still pond. The rebirth of your spirit carries with it deeds of past life.

We have paid for the last deeds and now the pendulum will swing back the other way. In order to step into light, we sometimes embrace darkness. Go now, girl. Go with the blessing of the God, or the blessing of all God's if that is what you believe. If one were to believe there is more than one God, it cannot hurt us in this world, it seems we may need help with the amount of strife we have."

In a way, Kadir sounded as though he knew something yet spoke in riddles. She processed what he was saying,

"You will not give me away, then? The girl portion? The other one seems too fantastical to believe. How does one know anything in this world?"

"It was ordained, written long ago, these events will come to pass. It matters not which God or Gods you believe. You must seek out the others. The Dragon-Riders! Together you will find and walk your paths. Strength in numbers, you know… As for the girl part, men only see what is placed before them. You mastered the art of visual distraction, yet I am afraid, you may not be in position to fool much longer, eh girlie?"

Kadir began to laugh which turned into a coughing fit and had her wiping the spit off his face handing him a cup of water. He drank, then thanked her for her care.

"I end my spirit knowing I helped to set certain events into motion. It has pleased me to be a small part of this. I will give a blessing to the God for your safe travels and adventures which await you. Go forward with a pure mind. Do not get bogged down with the machinations of men. Do what is right, not what is expected. 'Tis all now, my dear, I need to rest. God go with you."

Kadir was exhausted from his talking and coughing, and he lay down with Andic's help, closing his eyes.

She thanked him for his teachings, noticing after a few moments soft snores were coming from his throat. She quietly left returning to her rooms to ready herself to leave. There was nothing left here for her.

No need to enter the caverns if there is Dragon lore in the catacombs under the Hall of Learning. The tomes I was copying seem to be nothing of import. Why did I not know there was a secret building beneath the Great Hall? This makes me wonder if the other Halls have secrets below them. I will pass this onto Laza in case he has a curiosity. I will read and learn what I can. Secrets are what I do best.

Andic wondered at his declaration she was a DragonRider. Wondering about the health of his mind, mayhap someone slipped him some magic mushrooms. Those things in the right, or wrong quantities, could send the user on quite the mind journey.

Andic did her morning chores, gathering a few stores from the herb room. She said nothing to the other boys, quietly doing what needed to be done. Finding the most opportune time, quietly collecting her meager things, she stole out the gate and down the path. Her goodbyes were spoken to Kadir when she finished helping him. After his breakfast when he spoke to her all nonsense, he lay back down and fell asleep. She noticed his complexion was a wee sallow and knew he may be dead by summer.

Stepping out onto the trail, she found herself contemplating the past months.

I learned what men would have us not learn. It opened my eyes to another world, another life. There is so much out there I wish to know. I will assume the catacombs will have many items and there is much to learn. Especially about what the FirPader does not want us, as poor folk to know. Will it be enough?

I must also think on how my body is changing. Will the boys let me lead? Do I even wish to. I see a few would resist a female, especially if I look like one. Looking like a young boy was my redeeming feature however, I am sure if I grow breasts, it will not sit well with them.

Soon she arrived at the main thoroughfare and headed to the river and along the paved path. She viewed her surroundings in a new light and glad to be returning to her home. She missed her mentor and few friends. Now she had another tool in her belt, the gift of knowledge. She would be able to read signs for herself and knew she would keep this knowledge to herself as long as possible. She would find her head off her shoulders should it become known. It was law women could not have learning of the written word, or writing. It meant death.

How should I enter this chamber? I heard the Hall guards its secrets well. I may have to use bribes, which means I should pad my coffers some. I have many things to think on.

Oh, my stomach hurts! A woman's monthly course is sure awful! I see what others moan about. This happens every month? Why? Why cannot men go through this? I hope I make it in one day. Ughh!

The trip back seemed shorter than the way to the monastery. Andic knew where she was headed, and she was not stopping to look at stars. She travelled all night arriving at the brothel of her favorite girls by early morning. She brazenly walked up to Delma in her office. The older woman shocked at first, gave her the biggest hug.

"Me being so glad you are back! 'Tis been hell since you were gone! Them boys do not do anything I ask, Ayse left her spirit, after I asked and asked them to find a tonic for me, they did not know where to go. Oh, deary, look at you. I swear you have gotten taller."

Delma held her back then hugged her again.

"Your room has not been touched, would you like some bread and cheese, my luv?"

"Yes, please. I have a few herbs and tinctures I made while upriver. I may have acquired some, but most I did make myself. My time away was most informative. I will trade you those for the meal."

Delma beamed at her. "Good lass, you are, knowing what I need."

"I will get all the other items you need, after I have a good rest. Could you place word to some of the boys for a meeting? The next night or following? I am bushed. Could you wait until end of day? No need for unexpected company."

"I will. I will send one of the boys tonight, you get yourself some rest, dearie."

Last thing Andic needed was a knife blade tickling her, when she was bone tired, and not fully awake.

Going upstairs, quietly, as she always had, she found a few animals had taken residence in her space. She shooed them out, too tired to worry about fur and dried droppings strewn about. She saw Delma was telling the truth. Dust was everywhere, and linens left exactly where she dropped them.

How nice would it be if this place cleaned itself, mayhap I will get one of the girls to help me. Andic's vision became focused, and dust began to swirl and dance, working itself into a mini dust tornado. *This is a grand trick; I can order dust about, however, what to do with it?*

She looked at the hatch in the ceiling; it opened back with a clap and her little swirling dust devil left out the top and dissipated once it cleared the peak of the roof. This left her more exhausted. She reached up, quietly closing the hatch, hoping the noise had not woken anyone. Then she lay down, closed her eyes, and dreamt about absolutely nothing.

Due to her little experiment with magic tiring her, Andic soaked up a good day's rest. Upon waking she rose, had an evening meal with some girls, and met a few new ones. She caught Delma's gaze, nodding toward the girls and Delma nodded back, meaning the Matron would inform the girls about Andic. Andic needed linen rags. This was rather bothersome, becoming a woman, but she was not going to let it stop her. The stomach-ache she could do without, though.

"Delma, I have started the curse of women."

"Some women call it a blessing, especially in this line of work. Ahhh, lass, you have become a woman at last. Come here." Delma grabbed Andic into another huge embrace. "Let us get you some linens, from the laundry. You wash your own rags. You know this."

"Yes, thank you."

Andic took what she needed, and headed back up to her space, changing rags for new ones.

Heading out her roof hatch and looking into the sky, she noticed the star brighter than before. Andic wondered how long before others saw. Heading out to the warehouse district, legs a bit sore from the use, she never felt like this before.

Is this lack of exercise? Or the woman thing? This I cannot have. I am becoming soft.

Slowing down a bit, she tried to get her head back in the game, stopping periodically to listen, and focus in with her eyesight. She was intent on honing her skills, at the last stop before dropping to the ground, she did not hear Laza sneak up behind and felt the touch of a blade against her throat.

"Little sister, getting a bit sloppy, after your little vacation?" He chuckled as he placed his blade in his waistband. She turned giving him a wrist shake.

"Nice to see you, brother, you are more diligent. What news?"

He told her in short, the happenings in her absence.

"We have no choice, but to glean where we can, the Delight Houses included. The FirPader's Obans have tightened their hold on cargo's. With the soldiers coming back for winter, more were looking for work and cargos are well guarded. This should be changing soon, the first ships have set sail, and another regiment is due to go. A new Captain in the pit district does not cooperate well with us. Trying to establish his own empire, so you came back at the best time. Let us speak with the others."

He jumped down a few levels until he reached the ground, and she followed suit. Not as graceful as before and knew she would have to get herself back into shape. His lieutenants stood outside, several staying there while Laza and she walked into the building. Andic noted, more guards than usual.

She talked with her deputies. While most were happy to see her, she noted a few sour faces. No one took over her district while she was gone, and Laza stated the next meeting would be a while.

"I will get some goods; we are getting a little low. I will use the children as couriers and send word when I need them."

"That is what we need. Pad the coffers, there have been some unexpected expenditures. There should be lots in the Oban's storehouses. I will leave that up to you. Let me know when you need them."

She needed to catch up on news, view her empire, and set a few things straight. They adjourned the meeting and not too soon, as they dissipated, a dozen guards came patrolling the streets.

She gazed down at the patrol hoping with the beginning of the next campaign the street patrols would diminish. They did make stalking more difficult for the others. She rose from her perch wandered around for a bit, then went back to the House of Delights. A bit bored with her life, and a bit unsure of where to begin.

Andic entered Delma's office, sitting in one of the chairs while she waited for the woman to organize the new girls, as business began for the night.

"What are you doing here?"

A new girl poked her head into the office and barked the question at her. Andic thought she seemed a bit full of herself.

"Minding my own business, that is what. What business is it of yours?"

Andic spoke softly with no tone in her voice, she wanted to see where this was going to lead.

"Well, if you are one of the new girls, you need to get ready, Delma wants everyone washed and dressed. Damn you do not look like much. You can cater to the ones who like boys... Hurry up, no dawdling."

Andic did not move staring at the girl, who was trying her hardest to look like she was in charge.

"What are you waiting for? A smack? I spoke. Get a move on."

"I am thinking you may want to think about who you are, and where you are, dear…?"

"Avalen. Not that you need to know who I am."

"Well, Avalen. I am going to sit here and mind my business, and I suggest you mind your own. What I do is none of yours."

Andic told her quietly and saw what she said had the opposite effect, but she already knew that! She was beginning to enjoy this exchange and grinned at the thought which enraged the girl further.

"I will make your life miserable; you whelp. If you do not get upstairs and wash and dress for the night, I will…"

"You will what?"

Avalen moved forward lifting her hand to strike the woman in front of her who was not moving a muscle as Delma entered and boxed Avalen in the head.

"What are you doing in here, Ava? I told you to get upstairs and get ready. Were you trying to boss the Little Dragon around? Heavens help you then, you are lucky she did not gut you where you stand. Maybe you have a death wish! I should let her have at you. Now git, before I smack you again..."

Delma raised her hand again at the girl who scowled at Andic, who could not stop smiling. She thoroughly enjoyed this. Avalen left in a huff stomping her steps up the stairs.

"You better watch out for her. She is from Du'Lanay, new girl, thinks she is someone here, I think after a few weeks under several men, she will change her tune. She was somebody's wife back in her land, she is too good for this life it seems. What's new with you, lass?"

"You should give her the rough ones, give her a bit of a welcome, then. Maybe she will manage them if she is used to a husband. She does not come across as fragile; she might set a few men straight. But be careful, she will want your position, if she craves a way up, or a way back. I do not believe she realizes why she is here yet."

"You are probably right. You usually are."

Delma sat down at her desk opposite of Andic and opened a drawer on one side, bringing out a deep brown glass bottle with a stopper. She set it on the desk, reaching back in, retrieved two small glasses, placing them beside the bottle. She popped the stopper out of the bottle, poured an amber liquid into both glasses, and handed one to Andic.

"Here you go, girl, try this. One of my client's graciously gave this, as a token of satisfaction from the service he received from Verema. Seems she can work magic with her tongue. Ahhh, now 'tis some good swill."

Both Andic and Delma downed the contents of the glass they held in their hand, Delma smacking her lips and Andic trying not to choke. Delma began laughing at the expressions Andic created from the harshness of the liquor which trailed down her throat.

"You have not tried a good fire water if you cannot swallow this. This is one of the best I have had, and I have had many over the years. We will give this man the royal treatment, if one night with Verema gives this result. Ahh, that is much better, Avalen. You get into the main receiving room then, make your self available, and take that scowl off your face, or I will give you something to scowl about. Go on, git."

Delma raised her hand waving off the girl who returned down the stairs. Cleaned and dressed in the skimpy clothes another girl lent her; she had not done any business to pay for her own. Avalen peered at the young woman sitting at the desk, enjoying a glass of spirits, her face spoke volumes. Andic kept smiling. The girl retreated down the hall, her back speaking disapproval of what she was about to partake.

"She is going to have joy tonight, if I know you, Delma. Well, I should get my arse moving, do something useful. You better tell the girls to leave me alone, I see from dealing with Avalen you did not have the time. I think I will get myself some coin or trouble or both."

"Speaking of trouble… stay seated for a moment. Your childhood friend was here several times."

"Oh? To avail himself of one of the girls?"

"Yes. Him and a few of his friends, celebrating a name day. Not sure if it was his or not."

"Brecu is his own man. If he wants to have relations, what is it to me?"

"Just letting you know, lass. It was…quite interesting."

"You seem to be busting to tell me. Did he harm any of the girls? I will bust him if this is so."

"Oh, no. Nothing like that. He is the kindest young man I know. I have watched him grow, he is very courteous, and gentle."

"Then what, pray tell, is this tale you wish to tell."

"His companions were most adamant he partake of a girl, if fact I am thinking he had several vying for his attention."

"He is most handsome, I never noticed before, however, I grew up with him. So, he was quite the catch? Who was the lucky girl?"

"None."

"None? I find this difficult to believe. He chose none of the girls?"

"Well, several tried. He was not able…"

"He was not able…? Oh, is this a problem?"

"Only for the man. Your friend was not able to maintain…and it was soon a challenge for the girls to see who could get him…"

"Oh, and…?"

"He left here quite disappointed."

"You mentioned he was here several times."

"Yes, he came back on his own. He tried again but could not. I spoke with him privately, I felt it was warranted. He spoke of his affection for you, he feels he has a spot in his heart for you."

"We have an unspoken bond, yet I have always thought of him as a friend. You are saying he feels more?"

"Just warning you, should he pay you more attention. His inability to perform with another girl may be because he wants another."

"He is more than welcome to. I have never entertained such thoughts. I have many other items on my mind, I need to build up the coffers, then deal with another recruit. I have just started this curse, ugh. To be entertaining joining… not on the top of my list."

"You may not be given the choice… remember who you are. Many a man would be pleased to relieve you of your maidenhead. You must watch yourself... more so now. I see the change in you, perhaps it is because you were gone for so long, I see a young woman now, not the little boy-like girl who left last year."

"Ugh, do not remind me, do I look like a woman? Even with my short hair?"

"It accentuates your eyes, dear girl, making all your features stand out. Your cheekbone's prominent and are quite striking. You would bring in a good coin, should you…"

"No. Nay, nay... Do not even go there… I am not one of your girls… Do not think of it. I will leave here, not return."

"No, lass. I was not suggesting. You are fine. You be aware of what others may be thinking, it may be the men you deal with, may have these thoughts. You watch your back; I can only protect you so much. I am saying your friend may not be able to perform with another girl because he likes you."

"Oh? I never thought of him in this way…"

"He may. It does happen. If another consumes a person, it leaves nothing for any other. It is good if it was to be a permanent situation."

"We have not spoken about what happens down the path. We have our own lives. He is a guard. I am… well I am a free person. I should mention, keep this to yourself…"

"Yes, child, what is spoken will stay with me."

Delma rose to shut the door; the noise of girls entertaining beginning to enter the room. She returned, poured herself another drink and Andic shook her head, she would need her wits when she left the Delight House.

"If you need assistance with the written word…"

"Oh, is this what you were getting up to? Why, yes. If you can spend some time here, in my office, I need assistance. Then I do not need to ask Jiet. I know he is not honest, I will keep your secret, child. 'Tis a blessing."

"When is the best time? I do not wish to be interrupted."

"The morning hours, after the girls go rest. If you do not mind, spending the mornings…"

"I will try. I may not be able to some days."

"Let me know if I am indeed getting all my funds, I need to know if my payments to the Hall are correct. The costs to operate continually rise, I am not sure if Jiet is skimming…"

"Most guaranteed he is, Delma. 'Tis our life."

"Yes, but he seems to be taking more and more."

"You do not want to make an enemy out of him. He has the Oban's blessing. You cannot do business without his consent."

"You are correct. I do not seem to have enough every week. He takes all."

"I will inquire around, speak with some of my associates and find out a few things, then we can address them. You need to have more information to confront him with any accusations."

"I have the Oban's blessing. He will not close me down, I know too much."

"Well, I have no desire to see you expired."

"Oh, I did not think of this. Yes, we will tread lightly. Help me if you are able. I will not cause trouble if I do not see the need."

"Now I am going to do some rounds, I have many things to address immediately. Please keep my activities to yourself, it means my death, and probably yours…now that I think of it."

"Lass, your head is my hands and mine is in yours. I have always looked out for you and you have with me, of course I will not say anything. Now I must make sure all the clientele are happy. You go take care of your business."

Andic rose, Delma came around and gave her a hug.

"I am relieved to see you. Now I can sleep better, knowing you are close."

Andic left and went about her night. She wandered all around her empire. Into the Harem, around all the Obans villas. Most were quiet. She snuck into the warehouses, into the special areas not well known. She perused them all, gleaning where she could. She sent a few boys off to Laza with strict instructions to give items over to him only. She went down to the river. She came back up and climbed onto a rooftop of one of the storehouses, to stare at the advent of the sun, the sky beginning to lighten. She gazed around at her surroundings, smelling the scent of the river and watching the few skulking people down below her. Watching as men returned to their homes, as drunks vomited in alleys and a few stray dogs lapped up what did not soak into the ground… she watched this all with a smile on her face.

Ahhh, 'tis good to be home.

CHAPTER 19

Damara

Darkness will Light the Way

It was fortunate Damara's horse knew the way back to the villa, she was so buried in her thoughts, she did not notice they were home until the horse halted, a groom repeatedly asking her if she was dismounting.

"Nada, Nada, are you getting off now?"

Her escort arrived back with the dinner she bought, and she absentmindedly spoke consent, removing her body from the horse, and walking into the front entrance of the villa. She was all the way to her room before registering, she was home, then rational thought took over, *I am not really upset... Should I be? 'Tis as though I have always known. Ramis has a woman on the side. Do I even care? Any other woman would be crying and wailing. When had my heart stopped beating for Ramis?*

She still loved him, but if what she saw was correct, he lied to her about fishing and was visiting someone. *Have I changed? How? Have I always known? Has Ramis always been like this? Before I accuse Ramis of infidelity, I need tangible proof. Only then, will I have a potential case to divorce him.*

Because of whom she was, and who she was related, the courts may rule a divorce in her favor. Very rarely had the courts taken the side of a woman. Usually, it was well padded with coin! She knew of only two cases in her lifetime, and it was never spoken of. At least not in the presence of men, who might feel their masculinity threatened with mere mention. Women were beaten publicly for less.

Peylin knew something was troubling her, but kept herself quiet, knowing when not to ask questions, Damara appreciated her maid more than the woman knew. "Have I been blind, Peylin?" She told her maid all she saw in the few seconds her horse walked past the roadway.

"Mayhap you should hire someone, to confirm or deny what is roaming around your thoughts. It does you no good to worry about a thing if 'tis not correct. You may be harming your spirit to entertain negative energy. I can inquire for you; I have a few options I can pursue if you need."

Peylin did not tell her Mistress when she began working for Damara her brother worked for a time for one of the men Ramis and Davian associated with. Her brother had all sorts of contacts, some not so pleasant. Peylin reached out to him to find whatever she needed. It helped Peylin would find him things he needed through her association with Damara, which her Mistress also did not need to know.

"Thank you Peylin, I will consider this and will let you know what I decide."

As Damara pondered all this, she followed her normal routine taking a bath, and dressing for dinner. She heard the sounds of Ramis coming home. All too soon she would have to greet him. She agreed with herself to not accuse him or let him know she saw him. She made herself look exceptionally beautiful that night and partook a couple glasses of wine as she did so, to calm her thoughts.

"How was your day, my dear Mara?"

"Eventful."

Ramis greeted her with a hug and a kiss on the cheek as they entered the dining area at the same time,

"I see you thought to get dinner. Did I not say I was fishing?"

"I know you sometimes are gone longer, and I am famished lately, after being so ill. I was not taking the chance, I went to the shops, and had a particularly good day, matching up the orders, I am pleased with what you brought in the way of orders, I could not help but begin. How was your fishing, did you catch all you wanted?" She could not help but get in a dig, without him knowing, leaving the expression out of face and voice, asking as innocently as she could muster.

"Yes, I have given it all to Cook to prepare, I am afraid we will have fish for a few days, though, must not let it all go to waste."

He must have someone catch it for him. She became sad, he would lie to her face, as though he was ordering dinner or the horse to ride. He saw the expression on her face change and spoke.

"Do not fret, dear, Cook always exceeded our expectations with his inventiveness. We never have reason to complain about his talents. Did you attend the orders? When you have them complete, I can take them into the Capital for you. I would like to see if the lads have any leave from the battlefront." He sat down motioning for her to join him at the dinner table.

"That is an excellent idea, my dear, I think I will join you, if you let me; I would love to visit some shops, purchase a few items, and it would be lovely to see the boys again." She beamed at him and watched his expression flicker from annoyance to joy at the news. *Annoyance, at what? That I will be with him in the Capital? I never noticed this attitude with Ramis before. Hmmm.*

She knew then she would hire a man to investigate his affairs. She would not make the same mistake she did many years ago, by hiring someone underwritten by her husband. She made her decision, Peylin's offer to help, had her confident she would not make the same error again.

A month passed quickly, she kept busy once again at her shop, working on dresses, finishing orders, and working on new orders received from some of her clients here in Kara. The week following her startled horse incident, she asked Peylin to arrange a meeting with the man she recommended, Ash was his name. She met him in a quiet back alley behind a few of less travelled streets. She explained who she was and who Ramis was. He inclined his head in greeting. Peylin had filled him in on her employer. Damara asked he not double cross her like the last one and would be rewarded handsomely.

"I wish to know everything, good or bad. If you can determine how long events were happening, even better. Any extra expenditures, inform Peylin and I will give you funds. Coin is not limited, you need more, I will provide. If you inform Ramis and he divorces me from your actions, this…" she indicated the coin given him, "…will be gone. I will be destitute and will not be able to provide a piss pot for you to go in."

Ash agreed to her terms, and they arranged the way to communicate, mostly through Peylin. Following hiring Ash, she spent the next month collecting orders and dealing with cargo which sank with one of her boats. The winter storms had begun. This ship carried a vast number of silks, which meant a portion of orders could not be filled. In chatting with her husband and deputy, both agreed they had no luck with the other continent, and they should look at other sources of retail, as one should not rely on only one source. The business was growing steadily these last few years, Damara agreed with their logic.

"It makes sense to have another avenue of product. We have the Captains inquire next they sail to each port. Then report back to us, their findings. Once we have enough to decide, then we begin negotiations."

"This sounds fine, Ramis. I trust this to your expertise, I know I cannot get orders done with no fabrics. I believe we begin storing some, for when ships like this one are sunk."

"Stored fabrics. Hmmm, we do not need a surplus, if we were to not get orders…"

"I am steadily getting more the last five years. I believe we can afford to stockpile a small amount. If you recall, almost every year, one or two ships sink from storms. I am always in this situation, every spring."

"You are right, let me think on this."

A few days before their trip to the Capital, Peylin handed her a note Ash wished to convey information to her. Damara and her maid went to a flower shop to meet up with Ash. As they met in the back alley, she handed him a bag of coin for payment.

"The house at the end of the poor women's alley is owned by Arno, Head Judge. His former wife Lana lives there, since you hired me, your husband has visited her once a week, and his man pays a fisherman to bring a catch before they return. She also sees other men on different nights, always the same ones. These are their names."

He gave her a list. The fact her husband visited another woman, for what she assumed was sex did not seem to faze her. That it was Lana, also did not shock her. The other names he gave her, were though. One was the woman's former husband, and the other was the regimental Captain of the Guards. What Ash told her next, made her eyes begin to glow.

"There is one more thing, I did watch through a window drapery, like you asked. He does have sexual relations with this woman, and…."

Here he stalled, clearing his throat a couple of times.

"Yes. You can spit it out."

Her eyes gently glowed, and Ash backed up a step and hesitantly spoke.

"There is a child, three years of age. I saw the child sleeping on a mat, he, your husband, patted its hair while it lay sleeping."

The magnitude of what this man told her sunk in, her vision turned the world in the alley red.

"I will meet with you later…in the Capital… I must go." He hurried out of the alley, Damara sank to her knees, afraid of processing this information. She took a couple deep breaths, closed her eyes. *All right, what am I to do next? He has another's child, yet we are good, we never fight, is it me?*

Damara felt the feeling of being watched come over her, opening her eyes, the redness infringing on her vision was gone. Glancing first down one way of the alley, and then the other, there was no one. She gazed up to the roof tops and at each roof at either end across the streets, still she saw no one. She was not afraid. This feeling was warm, like a hug and kiss from her Mader when she was still a child. Comforting, but still enough for her to rise to her feet and breathe in a couple long, deep breaths,

I will acquire more evidence, before I confront him, he could have a very good reason, and it could be charity. Satisfied with her own synopsis of the situation, she exited the alley. Making sure she was not seen, she entered a few stores and bought frivolous things to verify her whim of going into the city.

Late afternoon saw Damara and Ramis sitting in their parlour. Damara was sewing embroidery and Ramis was at his desk, looking at accounts.

We are sitting here like nothing is different, yet it is. I know now Ramis has not been faithful to our marriage. He is very…giving… of himself. He is over there, thinking what? He has the right to do what he wishes. While I sit over here, knowing more about his spirit. He was with Lana, she was my friend once, she was Davian's betrothed, so long ago. Was he involved with her when she was joined? I think not. She has a boy, so at least the last four years. I was terribly busy with my clothing for the last five. Did I drive him away? He did encourage me to work more. Was this to keep me busy and unaware? Hmmm.

A messenger arrived with news their lads had leave and would meet them in the Capital the day after their parents' arrival, and they had a surprise for them.

"Mayhap, one of them has met a girl and wishes to contract a marriage."

Damara was excitedly speaking aloud. She wanted her boys to have children, even though they had begun their careers in the army, there was always time to procreate.

"I wonder which son and who they may be bringing home."

"We do not know this, dear, and when would they have time to meet any eligible girls of rank out on the battle front? It would have been while they were at home, here or in the Capital. If 'tis marriage for either of them, 'tis time we address it. I hope 'tis one of the girls we picked for them, they do have to think about the political ramifications of marriage."

"You have their best interests at heart, Ramis. I am sure you will have them placed where they excel. Well, let us set out tomorrow, I will order the household ready and us packed, if you would take care of the orders at the warehouse, we can task together."

"Why certainly. You have dinner without me as I may be a little longer than the dinner hour to get organized. I will confer with Tovah. She can give me what is complete. She is very thorough, organized and has a firm touch. She is an asset, Mara."

"Yes, she is. Which is why I trust her to work with you. I will have a light dinner then, nothing too grand. Ramis. I can certainly do so."

She turned to the hall leading to the kitchen area and servant offices, all the while knowing exactly where he was going.

That is why we have servants, to do the work, while you play. After her initial bout of anger in the alley, she was surprised she did not feel more anger.

Lana had thrown things at her late husband, the gossips had a field day, recounting all which transpired with her marriage breakdown. The shouting and arguing, many heard curses coming from the woman, who did not like the fact a man could have a paramour, but a woman could not. Damara remembered when she heard the rumour repeated, she would not be this kind of woman. Damara remembered back before she was joined, the stories her maids would tell her of what her brother Davian and his friends would get up to. Ramis was part of this group. They would play pranks on each other, the odd one would get a girl with child and either the girl or the baby would disappear, or both.

Had Ramis been one of those boys?

She organized with her servants, and they scurried about, getting their Masters' things ready for the following day.

The next morning, she woke with the cresting of the sun,

What else? What else? Is this merely the beginning? Is there more to Ramis? Should I ask Ash for more? Maybe I should ask Peylin what she thinks.

Her sons, she was not worried about, however, what else could her husband do to surprise her? She felt this life as she knew it was ending, and she was not done yet. She sensed there was an adventure out there waiting for her, more exciting than traveling for dyes. More surprises awaited her; she knew this for sure. She wished she had the foresight to know what.

She rose, expecting the red haze in her eyesight, as it happened a few more times, usually first thing when she awoke. She would lay there until it left, but today was not that day, and she gave silent thanks to their God. Her maid servant laid out her travelling clothes. Quickly dressing herself, she was struggling with the ties of her bodice, when Peylin entered apologizing for not being there and helped her finish dressing.

"'Tis fine, Peylin. I woke early and had nothing else to occupy myself with. I am more shocked at my lack of response to what Ramis is doing, than the fact. Am I indifferent to all this?"

Damara lifted her arm and waved it in the direction of her husband's quarters in the other wing of the villa.

"'Tis expected, he is one of the noble houses. 'Tis a learned trait, expected almost. His Pader was well known, among the lower houses…of ill repute."

Damara turned to stare at her maid. "How would you know this?"

Peylin covered up her slip with a blush. "My brother told me tidbits from time to time. I was to know everything about the House I served to not err in service."

Damara looked eased. "You have not erred. I do the same with my clientele. You see my ledgers. When I hear 'tidbits' I write them down. In fact, those books should be placed in a safe place. Where are they now?"

"They are in your office desk. Only yourself and Tovah have the keys."

"Yes, thank you, dear. I wonder if I should take notes on what I find out. To keep myself straight, regarding Ramis."

"It could save you grief, to get your facts in order, however, it can be a detriment in the future… if he finds it."

"Well, if he finds it, then he is welcome to refute. I think I will begin a tome on my findings. I will keep it down at the shop, with the other ones. Perhaps on your next outing, you find me a slim book, half the width of my clientele book. It should not take up too much room."

"I will find one for you, Nada, yet you may find you fill it fast."

"You know something I do not?"

"No. You write every detail; it will prove to be too small. That's all."

"You know me best. Very well, purchase something, you think I will not fill. It must fit in the desk… the locked drawer. I do not want Ramis finding it."

"Do you trust Tovah with this information? Perhaps, it should be you, and I… for now…the less others know…"

"You are again, correct. Thank you for pointing this out. Best 'tis us…then it can be bigger. I will lock it in my desk here, in the villa. I am sure Ramis does not use my desk."

"He does not. At least, I have never seen him in there without your presence, Nada. I have never seen his man in there either. It would seem to be a better resting spot for it than the shop, too many chances of it being seen and read down there. Here you can control who is in your room."

Damara heard the sounds of her husband's boots on the marble. She peered at her image in the mirror, she looked tired.

"Ahh, well. I am as ready as I will ever be. We should go, Ramis will be upset, should I cause a delay. Shall we?"

She would take the carriage. Ramis preferred horseback, and for the first time, Damara was not annoyed about the arrangement. The overland travel took a few very long days, with a couple overnight stops. They travelled without any mishaps and arrived at a late hour. Their servants were already informed, and there was a small meal waiting. Ramis gave her a short hug and a kiss on the forehead, and they parted ways to go to each others separate rooms.

It was an arrangement up to now, she protested, but now with all she knew and being so tired, she welcomed. She disrobed as she walked in, entering straight into the bathing waters, her servants made ready. After her cleansing wash, she put on a sleeping robe and welcomed her bed. Laying down she remembered the day her parents told her she was contracted to Ramis.

"Oh, I am! I am so excited! Thank you, Pader, and Mader! He is so handsome. I have strong feelings for him. Ramis has expressed his caring for me also."

Her Mader looked at Damara's face and saw her innocence of worldly happenings on it, smiled sadly then corrected herself to express more joy.

"As long as you are happy. Damara, you must make the most of your joining. Bear him a few sons, a few Daders and enjoy him. Be available for just him. Keep him happy."

"Oh, I will. Thank you! You have made me the happiest of Daders! When should we join?"

"As he is busy with the war going on, we will have this ceremony soon. He may not get much time to spend with you. You provide him with a blessed home to come home to, and he will not stray."

"Oh, I will. He says I light up the room he is in. I want what you and Pader have. You have only seen each other."

"I am sure of your heart, Damara. You must make sure of his. I have always known your Paders, he proved his love and caring for me many times."

"Yes, he does love you. We can all see his eyes light up when you enter a room. I will cater to Ramis' every need."

"I am sure you will, Dader, you will."

Damara fell asleep, thinking of what her Mader said and how she said it. Damara thought her Mader knew exactly Ramis's character. Damara's Mader knew people. She knew exactly what each person who crossed her path was capable of. Her friends were few, but they were stalwart. Few opened their homes to Damara's Mader. They had no choice but to, given who her Pader was. Damara's Mader told her when she was near her end of life, she had a very rough start. She did not have many friends. She chose to keep to herself and it was very lonely. She was kind to her servants and in the end of her life, she only made a few close friends.

"You keep your heart close. Only give it to those who deserve your love. Some will trample on it, and you will not know it until too late. Do not let them in unless you are sure of their spirit. Listen to your gut, it will not steer you awry. If it tells you something is not right, you back away. You do what makes you happy. Not anyone else. Not even Ramis. Your spirit needs to have happiness, and you need to love yourself."

"Oh, Mader. Ramis makes me happy. I make him happy. He gives my spirit so much joy. He told the children they must listen to me, now. It was difficult in the beginning but they are respectful now."

"This is good to hear. Ramis had a different upbringing than you and Davian. In bringing your concerns to him, he listened to you and brought the children to heel. We were worried about you. It relieves us to know he does care for you."

Damara drifted off to sleep, her Mader gave her much advice regarding Ramis. The more she thought about her Mader's advice, it made more sense now. Her Mader knew what Ramis was. Given she was a courtesan in her early years. Given she dealt with that type of man, for a time. Damara missed her parents, however, now they were both gone, she knew they were together in spirit.

The next morning saw her awake early. Today was the day one of her sons would present a bride. She could not think of anything else it could be, this was the only surprise she could fathom one of them would have. She dressed warmly. Winters in the South of the Du'Lanay continent were not always the best weather, yet better than if she was a Northman. Damara heard tales of heavy snowfalls and freezing weather. The most they had was fierce winds coming off the ocean with heavy rains. today was no exception, the wind, while not blustering, had a bite to it and the dark clouds heading their way promised a good downpour.

She sat to a fruit and cheese breakfast; she did not care for heavy meals first thing in the morning and was finishing when Ramis came in from his wing.

"Good morning, Mara, you look radiant. Excited for our sons arrival, I see."

"Yes, I do hope 'tis a marriage we will be discussing. You are right, this needs to be addressed soon…with both."

Ramis sat and his man served him a larger version of her own breakfast with the addition of bread baked this morning. His name for her from the beginning, he liked to use it when he was in a jolly mood. Once, it made her smile, but now it seemed to irritate her. She schooled her expression back to one of neutrality, glanced up and smiled back at her husband.

"Yes, I believe they will arrive soon. They spent last night at the Barracks. I saw the message this morning, they hope to arrive mid morning, and I have their rooms readied. If the storm coming in breaks, they will not be returning to the Barracks in comfort until it abates."

"As always, my dear, you think of everything."

Ramis smiled at her between chomping his breakfast. Even the sound of his chewing, which she never noticed, irritated her. She gazed at him thinking this, and Ramis stopped to look at her,

"My Darling, with the sun coming in and its light hitting your face, you are glowing with beauty. You will always be my beautiful wife, Mader to my children." He beamed a big grin at her, placing attention back to his meal.

By the Pader! I hope my eyes are not glowing! She picked up her silver chalice of citrus juice, trying to look at her reflection she saw the rim of her irises slowly fading.

Oh no, not now! I do not need him finding an excuse to divorce me and marry the other woman. I would be ruined! She wondered, how she could stop this thing happening to her eyes? *Please, do not do this anymore.*

She had a quick feeling of being observed and an acquiescing to her wish, her shoulders eased. Damara felt more comfortable with the cessation of the feeling. They chatted about the day's events, and other things. A couple of hours passed quickly. She was about to rise, as she felt a need to rest, when her ears picked up noise coming from the entryway. The sounds of laughter and horses.

"Oh! I hear the boys!"

Standing up facing the doorway, a smile beaming from her face, her glass in hand waiting for the boys to enter. Her eldest, Baron, then her second born, Jaidak came in, laughing at some joke the other spoke. They turned to another behind them, the young lad following them into the room.

She stood there looking, seeing a replica of her husband, almost exactly like the day she joined with him! The metal chalice slipped from her fingers; it seemed like time stilled. The smile left her face as she saw her husband was indeed busy all those years ago. Her boys were laughing,

"Look, Pader and Mader. We found a new friend out on the battlefield; he looks like us!"

She did not hear her boys laugh turn to concern as she felt the room close in and the darkness reach to embrace her. First the cup and then its Mistress fell to the mosaic floor. The boys and her husband racing to get her. Ramis picked her up saying to his sons,

"You could have warned me, bringing Rohut here like this. You did not think the likeness too close? Your Mader will have questions, he is just your friend, for now, until I can think of how to break this to her. She can divorce me if she does not accept the lad."

"Sorry, Pader, we did not think. We thought it astounding and thought she would too. Rohut informed us on the way here, of his connection with you. It slipped my mind, of the magnitude of such relationship. We forgot about the consequences, shall he leave?"

Baron spoke softly to his Pader, the other two lads behind their Pader as he gently placed his unconscious, or so he thought, wife on her bed. As soon as Damara hit the tiled floor, yes, the room went dark, but behind her eye lids, she saw the red haze. She knew if she opened them the men in the room would be terrified and have her locked up. Who knows what would happen after. He would be in his right to divorce her or worse have her killed.

Namanists would have a field day with her, regardless of her rank. Whatever was happening to her eyes, now was not the right time to announce the change in them. She felt the redness disappear, as she listened to the conversation between Ramis and the three lads. She heard them speaking as they left the room and heard her maid entering.

"What about Mader? She will ask when she wakes. Will you tell her?"

"Your Mader will be told he is just a friend, perhaps a long-lost offshoot of one of my cousins, he has no formal house, but for now…."

"Mader is very astute, Pader. You will have to convince her."

"Shall I leave? I am sorry to have caused this unrest. I did not mean to…"

"No, Rohut. It was not your fault. You can go; I would not have her distressed any more. Boys, your Mader was unwell for a while. We do not know what ails her. Let us speak in the parlour when Rohut leaves…"

She lost the rest of the conversation as they moved down the hall.

They plan to tell me a lie. I understand Ramis doing so, but I wish he would leave the children out of his machinations. 'Tis not their sin. She opened her eyes to see her maid standing close by, her head facing the doorway, a look of astonishment on her face.

"Oh, Peylin. Did you see? Did you know? The lad looks like Ramis, a twin to him. I am at a loss."

"Nada, I did see, and you are right, he looks like his Pader. I did not know until I saw with my own eyes, 'tis obvious. What will you do?"

"Nothing for now, I wait to see what he tells me. I cannot believe all these years, he has another son, no wait, two more. So the man I hired when we were first joined spoke truth. Ramis must have paid him to lie. All this time, Ramis has been the one to fabricate lies. I feel empty inside; this sets me into my mind. I must be smart about my next steps. I cannot get over he lies. I thought him to be a pinnacle of the best sort of man. Now I know different."

She would accept the story they told her and see what her hired man found out. She wanted to know who the Mader of this young man was and gather her case before addressing her husband. She saw her husband in action with other dealings. He always twisted words to reap the benefit of any situation. If she did not deal with this right, it could mean her end, not his. She fell asleep to these thoughts and the quiet bustling of her maid. Damara slept as though her spirit left for the rest of the day and night. Enough that several times, Ramis checked in on her. Peylin believed he was worried for himself, not her mistress.

Damara woke the next morning, laying in her bed without opening her eyes and thinking about today. Her dreams of marrying her boys off were dashed for now, but she would pursue them anyway. Always deflect, Ramis told her. He would tell her his secrets in dealing with other business, not realizing she listened to his council. In deflection, she would ease their minds, until such time she could officially take a stand. She heard voices in the hall, her maids entering quietly.

I am done. I do not even care about the business. I thought it mattered, but for whatever reason, now it does not. It served its purpose, keeping me busy while my husband kept himself busy. He has stolen the joy from me. He used my business, while he used my ignorance.

All his offering to help was in his favor. His trips to the city, every year, sometimes several trips, always an excuse for the business. At the sound of his voice approaching, she opened her eyes and sat up, as Ramis entered the room, concern covering his facial countenance.

"My dear, you should stay in bed, the lads found this young man on the battlefield and took him under their wing. I have a man investigating into his House; however, I believe it may be one of Farzan's dalliances come to fruition, he almost said as much when I questioned him. I sent him back to the Barracks for now, the boys are not up yet, they had a few cups of wine last night and went to bed late. 'Tis storming, so just lay back, that is right, I will attend to you for your meal. I checked on you a few times, I was so worried, you slept a full day's worth."

"Thanks, my dear, I admit, I was quite shocked, but I will lay only for a bit. Travelling must have taken my energy; I seem to tire more now. I do want to see the boys when they rise. They will soon go back, after the storm abates. They must have other stories to tell. And I do think we should press them about the necessity of marriages."

The mention of marriage for the boys had the immediate effect she hoped. Ramis began speaking about suitable brides for them, and they spent an hour or so talking. Her tactic of brushing off his explanation as the truth and not questioning his reason, had the desired effect she wished. He believed that she believed. She rose after Ramis left to see if the lads were up. She had a quick wash and chose a bright yellow dress. It cheered her up and she wanted to show a good temperament to her boys.

When she arrived at the parlor, all her men were there, and she embraced her sons one at a time. They said good morning but did not mention the other boy, so she confronted a problem head-on and addressed what they felt uncomfortable doing so.

"I am sorry I looked upset and wrecked your evening. That young man, I understand, you took him under your wing, and while he looks a little like you boys, I believe in happenstance. I am sure he will become a great friend. You can bring him back here someday if you like. We must not deny you your friendships. I really thought one of you formed an attachment of another kind, and your Pader and I believe it is high time both of you begin entertaining those ideas. We have a list of potential brides; you choose one. Let us say, by summer solstice, you return with a few candidates in mind, and we can work from there."

Her nonchalant view had the lads relaxing, she saw it from where she was sitting. Ramis's face looked relieved as he took charge of the conversation after her little speech.

What have I done? I denied this boy in front of three men. If I try to use this as evidence against Ramis, it will not hold up in the Hall. Theirs are three voices to my one. Yet, to acknowledge him, would cause more upset. I hope I have done the right thing. I know now I need something more substantial, something unrefutably solid. Ugh, perhaps I need to catch him in the act... 'Tis below my station to follow him, furthermore, he has his man with him always. I will bide my time; the Universe will sort it out.

She sat in her loveseat, smiling at the men having conversation, putting in a word or two when required. Her boys, even in the brief time they were out on the battlefront overnight become men.

My beautiful boys. Men now, how they have grown up so fast. Baron looks much like me, a male version. He has my dark hair and eyes, but he is Ramis's height. Jaidak looks hmmm, he has Ramis's hair colour and height but he looks more like my Pader in his younger years. That young man, on the other hand, was the perfect likeness to Ramis, the same large nose and the cleft in his chin! Was I the only one who saw this?

Jaidak was leading the conversation when he did not have his nose in a book. He would either have one in his hand or by his side. Or several. When he found an interesting subject, he would find all he could and cross reference until he was satisfied with his findings. *Ah, Jaidak. So, like his Uncle. I see the same thirst for knowledge.* Her musings were interrupted by conversation.

"Hey, Baron, let us off to Menonn and Sohm's, we have not seen them for a while. We can always discuss potential brides, Sohm is newly betrothed, he may have an insight."

"Yes... Mader, Pader we will remain there for the dinner hour. I am sure we will be late in the evening, please do not wait up for us."

"I will not, in fact I will retire early. I still do not feel my usual energy. So enjoy yourselves."

"If you are retiring, Damara, I will head out with the boys, I have not seen their parents for a time."

"Do as you will. Have a good evening. Tomorrow we should head to the shops and begin some of the local orders."

"We certainly can do so. If you do not feel up to it, I can begin. You need not worry, I want you to recoup your strength, you have me worried."

She smiled at him and her sons, giving each a kiss and then left, heading down the hall to her rooms. Damara had tea, a hot bath, thinking the day's events went well.

Ramis was so attentive over the years, how was I blind not to see it was his subterfuge. He convinced me he loved only me. No. Wait. I wanted to believe in him. I only saw what I wanted to see. It was there all along. Have I always been so easy to believe? I guess seeing the hardship my parents went through, I was eager to have the same love they did. Ramis must have seen this in me, he was always a glib talker. We had some good years, at least on my end. I would not trade it for anything else. But now, I question my own thoughts. Is this enough for me now? Will I be happy, knowing he has children from other women and why do I feel not as bothered as I should be? 'Tis as though I shut the door already.

She spent the next week seeing her men in the morning, spending time relaxing with needlework in the afternoon, and leaving Ramis, all too eager to conduct her business for her, to his own devices. Soon it was time for the boys, she still thought of them as her boys, to return to the Barracks and back to the battlefront in preparations for the next campaign.

After the boys headed out, she cried more tears. *My boys, so grown up. The other lad, they will no doubt bring him with them. Which means they are aware of their Pader's indiscretions. Baron said as much in his speech to Ramis. This world caters so much to men, and we women have so many rules to follow. Even the clothes I make cannot be too revealing. Not that I wish to wear such things. We cannot go out alone; we can not have a lover. Men hold positions, I am allowed to own a business, by the grace of my family name, other women cannot. So many rules. How I wish, we could be free to do as we wished.*

They continued their usual routine of attending parties at the other nobles' Palaces. For the next month, she all but forgot about the man she hired until she found a note on her pillow, on her way to change her clothing one morning. *Perfect timing, I will buy trinkets to wear to the next gathering. I feel the need to buy something.* She was a little bored with the mediocrity of everyday being the same.

"Ramis, I am going to the markets to purchase some sundries and will be back in time to dress."

"Yes, dear Mara. This sounds like a wonderful idea. Get some air. Be generous with your purchases, dear. You deserve the best. Pick out whatever your heart desires, nothing is too good for you. We may want to entertain the thought of expanding our empire. The orders lately are such we may need another warehouse. However, we can discuss such, perhaps on our way home in a couple weeks."

"Very well. I have a few ideas of my own. I will not be long, just a few things."

Did I not say this last month? Ramis seems to glorify himself, it is his idea. Not that I care... Mader told me, my happiness is paramount. Will I be happy, divorced? Knowing Ramis has other children. What if he joins with another? Will I have to meet her? Ugh, I hope not.

She took the carriage this time, she knew it would draw eyebrows if she were to ride a horse in the Capital. Since she planned to make a lot of purchases, well, it served a dual purpose. The meeting was in the back of a jewelers, and the man was posing as hired muscle for the store. She ended her shopping spree with the jewelers as his request was for mid-afternoon teatime. Damara looked over the stores premade necklaces choosing several different gems but took a special liking to a ruby necklace the older man brought out of an incredibly old case.

"This came across my path. An Aramite did not wish to part with it, and I knew from looking, it was special. I immediately thought of you and your love of rubies. There were some missing gems, and the clasp was missing as well. I hope the repairs are to its original splendor, do you like it?"

"Yes, I do. You know me very well, and pleased you remembered. What would you like as payment?"

When she really liked something, she never bartered. It was a matter of payment for services; everyone was trying to live; she could at least help alleviate hardship in those less fortunate. This had her loved among the tradespeople she dealt with. Her maid went to the carriage for the payment box, bringing the guard with it. Damara went into the back room to quickly meet with Ash.

"I will be quick, the boy belongs to a woman in the trade district, she is a herbologist and your husband was there quite a bit. They look like they are familiar with each other. He is also familiar with the boy. There is also another woman, who lives across the river proper, and.... he also visits a brothel. That is all for now. When you leave for Kara, I will follow you a couple of days later and we can settle my account. I have done all you required of me, thank you for payment, I must go."

He said the last in a rush, disappearing around the back wall and she heard a door softly close. She heard her servants come in loudly through the front door. Damara came around the middle wall to see the guard place the chest down. She knelt in front of it and opened the lid, taking out six bags of coins and giving them to the owner. Carefully placing the ornate box with the necklace inside the chest closing the lid, Damara rose thanking the old man for his business, motioning for her servants to go to the carriage, she followed behind them.

The trip home was uneventful; she had the guard place the chest in her room when they arrived. Damara knew the necklace would look exceptionally good with the dress of red. She would wear it for her own enjoyment. It was an antiquated necklace and while it suited her tastes, she was not sure it would compliment the new styles of clothing she was inventing. She took it out and caressed the stones, with the delicate filigree.

There were some things in her life she would not share and they were ruby red.

CHAPTER 20

Meera

The Many Become the Few

We started off North again, Nejan sometimes leading and sometimes trailing behind us. It was not until the third night we heard what was following us.

We would sleep in short shifts, always packed and ready to go at moments notice. When I was pulling my duties in the early morning hours, I heard rocks tumble down the embankment we took all day to traverse. I reached out to touch Kiem's sleeve, but he was already awake, pulling his pack on, I followed suit, flattening against a rock I leaned against to let Nejan sneak by me. She padded past and a minute later I heard growls and snarls coming from the trail behind us. Some rocks tumbled down, a yelp was heard and moments later she bounded back into view,

"Let us move, this will not keep him distracted for long."

We moved as fast as two-legs can, Nejan doubling back more than once to check our visible trail. We climbed using rope in a few spots, which she would leap to. One point high enough snow and ice were underneath our boots at a continual rate. We scaled the ridge of a mountain peak and if I had not been in such a rush to quit it, I would have admired the sheer splendor of the vista all around me.

The side of the rock face we were on, was one of many. Through openings in the jagged rock, one would see a land of blue green, and browns, with the occasional glimpse of a smoking lone mountain, so distant the smoke looked as though it connected itself to the clouds. I may have looked once or twice; however, I was distracted by the moment at hand. The sight was tucked away in my mind for another time to process. Now was not the time.

Kiem and Nejan stood looking ahead, "We find ourselves a ridge or somewhere below where we make a stand. Whatever is chasing us is getting close and we do not wish to be boxed in where they have advantage. Whatever happens you will need to get through to the other side, look for a u-shaped canyon to the east, which is where the yearly caravans stop for winter. Plenty of water and game there."

He began his way down skidding and sliding not caring about the trail, I followed suit and nearly ran into his back from the velocity of my decent. Near the tree line we came across a small plateau sheer enough nothing could scale three sides.

"Perfect," Kiem put down his pack in the roots of an overturned tree. I placed mine beside his and followed him to the plateau and began picking up branches as he was doing.

"A strange and wild animal is always afraid of fire. Most at one point have felt its sting. We get a fire blazing, use it if needed to tend any wounds and destroy their night vision if we are fighting after dark. Nejan says there is only one. An older male with many scars, which means he will not be easy to kill. He may have been around when there were Dragons and may have knowledge of men. I do not know; all she says is he is starving and will not rest until he slakes his thirst."

"If you collect the branches, I will start the fire. This way we are prepared should it be soon."

"This sounds like a solid plan, Meera. This wood is dry. Frozen but dry. Once the moisture is wicked off, it will blaze."

I started the fire with two slate stones, and it soon blazed. Kiem had time for one last foray, and he returned with a huge armful, carefully dumped it and I began loading the fire. We heard a fast-moving animal coming over the stones. Nejan stood to one side with her back fur slowly raising to stand at attention, her tail twitching and then still.

"Stay behind me, lass. Nejan will try to take him down."

A very tall and lanky orange striped feline emerged from the woods padding to a stop. He stood and sniffed. I knew he was sizing up his prey. One of his ears was ripped halfway down and the flap vibrated in the slight wind. Even through his fur coat, which was unkept, I saw hip bones protruding, he looked very emaciated, eyes large in his head. It gave me a feeling the mind was not all there, especially if viewing us three as food.

"He does not look right in the mind and starving, Da."

He was taller than Nejan by a few hand spans, his weight easily less from lack of food. I felt my pulse race in my chest as I thought about what I could do against such an aged and experienced foe. There was always grabbing a large branch from the fire. I eased my knife out of my belt slowly, but it seemed small when compared to the claws on these beasts. My Pader already had knife in hand.

"He probably is, starvation will do mad things to the mind. He will go for the strongest first, being Nejan, and then pick us off one by one. Stay out of her way. When they fight, they may do us more harm if we are under foot."

I edged closer to the fire, looking for a stick to grab, should I need it. The two cats growled at each other, they began pacing out in a circle, facing each other. They tensed up, then both sprung at the same time. Up in the air they clashed, claws and fangs out. The attacking male clawed Nejan in the shoulder with his forward swipe. She let out a pain filled screech which set the hairs on my arms to straighten. She stumbled when landing and was limping as they sized each other up again. Blood welled up and coursed its way down her fur, dripping onto the rock.

Again, they jumped at each other, clawing and biting, rolling around in front of us, we backed up as much as we could to not be caught underneath their warring bodies. They parted again. Nejan wounded the other feline in the neck, however, his fur was loose, and we did not know if she connected with any muscle. They began to circle each other again, and we waited for the next battle.

"Yes, good call, feed the fire. She does not look good. He is having her bleed out to weaken her; it is a tactic animals will use if they are unsure of their combatant. I will try to distract him."

"Are you sure you should try?"

"It may give her an advantage, lass. I cannot bear to see her bleeding, if there's a chance, I am going to give her one."

I picked up the remainder of the branches, throwing them on the fire and grabbing a burning branch, holding it before my person. Kiem grabbed a large stick burning at one end. He stood waiting for the male to circle closer and stabbed him in the male parts as his hind end came between us and Nejan, who was favoring her side which had blood flowing freely down her shoulder.

The beast whirled around and sprung upon Kiem faster than any animal I had ever seen, he clamped his jaws upon his shoulder and bit down. My Pader let go of the stick and I watched as it fell to the ground, as though time had slowed... It seemed to take forever to fall, all the while, I felt anger rise. Who did this large cat think he was! This was my Pader he bit!

Oh no you do not!

I felt heat build and rise in my stomach; I saw a white haze covering my vision as though a film of linen placed over my eyes. I let loose the contents in my stomach. The pressure built up, I opened my mouth and formed the word, "Nooo." This time I did not pass out and was very aware of my surroundings and the passage of time.

Time seemed to move ever so slowly; a projectile spume of acid came forcefully out of my mouth, landing on the male's face closest to me. He was three feet in front of me, it splashed up and out, catching him directly in the eye and inside his ear. Some splashed onto Kiem's torso. I knee jerked the branch up and then the plume set alight. He let my Pader drop shaking his head, rolling, and screeching in pain as acid and fire ate into his face and head. I closed my mouth and dropped to my knees dizzy and lightheaded but still awake. Crawling over to Kiem I could see bones and torn muscle and so much blood.

He was still conscious saying, "well done girl," before closing his eyes and passing out.

I tore my furs and the shirt off my back wrapping it around his torn shoulder. Paying no attention to the screaming NightStalker whose head looked like a burning mass of red Jelly. I smelled burnt fur and meat, and it made my stomach growl in hunger, maybe not so much the smell of fur, but charred meat, mmmm. Nejan picked herself up from the edge of the Cliff and limped over, her side drenched in blood,

"I will watch over Little Uncle, you must end to the screaming male, or he will draw more predators."

Picking up my knife, I stood and walked cautiously over to the male. He stopped shaking his head and rubbing it on the rocky surface of the ground, gazing at me with his remaining eye. He quit his tirade of pain filled howling, and I heard a gruff sound in my head,

"I am so deeply sorry, Little One, had I known who you are, I would have let you pass. I did not know until you shot fire, as the Dragons of old, you are the one to bring us life. Forgive me and make it quick, I cannot stand this pain."

He lifted his head up so his neck was exposed. I drew the blade quickly across his neck and forgot to move out of the path of blood which sprayed me from head to foot, I did however remember to move as his head came down where I had been standing. I glimpsed orange iridescent sparkles rising from the shell of his body, they rose and formed a figure I can only say ran away into the evening sky. I would process what it was later. Rushing over to Kiem, Nejan spoke to me.

"Whatever you learned from your time with the healer, you need to make it quick, he is losing his life blood."

I got to work; my training took hold. When I tried to tie off his wound with his leather belt, the flow eased but did not stop. Asking Nejan to bring both packs over, I tore my shirt and his into strips to use later. Nejan first dumped my pack, so I tore it open to find my healing bag, grabbed the first thing from it which was an herb I stuffed in my mouth and began chewing. Meanwhile Nejan brought the other pack over and dumped it beside me on the other side.

"Can you gently tear the leather ties, to open the packs and get the furs loose? Drag them to the fire and try laying them out."

"I will do my best, but I have tooth and claw."

"Try. Get the ones on my packs also. Here."

She got to work, and I took the wad out of my mouth packing it into the wound and around the edges of the torn skin. Grabbing more, I stuffed my mouth and kept chewing. This herb would help numb and restrict the flow of blood for a time. Hopefully, enough time for me to repair what I could. As it began to ebb, I knew it was working, and I grabbed the leather skin of water pouring it into the wound so I could ascertain the damage.

The shoulder socket and arm bone were separated but were still intact. I began by placing them together, then tried to gauge which muscle went where and I began to sew with silk threads brought up by traders from the Capital. I knew there was a chance of them not holding, but I had no choice but to try. The wound was such, when the feline chomped down upon Kiem's shoulder, it almost severed it from his body. I had a puzzle to piece together. The teeth narrowly missed his lung. I saw the edge of the spongy mass through the blood oozing with the pulse of his labouring breathing. This set my determination. I would not lose Kiem. Not today.

The Numbweed had more than done its work, there was very little blood in the immediate area, once it wore off though, it could potentially swell to where it became a harm to him, I would have to consider all possibilities. I thought about what some of the vessels to carry blood were and found some ends. My vision narrowed in and I found some and connected them with another needle. My smallest one. I hoped it would all hold. I was feverishly working with a mass of torn muscle and some white harder tissues. It frustrated me, but I kept going.

"I do not know if this will work. I have never worked on such a mess. Honestly, I have never done anything like this before. I hope I do not make things worse. I can not imagine Kiem without his arm, and I cannot think of losing my Pader so soon after finding him."

My eyes flooded with tears, and I had to wipe them with a corner of a cloth, smearing the middling mess on my face. My arms and torso still covered by the felines blood and my hands with Kiem's.

"You do the best you can for Little Uncle. That is all you can do. We will deal with the result as we must. You are doing fine, Little Cub."

I placed muscles together, looking at his other shoulder, Kiem was not a bulky man, and his musculature was defined enough to get a small idea, of where things went. His arm muscles had taken most of the chomp, I was hoping I fixed them. Sewing gaps, and tears. Weaving and twisting in and out I salvaged what I could and before I drew the flaps of skin over, double checked there was a minimum of bleeding, this took me a long time and I did not realize the sun was dropping, and I was losing the light.

"Can you grab the burnt ends of the sticks and throw them onto the fire? I may need its lights to help me see."

"Yes, I can do that for you, Little Cub."

The edges of his injury were punctures from the outer canine teeth and I rinsed them out, stretching the skin and muscle to cleanse as best I could and made a couple stitches to close them.

Finally with the skin flap sewn together and the pieces of silk exposed for later removal I was satisfied I had done what I could.

"I will need your assistance to moving Kiem, closer to the fire. If you could be careful and grab him around his torso, I will grab his head. Yes, like so, all right. gently down. Perfect."

I realized this must have been how she carried me up the mountainside. With his legs dragging on the ground, she gently lowered him, and I covered him up and padded cloth around his shoulder tying it on and around his torso. Finally satisfied I stood up, bending back I gave myself a bit of a back stretch and heard a few crackling sounds from the effort. As I stretched, I opened my eyes to see a wonderous sight. The stars were moving overhead, zooming past our place on the mountain, I felt I could reach out my hand and touch them. I noticed but was distracted only for a moment, I had more to do. I felt the pain emanating off the great cat. Noticing Nejan's side was still oozing blood,

"Can I look at your wounds, Great Mader?"

"Yes."

I looked at the flaps of skin and fur hanging down. I saw four distinct openings with some muscle damage.

"May I sew up the deepest? It will slow the blood flow."

"You know best, Little One."

I closed what I could, but after I did, I had another thought,

"I have used what silk I have, but there is a chance using your leg will open the wounds. I should cauterize them. It will hurt more, but I can lessen with another of my herbs. It will thicken the blood some, so there is less flow. Are you wanting me to do so, Great Mader?"

"I rely on your knowledge of wounds. You may apply fire to them if it will aid the healing. We have more of our journey to travel and may not have the means to address our wounds."

I placed my blade into the stoked coals and held it while the blade began to glow.

"This will hurt, but Numbweed should lessen it."

I lifted the blade.

"Prepare yourself. This will sting."

I pressed the blade against the first cut. She flinched and exhaled sharply.

"I am sorry. The first one is always the hardest to bear."

That encouraged me to finish the others, and as I completed the last one, she whimpered, and I apologized again.

"I must not have spread the herb as much on the last one, I am sorry. If you can clean this wound when you get the chance, I will watch it for infection. You need to be incredibly careful in the first few days. If you feel not yourself in any manner you tell me. I will feed the fire, so we can take care of the carcass of this old one."

Walking over to the male… *"He did not mean to attack but his hunger drove him to it. I do hope there are others like you, so you are not at all lost."*

"Yes, there are others but not many and we are spread out to not encroach on each other's hunting grounds. It will be many seasons before others realize this valley is empty and inhabit it. This will be beneficial to us as the game and little predators will come back in droves."

Looking down at the carcass, *"Great Mader, may I have the fur from this Li'on-sa, if only to cover Kiem? I will honour him and ask his spirit find another in the next life."*

"Thank you for the asking. I understand the need…it gives me ease you would ask, I would be honoured to have Kiem use it."

She lay down watching while I began the laborious task of skinning him. Once I removed the skin from the skeleton of the feline, she rose and dragged the carcass over to the edge of the woods. I spent half the night scraping and preparing the inside of the skin as best I could, stopping to tend to Kiem, giving him mashed herbs to deal with the pain and help ease his sleep.

"Great Mader, when I killed the Li'on-sa, I saw sparkles rise from his body."

"'Tis our spirit. You are blessed to see the rebirth of our kind. Our spirits rise into the sky to wait for rebirth. I only hope to see his spirit again. He was a great male. Driven to kill by hunger."

"Do all our spirits have the sparkle?"

"I have not seen such from your kind. Only those worthy are reborn. 'Tis a gift, it should not be given or taken lightly. 'Tis part of the religion of old. To strive to do good works, to be reborn into something greater… the cycle of life."

" 'Tis wonderful. I have lots to learn. About Vendar. Aunt Nena told me what she knew, it has peaked my curiosity more, Vendar is love, the Pader of all, and the leader of the Gods. Love, honour, wisdom. So many things to learn."

"Love is an effective way to start. There is much hate and war since my time with Little Uncle. It has grown into the being of your kind... 'tis time for love to return."

"Will it be enough? Many men feed off hate. I saw much in my childhood, they mock women because women love."

"This may be your challenge to overcome; you are the female of your species. Showing others love conquers hate, is part of who and what you are."

"It sounds difficult, in a world not receptive to love. I do not know how I begin."

"You ask others for assistance but form your own mind about love. 'Tis not going to be easy, however, the reward when complete will be worth the effort. If it were easy, others would have tried."

"No one has stood up since?"

"No one. The Great One was waiting for you. You have the strength to overcome all adversity. He would not have chosen lightly."

"I am honoured, however, am overwhelmed at the moment... This display in the sky is beautiful yet terrifying at the same time. Who knows what it portends."

"It could mean the ending of one age and the beginning of another. Time will tell. You must choose, which path you follow."

"That is easy. I will chose moving forward. I will not look to the past. What ever the Great One would have me do, I will do it. I will get us to the other side of these mountains and my Pader better. I will not lose him now, not now. I have just found him...and you. I would not leave you either."

"I give thanks, Little One. The Great One has chosen well. You will become a great leader of men; you have but to see it for yourself."

"Well, being a leader can wait. Let us have you both hale. I need to get this skin prepared as much as possible."

Meanwhile the stars continued to fly by. Several times I saw explosions of light as some hit the atmosphere, and broke apart, I would glance up, but soon it became a distraction and I was busy, trying to mend all. I chewed dried berries and meat as I worked. Some of my meal flew out of my mouth, so I tried to eat slowly. The chewing of the herb for Kiem made my mouth and lower jaw lose feeling.

As the sun was beginning to show its rays, I finally stopped, sitting down hard on my arse. Nejan padded out from the woods.

"Rest, Little One, I will watch over you. We deal with the damage later when all have rested. I found a water source and rinsed off what I could. I stayed in the water as long as I could bear it. The coldness of the water felt good on my warm fur. You will tell me if I cleansed it well?"

"It looks very raw, some of the areas are oozing blood. I will sew a bit here and put some more Numbweed on it which should help with pain. If any of these

wounds reopen, I will cauterize them again. You can wash again before we set out, it can only help if it eases your pain."

I rested my eyes against a fallen log. I woke to Kiem moaning, rising quickly I went to check. He awoke seeing me gazing down at him and cracked a weak smile,

"How bad am I? I cannot feel my shoulder."

Looking down at him I spoke bluntly, "I repaired what I could and packed it with Numb weed, the effects will wear off soon. I used almost all my supply and will have to find more, or you will not like what you feel. Your shoulder was torn and dislocated. All the muscles were torn around the bone, and I am unsure if I managed to salvage them. You may never gain use of the arm again, but this is the worst, no wait, the worst is you may lose the arm altogether if infection sets in. I will wash it when we find moving water, for now I will bind it close to your body and you cannot move it, or it may tear open, then all my hard work will be for naught. I will pack up, and we will move on. The carcass of the old one will stay here for the circle of life to take what it needs. I did, however, gain a cloak for you, with permission. It will help keep you warm as you will need it more than I."

Kiem smiled at me, but I saw in his eyes, the pain he was feeling. Masked by the weed, it also marked the eyes, with a huge pupil. His green eyes looked black.

"How quickly you have grown into a leader, yes ma'am!"

Closing his eyes he fell back into an herbal induced sleep, Numbweed, not only numbed the area affected but also allowed the mind to drift on the currents of darkness, with no ill effects. I spoke to Nejan.

"This water source, is it accessible for me? I would like to get fresh water and any weeds which may be near."

"Yes, there is one area you may be able to access, you should take the rope Little Uncle has. You will have to lower yourself down to the water. If you find yourself in trouble, call me. While you are gone, I will watch over him."

I tied all my furs on my exposed body parts again; the bite of the frigid wind had me shivering after adrenaline wore off. I headed out in the direction she came from; it was more treacherous than she said. When I reached the point, she told me about, I tied the rope to an outlying tree trunk, hoping it held. I assessed the knots I tied in the rope, and with a final conviction, of do or die, I started down the cliff face.

Inching my way down with the rope my feet walking down the sheer rock, it took me a good hour to descend. I finally touched my arse down on a wet rock.

I was so focused on watching what I was doing I did not look down, until I felt the damp rock hitting my behind. Sitting down I turned to face a huge raging current. I filled the skins with water. It was almost too cold to drink; and burned down my raw throat. I paced myself, after I swished a mouthful and spit it out. After I sated my thirst, I filled the skin back up.

I walked along the gravel bank until I lifted myself onto the dirt embankment and hurriedly picked the half dead weeds I needed. They were past their prime, however, I would see if I could make them work. I tried a small mouthful, chewed, and felt the effects of my mouth numbing and spit it out. I picked as much as I could fit into the satchel I brought down with me. It was not very heavy, and I would also have the weight of water to contend with on the way up.

Many times, I rested, I made it a third of the way up the cliff when I felt the burn of my arms. It took me twice as long to go up than it did to descend. I finally crested the top after throwing the skins and the satchel up, then very slowly getting my body onto the rock face where the rope was tied.

"I will still be awhile as I am exhausted. Let me catch my breath for a moment."

I closed my eyes but opened them up when Nejan sniffed my face. She came to me grabbing the water skins by the straps quietly leaving to go back to Kiem. I thanked her rolling over rising to my feet. I walked over to the rope only to see in untying it, I barely made it up. One of the outer knots worked its way loose. I would get Kiem to show me a better knot to use next time.

I easily untied the rest of the rope, wound it up, placing it on my shoulder with the satchel and headed back to my companions. Kiem was still sleeping, and I thought I would let him rest. The flight of stars was still going strong; I began to not see them until they hit the sky. Several hit at once, the sight and sound had me glancing up. I would ask Pader if this was a sign of the Dragon Age, he told me a little of. He admitted he saw a portion of the Prophecy, but it was not something he remembered.

I lay down after I packed her and Kiem's wounds with the chewed weed I collected. I would save the remainder of herbs I dried for last, use the fresh first.

I closed my eyes but for a moment, and the day disappeared.

CHAPTER 21

Natan

The Ebb and Flow of the Seas

Natan stood, stretching out his back from his hunched position over the wooden table slab. It was covered in books, scrolls, and paperweights. His lower back throbbed from the stretch, he felt older than he was, and wished the day were over. The glow from various lamps and wall torches flickered with the occasional air movement. Other than that, they burned straight. Guards would come down periodically to change them and watch him do his work. He would chat with a few friendly ones from time to time.

He first began his research by sitting in the chair behind him, but after time, he would stand in front of the table and lean over maps, one covering the other, some etched in skins and some in papyrus. There were piles stacked of open books, weights holding down scrolls and he scratched the irritated skin on his chin, it was a bad habit he started when he felt overwhelmed.

Natan was one of many scribes in the Hall of Learning in Aram. One of many who gained permission to look through the great glass. Having earned his right to do so, by his sharp mind and quick responses, he was also commissioned to set the information spread before him to rights. Catching the attention of the Oban of Learning, he was told to come down here and figure out the jumble of maps, papers, and artifacts, to catalogue, organize, and repair if needed. He had an assistant, a young man, but he only lasted a day. Natan found out the young man had gotten into his cups, visited a house of ill repute, and bragged about all the things he saw. Then the man disappeared.

Natan knew he was followed for a while. However, this diminished as the person who must have hired the man, was satisfied Natan was true to his oath.

He was a middle-aged man. Black hair and brown eyes, a little silver showing under his headdress, a small belly under his tunic. He looked like every other man of Aram. No wife and no children, that he knew of. He was dedicated to his work so much, he often would sleep here without returning to his home, which housed his dear Mader. He was frugal, never spent needlessly, so his Mader could have all she required. Having given up so much to ensure her son had an education; he spoiled her as much as his meager earnings could afford to.

Ever since the meteor shower, he was poring over any scrolls he could. Trying to find out if there was any mention of this event in historical texts. He was told and given permission to read and look at the forbidden texts, which were in lower areas in the Great Hall, in the hope of uncovering the meaning of these objects in the heavens. He was to give answers to his superior, who had to report to the FirPader. He found nothing to explain. Yet!

His skin was dry. The air in the catacombs was even dryer than the air outside, and his constant scratching at his chin broke where sparse chin hairs emerged. Some of the scratching was infected and he tried hard to not irritate it further. By the Gods! Sometimes the itch drove him crazy!

He was astounded at the amount of information he did not know was available. He was warned if he were to speak of this to anyone, he would earn his death. This did not stop him from questioning what he was raised on.

A singular deity. The FirPader was the Almighty God on earth! It had always been so. At least for Natan. His upbringing was reading the works of their God and his predecessors and was satisfying… up till now.

This information was contrary to his beliefs, it kept his mind busy, thinking to himself the world was bigger than where he lived. Other lands had other religions, and he had their beliefs right in front of him. All this information was dangerous to the wrong people… it meant death. The scribe who had broken in to see the lower catacombs on a dare lost his eyesight and ultimately died from his wounds. It served as a warning, to all.

Being an astute man, he swore on the hand of the Head of the Hall, he would not speak of or copy anything he saw. As the FirPader commanded the Hall scribes to find an answer, he was given access, and only him, after the assistant proved to be worthless. Natan was a quick reader and could speak and read in the other languages of this known world. His Mader's intuition at having her only son educated paid off. His advancement in duties came with an amount of money he all too readily gave to his Mader, being a loving son.

When in an attempt to step away from his readings, he on a whim, one night during the winter solstice, decide to investigate the glass to see the heavens. To his surprise, he saw the star with a tail. Having several other scribes confirm his viewings, he hurried himself to the Oban of Learning to tell of his findings, not caring he woke the aged man from his sleep. This set off a dozen scribes told to find answers. Natan oversaw this new contingent of learned men. Men who were also compelled to swear on their and their families lives not to speak of the forbidden texts they would view.

He knew one or two of the men would not adhere… several loved their drink. Loose lips and the sounds of their own egos in the telling would have rumours happening sooner than later. His ability to know their future came to pass. Soon enough he was the only one left and he preferred it this way. He was not very social anyway.

In his initial readings, he was incredulous. There were documents supporting the very heresy of Dragons and he kept reading. *Oh my. This is astonishing. The Islanders are deeply rooted in their belief of Dragons… and their Gods. There is no proof they existed… Or is there? If I say anything to anyone, I will be dead. I hope I finish this work by myself. I feel like not sharing this information, not to anyone. Who would believe this anyway?*

The Dragon texts he was very possessive of, he placed them in their own separate room. As he read them, he had questions, but no one to ask them of. Natan poured over each one, absorbing the information each held. He hardly believed this was their world so very long ago. It would not be written, if there was not truth to it all. He kept this all close to his heart. He had questions about his own religion and that of the one on the other continent, but he kept mum. Asking questions was a sure way of dying, he did not wish to die just yet, too much to read and learn.

The possession alone is heresy. This is as much as our history; I saw the Great Library. We have many tomes of FirPaders before. But this… this is a revelation for sure! This must have been truth. I have, five storerooms of information to organize. I will be down here for years. Ughh!

Dragons existed, he found several texts on the care of, the ministrations of people in charge of the care, housing, feeding, and reproduction of Dragons. There was only one text devoted to the care of eggs. The Dragons were by all means an exceptionally large flying lizard or snake with wings. One scribe of old thought to compare and apply his knowledge of such, and to document findings.

He found beautifully coloured drawing renditions of these beasts. In his readings, he learned there was one dominant male, and the rest females. They would lay eggs once every one hundred years or so. Dragons would bond, (not a mating ritual, but similar to a joining?) with one to three humans in their lifetime, as their lifespan greatly out lived those of their counterpart.

This painting, done by… oh! One of the great Masters. This rendition would create waves if known he painted this. This is one of the greatest painters. All his works are in the Capital of Du'Lanay. I wish someday I can go to Merida and see his works in the Palaces before they disappear or ruined. This is a beautiful painting. Look at the colours, these beasts were assorted colours. Interesting. Looks like the black one was dominant, by his size, this must be the male, he looks bigger than the blue and green one.

Natan placed the lantern down and picked up the painted canvas to look closer at the painting. The oil was dry and cracked as he unrolled it, it threatened to roll back up as he held it close to his face.

Hmmm, I see other figures in this. A figure holding what looks to be a sword. This a light, or is it a reflection? Then it looks as though there are figures on the backs of the others. Hmmm, DragonRiders? Oh, and look! I never noticed the ones in the background. One, two three… there are many more. Ten. I wonder what happened to them all. Was there a great war? Why is it not told? What is being hidden? I need to find this out… even if 'tis just for my knowledge.

Natan gently placed the painting down and weighed the corners down with books. It would eventually disintegrate unless he rubbed it with oil.

I will bring some down next trip outside. If I remember.

He kept reading one of the scrolls he laid aside. Humans would have to prove they were worthy. Have an incorruptible code of honour and conduct themselves in leadership with a neutral demeanor, not taking bribes or being corrupt. There were several texts on the attributes of humans deemed worthy.

Ha, try finding a man worthy in this life. Everyone is corrupt. This is our life. A man who does not take bribes. Well, will not find a man here in Aram like this. We all take bribes; this is how we live. Oh. Here is a good one. Unbiased. Hmmmm, again not here in Aram. We are deeply rooted in our worship of the FirPader. He is all knowing, all forgiving. One would have to have an open mind, to all ways of life and worship. Let us keep reading... maybe I will find more to amuse myself...

Natan read everything in the lower rooms, cataloging the Dragon texts in his own system. The more he read, the more he discerned the Dragons' humans did not live up to their duties. Several riders were killed by their own Dragon's, with horrific details written by the author. He found scrolls written in the other languages of Pelin'Dun and Du'Lanay which corresponded with ones in his own language.

There would be another Dragon Age, another round of Riders, beginning with the advent of falling stars. Finally, he found what it was he was instructed to find. He knew the information he was about to relay was not what the FirPader wished to hear. Theirs was a history of the after years, the Temple acolytes and scribes kept excellent records of the advent of their rule, and adamant about not repeating the mistakes of the Riders and their beasts. He placed those to the side, not sure if he should even mention it to his superior. He knew he would have to, but for some reason, he stayed silent. The timing was not right.

Pelin'Dun was the only land which kept the old religion fluent. They kept the rule of the Riders, which had its own mystery surrounding the Ceremonies and Rituals. They did not mingle with other lands, keeping to themselves. They were content to not expand the empire they had and kept invaders away, by marriage or by negotiations. Not that Aram did not try, for some reason never gained a foothold.

Aram was waging war periodically with Du'Lanay, taking the fight to them. This latest war was raging on for over ten years, and every year, they gained and then lost what they gained. They could not maintain the areas during the harsh winter of this land. Natan did not have to read to know. It was common knowledge, and some of the men he worked with were very good at gossiping.

The FirPader had a holy duty to convert all the world. Even though Du'Lanay had broken the wheel the six Gods were the ultimate religion, it still existed on the Islands. The advent of Namanism was one God. Thing is, it was the wrong one! According to the FirPader and his beliefs, he must bring order to the infidels, by waging war, gaining land bit by bit, converting those who would accept, killing those who would not. His methodology was to bring back slaves, children and raise them in the religion of Aram.

So historically speaking, the oldest religion to date that Natan could discern was the Vendic religion of the DragonRiders.

So, would this make the religion of my Pader and Pader before him, the wrong one?

He had so many questions, it made him want to rip out what little hair he had left.

Was the FirPader's war based on a Prophecy?

The more he read of the Prophecy, Natan saw the meteor shower and now the advent of the soon to be seen star meant a different beginning. A very controversial one at that! He placed the last scroll in its place, rolled up the maps, putting them in their special place, and the last piece of controversial material was stored. He gave one last look, shut the heavily ironed door, locked the bolt, and returned to his office upstairs among the rest of the population, hoping his findings would not see his head leave his neck.

Little did he know his work had just begun.

CHAPTER 22

Solina

Bring Purification to Amend

Solina stood there, a bit unsteadily on her feet, the creation of the intense winds used some of her energy. She wobbled a bit, watching the fumes leave the opening into the mountain. Reaching out with her mind.

"Are you able to walk if I get the chains off?"

She asked of her voices, now they left her mind alone for her own thoughts. She was unaware of the turmoil behind her. The horses scattered, various men took off to round them up, and the young Captain and his second stood behind her, at the ready should she fall. They stood silently, unaware of her talent of mind speech. Respectfully waiting.

"We must gather strength, but it needs to air, the air in here is extremely dangerous to your body, however, you have another pressing matter to deal with. There is another DragonRider, brought to you, the Mader of the Seas. You must go meet her. We can wait for our freedom for a little while. She may be able to help you with us when you bring her here. We see the light and it gladdens our hearts. We will bask in its glory while you greet your sister."

Solina did not question them, turning she began walking, unsteady at first, but gaining strength as she descended the mountainside. The two men turned and followed her, still silent, still in awe of the raw power they witnessed coming from this small slip of a woman. Her eyes lessened their glow but still whirled with Dragon sight as she walked more assuredly, passing by a few of her guards, some holding horses, standing around unsure of their instruction. Seeing her walking down the path, they saluted and fell into line behind her. The ones without a horse kept up with her. She heard the young Captain.

"Kallen, you take a cohort and guard the entrance up the mountain. Do not let anyone near. I will return when I have instruction."

She arrived at the Temple, only the Temple attendants were there. Walking up to the Pader, she asked him where her GrandMader and the others were.

"They went to the Reception Hall, it seems a young woman was brought there, she is said to command sea creatures and has blue eyes. What did you find up the mountain? We felt the earth shake."

"My Dragons, of course, locked up. There will be some explaining to do, however for now, I will go meet this woman. I want all attendants to be here in the hall when we get back. No exceptions." Solina was not mad, just matter of fact. He bowed his head as she walked past.

"As you command, High Dragon."

She continued to the Reception Room walking in, her head held high and her anger in check. What she did not know was her eyes were reflecting her Dragon connection and everyone she crossed paths with, bowed, or knelt bending their heads. She kept walking up to the chair, her GrandMader wisely was not occupying. Sitting down, her GrandMader and the other Rulers quietly kept their mouths shut, not knowing what she would do. She cut right to the chase.

"There are Dragons. They are kept chained and were drugged to keep them docile. The elixir in the Rituals is their blood. Well, no more. I opened their prison. Things will be changed from now on."

She paused, picking up a glass of water placed on the stand beside her chair, sipping it slowly.

"What do you plan to do, GrandDader?"

It was at this point, a guard entered the room, a poorly dressed woman following him but staring at the doors, running her hands on the wood, and gazing at the glass windows, her mouth open and she stopped walking into his back.

Solina giggled, and the woman glanced up, their eyes meeting. Dragon met Dragon. Solina's eyes hadn't changed from Dragon state and at the contact, Atin's eyes began glowing blue, her iris not changing. Solina stood up and held out her hands stepping down to greet her new sister, the hugest smile on her face.

"Welcome, you are…?"

"Atin, Your Grace."

She was shy and quiet, Solina knew the surroundings intimidated her.

"Not Your Grace, Atin, we have no rank between you and I, I am Solina, come I have need of your assistance. Our bonds need us."

Solina grabbed Atins' hand leading her out the doorway, stopping as her GrandMader asked what was to be done. Solina stopped and glanced back at her GrandMader, risen from her seat.

"For now, we keep this quiet, word will emerge soon enough. I want guards who are loyal, I need goats, sheep, and someone to figure out how to get water in the Temple basin again. There are Dragons again, and I must get them healthy, or there will be no Riders ever again. GrandMader, you look after the government and delicate details of everyday life. This is still your government, and leave the Dragons to me, they are mine. Now, Atin and I will be going up the mountain. Please see the livestock is herded up the mountain and use servants who will not talk. Oh wait, I can deal with that. Come Atin, let's go for a walk."

Solina spoke with a newfound strength she didn't know she had before. She felt her purpose was being fulfilled. She found her voices, and her voice, walked with purpose, spoke with authority, and stood taller for it. Though she hadn't ever seen a live Dragon before, she knew this was her mission. That and the blonde woman with her, looking very intimidated at the moment.

Solina looked at the woman. She was young, maybe her age, perhaps a bit younger, and marveled at her blonde hair and blue eyes. She was shy but when their eyes met, the shyness seemed to dissipate.

"I, am..."

"You are..."

They both tried speaking at the same time, laughing aloud at the attempt. Solina hadn't let go of her hand as they went down a vast hall to a huge set of doors. The women left the hall walking out into the sunlight, still holding hands.

"Where do you call home, Atin?"

"I live with my family on the Northmost Island, and I gather pearls for our livelihood. I seem to have gained some talents, lately. My parents seem to think I may be, well, a DragonRider? I am not certain, but all evidence so far, with my eyes glowing points to it. I never wondered at staying underwater longer than my family, but I am almost at ten minutes underwater."

"That is quite the accomplishment. No one I know has breath that long."

"I can communicate underwater also. The first time I noticed was asking a turtle to help me rise to the surface. I helped him seasons before with an errant hook in his fin. His help was needed. The second time was maneaters responding to my feelings of anger. I did not understand until I erred over my special place I am stocking for my family, of sea creatures from which to harvest pearls. Because of my feelings, maneaters killed a man trying to harvest in what I called my 'cove.' I realize now I was acting in anger. It was wrong of me. Why do your eyes glow, however, look different like a creature?"

"I am not sure, I bonded with all the Dragons here on the Island and when I am in their power, my eyes change. Have you heard voices?"

"No, I haven't. I have thought underwater, and it seems they follow my suggestion?"

Atin asked, hesitantly. The women had a dozen guards following them now and Solina stopped in the middle of the path, turning around. The men also halted, as she spoke.

"I have no doubt you are aware of what is in the mountain. It will not be repeated to anyone on pain of death,"

Here her eyes glowed a bit brighter, the men falling to their knees. All affirming their obedience to her.

"I will require assistance from some of you, I hope you all have strong stomachs for what you are about to see. Here with me is Atin, another Dragon, you will accord her the same respect as you do for me."

Atin looked uncomfortable with the accord, and Solina looked at her.

"You are also a DragonRider; my voices confirmed it. I need your help. I have opened their prison, but do not know in what state they are. I heard their voices since I was a child, had these eyes since I was a child. They called out to me over the years, but every year the voices became less. My voice told me they leave the carcasses where they perish and are left to rot. They are also covered in their own feces. I don't know how many are left, not many. We must bring them outside and get them their first real meal. I have people bringing up goats and sheep."

This last sentence she relayed to the Captain who had not left her side since this morning. He had stuck to her like a butterfly hovering, but she did not feel he had overstepped his presence. He was genuine in manner. His red hair was closely clipped under his leather helmet, and his handsome face was attentive to the girls. She could read nothing but respect for his charge.

"What is your name, Captain? You have been diligently by my side, this whole time."

"Veren, DragonRider."

He came closer bowing his head. He was a good head taller than them. His attire was the standard uniform of the guards, with a gold torc clasp keeping his red cape on his broad shoulders. It snapped back with his motion of his arm.

"Anything you command, it is done."

"Veren, I need you to take charge of your men and the herders bringing up the goats. Have them brought to the field just North of the basin, where most of the horses stopped. Then have the herders leave. Have one of your men to take that charge. I need you to come with us. The air should be cleared somewhat. Follow us when you have directed your lieutenants."

Solina and Atin, continued walking up the path to the North face of the mountain. Atin braved a question when she wished to clarify what she thought was happening.

"What exactly are we doing? And who have you released from prison? I am not sure of what you are talking about?"

"Why Dragons, of course."

Atin gasped. It was all fine and dandy to talk about them like they were real, but they were... actually real!

"And we are going to...?"

"I opened the door where they have been kept, for hundreds of years, I am hazarding a guess, since the last one disappeared. I have not entered, as you arrived. They said the air inside was not fit for us to breathe. So now hopefully it has aired out enough, and I would like you to come with me to see what we are up against. All I know is they are chained. You are up to the task? I would not ask otherwise. You are another DragonRider like myself, you have different talents, from what you have told me."

"By the Gods! Real Dragons! Oh! This is all happening too fast. It was just the past few days my parents mentioned I may be one. I never thought I would be one. Now we are to see them. Real. Oh my! And they speak. Real Dragons...You said you always heard voices. For many years! I have only started to notice the changes in me. Like thinking to the sea creatures and my eyes have only recently begun to change colour. It is almost too much to take in."

Atin felt so unsure of herself. Solina could tell it was a bit overwhelming. She gave Atin's hand a squeeze.

"I know. Sometimes I cannot believe it. That they are real. Many years I have heard voices. Somehow, I always knew, but to see one in the flesh... And I am glad you are one. I have always wanted a sister. You do not mind if I call you this?"

"Oh, no! I have always wanted a sister. I mean, I have them, but one my age. We can talk about boys. Oh. Maybe not. I am not interested in that. We can talk about Dragons if we are to be Riders. I have no idea what one does. Do you?"

"Well, we ride them. However, I have no idea how to manage this either. Shall we find out together? Once we see what is in the mountain? We may have our work cut out for us. They were imprisoned for many centuries. They told me they are chained, drugged, and left to rot."

"Oh, that does not sound good. Like an abandoned animal, chained and left to fend for themselves. Drugged? How?"

"I have yet to find this out. Obviously, it would have to be in their water or food. I have not pressed the Temple yet; they were the ones to care for them."

"Then they would know more on them. Good to know. I am sure they would have documented their care."

"I never thought about this. You may be right. Let us just see what we have before us. It may be daunting."

They were walking along the path, evidence of hooves in the soft packed grasses. The churned gravel, their feet making noise as they walked along the side of the mountain. Solina was hesitant for a moment, but knew this young woman was feeling the way she had just recently.

"After we deal with our bonds, would you want to live here with us? I could read some of the history to you, and we could have some incredibly good conversations. You could learn from Gran what a DragonRider is."

Solina asked Atin, somewhat shyly, as the magnitude of what was happening at that moment was sinking in. Even she had not considered much on what transpired this very day. It somehow did feel all too fanciful. Yet she knew it was right. Saving an animal from horrible conditions, had her ire up. She had yet to find these conditions. From what her voices told her, they were not ideal. Atin's shy voice broke into her thoughts.

"You know, my Pader said my life would change if I was a DragonRider, I didn't believe him, but now I do. If 'tis fine for now, I would like to return home for a while. My little brothers are still too little to help them survive. You would know where I am, and we can visit each other. When the time comes to move on, I will know I have helped my family adjust to my absence. He has lost five of his brood, and to lose another so quickly would devastate him."

"Lost five? This sounds drastic and devastating. Was it sickness?"

"Oh, no. Not like that. My eldest sister just joined, and four of my brothers have gone to the war. My Da is heartbroken, it was all his eldest. I have two younger brothers and three younger sisters."

"You have a large family. Your pearling keeps you fed?"

Solina was unsure of how to ask, but she was curious to learn more.

"Yes, we are a large family. The five eldest were from my Da's first wife. My Mader was asked to care for them, when the other passed. She had many children, but some have passed. May they be Blessed."

"May they be Blessed. I understand. Dame Metina, my GrandMader, and the High Magistrate have explained to me to appease the continents, we have to send tributes. She said sending men, to fight has kept them distant, but she fears it may not be enough. The Namarch keeps asking us for more than we can give. It may come to an impasse soon. She is filling my head with everything. It is so overwhelming. Then to add fuel to the fire, this. You will help me?"

"As much as I am able. I am just as new to this as you. I had no idea Dragons existed."

"I somehow always knew. I had voices in my head since I was little. Once I could master the clamour, I began to read. Reading tomes on Dragons, they would correct certain things. It wasn't until I partook of the Ritual, that it began to sink in. And now, you and I will release them!"

"Oh, this is monumental. Just how are we to go about this?

Atin said this with a question in her voice, not wanting to offend this new friend, who spoke to her as an equal. She waited for Solina to answer, and after a few more seconds, Solina replied.

"My voices say you are welcome to stay but understand you are caring about your family. We can figure out the later once we get them out."

"Oh, you can talk to them? How? In your mind? Why can't I, is there something wrong with me?"

Solina laughed, holding on to Atin's hand again.

"NO! There is nothing wrong with you, you don't have a bond yet. That is what mine says. The Dragons are too few and some won't survive much longer. I do not know how this will all work out. I do know, though, that we, you, and I, must get these ones out of this hole in the ground and get what we find hale and hearty for the next part in our lives. I can speak to them in my mind and that's where they speak to me. All I know is there are other people, like you and me and we will all meet at some point. Ahh, here we are."

They reached the opening where Solina blasted the doors back. Both girls stopped in their tracks. The doors look like someone huge had taken a hammer and struck them hard. The wood was splintered in various areas and the rusty metal strapping and hinges were bent in all directions and peeled back as though a banana peel.

"By the Gods! You blasted these open?"

"Verily."

"How? With a big hammer?"

"No, I command winds, much like you command water."

"I can? All I have done is ask a sickness to leave my Pader, while he was floating in the sea. I guess that is commanding...that is smoke? Looks like a green, brown, like sickness..."

"You can see colours in the air?"

"I was seeing auras around people, colours in their skin. It is the moisture which surrounds them. Not necessarily the air, but if there is moisture, it does accentuate the colours. I see what makes a person good or bad. I saw my Pader was sick, as he became more ill, the colour surrounding him grew deeper in colour. I have seen dishonesty in others when we bargain for pearls. I have looked at my family; the little ones have the best colours. More innocent spirits, I am guessing. Adults have the worst auras. I saw a lot in the markets. It gives me headaches to look. So, I try not to."

"You will have to tell me more on your talents. We should get inside and see what we are up against. Are you ready? This is a new beginning for us all."

As they approached the opening, only a small amount of foul air was still leaking out the top of the opening.

"It looks like we may be able to enter, let us help them to freedom."

"It looks very dark inside, but somehow, I can see. Can you?"

"Yes, we are Riders, we have the use of Dragon sight. Watch your footing. What is this?"

Solina and Atin gingerly stepped into the cavern. The opening at the doors was vacant but as they walked in further, the walls looked to be closing in. Reverse stalactites littered the area and close to either wall were mounds of rock, which both women realized at the same time were the remains of past Dragons. Somber now they plodded on, until they came into an exceptionally large cavern.

"Oh, Solina. There are so many. How tragic. Look at these ridges. Oh!"

They could see in the dim light. Both seeing with their Dragon sight, there were mounds all along the wall, and chains! The links thicker than their thighs, all bound together. Atin had tears well up in her eyes, and she absently wiped them with her ragged sleeve. She looked at the fused chains, then realised Solina had moved forward. Solina walked to the furthest wall to a mound, larger than the rest with a long neck and a head resting on the ground, but it was only how she could tell it was a head by the glowing eyes which opened, and closed at the same time she heard her voice, say to her,

"Many blessings, Little One. Any thoughts on the chain? It is solid on the ground, and I have not been able to move for many years now."

The chain he spoke of, looked like a log with what she assumed was petrified feces, and she saw his leg, raw and oozing with green and brown mucus around the area which seemed to be attached to the log, which also smelled like rotted fish.

Atin, came up beside her and spoke,

"I see the aura around him, it is sickly, but also there is a yellow, which is also your aura. I am guessing this is your Dragon. I do not see how we can get these chains off. I am only learning what talents I may have; I helped my Da get well, yet there was an ocean of water to do so. What are you thinking?"

The Captain, Veren had braved the dark to follow them, however, had a torch in hand, which only affirmed how dark it was inside the cavern. He came up behind the two girls looking at the leg area.

"I could find a smith and have him hammer the chain. It may take time, though. What a god-awful smell. I don't even think swine are kept like this."

He bowed to the Dragon, Solina laughed and answered the Captain,

"He appreciated your candor, but a hammer would just damage his already diseased leg. We must find another way. Can you show me where the pin is?"

She asked Veren, who showed no signs of fear, for one so young. His curiosity was such, he was more upset any animal would be kept in such conditions,

Dragon or not. This man had a heart for the downtrodden, for sure. He tried to look but without touching the feces, he merely pointed to where he thought it was.

"I am thinking it is here, but this looks like it is solid mass and hard as rock, I don't even think you could wash it off."

Atin looked at both. Her mind was busy thinking and she smiled.

"Wait, if it was bone dry, do you think you could chip it off?"

She asked the Captain, who nodded his head.

"I think so, but it still looks very moist."

"Well, by the strength of the Aunt then, I have an idea."

Both Solina and the Captain took a few steps back looking at Atin. She closed, then opened her eyes, her blue eyes glowing brighter when she opened them. Focusing on the leg and the solid mass around it, she stared, raising her hands to the Dragon. Her companions saw a mist, brown in colour rise from the leg and the mass, which began to shrivel and darken in colour, if that were possible in such a dark space. The mist rose to the ceiling and made its way to the opening behind them, but they were focused on the outline of the chain emerging from the hardening mass.

Veren left to go outside,

"I am going to see if I can find something to chip away with."

"No, wait, Veren, I can help with this part."

Solina touched him on the arm, and he stopped in his tracks.

"As you command, my Dragon."

They watched as Solina closed her eyes then opened them and a sliver of air, solidified. She motioned with her hands, using a chisel of air to chip off flakes of petrified Dragon feces. This worked very well, and Atin and Veren stepped back as Solina focused working harder. With more than one air chisel going, soon the outline of the metal chain was visible with the huge pin which held the shackle around the leg, also visible. Feces flew in all directions, hitting all the spectators, but no one cared. Soon the chain was bare of excrement, and the dilemma of getting it open presented itself.

They pondered what they would use to open the shackle. Atin walked up to it pulling the pin straight out after tapping the corroded cotter pin holding the larger pin in place with a rock. This had the desired effect of unlocking the shackle. Veren came up to the Dragon and bowed.

"My sincere apologies, Great One, if I am to cause you any pain, but I need to brace against something solid and your body is the only thing available. By your leave?"

"You have permission, Veren."

The guard took a hold of the shackle, tried but couldn't budge it at all. He looked closely at the shackle.

"If you were to form a wedge just about here, High Dragon…"

With a loud crack, the shackle split and fell onto the dirty rock floor on the outside and against the body of the Dragon on the other side. Veren grabbed the split pieces and with the girls help they slid the heavy iron away to the side.

"All right, everyone. Let's head to the opening. There is going to be a massive Dragon trying to get outside."

They backed away but didn't leave. The Dragon shuddered trying to rise, the bad leg would not get under the mass. The leg slid and could not find purchase on the littered stone floor, the dried excrement made it slippery and fine dust rose from the efforts. The huge animal lowered its chest back onto the ground.

Atin turned to Solina,

"How about pillows of air under his body to cushion it and then mayhap make the cushions move?"

This was the only way she could describe what she was trying to explain. If water were present, it would make a good lubricant, but pillows of air sounded the same. Solina looked at her with a grin, turning to the heaving giant lizard.

"You are a genius! Why did I not think of this?"

As he tried to rise, she gathered pockets of air, coloured yellow particles and all three of them backed out as this seemed to work. The Dragon's head was barely above the ground, his one leg barely functioned and the other dragged behind, under the slowly moving mass of flesh. At one narrow point, there was only room to go up, so Solina had the whole underside of the beast cushioned by yellow air and it rose high, almost to the ceiling, but trying to not touch any of the stalactites which graced the roof.

It lowered, and once Solina stumbled, so Atin grabbed her shoulders.

"I have you. You worry about the air and I will worry about your steps. We are a team."

The women and the Captain backed out of the doorway, Atin guiding Solina back with her hands on the other shoulders, as Solina was focused on moving the barely conscious mass. The men on the outside gasped as first the head and then the mass of the emaciated Dragon gained the light. It was a sorry sight. Not at all majestic.

Raised bulges which could only be wings crusted to the body with the solid coat of dirt and excrement covering it. One could not see the true colour for all what covered it over the hundreds of years it remained in the dark. Solina guided it to the shade on one side of the basin in front of the opening gently lowering it to the ground. Atin caught her friend as when Solina finished, she almost lost her legs.

"Alright, Veren, we must get him water and meat if it is able. But slowly. water first. Do we have any basins?" Solina sat down not too gracefully, requesting water for herself as well.

Atin said, "If you find me barrels, like for wine, but with fresh water, I can help with this."

Veren rushed to do her bidding, approaching his men, standing, and gawking at the beast of legends which just materialized out of a hole in the ground. No one had ever seen one alive before, only the effigies in the Halls of Worship, so what they were seeing for the first time was nothing short of a miracle. There was a heavy silence, no one dare say anything, shock at what emerged still capturing everyone's speech.

The starved Dragon was covered in dirt, dust from the mountain, and its wings were nonexistent, they were adhered to its body along with its tail. The layer of dirt was combined with the solids of its feces, and there was no evidence of scales. The only thing which made it look different than that of a drowned rat was its elongated neck. More like one of the geese which inhabited the inner lakes on the other side of the Island. It looked nothing like the statues.

The size of it was larger than any beast or animal on the Island. It had to be the size of one of their sailing ships if one were to compare it to anything. The height alone was twenty feet. The length was thirty. Well, then, maybe not as big, their ships were a hundred feet long. Solina looked at the mass of animal. It had bumps on its head and neck which would look like steps once it could raise its head. There were other lumps and bumps which made it look misshapen. It was not looking very noble now. The creature looked nothing like any animal that roamed their Islands. Other than a barely open eye, one would not know it even had a head.

Veren found his voice. He ordered his men to get what was needed. They rushed to do his bidding, Solina projected her voice and said very sternly.

"If you mention any of this to anyone down in the Temple or elsewhere, you will die."

The men stopped, bowed, and reaffirmed they would obey all the Dragons commanded, to the death. Then they hurried off, while Veren returned to the women.

"Is there more than one, High Dragon?"

He looked at the beast but directed his question to the now trying to stand woman. He offered her his arm; she took hold pulling herself up.

"Yes, there is, but I do not know if I have the strength right now to do that again." She looked to the Dragon, who was shallow breathing but had one eye facing them open.

"We are to try again tomorrow. We must retain our strength and use our skill on the others. This one will help but first let's get some thing in its belly."

A horse and cart were coming up the path, the horse blindfolded but still acting up.

"Marshall Diem, a cloth should have been placed over its nose, maybe with molasses, to mask the smell of the reclining beast. It'll rip your arms out once it gets close and its fear up."

"Sorry sir. Next time. I have my hands full with this one."

They managed to get the cart stopped for a brief time and most full barrels rolled and carried off by several guards who remained, before the horse took charge and left with his handler barely hanging onto the driving reins. Atin asked the Captain for his cloak, which he gladly took off his shoulders. Taking it from his hands she walked up to the alert but still laboriously breathing Dragon.

"Could you please try to raise your head, sir."

She looked at the Dragon's maw, his eye whirling gold. The Dragon tried, succeeding in raising it a few feet off the ground. It weaved a bit and shook with the effort. Atin placed the cloak under where the jaw sat and laid it out open on the ground. No sooner she did so, stepping back than the head came down rather forcefully. She remained on her knees in front of the jaw saying to Solina,

"If you could put some air pillows under all four corners and edges, and Veren, if you could roll a barrel close and open the cork plug, please."

Solina said, "Ahhh, I see."

The corners raised up, cradling the jaw of the Dragon in a bowl of fabric. Veren tapped the plug out of an upright barrel with a stone and motioned for another to be brought close by. Atin focused on the barrel and soon a stream of water was making its way over to the cloth basin and splashing down and filling it up, it soon covered the bottom lip of the jaw. As she emptied the one barrel, she watched to see if anything happened. Nothing. Then she saw the water slowly disappearing, and the level going down.

"Should we try a sheep or goat next? I don't think we should feed too much at once, it could reject food especially if it hasn't been fed properly for so long."

Solina agreed, and Veren telling his guards to get a goat but to mask its nose with a cloth.

Solina addressed Veren,

"If you could also ask that a repast, be brought up for Atin, myself, you, and the men, we will be here for quite some time. This I entrust only to you to do. Go down to my GrandMader and let her know what we are about. Just her, no other Rider! She is to conduct her business of the government, there is to be no interruption, she already knows, but I want to reassure her I am not going to interfere with her duties. Make sure your men are solid, no wavering, I also want Sheyna up here. She should be at the Palace by now, GrandMader was to fetch her. I am guessing we will need some torches for you and the men soon. Also, more kegs of water, and bring sheep, or the smaller goats, hobble them if necessary."

"Yes, High Dragon, as you command."

Veren walked down the path and leaving a couple guards at the entrance of the pathway.

Solina looked at Atin,

"The water helped a lot, and Nannosh says thank you. Also, she's a girl! I feel so bad, calling her a male! And she agrees, a little goat will keep her until the morning while her stomach settles. She says we should try to help the two other strong ones with at least water tonight. A meal may not stay in their stomachs unless its just a hind quarter or little bits. You and I are about to get bloody!"

The goat was brought up by one of the guards. He carried it on his shoulders, not willing to fight with the animal when it smelled its death nearby. He was just to do so. The goat started bleating when it neared the now alert Dragon.

He placed it on the ground but held onto the now frantic beast.

"Do we kill it?"

"I do not know."

"Well, I can't listen anymore to its pleas."

Solina directed the guard to bring the goat up closer to the Dragon. He held an extremely frantic goat as it neared, Atin grabbed a rock, clubbing it on the head and knocking it senseless. It went limp, and the shaking guard was hesitant to go any further.

"Its all right, the Dragon won't move while you place the goat before it. Atin, if you would grab the cloak, we can use it inside for the others."

Atin grabbed the cloak when the steadier head of the Dragon raised a little faster this time, the guard dropped the goat, and Atin moved it closer by dragging it by its two front legs to right under the jaw of the Dragon. She backed off and the Dragon raised its head even further, pointed its maw directly down, opened its jaws, grabbed the goat in its teeth closing them with a loud chomp! The jaws moved a couple of times and then swallowed. Her movements were more vibrant, but she lay her head down, closed her eyes and sighed out of her nostrils. The breeze from her breath reached Solina and she could smell the scent of the herb she had not been able to place. This just reminded her she would be having a chat with the Pader and his Temple helpers.

Veren came back up the path, with more guards and a small woman, and they were carrying cloth sacks with them. The woman saw Solina, smiling they hugged, and Solina introduced Atin to Sheyna. Then Sheyna's eyes saw the bulky mass laying on the ground behind Atin and gasped.

"That's a, that's a…"

"Yes, Sheyna, it is, we have rescued this poor beast from imprisonment. I requested for you to come up here to help us nurse it back to health. She won't hurt you, but you must not tell anyone what we are about. Our first order is to eat, Atin and I have been busy. Here Veren, come sit with us and we will discuss what our process of business will be."

Veren first passed the women some bread and cheese. One of the cloth bags was fruit which he placed in between the triad of sitting females. Then he sat down behind them having a slice of both, eating while Solina thought about what she wished to say. Other guards were placed along the path to deter any interruptions.

"We will most likely be at this well into the night, if you would like to get a replacement for yourself, Veren."

Solina looked to the young man. He smiled back at her and shook his head.

"No, my Dragon, I will stay with you until our business is done here and then we can appoint another cohort of men. We must think about the others inside and where we will place them when we have them out. Then there is the question of their security. Once word gets out, people will either want to see them or kill them. We need more men, which I will get, with your permission. The Dragons need to build their strength so they can take flight if threatened. I can certainly stay up here with them. I will guard them with my life if necessary."

"You have the right of it, Veren, thank you for your vision. I must admit, I was more focused on releasing them than the aftermath of release. Your thinking ahead has my utmost thanks. You are now the "Admiral of the Dragons," and I give you full authority on my behalf. You will oversee their security and nursing them to health, here with Sheyna, she knows herbology and has compassion like yourself. You will be duly rewarded for your insight and devotion."

Veren bowed his head rising to his feet after he finished his meager dinner,

"With your leave, I will get more kegs and a few more animals. How many should I get, High Dragon?"

Solina tilted her head,

"Two more for the two inside, and Nannosh requests another for herself, she says it will stay down, and she feels more alive for the care we have bestowed upon her. We should get ourselves up and inside so we can get the others watered and fed. Tomorrow we can worry about the shackles, since Nannosh says she can help with the breaking of bondage."

Solina smiled at the two other women, grabbing an apple from the pile and biting down on it.

CHAPTER 23

Atin

In Eternal Springs the Life Source

Atin picked herself up off the grassy embankment after the light repast. Gathering the discarded cloak off the trampled area she had dropped it on. Having listened to her new friend, Solina, take charge of the situation she never thought to be in, her mind still not processing the events of the last twelve hours. She lived in the now, which was to get the remaining beasts inside some water. Trying hard not to gag on the foul stench which permeated from the pores of the cavern, Atin ventured back into the dark opening, with Solina, Veren and the tiniest of women, Sheyna following.

"I feel so much better for the food, shall we find the others?"

"Yes, let's find them. Veren, have this shattered wood cleaned up, take it elsewhere to burn. We will need the room outside for the others once we get them mobile. There's not much room out here. Hmmm…"

"Meric, you and a few others, you heard the High Dragon, cart it down to the Temple, dispose of it somewhere, fireplaces in the Palace. Don't take it further than that, less questions to answer. Place guards along the path and below this ridge. I am sure few will have some questioning minds already at the Halls. We will deter the most inquisitive, who do not want to wait for answers. Even place a few more men along the lower ridge line. Kallen, you find more men. Even the recruits if you must. No, wait. Not recruits. Get the Lower City Guard, they can keep secrets like no other. Tell them, on pain of death. The High Dragons orders and they will be killed if they utter one sound. Now."

The Dragon they were leaving outside seemed to have regained substance, but it would take some time to repair the damage hundreds of years in captivity had produced, Atin saw the ribcage as she walked past the reclining beast.

The poor beast, to be in this condition, barely alive. It breaks my heart. But everything must have a beginning.

They went inside back to the area Nannosh vacated and veered over to the immediate left. Walking up to a mound, looking for signs of life, but this mound had visible signs of decay. A hollow just a bit higher than Atin's head was an indentation of rotted skin between ribs. She shuddered and tried hard not to tear up.

Who would be so callous to keep creatures locked up in such conditions? Is this what slavery dictates? Having only seen slaves and servants in the marketplace, Atin never wondered about their living conditions. Being poor herself, until seeing the appalling conditions these beings were subjected to, made her ire come to surface. She stepped into something soft and a smell reached her nose, it was foul.

"Oh, how could this have happened? Look at all these mounds. These were all Dragons. How cruel! I don't even want to count them all. This is horrendous!"

Not realizing her eyes had begun to glow, she kept on to the next mound and saw fresher signs surrounding the beast. While she and Solina could see in the dark, Veren, Sheyna and the two next bravest guards following the four into the cavern lit themselves torches. Those cast a glow upon the barely alive creature. Its silhouette indicated it was much smaller than the large creature they just released.

"Solina, are you able to see if this is one of your voices?"

"Yes, this is Atalay, she is on the brink of expiration, let's try to get water to her. She may not be able to drink. I hope you have more ideas to share."

Atin dropped the cloak near the maw of the Dragon's head, but the creature did not open her eyes. There was only the murmur of a breeze coming out of a slit of a nostril indicating the creature was still alive. Veren motioned for the two men who had brought a keg of water in with them to stand it up and uncork the stopper. Atin knelt motioning for the others to come close.

"I can bring the water to her, but we may need to open the jaw to get water inside. I do not want to force it open, but if we can get even the smallest crack, I can trickle water in. Can you let her know we are here to help, Solina?"

"Yes, I did so, she is too weak to hold her jaw in such a way, so I will use your 'pillow' idea to hold the part open."

Sheyna spoke up, "When it comes to extreme dehydration in a patient, it is ideal to not rush the intake of fluids, give it time to absorb back into the flesh."

Solina smiled at her young friend, and told her, "Thank you, Sheyna, you have the right of it. I would like for you to oversee nursing these creatures back to health if possible. Whatever you require, it is yours, I will get the Temple acolytes here to assist you and serve you in every capacity. They obviously already know of the Dragon's existence but first let's get this one and there is another we must find."

She turned back to the beast in front of her.

Atin had the water stream floating in the air and managed to direct it into the crack in the jaw, stopping the stream when she saw water flowing back out. Then very slowly directed a smaller stream inside, as she saw movement underneath in where she assumed the neck was, and as the keg depleted and was finished, she stopped.

"Let's give her some time to process the water, we can move on to the next, get water for it, and then we see if this one would keep some sheep down. Then we try again in the morning."

Atin yawned. They were with the creatures well into the night and none of them realized the horizon would be lightening once they emerged from their toils.

Veren was searching around with his guards, and they called out from a recess in the far wall.

"Over here, High Dragon."

The three women left their patient, Atin took a moment, to lay her hand upon the head of the creature she was leaving.

"We will come back and see how you are doing soon." She spoke softly.

Solina looked at Atin, her smile lit up in the dark space.

"She thanks you for your kindness and care, and to you Sheyna, non-Dragon!"

Here Solina hugged her little friend. "I am glad you came from my summons; I have missed you!"

"Same here, Solina, I never thought when I did, I would be seeing creatures forgotten by time and alive! And you! Everyone is calling you 'The Dragon,' and Atin here is also a DragonRider. There are no rumours about her yet."

Walking around the mounds they finally made their way to another mass of emaciated flesh. They could see a reddened orb gazing at them, pus oozing from the opening around it. A milky film covered the whole eye. Atin saw cracks, in the white, it was dehydrated from being open for so long, she hoped she would be able to help.

Atin softly spoke to Veren, she was tired and still overwhelmed. "If you could get another cask outside. Soak cloths and bring them in, in buckets, this eye needs attention." Veren, rushed with one of his helpers to go outside, their torches weaving a broken path over the ceiling as they left.

This creature looked more alive than the last and lifted its maw to give the girls access to lay the cloak down under it. Solina lifted the corners with her pillows of air and Atin streamed water into the 'bucket,' and the Dragon depleted the volume almost as fast as Atin could get it in.

"Let's have this one settle the water. We will get a sheep or goat for Atalay and see if she will eat one. We may have to butcher it for her."

Solina stood up slowly, yawning.

"We have almost finished, I am so tired, I could just lay here, and sleep."

"Well, why don't you and Sheyna deal with Atalay and her meal, I see Veren coming back with buckets, I would like to address this eye, see if I can help the infection I see. Then we can get...." Here Atin paused,

"Analaria, her name is Analaria." Solina put in.

"Analaria, some meat and then mayhap we pause for a time. I also could drop down and rest, but our patients need us more."

Atin smiled at Veren as he crossed paths with Solina and Sheyna working their way outside to get an animal for the weakest Dragon. She directed him to leave the buckets near the head of the oozing eye, and she spoke to the Dragon.

"I am going to lay these wet cloths on and around your eye. Try not to move, From the looks of you, you can't anyway. I am going to extract the infection into these cloths, Veren?" Atin turned back to the man,

"Are you able to get us a few sticks to remove these cloths? I do not think our bare hands should touch the contaminated cloths. We should probably burn them after. It may not be something we catch, but better to err in caution than to deal with repercussions later."

Atin turned back to the Dragon head, pulling sopping wet cloths out, unfolding them and laying them first on the lid mucous membranes. Then as she covered the circumference of the eye, laying them gently over the eye proper.

"Stand back, Veren. I do not want any of this ichor to touch you."

Atin stood up, moving the buckets over to her side. She then looked back at the cloth coverings, her eyes glowed brightly, and the cloths began to change colour, greens, yellows, red, browns and blacks. She finished her concentration and motioned to Veren, who handed her a stick his lieutenant brought them. She picked off the first cloth slowly from the eye. Fumes arose from the raised cloth, as she slowly swung it around and dropped it into the empty wet bucket and continued until all cloths were removed. The eye looked clearer, some of the milkiness had disappeared, but the membrane in the corner of the eye still oozed grot and had darkened from being irritated.

"I think maybe a little bit more extraction, then it will have to air and heal," Atin had Veren grab the noxious bucket of cloths, gently to not upset the contents.

"We will torch this outside; here is another bucket for the offal."

"Thank you, Admiral Veren."

She was already grabbing cloths and applying them to the areas which needed another go. She extracted more pus, the cloths discoloured again. She was careful removing these ones into the awaiting bucket as well. Veren returned with one of his men and the man carried the bucket away. Veren stood there, a goat on his shoulders, knocked out but still alive.

"I brought Analaria some meat, if she would be hungry."

The eye blinked slowly at his speech, and they both laughed. He spoke,

"I don't speak Dragon. but I will take that as a yes."

Atin backed away as Veren crossed in front of her laying the unconscious goat in front of the raised head. The Dragon grabbed the goat into its jaws and chomped down and chewed quite a few times before it was able to swallow. She lay her head down and blinked her eye twice before shutting it.

"All right, DragonRider," Veren addressed Atin, "Both beasts inside have been watered and fed, you and the High Dragon must rest, let's go outside and see what she wants our next course of action to be."

He directed Atin to precede him to the outside.

Atin left the fume laden cavern to the opening where some of the doors had been dismantled by guards and carried away. She saw Solina and Sheyna beside the reclining Dragon and walked up to the two.

"You both look how I feel," Atin dropped to her knees, "I could go to sleep right now."

She leaned against the belly of the dusty dirty Dragon, rested her head back and closed her eyes. Solina laughed. "That looks like a grand idea… Atin?"

But Atin had already fallen asleep. Solina motioned to Veren to get them all some new cloaks, not the one they used for watering. He came back with three clean cloaks.

"We will rest here for a bit, and I suggest you get some as well. If you head down to the Temple, please relay to the Pader when we come down, I want all Temple attendants, the Rulers, especially my GrandMader, and any guards you think are loyal and up to the task, to be in your Dragon Guard, to attend. We will be down when we have rested. Also, we probably will be hungry again. Thank you Veren."

Solina laid herself down against her Dragon. Sheyna spoke softly.

"Solina? If it is suitable, I would like to retire down at the Palace."

"Go with Veren, here. Have yourself a bath and a meal. If you would also relay my messages. Thank you for your help, today. I am so glad you are here. I hope you will like being here. I have need of your calming presence. We will reconvene when we've had a small rest."

Solina closed her eyes, pulling the robes over herself and Atin, too exhausted to care the sun was coming up over the horizon. The girls slept only four hours; when the sun crested the hill and gazed full force on first Atin and then Solina they came to awareness of their surroundings. Atin heard whisperings of guards, felt the rise, fall and heartbeat of the Dragon she rested against. She thought about this, sitting straight up, bringing the guards to attention and silence. Her robe someone placed on her fell into her lap, she looked over at Solina who copied her example of resting against the belly of the Dragon and was now coming to. The women smiled at each other and then at the belly of the beast which emitted a low rumbling, Atin laughed, and they helped each other to stand.

"I just slept on the belly of a Dragon,"

Atin could not escape her awe, Solina nodding in agreement.

"I would like to address this leg the shackle has damaged, all I can smell is an herb which has eluded me, and some decay, if I can do for Nannosh what I did for Analaria, before we get started, then I will be happier."

Atin beckoned to a guard to bring a couple of buckets with wet cloths in them. He mentioned the other buckets of cloths were burned and when lit, almost exploded, burning for a good hour. The contents had proven more than noxious but highly flammable too.

"Once we finish here, we are going to the Palace for a bath, and food. I have called together a meeting to address our moving forward with Dragons in our lives, you will join me?"

Solina asked her questions of Atin, as she did not want to seem like she was ordering the other Rider. That was not her intention at all.

"Oh, most definitely, I would LOVE a bath! Especially one which didn't include sea water! And food!"

Here Nannosh's belly rumbled again and Solina hesitated, but the guards had already gone down, bringing two goats this time and placing them in front of the alert Dragon. The Dragon proceeded to demolish the meal in front of her. Solina requested Nannosh would be fed one or two goats every four to five hours. The guards bowed, asking about the ones inside. Solina looked at the Dragon outside and for a moment said nothing, then addressed the guards,

"One more each for now, and we will get them outside when I come back. Can you manage this?"

"Yes, High Dragon. We will remain here and care for our charges until relieved of our duties."

Atin finished drawing out corruption into the cloths, removing them with a stick, placing them into the bucket for removal to the burning area. The flesh revealed underneath was green and oozing red ichor, which she assumed was the creatures' fluids. She closed her eyes, weaving her arms in front of her and the flaps of skin or scale drew up to position but wouldn't stay in place.

"Could you fashion a bandage of air? Solina. I can try to mend but it won't stay put, this would be only until flesh adheres itself, and blood can congeal. Thank you,"

Atin drew in a deep breath, as she finished, the leg still looking raw, but better with no infection visible. Atin got to her legs, doing a wobbly turn, her clothes covered in all sorts of fluids and solids. Not even a colour anymore, she looked like she wallowed in a basin of dirt.

"Let's go get clean, Nannosh can the others wait for us to return?"

Atin addressed the Dragon, and Solina nodded her head.

"Yes, the others, are willing to wait a few more hours, compared to the hundreds of thousands they were contained. We need to address people who will help us with this next stage of life. Come, Atin, lets us walk down to the Palace."

Solina held out her hand to Atin and the two women walked to the Temple with the glory of the full sun upon their countenance. Not realizing their eyes were still glowing and all who saw them, the guards, then the groundskeepers, would kneel and bow, murmuring, 'DragonRiders.'

The girls arrived at the Temple first to see the basin was filled with water. Atin almost dove in,

"That's not the bathhouse I had in mind!"

Solina laughed. Atin followed Solina into the halls of the Palace, an older woman with low glowing eyes meeting up with them.

Solina kept walking, holding Atin's hand, walking past this woman who had to turn to follow them.

"GrandMader, we are tired, and going to bathe, then eat and then I want everyone from the Temple, loyal Palace guards who I have placed a Captain named Veren in charge of, and any who you deem to keep their mouths shut, in the Hall within the hour. We will talk then, but for now, unless its pressing, can it wait?"

"Yes, my Dragon, I was just going to ask what had occurred, but I will wait for you to address all, thank you."

She bowed to the women, who didn't see, and they kept walking.

Atin went with Solina into her rooms and followed her suit as Solina took her clothes off, walking into another doorway naked, not embarrassed at all about it. Atin soon divested herself of her now dirt covered rags and stepped down into the warmest water,

"Ahhh, I never felt such warm water. You bathe in this all the time?"

Solina nodded her head. Her maids had followed her and proceeded to wash their Mistress's hair. After some discussion, Atin let the maids wash her hair and body, being slightly uncomfortable about it. The maids exclaimed about her sun-bleached blonde hair. It was a soft gold colour and very shiny being clean at last.

"Is it possible to get a message to my Pader and Mader, they might think the worst has happened?"

Atin asked Solina as they emerged from the murky bath water and were being dried off with soft fluffy towels.

"If you could stay one or two more days, I cannot see why you could not go back yourself. I would like to wait until we get the others outside and we assess their health. If you could help with this, I think we can manage the rest."

Careful to pick her words to not reveal too much in front of her maids, she did not want to give more fodder to rumour.

"Tamran, could you find the Sea Dragon an outfit, hmmm, I think a blue green to match her eyes. Yes, that would look gorgeous on her."

"If I could get a tunic and leggings, if 'tis not too much bother. I am afraid I am not comfortable in gowns."

"Either am I. Tunic and leggings it is."

The girls now dressed, headed to the dining room. Atin had another moment of awe. She tried fruits she had never seen before, and nuts, and cheeses on freshly baked breads, and ate a little too much, with a drink of citrus juice which was heavenly to her limited palate.

"Oh my, I have never had such a repast, I think I might have to come back, if just for the food."

Here Atin could not help but edge her voice with light teasing, as she was so close with her male siblings, she felt the same way with this new friend. Solina caught on to the jest, laughing most heartily,

"Mayhap, I will let you!"

She couldn't help but tease back. In just a brief time, the two women felt at ease with each other. Working together in the cavern, they did not need many words to figure out their path. Solina made Atin feel like an equal, and Atin was hungry for a friend. The fact they were Riders solidified the beginnings of their relationship.

"If you are done stuffing yourself, let us go to the Hall. You sit beside me, and we speak to the assembly. Girls, I would like you and all the Palace servants to follow into the Hall, I need to address everyone in the Palace proper. Please tell everyone, down to the kitchen servants. Thank you, you have ten minutes."

This last bit, Solina addressed her maids leaving ahead of them, they retraced their steps down the hall they had come in from.

Atin and Solina went through the Blackwood doors only less than twenty-four hours before, Atin was admiring. Together they walked into the Hall and up to the dais, where one chair was placed.

"The Sea Dragon requires a chair. Like mine. Right beside it."

"Yes, High Dragon, right away."

Once the chair had been placed, Solina walked up, Atin following her. They both sat down together, the Rulers sitting down in their chairs and the Hall slowly filling up with guards, servants, Temple workers, and everyone who dealt with the Palace.

"Close the doors."

Her eyes brightened their glow and transformed into slitted eyes. Atin felt the change in hers, glowing blue. The crowd knelt, bowing and chanting.

'DragonRiders,'

"Please rise. I would address you now."

Silence reigned amid the shuffling of leather and cloth sandals and slippers. One knew from Solina's demeanor this was no ordinary council. No one said a word. Atin was not sure if Solina would speak, and she gazed out of the side of her eyes to the woman beside her. Then Solina spoke.

"Many changes are upon us, as you can observe, I have come into my power as DragonRider, also I have beside me, another Rider, she is Atin, and she commands water." a murmur started amongst those in attendance.

"Yes, we are changing. Now is the advent of a new Dragon Age. The time of true DragonRiders is upon us and for the last 24 hours, Atin and I were busy and have released three Dragons."

The volume increased, Solina stood up holding out her hands.

"You have all been deceived, over the years and centuries, told Dragons did not exist."

Here Solina looked directly at her GrandMader,

"But! This was to protect them, to keep them safe. That is no longer possible. We have released them, and I need your assistance to keep them safe. When the rest of the world finds out we have Dragons, they will come for them. They will bring war to us. They will try to end their lives. So, I need you my people, here, to keep this secret as long as possible, I need help to bring them to health and to keep our way of life safe. I have elevated Captain Veren, here,"

she pointed down into the crowd,

"Veren is now the 'Admiral of our new Dragon Guard,' any attempt to destroy or diminish our efforts will have to answer to him. He has my full authority to ask as he sees fit, to merit any punishment he sees fit. If he delegates any cases over to me, it will mean death. If any is found to be the root of any rumours, it will mean death. If any attempt to impede the reconstruction of this new era, it will mean death."

The air around Solina was charged with yellow, it swirled and turned. Many gasped at the sight. Those who had seen it already were awed again.

"Pader, what is the herb used? Do not pretend you do not know."

Solina addressed the Head of the Church, who stood with his novices and other Temple workers. She sat down patiently waiting for his response.

"It is the Matrine flower, my Dragon. Picked when in full bloom and boiled until a paste, then dried and powdered, placed into the meat the Dragons were fed. Harmless to us."

He looked extremely uncomfortable at the admission.

"That is neither here nor now, obviously it is not all on the Church, as this was passed down over the ages."

He started to look better; his shoulders began to straighten but slumped at her next speech.

"But it doesn't excuse the conditions we found. Slaves in the lower market live better. The Church will be responsible for the clean up of the caves where they were kept, when it is chosen to do so. Also are all those fields, this flower?"

The slopes of the surrounding mountains were covered in these fields, Solina loved to look at the delicate pink flowers when they were in bloom.

"Yes, my Dragon, and it would be a great waste to destroy these fields."

"Oh, and what if we wasted the fields?"

Solina's voice rose, and her eyes began to glow and whirl in her growing anger. The first row of people dropping to their knees. The air which settled, started to whirl again. Her agitation made it move quickly.

"Umm. High Dragon if I may?"

A quiet hesitant voice came from a novice at the back.

"Yes, proceed," She sat back down as the novice spoke.

"I'm sorry, you need to come closer, I cannot hear what you are saying."

Reluctantly the young man came forward. Bowing his head, not sure where to look. Solina bade him look up, speak his mind, loud and clear for all to hear.

"The Matrine plant has more than one use, High Dragon. If it is not allowed to come to flower and is harvested prior to this, and let to dry on the fields, it can be use for fodder for animals, not unlike the hay and alfalfa which is harvested on farms. We have not three weeks until the flower buds form, and we may be able to get a good yield if there are no heavy rainstorms to destroy the crops."

He finished speaking looking very relieved he was still alive, bowing again and backing up a step.

"Thank you, young man, this works in our favour. This is what is going to happen, we will harvest the Matrine plant, and those fields next year will be taken over with other crops. The Matrine plant and flower will be forbidden moving forward. We will begin breeding and raising more sheep and goats, we have these animals graze down the fields of Matrine after the harvest has been reaped. We will also raise more fowl as a short-term solution for the appetites we will be serving.

Sheyna, from Nashta Church will oversee the nursing and overall feeding of the Dragons. We will also need to clean them, I think it only fitting, the basin at the Temple resumes its former use, as a wallowing basin for the Dragons. The Dragons will not harm you, but if they or we see any untoward behavior you will die. No debates, no law will save you. Atin here, can see your aura and tell if you mean the worst. I will pass sentence, if needed. I hope I never have to, but to preserve our Dragons, I will do everything in my power to protect them.

My GrandMader and the other Rulers you have, will remain the leadership you have always known, but once they are done their time, there will be no more Riders. Riders without Dragons that is. Atin and I will be searching for our brothers and sisters, but this won't happen for a very long time. For now, the laws remain intact, I make no changes. They retain their positions, the two who are not here, their positions will not be filled by a Rider, but an appropriate candidate will apply and be chosen to fill their position at such time. I am sure that you can do so, GrandMader?"

Solina's GrandMader looked relieved, annoyed, and angry, all at the same time if Atin could tell by the colours of her aura swirling around her. She leaned over, whispering as much to Solina, who nodded back.

"If there are no questions, we will adjourn for now, please remember what I have said, no rumourmongering. All you would be doing is bringing us war before we are prepared. That will be another meeting in the future. For now, we have our immediate future to address. Thank you all for your service and please do not fear to come to either of us if you have questions. There is no wrong question."

Solina stood up saying to Atin,

"I think we should grab a quick bread and cheese repast to eat on the way up. Now that we have everyone informed, we will have plenty of help. I really want to see our bonds."

Atin agreed but held back as her friends GrandMader came up to Solina.

"You have really released the Dragons?" she asked this bluntly.

"Yes, we have. Does it not have your blessing?"

"I am trying to process this, and the ramifications which will reverberate throughout the world. You are right, war will come to our doorstep, and all the evils associated with it. There are only three Dragons and two of you. We are a long way to being ruled by Dragons again, my GrandDader. We must plan for the future."

Bowing her head she waited for Solina.

"You are of course correct. But we cannot repeat what past history has given us, therefore, I believe you must lead this nation into the next chapter. I and my sister here will take care of our charges; you will do what you see fit to plan and execute to protect us from the outside world."

Her GrandMader nodded joining the other Rulers, the five of them leaving together. The rest of the servants dispersed and that left the guards. Veren walked up to the two of them, Sheyna by his side.

"My Dragon, you have not had enough rest, Sheyna and I can go address their needs."

"Thank you, both, but there are still the shackles on the two inside, which need to be dealt with before I rest. Once we have done this, and Atin is happy none are beyond her care, she would like to return to her family for a time. Can you have one of your lieutenants go down to the market district to find Kaisan, an Aramite, who Atin says is very colourful in his attire. Hire him and his boat to wait in the port for my summons. I have need of his services."

The women left their attendants and walking through the Temple, through the farthest gate up the path to the smoking mountainside. They passed a few guards past the pen which cropped up to house the next round of meals. They arrived at the mouth of the cavern to see Nannosh standing on her two legs, a bit shakily.

Atin walked up to her admonishing her like she was a child.

"Not so fast, girlie. You need a little more rest, some more food and then you can try those legs of yours! Baby steps. We must get your siblings out and we must figure out how to get you clean. I can try to dry it out and we can dust it off until you are able to get yourself down to the basin. I'll be damned if any of us can carry you!"

She looked at her friend, Solina who was trying to keep a straight face. The shaking Dragon lowered her bulk to the ground, albeit a bit hard and Atin felt the earth shudder under her feet.

"Nannosh, says apologies, she wanted to stand after so many years of not. She says it will be a while before she will be able to walk. And any attempt to rid herself of this filth would be greatly appreciated. But you are right, let's get these others outside so they too can enjoy the sun."

The girls went inside. Some of the men, following them bringing more goats and sheep, periodically feeding the three Dragons who insisted their stomachs could manage it. They managed to remove the shackles and with Solina's air cushions, each one was brought out into the daylight. Both of their shackle legs were raw and oozing. Atin did the same thing she did for the eye and leg treatments. Atalay was the worst off, she would not drink without assistance, so Atin had another blanket bucket made. It wasn't until she saw the level of water lower by itself, she knew Atalay would be fine without her.

Atin stood, going over to chat with Solina who was standing with Nannosh, relaying she would like to set off. Solina sent word for the ship to take her home.

"I have a request of sorts. I know you have relayed your circumstances to me, and I know from reading, the level of life you have. I would like to know if you, or more your Pader, would accept a gift from me. I would like to send to your Island gifts of building materials and gift your Pader a new skiff. It is my thanks, for without you, I do not know if I could have done this all," her hands waved to those around them, "by myself."

The women walked down into the Palace, having another cleansing bath, a lunch and Solina walked with Atin down to the lower city. On the way, the two girls were cheered and followed. Chants of 'DragonRiders' followed them, they waved and the guards closed ranks as more people entered the streets. When they reached the docks, Atin gave Solina a great hug and her thanks,

"I am sure my Pader will appreciate your gift. His repairs took longer than usual last time, and he is probably thinking I am gone for good. I will return to see you as much as I can, we have constant customers with the pearls I find. If I find any, I think will compliment you, it will be my gift back. Until then, thank you and best of luck with the Dragons. Hopefully one day, I will be bonded."

"I thank you for sharing this with me. I must admit, I am a little overwhelmed with all which has happened these last few days. Even my Ritual of the elixir is nothing compared to this. It has opened my eyes, and I am so glad I have found another of my kind. You have a turbulent future, as do I. We will need to find the others like us. But all will be revealed when it is deemed time. I will send you on your way, your Captain is waiting at the docks for you, I think you will know him. Return when you want, and if I have need of you, I will send for you. If you have questions, we will find the answers together, if I can not immediately provide one. I am so glad we found each other."

"I am glad also, I feel a kinship, and I am relieved I am not alone with my talents."

In the shipyard district she was incredibly surprised to see the Captain taking her home was Kaisan the Aramite. She heard Solina tell Veren, but she was only half listening with her mind on the task up on the hill.

Her heart skipped a beat! She greeted him, looking him in the eyes telling him she was glad it worked out to be him, as then she could show him the way to her Island, then he could not possibly get lost. He smiled at her, looking her in the eyes back, and she suddenly felt shy and unsure of herself. They held eye contact for a moment too long; she felt sensations of heat and cold running through her body. It made her uneasy, only for the fact it was a feeling she did not know until now. A cough from his acting Captain interrupted their contact. They set off with the tides and an escort of two other ships.

Atin smiled to herself,

Da is sure to think he is being invaded.

CHAPTER 24

Andic

Bringing Desolation to an End

Andic settled back into her routine, ferreting at her rich folks' places, listening to their conversations, gleaning every bit of information she could. As scrolls and books were not readily available to the general populace, she got inventive and would sneak into homes when their occupants were otherwise occupied. Especially the Obans of Law, learning every bit she could from whatever their libraries held. She found she had an insatiable appetite for learning and knowledge! It was in a lull of exploration she remembered what the old man Kadir imparted to her just before she left. There was knowledge, she just had to find it.

Andic loved to wander through the halls and rooms of some of the villas where these objects of her observations lived. The exquisite murals on the floor of one, held her spell bound, she was nearly caught in her musings by a wandering guard. Who from the smell of him, had been visiting a female in another quarter.

The designs had her mesmerized, inlay tiles of beautiful colours. She heard the Master of Tile had his own luxurious home but was never there as his demand reached to the other coastal cities to the west. There were murals on some of the walls. She noticed the older ones, with colours faded. The owner had not repaired the damage. They were still fine; it just made her sad these lacked the attention they required. This occupied her for a while, until she remembered her quest.

One day she went down to the Hall of Learning waiting in line again to see Zenzol. Dressed like a woman again, she found she was growing certain body parts which kept her tightening the bodice, hoping that would make them disappear. It had the opposite effect. In her garb, she looked like any other woman of respectability. If it weren't for her voice, Zenzol wouldn't have known it was her, and he said as much when she sat down at his table.

"Dear Zenzol, how have you been these winter months?"

"Andic, this is you? You are certainly carrying yourself differently, how have you been? Did you find the man I last spoke of?"

"Yes, I have. I spent the last few months learning to read and write. If I weren't a female, I could do your job! Probably better than you! Do you have any gossip or news you can pass on?"

"Well, actually there is," he leaned forward to speak a little softer, "talk is, there's a new DragonRider announced from Pelin'Dun. She's young and more powerful than all the previous ones who have partaken of the yearly Rituals. Apparently from one of the older houses, she grew up in secret. Not sure how this affects us here, as it is sacrilege, but we will keep our ears to the ground, times are changing for a certainty."

He was scribbling something on a papyrus as he talked, to give the illusion substance.

"Where might I find tomes on Dragons? Is this what prompted the removal of Jeral's eyes? He saw hidden texts?"

"Well, yes, but since then, and since the shooting stars this last fall, there is access given, by order of the FirPader, to a scribe of the name Natan to find answers and their portent. If you were to find this man, I will leave the rest to your imagination." His voice lowered even more. "Keep your ideas about Dragons to your own council, the Guards are on edge. The more this talk goes on, 'tis like a volcano waiting to blow. It may come eventually; the FirPader won't let this rumourmongering linger."

He finished his writing, waited for the ink to dry then rolled up the paper giving it to her and forgot to take payment. She remembered this as she had almost left the hall. She unrolled the papyrus laughing aloud and drawing stares from everyone in the area. Zenzol had written a shopping list of a woman of the courts.

Andic spent some of her time exploring the Hall district. First going to her Captain Laza, explaining she had a mission of sorts. Without giving the man's name, she said she had some business to do with this man but wanted to observe him first. She noticed the patrols hadn't diminished by much. Of course, in the richer area on top of the hill, their uniforms were cleaner and crisper, but they were much less attentive. More apt to be gambling than watching for anything.

She spent a couple of nights roaming around, trying to evade the guards, and learning their patrol patterns. By the third night she had devised a pattern of sorts and saw that like the ones in her area, these also had some gambling issues. Usually when they received their pay and for a few nights after. In casually wandering close to the gates, she looked for any guards she recognized. Lucky for her, on the third gate, the one closest to the Hall of Law surrounded by a high stone wall, she saw a familiar face. She approached the men and was shushed away.

"Oi, you, git yourself gone. Ain't no hussies allowed up here. Goin, git, ain't time for your kind."

The young man brandished his sword at her. She remembered she was still in the feminine garb and the head scarf covered her hair and face.

"That's not nice, Brecu. How about I take that sword from you and give you a closer shave, eh." Andic kept on walking towards them.

"Andic, by the God! You look like a girl!"

"That's because I am, silly."

"Well, you truly look like one. Where you been? I've been promoted recently, can't you see? Haven't seen you for a bit." Brecu put his sword back in his scabbard leaning against the wall.

"I've been away on family business. Took a trip upland for a time. I was wondering if I could ask you a question."

Here his comrades started who-hawing and ribbing him, and he just responded.
with a "Fuck off" and looked down at the short woman.

"You know, if one night you aren't too busy, you could come back here and
we could chat for a bit,"

"Fuck off, you bugger, I'll shave something off of yah if you think for one
minute, I'd…."

"All right, all right, no need to get nasty! You look like a real girl now, never
noticed you when you looked like a boy. That's all, don't get your loincloth all
wedged up. Now what did you want?" Brecu threw his hands up in defeat, smiling
anyway. He only had eyes for his friend. She noticed with his smile, he was indeed extremely attractive. How had she never noticed this before? "Do not blame
me for trying."

"I am curious about the scribe Natan, you know where he lives?"

"Now why you curious? Can't be good if the Little Dragon is looking for him.
You sure like your scribes, don't you?"

"Well," here she moved a little closer to him and trailed her finger up the front
of Brecu's uniform, "I hear the scribes are talented…. With their quills!"

She could not resist bugging this boy. She had known him ever since they
were young. He worked for his Pader in the bake shop until he joined the city
guards and Andic an errand boy for the brothel where she spent her childhood.

"Not fair, try that again, and I'll show you, my quill!"

Brecu stared at the girl standing in front of him. Her front just grazing his
buttons on his uniform. His gaze intensified as he looked at Andic. It started to
change the energy between them. It became charged with an electricity which had
her very aware of his person. She could smell his body odour. It was pleasant, a
bit heady. She started to lean toward him, but caught herself, backed up a step.
The smile leaving her face.

"Sorry, I was just teasing. Just like when we were children."

"Well, don't. If you haven't noticed lately, we are no longer children. Anyway, the scribe you are looking for, he is favoured lately. He lives with his Mader
down the Path of Learning, but he's never there. He sleeps mostly in the Hall;
he's been charged with finding answers since the show of lights a couple of
months ago. Did you see them? There's been talk, and I never said this. This
heralds a new age! Especially since it's been reported there is a new DragonRider
in Pelin'Dun. Have you heard this one?"

She voiced she had, clearing her throat which had stopped working. Andic
bade him goodnight after she weighed his palm down with a couple of coins for
his information. She never took any information without payment. That would
not serve her interests any. Nothing was ever given for free!

*Well, I think I diffused that situation, but I should take more care. I didn't
think I looked more like a girl! By the Gods! Now I will have to fend off hands
and cocks. Brecu does look handsome in his uniform!*

Andic knew all about cocks. She was curious when she was younger and had
watched a few of the brothel girls through peep holes. She saw what they did, for

what men paid. She didn't know why men liked getting their cocks sucked or putting it inside women. She hoped she never had to deal with that. But with what Delma imparted on her and seeing her friend again after her time away, she may have to reconsider changing her views.

The way he looked down at me, it made my skin alive. I could feel his intent, like he wanted to gobble me up. How did Verema put it? Oh, yes, she could get with child with just a look. Hmmm.

The girls in the brothels had to drink potions, to prevent a child. Sometimes it didn't work, and they would go to an herbalist in the dead of the night, to get rid of the child. Sometimes that wouldn't work. Andic more than once would have to deal with the body. She had lost many a friend, to that. Not very many had the child, and if they did, the child would disappear.

Andic hated that part, she had to "disappear' a couple of those. It earned her the name, 'Child Killer.' It hurt her to the core but also helped to boost her reputation on the streets she called home. Being feared helped her to walk the streets at night. Only the very inebriated or the less informed would attempt to accost her, and she could easily deal with those.

The spirit manifests itself in mysterious ways. I have heard of people becoming ill from their thoughts, and if Verema tells me she had to be careful with her clients. What about the convictions I feel sometimes…?

One night, months ago, on one of her reconnaissance missions, before her travels upriver she swore, she would never have to kill again. A feeling came over her, as she finally got to a vantage viewing point, hunkering down to wait. The hairs on her neck and arms had stood up, with their own power. She felt it was more than her usual wariness; it felt more like a conviction. She repeated it to herself, just to make sure. It was like the world stopped and time stood still. There was complete silence and then it began again. She could have sworn, she spoke to herself inside her head, saying,

"I will someday, hold you to that promise."

All these thoughts came with her as she walked with a purpose, skirting the crowds of homeless and rough hands, boys who would beat anyone, for the sheer pleasure. Some would watch the others, and if a woman were available, many would take her while they watch a fight. It was the world she lived in. It was rough. Not for the elite on the hill. She kept on her path, occasionally taking to roof tops.

She found Natan's home, giving herself a vantage point where she could see several avenues of escape if needed. She waited a week before she saw the man she was looking for, He came home one night, having not been back the whole time she was watching. She saw nothing which made him different from any other man. He was middle aged but walked like he was older. She thought about how she would approach him. She obviously couldn't approach him during the day; he collaborated with many other men in a crowded hall.

Making up her mind, she decided she would have to approach him privately. She watched a few more nights, but he didn't come back. Andic found a way inside, while his Mader was sleeping, had a good look around, and found his room by the amount of literature inside. She continued to watch for him and was almost going to quit to try another way when she saw him shuffling down the path.

All streets, or roads were called Paths. There was the Path of Law, Path of Learning, Path of Delights, to name a few. That's where she would hole up, and where she spent most of her childhood. Her childhood was lived roaming the streets. She knew them inside and out.

Its not like she had parents to tell her otherwise. She didn't know who her parents were, and she never really cared to know. She did ask Delma once, her Mader was a working girl, and who knows who her Pader was. Girls never knew, unless one man favored them, and he paid for the exclusivity. So, she never asked again.

To her, Delma was a motherly woman, and she had many 'brothers' on the streets. She would watch her subjects inside their villas, and most oft the Paders were rude, mean to their women. She liked her life, her family, such as she called it. They were the people she spent her days and nights with. She was content with the family she had and the life she knew. She had no need to live the cushioned life of the noble. Many women had no rights, so why would she want such restrictions?

She had enemies. Who didn't? But the biggest enemy was starvation. When times were tough, people banded together, and their FirPader would always feed his people. She dealt with her enemies as she needed. Andic had a knack for acquisitions, so she never felt poor in any sense of the word. Now, gaining the knowledge of the written word, she felt rich indeed.

'Ahhh, there he is, finally.'

Natan walked slowly, hunched over like he had the weight of the world on his shoulders. She waited for him to have his evening meal and from her vantage point, on the roof next to his window, she saw his candlelight flicker inside then get extinguished. Andic waited for a little bit, before she padded down on soft soled feet to his bedchamber. She saw the man, gently snoring in his lightly sheeted bed. She very carefully snuck up to the bed, placing her sharp blade against his throat.

She quietly called his name, until he started. After clearing his throat, he quickly realized a blade was pressing at his Adam's apple.

"What do you want? I have no money; I am but a meager scribe."

"I have not come for money, Natan. Yes, I know who you are, and more importantly what you do."

"How do you know who I am?"

"An old, wise man told me to find you. You have information you want to share with me."

"I do?"

"Yes. Dragons."

"I can't. You know the last man to go down there unexplained lost his eyes and then his life. How would I explain you?"

"As a matter of fact, I did know the last man. Jeral was his name, and it was he who set me upon this path. I have spent the winter months learning how to read and write from Kadir, who sent me to you. You can hire me to assist you, as I am a woman and couldn't possibly know how to read anything. I would of course be the perfect assistant; do you not think?"

She retracted the blade, after he promised to not try anything, he didn't look like he could wield anything larger than a quill and use it effectively anyway.

"You must be Andic." She looked at him, shocked. He smiled.

"I have received a letter from Kadir, at least it is his words. He praised you greatly, saying you remember everything you read. He said you also organized the bulk of the library at the Mosque, and it has proven to be most effective now. He also said…. You are someone incredibly special, I dare not repeat it…"

"Yah, that last bit, I don't know what the old man was babbling about. He was doing poorly when I left him. Given they would have found out I was a female sooner than later, my time there was over. Pay no mind to his ramblings, but I would really like to see what is written. I can be very obedient when it suits me."

"Let me see what I can do about this. I will have to put in a request, and it may take time. They don't want anyone to know what is written on these tomes and scrolls. It may work, your idea, and you are right, no woman is allowed to read, but if they find out you can it will mean both our lives. Now if you are finished with me, I do have to get some sleep, I am exhausted already thinking about to-morrow."

Natan rolled over onto his side and was gently snoring before she had left his room. *Pretty trusting man, either that or he's just too tired to care,*

She left the way she entered and made her way back to the Path of Delights. She went into the kitchen from the backyard, heading straight into Delma's office, only to find Delma was out in the front reception room. Andic sat in the older woman's chair, placed her feet up on the desk, and in waiting, fell asleep. Delma gently shook her awake, casually mentioning if she were to put her feet on the desk, it would mean she was ready to manage the girls.

"Not on your life!" Andic looked horrified. Delma smiled at the girl's expression then laughed.

"What are you up to lass? Come to try a few men out? You are starting to look like a girl with your breasts growing. We could auction off your first night. Many a man would love to have a go at the "Little Dragon." A virgin prize is very sought out and would fetch an exceptionally good payment."

Andic's face paled visibly, until she saw the humour in Delma's face. But she also knew the business side of the older woman, would not pass up an opportunity like herself. She would have to tread lightly.

"Didn't you just get a bunch of new meat? Are they large disappointments already? I wanted to let you know I am going to get a day job, assisting a scribe at the Hall of Learning."

"Have you been drinking again? What have you done with Andic? That means you need quiet during the night. Won't be 'appening here, lass."

"Yes, I will have to hole up elsewhere for now. Just didn't want you to worry none."

"Well, do what you must do, then. Although I do not understand why you want to work for a man, when you could work under a man. Make more coin, but each to their own." Delma ruffled her hair as Andic got up to leave the room.

Andic went back to Laza's lieutenant telling him she would be switching to a daytime job. She would be working in one of the Hall's, under the guise of obtaining information. Then she did her rounds until the early morning. Before the horizon began to lighten Andic thought about where she would go, deciding on the farthest corner of one of the Obans of Knowledge's gardens. It was left to its own devices, and after a time, refuse from the gardeners was piled high. She had slept here before when she needed a good sleep. She kept herself out of the sun and there was a fountain in the garden where the water still flowed but no one cared for it. She could use this to bathe herself. She paused to take a few items from the vacant kitchen, snuck off to her resting spot hunkering down to get some sleep.

Andic managed to sleep until mid sun. It had become too warm to continue with sleep. So, she rose and saw she would not be able to bathe until dark. There were men working in the garden, so she put the cowl over her head walking into the Law district, stopping in to see Zenzol, who said he heard nothing from the Hall and Natan. Andic and the scribe arranged if she were hired, she would check in with Zenzol for the confirmation of such. Zenzol suggested she come back, same time tomorrow.

The next day, she tried again. Nothing. Andic headed to the Delight House and was washing herself in the fountain when Delma came out. Walking towards her, Andic shook her hair and the short ends fell onto her forehead. She wiped her face with a linen towel, as Delma stood before her, a look of concern,

"There's a guard here to see you? Are you in trouble?"

"Not that I am aware. What's he look like? Dark hair, handsome?"

"Yes."

"It's Brecu."

"Yes, and he is in uniform, so this is not a personal visit."

Delma left to go back inside. Andic thought to make sure her shirt front was not too wet. It was slightly, but she knew it would dry fast. She went inside to see Delma animatedly talking with her friend. "…it has been a while. You are well?"

"I thank you, yes. The Barracks keeps me busy…oh, there you are. Can we speak?"

"Sure. Delma, can we use your office?"

"Yes, I will be around should you need me."

"Actually, Delma, this concerns you, also. If we could all go inside."

Delma led the way and the two young adults followed her in and Andic shut the door behind them. She stood beside her friend, who in the small room took up a fair bit of room. He smiled at the two women but lost a bit of the smile.

"I will get to the point. You will need to be cautious, in your dealings. In what information you glean and repeat. I have instructions, our cohort and others who patrol the streets will be dealing out punishments for any heresy spoken."

"You are meaning the rumours we have all heard?"

"Yes. So, you have heard them too? Well, it is not to be spoken. Any words you hear, keep to yourself. If any guards hear of these rumours, another person could turn you in. There are rewards for these rumours."

"You came here just to warn us; I thank you lad. Andic, I will leave you two, I should go tell the girls. Was that all, Brecu? I thank you for the warning."

"I thank you, and yes, that was all I was wanting to tell you. I bid you good day. Andic?"

"Yes?"

Delma left Andic and the very handsome man in the office while she went to tell her girls. Andic heard her steps on the stairs. Andic turned to see Brecu looking at her and smiling.

"What? Why are you smiling?"

"You have a spot of dirt on your nose."

"I do?"

Andic began to wipe her nose with her hand. Then she looked at her male friend. "You bugger. I don't, do I?"

"No. I just wanted to see what you would do. It was fun watching you."

Andic slapped him, then poked him twice. It was something they had done as children together. They would play small pranks on each other, then when one bested the other, it was two taps for the loser. He smiled.

"How are you keeping?"

"I am good. I am starting a job of sorts. As soon as I get permission."

"What kind of job? Not the death kind? If so, do not tell me. Every time you end a life, they call me over and ask if I know anything about it. I tell them I know nothing, its been quiet since you left to go…wherever it was. I did miss you though."

"A real job. During the day. Assisting a scribe…no! not again. Don't give me that look. Its to assist in the catacombs under the Hall of Learning. I am to help…move books."

"Why would you want to do that? Have you been drinking? Did you send a twin back and the Andic I know is still somewhere else? A fair-looking twin…"

"I need to hide out…what do you mean a fair-looking twin? Was I not before?"

"You look different, Andic…more feminine, and yes, I said fair-looking. The Hall of Learning you said? I am going to ask for a transfer of duties then. Well, I must be off. Remember what I said. Keep your mouths closed on all that is heretical. If any were to hear such from you, I cannot do anything about it. I would hate to lose you. Good path, Andic."

"Good Path, Brecu." Brecu opened the door and let himself out, Andic could hear him say good path to others, then a door closed. She stood there with her mouth partially open as Delma came back in.

"I have told the girls, the ones who were awake. They will pass it on. I have instructed they change the subject should one of their clients were to speak on these…Dragons. What is the matter? You look like you haven't seen a man before? What did Brecu say to you to make you stupefied?"

"He said I was fair-looking. And feminine. Shite!"

"What? He obviously likes you. It would not hurt to have a guard watching your back."

"I like him too. But I do not want to look feminine."

"You haven't seen yourself in a while. Here, look in my mirror."

Andic walked over to the mirror on the wall. She looked at her face, seeing a small face with stubbly brown hair sticking out like that of a brush. She shrugged. "I don't see it. It's just me, with my hair getting longer."

"I am sure he sees you differently. He has known you almost all your life. He would see the changes. This last while had been the greatest. You are showing more female signs; your breasts have gotten bigger lately. Plus, the fact your tunic is slightly damp, and one can see your breasts, hmmm, they are very shapely, right now." Andic looked down to see what Delma was talking about to see the still damp tunic clinging to her body. Andic swore.

"Ox balls! Delma! Why did you not say anything! He may think I am for the taking. Shite!"

"Girl. If you haven't noticed, lately you are less a boy and more a girl. Hiding in clothes may not suffice."

"Well, I must hide in clothes. I must look respectable. I am trying to disappear and fit in. What can I wear outside?"

"You can borrow some of Verema's outerwear. She is an expert at hiding in plain sight. She has all you will need. And a proper bodice if you plan to hide your breasts. But those are uncomfortable and will only hide them for a while. If they get too big, we have clients who love big breasts. They will pay just to touch."

"I am going now, Delma. Do not get any ideas in your head, I am a street rat. That is what I do. Not…this."

Andic waved her hand around and headed up the stairs to chat with the woman of their discussion. She needed something to hide under. Once attired, she headed out into the heat of the day before the sun lowered itself and hid. She walked to the scribes place in the Hall's open patio's where she had first questioned Zenzol. Nothing, she walked back, trying to avoid guards and men, looking for errant women. She felt the garb was beneficial to hide her identity and with all her face covered and the colour of her robe, it was very demure and a blessing to cover what she felt was a new her.

I cannot believe that Brecu said I was fair-looking. Why would he say that? Is he intending something more? I have never thought of us in this way. I find him attractive… well… I do. He is very handsome, and intense. We have always been there for each other. Just with him giving us advance warning, shows he cares for me, us. I don't know… what happens now? I need to see what is in these catacombs. That is my priority. Joining should be on the back side of what I need to do. I will wait for permission. If I do not get it, then I will sneak in.

This went on for another week, until Zenzol conveyed Natan was given per-mission for an assistant, and if she told anyone she would be stoned, killed, and thrown in the burn pits. Andic was to begin tomorrow at sunrise at the side gate on the west side. A guard would meet her there to show her the place she would be going.

She was there before she was supposed to. Andic had her routine, she liked to gauge and assess possible escape routes. She knew there were gates at three compass points, and she noted areas where she could scale the rock wall. At least from the outside. The North wall face was more of a mountain side she could see.

A guard appeared at the gate after a while. She walked up to it, wearing her head gear and a plain, tan robe, following him after she confirmed who she was. She was brought before a group of men, one very elegantly dressed, who she knew to be the Oban of Learning. She had of course, observed him in his home with his family. She bowed, keeping her head down.

"You have been given permission, by me to go into the catacombs. Natan has told me you would assist him with moving scrolls and books. You will see artifacts and items should you repeat any to any other, you will be stoned. After you have been raped and your body would be left for the wolves to tear apart."

"I understand. I am to help Master Natan."

She was led to a back stairwell inside an antechamber at the back. Following the guard, down a stairwell, into a tunnel lit with the odd torch on the wall, she finally came to a well-lit chamber. Natan was inside, hunched over a table covered with scrolls, books, and maps. The guard told her to behave and left. She bowed to Natan saying, for the retreating guard to hear.

"What is your command, Master?"

Natan looked up and smiled,

"Somehow, that must have been difficult for you to say."

"Not really, I have been looking forward to doing something with my mind and hands. How would you like this to be catalogued?"

The rest of the morning, he showed her the chambers and they discussed the best way to store and organize the information. Natan listened to her ideas and while he agreed with most, she tried not to argue when he refused others.

"Do not get caught looking at the books. Guards come down periodically to watch me."

"We should have a signal then. A signal word if we hear them. Let's talk about getting food."

"That sound reasonable. Sometimes they bring me down food. There is a chamber pot in the corner of the room next. I use it as a sleeping chamber when I work longer days. We are not allowed up during the day. There is fear that I, we would be passing on information that we find."

"What is down here that is needing such attention."

"It not so much what is down here, well, there is that. It is my journey to catalogue everything, organize it accordingly. My main objective is to find scripture and Prophecy about the star which is now visible at night. The FirPader has demanded answers. I am of the opinion; he needs to have answers for the people. All this information down here, is not from here. It would be sacrilege to have the masses know of it. You know there is a special looking glass?"

"The Mosque of Remembrance has one also. I saw the star in the sky when I was there this last winter. It is interesting to view."

"What do you hope to find down here? Besides information on the Dragons."

"I am looking for answers, Master Natan. But I am not certain what the question is."

CHAPTER 25

Damara

Lay Hidden Our Mader

Damara felt a disconnect, a little bit lost and not sure what to say anymore. She saw Ramis had noticed her discomfort, which made him try even harder. He would greet her every morning with his usual kiss and poetic salutations. It just made her withdraw more. After another week of this, Damara made the excuse she felt exhausted from the bustle of the Capital.

"I am tired, I would like to retire to home in Kara. If you give me leave."

She was speaking truth. She felt worn out and it reflected in her countenance. She had dark circles under her eyes, and of course, her weight loss had given her an aged look. Ramis said he would finish at the shop one more day, collect the new orders and they would set off day after tomorrow.

"I will take you home, you have me worried. I can always come back later."

"As you wish, I would like to relax at home. Less people there and I would like to consult the physician; they know me best." She agreed going back to her needlework, knowing her indifference had Ramis on edge, but she didn't know what to say or do to fix it. She felt indifferent towards him. He no longer was her sun, moon, and stars. She felt the Universe shift, feeling a little awkward with what her next steps would be.

I seem to be in a stream. Stuck on a sand bar, neither flowing down nor going up. Just stuck while the water still flows around me. How do I move off this obstruction which holds me here?

It seemed Ramis was terribly busy over the years, but had polished his ability to cover his tracks, using his assistance with her business to his advantage. While she applauded this duplicity, she had made it easy for him. Not questioning his actions, blind to all but her business. She had created the very thing he used for his intrigues.

I could not see it then. But of course, I was not looking. Now I see in hindsight, his deception was partly my fault. I gave him the means to hide his actions. Other husbands have not, but then, I know of two other wives who accept it. They just do not love their husband as I once did. Oooo, I just said it to myself. I do not love him. Just saying such to myself makes me despondent.

And her trust. That was the conundrum, she trusted him with her heart, and that's what made her melancholy. He had betrayed her trust in him. He had not been exclusively hers, while Ramis was her one and only. She was willing to believe he was of the highest standard of man, faithful, cleaving only to her. He was a wonderful Pader when he was present. She would not disparage him on that. Her heart felt fragmented.

Damara didn't want to dwell on this now, it really grieved her. She did not want to walk down this path just yet. She knew to move forward she would have to place it aside for now and focus on deceiving Ramis, while she gathered her evidence, knowing divorce would be her ultimate goal.

He came back early for once, and they sat down to dinner together.

"Darling, we have several new orders, we can address when we return to Kara. There's been one for your favourite colour, pink. She has given you full discretion to create the colour. You have done this before for Noma Kavena, she is excited to see what you create this time. And news just came, have you heard? There is a new DragonRider in Pelin'Dun. A young girl, of one of the older houses. She's stronger than all the others combined, apparently. There is talk she can breathe fire; she burned a servant in the Ritual."

Damara's head shot up in shock. "Really, how is this possible?"

"I do not know; this is just what I have heard. There is also talk her eyes have changed. You know the Rulers' eyes also glowed with light, apparently hers are the brightest they have ever seen. One account says they are slitted like a cat."

Damara found this information intriguing and something was niggling at the back of her mind, but she pushed it aside to glean more from her husband, who was only too happy to engage her attention.

"I wonder about the ramifications of this, I know they keep the old religion, in their country of Islands, but what will the Church say to this here? Will they wage war on Pelin'Dun? We can't fight war on two fronts. Aram has been a thorn in our side for too long now. Are we not stretched thin as it is?"

Her questions on war had them discussing these points for the next hour. It almost felt like old times. He never hesitated to discuss politics with her, as she had an insight being a member of the Royal House accorded her to have. At least a working knowledge of current events.

"Well, now I am excited to return and gather items for a new dye. I may have to take a trip to the mountainsides of the Northern Reaches, as the season is changing, and I have a few ideas to make it original. I am going to buy a few more things here and get to packing. Maybe we can stop at the Falls halfway and I can get some supplies there."

They made the trip between cities so many times they liked to push through now and could make it nonstop in two to three days. They had various stops where they placed horses and carriages to help facilitate this. The townspeople were all too willing to take their coin bond keep the animals in the ready. Some trips were a seasonal given, and in the beginning of their life together it had taken a good week to navigate the trip.

Almost halfway in between there was a small hamlet tucked away from the main thoroughfare. It was at the base of an enormous waterfall emerging from the mountains behind it. They had spent an idyllic week there once. It was so romantic and just by accident, she discovered a flower there which produced the most beautiful colour of pink.

Ramis commissioned the woman there to gather these blooms and he presented her with a room full of flowers. He was so romantic in the beginning years, he still was, just not as frequent. They hadn't left the room for three days. Damara smiled to herself at the memory. By the God, they had captivating relations!

She had taken some of the flowers back and dried them, as a memory. She hadn't started her business then; this came later after her children were born and were being taught by tutors. She remembered one year during a horrific winter rainstorm; it had blown through the shutters drenching her bedroom. The dried flowers on a shelf bled down the wall, and to this day there was still a stain there. It had not come off, despite all their scrubbing.

This memory of those flowers becoming her most favourite colour and the start to her business, made her smile. But her smile didn't last. Ramis saw her smile, rose to give her a kiss on the forehead, stating for a certainty they could stop at the falls. He placed his hand on her shoulder as he turned to walk out, giving it a small squeeze.

This helped erase the smile off her face, she did not feel the rush of excitement the squeeze indicated. He still wanted physical intimacy from her, and she did not know if she ever wanted him to touch her again. The thought of his hands touching other women, lots of other women, gave her the thought of feeling unimportant to the only man who ever touched her. She had a rush of anger, and saw the room turn red, blinding her for a moment.

Her maid had the misfortune to walk in at this instant. Peylin stopped mid step, to see her Mistress sitting in her chair, her eyes glowing red. She dropped the tray she was carrying with tea and fruit. The clatter had Damara closing her eyes and grabbing her head, there was an instant of sharp pain. She opened her eyes to see her maid, crying and bending down to pick up the pieces.

"What ever is the matter, Peylin? Did you trip?"

"M, m,m, mistress, you, you, your eyes, they were red!"

Her maid was visibly shaking trying not to look at her and busy picking up the pieces. Damara felt the energy of her maid, scared witless and ready to bolt.

"Yes, I know, this has happened before, I don't know what is happening to me," Damara sighed closing her eyes, leaning back into her chair.

"I don't feel different, and I am scared, Peylin, please don't fear me. I couldn't bear having you leave me." She began to cry. Her maid put down the tray coming over to her. Placing her hands on Damara's knees she said.

"Please don't cry, mayhap we should go to an herbalist when we get back. There must be a reason. Mayhap too much of this tea? You are consuming enormous amounts of it."

"You could be right, but 'tis holding this anxiety at bay. Please don't mention this to Ramis, he would get too worried. And with all he is doing right now, I don't need him to know something is wrong. I must tread carefully this next while, I cannot give him an excuse to divorce me, I would be ruined."

Her maid agreed, standing to pick up the tray, she said she would return with some citrus juice and a small repast. Damara managed to get through the rest of the day, by pushing thoughts to the back of her mind, to process at another time, once she was alone.

They set off for home and while they weren't in a rush, they stayed the night at the Falls. Damara had the sense to fake extreme exhaustion when they arrived, to dodge his question of being intimate. She looked pale and could not keep food down. Ramis was extremely attentive and caring. Damara did not get sick often and her health was important to him, or so he said to her maid, within her earshot. Damara knew it was the thought of touching him and him touching her which upset her stomach, the contents which came up burned her throat, and her belly was very sore. She slept alone that night, and her maid quietly woke her up the next morning, to help her dress, saying they would set off after her Mistress tried to eat.

"I'll have some bread and cheese, my stomach feels much better after last night, but 'tis also empty." Her belly rumbled to help announce the truth to her statement.

They set off for home. Her maid had gathered the needed flowers, dried by the Matron, who had over the years, supplied her with this product. There were no more instances of her randomly changing eyes.

Damara got to work right away when they arrived home, leaving Ramis to his own devices, while she busied herself with creating a dye which would stun her client. If anything, Ramis stuck to her like glue, when he wasn't 'fishing' or down in one of their many warehouses or dealing with shipments arriving. Spring was busy. The winter storms made sea travel precarious, many ship Captains, would set out after the last great storms of winter. Spring saw the many ships coming in, silks from Aram and some different perishables from Pelin'Dun, and of course the travel of information. She forgot her troubles for a while.

After a couple of weeks, Ramis calmed down his attentiveness towards her. They would have interesting conversations during the dinner hour. The few times he made remarks of an intimate nature, she would beg tiredness or stomach upset, and as she showed signs of both, Ramis would not pursue it further. She knew he would eventually tire of asking. He started to stay 'late,' and she knew he was back to his old habits.

"Ramis, I am heading into the city today, I would like to continue working on the pink dye, and I am thinking I will do a little shopping. Will you be home for the dinner hour?"

"No. I do not think so. There are multiple ships and cargos which need to be organized. I will be busy with this, and I do not know when I will be done. You repast without me; I am sure I can stop at one of the inns if I am late."

"Yes, yes of course."

Ramis finished his morning meal, excused himself, and left the dining hall. Damara was contacted by Ash, which was part of her venturing out. Damara thought he was abrupt in his response, and she for a quick moment wondered if Ramis was watching her.

As if I have an exciting life like his. It must be something else. Mayhap one of his women wants him for herself. He would always be curt with her if she asked him something which did not suit his way. She knew enough of his moods to see when something was not right.

She dressed for the day hiring a carriage. She would leave it at the shop and walk into town with her maid as her companion. Peylin was by her side for ten years now and knew everything her Mistress told her, and some things that she hadn't. After Peylin saw her with her red eyes, Damara had a heart-to-heart talk with her, and Peylin confirmed some of the things Damara had found out.

"Nada, I have taken a walk like you asked. I have found out this woman, Lana, whom you used to know, is quiet and makes simple soaps which sell in the lower markets. She does enough to keep herself and her son fed, but I am of the mind the men who visit bring her presents. Her past husband brings a food basket occasionally and Ramis will buy extra fish. She is comfortable enough in her home. The boy goes with her into the markets, and she does have him learning his languages. She is teaching him herself. The boy does have a few toys which look like gifts, she would not be able to afford on what business she does. This is just what I have observed."

Peylin did not mention Ash had filled her in on his scrutiny of the woman.

First thing, while her husband was bustling around the docks and warehouses, she worked on the dying of fabrics, organizing her workers and worked on the first batch of silk. Then while this portion was drying, she and Peylin walked with a guard to all the stores she wanted to buy at saving the bakery for last. She asked Peylin and Orlan, the guard she asked for specifically as she knew Peylin and he were sweet on each other, to wait outside while she chose some baked goods, sweet treats, and such. Of course, both agreed.

Damara went in picking out what she wanted. While she waited for them to fulfill her order, Ash came in and in a nonchalant manner he told her what she already knew. Ramis had even more visits to other brothels, while not on a constant stream, he seemed to habitually visit several repeatedly. He visited the woman, who lived in a trade area, once a week while they were in the Capital. Ash saw the young man come in while the men from the war front were on leave, the woman was definitely his Mader. He also said from her husbands' actions when the young man was there, and then the mirror image, it confirmed Ramis was his Pader.

"You followed him to the other places, are there any other 'homes' he visits?"

"Not that I could see, my Lady. There are three brothels he seems to have on rotation, for lack of a better word. Do you think you can relieve me on my charge? I have done what you asked. I am afraid another of my clients would have me travel soon."

"If you could please continue until such time, I will pay you in advance."

"That is only until I am bid to go. I am afraid I have another client I must do his bidding, or I would be imprisoned for my refusal, you understand?"

"I guess I have too then. Also, if you were to be seen, cease all observation and send a note through my maid, and I will consider my debt paid, until such time I need you again. Thank you."

He bought himself a roll and left through the front door, eating his meal. She collected her goods going outside where the two servants stepped back from each other guiltily. Damara smiled giving her packages to the guard to carry. She finished her purchases and they left to return to the villa.

She arrived at the villa tired, Peylin took one look at her and ordered a bath for her Mistress. Damara soaked in the bath and once she felt somewhat restored, she dressed and headed for her favorite spot in her garden, laying on her chaise, she fell asleep. She woke suddenly with a thought of fried meat. She swore she could smell it. As she closed her eyes in the fading light of the sun, she heard sounds of her husband walking towards her through the clipped grass.

"Oh, here you are. Are you not feeling good today? I looked for you in the shop this afternoon, I thought you would be coming back for your dyes."

"I am tired, Ramis. It could be from this illness; I have not the energy I once had before I fell ill. I have headaches, and I seem to want more sleep. The physicians say I may have eaten something, but I can not think of what would make my stomach hurt as such. They are just as puzzled. How was your day? Were you not going to be later?"

"I was, but things were completed sooner, so I came home. I am worried about you. You do look tired. Is it just the illness? Are we fine? I must ask, as you seem… distant as of late."

"We are fine, Ramis. I have not been feeling as good as I would like, the trip to the city did wear me out. I am very appreciative of your assistance, and the work and diligence of Tovah and Raqia, without the three of you to get me through these last few months, I do not know how the business would have survived. Why do you doubt?"

"You have not been the same since our boys came to visit. I have been informed the young man is indeed an offshoot of my cousin, a lad of dubious name, his Mader is a woman of…"

"It is fine, Ramis. No need to explain. He has the look of your family. I am sure he and the boys will be fast friends. I am not concerned." This statement seemed to place her husband at ease, he leaned over her, giving her a kiss on her forehead. She knew without looking he was smiling to himself.

"You just rest, I'll have Peylin bring you some repast."

"Thank you. Rest well."

Ramis left to order her maid, and Damara thought about what transpired. She had lied to her husband. But then, he lied to her about the boy, and he said it so easily. She did not feel comfortable with what she said to him, but she also knew to raise the question of the lad's paternity would set in motion, what she did not wish to expose just yet. She needed to be certain the law would be on her side in this. She would not stir the coals until she was ready to.

I wonder if he even loves me. He seems to care, but he also "cares" for other women, the thought of him touching another woman makes me angry. How would he feel if the tables were turned? If women could have more than one lover? Men would be battling for our favor. Oh, if only there was such a world. To be fought over. I am no better than a used, old woman. I have only known the touch of one man. I cannot fathom another touching me. How weird would this be. I shudder at the thought. I have never ever had thoughts of other men. I wonder if that is why there are such strict laws for women. I wish there were a way to investigate this. If I were to even ask, it would get back to Ramis. I better not. Harrumph! I can't even ask for information. This is so frustrating.

The next day saw Damara back at the shop, perusing the pink fabric, she thought it looked the same as other batches. Looking up at Tovah, she brushed an errant hair behind her ear, under her snood.

"I am going for a walk, along the beach. I need some air to clear my head."

"Are you fine? The smell is getting to you? Make sure you take a guard."

"Thank you, Tovah. I need to think. this pink is not…vibrant enough. I know Kavena would like something to fill her with awe. I feel the same."

"Perhaps some Matrine? Or Pana?"

"No, I've tried this. It will just make it darker. I want something…vibrant."

"Hmmm, I will think, and you do the same. What do you want me to say if any come looking for you?"

"Just send them out to me, you know where I am, and I will have a guard."

"Very well, Nada. The Captain was looking for you earlier. He saw you were busy and went for a bite to eat. When he arrives, I will send him down to you."

"That sounds fine."

Damara nodded her assent, and left motioning for one of the guards she seemed to have more of. He followed her as she left the shops and wandered down to the beach. On the North side of the docks, was a small beach. She would often come down here when she needed peace. The sounds of the waves and surf would sooth her and she would either stroll or pick up seashells. Or she would sit and stare at the ocean. It would help to ease her angst and calm her down. Her Mader had done this. It was a memory she would keep with her always.

She was sitting down and staring when she heard footsteps. Her guard, who knew to stand aways from her, stopped the footsteps.

"It is fine. Let him pass."

She kept staring out at the waters. Not much of a breeze. The steps came close.

"Captain."

"Nada. You knew it was me? You have not moved your head."

"You have a heavier tread than most."

"Very good. You listen to a person's footfalls?" Damara smiled sarcastically. Then looked at the man before her. His silhouette took up a fair bit of space. She threw the shell she was worrying back onto the shell littered sand. "No, Tovah told me you were looking for me. Why were you looking for me?"

She hadn't moved and sat looking back at the surf.

"You seem troubled."

"Ah, it is just a dye giving me grief. I have no idea how to make it more…spectacular. But I do not want to bore you on this subject."

The Captain had bent down to pick up the shell she dropped. He turned it over in his hands. Then he looked at her. She was still looking out at the seas; she did not notice his intense knowing gaze.

"I thought it might be something else… I have traveled to many places, Nada. I have spent many a day, and many a night speaking with other women, on their pursuits. Did you know if one were to grind up pearls, you could get the vibrancy you may need?"

"What?"

Damara bounded up of her perch. She brushed her backside off, the sand which was on the rock face. She almost toppled over and the Captain reached out to steady her. Damara grabbed onto his arm. Gripping it tightly she spoke to the guard. He started to rush towards them, his hand on the hilt of his sword.

"Its fine. We are discussing business. Continue." She looked up at the Captain. She did not notice his stare, or his smile at her touch.

He nodded down at her. "If it pleases you. I will assist you back to the shop. So, you do not fall, Nada. I will tell you what I know."

He led the way; Damara was only too appreciative of his assistance. In bounding up too fast, she had gotten quite dizzy. She was extremely interested in what this Captain had to say. They walked back and she kept looking at the man helping her walk. He was tall. Much taller than Ramis. Blonde where Ramis was dark. She looked at the blue eyes staring down at her, the corners sporting wrinkles in his tanned face. She was intent on what he spoke.

"So, pearls? Is this what you said?"

"Yes, I heard it from a woman in Pelin'Dun. She would dye fast with ground pearls; she said it lent a vibrancy to the fabric colour."

"Ohhh, this is remarkably interesting. What can I use?" Damara thought for a moment. "Will you be upset, Captain? If I were to use the set you brought back from Pelin'Dun?"

"You remember the pink set? I thought they would have been on the bottom tray of your jewelry box or placed aside." Damara laughed and looked towards the shop and saw a figure step down the stairs to the beach.

"Well, dear Captain. For one, pink is my favorite colour, which you knew from when I received them from you. Therefore, I do wear them often. I am loath to use them, but those are the only pearls I have. I am asking you as you were the one who gave them to me."

"I thank you. I will find you another. I saw a blue, quite like the depths of the seas which would look great with your hair colour, ravishing truly."

She looked up at him with that comment but did not answer back as striding towards them was her husband. His face looked grave, and she forgot about the man who's arm she now let go of. She looked at her husband who was shooting daggers at the man beside her.

"What is it, Ramis? Is it the children? Has something happened? You look grave." Ramis's face took on a whole different demeanor. He smiled at his attentive wife and offered her his arm. She took it and looked back at the Captain.

"Thank you for this information and for the assistance. I bid you good path. Now, what is it, Ramis? The Captain assisted me, as I felt faint."

"Are you certain you should be exerting yourself with a rigorous walk? You may fall ill again. Thank you, Olent. I will assist my wife from here." Ramis nodded at the other man and led Damara back to the shop. She forgot about the Captain and his attentiveness, but not about the pearls. Ramis spoke to her all the way back, and she forgot for a time the reason she had gone to the beach in the first place. She was led into the shop, only to see her maid waiting for her.

"Ramis, I will go with Peylin. I am feeling the effects of the sea air. Have I leave to go?"

"Yes, Dear Heart. You go. Rest and Tovah and I will see to some of these orders. I can be her arms for the heavier lifting." Ramis gave her a peck on the cheek and Damara left, with Peylin walking behind.

Damara entered the carriage with her maid sitting across from her. Peylin made to speak and Damara raised a finger.

"No. Let us away. Not here." She rapped on the carriage roof with her hand, and the carriage set off. A few minutes later, she burst out.

"By the Gods! What the blazes was that?"

"Nada? I saw Ramis's face when Tovah told him you were on the beach and Olent had followed you down there. He was quite irate. Not that he verbalized it, but one saw it in his face."

"Of all the insecure husbands, I would be stuck with the worst. Ramis is jealous on a Captain! Like I would!"

"You think Ramis would be jealous?"

"You did not see him shooting looks at the Captain. I would not stoop to give him this reason! He sees nothing! Nothing wrong with his actions. Yet I am to be pure! Oh, I should. Just to spite him!"

"You should not."

"No, you are right. I should not. I have not thought in that direction. There are too many accounts of women being beaten and killed for doing so. I would not become another." Damara calmed down some. She remembered Olent's idea.

"Peylin, I need you to find the pink pearl necklace, and we are going to smash it." Peylin looked shocked.

"Nada. That was a gift. Are you sure?"

"Peylin, I asked Olent if I could use it. He told me crushed pearl in my dye would lend a vibrancy to the colour. That is what he came down to the beach to tell me. He said the Islanders use it. If it works, then I may have to purchase some more, just to use in assorted colours. He may be onto something."

"Or he had other reasons for telling you."

"What do you mean?"

"He is very attentive where you are concerned, and he does not like Ramis."

"Really? I have never paid attention. You have seen this?"

"Like two alpha male dogs, Nada. They do not say, but one can tell when they are near each other, there is tension."

"So, you are saying I am the bone they are fighting over? How nice."

Damara lent her voice to sarcasm.

"I am sorry, Nada. I did not mean offense."

"No. I am fine with this development. It is nice to be wanted, Peylin. I am not sure about Ramis. He has no cause to be. I have never entertained thoughts of beyond joining. I would not give him this. I am a Du'Landan, I am better than him."

"Yes, you are, Nada. Much better than him."

The women arrived back at the villa, and Peylin went inside with her Mistress. Damara opened the box where her jewelry was kept and grabbed the pearl necklace.

"What can I use for crushing?"

"How about we go into the kitchens and speak with the Cook. He must have tools for shellfish and whatnot."

"You, my girl are very clever. Let's go." They went into the kitchen and after explaining what she desired the Cook helped her to not only crush but to grind up the pearls. Thanking him, she let him finish preparing the meal and gave Peylin the clay cup of finely ground pearls. It was powdered.

"I want to try this right away. Can you get the carriage for me? I want to change into another tunic and leggings. My bottom is still wet. I do not want to catch a chill. I will be right out. Don't spill a drop!"

They set out back to the shops. Arriving in a rush, Damara alighted before the carriage had completely stopped. She strode forward while Peylin instructed the coachman to rest the horses. Damara would be a while. Damara turned and took the clay cup from her maid. They walked into an empty warehouse.

"That's strange. Where is Tovah? She is usually here. Mayhap she had somewhere else to deal with. Peylin grab my apron for me please."

"Yes, Nada. I will assist you."

"Certainly. I am so excited! I cannot wait to try this." Damara set off to the vat room. The room for dying. She waited for Peylin and set the clay cup down. Peylin came in with her apron and another.

"Tovah's cape is still here, Nada."

"That's fine. I will tell her later. Can you tie my straps?"

Peylin watched as her Mistress poured the finely ground pearl into the vat. Damara grabbed the stirring paddle and used it gently to mix in the abrasive. Too fast would have both women covered in dye. Tovah came in while she was mixing. Damara did not look up, but Peylin did and saw the other woman a bit flustered and tucking her hair into her snood.

"What are you about, Nada Damara?"

"The Captain told me of mixing in pearl dust to dye fast the pink. Just my luck I had pink pearls. I hope this works."

"I have never heard of this. I hope for his sake it does."

"This is an acceptable loss. If it doesn't work, then I will use it for myself. Pink is my favorite colour. After all, I will not waste it, should it be not the right colour." Damara glanced up at her assistant. She noted Tovah looked flustered.

"Where were you about? I did not see you when I came in."

"I was in the back, Nada. Directing Ramis to attend some bales."

"Oh, Ramis is not a dock hand, Tovah. You need to address him as Nadan unless you are on familiar terms with him. Are you?"

"He bade me to address him as such and he offered. I can not refuse. Now, if you excuse me, I will direct him to desist." The blushing woman left in a fluff, and Damara was distracted by the changing colour in the vat.

"She seemed…"

"Oh, Peylin! Look!" The pearl dissolved into the dye and one saw a pearlescence about the vat. Damara stirred, her face excited and giddy.

"Oh, my! If this is what happens, I hope it remains. Oh, my! I am going to cry!"

Ramis poked his head in. "You are going to cry? Are you fine, Damara? Peylin, grab the paddle, she should not exert herself."

Peylin went to take the paddle from her Mistress, and Damara looked through her tears at her husband. "I am fine, Ramis. I am happy. This fabric, if this works will be another achievement, and it will give us more orders."

Ramis came over to look down. He turned his head one way and the other. Looking closely while Damara stopped the stirring. "Its shiny. Like a pearl."

"That's because there is pearl in it. I used my pink set. Ground it down and stirred it in."

"You did?" Ramis looked incredulous.

"Who gave you this idea? I thought that was your favorite necklace. Were those not a present?" Damara was looking at her vat of dark pearlescent pink fabric and did not see Ramis's face when she nonchalantly spoke.

"The Captain gave me the idea and as it was his gift, I thought to use them. It seems to be working…"

"Well, then. I will leave you to it. Please Peylin, do not let her remove the heavy fabric, she may feel faint from the exertion."

"As you command, Nadan. I will not let her."

"I can."

"No, Nada, your husband is right, let us remove while you direct." Ramis left while Peylin started to grab the paddle.

"I will see to the stirring for a while." She whispered to Damara. "He was not pleased to hear this was Olent's idea, and it was his gift. He looks like he will have words with the Captain."

"Thank you, for your observations, my dear. Now keep stirring, I will find Tovah, you both can remove the fabric. Poke it under for a bit. Then let it rest."

Damara walked out of the vat room and looked for the others. She looked in her office, nothing. Then the back where there were bales. She wandered around looking for signs of people. Not seeing the corner bales which looked they had been sat on… She wandered around some more and thought to look on the docks. There she found all three. She saw Tovah bob her head down and curtsy while Ramis stood over her a little too close. She wondered at what he could have possibly been saying to her assistant. Then she turned to come back and saw Damara watching. She looked down as she came close.

"Can you help Peylin with removing the fabric, Tovah?"

"Yes, Nada. Right away."

Damara stood there and watched as Ramis walked up to the Captain who was readying his ship. She knew Ramis had every intent to tell the Captain to stay away from her. She thought to set him straight on this. She would not see her best Captain fired or demoted. She strode down the ramp to the two men who one of them was paying deference, but barely. They turned as the sound of her footsteps and the vibration on the boards gave them notice another was coming towards them.

"Good. I find you both here. Captain, your idea was an excellent one. Ramis, I do believe we should award this great man with a promotion."

"We should? What did you have in mind?" He looked flushed and agitated. Her arrival seemed to have deflated his speech. He did not expect an audience to his anger at another man. She ignored his temperament and looked at the Captain who had his eyes lowered.

"We reward this Captain with the Admiralty of our fleet. He certainly seems to know much on our business. I thank you, Captain Olent on the pearl tip. If this works, which I am sure it will, you will have brought us more business."

"I thank you, Nada. Once it dries, you will see. I will strive to serve you well. Nadan?"

"Why, let me think on this… Damara?"

"What is there to think about? The ship that carried our Admiral has sunk, with him many silks. Olent has proven his worth. I can imagine he will be quite busy in the future. Captain, I hope you are up to the challenge. You will be extremely busy. I am sure we won't see much of you. We will need you to oversee all our ships and sail to the other lands. I will need a new supply of dyes soon. You may not see much of our new Admiral, Ramis. I am certain he will serve us well."

At her speech and when her words sunk in, she saw Ramis's countenance change as he digested indeed Olent would be busy. She knew exactly what he was thinking. She also knew the Captain knew what she was about. But for him, it was indeed a promotion and much stress. He straightened his shoulders and took the hand Ramis offered.

"You are now the Admiral of our fleet. I will expect reports when you dock, do not let us down."

"Thank you, Nadan, Nada. I will serve you well."

"Now, I must get back to my dye. I want to see this fabric." Damara walked back to her shop, satisfied she had just saved Olent from the wrath of her husband. She also helped Ramis make a decision which would only serve them well. She smiled, as she walked into the vat room and saw the result of the fabric. The girls had grabbed some helpers to deal with the raising of the fabric. The light coming inside the windows were hitting the hanging pink swatches. She saw the sparkle in the fabric.

"Oh, yes! Three for three!"

Peylin looked at her. "What was this?"

"Oh, nothing, Peylin. Just… I will tell you later. This is beautiful!"

"Yes, hopefully after washing it will retain the sparkle. We will see."

"I am suddenly tired, Peylin. Ready the carriage. Tovah, I will be down in the morning. Please tell Ramis I have left. I am sure you will see him before I do."

"Yes, Nada. I will. Rest well."

"Oh, I will. Barely. I am excited for this fabric. I am sure I will not sleep a wink." The next morning had her rise early and with Peylin's assistance, they left for the shop. She was more than pleased to see the sparkle stay after the final rinsing. Fabrics had to be washed after they dried, to ensure the colour did not run. Satisfied it was set, Damara returned to the villa to find Ramis had just eaten. He was rising from the table when she arrived.

"May I be seated?"

"You look incredibly pleased, and yes, you may. Have the Nada served her morning meal."

"Right away, Nadan. Your usual fast, Nada?" Their Head of the House deferred his head when Damara told him yes. She sat down at the table and smiled at Ramis. As much as she was not liking him, she found it quite easy to pretend they were still happily married. He seated himself and motioned for another tea. He liked his strong.

"I gather you did not eat before you left? You should take care of yourself better."

"I was excited to see the fabric, and it is better than I expected. I need more pearls. Every colour."

"Most women would wait for their husbands to gift them. You my dear, are slightly more demanding."

Damara could tell, Ramis was in a good mood. The one thing they had was a good repour with each other. That is why she had never thought he would stray. He would cater to her whims, and she hoped he would with this one.

"Well… if Kavena takes all this fabric, and I believe she will, she will be a shiny pearl. If the Namarch gives his blessing, then the Empress will want some. I need to get started on red. I am wondering if Aram uses this in their gold…" Ramis looked studious for a moment. Then he smiled.

"You may have something here. We can have our Captains gather some supplies from the Islands. We must wait to see, though. If he does not…"

"If he does not, then Kavena will be most angered. She is the perfect Noma to give us patronage. You know he does whatever she directs, and if the Empress wears a red, then we will have to find more pearls. However, I understand. Give Kavena the fabric first. Then we sit back. We need to find something for Kavena, a thank you for her order. She will know, once she sees this fabric it will be her word which gives us more orders. Has Captain Olent left yet?"

The sound of his name wiped the smile from Ramis's face. He looked at her, a question in his eyes, she kept her face neutral. "I need him to get more pearls. He also needs to get the others organized. I wish to be ahead of these orders, at least prepared to dye. I am going to need more dyes. Can we send him to Aram?"

Ramis smiled at the thought. He looked at his wife. Seeing the thought processes in her face and he felt reassured Damara was only thinking of her business. "I am afraid he has sailed to Merida, but I can send a rider to catch him before he leaves there. What would you have him do?"

"Hmmm, have him return. He needs to organize and send others. We should have him at our disposal. We have trading rights on the Islands. They have the most pearls. What can we use…?"

"We can certainly do so. I will let you organize your dyes. Make up your list. We may have to attend back at the Capital. The new heir is due soon. Mid summer I hear."

"I will be ready. This has given me a new life. Much to plan. I will see you for dinner?"

"Perhaps, do not tire yourself. Let the others make your lists."

"That sounds like a very good plan. I have many lists. I have your leave to go?"

"Yes, have a good day, dear Mara."

"You also." They rose and went their separate paths, hers to her room to gather her writing utensils, and Ramis for whatever he planned. Damara for once, gave not another thought to what her husband was about.

Not another.

CHAPTER 26

Meera

Weary is Her Breast

I packed up our packs after two days of rest which I was glad for, I regained my energy, and I packed both wounds with weed before we set out. Nejan was down to the water a couple times and washed her wounds which were red, but I saw no infection setting in. I had gone down again, tying an extra knot, and gathering more of the very limp weed. I tried to compress it, not knowing how much longer our travel would be. It would be needed for both injuries for a while.

I tied the fur on my Pader, and we set off still moving in an upward direction, across the peaks of mountains. As we started to trek, snow began to fall, It snowed a little during the battle of the cats, and after, but I was too engrossed in what my task was to notice. Plus, the falling stars distracted me for the few Days they showed their lights. They slowly stopped the morning past. I tucked this memory away to analyze later. My Pader was my main worry, and I was trying hard not to.

With Nejan leading, her body cutting a path through the snow, I would cut another swath, so Kiem could walk as uninhibited as possible. The next month of travel was laborious and sometimes treacherous. One day we only made it from one side of a mountain to the other, trying to find a way across which wouldn't be too painful for Kiem.

His arm began healing after a short bout of infection which kept us stationary for another two days while I rummaged for the herbs in our packs to take down the fever and kept water down his throat. After he conquered it, it seemed he lost some of his zest for life. He would be muttering under his breath and many times Nejan would walk beside him when she was able. I know they had conversations about me as one or the other would look back at me from time to time.

The mountains were fatiguing; there was so much snow. I was cold, every part of me. My furs I unpacked and tied on with leather straps but the areas I could not cover I suffered through it. I made sure Kiem was bundled up, the cloak from the Li'on-sa was a redeeming quality, it kept his back warm just from sheer volume. We would stop and sleep standing up together, holding or leaning against each other. Most times we could snuggle together with Nejan, she proved to be an excellent source of warmth.

"Kiem, Da. Are you feeling better?"

"Better than what? My shoulder and my arm are throbbing. I hurt from my chest up."

"Let me have a look. Let's put the fur over our heads. Hmmmm, it's a bit red and swollen still. I can pack it with weed again."

"Mayhap not yet. It has given me lucid dreams. I barely know what we are about."

"We are high in the mountains. Nejan is leading us higher, and it is snowing pretty heavy. I am thankful for this fur, it serves as a covering for you and me, combined with Nejan when we stop, it has kept us dryer and warm."

"Yes, 'tis the fur from the other?"

"Nejan let me take it. I saw the spirit rise into the air. I did not know about the spirit rising. Have you ever seen one?"

"No. You have witnessed something not seen in an exceptionally long time. there have only been a few written accounts of a human's spirit rising. One was Noster's. I remember reading a tome of the last days. A scribe thought to put it down. It was not well known."

"So, peoples spirit's rise also?"

"Yes. From what I read. But not lately I am thinking. To much evil in the world. You have much to clean up."

(Sigh) "Don't remind me. I have not the slightest idea what I am to do."

"Well, you start each day with a clear mind. Do not fall asleep with troubles. That will affect your dreams. Waking up, putting forth your intent for the Day, is an effective way to begin."

"You have some clever ideas…Pader. What else can you impart on your Dader?"

"Ahhh, lass. It gladdens my spirit to hear those words from you. I watched you from afar, always longing to tell you. However, I knew to have told you sooner would have consequences. You and I for that matter were not ready for this revelation."

"I am glad you told me. I was beginning to feel lost again. I was looking for something, listening to all the stories of old, made me feel there was something out there, I knew not what."

"There are lessons in some of the stories. Perhaps take a lesson out of Noster's life."

"I know nothing about these last Riders, other than the tragic tale of his last days. He was murdered by one of his own. Should I be wary of the other Riders?"

"There is more to his life than the end. He was a stalwart figure. Above reproach. He was just. I read a few tomes on his life. Let's see… he gave many people second chances, to repent, to bring good into their hearts. He let more than a few Dragons decide for themselves where they would live, under Vendar, or turn away."

"Mayhap we do not need that. If Naman would rule with fear, I can not see this as a good thing."

"People who are afraid will go with who would give them a reprieve. Naman has proven themselves a hard master. They will give with one hand and take away with another. The past Commanders of the North were hard pressed to keep themselves from having an infiltration of Naman influence."

"How did they manage then?"

"Easy. Snow. The cold. Many Naman Secondaries cannot manage the cold. Only a few remained more than one winter. A few were found frozen."

"Deliberately?"

"Nah, lass. Naman men are arrogant. Few listen to the North. When told not to do something, they take the other path. Being told not to venture out, in the heart of winter…well… some did not listen."

"Sounds like the North knew what they were about. Pader Reudin has been here many seasons."

"He has a pupil in Vandrin. Your brother…"

"He's not my brother though, is he?"

"Well, Vandrin then. He has a different agenda. He is Naman to the core. His Lordship may have been able to keep him out of the Faith's clutches, but with his absence, the Secondary is able to mentor him. Lord Bodan will have his hands full when he returns from the warfront."

"What if he doesn't?"

"Then Vandrin becomes the next Lord Commander, and the North will become a vastly different place. Now, if you could give me some weed, I am feeling the pain more now. I would like to rest."

"Here…I will let you rest. Let's slide down and lean against Nejan. I will step out for only a moment, to give her some dried meats."

I left the comfort of the furs to give the great cat some dried meats. She thanked me and I climbed back under the furs to see Kiem had fallen into slumber, we would often use Nejan's belly to sleep against. It was a system which worked for us. I shook off the snow which collected on my back. I did not need it melting into my clothing. I lay down and held Kiem upright with my body. I tried not to think about the cold outside. It was only the advent of winter. I was hoping we would see the other side before the temperatures really dropped.

Its not like I wasn't used to the snow, the winters in the Aerie were no less cold, I never stayed out in it for so long. I also transferred as much as I could from his pack to mine, I knew it was placing pressure on his shoulder, but with a forehead strap, I tried to alleviate the pressure. It seemed to work, or he did not complain that it did not. Then one day amid the falling snow, I realized we began our descent, we travelled for several days always going down and were careful where we went as to not start an avalanche.

"Is this the way?"

"Yes, if I have not been directing you, Nejan knows the way. She has travelled with me many times over the years to these far lands."

Nejan picked her trail carefully, and we followed her. We kept onward, and I could not help but wonder how much longer we would have before we were out of the snows. No sooner had I thought, the falling snow reduced in volume and then diminished as we continued travelling in a downward direction. Soon enough the snows ceased, the cloud cover lightened as we kept walking. We broke into sunlight; I saw the size of mountain peaks around us diminishing. We came out onto an escarpment, to see the way before us. I was amazed to see less of the rock faced mountains, more of treed rolling hills, and a haze beyond on the eastern horizon. I was curious as to what it was, Kiem spoke out of his bundle of furs.

"If you think traveling through mountain peaks is hard, you have no idea…"

He would mutter to himself, at night I would ask him trivial things about his homeland, trying to keep him engaged in some form of conversation. His fever set him off to muttering, half of the time, I wasn't sure if he was lucid, or fever-speech. I thought if I could keep him talking, even about non-essential things, then I could keep his spirit alive. He talked about people I didn't know, as if I should ever get to know them. One thing he said stuck with me.

"You will see what they want you to see, but if you listen with only one ear and with your heart, you will see what they are trying to hide from you. It is not all as it would seem. Your Mader knew, and she left with me, because she did not want to support such a corrupt system. If you go back to the Maderland, and you may have to, only you could put a stop to it."

When I asked him what he meant, he would say no more on the subject. Other times, he would tell me about the city he grew up and worked in. Describing the streets, the markets and all the flavours of spices and where each one hailed from. I had a sense of largess, the world had so many things to offer, not my narrow view as a citizen of the Aerie. I felt then I wanted to travel it, only to see what each region had to offer, if only in the way of food and spices. I felt intrigued by his descriptions. He spoke as if he had been to all these places, but he said it was all from reading and exploring the markets themselves.

We conversed while we walked, it helped to pass the time, especially when we could not see where we were going. Having Nejan was a blessing. She knew unspoken where to go, and travelling through this woodland forest, I was not sure of my direction. There were no Ravenwood trees on this side of the mountains. The trees were just as big, but a bark of burnt red, the leaves deep green and other trees were broad leaf and a brown bark, some had needles and I broke off a branch as we walked so, I could study it.

"What is this tree? It has needles instead of leaves."

"I am not certain. I will have to study it for a time. I can always speak with the Medijan, I am sure they would know."

"Who are the Medijan? I have never heard of them."

"They are Wanderers. You would have never heard of them, because they do not pass over the mountain range which separates the continent."

"You can tell me more on these people later, but can you explain this land? This mountain range we traversed separates this continent?"

"Yes. The mountains lead down into the South. They stop midway. The South is rolling lands. This is the seat of power of Du'Lanay. I have not been but I had pored over maps before I came here, and his Lordship had a few in the Great Hall. The Aerie is almost the pinnacle of the North lands. To the South are rolling hills."

"I remember seeing lights from Hoil and a few of the smaller townships. I climbed the tower one night, I was curious. I nearly froze up there. Even in the spring, the winds coming in from the west are very cold."

"Ahh, yes. I have only climbed the tower once. I am not good with heights. But the view is spectacular. This I remember. Past the rolling hills on the other side of the mountains is the swamp lands which separate the North from the South lands. It was said to have been the best for grains, at one time, but now the waters of the seas have taken over."

"How is this possible?"

"There may have been a change in climate in the time of the last Dragons. An earth movement, which claimed it. I read that the mountains closer to the South are rich with minerals and ores. The movement of the mountains unearthed more of its wealth. The South use much from the Southern ranges. They do not look further."

"What about the eastern shore? The other side of the central range?"

"Well. We are headed to the other side of these mountains. That is where we find the Wanderers. North of here is Lanthia. It is most likely where you need to go. It is the North most land, after that is ice. At least from what I have read. That land is bare rock. A harsh land, Naman is not interested in a land such as this."

"It seems Naman only cares for itself. Very self-seeking."

"So, you are beginning to see. It is. Naman only cares about something if it serves its own self interests. Very closed minded."

"So is Lanthia part of Naman?"

"From what I know, yes. However, there is not much written word... the Lanthians have kept to themselves. It may be self preservation, or it may be what is written. You may have to find out for yourself what it is."

"Is that what I need to do? Keep going?"

"What do you feel, in your spirit?"

"I feel...I am still feeling a pull to the North, Pader. I guess I follow this?"

"You must do what you feel you should do. I cannot tell you. It may be what is needed. Once you get to where you need to be, another revelation may present itself to you. As for the rest of the eastern shore... South of the lands of Lanthia are the Burnt Lands. It is a barren wasteland. Nothing grows there. Yet from an ancient map, it was once a thriving place."

"How did it become barren, Da? I have a feeling you read this somewhere."

"I did. There was a tome, it was once a busy trading port, there was a thriving river, it led to a city where I think it may have been the capital of Du'Lanay so many centuries ago. I was curious as to what happened myself and it took me a year of asking questions, not getting the answers, and finding them myself. It was one of the many things your Mader and I found out. We were incredibly pleased when we discovered the one book which told us. A Dragon burnt it; there was a war between Dragons. Some had become complacent or started to become Naman. It was an argument which ended with Dragon fire."

"Oh. Dragon against Dragon. This does not sound good. I do not even have one and I am shuddering at the thought. I hope I get along well, with my brother and sisters, whenever I should meet them."

"You will find out many things. If you are to rule the others, you may have to be firm in what transpires. I read the Dragons may have had more than one Rider. It seems they have a longer life span than humans. The human Riders, the last ones, had an extended life. It seems your bond will have you living longer than most. You may see several lifetimes."

"Oh! Am I ready for this? Living longer than most. Learning to rule others. I have no formal education. This seems daunting."

"Well, then. You learn. All you can, from who ever you can. Make sure in your heart, and your spirit, it is the learning you need. More than who. You learn from those who have no agenda than to serve you. We do not need a DragonRider who thinks Naman."

"No! You are right on this! I will never be Naman. I will have to tread carefully on learning, then. Perhaps my Dragon will guide me."

"Perhaps, but he has left you to make your own decisions, has he not? You already have a sense of what is right and wrong. Use your gut instincts. It has not served you wrong yet."

"Thanks, Da. You have me wishing to know more. I will find out all I can. There is a break in the canopy above us. I wonder where we are coming to, now."

At last, after many days of walking on semi level ground, we came out of the lower woodlands and onto rolling hills as far as the eye could see. It was grasslands, almost like looking at our lowlands, the grasses looked the same. Mayhap a different variation? I had grabbed a handful to peruse while we walked. I could imagine the uses for the stalks and leaves would make excellent baskets. I saw the haze closer, looking like the sky and earth met in an indistinct line, one merged into the other. I was very curious, but my attention was then caught by a plume of smoke far off in the distance to the North of us.

"We will be headed there, and I think that is where we will part ways, I cannot finish your journey with this injury, but Nejan has volunteered to take you across the desert and then make her way back."

Kiem would say no more than that, so I tried to converse with Nejan.

"Pader says he is staying with these Nomads."

"You need me more. He will be in safe care with the Travellers. They know many medicines. The Great One told me to take care of you and I live to serve. We will stay and prepare for the travel; there are different difficulties with the terrain. Different than the high mountains."

"Everything has its time bond place, Dader. We will be received with opened arms; there is need to worry about what lays ahead. The Wanderers will help prepare you."

"Yes, Pader." I took his word as such, trying hard not to bother him with too many questions. I learned to observe when Kiem was willing to talk. Usually after I gave him Numbweed. When he was in pain, he closed himself off. I sensed all these things like I had always been with him. Though my heart would skip a beat with joy, he was my Pader of blood. I was content.

At one point I called a halt at midday at a slow meandering stream. Kiem was only too happy to slide down onto his knees. As the weather was holding its own, and not too cold.

"We should stop and rest here, we can bathe, and I will start a small fire. I found a meal package hidden inside my pack. Let's have a hot meal and recoup some energy. It will do us all well. I will prepare a spot for you, Pader, just hold fast."

"Thank you, I will rest. I feel very tired. Wake me up when you are done."

"Just let me get you something soft to lay on." I dug out a pit as to not ignite any of the tall grasses. I tamped down a few areas to make a pile of grass to lay some furs on, for Kiem's delight at having a softer than usual place to rest on. He lay down and fell fast asleep. I covered him up with an errant fur and let him snore on, while I unpacked our packs and tried to organize our meager supplies. I bathed myself and washed as many clothes as I could find, laying them in the still hot sun to dry, I set out to fix a fire. Looking around a bend in the stream, I managed to find myself the odd piece of stray wood which floated its way down and soon had a rather large bundle even dropping them together on the ground did not wake Kiem. At one point I must have looked worried, but Nejan reassured me he needed this rest to recover from the wound he sustained.

"Even though it looks like it is healing well, his mind also needs to heal, he feels responsible for you, and feels he could have done more."

"Well, not at the speed in which the male moved. I have never seen such quickness. There was no time to react."

"You reacted quick, the male had barely bit into Little Uncle. You must be garnishing your speed from your bond with the Great One."

"Is that what this was? It felt like time slowed for me. I shudder to think if I had moved slower. Kiem would have lost his arm or his life. The acid which came out of my mouth. It does not affect me. Yet it ate through the male's fur and skin easily enough."

"You are a DragonRider, Dear Cub. You have a destiny to fulfill. I am sure you will gain other talents from your bond. These are but a few."

"Do you know what the other Riders can do? Aunt Nena told me one of them saw the truth or lie in another. The Air Dragon commands the winds. Good for sailing. I am thinking the Sea Dragon commands water. The Earth Dragon could command plants and one story I remember, was the Earth Dragon moved stone. The Earth Dragon partially built the Aerie. The Fire Dragon is obvious. The Mind Dragon. The stories say he was arrogant and was the downfall of the Great One."

"Yes, that is truth. It was a terrible time. You are the greatest of them all. You have all the talents the others have. You will discover in time for yourself what they are, and you must meet your Dragon."

"I am terrified I will fail. I do not want to be a disappointment to him."

"Keep this thought in mind when you set yourself to a task and you will never fail. You will not be a disappointment. Keep yourself humble and not proud. His

last Rider was a pinnacle of character. The Mind Dragon was proud. However, there were also outside influences which helped to shape the events which happened. You will have to ask your bond, or a learned person for the full facts. I have no knowledge of your history."

She lay over the stream trying to fish with her paw. At one point she moved so fast I didn't know she had caught one until its smacked me in the face, laying at my feet struggling to get back into the water. I bent down, picking it up by the tail and smacked it on a rock.

"Nice work, here you go, you have excellent fishing skills, your speed is apparent."

As I tossed it back in the air, she rose to gobble it up in one bite. Laying back down in her spot, patiently waiting for the next victim.

I managed to get a fire going, borrowing Kiem's slate stones, first shaving one of the sticks of pale brown wood into angel feathers, or as he called them, Dragon scales. Kiem demonstrated at the cabin, ways to start a fire, using stones and shavings. Slowly at first and with lots of smoke, but it soon blazed with some of the dryer wood I found. I gathered stones from the bank and made a rim around it, pulling the grasses away, churning up dirt. Last thing I needed was a rogue grass fire. Occasionally, in the lowlands, someone would err and if one of the hills caught on fire, it wouldn't be until a natural break of a stream or the stone fences erected which would stop a fire. Everyone in the Aerie were trained from an early age the dangers of grass fires. Soon, I had a good pot of stew going and I turned to see Kiem stirring, waking himself up.

"Good to see you rested, Pader Kiem." I smiled at him. He still looked off, but at least he was smiling up at me.

"Call me Kiem, less questions will be asked, no one needs to know about our history, and I see you are more comfortable with my given name as this is how you know me. I see into your heart, Dader, and you see into mine, we are family, now and always." He smiled at me. "I feel as if the last month has been a very bad dream, did I see what I thought I saw you do, Dader?"

He asked the very question I was dreading. All the way here he had been looking at me, in and out of his infection and I knew I would answer this eventually.

"I am not sure what I did, this is the same thing which happened when I was attacked by the young man long ago. I stayed awake for this, and I did not hear any voices, just a feeling I was not alone. I felt a pressure building up inside me and my stomach spewed a fluid which ate through skin and bone. This time I accidently set it on fire, with the stick I had in my hand, and it burned the cat alive. I also did not get sick after, although my waste the next day had a putrid smell to it. I am not certain, but I would say I reacted out of fear."

I sat down passing him a bowl of the stew I cooked. Trying not to look at him and see his disgust for me, I ventured a glance, and he was still smiling.

"I could say it was not out of fear this time, but a need to protect, and for that I am eternally grateful." Hanging his head slightly. His smile saddened, and I wanted to make him smile again.

"It is I who should be grateful. Grateful for you saving me when I jumped off the neck," Here I had to smirk at his initial comment.

"Grateful for your care, grateful for your teachings, and grateful for your name, where I thought I had none."

A tear slipped down my unblemished cheek, only for me to wipe it away back-handedly. In the saying of I suddenly got emotional. He reached out and patted my knee.

"I am grateful too; you know the truth and have a family name. I cannot give you mine as your Mader and I did not say the vows, but you have hers. Mine is of a lower caste and is not recognized by the upper families. Your Mader is from one of the original ruling families, and most DragonRiders have been from one branch or another of this family."

"I have my Mader's name? Not yours?"

"In the old ways and still on the Islands, all children have their Mader's name. it is only here and in Aram I think the Pader's name is taken. That was just another difference they changed when they took over."

"So, what is it?"

"D'un."

"As in Pelin 'Dun?"

"Yes. Your Mader's family is the primary ruling family. They have held more DragonRider positions than they have children, it seems. Your Mader and Aunt would have sealed all the positions, had they partaken of the Rituals and passed the ceremony. It was your GrandMaders goal. It was common knowledge among the lower caste's; all scholar's talked about the elites. I had no interest in gossip, mine lay in reading manuscripts. It was how I met her.

Our meeting was by chance, she was an avid reader, absorbing all she could of all the great teachings. Always looking for more, much to her Mader's disappointment. We had a common interest; it was what attracted me to Miiele. Her Mader was grooming her to become a Rider, but Miiele didn't want to give up her passions. She felt it should be her choice to make, and she saw something she would not talk about, not even to me, as much as I pressed her. It was horrible and she made the decision to not become a Rider. After your Mader made her decision, her sister followed suit, and they both had words with their Mader.

We have been taught, Dragons as such do not exist..." Here he gave pause, and a thought crossed his countenance.

"Dragons no longer exist, but Riders go through a ceremony and are still being groomed, not for the riding part, but the advocation of the ruling and lawmaking. The only explanation is they do exist, given your experiences up till now. But where? This is what you need to find out. You may need your Dragon, but he may also need you. You have a long journey ahead of you. I will get better and meet with you in the future. Of this I have no doubt.

In the far South is a port of all lands. It is a free port; you will have to travel through the vestiges of war and the infidels. You will find a ship to take you there but not during winter, the storms are too great. We have travelled North; your Mader was adamant North and west were your destiny."

He raised his hand to shush me. I was going to protest, and he knew it by the look crossing my face. "Don't ask me what your Mader meant, she did not tell me, but she knew something, either from books or from her family."

"Well, given that I feel a pull North, perhaps she did know something. Perhaps her spirit is guiding me."

"You could be right. Although I have no knowledge of guiding spirits." He rose to his feet. He was slow to rise but he managed it on his own but given that he hadn't moved his arm in a while, I thought he did so remarkably well and told him so.

"Now help me please, I would very much like to bathe."

I helped him to unwrap his bandages, untying his shirt straps I created to make undressing easier. He left his pants on for modesty's sake. We took his boots off, and he sat down on the bank and slipped into the water.

"There is a clean pair of trousers over on the grass, Pader. They should be dry by now, you did sleep for a while and the sun was out, nice, and warm. Why does it feel like a different season here?"

I was curious about the change in temperature. Coming out of the frigid cold of the snowy mountains into an almost tropical warmth had me perplexed. Back home was heading into winter; this was like winter had already passed.

"It is always sunny here, this is their winter, it gets rainy in their summer on this side of the mountain range. Opposite of ours over the mountains."

"Why and how do you know all that?" I asked very curious. Kiem was a walking fount of knowledge, for someone I had only known as a Hunter-Ranger in the mountains back home.

"Well, I did study in Pelin'Dun, I was after all a cleric, scribe, and I would look at tomes and learn about all the different lands in all different areas. Your Mader and I would read sometimes together, when we could sneak off, having a passion for learning all we could. One such tome spoke about the bond between beast and man, and how as it strengthened, the eyes of man would glow brighter than the sun, each person…"

Kiem came out of the water and motioned me to turn around, I heard muttering and cursing and almost turned around, "Unless you want to see your Pader in all his naked glory you had best not turn around…oooff. Yes… just wait… ahhh. I am good, you may turn around now. If you could me help with a shirt?"

I picked up the dry linen as I turned to help. Kiem was speaking quietly, I was not sure if it was to me or himself. "Now I reflect upon it, the leading house culled what they called Riders, but no Dragons present. Those chosen became part of the Rulers, their eyes opalescent and glowed. Hmmmm…They maintained our laws. However, there has never been a question as to how their eyes changed. The few who would question would always disappear."

He looked at me. A far-off look to his eyes, somehow, I sensed he was reliving a memory from his youth. His smile was sad.

"I have often wondered, not lately until I saw your eyes, how this can be, as you have not partaken of any Rituals. Now I am thinking it may be your destiny to solve this riddle for yourself."

He grimaced as I tied bandages around the red inflamed scars on his shoulder and back.

"These are healing, but very slowly, I am not sure I have done a good job, enough you will have use of your arm." I pursed my lips into a line. I wasn't satisfied my stitch job would lend him use of his arm; in fact I was fairly sure I hadn't done it right. Kiem was not able to raise his arm from the shoulder, it had no strength at all. The bandages held his arm against his body, or else it would swing freely. He smiled down at me.

"The Medijan peoples have other healing practices which may help me, which is why I am choosing to stay with them for a bit. I saved a son from a rogue wolf who strayed too close to the caravan, and they are eternally grateful for my intervention. So, I have no doubt they will welcome us, in fact, I am sure they already know we are here and are sending a welcome committee."

No sooner had he said that Nejan looked over at Kiem, fish tail dangling from the side of her jaw before it got slurped up, then went back to her meal finding. Kiem said,

"So you know, there are hunters all around us, don't act surprised. Let's finish and sit by the fire to wait."

We sat by the fire and Kiem talked about the flora and fauna of his homeland. I could hear the homesickness in his voice of the land he left behind 19 years ago.

"The North has plenty of Ravenwood, but the Islands have Redwoods. Their strength is second to that of the Blackwood. The ships which grace the waters are built from the hardy Redwood."

"Is this the forest we just came from? I saw a few red barked woods."

"Yes, they have made their way to this land. I read the Southlands have plenty of Redwoods. Various species, in fact.'

"I saw some other woods. This seems a truly diverse landscape, with a few species being dominant. How do the Islands keep up with shipbuilding, do they not run out of wood?"

"It has been a mandate, law, for every tree cut down two are planted. The Northern Islands were used first. Even though their function is the sail cloth and rope grasses, there is still a portion given over to trees. It has proven its worth. Only a dozen ships are built a year. This system has proven over the centuries to be most effective. Ships are lost during storms, but not every year. Pirates have stolen some, but others are bought."

"Why would the Islands sell their ships? Would they not be used against them?"

"Everything made has a price attached. Ships were a bargaining tool in the past. It has kept the other lands at bay. One ruler, hmmm, I think it may have been a…no…ninety years ago, the Rulers let too many go to Du'Lanay. It caused a bit of an upset. We almost lost the Islands. When your GrandMader came into power, she started to turn the economy around. The Islands prior to this were slowly recovering from that one blunder. I think her Pader was a Ruler…he taught her everything she knows."

"My GrandMader. It seems too good to be true. I always believed myself to have no family. My Mader died when I was a child. My Pader I knew to be mine, was gone fighting in the South. I never really thought I had family. Then you tell me that I am yours, and I have my Maders family on the Islands. Now I may have more family than I know what to do with."

"You will always have me. Dear child, I am sorry for your sense of loss, in growing up. You can dwell on the past but use this loss to move forward. I will be here, until I cannot. The Universe has given you a path, it has led you up to now. Believe it will send you into places you have never been, and people you have never met. Knowing where you come from…well, I can only hope I can tell you of who you come from."

"I was not meaning to disparage you, Pader. I am happy knowing you as my Pader of truth. I have pleasant memories of you. You have always been there for me. I always felt it inside, here…you looked out for me the most. How can I not think of you, but with love. Just thinking there are others who share blood with me…'tis nothing I would have ever imagined. I find it…"

I sat up and Kiem nodded to me. I heard the tall grasses move as though there was a wind blowing which there was not. One by one, five hunters came into our clearing. The oldest one, which was a man of advanced years, held out his hand to Kiem as he walked forward. Waiting for Kiem to rise and speaking in a dialect which sounded like our speech but different. They were simply dressed in leather loin coverings, their skin tanned, and they sported strange markings on their skin, be it dye or paint. Most, other than the elder, had black or deep brown hair, shaved on the sides, and braided in the middle.

The leader glanced over at me and started when he looked at my eyes, then said something to Kiem. Kiem, without looking at me, reverently spoke and gestured in my direction. I had slowly risen while the men were greeting each other and stood silently waiting. The leader came to me and bowed, at which point the rest bowed to me. I nodded my head, putting my hand to my heart and touched my forehead with two of my forefingers. Kiem started at that, looking at me closely and asked,

"How did you know to do that?"

"I remember something Aunt Nena spoke about before she settled in the mountains. She spoke about leaving a great love and the formality of the gestures of different races she encountered in her travels. This man with his piercings and lines, looks like he may have been such a man, she spoke with great fondness and caring, I thought to try it. Did I do wrong?"

"No, not at all. In fact, I think you may have asked the elder for his hand in marriage, which he has gracefully declined."

At this, all the men broke out in laughter, much to my embarrassment I turned a bit red in the cheeks.

"You may want to wait or ask, next time." His expression said he found my gesture more than amusing; he was holding his laughter in check. Kiem gestured for the men to come sit by our fire with his good arm.

The men all came forward from the edge of the clearing I noticed one was but a young boy learning the ways of adulthood. He stared at me until another barked something at him. The lad bowed his head sauntering off in the direction of the stream, standing at the edge in what I assumed was punishment, or to stand guard.

Kiem and the elder chatted in the guttural dialect, which I would pick up the odd word occasionally. Then they all stood up and began collecting our packs. One put out the fire and covered it with dirt. When I rose to protest, Kiem said,

"We will go with them, and they will care for me while you prepare for your journey across the sea of sand."

"Sand, like the bottom of the stream sand?" As I could not fathom what a sea was, all I could envision was a handful from the river bottom.

"Oh no, little Dader, much, much more than a handful!" He smirked, and I smiled back, because I saw myself in his expression.

"They do not want the little Mader to task herself, so they will carry our things, and they also revere Nejan, as they know in protecting you, she will also protect them for a time."

When one of the men saw the hide of the Li'on-sa male, he started gesturing and talking rapidly. Kiem told them I alone had killed the male, they stopped and bowed, touching their first finger to their foreheads. I was perplexed,

"I thought you said I asked for marriage. Do they all want to marry me now?"

"No, certain ways of gesturing mean different things. They are your protectors if you have need of them. It is a sign of respect."

It was a good thing he didn't tell me then it was more than that. It was a sign of reverence. I would have argued the point. Later in life, I would get used to it. But for now, I was glad I didn't know everything. We moved west through the tall grasses and scrub. Crossing shallow streams and one exceptionally large river they seemed to know exactly where the sandbars were to facilitate easy crossing. All the while the smoke plume became larger, then broke into several, soon cliffs of red stone came into the view. As we crested the last hill, below us was a massive village of grass huts and a large one in the center, before the huge entrance to a canyon.

We were spotted from below and one of the men motioning to the young lad and he raced ahead. Yelling something, I gathered it was announcing our arrival, I did not expect the welcome we would receive when we descended to the bottom of the hill. Folks of all ages, men, women, and children lined up and made a tunnel we would have to walk through, when we were close enough, they genuflected and bowed, and a murmur rose.

"Manuman," was the cry, which when I looked over to my Pader he whispered, "It means, Little Mader."

I nodded and nodded so much, by the time we reached the main tent where an older man stood with his (I will assume) wife slightly behind him, I had to shrug and crack my neck, it was so tense. The older man dressed a little fancier than the others. I assumed him to be the leader of this people. They wore thin garments, a type of linen or maybe silk, and while some of the people wore colours to blend with their surroundings, the fancier dress had some bright colours.

Kiem put his left hand out for an arm grab and said, "Lo'nan, greetings,"

To my surprise the older man answered in our language!

"Welcome, Woodsman Kiem, you brought us Little Mader, May she Bless us."

I started, startled I was expected.

"Our journey was quite eventful as you can see, we seek refuge here, if you would honour us." Kiem answered back quite formally.

"It is you who would honour us, and what is ours is yours." Lo'nan gestured his arm around the camp. "Speak and it will be yours. I will have our healing woman look at your shoulder. You and little Mader can rest and tomorrow will be another day."

He waved his arms, and several women came gesturing for me to follow. I was so exhausted I placed one leg in front of the other and did not even look back to see where Kiem had gone.

The next thing I knew I was in one of the grass huts. The women and young girls were nattering, pulling off my tattered clothes and at one point there were so many, the eldest wife ordered most of them out, but a few still looked in through the doorway. They took off the remainder of my clothing and I stood there, naked while they bathed me with warm water smelling like lavender flowers which grew wild on the mountainside and in some of our gardens in the fortress.

One woman clucked when she saw my hair and gestured to me, I nodded, and she set to trimming my hair so it looked less wild and matted. Their hair were the colours of black and browns, braids with beads decorated most women. Another woman showed me what I assumed were clothes, several tunics, and I gasped when I saw them, and I moved closer. "Oh, my, beautiful!"

Putting my hand out to stroke what to me was the softest and thinnest fabric. And the colours! It was so beautiful I did not realize tears were streaming down my cheeks. One woman started to dab my cheeks with a cloth. The blues and greens were so intense and vibrant I looked up with the biggest grin on my face and everyone in the room laughed and chatted merrily.

They dressed me with a loincloth of the same soft material, then beautiful dark green leggings, which reminded me of the foliage of the Ravenswood trees. The tunic they put over a small top lacing up over my breasts which was quite functional. I did not pay any attention to my body, but now I wore this laced up item, I realized I did have some substance there to fill it.

Hmmm, guess this is what men are always looking at.

Then I heard a musical chuckle in my head which I knew was Nejan. She was being fed lots of tasty morsels she told me,

"I could get used to this."

I smiled and the women laughed some more. The eldest shooed all but three of them out and stoked the fire in the center of the room ushering me over to a mat and several bowls. I sat down cross-legged, all the while feeling the fabric caress my fingers. They showed me bowls of prepared food, I nodded my head, and they proceeded to feed me. I let them as I was unprepared for such treatment and did not know if it would be rude to refuse. One dish I refused as it tasted like old sweaty leather bits. I shook my head not one, as my stomach let out a gurgle of protest. After I put my hand up to stop the influx of food they handed me a wooden bowl of fluid, upon tasting, was a bit like wine.

The building or hut I was occupying was quite simple; the walls were woven grasses. Upon closer inspection, when I had such a moment, it was much like a basket, woven as such. I learned from Kiem the huts were left to the elements, and when the roving bands of traders used them, they would repair and brace up what needed to be done, use for the season, then leave them for the next group. Each layer of repair would add to the stability, and some of the huts were so sturdy the elements could no longer enter. Only in the worst of storms would extensive damage be done. For such a simple and readily available building material it was very hardy.

After tasting, I realized I was very thirsty and drank the whole thing down to which a few were very astonished. A little while later I could not suppress my yawns and they ushered me to a padded mat behind me on the ground, I rolled up and over to the mat where no sooner did I lay my head down than I fell into a deep sleep.

I woke up from a dream I could not remember but I could not shake a feeling of hopelessness. What I assumed was morning was midday. I rolled over to see several women grinning at me. I must have looked puzzled until a young woman my age made snoring sounds, then I smiled and shrugged. I rose and the young woman grabbed my hand taking me to a small stream where other women were in the water dipping down while holding their tunics up around their waists. She had the same bronzed skin, black hair, and dark eyes like the rest of the populace who surrounded us. Kiem and I were a sharp contrast to the Wanderers, with our red hair and paler skin. They were always smiling, and I could not help but feel a relief and happiness that we had arrived in a relaxed and joyous environment.

No one had to tell me what was happening, I shoved my leggings and loincloth off and stepped out and walked into the water gathering my tunic as I walked. The young woman was right behind me. As I dipped down, bubbles rose up and she giggled, as she did the same, we looked at each other and laughed. I pointed to my chest and said my name, "Meera" to which she did the same saying, "Si'Sue."

I made a friend, she was with me all the time, I am not sure if she was assigned to me, but I gathered from the looks of others it was a great honour to be with me. She went with me everywhere, or she led the way. I saw only half of the encampment when I felt an acute loss, not knowing what it was, I turned to my newest friend.

"Where is my Uncle? Where is he? Kiem?"

Si'Sue grabbed my hand and led me to the other side of the village where I gathered was the unmarried men's side. She looked everywhere and giggled when men would speak to her. She spoke to whoever was in the tent and Kiem came out followed by several men of various ages. I saw now that his hair was the same curly mop I had with his red a bit deeper in colour, dark enough to be a rich wine, if one were thirsty. Someone had taken a knife to his and fashioned it in the style of the men, shaved on the sides, and braided down the center.

"That suits you, old man, shaving the sides gets rid of the white I saw close up."

I smiled as I took stock of how clean and smartly dressed, he was in leather leggings, a pale green shirt of the same fabric I had on, with a leather vest with beautiful stitching decorating it. I exclaimed over the stitching while he tried and failed in boxing my head, with his good arm. I ducked laughing while some of our audience exclaimed in shock, he would try to hit me until they saw we were laughing.

"That's not nice, young lady. Did no one teach you manners?"

"No!" We both laughed.

"The healer woman looked at my shoulder, and while some parts she said were good, there is an area in the front which doesn't want to heal. She said the only way is to open it up and see what it is. But she can't do it until the rest heals up more. This woman was quite impressed with what you did in such a fleeting time under such extremes, with that kind of wound. So, I will have to stay and get this fixed again. The young men will double up their hunting and they will prepare your pack for the crossing. You do not mind if I keep the furs here? You will not need them where you are going."

We walked through the huts to the clearing in front of the large tent.

"Just where am I going?" I asked, still not sure of leaving so soon after meeting these kind and attentive people.

"Here, Si'Sue, Lo'nan and I will take you to the edge of the fields and you will see what it is you need to see."

We all walked for three hours to the east through diverse types of grasses, and I noticed they diminished as rock underfoot was what we walked on. As we walked, the haze I so admired became an endless vista of yellow. The indiscrete line now changed to a sharp contrast from blue to yellow. I now started to sink in what I learned was sand, fine grains of rock, too fine to hold in my hands as I picked up handful after handful.

"Its very warm, is it always such?" I asked as I knelt and ran my hands through it.

"It gets very warm, sometimes too warm to walk on, you must travel at night when its cool and rest when the sun is over head, the heat of the sand will burn Nejan's paw pads, seek shelter when the winds blow, you may suffocate in the blowing sand, and so would Nejan. There is a plant the Medijan dry which will sustain you, it is light to carry and upon chewing provides you with moisture, but long-term chewing will take its toll, you will carry water and only drink once every two days.

The walk will be a long one, many moons, and you must follow the pale sun of the night, we will explain this later. This is a harsh environment, and there are different animals which kill with just a bite."

Lo'nan told us of several animals on our way back I could not fathom, a large bug which walks with its tail up in the air and bites with it, and poisonous. We returned, following the same routine as our first night, with me commenting to Nejan, that I could get used to this.

Over the next month, I was pampered and began to learn the language by pointing and repeating sounds, a lot of sounds were very similar but with a guttural sound added, I soon became proficient, enough if I didn't know something, I would just point, and everyone would laugh and tell me. I was also busy, gathering plants from the neighbouring woods on the South side of the canyon and learning how to harvest others which were new to me.

Even on this side of the mountains, wild onion and garlic grew, it was a staple of most diets. Some small flowers were edible, petal, and leaf, dried made a good tea. There were berries, wild strawberries, and small blackberries. A hardy bush with small round pale pink berries which made an extremely sweet jelly when processed. I found various root plants, tubers which were eaten, but had to be cooked to be palatable. I learned a lot from harvesting food for preservation, by the Wanderers. Aunt Nena taught me much, but with different plants on this side, it added to my knowledge, and I was grateful to them. Somehow, I knew everything I was doing was preparing me for the future. How could it not.

One night we were both sitting around a community fire. There was story telling happening, I surmised it was for the small children, as a few adults were chatting quietly among themselves. I turned to my Pader asking him the question which was in my mind on the trek over the mountains and had just recalled.

"I must ask you, Pader, how did you know I would be in the God's River at that moment? How did Nejan know? It weighed on my mind for a while now."

I looked at his face in the firelight.

"Well, it may have happened when you touched the sword, I was cleaning a skin outside the cabin, and Nejan suddenly became alert. I thought it may have been another animal, but she confirmed a relic of old was… touched or set in motion is a better way. She felt the vibration through the earth. I kept on doing what I was doing until she spoke in my mind. I looked up to see her pacing and facing down the hill. When you hit the water, we felt more than heard the concussion and it wasn't mere minutes before the wind reached us. She said something happened and took off down towards the river, I don't know how she knew, but she did.

She found you in the river, unconscious and bleeding, mostly from the cut on your face. She swam into the current in a bend of the river, fetched you, picking you up in the shallows and carrying you out. She only stopped long enough to lay a false trail. Nejan is a very smart feline, she knew whatever or whoever tried to kill you may come to finish it or at least confirm your death. So, she took bits of her meal she hunted, and some of your hair and clothing leaving it there to be found. It was meant to be found and reported back a wild animal finished you off. The size of her paw prints would have confirmed the lack of evidence to those who looked, Nightstalker's are known to not leave much behind.

She picked you up as gently as she could, but you were leaking lots of blood. She was worried you would lose your spirit fast, so she wasn't gentle the rest of the way up the hill to me. She warned me you were bleeding, so by the time she arrived with you in her jaws, I had water, cloths, needle, and thread waiting. I did not know it was you until I saw you. She told me the Chosen One. I was terrified and happy at the same time. The rest you know."

Kiem took a long drink from his wooden cup, which was the same mead I was drinking. We sat for a few more hours talking about people we left behind. Recounting stories of my youth, Kiem told me of a few I didn't know.

"When you were three, you were a handful. Your Mader told me she was pregnant again. Lord Bodan was busy gearing up for war. The treaty with Aram had disintegrated, and the whole Empire was busy. The smithies rang night and day, hunters gave over the hides for armour, saplings were being prepared. He could not keep you entertained enough. You had other minders who would be losing you. Or maybe you were losing them. You ran everywhere. And you had incredibly good balance. You know the beams in the main Hall?"

"The ones which cross the length?"

"No, the ones above those. You were walking across those. You scared the spirit out of Lord Bodan. I don't think he ever told your Mader."

"I think someone did, though. I vaguely remember I was not scared of heights. I was laughing; the people below were so small. Then after, I remember being smacked on the bottom, and a woman squishing me in a tight hug. She smelled of… roses… hmmm, a different smell… I think wild roses. Its less fragrant than the larger ones in the city."

"You do have a good memory, lass. Mielle loved wild roses. I would pick them for her; I had to have another give them. I did not want her or the Lord to be uncomfortable with me when I visited. You were punished, and it was his Lordship who spanked you. He made you promise to never walk those beams again."

"I never did. After I did it once, it lost its appeal. I walked the edge of the Aerie tower once. It was beginning to snow; the stone started to get slick and I nearly went off the wrong edge. That scared me enough to not take the chance again."

"You did not! I am glad I was not there to witness. I would have smacked your bottom myself. That is a terrible height."

"I think the God's Neck might have that one beat. I am not wanting to go back to measure them both. See which one is lengthier. One day, I might."

Kiem laughed. Then finished the remainder of his cup.

"You may be right. On both. The God's Neck is quite the drop. You have other things to do. Another quest. The Aerie can wait."

"I used to sneak loaves from the kitchens, not sure if the Cook knew, I was never caught."

"Oh, she knew. She told me once. She never said anything to anyone else. She knew you were not in any favour with any of the other servants. Many would have given you over to the Church if it weren't for their love for his Lordship. He made his servants swear they would care for you. Mila brewed the walnut rinse herself."

"Yes, I remember this ordeal. I had to use it once a month. She made me a special tart, it was my favorite for several years… it was Mmmm, Ravenberry. Oh, how I miss those… she would always use those to get me to cooperate. I hated that smell. The tonic for my hair was disgusting. She always told me it was for my safety. She used to use Mader's name, and when that didn't work, Paders… I mean, his Lordships."

"Its fine, lass. It'll be on your tongue for a while. It does not bother me."

"You did not hate him? For stealing Mader away?"

"He did not steal anything. Mielle and I had grown apart. You cannot force someone to love you. That's not how it works. She later admitted she used me to get away from her Mader. She knew I loved her. I always will. That's just who I am. She apologized every time I saw her. I came to terms with it. It was hard to do. She told me she loved his Lordship, and I believe you can love many people at once.

And she knew I would always love you. I promised I would not interfere with his Lordship, with your upbringing. She said to tell you when the time was right. I did not know until Nejan brought you unconscious and dripping your spirit's blood, the time was now."

"The Universe let's you know when the time is right."

"Oh, where have I heard that before?" Kiem laughed.

I loved spending time with him. We were very much alike. Comfortable with each other and not needing to say much. This trip down memory lane was what I needed now.

"Oh, yes. Healer Nena. This is one of her favorite sayings. She pretty much raised Lord Bodan. She was his nanny for a time. She was quite the bonny lass when she was young. She used to say, she broke more than enough hearts when she was young."

"Oh? She never told me this story."

"She had many suitors. I think one she loved, went to war, and never returned. She lamented she never could have children. Maybe that's why she had many 'other' children. She would look after everyone else's."

"She knows a lot. She likes her privacy too. Living out in the woods, she told me, was the peace she needed. The city holds too many. She was fine with her solitude. I quite agree with her reasoning. I could live a quiet life."

"You do not know what the future holds. You may have to rule people. Be among people. Not be able to live a quiet life. Be prepared. The Universe may have other plans than those you would rather have."

"Well, I hope I have many to help me with ruling. I have absolutely no idea how to rule. What makes you think I will be a ruler?"

"Well, Noster's sword for one. He was the Purity Dragon Rider. His was the white diamond in the sword. He was the last Rider; his death is what set the Great Dragon to disappear. You may have found the sword and may have triggered it to glow. Nejan felt the occurrence, remember? The Great One ruled all the others."

337

"Why does one have to rule the rest? There are six Riders in total. I am perfectly fine with sharing the responsibility. I don't want to lord it over the rest. Maybe it can be shared."

"Maybe, dear Dader, this is what is needed. You can make these changes, if you are the Purity Rider, you can do anything you want!"

"How about I get us some more mead, dear Pader. I can start with this."

"I am not about to disagree with your logic. How wise you are!"

I spent another month of my time with this roaming group, which remained stationary while they said they would see me on my way. I learned how to make the grass baskets and collect the strands from the river side. Kiem began to heal after the healer opened his shoulder up again. She packed it full of Numbweed as she cut, but an interesting salve had me asking her what it was. She spread it on the skin, leaving it on for a time before cutting. She said it numbed even better than the mashed weed I had used. It was from the root, and it was boiled for days, until it created a paste, then dried. After it was dried, it was ground up, sieved, and mixed with a gel from another plant to create the most powerful numbing salve. She told me all this, and I stored it away in my mind. She said she would teach me before I left and send some with me in a clay jar, I may have need.

Kiem after his operation, started using his arm a week after. He could finally raise his arm,

"You should not rush activity; it may tear and then take longer to heal."

"Everyone contributes to the tribes needs. Even guests. I am expected to help."

"I understand, I am saying, don't overdo it. Take it slow."

"When you get my age, dear child, you will understand more about life. We give of ourselves, to receive."

CHAPTER 27

Rowan

Strife and Conflict Echoes the Halls

On one of her husbands many trips home, she heard the most interesting item of news.

Rowan heard shortly after the time of the shooting stars, it heralded the advent of a new DragonRider in the land of Pelin'Dun, the Islands which harkened to the old ways. She was intrigued. She knew nothing of the Islands and their religion. Just another thing she was ignorant of during her upbringing.

The Namanists could not take root there, she knew this much from her studies. As Du'Lanay was busy warring with the farther off land of Aram, the Faith did not think to extend their efforts in Islands which had no value. The people there were deeply rooted in their beliefs of the Rulers and their systems. Du'Lanay had tried before. She wondered about this so-called DragonRider. What was a Dragon? In all her fifteen years, with her education coming from her tutors, she was not instructed in the Vendar faith, just the Naman way.

Is it an animal? Like a horse? People ride horses. A special animal to be sure if no one has pictures or written word. An animal no longer seen in all the lands. Hmmm... but one that has our religion scared of if I think about it.

The Namanists had tried their infiltration over a hundred years ago, to no avail, and lost a third of their brethren in the efforts. She read history of the Faith's slant on the last hundreds of years. How their prophet, Narman had given them new meaning to life. How they saved the people of the land from idleness and faithlessness, how they banned worship of the six old Gods with threats of death or worse and how they carried through on their threats. Many people were scourged from the land; many had no choice but to convert. Rowan also heard in whisperings there were a few pockets of land further to the North and the eastern shores who still catered to the Gods of old, but no Northman would admit such, and she had never met any of the famed female warriors.

She was sitting in her garden, she called it such, the Blood Roses emerged from the ground, the bulbs of various other flowers she planted around the garden were close to bloom, and spring was in full force, they had the occasional rain, but Tannah was pretty good at watering her garden when it didn't.

It was late evening, she had eaten and was sitting there, in candlelight, enjoying quiet solitude. She heard her husband enjoying himself with a few comrades he brought with him. They would stay in the wing closest to him, and he warned her to not show herself unless he expressly asked her to.

"I do NOT want to see you. These are my friends. They have no interest in you. If you think to disobey me and appear, I will be wroth. You are not welcome in my wing. It is to discuss the war, anyways."

He would entertain his friends, and never once would they entertain together. She would find out very much later he made continual excuses her childbearing was taxing on her strength, and she was not well, to all invites for the couple. She heard their voices rise with drink, and if she sat there and focused, she could hear as though she was right there.

"What do you think on the news from Pelin'Dun?"

A voice asked, slightly inebriated. A rich baritone, if ever there was a voice to sooth the soul and make her heart pound.

"I think 'tis bullshite," Her husband was well into his cups of drink.

"There's no way there are two DragonRiders. There are no Dragons, you can't believe everything you hear. If there were Dragons, the Namarch would have sent emissaries to kill them already."

"Oh, come on now, Kavus, the rumours are flying around, there are Dragons. Sickly ones though. They say the High Dragon released them with the help of this other girl. It is said their eyes glow, and the High Dragon hears their voices. As for our Namarch, how do you know they haven't sent people already?" The baritone questioned her husband, and she heard the anger start in his next barrage.

"You believe this? Its bullshite I tell you! There have been no Dragons for hundreds of years. Just Pelin'Dun playing at their little games. Now suddenly there are two Riders and a handful of sickly beasts. The Riders are girls to boot! Never would they be able to rule anything. You can get your head out of your arse, Bartok, we need to discuss our next strategy on how to eliminate the next round of Aramites who are sure to be on their way to our lands. We cannot fight wars on two fronts. Let us worry about the enemy on our doorstep."

Her husband's dismissive tone brooked no argument. The men started talking about war strategy, and quite bored her. Rowan started reading tomes from her husbands library, in his office. She was bored and as it was all he had, she read a few.

"Where do they get all their men? I see a few mixed races. They look like they are slaves."

"That's because they are. Every time they take one of our towns, they ship the inhabitants back to Aram and then in the next season, they are back, fighting us."

"Our own people. What do they tell them, to have them fight alongside. It must be something good."

"Well, probably they get to live. Their lives, Bartok. That's what the FirPader gives them."

"I don't know… they are fervent. I've seen a few in action. They must tell them something other than that. To come back and fight their own countrymen and kill them."

"Well, perhaps we should wound and capture a few, to interrogate them and find out the answers to your questions. It would serve the Empire do you not think?"

"You know you may have an idea there…"

She thought about what the baritone said.

The DragonRider Ruler heard voices. I hear a voice. Maybe I should find a way to meet this girl, but how? Should I send a missive? No that would be my end. But I am right, judging by the distain I can hear in Kavus's voice. These beasts are real, and real enough to scare men. Even if they are sickened. How I wish I could help them. I cannot stand an animal to be suffering. I hope they thrive and get better.

She could not travel, she was pregnant with the heir to the Empire, and she was a prisoner here. Her husband would find out; she was sure of his capabilities. He would also come after her if she were to attempt to leave. She would bide her time, first she needed to give birth, then she would plan something. Who knows what else would have happened by then. She picked herself up off the bench, went to her chamber and fell asleep. At peace she wasn't going crazy, there were others like her.

The remainder of her laydown was dealing with her husband when he was home and enjoying herself in her garden in his time away, which seemed to be a routine schedule of staying home one week and gone for two. She barely saw him. He did not go out of his way to visit her, for which she was glad. Tannah occasionally would have bruises, which she reassured Rowan, was bearable.

Her garden was flourishing. Even the cook was amazed at the harvest of each vegetable as it came time. She made sure she checked on her plants, walking in her bare feet in between the rows, and plucking at the few errant weeds which would try to present themselves, bending on one knee as her growing belly made it hard to bend at the waist. As the amount of harvest was more than he saw given from this 'cursed' soil, he tried preserving the excess, still astounded at the sheer volume of gleaned greens.

She was walking barefoot one day and humming a tune, when the cook approached her.

"Are you sure you should be barefoot, my lady? You know there's horse shite in the dirt."

"Nothing which can't be washed off, Ryff, and it feels good to connect to the earth, and 'tis cool in this growing heat."

She was sure to add this last part, the staff already thought she was different, and hopefully not wrong in the head. A few times other maids heard her talking to her voices. She told them she talked to the child inside her. This reason sounded so much better than talking to herself. They seemed to relax after her exclamation. All she needed was the Namarch to grab her and put her to the rack or worse.

"The plants are thriving in this soil, you have brought us a very good bounty, I am finding jars to preserve what I cannot dry."

"Maybe all it needed was more shite." She couldn't help but add this dig, but she also didn't want to piss off the cook.

"You are busy enough, and I have been idle, I do not mind spending all my time, tending to the plants. The soil has been absorbing the water very generously; I can imagine the addition of the horse manure may be what's keeping the water from draining away too fast."

Ryff agreed with her by grunting his reply and walked back to the kitchen a basketful of blue beans he picked while he was conversing with her. She knew she wouldn't win him over with words, but maybe the garden would ease his dislike of her. But then, probably not. Frankly, she could give a rat's arse what the man thought.

She was still not allowed to speak unless her husband directed a question to her, and she was careful on how she answered him. His appearances were minimal, and she was very much aware of not angering him. If she angered him greatly her maidservant would have new bruises appear. He was taking out his frustrations on her maid, and he seemed increasingly focused on the war. She knew he was trying to advance himself and would someday take his Pader's place as head of the army if he didn't mess it up. And while it upset her he was probably beating and raping her maid, it did save herself from any harm he may want to inflict on her own self. And like the leeches when she was a child, her saying anything to the contrary would not change the outcome.

So, she tried to be kind to her maid, Tannah had more burdens here than at the Palace, with the added beatings she had to endure because of Rowan's husband's mean and ugly demeanor. "How can one live with themselves always being mean?"

She would often ponder this as she didn't think she had ever been cruel to her maids. So, she asked Tannah once. "Have I ever mistreated you? Back when we lived in peace at the Palace."

"No, my lady. You were the kindest. But…"

"But what? Have I ever mistreated you? I am terribly sorry if ever I did. I have realized in these last months, by my marriage that life is not always fair. I had never imagined I would be a prisoner, not allowed to do anything without permission, not allowed to go anywhere, not allowed to speak, getting beaten for asking a simple question. What is it that makes people so mean?"

"My lady, you may have been entitled to your position back at the Palace, but you were never mean. Some of the male servants would take it out on us females. We were powerless to say anything; it would not change the outcome. We learned to put up with it. The Headmaster in the kitchens would beat and rape each girl who caught his eye, he got several with child and they would end up disappearing. He had his rounds with me, but if I did not fight him, then he grew bored. And he did, when new girls showed up, he would latch on to them. He had power, and he used it for his perverse addiction. As far as why they do it, some of it is learned behaviour, some of it is the power they feel, but I have also thought about it some. Mostly it is because they fear us."

"Fear? Of us? What do you mean?"

"We are women, and most men do not understand how after all the things they do to us, we are still standing. We are given nothing, and we can survive. We are beaten and still we get back up. We take their restrictions and still we remain optimistic and sometimes see the happier side of things. They do not understand us. They do not try to. Men are baser beings. They are given nothing, and they stay nothing. Many do not strive to better themselves when given the opportunity. Some expect to be handed their roles. We expect nothing from them. Yet we thrive.

This scares them about us. Scared men react as it gives them a false sense of power. This I have found is also because they fear the possibility of retaliation. If women were to be in power, would they do the same? Every man thinks this, and they think if they can beat us into submission, we would be less inclined to fight back. Also, this is what is preached by our religion, do you not find?"

"Yes, it has always been. Women are to be submissive. I often wonder at the old Vendar religion of the Islands. If this is what is told. I would be interested to find out about the old religion."

"I don't think so, my lady. I have a few acquaintances from the markets in the city. One woman from the Islands had married into our way of life, she did not know what to expect, but she loved the man she married. It ended up being the death of her. He beat her so bad she died from her wounds. After a couple of years of her questioning him, he finally snapped and beat her to death. His friends goaded him into it. He loved her back, but he was driven to it in the end."

"That's tragically sad."

"Yes, I asked her to stop questioning him on everything, and she told me women were revered and treated as equal as much as possible on the Islands. They had a voice there and some of their leaders are women. In fact, the main Ruler is a woman, and to hear Sora talk of her, she more than admired her. The Ruler was fair and Pelin'Dun's economy was thriving. Sora only said once she was regretful of leaving. She did love her husband so."

"I grew up believing in our way of life. But in hearing what you have told me, it would be a better world if women were treated fairly. I never had any literature other than what was given to me to read. I see now it was strictly biased. I would love to visit these Islands one day, if ever this was possible.

How I wish I knew what made Kavus tick. Then I could at least be prepared. I don't want to live like this forever; it will eventually wear me down. Every person needs love at some point."

"You are right my lady. I must get on before I get reprimanded. However, think on this. A beaten dog will eventually bite back because that is all it knows. It will eventually turn on its master. But a dog treated with love will always be loyal even giving its life for its master if need calls for it. Which dog do you think will survive the longest? You would think this world we live in would be the latter. Times will change, you'll see. Now, I really must be off."

Rowan enjoyed talking with her maid when they had the chance. It opened her eyes to the world that she had lived above in the Palace. She hoped someday the world did get better; it would be nice if it began with hers.

But it never did. This behaviour continued, she found out the war in the low-lands was intense, and the infidels captured another seaside city port. This seemed to anger her husband a great deal; she would make sure to rub her now large growing belly when he was nigh. She noticed Tannah had more bruises on her arms and legs, and when she confronted Tannah, she just said that Master would not hit his bearing wife, so he would use her maidservant. Rowan made a mental note not to say or do anything to upset him, as she knew her maidservant was more disposable than she.

"Aram seems very intense this season, its like a plague that won't disappear, like a prostitute infesting every man she lays with, they won't go away."

Kavus had another night with his cronies and Rowan sat in her garden again in the evening, drinking mint tea from freshly dried greens she picked herself. It gave her a sense of well being she could do things now, maybe that is why she was so bored at the Palace, watching her servants do her gardening for her. Here she had no choice but to do some of the gardening, what she was able to do, and allowed. She felt a sense of satisfaction in her own toil. It gave her peace inside. She recognized the baritone again, how she loved listening to his voice, it gave her shivers, in a good way.

"We are losing ground again. Do you think they have any of our people working for them? How else would they know where to press forward and where to concede."

"Given they most likely use the ones they capture for information, I see this happening. Why don't you just ask them?"

"We have captured a few of our own people, like you mentioned. They will not speak. Not even under torture. They are brainwashed; I am thinking. What makes them not want to speak."

"Perhaps you are asking the wrong questions. Let me know, the next time we are fighting, I would like to ask my own questions."

"I know how you operate; you would have to take it easy on them."

"Easy? Not a chance. My easy is not your easy."

"I was not meaning, be soft, Kavus. Just don't be…brutal. I have seen you on the battlefield. No berserking."

"When I get my bloodlust up, I cannot control what my sword arm does. It has its own agenda."

"Go in easy, then let them have it. That's all I meant. We could try to have turns. I could ease them into it for you."

"You? Hah! Bartok, you need a good arm to hold you back. I have seen your easing…"

"Men, you can talk about each other's tactic's or you can figure out what we are going to do. We are losing ground. The Northmen have managed to hold the North, but barely."

"They are being driven back, look. This spring, we were here. Now we are here. Why is Aram not driving us South? If they take this pass here, and that is their intent…see the pass and the valley beyond will cut us off from the Northmen." Rowan could hear a man's low whistle. It was one of the other men who she heard with Kavus.

"You should tell your Pader this. If they take this valley, then what's to stop them from coming South?"

"Exactly. They divide us, then they will sweep down and there is nothing in the way between them and the Capital." Kavus took a sip of his drink.

"What if they drive North?"

"Let them. Aram can house themselves for a winter. It might bleed them off. They leave every winter; they cannot manage the cold. I would kill to see an Aram manage the snows and the cold."

"Have you ever wintered up at the Aerie?"

"No, and I have no intention of ever going. I heard from a few Northerners how cold it will get. People will freeze standing up if they get caught in the heart of winter."

"I've heard this too. They've lost digits also. The fingers and toes will freeze, turn black and fall off. One of the older Northmen showed me his hand, he was barely able to hold onto a sword, but man could he kill! I saw him out on the field, he could move just as quick as you, Kavus. However, an arrow got him, several. It took many before he dropped."

"I do have to hand it to the Northmen. They are fierce fighters. Their Black bows are God given. Have you seen their range? Its perfect for getting at the riders Aram has in the back." It was odd to hear admiration in Kavus's voice.

"Yes, have you tried to pull one of them? Its taxing on the arms, I was only able to pull twice. They go all day."

"That's why they are essential to us. If the North gets separated from us, I can see us losing more ground. We should think of some more ideas."

Rowan heard a clink of glasses; liquids being poured and a few sounds of satisfaction. She smiled, she knew they were taking a break with their drinking. Then she could hear an intake of breath.

"Too bad we couldn't have a man or two infiltrate their army, find out what it is that makes them so sure of themselves." The baritone gave her a shiver.

Rowan was astounded at her hearing, she could be in the room with these men, if she heard this well…

"You may have something there, Bartok, but who and how? Not an easy task, especially if one is not Aram. Maybe we should just concentrate on holding fast where we are and see if we can gain back what they have taken, anything else?"

"How about another bottle of this fine stuff you have. I'm in love with your ability to find such delights. I am going to find out where you get your swill from and buy it all for myself."

"Ha, good luck with that. But yes, let's have a few more drinks and maybe we can get a few more ideas flowing…"

She finished her tea. Their talk of war was more than enough to put her to sleep, so she left her garden, going back to her sparse chamber and went to sleep. Before she lay her head down, she sat on the edge of the bed, looking around her room. Devoid of decoration and very plain, thinking that it did not matter any-more.

I am beginning to realize it does not matter how much or how little one has, 'tis what you make of it. I was not happy in the Palace, surrounded by all the wealth of my Pader and Mader, and at least here, I know the reason for my unhappiness. Kavus makes this easy to decipher.

But even the sparseness of this room does not control my mind. If anything, I like the bareness. Possessions do not dictate my sense of well being; they are after all just things. You cannot take them with you when your spirit says its time to go. I would trade all the possessions I own for a happy life. All the jewels, everything material. They mean nothing if one is not happy inside.

I wonder why Kavus is so mean. Was he always like this? Or did something happen to make him want to hurt another being? I thought I hated him, but somehow, I feel sorry for him. He has no love in him and no one to love him. I do not think I could go without love. I am sure my child will love me as much as I will love it. Everyone needs love at least once in their lives.

With those happy thoughts, of her child and the love she already felt for it, she laid down on the hard bed and fell into a dreamless sleep. One day she woke up naturally and stretched on her bed. *My body and my mind seem to know when Kavus is not here, I have noticed a pattern, I get good sleep when he's gone, I'll have to ask Tannah when he left, but if I count back, I will say about four days. Interesting.*

One day she was helping Tannah with laundry, washing, and hanging linens up.

"Noda, I have noticed a humbleness in you, either from the child you carry or your circumstances. You have gone from a Princess to a wife of a man who would break most women in half. I see a strength in you. I hope you do not take offence to my words, but I hold you in high regard. Not because you are my Noda, but because you have not let all this… wear you down. Keep holding your head high. No matter what comes your way. The Universe may assess you again."

"Awe, thank you Tannah, I take no offence, you spoke kind words. Wait… can you hear that? It sounds like a battle coming to us."

They could hear a roaring outside the villa. Shouting and horses neighing and a general noise which was rising. Rowan had one of the servants go outside the gate to see and ask what was going on. He was outside for a few minutes before he came back. "A lot of soldiers are coming this way, Noda. I see our colours. It does not look good."

No sooner he told them than a group of wounded arrived at the courtyard. On the back of a carriage was her husband, bandages on his legs and arms soaked in blood. He was in and out of consciousness.

"Quick. Grab him and bring him down. You, help the other and bring him inside." Rowan led the way.

"Lift him up, gently. Place him on the table."

Tannah followed and started barking orders to the females. "You, get linens and start tearing them into strips. Kuna, get boiling water. Now! Tell the cook to keep the fires going and we will need continuous hot water. Every pot!"

Both women started to unwind the bandages on his leg which looked worse than it was, a slice from a sword was stitched but stitches looked hastily done and there was infection setting in. As much as Rowan did not like him, she was still bound by law to him (for now) and felt duty bound to take care of the wounded.

They got to work, her maid servants lingering back, bringing linen strips forward,

"Bring me my sewing box. I need needle and thread, the white silk. Thread several, about an arms length each. Go on, I will need one soon. Can one of the men bring me Kavus's firewater? Tannah, I will need your help. Lara, you hold a needle to the ready and this water jug. Now, I am going to look and see what the extent of his leg wound entails. I will have to open it up. Knife please. Wash it with liquor first… thank you."

"Here's a leather belt, Noda."

"Thank you, Tannah. Lift the leg. Yes, there. Higher. Now tighten it. Perfect"

Rowan thought perhaps Kavus would die from his wounds, infection would take him in the end. However, she told herself, that wasn't her to wish this on even the man who treated her like dirt under his boot. She was better than that.

"Knife."

"You. You. Hold the Nodan down while Noda is going to clean the wound. This is going to wake him up. Great. Grab his shoulders."

Rowan cut the stitches which were barely visible and gently drew them out of the inflamed flesh. She had Tannah hold the sides of the thigh together until she removed them all. Then she asked her maid to slowly release pressure. The maid did as she asked and as the wound opened up, she saw debris inside, and she held her hand out.

"The firewater please. Now hold him. Hold him hard."

She poured the fluid into the wound. All of it. Blood welled up and he woke with a start and started to thrash and yell at her. The men struggled to keep him down and others rushed forward to grab his flailing legs. Then he fainted.

"He's out. Tannah, I need you to open on that side, yes, I see some dirt, and that looks better. Now let's push it back together. Yes, there. Needle. Let me just get this here… here… and here. Now close. Your hands slipping? Wrap a linen around his leg. Cross it over. Hold onto the linen tight. See? Easier. Needle. Thread two more. Lower the linen. Can we switch spots? Hold there. I will start on the other end. Fine, done."

"That looks so much better, Noda. I will wrap with clean linens while you wash your hands."

"Clean the seam with liquor first."

"Yes, Noda."

Tying the linens off, Tannah released the tourniquet in the nest of Kavus's groin, he was still unconscious. Coming back to the table, Rowan checked his breathing. She was partially aware of the servants helping the other wounded into the villa. There were soon sounds of the wounded over the words of the servants.

"Let's now look at his arm, here. Tannah, the belt, please."

Rowan moved up to his arm and cut off his linen shirt at the shoulder. Placing another leather tourniquet between the shoulder and bicep she tightened it up and unwrapped the bandages on his arm. She saw he had taken another sword cut but this one bit deeper into the bicep muscle. This one must be more recent as there were no stitches in it.

He was still passed out, so she cleaned out the wound with the liquor just below the tourniquet. Her maidservant was gathering supplies on another table.

"Two needles for this one."

This injury was a little bit trickier. She ended up sewing three muscles where she thought they should be, having one of the men demonstrate with his good arm. She ended up having quite a few ends of silk coming out of it, but she was satisfied with her sewing. Now it was essential to keep infection out of the wounds.

Rowan tied up his arm with the linens and the rest of the night all the servants in the villa were busy tending to the wounded who were brought.

Once her husband was finished with, the menservants gathered around him.

"Take him to his rooms, clean him up and dress him appropriately. One man is to watch over him. At all times. If his body should get warm, come, and get me. Only cover him with a linen. Nothing more. We are watching for fever. It indicates infection. Do you understand?"

"Yes, Noda."

"Who's next?"

After the dining room table was cleared another man took his place. Rowan and the household servants worked all night stitching, cleaning wounds, and at some point, using a hot knife to cauterize some. They finished as the sun was cresting over the horizon, she looked down at her clothes to see she was covered in everyone's blood, but then so was everybody else.

"Well, that's all? All right, excellent work everyone. Let's get ourselves cleaned and fed before we rest. Who'll take first duties. Yes…thank you. If someone can take over in about four hours. We will do short duties, then we all can rest. Once we establish a routine, let's have short duties. Tannah? I am going to wash, then I am going to bed. I am too tired to eat."

"Yes, Noda. Lara, let's go, we will see the ones on duty get fed, then we can rest. Noda, I am washing up first also."

"Yes. Girls, let's get ourselves clean first. This way 'tis not tracked all over. Who ever stays if you can tidy up in here."

"Yes, Noda."

"Yes, Noda, right away."

She went outside into the front courtyard to take in the rising sun and stood there in quiet contemplation. She heard when she focused on other sounds, and she realized the whole city was buzzing with sounds indicating they weren't the only ones with wounded.

She went back inside and straight to the bathhouse, threw her clothes off and stepped into the water which had several of the maids and Tannah already bathing. After they all helped each other clean their backs and hair, some of the girls exclaiming over her enlarged belly. Rowan emerged not caring that she was naked, walked to her room, put on a clean set of clothes, laid down on her bed, and fell right asleep.

She only slept for about 5 hours as sounds of moans and groans, wailing and crying invaded her thoughts. She rose as her maid came inside her room. She was carrying a tray of food which Rowan didn't even look at as she gobbled it up and then walked down the hall to her husband's room still eating a hind of bread. She took over for the man servant, sending him to bed while she tended to Kavus who was still in and out of consciousness. When he was awake, she would give him sips of water and she had one of the girls brew a tea of certain flower petals in the garden, ones she knew once brewed would help ease his pain and help to stave off the infections.

She stayed with him all day, only eating when she was brought food and then had one of the maids sit with him so she could see how everyone else was doing. For the next two or three days until they got into a routine the whole household worked together as a team under her direction to care for the wounded. Out of the twenty men they cared for three died of the wounds they sustained. These twenty men were all who were left of the fifty-five men her husband had taken to the war.

Kavus began to recover after two days of fever, it broke, and he began to regain his wonderful demeanor. As he could not walk on the leg, which was wounded, she had one of the men fashion a crutch for him to lean on using his good arm. It took him five whole days before he walked around and saw each of his men she and the servants had made comfortable as much as they could on the floor of the dining hall.

Not once during his recovery, did he so much as thank her for the care of himself or his men. After a week of checking his wounds, she saw they were healing quite well. She told him the threads needed to be taken out, so they proceeded. Once again Rowan used the alcohol to clean the area before she pulled the threads. He grimaced in pain but did not cry out and she managed to remove all the threads, cleanse the wounds, and rewrap them with clean linens. The next day a message came from the Emperor's Palace he was to attend her Pader the Emperor and his counsel as soon as he was able. Feeling brave she asked him.

"If you send a response back saying you will attend tomorrow, I will brew you a tea which will help you get a full night's sleep. It will ease your pain, and you will be more refreshed tomorrow. It is late in the day; you would be best to go tomorrow with a clearer mind."

"Hmmph."

He sent his response back, for the following day.

The following morning saw her and several servants helping her husband into the baths. He was thoroughly washed, and she rewrapped his wounds before he was dressed in his regimentals. As he was unable to walk far, she sent him up to the Palace in a carriage with his manservant and two others to help him. He was gone all Day and when he returned after the dinner hour, he looked very tired.

She bade him retire to his room and food would be brought to him. His servant undressed him and robed him for bed, to which he fell asleep promptly. She went into the kitchen and listened to the men who had gone with him chat with the others not bothering to ask them anything. She sat quietly in the corner,

"We were set upon; they were waiting for us. The Lord Commander had us form up on the left flank; we marched close to a hill covered by trees and low brush. As we crested the low side, the enemy came out, screaming and we shifted, but they had the element of surprise. Nodan Kavus wheeled around and led the charge through us to the hill and he fought like a mad man. We were pushed back, we lost ground. It was a huge loss for the Namarch, we lost the Veavon Valley and much of the headland leading to it. We are losing a fair bit of the lowlands; it's a good thing the Sohm Swamplands are not passable. We had to come back, once Nodan was injured, the Lord Commander had us bring him home. He is expected to go back once he recovers from his wounds. We need all soldiers to be fighting."

One man did say thank you to her face and she bobbed him a nod and quietly went back to her room. The next day her husband called for her.

"You need to help with the running of the household. I cannot do everything. You will document here, in this ledger. I can not write with this arm. I will watch you to make sure you do it right. You will report everything to me, everything, everyday. Until I am able. You will have to make trips into the city for the supplies I need, and you will be well escorted. You will behave yourself. You carry the heir, others will attend to you, and your direction."

"Yes, Kavus. It will be as you command."

Several days passed and she was informed some of the supplies were running low. She was given permission, under a heavy escort, to go into the city markets and find the things needed. He had his brand of liquor he liked; she used a fair bit cleaning wounds. There were other things he also wanted. Thus started her exploration of the lower city markets.

Until then she had not thought about after she gave birth, but she remembered what her voice told her, she would not be staying and she would be going out into the world. She thought this would be the perfect opportunity to find her bearings and explore areas as she was able.

She went into the city as often as she was told and soon had all the places memorized and the routes. They would go to the butcher and get the meat; go to the apothecary and get the supplies she needed for fever and treating wounds. Also, to the fish market where she saw the ocean for the first time, but she made no remarks she did not want to lose any freedom of what she was being allowed. She was glad for the escort as people were starving and she was jostled by waifs and emancipated people. No one paid any attention to them, and all she saw was the freedom they had. Her freedom was not to last, as soon as he could walk without the crutch, it was like the old husband was back. She was no longer allowed to go out and he left to go into the city for a couple of weeks.

Summer was soon to start rearing its ugly head, and she was not in the Palace this time, she would feel the heat more. His location of his villa, situated not on the top of a hill but nestled between in a valley which ran east to west, took geographical advantage of prevailing winds. They funnelled into the valley and cooled them down. Her garden courtyard also had a few citrus trees, in full foliage, kept the garden quite cool in the shade, many of the girls and staff would come to rest there. She did not deny them that.

Her growing belly made her very awkward in her ability to move, the baby kicking a lot, and she would sometimes sit under the trees on her bench with her hands on her belly, smiling at absolutely nothing. Tannah found her one day sitting there in her solitude. "Noda, are you fine? Can I get you anything?"

"I am fine, Tannah, thank you for asking. The baby is moving vigorously. It wants out. I certainly cannot wait! How wonderful it will be to hold this child I helped to create, and give it love. Oh, here, give me your hand. Do you feel this?"

"Oh, yes! How wonderful! It is for sure a boy! You will have the heir to the throne! What's wrong? Do you not want a boy, Noda?"

"Oh, yes. Yes, I do. I do not want him to be like his Pader. I want to give this child as much love as I can, but I am uncertain of Kavus. Will he be a good Pader to his children? Then there is the after. He will want his rights again. I do not think I can bear it. It is not comfortable. He is so cruel."

"Hush, Noda. Get through the birth first. Don't worry yourself about something which may not happen. Just focus on the now. Oh, he kicked again! Cherish the moments as they happen. Tomorrow is another day. Thank you for the time, I must get back to work. Noda."

Other days she would wander in the early morning hours in her full garden, the vegetables being continuously harvested by the cook and his servants. She would pull the odd carrot, brush it against her skirt and crunch down on it as she viewed the rest.

The blue beans had finished, and those rows were bare, the cook stated, it was possible to get another crop in, before the winter storms, if they had the grace of their God. She had the rows prepared and planted. It would be soon the new growth poked their shoots through! She smiled to herself at the thought.

She realized it had been sometime since she heard any voices in her head, maybe she wasn't crazy after all!

CHAPTER 28

Solina

Adjoining and Aligning put to Rest

Solina saw Atin off at the lower Palace gate with one of her newly appointed Officers. He was ordered to take a couple ships of supplies and pieces of timber for Atin's Pader to use for his building of whatever he chose. Then she wearily walked back into her Palace with her guard detail. A crowd had gathered and followed her back to the Palace. She waved to the dispersing throng.

Her GrandMader met her halfway, and walked back with her, Solina too tired to say much. They walked in silence for most of it, and once inside the Palace gate, her Gran spoke to her. "Is the newest DragonRider just leaving?"

"Yes, GrandMader, she wants to go back to her family for a bit, reassure them she is alive, and help them learn to survive without her, when the time comes. She won't return for a bit."

"Her identity should remain secret for now,"

Solina nodded her head in agreement to the logic of her Gran's words.

"There are people out there, mostly from other countries who would love to kill any new Riders, we have always maintained neutrality, because we have never posed a threat, we had no Dragons. But you have changed all this. Word will get out; this won't stay secret for long. They will seek out to destroy the Dragons and anyone who has the bond of Rider. Do you realize this?"

Her GrandMader was trying to be diplomatic, but Solina could hear the rebuke in what she wasn't saying.

"I did not think of what the future may hold, thank you for reminding me, I do appreciate you are thinking about this and will tell me. I can only learn from you, as you have been a Ruler for many years."

"I have ordered more guards. For you, for the Palace, your safety is paramount. If when the Sea Dragon comes back, have her view auras, especially here. It is the thief we have against our breast who will strike unawares. We must make sure all who serve are true."

"I noticed the influx of guards. I will ask her, but as she may not come back for a time, it may be a while. Can any of the other Rulers, or yourself use this talent?"

"I will have one of your Uncles wander through here. He is finding it taxing, or he will once the elixir wears off."

"How does this work? I have cut you off, no more Dragon blood."

"We did partake, before you did. I understand more now, your decision. Up till now, I did not."

"If we can at least keep the Dragons a secret for a while until they regain their strength, it would be to our benefit. Right now, though, I have great need of sleep, I can take you up there when I wake if you would like to see them. No one is to go there without express permission."

Solina and her GrandMader had reached Solina's chambers first and she turned to her GrandDader. "Tell me quick, why did you release them?" Solina's GrandMader was not one to beat around the bush.

"They are dying, GrandMader, in the conditions they were in. Dying. Have you no idea of the conditions in the mountain? If you knew about the elixir, you must have seen them in captivity." Solina looked her GrandMader in the eyes. All she could see was tiredness and concern.

"I did not know the conditions of what you speak. When I partook of the Ritual so many years ago, I received advanced Dragon sight, much like yourself but I was thrown into the politics of the realm as there was two positions which required, I fill them. I hate to say I was too busy for an exceptionally long time. When I had the time again, I never really questioned the where or why of it. I accepted it for what it was.

I never was curious about them or where they were housed, and I was never blessed with their voices, or I would have known. I am sorry I didn't make it a priority. After your Mader and my other Dader died, I immersed myself in the running of this country. It was my life… my one focus. One until now, I never thought to question. Having you here with me has made me question my life. What I thought were my values. How things would be if certain things never happened. It has made me question our way of life, and yes, the Rituals. Now if you excuse me, I would also like to retire for a time."

She bowed to Solina and headed back down the hall to where her chambers were. Solina entered her chamber walking slowly to her bathing chamber, stripping her clothes off, walking into the waters, and dunked her head and whole-body in. After a very long moment, poked her head up and waited for one of her servants to wash her hair. When no one showed up, she went ahead and did it herself, washing her body and stepped out. Her servants finally arrived and handed her a robe which she belted on and grabbed a quick bite before she headed over to her bed. Laid herself down and fell fast asleep.

Solina slept almost the entire day and woke up as the setting sun shone into her eyes, the brightness waking her. She yawned, stretched, and stood up, suddenly very ravenous. Her servant girls went to get her a meal, which she devoured then dressed in a serviceable tunic and leggings and draped a large cape over her shoulders.

Solina then headed up through the Temple. On the way up she met Veren coming down, "High Dragon, you have rested?"

"Yes, Admiral Veren. I feel quite well. How are you?"

"I have come from the Dragons, they look like they have colour coming out, remarkably interesting to see. Are you on your way up there? I will come with you."

"This sounds interesting indeed. Let's go!"

Nannosh looked good and Solina could see a navy-blue colour to her emerging scales, and Analaria looked less robust yet more than lethargic, it was Atalay who had no energy to lift her head but could still take in food and water.

"When you are all able and can walk, we will take you down to the basin. I would like to get the centuries of dirt and offal rinsed off your scales so we can get your scales back to recovering," Solina thought this to Nannosh, *"You will need to get your muscles back and get your wings unfolded and strengthened. Once word gets out, you three and probably me and Atin won't be safe for we threaten the existence of the ruling Churches on the continents. But first, is there anything we can get, or do to help you now?"*

"No, Little One, we are content. We are better now. You have given us hope."

Veren stood beside her while she looked at the three Dragons, still covered in dirt, and looking like ragged birds.

"They are fed and watered and Nannosh has been restless, it would probably be best to have her walk down to the basin under cover of night and we can help her get clean, then bring her back up here and wait until the others feel better to get them down there to get clean."

"Kallen, come over here for a moment, please."

"Yes, Admiral, I am at your service, High Dragon."

"Let's plan to have Nannosh walk down to the basin tomorrow night. Feed her all she wants all night, letting her get up and walk around. She does not have a huge area here, so make sure there are no torches which could lend shadows that can be viewed from below. We don't want to bring attention any more than we must."

"Yes, Admiral, right away. We will bring more to the stock pens below. In anticipation of the others, we will bring more the following nights."

"Good thoughts, Kallen."

Nannosh confirmed she would be wanting to try out her legs.

"I am worried about Atalay though, she doesn't look like her spirit is very strong, will she recover?"

Veren asked the question Solina was scared to ask.

"I don't know, she may have had too much of her source drained from her, the last Ritual was all from her, and they let it spill out needlessly, we will try to extend her life, but I cannot say for sure, if we can."

Veren excused himself, he left to go down to the Palace. He would send Kallen back up the hill after Veren talked to his subordinates. Solina stood for a while, talking with her Dragons. She took a cue from her GrandMaders conversation earlier and asked Nannosh what the future looked like.

"We must first get strong, and to keep ourselves alive. We will have to leave, we must find the greatest of all, he is waiting for us, and we will procreate. If we don't, Dragons will die out. We used to procreate every, one hundred years or

so, but since being in captivity and dying slow deaths, we have not done this for an exceptionally long time. There is a chance we are infertile. We have missed four opportunities to do so, I believe. If we are successful, you and the others like you will then have to help the new Dragons learn and protect them. Atalay states others are in another land, she feels their presence, she has far-reaching energy, but it wanes her strength to try.

Do you know there are six of you? You are Air, the blue eyes are Water. Each element is represented by colour, red is Fire, green is of Mader Earth, purple is of the Mind, and magic some would call it. She is most active of late, and white is Purity, she is bonded to the Great One and has already begun her journey. You will all find each other, some quicker than others, you must protect each other. The world as you know it will be quick to judge and quick to pass sentence. Should one of you perish, it would be some time before another is born into this world. But the cycle would repeat, and you would be at a slight disadvantage until maturity was reached.

You will meet others like you, and we have selected females this time, given the arrogance of the last Riders. The Great One decided on giving the nurturers of your species a chance at redemption. Now I must rest, I will gather my strength to try the long walk to cleanse myself tomorrow in the evening. I bid you good rest."

After that long speech, Nannosh had paled in what colour she gained and Solina beckoned to her night Captain.

"Please see her every need is met, as Veren stated, when she wakes, feed her until she refuses. Water till she stops, I will be back in the morning with Veren, and we will discuss tomorrow's activities. See your men do not talk with others, keep them sleeping close by. Send out for more livestock, to the other Islands if necessary."

"As you command, High Dragon."

Solina saw Nannosh had fallen asleep, and walked over to Analaria, to see she regained some of her strength and darkened to a green in shadow colour. The men were busy feeding her and her leg looked like it was rid of infection, and the skin was no longer oozing ichor.

She walked over to the third Dragon, Atalay, and saw the heaviness in the head, resting on the ground. There was not a colour to the scales, the dirt and offal gave her a somewhat brown tone. Solina got to her knees and rested her hand upon the Dragon's head, the once proud scaled head devoid of horns. There were not as many indications of horns, quite unlike Nannosh's nubs. Solina saw small indicators, and this Dragon was even smaller than Analaria. The nubs left would take a long time to regenerate. The eye closest to her slowly opened a sliver and then shut.

"My love, oh Saviour, you have brought me such peace. My spirit rejoices in the brightness and warmth of the sun, and I praise your worthiness to raise the next generation of life. I will not be long with spirit; I will grace the currents to await the next generation. Our spirit lives on, and we share it with whom we think worthy.

You are so worthy, Little Dader. I gift you with my everlasting thanks. My bond is a handful, I cannot extend my spirit to her, not until I am born again. She will find other ways; she is already very resourceful in this aspect. She is soon to be tested. She resides in the land of hot, the others in the land of diversity, they will soon seek out that which they need."

Atalay's voice was a mere whisper in her head, and Solina knew it took all her strength to speak as such. Solina rose to her feet and heard restlessness behind her. She turned to see both other Dragons awake and looking in her direction, their eyes whirling extremely fast.

"Little Dader, stand back, I pray you never have to witness this again, but Atalay's spirit will take flight soon."

Solina backed away from the Dragon on the ground and the men stopped what they were doing at her direction. She motioned them for silence.

The sound of breath stopped and a great exhale. The body of the small, emancipated beast diminished into itself as a cloud of tiny iridescent fuchsia-purple sparkles rose from the shrinking shell. It formed into a flying beast and circled each of the other Dragons and spun once around her before it rose to the sky and headed to the North. The remaining Dragons humming a deep tone which vibrated through the ground beneath her feet. Once it disappeared the men behind her whispered to themselves. She told them, in reverence, it was the spirit going to prepare for rebirth.

"This is the way of Vendar, we die, and our spirit is reborn. May it be Blessed to find one so worthy to shape itself again."

"May it be Blessed."

The men repeated the litany many repeated at Celebrations of Spirit. They quietly went back to work. Solina could not help but ask, her curiosity begged it.

"Umm, just wondering... what do we do with the shell of the Dragon? It is too large as it lays, and would it not be a sacrilege to destroy it?"

She quietly asked Nannosh as the Dragon was being fed more livestock, the animal going down faster than the previous night.

"In the wild, it would be left to the elements. It would disintegrate in time or be ravaged but I understand your concern. Other Dragons would choose caverns of old as their final resting place. Leaving it as such would create questions you prefer not to answer. You may cover it with earth; it will speed the process of degenerating and keep a prying eye from curiosity.

I would love to try to walk down to the wash basin tonight if feasible. I have this urge to stretch my wings; however, I do not want to tear the membrane, it takes too long to heal as it is. I am afraid it may be damaged beyond repair, but we won't know until I can clean this accumulation of filth off. It itches like crazy underneath them, and I cannot take it much longer."

"Just let me make arrangements and wait for me to return. I must clear the areas needed for you to travel down and the basin area. Meanwhile eat your fill, it will help you regain your energy. I will return soon."

Solina bowed to her Dragon and left with Kallen. His green eyes were focused on the distracted woman.

"Nannosh would like to be washed tonight. The less people the better, but more guards to make sure we execute it seamlessly. Wake Veren, I will go wake Sheyna, I know it is not fair, but we need them. I will acquire some servants and get supplies. We will remove any unnecessary people from the grounds. If you see any Temple acolytes, gather them to assist."

"As you command, High Dragon."

They arrived at the Temple and saw the water flowing into the basin and the immediate area surrounding it was cleared of all ornamentation and stonework. A few torches were still lit and not soul in sight. They parted ways once inside. Solina walked down to the room past hers and into the chamber she set aside for Sheyna. As she did so, the small girl was already risen.

"Is something amiss, Solina?"

The worry was quite evident in Sheyna's voice, and she threw her tunic on as she spoke.

"No, but we lost the weakest Dragon tonight. I watched her spirit take flight into the heaven's. It was the most glorious yet most sobering thing to behold. It feels better she is no longer suffering in body. Her spirit will grace the heavens until it is ready for rebirth. I cannot help but wonder at it all. The glory of the Mader is upon our very beings. Our Gods are real! It brings a fever to my blood! We have Dragons! Sometimes I need to pinch myself this is happening right now!

We have a very restless Dragon tonight; she wants to extend her wings but is afraid of ripping the very membrane of them. We need to get her clean tonight to do so. I feel her urgency also, don't ask me why, but I feel events may happen sooner than we wish them to. They need to get airborne as soon as possible. At least up in the sky, they would not be prey to man. We need to gather soft brushes, cloths, and buckets. We will get everyone to help who is helping already, more hands make short the chore."

The favorite saying of the Sisters of the Church where they both came from had Sheyna smiling and the two girls strode down the hall. There were a few servants in the halls when Solina and Sheyna beckoned, and they began to follow them. Solina turned and told them if they were going to be a part of this ceremony then they needed to get the necessary tools. They hurried off and the two women met Veren and a handful of guards at the entrance of the Temple.

"Kallen tells me we are washing the largest one tonight?"

"Yes, we need to get her clean, she wants to stretch but is afraid of tearing her wing membranes. She does not feel confident as they are still adhered to her body. We will have some of your men keep watch, the others will help scrub. Gently of course. Her skin, or scales will be soft and spots of injury, will pain her greatly. I feel the urgency with her request, we will labour all night, if necessary, Analaria will have to wait another day or two for her turn, and we lost Atalay. Her spirit rose into the heavens to await rebirth."

"I am sorry for the loss. May her spirit be Blessed."

They started back up the path after Veren left half his men surrounding the Temple grounds with instructions.

When they arrived at the two remaining Dragons, Nannosh was already standing and Veren had his men go back down the path to the Temple.

"Great One, I am sorry for the loss of your companion. May she ride the Skies. May she be Blessed. May she be Reborn stronger. You are to get cleaned tonight. We will walk ahead of you, and I have a couple of men behind you. Try not to extend your tail until we clean it. It also looks adhered to your body."

Veren looked directly at her and spoke like he would to a person. Nannosh blinked her eye in assent, and he continued.

"If you feel weak or your legs are going to give out, please lower yourself down. If you were to tumble down the rest of the way, not only would you crush us, but it would look most undignified for a Dragon."

His smile said if she were to do so, he would have something to rib her about. They started off slowly, stopping to see the Dragon take first one step then another, her pace picking up as they descended. She stumbled at first but found a rhythm. Slow and steady. It was like watching a waddling swan or a newly born colt.

After a short distance, Solina called a halt. Nannosh lowered down and rested for a time, then stood up again, a slight shake to her legs. They had many more rests before arriving at the basin. Solina saw the fear in the few servants who had brought the cleaning supplies, as the bulk of the Dragon came into view of the torches. A few came forward as the legs of the Dragon slowly walked forward, shaking and wobbling.

Her head was the size of a bovine, and the neck three times the length. It was the size of her body which had a few servants gasping. None had seen anything as large as her. Even the largest statue was half her size. The Dragon's head was barely gracing the surface of the Temple floor, heavy with weariness. The more sympathetic servants were not afraid; they saw the beast was in poor condition and posed no threat.

Solina wished Atin was here, she could read the auras, then tell Solina which ones were genuine. Solina saw the faces of the few who were there. What she saw reassured her. The servants who were in attendance were there to help a suffering animal. She trusted her guards and Veren to keep order and keep the more curious of people away.

Nannosh came to a shaky halt at the edge of the basin and lay down and placed her head down onto the water, nose, eyes and whole head, bubbles rose to the surface as water lapped outside in various areas as she took in the much-needed moisture. She finally rose to the surface, her eyes whirling and water dripping off her blunted horns edging her head crown.

Solina stood and faced the bulk of her people,

"We are here in quiet servitude to this wonderous animal. We will work quiet and efficiently, softly scrubbing and I will relay any requests from her. If she flinches from any touch, stop on that area, we will wash her again in a couple of weeks once her scales have healed more. This is to get off as much filth as possible in the time we have. Kallen, will you take a few men and get some goats and sheep and pen them nearby, she will need strength to return up the hill."

"If I may, High Dragon, there is a small alcove around the base of the mountain in the other direction. It may prove to be a better habitation for them to rest in. It is cleaner, and closer to the Temple and not as visible to the valley below. We risk being observed during the day in the other location. We had some questions regarding what may be going on, some have seen the torch light. If the Dragons care to extent their wingspan, they will be seen where they are now, the other location is not visible, and they can rest in privacy."

Kallen spoke up, he had his men searching for an area more viable for the future care of the Dragons, after Veren asked him about security concerns.

"We will go there tomorrow or when Analaria gets clean. It doesn't serve us to separate them as we don't have the manpower to serve both separately right now. You will see to preparing the area?"

"As you command, High Dragon."

She turned to Veren and Kallen and saw both watching as Nannosh slid down into the basin slowly as to not displace water too fast. The body was almost too large for the basin, but as it settled into the curve, Solina saw it fit perfect. As it was, everyone got their feet and ankles wet, so Solina kicked off her sandals, grabbed a brush, and moved forward.

"Sheyna, you are the tiniest. Nannosh has granted permission for you to attend to her back ridge. The rest we will start with one side at a time, and we are only concerned with the bulk of the filth, we can adjust it later."

The Dragon rested her head on the opposite side of the basin and rolled onto her right side, the water already muddying with the entry of the beast. Solina moved forward getting right into the water with her Dragon and began scrubbing her neck. The scales came clean after she grabbed a bucket a servant handed to her, and she rinsed off as she scrubbed. The rest of the people hesitant at first, but more fascinated as first Sheyna crawled on the side of the Dragon with her cleaning tools and then it was a rush to clean. Some areas were raw, especially where limbs were adhered to each other, the scale was all but gone and the flesh skin very fragile.

"Nannosh, I have a question..."

"I can sense that, ask Dear One."

"You could sense I had something to ask?"

"Yes, I am very...aware of your feelings and can surmise what you need to ask. You want to know about our growth."

"Well, yes. But I wanted to be more specific. Why are you bigger? Atalay was the smallest, by far and Analaria in between, are you not once connected with a Rider?"

"There were...difficulties in the end times. But you are observant, Dear One. Yes, Atalay was newborn, newly hatched. She had just begun to grace the skies. Her bond had...to begin again. Much like Analaria. She is a little older, ready to clutch. Her bond was begun anew."

"Why is that?"

"The end days were turbulent. Many wars. Much fighting, between Riders and Dragons. The Mind Wielders first bond was found, by me, to have been poisoned. She was reborn, luckily right away."

"Poisoned? How? That would have been a lot of poison. Can it be done?"

"It was done. The Mind Wielder was distraught. This started him spiraling to towards the end result. When he received his Dragon again, his impatience was noticeable to even us. We could tell there was something not right...however, the Great One was patient. He should not have been."

"So then, a Rider could have more than one Dragon in their lifetime? Much like a Dragon could have more than one Rider."

"Yes. Barring a natural death, a Dragon or a Rider could have more than one. But it is a timely process. For a Dragon, it must wait for the Rider to reach maturity, in the mind. The Great One did choose humans who were not mature and the Riders did get influenced by the times they lived in. It was a mistake he had to live with. A Rider on the other hand, must wait for a Dragon to physically mature. It takes several years."

Solina was interrupted several times by others wanting to make sure they were not too rough. She had to direct them before she could listen to Nannosh's narrative. She was intrigued by life Nannosh was regaling her with. Once the questions were answered and all were steadily busy, she went back into her mind...

"There is hatching. And are the Dragonettes much like chicks?"

"Your fowl? Yes. We have growth cycles. The scales molt much like feathers. The new Dragonettes will itch with each molting. They need to be oiled regularly. Once I am clean, I would benefit from some oil. I feel very...dry...we absorb the oil into our scales and flesh and it will keep my wings supple. In newborns, however, they grow extremely fast. The skin stretches, and if not oiled, will crack and fester. I have seen only one Dragon die from infection. It was one of my first clutches. Before Riders became bonded."

"The bond? What does it entail?"

"Why, one who is worthy. One who is pure of thought."

"But if I remember what I read, the Mind Wielder and others became not worthy."

"Yes, there is this. Humans can be changed by the times they live in, or outside influences. Events which take place. There are many variables. The Great One is hoping the six Riders he has chosen will overcome the obstacles placed before them and help rid this world of the evil it has become."

"Not a small task, there will be many outside influences to overcome."

"Yes, but somehow you will prevail. We have been with you since your childhood. We have watched you mature."

"But when I began to hear you, I was not mentally mature. I was but a child. How was I able to bear it?"

Solina shuddered, she remembered she had been almost ready to do something drastic several times. She had been remarkably close.

"I was not mature."

"You were descended by your blood by one of the Riders of old. In keeping the old ways, your people have kept several houses together in joining. The bonding of your marriages. Most of your Ruling houses are all related to one another. Your blood recognized the bond; your mind may have been overwhelmed. We tried so hard not to, but each year we were diminishing. As you grew, you became stronger. I am proud to have you as my bond. You are worthy!"

"I thank you for your belief in me. I think we will have to continue this later. I see we are ready to begin on your wing. I do not want to hurt you."

"It will sting for a while; however, I am prepared. Once it is removed from my body, the air will help to heal the scale underneath, it was one of my first areas to lose scale. It may be raw. I will bear it."

They all worked on the separation of the wing from the body, and managed to get it clean, but Sheyna suggested they just clean for now, and not extend it very far, and an application of oil to the wings would help the membrane stretch out when it was time.

"I'll massage the oil into the flesh, it will help to lubricate it and we can slowly stretch out the wings, no need to rip the membranes any more than they are."

"Nannosh was just telling me oil was used. To hear you repeat it makes me wonder if you cannot hear what she says."

"I wish! The area underneath is very fragile. The skin flesh is very thin. We will not touch it for now."

"You seem to know everything, Sheyna. You are correct. Nannosh says it will harden up with the air and will scale up. But it is sore for her. She says it will be better to touch in several days."

"We will oil her and her wings, so that they do not crack and bleed. I see several areas will need extra care. There are a few cracks here, where scale have left. Many scales have fallen off into the basin."

"Yes. These need to be picked up and not left for persons to find. I do not need to see these in the markets. Veren, you will see the removal of the debris."

"Yes, High Dragon. What shall be done with the pieces?"

"Place them in storage for now. Until we can find a use or a means of disposal."

So Nannosh rolled onto the clean side and into the very dirty water, but clean water was being pumped in as they worked from hidden holes in the sides of the basin, Solina didn't remember seeing them at the time of her Ritual. They were filled in, but as the material had softened over the centuries, it was easy to chip it out and get the water flow hidden somewhere to operate again. She would try to visit this at a later date.

They made easier work of this side, taking care of the wing membranes and the soft areas underneath, the tail was washed and uncoiled and cleaned with buckets of clean water poured on top by various persons.

Soon they were done as best as they could. Solina called a stop to the cleaning, and they let the Dragon lay there as clean water soon replaced the muddied waters.

"Let's get her fed some more and then we will walk her up. Thank you to all that participated. Please tidy up and you may all sleep late and rest. We will need you again tomorrow for the other Dragon."

"I'll have a few guards, pick up the scale. Could you get some baskets?" Veren instructed a few guards already soaked to start picking up the scale. Once the waters cleared, Solina saw a blue bottom to the basin. Had that many fallen off? Several servants left and came back with baskets. Solina reached into a basket and picked up a scale. She tapped it against the stone. It was a hard substance. She grew sad at the amount they removed from the basin. Veren directed them to take the baskets to a storeroom in the Palace. She kept the one she had in her hand and put it down in her room. It was a beautiful blue, reminding her of Atin's eye colour.

The next night was a repeat of the previous. Solina had everyone ready to go as the smaller of the two Dragons arrived on even shakier legs and almost fell forward into the basin. Analaria drank first, much like Nannosh did, but not as long. She entered the pool and lay on her side. She was smaller and fit into the pool with room to spare. The same operation happened, but as everyone was more comfortable with their chore now, it went faster.

Solina had a few men go up to Nannosh and lead her to the newest area for their recouperation. They would lead Analaria as soon as she had eaten and felt ready to make the short walk. As they were finishing and letting the water clear, Solina's GrandMader emerged from the Palace entrance to the Temple.

"Would you like to meet her, GrandMader?"

Solina walked up to her GrandMader, soaking wet and not caring one jot.

"Yes, this is one of them?"

"Yes, this is the smaller of the two. We lost the smallest one the other night. She was used for the Ritual and was carelessly allowed to bleed out. She had not the capability to recover. I watched her spirit rise to the heavens to be reborn in the future."

Solina led the older woman to the resting Dragon. The Dragon, now a dark green, lifted her head and opened her eyes and stared at the two humans on the ground.

"She says you should have known what it was that made you what you are. Avoidance is a form of ignorance, and she says, you are not an ignorant woman. Analaria commends you for keeping to the old ways, and for keeping me safe. For your service she gives you this piece of knowledge.

Another of your line is a DragonRider, she wields Purity and is on her path. One day, if the Gods decree, you may meet her. She is the one who will bring balance to the chaos of the world, but not before ruffling a few feathers."

Solina's GrandMader grabbed her arm and stumbled a bit. Tears formed in her eyes and threatened to spill over.

"You mean the Dragons know of the other Riders?"

"Yes, the one who passed could feel their energy in other parts of the world, but in doing so, she extended herself too much and perished. She felt one in the hot land. Which could only mean, Aram, and three on the other continent of diversity. Which could only mean Du'Lanay, and what does she mean, another of your line? Do I have a sister?'

"It could only mean that my other Dader, who disappeared must have had a child. Oh my, I need to sit down."

Solina placed her GrandMaders hand on her arm and led her to a bench near the Palace walls. She helped her to sit down and had a servant sent for some refreshments. The older woman let the tears spill over her smiling face.

"I am thinking you have more to share about my Mader and her sister you would like for me to know, now."

Solina asked her very gently. Her Gran wiped at her tears with her hands which were shaking a bit. She placed them both in her lap.

"I always thought of both of my Daders as perished. Your Mader died of natural causes during childbirth, that you know, and you know your Aunt ran off with a man she had fallen in love with. Mayhap just to spite me but ran off she did. We had words, heated words. She discovered the Ritual, I don't know how she discovered the machinations of the formulation of the elixir, but she refused to partake. Once she refused, your Mader refused also.

I was in a quandary, I had two candidates who would be more powerful than I, and they didn't want to go through with the ceremony. This refusal diminished my own power, and I could not see past that. I had word a year later the remains of the boat they sailed in, washed up on the shore of Du'Lanay, no survivors. I sent a couple of Ambassadors; in the hopes it was untruths. So, someone must have hidden her and hid her well. Not just from us, but from the Namarch. I am hoping I see this child. I feel in my heart Miiele is no longer here in spirit. If her child is the Purity bond, then my heart is full again.

Your Mader and her sister were inseparable; they did everything together. Like two flowers on the same stem, two peas in a pod, in life, and obviously in death, it seems."

"Nannosh told me all the Riders this time are female. So, then the Purity Rider would be female also. I have a cousin, a sister of blood."

"Well, perhaps you will know each other right away, she may look like you. Your Mader and her twin were identical in looks…"

Dame Metina smiled at her memories, lost in thought. The servant brought her a drink, and now approached the two women, handing both a cup of citrus juice.

"I would love to hear more about their childhood together, someday when we have a respite to this craziness! Now I do need to see this magnificent beast back to her resting spot so she can regain her strength for what is to come."

Solina rose to her feet and turned to her GrandMader.

"Word has certainly left the Island. My guards say questions were asked, lights have been seen on the mountain, and I am sure any small street rat could have been paid to sneak up there. Winter solstice is upon us, Aram will be resting up and preparing for their spring campaigns. Du'Lanay may not send a force, but the Faith will certainly send someone. We, I, must be prepared. I must get them rehabilitated soon; they are only safe if they are not here when the storm hits us.

Now, I must really address Analaria, she is rested and ready to go back to her resting spot."

Solina walked away accompanying the sturdier Dragon who shone in the torchlight, like black ink, the green would only be visible in the daylight.

They went back up the hill but veering off to the left this time and out of sight in the darkness of the night.

CHAPTER 29

Atin

Upon the Breath of the Wind

Atin was extremely excited to tell her family how she had spent her time with her new sister. Excited to have them see her again, alive, and well. She could tell Kaisan seemed to be very congenial towards her. She smiled even through her tiredness, the sea breeze very bracing and crisp.

"Its very good of you to take me back home, Kaisan."

Atin looked over at him with a big grin on her face. Kaisan was struck by how he hadn't noticed this small slip of a woman before. She had made herself known when he was bargaining for pearls, but now she stood even taller. Her blue eyes sparkled with joy. He was smitten.

Her last day opened her eyes to another world. One she never, ever thought could be possible and with it brought a new confidence. She stood straighter and did not bow her head when she spoke to men. Her blonde hair and her very bright blue eyes captivated him. They mesmerized him, when she looked at him, he thought his knees would buckle, and he would drop to the ground. He engaged her in conversation all the time they took to get to her home. It was probably a good thing he had a Captain who did his job, because he could not remember anything other than her.

"It is no problem at all. Your Pader requested it was best to do business at his home and you are here to direct us. You have earned the admiration of the Rulers, and they have rewarded you. I do hope you will not feel it untoward if I were to stay a day, to make sure you get all what you need, of course."

Here, Kaisan ducked his eyes downwards, suddenly feeling shy, and Atin noticed this and felt herself looking at him in a different light. When had she not noted he wasn't very old! She always assumed he was a man of many summers, and he treated her with respect, not jeering at her, like many men in the markets would. She noticed he may be even younger than his manner of dress hid. She did not see any gray in his hair which was visible under his headdress, and he had only smile lines in the corner of his eyes when he was talking with her or maybe it was squinting from the sun.

"Maybe one day, you could come out to the shoals, and I could show you how I pearl,"

As she said this, she wondered what prompted her to say this unexpectedly. She wasn't one to invite a man, especially with her being unmarried, and she almost never said anything without thinking about it first.

"With your Paders permission of course, I have always been curious about how you acquire your catch."

Kaisan smiled at her, as she piqued his interest, not only for the mere mention of pearling, but also for his building interest in her. She didn't shy away from conversation, and she looked him in the eye as she spoke back. Much different than his upbringing.

Just then the sails caught the wind, and the ship jerked to the port side throwing Atin forward into Kaisan's arms. His quick thinking had him catching Atin with one arm and a rope connected to the mast with the other.

"Oh."

"Are you fine? I should have warned you about the sudden shifts with the wind. It took me a while to get used to it."

"That's fine. I am used to it, but on a smaller boat."

Kaisan stood there holding onto Atin, and was content to do so, the placement of her body felt all too natural to him. In fact, his trousers were getting extremely uncomfortable in the front, he was glad for the robes he was wearing. He looked down into her upturned face and she saw the look change in his eyes. It was very intense, and she felt very warm in his gaze. She remembered where she was, beginning to pull away. Kaisan dropped his arm from around Atin.

"I apologize if I was too forward."

"No, it is fine, you saved me from an ungraceful fall. I thank you for your quick thinking."

"You are most welcome."

The two continued to talk, awkward at first, but with the memory of the embrace behind them, it became more natural. Until he asked…

"You have no intended?"

Kaisan went a deeper shade of his tanned face, which was his version of blushing.

"I am sorry, I did not mean to be so forward, I don't know where that came from."

Kaisan looked down if anything he was unsure of himself now. She smiled at him and understood his shyness; she was just coming out of her shell.

"I have not. I was busy with my sister's nuptials, and I have not had thoughts in this direction. It was busy enough with my brothers heading off to war and getting the pearls for my family's survival. I am afraid my family needs me more now, and when I am ready to, I will entertain such thoughts. Tell me of the markets where you hail from, you must have plenty of different items and spices."

With not intending to, she deflected his train of thought, and Kaisan spent the next few hours telling her of his homeland, with Atin asking key questions, she was genuinely interested, she had never left Pelin'Dun.

"We do. The lower city markets are very…ripe. Once inside the city, the markets are regulated, there are plenty of guards to keep things peaceful. Canvas sails over the paths keep the heat of the sun off, but it still smells. Here, in Peli, it is much cleaner, but some of the smells are the same. Markets come alive, more at night, than during the day. Most will close during the hot days; it is too hot during the summer."

"Too hot? How so?"

"If I was to stand in the direct sun, even my skin would burn in the turn of one torch."

"Oh, that is very hot."

"I have seen a duck egg cook on a rock, in less than five minutes."

"How do you live? If its this hot."

"Well, we have a large river, which feeds us, and every year it floods and we channel the water into fields. This gives us our grains, and our silk. We have mastered the heat, we will rest in the midday, mornings and evenings are when we gather. Some trades work only at night. In winter, some evenings are very bracing."

"We have some chilly winter nights here."

"I have been in some fearsome storms. Once we were blown onto shore, but this was in the Southern part of Aram. It was still hard for us; we lost many men and had to wait it out and until another ship came by."

"Oh, what is on the South part of Aram?"

"There are several different townships. Another large city on the western shore, we trade our silks with them, and many other spices. Cyntilla has various spices we cannot grow; they are also on the mouth of another large river. They grow the Sargal Safran spice, Vuz has the Pusholi Safran."

"I thought this spice came from Du'Lanay?"

"Du'Lanay has the Karamir Safran, it is less red, more a yellow, but it is more robust in its flavour and aroma."

"You know your spices."

"I love the treats that various…vendors create with this spice, some of them are unbelievably delicious. I will try to bring you some, next time I go back to the homeland. They may not last though, I have a bit of a sweet tooth and no boundaries. When I start eating those, I can't stop. I almost always have a stomach-ache after, but it is worth it."

Atin laughed at Kaisan's admission.

"I love my Mader's pearl drops. They are sooo good."

"Pearl drops. What are those? They look like the pearls you sell?"

"Yes, but they are food. Much bigger and made from a tuber. A wild plant, we harvest on the Island we live on, it grows in shaded areas, and we try to cultivate them, but they still must grow wild. We pick them, very carefully, the root, tubers are connected to each other, and if we aren't careful, we can kill off a whole area. The tubers are gently washed, and we boil the tuber until it is soft. Then while it is warm, we mash it up. Flavour with a little black salt, and rolled in some cane sugar, we don't use much, as sugar is dear. Then it is rolled in dried flowers."

"Dried flowers?"

"Yes. much like the Safran, but this one is…delicate. I cannot think of the name…"

"The Kiella flower?"

"Yes, how did you know?"

"I have a passion for foods. More like treats, but I have studied various plants from all over the world. I would like to have a bakery one day and make every treat imaginable."

"Oh, a flavour from everywhere kind of bakery?"

"Yes, where a person could taste something from every land without having to go there."

"This sounds delectable."

"I will have to talk with your Mader and find out her secrets."

"I am not sure she would give them to you; you might have to charm her."

"Well, then a challenge it is."

With her direction, the half day seemed but like a drop in the oceans, they talked about other various foods, Kaisan kept his captivated audience laughing with his anecdotes from his travels. They rounded the hill which sheltered their little cove on the North tip of the Island. As they came into view of the huts which housed her family, she saw her Da and Ma and some of the children come out and stare at the approaching ships. Having a deeper hull than her Paders skiff the ship could only go so far, and an anchor was dropped, and a smaller rowboat lowered. Kaisan, Atin and four crewmen, for rowing, descended into the small boat with some of the goods Solina thought to gift her. Another crew was to bring other wood stuffs and the skiff which sat on the deck for the trip there, while she and Kaisan were busy with her Pader.

As the small boat came closer to the shore, her family saw it was her. Atin saw the littles joy and heard her Mader and Pader's expressions of joy. She waved and smiled, and before the boat stopped by means of the sand beneath it, she had jumped out of the boat into the surf wading to the edge of the shore. Her little siblings running at her and giving her countless hugs nearly toppling her over. Her Pader and Mader were slower but shooing the littles away, they also gave her hugs.

"We thought you were doomed! The Rulers have been known to be fickle and have put countless fake Dragons to death; we assumed this was your fate."

"Shh, Pader, not so loud. None with me, know of what you just spoke."

Atin turned to see Kaisan coming along the beach. Then back at her parents.

Her Pader looked worn but happy, and her Mader could not stop the tears coursing down her face.

"Not at all, Pader, she fed me, bathed me and she has given you a gift of a new skiff and some building materials, and for Mader, some fabrics and laces and various other things for the littles."

"What have you done to be so recognized, Atin? I see you have brought a guest. Sorry sir, we do not entertain guests much."

Atin's Pader addressed this last bit to the man standing behind her, the crew were already halfway back to the ship, leaving the two of them on the shore.

"It was requested of me by the High Dragon, my friend. It was perfect timing and providence I could join the two missions into one. She had bestowed gifts upon you for the services Atin has provided for her and saw fit to reward her. As to what service, I do not know, this is for Atin to tell."

Kaisan bowed his head to Atin's Pader and motioned to the skiff being lowered into the water and planks of wood being dropped off the side of the boat to be lashed together to tow into shore.

"So, what is this service you provided, dear girl?"

"I would rather not say just yet, Pader, perhaps later after dinner, Master Kaisan would appreciate a light dinner and some conversation, he has so graciously brought me here."

Atin tried not to sound too appreciative but felt her face heat up and she bowed her head, looking too uncomfortable. For the first time, she didn't know where to go. Her Mader grabbed her arm and steered her towards the hut.

"Let the men unload the goods and you tell me all about the Palace. This clothing they put you in, is a beautiful colour on you, child."

Her Mader knew how to take charge and Atin could sigh a touch of relief at leaving the uncomfortableness and the sudden tension she felt, not a bad tension, but one she couldn't quite put a finger on. She felt a connection with the young man on the trip home but did not entertain anything past this as they were from two diverse levels of society. No one ever crossed those boundaries.

The children followed the two women back and Kaisan and her Pader discussed the incoming skiff and goods.

"Ma. I cannot say in front of Kaisan, it is not to be known, so later tell Pader, I helped to release three extremely sick Dragons,"

This last part of the sentence she whispered into her Maders ear, as the children could potentially hear and repeat. Atin did not want this. Her Mader started at that but kept walking.

"You what?" she whispered back.

"Yes, three, exceptionally large, extremely sick, and emancipated beasts. Kept inside the smoking mountain, apparently for hundreds of years. This is what the Rulers used to boost their abilities. They drained the blood and drank it. Apparently, you and Da were correct, I am another DragonRider, although I am still not believing it. Seeing the Dragons in the flesh helped, though. I do not want to say it in front of the Aramite, as I am sure his allegiance is with his homeland."

Atin and her entourage reached the hut. When she turned around, she saw the arriving skiff, and the men ran it onto the shore, bringing the remaining wood. Her brothers helped as best they could but most of the work was being done by the crew. Atin's Da was standing there, directing the men. She knew he was still unbelieving by the height of his shoulders and set of his back.

"Do we have enough to provide a meal for the men on the boat? I do not think we can provide anything other than fish."

Atin looked terribly worried, and her Mader noticed her distress.

"I am thinking you would like to impress this young man. He seems extremely interested in you. Have you told him anything of what you can do?"

"No, Mader, I do not know if I can trust him yet, and it was expressed the release of the beasts to remain a secret. I do not wish to be the one to have let the fish out of the bucket."

Atin helped her Mader to prepare a light feast for the men who would stay for the night and leave in the morning. They prepared a hut also with bedding. Atin looked around the hut which housed her brothers. Her Ma looked sad also.

"I find it strange, Ma. We are hosting Aram for the night. Here, on our Island in our home. My brothers are fighting for Du'Lanay, against Aram. Yet I feel no conflict inside. Why is this?"

"It does you well, to not feel conflict. Others are very opinionated in their views. Soren says the markets are a melting pot of opinions, and there are many skirmishes and deaths from those who insist on our differences."

"Yes, I saw it myself. Many fights break out. But the markets have all peoples. I find it difficult to understand why our men must fight in a war not of our making. I know Da is still upset."

"Your Da is coming to terms, he won't let it fester inside. We have had many talks, and he has shed tears. He does not wish to fall ill again. We give you many thanks for what you did."

"I can heal, Ma. The Dragons were… infected. I can heal with water."

"You are blessed. Atin. Healing is a gift from the Gods. I am so proud of who you have become. Not that we weren't before. You have always walked in the path of life. Being able to give to others, has always been your temperament. Now, if these men stay, this should house them. They may also stay on their ship. We can send some sustenance out to the ships."

"That's a lot. Do we even have enough. Won't that set us back?"

"We show our hospitality, Atin. And besides, your Pader will want to use his newest acquisition soon enough. We may not be able to peel him away. It came at a suitable time. The other has proven to be less seaworthy of late.'

"Perfect. Let's get back and I will assist you with serving the men."

Later that evening after dinner was eaten, and the littles were shipped off to bed with her younger brothers staying around the fire with the adults, discussion came around to the goods Atin brought with her.

"So, Dader how is it you acquired this gift, from the High Dragon, this is her title?"

"Yes, Solina is now the High Dragon, her GrandMader, is Dame Metina. Her GrandMader insists on the title."

"Soren, leave it be. Atin, why don't you take…. Master Kaisan…"

"Just Kaisan, I am no Master. We have no titles here in your lands."

"Kaisan, then. Why don't you take Kaisan for a light walk along the shore. With an escort of course. It is a still evening, and a walk would help with digestion."

"Yes, Ma. Certainly. If you would sir, we can walk along and watch the colours of the setting sun."

"After you. Men, if you would."

The two of them rose with the two crew members, as by standards, two un-married people could not be seen together unless chaperoned. So, the four of them went outside, and Atin knew that her Mader would appraise her Da with the news she had told her Mader. They walked for a while. The sun was disappearing quite rapidly and the two of them did not speak for several minutes. She saw he was wanting to speak.

"You and your men enjoyed the meal?"

"Yes, I have enjoyed different meals, your family has given us the best of yourselves. I find it very palatable. Pelinese dishes have become some of my favorite."

"You have an extensive range of taste. What other tastes have you tried?"

"Well... I had a small taste of Layanese. Their foods are heavily spiced. I find the dishes harder to digest. Some of the coastal towns are less..., more to my liking. Aram uses different spices, but some are universally used in all countries."

"You have travelled a lot, then?"

"Yes, but Aram traders are not very welcome lately in Du'lanay. We need a special pass, or authorization to dock. It is extremely strict. Much like what it is like for them in the homeland. It is still done. Just very regimented. I am one of the Captains who has special permission."

"How do they tell it is you? Do they not try to sink your ship?"

"We have been given a special flag to fly. This gives them notice we are one of the select. It has given us grief though. Others of my country have tried to take it from us. There are pirates of the seas, who would stop at nothing to acquire it. That is why I have three ships. Safety in numbers."

They kept walking and Atin realized they walked out of sight of her home. The sun had gone down and the moon was beginning to lend its light. The light of the moon was incredibly bright in the clear cloudless sky. They stopped and the men behind them passed by and set up behind the two young adults.

"I see by your men we should begin to head back. It was interesting having this time to chat. I have not left the Islands. Hearing about where you have been very intriguing. One day I hope to be able to see more if the Universe allows it."

"Perhaps you will. Your belief in the Universe may have you travelling before you know it."

Atin turned to her companion, they stopped on the beach, the surf gently crashing behind her.

"You speak as if you know my future, sir. Do you know of something I do not?"

Atin was puzzled. He was alluding to something; she hoped she hadn't let it slip about the Dragon's. Solina was adamant no one find out just yet. Not until they had time to get the beasts to a better health. Atin stopped her forward movement, turning to the man who hadn't even taken a step. She saw he was struggling for words. She waited patiently while he gained composure.

"I was hoping to ask you something, and this seems like the opportunity to do so."

The crewmen were five paces behind them and could not hear what Atin and Kaisan were discussing. She let out the breath she was holding in. Somehow, she knew he did not know about the last couple days events.

"Oh, and what would you like to know, where I do all my pearl farming?"

She could not help but lightly tease this admirable young man she seemed to like, but their differences in nationality stopped her from pursuing her admiration further. What he said next was a complete shock.

"No. Actually I was wondering if you would let me address your Pader, as I like you a great deal and would like you to consider joining with me, in marriage."

He said this quickly and quietly as if he were in a hurry and the words would disappear into the night.

"Is this even possible? You are of a different race and religion; would you even be allowed by your family? Would you not be shunned? Would I even be welcome? I am sorry. I seem to have more questions; we would have to discuss this at length."

Atin stopped in her tracks and knew her face was flaming hot, but she looked him in the eyes. She hoped he couldn't see her face in the torchlight. He stared back at her. His smile hovering on her words.

"I felt you have respect for women, and I respect how you have asked for my Paders permission. Is this how it is done where you come from?"

"Not exactly. It is done by the head of each family, usually without the persons knowing each other, until it is done. I have always been my own man. I have conveniently made myself absent from my home and indispensable to my employer as to not get drawn into a marriage.

I believe two people should at least be compatible with each other. I believe we could get along fine. I knew you are not prejudiced to my race and have a caring countenance. Our discussion on the way here, I felt we both have the same tastes. But, for me, I feel more. You have bewitched me. I have not had many encounters with a woman who would look me back into my eyes. I see a strength in you. I love the colour of your hair, like the wheat at harvest, and your eyes, I could lose myself in the ocean of them."

He blushed at the last bit, Atin blushed too and bowed her head, digging a trench in the sand with her toes. She thought for a moment on her reply.

"Well, if you have your family's blessing, and I think you will have Pader's, I will accept you. I feel natural around you. When you get back from your spring sailing, I will have something I need to tell you, and if you are accepting of me, then I will become your wife. I do not know what the future holds for such a union, I do not want to live with your family if they do not want or accept me, you understand this? We would have to work through the difference in religion, and I am no woman to obey a man who does not respect a woman's opinion. I am very full of opinions."

She looked at him in the eye.

"You would of course, be welcome here."

He agreed, they walked back to the huts in a comfortable silence. She looked up to see her Pader standing in the doorway,

"If you excuse me, I will have this discussion with your Pader and see if he's agreeable."

"Yes. I will leave you to your discussion."

They arrived at the hut and Kaisan gestured to Soren to go for a walk. Atin walked in and her Mader telling her quietly she told Atin's Da,

"I tried to be quiet, but the boys heard. We have instructed them to remain quiet. At least while the Aramites are present."

"Thank you. It will be known eventually. I wish it not to be myself or my family who lets it out. Ma, the Aram Kaisan asked me to become his wife. Is this possible?"

"It has been done before, but there are more success with Aram living here than Pelinese going to Aram. Few survive going to Aram. You would have to convert to his religion. That is the hugest change."

"I don't think I could do this. This is doomed to fail before it begins."

"Do not have this way of thinking. The Universe has a path for you to follow. This may be something you have to try. Let yourself be open to change. Mayhap, he will change his ways to suit yours. I am incredibly happy for you. I am sure your Da is also, but it will change us once again."

"Oh, Ma. I hadn't thought of that. Like you said, lets see what transpires."

"Well, some of this new fabric would suffice as a wedding tunic. I will have to see…"

"But that is for you! I can always find something else. Would I have to wear the garb their women wear? It looks stifling."

"If that is where you go, yes, however, this may not happen. He is of another culture, his religion has strictly forbidden marriages of mixed races, he may even be killed for suggesting it. I am only saying this, so you do not get your hopes up completely. But love can win out. He seems to be a man of his word. Here they come now."

The men entered back into the hut and Atin could tell by Kaisan's smiling face her Da had consented. Kaisan spoke up first.

"I am afraid this has sped up my timeline for returning to Aram. We will not spend the night, but head back to Peli, as I need to prepare my ships for travel. I thank you for your hospitality and for your consent. I will return in about a month's time, and we will have plenty of celebrations. Dear Atin, I look forward to seeing you and will dream about the day we meet again."

He bowed first to Pader, then Mader and lastly to Atin, then Kaisan and the crewmen turned and walked back to the small rowboat and set off for the ship. Atin turned to her Da,

"Ma said she told you."

"Yes, she did. See, I told you, you were destined for something greater. I do not think this marriage will happen. If what I hear about Aram, they do not marry outside their country or religion. They do not hold to the old ways of our people. But I could not seem ungracious, and he is such a pleasant young man. If it is ordained, then it will come to pass. So, tell me what exactly happened with your time on Peli?"

Atin told both her parents about meeting Solina and about the Palace and all its glories. Atin's brothers had been shushed off to bed and she talked well into the night. Her parents discussed her marriage to Kaisan. While they were happy for her, she could tell they were thinking of the future. Of life on the Island without her helping hands. And of the pearling. They relied on her pearling for almost all their well being, and she hoped to remain for a bit and get her brothers more comfortable with it. That was another reason, deep down she transferred the shells to a special cove, it was shallow enough to facilitate shorter dive times. As long as no one disturbed it from the outside.

"What if we were to live here? Kaisan could help Da with the fishing, and I could still pearl. Teach the boys more on how to extract without damaging the host. From what you have told me, I cannot see me living contented in Aram."

"We will wait to see if he comes back and what his answer is. You will have to tell him who you are."

"I know. I am not sure if I can. I should maybe go and ask Solina. This will impact her as well."

"If he comes back and lives here with us, then he has no choice but to accept you as you are. He will have to adapt. We can teach him about the Gods."

"That makes me have so many more questions. What if…"

"Atin, we accept what the Universe puts before us. Worry not. If it is meant to be, it will happen. If he comes back, then you take him to Solina and see what may happen. Don't fret about something which may not transpire. You have a turbulent future ahead; a marriage may be what you need to be grounded. It may be what you need. Take and accept what is placed for you. Now, let us off to bed, it is extremely late, child."

"Thank you, Ma, Da. Rest well."

Atin was awaken earlier than she wanted, by one of her little sisters jumping on the bed and then joined by all the rest.

"Oomph, you would think I was gone a very long time, instead of just a couple of days."

Laughing, she started tickling the closest until they all ran away from her grabbing hands. Her little sister Soya chirped up,

"Well, we all thought you were dead, biggest sister, Da said you would not be coming back."

"Where is Da, anyways?"

"Outside, since early, drooling over his new boat. Are you rich now? How come you brought Da all these gifts? Is there any for me?"

Soya could not help herself and Atin laughed.

"Ah little sister, I will find you the most beautiful pearl, maybe to match those sea blue eyes of yours. How about that?"

Atin rose and pulled her new tunic over her head and headed out the back to use the wooden chamber they had set up. She did what she needed to do and headed to the shore to see her Da crawling over his new boat and making adjustments, the boys helping him.

"Not there, over here,"

Her Da was instructing Tarik in the position of one of the sails. He looked up to see Atin approaching.

"And what are you getting up to, today."

Her Da was preoccupied with setting up his new boat and Atin knew this sparked a new life into him.

"I think I will go pearling; I missed my time here; the Palace was too grand for me. I much prefer the ocean and its quiet tranquility, to the grandeur of marble floors and great wood doors. You should have seen the blackest wood, three times taller than a man, smooth and glossy, I have never seen this before.

I would like to swim and pearl a bit. If you don't need me that is. I would like to go by myself; you seem to require the boys for outrigging your new catch!"

Her Da agreed, his smile at his new boat gladdened her heart.

"It needs some tempering first, sealing and tacked out. Then we will take it out for a small voyage, make sure there are no leaks and she's seaworthy. You go out, my child, take all the time you need."

"Mader, I am off, could I get a few baskets?"

"Here you go, need you help?"

"No, I would like time to myself. I want to contemplate all which happened these last weeks. You know I will be fine."

"Yes, we are reassured even more now. Take the time you need. Your Da will be busy with his new skiff."

Atin set out to her boat in its cave. She set sail and travelled to her two coves and spent the day diving and enjoying the peace she felt in her own world. Many sea creatures came to observe her, mantas, sharks, turtles, and a couple of great gray whales hovered outside with their pods.

She took a fresh look at her habitat, thinking eventually she would leave this behind. She saw the corals, the vibrant fish who swam with her, and the eels which would hide away. She hadn't befriended them as much. She gloried in the fact she could last much longer without strain and none of the underwater denizens were frightened by her. They felt her joy emanating throughout the water, pulsing with a vibration. She did not realize she was expressing herself in such a way until her last dive. She had gone further than before, and she felt their presence.

They can feel my happiness. It must be an underwater vibration of sorts. Just like the maneaters felt my anger. I can move water, also. And use it to heal. Given our bodies have blood in it, which is a fluid. I wonder at what else I can do?

She floated in the depths and smiled underwater at her audience and then rose to the surface. Her net loaded but bearable, she unloaded it in the shallows. With an unspoken request, she shucked the shells of their bounty, and after she completed her task, she grabbed her net and ran over to her cove dumping the net into the shallows.

She ate a small meal of nuts and plants she packed and went back to her boat turned it over onto its side, propped it up and snuggled under and fell promptly asleep.

She woke in the night, not two hours later, to her senses having her rolling out from under the boat, in time to see a light phoenix fly over head.

"By the Mader!"

It banked to the left and headed straight for her. "Oh, my!"

She jumped to her feet and stood very still. She wasn't sure until it came close to her what it was. The spirit of Atalay, she somehow knew, flew around her and back up to the sky heading North.

Ahhh, the little Dragon expired. This must be her spirit, which was the most beautiful thing I have ever seen. May you be Blessed. May you ride the Skies. Find your peace.

She thought this to herself, sat back down on the sand, and then rolled back under her boat to fall back asleep until dawn. She dreamt that night of flying through the air, of diving into the seas and bursting out into the air only to keep doing so, not unlike dolphins and whales she would see from time to time. There was a feeling of peace she felt when she awoke, and she sat on the beach and watched as the sun gave its light to the waves of the ocean. The ever-changing colours gave her some joy to behold, and she wondered about the differences between herself and Kaisan.

I saw Dragons. Poorly, but still alive. What does the future hold? Will I marry a man, I barely know but feel like I do? I certainly find him attractive. He looks at me with admiration. I certainly feel attraction to him. But our biggest obstacle is our beliefs. Will he change what he knows to suit the Gods? I cannot see myself changing. Plus, I have talents. I am one of these DragonRiders. I know enough to know that if I were to go to his homeland and this is known, I would be killed. Even Du'Lanay is not an option. There only seems to be here. Does he love me enough to defy his family?

Would love be enough to marry their differences?

CHAPTER 30

Andic

Whisper of Strife And Decay

Andic settled into her routine every day, and sure enough a guard would come down once or twice and watch her for a time then leave.

Natan and she would organize the rooms, sections by date, country, or by sheer volume of written word. Artifacts were another matter. She entered the room with the Dagger on the pedestal and felt an energy pull her towards it. The gem in the hilt reflected some of her torch light, and she was very tempted to palm it into her waistbelt. She swore on her last day, this treasure was going with her. Until then, she would ignore the urge.

She had other things she needed to worry about. The guard for one. He was watching her and would try to get cozy when he brought food down to them. He would stare, then he would get braver and make comments. Barely respectful. Finally, she had enough.

"You want something I cannot give you. My heart belongs to another; I must remain pure for our love."

She told this guard with her head bowed, but the guard laughed and said who would have the likes of her. His smirk at her demure remark gave Andic the impression the guard knew exactly who she was. Word travelled fast in the lower city. She should know since most informants were hers.

"Why Brecu of course. Shall I tell him that you have taken really diligent care of me and Natan? He would be most appreciative."

The guard backed off and Natan spoke up.

"Isn't he the genuinely nice guard at the third gate? He is very respectful; you could do worse for yourself."

The guard left and the very next day, who should she see but her friend of old. She greeted him with a smile, and the days seemed to pass quicker for the conversation. Brecu and she would talk about life, what each other was doing. Catching up on life, laughing at some of the fun things, one or the other had done.

"Do you remember the mix up with the spices? Your Da was incensed!"

"I remember all too well. He beat my arse black and blue for this."

"Why? Not like it was your fault."

"Oh, yes it was. I should have smelled the flour before I poured it into the vat. When it began mixing, he came to the front and gave me a slap on the head which rang my ears. He told me, I should have known better."

"I guess I should not have had the bags changed. I thought it would be a good lark."

"Well, you saw me afterwards…when I could walk. He almost throttled me. I was on eggshells until after it baked. When he set the bread and rolls out, he swore if it did not sell, I would eat it all until it was done."

"Yes, but did it not end up selling? If my memory serves me, it did quite well. Your Da should have paid you the surplus profit."

"You know, it did start a new loaf. After that mix up, his bakery was well sought out. I had so much work to do. Thanks to my mix up."

"Ahem. That was my doing, so I should get the credit. It would not have happened if you hadn't tripped me on one of my rounds. My knee still bears the scar from that."

"Well, if you hadn't put that rat in the bakery, then I would not have tripped you!"

"Well, I was put up for this. You forgot to give the girls their rolls."

"Yes, well… we could go on about this. We had some good laughs. My Pader was sad to see me enter into the guards, but I could not see myself baking for the rest of my life. I always wanted to serve my country. It is my duty and my honour to serve my FirPader. He is all knowing."

Although Brecu knew some of what Andic did, she glossed over some of her activities. They had always been in each others life, and had an understanding they always would be, but no one knew what the future had in store for them. Natan would leave them alone as he heard their conversation and was almost always in the next room anyway.

"You missed the winter solstice festival."

"Just a bunch of blue temple guards bowing to the might of our FirPader. I missed the coffers and lightening of pockets."

"Please don't tell me what you do."

Brecu sighed, he raised one eyebrow to the woman in front of him, moving scrolls. While Natan and she had company, she would move scrolls from one room to another. She did not want even Brecu to know she could read. The less he knew…

"Why? Would you have to…restrain me?"

She could not help but tease him. She was sure he would not. But he was one of the guards looking for advancement. They all were.

"MMmm, restraints. Is that what you are into now? Would you like me too?"

"Are we talking about the same thing here? I meant the kind, in a dungeon…"

"Oh, I thought you were talking… well, this is a dungeon, kind of. I'll be right back." Brecu left with his torch, walking in the opposite direction of the stairs. Natan came into the room.

"Where is he going?"

"I think he needs to find arm and leg irons. He said this is a dungeon."

"Did you put him up to it?"

"No…I am not sure what he is doing. He does like to know things… and not be wrong. This could be it."

Natan spoke softly to his apprentice. "I think you may intimidate him, just a little." His two fingers on his hand joined tips barely, at his words.

"I did not think I did, and I haven't told him anything."

She could hear Brecu's footsteps shuffling back, so she also whispered back to Natan. Natan left to go back into his main room, full of maps, books, and scrolls. Littering the room, it left not much room for moving, but they would read several, when they had no guards. Brecu came back, a smile on his face.

"I found one room at the end with leg irons. Several other rooms have the rings in the floors. So, I am right, this was a dungeon long ago."

"Hmm, a dungeon under the Hall of Learning. It must have been for errant scholars. Perhaps they were locked up if they misspelled a word."

"Could have been an overflow for the regular Barracks."

"Well, I am sure you will find this out. I know you well enough, to know you will not rest until you know what these catacombs were used for."

"I know you well enough, not to ask you where you were. Why did you not tell me, you were going away?"

"Was I supposed to? We have our own lives, Brecu. I had a mission to do. One which took me away from here. That is all."

"You have given me joy at seeing you again. I did miss you."

"Well, you are seeing me now."

"Did you not miss me? Think of me?"

He picked himself up off the wall and took the scroll she held out of her hand while she straightened up. His look was intense and she remembered what Delma told her. Her childhood friend liked her, and she did not know what to make of it. Other than he was very handsome. She looked at him back. He smiled down at her. "Not even a little? I thought of you, a lot."

"Why? Have we changed? I am still the little Dragon. You are still Brecu."

"You have changed. You are more…mature and…female. We've known each other almost all our lives, but lately, I feel very beguiled by you. If you do not mind me saying so. We have always been honest with each other. Do you not think so?"

"You can have any girl you want. You are handsome enough. Why would you want me?"

"You think me handsome? Well! And I want you, more because you know who I am, inside. Not for what I look like. Some girls only see my shell, not my spirit. I am most comfortable here with you."

"Well, I am comfortable with you, but I must continue my work. Can I have this back?"

Brecu handed her the scroll and winked at her, then left to finish his duties upstairs. Andic wondered at his intensity. Would she have to cover up more? Even at night? *Oh, I hope I do not. That would make traveling and hiding so much harder, many a person got caught, because their robe got hung up on something. I certainly hope Brecu doesn't want more… I do not even think I am ready for something like that.*

Andic went back to the Delight House to speak with Delma and to have a quick look at her bookkeeping if scratches were words. Delma knew enough to mark down what each night brought in, Jiet would make his marks beside hers. Andic was lucky enough to pass Jiet on the path outside the beginning of the Path. She did not see he recognized her. He would have been looking for a boy, Andic had changed!

"Delma, do you recall exactly what you received tonight?"

"Yes, and Jiet took almost all of it. This is all he left me." She held up four coins.

"You made fifty coins. So, he took forty-six of them? What is his reasoning?"

"He said for nights when I have dignitaries, he must hire extra guards. But I looked. There were no men outside. Not that I could see."

"Do I need to say something to him? I thought your agreement was for half? He is taking more than this."

"Yes, you can see the quandary I am in. He is taking more. I cannot survive off this. I have not enough to purchase food."

"I will find him. This is ridiculous. Where is he holing up?"

"He is well guarded down by the North harbour. Do not get caught. I will not be able to help you out."

"Well, if I do not come back, feel free to share with Brecu. You were right. He is extremely interested in me. Seems he is very attracted to me. I am not sure…"

"Lass, you do what feels right for you. You have been strong with your convictions. If you want to have relations, then do so. You are comfortable with him, and I cannot see you giving your maidenhead to a stranger. No matter the coin."

"You are right again. I am not one of your girls. The thought of a strange man on top of me, ugh! Not for any coin! I will be right back. Or I won't."

"Be safe, Andic. May the might of the FirPader's arm be with you. Don't let it ripple back to here."

"I won't."

Andic left and went down to the harbour, but the South side. Laza was the director in charge of the harbours and she felt obligated to tell him of her mission. He was in a drinking house, and when she told him why she was there, he came alive.

"Jiet! So, he is skimming off the girls. Out of forty-six coins, he only gives me twenty. Half should be twenty-five and he is supposed to take only five. So now he is taking more than double. Hmmm, how do you want to work this? I will support you, just let me gather some men together."

Laza swirled his arm and bond in the air, the room stilled. Most in there were his crew. Andic looked to see his 'men,' mostly boys, but a hard bunch. She spoke to the man, downing the liquor in one shot.

"Do you want this to be a lesson from the 'Little Dragon' or yourself? I am trying to make sure Delma has enough to eat. He is robbing her blind."

"You are right on this. How about I take care of this? You can deal with him if he does this again. I will tell him that this is a warning from you."

"He will take that as such?"

"Many fear you, little sister. Many tremble at crossing you. All I must do is mention what you did at the last winter festival. Those men who were found, no balls and their cock stuffed in their mouths…well, lots know it was you."

"Yes, those men raped one of our girls. She had begun her cycle and was given permission by Delma to have a few nights off. They were wrong to accost her, the man who beat her was obsessed with the girl. I have no patience with men of this temperament. If it is a deterrent, then by all means. Use me. Now that you've made me angry with this memory, I think I will stand in the shadows, and watch. If he thinks to not listen, I will let him see me."

"Yes, that sounds even more sinister. I will have one of the boys shadow you, with a shaded lantern, let us convey a message!"

Laza knew the dramatic flare would keep his man in line. They would sometimes watch the pantomimes at the festivals, while they were working the crowds. Laza and Andic had spoken over many a drink on the benefits of a well-honed drama. She had done jobs which many thought a spirit had done, but when Andic explained her methods to Laza, he saw it was a simple trick of the mind. He would use such methods for his own and was amazed at the results. Which only benefited them all. Laza called his men together and explained what and who they were going to see. He told each one what they could and could not do. He nodded to Andic; she nodded back. Laza and his group of men got up and left. She waited a few minutes and followed him down to the docks and across a bridge. A shadow came out to meet her.

"You are Laza's?" The shadow nodded.

"Then walk with me. I see you have your lantern; you know what to do?"

"I think so. He just said if he gave me a sign, I would open up one of these shutters. What will this do?"

Andic smiled at the young lad, barely eight, and trying hard to be tough.

"When Laza gives you the signal, you open the shutter. You must be behind me, it gives a dark sinister look, and it will cast a large shadow on the wall. I will try to look as menacing as I can. You understand?"

"I think so, Little Dragon."

She nodded back to him. She knew the less said the better. The lad was in awe of her. She tried to remember when she was this age. She and Brecu were thick as thieves, when he had the time away from his Pader's bakery. She smiled at the thought. Soon enough the two of them could hear sounds of a scuffle coming from outside a warehouse on the Northern shore. She motioned for the boy to get behind her and she peered around the corner. Laza was giving it to Jiet, the others forming a circle around the man, crying and on his knees.

"You have no right to take what isn't yours. Those whores you glean from, they must work. If they can't eat, they can't open their legs. If they don't open their legs, especially for the Obans who frequent their house, then they can't make the coin. Are you starting to see the picture here? You were told exactly what you could take. There is no room for you if you can not take direction. Do I need to replace you?"

"No. I swear I will not take anymore than you tell me. The old whore can't tell how much I take. Was it she who told you?"

"No, the Little Dragon."

"What does she know? She's just a girl."

The man spit the blood in his mouth onto the blood splattered stones he was kneeling on. Laza looked back at the boy, who was not looking. Andic hissed and the boy looked up and tried to raise the lantern.

"Just open the shutter, a little bit. You can do this." Andic whispered to the boy trying not to shake his arm. The lantern light shone and cast her shadow over the group of men. They looked up.

"Good job, now walk slowly away a couple steps and to the left, no. The other way." She kept whispering to the lad, and he followed her direction. Laza was speaking. She started to wave her arms and gyrate into a pantomime, and it gave the illusion of a giant bird in flight. Laza had thoughtfully had another of his boys, take a musical instrument, a low tube, and blow into it. It gave off a low growl. She waved her arms; the boy got into it and walked slowly back and forth.

"There are Dragons on the Islands, you've heard? Perhaps, Andic is one."

"I swear, I won't do this again. I'll give it back."

"You will. You are to give all you took from that house."

"I cannot. I can only give a portion. Don't let the Little Dragon loose, I swear I will not take anymore than half."

"The Little Dragon will not hurt you. For now. Should you try this again, even I cannot save you from her wrath. Should you tell the Oban, the Little Dragon will use you as an example. I think you may want to keep your cock and balls intact."

"Yes. Yes, I do. Do not let her near me. I will do as you say. Thank you, Laza." The man was left crying on the ground. Andic turned and motioned for the boy to shutter the lantern and she and the boy backed around the alley. She then walked back with him to Laza's warehouse. The others came in a few seconds after.

"That was exceptional. How did you make it look so real? I could have sworn you were a serpent. Like one of those lizards, you know the ones which stand up when threatened, even I was hard pressed not to piss my pants."

"Practice. It was nothing. This boy here, did exactly what you asked. He should get an extra ration, I am thinking. Perhaps he can do more for you boys."

"Thank you, Little Dragon. Maybe one day I can work for you." The boy was trying hard not to be in adoration, but she saw it in his eyes.

"You keep working hard here, for Laza. Be a fast runner, do not get caught. And stay alive. Move up the ranks, then if I have need of you, I will ask for you."

The boy nodded and left, after Laza motioned for all to leave. Several boys moved away but stayed within eyesight.

"You expect trouble?"

"I have learned to always expect trouble. While you were gone, I was jumped, after a meeting. I take no chances now."

"Well, if I weren't doing my day job, I would have your back. Tell me if you want me to take care of anything for you. We stick together."

"How long will this job take? I heard you are down in the Hall of Learning. Are you learning anything? And how'd you know about Jiet's light fingers?"

"I know enough when girls are starving, Laza. Before I left, the girls were happy, everyone was happy. I come back and even Delma's clothes are loose. The signs were there if one were to look. She did not want to cause upset. If anything comes back to her, I will wreak havoc. Jiet better know this."

"He will."

"He better. No one touches Delma. Or her girls. No one, she has always been under my protection. How did Jiet figure he could get away with this?"

"This is what happens when you leave, Andic. It's like the tide that comes in. It takes away some things and leaves others. Many thought you were gone for good. I am stretched over many areas; I cannot watch them all."

"Sorry for this. I'll skim more for you. Send the boy if you want. I will only send a portion at a time; in case he gets jumped."

"Good plan, you better get your sleep. You'll be tired tomorrow. Good Path. Thank you for the show, I don't know how you did this. It looked very real and something I would not want to see in a Dark alley."

"I have my secrets! I will get going. I will try to get some coin soon."

Andic walked away and ran after she turned the corner. She was using up some of her sleep time, she knew she would be tired for sure, but this night had been exciting. She recalled the little show she had put on. It looked very real, even she was amazed. In her little shadow play, her arms and hands cast shadows on the group which did look like an animal. The sounds which came out of the musical instrument did sound like roars.

Hmm, that was better than I thought. I will leave this night to Laza and I really need to get some sleep. I hope I do not sleep late.

She went to her spot and hunkered in and thought to face the east. Sure enough, her sense of timing had her waking upon the lightening of the sky. She washed her face, and straightened her robes, covering her face, and left for the catacombs. She was not late, but she was not early.

"You had something to do last night?"

"Why do you say that Natan?"

"Oh, you are usually here, before me."

"I had something to do. Take care of my House. Nothing to worry yourself about."

"You have a house now?"

"Well, of course. It is mine, not that I own it, but it is under my protection."

"You will need to tread carefully. Questions were asked about you."

"Others are wondering what I am about, aren't they?"

"Yes, I have feigned innocence about who you are. It may get out. Just watch yourself."

"Thank you, Natan, I will watch where I place my feet."

She wondered how she would work at learning about Dragons if she was caught out. Andic hoped her days would be mundane and not exciting. She went back to Delma's a couple of nights later, to find there were sounds of laughter back in the halls. Delma smiled at her when she poked her head in.

"Thank you, lass. Jiet knows not to take more than half. I have tried to count out all. I watch him and he is sure you are out to get him."

"I will if he dares to try this again. I have no patience anymore for men."

"Not even for your guard?"

"Well, for him I would probably take him up on his offer. How I wish life did not have these kinds of surprises."

"Lass. This is what life is. We are given what the Universe thinks we can manage. You are incredibly good at what you do. I heard from one of the girls, who has a man in Laza's group, you gave a good show. He was sure it was fully alive. What did you do?"

"I gave them one of those shadow shows. Apparently, it worked well. I may have to try this again. I even surprise myself."

"You may have to show us, one night. We do have a night which is noticeably light, work wise."

"Perhaps you should think about shutting down one night. To keep the girls…less conditioned."

"Lass, each girl already gets one night off. I rotate them. I have a system in place. Girls wear out too fast if you work them to death. That's why my girls are so sought out. Because they give their all to their clients. Verema gets two days, she knows how to work the best clients. A few have asked for exclusive rights. She is feeding off both right now."

"That's grand until they find out."

"She'll have this figured out before they do. She's smart, that one."

"I should go ask her what to do about…Brecu. I am interested in him, but do not want things to change between us. I want us to be friends, forever."

"I am sure you two have something special. You have always been in each others lives."

"I hope so, I don't want things to change. I am happy with where I am now."

One day a couple of weeks into her work this all changed, in a most unexpected way. One she was not prepared for but accepted with open arms, or in her case, open legs. She was on a small step with her attention taken by scrolls above her head, her arms reaching for two which had tucked into the back, she heard Brecu talking to Natan, and she stretched up higher and sent a bundle careening off the shelf.

They fell all over the floor, flying in all directions. The sound of the scrolls hitting the floor sounding like a horse running on the cobblestone paths she would walk on. This caused her to lose her balance, and she tried to catch the edge of the shelf but missed.

"Oh, ox's balls!"

She fell backwards and uttered another curse aloud as she dropped onto the floor with her right leg and felt herself falling, but strong arms caught her and took her falling momentum and blocked the fall. "Ooooff!" The arms turned her around but not letting her go. She looked right into the face of her friend Brecu, and before she could utter a word, he took her voice right into his own mouth and kissed her. The shock of it, left her breathing in his breath, and the sensation of his lips on her, ignited her mind, and she did not want to not feel the sensations running through her body. She automatically proceeded to kiss him back and the two of them kissed each other hard. She brought her arms around his neck and grabbed his hair with her hands, not willing him to let her go or stop.

The sensations going through her, had her craving more and she moaned again at his tongue sneaking into her mouth, and she felt alive. She felt a pressure building up, it felt as if she wanted to drown in his embrace. One thing she knew was she didn't want this kiss to end. He grabbed her by her hips, pressing her into his body and she felt his hard length against her belly. With every move she made, he was growling into her mouth. This guttural sound made her feral and it sent her into a dizziness she welcomed. His hands were warm, and he was grabbing lower until he grabbed her bottom, cupping her small ass and she moaned again.

This was all ruined by Natan, coming into the room.

"Are you sure you can breathe if you can't draw in air? You both look like you are attached by your heads."

This had the effect of both pulling apart, which was exactly what Natan had planned. Andic saw Brecu was affected by this new development in their dynamic, and she stood there, lips swollen and parted with her heavier breathing. Brecu blushed.

"I'll see you tomorrow then."

He spoke to Andic, bluntly, his voice a bit deeper in tone than normal. He turned around and walked down the hall, his step brisk and his arm tugging at his uniform front as he disappeared around the corner.

"If you have plans to be joined in matrimonial bliss with this young man, wonderful, I am happy for you, but this didn't look like a chaste kiss at all. Not that I am trying to be your Mader, but I don't want to lose my best assistant to date, you have no idea how many I have gone through before you showed up. You better take the necessary precautions and maybe let me know so I can absent myself. I really don't want to watch; it makes me sad about my own shortcomings."

Natan was very nonchalant about the two of them kissing. He was a man who had seen everything in his lifetime and was not easily shocked. He would not report them if that meant he could keep his assistant; she worked quietly and efficiently. She read when the guards left them and had this knack for knowing when time for the arrival of the next guard was near. Plus, he had the other reason, the one she didn't want to acknowledge.

"I am sorry. I did not expect this. I do not want to leave the work here. It won't be necessary for precautions, we won't be doing… ummm, what you think…"

"Oh, yes you will. I've seen this before. I am not that old." She blushed and bowed her head.

"Let's see what we can get done today before we get interrupted again. Shall we?"

She learned what she could when she could. The guards did not come down as often as she thought they would. Brecu must have had a hand in that. If it wasn't Brecu, then the other guard would come down, he remained silent but would stare at Andic and follow her from room to room. She just ignored him; she knew the type. He would not touch her while his cohort threatened him. She hated to think what may happen if Brecu wasn't around. Little did she know, it was her reputation which had the other spooked.

Andic learned the history of Dragons, the last Rulers consisted of four men and two women, and the egos who ruined the existing peace between countries. The growth of the Namanist Faith and the conflicts which arose from such. It was so fascinating to read, she nearly was caught a few times. She absorbed everything!

"Natan, listen to this. It seems, Narman was planning this coup for years. This letter to his brother, speaks of a hidden secret. A love triad? Hmmm, anyways, he alludes to having Dragons on his side, and one day in the future he will rule the land. But not directly. I wonder what this meant?"

"Well, Narman did rule. Indirectly, was his intention, but I have read other tomes. They state Narman ruled for twenty-five years after the last Dragon left. His rule is what the Naman faith is based on. There was a cleansing, his followers swept through the land like a scourge. Here is an account of the laws they issued. No woman shall own land. No woman shall have direct possession of a property, even by inheritance. No woman shall carry forth her name but cleave to her husband. No woman shall direct or own a business. No woman shall carry outside of a marriage contract. No…"

"Is that all on women? Seems harsh."

"Yes, there's a whole itemized list here…"

Natan sifted through the scrolls in his hands.

"Three scrolls of restrictions and laws. These are the original laws set in place by Narman. This is historic. Hmmm… yes…ahhahh…still… most of these laws are still in place. Women shall cover their hair and not incite desire in a man not her husband. Women shall not hold a conversation with another man not her husband or Pader. Well, that one is a bit lax, now. Men have the right to take a woman outside the bonds of marriage. Yes, we see this one is still in place. Although here, our FirPader has designated houses for pleasure."

"Yes. Seems Aram men are perhaps more respectful of women. Only using women in the pleasure houses for their baser needs. A few Obans visit the one I utilize; interesting conversations happen there."

"I'll bet. But on the Islands, I read and have discussions with other scholars, the women there hold property and their Rulers are women. That is how our discussion began… and ended, no one could fathom a woman ruling a country. It's a cause of disagreement among our scholars."

"And what is wrong with a woman ruling a country? If she can do it, why not?"

"It is not how Aram and Du'Lanay see it. A woman should know her place."

"What? Under a man? What if the woman wanted to be on top?"

Andic thought about what she said, and immediately blushed. Her mind had taken another route of thought.

"That's not what I meant. I mean if a woman can do what a man can, why should she not? The Islands have kept their Gods and way of life intact from ancient times. It seems to work for them…"

"Yes, it has. The Ruler they have now, the leader of their system is a woman, she has been ruling for many years and is a force to be reckoned with. Aram, and Du'Lanay have had no choice but to deal and trade. The Islands have the monopoly of Salt and other precious items. It is a sore spot with many."

"I don't see the point. I have my business…if one can call it that. Many know not to mess with me."

"Yes, but you have proven yourself, as a skilled fighter, as a leader. You will support those who support you. I've heard a few tales of your exploits. Even some of the higher leaders, while not openly endorsing you, respect your skill set."

"That is because they need me when a certain… finesse is needed. If I spilled what I know, it would collapse the system… well, maybe not. Our land is ruled by men, after all. But I do deal in secrets. I know many secrets. Not the kind which would topple our government and the rule of the FirPader, but enough to rock the boat. However, I also do not want to wind up dead. The secrets I know would anger a lot of people."

"Then you keep those secrets, no need to bring attention to yourself. The Oban of Learning found out you are down here. He knows who you are, and he is inquiring as to what you want. You need to be careful."

"I can guess as to who let that slip. I will watch myself. Maybe someone can let it be known I am hiding out. Someone wants to kill me."

"That might work. You may have to hand over some coin, to help them look the other way."

"Hmmm, yes. Maybe this will ease a few minds. What else can we discuss? Shall we keep looking at this stack here."

"Andic, listen to this. The DragonRiders have special weapons. Or more specifically gems which only glowed when they used them. Oh… it states they had weapons with gems in them. Very interesting…"

Andic stood beside and read the scroll he was holding. Each of them muttering under their breath. Natan would snort a few times. Andic knew from his mannerisms there were accounts he did not believe, or thought was ludicrous. She smiled to herself, he was easy to read, she found herself at ease with this man. He treated her with respect, and she saw his mind was at war with itself. The information they were reading was heretical. But it was someone's truth, which made it difficult to digest. She grabbed another scroll and leaned against the table while she unrolled it.

Gems, each had a specific gem they channeled their power through, be it in war, or in ruling. Clear or white, was purity, the wielder free of prejudice, and pure of heart. This she learned was Noster, and it was through his trust in his comrades which led to his betrayal and death. There were other colours, but not descriptions. *Not yet anyway, I'll find them in this mess.*

It was several weeks before Brecu came down. He watched her for a bit and she felt the tension rise between them. The energy in the room lay thick in the air, and she became on edge. Finally, she turned from her position at the table and looked him in the eyes, he didn't say a word and walked up to her, close enough to almost touch noses. His chest touched hers and she could feel his heart beating fast against her breasts.

"You know I want you? You have grown into a woman, and I see you in a much unique way. I will leave you if you say you do not want me. I was put on other duties for a while. I am on duty here for a time."

His voice was huskier than she remembered, and the sound of it sent shivers down her spine, and a warmth between her legs.

"I do see you differently also. I enjoyed the kiss. Very much, Brecu. I would like another if you wanted. You are down here for a time? Good. I missed seeing you. We can talk some more...or kiss. In fact, shall we see where it takes us?"

He slowly lowered his head and lightly kissed her on the lips, and she parted them, sighing, he then pressed his lips into hers and proceeded to kiss her heavily like before, but she knew this would not end there. The change in their relationship took an immediate spin. She felt heady, like she had to get everything all at once. She took the initiative.

She started to unbutton his trousers and could feel his arousal against her fingertips as she tried to get at the buttons and ties. His response to her fumbling's was to groan and she deliberately brushed them across the hardness through the fabric. This had him groaning louder and pressing himself into her hand. So, she rubbed her palm across him several times. Brecu's response was to grab her bottom and press his hands around each cheek and squeeze them with his desire pressing into her hand and belly. His breathing when they parted was raspy with his need.

"Girl, you should not have done that, I want to ravish you right here, now. I need to feel you around me."

"Mmmm, I think you know what my answer is."

She undid the ties of her leggings with one hand. He grabbed the back of her leggings and ripped them over her buttocks down the back of her thighs, and she stepped out of the falling fabric. He unlaced his breeches, and he grabbed her bum, lifting her up onto the top of the table. She grabbed the fabric of her tunic, instinctively lifting it as he stepped forward into her now widening legs. He grabbed her hips as he pressed his hard cock into her wetness. She gasped with the smoothness of his entry; a small resistance parted with a small moment of pain. As he filled her completely up, she pressed herself into the motion. He retreated and she groaned with the loss, wrapping her legs around him. She then gasped again as his hardness filled her. This was repeated several times, before she urged him to go faster, and he obliged twice before he shook and pressed twice quickly and stopped. She felt the pressure building inside her, stop and diminish but she still wanted more.

"Can you go more?" She whispered to him. "I want it more."

He laughed softly. "I can, but not until I recover from this, you were so tight, girl, I could do this again, but I must regain my energy. You took it right out of me."

He backed away and pulled his now softening cock out of her very wet core and there was a touch of blood mixed with his seed and her juices on the surface. She ached with the withdrawal, but she wasn't sure if it was from the hurt of the deed or from wanting it more. She really enjoyed the movement of the act, the sensations of the hardness inside her had her craving it. She told him as such.

"Until later then, if I get the chance to come back, I will. You have such a sweetness; I will fill you up all you want."

He finished putting his uniform back to a semblance of order, and turned to leave, giving her a big smile, but looking tired for the pleasure of it. He left and she got off the table and bent down to pick up her leggings and heard Natan from the next room.

"You two weren't quiet at all. I think I will just leave and go down the hall next time, thanks for the warning."

His dry sarcasm had her smiling more.

"Sorry, Master. I did not have time to warn you. It was…unexpected."

"Really. I saw it a while back. I did warn you. But you know more than I, oh Master of Secrets."

"No need to be jealous."

"Hah! Jealous I am not! You are barely old enough to be my Dader! I do not think of you in that…other way."

His statement had Andic smiling as she picked up a scroll and laid it onto the table. Not where she and Brecu had just been. There was a dark stain on the wood surface which she realized was her body fluids and her blood. She had just given her maidenhead up to her friend.

Brecu didn't come back until the following day. After their timely exercise, she left the catacombs early, washed herself in the fountain and had an exceptionally long sleep. Waking up early the next day she felt refreshed and ready for either more reading or more fucking. She wasn't particular.

She greeted Natan, who didn't seem to leave the catacombs, his drive for information, benefited the FirPader's need for the same. He had set up a small corner in one of the emptier rooms which served as his makeshift bed and home away from home. He explained it saved him time, to not have to walk home. His Mader would send him meal packages from time to time, which he shared with her.

"Good morning, Master Natan. Did you sleep down here again? You are going to get pale, like one of those Islanders, they look like they don't see the sun at all."

"Enough of your teasing, we still have this room to sort. What I accomplished before you arrived was nothing compared to these rooms. Let's start here and work on this wall and we will sort a bit then transfer to the other rooms we've designated. My Mader sent enough for you this time, she thinks I have an interest in you. Hah, if only she knew, she'd slap me for sure. Here, take this book."

Their mission on that day was to find and set aside anything on the care or historic information on the pre death of the last Rider. She set to work and was busy stacking books when she saw first Natan walking down the hall and then Brecu entered the room where she was, grinning ear to ear.

"You look happy, is it because of me, or something else?"

She stood up and stretched out her back, the sound of it popping, filling in the silence.

"You, of course. I have been fantasizing about you, and would love to have another go at it, if you aren't too sore from yesterday. I did not realize that was your first time. You were certainly eager for it. Fancy a go? Natan has made himself scarce."

His not so veiled hints got her smiling. And she led him back into the room where they had used the table and turned and dropped her leggings in one fluid motion.

"Not eager at all. I see that you aren't ready for me. At all."

"Well, I am a little bit sore, but I have thought about what we did yesterday, and I want to feel you inside me. Your…manhood filled me up, and I want to feel this sensation again. But I did not reach the top… is there more to it?"

"I am sorry, I did not expect to feel so complete being inside you. There is more. I will try to last longer, to give you pleasure."

"This is not what a man does. Give pleasure. This is what the girls do. They give the man pleasure."

"Well. I am different. I want to please you. I have only ever wanted to please you."

"I know. You have not been very subtle in your gifts. I was not ready until now." His response was to lift her tunic and undo her bodice, grabbing her small breasts in his hands and rubbing her nipples with his thumbs which had her gasping at the sensation.

"I was willing to wait. When you left for a time, I was distraught. Having you back here, well, I was not going to wait much longer. This is working out, me guarding you down here. I may have to perform other duties soon. We are on rotations."

"Well, I know one duty you can perform. On me…oh!" His breeches seemed to drop on their own and he bent his head as he then grabbed her bum and lifted her to the table again.

She watched as he took first one nipple and then the other in his mouth and lightly nibbled them. The pressure she felt the previous day started to build, she was reveling in that when she could feel one of his hands reach between her legs and start caressing her nether lips and finding the button of her pleasure. He gently massaged that, and she started moaning with the pleasure she was feeling.

His fingers were magic. He would rub the button and then insert his finger into her wetness and rub her there, this didn't go on too much longer as she felt his hard cock waiting eagerly, slapping against her thigh.

He withdrew his finger, and his cock took its place. He then raised his head to look at her and smiled.

"You would like to feel something a little bigger?"

He was only letting the tip penetrate and she felt her hips moving forward to help entry. His response was to withdraw, and she moaned.

"Yes please, I want it, I want it all. Inside, like yesterday. Fast and hard."

He could not hold back and thrust inside her and she gloried in the sensation. He thrust fast and hard like she asked, and Andic felt the pressure building fast. Brecu held onto her back with one hand and braced himself against the solid table with the other, getting himself into a quick rhythm which had him breathing hard, and her making small sounds of pleasure.

The feeling she was going to explode rose and she crested the hill and could feel nothing but her spirit vibrating with its own pulse, every nerve alive.

She felt his quick two small thrusts which she could tell was his way of ending his routine. And routine it became, almost every day for the next few weeks. They did not let up. Andic was smiling much more, even Natan smiled at her smiling.

This exercise had Brecu breathing hard, and he rested his forehead against hers while he grabbed air and his breathing slowed, his cock gently jerking inside her while her orgasms still squeezed his member dry, and he smiled and spoke.

"If this is what this is going to be every single time, we are going to be very tired. I'm bushed. Did you like that? I'm thinking by the noise you were making; it wasn't too bad."

She smiled back at him and gripped his cock still inside her with gentle squeezes which made him gasp. He left it there and after a few more squeezes she felt it get hard again. She raised one eyebrow, and he smiled sarcastically back.

"Just keep that up and we will go for round two,"

So, she did. She leaned back against the table on her elbows and let her lady bits squeeze his hardening cock until he grabbed her bum and stood up with her in his hands and used momentum to thrust again. It didn't work as well as she liked, so he placed her back on the table, but he slowly thrust this time, not listening to her pleas to go fast.

The slowness of his thrusting, pulling it almost all the way out and then slowly pushing it all the way in had her begging.

He then took one of his hands and placed it between them and used his finger to gently rub the button he found earlier. This drove her to beg more, and she gasped with the pleasure building up again.

She then begged him not to stop what he was doing as it was giving her the same crescendo of feeling the first time had.

"By the Gods. Don't stop! It feels so good! I can't get enough of you!"

He was more than happy to comply, the first efforts had left him short of breath and this worked just as well for both, his slow movements and his talented finger had her legs shaking and her head threw back as she came to orgasm once again. The movement of her inner muscles grabbing him had him reaching his orgasm right after she began flexing.

His body was covered in a light sheen of sweat. She did not remember his shirt being removed but she saw his lightly hairy chest gleaming, and she reached up to run her hands through the hair and grabbed his muscular chest. Her fingers traced the newly inked tattoo of service on his left pectoral. His right chest bore the mark of manhood. He let her explore and smiled down at her.

"Mmm, how was this?"

"Very fine, I think I could get used to this. The feeling at the end is very... ummm... nothing I have ever felt before. It makes me want more. And you? Do you feel the same?"

She suddenly felt shy and looked at this boy that she grew up with, with a different lens. He had woken in her an almost insatiable hunger for what they were doing. They had a couple of girls at the Delight House who could last all night with various men. She thought she could probably be one of those, if this were what it felt like, she could take more. Much more.

"Yes, I have never felt so tired but with a complete purpose, if this makes sense."

He then looked at her and leaned in to kiss her, gently and thoroughly.

"Almost forgot the beginning part, ah well, better late than never, eh?"

He smiled as he backed up a step, his cock now limp, dripping fluids on the rock floor, a testament to the now finished sex the two enjoyed. She looked at his flaccid member and smiled.

"You have quite the large piece of man flesh, it certainly knows what to do."

Her observation had him smiling back, his chest now dry from the dry air inside the room. He was busy putting his uniform back on, and she just sat there, her legs spread, and he looked at her and spoke.

"Maybe if you don't close those legs my tongue will have a go at that fine looking piece of girl flesh."

He looked at her dripping honey pot and licked his lips.

"I'm not the only one who can't get enough it seems."

She smiled and pushed herself off the table, landing on legs a bit wobbly, and reaching back with her right hand to brace against the table.

"Let's save this for next time shall we? You look like you were chased hard by the enemy and could use a rest. I hope this isn't too taxing for you. I could always get on top if you like."

Brecu finished putting his uniform to rights and walked up and grabbed her close. His hand grabbed the back of her head and she leaned into it to look up at him. She saw the shine of sweat rapidly drying on his forehead, his brown eyes alit with his happiness.

"Mmmm, now there's a thought. If I weren't so tired, I would love to have another go at it like this. Maybe tomorrow, you can ride me. You can go as fast as you want then. And then if you want, you can suck on him too, I would love this. I better get going before you make him hard again, by talking about what you want to do to him. Thank you, by the way. I never realized we would have such a fierce connection. You are mine. No one else will touch you. I have let my comrades know you are off limits. Are you in agreement with this?"

His method of nonchalantly admitting his attachment to her had her smiling.

"Yes, I'm good. I didn't know you liked me this much."

"I have always looked out for you. No one messes with you, or they would have me to deal with. When you left, no one would tell me where you went and I finally heard you were upriver, but again, no one knew what you were up to. I must admit, I felt like someone had ripped off one of my arms, and I was not at my best."

He bent forward and gave her a gentle kiss on the lips.

"Until tomorrow then, we can enjoy ourselves some more. If we are caught by my Superior, I'll be reassigned, and you, may be sent away or worse, killed. We may have to pace ourselves. It's good Natan is understanding, and I should really go now."

He gave her another kiss, turned, and left. His light hum as he walked down the tunnel to the stairs had her smiling to herself. She busied herself to putting her clothes back on, not caring about stains.

Well, he certainly has no issue performing. Perhaps Delma was right, he was waiting for me.

She looked for Natan in the next room and not seeing him, walked down the hall to the room at the end containing the artifacts, chests, and armor. Here she found him, sitting on a chest and holding the jeweled dagger, turning it over and over in his hands.

"Natan? What are you doing down here in almost dark? I cannot think this lack of light good for seeing anything."

The light from the one torch barely illuminating the room. He looked up at her, startled out of his observations, and stood up.

"You do not realize who you may be?"

His whispered voice contained shock and disbelief. He sat back down abruptly. Almost like his legs would not hold him. Andic looked at him oddly.

"What are you talking about, Natan. I am but a woman, raised on the Path of Delights, in a House of Delights, by an overseer of women of Delights. That is who I am. What makes you think otherwise? What else would I be?"

She really didn't want to know anything, other than the dagger would be leaving with her when she was done. She saw the reflection of the torch she held in her hand, in the gem at the hilt as Natan placed it gently on his knees. She resisted the urge to grab it and busied herself by sitting on another chest adjacent to him.

"When you and your friend, ahem, started engaging... I was busy in this room and sorting through one of the chests, the one I am sitting on, and I saw this dagger begin to glow. Turning around I watched it and as you both reached crescendo, it shone most brightly. Radiantly in fact. I knew this because you both were not quiet about it. I am surprised others could not hear you. It diminished, and when you began up again, it shone most brightly with your completion. We must focus on finding documentation of the gems, I believe you are linked to this one, but do not know the meaning of such."

"I think you quite daft, old man, but I will heed your council. Perhaps we should venture further down into the depths, so we will not be discovered, and how about this Dagger? It glowed? You have been sneaking spirit wine down here? That is the silliest thing I have heard, yet. May I have a look?"

She reached out her hand, not being able to resist a chance to hold the precious and beautifully crafted item of antiquity.

Her hand folded around the hilt as Natan lifted it up by holding onto the leather clad blade. The gem in the hilt, began to glow and it shone bright as she closed her palm on the hilt. The both of them rose to their feet in shock and were startled when they heard footsteps pounding down the staircase. Andic hastily handed the Dagger back to Natan and the gem went Dark, and he placed it back on the Dais it was sitting on. They both turned and rushed out of the room and met the owner of the footsteps at the doorway of the room where the bulk of the cataloguing was done.

It was another guard, the first one she dealt with before Brecu was assigned to this detail. He grinned at her, and she saw he knew precisely what Brecu and herself were doing.

"Well, pretty girl. Here I am, are you going to satisfy my curiosity also?"

His matter of fact, assessment she would entertain his delights, made her first angry and then she smiled.

"And why would you think that dear….?"

"Matteo, Little Dragon, Matteo."

"Matteo, I do not think you would be as fully equipped as my dear Brecu. He is so well endowed, anything less, I am sure, I would not feel inside me. It would not be worth your time and effort. He is so big, he nearly ripped me apart. His cock so big, and so hard, I can barely walk. How is it that you think you could compare? Have you come to show me? And where might my big man be? He is not on duty? And I am quite sure he told you hands off; I am his only."

She took a step toward him which had him stepping back, the grin disappearing as fast as it had appeared.

"You fair plumb wore him out, girl."

Here Matteo had the decency to blush, backing away at her thinly veiled challenge. He obviously was not up to the comparison of size matters, and to tell the truth, she intimidated him, she intimidated everyone.

"He begged a day off to rest and barely could stand upright. You must have had a great deal of sport; he looked pale and staggered off when given permission. If the Commander knew the why of his reason for his request, you would both be hung. I am thinking when you had your fill of dear Brecu, and if he cannot fulfill your desires, then you do not have far to go. I will gladly step up to the challenge."

He said he would have a seat and watch her ass as she worked.

Her response was a big 'fuck you' and he then recounted with a 'you will.'

She spent the rest of the day, sorting and putting away of scrolls Natan handed to her. She knew without his verbal commentary he had a new mission, finding documentation about the gems. Which was also her goal, the gem glowed when she touched it, what did it mean?

Holy sheep balls! What does that mean? Am I possessed? I am smart enough to know not to tell anyone. Natan looks like he will keep this between us. I think I can judge his character. All this information down here, for us is heresy. But someone took the time to write it. Which means it was once real. There are pictures. Tomes on eggs, the care of young. Why does our FirPader have it?

She was lost in thought, ignoring the guard who looked more put out she did not acknowledge his presence. Soon enough Matteo left, and they both stopped and looked at each other.

"I am sorry about the whole… you know… ummm screwing Brecu encounter. I did not plan this, it just happened. I have known him all my life and up till now, have always thought of him as one of my many brothers. I can not explain what is happening to me, this whole woman thing has me fuddled."

She had the decency to blush, and she spoke truth, before the whole blood and soreness and breast developing, she always thought of herself as a boy, she pulled it off excellently, not very many knew she was a girl. She had so much more freedom, and her reputation as a killer not to be reckoned with granted her many freedoms as a girl, she would not have had.

"Your apology is accepted, you feel things in excess, granted, but this glowing gem, we need to find anything which speaks of this, here you look in this pile where we found the last scroll and I will look over here. Mind, you we will do this methodically, and neatly, organizing as we go. We may not be able to finish. I was told the FirPader heard rumours from beyond, you heard of the new Dragon? I mean, who hasn't, but there's more. And I do not know what it is, so we need to be mindful we may not be able to finish our task."

"I will find out some of these rumours. The girls heard things also. I agree with your logic. Let us see what information we find. I may have to distract the guard, so you can read in peace."

"You are going to distract him? Not by…"

"No! Not this way. Brecu has told his companions I am hands off. I certainly do not like the other guard. I meant to verbally distract him. So, you can organize in peace. No. No. No. I do not want what you were alluding to. Not from him anyway. Brecu is enough for now. I am not one of the girls."

They sorted, and stacked, putting aside, tomes of history and care, the tomes of the Faith, those were well documented and the time after. Trade agreements had their own shelf, but it wasn't until she reached the bottom of the pile she found a scroll that looked like it was in another language. Looking like Pelinese.

She called for Natan, and they unrolled the scroll together on the table she and Brecu fucked on, the stain dry but visible from their enjoyment. He did not say anything, so hopefully he didn't notice it, she was silently thinking to herself, holding down the corners with rocks, Natan poured over the writing while she held the lantern over his head with the shutters open for maximum light.

"Here, this states, there are six gems for six gods, and six Dragons, which chose six Riders. White, or clear, a diamond, symbolizes purity, Ruler of the Riders, a personality of equality and fairness, never prejudiced, never swayed by politics of the time, always just. This is empowered in a sword, which was wielded in battles, see here, the gem would glow with the strength of the Rider who carried it. Always just. This seems a tall order. I have never seen such the like in any man…hmmm, yellow, or Citrine, or it can also be Topaz, Ruler of air, this seems to be what Pelin'Dun has in its newest addition to Rulers, seems she can control air, breathe fire and her eyes have changed to glow yellow. I do not know if this new Rider of Pelin'Dun has a gem or item of power. It would have been noticed or spoken of. Hmmm, let's see, next.

Blue gem, Ruler of water, can wield power over the depths of the seas, hmm interesting…. Green, emerald, power over the plants and animals, and maybe, the earth itself, that seems to be also in a sword. Red, now this is interesting, ruby, of course, a necklace worn by the wielder, can draw fire from hands, and flames from the mouth. Lastly, purple. dark Amethyst. Wielder of magic, mind control, encased in a Dagger. This seems to be the one we have in the next room."

Here he looked up at her.

"You have a connection with the dagger. If anyone were to find out, you would find yourself dead. Speak of this to no one. This scroll when we are done with it, needs to be buried beneath the rest. I will hold off reporting this back to the FirPader and my immediate superior. You realize what this means?"

Natan looked at her, and she stared back at him blankly. He repeated his question, and she shook her head no.

"You are a DragonRider, dear child, you have the power of the purple gem."

"No, you lie."

"Sometimes I do, but Kadir told me his thoughts, and that man is a devout follower of the FirPader, he does not lie. What reason would I have? You touched the dagger and it glowed! It did not glow for me. We need to sort through the rest, read what we can and then you must go. There is no mistaking what the both of us saw. We need to keep this information to ourselves. Until the Universe tells us what next to do."

Andic could not believe what this man was telling her. She sat down on the floor, her legs not holding her up anymore. She looked inward and sifted through her thoughts. She could not fathom what this meant, she was just learning about Dragons! Yet it all seemed to feel right. She felt the connection to the gem, it had lit up when she was touching it, but she didn't know everything yet. She was smart enough to know if this were known, her life would be forfeit. The history of their land brooked no other God, and yet, these scrolls stated once all lands, had six Gods of worship. And all were ruled, quite effectively until these new religions, destroyed what remained of the Dragons and murdered the last Rider.

Natan bent down and hunkered beside her and whispered.

"Dear child, say nothing. Do your business with Brecu but tell him nothing. Nothing. Your very life depends on you, let us finish gleaning what we can from these catacombs. The only other place I can think of who has documents which may serve you would be the very soul heart of Pelin'Dun. And there you may find more answers to the questions arising on your mind. The dagger we will cover with a cloth. If any other should see it, even Brecu, he would not hesitate to mention it to his Commander. It is what he is, a soldier, and his life belongs to the state."

"No. You are right. No need for Brecu to know anything. He loves what he does. Probably more than he likes me, it would be an easy choice for him. Give me a hand?"

Natan stood up and held down his hand for her to grab and he helped her stand to her feet. They finished reading the scroll and she left the catacombs, head covered and bowed, this time she was silent and more aware of the outside world. She went through her usual washings and fell asleep wondering about how this life as she knew it was changing.

This is all too fantastical to believe. Yet the gem glowed when I touched it. Natan said it glowed when Brecu and I were together. So, it relates to me. But a DragonRider? What the hell is a Dragon? People already call me the Little Dragon. Is it a fierce animal? Kadir believed I was and told Natan. Who else knows? I should be careful. Maybe screwing Brecu down there is not such a great idea. But he is soo good. I can not get enough of that man.

All this information... The FirPader has it and is keeping it hidden. He has a purpose. Because it would mean too many questions, I am thinking. There is a Prophecy, out there. There is the star in the sky, and a DragonRider on the Islands. And if I am one, then there are others. Perhaps, our history is wrong. Oh, stop thinking Andic. Go to sleep.

Two weeks later, Brecu came back down, his countenance still looked tired, and he commented maybe he caught a cold. Natan not even looking at them, strode down the hall and she knew now he would be watching the dagger again. She took Brecu down another long hall with just a lantern to guide their way. She had prepared a room for them, just a ragged blanket on the rock floor she had swept, but it served their purpose and Brecu was gladdened by her efforts.

"Natan will keep an ear and eye out for any unexplained guests."

"My comrades know about my business down here, and if there is anything happening Matteo will come down. You know he wants you, don't you? He pesters me all the time about sharing."

"He can wish all he wants. You are all I see. You are all I have ever seen."

Brecu held her in his arms and gave her a deep long kiss, which had her heart pumping hard. She broke off the kiss and helped him to open his jacket and take it off. He rolled it up and placed it on the blanket. She then took off her clothes as he took off his, each other knowing their own clothes best.

When they at last stood before each other in their naked glory, she couldn't help but take a good look at him and his body. While he was not as tall as other men, he was big, broad shoulders, thick of muscle, legs like trunks, and like her, he was also of black hair and brown eyes. He had the makings of a beard, but the soldiers were not allowed to have one until they rose high enough in the ranks. His appendage was very ample, not that she had seen very many. It waved at her, rising at her attention, Brecu licking his lips as he saw her gaze.

Her knowledge of such was as a child, this was much different, she was viewing now as a woman. She took a step towards him and as he bent to kiss her, she just smiled and put a finger on his lips and shook her head no. She ran her hands upon his chest, lightly brushing his nipples with her fingers and following them with her lips, kissing, and then licking them with her tongue. His arms lay at his sides but then he put them in her hair and held on as she lowered herself onto her knees.

She teased him a little, licking beside his now extremely hard cock, it stood out in front of him begging and shaking with his desire. She licked the shaft and his hands tightened in her hair, she looked up to see him watching her his mouth slightly open and his expression one of want. His eyes were heavy, his gaze held hers as she brought her tongue to the tip and flicked it over the wet spot. She watched him as she licked one side then the other, her small hands holding the base of it, and then she thought to take the whole thing into her mouth, he groaned with desire and she sucked for a bit, but he was way too big for her to get very far down, he stopped her and motioned to the mat. She nodded.

"You lay down. Its my turn to ride. And ride you I will!"

"Yes, Master!"

He lay down on the blanket and she straddled his staff, it was glistening with her saliva, and she had to raise herself up to put it inside her. She sank down upon it, and he thrust up.

"Easy, boy. Let me do the work for once. You can just lay there and enjoy this."

She did not know how to start so she just rocked back and forth.

"I, umm, may need your help, though to get started…I, umm… do not know what works."

"Here, let's try this."

He put his hands on her hips and helped the rhythm.

"By the God, you fill me completely!"

She found if she got onto her feet, she could get him further inside and she felt the same pressure building up. She kept rocking faster and faster and soon lights exploded behind her eyes. As she came onto him, her tightness pulsated and he came violently inside her, his hands gripping her hips so tight, and he groaned very loudly.

"By the God, girl!"

She rested back onto his hips and had to peel his hands off her. They dropped onto the blanket, and he lay there with his eyes closed, but a dumb grin remained on his face.

"I don't know girl, that felt good, but damn, I feel like I did all the work. You are tiring me out; I may have to rest another day. Do you know I slept like the dead for a day and a half? By the God, I may have to pace myself, take longer between times. No one has ever told me it would feel this good, though. Those titties feel good too."

He raised his hands to grab handfuls of breasts, and pulled them forward to his mouth, his eyes twinkling at her, pulling her off his now flaccid cock, but so, so, wet. He leaned her forward and teased her nipples with his tongue and then scooped up her bum and brought her wetness to his mouth. The momentum had her on her hands and knees with her wetness on his face. She didn't care; the sensation he was giving her made her forget who she was.

He licked her button and made it hard and used his hands to part the skin of her opening, using a finger and his mouth to make her feel the pressure rising again.

Her legs began to shake a little. She felt a mild explosion happen when she could not stand it any longer. She sank down.

"I can't breathe, Mmmmm. Get off."

Laughing she dismounted him and scooted beside him to have him cradle her in his arms. They lay like that for a time, then she lifted herself up to look at him, he began to gently snore. She noticed he did look worn out. His pallor was a bit sallow, there were wrinkles at the corner of his eyes, and look, a few gray hairs in his temples. Brecu wasn't much older than her.

Mayhap men aged faster than women?

Her gaze went back to his face, and she saw his eyes were open and looking at her.

"I love the way your eyes, wander, always thinking, what are you thinking about?" He spoke quietly, looking at her.

"Wondering where this takes us. What happens when we are no longer able to have our fun down here, away from all the world?"

"I don't know, Andic, I would like to just enjoy what we have, right here, right now. We can figure out later when it is time. Unless you are done with me."

He smiled, knowing damn well that she wasn't.

"You know perfectly well that you have uncaged my beast. I want to have you all day if I could. You have opened my eyes, and I want to ride you like there was not tomorrow." She gazed down at him,

"Grrr," Lifting himself up and tossing her gently down and he pushed her legs open as he rolled on top of her. "Well then, shall we start this study, then? Is that not why you are down here?"

And he proceeded to ride her hard, and she could not keep her voice from exclaiming her passion.

He had to cover her mouth with his hand to keep the sound from echoing down the hall, and this brought her back to her senses. Smiling she pursed her lips together as he finished his hard and fast paced thrusts until this time he came first, and she felt his cock pulsing inside her. She didn't feel the same thing this time, but she didn't care, he had more than pleased her prior. His body glistened with sweat as he finished and gently lay down on her.

"Ooooff! Help, I can't breathe!"

His weight was more than her slight body could manage. He laughed and rolled off and lay there, breathing in deeply.

"I am afraid I have been down here too long; they may send someone to look for me. I am sorry it seems like we just pleasure each other, but it is all the time I can spare, right now. Are you good? And by the God, am I winded. I may not be back for a day or so. I may have to rotate out, for another two weeks. This is flattening me."

"Yah, I am good. I must get this cataloguing done, and you rest. Maybe see an herbalist if you think you are getting sick. I would rather you take care of yourself, be healthy, so we can enjoy our relations."

Andic picked herself up and lowering a hand he grabbed it and lumbered to his feet, swaying a bit with the effort. She grabbed his clothes and handed them to him one by one as he put them one, leaning against a wall to pull on his pants. As she handed him his jacket, she reached for her clothes and hurriedly put them on. They walked down the hall, and he kissed her on the lips, his face reflecting his tiredness, even through his smile to her.

"I do care for you, whatever the future holds for us, know that. You will always be a part of me."

They both looked towards the stairs as bootsteps sounded and approached them, Matteo rounding the corner, and addressing Brecu.

"Captain Kadir is looking for you; you know it's been a couple hours, right?"

Brecu started at that, and took off without a goodbye, following his now retreating comrade.

CHAPTER 31

Damara

Wings Raised High and Mighty

Spring was slowly showing its head, the rains slowed, and buds began to form on green leaf trees and bushes, Damara finally noticed one day on her way back from the city and her workshop.

She mastered the new colour of pink and the dyes on the silks she had finally gotten a hold of proved to be so beautiful she had enough fabric done to warrant a dress for herself and she would store the rest, if her client did not want it. However, she was sure once Noma viewed it, she would take it all. The pink she created had such a depth and vibrancy, it took on a life of its own, she wasn't even sure she wished to share. The sparkle from the pearl had proven its worth.

Guaranteed once this colour was seen, others would request it. She had a wide range of paying customers, and her clients knew if they wanted a colour all their own, they only had to pay for the privilege. This was a strategy she thought of, in her early years, all thanks to her Mader.

"Dader dear, back when I was just a little older than you, when I was a courtesan, before I met your Pader, if a man wanted a mistress all to himself, he paid for the privilege to have it so."

"Did they not pay already?"

"Over and above what the payment was. Your Pader, May he be Blessed, paid handsomely for exclusivity. He paid an entire year before we stood before a judge. If it weren't for his Mader being who she was, the judge would not have done it. So, you use this formula in your business, and your name. Take Ramis's money and you make something of yourself. You are smart, Damara. Smarter than Davian. But use your brain wisely. Know when to not say or do something.

Especially around your husband. He is a very jealous man, and we only agreed to this marriage because I saw you were in love with him. He loves what others have. So, watch what you say and how you say it. Pick your battles. Plan your strategy. Then execute them. Use this in your business, raising your children, dealing with Ramis."

"Ramis loves me, Mader, I will have no issue with him. Although he lets the boys run amuck. They will not listen to me sometimes."

"This is the world we live in, Mara. You find a way to curb them, or you will never be happy. Then, when the time is right, you live for yourself. Your happiness is paramount. Your Pader is my happiness; he risked all for me. I am incredibly happy with him."

"Ramis makes me happy, Mader. He is very… attentive."

"I can imagine. Be wary, he likes what others have, and this is a man's world we live in. You make sure you do not bring Naman's eye onto yourself. The Church has ruined many a woman. Over a word, or even or a look. Make sure your attire you create has their blessing. Then you will thrive. Mayhap Davian can help once he has risen up the ladder."

"He has a way to go, Mader. He only became a Third. I will remember what you have told me. Always." Damara applied this concept to her business. It had proven to be very lucrative. Now she had a warehouse of stored fabrics. She sometimes would redye a fabric and add to the colour to sell, but she only did this when orders ran thin. She wasted nothing!

Damara rode into the villa and saw Ramis rode in, ah well, another dinner where they would have to talk to each other. Both were busy of late. She hadn't thought about what he was up to, she knew, but now she didn't care. She dismounted and handed the reins to one of the groomsmen, strode in and went to her rooms to bathe and change for dinner.

She dressed in an orange dress, feeling a bit citrusy and energetic, and it went well with her now graying hair. She wore topaz jewelry, Ramis gifted her on their anniversary of ten years of being bonded.

Our ten years, Ramis did like to show off his gifts. I remember this night. He gave this jewelry to me in front of a gathering. Like he was exceeding his expectations. I remember now that I think of it, he basked in the adoration I got for the jewelry. Maybe Mader was right, he wanted to be seen, adored, and craved more. Now that I reflect on it, this bond of marriage, is more like bondage. I have nothing without him. How will I make it beyond this marriage? Will a divorce end my business? I have so many uncertainties.

She also was feeling a little frisky or agitated. She had energy she wished to burn off, be it sexual relations, or to do something. Working kept her mind busy but of late she was craving the intimacy of affection. She wasn't sure which, but she did love a good romp in the bed for the sensations it gave her.

If he wanted it, then he could have it. She had needs too. It was beneath her to look outside of her marriage, no matter how great her want. She would not give him the satisfaction. It seemed unfair men could look outside the bonds of marriage for sexual satisfaction, but women could not. Women were killed for even voicing such.

Ramis has shown me his jealously, by that little spot of attention the Captain showed me, even though it was to impart knowledge to me. Ramis did not know from his view of the beach. What if I was absorbing the Captain's attentions? Would he then divorce me? Would he? He has his paramours, and the business is his method of acting on his…lusts…or his addiction? What else can one call it? I will think on this. I wonder if I can ask Davian a few questions… It was not a fair world she lived in, and she wanted to shout it aloud, it irked her so.

He was waiting in the dining room when she walked in, and she smiled as he rose to greet her. "Darling, you look so beautiful tonight, any special occasion?" *Suave, still so suave, in his manner*

"I thought I would look good for you My Dear, we are so busy, we have not had a moment together in such a long time." It was in fact, since the meteor shower they had lain together, but who was counting.

"I look forward to having a wonderful evening with you My Dear, in fact, I brought a new wine, light body and a citrus fruit undernote, I thought you would like to try."

"Ooo! You know I like my wines. I need to be gentle, my stomach has not recovered, fully."

"A little bit to ease you. The Cook agreed it would pair well with his dinner."

He smiled and motioned for the servants to serve the meal. They ate their dinner, sometimes in silence, and sometimes speaking of trivial things, Damara stating she had the fabric all dyed and ready for designing. As he was asking her about the various other orders, the door servant came in with a note on a silver tray. He handed it to her husband, and she waited quietly while he opened and read it. He read it again, placed it down slowly and looked over the table at her, his mouth slightly open in disbelief.

"Well, what is it? Its not the boys, surely 'tis not unwelcome news?" Damara half rose from her seat, and he motioned her down with his hand.

"No, 'tis different news all together, we have nothing from the war front. This came from overseas. One of our Captains was at Pelin'Dun, he brings me news of anything of import. You remember the news of the new DragonRider?" Damara nodded her head.

"Seems there are rumours of another girl, with glowing blue eyes, she commands water, and the denizens in it. Seems she had a run in with men who wanted to farm pearls in what she called her spot. One man was killed by the man eaters in the water and the other made his way back to port with an 'escort.' He was bought off for a considerable sum of money and she was brought before the Rulers, stayed for a few days, and sent on her merry way. I had to part with an exceptionally hefty sum of coin to pay for this information, my Captain tells me, but this is exactly what the Faith would pay even greater favours for. Your brother would love to hear this information for himself."

She started at the mention of her brother. Her Pader had given the Church his eldest and only son to placate the Emperor his house was forever loyal. Her brother had risen in the ranks by his own merits, but not always by doing honorable deeds. She had not spoken to him in several years, leaving any communication between the men. She had no ill will towards him, but he also only tolerated her business ventures as she was his sister, and she donated large sums annually to the Church. She knew Davian used her for information. He as much told her when she asked him. They had words, and she stayed away for a time.

"But here's the conundrum, there are rumours exceptionally large beasts are on the mountainside, larger than any seen and some have called them Dragons.

But this information has not been confirmed. You know what this means, if it is confirmed, then we will be going to war with Pelin'Dun."

"Dragons. This sounds impossible. Where would they have come from? And war? With Pelin'Dun? Over the centuries the Faith have tried and failed. We cannot fight on two fronts. It would mean losing our lands here to gain what? Little Islands, of no real economy. It would ruin us here."

Damara began thinking of what he told her.

"But you don't see, my dear Mara, the war here would end. Our Emperor would have no choice but to broker a peace with Aram, maybe join forces and then both lands would crush Pelin'Dun between them like a hammer crushes a nut on an anvil. The Islands adhere to an old religion, and Aram has only one god, like us and not the six the Pelinese worship. That is the pearl the Faith seek."

They spent the rest of the evening talking about the importance of the news, how it would affect them as a country. After many glasses of this new wine, Damara begged to go to bed as she had a raging headache, her head spinning with wine. Ramis indulged as well, and he had many arrangements to make, he would set off for the Capital in a few days. She completely forgot about sex; her mind was going in all different directions.

Another girl with glowing eyes, but blue. Does this mean I may be one of these 'DragonRiders?' I must not even mention it, even to my brother. It would mean my death. I must glean more information, but where?

The next day she woke late, her headache lingering, and she took a tonic to alleviate the dull but otherwise still there thumping behind her eyes. She walked slowly into the dining room to see Ramis seated there. She smelled the strength of his tea and ordered one for herself. She sat at the table and had eggs and bread toasted for breakfast, the fruit she passed by.

"May I attend with you in the Capital?"

"I was going to ask you to come anyway, we should see your brother together, this is too important to not do." He stared at her over the length of the table. "Are you feeling up to going for a walk in the gardens? Your head is not pounding anymore?"

"Yes, I am afraid the wine was very good, and I indulged a little too much." She motioned with her fingers at this, and her husband laughed at her expression.

"Oh, my Darling, you will have to watch this one, it doesn't agree with you if you are so affected by a mere bottle."

"I used to be able to manage my wine. I can't seem to enjoy as much as I want to, since I was ill. Ugh!"

He rose to his feet and walked down to her end, offering her his arm. "My Dear, let's take a turn in the gardens, it is not too bright and there is something I need to ask you."

She looked up at him, worry in her gaze, took his arm, and rose. They walked out onto the patio down the steps onto the greening grass. They walked looking at the budding plants, and finally Damara stopped in her tracks and spoke.

"Alright, your silence has me wondering what you may speak to me about. What is on your mind?"

He turned to her and took both her hands into his. "Darling, we have a double purpose in going to the Capital. Baron has asked for us, I have a feeling he has brought us a viable prospect forward and will wish to be joined. It can only be one of three girls, and I know you are partial to the lesser of the three. If it is not her, you will behave? The other two have better political positions."

"Do you know something you are not telling me?" She looked him in the eye and could see a flicker before he said he did not.

"There is one more thing, though. Your brother sent me a letter this morning, it seems he already knows we are coming to the Capital, which means he has spies of his own and knows what we are coming there for. He asked for one of our sons to be indoctrinated into the Church. This only leaves Jaidak, and we need to convince him of the benefits of such a position."

Damara gasped. She wasn't sure how she felt about this piece of news. "I did not think our loyalty was under question. We have always done what is best for the state, our boys fight for their Emperor."

"I do not think it a matter of our loyalty, My Dear, I am thinking your brother wants a man who is loyal to him, so he can groom him for his successor. Your brother is Second in Command; there is only one other position he has not held. This one cannot be held forever, as our volatile history has shown. Your brother needs men who he knows will cleave only to him. I consider this a great honour. One of our sons in the Army, close to the central hub of command, the other rising in the ranks of the Church. You could not ask for a better legacy than this. Do you not agree?"

She saw his reasoning and nodded to his thinking. As a house they had come a long way from her Paders disgrace and gradual rise in the ranks beside the Royal houses. Her sons were guaranteed positions of power.

"Only if they are smart enough to keep them, you must emphasise the futility of refusing such meaningful offers. They may listen to you more than I. I guess none of my orders are complete enough to bring, depending on how long we entertain in the Capital. One of us may have to come back for those."

She realized she was thinking aloud and they turned and walked back. Her headache all but gone and her mind whirling with all she had to do to prepare for the trip on the morrow. They parted ways inside, each going their separate ways, both thinking different thoughts of preparation.

Damara informed Peylin, they would be leaving, but she had begun packing, having already chatted with Ramis's manservant. "Prepare a horse for me, I want to collect a few things to take with me. I will bring a sample for the Noma."

"Yes, Nada, right away."

Her mind thinking of the orders and thought to take Noma Kavena a sample of the pink fabric to whet her appetite, however, the Noma was one of the biggest gossips. She could catch up on her news of what was happening in all the noble houses, and what marriage contracts were being written. The Noma's husband was none other than the Head of Law, in the state. She was privy to all sorts of information and could be convinced to part with information for the right price.

Damara had the right price. This fabric could buy her whatever the Noma thought would serve.

She rode into the city down to her shop and gathered a small sample of fabric to take with her. Damara thought to acquire a few items for her brother, as she knew he was frugal in his attire and daily habits. He hadn't changed in the twenty years he was in the Namarch's grasp, so over the years she would time to time bring him sundries and things she knew he liked. So, she decided to walk to the candlemakers and soap makers shops. She knew he would like this small gesture from her. She was still smiling as she walked out of the soap shop, and almost ran into the woman coming in. It was Lana. "Oh, excuse me, I did not see you, the sun was in my eyes."

"Damara. Hello, it has been a few years since we last spoke. How have you been? Your business has really taken off."

Seeing Lana caught her by surprise and Damara was at a loss for a moment at what to say. In the split second it took for her to register the woman in front of her was her former friend, she arrived at the conclusion Lana could damn well have Ramis and she smiled at the woman before her.

"Actually, it's been more like four years. Ramis told me you were otherwise occupied on a different trajectory than me and to not see you anymore or it would hurt my reputation. My business has in fact kept me terribly busy. How are you?"

Damara moved into the shade so others could get past, and she was not squinting into the sun. Seeing Lana again, she saw the woman looked older but happier. Lana's attire was well worn but respectable for a matron. She did not give Damara any reason to suspect she was a 'kept' woman. Damara was actually extremely glad to see her; she had missed her friend and did not feel any hatred for the woman who was keeping Ramis busy. "Is that what he said to keep you away, I always wondered. A different trajectory?"

"That's just a subtle way of saying you were entertaining other women's husbands to keep food on your table. He was thinking you might influence me to do the same, just a guess."

Lana looked uncomfortable at Damara's forthright admission. "Mara... I... I have something to tell you..."

"Lana, I already know. Frankly, I am past hating you. Believe me I did at first, but since then I have found out Ramis's cock is everywhere, so don't think you are his only secret."

"What? He said he was in love with me and was going to divorce you to marry me. Do you know about Ramoth then? I didn't know what to do, Ramis said he would always take care of me. I wanted so much to tell you, and I was going to, but then a man came and gave me a huge sum to not tell you. I don't know why I am saying all this to you now, but I have felt guilty all these years. Even after Ramis said you hated and wanted nothing to do with me after Arno divorced me. Can you forgive me, Mara? I was in such a tight spot for a while. I had to do unspeakable things to survive."

"Its quite all right, Lana. You have had a tough time; I can surely imagine. It seems Ramis has told each of us different things to suit his needs. I am not angry with you and if I have time when I am not busy, I would like to meet your lad and catch up. It might be wise to not tell Ramis of our meeting. I would like to not get divorced right now."

"I would not want that for you; life is challenging. It has not been easy. You are right, Ramis need not know, it can be our little secret. I must get this order inside, so I will see you again?"

"Yes, I will send Peylin with a message when I have some time and we will set something up. It was nice seeing you again and I wish circumstances were different, but everything has a time and place. Take care, Lana."

She strode off before Lana could think to hug her, Damara was happy to see Lana again, not quite this happy. She went into the candlemakers and purchased a few beeswax candles one could only get from their locale. The wax had an underlying scent from the flowers the bees pollinated in their one area of the country. She knew in Davian burning those candles, it would remind him of home and their Mader.

Her gifts to her brother were from the heart, she was never the kind to buy anyone's love, but it never hurt if it did grant her favours when she needed them. She kept smiling as she walked back to the shop and the stables, her arms full but not overly, she could manage the walk back, she thought. The saddle bags could carry the small amount she bought without any damage, and it was not far of a ride, she glanced up at the sky and as she looked forward a shadow in the alley beside her caught her eye. She put the satchel onto the saddle where it was tied on and left the horse tied up and went forward into the alley and once around the first corner, she came face to face with Ash the man she hired. He was standing there waiting for her.

"You did see me then, I have extraordinarily little to tell. Your husband has visited the woman in the house a few times and to a few brothels, never the same girls, that I can see. At some point I may have to cease, I have other clientele and other jobs which may take me away, you understand?"

"Yes, I do. We will keep on our arrangement, you provide me information periodically, and if I need anything, I will seek you out. For now, continue as you have, and we will deal with any unexpected developments as they arise. Thank you. Do you require any more payment?"

"No, you are more than generous. If that is all?"

"Yes. We will be travelling back to the Capital, and I will wait to hear from you when you have more. I will see you then. Thank you again." She turned and walked back to her horse, mounted, and rode up to the villa to finish her preparations for the following day. She talked with Peylin who was packing her clothes into small chests for the transport carriage to Merida.

"You will never guess who I saw and had a small chat with today?"

"Well, judging by your expression which still has the remnants of shock, I would hazard a guess that you saw someone you never expected. I will say, the woman Ramis is keeping in the city? Am I right?"

"By the God, you are! How astute you are! I'm impressed, Peylin. You don't mind if I keep you?" Damara was sarcastic to her maid which had the girl smiling at her Mistress.

"Only if you must, Nada. What did you do? Did you hit her? Rip her hair out?"

"No. Unfortunately nothing of the sort. I was glad to see her. I have resolved Ramis is never going to change, and I can be bitter about it, or move forward, safe in the knowledge it all reflects on his spirit, not mine. She can have him. Good riddance. Once I divorce him, and I will make sure I can, without too much bother, he will be her problem, not mine. She admitted to me he told her something to not have her question me, and it worked. But she said she never felt right about it, and she would like to have a chat with me and catch up. She also would like me to meet her son, which is strange, but I felt like time stood still and we were still friends. Is this not strange?"

"You are a good woman. I would have beaten her to a pulp if she were having a dalliance with my man. Not I have one, but I feel like men should only cleave to one woman and not have the Church's blessing to do what they wish. It isn't fair, this world we live in. I know many people who love the one person they were married. Look no further than your own parents, they had many wonderful years together."

"Yes, you are right there. My Pader loved my Mader very much. He risked death from the Emperor to marry her and proved to her everyday of his life she was the only one he loved. Other than us, but yes. No, not the yellow dress. It needs cleaning, grab the red and deep pink, and the dark blue, and maybe the green. You have all the corresponding jewels?"

"Yes, Nada. I'll pack a few more, just in case. You never know how long this time in the city will be."

"You are so right, again. I will head off to the bath, thank you for your efficiency, dear girl." Damara peeled off her clothes, soaked for a while ate a small dinner and went to bed feeling light of spirit, almost as happy as before she knew what she knew. She was not going to let her husband rule her life, she would take charge, little by little.

The travel to the Capital was uneventful. Damara thought about her life.

My boys. Ramis wants them placed high up, he wants for them what he could not achieve. This can only be the reason. Should they not rise on their own merits? However, once placed they will have to. They will fail or succeed entirely. Ohhh, I hope they survive. They know not the struggle to rise from the bottom. They will have an easier time of it, having better placements. I do wish Baron does well, one misstep and he could be killed. Jaidak will have a harder time. From what Davian told me of his rise, it was more cutthroat. Jaidak is a gentle soul, he loves his books. He's more the scholar, I hope he thrives. The next generation is about to embark on their life quests. Jaidak will become a man of the cloth, Baron a warrior. (gasp) They will be on opposite sides, and they are different enough to be at odds. Peylin looked at Damara when she gasped and saw the tears forming in her Mistress's eyes. The carriage ride was quiet, Peylin was nodding off when she heard her Mistress.

"What is it, Nada? Is it your stomach? Do we need to stop?"

"No, Peylin. My stomach is fine. I was thinking on my boys. One is in the Army. The other is requested for the Church."

"Yes… does this not give you pleasure? Your boys will have high positions."

"I am pleased. But then, I thought about it more. Baron will be serving the Empire. Jaidak, the Namarch. One man on either side. What if in the future, they are placed against each other? What then?"

"Well, one cannot worry about events which may not happen. Do you think they would serve well in each capacity?"

"Well, yes. but if they must fight each other?"

"Then, you just think of how well they will do. You and perhaps even I, may not be alive if and when there is a future conflict. Why think about the future. Negative thoughts like those do not serve you. You are still recovering from your stomach upset. Do you want a reoccurrence?"

"You have the right of it. I should not dwell on the negative. I see myself and Davian, our lives…"

"You and your brother have never been at odds. He is risen in the Church, enough to give you, his blessing. Your business has thrived. There is a blessing in everything that you touch, Nada. This fabric, will have you busier than you may want."

"Yes, I see this happening. I remember my Mader told me to do what makes me happy. With all my children having placements, now I should think about myself."

"Your Mader some exceptionally good advice. I remember in her latter years, she was well respected. Kara lost a good citizen when she passed. May she be Blessed."

"May she be Blessed. Yes, I loved her, but Davian was crushed. He was her favorite; she doted on him, until he entered service. She told me she was lost without her scholar. They used to debate over tomes and books."

"Perhaps this is a suitable time to tell you. When I first entered your home, to become your maid, your Mader pulled me aside."

"Oh. I never knew this. Mader told me plenty of things, but she never told me she had spoken to you. What about?"

"Your Mader told me to cherish you. To serve you, but to also mentor you. I did not understand it then, but I see it now. She wanted you to have friends, I hope I do not overstep my position, but with all happening, I see you need an outlet for your worries. You cannot voice to Ramis, so I wish you find myself as a recipient of your findings. She may had an inkling of what Ramis was about."

"I am thinking you are correct. She told me before she passed, the only reason she agreed to my joining was because she wanted my happiness. Most definitely, she saw Ramis's true character. I didn't see it. As for your friendship, I treasure it, you have nothing but good advice for me. You have served me well, and I do appreciate your silence and your candor. I find as I age, I value the friendship of women more.

Women need to bond together, in this world which caters to men. If we don't, the men have won. We fight and win the small battles. Even in what I do, the Namarch has the power to have me succeed or fail. I know well enough which clothing will win out. Living my childhood life, I see the struggles my parents went through, I have struggled with my own marriage, but made it work. All the while, catering to men. Having women who support each other, in this life, well this has value. I care not for a man's support. Ramis is proving to me, he only values his life, not mine. He is duplicitous, and exceptionally good at it. I was very blind. Now I am not."

"Well, you do need to make yourself happy and place your needs before others. I see the change in you. Very slowly, which is good. Too many women would break or be broken when changes happen too quickly. Your friend Lana, she has had a rough go of it, but she is surviving. You mentioned she looked well?"

"Yes, surprisingly so. I saw in her, pride. It was in what she was doing. She was surviving, on her own merits. A weaker woman would have been working the baser needs, the…you know. I wish she hadn't picked Ramis to have relations with. I always thought she was better than this."

"She may not have had a choice. Ramis may have picked her."

"Yes, now you voice it, you are probably right. His choice of women, why does he do this? He is very giving…why does a man need to find pleasure with so many different women? How does this satisfy him? I have no thought of joining with another. Ramis is the only one."

"Perhaps he is looking for completion. One searches for something one cannot find. He may be not satisfied with not finding it."

"Is this not called an addiction? He is addicted to joining. Because he is searching for, like you said for satisfaction? He was always satisfied with me. I am sorry, this is more information than you need to hear right now."

"That is fine. I take no offence. You say he found his satisfaction with you. Every time? Have you been satisfied with him?"

"Ohhh, Peylin. Is this something women feel? (sniff, sniff), I feel so let down. I do not know what satisfaction is then. I cannot remember the last time I felt …satisfied."

Peylin came over to the other side of the carriage and held Damara while she let out her sadness with an incredibly good cry. "There, there, Nada. I did not mean to make you upset. it was not my intention. Hush."

"(sniff) 'Tis fine, Peylin. Having you here, like you said to voice my frustrations, I do not know what I would do without your friendship. Having voiced this aloud, well has made me think. Perhaps I should take a lover. The Captain, perhaps."

"You must think very carefully on this, Nada. Ramis has already shown you, his jealousy. By simply being near another man. A nice looking one. Having relations with one not your husband will have dire consequences if you get attached. Being found out, you could be killed."

"You are right. I should not entertain such thoughts. It just burns me up, this world we live in, is not fair in any regard. I must hide my business behind Ramis's name. I do all the work. He plays."

"The Universe placed you exactly where you should be, do not trouble yourself with being stuck with a petty man. Ramis will be the end of Ramis. You will not have to lift a finger. His dalliance's will prove to be his downfall. Spreading himself out too thin will have the fire extinguish. He can only manage to bring this upon himself. You will see. Just focus on yourself, Nada. You are what matters. Do what makes you happy. Perhaps not a dalliance, though. Not until you are sure there will be no repercussions. No need to give him fuel for his fire. He would burn you down and out. I would not want this for any woman. Especially not you." Peylin gave Damara another squeeze and left to sit back on her side of the carriage. She plumped up the pillow she was using.

"I thank you for the council. I see my Mader saw something in you. I am glad you are in my service. You have some sage advice. The thought of a dalliance makes me tired. I will not pursue. I cannot fathom having one."

Peylin smiled through her closed eyes, "The Captain, though, he's very easy on the eyes, do you not think?"

Damara laughed and she picked up her pillow bolster off the carriage floor and plumped it up before leaning into its softness. "Yes, he is. Very intent, and very nice on the eyes. Ramis should be jealous!"

Damara closed her eyes and the two women tried to sleep amid the bouncing route. They talked some more along the route, stopping where they usually did, sleeping in the inns along the way. Damara emptied her heart out to Peylin, voicing every deed, and every nuance of what she could recall. It felt good to express herself. Speaking quietly, a few times, she knew Ramis could hear his name spoken. Damara would wait until Ramis rode ahead. She did not want him to hear every complaint she had. They soon arrived at the villa in the Capital. Damara found herself tired, but lighter of spirit.

Ramis went about his way, and she settled in to wait for the summons to the head of the Church, nothing was ever done without great ceremony, she hoped that she could have a moment of her brother's time, as she had a question, she wanted to ask him, but of course with no witnesses. There always was an abundance of ears hanging about.

The summons came sooner than she thought.

CHAPTER 32

Meera

Diminish Disbelief Where it Lay

I settled into a routine of learning all I could from these over friendly nomadic people, who wanted so much to please me, 'the Little Mader.' I had some difficulty with the language, but caught on to the words which sounded familiar, and of course pointing always helped.

Having a girl friend my age also helped, Si'Sue was all too eager to be my shadow. She taught me how to harvest the reeds used for linen making, and I spent many a day, in the sun getting blisters on my hands and an ache in my shoulders. We became inseparable, and I was grateful for the company. Si'Sue was my first friend, a woman my own age, even though she saw me on a pedestal, after we knew a little more of each other, in our limited means, she and I were a lot alike.

Si'Sue showed me a remarkably simple way of life, the Nomads lived life with a giving attitude, different than how I was raised. Or more to the point, the way of the Northmen. If one wanted to be truthful, I raised myself. It was a most peaceful way of being and I was finally smiling. Kiem remarked more than once I looked like my Mader.

"What are you smiling at?"

"Oh, nothing. Si'Sue has a crush on one of the young hunters and I expect they will have the joining ceremony soon for the two. Why?"

"Seeing you, at peace, reminded me of watching Miiele in one of her calmer moments. She was reading a book in one of our spots. It was a hidden patio in one of the Temple gardens, one of our regular hiding spots. All worshippers of all castes could use the Temple at any given time. She was reading, the sun was setting and caught her in the eye, I said something, I cannot remember what, she looked up at me and smiled. It was then, that very moment when I knew I loved her. It was the faraway look in your eyes which reminded me of her. How I wish I could go back in time and see her again."

"If seeing me makes you sad, Pader…?"

"No, I am only feeling sorry for myself. I do miss her, but she also did not love me as much as I did her. You can't cage a bird which doesn't wish to be caged. I could not do this to her. I loved her in my way, and she gave me you. The best gift I could imagine. I knew my life wasn't good enough for you until you were old enough to keep yourself alive. I am sorry it wasn't all a pretty garden."

"It wasn't all bad. I know it will take me some time to get over the feelings I have about being abandoned and alone. Nena helped me by getting me to put a voice to all. It was not until the last three years I have come to terms. Knowing what you told me about my Mader and you, everything you read and know, it is making up for my childhood. I guess in my lack, it has given me certain survival skills, a lavish upbringing couldn't.

My battle with Vandrin was bound to happen eventually, he is a very bitter man, and I am happy to not be around him. As for… ummm, what's her name… ummm S S S ara, no, S Saliene, yes, I knew it started with an s! I never was allowed around my sister, guess they didn't want me to taint her, and the few times I did see her, well, by then she hated me.

I am not sure what they told her, but she insists we aren't blood. She looks like Vandrin, black of hair, like their Pader. As I grew out of my childhood and into a woman, I was past all this, and it does not bother me. Family is the people you surround yourself with who care for and love you. It doesn't have to be blood, but in your case, it does help!"

We were alike in so many ways; humour was one of them. He laughed at my last comment. "Oh, you are without doubt my child. I hope we have many more years together, but you will have to leave me in the capable hands of the healer here. I cannot help you if I cannot help myself. I did not plan this to happen, and I am upset with myself for goading the Li'on-sa in the balls, I did promise your Mader…"

"I think you should get yourself better first, you can not help me forever. And this gives me a definite reason to come back from wherever it is I am going. Do you have an idea?"

"Well, you must cross the desert, I have an idea of what's on the other side, but I have never been there. Lo'nan has, once. His hunter's make the trip across the burning sands, to trade and keep up with news. As for what it is you will do there, the Universe will present you with the next step. You must find it yourself."

"That's not really helping me much."

"Nothing in life worth keeping is easy or handed to us on a shiny platter, dear child. You must earn it honestly, or it will not have value in your eyes. You will find every lesson learned will shape you into your spirit. You must always choose good, even if it's the hardest thing to do. You will be tested. Life is never always easy, I know. I had one of the worst decisions to make, and this was to give your Mader up, however, it has given me you. So, I will leave you to keep on your path with the knowledge of my love for you. You will always have it."

I stood up from my pile of reeds I was striping while we chatted. He and I hugged while I tried not to cry at his admission to me. It was bittersweet, I had found my Pader. We got along so well, and here I would have to leave him behind. At least he hadn't perished, even if he never had proper use of his arm again, he was still sound of mind. I knew leaving him in the hands of the nomadic warriors with the gentlest hearts was for the best.

"And I will always love you as my Pader. Even if I know you as Uncle."

"Well, lass. Sometimes those are the best friendships. Beyond the bond of blood, do you not find we have a friendship?"

"Yes. Yes, we do. Not until you voiced it. I was wondering. So, because I still think of his Lordship as my Pader, however, you have shown me more caring. At least what I can remember, from growing up. You were distant, now I know the why, but you cared more. In the trivial things you did. Like the bark juice and the clothing."

"It was all I could do, anything more, would have others wondering."

"And his Lordship never thanked you? He must have known you would tell me."

"I do not know if your Mader ever told him. So why then would he thank me? And if he did know, why would he acknowledge my care? It would make him less. His primary thoughts were on trying to rid this land of the enemy. With it continuing over the last ten years, he was constant in his role."

"Well, I thank you. If not for you, I would not know the care of Nena, and it was she who rid me of my anger, my shame, and told me many things, I have the greatest love and respect for that woman. As I have for you."

"You are much like your Mader, she felt things deeply. I will let you finish this… and I will find myself the healer. She wanted to have a look at my arm."

He left to go back to the village, and I sat back down to finish helping Si'Sue with our daily task. She comment while my Pader looked sad, he would be well cared for.

"How do you know he is my Pader?"

"Any one of us, can see, you look like same."

She spoke to me so I could understand, sometimes when she got excited, I could only catch every other word, but most times she spoke like I was a little child. We finished and left the ends which would in time, rot and give themselves back to the soil. I knew what she meant, and we carried our bundles back to the elders. The older women who would process the next step. I had a few more weeks of learning, and at the end I knew how to make a rudimentary linen.

Not a bad skill to have.

Eventually the time arrived for me to embark on the next portion in my journey. I ate my morning meal with Si'Sue and met up with my Pader and the elders. I asked Kiem what my Mader had meant, for me to go North.

"Well, the only thing North of here is Lanthia. It must be in your path to go there, and what you need will present itself when the time it right. Your Mader must have known something. She was an avid reader, so perhaps she read of something. Lanthia is seeped bon mystery." All he could tell me about the people that lived in the hot arid desert was what he heard from a far-off traveler of those lands.

"They are darker skinned, fierce warriors and they do not treat their women as equals unless they prove themselves in combat. Their armies consist of both sexes and the women who fight give up their right to bear children. They only have one God, who dictates all they do in life, so don't disrespect anything! They might see you as an adversary or they might not. Nejan will provide them with a distraction, but you need to find your path with them before you move on, hopefully one day we will meet again and if we don't, I will give you this."

As he spoke, he rummaged in his pant leg which I realized was an inside pouch attached, quite ingenious, held out his hand to me and opened it. On a fine gold chain was a ring. Small and dainty it was. Set into it was a Redstone surrounded by amber ones.

"This was your Maders, she gave it to me, the last time I saw her and made me swear to give it to you before we were ever to part ways. This ring was given to her by her Mader, and there is only one other like it, these were made specifically for her and her twin sister. Each generation of D'un children were given a talisman of sorts to distinguish where they were in the pecking order of the hierarchy. Red stones being the highest, only the Ruling House could wear these. Keep it safe, this is your only link, other than your red hair and eyes which link you to the D'un family. You look like your Mader, but the Maderland is well…, everyone looks the same there. I had the chain made, you can hang it on your neck under your tunic or when the time is right, wear it on your finger."

Tears were in his eyes as he gave this to me, and I heard Nejan softly in my head,

"This was his last link to your Mader," to which I blurted aloud, "You have me!" And I gave the biggest hug I could muster without hurting his shoulder too much, we stood like this for the longest time, before he pulled away and smiled down at me.

"Indeed, I do, you are the greatest gift your Mader could have given me, and also you gave me purpose, for after your Mader left her spirit, I was floundering."

Just then, I had a feeling come over me and I must have paled incredibly before I sunk onto my knees, to the packed dirt in front of my hut where we were standing. It was of such hopelessness and despair. I must have cried aloud, as others and Kiem tried to get me on my feet. Concern in their eyes showed, and I must have been crying, because Kiem began wiping my face,

"It's not that bad, we will see each other again!"

"That's not it, I mean, yes but, I felt death and despair. A loss of life." I told him of the despair I felt. Kiem said, my Dragon could be projecting his feelings to me especially if they were strongly felt.

"You must try and connect your minds and open this means of communication."

Maybe it was the distance between us which stopped us, or maybe I had to keep practicing with Nejan, so it came automatic without hesitation. "I am trying to, Pader. But sometimes the bond is not there. Like there is something blocking it. I feel connected, but not. I know this is crazy."

"Well, all in suitable time. We should start your journey. I will hold you close to my heart. Always."

The day progressed with the ceremony to bring safe travels and good fortune. There were prayers and offerings, and they prayed to the Pader and Mader for safe travels. I had never seen or been part of any ceremony which involved the

Gods of old. I was intrigued and listened intently. I had plenty of questions, but Kiem said they would have to wait. A pack for me and a pack for Nejan was produced, who although wasn't impressed with being a packhorse, understood it was necessary to our survival.

We had water skins, packs of dried water herbs, and some dried meats, which were easier to chew than the ones Kiem and I had dried. Also given, after it was demonstrated, was an exceptionally large sheet of light fabric with an oily substance on it, it was rolled up and put inside a leather tube tied on both ends.

"This is to protect both of you in a sandstorm, put the sheet on top of you and sit on all the ends, the oil will prevent the sand getting in through the fabric. Make sure you shake what you can off before rolling it back up, and it may only work twice before the coating needs replacing."

Si'Sue gave me a bulb of a plant I had never seen. "Break this open and rub it under your eyes. It will sting for a moment, it will cut down on the glare of the sun, or you will be blinded. You can also wear a bandage over your eyes with slits to see through, the plant would serve Nejan better."

She gave me a big hug and began to cry, "I will miss you great Mader."

"We will meet again. I have learned a lot from you and your people and have enjoyed every minute of your teachings. Take care."

I hugged all of those I had gotten to know. We packed up all we would need and harnessed up Nejan, amid some growling and huffs. It was late day before we headed over grass to the edge of the sand sea. Walking through tall grasses was endless, it took us several hours of walking, and I knew we were close when I saw the ground, begin to change into a sandy skin.

"Walk with the moon on your right shoulder at the beginning of the night and end your night walk with it over your left."

"*I am sure I can manage.*" Nejan huffed.

I turned to Kiem, we hugged and I squeezed him tight, not wanting to let go of my newfound Pader. He looked down at me, leaned down, and kissed my forehead.

"I am loath to let you go, now we found each other, know my heart is always with you. We will always be connected on a deeper level. You follow your path; we will meet again. I am proud of you, Meera. Remember, I do love you. I loved your Mader; you are my gift from her. Just like you are the gift for this world. You be strong, find your sisters, and find your path."

"Oh, Pader! I do not want to leave you either. I wish for you to heal your arm, and to find me again. Or I will find you. I want to have you constant in my life, wherever this will be."

I tried not to cry but I did. He wiped tears from my cheeks.

"Lass, you have a great responsibility ahead. Focus on this. We will be together again; I have no doubt. You cross this ocean of sand, find what it is you need to do. Now you should start out. I love you."

"I love you too, Kiem. I will make you proud."

"I know you will. You already have."

We parted; I hoisted the pack onto my back and listened to the words of Lo'nan. There was an Oasis halfway to the ones who knew where to look. It would provide us with more water and some plants there were edible. As we were about to leave, a wind picked up and swirled around us. We all looked around; it was still before. Then Kiem shouted. "Stand still, there is something coming at us."

I looked around and spotted a colour on the wind. It was purple, then as I could see the wind advancing, it became darker. It looked similar to a winged bird yet was iridescent and I saw the sky through its shape. We all held still as the shape came closer. No one spoke.

"Nejan, what could this possible be?"

"Little One. This may be the spirit you felt earlier. This is a Dragon, the spirit is flying, possibly to await rebirth. Few have seen this. It may be going to rest, awaiting rebirth somewhere. Stand still, 'tis close."

We stood very still as the flying sparkles came towards us, it circled around Nejan and I, twice before heading off in the direction we would be heading. Lo'nan knelt before Nejan and I.

"We were blessed to see a Dragon spirit. May it guide you on your path. It may pave the way forward for you, Little Mader. Many blessings."

When I glanced at my Pader he was smiling.

"You saw something few people have seen. This is the first time for me. It portents a great journey for you. This is your path forward, the Dragons blessed it. I will miss you, Dader. However, I will sleep better, knowing you have the blessing of the Gods. May I see you again. May you be Blessed. Safe Path, Little One, and you, Great Mader."

After some last hugs and kisses, Nejan and I set off, her paws bundled up in leather socks. Which only lasted one day before she lost one and threw the rest off.

"I saw two spirits now. Does this make me special?"

"You may find it a burden... or not. The last Rider saw many, especially in the last times. It grieved his heart."

"Oh. I am not sure I like this 'gift,' not if it is going to give me sorrow."

"It may not. You will figure out how to deal with it."

"Look at it in a more positive way? Perhaps sing songs of the departed? Like the Northmen do?"

"Perhaps. You will find your way. Every culture has a different method when it comes to end of spirit. You find what works for you."

"I gather, from what I know of life, there may be more death, before the world stops. Or war. War always means death. (sigh) I get a feeling; I should get my thoughts on death figured out foremost. So, I do not let it affect my spirit."

"You will see much death and sorrow. You are thinking ahead. This will aid you. You will be the stick others will measure themselves by. You may be raised up and placed on a hill, so all see you."

"Oh. I never thought of this. I am hardly a leader to be revered. I have many things to think on."

"Yes, you do. Having your ideas formed, before you start, is an effective way to begin."

"Well...we are beginning a journey. How long will it take?"

"A couple of moons...however you tell your time. The moon ebbs and wanes a couple of times. One time it took me three, but I had to hide from men for part of it..."

Nejan spoke the rest of the night and told me of her travels. For a large feline, she saw much of the North, before she hid in the mountain passes. We walked long into the night and saw the moon rise on the right side of me and soon it was overhead, the sand was hard packed and cracking. Many times, I stumbled from not picking my feet up high enough. Nejan and I conversed more to pass the time, I was learning about Dragon skins and scales, plants used to condition, different plants used to treat wounds, where to find and how to apply them. My Dragon education continuing as we walked.

Soon the moon was on our left, disappearing over the horizon. I saw the sky slowly brighten on my right and I realized we walked all night. My body was weary from effort. I looked for a spot to camp but as the terrain was flat, no areas looked good enough. I brought a couple sticks, one which I used for walking. I grabbed the cape I was shown to use in numerous ways and made a makeshift lean-to for both of us.

It was only big enough for me and Nejan's front torso. Soon as the sun rose, we realized her comfort was essential. She fit herself underneath the cape and I ended up cradled in her paws, tucked against her torso. This became our daily routine, and as uncomfortable as it was, I saw no other way. She tried to lick me once and nearly took my hair off, her tongue was so rough, my hair got stuck on it. Laughing, I tried to get my hair off,

"Great Mader, I don't think your affection would...ugh... help me... ooohh... with keeping... my hair in place...while I appreciate it. Your tongue is very... rough...maybe just nose bumps, what do you say?"

"Sorry, Little Cub, I forgot for a moment, you have no fur." and she did not try again.

Many nights became many days, the sand became soft, and we struggled to make our way through it. My calves and my feet ached from trudging through the soft sand. We climbed one hill only to reach the top and see many more ahead of us. It was all the same, hill after hill of soft sand. I ventured a look back the first night, the sea of grass had disappeared. A week in and I had a complete circle view. There was nothing but hills of sand in all my sighting. If I had not the moon to guide us, I would not know the direction in which we were headed. One time I thought I saw trees but the further we walked towards them the further away they got.

"'Tis the mind tricking us. 'Tis still farther than it looks. Seeing means it is there, though more nights to walk."

One day we were resting, after we ate dried plants and meat for Nejan, and it seemed we closed our eyes, when a quick breeze nearly pulled our makeshift canvas from Nejan's paw where she placed it over the edge. The sky disappeared, and a wall of sand was heading our way. The air became contaminated with sand particles, and I was glad I did not open my mouth to speak with my companion.

She did not explain what was happening and I jumped up and raced to remove the tube of fabric and shook out. I tossed it over Nejan who in trying to help kept hampering my efforts.

"By the Gods, stand still. You keep moving and pfft, this sand wall will be hitting us soon!" Once I covered her, I tucked the edges under her paws,

"Can you extend your claws into the fabric while you drop down? Good, let's get one of your front paws into the fabric. Let me get these packs under. There. Now myself." I grabbed the last edge, tucked it under her chin, and secured it under her last paw. By this time, I did not say anything, she secured it as we were hit by fierce wind.

The voice of the sandstorm really began howling and we were bombarded with sticks hitting us, continually, until I felt drowsy and fell asleep nested against her body. We woke up several times but always heard the wind howling louder then becoming muffled. After several hours or more of slumber, I woke up to something pressing down on my head, and complete silence.

"I think it is past, but something has weighed us down, watch yourself, I will try to stand, Little Cub." After a couple attempts, she was successful but oh what a mess, sand blew into my face and mouth, and it went into my clothing. We managed to emerge from our tent, into a vista which looked exactly the same!

The sun was still overhead, and we would have a couple more hours of light so we struggled and retrieved the length of material out from under the sand, and I tried to shake out what I could. The packs we nearly lost but dug them out also. I dug inside my pack and found one of the bulbs and broke it open and applied the resin to our faces and tied a scarf around my head and eyes. It did cut down on the glare. We set off again after preparing ourselves and as we walked, I apologized to Nejan about snapping at her. *"I am sorry, Great One, about barking at you before. I did not mean to be cross. I felt the urgency of timing."*

"I understand, we will work better as a team, if there is a next time. The sandstorm is not something I wish to experience without the cloth. My skin itches something fierce."

The sun set, with beautiful colours and we walked half the night before I realized the ground was hardening. Over the next hill, we saw before us trees and scrub.

I remembered Lo'nan said, trees meant water, but he said it could also mean predators. As we descended the hill down to the edge of the tree line, an odd-looking dog came into view, and then another and another until there were five standing before us. They were canines to be sure, but the fur on their shoulders stood higher than the animals I knew back home.

The leader yipped and the rest followed suit, until Nejan let out a very deep throated growl and the lead dog yelped and ran back into the scrub, with the rest following suit.

"Well, this may scare them off for now, I wouldn't be surprised if they shadow us and tried again. Maybe while we are distracted. Best to be on guard." We

moved forward together and heard the animals coordinate with us as we approached the edge and moved along the low-lying scrub.

"I hear them, Nejan, as though they are right beside us."

"Your hearing will amplify what you focus on. As you have an...intense awareness of the canines, it will sound louder than it should be. If you relax your focus, it will diminish. This would be a good moment to practice both and be aware of the differences. Try as we walk, it will help you in future endeavors."

Soon we came to a muddy bank, a pool of water which looked very murky in the moonlight with a strange smell emitting, as a smell of rotten quail eggs. We moved along the edge until we passed by the pool and kept moving through the scrub and trees. Finally, it opened to a larger pool, not smelling quite so bad, I knelt and scooped a handful of water and brought it to my nose to smell.

"Do not drink, while it does not smell bad as the last pool, I see bones inside the water and some on the banks, 'tis poison to all who partake. I see why the dogs are starving. We should continue; our journey is but half done. Lo'nan said nothing of the water not being good to drink."

"Perhaps he did not know."

"We will keep ahead of these canines. They may follow us."

"Let's hope they give up."

"You may get some practice with your knife, Little One, if they attack me all at once, I do not think I can fend them off. I am weakened by our trek, as are you. If I were in my health, this would not be a problem. There was a male of our species, a great fighter. He fended off six wolves by himself to get his mate to safety. He was glorious!"

We skirted around the pool and kept walking, ever walking. My feet were aching, somewhat. *"Are there many of your kind still alive?"*

"There are a few. Once we were many. We mated for life, so when one passed spirit, the other would tend to the pack or go serve the Dragons. We would have cubs, but with the last Dragon leaving, we had only another season, before we knew something was wrong. We travelled far into the hills to survive. Those closest to humans, did not listen and they are gone."

"What about you, Nejan? Did you have a mate, once?"

"I was on the cusp of searching for a mate when the last Rider left. I had to travel into the mountains, far into the wilderness. I went as far as I could, to find my own hunting grounds. In the beginning, there were battles between our kind as we were many and several placed dominances over others. I knew the further away I was, then I had a better chance at survival. It wasn't until the Great One spoke to me I travelled back to Little Uncle. He told you the rest, I am to help you on your path; in helping you, I help my kind. Once the Great One is once more, then I will seek out my own kind. Many blessings to you, Little Cub."

"I thank you for the knowledge you have given me, how will I know when all you say comes to pass?"

"The Great One will make himself known when it is time. Before the Great One faded from all thought, he sought out a scribe, to write down his words. You know it as a Prophecy. There will be a great sign, I know not what, mayhap your

sire knows. My kind know not of words, we live in pictures, in our minds, and of simple scents. Now the scent of rotten eggs is past us, I am picking up the scent of the little canines. We should keep on."

"You have the right of it. We keep going. Kiem told me the pool was more than halfway, so the next portion of our journey won't be as long."

The rest of our trip across the barren land was a different vista but no less difficult to travel. The ground would be hard in some areas, sandy in the next. I lost track of the days and nights. I watched the moon ebb, disappear, then reappear, fill, be full and then slowly become a sliver again.

We travelled around huge mountains of rock, and I imagined the wind hitting the mountains with such force to create the sands underneath our feet. The rocks were solitary figures, only once did we find one which was so big we climbed instead of navigating around it. When we reached the top, I saw behind us the sea of burning sands, and forward, I saw a stark forbidding landscape dotted with rock mountains. It was difficult to tell in the waning moonlight what lay ahead, but I noted the horizon was going to be ever changing.

We descended carefully from the sheer rock to walk upon sands making way to packed ground. Soon, there was hard packed ground, then cracks riddled in the hard ground which became larger and large, Nejan was careful of paw placement, the edges were sharp. She cut her pads on a few sharp stones, and I hoped for her sake they did not invite infection. The ground underneath hardened even further with small rocks; it was difficult to walk without falling over from loose footing. They became larger boulders, and we began weaving around them to move forward. We began an uphill climb which had us walking around rocks until we could no longer climb and reached a dead end.

Nejan spoke, *"We best get ourselves out of here, those canines followed us and we are not in a position to defend ourselves; I do not have energy right now."*

We returned to an open vista and Nejan jumped onto a boulder and said she saw a way through but would take us off our path for a bit. As she was turning, we heard the pack behind us. She jumped down and asked if I would be comfortable to climb onto her back.

"I suppose, you can carry my weight?"

"Yes, you have no choice. I can run faster, and I can not leave you behind. Get on now!" Startled I climbed up the harness which was made to accommodate her and the packs she carried, and I had no sooner settled onto her back,

"You had best hang onto something." I grabbed a handful of the strap across her back as she set off east at a quick lope. I felt her ribs under my bottom as I tried to grip with my knees. I turned to look over my shoulder and saw glowing pairs of eyes receding into the darkness. As she galloped forward, I heard her breathing shallowly and rasp.

"Try to pace yourself. Mayhap you stop for a drink, we have a little water left."

"Not until I distance ourselves further from those who follow."

The direction we headed made it easier to see shapes and I saw the sun making its appearance. I saw the wavy horizon ahead as the sun was rising, we came upon a plateau, across a gorge were hills leading into mountains and behind us to the South was the outline of a city.

What I failed to see across the gorge was the outline of a man watching us. Nejan stopped suddenly and laid down panting heavily. I dismounted, grabbed a skin, and poured the tepid warm water into a wooden bowl we packed for the very purpose of placing drinking water in it for Nejan.

"Many thanks, Little One." Nejan drank the contents and closed her eyes for awhile.

Meanwhile I walked to the edge and gazed down into the bottom, to see a silver stripe down which I knew was a river. I followed it Northwest and saw nothing but the gorge. I knew we had to cross and looked along the edge, however, saw no way down. Directly past the gorge and canyons were hills, and behind us flat plains.

"Best we move forward to move back." I startled Nejan out of the nap I knew she needed; however, I knew we were probably still being stalked by hungry dogs, we needed to move forward and try to cross the river and gorge.

She rose and I grabbed a package out of the pack, handed her a piece of dried meat. *"Can you chew as we walk?"*

I continued to hand her dried bits until the package was gone and I saw her energy return. We walked along the ridgeline until we came to scrub, then short trees and then into a forest proper. The trees were a different kind than I knew. Broad leaves, a green I likened to grass back home, and vines of a nature I had not seen before. We made our way through ferns so big and tall they dwarfed Nejan but provided us with shelter from the sun. The canopy of trees higher up, so high one would think the sky was green.

The sounds of animals and birds filled my ears with chatter. We climbed up an embankment, all the while keeping the edge of the escarpment in sight. Soon we noticed the other edge getting visibly closer, but still far enough away to not attempt a crossing.

"Awoooo, yip, yip, Awoooo!"

"Get back on, Little Cub." I did, all the while hearing continuous howling from the approaching band of canines. We set off, I had to lay down so I didn't get hit by branches and brush so didn't see when edges became close enough, but I felt when Nejan swerved and ran to the left and stopped.

"Hang on tightly, Little Cub."

She spun around; I didn't have time to respond before I felt power in her stride accelerate. I lay flat on her back and grabbed the leather strap in front of her shoulders. I felt muscles working beneath her fur. They tensed and stilled. We sailed through the air onto the other side of the Canyon! She stopped suddenly, the muscles under me, jarred with descent and a halt, I fell off and rose shakily up off my knees and turned to look across the gorge.

"By the Gods! We jumped that?"

I could not quite believe she successfully leapt over a Canyon gorge ten times her length (I'm guessing at least one hundred feet.) As I looked across, I saw heads of a few dogs sniff around, then we connected eyes, and they disappeared into the brush. I turned to Nejan to see her collapsed onto her side, sides heaving heavily.

"Are you all right, Mighty Warrior?" I asked as I quickly untied the leather sides of the harness.

"Ah, much better, yes I need to catch my breath, then we can go." She sat upright then stood while I removed the leather completely. Her sides still heaving.

"I am going to condense these packs to one I can carry. You have the rest of the water; we can find a stream nearby?"

I busily emptied the last of the water skin into the wooden bowl for Nejan and took stock of our supplies, all the while talking to myself, not caring if she answered.

I stopped my labours to project my hearing outward to hear running water. I slowly cancelled out each animal noise I heard until, to my astonishment, I did hear the tinkle of music I knew was a brook or stream.

"Good work, Little One, you are a natural at this. I didn't even have to coach you on the narrowing in on what you wished to hear." Nejan laid back down.

"When I hid under the busyness of the city, hiding from whatever bully was chasing me, I used to listen to the sounds of the tunnels. I heard the music of the miners, the sounds the walls made when they moved. There were always earth shakers and groans, and I was able to always find my way out by listening. I did not think about this until I focused on the water. I will fill our skins with fresh water; you rest and gain back your strength."

She sighed and laid back, her breathing now a steady movement. I gathered the four skins we brought and moved along the underbrush until I came upon a tinkling stream rushing over mossy rocks which had glitter to some of them. I filled the skins, honing my ears to listen for unusual sounds other than the busyness of the jungle forest.

After I filled the skins, washed my hands and face, and laid down to slake my first, I rose and followed the path I made back to Nejan.

I dropped the packs, laid against her, and close my eyes for a moment. That was a long moment. We rested for most of the day and at one point, she moved enough to have me slide to the ground, and I did not wake. She rose, found the stream, and followed it until finding a small pool, where she could rinse off some of the dust.

Meanwhile I snored peacefully unaware we were being watched.

CHAPTER 33

Davian

Inside the Spirit World

Well, God be damned, Davian thought to himself, looking down at the message in his hands,

His Eminence, the Grand Namarch is going to have a fit over this little piece of news. This might send him over the edge.

He rolled up and tucked the message scroll back in its cylindrical case, placing the lid back on, rising from behind the desk in his office, his signet ring clinking against the gold cylinder in his hand as he transferred it from one to the other. His attendant stood in the doorway and probed for information.

"Bad news, Your Holiness?" Geravon, the middle-aged man with dirty-blonde hair who was his scribe and understudy, tried not to sound too inquisitive, but Davian could tell he was itching to know what the missive contained.

"Oh, you have no idea, and as soon as His Eminence reads this, the entire world will know, all the way down to the lower quarter. I am sure he will shout it to the heavens, and I did not just say that. Follow me, we are about to unleash chaos."

Davian stood up from his desk striding over to grab his ceremonial robe from the hook on the wall. He liked to work without sweating too much in the heavy fabric and always wore it outside of his office. The heat lay heavy this last while, the fabric would trap his body heat and he hated wearing it inside. He put it on, belted it, placed his chain of office over top and checked his image in the mirror on the wall before he continued. His graying dark hair was still neat, even with his hands running through it, on occasion. Everything looked to be in place, his face wasn't too sweaty.

There was a slight breeze coming in through the open shuttered doorways of the Grand Palace of the Namarch, his office caught the winds exactly right, which is why he liked these rooms. Davian strode past the waiting scribe his soft leather sandals barely making a sound on the marble floors. A light flip, flop, as he marched down the hall to the small reception area his mentor the ruler of the Namanist Church used as his main working office. Thinking, always thinking…

This is monumental news. Is it real? Of course, now our life will change. What to do? How to do it? Guess I should ask my mentor if I can begin reading in the Sealed Archives. I know this is what is needed. Reading the forbidden texts. If this

is truth, then what else is there? I cannot believe it either. I am going to have to send others to confirm, to make certain it is not propaganda.

The Small Council, the Emperor and His Eminence were the only ones allowed in the small office. But small it wasn't, neither was the council. Each province or geographic area had a representative, one or two personal assistants, and it became quite the busy place. War would do this. One half of the Hall was designated to the war, an exceptionally large table of blonde wood, held maps and figurines to depict the areas of Aram and themselves. This table was almost always surrounded by the heads of the armies and different divisions.

The other side had the large desk of the Head of the Church off to one side. In the middle of the Grand Hall a Throne Chair on a dais, for when the Namarch wanted pomp. There were many smaller tables with three or four chairs around, which was usually where the religious representatives sat when there were discussions to be had. Right now, it was full, and lots of murmuring, low and steady.

Davian strode in, his expression blank, his scribe scrambling to keep up to him without looking like he was running. Some of the men at the war table looked up from their discussions, watching him stride by. Only the Lord Commander of the Army knew this look, and as he remained standing the others stopped talking and followed his eyes. Soon the room became quiet as Davian kept walking all the way to the Namarch sitting on the Throne Chair, in its pillowy softness, his attendants parted to the side, as they looked to see the reason for silence.

The Namarch was in his latter years, what hair remained on his head, circled his ears, the top bare with a few pieces white and straggly. He was a hefty man, he liked his sweetmeats, it showed in the paunch no longer hidden by his robes.

The Namarch saw his Second-in-Command walk towards him, not a hint to what he wanted, his gaze dropped to the cylinder Davian was holding in his right hand, the gold glinting occasionally as it swayed up into the sunlight with the motion of arms swinging. The Namarch motioned for the attendant in direct view to move aside and Davian took a step up onto the dais and wordlessly handed his leader the contained missive.

"What's this, Davian? News from the front?"

Davian said nothing. The Namarch took the cylinder, opened the lid, and handed it absentmindedly to the man at his right shoulder, who took it from his hand. Meanwhile behind Davian, like hunters scenting their prey, the others in the room followed him to the seated Head of the Church. Davian heard the movement of the crowd but his eyes remained on the man before him.

The Namarch unrolled the scroll and began reading the message, and as he read, he slowly rose to his feet, his facial expressions travelling from curiosity, to shock, disbelief, and then one saw the anger threatening to erupt. Many close to him, shuffled back a step, knowing his temper would soon be unleashed, and if they didn't know the cause, many didn't wish to find out, as he had quite the temper and didn't hesitate to vent it on whoever caught his eye.

"Who in the God's hell do they think they are? It's impossible! Not in my lifetime! This is a hoax! Davian!"

This last word was shouted from the spitting mouth of the now red-faced man. His countenance spotted and flushed, as he threw the scroll at Davian who had the forbearance not to flinch. The scroll rolled up as it flew airborne and struck the middle aged, handsome dark-haired man in the chest and bounced to the white marble floor. Not a person bent to pick it up.

"What is the meaning of this? We have tolerated their childish antics long enough. Why would they spread these rumours now? Do they think to cause us grief while we are retreated from the pressure of Aram? By the God!"

He sat back down heavily onto his generously padded throne. Sweat covering his face and head, the shine from the candles nearest to him, bouncing off the top of his slick head.

"I am afraid my man on the Island is to be trusted. He has never given me incorrect information, as unbelievable as this is, there must be truth to it."

Davian spoke in a level voice, as any emotion in his words would continue to irritate his mentor.

"Unbelievable! Its Ludicrous, this is pure bullshite!"

"I am afraid not. We can wait, for more confirmation, or we can act."

"Act! If we do anything, anything, the entire world will know, sooner than we want. Davian. What do you suggest?"

"Quiet. We keep this concealed while we investigate. I have sent another to confirm this information."

He hadn't, but it was something he would do. It was too incredulous not to have another account to verify. Davian's scribe bent down and snuck back with the scroll and some of the others closed in as if to shield him from the other prying eyes looking in their direction. The gasps travelled around with the scroll, it ended back up at the Throne, the Namarch's assistant held onto it after reading.

"Your Eminence," the Namarch's scribe Nader spoke up.

"The first thing we should do, is send a small contingent of highly trained men, to end the root of these rumours. Men who know the Island, have been there before, and know how to kill."

"Obviously." The Namarch calmed down a bit and Davian saw his mind was travelling.

"I suggest caution, one person. A cohort of men are too visible; they would draw too much attention to themselves."

Davian always erred on caution, and it always acted in his favour. The other man jealous of his position, Davian knew, and would always take the other road, trying hard to undermine the second to the 'Throne.' This is what Davian expected from Nader and he knew an open assault was not the direction to go about it, but if Nader would see to his own demise, Davian would assist him along.

"One person could easily fail, and we would never know. Meanwhile, they would get stronger, the Islands would wage war on us, join forces with Aram, we would not see it coming until it was too late."

Nader's narrative had the room buzzing with conversations, low enough to not cause the Namarch to raise his voice. Davian laughed at Nader, a short derisive bark.

"The Islands will not join with Aram; we have already gotten our tribute from them. We bleed them dry, where do you get these ideas? We go in quiet. Not blazing, shouting it loud."

"A small group of men is not shouting, Davian. Best to get this done and done now."

"I have a few men who would get it done with less… disruption."

"If we do it your way, no one would know it was us. We need to set a precedent. It will be expected, and we cannot disappoint."

"That is the point, they would not know who. Keep the enemy guessing. They might think it was Aram. Never show the enemy your position. Do you not study war tactics, Nader?"

Davian wasn't always here in his position; he worked hard to get to where he was. He built his network of spies, assassins, and informants since the day he was told to join the Church. The few he trusted to do exactly what he wanted, he had over the years, threatened, paid or had them in his grip. The most loyal ones were the ones who owed their lives. He made sure he kept the wheels very well greased and gave back good on his word. Those who knew him the longest left him to his aspirations, they either saw or been on the receiving end of Davian's wrath. He was not someone to be trifled with. Most of the men in the room avoided him.

"Give the Islands a thrashing."

"This is an abomination, kill them. Kill them all"!

"Show the might of Du'Lanay."

Others joined in, the most fervent were getting loud, and Davian saw the pain of a headache beginning behind his mentor's eyes. The scroll worked its way to the War Leaders and Davian saw them whispering among themselves. At least they were willing to figure out strategy. The army, now this is where he belonged.

He always wanted to join the army, but this was not his destiny. He still remembered the day his Pader came to the Barracks whereas a hopeful candidate for the army he was hanging around, usually being helpful and then learning sword and combat tactics. He remembers the anger he felt, until his Mader pulled him aside, to explain the potential. His Mader had risen from prostitute to courtesan to marry a member of the Royal Family.

"You can do whatever you set your mind to do, Davian. Think about your future. You were asked to go into the heart of the power behind the power of the whole continent. The Emperor may rule the world, but the Namarch rules the Emperor. You begin at the bottom, and you will, but you can only rise like bubbles in water. Let nothing keep you down. You are very fluid; you can absorb your situation and rise behind the shadows. Keep your own council, don't ever give anyone the power to destroy you. People will always wish to kill you. Sleep at night with this in mind.

You cover your tracks, leave nothing to chance, give yourself more than one option to a plan, always have an out. You can become the greatest power of the land if you are patient and work hard. Build your network, pick wisely, and always pay your dues. Coin does not always buy loyalty, deeds do. Be a man of your word. This will speak for itself."

His Mader gave him the best advice anyone could have given him, and he knew she rose to where she was now by sheer determination to not stay where the system would have her. He knew his placement was the last brick to be laid to cement his family's loyalty to the crown. Her death devastated him when he witnessed it, even though it was ten years since, this always made him sad.

"Davian, hey Davian, you sad for this girl?" The sound of his name broke him out of his musings; a tear snuck out and was travelling down a cheek.

"No, sorry to disappoint you, Nader, I am sad for you when you are proved wrong." Davian smiled at the ambitious man who several times tried to knock him off his game.

"Children, no fighting. We send men to Pelin'Dun, get rid of these animals, while they are weakened, this is what the missive said. They stand less of a chance of fighting back. This will end talk of a new Dragon Age. Davian, we produce a plan to rid Pelin'Dun of their rule. They kept that ludicrous dream alive, and we let them. First we rid the snake of its head, the rest will follow."

The Namarch rose, stepped down, and came up to Davian and placed his hand on the other man's shoulder.

"I wish this didn't happen in my lifetime, but it has. There was always a chance of this happening. The heretics Prophecy written so long ago was never specific with a timeline, the shooting stars may have announced it. I need you to study more, you always have clever ideas, I need your brain right now. Right now, mine is hurting, I am going to retire, you deal with this mess."

The Namarch strode off, his attendants following behind him. As he left, more men filled in the gaps and volume in the room rose until Davian stepped up onto the dais and bellowed for quiet.

"Everyone! By the God, please be quiet!"

Davian when he yelled, everyone shut up.

"For those who don't know or haven't read the missive, we know Pelin'Dun has a new Rider. The most powerful Rider they have. She burned a man alive at the Ritual; her eyes glow differently than her predecessors. Well, now it seems there is another. Not from the Ritual, this one has blue eyes and commands water. There is talk they have Dragons."

The volume in the room rose. Davian waved his hands.

"That's enough. We must think of the next step forward while Nader's plan is executed. We have finished winter solstice, we focus on celebrating our spring Rituals, getting people more involved, and squelch rumours, quietly and efficiently. We will be watched, and our every move dictates which way the wind blows. We must revive our ways; this is time for our God. Our faith will prevail! This is our time; no Dragon will take this away from us!"

He aimed his fist into the air above him and the whole room cheered.

CHAPTER 34

Solina

Great Strength Brings Death

After her conversation with her GrandMader, Solina had nothing but questions, running through her mind.

The days were spent with Sheyna and Veren, walking up the mountain to see the blooming Dragons. And blooming they were!

"Sheyna, I swear these two changed again overnight. Nannosh has changed again, this cobalt blue of scales is even more glorious! The colour variation into her breastbone and underbelly! I love the transition to white."

"Thank you, Little One. When I was younger, I had no white. It has come from many centuries, ahhh, years… hmmm, and clutches." Solina turned to Sheyna and repeated what her Dragon told her.

"So then, do you change colour more? Will you lose the blue?"

Sheyna directed this to Nannosh as she walked underneath and touched the scales, while the Dragon stood under the gaze of her adoring humans. Sheyna was not afraid of being under, on, and around the two exceptionally large beasts who would not think about harming their little Mader. Her hand caressed the white scales.

"Some of these still need to fall out. Like molting in fowl? We should get more oil. Will this help?" Sheyna was busy talking to herself.

"Tell Little Mader I will always have blue scales; I have reached my prime life."

Solina repeated what Nannosh said, the small woman was busy looking at the three-claw foot of the blue Dragon. She grabbed the back of the first elbow joint of the foot or leg and peered closer to it.

"You are developing a dew claw. See, Solina right here! Amazing!"

Sheyna was rubbing and peering closer, and Solina and Veren came around to the side while Sheyna was in-between Nannosh's legs. They took a good look and agreed it was indeed developing. Then Sheyna walked out from under the brilliant blue Dragon the other two following.

"Nannosh, can you lower yourself? I wish to show Solina your neck ridges and horns. If you are allowing me to do so."

The blue Dragon turned her head and made sure the humans were clear and then lowered down to rest. Her belly and breastbone resting on dried grasses and straw the temple acolytes changed periodically as weather dictated. Nannosh lowered her head on the straw, closing her eyes. Sheyna pointed to the horns, emerging from the crest.

"See the double crest here? Analaria has only one, which we can look at in a moment, I want to show you Nannosh first. Her face has filled out, and we can see the scales are tighter knit, and more flexible. We are busy, trying to oil them every two days or three, to keep them supple. Then, less itching for these two girls."

Solina heard the fondness in Sheyna's tone and she smiled over to Veren. His intense look of adoration was directed at the small woman who paid him no mind. Sheyna was focused on the Dragon under her hand. Solina saw the man whom she raised to Admiral was admiring her friend, so she turned back to the woman who kept on talking. Not caring if her audience was listening.

"I'll show you the neck ridges. Veren?"

Veren walked forward, bent down, and cupped his hands together beside the Dragons neck and directly in front of Sheyna. She placed one foot into his palms and he hoisted her onto the neck of Nannosh. He placed her behind the crest of horns.

"Oh, I see you have done this before. Nannosh doesn't mind?"

"Oh, no. Once I explained to her what I was about, she lets me crawl all over her."

"Yes, I remember her telling me, she cannot even feel your weight. You have no fear of heights?"

"None. If I fall, Veren is here to catch me. Right?"

"Yes. I will guard and protect the Dragon's 'Little Mader' and catch her should she fall. But, High Dragon, she has not. So, I just stand here and get a kink in my neck from watching."

"You both have worked wonders; they have the best of attendants. You work well together; I am so pleased our Dragons are looking so robust."

"So, these ridges in the neck, they function as a wind breaker… Veren took me to the shipyards one day and explained what sails do on the ships. If I…just go further to her body… and her shoulders…this is where Riders used to sit."

Sheyna walked down the ridges of the reclining Dragon and Veren walked on the ground beneath her. Solina backed up a step to see properly what Sheyna was pointing at.

"Oh. Yes, I see now. Is it comfortable?"

"Well, Nannosh is a little big for me. I fit better on Analaria; however, I assume the Riders of old had saddles?"

"Nannosh says yes. It will take some time to get fitted. She also says 'tis possible to sit wedged in there. Like what you are doing."

"Yes, and there are two horns, here, onto which one could grab. Now, I will slide down her shoulder, and Veren has never failed to catch me. Ready?"

"Yes, I am, Shey."

Solina looked at Veren, using a familiar with her friend. Her eyebrow went up, as the Dragon shifted her wing, to accommodate the woman who slid down the main 'arm' to the man waiting to catch her mid way. The two were laughing and he placed her on the ground with a bit of a twirl. Solina smiled at the well rehearsed dismount.

"Oh my. You have much practice! Almost like dancing partners. Oh, Nannosh says with your movement on her back she is now feeling a bit of irritation in the joints. Is there something we can do?"

"Well, we oiled the girls up quite well. If there is another suggestion, I would welcome it. Let's walk over to our green goddess!"

The trio walked around Nannosh to Analaria skirting around the wing now being tucked in by the resting Dragon. Solina gasped at the sight of the now fully green Dragon, who opened her eye when she heard the sound.

"Oh! She's gorgeous! Look at that beautiful green! With these two colours, it reminds me of the peacock tail feathers. Oh my! The colour on her chest! It fades to a lighter green, not unlike the colour of new grass."

Analaria rose up a bit under the admiration of Solina, then nested back down and closed her eyes. One felt the breeze as she let out a big breath through her nostrils. It ruffled their hair, and Solina sniffed.

"I cannot smell anything other than the scent of animal. Thank the Gods. I give thanks to Vendar we got them out of the mountain in time. It gladdens my heart and spirit, we will prevail. I notice Analaria has only one crest on her crown. Oh… she says she has less… oh, she has never clutched! Oh, Analaria tells me that when the Great One banished them, she was newly hatched. But full growth? No, she said she had just learned to fly. So that would explain her size."

"Will she get full growth?"

"It remains to be seen. Nannosh tells me having never clutched it may be she won't be able to. If she starts to grow a bit more, then she may. It has something to do with their spirit. Nannosh says 'tis a Dragon trait. The spirit needs to be receptive…? To be able to clutch. She's right, I do not understand."

"I wish I could speak with them; this is so intriguing. I want to learn all I can about their reproductive process. It sounds very mysterious, yet perhaps 'tis quite simple."

"I think you communicate very well with them. Anytime I can help you…?"

"You are busy… I would not wish to bother you. You have matters of state to tend to. Veren and I have our ways of talking with them. If we need a yes or no answer, they blink their eye for us."

"That sounds like you need me less. Why are you smiling at me, Sheyna? Is there something else?"

"Oh, waiting for you to notice something…"

"What? These two look magnificent. What should I notice?"

"Take a closer look. Girls. Look at our High Dragon, please."

The two Dragons raised their heads and looked at the trio, waiting patiently for Solina to make a sign she knew what it was she was looking at…

"What am I looking at? They are different sizes…their scales are distinct colours…they are looking at me… oh wait now I see it! Nannosh's eyes are yellow, like mine, while Analaria's have, can you come closer? Yes, oh, she has a red vibrancy in the iris. So this would make her the Fire Dragon. She says yes."

"That's what we were thinking. I have a question for you or perhaps Nannosh can tell me. You have a connection with both Dragons. I thought one Dragon cleaved to one Rider. Why do you hear both?"

They waited while Solina listened to the Dragons. Then she turned to the two others, waiting for her reply.

"Nannosh tells me when they reached out to me, when I was a child, the Great One said I would be able to manage the volume of chatter. I was…receptive… ummm, it seems it is part of the bond, acceptance is needed from the human to bond with the Dragon. My sister and I, or cousin in this case, we were…not forced… ummm, we were more accepting because of our blood. We were de-scended from some of the original Riders.

We know we are Riders. The others, in the lands of Aram and Du'Lanay do not. Atin knows she is a Rider now, but she has no Dragon. The Fire Dragon does not, so they are reaching out, periodically to… assess the waters… ummm, ease her mind to the possibility of a bond. They need to be gentle; there is a chance they overstep and the Fire Dragon is caught or rejects the offer. Nannosh tells me Analaria was a bit eager. Another female questioned her Rider, Nannosh is men-toring Analaria in the bond process."

"Oh, this is so interesting. We should sit in the shade over here and have a bite to eat, keep going. We must continue this discussion!"

They sat down in the shade. Solina grabbed an apple and took a bite. They were quiet while they ate some bread, cheese, and fruit.

"There are other ways to bond, as in hatching, however, she will explain if we get this far. What I gather the most important is the Rider is responsive to being a Rider. An open mind and spirit. This may be difficult for the others, living in lands which do not believe in the Gods and the Dragons. Nannosh tells me the Great One would have taken this into account when he chose the Riders. So, they will become Riders when they accept the bond.

The Great One can speak with all the Riders, but each Rider only bonds with one Dragon. So, then there is no crossover, and confusion. Which makes sense. The clamour in my head when I first heard voices, was horrific. I tried to jump off a tower; I tried to cut myself. All the time I was thinking I was going mad."

"Oh, Solina! This must have been so terrifying. I remember arriving at the orphanage. I was told you had a sickness at first, but when I saw your eyes, I was told you were a bit mad. How did you manage?"

"It wasn't until I began to read these hidden tomes, in a secret room at the Church I began to realize my voices were in fact beings. When GrandMader came to see me earlier this year, it set all this into motion. I realized my voices were Dragons, yet seeing our beauties in the flesh have made me more determined to see this to fruition. The voices do not bother me in this way anymore, mind you, I have only two to contend with."

Solina bowed her head in sadness and grabbed another slice of bread. She looked up and saw the Dragons were getting their midday meal also.

"Veren. You are incredibly quiet. You wish to say something."

"Yes. I do. You are very astute."

"I seem to be able to sense energies. Or the air around people. Much like Atin can sense aura's I am guessing. What is on your mind?"

"Word has most likely reached the Continents, by now. There are sneaks in the night we have caught, but it only takes the one we miss. We must plan for the future. Du'Lanay will send assassins, which is almost guaranteed, and it only takes one person to try. Can I suggest something, High Dragon?"

Veren was a very direct man, who called as he saw it. Solina nodded her head yes, as her mouth was full of bread.

"Can I suggest we make this known to the land, a great advent of a new age, and have the whole Island keep watch for any suspicious activity. The reward could be a glimpse of the Dragons, so people know what they guard. We have not the manpower as it is, to guard them night and day as well as the ports here and to the North. I mean, we do, however, now we must watch the western side where the Dragons are. It has stretched us a bit thin. Our first line of defence is the ports. Many eyes would add to our advantage. We can then concentrate on getting these two airborne. This is what we must focus on. Then they can travel, hunt and forage beyond our borders."

"I like your ideas, Veren, let me put this to GrandMader, she will have other ideas to add, I am sure. I am sure also the word is out. We must plan accordingly. Sheyna, you have worked wonders. They are healing nicely, and the oil idea is just what their scales needed, but the wing membranes are still damaged. They won't fly unless they have the ballast they need."

Solina stood up with a thought, she strode over to Nannosh, asking her to extend a wing out to the ground so she could explain what her idea was. She motioned to the other two who followed close behind her. The wingspan alone took up the body length of the Dragon and then some.

"This is what I was thinking. The wing membrane is a lot like sailcloth, thin and a bit see through, yes? What if… we glued, fabric underneath, for added support while it healed. Or on which ever side, but I was thinking underneath, and somehow pull the torn ends together, we might have to sew some, and would this help?"

"Yes, I like this idea, using something organic, honey?"

Sheyna could visualize Solina's ideas, but her knowledge of herbs was not as extensive.

"Hmmm, what about pitch, the stuff sailors use to seal boats? A little thicker, it would help hold longer, we could wash it off later with oil."

Veren added his ideas and the three of them sharing ideas with the Dragons adding what they thought.

"Great One, there are a few large tears on this one wing. They might require sewing them together to heal, would this hurt you?"

"Little One, after the pain and suffering over the last hundreds of years, a little more pain would be a drop in the ocean. The fluid vessels in our wings are minimal. The largest tear may require cleaning or cutting the edges to bond them together. I can bear it if you were to try mending them. I trust you, Little One."

Nannosh had various gashes which gaped wide, on the wing they were looking at. The other wing was not as bad. Analaria was in better shape, she had a couple small ones on either wing.

"Well, I will leave you two to collect what you need, we should have others to help with the application of the clothes. I am thinking we three should combine our efforts to do the sewing. Veren for his strength. You for your skills. Me just because I can communicate with them. Let me know when you are ready, the sooner we get this done, the better. I am going to talk to GrandMader and see what she has to say."

Solina said goodbye to the two young people already turning back to the Dragon talking over the ideas.

As she walked through the Temple, she saw the Pader who blessed her at the Ritual. He bowed his head to her. "High Dragon."

"Pader, how are you doing this fine day?"

Solina held no ill will towards the Head of the Church. Other than the wrongness of captivity of helpless animals, she refused to let her mind wander past this thought. It would serve no purpose. Just the thought had her getting angry. She did not want her eyes to glow, if not needed. She walked taller lately and spoke out more often. She was opinionated and Solina was still getting used to not being rebuked for her forthrightness. She did not respond much to the adulation, which was allotted to her, it was a heady feeling, and one she still wasn't used to.

"Quite well, thank you. And your charges? I am sorry for the loss of the little one, the others are better?"

"Yes, thank you. Pader if you would come with me, I have an idea to run past my GrandMader and I would like your input, if you have the time?"

She knew damn well; he had nothing but time.

"Why, yes, I do. Shall I accompany you now?"

"Yes, please, do."

They both walked together and discussed the cleansing of the caverns. Solina heard the swishing of his robes, heavy ones, she wondered at the utility of such in their clime. Out of the corner of her eye, she noticed the amount of gilded thread. A little too ornate for her.

"The caverns. What could we do with the offal inside? Do you think there is a potential for use as fertilizer?"

"I will have the acolytes investigate the uses, and I will personally bring you the results, High Dragon. You can decide what you will on the matter."

They reached the Throne Room where Dame Metina spent all her waking moments. She blossomed even more with the news she had another progeny out there, quite possibly the most powerful of them all. It was all Metina needed; it mellowed her temperament.

Metina greeted her GrandDader with a smile. The Pader not so much but smiled a political smile anyway. Solina requested the room clear so she could have a discussion privately. The room emptied. Solina sat next to her GrandMader, and the Pader took the chair on the other side.

"I had discussions with Admiral Veren. He suggested the number of soldiers we have is not sufficient to protect the Dragons as he would like. The consensus is, we think the word reached the continents by now and it is only a matter of time before they send someone or someones. His thought is to make an announcement to the masses. Have the whole Island on our side, and they can be our eyes, while we work on the Dragon's health."

Solina looked at her GrandMader, the question in her eyes. Her Gran smiled back at her.

"I see you are beginning to think ahead, good. Veren is right. We need our people to be behind us! It lessens the chances the continents succeed. We have not kept our religion, our way of being alive for no reason. This is where the entire world begins anew, and we can't take the chance it fails before it begins. What does the Pader have to do with this?"

Ever so blunt, Dame Metina was never one to beat around the bush.

"A new awakening, this is a chance, a big chance to revive the ways. We begin reciting the Prophecy, encourage worship, encourage protection. I see where the High Dragon is going with this. We light the spark, fan the flames and the entire world will light up. Our best allies, beyond our borders is the Northmen, Lanthians and the Wanderers. They can spread the word faster over there. Aram may be an obstacle, but Du'Lanay will be the toughest nut to crack. If we begin with our own people, the word will spread outward and blossom. This can be the rebirth of our faith, instead of it being under a hooded lampshade. We can finally take it off and let the light reach everyone!"

The Pader certainly had a vision.

"Hold on to your robe, Pader. Little steps. Let's get our Dragons healthy first and keep them alive. I love your vision, but we won't be anything without them. If we fail, we are doomed. Du'Lanay will not stop at anything to eradicate us now. They left us alone for far too long and we are now the thorn they feel in their heel. We won't be able to buy their patience now."

Dame Metina was always thinking about the next step.

"Let's aim for the advent of spring. We expand the ceremonies, hand out some coin, some wine also, and make the announcement then. It would be the crown on the head if one the Dragons was keen to show her countenance. But let's see which way the wind blows before we get there, shall we."

"I thought of something and it's not going to be easy to bear."

"What's this, dear child?"

"The tribute of manpower we sent, to boost Du'Lanay's army against Aram. Is there any way to get them back? Do we know how many men we sent or are still alive? Atin has four brothers over there we have sent. She will be upset if we don't try to arrange for them to return."

"We may have to accept the loss. I will see what we think of in the way of getting them back. We can not ask. Once the entire world knows of the Dragon's they may be as good as dead. We do not know how they will react. Well, we do. Du'Lanay will froth at the mouth. Aram will deny, deny, deny. Always expect the worst and be happy if the result is better. Knowing about her brothers, we cannot let this piece of information get out. The Empire would for certain use it against her. Four brothers you say. No wonder she did not want to leave her family. I would not be surprised if when the word is out, Du'Lanay sends all our people to the front of the fighting."

"How can you say this? That's not a tactical move? Or is it?"

Solina did not know everything about war she knew she should. Listening to her Gran explain things, she understood better how to plan for all scenarios.

"'Tis what some war leaders will do. Send the men who do not mean much to the effort, while they figure out strategy. The Namarch will be livid when he finds out, this is for certain. It will be a message sent; our people are expendable. We must produce ideas. Let's meet in a while to discuss them."

Dame Metina beckoned the guard to open the doors and let the servants in. She wanted her tea, and Gran had her schedule she lived by; one mustn't deviate.

Solina stood up and so did everyone else, Dame Metina reached over to hug her GrandDader, which took her completely by surprise, but she accepted the hug and hugged back.

"I am proud of you, Solina. Your Mader would be also."

"Thanks, Gran. This means a lot to me. This has been an eye-opening experience to be sure. I have so much to learn."

"Yes, you do."

The Pader left to make his own preparations. Solina left the hug and ran to catch up to him, calling at his back.

"Pader,"

He turned, almost at his door to his office.

"Yes, High Dragon?"

"I was wondering, this Prophecy, is there a copy I may look at? I am afraid I am a bit ignorant of the whole thing; I have only heard a few lines. I am very curious to the whole."

"Why yes, my dear. We have a whole library dedicated to the teachings, and all Dragon lore. It is not widely known we still have documents. To appease Du'Lanay, we had to ceremoniously burn a lot of knowledge, however, we hid the most relevant. They did not know the bulk of what was destroyed was trivial knowledge. Your GrandMader has the most precious piece of them all, you should ask her some day. When would you like to have me show you?"

He smiled down at her, and she smiled back.

"Let me get sorted up at the hollow, and I will get back to you. Thank you, Pader. Let me know your ideas for the announcement ceremony and the three of us can arrange a grand spectacle the entire world won't forget."

He agreed and Solina headed back up the mountain to speak with her friends.

She found the two of them still talking around the Dragons.

"Veren, Sheyna, I am glad to still find you both here. We are going to celebrate! We are going to announce the Dragons to the world. Gran liked your ideas, Veren. She says you are an Admiral to be proud of. Give me a moment."

"Your male companion is caring of our wellbeing; he and the small female have cared for us well. It is better than trying to remain hidden. I can not grace

the winds with my poor wings. Analaria could but if we could be bathed again, Little One, then repairs made, then we may again soar! You may do as you see fit to repair our membranes."

"Nannosh is suggesting another wash in the basin, her scales growing in are causing some itching where we haven't cleaned the first time. Her skin covering will be able to manage some scrubbing. We will get them cleaned, use smaller brushes and many more…"

"Make light the chore!" Sheyna finished her sentence and both girls laughed.

"We will wash them tonight then, if tomorrow we mend. Let's get prepared with supplies and helpers." The three of them headed back down, each to prepare and get the necessary help.

Later that afternoon both Dragons were washed, most thoroughly! More servants wanted to help, and as there were less injuries, it made for a faster wash. The brushes they used were smaller and they made sure to get under each newly growing scale. Sheyna knew the job of oiling would take just as long to perform; she informed Solina she would need more helpers for this task.

"You tell the Pader you need more, I appreciate you letting me know, but I have given you the authority to command. Anything you need, you get. These two are our highest priority.

I know your size has a few thinking of you as a child, you tell them like you expect it to happen. You shouldn't have problems, there are a few that are awestruck by them, like myself. But I will say a few words, so all know."

Solina stood up from her washing and walked out of the basin and addressed the people helping.

"We will need as many hands as possible tomorrow for the oiling of the Dragons. It will be messy, but many hands will make this chore go faster. Please see Sheyna for direction, we will commence oiling after we get the wings mended. Now let's get the other creature of ours clean."

The water was as muddy as the first time, but Nannosh sighed inside Solina's head, and she knew this time they had gotten her sparkly clean. They repeated it with Analaria, with both Dragons clean at the end,

"Tomorrow we will set the wings, and oil the remainder of the body, however, some of it will have to be whale oil. We have an abundance of this in the Harbours storehouses."

"Very well, Sheyna. You have worked wonders on our two charges. Keep up the excellent work."

Solina left to go back to her apartment in the Palace, she was tired. It was a very productive day but tomorrow would be monumental. Trying not to overthink the next day, she fell asleep to Nannosh in her head.

"Little One, I can feel your angst. I will hum for you; it will ease you to slumber."

"Thank you, I am worried we cannot repair the damage."

"Do not worry yourself. If it doesn't heal, I can still fly. It will just be more of a challenge. The Great One has many tears and cuts in his wings."

"Was he not repaired like we are attempting tomorrow?"

"He was not. He was on a rampage before he left. He may not have healed from wounds he may have sustained. I do not remember those days well. Too many things happened at once. I prefer not to remember."

"I do not want you sorrowful. Let us think about the future. There will be happiness again."

"You are right, Little One. Now, listen to my sounds, it will sooth you to rest."

Solina fell asleep quickly and woke up refreshed and ready to repair her Dragons. Walking into their resting area, she looked at both when Nannosh and Analaria rose. They left the nesting area to the grass below, to give the acolytes space to clear out the crushed straw and replace with new. She smiled at their mobility in their pace.

Both Dragons were walking very well, as large waddling ducks could be, they had huge appetites and were filling in. Ribs were disappearing, divots in the legs were diminished and the largest visual was the colour coming back into their scales. Nannosh was easily double the size of the green Dragon, and her ridges were growing larger to make an interesting figure. Solina saw the effigy in the Temple to the Mader resembled her the most.

"We have different growth to differentiate maturity... I have more horns, you call them... the Great One is older than I. He has many horns. My scales are harder. It is our armour. Many younger ones, died easier, they were quick to anger... it was a blood bath before our imprisonment. Many died."

"I am sorry. Now with just the three of you left, I promise to do everything I can to see you do not expire. I am sure the Purity Rider will be of the same mind. You have woken up way of life, shaken the rest of the world to the core. I will protect you; I swear this."

"Many thanks, Little One. I see your mind and spirit; I give thanks to the Great One you are my bond. I watched you when the Great One gave me my choice, I knew you would be strong. You managed to accept all the Dragons at once. It was a test to see if you could manage the clamour. You will be evaluated in the future."

"This was a test? I thought many times I would go mad. I was so tempted to harm myself. I realize now the voices were leaving because of the yearly ceremony and because I was testing out my talents. I am sorry I was contributing to their deaths."

"All happens for a reason. You are stronger for it. You may have to be strong for your sisters. They may also have to be strong for you. Through you, I have seen the females of your species, stand together when times are not favourable. It seems the Great One may have chosen well."

"You see through my eyes?"

"Yes, the times when you were feeling more... disorientated. Or emotional. It is the nature of our bond. What one feels, the other feels also. I hear with your ears, see with your eyes, feel your emotions. You see what I see, but it will take practice. I must preserve my energies, the Great One says, to bring forth our future. Perhaps later we can merge and learn this. All Riders can learn many things. But 'tis only if the Great One allows and ordains it so.

He may not, until the time is right. The last Riders abused the gifts. He will be cautious moving forward."

"I understand. I can wait, I have much to figure out, on the human side of things without adding Dragon talents to the mix. I have to say you look more vigorous than when I first brought you out of the mountain. I love your colouring. Your scale growth is almost complete?"

"Half. The scales I still have will drop and I will grow all new scales. Some will be stubborn. They were my full growth armour. Being drugged and kept in the mountain did loosen them up, I have lost most, but not until I have lost all and regained all will I be armoured again. I may not regain them all if I need my energy for procreating. Time will tell."

Solina had a better look at her Dragon. Noticing other details she overlooked the other day. The three claws on their wing joints had sharpened. The shoulder muscles had bulked up, leading into their wings. Both injuries on each shackled leg was healed, a scar remained, one saw the muscles underneath. Nannosh's scales had started to grow. When they washed her the first time, many had fallen into the basin. In their nesting area, there was evidence of many more. Solina noticed her flesh regenerating new scales. The blue of the new growth was quite dazzling. Not to mention the voracious amount they were consuming. Their humongous appetites had Veren send out to the other Islands to buy every animal he could get firsthand.

"Once our wings are mended, we will begin getting our muscles in use. It will help once we are in the skies, but our captivity has lessened them. I feel it when we try to use them."

"Once you feel comfortable, Great One, you can use them all you want. But let us first repair them. I do not mean to cause you pain."

The wings with the pitch were an ordeal, very messy, and Nannosh did cry out in pain when the largest of her tears was recut. It took four of the men who were not too frightened to push the flaps together so Sheyna and Solina could hurriedly sew them together. The cloths soaked in pitch were applied and Sheyna pointed out they should have applied them first. This technique was used for the other wings. After they finished, they were all covered in sap and blood. They had to be cleaned with whale oil first before Solina suggested they use the basin to wash themselves before using the bathhouses inside.

Once the Dragons were in recovery, Solina excused herself for a time,

"I must read some manuscripts the Pader mentioned. I will be here if you need, but I want to focus on learning."

"Don't worry, Lina, Veren and I have these two under control. They can build strength in their legs and shoulders. I have all the herbs I need for poultices, and it may take a month to heal the largest one. Analaria may heal first. We have the field below the nest for them to wander and build leg strength. You do what you need to do. We will be here."

After her initial shock at the sheer volume of the library the Pader showed her, Solina got to work. Her days and into some nights were busy reading, more discussions, and learning about Dragons from Riders of the past. The oil was a good call; it was used all the time. One such book reported oils were combined to max-imise effectiveness. Plants like olive had different healing properties while whale provided essential properties for moisture. If one were to extract seed and nut oils, these were also added when found. All oils were used to keep the skin under the scales supple. Growing Dragons needed the most care as they grew fast. Their skins stretched, and they itched all the time. Solina thought to put in a pile the books on Dragon care to give to Sheyna for her small library she was amassing.

She read the Prophecy the Pader gave her but felt somehow it did not sound complete.

When there is naught but shadow
A glimmer in the sand
When the advent of fire
Sweeps across the land
Thru dust and ash
Arises new life
A time long forgotten
Fraught with pain and strife
From the heavens descend
The six-pointed star
From darkness comes the light
And love comes from war
From old comes the new
The six shall rise again
Beated wings adrift
Thus ends the one man
Let fire cleanse the spirit
And reverence begin anew
Darkness will light the way
The many become the few
The ebb and flow of the seas
Bring purification to amend
In eternal springs the life source
Bringing desolation to an end

That's it? It leaves me with more questions, now. Hmmm, maybe I'll ask GrandMader when I have the chance, I mean it sounds good, we've seen the stars and their light and the six shall rise again, we have two of us so far. Let's try to decipher this later.

Solina had Sheyna brought in for when she read the tomes on care, and they had lengthy discussions well into the night. When she asked her GrandMader about the one tome of Dragons, her GrandMader said for sure she could, but it would be at her home she could read it under strict privacy.

"I do not want it known we have this manuscript, the Namarch would become livid, if he knew there was a book of this calibre out in the world. They destroyed everything the Church could find direct, and while you may read it you may not understand it all. It is meant for the wielder of mind magic, the purple gem. She may have better use for it. We need to be careful. We almost lost everything in a fire, a Namanist stole in under our noses, claiming to be Vendar, and lit a fire in our Great Library. Little did he know I have the most precious of all and almost everything the Great Library has.

Perhaps you could stay at my apartments for a couple of nights and read what you need. My servants are all loyal, I have made sure of this. The wheels of time are moving faster; you glean what knowledge you can. We will protect our library, but it may not be enough, if we have war brought to us. I tell you I have copies made of everything and hidden them in an unlikely location. Everything but this book. This book I will hand over to the Mind Wielder or the Highest of all Dragons, who would be your cousin."

Her GrandMader smiled at the thought.

Solina had never seen her GrandMader so happy in the time she was with her. While she knew her to be calculating, always thinking of the future of her house and the future of Pelin'Dun, one night at her Palace while Solina was reading, Dame Metina confided in her she always regretted the way she managed her Daders. She hoped to repair familial relations, starting with her GrandDaders, and was proud of the woman Solina had become.

"You have developed into a fine, level-headed young woman, you analyze everything before acting. You remind me of myself when I was your age. Your Mader and her sister were also very clever, I remember Miiele absorbed everything she read, and your Mader loved beautiful things. Always think two steps ahead of the enemy, always have two outcomes to every problem, and expect the unexpected. This is the only way to rule and succeed.

Carry this into the future, only use your gifts if necessary. Your gifts, if not properly bonded use the power of the Dragons and leach their essence. That is why over the years your voices dropped off one by one. And yes, before you ask, I know this, I read every scroll in the library twice. I had reports about you every year. Yona kept me informed.

There is one here which mentions it specifically. Not just you, the other DragonRiders, out in the world, may use their developing gifts, and it could impact the remaining two Dragons we have. The Dragons must regain their full strength before another of you try to wield their magic."

"Thank you, this would explain why, I never thought of it until the last year, when Nannosh urged me to hurry. So, the plans need to escalate, we get our Dragons fit and healthy. They need to get airborne, but their wings need to heal first. We need all the people to be our eyes, our ears, and our swords. We need them to be proud of our history and proud to be the people of the Dragon. Maybe we should capitalize on this. Give gifts to the people, so they have more pride and readiness in what is to come. Have training sessions, distribute food, and clothing, get everyone in agreement with what is coming. A celebration to out do all celebrations, one to be talked about for years."

"I like the way you are thinking. Buy the people with kindness, but always with the intent of protecting the Dragons, while protecting themselves. We don't necessarily need to send Du'Lanay tribute anymore. Let's not waste our riches on them, they would only be using it against us anyway. It is a moot point now. Private broker's we still invite, this is how I have gleaned my information over the years, I have a few Captains on my payroll, which will spill for the right price. Of course this will set them over the edge, the current Namarch is an old and unhealthy man. It's his successor we have to worry about. I have my run ins with him before. He's smart, and devious. And very devout."

"Mayhap this will be his undoing. The most devout are always the hardest to budge from their ideals. This would dictate his response, would it not?"

"Yes, however, you need to understand more to the equation. There can always be variables added to the mix, which would change outcomes. Like a pendulum which swings. His devotion to the faith may crumble and he may surprise us all. There are many factors, and we need to discuss them all."

"I cannot see this happening; however, I hear what you are saying. Prepare for all outcomes. This is mind boggling. You know so much, Gran."

"Which is why our economy has flourished. I am not too proud to say, we have the best trading since I first began. With the advent of Dragons, it may diminish."

"If anything, it may not. Many would flock here to see them."

"And not all will be sympathetic. Many will be commissioned to kill them."

"Yes, we will tighten our security. Veren has already begun working on this, so he tells me."

"He is a quick mind and loyal. I knew his Pader, and his family has always been above reproach. You were right to promote him. If you hadn't, I would have. Now let's discuss further plans."

Dame Metina nodded, pacing around the room, her study fully lit with torch sconces on the walls and various candle stands around the perimeter. Her plain red house robe unadorned except for an embroidered edging in gold thread, all the while thinking, the woman never stopped.

She stopped her pacing and turned to face her GrandDader,

"We best do this all at once. The spring celebrations, we distribute the coin, food, announce the Dragons, bring them all into the fold. Explain the importance of protecting what is ours. Capitalise on the new Dragon age we are beginning. You will, of course, be the one making the announcement, My Dear, the people will want to see you."

Solina gasped and began to protest, her GrandMader raising her hand,

"No, you are the new, I am the old. We prepare, I will instruct you on what to say and the best way to project your voice, but you will be the one. It would also be beneficial if your water sister were here to stand by your side. The topping on the cake would of course be the Dragons. We would have to have our soldiers disbursed among the people on high alert for any mischief. This we have Veren work on.

This is a pivotal moment in our history, let's announce it to the world and watch them quiver. The Prophecy is happening; Dragons are alive again! You and the others will come into your power and bring much needed peace and harmony to our lands. Oh, how my heart is gladdened!

You must expect that once we muddy the waters, Du'Lanay will respond. We have drawn the line in the dirt, and they will come. Maybe not in force, they are dealing with a strong Aram this campaign, so I heard, and will not be bringing any troops. I predict one boat, a handful of special trained men, and most likely at night."

"How do you know all this?"

"Why, because it is what I would do." Her GrandMader smiled.

"You need to think like the enemy, My Dear. You need to always think of every possible scenario when solving problems. The Namarch will not live forever, and you must think of who would take his place. His Second-in-Command has made his way up the ranks. I have spies over there who feed me information, over the years, and he is a force to be reckoned with. The first wave of attack will not be his. This will be what the Church's first response will be, an open declaration, it's the ones which come after. I have repeated myself, but think about the future and the various outcomes, and find out all you can on your opponents. Now there is also Aram…"

"How do you know all this? It quite boggles the mind. Do you have informants? Do you trust them?"

"Yes, to a point. I have over the years had ones who were devious, but they have fallen away to the side or disappeared altogether. I pay handsomely a few who would of course, turn on us for a mere coin, however, I know who they are and of what they are capable. One must always know the enemy, even ones close by. Always expect there are informants for the continents in our servants."

"This is why Atin would be so useful. She sees auras and could tell if anyone was duplicitous. I would like to have her here and clean house, so to speak."

Her GrandMader spoke on this subject for the rest of the night, and the following day. Solina soaked up what her GrandMader was teaching her. Making her think, uncomfortable as it was, grilling her on problem solving, from war, to harvesting, to dealing with crimes and punishments.

"You will have to deal with death, my dear. The first time will be the hardest. Furthermore you may find you have no choice."

"You mean killing someone? I don't know the first thing about a sword."

"You don't? Oh, right… You don't. Well, we should have you begin lessons. No, don't shake your head at me, young lady. You will know the fundamentals of sword and dagger. There may come a day you need to defend yourself. All of you should know the rudiments. I'll speak to Veren about starting your training."

"I am not sure I want to begin. I don't like the idea of killing someone."

Her face fell, Solina remembered the assistant she burned alive in the ceremony which started her on her path.

"That is not the way of our Gods. Vendar is a God, of love, it says in the tome of…"

"Spare me the rhetoric, Lina. You will learn at some point, and it may not be a physical altercation. You may have to pass sentence. You will live with commanding someone to die. There are many ways, that as a leader of men, you will have to deal with death. The best way is to face it directly. Do not shirk from your duties. People will see this as weakness. They will undermine you, every chance they get."

"Ruling is not easy, is it?"

"No, it is not. I have hardened my heart to it. But I have to say, now in my twilight years, having you here, knowing I have another GrandDader out there in the world, I have softened my resolve to being happier. I will mentor you, instruct you and direct you to lead your people. You are the future, with all your sisters, and most importantly the Dragons. Oh, I am so happy, Lina! You make life so much fuller for me!"

"Oh, Gran. I am glad. I really enjoy our conversations. You have taught me so much."

"There is so much more you need to know. Never be indecisive in public, be prepared where possible, do your research before hand…"

Time flew by, and Solina's head would spin with the amount of information, not only by the tomes and scrolls but the knowledge her GrandMader passed onto her. Many long nights Solina would spend pacing in her Gran's apartments, while Metina quizzed her, debated with her, and forced her to make challenging decisions. All in the name of ruling. It made her stop and think about what she may say, had her mind always planning and she began to emulate a calmness, her demeanor was becoming polished. Her GrandMader was smart, very smart, and Solina saw everything she was telling Solina had years of trial and error behind it. The woman never stopped calculating; it made her dizzy trying to understand all of what she was being told.

"I really hope you are around for a very long time; I don't think I could ever step into your shoes anytime soon."

"One day you may have to. Or delegate someone to rule while you attend the Dragons. The effects of the absence of elixir are beginning to show in the Rulers. Two are bedridden now, they won't see the summer. I am extremely tired but am managing. The others have similar issues as me. We will work through this. There may come a time to have others replace those who perish.

Either way, you need to know everything I do. I mastered this over the many years I have been in office. You may not have as much time as I did to learn. This is why I am telling you as much as I can, while I can. The future can change on a heartbeat. However, I am confident you are on the right path. From what I see you become in the brief time you are here; it makes me nothing but proud. I say this… I love you very much. I hope I meet your cousin and get to know her, as well I have you. I can let my spirit rest, when it is time, as a happy woman, knowing I passed on my knowledge to the next generation. Wait before I forget, I have something for you… It was your Maders."

Dame Metina went forward to a small desk and opened the drawer in the front face, cleverly hidden. She reached in and brought out a small dark cloth bag.

"Hold out your hand, Dear Child."

Solina came forward to her GrandMader as the older woman turned and dumped the contents into her palm. It was a dainty ruby ring. She gasped.

"Its so pretty! And tiny. This is for me?"

"Yes, it was one of two. I had them created for both girls as a Ritual present. I had no doubt in my mind the girls would pass the trials. So much so I gave the rings to them on their name day. I am glad I did. If Miiele survived long enough to bear a child, then maybe her ring was passed on to her child. This is a sure way to know the identity of the wearer is your cousin. In old Days, only those of the Ruling House could wear ruby. I am afraid I let some traditions slip by the way-side. Some traditions are too painful to bear. Seeing you bloom into a leader has sparked new life into me. I hope you will wear this and think of your Mader."

"I will, thank you dear Gran. I will cherish this the most!"

"You are very welcome. Now, I will retire. I am happy, but also tired. Good night, dear."

Dame Metina gave her GrandDader a kiss on the cheek and went to her sleeping chambers. Solina placed the ring onto her third finger, looking at it from time to time. Smiling to herself, she walked back to her sitting room, picked up a book, and kept to her reading, into the wee hours.

Solina spent long days reading, and when Sheyna beckoned her to come to the hollow to see Nannosh stretch out her wings, Solina realized the spring ceremony was fast approaching. She would send word to Atin to return to stand by her when she spoke to the people. She walked up the mountain and arrived to see Veren, Sheyna and a few of the guards milling around talking. She noticed Nannosh and Analaria spaced out from each other and walking around, wings agape from their bodies.

"How are you feeling, Great One?" Solina thought to Nannosh.

"Eager to see if I grace the currents, little Dragon."

If Dragons could smile, the teeth baring grin Nannosh showed her, had the others around her stepping back. Solina laughed and told them Nannosh was incredibly pleased. She wasn't going to spout fire!

Sheyna strode forward and addressed Nannosh and had to speak loudly as the Dragons were many paces away.

"You take it slow if you feel any tearing, at all, you stop. I mean it, that large seam is a concern. If it doesn't hold, you will have to wait another month to heal. Don't over tax it."

She stepped back as the Dragons, wings beginning to flap, churned up wind and a little bit of loose dirt.

Analaria proved to be first to grace the air, her legs bunched, and she launched her body up into the air, flying around the little valley. Solina felt her happiness.

The Dragons' thoughts flew at her, of boundless joy. Nannosh on the other hand, exercised more caution, her legs bunched up, but in testing out her wings, one knew she was cautiously favouring the one with most injury. She launched into the air, did a small circle in the immediate area, and came back down. She landed heavily on her legs and folded the wing back in. Sheyna and the others strode up to her, and she unfolded the wing, showing a couple of areas a bit raw.

"You didn't open the tear completely, perhaps in a couple more weeks you can take flight without fear of tearing it. It looked good otherwise. We will use more oil and some herbs to reduce the swelling."

Meanwhile Sheyna yelled up at the circling Dragon to return and not overdo it this first time. Analaria could practice every day but only if she didn't fly too far and too long. The Dragon listened to the young woman, as they respected her for her genuine love of them.

"We listen to little Dragon Mader; she cares for us like we were her brood."

"Yes, she has a heart of pure selflessness. She is indispensable, I do not know what we would do without her."

"We will gift her, when the time is right."

Analaria descended, more graceful than Nannosh and unfolded her wings when Sheyna came near, and Sheyna gave her a nod.

"Yours have healed quite nicely as you were not so injured. You are hungry now?" The Dragon lowered her head and Sheyna turned to the men and bade them feed the Dragons. Then walked towards her friends.

"We are going to have to think of another food source, as the volume increases, we won't be able to feed them like this for much longer. Do you have any ideas?"

Solina spoke up.

"Nannosh says while she is still grounded, Analaria can fly over the seas, and get her sustenance from the fish which live there. It will hone her muscles, get her scales cleaner, and ease the burden of what you are feeling. This hidden valley is perfect. The way to the ocean is uninhabited and the chance of being seen close to none. Nannosh's diet could be supplemented by the fishermen at the markets. They would be extremely happy for the coin. Now the ceremony is around the corner, I must take a small trip to see Atin and bring her back. Magnificent work everyone!"

She smiled back at the Dragons and left them to go back to the Palace and prepare for her trip. When she returned to the Palace, her GrandMader suggested that a herald would be more suitable.

"You need to prepare for the ceremony and here's a list of things you should consider. I have also begun a speech; you may add your own ideas. This is what I would say, given the magnitude of the occasion. You must also consider, outside the city. Veren can help with protection measures. There are still enemies close to the gates. Then there is the presence of the Dragons. Will they walk, will they fly? You look over what I have prepared, we can discuss any points you have questions on, or if you have some of your own. You may still be working on it when Atin shows up…"

"Yes, Gran. You know best. I will send for her then. Head Chamberlain?"

"Yes, High Dragon?"

"Please send Marshall Vorna here to attend to me."

"Yes, High Dragon, right away."

She instructed the herald in what he was to tell the Sea Dragon and handpicked the gifts for the family herself. They were to set sail within the week. She then took a good look at the list; Gran was thorough to the smallest detail.

Who knew ruling was so hard!

CHAPTER 35

Atin

Mastering the Living Spirit

Atin returned home after a couple of days and saw her Da had taken out the new skiff so she settled down to help clean the pearls she found and help her Ma around the hut. Both boys were out with her Da, so it was a good day to have some female bonding. She talked to her Ma about marriage and said she changed her view of the institution. She quite liked the young man who had treated her with respect. She blushed when she told her Mader she found him quite attractive. Her Mader told her about the country Kaisan came from, at least her knowledge of it.

The women are not permitted to show their hair, or learn to read, or hold any positions of wealth. Men determined everything. Quite unlike here, while they had not the means to teach their children to read on the Island, they taught them the ways of the fisher folk, respecting the world they lived in, not to waste need-lessly and to cohabitate with animals they shared the land and waters with.

"Women have a voice here; we live with our men equally for the most part. Aram and Du'Lanay treat their animals better than their women. Once you step off the Islands, you must be invisible, and that's extremely hard to do sometimes. I give thanks to your Pader for bringing me here, I love the tranquility of the simple life. I was not quiet in my youth; I caused a lot of strife to my parents. This was a way to shut me up, one day I will tell you, when you have children of your own. Only then will you understand. However, enough on this, Aram has many differences, the main one is their leader, the FirPader believes himself to be a God, the God of all."

Then there was the difference in religion her Ma said once, in the time of Dragons all lands were united in worshipping the six deities, but two brothers saw it differently, saying there was only one. One brother settled in Aram, claiming to be the all-Pader, God incarnate, the other brother traveled to Du'Lanay and claimed to be the representative of his God. One ruled with love, the other with fear, and both succeeded in swaying the masses.

Over the course of the four centuries Dragons were absent, the continents, had different views on how to rule their people. The Head of the Church, the Namarch was the power behind the figurehead of the Emperor. The two had butted heads in the past, but the Church won. He had the strength of the army behind him and the Emperor and Namarch came to terms. Atin's Mader told her of some of the horror's the Church inflicted on their people, and the narrative of rule was largely against women.

"The very beginning was a blood bath, but it was won by strength of numbers. The more territory they crossed, they gained more than they butchered. It sent the message loud and clear they were there to stay. The people did not have any Dragons to stand behind. Once the last one was gone, people gave up and gave in. There was nothing to save them. Quite a few thought the Gods had left with the Dragons. Some thought the Riders were Gods. Only the last to stand ground was the North and that land was bought, by marriages and bribery. The land across the continent, of Lanthia is still to this day shrouded in mystery, they do a tribute tax also, to keep the Empire out of their lands. Its going to be interesting what happens in our lifetime."

She continued to tell her version of history, as she knew it. Only Pelin'Dun remained true, and only by the wiles of the Rulers had they survived. Her Mader stated she was not sure how a marriage between the two of them would survive if either went with the other, she would not survive in Aram, she would wither and die, yet if the young man were to stay with them, he may have a chance. However, it all depended on his adaptation to their way of life.

"What if he never comes back?"

Atin didn't want to think when she may have a different outlook and future it would disappear just as fast. What her Mader was retelling her now, had Atin thinking the two of them were doomed before they began, she grew saddened at the thought.

"Then you continue to do what you are doing, and maybe the High Dragon will have things for you to do in the Capital. With the presence of Dragons in the world, there are going to be other wars. Vastly different ones."

"You are right Ma. It may not be the right time to marry into a controversy of religion. I should not worry either way. I am going to go and wait for Da to return, the boys should be home soon."

She went outside and waited for her Da to dock, she saw the outline and it took a short time for him to draw closer.

As she waited, she wondered what the future held, two Dragons and two Riders. What she knew about the continents was they were adamant about there being neither. She stood lost in thought until her Da hailed her out of her revere.

"Hey lass, grab the line." He threw the rope at her, smacking her in the face about the same time she reached up to grab it.

"You looked very thoughtful, are you daydreaming about your young man?"

Her Da could not help but tease. Even though she heard the jest, behind the humour was a sense of sadness.

"How were the boys?"

"She handles like a dream, cutting through the surf like a raw oyster… oh you mean the boys, yes, they are getting quite proficient."

He told her later that if it weren't for his quick thinking, they would have capsized, the skiff handled almost too well. She helped to tie it to the wharf while her brothers brought in the nets of fish.

"What do you think I should do, Da? Ma just gave me a history lesson, and it sounds like Kaisan and I will be struggling. With our religious differences, to name the biggest one."

"Lass, grab this and tie it on… you are strong. In the mind. You are stubborn like your Ma; she was the one who convinced me to bring her here. I was looking for a woman to help raise my boys, she was young and inexperienced, yet she has shown me much. She is resilient, and opinionated, to name off her best qualities. She also thinks ahead. She told me, she would make me happy. I am glad I listened to her. She has made me incredibly happy and I love her dearly.

We had our differences, not to the extreme you and the Aramite will have, but we made it work. It was not always easy for us. But talking about what it was which came between us, has made our bond stronger. You make sure whatever comes between you does not fester for too long. This can cause more strife. Address it as soon as possible, like your religious difference. First, we see if he comes back. One thing at a time, Atin, one thing at a time."

The next day was the family preparing fish for drying. It was how they survived, and the next day, and the day after that! The routine of daily fishing and pearling began again for her and several weeks went by. The routine of getting out after storms became her routine. One day, her Da said they would all go with Atin to pearl and enjoy the day doing something different.

"You want to go with me, Da? This is unexpected."

"Well, I would like to see firsthand your cove. I have not been in a while. Fishing can wait a day. We can take the new boat out; you can get a feel for her."

Atin saw her Da was in love with his new skiff and grinned at her Da's obsession.

"I have no objection. I'll help Ma with the girls."

The family packed up and sailed up the coast to the cove where Atin would extract her findings. They had a good morning, they would watch as Atin would dive down and bring up her nets, and almost always there would be an odd shaped one.

"See here, Da. In extracting, having little hands and fingers help. I always have the shell in the water, half in, half out, so the creature inside is not harmed. I ask for assistance from the Gods, if the pearl is minimal, I will leave it inside. I have found several not valuable enough to extract."

"You have mastered this almost to an art. I am not sure we will be able to keep up the volume."

"Well, Da. If I am a Dragon, you may have to move. I won't be able to protect you."

"Atin, lass. Your Mader and I have discussed this to length. The future has not been written yet. We will deal with adversity when it happens. For now, we will not worry about something which has not happened. What have we told you?"

"Not to worry."

"Yes, and do you not command the inhabitants of the seas?"

"Why doesn't Atin tell the fishes to protect us Da?" Soya piped in. Atin was using her sister to help with the extraction with the smaller shells. Atin gazed down at her sister, her mouth dropped open and Soren observed the beginnings of an idea take root.

"Why yes, Soya. Why did I not think of that? Good sister. Da? Can I have all of you come to the edge of the water? Ma?"

Atin shouted to her Ma, who was in the shade of the only large rock on the small Island with her littlest sisters. One of her brothers had fallen asleep and she saw her Mader shake him awake.

"Can everyone come here. I want to do something."

The group came to the edge of the water. The little girls were busy chasing the gentle surf on the small sandy beach.

"I am going to ask my sea friends to come here and I want to ask if they will look out for your well being. They can only protect you in the waters, so of course, on land will be another matter. Not knowing what the future holds, this would help to ease my mind I have done what I can to protect you from harms way. Are you fine with this?"

"What ever you want to do is fine with us, Atin." Her Da said very quietly.

"This way Da, you see what it is I can do. I am still in awe of it myself. If there is a man eater, do not be alarmed. They will not hurt you. You will all need to stand in the waters; the shallows are good enough. They need to sense your presence, by the vibration your body makes."

Atin turned to the vast expanse of the open waters and dove in, she sent a pulse of intention out to her sea friends and was incredibly surprised many answered. She asked them to protect her family. In the event of a storm, or invasion from one who may be an enemy.

"I am not sure how you might be able to sense intent, but if there was harm indicated, can you protect them in your way?"

There were three maneaters which came close and she rose to the surface. Various creatures surrounded her. They came out in droves.

"Selim, Da, Tarik, do you want to come out here? Touch a shark?"

Soya ran out into the surf. Her Ma trying to catch her and failing. "Can I? Can I?" She dove into the shallows before Atin could answer her, her brothers and Da walked slower, not sure about what they were about to witness. Atin dunked her head down and watched her sister swim directly to the smaller of the three sharks and run her hands on the top and grab its fin. Atin asked for the maneater to take her around for a turn, but to be mindful she could not hold her breath as long as Atin could.

The maneater rose up so its fin broke out of the water. Soya had grabbed on with both hands and her face was lit up with a huge grin. Atin broke surface,

"Hang on Soya. You are getting a ride!"

The shark slowly began swimming around the cove. When she had done a lap, she yelled to her older sister. "Can I go again? Please?"

Atin did not even have to say anything, the fin made another lap. Laughing the little girl let go and dived into the water and she kissed the shark on its nose. Then swam back to her sister.

"That was wonderful. Can I call them on my own?"

"I am not sure. They listened to your question. It may be because I am here in the water with you. Please do not attempt this without me. Please promise."

"Would they eat me?"

"I am not sure, Soya. I do not know for sure. Tarik, Selim, do you want to get close?" Tarik nodded. He dove down and swam to a shark and ran his hands on the snout of the double row toothed beast. He rose to the surface and swam back. His face said it all.

"I'm good." Selim was cautious, and Atin did not press him.

"Da?"

"As much as I don't want to, I am afraid this may never happen again."

"Would you wish to see the whales? They are further out, and we can go by maneater. Much like Soya's little swim."

"Yes, I would. Let's just tell your Mader. Boys, can you take Soya back to shore and let your Mader know what we are about. We won't be too long."

"Yes, Da. Soya, come on, Atin is taking Da out of the cove, we will wait for them with Ma."

"Awe, why can't I go? No fair!"

"Sorry, Soya. When you are a stronger swimmer, perhaps we can do this."

"Oh, all right. You promise?"

"Yes, I promise. Now go and help Ma, she looks like she has her hands full." Atin looked at her Pader. "You ready?"

"Yes."

"We'll just swim aways, grab onto the fin when it rises."

"I won't hurt it?"

"No, Da. They'll be fine."

The two of them swam out into the deepening waters and two fins rose beside them. After grabbing onto the fins, Atin's family watched them shrink as they travelled out of the protection of the cove and into the dark waters. There was a bit of chop starting up, the storms hadn't abated fully. Hanging onto the fins, Atin could see her Da's face as he noticed the spouts rising in the distance.

"Will they get closer? Won't the sharks go after them?"

"Not while we are here. I seem to have the effect on them; they remain harmonious while in my presence. Plus, I asked them to not eat each other."

"Oh, that's good. I don't want to be in the middle of a sea battle."

Soon the whales were just below them and slowly rising to the side. Atin saw and felt the vibration of their presence.

"Just hang on Da. Unless you want to let go for a bit. I am just going to dive down for a view. I have never been this close. I want a good look."

"I am good to hang on, lass. I feel like my arms are like jelly. I can look from here. If your maneater friend is fine with me doing so."

"Yes, he will stay afloat for you. Do not worry."

Atin dove down to see a small pod of whales. It was a male and female and their small baby. Except this was the largest whale species she had ever seen! The baby alone was larger than her Da's skiff! She swam up to the male who rose to the surface, she ran her hands on the barnacles which crusted the scales of the male. She brushed a few off and then began to take off as many as she could. She felt the thanks emanating from the male and almost forgot about her Da. She rose to get a breath.

"Atin! There you are! I was beginning to worry."

"Sorry Da. I was cleaning this glorious male, from crustations. He is covered in them."

"Perhaps you could do this service another time. We have been out here a while. We should get back to your Ma, and the lunch she prepared. You have given me an exceptionally fine gift today."

"You are right, Da. I'll be right back." Atin dove down and hovered while she thanked the whales and her ride came back to get her. She rose and grabbed the fin.

"All right, Da. Off we go!"

They arrived back in the cove and Atin and her Da let go of the maneaters wading to shore. Her siblings already eating. Soren sat down heavily and Atin's Ma handed him a salmon sandwich. He took a few bites before he spoke.

"Atin. That was wonderful. Thank you for the gift you shared with us. You have shown what true bonding is about. Seeing the great whale up close in his habitat was amazing. I will cherish this time spent, and your talents with the aquatic creatures. You have a gift. A precious gift."

"You are welcome, Da. I have much to learn. Solina says each Rider has unique talents. She is just learning about hers. I can direct water to move through air; she can manipulate air. I can speak to all the creatures of the oceans. She can speak to the Dragons."

"Will you be able to speak with a Dragon?"

"Not until I get one. There is only two remaining…and the Great One, but he has his Rider on the continent. It seems one of the Dragons, needs to procreate first. I may not get a Dragon right away. So, I am not sure. I will have to wait. Thanks, Ma."

"Well, you may get your husband first, if he is able. You will have to tell him."

"I know. I am not sure how this will work. If I go with him to his country, will I be welcome?"

"You may not be able to marry him. You must think about what you are. You are a DragonRider, Atin. There may be grave consequences to you going to Aram."

"What do you mean?"

"I am talking about you being a Dragon. Aram only believes in the FirPader. One God. Atin, think closely on this. You will be an abomination."

"Oh, I never thought about this. I was only thinking about our religious differences. Not the Dragons. I guess I can't go there. At all."

"That is correct. You would be killed. Regardless. If Kaisan was the FirPader himself, you represent something in which they do not believe. You probably would not be even allowed to set foot on their soil."

"That's a bit harsh."

"Their culture is harsh. They are stricter with their women, but in some ways, they do revere them more. More than the Layanese. You hold a position of power. Power to an Aram means only men are possessing of power. That's two strikes against you right there."

"I guess if Kaisan comes back, it would be best to find out his intentions and we have this discussion before we wed. If we wed."

"Yes, you need to talk with him. All good marriages start on a foundation of communication. If you cannot talk out your differences, then it is not even worth considering moving forward with the union. It would be doomed before you started. No need to break any hearts if it was not fated to be."

"Thank you, Pader. You always have the best advice. I love you, and Ma, very much."

"And we love you, lass. Our very own DragonRider."

Atin and her family spent the rest of the day, gleaning pearls, they sailed home with their bounty. She was happy in her surroundings. She was at peace. For about a day, then her fears began to creep in like the tide. Little by little, eroding the sands of her thoughts.

Will he want to live here? Will he be arrogant? Oh, I hope not. One thing I cannot stand will be a man to tell me what to do and how to do it. Someone like Da, at least he listens when Ma has something to say, and she listens to him. I would like this. I hope Kaisan does not have the unpleasant habits of an Aramite. Oh. Who am I fooling? He is an Aramite. He will have his ideas of a woman's place. Maybe it will be for the best if we don't try. I must be dreaming. He probably won't even come back.

She began to wonder if her man asking for her hand had been but a dream. One morning her littlest sister bounced on her mat,

"Wake up, wake up, Atin! There are big boats in the harbour! Wake up!"

"I'm awake. You can stop bouncing on me. Oooff!"

It was not even daylight yet, the sky was just showing its colours, her Da and Ma were also rising from their mats. They all rushed outside in their tunics and leggings to see the silhouettes of two ships, sails down, and anchored. She assumed them to be with a small boat already halfway to them. She looked at her family.

"No one says anything about Dragons in front of the Aramites. They might kill us."

Atin looked at the littles. Her Ma bent down to the little girls and Atin looked at her brothers.

"Say nothing. The Aramites might harm us or kill Ma and Da and take you hostage. And your sisters. Their way is harsh, and we do not need them to know about me. Have I your word on this?"

Both boys nodded. She looked back at the ships. She saw an arm waving. Atin knew then it was Kaisan. She smiled and ran out to the boat when it grazed the bottom on the sand. Kaisan jumped out with a few crewmen, helping to pull the boat in, then turned to her, grabbing her hands, bringing one to his lips and kissing it.

"My dear Atin, it has been a very long month, but here I am, and all is well."

He then turned to her Pader shaking his hand and asking if he could talk. Kaisan turned requesting that the men return to the boat and bring back the goods he brought. Once his men had gotten halfway back, he spoke to Atin and her family.

"I was denounced from my family for saying I would be marrying a woman of Pelin'Dun. They do not want me back. My employer also let me go, as much as he did not wish to, but his hands were tied by protocols, and he did not want to break traditions. So here I am, with all that I own, the boats will return to Pelin'Dun and continue under a new Captain, however, if I am to call, he would answer my summons. He is like a brother to me. He would also like to continue the pearling business we established together. Am I still welcome?"

"Yes, yes you are."

Her Pader embraced him stating he could marry the two, once Atin said her piece. Kaisan looked at her, Atin looked at the man, worry etched in her face.

"If you would walk with me to the falls, I will say what I need to say. You can decide whether you stay or go."

"Yes, you sound very serious, I hope there is no impediment. One which cannot be fixed."

"Just wait, let us get there and I will say my piece."

She grabbed his hand, pulling him along the trail not saying a word. Kaisan glanced at her from time to time along the short walk until the trail ended and opened to a small grove where a beautiful waterfall careened off mossy rocks. It was so serenely quiet the surf was no longer a contender to the sound of the water tinkling gently into the pond. She led him over to a couple bare rocks by the water's edge. She sat down, and he sat on the one opposite her. Kaisan looked at her, a little concern showing in his face.

"You have second thoughts of marriage? I can convert to the old ways; I do not care as long as I am with you. You are in my dreams this past month; all I have been able to see are your blue eyes. I understand women pass on the family name, and I am prepared to fully do so. I will do whatever you ask of me. I have nothing to offer you for a dowery. I do have some goods. I could help your family with fishing. I am sure your Da could teach me."

He looked so sad and forlorn that Atin smiled, "No second thoughts, but you might when I tell you this. You say the old ways, but for us it has always been THE way. There have always been six Gods, always six Riders, or Rulers, and at the heart of it all, we've always believed in Dragons."

She paused for him to fathom what she may say next. He looked at her puzzlement in his face; he opened his mouth to speak but she held up her hand. He closed it again and waited for her next revelation.

"We have never lost faith in what we believed. It is our foundation; our Gods have never let us down. We have never changed our religion to suit man's belief in himself, so when I helped the High Dragon release three Dragons and help them to health, I was humbled."

Kaisan's gasp at her admission had her smile sadly,

"Then what is the matter, my dear? I heard the rumour come to Aram soon after I arrived, but I did not know you were involved. And yes, it has stirred the water in the pot. Discussions on what to do next are on everyone's tongue. It will change everything as we know it."

He grabbed her hands and held them lightly. "There is more you wish to say?"

She stood up still holding his hands and he rose with her. Gently disengaging her hands from his, she walked backward to the edge of the pool.

"You see, dear Kaisan, I am also a DragonRider, I command water." The water swirled around her feet, and she had the spray from the waterfall create swirling patterns and dance as birds in flight and dolphins jumping waves.

His expression was to stand there with his mouth agape, and he sunk to his knees in the sand, little bit there was at the edge of the water. He watched as the water danced in front of his eyes. He looked back at the blonde woman standing, feet in the pool and her eyes glowing brightly. He was dumbfounded, and enchanted. A smile erupted from the amazement; it lit up his eyes. She noticed his eyes were a lighter hazel shade, she was mesmerized at his undivided attention and she began to flush at his next comment.

"I always knew there was something special about you the first time I saw you. I didn't know this was it. We were brought into each others life for a reason, I have always been drawn to you, respectfully and with admiration. This last month I analyzed the feelings I have in the brief time I have known you, and I do adore you. You being a DragonRider and having these talents only makes me adore you more. I accept you the way you are if you will accept me for who I am. We can only be in each others' hearts. Whatever the future holds, I would be proud to be by your side."

He stood up and moved forward to grab her hands. As she came out of the water the dancing waterfall spray ended.

"Do your eyes always change colour like this? I loved your blue eyes before, however, now I think you bewitched me. 'Tis like watching the silver of the moon Dance on the waves of a daytime sea, I will love you until the day I die. If you will allow me to love you as such."

He pulled her close staring down at her very intently, she flushed even more. Her heart was beating at the bottom of her throat and she cleared it somewhat noisily. This action had her face flaming hot, she knew he noticed her discomfort. He was leaning towards her by pulling her hands towards him, his voice softened as he drew her close, he asked,

"Will you let me seal my oath with a kiss?"

"Is this the way of your people?"

"No, this is how I want to barter a deal with my very own pearlier."

She smiled, their faces were barely inches apart, she felt a pull towards him, it was a natural force, and she did not fight it.

"A double handshake doesn't have any value?"

"Not under these circumstances, no."

He lowered his head and gently kissed her. She leaned into him as she returned the kiss. They broke apart as they heard someone calling her name, he saw the blue in her eyes brightened and then watched it fade away. He took her hand, and they proceeded to the path as one of her brothers came pounding through nearly running into them.

"The sailors have finished unloading the goods you brought sir. They are awaiting your next instructions, Da sent me to find you."

Tarik did a slight bow to Kaisan, Da was teaching the courtesy of manners, as in all business dealings. Atin smiled, ruffling his hair, which had him shrugging and ducking out of it, racing back the way he came.

They walked back hand in hand again, smiling and emerged to see the crewmen, her parents and siblings waiting by the ship's boat.

"What are your orders, sir?"

"I will be staying here with this family. You are now the Captain of my fleet. You may return after a month for pearls and continue the trade I have secured. They will be ready for you then."

"Yes sir, thank you for your faith in me. I will treat these vessels like they were mine own."

"If that is agreeable, My Dear?"

Kaisan addressed Atin, which shocked the crewmen, but they said nothing.

"Yes, we should have some for trade, but we will have to satisfy our other clientele. There cannot be a monopoly, or others will come here seeking their own. I do not want a repeat of the last man who tried."

"Ohhh, then this rumour was truth. We thought the man was in his cups a little bit too much." He looked at her with genuine care. Atin smiled back at the man she was beginning to admire.

"I hope I can be there to protect you next time. Sir, before my men go, I have a request to ask, may we be joined now, in front of my men, so they can take what they see back to my Patriarch? I want there to be no doubt as to my marriage, and they will not bother to send someone to bring me home."

Her Pader and Mader looked startled and as her Da said yes, her Mader said to wait just a moment.

"Come, dear child, we will have you joined in some finery."

Atin and her Mader hurried into the hut then hurried back out, Atin changed into a tunic her Mader finished sewing and a few shell and pearl necklaces she was making. As the two women approached, Atin was busily finger combing her hair out. It hung on her body in gentle waves, and she was receiving a few looks from the crew. Few Aramites saw different races and she was a beautiful distraction from their normal. The men were careful to school their faces to neutral when Atin and her Mader finally stopped in front of the small crowd of men.

Oh, my. By the Gods, this is happening! I am not even prepared. Oh, I hope he likes me. Oh, my. Breathe Atin, breathe.

Atin smiled hugely and the congregation watched as her Pader said the old words of marriage.

"The Pader blesses the joining of these two who have expressed their desire to be one. We have gathered on this beach to witness the union between Atin and Kaisan and give our blessing as well. May the Mader bless the couple with a healthy and caring marriage. May Viana bless the couple we have before us with many children, Vandric give them strength and perseverance to battle any discord from outside influences. May this young couple serve themselves and Vuzian by keeping their oaths to each other, may Ilyan bless them with forgiveness, and hope when there are storms. All here today add our blessings to that of the Gods we worship, may we keep our faith in them and the young couple who have come before us. Who is here that would take this Dader of the Gods as a wife? To care for, be one with and love for the remainder of their natural life?"

"I, Kaisan, formerly of Aram, do take Atin of Pelin'Dun as my wife. To have and to hold and to love with all I am, as a man. I have denounced my religion, my country, and embrace a new life with Atin, and take her name as my own. I will love her with all my heart, care for her and protect her from all harms. This I pledge before these witnesses, of both lands."

"I, Atin of Pelin'Dun, do take Kaisan formerly of Aram as my husband. I embrace his willingness to marry outside of his country, to love him as I know, and to protect him from all harms. As Iris blesses this union with health, I also pledge to keep our marriage healthy and serve him in all I know. May it be Blessed with the fruit of our loins, and may we keep it in all faith, serve each other in love. This is sworn before witnesses from each land today."

The men spoke words of the witness, and then Atin's Mader spoke hers. The crewmen started again at this. Kaisan later explained women never spoke in the ceremony in Aram, her representative was always a man.

After the ceremonial words were spoken, and the crewmen returned to the ship they would sail to Peli, Atin's parents welcomed their new son by law, with hugs and then her little siblings, the boys shook hands, but the littles all gave him hugs. They had a lunchtime feast. After the feast, Atin's Mader began packing food in a basket, and Atin asked her what she was doing.

"Why I was thinking you take your new husband to your Island to show him your pearling farm and show him how you do things. It will give you privacy away from curious, prying eyes. Vandric knows we have many of those here. Stay away for a few days, get to know each other. I am sure your Da will want to steal him away to fish, you may be fighting over him in the future."

She smiled a knowing smile, and Atin would soon know what the smile would mean. Atin looked at her husband, suddenly shy, and he grinned, and taking the basket from his Mader by law, thanking her and grabbing a pack from his pile of goods on the beach. Turning to her Pader he asked what he should do with his goods.

"Most of this is clothing, which may not suit this clime, but I brought all that I own. Is there a place where I may place it before we leave?"

"Don't you worry none. My boys and I will carry it to the new hut we have been building the other side of the waterfall Atin took you to. While it will afford you two the privacy newlywedded young people will need, we are not so far away to not be heard. We will finish the roof while you are gone and move all Atin's things there along with yours. Your new home will be ready for you when you get back. Take your time, glean lots of pearls, we will understand though if you come home empty handed."

He grinned at Kaisan, and his wife punched him gently in the ribs.

"Soren, please, the littles, you'll embarrass them." She smiled too. He looked at Atin's Ma and Da.

"Thank you, for the gift of the home. This means a great deal to me, welcoming me with open arms and with no prejudice. I will do good by your Dader."

"Of that I have no doubt. If you were to wrong her, it's not me you would have to answer to."

Atin gave her Pader and Mader big hugs at the mention of the home, this was too much to take in and she didn't hear what her Pader had said quietly to Kaisan when she was hugging her Mader.

Soon they left, Kaisan carrying the pack and Atin the basket. After they emptied it of its edibles it could be utilized for pearls. She looked forward to showing him what she did. It was her way of accepting him as part of her family. They grabbed the canoe from its hiding spot, checked it over, and then set out for the other Islands. Atin explained all what they did for fishing and Kaisan asked so many questions she was truly at ease with him, her now new husband.

When they arrived at her place they carried the canoe up onto the beach, she noted it was easier to manage when the strength on the other end matched her own. They placed it on the hard packed ground where she had created an area to sleep. It was behind the large rock which provided shade and a bit of a windbreak. Kaisan unpacked a blanket laying it down on the packed earth, Atin commenting she slept bare on the ground, no bugs dare come into her circle. Kaisan explained it was there if needed.

"I am uncertain as to what we should do next. I, ummm, dive naked, to pearl, and I ummm, feel a bit awkward right now."

Atin looked down at the sand beneath her feet, not sure where to look.

"Would you feel more comfortable if I were to disrobe first? Then this may make you feel more at ease?"

She nodded, watching as he removed his headdress first. He had longer hair than hers, all wound up in the fabric of the turban. Her curiosity peaked, and she didn't notice when his tunic was off, he stood there in his cloth pants and she, focusing on his long black hair, asked him if she could touch it. He said by all means and she took a step closer, running her hands through his hair, not realizing he was watching her.

"You have beautiful hair, Kaisan, it is so long, why is this?"

"It has to do with our religion, but if I am to renounce it, I could cut it off."

"Oh, no, I love it! It is beautiful. It would be a shame to cut."

"Not as beautiful as your glorious blonde hair, you look so... I am spellbound!"

She looked at him in wonder as he gently bowed his head to give her a kiss on the lips, not caring her hands were still wound in his hair. She returned his kiss and finding it was quite pleasurable, deepening into a need she wanted more of.

The kiss broke apart, his hands on her waist, hers still trailing his hair and then his chest. She looked at him, running her palms on his muscles, never having touched anyone's skin before. His skin was a bit browner than hers, and his muscles while not overly large were well defined. She unknowingly licked her lips, Kaisan took her mouth once more in a more searching kiss, deepening it and making Atin moan in pleasure. He picked her up at the hips, sliding his hands under her bottom turning back to the blanket he had laid down, slowly kneeling, he lay her down.

Ahhh, she thought, he planned for this! The thought made her smile, and he broke the kiss off.

"What makes you smile?"

"Ohhh, the blanket, you knew."

"Umm, yes, I always come prepared."

He smiled back down at her.

"Actually, I come from a land made purely of sand. I know what it feels like when it gets where it shouldn't be. Very unpleasant when it gets in the cracks."

Bending down he engaged her in another kiss. This time his hands crept from her hips onto her stomach and then her breasts, reaching under her bodice to tease her nipples making her gasp with pleasure. He stopped and she tried shucking her tunic off by wiggling her body. He raised himself up, helping her up and off with the tunic and to untie her bodice. He helped take this off then reached out and put his hand on her breast, massaging it as she lay back down. He bent down, taking the nipple into his mouth, rolling his tongue over and around it and then the other, her back arching with the pleasure of it.

He undid her leggings, and she raised her hips so he could pull them down, and off. He then pulled her loin cloth off and kissed her lower belly. She closed her eyes, and after a moment of rustling realized he had taken his trousers off too. He came back to her lips. She opened her eyes, watching him looking at her as he kissed her. It was the most incredible feeling. He broke off the kiss.

"Your eyes are glowing. This is the most glorious thing I have ever seen. It makes me want you even more."

She said nothing just smiled and gasped as his mouth kissed her neck and then lower to her breasts.

"I want to taste every inch of your body. I will worship you with everything that I am."

She moaned as her nipples were sucked, massaged, and licked. Atin realized he was going lower and lower. He parted her legs, with his hands and parted her nether lips with his lips, tongue searching her lower region out until he found the very thing he wanted. Licking her nub until it hardened a bit.

She started to moan with a feeling of wanting something, her energy was charged and she looked at her new husband with lidded eyes.

"This will prepare you for the union of our bodies. It will only hurt the once, and then you will feel pleasure like no other."

He rubbed her nub with his finger and inserted it inside her, gently stroking her insides. She writhed with an unknown pleasure; unlike anything she had known.

"Ooh, what…?"

As she began to ask him what he would do next, he raised himself up to her face kissing the very question away. He looked at her intently. She looked puzzled but then something larger was gaining entry. She felt him enter her, not feeling any pain, she felt the pressure building again. As he withdrew from her, she moaned…

He slowly went back in. She moved her hips, bending her legs and adjusted herself as he moved in and out. She began to move with him,

Moaning all the while. He began to move faster, and she moved with him, panting and grabbing the sand beneath the blanket. As the pressure was building with his movements. She crested the peak, grabbing him with her legs, riding the wave of pleasure, he was giving her, not caring that her moans were loudly echoing in his ears.

He kept on until she began to ebb, and his pleasure came soon after hers. The pulsing of her core, binding him until he exploded inside her, releasing his seed.

He shone with a light sweat on his skin and he gently lay on her. When his manhood finished its dance inside her, he pulled out and lay beside her. Atin faced him, he saw her eyes were fading their glow. Moving his body onto its side, he placed his hand on her hip, then ran it along her side from waist to hip to bottom.

"Was this fine, My Dear? Your eyes were very bright. I hope that I can always make them glow with desire. It makes me feel very virile and eager to please you."

He then kissed her gently on the nose.

"Is that what pleasure is all about? I feel different, like riding on top of a wave until it lessens at the shore."

"Yes, I hope to always make you want to ride waves with me."

He pulled her on top of him. She felt awkward until he palmed her breasts in both hands and began to massage them. She could feel his manhood beneath her, mingling warmth with wetness, and she adjusted her body down a bit which had him gasping. So, she wiggled again, his hands leaving her breasts to hold her hips. He showed what movement to do. A back-and-forth movement, which soon had him hard between her legs.

"Now if you raise yourself up, we can put him in again and you can dictate what you want to do to me."

She did what he suggested. As she lowered herself on his large and wet manhood, she felt a stab of pain, but it quickly disappeared when she raised herself up and his hands guided her into a rhythm that she lost a few times…

"Let's try a different position, like this…"

They spent the whole afternoon, making love and trying all sorts of positions which had her begging a reprieve after a couple more hours. Not that she didn't want to, he opened a whole new world to her, and he gloried in her orgasms, but she was beginning to hurt in the area he made love to.

They ate more food, she was ravenous, and watching the sun set, they curled up in each others' arms to sleep the night away. Waking up at the rising of the sun to join some more, her moans waking the nesting birds nearby and setting some of them to fly off. This made him howl with laughter which only set the rest of them to rise, and she called a truce, for the time being.

"I am a little sore in the lower region, lets wash and go for a swim. I would show you, my craft."

They rose and she walked naked to the water. He followed her and after her first dip into the ocean which stung on initial contact, for the next couple of hours she showed him her pearling methods, not realizing he couldn't stay down as long as she could.

Staying down too long she came back up to find him on the shore pacing, and a little bit angry at her for scaring him. Grabbing her and hugging her,

"I was frightened. Now I have found my other half, I don't want to lose you."

"I am sorry, this is normal for me, I did not realize…mmmm," which turned into another couple of hours of activities. After another food feast, she picked herself up, telling him she wanted show him the other area she considered hers. Gathering the shells they emptied of their bounty, he most graciously carried the net for her, walking past the bird nests her voice had disturbed.

Atin and Kaisan tossed off what little clothing they had on, wading into the pool, then diving in. She pointed out the areas she dropped the shells and he let the net open, the shells floating down to rest on the bottom of the shallows, as she motioned for him to rise. When they both broke into the air,

"Do you trust me, Kaisan?"

"With my life,"

Not knowing what she was referring to. She motioned for him to take a deep breath, and they dove under again. She held his hand, and they waited. To his amazement, the denizens of the ocean came from the deep to pay homage to her. They swam close, hovering in clusters around them. He saw turtles, a white whale who could not come too close as it was too shallow, several types of colourful fish, and the one which had him hide behind her shamelessly was the eaters of men, sharks! They came close enough for him to see their double rows of teeth and his hands tightening on her shoulders reminded her he needed air. They rose to the top and as he breathed in a breath of air and turned to face the ocean, he saw the fins turn and swim away.

They swam to the shore wading out of the shallows, his expression of wonder, his dark hair, laying down his back dripping water onto his naked body. Looking at him,

"You are the most beautiful man I have ever seen. You are mine!"

"You are beautiful, my love. That was the most wonderous thing I have ever witnessed. I will never forget this moment for all my life; you have a gift. You are my beautiful wife, and I have never wanted you more than now."

In a fit of lust, he grabbed her by the bottom, lifting her up, placing her on his cock. It knew exactly where to go, he leaned her against a large rock and drove her against the smooth surface, his feet sliding constantly in the sand and his hardness almost popping out. They managed to climax together, and they held on to each other for a while her hand trailing in his wet hair.

"I am not sure we have enough food to last a few more days if we keep gorging it down, you made me ravenous with all this exercise we are doing. Not I'm complaining. Not at all. You made me the happiest of women, but I am very sore now. I would hate to not share our pleasure together because we made it such."

"I agree, but I can not keep my hands from wanting to touch you. You are my golden angel, and when you reach climax your eyes glow so brightly and I cannot stop, knowing you enjoy our love as much as I, makes me the happiest of men. I have fallen deeply in love with you, my water angel, you have my heart. Forever and always, as long as I have breath in my body, it is yours. I will strive to be worthy of you and keep you happy."

They walked back to their camp, only to learn the local winged inhabitants had flown off with the rest of their lunch packages.

"Well, I guess it is decided for us. Shall we go back today? With only a handful of pearls, what will they think?"

"I am sure they knew well we wouldn't be doing much in the way of diving, at least for pearls."

Here he smiled remembering how they had pleasured each other with their mouths. She blushed at the memory, punching him lightly on the arm.

"What happens if the world turns over on its side, with the knowledge of Dragons? What if they come after me?"

She could not help but wonder about the future. He drew her into his arms and told her.

"Whatever gets thrown your way, I will stand in front and protect you as best as I am able. This I swear. I have never loved anyone as I love you, and I never will. You are my heart."

Placing her hand in his over his heart, she fell asleep cradled in his arms.

Later that day, they packed up what meager items they had, put on their clothes, which after a couple of days not wearing much if anything, felt a bit constraining, and left to return to the homestead.

As they arrived back in the setting sun, she saw her Da hand something to her Ma. When she asked what it was, Niena laughed saying she and Soren had a bet on when they would return. She won and he had to pay up. Atin grew embarrassed at the fact her parents would bet about something like this, but Kaisan laughed with them.

"I have gotten your home ready because I knew, not just from the bet, that you would be back early. Your Ma doesn't know everything."

This last bit he directed at Niena, she laughed back at him.

"Here eat first."

They sat down to the evening meal. When Atin brought out her small bag of pearls, her Da just laughed even harder. Atin excused herself, Kaisan following, telling her she would have to get used to the ribbing of males, their sense of humour was different.

"If you say so,"

She said in a huff, and they walked into their hut exclaiming at the thought and care. When Atin saw the sleeping mat she sighed, laying down with Kaisan crawling in beside her and holding her in his arms as they fell asleep together, exhausted.

The next day, just like her Ma had said her Da stole her husband, the men went out to do a day of fishing with the two eldest boys.

"I don't mind the rest, Ma. I am so sore down there. We had a lot of activities…"

"It will pass. The first time is always the worst. Give it a moment of rest. Your man is very pleasant. His manners are flawless; he must have a good upbringing. I was always believing Aram men were arrogant and rude. Your Pader had dealings in the market with others and left him with a different opinion."

"Yes, he is very pleasant. Very pleasant, indeed."

The next month passed by quickly. Every couple of days, the two of them would go 'pearling' and then after, Atin's Da and Kaisan would go fishing, she barely brought anything back and one day she commented that when the ships came back, she would not have enough to sell. Kaisan pulled her aside later.

"I have enough funds to keep our family without the pearling."

"That is up for my Da to say. Until such time that we move away, he is the Patriarch, and I have worked hard to ensure they have the means to survive should I ever move to the Capital."

"What do you mean by this?"

"When people know I am a Dragon, I do not want them coming here and harming my family."

"I will stay at your side. I swore to protect you with all that I am. I will stand…"

"Atin, Atin, Kaisan, there are boats arriving. Hurry." Soya came running into their hut. They walked out to the shore, watching as the ships came closer.

"Are the ships yours, Kaisan?"

"Yes. Yes, they are." The ships dropped anchor, and a smaller skiff was dropped.

"The colours they are flying. It is Pelin'Dun business… it seems to be red and gold, Atin. It must mean they are here for you."

"You may be right. I wonder what Solina requires."

"We will find out, Dear Heart."

The boat docked and the herald walked up to Atin handing her a rolled-up scroll. As she could not read it, she handed it to Kaisan.

"I can only catch a few of the words. I do know your language, but I had difficulties in childhood grasping the written word." He began to read but hesitated on some words, putting her hand on his arm, Atin addressed the herald.

"Do you know what the message contains?"

"Yes, Sea Dragon. The High Dragon invites you and any family member who cares to attend the spring celebrations which she will announce the advent of the two Dragons which live on the mountain. She would like to have you at her side to make these official announcements. We are to bring you; hence the celebrations will begin in a week's time, and she would like you to be well rested beforehand. You and your family will stay with her at the Palace and be well looked after. She has also included some gifts for those who choose to remain behind."

Looking at her Ma and Da and at her husband, they all started talking at once.

"If one goes, we all go."

"Soren, how will we manage? We can not leave our home empty. It invites anyone to squat and take over."

"Sir, ma'am, the High Dragon has prepared for this. I am instructed to inform you a small regiment will remain behind and protect your home for the time you are in the Capital."

"Well, I guess 'tis settled then." Atin looked at her parents smiling, "I hope you like it, it is very grand, but not my style, I like a simpler lifestyle myself."

Her husband gave her a squeeze, kissing her on the cheek. "That is one of the reasons why I love you, Dear Heart."

They packed their meager belongings, and all clamored into the small boat with the crew, heading towards the bigger of the two ships where Kaisan's Captain was waiting. They arrived on the deck and a dozen men set off back to shore, with strict orders to not Damage anything. They would be back within the week. As they set off Atin called down to them,

"I thank you for your service in this endeavor. I regret you will miss the ceremonies and give you my thanks for your sacrifice." A few nodded back at her acknowledgement.

The trip to the main Island was uneventful. They talked about what the ceremony would be like and Atin said nothing about the Dragons. Her brothers were chatterboxes, and she wasn't sure if the beasts were common knowledge to the sailors. They arrived at the Capital dock and two carriages were waiting for them. The family was big enough; her two brothers sat with her and Kaisan in one while her Da and Ma managed the rest. As they arrived at the courtyard, Solina was standing with a few people. An older version of her, the young man and the very tiny woman who helped with the Dragons.

She alighted, waited for her husband and brothers to alight, and then waited for her Da, Ma and the littles to come out of the other one. She couldn't help but notice how worn their clothes were compared to what everyone else was wearing. She shook off this feeling, greeting Solina, who came forward with a welcoming hug.

"Sister, you have brought the whole family. Welcome, you can make yourselves comfortable, and we will shower you with delights. Come, Atin, make your introductions first." Solina looked so happy to see her Atin smiled right back at her, she introduced Kaisan first.

"Oh, you have been busy. You are an Aramite? Your name is not." She directed the question right at Kaisan, looking him right in the eyes.

"Yes, High Dragon, I am, I denounced my land and my family for this woman who I love. My Mader is... was a Layanese. She named me such when I was born." He bowed, gracing Solina's hand with a kiss. Then he backed away and

Atin then introduced her two brothers. Both bowing and when Tarik kissed her hand, he looked at her,

"Your eyes are the colour of the sun, much like Atin's are the colour of the sea. You are so beautiful." Atin shushed her brother, but Solina held his hand longer.

"You are a very courteous young man. I don't suppose you would want to see a Dragon up close later?"

That made him open and close his mouth. Selim took the opportunity to belittle the starstruck brother.

"You look like a fish gasping for water, brother. You look so silly."

Atin introduced her Pader and Mader and her little siblings. The sisters again telling Solina how beautiful she was. Solina laughed introducing Atin to the elegant older woman, as her GrandMader,

"You did not have time to be introduced last time as we were a bit busy. This is my GrandMader, Dame Metina." Atin curtsied and bowed at the same time.

"You look the same, and I see an aura of the same colour surrounding you both,"

"Oh, I forgot about this," Solina hugged her again and whispered in her ear,

"I could have used your talents a while back."

She went on to introduce Admiral Veren of the Royal Dragon Guard, in charge of security of the Dragons. The little woman was Sheyna, in charge of the health and well being of their charges. Even though Atin had worked with them to release the Dragons, she couldn't remember if there was introductions. This cemented their names into Atin's head. Not being overwhelmed and tired helped.

The introductions done, Solina gestured for them to walk down the hall. She showed them where they would be staying, telling them who would be seeing to their needs. She spoke to one of her attendants who rushed off.

"I did not know you acquired a husband; they are making a suite ready for you both, if you care to be parted from your family." Atin agreed with a smile, she knew there was a bit of sarcasm and inuendo behind the remark. She was already entuned to Solina and Solina smiled back. Solina then addressed them all.

"If you care to bathe and change into clothes I have placed aside for you, we will dine in an hour. Then if all are agreeable, we will go for a walk to meet what is now the future of our world."

Giving Atin a quick hug, Solina whispered in her ear, "Gran would like to chat with you privately at dinner if you are agreeable. I will deal with your family during such."

"We have time to wash?"

"Oh, yes. We can meet in say, an hour. I will have a servant come and fetch you at the time. It'll just be us for dinner." Solina then left Atin and her family, walking out of the large room.

"I wonder what this is about?" Atin repeated what Solina had told her to her Mader and Pader. She did not want to start worrying but the intimacy of the remark, had her a bit on edge. She hoped it wasn't something she could not manage.

"Do you have any ideas, Atin?"

"I am not sure. I suppose it may have something to do with being a Dragon. It must be of some import if the Supreme Magistrate requests a conversation."

Atin helped her family with their needs, helping the littles to bathe while the men sat around and looked at their suite. A servant then entered, asking Atin and Kaisan to follow her as she showed them their own suite. After the servant left them, Atin shucked off her clothes quickly, heading to the bathing room. Kaisan followed her in divesting himself of the same. He ahhed as he walked into the sunken pool. They helped each other wash before it turned into a quick joining on the step going in. She felt so much better and the way he knew how to please her had her panting his name.

After their quick activity, they got dressed in the clothes Solina placed for them. He was elegantly dressed in dark blues to compliment her in her cobalt blues, complimenting her eyes.

"Would you be wishing a head wrap for your hair, Kaisan?"

"No, 'tis a religious item, and as I have denounced all which is Aram, I am no longer required to wear one. To tell you truth of it, I am glad. It is freeing to be no longer shackled by the rigors of Aram. I would like to trim my hair though if you allow me. It is quite long, and I find it cumbersome. I am also free to cut it, as I am sure my manhood will remain intact, if I were to do so."

"Oh, is this what happens, should you cut your hair? I did not know. I do love your length but as it is upon your head, and you must deal with it, I understand. Let me braid it for you though. It can get quite windy on the mountainside."

Atin braided Kaisan's hair quickly. It was so much easier to braid than her own. She talked while she braided, telling him of the Palace and the wonders she saw.

"Da and the boys…"

"Sea Dragon, my Lord, the High Dragon requests your presence in the Dining Hall at your convenience."

"Yes, thank you, we will arrive shortly. I will go inform my family."

"This way, Sea Dragon, if you will follow me."

They exited the suite seeing her parents coming up the hall with all her siblings. She hung onto her brothers' hands and Kaisan without asking picked up one of the girls and hoisting her into his arms. Soya didn't mind as she already declared her crush of Kaisan and she was going to marry him one day. Her parents voiced their thanks, and they made their way to the Dining Hall to see it was just them and the people they met earlier.

Atin was placed beside Solina's GrandMader, of course, and the littles had their own table. Solina explained the littles would have entertainment to keep them occupied, while the adults dined together.

As dinner progressed, Solina kept her parents and Kaisan engaged, and the littles had servants catering to them while people were doing antics to keep their attention. One such man juggled which had the children enraptured for the longest time. Dame Metina looked at Atin.

"How are you finding your quarters? I hope you have all you require. How has your family been?"

"Very well, Supreme Magistrate. I joined in union with Kaisan, and my family is adjusting very well. Thank you for your concern."

"You may call me Dame Metina if you care to. Solina's sister Dragon need not be on ceremony in private."

"Thank you, Dame Metina." Kaisan had one ear on the conversation, which Solina saw he had every intention listening to.

"The ceremony we plan for the advent of Spring would also announce to the world the presence of Dragons once more. We will be announcing your presence. It would proclaim without a doubt the Prophecy was truth. You would be more protected if you were to reside in the Palace alongside your sister Dragon, Solina. With your new husband, of course. Once Du'Lanay and Aram hear the proclamation, they will be sending assassins. Of that I am certain."

Kaisan who was listening, spoke up. "I can protect her."

"Yes, but can you also protect her family from the thief in the night? Once it is known, their lives are forfeit. We wanted to bring you here, so they saw the Dragons for themselves. Privately! Then send them back. The less people who see you all together the better. The state cannot afford to have protection on your Island, you understand?"

Her Mader and Pader were now listening in, and her Da spoke.

"Yes, I understand, and I appreciate your candor and caring. We see what you mean. Kaisan can stay with her if this is agreeable. They are newly wed and don't wish to be parted. You have taken us under your wing, and I appreciate your hospitality. We will depart when you give us leave to go. Atin will keep us appraised of any updates. We understand she has a role to play in the future of our people and have accepted thus. Thank you, High Magistrate."

Dame Metina inclined her head to Atin's Da and husband, Solina spoke to Atin. "We will discuss the ceremony details later; it would be quite monotonous to your family. As the midday meal has finished and your siblings seem restless, shall we take a walk?"

The children jumped up. The boys, being boys, would not stop running around, not listening to their parents.

Solina laughed it off telling the adults to wait for the walk, it would settle them down. The group of people, adults, and littles, Solina taking hold of one of the girls and carrying her, made their way up the mountainside. The way had guards posted around and Veren stopped to speak with a few, as they continued up.

Atin grabbed onto her Pader and Maders' arms as they rounded the corner at the top. Even she gasped, they looked different than the beasts she helped to release. Her family was silent and awestruck as the largest one swung her head to look at the approaching humans. Atins parents gathered the children close and for once they were quiet. Atin asked her husband to remain with her family as she and Solina walked forward.

"Amazing, they are easily double the size they were when I first saw them, what, two months ago? And look at the beautiful colours. Nannosh is a beautiful ocean while Analaria looks like the darkest depths, dark and mysterious."

Analaria raised her head to look at Atin and lowered her head to the ground close to the approaching humans.

"She says thank you. She has been in the skies. Nannosh was up too, but small bouts her wing here is almost healed. It is more than two months. Easy double that."

"Has it? I guess I've been busy."

"Busier...I am thinking!"

"Hah, you have no idea!"

"Oh, I think I can guess. He is very...striking...for a Aramite."

"You think so? I think he's divine!"

"I am glad you are happy. He knows, I take it."

"Yes, I told him before we wed. Is this fine? I guess I should have asked you."

"Whatever for? You are your own person." Solina looked at Atin, the question in her face. Atin looked at her newest friend.

"Because you are the High Dragon...and the newest ruler of Pelin'Dun... did I think wrong?" Solina stopped and hugged the girl who looked like she had eaten a sweet only to find out she shouldn't have.

"Atin, I am not your Ruler. You and I are equal. We are sisters. Sisters of the sky and we do not have...a position over each other. Yes, I am learning to rule. Yes, it is very daunting, however, I will not bore you with the details. I am learning before you, it is my placement. I will be able to guide you when you get your own Dragon, but I do not place myself over you. If you want to join, then it is your choice. Not mine. You will have your work cut out for you though, I hope you can manage."

"He denounced his land and his family cut him off."

"That is harsh, how did he present it to you? May I ask?"

"Hmmm, he said he was taken out of the annals of history. Something like that. Why? It seemed a bit dramatic, but I was busy getting wed."

"Oh, just the wording. It seems, like you said, dramatic. Speaking of dramatic, would you like to see our healed wings? We had quite the ordeal. It would have been nice to have your healing power to mend the wings. We did the best we could, with what we had. Nann?"

They walked around the smaller of the two, forgetting they had onlookers. They had a good look at the wing in question, Nannosh very politely stretched it out and Atin saw a raised scar but no redness. They discussed how they fixed the wing with sap and cloth, Atin suggesting a fishing net would have worked as well, wrapped around the wing, and tied to itself, it would keep pieces contained.

"Yes, but your talents would have cut the healing time in half. We did good."

"Do you have healing talents?"

"I do not know. Nannosh said our talents would be given by the grace of the Great One. She mentioned the past Riders misused theirs. I can wait; I have enough to contend with." Solina and Atin walked to Nannosh's head which she lowered.

Atin spoke to Solina, "Not like I would want to steal your thunder, however, for the ceremony, what if your GrandMader spoke first and you and I rode the

Dragons in? So there is no question as to what our intent was? 'Tis a thought...
You could address them from the Dragon's back. We are DragonRiders, are we
not? Just thinking aloud. It would certainly make a statement."

Solina looked at her in amazement and then at Nannosh, "It could be done, if
Nann here could fly. You are right, it would make tongues wag! I will present
this idea to GrandMader. Right now, your family is becoming restless."

Atin turned to see the boys, having recovered from their initial shock acting
out again. Turning back to ask Nannosh if she could bring them forward. Solina
agreed. Atin walked back to the restless boys saying if they behaved like the
young men, she knew them to be, they could hold her hand and she would bring
them up to the largest of the Dragons. They grabbed her hand, one pulled, and the
other was more cautious. She stopped in front of the Dragon's head resting on the
ground and Tarik being the curious child he was asked if he could touch.

"If you promise to behave like proper young men and promise to forever look
after your parents, then you may touch the Dragon on the head. Kaisan, would
you please lift the boys up?" Solina came up behind her with Kaisan by her side.
Kaisan looked just as dumb struck as the boys. "Why, yes, yes, I can. Tarik?"

Kaisan even got to touch Nannosh on her scales, Tarik grabbing a larger horn
than the last time Atin saw on her crown. The boys were awed. Solina thanked
Kaisan and Nannosh and the company of people headed back to the Temple and
Palace, the boys still awed by it all. One of the youngest girls fell asleep in her
Da's arms, missing the whole thing.

"I hope your sea Captains are all aware. When you send my family home, the
boys will not keep their mouths shut the whole trip home, they don't know the
meaning of discretion." Atin walked side by side with Solina, Kaisan on the other
side holding her other hand, he was strangely quiet, having seen something he
never thought to see.

"I don't blame them, after next week, it won't matter anymore, I am sorry if
this causes you and your family difficulties, but to protect them, I need my people,
behind us. They need to believe again. We will fight, hopefully never, but if war
is brought to us, well, we must be ready. Sorry, Kaisan, I do not mean to discredit
your people, but Aram would not hesitate to change their focus and wage war on
us, especially if the continents were to make a peace pact and come after us. But
enough about this. 'Tis what GrandMader is for, she's the genius behind this
country."

Solina smiled at them. As they reached the Palace, Solina led them to their
rooms, "I will let you rest. If you require anything, there are servants placed outside to do your bidding. Atin, would you walk in the gardens with me, for a moment?"

"Yes, I certainly can. Kaisan, I will be but a moment. You will help my parents, with the little ones?"

"Yes, Dear Heart I can."

The women left Atin's family and her husband and they walked into the gardens which faced the mountain. It was private enough and Solina led Atin to a

bench by the largest fountain. Solina sat down, Atin facing her a worried look to her face.

"You have been busy, sister. You married an Aramite."

"Yes, he is or was the Captain of the ship you sent me home on. It was rather sudden."

"You know him well? I ask because now we must take into consideration, his allegiances. Gran says we must consider all aspects of our lives. I am only concerned, where this will go."

"I met him in the markets when I was helping Da sell my pearls. I felt the attraction before I knew, and before he knew I was a Dragon. He was surprised when I told him, but he did not reject me for it. It has been quite enjoyable..."

Atin blushed, in admitting the joy of her marital life with her husband. Solina smiled at her and took her hands. "I need no details, sister. I am sure it is all for which you could hope. Gran wants to make sure we do not bring a viper to our breast."

"I understand. I saw his aura. In fact, I have watched it from the moment I met him. He is not my enemy and should not be yours. It never changed since we have been joined. I see nothing but truth from him."

"He may not be the issue. Have you asked him anything about his homeland?"

"He told me many things, the way of Aram. We discussed many nights on the differences in our lifestyles. As he renounced his culture and religion, our family are instructing him in our way of life. He seems to have taken our marriage seriously, he has not tried to, ummm, be an Aram regarding being more than... a dominant man."

"Well, sounds like he is trying. Few men adapt to having a female stronger in the marriage than the man. I will let you go back to your family, let me know if I can help you in any way. I can have a repast sent to your rooms if you wish."

Atin and her family talked into the evening about the glory of the Dragons they witnessed.

The next day a very tired Atin and Kaisan emerged to see her parents walking down the hall with the littles to find a morning meal. They caught up to the group,

"This is all so grand, my child. I would very much like to return home. This is not my place, and I feel a longing for the simple life we have."

"I understand, Da. Believe me, I do. I will speak with Solina and pass on your request."

After they were all fed and Atin had spoken with Solina, who agreed with her reasoning, Kaisan and Atin went with her family down to the docks. She hugged and kissed them goodbye,

"Farewell, Pader, and Mader. Safe Path. I will see you soon."

"Many blessings to you and Kaisan, Atin. You have a future together, and as a Dragon you will be busy. Do not worry about coming back. We will understand. Send us word, time to time. That is all we need."

Atin and Kaisan returned to the Palace, holding hands the two of them went exploring, accidently walking into the Great Hall where Dame Metina was holding court. Begging her pardon, they tried to leave, and Dame Metina called them over asking them to sit.

"Solina told me of your idea, and it has merit if the Dragons can hold your weight. This would cement it in the eyes of our people, and we need to encourage a renewal of our ways. You should probably have a practice run first to make sure you don't fall off. We will take care of your husband for you."

Turning to Kaisan she asked him. "Do you have any special interests; we can indulge while the Dragons go about their business?"

He almost forgot to answer back. "Oh, yes, Dame Metina. I love works of art. Especially by the Greats. I also love an exquisite piece of jewelry. In fact, I would love to honour my bride with such an item. This is one tradition; I do not wish to lay aside. If you would know of such a place to acquire an intricate item, I would be honoured if you will take the time to show me."

"Then 'tis settled, I have various shops I like to visit, and I will take you personally if you are agreeable. The girls will be busy with their charges; you met them?"

"Yes, I have. I thank you for the invitation."

The two of them got up, bowed to the Dame, and left the hall.

"Do you plan on riding a Dragon?"

"Why yes. 'Tis a momentous event. It will usher in the Age of The Dragon's. It may only be a one-time occurrence. At least I can say I rode one. You will be with all the noble houses as Solina, and I fly in. It will be grand!"

"How can I protect you, then? I swore I would protect you. I love you more than my life."

"I love you for loving me as I am. However, I did tell you what I was before you agreed to marry me. I will have duties not normal to a man with your background. In Pelin'Dun, women have more responsibilities as the old ways, the Mader is respected for her wisdom and head of health in the family unit. If you feel I am overstepping, you have but to ask and we can discuss. I know some of our ways are different than what you are used to."

He smiled after a moment of thought, reached for her wrapping her in a big hug,

"I have to admit, I never thought I would be sharing you with a Dragon."

CHAPTER 36

Andic

Upon Taking the Last Breath

Andic did not see her paramour for another rotation of his duties. It was a good thing because they found more information pertaining to the gems, the talismans which held them, the Riders, and specifics on the Dragons. This scroll was tucked inside another, almost like it was meant to be hidden. Natan mentioned they should carefully watch for all the lower scrolls on this pile. They found more to place aside before the other guard, Matteo came down. He taunted Andic whatever she did to Brecu, he would be happy to accept the same treatment. The first day he came down, he commented how ragged his cohort looked. That he paid to have two meals out of his wage and scarfed it all down.

"The Commander is a little suspicious, Brecu said he felt like he had a grippe coming and our Captain gave him two days off. We don't need another scourge to wipe out more people, like the last one."

The last one had indeed wiped out both of Brecu's parents. She held him in a moment together as he cried in her arms. She never mentioned it after this, never held it against him. Back then, she thought of him as an older brother, now she knew very differently.

Ignoring Matteo's attempts at conversations, she busied herself with moving scrolls. Natan directed her, to another room. After a time, Matteo left, only to come back the next day, fresh and full of new taunts. Again, she ignored him, did her work, and as soon as he left, she and Natan read the scrolls they set aside.

"This one is more on the use of the talismans, which were created by previous DragonRiders with an infusion of Dragonmagic. It seems, the crystal in the purity sword was created by the man who wielded it. Each of the gems in the others were also created by the DragonRider it was meant for. Hmmm, this is interesting. They were created by the DragonRider themselves. What we have in the other room, has already been created. The Riders' eyes reflected the gems as they used their talisman but were not always in possession of them.

Here's a reference to other documents, held in a library of sorts. It seems there is a main place these documents…" Natan's arm swept around him, "…were kept. These must have come from there, which would explain why I am down here, to make sense of it all. The only place which comes to mind is Pelin'Dun, however, there could be other places of importance. You keep reading and see if you find anything, of import, and we can reroll these up inside the annals of farming and feeding."

They got to work reading while they could, and discussing what they learned, each Dragon had a specific area where they went to lay eggs and the great male would visit to fertilize them. It seemed the male was with the man who wielded the Sword of Purity, and he was the leader of the human Riders. He was called the Pader and corresponded with the Pader deity who was worshipped. Another was the Dragon and Rider of air, yellow, last known talisman was a woman's ring. It was wielded by a female Rider and known as the Sister deity. The next one was the Aunt, deity of fertility a green gem, was in a tiara, another female Rider, commanding earth. Uncle, God of war, and of commerce, red gem, a torc or necklace.

The Mader, Goddess of Health, childbirth and love, commanding water, with a blue gem. The gem was a sapphire, set into another sword, and lastly, the Brother, wielder of the purple gem, set in a dagger, keeper of knowledge, art, songs and literature and the ability to manipulate minds, and energy.

"This one is interesting… if we assume, hold on, you, yes, let's say you…" Natan had the bit in his mouth now and she knew when he set his mind on something, he didn't back down, "…were the Brother, you are on the path of learning. You mastered three languages, in a brief time. You remember everything, your emotions are linked to the gem, I monitored it while you have, ummm, expressed, ummm, desire. The manipulation part I am not sure about. I am sure there are more books, more in-depth tomes about the specifics of each DragonRider. What we have here, is what was gleaned from the Riders before they were murdered. All you can do is learn everything, while you are given the chance, and use it. I only suggest going onward, a journey to Pelin'Dun, to meet with the Dragon there, and see what the path has in store for you."

Brecu came down the weeks passed without her realizing. She was glad to see him; he seemed reenergized but looking a bit ragged. While she couldn't see the signs in the torchlight, outside in the daylight, he aged. No other way to put it, he looked older, creases in the corners of his eyes, dark circles under them, and his hair was sporting a few greys.

"Greetings, Natan. Andic, may we speak?"

"Greeting, Brecu. I will make myself scarce. Do not worry, I know where I am not needed." Natan left, walking down the hall, muttering all the way. She gave Brecu a kiss. "I missed you, and I miss your touch."

He held her in his arms, kissing her back, but after a time he pulled back to look down.

"I don't know what is happening to me, girl, my closest companions say I look worn out and suggest 'tis because of you. I don't know how rounds of joining can do this, so I told them, they are full of shite. I think we should pace ourselves, but holding you in my arms, I want to rip your clothes off and pound you against the table of ours."

"I would definitely love this, I missed your hard cock inside me, Matteo was beginning to look good." She couldn't resist teasing him. The look on his face was priceless.

"Haha. You should see your face. I am teasing you. Brecu. I did not mean it. Brecu?" He looked hurt, but when he realized she was jesting, he lightened, but then he furrowed his brow and asked her.

"You are taking, ummm, precautions, you know, to prevent a…"

"Why, yes, yes... of course." She wasn't, she absolutely forgot about this. As she thought back some, she realized she hadn't bled in a while. Hmmm, she should probably see Delma, and make sure she wasn't with child.

"Because I don't want any. I don't want to bring anything into this shite life. I have things to do, and while I love joining with you, I don't see this lasting forever. Nothing does. I'm sorry, but 'tis my take on things."

Andic knew his parent's death and the plague which took many lives impacted him in a huge way. It was the way of the poor, live life as though it was your last day. She felt the same and gave him a squeeze.

"Hmmm, do you want to get out of those thoughts and do some joining?"

She opened his jacket and was teasing his nipples through the fabric of his shirt. He kissed her hard and lifted her tunic over her head. He played with her nipples which helped to accelerate the removal of clothing. Grabbing her by the bottom again and lifting her onto the table instead of putting his cock inside her, he got onto his knees, kissing and licking her until she was begging for his cock inside her. He didn't say anything about it taking this long to harden, and he wondered if his friends didn't have the right of it.

He stood up and undid his trousers, letting them fall to the ground, holding his manhood while he guided it inside her. It was not as hard as the previous times but once it entered her tightness, he thrust into her fast and hard, and she peaked way before he did. He kept going and eventually exploded inside her. His breathing deep, the sweat poring off his face, he had to work hard to peak this time. Brecu rested his head against hers, hands upon the table on either side of her.

"I don't know, Andic, I must have something wrong with me, I can not seem to keep going, like this, you wear me out, physically. I am spent."

"Are you eating properly? Have you eaten anything to upset your stomach? I hate to ask, but drinking more than usual? I've seen effects like yours at the delight house where I frequent. Anything out of the ordinary for you could have a tiring effect on your day-to-day life. I hope its not me, I love when you come to see me, and when you are inside me, you make me feel alive." She got off the table after he backed up to pull his trousers up and put his uniform back together.

"Well, that's one of us at least. I do remember having a fish dinner a couple of weeks ago which set me off, and I am playing dice with the boys more often, you could be right. I could be indulging in all sorts of delights all at once."

He came forward giving her a hug and a quick kiss, backing off the kiss when she pressed for more.

"Not again, love, I am going back to the Barracks, I can't stay. I am being monitored down here. Can't have a two hour stay like last time, nearly had you buried. I will see you when I can. Stay away from Matteo, he's hot for you, and if it weren't for the thrashing I gave him the other day, he'd be after you. Don't encourage him. I told you; you are mine. I'd be pissed if you screwed him." He was dead serious towards the end, and she looked at him closely.

"I have absolutely no intention of joining with your cohort. I am sorry I teased you; we used to tease each other all the time; I didn't think this changed. He comes down here and is always pressing me, I can only tell him to piss off so many times. I think the only reason he doesn't pursue it, is because he knows I would gut him without a second thought."

"I will rest easy with this thought. In fact, I'll tell him you need to practice your knife work." He smiled, giving her another peck, leaving her, fulfilled but craving more.

Natan came back a few minutes after Brecu left, "The gem glowed again."

"Of course it did. Do you think I can have the rest of the day off? I need to do something."

"Yes. But no more than this. If you were to take more time, I do not know if you would be allowed to continue. There is no need to make anyone in the Grand Hall suspicious. They may think you mean to send missives or share the information we glean down here. You are known to them."

"I need a bit of a rest, it is much to absorb, and it is taking its toll on my body."

"Harumph. I am sure 'tis not what's taking its toll. You are too young to talk like this."

"Thank you, Master Natan, I will be back tomorrow."

She left early heading down to the brothel, catching Delma rising, preparing for the night. Andic asked her what signs of pregnancy were, she was feeling tired and a bit off. When Delma asked her when the last time she bled, Andic had to think about this one. It had been at least six weeks prior.

"Hate to say this, luv, but given you are active with your man, best guess is you are going to have a child. It this what you want?"

"I don't know, I never thought about it."

"Have you told him?"

"No. We just had this discussion. He does not want a child. I do not know what to do."

"Well, regardless, you will have to tell him at some point. I have never known you to shirk from anything. As it is inevitable, you delay it until you show, but other symptoms will probably give you away, or you get it over with and deal with your man. 'Tis your call."

"Yah, I hear you. You are right, that's why I came to you. I am going upstairs to rest for a bit; can I have a cup of your night tea?"

Delma's night tea was brewed when someone needed a deep uninterrupted sleep. It was extremely hard to wake someone up from it, although possible. It was a tea made from leaves of a plant if not diluted enough could also cause death, but it was so versatile, used as painkiller for injuries, among other things. Andic read up on the Toi plant, a weed to some, but for the intelligent, a way to heal and kill, all in one tiny leaf. Delma left to brew it returning with a cup of what looked like yellow urine and tasted much the same. She drank a sip or two before she shook her head telling her friend she would be going to her loft and sleeping for the night.

The next day she was up, with the birds before the sun. Washed and dressed, she took herself off to the catacombs, not stopping on her way through the Hall. She felt off, and Natan mentioned she looked worse than when she left.

"I did not get a good night's sleep, where I lay my head." Brecu entered at this moment, "Busy night?"

Natan ducked his head, taking himself out of the room after he spoke mumbled greetings and muttering something about not getting any work done lately as he strode down the hall. She looked up to see Brecu leaning against the door opening.

"Not for me. It was a bit loud. A few girls don't know how to be quiet when they are working their clients."

"Hmmm, I know how that is." He smiled and casually strolled in with his arms crossed.

"You all right? You don't look very, let's see, happy to see me."

"Oh, I am, but I don't think you will be."

"Oh?"

"Yes. I think I am with child."

There, she said it. She stood up to see Brecu's face change from disbelief to growing anger. She thought for a moment there might have been a spot of joy, but she could be imagining it. He took a step toward her.

"What did I tell you? I do not want a child. How can you stand there and calmly tell me this? I thought we were having fun for now."

"We are, we were, what do you expect? It happened. I did not think this would happen this fast." She became angry, he was blaming her, when he was as much to blame!

"Well, you need to get rid of it. You aren't called the 'Child Killer' for nothing."

"That's low, even for you."

"I'll tell you this, Andic. Either it goes or I go."

"Well, if that's your stance, goodbye."

She turned away from him, her anger flaring, afraid she would say something worse, and she did not want to go there. She feared sayings things later she would regret, words once said, could not be taken back. He stood for a moment, turned, and left. Natan returned after a couple of minutes seeing her anger had turned to sorrow. She had tears running down her cheeks.

"I think I did mention at the beginning to take precautions. You are in a bind. When it is known you are with child, you will not be able to stay. We are halfway through our task. If you leave it will take me double the time to get finished. Not I can influence your decision in the matter. Oh, in your anger, the gem lit up again. It reflects on your emotions, not just pleasure, but also in anger, intensity is the key, I think." Natan commented he wished he could document his findings but didn't want them to be found out.

"Yes, yes, Natan, I have other things to worry about right now, like what I'm going to do."

"Brecu didn't take it too well?"

"No, he told me he didn't want to bring any child into this shite life. I didn't think life was shite, until now. I am going away for a week or so. I am weary of staying in this dungeon right now. By your leave?"

"Yes, of course, but I am not sure about the Masters. I will make up an excuse for you, but you may have to explain when you return, be aware. Whatever you decide, make sure 'tis what's best for you. Not anyone else. Do what your heart tells you. Then, you will not have regrets."

"Many thanks, Natan, I appreciate your insight. You are a good man." She gave him a quick hug, leaving the room, her eyes now dry. She exited the catacombs, into the hall, and left thru the front entrance, walking right past Brecu at his post without even looking in his direction. His comrades began to pester him until he twisted the arm of one and told them to shut the blazes up or he would kill them. She heard all this as she kept walking, ignoring everyone and continuing until she arrived back at the brothel.

The brothel was a buzz with girls chatting. It being a bit early in the day for them to be up. Andic stopped, learning Dragons were alive in Pelin'Dun and there were two Riders, Air, and Water! They rode the Dragons in the air! The Rulers announced it amid their spring ceremonies a couple of weeks past and Aram was getting the news. News always took a bit of time, depending on the weather and speed of the ships which sailed the seas. *Three if Natan wanted to include me in this mess.* She thought as she sought Delma sitting in her office, in quiet contemplation.

"Delma." She didn't say anything else, just sat down opposite of her mentor, in the chair provided.

"Andic. You've heard the news? This is remarkably interesting, indeed. Is the FirPader going to call off his war with Du'Lanay to go after the Dragons? Do you wonder? What brings you here at this hour? Ohhh..."

The expression on Andic's face spoke the words Delma heard many times before. Sorrow, disbelief, fear, and resolve. Andic hid nothing from the woman who raised her, who cared for her, in her fashion.

"So, you are going to go through with it?" Andic nodded.

"Best you do it now before it quickens. Less chance you die from what you know is more difficult down the path. I will make the necessary preparations."

Delma rose, going into the kitchen to brew the tea. Almost the same, but the strength was different, a little more leaf and some others, to help expel the fetus. Andic knew what it involved; she often helped girls with this elimination. They had a special room built into the ground in the back of the yard which was mostly soundproof. It helped for the business, when clients weren't joining with girls in one room while in the next one, a girl was screaming from aborting a child.

Delma returned with the tea, and both walked to the back of the yard where the small hut stood. Delma unlocked the door and swung it open, handing the tea to Andic giving her a hug.

"I will see how you are in a couple of hours. I have things to do, and I sense you don't want anyone here. Please feel free to clean up after yourself, all items are there on the shelf, you know the way of it." She gave Andic another quick hug. Andic stepped down the stairs the open door revealed. She needed no lantern. None was given, especially after one girl lit herself on fire after being locked in.

She sat down on the one stool, watching as the light disappeared with the closing of the door, hearing the padlock click shut. Delma took no chances, not even with her protégée, she was a wiser older woman who had seen it all.

Andic took a deep breath, drinking down the vile tea. She tried not to bring it back up; it would have no effect if it were not in her gut. Almost immediately her stomach cramped. She quickly remembered to shuck her leggings off to not get them dirty. Not only the blood, but the shite she knew was going to happen, and very quickly. She quickly gathered them, hanging them on the one hook which sported a well-worn towel. She bent over as the first wave of pain hit, feeling something run down her leg. Judging from the smell it was indeed shite. She fell to her knees as the second and quickly the third hit. She tried not to cry out too loud.

She grabbed the stick on the ground beside the stool. It had teeth marks in it from previous users. She didn't care it was on the floor and was dirty. It was Blackwood, the hardest wood there was, from the other continent they were trying to conquer. She shoved it in her mouth as waves of pain, came so fast she began to feel blackness around the edges of her vision come together. She let out a silent scream, as the hardest and strongest shot of pain took her pulling her down into the pit of deepest sorrow.

Waking seconds, minutes later? She didn't know how long, but she felt fluids against her legs and in between. She gradually rose onto her knees, blood, clots, and a lump of tissue sat on her thighs, shite and urine combining to make a very fetid smell. She saw what it was, as the door was gaping open. She tried to fathom the why, when it darkened, and she saw Delma's incredulous face looking down at her.

"Andic... Lass."

The older woman rushed down the stairs, to help her rise, grabbing the towel, dipping it into the bucket in the corner, water Delma brought by earlier. The older woman supported the young girl, wobbling on her feet, cleaning up the mess on her legs, and in between.

"Sit yourself down. There. Now open your legs. Yes, that's a girl."

It was a bit tender, but not as sore as when she had first had sex, with Brecu. Delma was muttering to herself, and Andic broke herself out of her daze to ask what was going on. "I don't know, deary, one moment it was like a silence came over everything and then earth shook, and the house rattled. I came out here to see the door blasted clear off and its across the yard. Did you break it?"

"I haven't moved. I took the tea and it worked, right away. It was the most intense pain I ever experienced. I hope I never have too again. I now have more respect for women who have this done. What do you mean the door is across the yard?"

Andic stood up after Delma cleaned her up. She limped over to the hook, taking her leggings and pulled them on. Delma emptied the bucket over the mess on the floor, usually she would leave the door open for whatever wild animal chose to clean up after an episode, coming back to close and lock the door, after preparing it for the next victim.

"Come see for yourself." Delma threw the soiled towel into the bucket and Andic slowly went up the steps, every step she took, the ache lessened, until at the top she came out into the yard. Looking at amazement at the door, laying ten feet away, and broken at the hinge placement, the warped hinges, still clinging to the building, one slightly askance at the bottom. Delma came up behind her a minute later, holding two pieces of Blackwood in her hand, the look of amazement still on her face.

"Look what you did. I have never heard of this; you bit clean through a piece of Ravenwood. This has never been done. You have a jaw of iron, child, look at your fresh bite marks." Andic looked at the two pieces.

"How is that even possible?" A few girls came out back.

"Shoo, shoo. Get back inside. Nothing to see out here. Go on, git." Delma flapped her arms.

"The girls will chatter like birds. Let's keep this piece of wood between us, I can't do anything about them gossiping about the child you got rid of. Is there anything you wish?"

Andic swayed a little on her feet. Delma grabbed her by the arm taking her inside to her office, sitting her down on the very chair she vacated only one hour prior. "You sit down here, how are you feeling?"

"Surprising well, physically. Mentally I am angry. I didn't have time to come to terms with this. (Sigh) I guess I shouldn't have regrets; 'tis done now. It will be a while before I get back under a man. I've learned my lesson. So, what else about the Islands, there are now how many Dragons? And Riders, I heard about the yellow eyed one. They say she's the long-lost GrandDader of the High Magistrate?"

They spent the rest of the day talking, then Andic went upstairs early to rest. She thought about her week off and changed her mind. She would return to work; she had nothing better to do. She would face Brecu also,

Oh well, I can run from my problems or face them head on. Prolonging the next confrontation is not going to make it better. Brecu was terribly angry with me. 'Tis the end of what we had. I wish it had not come to this. I will miss his friendship even more that the sex. Well, perhaps the sex was better... no, I think it was our friendship. Oh well...

She woke early, rose, had a wash in the fountain, looking all the while at the blown off door, wondering what else happened in the city, and only felt like she had rough sex. Other than this, she felt fine. *Back to normal, as normal as I can be.*

Andic walked back to her job along the Path of Learning, not seeing any damage to anything the closer she got to the Hall. Outside the House of Delight where her nest was, there were cracks in the closest buildings, but the further away she walked, nothing revealed a quake even happened.

Matteo was at his post; he took one look at her eyes and let her through. He made a comment and Andic stared blankly at him with no expression on her face. She hardened her resolve and the old Andic of street rat Days was back. She felt a huge detachment, her survival method while she worked through the thoughts rambling around her brain. She was let in and Natan was surprised to see her. He had her sort through a pile of scrolls while her escort was there, but as soon as he left, Natan grabbed her hand and took her down the hall.

"You won't believe what happened yesterday. This." He took the cover off the dagger to show the gem shattered. The pieces lay under the cloth, the piece of cloth showing signs of wear and tear in it. She picked up a few pieces of gem, sharp and purple lifeless in her hands.

"What happened?"

"I'm not sure. I heard a large shot, like a stone had fallen from great heights and I came down to investigate. The cloth was on the floor, pieces everywhere, I picked it up and placed the cloth back over it. I am afraid I had to report it. Did anything happen outside? Someone said there was ground disturbance, but I did not feel anything here."

"About what time did this happen?"

"Sometime right before the evening mealtime, I believe, I finished eating. Why?" Natan peered at her closely. "Did something happen to you yesterday?" He looked at her expression, which saddened some. "Ohhh, so you did do something. About the same time, I am guessing?" She nodded, "I am truly sorry, but better than the alternative if you are not prepared for this life."

A tear slipped down her face, and she roughly brushed it away.

"You are beginning to see, then. You have a destiny to fill, and not here. You have my word; I will not say anything to anyone. I am thinking your time here will need to end. You heard the news? There are two Dragons. Dragons! The FirPader will not stand for this. It undermines the very foundation of his existence. I had to report on our findings thus far. Now with this new finding, I may not be able to finish. One Oban wanted to burn everything, however, our FirPader has more respect for history, even if it's the wrong one."

They walked back to the main working room, Andic began back where she left off. Sorting and piling scrolls in the room where they were meticulously organizing, she didn't hear Brecu come down. It was a time before she realized he was there; the lantern he was holding moved and cast a shadow on the wall beside her. She looked up and he tentatively smiled. She ignored him, turning back to her work, she felt anger slowly touch her heart.

"Hey, I heard. You fine?" Brecu stayed where he was, he instinctively knew it wasn't.

"No. Fuck off."

"So that's it then? Just like this, we are done."

"Yes. Just. Like. That." She placed scrolls with each word for emphasis, kept herself busy, getting angrier by the minute.

"All right." This was all he said, he left going to the room Natan was in. She heard their voices, Natan leading him to the room the dagger was in. A few minutes later, she saw Brecu walking past her doorway, carrying a cloth wrapped parcel in his hand. Not glancing in her direction, he left. Natan came to her doorway,

"He has orders to bring it to the Oban. I must go also. They want my report on what I know. You are here on your own, keep doing what you are doing. I will be back when I have told all."

"Yes, Master Natan. I will do as you require." Natan left and a few minutes later Matteo came down standing in the doorway watching her. She ignored him too.

"We all heard what happened. Brecu was quite embarrassed by the openness. The girl from the Delight House doesn't like you much, she practically yelled it out for the whole Barracks to hear. He was reprimanded in front of us all for dereliction of duty. Guess one can't play and work. Do you fancy a go? You and Brecu are off each other now?"

"Fuck off."

"That's not a nice attitude, girl." He stood up from his leaning; a mean look on his face taking a step forward. She stopped what she was doing and turned to look at him.

"Go ahead, try if you dare. I am feeling a bit like taking it out on someone right now and couldn't give a fuck if it were you, Brecu, or anyone else. I have this urge to see someone else's blood."

She palmed a knife and held it in her right hand, loosely waiting to pounce. Matteo took one look at her blank expression, and backed away, putting both his hands up, stating he didn't want to be in Brecu's boots at the moment.

"What's wrong with my boots?" Brecu walked in as Matteo brushed by him. He saw Andic with her knife in her hands. He looked at her, sadly but as determined as her to not interact with the other. He turned going down the hallway, and then a while later, walked right by again, not looking in her direction.

Natan didn't return for an hour or so, she almost finished her pile of sorting when he showed up.

"Well, this was interesting. I had to report on everything. Well almost everything. They wanted to know all about the dagger, had I touched it, had you touched it. I told him I let you have a day of rest, you weren't even here, which pleased them to no end. They were looking for someone to blame. They looked it over and proclaimed it to be worthless but will hold onto it to not incite substance to any rumours. Then I told all I have found. They know of the maps, and all we catalogued. I am afraid our days are numbered here, you most of all. They say I can do the rest on my own. So, I would say by the end of the month, let us part friends."

"I'm fine with this. Like you said, I should head out and seek more information. While I don't agree with what you are saying about me, I do know I must find my path. It won't be here. Thank you for your care and discretion, on the, ummm, other thing, you know."

Andic had gotten to know Natan a bit and blushed at her admission.

"As to that, I was young once, made a few wrong decisions myself. You listen well. You have a huge part to play, in what comes next of this world. Do not go into it without knowing your options. Knowledge is the key. For the Pader's sake, you find another of your kind, there is strength in numbers. You will be hunted when revealed. No. Don't deny this. You are another DragonRider, this was told to me by Kadir, and I trust his judgement. You proved him right by the gem in the dagger.

Find your path."

CHAPTER 37

Damara

Through the Lives of Many

Damara had just woken up on their second day in the Capital when Peylin handed her a note which was delivered to her husband just ten minutes prior. Her brother requested their presence on the top of the hill at the Temple in his office. "'Tis official business. Peylin, I will have my full regalia. My state robe with my red dress underneath, all my ruby rings. One must show I am still of royal blood."

"Yes, Nada, I have the bath waiting. I will prepare your robe. Nanya, Venae, assist me please!"

She finished dressing, when Ramis strode in, dressed in full military regalia, he hadn't worn it since the Royal Wedding last year. She had to admit, which she did, he was very handsome in it. He used to get her wet every time he wore it when he was actively serving. Now she was indifferent to the charm of a uniform.

"You look fabulous, Ramis. This is very excessive; do you not think?"

"You look very official and beautiful My Dear, as well. No, I don't. We must represent the family. Let's set off now." They had a carriage take them up to the Temple Palace. It was a covered carriage, and Damara was glad for it. They started off into the city, and she noticed there were more people than usual in the streets.

"Do you know what is going on? Is there a celebration?"

"I am not sure; it could be for a religious ceremony. There seems to be lots of revival lately. I'll ask the driver to skirt around if he can." Ramis knocked his cane on the ceiling of the carriage behind the driver's spot in the front. A small hidden window opened, and a disembodied voice called down.

"Yes, Nadan? What are your wishes?"

"Do you see what is going on? Is there a way to circumvent it? We have business at the Palace. We do not want to keep the Namarch waiting."

"I will do my best to get around this. There are droves of people going to one of the main squares. We may have slow going for a while. I will do my best."

"See that you do." Ramis lowered his arm, his cane was a gift from Davian when Ramis left the army. It was a subtle reminder of Ramis's connection to his brother by law. Damara thought it was not necessary, but Ramis would always have a method to his dress, a connection to the host. The carriage began to move, but it was slow going and at another intersection they halted. The sounds coming from outside were beginning to enter the carriage.

"What is happening? It sounds like shouting." Damara made the move to open the curtains.

"Careful, Mara. We do not want to draw attention to ourselves. There is unrest lately."

"I just want a peek." Damara peeled a little bit of the curtain back. What she saw shocked her.

"Oh, Ramis. Get this carriage going. Going, now!" The sound of a whip connecting with flesh, and a female crying out met their ears. Then the sound of the crowd cheering, Ramis took his own look, and rapped his cane on the ceiling again.

"Move this carriage now, Damn it! I do not care who you run over. This mob could become fickle." The carriage jerked forward. They heard sounds of the driver cursing and yelling for the crowd to part.

"Move for the Church, move, out of the way! Hie, hie." Soon the carriage was travelling without stopping.

"Are you fine, Mara? You should not have seen this. There must have been reason for such a public spectacle. The Namarch must be setting an example."

Damara nodded, too upset to reply. She placed her hand over her mouth. *An example, hah. The Namarch is punishing women like they were the cause of all which was going on in the world. That poor woman.*

In the glimpse out the window, she saw a stage in the middle of the square. A robed man of the Church with a book in his hand, speaking with animation. A woman, her hair blonde. It was chopped, the ends poking in complete disorder. There was blood on one side of her face, and Damara saw streaks of red down the woman's neck. The face was one of resolve, the woman was crying, and Damara saw the whip arm of the man standing behind her come down.

They arrived at the Namarch's Palace, Damara took Ramis's arm after alighting from the carriage, he patted her hand. He spoke to her softly as they were let into the Grand Entrance.

"No need to mention this to your brother, we do not want any attention brought to our family. What happened in the square is the Church's right to perform. If there is unrest in the city we should take more caution. I will hire more soldiers. At least here in the city. Back home doesn't seem so volatile. I will protect you and our family."

"Thank you Ramis, I have caught my breath now. Yes, no need to tell Davian. He has other things on his mind. Let's see what he wants."

All white marble, they walked down the long, tall hallway. Columns of marble every ten feet against the walls, flanked by soldiers of the Faith. Their uniforms merely decorative, Damara didn't think they actually fought in such ridiculous outfits. Ramis saw where her gaze was, and spoke in a whisper, "No, they don't," which had her smiling and that's how she greeted her brother when they rounded the corner to enter his office.

Davian dressed for the occasion. His golden robe was elaborately decorated and wore a flattened chain of many links of silver and gold. His black hair was like hers, graying at the temple. His was just a little more, brother and sister looked very much alike. Davian used it to his advantage with the ladies when he was young, until his 'calling.' All men of the Church were not allowed to wed, many had ways of skulking around in secret, many were brought down by a skirt. Davian had not. He kept his cock in his pants, in this case his robe.

He used the rules of the Faith to his advantage and knew when to not. He was a man of the Namanist Faith for twenty or so years. Many of his brethren had fallen by the wayside, either deliberately or not. He had risen by his own merits. So, he told himself. He was not a man to have many friends; often buying his information.

Today was not one of those days, he rose, coming around the desk when Damara and Ramis entered. Plastering a smile on his face, he greeted each with a hug, his smile diminishing as he asked them to sit.

"I am sorry for the haste, of my summons, I understand you have information from the Islands, Ramis?" Damara started until she realized this was not why he called them here; everyone knew this news by now.

"Yes, one of our Captains, was on the Island, paid for inquiry on suspicious activity. He headed out to bring this to me when he found out what it was. You received my messages?"

"Yes, but I heard one better. It seems they have announced it to the entire world. During their spring celebrations, both DragonRiders flew into the city, landed, announced they would be gearing up for war, to whoever would think to take their Dragons. They have two DragonRiders, which control water and air. We won't be able to get near the Islands now." Damara and Ramis sat in complete silence, until Damara spoke up, "That's only two, Davian, what about the other four? You do nothing without thinking this through."

She and Ramis had a discussion over one of their many dinners and Ramis divulged to her some of the heretical Prophesy. It only made her wonder how her husband acquired this information; he was even more secretive than she originally thought.

"I haven't time to think about this, I received this news before you arrived here... what did you wish to say?" Many times, when Davian and Damara were younger, they would plan and execute games. Play tricks on their friends and the two of them, would bounce ideas off each other, like they had an unspoken connection. This is why he had them come here, he needed her calculating mind, to bounce ideas off.

"Well, we know about two, the others must be around this world of ours. Soon enough, they will make themselves known, by deeds or whatever makes them, them. The Faith need to be ready; you send someone to take care of the two, but they will be expecting this, and what you told me of Nader, it will already be happening." Davian nodded and asked her to continue.

"Obviously, you wait in the shadows. When the attempts fail, you have someone pick up the pieces, and work by subterfuge, when they least expect it, Have them pick up the ceremonies, and festivals, they will hide in the crowds," She grew quiet and Ramis asked the question he, and Damara discussed plenty. "Will the war between Aram and us end and join forces against this new threat?"

"That is good question. 'Tis being debated while we are speaking. Aram will have the same issues we have. I heard the water witch married an Aramite. He attended the ceremonies. This may be their way in, we have none."

"I have ships. We could use my business as an in, they can't close off all their routes for the sake of the beasts." Ramis looked at her in shock. She looked back at him, just as determined as ever. "What? We are giving the Faith one of our sons. Our ships aren't good enough now? I could give it validity and go myself; I need more dyes. They have the only plant which gives the orange hue. I have the monopoly on it here. What better way in?" She had risen out of her chair and sat back down.

"I apologize Your Grace, I forgot myself."

"No need. This is an excellent idea, let's leave it in a back corner until we need it. I appreciate your enthusiasm for helping, and this brings us around to your son Jaidak. Yes, I asked for him. I need one I trust, in here with me. I need to groom him to step into my shoes. All I trusted in the past were eliminated over the years. There will come the day when I rise once again. He could have no better career path than this."

"We do appreciate your placement, and I am sure Jaidak will thrive." Ramis rose, bowing to Davian. Damara remained seated and stared at her brother, concern, and determination set into her expression.

"Sister, I know you have something to say."

"Please promise you will watch out for him and keep him safe. Promise me, brother. Or I will not give my blessing, to your venture." Damara rose, looking at her brother, intensity covering the words she spoke.

"I promise. I promise I will protect your children."

At this very moment, thru the open windows a small breeze fluttering the gauze curtains hanging from ceiling to floor. It stopped! A silence reined! Enough to have them glancing in the direction of the curtains. Then a horrendous breeze blew in. Blowing the curtains up into the room, smaller ornaments fell off shelves, scrolls and papers blew off his desk, flying in circles.

Damara grabbed at her head; it felt it was splitting in two. She thought for a moment, she heard a cry on the wind of pain and anguish. She fell to the carpeted floor in a faint.

She woke up on a couch in her brother's office, tried slowly to sit up and take the drink Ramis offered her. She saw various servants of the Faith on their knees picking up papers and items which were knocked over, cleaning up bits which were broken. She knew it was not a long time she was out.

"What happened? Was there an earth shake? The wind?"

"I don't know Dear, what made you to faint?"

"It shocked me, I guess, I really am not sure. I don't usually faint, but since my illness, I have not been the same. I am getting headaches more frequently." She looked up to see her brother striding back into the room.

"No cause we see as of yet. The oceans are calm, and the air is back to normal. I called some men of learning to investigate the matter. Sister, how do you fare?" Walking up to her, looking with concern in his countenance.

"Yes, I was telling Ramis since my illness I have not been feeling my usual self, more headaches, I am afraid. However, I am feeling better if I could return to our villa?" She rose with the help of Ramis, her brother saying. "If ever I have need of your offer, dear sister, I will be sure to reach out. It may happen; I do. I thank you for it. It was a pleasure, Ramis. For now, rest assured I will do all in my power to take care of your son. He is after all soon to be mine, in this family of Faith. We take care of our own. Remember the tree when we were kids, Damara? I make you the same promise today I made when we were young. I will watch out for him."

Davian gave his sister a hug, shook Ramis's hand and they were led out by an attendant, back to their waiting carriage. Ramis walked slowly while Damara clung to his arm with a death grip, scared she would fall again. He waited until they were in their carriage to say anything.

"What were you thinking, offering our services in what could only be a Dangerous mission?"

"We are always being evaluated dear Ramis. Do you think I like the idea of one of our sons, becoming like his Uncle. I love my brother, but the Faith has changed him. Davian was so carefree when he was a young man, heading out for a career in the army. At least he would have been able to see his enemies face to face in battles. He would have married, and Lana was devastated when she heard. They were promised since infancy. They genuinely loved each other. That is most likely what caused her divorce, she never did get over him." She forgot for a moment Ramis was currently screwing Lana, but after she said it, she thought to herself, *good, let him chew on that thought for a minute.*

"Our son is going to have the same life. One of always looking in the shadows for the next blow. Davian can only protect him so much. He will fail or succeed entirely, and I much prefer him not to be having to make those choices. If offering one of our ships, is not another way of stating our loyalty, then I don't know what is. I am sorry."

"You have no idea what Jaidak will be doing. You are having nonsensical ideas, and Davian said he would protect him. He is smart and will be able to hold his own. The Faith would not be asking for him if he were a half-wit, Mara. And I am angry about the ship and the offer; you did not discuss this with me first."

This was perhaps their first argument in an exceedingly long time, and it wouldn't be their last. She would find Ramis had his own idea of how they should be living their life. She leaned back in the carriage, closing her eyes for the rest of the trip back to the villa, her head pounding beneath her temples.

She took a tonic when she returned and took a meal in her room. When she asked Peylin what Ramis was eating, Peylin stated Nodan had left almost right after. *Of course, he did.* She expected he would be out a lot in their time in the Capital, and he did not let her down. The month passed slowly, she didn't get any more headaches, Damara remembered she had the fabric sample. She sent a message requesting to visit the Noma at her convenience.

A message came the next day to meet the Noma the following day; Damara knew by the brief time it took for the reply her client had interesting news she wished to share. She packaged up the fabric in a decorative box, as she knew the box would be the gift. The sample, she knew was the icing on the cake.

Damara dressed carefully; in a new colour she made for herself. A reddish orange, the colour of deep flame, or 'tis what she called it. She had begun naming her most difficult dyes. She would name the colours on how her mood was or what the resulting colour inspired her to think of. She wore her necklace and both hands were full of rings. Her favorites and most were ruby red. She brought Peylin, and her maid could glean gossip from the Noma's servants who would have more than what she heard from the older woman. They took the carriage up the hill and to the east of the Palace, where the Vezyr of Law had his formal residence. The Halls of the Vezyrs where they conducted the laws of the country were on the lowest hills which led out of the Palace before the bridges cresting the rivers.

They arrived at the courtyard. Alighting from the carriage, the doorman leading Damara to the patio past the dining hall where the Noma was waiting. Peylin went the opposite direction to the kitchens where she would find most of the servants. The Noma had a grape arbor over most of the upper patio, which functioned as shade in the summer heat. This is where she found her hostess waiting for her at a delicately crafted glass table on iron legs.

"How genuinely nice to see you Damara. You are well? I heard about your illness. How are you feeling?" Damara sat down at the seat across from the Noma who hadn't risen from her chair but beckoned for a servant to serve a citrus based tea to her visitor.

"I am much better, thank you, Kavena. I was taken terribly ill for almost a month. an illness of the stomach. I so wanted to be here for the joining; I was looking forward to seeing the fashions."

"Ah yes, the fashions. You have a sample to show me?"

"Yes, here it is."

Damara motioned to the servant she gave the box to when she arrived. The man followed her out to the garden area and stood by the wall holding the box until he was directed to bring it forward, placing it in front of his mistress. She exclaimed over it, a Ravenwood inlaid with Mader of Pearl in a flower design. The box was unique. It cost a dear chunk of coin. Damara hoped the fabric Kavena was about to pull out of it was as jaw dropping. She held her breath as the other woman slowly opened the box lid.

"Oh my! This is gorgeous. This is all mine. I will take it all!" The Noma lifted the fabric, holding it up and running it through her hands several times. She smiled at Damara when she said it was hers.

"I am glad you like it. It is one of the most satisfying colours to date. I have a fair bit ready for your order. You have to tell me what you would like made or I can send you the whole works."

"I will have to think about what I would like commissioned in this fabric. I want it to be spectacular, unlike anything ever seen before. I have never seen such sparkle."

"It was an experiment, which turned out better than I hoped. You are the first to receive this fabric, I am hoping you will wear it well. I am toying with innovative designs and embellishing on current ones. I know the younger women have been trying for years to procure dresses which show more... skin and are not received well. I am adding some more to the sleeves, a flare if you will and I have a dress of my own with slits in the skirt upon twirling, have inlays of a complimentary colour underneath. I can show you if you would like to come deal with me at our villa."

"I would love to, I don't like to bend the rules much, and your dress ideas sound intriguing. Speaking of intriguing, I heard the most disturbing news from some of the other matrons in our circle. Do you know of the young man the Princess joined? Surely your husband knows him, Kavus his name is."

"Yes, Ramus and his Pader are best of friends. He does not speak much about their family. You know Nimai and I had a quarrel several years back and I let Ramis deal with his friend and family on his own. I am not very welcome there."

"Oh yes, I do remember this incident, the whole city was whispering about it for months. Did she ever recover from you hitting her in the face?"

"I haven't been invited back since, so I would think not. I was not looking forward to seeing her again after all these years. I would have to behave myself. I don't like to behave myself if I am in the right. She was wrong to slap my Dader. I still smile when I think of the blood which came out of her nose. She deserved more than this, but Ramis held me back. I would have done more. But that's all in the past. What is it you were going to say?"

"Oh yes. It seems... there are rumours going around... this Kavus... is a bit of a bully."

"A bully? You have described half the men in our circle. Can you explain further?"

"Oh well, you have seen as much as I over the years. It seems the young man likes to beat up women, while he is having his rights."

"Oh, you mean he likes to strike them some, while he..."

"Yes, you don't have to come right out and say it."

"He is like some of the men from the lower city. We are warned to stay out of the lower markets for this reason. I send my maid to go there if I need anything."

"Well, it might be more than this. My head maid was talking with one of the girls in the market who has a sister who works as a maid in the home of the young man and his new bride. It seems there is much screaming from both the Princess and her maid she brought. Both women sported bruises. She also says the Princess was bedridden for weeks, he beat her so badly."

"Oh, 'tis not noble. Have the Emperor and Empress heard these rumours?"

"Surprisingly, The Empress is reported to heard these rumours and stopped them from reaching the Emperor. She had the man killed who was bringing the news."

"So, it seems the Empress really wanted this marriage. But why? The Princess had her choice of suitors. She could have anybody."

"That's just it. The Empress wanted it. That is her favorite family. She always favored them, and now this is known, it did not sway her from her goal. Get the Princess married and with child. The poor girl. It seems she may talk to herself."

"Do you blame her? I probably would, but then, I would probably do worse than this. Tell you the truth, I have a hefty right hook."

Damara smiled and they chatted more about other gossip on other members of the nobility. After some time, Damara excused herself. She was used to using her illness as a means to leave or get out of situations. However, for the most part, she was speaking truth. She felt tired after the days highlights with the Noma and looked forward to relaxing in her villa and gardens. She thanked Kavena for the visit, with her friend saying she would be in touch with what her decision would be concerning the material. Peylin met her at the carriage, and they set off together.

"Did you learn anything?"

"Yes, the young Lord Commander's son is a prick, likes to beat his women when he fucks them." Peylin was visibly upset, and her language showed her upbringing through. Damara agreed the man was not a true noble son.

"The poor girl, the woman telling this story says the person who saw and heard what is done to the Princess, says the Princess is one strong woman. She has come through this, she's with child and he is leaving her alone, however, taking it out on her maid. He has a problem with getting his prick hard with a normal relationship... something to do with his Mader. I don't know what, this is what was told."

"I wouldn't put anything past his Mader. Nimai is quite the tyrant. Maybe she beat him as a child. Who knows. Ramis and I will be seeing the Princess soon to give them our gifts for the birth of their child. I hope that its an easy birth. When we return, I would like to bathe and rest. The Noma is quite the ordeal, I am tired. I will just have a light meal, read a book for a while and rest."

Arriving back at the villa, she had her quiet evening, Ramis was off doing Ramis things. She did not care at all.

Ramis came to her one day, shortly after, saying to honour the upcoming birth of the newest Prince or Princess, and potential heir to the Throne, they were invited to a dinner in the child's honour. Ramis was letting her know ahead of time so she could plan a birthing gift. Good thing she already heard from Kavena who was going. Damara let Ramis bask in his own glory, she was too tired to pick a fight. Glad he was back to speaking with her, she asked what sort of gift would be appropriate. It had been an exceedingly long time since a Royal had given birth.

"You know best, My Dear."

"Well, I have some excess silks, I will get to dying the colours of the Royal House and of your friends. How much time do I have? The birth should be soon, I am thinking. Is not the birth around summer solstice?"

"Yes, which is not very far away."

"May I return to Kara, then? I should make haste. Sometimes first births can come early. I can get any finished orders and bring all back."

"You have leave to go. I will stay and meet with Baron. See what it is he wants and who it may be he has chosen."

"Send me word when you require me back. I may come back when all is dyed. I will send you a missive if I do."

"Thank you. I bid you safe travel. We will eat together tonight if you are to set off tomorrow."

"I will let the Cook know for tonight. Are you fine with duck with citrus?"

"Yes, that is fine. I will find a wine to pair with, and I need to be out. I have a few purchases to make. Good afternoon."

Damara watched as Ramis left, he was dressed for riding and taking only one man. Curious as to why he would say the city was in unrest, and he would hire more men, but then only take his man with him. Then she remembered he had paramours; he must be going to visit one. The thought made her sad. She remembered their courtship, how he would arrive at her Paders home via horseback. He cut an elegant figure back then, in his formal dress, then later in his uniform. Once the marriage contract was signed, the visits diminished.

I was so in love with Ramis back then. I did not know his character, now I know his character, more being revealed every day, and I do not love him. I was so blind. However, 'tis not something I lament. I do have three wonderful children from this man. I do love them, even if I find their Pader less of late. I only wish my boys do not follow in their Pader's footsteps.

As a marriage contract only needed the Patriarch's approval, to be considered valid, her presence was not required. She knew Ramis knew exactly who it was Baron planned to be joined with. Out of their list of potential candidates, Ramis put forth two and promoted them heavily to his son. Damara was at the point of not caring.

First, he involved them with his infidelities, and machinations of where they would serve the Empire without so much as discussing with her. Then he had the nerve to become angry with her when she offered one of their ships. She knew he was angry because it wasn't his idea. He hated when she showed him up, and Damara and her brother had a relationship which bothered him, because Davian would always ask her what she thought and not him first.

Ah, Davian. What a mess with which you must deal. With the advent of Dragons what will you do? Our world, our religion will change. Can you not see it? Will it bring more strife? How can it not? I only hope the Church will not punish women more than they have. Oh, who am I to think that, of course they will. They have already begun. The beating in the square is only the beginning, I should watch my actions, I do not need Ramis punishing me. He would do so, if pushed. He does follow whatever he is told.

Ramis competed with her, in her business, in her day-to-day life, with her sons, and with her brother. She was so tired of his actions. His ability to lie to her face and not think twice, Damara wondered if Ramis married her because he wanted to hang around her brother. He was very attentive to her, when he first began his courtship, but then Davian was living at the family home. He never got anywhere with Davian, and probably never would. She was so done with Ramis, and she forgot to ask Davian her question.

She could leave him now but it would ruin her, Ramis could take the business, and leave her destitute, she wanted to ask Davian if she had enough evidence to divorce him. Only then could she keep what was hers and he could go wherever the fuck he wanted. He had his own fortune she was sure he pocketed away somewhere, and the ships were all his. So, she packed up and left, wanting to return within the month with everything she needed.

Summer promised to be a hot one.

CHAPTER 38

Meera

Being Still of the Heart

We rested the remainder of the day and into the following night. Eating, drinking fresh water, and I took the opportunity to look at my surroundings. The fauna was so different from one side of the mountains to the other. I had never seen the like. The trees were like tall sticks. The leaves skinny and green as the colour of grass. The trunks segmented and I knew one could not climb these. I found a few deadfall ones and saw the inside was hollow. Interesting.

The ferns were different also. They were tall, the leaves wide and flat, like a dinner bowl. Ours, home in the woods behind the Aerie were shorter and the leaves skinny arms, and darker green in colour, Swordferns, named for the shape they were.

I ventured for a wander and heard animals in the forest behind us, the call of strange birds, and a glimpse of some flying fowl, in glorious greens, yellows and reds. This was a land of colour! It was spectacular, and I wished I could have the chance to explore more. Or at least learn from where we were headed, the animals which inhabited the area.

The soil was diverse and distinctive, reddish tan, with finer grains, a mixture of sand and silt. I picked up a handful and filtered it through my hand, coarse and dry. I was on the cusp of the desert and the woods I was currently in. I wondered how plants survived in these soil conditions, but life adapted to its environment, like I would have to.

Nejan hunted for herself, and she kindly brought me a creature I had never seen the like. It was small and scaly, and the skin was leather. The meat was also; I handed it to her and thanked her… I would finish the dried meats. I had a handful left; it would be enough for the next while. I adjusted to the lean meals while travelling, my stomach flattened in, and I honestly did not feel hunger. I lost weight, I knew from the loose skin on my belly and arms, it also gave me great definition, especially my legs which muscled up from all the hiking in the mountains. The resistance of the sand was also a muscle builder. I had a terrible time walking through it. Nejan many times waited for me on the top of a dune or two.

"I'll just finish off this dried meat and berries. We find more strange animals as we go along. I think we're headed to the city which is a day or two away. I am surprised we haven't seen any people yet."

As I made this statement, the feeling we were being watched struck me.

"It's about time you realize this. They have watched us for two days now. They will come forward but are waiting for something. Maybe for us to show ourselves? We should travel Southeast along this ridge until we come out of the jungle forest and then see if we can spot them."

My feet hurt something awful, and I was scared to take what remained of my boots off. I figured I would wait to see what it was. As it was, the leather had worn in areas, I tied straps around my ankles and calves and I was not looking forward to the mess I knew was beneath all the leather. I rose slowly to my feet, gathering the harness and folding it into my pack. The rest of my body ached too, but it was from the long days of walking. I could use a rest, but not until we finished and arrived where our quest sent us.

Everything else I carried. We consumed most of our supplies and there was only enough for one laden pack, which was more awkward than heavy. I hoisted it up, tying the straps and following the great cat already padding away. Nejan led the way. The sun was directly overhead when we finally emerged to the barren landscape we had known for the last two months, leaving the shade of the canopy of strange trees behind us.

We rounded a corner of the cliffside we were following. The gorge was to our right now and receding the further we walked. We were surprised by a group of warriors, some male and some female, standing in formation of a semicircle waiting for us. They stood at the ready but did not have their weapons presented like they were going to attack. They were of darker skin than the nomads I left behind on the other side of the burning sands. There was one who was lighter than all the rest. It seemed an eclectic mix. The garb on the women, was tight tops of leather material. Some of the men wore loincloths while others wore short leggings, they all had knives of a shiny material and very long spears, with gorgeous feathers decorating them.

We both stopped and I am assuming the leader came forward. She was the center of the semi circle before us. She spoke a language I did not understand. As I did not reply or look like I understood she gestured with her hands for us to approach, holding her palms up and out, the universal language for "I mean you no harm." Walking forward we passed the outer edge of warriors; they bowed at the waist to us. The leader walked ahead, the remainder fell behind as we passed by. We walked most of the day. My feet turning to an intense ache with each step. The ache was a reminder that there was something wrong. Our entourage was strangely quiet, and a bit unnerving,

"They are disciplined warriors,"

"Do you think they speak our language?"

"They may think that we, or you speak theirs. They may be cautious and we will wait until we arrive at the end of this path."

"They are erring on the side of caution, like you believe. I can wait; the silence is not too unnerving."

It was leading into evening as we finally approached the outer wall of a great city. They slowed their pace, I had begun to limp, and every step taken with great resolve.

'Oooff.'

I tried not to wince, but occasionally my breath would labour and I was making small whimpers without realizing it. One warrior saw my struggle and gave me her spear to use as a walking stick, I gratefully placed my hand over my heart and bowed my head to her, she bowed back. It eased my efforts so I could continue. We arrived at our destination.

How to describe this? I have never seen larger walls than Ravenswood Castle in such a different landscape. They rose before us, as high as any cliff, and stretched to either side as far as I observed. An imposing and bare, devoid of ornament, vista, but one to take stock of. These walls were very thick at the base. We walked through the gates made of a bleached wood I had never seen before.

The walls of the city were made from the natural landscape. A faded version of the soil I looked at, by the edge of the gorge. Pale orange-yellow coloured rock or brick with no visible gaps. It appeared seamless from the quick glance I had before I walked inside. I was not given the time to look further as we soon walked through crowds of unwashed people, gasping, and chatting in their own language. As they saw us, some genuflected and bowed. Silence followed us, when Nejan passed through, it remained until we left the crowds, then I heard the sounds of chatter rise like a wave, lots of excitement.

"You are quite the crowd stopper."

"They have not seen my kind before I believe. There is a feeling of reverence. I will bask in their admiration while I can. Once you are known, it will follow you."

"I can wait, Great Mader. You bask for now."

The crowd parted easily for us as two more of our escorts walked past us to head off the crowd and two more moved in beside us. We walked up a slight incline under another battlement and through another gate. Here the avenues were farther apart, and people wearing cleaner garments. There was less dirt and less sound. The clothing in the first entrance was muted, the colours matched the landscape, browns, and tans, but once inside this next gate, it was as though flowers bloomed! The citizens wore every colour, and it was bright! I had to shield my eyes; it was like walking into a garden! There were markets we passed through with exotic smells which I longed to investigate but we walked on.

"The people look friendly enough."

"I feel no aggression from any, we look to be expected, I feel a waiting energy, if this makes sense."

As we passed through yet another gate I wondered where our journey ended, then our escort halted. We were in a small courtyard of golden stone walls and a fountain playing wonderful water music. I must have made a sound, as the leader motioned us to an opening which we followed. The rest of our escort was taking off their gear, handing their weapons to others dressed very simply in robes and loincloths. Here was an open room with tables, benches, and the smell of food, strange to my nose but appetizing. My stomach let out a growl which seemed loud to my ears. The inhabitants of the room gasped when they saw the size of Nejan. Almost all bowed when they saw her.

I saw every shade of skin; this was a land of diversity. It was refreshing. There was almost midnight black to even more fair than me. There was blonde hair, almost white to braided black hair, and a few wine reds. No one had my bright locks which looked brown with all the dirt and sand in it. I was looking forward to cleaning my scalp which itched something fierce! It felt good to not be an oddity, standing out because of the way I looked. I looked around at my surroundings and was motioned forward by the man who seemed to oversee the servants.

Nejan padded over to a bare spot against the wall laying herself down. I went to the front section beside her and found a spot on a bench. Right away we were served foods of an exotic nature and some of the servants approached Nejan with platters of raw meats, placing them on the floor in front of her grinning and chatting. She raised herself up, sniffing around the platters and then gobbled down the meats. I grinned at her, turning to my plates and began to sample everything they served. I also had a light wine and sipped it occasionally. I made sounds of thanks, bowing my head and the servers smiled back. Some things are universal and don't need translation.

We finished our repast and as I looked around at the people who were gathered, the leader of the servants came up to me, touching his garb and making a motion of shaking it out. I rose, following him through another doorway with Nejan padding behind me. We emerged into a courtyard of pools, with several people in them who began speaking as soon as we entered.

The leader said something, everyone getting out, all of them naked. I gathered this was a cleansing bath area. There were walkways in between and several raised flower and shrub beds with the most stunning trees and flowers in them. The trees were tall enough to provide shade. These were different from home and different from the forest we had departed outside the city walls. They had broader leaves which provided shade, and the bark was a lighter brown than what I left behind. I wondered if this was the wood I saw on the gates.

He motioned to my clothes, and I did not think twice. I ripped off my clothes, but I had to sit down on a stone bench, trying to take my worn boots off. Struggling with the strips of cloth I tied around the leather of the boots, one of the warriors who met us out by the gorge came towards me palm's up with a knife in her hand. Making cutting motions and motioning towards my boots. She was asking to cut them off.

I nodded my consent, and she proceeded to gently cut them off my calves cutting the leather off at my ankle. I saw the rawness from the sand which rubbed against my skin and leather. While it provided some relief, it also set them off to hurting. When the fresh air touched my raw skin, it burned! I was not looking forward to seeing what my feet looked like.

She gently cut one boot off, then the other and I saw the devastation of my feet. The sand which remained inside the leather of the boot had scrubbed the top layer of my skin off. They began throbbing.

She motioned for another person and holding out her hand for me to take as she helped me to rise. My face said it all. Another girl came to assist. They both placed their arms around my waist, and I instinctively put my arms around their shoulders. It was a good thing I had done so, because when I went to walk my feet burst into flames of pain.

It hurt as though I was walking on fire coals. I tried not to moan too much, but my breath with each step gave me away. The women smiled sympathetically at me.

They literally held me up, walking me to the first step of the pool. I gently dipped first one foot in the water and then the other. They walked me in slowly. The coolness of the water helped ease the pain of my throbbing feet. I relented and let them carry me by the end. I was thinking they saw this before.

Nejan made to follow but I shook my head and motioned to the adjoining pool beside me.

"Ah, no... Great One. With the addition of you, there would be a huge overflow of water. I think you will want your own pool."

I did not want to think about what was trapped in her fur. As the water swirled gently, I floated around the edges seeing openings in the base of the pool which denoted a current of sorts. The girls stayed in the pool; I was guessing to assist me if I should require it.

Good thing the Great Cat had her own bathing pool, because as Nejan walked into it, it overflowed. As she began to move around, I saw she was contorting herself, debris, sand, and other questionable things were making their way to my pool in the small tidal waves she was creating. She was enjoying herself! I felt her happiness as I dunked my head and rinsed my hair.

As my head came up out of the water, I heard gasps and chatter from the servants and warriors who stayed. The two women who entered the pool with me taking what looked like a block of soap and motioning to my hair, I nodded, and they helped me to wash. I was very thankful for the help. Smiling, I placed my palms together and bowed to them. I tried to stand but the two women took to either side of me, helping me to exit the pool.

They sat me down on a cool stone bench, another servant coming forward with a thin cloth and made to start drying me off. I smiled, putting my hand out for the towel which she placed in my hand, and I began to dry myself off. I started with my torso and back, being careful not to break the chain around my neck. I looked around for my clothes but could not find them. Then another servant came forward with a robe of the finest silk fabric. It was a golden colour with fine detail stitching. The two girls stood me up on my painful feet, helping fit the robe around my body, then sat me back down.

Two female servants came forward with towels and a small basket with tonics and lotions. I took a better look at my feet. Around the base and sides, I had blisters and callouses. In being released from the cage of my torn boots, my feet had begun to swell. One of the girls sat on her knees taking my foot gently in her hand, using a very sharp knife began shaving off the callouses and blisters.

Being interested in what they were doing, I watched closely as they shaved open blister pockets which contained gel-like pus with some of them being black and some of them being white with black dots inside. I gathered during my trip across the sand I gained some bugs which burrowed into the thicker skin of my feet. As they finished the shaving, one of the girls applied a cooling ointment on my feet and they wrapped them in clean, soft linens, tying them off.

Realizing they were finished, I let them help me to my feet. Belting the robe, I waited for Nejan to finish cavorting in the pool smiling at the chatter. They gasped as she rose out of the pool shaking herself like a dog, getting the closest to her quite wet. We were led through several passageways to an inner courtyard, with me walking very slowly unassisted, but walking none the less. It did not hurt! Whatever was in this ointment took the pain away.

Nejan found herself a sunny spot, plopped herself down, proceeding to lick herself and stretch out for a nap. Looking around, I saw a bed of sorts, raised up off the floor in an alcove. I went towards it, motioning to the leader who nodded, and promptly fell asleep as soon as my head touched the pillow. Waking the next morning, I rolled over opening my eyes to a large retinue of people. I assumed they were servants apart from one impeccably dressed woman, who as she saw I was awake began giving orders.

One held out a pot, motioning me to go behind a mesh screen. She held out her hand, helping me up and I noticed the wrappings on my feet were new and a new application of ointment was applied. I found when I stepped down onto the ground my feet did not hurt as much as they did the day before and the swelling had abated. I walked to the mesh screen. Behind it was a chair with a hole in the seat. She placed the pot beneath the chair and motioned me forward. I exclaimed in delight, smiled, and sat down and did what I had to do. She picked up the pot as I rose, made a comment to which the others ohh'd in response.

I was led back into the main room area, then directed to a table where there was an assortment of fruits I had never seen before. The girls stood by me and waited. I realized they were waiting for me. I pointed to a fuchsia-coloured fruit, and a girl came forward, picked one and began to cut it open. Inside was a soft white flesh with black dots. She spooned some onto my dish and I picked up a gilded metal spoon sampling it. It was so delicious!

I ate all placed on my plate and noticed some fresh bread of sorts coming in as I smelled it throughout the room. I motioned for the bread the same girl cut a slice, wiping a pate on it, which as I tasted, realised to be goat's milk butter.

I made sounds of delight as I ate, to which all the girls were giggling until the older woman frowned. I ate several pieces of bread then sat back, rubbing, and patting my belly.

Nejan rose to do her business on the lawn outside in a corner to which the men servants rushed over with a large Wicker basket on wheels and some shovels, picking up her waste. They also goggled over it. The garden lawn was a delicious shade of green. I saw they meticulously trimmed it by the men in the background on their knees with sheers doing just this.

"Umm, Great Mader. What is the fascination with our waste? It seems we have spectacular dung?"

"We could be Gods to these people. I do not know. Other than myself, mayhap we are expected to be Royal? We will find out in time, Little Cub. I would expect we will know in suitable time."

Nejan was fed another wicker basket of raw meats blood still dripping, until she was satisfied.

"You are being spoiled here; you may not wish to leave."

"They are very generous and have treated us well. I have enjoyed having fresh meats. You are taken care of well?"

"Yes, I did not realize my feet were so bad. Taking out all those burrowing bugs made my feet look like someone was hungry. They are raw, but whatever was in this lotion made them feel so much better. Once I communicate with them, I really wish to learn what some of their plants are."

"I am sure you will be here long enough to learn their language. You have more to do after spending time here, but learning is how we grow, mentally and physically. You learn everything you can from everyone, and you will grow to be who you are meant to be. The Universe will place people and events before you, not only to test you but to make you learn and grow. You have choices whether you do good or bad, and that shapes your path. We all have choices, mine is to eat until my belly is full."

If a cat could smile, I imagined Nejan doing such. She had a direct manner, and we both starved our way across the burning sands. I felt the same way as Nejan, she put it into words.

I kept smiling as a formally dressed man came in barking orders. I stood there looking at him until the woman came forward touching my arm to direct me back to the sleeping chamber. He followed until she shooed him away, leading me to a room on the other side with an assortment of fabrics hanging up. There were hues of every colour, and some I never imagined!

I fingered all the assorted colours I saw, finally picking out a deep emerald green which reminded me of the trees at home. She proceeded to wrap me in it. The woman and her assistant finished with a tie of sorts and presented me with a tray of jewelry in an assortment of colours. I selected some emerald and Ruby pieces to compliment my ring which I placed on my index finger as this was the only one it fit. The fabric lay on my skin like a soft kiss. It draped on my body loosely from two clasps of gold which sat on my neck muscles. I felt like I was wearing nothing.

"They are dressing me in fine cloth. You may be right. We must be going to meet their leader."

"Of course, I am right. I am rarely wrong."

One of the girls bade me sit on a stool. She brushed out my hair which several other girls had to touch until the older woman smacked a few hands away with a curt admonishment. She styled it away from my face with fine chains and showed me a reflection of a woman in a glass mirror. I was astonished! I had not seen my face in a mirror for at least 7 years since running amok in the castle.

I had not the slightest interest in my appearance. The face staring back at me would be what people might call attractive if it weren't for the white scar from my brow to my jawline. I thought it made me look formidable, which wasn't a terrible thing, I guess.

I noticed my eyes had a luminescence occurring. Flecks of glitter is the only way I could describe it. And my hair! I had curls which sprung and coiled down my back. But what really had me in awe was the colour it had become. My hair was a vivid red! I don't remember it being this bright. I always thought it to be darker like Kiem's.

"It was darker, Little Dader. I watched it brighten after each time the other voice spoke to you and after you killed the elder. I suspect it will get even more bright like the flames of fire."

I must have looked like I was staring at myself, I started when the elder woman touched my arm. She gestured to me to follow her and also to Nejan with her hand gestures. We padded softly after her, me in a pair of slippers they provided. The swelling and redness diminished overnight. Whatever was in this salve, I really wanted to know. My feet were feeling better, they looked like mice had eaten little bites out of my soles.

I gazed around the courtyards we traveled through; people would stop and stare and a few bowed. Then conversations would begin as we left and very soon, I heard the conversations following us. We went outside walking up along a garden path, towards a huge building which I realised housed their leader. There were soldiers every ten paces along this walkway and up steps into a Grand Hall.

The soldiers were in formal dress. The white linen tunics embroidered in gold thread, with trousers of purple, purple sashes draped on one shoulder and around their waists. There was visible signs of swords over one shoulder and another around their waist with the leathers which accompanied both. They had bronzed helmets with a purple fabric draped from them. I saw it helped to keep them cool while being decorative.

At the end of the path was a robed man, dressed elaborately with an ornate headdress of linen and jewels. Purple was a royal colour, then. Beside him was a woman of latter years, too old to be his wife, I assumed she was his Mader, but since I didn't speak the language, I didn't worry about making any mistakes. He looked to be middle aged maybe younger, but as I did not know how to determine age by looking, I was merely speculating.

We were ushered forward by our escort. The man stood up from his Throne and made a gesture. I bowed a little and a gasp came from a few people. The man was startled but nodded and spoke, I asked Nejan if she understood. She said she didn't, but there was a servant here who could translate. She turned around at a commotion in the far doorway. Padding down the aisle, the crowd parted before her to the door where a few people were arguing quietly.

I turned, watching on, as the soldiers would not let a poorly dressed girl pass. The others were arguing softly. Nejan strode down the aisle and roared out to which everyone lowered to their knees and then genuflected onto their fronts. Striding over to the girl placing her paw, with claws extended over the shaking girls head, who along with everyone else was laying prone on the floor. The great beast then roared to the crowd; removed her paw and then licked the back of the girl's body which had the effect of rolling her over.

Nejan stood staring at the girl, the girl speaking, in their language.

"The Great Lioness wishes me to translate her wishes to the Amman and assembly."

One of the soldiers came over, helping the poor girl up, giving her his cloak to cover her rags. Another came forth to offer his belt and they fashioned a robe for her to come up the aisle with Nejan. As they reached the dais, the girl first bowed, then got on her knees and faced down on the carpet in front of the Throne. Staying like this until the Amman spoke to her. She did not look at the leader as she went still and Nejan looked down at her. She then spoke quietly in the Amman's direction. The Amman spoke, spreading his arms to his people in the Great Hall, a cheer went up and clapping of hands. Nejan saying to me as she turned around to face the members of the audience and I followed suit,

"They welcome us with open arms and will hold a great feast in our honor. They seem to think I am a God reincarnate and you are my familiar. The girl is now ours. I claimed her as mine and she can hear my thoughts as you can, but I do not think she is a DragonRider. I will question her later when we rest. She will need a bit of cleaning. We are to go back to our rest area and prepare for the feasting."

"A God? That's spectacular!"

She walked slowly through the masses with the girl following behind us, Nejan slowly looking over the crowd as many bowed and exclaimed themselves with arms raised and voices crying out.

"One must have a sense of calm dignity and patience when dealing with adoration. We mustn't rush ourselves. They are here to see us; we will let them see all."

I just smiled. She was feline elegance.

"But, of course."

In time, we walked out of the Great Hall and back down the way from which we had arrived. As we arrived at our doorway, our same attendants were there waiting. Softly talking with the young girl, she bowed her head and walked off until Nejan stopped and roared again.

The girl scooted back, the man and woman made motions asking for forgiveness and we started back to our courtyard. There the girl was motioned to the baths, given a robe and then brought to us. They had dressed her in a white robe, which was unadorned until I rose, going to the room, bringing back a glorious bright blue fabric which I motioned her towards. The older woman looked at me and I gazed back and kept motioning towards the girl. She then took the fabric from me and dressed the girl in it. The blue went so well with her hair and her brown skin, I chose well, I thought.

I motioned for ears and throat, and the older woman retrieved a blue sapphire set I nodded my approval to and put it on the girl. I tapped my head, pointing to the girls' wet tresses of the bluest black. My attendant had her sit and did a simple hairdo, with a blue ribbon.

At last, I was satisfied and sat down at the table to have a drink of simple juice of berries. I motioned to the young girl to sit down. She sat and waited.

I asked Nejan to reassure her she was safe and would remain with us to translate. I pointed to the fruit and requested Nejan ask her what it was. The young girl said, "Bandon," which I found out later meant, Dragon fruit. I repeated what she said and began pointing to the other things and thus my education began.

We went over everything in the room, me asking and her speaking while Nejan napped in the sun. Then other girls joined in, and I learned a lot of words that day. This is how my afternoon passed. I would walk and point, others would tell me, and I would repeat. I had a group of six or more girls. As we walked around the whole gardens, others soon followed, chatting among themselves, and giggling when I pronounced something wrong.

The smell of flowers and shrubs were overwhelming; my nose was busy processing. I even picked up the scent of Nejan's urine from the far corner of the garden next to this one. Soon we had to bathe again. I had quite the collection of girls each doing a different task. One took it upon herself to wash my hair another soon joined in to wash my arms or body. I found out I was ticklish in a few areas and soon we had a water fight going on. It was fun and felt liberating to laugh again. I hadn't laughed like this in a very long time, if at all, and my stomach muscles were aching for a while after.

We ended up splashing quite a bit onto the deck and soon it was time to dry and get dressed. This time I was not inclined to robe myself; I walked naked to the dressing room and by the time I arrived there, all but my hair had dried. I did not feel self-conscious of my body in the company I was keeping. There were no feelings of negative energy from people I was surrounded by, and it was refreshing. I picked out a pale purple robe. My girls dressed me and gave me amethyst jewels to wear. I had one brush and dress my hair again with coordinating gems and chains of silver. As Nejan woke up and stretched I asked her if she needed anything, to which she replied,

"I need nothing Little Dader, I will hate to have to leave,"

I exclaimed in shock, *"Not yet surely?"*

"At some point I will, however, I will ensure you have a good grasp of knowledge of these people, who call themselves Lanthians. They believe a lot of good comes back if they do good themselves, yet they are also a fierce fighting nation. Their warriors are second to none for bravery and skill. Here I think you would do well to learn some fighting skills from them, if you stay."

"You know, I think you are right."

"Of course, I am."

"I feel this will be the right thing to do. I can not learn a skill from a society who doesn't believe in women fighting, let alone having equal status. History teaching women are to be weak and the men dominant. I must begin by being able to defend myself. If ever I am to wield a sword and find my Dragon, I will need some fighting skills. Hopefully, it will be a skill I won't ever have to use."

"Better to be trained and not have to use it, than to lament the lack when needed."

"Again, you are right. But how am I going to broach a subject if I do not know the language?"

"You are an adaptive learner, I am sure you will be able to grasp their speech in no time at all, Little Cub. You have learned great skill in tracking from me."

"Well, these things have a tendency to work themselves out, so let's just go eat," I responded turning back to her with a smile.

We followed the men up the hill to the Palace but took a side path to another Great Hall which held long rows of tables with a head table to which we were led. Nejan padded off to the side I was sent to and let herself down on a small dais which held her perfectly. The Hall was filled with all sorts of elegantly dressed people in all colours of garb. They all stopped talking when we entered, as we progressed past, they bowed and a few genuflected, all signs of reverence.

I was led up the centre to the head table, placed beside the older woman, my translator was placed on the other side of me, and on the other side of the older woman was the leader. My translator quickly told me his title was Amman. On his right were two more men whose garb was elaborate but not as fine as the Amman's. His crown was ordained with so many jewels, it looked like he wore a very heavy weight, over and above the gold. I did not envy him, I noticed he was looking at me without trying to.

Hmmm, I wonder what this is about.

As I gazed over, I notice one of the men looking at the older woman with a veiled look. His energy I felt was mixed and left me puzzled, I would not know until later what the look meant. I took my seat next to my translator, whose name was simply Chan'tele. She told me many toasts would be made to honour the great cat and myself, as my red hair meant I was of the flying Gods of old. I gave myself a start as a servant came between us filling my glass with a rich red wine. I noticed the pungent smell right away.

She stepped back and another took her place filling the older woman's glass with a rose wine. I observed thinking to myself if only I had a lighter wine than the heavier red. I focused on her glass. I narrowed in on it as she brought it to her nose, I could focus on the aromas emanating from the wine. I smelled the fruits and an underlining smell which set my stomach to edge. Where had I smelled this before?

"Nejan. Somethings feels not right."

"What is it?"

"The older woman's wine. I smell a rank smell. Like the pool in the middle of the sand. Like rotten, 'tis faint, but I smell it."

"I smell it also. You trained yourself to focus on the parts, not the whole. Clever work. The more you practice, the easier and faster you will get."

Halfway here, the smell was of a plant I crushed under foot by the poison water. The smell on my boot was enough to make me want to vomit I could make out a hint of it, but it was enough.

The Amman stood up and I could understand even without my girl translating he was toasting Nejan and myself, good health. As he raised his glass, all raised their glasses and began to sip at their vintages. The older woman began to take a sip; I brought my hand to her glass and smacked it away violently. I noticed the man across the way watching. The wine sprayed the Amman, the table laden with fruits and ornate decorations. His protectors behind him pointed their spears at me and the older woman cried out as I partially hit her cheek. Silence in the room reigned with expectation.

Motioning with my hands around my neck and making strangled noises, and Chan'tele told the Amman with her head down I indicated it was poisoned. The servants picked up the goblet from the floor and brought it to their Ruler, who gave it to me when I asked for it. I grabbed it and brought it to my nose. I could smell the fermentation of the plant explaining this all to Chan'tele who in turn told the Amman. His Mader sitting back was still in shock. The Amman called the servant who served the wine, and the girl came forward shaking all the while.

She explained the wine was given to her by another servant she had never seen before. As she was explaining this to the Amman, she lay flat on the floor, crying. I watched the man across the other side, saw fear in his eyes, and then arrogance crossed his countenance. I touched the Queen Mader's arm and motioned to Chan'tele to ask the Queen Mum who the man was, whispering softly while the Amman was interrogating the servant.

The Queen Mum whispered the man across the way was quite ambitious and had made overt advances to her. Her son refused the offers of marriage to his Mader. The man had other ambitions, which she noticed and all this was told to me in the moment.

"Can you smell or sense anything from this man? I get an energy from him; I am not sure of."

"I sense dishonesty, and malice, his pores emanate it."

"That is good to know, thank you Great Mader. Now you have spoken, I sense it also. I would like you to teach me once we have a moment."

"You begin with a circle of energy around a person or animal. Then draw the circle close in, making it smaller. Each time you do so, what you feel instinctively each time will give you an idea of intent. Do so until you close the circle inside of their body, at the core. The last point will give you the whole. The others will compliment or correspond with what you feel about their energy. Use this to practice on others. 'Tis what makes you special, and it will save you from harms others would do."

"I thank you again."

She rose padding over from behind the front table, paced up to the men standing beside the Amman and began sniffing around. Everyone hushed watching to see what she would do. She sniffed the first Vezyr, and then on to the next man. Which she sniffed very thoroughly.

"I smell the plant, faintly on his fingers under his nails, however I will let you determine this, so you can take credit, you need the boon from the Amman you ask a favor, and he will grant it."

Approaching the prone girl, the guards parting to let her by, Nejan sniffed the girl, telling me she was clean smelling, except for fear radiating from her. Chan'tele translated this part to the Amman.

She then padded over to the older woman laying down behind her. I rose from my chair bowing to the Amman and strode up to the man I watched, grabbing his hand before he could react.

He tore it out of my grasp, but the Amman said something softly and he held his hand back out. I held his hand and brought it to my nose; I could smell a faint aroma. Before he could react and before I could think about it much, I took his pointer finger into my mouth and sucked on it. I tasted the citric bitterness of the plant. After I took his finger out of my mouth, more like he jerked it back, I spit out onto the floor.

"I have told the girl,"

"Thank you." I heard her soft voice tell the Amman what Nejan said, but he already knew from my action what she was going to say. I backed away one step to the side of the visibly shaking man.

In one fluid motion the man before me lowered to his knees, laying down in a prone position in front of the Amman begging for mercy. I did not need a translator; the action spoke for itself. The Amman barked something out. One of the guards took hold of the motionless man raising him up. He was sobbing profusely and uttering denial. I fluidly moved myself back to the Amman's Mader's side.

"This is your opportunity. Ask the leader for your favour. This is what the Universe would have for you." I turned back to see the guard slice the man's head off with one swipe of his sword. The Amman then spoke to the crowd, and everyone sat back down. Turning to me he spoke.

"The Amman says for saving his Mader's life, you can ask anything of him. He is eternally grateful. This is your moment, Little Cub." I rose to my feet and stood in front of him, then on impulse dropped to one knee.

"I wish to serve the Amman, learn the way of the mighty warrior, become an asset to his army, in order to move forward in the Age to come." Chantelle translated after Nejan spoke to her. The Amman raised his hands in the air making an announcement to the whole assembly clapping and cheering. I returned to my seat as Chan'tele translated telling me the Amman wholeheartedly approved of my request, and I would make his army invincible.

He motioned for the feast to resume, the servants moving to clear away the remains of the Vezyr who made a fool of himself. I smiled at the amount of food and tried in our way to talk to the woman beside me. Several times I saw the Amman glancing my way. Once when I caught him, I lowered my eyes and bowed my head. He drew in his breath and I looked back up to see him smile and bow his head.

"Nejan, is he paying me deference?"

"It would appear so."

"But he knows me not."

"Practice your senses, I feel other emotions. What can you see?"

"Well, I see respect, right away. Then if I narrow in... admiration...and...closer yet...oh."

"Yes, Little Cub?" I began to blush and looked down and took a bite of food. I wasn't sure what it was, I wasn't tasting anything. Just chewing what was on my fork.

"He feels desire. I am not sure I wanted to know this."

"You are sure to have many admirers among your kind. Procreation is natural among humans."

"Yes, but I never thought I would be on the receiving end."

"Well, you gauge a person's temperament, the more you practice, the better you will get and it will tell you if one means harm or good. Desire is among good things, is it not?"

"As long as the bearer is true. Desire used in selfish means is not."

I looked up and took a deep breath to steady my mind, then I looked at the Amman. He had turned to the side, talking quietly to the man beside him. He was striking to be sure. dark skin, which glowed in the candle and torch light. His eyes, a warm brown which smiled by themselves, I saw he smiled a lot. He had creases on his face, which denoted some age or experience.

I looked to his Mader to see her watching me and smiling. I smiled back and she raised her glass to mine. Clinking them together, we smiled and sipped.

"What is the word for thank you?"

"It is 'Dad doe."

"Dad doe."

The older woman spoke softly and Nejan translated to me. *"She is asking why you are thanking her, when it should be her thanking you."*

"I am thanking her for providing hospitality in my quest. It is very welcoming, and she is an excellent hostess. 'Tis fitting, to thank the host."

"She says you are the one who is promised, and you have excellent manners. She is glad to provide you with anything you require. Her son will be at your command also. She assures you he will also provide you with anything you require. I am not sure why she would speak for him. He is right there."

"She saw me looking at him and I am sure she knows her son best. She is probably thinking of a union between the two of us. I have many things to do. I do not have time for a dalliance or joining. I leave all in the hands of the Universe. It will guide me on my path."

Nejan must have told Chan'tele a bit, she spoke softly to the Amman's Mader, who nodded her head and I saw the Amman heard it. His face lost expression.

"What exactly did you tell her, may I ask? The Amman heard it and it has made him sad. I would not want to be the cause of sadness."

"I merely said you left all in the hands of the Universe, it would guide you on your path. It would place you where you need to be. I thought to be opaque in the telling."

"Thank you. I will have to tell him myself when I learn the language somewhat. I want friends, I am not sure how my path includes a partner right now."

"You will be fine. You learn what you need to learn, then the Universe will set you back onto the path it wants you to travel. Some will travel with you; others

will stay in one spot. I will be with you here for a time, then I will move on. 'Tis what my path is."

I knew at that moment I was going to be all right. Training in combat arms was what I needed. I had to be able to defend myself, with the discipline I saw displayed tonight. This was where I needed to be. I would stay, learn what I could and when the time was right, I would move on. I smiled taking a sip of the red which wasn't all bad!

"Well, this was almost too easy. I will learn combat, and arms. Then I am better prepared for what comes."

"'Tis what you need to do. As a cub, I had to learn to defend myself from others. It wasn't easy, so I am thinking you may find your training as hard. Be prepared, you may find yourself getting trained soon."

My training began the very next day, after I had risen, and broke my fast, I was asked to follow the older servant woman. She led me through a different battlement gate into a training yard. Nejan walked beside me and as we approached a woman commander yelling at the training warriors, the swordplay ended. The sweaty men and women parted to let us through. We stopped when we neared her.

"This leader states you and the girl will be housed with others. There is no rank, no favoritism among those here. We are all the same level, rank. I am to lay wherever my gracious being desires. I will go over there while you fight."

"Of course." Nejan promptly lay her body in the shade of trees, lining one side. Servants came to her side giving her water. The woman pointed to the building on the other side. I followed another leader of the soldiers, and we entered a building with mats on the floor.

She pointed to two, then walked to the end, into a smaller room, us following her every step. She pointed at my clothes and handed us piece by piece of leather attire from hooks on walls, which I gathered by Chan'tele stripping off her robe and putting on the items handed to her we were to wear. I followed her lead. Stripping off my robe, I put on a leather skirt of strips over the loincloth I was wearing and a leather bodice vest, lacing it up over my small breasts. The sandals I was wearing were traded for tighter fitting leather lace up booties, which I hoped didn't let in the bugs and they didn't make my feet anymore sore than they were.

Both of us were handed wooden swords, beckoned to follow to a different section of the training yard, and given over to another leader. With this, Chan'tele and I began our training. It was hard. I was hit so many times, by another who had only been there two weeks but knew so much more. I learned unfamiliar words, commands and tried to communicate on my own but failed miserably. I became so many assorted colours, with my hair I looked quite colourful. The meals were meager, but I did not care, and I did not complain. This went on for a few weeks, my skin changing colour every day.

Chan'tele on the other hand, failed miserably at everything they threw at us,

"Chan'tele looks miserable, Nejan. Do you think you could have her serve you instead? I know a little of the language; I can muddle through on my own and will use the girl when I can't. I don't think she will make a good warrior.

Then she will be more grateful to not have all these bruises. " Nejan had Chan'tele translate, and she gratefully went to the great cat's side resting in the shade with her.

I ate, trained, and slept with the men and women in the yard. After a month of being battered and bruised, I advanced to another cohort. I had rudimentary language skills and finally some of the others were approaching, introducing themselves. All except one woman, who scowled every time I looked her way. A couple of the men said to ignore her, she was a bitch to everyone, including the men. However, she was their top fighter and to become one of the fighting ranking warriors, one would have to beat her in hand-to-hand combat.

The weather seemed to change, from extremely hot, to high fierce winds and then lots of rain. I trained in it all. I began to notice I had muscles, and my body was firming. I became quite proud of what my body shape was becoming.

"This is their season where the shoots come out of the ground. They will stop on a particular day and celebrate the creation of life. You humans call it a solstice. There will be an abundance of drink and food. It is very colourful, Chan'tele tells me. " The day came, training ceased, I was given more food and wine was passed around. There was lots of horse play and I made sure I didn't indulge too much; I remembered the headache I had from the liquor I consumed with the nomadic Wanderers.

Keeping my head is what saved me in the end, the grouchy woman whose name was Adini, approached me and saying, "You are not one of us, and you never will be. You should leave," All in the vicinity who heard, grew quiet waiting for Chan'tele to translate, but I raised my hand,

"I heard enough to know, "

I knew enough about bruised ego's, I had after all grown up, with a brother who thought he was entitled to have respect without earning it. I received the same sort of energy from this woman and knew what I said next, would be crucial. Chan'tele came forward and translating what my response was to all.

"I have no intention of becoming one of you. We are all Tamber pieces on the game of life. I would however like to be able to learn from the best warriors, walk side by side, with all of you, regardless of nationality, difference in speech, religion. We all have a purpose in life. Let me find mine, I promise you the future holds profound changes, and I would hope to move forward with you, not against."

Hearing the unspoken words, 'either you are with me, or you are not,' Adini glared at me and shrugged sarcastically, turned, and walked away, still scowling with a couple of her companions following behind.

"There is a different energy surrounding this female warrior, enough so, you should watch your step, she is not a threat, but 'tis something which has me puzzled. Her energy is different. Quite different. "

"I feel it also, but I do not know what 'tis. "

"She wants to fight you, but she wants to fight everyone. It is her focus. Her mental being. Her direction. "

"I have to work harder if I am to be good enough to beat her, advancing to warrior status, to be ready for war."
  "But go to war with who?"

CHAPTER 39

Rowan

Til the Death of the Spirit

As Rowan's birthing time came closer, summer came early, days were hot and unbearable. She harvested many vegetables, mostly in the morning hours and they had bountiful dinners. Men would hunt in the hills behind the villa, bringing in venison and other kills. It was a very fruitful time for them. Kavus was in grand spirits, he went on a few hunts. On morning, Rowan was resting in her flower garden where Tannah found her. Tannah was changing the sheets on beds and she sat down beside her mistress, placing the linens beside her.

"There are orchards behind the villa, Noda, and mountains beyond this. Your husband owns quite a large tract of land. It has been in the family for many generations. He has a large vineyard and olive trees. There is another valley to the North where the buildings are, the olive presses and winery are there."

"I wonder if I would be able to see it one day. I am curious about the processes."

"I think not. At least not until after the birth. He has patrols around this villa and I hear there are many men guarding the vineyards."

"Why, what for?"

"There is unrest in the city. More laws are being implemented. Some try to escape and are known to rob outlying towns and homes. The countryside's do not have the protection needed. Kavus knows this and he is granted more men, by the order of the Emperor."

"He really expects this child to be a boy. What if it's a girl? He will be sorely disappointed."

"You will bear it with dignity. Much like you are doing. You have an inner strength, Noda. It will serve you well, during the birth. Many women would have given up by now."

"Kavus is mean. I see this now. If one is to ignore what he says, and try to see why he says it, one sees he is not a content man. There is a wounded boy inside of him. It makes me wonder what happened to make him so."

"You are too kind. He is a cruel man. He does not care…"

"I know. I am sorry you must endure the most of his…relations. It grieves me to no end. If I could change your circumstances I would."

"I can bear it, Noda. He is no different than any other man in the city. I have heard accounts of worse happenings. Women are publicly beaten by their husbands, for as little as forgetting to wear a head veil."

"Veils are required now? I thought it merely ornamental, at least among the nobility."

"The Namarch has charged the nobility to set the tone and lead by example. Head coverings are mandatory. Much like what Aram women wear but not to the extreme of covering the whole face. Aram believes women cannot be seen as they would instill lust in men not their husband."

"Men are afraid women would instill lust? They are the lustful ones. I could not care if I ever have…that again. 'Tis a horrible act."

"It can be caring, Noda. Kavus has shown you the evil side of it. If a man genuinely loves his woman, it can be gentle and caring. A woman can enjoy it also."

"What? Enjoy it? How? It hurts so much. I am sorry, you need not know this."

"'Tis fine, Noda. I know of what you speak. You forget, I receive his affections now. My Mader told me when she first was contracted to my Pader, she was very naive and knew not much. However, she grew to love my Pader, and he loved her. After he passed, before I came to the Palace, she would think aloud about Pader. She told me there is such a man, furthermore, if he loved his woman, he would do anything to give her what she wanted. He would take the time to please her and not himself."

"Oh, strange. Is there such a man out there? He certainly does not live here. I would give up all to have such a man. However, I am contracted…no… I was sold to a man who has no heart. 'Tis what he is, a man with no heart. His spirit is so damaged, it has given him no heart."

"You have a great destiny before you. Ever since I came to the Palace, you were different. Letting the birds out of their cage helped me to see underneath your upbringing was an intelligence."

"You could see this, about me? How…nice, Tannah. I never knew, you had precognitive abilities. Tell me more."

"Well, this marriage is a test. The Universe wants to see your mettle. Will the branch bend or break? You are not broken, so whatever is before you, has not shattered you. I see you will not stay here. There is a journey ahead. A different path."

"How do you see this. In dreams?"

"Sometimes. Mostly. However, to say more means my life is yours."

"I will not speak of this to anyone, you have my word. Women must stick together and support each other. These are challenging times indeed if women get placed against women. It is bad enough men rule us. I will do all I can to protect you, Tannah. I swear on all I hold dear. On my unborn child."

"That will do for me. I see you are truthful and are honour bound by your oath." Tannah sat closer to Rowan so to speak in lower tones. Rowan knew what was coming next was not to become common knowledge.

"I have visions… not always in my dreams. I almost gave myself away when Kavus was having relations. I cannot control when I have them. I saw you, leaving this place. Alone. I saw you giving healing. You care, Noda. Not just about living but life. Lives. I saw so long ago, the release of your birds."

"You did? When?"

"When the Empress, gifted you the Purple Sennet. I saw it listless, and I thought it had passed, however, then I saw it fly away. I saw them all fly away. But the Sennet, did not fly away. It has some significance; however, I do not know what. Do not tell anyone, I would be killed for telling you."

"I will not say a thing. This is intriguing. You gave me your life; I hold it in my hands. I would share the same with you."

"Are you sure, Noda. Knowledge is power. You are more powerful than I."

"Should I be? Are we not equal in spirit? Does being born a Princess make me more than you? We are in the same circumstances, regardless of status, we are mistreated by the same man, in the same manner. You have given me your life, and I do not treat such lightly."

"Then I am honour bound to treat you as you will me. I will take such to my grave, Noda. You have my word."

Rowan took a deep breath; she was about to voice her fears. "I heard a voice."

"I have known you for most of your life, Noda. You always talk to yourself."

"No, Tannah. I have…heard… a voice. It responded back to my thoughts. I fear I may be…touched…"

"It could be a way to survive what you are going through. This may be how you have not broken. Women are strong, inside. We are weaker of the flesh. It could be your way of coping with the abuse by his hands, and his voice. I would not fear you are touched, Noda. Accept it for what it is, a way for you to stay strong. Your secret remains safe in the telling. I will not say anything to jeopardize you or your child."

"Thank you, Tannah. I feel better, lighter of spirit for the telling. I am glad of your council, and you have the right of it. Women should support each other in this land of ours. We have a hard path ahead, given we are about to get more restrictions. One day, I hope we have a say."

"I have other visions, Noda. There will be changes ahead, much turmoil. You know of the rumours of Dragons?"

"Yes, to speak of such is death." Rowan looked around to see if any others were close. She leaned closer. "Be careful of what you speak. There may be ears listening."

"There is not, but I heed your council. Some have not. There are rumours of beasts on the Islands. Do you know what this means?"

"No. I do not."

"I had a few visions in the last few months. I saw Dragons in my dreams. They are here. I am certain. My dreams have always happened, Noda. I am serious in the telling. Somehow you are connected. I have not seen past this."

"Tannah. I regret telling you. This is heresy to be saying this. You should not say much more. I will try to forget if you will not speak on this topic again."

"I will not. However, if I receive another vision, I will tell you. It eases my spirit to give you what support I can. We should perhaps get ourselves up and about before we are sought out by your husband or others."

"You have given me much to think on, you are right. You and I are connected by circumstances. We will be careful of future speech. I am going to rest; this morning was very fruitful. The cook and servants are preserving many greens and root vegetables. It will keep us in good health over the lean months."

"Yes, Noda. I will hasten to the laundry now. Your bed linens are changed and I will bring you a repast in several hours."

"Thank you, Tannah. Nothing too heavy. I feel like solid meals do not sit very well inside my stomach."

"You should try small portions several times a day. I will tell the cook. Your baby still needs the nutrition. You are getting close to your laydown."

"Yes. As soon as I get to my room, this is exactly what I am going to do."

Rowan and Tannah parted ways, and Rowan forgot the conversation with the activity of the baby in her belly. She found herself taking small naps during the day and implemented small meals. She found it helped with the aches she was feeling and although she felt tired all the time, it did help to change her schedule. Kavus announced one night they would be staying at the villa in the city for the arrival of his child.

"We will be receiving guests and well wishers. Up until you give birth. You would be well advised to not speak more than you must. If you were to cause an upset, it would reflect badly on my house. Also, your house. You are to conduct yourself with quiet dignity and poise. I expect nothing else. To disobey me publicly would bring great shame upon all, it would stain your child and such would follow him. I would not be pleased and I would have to discipline you and your maidservant. Obey me in such."

Rowan had no doubt he would stay true to his word. He was not kind at all, cruel to her and her maid. She only felt a deep burning hatred, which she masked when he was around. She dared not act on any of her feelings, she was raised to accept what her life was, but that didn't mean she had to like it. She hoped with the addition of her children it would buffer any unkindness and eventually soften his resolve. Her dreams of having a happy, satisfying marriage with children were dashed the first few days of confinement.

"I will obey you, Kavus."

Her head bowed; she could not hide the grin as she turned to go to her chamber to help Tannah pack. She began to help her maid, and with her guidance, was able to clean her own room. As much as she was able with her belly, which in the last two weeks had blossomed. Helping Tannah in her small way helped to alleviate her maid's workload, as the household was working her long hours.

Her maid was appreciative of the rest when she attended her mistress in her room. Many times, Rowan would let her nap on her bed while she partook of her midday meal, and she would clean up after herself. They became friends of sorts, as two in confinement will be, working well together in her chambers. After

Tannah gave her private council in the garden, Rowan looked at her maid differently. Rowan, while not having any friends growing up, did not know how to be one.

She was learning status did not have to be a deterrent to friendship. She was finding it hard to keep herself from changing her demeanor when Kavus was present. Rowan kept her own council for the most part. Her deepest feelings, she kept locked up.

Tannah helped her mistress to dress in a green gown with black and gold ties and accessories, to which her husband gave his nod of approval once she emerged. It was merely for his benefit; the smile did not reach his eyes when he looked at her. The transition to his house colours with a hint of hers, flattered his ego. They travelled the rest of the day to the villa in the Capital. She was excited, but also apprehensive, as she did not want to create any upset which would see her, or her maid punished.

It was quiet in the carriage; she dare not make a sound. He seemed irritated by everything she did, even being with her placed a scowl on his face. She did not look at him… He would not look at her anyway. She felt invisible. If ever the opportunity arose, she thought to take a chance and send a message out, but to tell the truth, she didn't feel overly optimistic as she didn't know who would be able to assist.

They arrived and Rowan had no chance to view her surroundings. They alighted, and Kavus walked ahead leaving her in the courtyard. It looked very much alike the one she left at the Palace. Same colour stone… different elevation. She quietly followed her maid inside.

Tannah got herself and her mistress settled into an adjoining suite with her husband. Rowan knew it was all about showmanship that she would have a luxurious room in the city. She sat down to view the room on a settee covered in a luxurious pelt of the blackest fur!

"This is what I call a suite! Kavus has expensive tastes. Not quite mine own, but expensive."

"Yes, Noda. I will return with a small meal. Is there anything you require? I must hurry; I have many things to attend."

"Oh, yes, some citrus… a small glass. I do not want to waste. Thank you."
Tannah was reminding Rowan this was not the place for confidences, and Rowan noticed the hidden message. She was tired and her back had begun to ache; the carriage ride was not the smoothest. She sat there petting the fur until Tannah came back with the midday meal; Rowan saw a remarkable difference in the food they served her here in the city.

"Oh my, this is heavenly. I did not realize how much I missed better food, until this meal. Its amazing how good a simple potato can taste with the proper seasonings."

"I would not know, my lady."

"Here, have a bite, I don't mind." Tannah took a bite of Rowan's potato, however, made a face, she did not like it and said so.

"It has too many spices, to be palatable. I like one or two. Not several, which for me is too much for my mouth to figure out."

Rowan thought about it some, she had grown up with excess and now with Tannah explaining her upbringing in such a way, made her reevaluate her tastes. She thought about it some more, and as she finished the remaining portion of the potato, changed her mind.

"You are right, it has more than less on it. However, this was what I have always eaten, I never thought about it until you mentioned this. A simpler approach, like what I am given since I married Kavus, now I have the opportunity to eat more luxuriously, it is excessive. You have given me something to ponder, thank you Tannah. Now I think I will nap for a while." She finished her meal, changed out of her travel attire, and lay down for an afternoon nap.

No sooner she closed her eyes, it seemed she was roughly shaken awake. She opened her eyes to see her husband standing at the side of the bed, his face opaque.

"Prepare yourself for this evening. We are having a dinner party with twenty people. My Pader and Mader will be attending and some of my family friends. It must be perfect. Your dress attire is in the dressing room, I have already decided what you are to wear, and you will need to speak with Cook about the meal. Get yourself busy, you do not have a lot of time, the guests should be arriving in less than three hours." Kavus abruptly left the room.

What an arsehole, he knows damn well Cook could manage without my input, he wishes me tired and compliant. Rowan saw the why behind his communication with her. She thought long with their minimal contact. His was a need to feel control, be it in public or private.

He must have been in a situation once, where he had no control. How else to explain his cruelty.

Managing to roll herself out of the bed. Which was the softest thing she was in for an exceptionally long time; Rowan was loath to move out of its embrace. She put on a dressing robe and tucked her feet into soft fluffy slippers. Again, courtesy of her magically attentive husband here in the city. The slippers made her feet seem as though she was walking on clouds. She managed to find her way to the kitchen first by the noise and by the smells. She saw the Cook, and he had everything well in hand. She confirmed the menu with him but left him to his business as the meal he served at midday showed he was more than capable.

"Housemaster."

"Yes, Noda?"

"Can you find Tannah and send her to my rooms. I am needing assistance to prepare for tonight. You have everything Nodan requires for the evening?"

"Yes, Noda. He already gave me instructions. It will be as he ordains."

"Very well, please have her attend me, immediately."

She tired very quickly. Rowan found the larger her belly grew, the less she wanted to move. She was feeling pressure in her hips these last couple of weeks and always seemed to need the use of a pot, even if she didn't drink anything. The child inside her would sometimes kick her in the bladder and cause her leakage. It was the most uncomfortable she had ever been, and she lamented she wished it were over. Listening to Tannah and the other servant girls who repeatedly told her it could be any day now, she really wished it were soon as she was craving a good night's rest. Tannah helped her bathe the travel dust off.

"How are you wanting your hair, Noda? You are not required to wear a hair covering inside. So, I can braid or place it up. The length 'tis now must be heavy. There is no time for it to dry completely."

"I will keep it long; however, can you frame my face with a braid? When I give birth, I will consider containing it in a snood. Or braids to wrap around my head. I do like some of the matrons styles, but I am restricted by traditions. It is quite heavy, and in this heat, it will dry soon enough. I cannot wait to bring it up. What has my dear husband picked for me to wear?"

Rowan was sure the walls may have ears, after Tannah's conversations. So, she opted to create a false persona of happiness. Some of the servants were permanently placed, and she did not want to begin any rumours. She would lead a pretend life while she was here. Especially if she was under observation, she did not know who may be watching or listening.

"You have this gorgeous green silk, Noda. Shots of gold thread adorn it. Nodan had this commissioned especially for you. It fits over your belly in several folds in a very stylish manner. I believe the clothiers he purchased it from will be here tonight."

"Do you know who is all attending? So I have an idea."

"I heard from the master of House 'tis of the status you enjoy with your husband. Not the nobility from the Royal House. His parents, some of their friends. Mostly their friends. Your husband has his cohorts from the war; however, most are in the field fighting. This is mostly the older generation."

"That is fine. I was only allowed to have tea with some of the older matrons. It will be sedate. I am fine with this. I feel too much noise would hasten a headache. This gown is exquisite. You are right, it feels light and not restricting, what a stylish drape. What jewels has he allowed me?"

Tannah turned back with a tray. Kavus was selective of what he thought she should wear. He certainly did not lack in ornaments. Some of them had to be generational pieces. She picked out all emerald jewelry with the odd topaz and a bracelet of black and emerald gems. The colours were predominately her husbands house with no sign of the red of royalty.

She felt the baby kick inside her making her extremely uncomfortable with the action. She held onto her belly, wishing the child to calm. She hoped it would not be a long night; she wanted nothing but to return to sleep. She hoped with the birth of their child many things would change. Somehow, she knew she was dreaming an impossible dream.

As this was a party of attendees of his choosing, it was a reminder her status was Secondary or didn't matter. Kavus had shown these last eight months his true self, his demeanor was a cruel selfish man. His small act of posturing bounced off her lack of caring. She was past his cruel words and began analyzing why he would be saying such, to her. She built walls inside, placing the words behind the walls and leaving them there. It did her no good to fret, as she did not carry any love for him in her heart. Her heart was now solely for her child. She rubbed her belly willing her child to calm.

Her husband entered to inspect, nodding his approval he held his arm out so Rowan could grab a hold of it.

"You will not speak unless addressed. You maintain a quiet dignity. My Mader and Pader have grand expectations of you. Do not give them cause to dislike you."

He made a show of escorting her to the front entry to greet their guests. She had this insane urge to scream at the top of her lungs, as people were arriving of the kind of man her husband really was.

The voice inside her head piped up, *"Now would this do any good?"*

She didn't answer back, but must have begun nodding, and her husband glanced down. Rowan covered it up by nodding and smiling as the first guests were arriving.

All through dinner and conversation she had a smile plastered on her face, asking the other wives about gossip happening in the city to which they were all too happy to tell. As the wives were chatting, she heard the husbands speak about the war, and the men they were losing to injury and death. Voices began to raise. The infidel managed to gain a foothold on the continent many years ago, and even though the fighting ebbed in winter months, they managed to not give back much of the land they gained. The men talked about recruiting more and even boys from some of the outer provinces.

When the talk turned to strategies, Rowan paid back her attention to the women's conversations. She noticed Kavus hovered around her more often than naught, she knew he was listening for her to say something disparaging about him or maybe ask for help. Oh, she wanted too so much, did she ever! However, she also knew he would be true to his word, and if he didn't beat her, her maid was as good as dead. He would take it this far. Her life was not fair. It was a prison.

She said little as her stomach seemed upset by the evening meal, or maybe it was the sense of being watched. One of the wives would stare openly at her, an older woman, she thought to be a friend of her Mader by law. But this notion quickly disappeared by their conversation.

"I merely said you look your age. Am I wrong?"

"Damara, don't."

"Ramis, I am not beginning anything. Not anything I can't manage. I am merely being truthful. Our dear Namarch says in his sermons, an honest wife is the best sort. Am I not the best of wives?"

"You are. Of course, Darling. Let us not forget about our hosts. You would be best to not bring dishonour on my house. Kindly retract what you said. Now."

"I am sorry, Ramis. Nodan. I am in the wrong to cause upset on such a joyous occasion. Nimai, I am sorry if I said you look your age. What I meant was, you look tired."

"Damara! Enough!"

"That's quite all right, Ramis. I can manage your wife. Damara. I may look tired, but not as much as you. I hear you were ill; I am sorry for this. It was unkind; you look like you've aged at least twenty years."

"Thank you, kindly."

Rowan wondered at the dynamics between the two matrons but did not ask. She did not want to add fuel to a fire which promised to blaze if she were to do so. She turned to another and asked about women in the court, had there been any other marriages lately.

The woman named Damara was intently watching the Princess when she could. She had graying black hair, and the kindest eyes, her smile when she laughed gave her a pleasant look. Rowan watched her back covertly out of the corner of her eyes when she could. By their mannerisms, this woman's husband and her Pader by law were the best of friends. She observed them all. She knew none of the people in the room, and they seemed to all know each other. She wondered if Kavus meant for her to be the outsider.

The rest of the evening was moved into the reception parlor after the dinner meal. Her husband hovering near was attentive to her needs. He would place his hand on her shoulder, and she was careful not to flinch. It took all of her will not to shrug the hand away. Rowan felt the room was watching to see what she would do. Expectation hung heavy in the air, as though fog which sometimes rolled in with rain.

She knew she would have no chance at any private conversations, with any of the women there, so she didn't even try. His kind attention set her on edge as it was so unlike his attention in private. It seemed an untruth to her. Her teeth clenched, her neck and back tightened and a headache threatened to erupt.

How I wish this night would end. I almost wish Kavus was his true self. This is so unlike his true character. I feel as though I am partaking of a pantomime, the puppets I used to watch as a child... any moment the play will end. I am so tense, my lower back and my shoulders ache something awful. I need a good soak with some relaxing tea.

After a couple of hours, the woman was periodically watching her, saw the level of Rowan's discomfort increasing, ended the evening for her. They managed to make eye contact when she knew her husband had his back to her. At the moment when their eyes met, she sensed a kinship, an understanding of sisterhood, and a sense of calm passed through her. Her voice murmured to her quietly,

"Your destiny with this woman is linked, you will both travel far, perhaps not together, maybe parallel paths, you will meet again. Take comfort in her energy, you both have destinies to fulfill. She can tell of your discomfort, she feels it."

Rowan ventured a quick smile of gratitude as she was helped to her feet, and they thanked all their guests as they departed. When the last one left, saying nothing to her, Kavus left for his room, while she headed back to hers. Rowan wobbled on her feet, tiredness and the pressure in her stomach dictating the use of the chamber pot, and straight to bed.

"I must have eaten something which didn't agree with me," Tannah smiled saying it wouldn't be long now.

Well, it ended up being that very night! She undressed for bed, her silk night-robe on, rolled into the bed, tossing, and turning trying to sleep. She hadn't slept very long, when she felt an excruciating pain between her legs and wetness. She screamed for Tannah, who was laying on the floor inside the dressing room, waiting for the call. Rushing in, fully dressed, Tannah grabbed a pot of water, and she placed towels close to the bed.

"Oh, oh, oh, Tannah!"

Her husband strode in. "Is it her time, girl?"

"Yes, Nodan, 'tis." He left shutting the door behind him. Slamming it, so much it rebounded open. He addressed the guard outside.

"Get me the Headmaster, and have the grooms saddle horses, there need to be messages sent. Right now, man! Don't just stand there. Move!"

Her scream must have woken other servants, a few girls trickled in. Tannah sent them off to assist in the kitchen with boiling water, one to relay messages and another to get more linens. The pain became unbearable, and Rowan began screaming in pain.

"Ahhhhh, Ahhhhh!" Tannah gave her a wooden paddle to clamp down when Kavus returned to scowl on the noise she was emitting.

"Tell her to stop this noise, its irritating."

"Yes, Nodan."

It seemed to help muffle some of the noise. It wasn't until she heard a soothing voice humming an unrecognizable tune in her head she calmed down. The voice would sooth during the bouts of pain, reassuring her the pain soon would be gone. *"Ummmmmm. Mmmmmm, ummmmm."*

She heard sounds of movement in the rest of the villa, picking out her Mader and Paders voices. *It must be important to get the Emperor out of bed,* she thought. She also heard other voices besides her husband's, but not one person came to see her. She screamed, another wave of pain hitting her as now the doctor was in attendance with his helpers, probably courtesy of her Royal status. It became terribly busy in the room.

"MMMMhmmmm, ummmmm, ummmmm."

She felt wave after wave of pain, the voice in her head became louder and continued chanting, *"ummm, ummmmm, ummmmm."*

Her pain ebbing and flowing, she felt a rhythm begin easing her somewhat. She felt intense pressure begin and the urge to push harder than before, a great rush of pain and then the pressure was gone. She may have blacked out for a bit, the voice gently and softly crooning to her bringing her back into being.

"Child! Earth Mader! You have work to complete. You are needed in the world of man; you may not travel the spirit world yet. You met the Fire Dragon, though she does not know it, your time to meet will happen but not yet. You must find your way. The path before you can help others."

She groggily woke to see the doctor holding her child in clean linens. He bent down to give her a courteous look at the child, before he strode out of the room and down the hall, taking the babe with him. She heard cheers and voices raised to praise the next Emperor-in-waiting. She lay there in her bloodied garments,

Tannah helping to expel the other bits still inside. This afterbirth would be planted with a dedicated tree for her son, to thrive and grow strong like the tree. Tannah removed the remainder and helped the girls to clean Rowan up dressing her in a clean gown.

She waited and waited, then sent her maid down the hall to see what the delay and where her child was. She could not shake the sense something fundamental was happening… time seemed heavy and still. Tannah returned ten minutes later, alone, crying and wringing her hands. Rowan knew instantly from her face all was not well.

"Your Lord husband, and the Emperor and Empress feel you are not well enough to care for the infant, which is a boy. As he is directly in line for the Throne, he will be raised according to the Emperor's wishes, and you will have no contact. They feel you are not right in the head and would corrupt the child. They feel justified, as you were chanting as you gave spirit to the child. 'Tis by the grace of Nodan you are not given directly to the Namarch. The Emperor has requested another child. I fear your life is to bear more pain, Noda."

Here Tannah's voice lowered to a whisper, and Rowan gasped as it all began to sink in, she was about to say something, but Tannah cut in, "You are to leave immediately, my Lady, I am to go with you with other servants back to the country estate to recuperate from birth. Do not resist, it will do no good. You are weakened by birth, and Nodan will not listen to your pleas."

At this statement, Rowan embraced the darkness, either from shock or the pain still inside her, waking as a manservant was carrying her into a closed carriage. She was placed unceremoniously inside. She protested.

"I want to see my child, where is my son?"

"Noda, come, you know they will take good care of him, let's get you home and feeling better."

Tannah's soft voice held steel in it, she would take no protests, and Rowan knew she had no battle left inside. Rowan was exhausted, and her sight was fading. Tannah followed her inside, and she lost herself to darkness again. She did not see the full regiment of soldiers surrounding the carriage, her husband was taking no chances with her escaping, but it was also his due as padering the next heir elevated his status. Her last thought as the darkness rose to embrace her, was she had not been allowed to hold her child, she would not be allowed to see him and the thought of this left a hollowness she could not fathom.

What have I done to deserve this treatment? My poor boy. Will he not miss me? How can this be? Will I ever get to see him? Will they take all my children away? Am I just a brood mare?

This must be the loss her voice said she would suffer. She thought if she didn't wake from this nightmare, she would be fine with it.

She would feel comfort in her darkness for now.

CHAPTER 40

Solina

Brings Together That Which was Apart

Solina spent more of her evenings with Dame Metina learning state craft and other nights they read tomes together. When Atin and her husband emerged from their rooms, she would spend time with them. She began reading aloud, the three of them learning more about their Dragons. Nannosh interjecting the odd time to set straight the odd minor mistake in the documentation. As the same as her childhood, she remembered.

This family time, as Solina liked to refer it, was something she embraced, not having moments like this in the Church setting she was raised. She and Atin became closer, like sister's. "I feel the kinship also. I have no female friends my age, my sisters were either too old or too young. I feel like we could be exceptionally good friends."

Kaisan most times would sit back and enjoy watching the two girls interact. When it came to discussions over some of the books they read together, he stated, "This is enlightening, 'tis all new knowledge for me; I have only the formal teachings of Aram. I struggled to pay attention and disappointed greatly in the written form. I am afraid I was not the most attentive, however, what you are reading to us, makes up for my lack. 'Tis most engaging! Please read on."

The two women became more comfortable with each other as time went on. After the initial flight, the two would speak about nothing other than being astride the Dragons. The ceremony was a momentous success. They dressed in finery. Solina chose red and gold of her House, but more gilt than red. After she explained to Gran she wished the sun to be reflected, and to be noticed as a Rider, her Gran approved. Atin felt blue was her colour, and deep blue to compliment Analaria's green, and stated it reminded her of the beautiful birds in the gardens when she first arrived.

"Remember the ascent, Atin?"

"Oh, yes. I thought I was going to get thrown off. It was not something I would have expected. However, once we were flying, the view was spectacular!"

"The sound of the people of the city, once they got over the shock, the cheers! I wasn't sure if I was crying or if it was the wind making my eyes tear up."

"How did you make your voice loud like that? It sounded deeper, like a man's." Solina's voice projected over the whole of the city when they flew over.

"WE HAVE ENTERED THE AGE OF DRAGON'S. LET ALL WHO REFUTE THEIR PRESENCE, QUAKE AT IT. WE USHER INTO A NEW WORLD OF LOVE AND PEACE. LET THEM BRING US WAR! WE WILL GIVE IT BACK! WE ARE THE PEOPLE OF THE DRAGON! LONG LIVE THE DRAGONS!"

The Dragon's banked low over the city and let out a few loud roars, trumpeting loudly. Then they let loose fire into the skies. The city hushed and awed… then roared! The girls heard it up above. Solina had a big grin on her face and tears streaming from them. Atin had tears too, but from the wind in her eyes.

Dame Metina told Solina after they alighted from Dragon-back onto wobbly legs it was exactly the flare to make all believe. Gran personally thanked the two Dragons herself. She was more comfortable now in their presence. Solina explained to Atin,

"My bond works both ways. I know what they think and talk to them, but they also use my voice to word what they think. Nannosh says when you have your own bond, it will be the same for you. Until then, only I and my sister of blood, which means the other woman in Du'Lanay, can use the bond. She is bonded with the Great One, the male of the species. You will have to wait. If necessary, Nannosh says she can temporarily bond with you, now you have knowledge and acceptance of being a DragonRider, you would not be damaged in the mind from such a union."

"I guess 'tis comforting."

They discussed all points of the celebrations. The people kept the wine flowing and feasting lasted for ten days. It helped the Palace gifted all residents with wine and foods for feasting. Coin was given and other gifts. The worship halls were filled every day since. The Pader and his other brethren were kept remarkably busy, and a revival of reverence to the Gods was ever present. People were happy, and joyful and marriages were contracted with a fervor. It was what they needed.

The one thing they discussed the most was the impending attack they knew was coming. "Veren, how are the new recruits?"

"We have every young boy wishing to enlist. We have to turn many back."

"'Tis good is it not?"

"We may need extra help from your Excellencies for the screening process. I have fears some may not be truthful. It only takes one Layanese to upset the proverbial waste bin, High Dragon."

"You are right. How have you done so in the past?"

"During the graduation ceremony, one of the Riders would 'inspect' the troops. He would pick out those of dubious or suspicious character. It was never something we brought attention to. Many thought they were being promoted."

"Let's continue this, and we do not need to train one who is duplicitous. Atin and I will inspect training. She can pick out those who would harm the Dragons. We will be discreet, of course. Pick weeds before they take root. Time is of the essence."

"I agree with your decision. Having the people keep their eyes open has caused unrest in the lower markets and parts of the lower city. Perhaps you could alleviate some by taking a stroll through the city. Heavily guarded of course. Then Atin could work her magic, and we see if any of our citizens are suspect. You can address all if you find them above reproach. They have need of reassurance."

"We can certainly do so. I never thought about our people turning on each other. I will confer with Gran; she has much insight on people. Thank you, Veren. You are much appreciated."

"Thank you, High Dragon, Sea Dragon, if you will excuse me. I need to get down to the Barracks." This was only one of many conversations they had. Veren would have many scenarios in mind. The man was cautious and spoke to the women with some familiarity in private. In public, he was very much a loyal subject. Solina respected him all the more for it. It gave her pause to do the same. After all, she still had a country she was learning to rule. Manners went a long way, Solina was told so by her Gran.

"Veren is correct in the backlash of the Dragons emerging into the light, it has caused some unrest in the city. We have many citizens originally from Aram and Du'Lanay, who serve us, however, the Island never forgets. Having you two traverse through the city, create a calm with the original Islanders and the rest of the populace, can only serve us well. Before it leads to more than unrest."

"We will do so, Gran. It would do us very well to have Kaisan with us, then."

"Yes, have Atin and her husband hold hands and show affection to one another. I am sure they will have no problem doing so."

"Yes, they are very 'vocal' in their affections. Sounds carry in this Palace."

"You could follow their example, you know."

"No, Gran. I have much to do, much to learn. I have no interest in a joining. It is not something I need to do."

"There is not anyone that catches your eye? No young Marshall? They certainly follow you with their eyes."

"Gran. When I say no… I mean it. This time we are in, is especially important. The next while will see us in turmoil. I have Dragons to attend my time with. I have no interest. What is more important, Dragons? Or joining?"

"All right, all right… However, do not let time get away on you. If you focus primarily on the Dragons, there may come the day when you are my age and it has passed you by."

"Gran, it will not come to this... Or it may. I will let the Universe choose for me. If it happens, it happens. My energies are focused on now and getting our Dragons healthy. This is a precarious time, for them, for us." The conversations continued, each putting forth their ideas, trying to plan for every scenario they could think of. In the end, it was exactly as her GrandMader had said.

It was a quiet evening, Solina was in one of the parlours, reading by herself. Atin and Kaisan had snuck off early after dinner. Solina had no doubt as to what they were doing. Atin wasn't quiet about it sometimes, and the energy sometimes had the Dragons trumpeting. The citizens were quite enthralled with their very own Dragons. The gifts bestowed upon the residents and the occasional visits up to the Dragons, had the effect they wanted.

It was in this quiet solitude which had Solina looking up and gazing into the dark night. She stood up, placing the book she was reading on the table beside her, and walked onto the patio. Looking up to the mountain, towards the Dragon's Nest. Veren named it such and it seemed to fit. Feeling the silence laying heavy on the air, she felt discomfort and pain piercing her head. Not knowing where it came from and not caring, she grabbed at her head and moaned, dropping to her knees.

That is where Atin and Kaisan, found her! They rushed to her with Atin dropping down and holding Solina by her shoulders.

"Lina, are you fine? I felt it too, although I thought it something else. What could this be?" They heard the trumpeting of the Dragons, as Sheyna was running fast into the Palace, shouting Solina's name with two guards running after her. For a small woman, she was fleet of foot.

"High Dragon, Solina! Solina!"

She ran into the room, careening to a stop sliding on the smooth floor almost crashing into Kaisan. He moved fast, getting out of the way of the hurtling girl, as she tried to stop. Sheyna turned it into a sliding kneel, colliding into Solina, who grabbed her friend on the arms.

"Sheyna, what's going on, is it the Dragons, what's wrong?" Solina and the other two women, rose to their feet. Solina functioning again now the pain stopped.

"There was this strange moment, like time stood still then a fierce wind rose. The Dragons began weaving and swaying and then let out a roar. Yah, a roar, and they kept swaying. I ran down here to get you, as quickly as I could. You need to talk to them, see what the trouble is." Sheyna was visibly upset and Solina stood there hanging onto the women as she asked Nannosh what was wrong.

"Another DragonRider was in pain. She lost a piece of herself and caused herself physical harm. She does not have a Dragon bond and was gathering energy from another source. When she was in the deepest dark of her pain, she projected it out into the world. We all felt it in unusual ways. She is of the mind, magic if you will. If man finds her, she will be killed, her growing power needs to be tempered."

"Are you both fine?"

"Yes, we answered the heavens with our voices, we were heard."

"Well, we are coming up there to see you."

"As you wish."

Solina relayed what the Dragons imparted. Feeling relieved, Solina said she was going to walk up to the Nest with Sheyna to see for herself. Atin volunteered to go with them. Solina taking one look at her, began laughing.

"You may want to put something on then!" Atin looked at herself and Kaisan realising they rushed out of their rooms, naked as the day they were born. Laughing, they excused themselves, going to grab some clothes. They left the room in a rush, laughing down the hall.

"Sheyna, is everything else alright up there?" Solina asked her friend about the feeding and general wellbeing.

"The Dragons are very well, and they are gaining strength in their wings. They practice every day by descending to the ocean during the night to consume a meal of fish and ocean meat. This has lessened the number of fowl and goats, we must bring them, but our supply is going to run out and run out sooner than we like. We may have to ask the other Islands for more supply. I don't see any other way. They may not want to survive off seafood alone."

Solina said they would produce a plan, as Atin and Kaisan walked in fully dressed. "That's much better." The four of them along with guards, who finally caught their breath, all headed up into the darkness carrying lanterns and torches.

They met Veren there, his men on high alert, the Dragons, while not swaying, looked upset, their eyes whirling wildly. Solina worried about their state. She stood there gazing at Nannosh and spoke to the others.

"They are here, a boat full of men, on the side the Dragon's fish on. They saw them earlier on the horizon as they fed, they will arrive soon. They will ascend through the trees and Nannosh would have me access my air magic. With her help, she says it would be good practice."

"Practice? High Dragon, we cannot protect you if you stay here. Kallen, you hie to the Palace! Get everyone up here. Now!"

Veren shouted out the last word and his men took off. Looking at Kaisan, Sheyna, and Atin. He addressed Solina.

"What about them? They should leave here too." Solina glanced at Atin.

"Atin will stay with me, the others can return to the Palace where they will be safer."

Kaisan began to speak, but Atin looked at him, her eyes glowing blue. "My love, I will be safe with the Dragons and all the men. Please go down with the others."

She gave him a kiss and he hugged her hard. He did not wish to leave, but as she was a Dragon, he could not argue with her, especially not in front of others. He wanted to. Solina sensed his upbringing was at war with his heart. She knew she would have to speak with him at some point.

The others left heading to the Palace, Solina spoke to Atin.

"Nannosh says for me to access my powers without too much effect on the Dragon's mental wellbeing, I should be on their back, with direct contact. You should join me in the air. Since our last ride, you know as well as I, we can sit comfortably in the crease between the two ridges on their back. Analaria says she won't do any maneuvers like the last time. She was a little excited about the whole event. We need to mount up, Nannosh says they are near."

Solina and Atin climbed up the Dragons' legs and onto their backs, wedging themselves into the ridge Solina spoke about. Solina graced Nannosh and Atin sat upon Analaria. As they managed themselves comfortable, men began creeping out of the treeline. Both Dragons bunched their legs, taking off into the air, men throwing spears at them as they rose. Veren and his men, stood their ground, waiting for the intruders to draw nigh. They had advantage of light behind them, it would blind the enemy, but it also made them targets.

The women felt wind in their hair as they flew high. Neither had been this high. As they flew side by side, Solina tried to yell over to Atin, to hang on. Atin did not hear exactly what she yelled but grabbed onto two horns anyway. The Dragons flew together and then Nannosh flew around while Analaria banked around and dove. Atin whooped and held on, her butt wedged tight and her legs squeezing tight as she could.

Analaria let out a breath of fire which caught the vanguard of men sneaking forward. There was twenty out of the trees but as it was dark, one could not tell if there were more waiting. The wall of fire lit about ten of them aflame, their screams echoing in the lower valley. Analaria rose back into the air, and Atin peered down to see ten figures writhing. The grass on fire, the other men were running back to the cover of the trees. The Dragons and their Riders hovered over the fire which slowly lost its fuel. Solina conferred with Nannosh about what she should do. The men brazenly walked out of the underbrush and tried again to volley another round of spears at the hovering Dragons.

Solina held out one of her hands and the men dropped one by one, each grabbing at their throats. At the signal, Veren and his men caught up to the intruders. Running past the burnt ones on the ground, they proceeded to run each of the kneeling and prone invaders through with swords. Solina saw Veren directed his men to scour the trees for any hidden enemy. She hung onto the Dragon, and they landed in the area of their Nest.

Getting off Nannosh's back landing upon her own wobbly legs, Solina noticed Atin suffering the same effect. They hugged each other, waiting for Veren to return. Solina felt tears on her face. "Hey, hey, Lina. Its all right now, they are all dead."

"That's my sorrow, I helped kill them, I took the breath from their lungs. I have only ever killed one person before. I don't like it." Solina looked at Nannosh for a minute.

"What did she tell you?"

"That sometimes to preserve life, one must take it. She said 'tis why the Dragons chose women this time. They hope all methods will be taken to preserve life before taking it. However, there will be instances when we have no choice. The previous Riders were all too happy to wage war. In their arrogance, they lost what it was which made them Riders. She says we are off to a good beginning."

Atin gave her another hug. "I too have taken a life, by trying to protect what I foolishly thought was mine but is not. The ocean does not belong to me, and I feel remorse over my action. We may always carry this in our hearts as reminders we are not here in this spirit to take life but to preserve it."

Veren and his men crested the outer area of lantern light. He walked up to the women and bowed, lowering to one knee, the other men followed suit.

"You are our Mader, High Dragon. We bow to your grace and give thanks you have given us our meaning of life. We killed twenty-two men, but we heard rustling in the underbrush, more than one. We believe they have gotten away."

There was a pause as Solina gazed at Nannosh, looking at Veren she spoke.

"Thank you, Nannosh confirms 'tis indeed two men. We will let them go. They will report back to Du'Lanay, the power and might of the Dragons and their Riders. I thank you for your service. We should set a perimeter in case they decide to return."

"Yes, High Dragon, we will make it so,"

Veren and his men rose. There were murmurs of 'High Dragon' as they left to do as instructed, "I will escort you both back to the Palace myself, your family will be worried,"

Veren waited for the two women to walk in front of him, and he walked a pace behind. They held each other walking arm in arm, chatting about being in the air and how giddy the feeling was. Atin piped up.

"Do you think if we had a strap around the neck of the Dragons, with a loop to hold onto, it would lessen our chances of falling off, if, say, the Dragon was to fly erratically? I feared for my life when Analaria pitched like that. I felt I was slipping a bit, but please don't tell Kaisan. He would try to forbid me from flying."

"He cannot forbid you; you are a Dragon. He comes from a land which made women less than what we are. I know, I know, he doesn't treat you as such, but there may come a day when he forgets love conquers all."

"Did you not say saddles were once used?"

"I will look for any references. They were, but if there were pictures from long past, then I can have some leather makers begin. For now, straps will have to suffice. I will have a few lengths made."

Solina said no more as they arrived at the Palace. Kaisan, Sheyna, and her GrandMader came rushing forward. Kaisan grabbed Atin, hugged and kissed her. Sheyna gave Solina a hug and to Veren's surprise the small woman hugged him. Solina sensed where this may be leading and smiled at the thought.

"Let us retire to the reading room to partake a light meal. I am feeling a bit of hunger. Maybe a glass of wine would be refreshing. Atin and I will then recount everything we experienced." They spent the next hour telling all and when Atin and Solina began to yawn, Dame Metina urged them to retire, and everyone disbursed.

Waking early Solina dressed and ate, then took herself for a walk to see the Dragons. Nannosh opened an eye but did not lift her head. *"You are fine? Not tired or taxed?"*

The lack of Dragon movement had her worried. *"Yes, we are fine little one, after the excitement last night, we waited for an hour then flew to the ocean and enjoyed some bounty from the sea. We do not mind if the bulk of our sustenance comes from the ocean. It is good nutrition for our scales and has made us fill out to our full selves. We may have had a bit of sport with the ship sailing away..."*

Nannosh said this so nonchalantly it took Solina a moment to think about what she said. *"You burned the ship?"*

"Mayhap a wee bit. The cloth on the top lit up like a huge torch. It will take them some time to return to Du'Lanay. We didn't burn it down completely; it was still floating when we were done. They will think twice before they return."

"Yes, but they will come back, 'tis what scares me. Like a thief in the night, GrandMader says, all it takes is one."

"Then we prepare. Not to burden you, but once we are full strength, the two of us must leave. We are the future of our species. You will still have power, although I am not sure how much it would tax us if we were far away. We have a duty to the Great One, and I truly do not wish to perish. We are the last of our kind."

"I understand. I have many duties here. Gran is teaching me all of ruling. Having you airborne and not here eases my mind none will attempt your lives again. I could not bear such. Not now, I have become quite fond of you."

"I am more than fond of you, Little One. You along with your sisters will help cure the disease which is hate. You will usher in a new age, one of love."

Solina sat down and leaned against the reclining Dragon. Analaria was resting by herself several paces away. The sun hiding behind the horizon and making its way through the cloud cover on the horizon. She closed her eyes and sighed.

"There may be many who do not want what we offer, and they will resist. It may get worse before it gets better."

"You can count on this. If it were easy, many would have tried, without Dragons. You will need all our assistance. Every Dragon, every Rider will need to be of the same mind."

"I guess finding each other should be our objective. Although I am not sure of how."

"The Great One will provide. It is his directive which will have us procreate."

"He told you? Is he around?"

"He has spoken to me, as our lives were in stasis, and once we were freed, many blessings to you…we are to regain our energy and to leave here."

"Going where?"

"To that which is hidden from man. We have many breeding grounds. However, I will return to mine before the Great Ones sleep."

"Did you not go into a 'sleep'?"

"It feels like it was, however… no. We paid penance for the others. The ones who rebelled and those misled."

"Misled? By their Riders? This does not sound promising. Are we not allowed allowances for mistakes?" Solina opened her eyes at the distressing thought. She was sure her life was not perfect and made many mistakes. Growing up, talking back to her Gran…

"Some were misled, those who were younger. Some of their Riders were to blame, but not all. There were many Dragons who rebelled against the Great One. He was trying to… implement our ideals. He was lenient, and it created more issues in the end. He is bound to be stricter this time around. If mistakes are to be made, the penalty may be harsh."

"You will guide me? Council me, so I do not make mistakes? I do not want to disappoint the Great One before I even begin."

"Ahh, Little One. I can indeed council you, but you will have decisions only you can make. To be conscious of the effect of your decision is part of being a DragonRider."

"I have many things to learn. I wish to assist the Purity Rider when I meet her, she will want a tight knit group."

"You are learning much from your Mader's Mader, she has much knowledge. The Purity bond, who is your sister of blood may rely on your knowledge. It can never be a dreadful thing. Unless you are the Mind Wielder."

"Oh, you speak of the past one, the one who killed his brother."

"Yes, he was arrogant. Perhaps not at first, however, with much talent, and with outside influences, he became...not one with his Dragon. He was able to block out his Dragon and still maintain the bond. It distressed his Dragon, not to be able to speak with its Rider. It weakened both."

"Weakened? I don't want to know. Will the new Mind Wielder be able to 'block' out its Dragon? Once she gets one."

"I am not certain. I have heard on the winds through my imprisonment whispers of one of your...'tomes'...ahhh...writings..."

"Do you mean books? Where we keep writings?"

"Yes, books. There may be a book the last Mind Wielder wrote; it was a relic from another. It may have been given to the last Rider. It was something, the last Dragon was in the end, scared of. She said her Rider gave thought over to evil deeds, which was how she worded it. I am hoping this Mind Wielder has more spirit...integrity than the last."

"I know what you speak of, I looked at it, however, some of the ideas are too fantastical to believe. Hopefully, like you said, the Mind Wielder has more integrity. We have huge tasks ahead of us all, finding each other and then becoming like minded. Given only two of us come directly from Vendar, the others come from countries and lands which have only one God."

"Do not see this as a detriment to your finding each other. You are all women. What else can you think of which you have in commonality?"

"Ummm, we perhaps are all young? Atin, I think is a year younger than I. I am thinking the Purity Rider is close to my age. Perhaps we have no experience?"

"Perhaps not this... You surmise you are all the same in age. What about experience?"

"How so? As none of us have experience being a Rider?"

"How about influences of location?"

"Oh, you mean the country of the others? Ohhh, you are talking about the influences of the rule of man. Well, one Rider is in Aram. She must be meek, or perhaps she is ready to be a Rider, from being beaten by their system."

"You know much on the history of Aram? Have you not learned of this? What if this Rider is devout? The people of the hot lands love their Ruler."

"Yes, however, to become a Rider does she not have to believe in Dragons?"

Solina closed her eyes again, their talk was interesting, but the warmth of Nannosh and the air, plus the cadence of the heartbeat was very soothing, Solina stifled a yawn, and smiled as she snuggled into the crease created by the leg and breast. Nannosh curved her neck and head around to shield her Rider. The men around them worked silently, after one saw the High Dragon cuddling with the blue Dragon. He quietly told the others.

"She can still be a Rider and still believe in her religion."

"Oh, I never thought of this. So, then the Riders in Du'Lanay may also believe in their Namarch and their God. This is all so intriguing; I am grateful for your insight on the others. The Purity Rider is already bonded. Is she not?"

"She knows of her Dragon, and the Great One has not confirmed his bond. She is on her path. You will all meet, find each other."

"The others? Will they find us? Or each other?"

"You will all meet. The Universe will provide you with certainty. One certainty is you will all be together at some point, like you and I will be together. Our bond surpasses distance. I can find you anywhere on this land."

"This land? The Islands are not noticeably big compared to the main lands."

"I meant the girth of all the lands, which are known. I feel your teasing little one. I like your humour. Laughing and humour makes the spirit lighter."

"You are right."

They conversed for awhile Solina rested against Nannosh's leg falling asleep only to be woken by Sheyna who arrived to see her charges. Sheyna found Nannosh curled against her friend and the movement of the Dragon moving to greet Sheyna had Solina waking. She rose and stretched raising her hands above her head, then bending down to touch her toes.

"Sheyna, my dear friend, I have not thanked you enough for your hard work and dedication to the Dragons, ask, if there is anything you want, I will repay you." Solina gazed at her friend who had thoughtfully brought the High Dragon a small basket of food. Sheyna handed it to Solina who lifted the cloth and sighed at the smell of fresh bread. Solina grabbed a slice and bit into it.

"Kallen said you were up here early; I thought if you weren't coming down for a while you would be hungry. As for anything, you have given me something I would never trade, these great beasts are like my children, my babies. However, I would like to document my care of them, I wish to make notes on everything I have done." Solina handed the basket back to Sheyna offering its contents to her friend. Sheyna shook her head no. She had already eaten.

"Excellent idea! You will have papyrus and quill, and I will grant you access to the written works of the others who thought to document their findings. Keep a written record, and keep it to yourself, these should be your journals, for your knowledge. Speaking of babies, would you think that one day, you would be able to take care of small ones? We may have a need of your skills with their progeny." Sheyna gasped at Solina's hinting.

"You will keep this information to yourself… do the math, though. We have two full grown Dragons. They told me the Great One, a male is somewhere, which was at one time, Noster's Dragon. He flew off and has not been seen since. So this makes three. The cause of yesterdays voice on the wind which set the Dragons on edge and caused my headache, is in Aram. She has no Dragon, we are two here, and there are three in Du'Lanay. Three Dragons, six riders. We have a duty to keep them alive. There is no other way, and there is something else, they will not say. We will experience something which will turn the world upside down."

"I thought Dragons have already turned the world on its side."

"I have looked at the Prophecy, over and over, it alludes to an event but won't say exactly. I thought it was the display of lights we had a while ago, but Nannosh indicated Atalay mentioned it wasn't. She felt things. She is the one who could feel the life spirit of the other Riders and where they are, but in doing so, she drained her spirit, she awaits in the heavens for rebirth, like the others before her."

"Oh, this is astonishing. I will do my research then; I will bring anything I find puzzling to your attention. How I wish I could speak with them." Sheyna sighed.

"Alas, you cannot. However, you seem able to gauge their temperament. They would not harm you. Wait, Nannosh says during hatching, one can bond through first sight. There were other Riders, but they had no powers like the first six. She says the six were jealous of this and had them disappear. I think we will also keep this to ourselves; however I believe, and I am sure Atin will agree, we are stronger with more numbers. I for one, would be proud to have you as a sister, in the sky. You are a sister of my heart. We will see what the future holds, shall we?"

Sheyna grinned; tears were leaking down her cheeks. and they shared a hug. Analaria brought her head over to the girls. Breathing on them, she looked at them, her eye whirling, Solina laughed. Telling Sheyna. "Analaria says she will gladly take you for a ride on the air if you are willing. But since you are so tiny, she suggests a strap be made to hold you on."

Veren came around the corner, gazing at the two women, laughing, smiling with tears streaming down their faces. A look of worry crossed his face. He was very aware of the well being of the two women. He had several cohorts stationed nearby, and now with the attack which came from the woods, a cohort was spread out in the woods along the cliff edges. He would not be so lax next time.

"Is everything fine, High Dragon, Sheyna? Kallen said you were up here. I came to check, to make sure everything is calm, and I have my men scouring the woods. I also placed several cohorts along the cliff edges and more inside the Palace apartments. Your GrandMader spoke to me on attempts made in the past. She agreed with me it would not hurt and assured me the Namarch may try on your life. So be assured, we will be more prepared for any such attempts."

"I am afraid this is not necessary; the woods are now clear. Veren, I thank you for your diligence in the matter, and, for the influx of guards. We can never be too cautious. I am afraid the two men got away, but not before Nannosh and Analaria had a wee bit of sport with them." She told them what the Dragons did and Veren and Sheyna had a good laugh. "Veren, you have been with me for this whole time. I would like to thank you for your service and your care of these two, ask, what you will of me, and I will reward you."

"I am rewarded enough, High Dragon, by being a part of our new history. You have given me the highest honour of which I can think. There is one minor matter, I would like to discuss, since we are all here."

"Ask away."

"Being in the situation we were in last night has brought something forward I would like to address. Sheyna, would you consider joining with me?"

Sheyna gasped and reddened, Veren turned to her, "We have worked together and seem to be on the same thought. We can finish each others' sentences, we think alike, and have spent countless days in the worst of conditions. I have become very fond; no, I have fallen for you. I would rather spend a lifetime alone if you do not consent to be one with me. Do you feel the same?"

Taking her hands in his, Sheyna tears running down her cheeks through the big smile. "Oh, yes. I fell for you the first time I saw you in the cave. You were the bravest and handsomest man I had ever seen!" She blushed even more if it were possible. They both gazed at Solina, who was also smiling and crying.

"Why yes, of course."

The Dragons trumpeted loudly, startling the three humans and the scattering of soldiers but making them grin. Veren turned to them expressing his thanks. Solina commented they already could communicate with the Dragons, who needed mind speech.

"I will leave you two; to make your plans, I have an idea, I would like to speak to Atin about. I believe the Du'Lanay ship may need a personal escort back home."

She smiled wickedly, winking at Nannosh, who seemed to wink back. Smiling to herself, she walked back to the Palace to share her idea with Atin, the couple were in the Dining Hall, Atin and Kaisan laughed when they heard what Nannosh and Analaria were up to. Atin wholeheartedly agreed to speak to her fish folk, but said while she could ask, it was up to them if they wanted to.

"I do not know if they feel humour." Atin reflected.

"But they can feel love," Kaisan said to her, his face reminding her of their first time in the water together. She smiled back at him, kissing him fully on the mouth, not caring Solina was watching. "How right you are."

"I would also like to walk around the city, the lower markets in a unified attempt to show we are all people of the Dragon. Veren told me there is even more unrest in the lower city. Perhaps after you ask for the escort, the three of us can walk down. Heavily guarded of course."

"Even me? I am not a Dragon."

"Especially you, Kaisan. You are from Aram. This shows our people all are accepted if they have Vendar in their hearts. Atin, you would have to be using your talents."

"I do not know how long I could do it for. I get some incredible headaches, after."

"Nannosh says she will bond with you, 'tis because you have no Dragon, which causes the headaches."

"Will it hurt?"

"No, Sea Dragon. Because you have accepted fully you are a Dragon, I will support you when you need. My bond will be by your side also."

Atin came to the present, her eyes glowing and Kaisan holding onto one of her hands. She smiled and tears were flowing down her face. "I heard a voice! Was this Nannosh? Oh, I am crying. Solina, this is so wonderful! Is this what it is like? Why am I crying, I cannot seem to stop. Thank you, Dear Heart."

Kaisan wiped her face with a linen; she took the cloth from his hands and wiped the last few which escaped his hands.

"Yes, see, 'tis nothing drastic, and yes, 'tis wonderful. Not so when I first heard them, however, having this bond, I have a great friend I can speak to, well, I have two, and 'tis a wonderful feeling."

"When would you like to do so?"

"After you ask your friends, perhaps tomorrow. This will give Veren and Kallen time to prepare the route. We will have guards with us and there will be guards along the route."

"I am guessing we will speak with the people?"

"Yes. Not all will have heard some of the speeches. This gives the mixed crowd in the lower city a chance to see how unified we are. Which is where having Kaisan with us will be a way to show them."

"But we have sent our men off to war against Aram? How is this unified?"

"I am addressing this with Gran. She says we will send no more tribute to Du'Lanay. We are not wasting tribute and payment when we will need all we have when they respond."

"I guess we have to expect they will."

"Yes, but I am not sure how. Gran has many ideas. It quite boggles my mind."

"She is deeply knowledgeable and very curious. She kept me very entertained when we went about, in the markets, I understand about the unrest. Several loud men were quite rude when I entered a few of the shops. Your Gran was terribly upset and had words with them. This idea can only help, or it may make it worse."

"How do you mean?" Solina was curious. Kaisan had some particularly good points in their conversation. Ones only the well educated could know, he did not come across as a man from a lower caste, his range of knowledge was vast. She had a curious look to her, and an attentiveness which had Atin wondering.

"People will only hear what they know. The lower markets are filled with people, mixed from all lands. Not raised here, they are not permanent. Expendable if you wish. They will do their business here and move along. It is those who do not care about the Dragons who will cause the most strife."

"Well, do they not, while they are here, pay docking fees and taxes on their goods?"

"Why yes. I had to pay those when I arrived from Aram. 'Tis part of the agreement we have, in order to do business."

"Just as you said, part of the agreement… if other lands want to do business in our markets, then they will abide by what we tell them. If I say all will be welcome, then those who disagree can leave. Simple"

Kaisan looked at her in astonishment. He had not seen Solina be so assured about her position and bowed his head. "This can only prove to be interesting. Atin and I can certainly help in our way."

"We will all do what we can. You are part of our family now, Kaisan. Having your insights will keep it fresh, I do appreciate your ideas. Gran says you both will set a good example of unification."

"I have nothing but love for my new family. 'Tis refreshing to be able to be free to say what is on ones mind and not be told 'tis wrong. I thank you."

Kaisan bowed his head to Solina, his smile lit up his face, making Atin love him even more, her eyes glowing still as she looked at this handsome man who was her husband.

"You are most welcome, brother."

CHAPTER 41

Atin

Like the Pheonix Arising

Atin loved Kaisan very much. He seemed to accept her being a DragonRider, however, was concerned the first time she rode Analaria, during the ceremony. She felt euphoric for days after, Kaisan said he really enjoyed the sex after, her eyes stayed glowing blue for days. He gave her the most beautiful sapphire necklace, earrings, and tiara, later in the evening when it was just the two of them. They made love, with her wearing nothing but. She swore it was the most beautiful thing anyone had ever given her.

Truth, it was, and she knew he loved her. His aura whenever she saw it, was a beautiful array of colours, nothing around him gave her any reason to doubt his words. He was more than upset when she rode the second time, he told her after, he felt powerless, it was armed men this time, and he wasn't there to protect her. She tried to tell him he may not always be in the right position to protect; she had a duty to fulfill and riding a Dragon was part of it.

She didn't want it to turn to an argument, and their voices were raising a bit, when Solina walked into the dining room. "Am I interrupting anything?" Solina sat down, a servant bringing her breakfast which she waved away, asking for tea.

"No, not all, we were just discussing yesterday's events." Atin tried to make light of it, but Solina knew something was bothering her.

"Well, have I a story to tell you," Solina told them what the Dragons were up to. After the three of them had their laugh, "Would you be so kind to request an escort for our friends? It seems they may need assistance. The Palace has their own private dock in an underwater cave. It was a secret I, myself learned of. It would be very private. No public display."

Very few knew of it, when Veren asked about security measures with the Dragon Council, a name they gave themselves.

"Why yes, I can. I will go prepare."

"I would also like us to have a walk around the city…" After Solina had spoken about the walk around the city, Atin rose to prepare herself for her underwater excursion. As Kaisan got up to go with her, Solina asked Kaisan to stay with her while Atin went with one of the Marshalls and a few men. "Yes, of course I can stay," Kaisan looked puzzled, and Solina smiled at him as Atin got up to leave.

Atin changed into workable clothes, asking her maid servant to collect a towel and a change of clothes to bring with her. Meeting the Marshall outside the great hall, she affirmed her readiness to him. Kallen was spending more time with Veren, rising in his rank to be Veren's second. He ventured to nod back and motioned her to precede him. "Marshall Kallen, Solina mentioned we will be walking into the city tomorrow."

"Oh? She has not told Admiral Veren, or I would know this."

"I am sorry, Marshall. We were just discussing this at the dining table. I am sure Admiral Veren will soon know. I was advancing this onto you, so you and he can prepare yourselves."

"I thank you for the information. We can begin planning, can you tell me more?"

"Yes, it is the three of us, Solina, myself and my husband, Kaisan."

"Very well. We have you and the High Dragon in between us men, your husband will be on your outside."

"I will concede to what Solina thinks, she may wish him in between us women."

"Your husband has shown himself to be very proficient with arms. He could better protect you if he were between you and the crowds."

"Oh…?"

"Yes, he has come to the Barracks and sparred with me and even the Admiral. He is well versed in combat. He is an asset to Peli."

"Oh, I never knew this. Oh, yes, I do remember. He went to the Barracks… he never said he sparred … oh well. Anyways, you plan the event, and we will show our people all can be Vendar. It will be good to see parts of the city; I have not the chance to explore."

"Perhaps, we show you the layout on one of our many maps. It is always a clever idea to know the layout of a city."

"How right you are." The small group walked down the hall towards the lower Palace. There were internal stairways, mostly utilized by the servants, but it did save time. The Palace was a warren. Veren lamented it was not secure enough. There was a larger presence of soldiers since Solina's commencement of High Dragon. Solina's GrandMader hearing many footsteps, poked her head out of the Grand Hall. Inquiring where they were going, upon Atin telling her the where and the why, she asked if she could come along to observe. "Of course, although there won't be much to see, I will be underwater."

"I am simply curious, about your gifts, lass, 'tis all. You are a good companion for Solina, and I had a wonderful time with your husband. He is such a gentleman, very well versed in art and antiquities. He loves beautiful things! When he saw that necklace, he had to have it. I am ashamed to say what he paid for it, so I won't." Dame Metina was smiling as they walked down to the lower Palace together.

Dame Metina led them to the opening of the tunnels and sea caves, as she had traveled them many times. "This used to be how certain men of rank, no names, used to smuggle in goods, contraband, and the odd paramour, when times were… less congenial between us and the continents."

"Only the men?" Atin could not help but tease her friends GrandMader, who had been nothing but friendly to her and Kaisan. Her comment had the older woman laughing so hard, she had to stop and place her hand out on the damp walls.

"Oh, my goodness! Its so refreshing having laughter in these walls again. I do hope you and your husband stay for an exceptionally long time. You will always have a home here." Dame Metina paused catching her breath

"I messed things up with my two Daders. It has weighed heavily on my heart these last many years. Having you young people here, the Dragons, has lifted the burden. I want to hear laughter and maybe one day, little feet running down the halls."

They turned a corner, which opened to a large cavern, with the surf gently crashing under a low ceiling opening to outside. The soldiers under Kallen's direction lit the few torches they brought with them. They stood at the ready, one walking to the entrance to stand guard. "This is low tide, so you can imagine what hightide is like. No one can really see it until they are right there and even then, many a boat has sunk because someone didn't manage the tides right."

Atin walked towards the water on a small beach, torchlight absorbed by the dark stone walls. It was a smugglers paradise. She addressed her companions. "I will be more than a few minutes. I must clear the caves and go out into the ocean. Please do not worry, if you think I am gone too long. I will be back soon."

She turned back, shucking her sandals off, walking into the calm water. Diving in when she was deep enough.

Swimming underwater and out through the opening, she saw the various remnants of past boats which hadn't been swept out to sea. She rose for air once she cleared the sunken doorway, looking back to see stone walls of the Palace reaching high up, up, up. 'Impregnable,' was her first thought.

Atin took a deep breath. Diving down into the depths, placing her thoughts out. Soon a pod of grey whales answered her, and a few man eaters as well. She projected her thoughts, *"I ask for your assistance, if you can find the floating wood ships, on their way back to the large land, on the Southern currents. If you could escort, ummm, follow them to the place where the seas meet the land. There is no need for death, just a presence. I thank you for your help."*

Atin watched as the assembly of aquatic animals left swimming to the east.

"Would one assist me? My fins feel heavy." She was feeling the effects of being down too long. A man eater came close enough for her to grab onto his fin. He took off quickly, fast enough she wouldn't lose her grip. As her vision began to waver, the surface to the cave came into view. She hung on while the fin broke through the surface, the shark staying with her while she caught her breath. She let go, diving back underneath the water,

"Thank you, May you be Blessed." Atin placed her hand on his scaled skin. The man eater then dove back down and left the cave. Swimming to the shore Atin rose to her feet. The glow in her eyes diminished as she walked out. Kallen stood there with his men, their mouths gaping open. Her maids came forward

with a towel to wrap around her, Dame Metina came forward, as she was drying off, and spoke,

"Now there's a sight, you don't see everyday. I was about to send for a boat to come around outside and look for you."

"How long was I gone for?"

"Enough for one torch to burn out. The men say it was a half of an hour, as the torches are built a certain size to determine time in the dark."

"Well, I guess my timing is getting better, then, that's good." Atin looked pleased with herself.

"This is how you did all your pearling?" Dame Metina was genuinely interested. Atin dried off, changed into dry clothes and they walked back into the daylight. Kallen and another walking ahead and the other soldiers walking behind. The security was enough Atin noticed. Atin told Dame Metina all about her pearling, techniques, and the area she determined was hers. A place she was preparing for her family to use when she was no longer there.

"I hear the question in what you've told me, I give you my promise, while I am alive, your family will never want for anything. I will offer my assistance, should they ever ask. You have my word." Dame Metina did not make idle talk or promises she did not keep.

"Da would always agree with Ma, you are the best Magistrate to date. You make the most favourable trade agreements, less taxes and the fairest of judgements. 'Tis the best economy we have ever seen. Ma would say it was because you are a woman. Da would smile and agree with Ma, no argument there, he would say."

Dame Metina told her, ruling wasn't all roses. "You have no idea of the sacrifices made to get this country to where it is now. My first sacrifice was the happiness of my family. A decision I regret to this day, but the Universe has a strange way of working out. It put into place the events of late, and I hope you and your husband and the other DragonRiders will call this place home one day. Not for me, but for all humankind. We need this now. The world is too evil, too unjust, and while I am frightened at the hell Dragons will unleash, the result will be worth it. Time to set things to rights. Equality should be felt in all corners of the world, not just ours."

As they walked, Dame Metina spoke softly. "I was told your brothers left for the continent. This is a huge sacrifice on the part of your family. I do not think we can ask for them back. We are not sending anymore tribute to Du'Lanay, and the backlash is yet to be seen. I am sorry, Atin. I did not know."

"Thank you for acknowledging it. The loss of his sons is what made my Da ill, it began when he received the news. He resigns himself to it, Ma is his constant. I miss them terribly, but we must make sacrifices. I pray to Vendar to spare them, and I pray someday I see them again. 'Tis all I can do."

"But if your Da hadn't gotten ill, you would not know who you are."

"Yes, you are right."

"May I be blunt, Atin? That is my way."

"Yes. You need not coat your words with honey. I have talked with my Da and Solina, for that matter. I know there is a possibility they will not return. She was very forthright in her speech. I know they may be placed in battle first. I pray they survive."

"Well, It seems my GrandDader has been listening to me."

"Oh, she has! She is telling us many things. You know so much about ruling and …everything!"

"Thank you, Atin. I will leave you now. Thank you for having me join you in your little adventure. I bid you good path."

"Good Path to you also, Dame." They reached the Hall of Law and Dame Metina left her to go in the direction of her rooms or Dining Hall. Two soldiers went with Dame Metina and Kallen and his companion went with Atin. Atin opted to go to her room as she wanted to wash the salt off her body and hair.

"Thank you, Kallen."

"Sea Dragon, you are welcome." They parted ways at Atin's chambers.

I am going to ask Solina what the extra guard detail is for. It is a little unnerving inside the Palace. She was halfway through washing her hair when she realised Kaisan was standing in the archway watching. "Do you like what you see? Do you always watch the girls in the baths?"

She couldn't help but tease. This was exactly what he needed to hear.

"Only the ones, I love, and the ones I wish to make love to." Peeling his clothes off to join.

"Oh, there's more than one, then?"

"Mmmm, why yes, can't you tell I've been sooo busy lately." He kissed her neck and pulled her wet hair out of his way. Scooping her breasts in his hands as he came up behind her, he pulled her close. She felt his hardness against her bottom, slipping into the space between her legs. Opening a little as he took one of his hands, trailed down her belly. Down until his fingers toyed with her lips, going further until he guided his manhood into her opening.

She moaned as she felt him gaining entry. Placing his hands on her hips, he thrust against her from behind until the movement caused too much water to be splashing out and over the sides. He stopped and withdrew, as she laughed at the mess, "Good thing its so warm out, hopefully this will dry soon,"

He just, "MMMMmmm'd," turning her around to penetrate her from the front and walked out of the pool. His cock still hard inside her, she wrapped her legs around his waist as the water was replaced by air, and he dropped them down onto the sleeping mat. They spent the rest of the night enjoying each other until the dark before the dawn. Atin woke first, to find a servant girl in the room, with a towel draped over her arm. "Can I help you miss?"

"The High Dragon would like your presence in the Grand Hall."

"Oh, did she say what it might be for?"

"She spoke about a procession into the city, Sea Dragon. You were to go with her."

"Oh, my! What time is it? Kaisan, wake up!"

"Huh… what?"

"It is almost midday, Sea Dragon."

"Oh, Kaisan, we have slept in! Hurry! Miss… can you get us a small meal, no. Wait. Can you tell the High Dragon we will be right there. Oh, no! Kaisan!"

"It's fine, calm yourself. Miss, tell the High Dragon we will be there shortly. Also have a small meal brought here and we will rise and wash and we will get there, when we get there. Atin. We won't take up much more time than we must."

"Yes, Master Kaisan. Right away." The servant girl left, and Kaisan rose after Atin had bounded up and was rushing around. He grabbed her and held her tight. Kissing her forehead.

"Calm, Atin. I can tell you are agitated by the glow in your eyes. If you take a deep breath in and hold it, then let it out slowly, then you will feel better."

"Oh, Kaisan. All right. (Inhale…exhale)."

"Better?"

"Yes. I can't believe we slept in so long. I am getting quite lax."

"You are allowed to, you are the Sea Dragon, you know."

"Yes, but I do miss my home. I mean where my parents are. This Palace feels not like home yet. I like to keep busy."

"I have kept you quite busy."

"Not that kind. I mean swimming in the seas, I miss this. One can only walk in the gardens so much."

"Perhaps we can go there. If Solina lets us."

"They want us here. There are more guards now. They fear an attempt on us. Solina and I."

"Yes, you are right. Ah, here is our meal. Let's have a quick bite, then we can get attired and set off. Atin, let's sit." Kaisan patted the chair opposite his at the little table for the meals they had privately. The servant set a small fruit and cheese repast down with citrus juice. Then she left them to walk into the dressing room. The servant girl began to speak. "Dark reds today, we must look somewhat royal. It will accent the High Dragon."

"Very Well, Master Kaisan."

"Well, Look at you! Coordinating with the Rulers!"

"Well, one thing I like just as much as food is a good wardrobe. One must either look Royal, well dressed, or both!" They ate, Atin trying to eat fast but had to slowly chew. Her stomach was not feeling like it wanted food. "I must be nervous or just upset over being late. I will eat more when I return."

"Make sure you do; you will get light of spirit if you forget."

"Yes, Master Kaisan, you know me best!"

"Are you mocking me? Sea Dragon! I know how to make those eyes glow!"

"Not now. I am done eating. Let's just get dressed." Atin and Kaisan dressed in dark reds; they looked very well suited. Atin did not paid much attention to what she wore before. They left and walked down to the Grand Hall where they saw Solina sitting on her chair and Veren and Kallen standing before her. They looked up to watch the couple walk in and Atin's eyes began to glow. She squeezed her husbands hand, they stepped onto the dais, and Atin sat down. "I am so sorry if we are late. We slept in."

"Oh, you are right on time. I had the servant girl go in early to give you ample warning." Atin let out her breath she had been holding. Solina smirked at her Dragon sister. "I knew you'd be sleeping late; the Admiral and Marshal have planned for us to walk down after the midday meal, so planned to let you sleep in. however, now you are part of our planning. Kaisan, Marshal Kallen says you have proved your mettle in combat training, so having you walk with us, we will be double protected."

"Thank you, yes. I had formal combat training, before I began sailing the seas. I have kept it up with some of my sailors. It helped to pass the time, plus kept us honed for any pirates."

"It does us good. Atin will walk in the middle. I will walk on her left and you can be on her right."

"High Dragon, now that we have a strong man in the procession, It would do well to have him in the middle of you women. Then, he can grab either one should it be needed."

"Very well. Kaisan you can be in the middle."

"I can think of no other way, to walk with two lovely women on either side of me! Many a man would be jealous." The planning went on for another hour, the girls were shown on a map, the route they would take and what they could and couldn't do. Kaisan in the middle was a good point. Not just an Aram in the middle of two Pelinese women, it sent a message, Solina pointed out, it may look like he was a prisoner.

"A prisoner of my own making. I can have you hold onto my arm, both of you. It is more formal, but also if you feel faint. This sounds like a fair walk."

"We will have a carriage at the end to take you back, we made allowances. We cannot have you out for more than a couple of hours, this would give an assassin time to plan an attack." Veren was planning for all kinds of potential scenarios. His face was given over to the seriousness of the outing, Atin saw the mind behind the eyes, calculating every step. She wondered if going out was a clever idea… "Oh, is this something they would do?"

"Oh, yes, Sea Dragon. I am surprised they haven't already."

"Oh."

They ate the midday meal, after they all walked down to the Barracks. A cohort of guards were in formation, and Veren pointed the trio into the middle. He would walk in front and Kallen would walk directly behind them. The other guards would surround the Dragons as they progressed. Atin glanced at Solina and nodded and Solina nodded to Veren. "On My Mark. Open the Gates!"

A herald was sent to the front of the procession and announced the Dragons on their walk. Soon many faces were seen, poking out of windows and doorways. "Hear Yee, Hear Yee. The High Dragon and the Sea Dragon make their way through the city. Make way! Make way!"

Atin heard cheers, and accolades begin in front of them and behind them. Mostly it was DragonRiders, but there were High Dragon, Sea Dragon, and Dragon. As they passed people, the voices lessened as they saw Atin's husband. She grabbed his hand in hers from her position at his forearm and she smiled at him. She heard Solina murmur something from her side and Kaisan bent down without breaking stride and kissed her cheek. Atin grinned, then she pulled his hand up and she kissed the back. "Is that necessary?"

"Why, yes. Have you not had your hand kissed before?"

"Well, yes, but not by you. It seems strange."

"Well, get used to it. I will be doing it a lot today."

"Then I will be kissing you a lot, in rebuttal."

Solina grabbed Kaisan's other arm and leaned towards Atin. Atin heard Solina's loud whisper. "This will be the only time I will not say anything. It seems to be working."

The group walked down the hill, into various squares, past fountains, and Temples, not stopping until they arrived at the middle point of their procession. It was planned they would stop and Solina address the crowd. Word preceded them and guards fanned out around a fountain in the middle of the square. Solina and her escort stopped before the fountain, because of the incline, they saw people around and behind them. A few of the guards left into adjoining alleys and watch the people. As Solina and Atin came to a halt, the crowd surged forward, but the guards had it in hand. Solina whispered to Atin, "Have yourself start viewing, Veren wants to make sure we do not run into problems."

"Certainly."

"What do I do?" Kaisan looked awkward.

"Nothing, just look happy." Solina began to speak, Atin began to look around. Both women's' eyes were glowing.

"People of the Dragon, we come to you, to see you in your homes. We give you our blessing, our people of Vendar. To be Vendar is to love. To be a Dragon is to love. 'Tis the Vendar way. Our very own Sea Dragon has her own love. She has chosen a man of Aram, to be hers. Vendar has embraced him, and we share our love with…" Atin felt something hit her shoulder and turned to her right to see a man with anger on his face.

"You know not love. You killed my brother." The guards on her right side pushed into the crowd and two held the man as he shouted. Kaisan was holding her left arm. "Atin. Atin…"

"What? Who is this man?"

"You killed him. We are poor folk, trying to make a living. You killed my brother." Atin looked at the man and saw a dark haze surrounding him.

"Veren, he…Solina, he has a dark haze around him. He was one of the men who came to my cove. 'Tis his brother the man eaters killed." Atin whispered to Solina who came up beside Kaisan.

"You see a haze? Oh, by the way, you have a knife in your shoulder."

"I do? That's what hit me? oh…" Kallen's voice spoke from behind them.

"If the Sea Dragon isn't feeling it, leave it in, we deal with it later. It will hurt when it comes out. Let's deal with this man…" Just then, he threw himself onto Solina, and Kaisan pulled Atin in front of him, and onto the ground. She fell onto her knees and Kaisan hovered over her. She heard shouts and looked at Solina, who's eyes brightened and Solina tried to pull the man on her, off. Kallen was bleeding over her from an arrow in his arm. It went right through the muscle. "Kallen. Are you fine? Please get off me."

Others helped Kallen to his feet, and Kaisan stood and helped Atin to stand. She looked at Solina who's eyes brightened considerably and she knew the bond jumped from her back to Solina. Solina stood and the yellow haze surrounding her pushed out and enveloped all of them in a huge circle. Much like a bubble. Atin saw bubbles form on the seas when algae were agitated. This covered them and a few guards.

"Nothing can get through. Kallen, your arm." The man was not fazed.

"I am good…for now. Like I said it will hurt when it comes out. Let us get you back before more try to end your life."

"Where's Veren?" Solina looked at the man who looked as though an arrow in the arm was an everyday occurrence.

"He left with a few guards. The arrow came from up there." He pointed to a roof behind them. Atin began to feel pain in her shoulder. Kaisan had not let go of her. He was holding and looking at the man who had thrown the knife. The crowd was quiet, but murmurs begun. Two guards still held him.

"I am sorry for your loss. I did not know what I was when you arrived. It grieves me, what I did. Would you offer forgiveness?" Atin wanted to make this right, however, didn't know how.

"I will not! You have no right to do what you did."

"I am sorry."

"Atin…"

"No, I will deal with this… stand away, Kaisan."

"You are hurt. He threw a knife at you."

"He had every right." Kaisan left her side but stood right behind her. She sensed he didn't want to; however, she had to address this. "How can I make amends?"

"You can die. Just like he did." He broke out of the guards grasp and leapt at her, another knife appeared in his hands, he had almost reached her and Kaisan grabbed her arm she started to raise.

"Let me GO!" Atin's eyes glowed up and she raised her arm with strength she didn't know she had and the man in front of her stopped at the yellow barrier. He could not go further. She stared at him, and all she saw was hatred in his eyes. He was trying to knife the air and failing. Then he stopped, a haze appeared around him and began to rise. He dropped to his knees and fell against the barrier. Atin saw the man shrivel and the dark haze rose. Then the man fell to the side. She saw he was dead. The crowd began to murmur, Atin looked down at the dead man, then at the crowd. Her eyes shone with brightness. Her face set with no expression.

"This man had no love in his heart. Yes, I was the cause of it, I did not know then; I was a Dragon. I asked for forgiveness, and to make amends. He did not grant me either. If one cannot change their spirit, then that person is not welcome here. It matters not if you are Pelinese, Layanese or Aramite. Vendar is love. If I find one who has no love, then I will seek to end the spirit. This is the new

Dragonage. There is no room for hate. This is what we wanted to see when we walked through here. Love, not hate."

Atin turned to Kallen who still hovered around Solina. He watched her. She pointed into the crowd. "The man with the orange headdress. The woman with the purple skirt, the man who's hiding behind the one in red. Those are the darkest auras."

Kallen told the closest guards and they left to search the crowds. Veren came back with another guards, his face flushed and breathing heavily. He entered the yellow bubble with no deterrent.

"High Dragon, whoever it was planned their escape well. We caught a glimpse of two men. We found their bows, but 'tis our equipment. So, it could have been anyone. I am sorry I failed you. Kallen! Your arm."

"We deal with this later. Shall we disperse the crowd? The Sea Dragon has given us a few who are not Vendar."

"Solina, can we walk over to the fountain?"

"Oh, certainly. You wish to drink?"

"No, I will deal with this knife and this arrow." Atin looked at Kaisan, who was trying not to hover. She smiled at him; through the pain she was now beginning to feel. "I am sorry if I yelled at you. I needed to deal with this situation."

"I was just trying to protect you."

"I understand. However, I am also a Dragon. Now can we get to the water please, I am feeling this knife."

They walked forward and the yellow haze surrounded them and moved with them. Once Atin reached the fountain she sat on the brick edge and put her hand in. Kaisan stood over her and watched the crowd. He did not see Atin place her hand in the water and he heard a gasp from Solina he looked down watching the knife back out of his wife's shoulder and robe and fall onto the stones. The crowd gasped at the clatter. She looked down at the knife.

"Kallen, come here." Kallen came forward. He looked at Atin and the knife on the ground. "I am afraid the arrowhead will hurt worse going back and the fledge of feather would hurt going through."

"You are right. will you be able to stand the pain if someone were to cut the arrowhead off?" Veren came forward as Kallen was nodding his head and with a quick chop of his sword the front of the arrow was cut. Kallen winced at the movement.

"Well, then, Marshal Kallen if you would be so kind as to take my hand in yours." Kallen blushed as he took the outstretched hand of Atin in his and all watched as the arrow began moving out of the muscle of Kallen's bicep. It got hung up on the fabric of his uniform, but Veren pulled it through the cloth and held onto it. Kallen felt his arm with his other hand and looked at Atin as he gently disengaged his hand from hers. "What did you do? I feel no pain. I feel no tear."

"Merely healed the wound. I have some talents; healing is one of them."

"I give you many thanks, Sea Dragon."

Veren was looking around at the crowd. His guards gathered the three Atin pointed out and Veren spoke. "What would you like to do with these three, High Dragon?"

"Atin, do they still have dark auras?"

"The woman has lightened up, the men not. Do you want me to…?"

"No, I will deal with this." Solina rose to her feet, she sat beside Atin while the other healed herself and Kallen. She stood and addressed the crowd.

"The Sea Dragon has the right of it. To be Vendar is to love. It is our way. I will not stand here and tell you otherwise. To be Vendar is to be love. These three have not love. They will have a chance to say a few words. You, orange head-dress, what have you to say?"

"You are but a woman. What can you do?"

"Well, let's see. I ride a Dragon. My sister here rides one also. I make winds and create diamonds. However, another talent I have, is to take the air you breathe, shall I demonstrate?" She did not wait for an answer and held out her hand. The man trying to gasp, his mouth opened and nothing happened, he made choking movements, then fell with guards still holding him. They gently lay him down and stood. The other man began begging. Solina glanced back at Atin and she looked around Solina's legs and shook her head. Solina watched the man, his mouth opened and the same thing happened. Atin placed her hand on Solina's leg.

"The woman's aura has lightened. She looks like another may have influenced her."

"You have a chance to remove hate from your heart, Mistress. The Sea Dragon can tell if you are Vendar. Go now, and I do not wish to see you again. At least not with hate."

"Thank you. May you be Blessed. Dragons. Thank you." The woman left and Veren spoke to Solina, "This has been an eventful day. Shall we continue or go back to the Palace."

Solina looked down at Atin. "What would you like to do? I can go for a little bit more if you like? I am afraid you will need to bond with Nannosh again. I want to make sure; we have no more deviant auras. Do you have a headache?"

"No, headache, but my stomach is swirling some. I can walk more. I would like to see a bit more of this city. 'Tis very fascinating."

"Are you sure? My Heart, you were knifed. Here, take my hand."

"Thank you. Kaisan, what happened, may happen more. Solina and I are Drag-ons. We have a responsibility to our people. If we turned and swam away from every adversary, then what does this say? My Da always said to face a rogue wave head on. Less chance of capsizing."

Atin shook her head at Kaisan who opened his mouth to start talking. "Less chance, it will happen, but at least you will know it. If we were to not address our worries, they will follow us."

"Thank you, Atin. Well said. Have you been listening to Gran? Those sound like her words. Then that's it. We keep going."

The guards formed up and Kaisan bent to give his wife a kiss on the lips. Atin hugged her husband and kissed him back. She backed off when she felt a tug on her arm. "There's enough time for this later, but it does have the desired effect we wanted."

Atin turned to Solina as Kaisan embraced Atin tightly. Then he let her go but held onto her arm. "Exactly. Shall we?"

They began walking around the fountain and with the guards surrounding them, they walked through the parting crowd to go along the path they planned. Solina kept the yellow haze surrounding them. Walking to chants of DragonRiders, they waved and shook hands and made the most of the rest of the walk. They arrived at the carriages, alighted and Atin snuggled with Kaisan while Solina sat opposite them.

"That tired me out, I am keeping my yellow air bubble around this carriage until we arrive back in the Palace. I have never done this before. I wish I put it in place before, then you would have never had the knife reach your back."

Atin looked at Solina and smiled contentedly. "You would have never known to create your bubble if I hadn't been knifed. I feel sorrow at taking the man's spirit. It weighs on me. I am not set out to be a Ruler."

"This is what a Ruler must do, set punishments, and sometimes pass sentence. Gran told me a good Ruler must conduct the sentence. Or people will not follow with a clear conscience. I don't like what I had to do either. If you both do not mind, I would take my evening meal alone."

"Are you fine? Not distressed?"

"I am only tired. Using my bond tired me, I wish to sleep."

"Me also, when I healed my Da, I slept soundly for a half day. I am hungry, ravenous, so I would like a huge meal then a warm bath and then bed."

"I will leave you to your meal, if you will let me hold you while you sleep."

"Yes, this sounds wonderful, as long as 'tis just holding me. I will fall asleep as soon as I hit the Dragon!" Solina laughed at Atin's reference to her falling asleep on Nannosh.

"I think tomorrow, Veren will wish to discuss today's events. Gran will also, once she hears what we did and said. Shall we meet in the morning, after our meal?"

"Yes, this sounds grand. (Yawn), you are too comfortable, Kaisan. I am not sure if I will eat now. I could use a sleep."

"Well, I will carry you if you like. We have arrived."

"Oh, we have. No, I will walk." They arrived in the courtyard and alighted from the carriage. Solina stayed a moment, and Atin left with Kaisan back to their rooms. She walked into the bathing room and her husband helped her to remove her robes. He was astounded to see a raised white line where the knife had been embedded. "This looks like an old scar. Does it not hurt?"

"It did when it was jostled a bit. I numbed the area. Or perhaps having a bond with Nannosh helped. I am not sure."

"Well, 'tis a wonderful talent to have. You have a gift from the Gods. Which one, may I ask?"

"Well, help me to wash…without any relations. I am too tired right now. Then when we lay down, I will tell you. Are you that interested?"

"Why not? If I am to become completely Vendar, I do need to start knowing."

"True." He helped her wash, robed her, and held her while she got herself comfortable. However, he was not surprised when she faded into sleep without even getting a full sentence out. He held her all night, and she woke to find Kaisan looking at her and smiling.

"What?" She said groggily, feeling a wee bit off but seeing him made her forget herself.

"You. Beautiful… I love watching you wake. You look dreamy. I love the way you look when you ride me, and we make love, and… you."

"Ahhh, and I love you. What makes you so sentimental? Oh, and what did you and Solina discuss when I was gone? I forgot to ask you in the wake of our eventful day." Atin felt wide awake now.

"You. She took me to see the Dragons and I spent time touching the biggest one. She looks like your eyes, but bigger. Solina told me times were going to get harder, and I had to be sure our love would traverse the tough times, not just the good. To make sure I understood the Dragons would not replace our love, I had myself a ride on the smaller one. By the Gods! What a heady marvel. I see how one could love flying in the air as though they were a bird. I will try not to be too jealous of your ability to fly, as long as I can get the occasional flight in."

"You proved yourself yesterday, you would give your body to protect mine. I do love you. We will get through these troubled times. I do have my duties to address. The Dragons are part of those duties."

"I understand. Having you show me, will only help more. I do want to be a good husband."

"Well, a good husband would kiss his wife, first thing in the morning." Kaisan kissed her, Atin wrapped her arm around his shoulder and pressed him closer as the other arm in between found what it was looking for… all hard and ready.

"Is that fair?" He asked in between kissing her lips.

"No, not at all. This is me, now. You have taught me all sorts of unhealthy habits. I would hate to disappoint my teacher." She rolled on top of him, placing herself on his hard length and rode him until he was the one moaning loudly.

The day would not remain as good as it began. Atin and Kaisan dressed making their way down to the dining room, it was quite common for Sheyna and Veren to join them. Since the announcement of their engagement, Solina insisted they be housed in the Palace with them. She said their little family would grow and the more they spent time with the others, the more the trust between them would be cemented. The two new lovebirds were eating at one end of the table, heads bent together, talking about how their day would be spent. Atin could not help but smile at them as she sat herself opposite at the table with Kaisan sitting beside her.

"Good morning, Veren, Sheyna."

"Good morning, Atin, Kaisan."

"We are to convene at the High Dragon's convenience, to discuss yesterday's events. 'Tis to be a council with the rulers attending."

"Thank you, Veren. We expected this."

The servants brought newly baked goods and a plate for each of them with a serving of quail's eggs which Atin relished from the very beginning of their tenure at the Palace. This time however, the smell was making her stomach turn and she tried to ignore it. "How are your plans for the joining ceremony coming, Sheyna? Do you have a date?"

"We are in discussions; we want the joining to happen soon. Solina says the Dragons will officiate, and we are very honoured. Atin, are you fine? You have a pallor to your complexion."

As Sheyna spoke; Atin stood up quickly and Kaisan rose to his feet also.

"Darling..."

"No, please sit, I'm fine, I'll be right back." Rushing out of the room, Atin bumped into Solina, mumbling as she sped off down the hall. He followed her but stopped at the doorway Solina was blocking.

"What's bothering Atin?"

"I will go see, then I will return." Solina grabbed his arm, "No, you will stay right here." Her eyes began to glow, the expression on her face brooking no argument.

Atin rushed down the hall, hoping she didn't empty her stomach until she reached their room. She sped in, grabbed the pot she used to pass water in and emptied the contents of her stomach, which wasn't much, just liquids. She lay on their bed for a while, not knowing what it may be.

Then, as she lay lost in her thoughts, she remembered seeing her Mader, partaking of her favorite herbal teas, and throwing up the contents when she smelt even the flower from which it was made. *No, it can't be.* But then, yes it could. They were highly active for the last couple of months. Terribly busy. Atin couldn't think, her thoughts in a jumble. As her stomach settled down, she remembered the assembly of her friends in the Dining Hall.

She rose to her feet, stood waiting. As she didn't feel nauseous again, headed back. She entered to see Solina standing behind Kaisan, seated on his chair, looking grave. Solina's hands were on his shoulders, and her eyes were full Dragon, whirling golden. The expression on her face was also grave. Atin slowed to a stop.

"What is it? What has happened? Is it my family? Have you had news?"

Atin dreaded what was next, but this wasn't what she was going to hear.

"Kaisan has something he would like to tell you. Kaisan." Solina backed away and Atin walked closer, knowing something pivotal was going to happen. Looking at Kaisan, her eyes began to glow blue. Veren and Sheyna had risen, standing off to the side. There seemed to be a few more guards in the room, their hands on their weapons for the ready. Atin took all this in as her gaze went back to her husband. Her eyes became brighter.

"Kaisan, Dear Heart, what is it?" Atin was scared to ask, however, her parents told her, when faced with a problem, one faced it head on, not run from it, as it would always follow.

"I have not been forthright with you. You have always been with me. However, I will explain. In Aram, family is right, or it is wrong, there is no in-between. When I left you in the spring to tell my family I wished to marry you, they cut me out. Completely. I have my name struck out of the annals of history; I am no more. This is why I did not mention it. I am without a nation, without a name, and I was ready to embrace yours, take your name as mine. I have always questioned my way of life, my religion, and took to the seas to escape. I had no purpose except to exist for the possibility I would be of some use to the state. I was expendable.

I did not agree with, and I was punished for my views, I have always embraced other ideas, while Du'Lanay was not much different from my homeland in their views, Pelin'Dun was where I was always drawn. When I first saw you, I had no purpose and your eyes had me mesmerized from the beginning. When I told my Pader, he begged me to give you up, I did not. He said while in his heart I would always have a place, he had no choice but to disown me. He told me never to return or I would be killed. I gladly chose to return to you. You must believe me." His face had a pleading look, he was openly crying, tears streaming down his face.

"I do."

"You have to do what is right for the Dragons, Atin" Solina spoke softly,

"He could be lying, a spy for Aram."

"How can you say this?" Atin looking at Solina, a spark of anger lighting her eyes more than ever. "I see his aura; there is no subterfuge in his manner. He speaks truth to me."

"Ask him who his Pader is." Atin slowly turned to Kaisan, the question burning in her eyes. Kaisan spoke very quietly. "My Pader is the FirPader."

Atin turned and walked away to stand staring out the open window and at the mountain. When she heard rustling, she raised her hand, then turned around. "And how is it you know this, Solina?" Her voice devoid of emotion, her mind, churning over the information she was trying to process.

"GrandMader thought it strange a mere trader had such exquisite taste in art. You know she took him around the markets while you were busy with me and the Dragons. She also told me the price for the sapphires he bought you, a small fortune. 'Tis traditionally a bride gift of the nobility in Aram. Also, his abilities in combat, not all are trained in various methods. Veren made a study of combat, Aram, and Layanese. Kaisan excels at combat, Veren was hard pressed and impressed enough to know Kaisan is a Master.

Then there is his name, not quite an Aram name. She had scribes bring up the names of all noble houses. There is only one Kaisan. He is well educated, well mannered, and she has a duty to this country to check out everyone who plays a part. Do not blame her for doing her duty. She has always placed duty first. I am here to make sure there are no secrets among us. To move ahead, everyone must be honest, past, present, and future. If we do not trust each other, then we are already doomed." Solina said her piece, her eyes calmed down losing some of their glow. Atin looked at Kaisan.

"Why did you not say, when we were at the waterfall? I told you who I was. I trusted you with my own doom. You could have rejected me and told the world or killed me right then and there for your Pader and his beliefs. You could have killed me!" Atin's anger came to the forefront with her last sentence. The fluid in all the glasses rose and all looked at the table. She knew she should calm down, but she looked at the man who she thought she knew.

"You could have killed me." She spoke softly and the fluids fell as she let her anger disappear. Not all landed back in their vessels and the table became, well, wet. Atin had tears streaming down her face. Her blue eyes glowing very brightly shedding tears openly.

Kaisan, still crying, stood up and walked slowly around the table, towards her, his palms up when some of the soldiers made to unsheathe their weapons. Solina motioned to stop them. He continued until he was directly in front of Atin, and he took her hands in his.

"You see my energy, can you not? You hear the truth in what I say? I am sorry I did not tell you, I had only you in my heart. The moment my Pader told me to leave, I put that life behind me. Aram for me is no more. I have only thought of you, since the moment I first saw you, I only want to make you happy, Be with you every moment I have spirit. Protect you from harm, although I know the Dragons protect you. I love the way you look at me; it makes me complete. There has only ever been you. I have never felt fuller of spirit when I am with you. More than any religious ceremony I had to attend, more than being the last on the pile of many sons, I knew my life had more purpose than waiting for a sword to the neck. You are my purpose now! You have all my love, now and forever. I give everything I am to you and to you alone. I would give you my life, my body to protect yours."

"Well, what you say has truth, but there is one small problem." Atin smiled tentatively at her sad husband. She was full on crying, the tears flowing with his admissions.

"I spoke truth from my heart, you are my Dragon, I will always cleave to you. I will always give myself to protect you, as much as I am able. This I swear and vow. Always. Now and always."

"Well, you will have to share your love with one other, my dear Kai."

He looked at her blankly. "I am with child." Kaisan looked at her, his eyes rolling back in his head, as he collapsed on the floor in front of her. She could not catch him in time. Veren rushed over with Sheyna and a few guards, and they carried him back to their room.

Solina came over to Atin while they walked behind. "You are not upset with me? I have a duty to the people while my family rules here. There must not be secrets among us, which includes those who serve the Dragons, all of us. I know he loves you very much, but as I knew of this information, I could not keep this secret from you. It was best to be told by him since it was his to tell."

"I am not upset with you, you did right. I am more upset with myself. Oh, how could I have been so stupid?"

"Love will do many things to our hearts and mind. Lighten the path we want only to see, not what we need to see. However, 'tis not something with which we cannot live. Better to be found out now than years down the path. Then, it would be more deceptive. One thing I learned from Gran, is question everything. And discuss with others, many minds have different perspectives, and combined, many outcomes. We will learn, if only by our mistakes. It is a lesson learned; do you not think?"

"Yes, most definitely. Your Gran is deeply knowledgeable and intuitive. I thank her for her insight. If, like you said, this was found out later in our journey, it would be more deceptive. Thank you, Solina."

"No thanks are needed; we look out for one another. You are my sister now. I want what is best for you, and Kaisan."

"Ohhh! I have only myself to blame, as I did not think to ask him about his family. He did tell me things, but not specifically his family. He may have had all the best intentions in the world, so I will try to think this from his side. He denounced all he was. To him it was a past he left, out of sight, out of mind. I never thought of myself as mesmerizing… just a simple woman, leading a simple life."

"And now you will become a Mader." Solina hugged her friend, "I am so happy for you both. I will relay the news to GrandMader and place her mind at ease about Kaisan. She does not dislike him; she was being cautious, she has made me question everything, if only for the good of our people. She will be so excited about the news. This only serves me well. She was hinting the other day about little feet."

Solina hugged her again, leaving to walk down the hall. Atin went inside their rooms to see Kaisan regaining consciousness. Sheyna and Veren left after giving Atin their congratulations. Atin sat on the edge of the mat, watching Kaisan closely while he looked at her processing the information of her announcement. "You are sure?" she nodded.

"You are having my child?" she nodded. "Unless you think I had time to have someone else's?" Here her sarcasm found its way out. He sat up.

"I made a fool of myself, didn't I?" She nodded again. She could not help but smile at him.

"You still wish to be joined to me? You won't send me off? You have the right to do so, in this country?"

"Of course, you fool, why would I not? You spoke truth. I am only a little upset you thought not to tell me at the beginning. We are to have no more secrets, from now on. I told you all that I am, you should think about doing the same. We talk and you tell me, or if you feel it is something everyone should know, tell us about your life and growing up. If we are to serve in the future, we must trust each other. I have given you my trust, but you will have to earn the others back."

"No more secrets, I will tell you anything you wish to know." Kaisan sat up and grabbed her in a hug. Pulling her back, he looked at her and smiled, pulling her back again to kiss her.

"You have made me the happiest of husbands! You are having my child! I didn't think I could love you more, but this, this is the best gift you could ever give. I will cherish the ground beneath your feet. Oh, how I love you. I feel full of spirit and eternal!" Later that afternoon, after Atin had a short nap with Kaisan, he gingerly made love to her, and she had to admit, her husband was gifted in all things!

"I'm not going to break, you know, I am going to have your child, 'tis still incredibly early. My Mader was making meals in the morning, had a birth in the afternoon and was back at the fire making more meals in the evening. I am made of sterner material than the glass figurines on the table. I do have to admit; I really enjoyed what you did. Can we try this again?"

"Oh, my Dear Heart. I was always told a childbearing woman had to be very careful in all things. You tell me differently."

"Maybe this was because the women you knew wanted nothing to do with men and their 'activities.' Do you not think? Is it not different in Aram? Women are not treated equal, are they?"

"You are correct. The only authority my Mader has is over the Secondary wives and the Harem. She answers to my Pader and to his advisors. She only has her status as the first wife of the living God. Nothing more."

"Why do your men need a 'Harem'? Isn't this a subtle way of saying a courtesan?"

"The Harem was the FirPader's women. No other man can touch them."

"How many wives and how many Harems does your Pader have? I am curious." Atin grabbed a couple pillow bolsters and placed them behind her, so, she could be comfortable. Kaisan sat up and Atin grabbed a couple more from the end of the bed to place behind his back. The bolsters usually ended up all over the floor in the morning and when they retired, the bed was tidy and pillows in their place. Atin enjoyed having this done for her. It was the trivial things she could get used to.

"Well, let's see. There is my Mader, she has two sons, myself and the heir apparent, and I have three sisters by my Mader. There is the second wife, she has my brother Tovan, and I have four sisters by her. Then there are ten women in the Harem, I have five more brothers and ten more sisters by the Harem women."

"That's a lot of family. Do you know them all? How does the line of succession work?"

"I only know my family by the wives. I was not close with my eldest brother. He is quite a bit older than me, by ten years and is kept busy with learning statecraft from my Pader and has several wives and plenty children of his own. I am closest to Tovan; we are days apart in age. We grew up together and he married a King's dader and spends his time between cities, in trading ventures. He has children also, but they are kept away, in another city."

"Why is that? You have me intrigued. I know nothing about your family."

"They are kept away because…"

"Is it a secret? You said we had no secrets from now on."

"No, it isn't this. Tovan is a second son. When my Pader dies my eldest brother Akishen becomes FirPader."

"So…. What does that mean? Do you not celebrate?"

"I… well, the man who assumes the Throne will murder all contenders who would usurp his ascension. This means my life and that of my brother and his sons, even my youngest brothers would be put to the sword."

"That's barbaric! How does this even begin to make a family love each other? What about you now? If you are erased from history."

"I am hoping the sword arm does not reach out to me. This is one reason I stayed as far away as I could. Pader is getting more infirm as he ages. He does not attend ceremonies anymore; he does not want the people to see him not glorious. Akishen has been hovering around the Throne for a couple of years, he has his army of men around him constantly, 'tis only a matter of time."

Atin looked sad, and she wiped a tear. "They, your brother would even kill his own brothers. How sad. What if Tovan became FirPader? Would he kill you?"

"Yes, 'tis what tradition has taught us. He would be sad, but there can only be one God."

"I am sorry. Kaisan, deeply sorry, but I do not want to ever go there. I do not agree with some of your country's traditions. This isn't even fair for the others in your family. How can anyone love another? I have nothing but love and caring for all my brothers and sisters, and I have great love for my Mader and Pader. I have the greatest love for you, and we are going to bring a child into being. I would fight tooth and nail to keep my child alive. I do not want anyone to murder my child because it was in line for a Throne. One which gave it God like status. Woe to anyone who tried." Atin's eyes began to glow and Kaisan grabbed her hands.

"No one is going to harm our child, Atin. Look at me. I will not let this happen. I am no longer Aram. I do not exist for them anymore, only for you, and our child. We need not worry." Kaisan's stomach growled at this very moment. Atin's tummy growled a reply. Both looked down and then at each other and grinned.

"I am thinking we should find our evening meal and continue our discussion after?" Atin agreed and they rose, dressed, and walked to the Dining Hall together. Atin had a thoughtful look as she processed all Kaisan told her. They found Solina looking worried at the head seat of the table. Both sat next to her and were served. "What is the matter? Is it the Dragons? Is everything fine up there?"

"Oh yes. The Dragons are fine. I had some distressing news. We had our council, without you both. In the wake of your exciting news, we discussed yesterdays events and… other things."

"Oh, care to share?"

"Yes, I have no choice, but to clear this issue up. Kaisan, you told Atin your secret are there others you wish to share?"

"I am unsure of what you speak. What others might you refer to? You have but to ask, I will tell you what you desire to know."

"It was brought to my attention your ships were sighted, hovering around the Islands. Were they not to sail back to Aram?"

"Yes, this is what I understood them to be doing. I have no idea what they would be doing, still here. You think I have information on their activities?"

"What else could I think?"

"Kaisan is speaking truth, Solina. What are you accusing him of?"

"I am merely asking, not accusing. However, considering what transpired yesterday, Kaisan will have to earn my trust. His ships being where they are, is not an effective way to begin."

"But Lina, they are not his ships anymore. He gave up Aram. Maybe this other Captain has other intentions."

"I hope 'tis all it is. Kaisan. If I am wrongful in my thought, I am sorry. However, if I am right…I do not want it to be so. You are my brother by marriage. Atin is my sister Dragon, I will protect her from all, even from those she holds dear. You understand?"

"Yes. I do. I will find out what his intent is. However, I can not do so until they return. I have no ill intentions, nor ill will for my new home and my new family, if I can call you such. You will see. It gladdens my heart you would look out for Atin, she is my breath, my spirit, and I have a lot of relearning, of your ways. Unlearning Aram ways. I will earn your trust, someday. May I retire?"

"Yes, certainly. Atin, can you stay for a moment?" Kaisan bowed, then gave Atin a small peck on her cheek, smiling sadly. He walked out to return to their rooms.

"Lina, I watched his aura the whole time. It was truthful. He spoke from his heart. I am sad at these events, but how much will he have to prove?"

"I believe you, and Kaisan for this matter. This was only brought to my attention, others are distrusting. It is suspicious actions by Aram. I will have to investigate, if only to appease others. This is what ruling is, I am pulled in different directions, by all. It hurts my head sometimes. This would have been simple if all were known before."

"That I cannot disagree with, 'tis my error. I can only learn by my mistakes. Information is the key to moving forward, having all would have eased my mind also. Please do not hold this against him, he is the most open with me now."

"I love you can tell by a person's aura if they are truthful. Yesterday was proof of this. It would help me in all aspects of ruling. However, you cannot be with me all the time. I should see if I can develop a talent of my own, it would save me these headaches."

"Your talent of the air bubble, and mine of healing. We are learning about what we can do. I am sure there will be more... like what your Gran is imparting upon you. Does not your Gran do most of the ruling?"

"Yes, however, she is training me, she says. She won't be here forever. The elixir effects are wearing off; the two eldest have passed spirit and now the others will expire from natural causes. She says it is a matter of time. I am to know all she knows; it is so much sometimes. She is like a walking library of many tomes, books, and maps."

"Sounds like you are well on your way to becoming a leader."

"It is so much to know. I hope the Purity Dragon does not take offense."

"Why is this? I do not understand."

"The Purity Dragon is the leader of all of us. She will lead as she has all our talents. I hope to step down when she does. I find it very taxing."

"I would hope all of us bring different talents to bear. It should not be on one to bear the bulk. If we are done chatting, I would like to comfort Kaisan. He looks as if you took his favorite toy away!"

Solina laughed and gave Atin a hug. "You go, I understand completely. Kaisan will have to convince us he is truth. I have faith he is, but Veren is not so trusting and my Gran even less. Not they are the only ones, but it has made me question everything and see other paths. His omission was a large oversight. You would do well to question everything also, see all sides of the gem, so to speak. I will see you later."

Atin walked back to her rooms, Kaisan was laying down, his brow furrowed. She plopped down on the bed into his outstretched arm and tucked right in, he tightened his grip and enfolded her into his embrace. "She told you to not trust me. I understand, I would be doing the same."

"No, not at all. I see your aura, you forget. I know when you are truthful. It is others are not as trusting. Solina trusts me, she says we must see all aspects of a gem to see the whole."

"She sees me as a diamond then. It could be worse."

"Mmmm, you are my diamond, husband! Every facet, every single side!" Atin could not resist leaning up and removing the ties which held her husband's tunic together. She trailed her finger down his stomach, bouncing it off the muscles as she said the last to him. He let her. She ended up with tucking her finger then her hand down his leggings to grab his member in her hand and gently squeezed and stroked him until he grabbed her hand and rolled on top of her and kissed her most thoroughly. They spent the rest of the evening and most of the night, exhausting themselves.

It was a glorious end for Atin's day.

CHAPTER 42

Davian

From the Shadow and Ash

Davian sat in his office, the breeze had left, the heat inside his room becoming unbearable. He leaned back, sweating in his light robe of white, unadorned except for fine edging in gold, the only thing to announce his position. Looking at the same scroll for an hour, wondering what else could happen. He felt angry at the world.

What is this blasphemy we are hearing? How is this happening? I feel underprepared. Dragons... was this predicted? How do we react? Do we react? Hmmm, maybe I need access to the hidden library. I have not access... yet. I will ask my mentor; he may let me this time. I wonder what it contains. I hate not knowing things. If forbidden manuscripts are hidden away, they must contain information pertinent to what is happening now. How can I justify anything, without knowing key points. I will insist when I take this to him. If he doesn't blow up again.

Things which should remain hidden were happening in his time. He wondered what the next development would reveal and if he was ready. A moment of uncertainty crossed his thoughts then quickly left.

Our God has written Dragons and the Riders are demons, and now we are faced with them again. I should prepare our tactics and begin reading again. I will have Geravon finding me tomes on our history. See if we can sort out what they did after the demons were slain. A revival of sorts, time to begin cracking down again.

Just then Davian heard something, as though someone had said, *'my Lord.'*

Thinking there was a conversation nearby, Davian rose and looked outside each of his windows. Nothing. Other than his view from above the gardens, several lengths above them. He saw Thirds, some busy pruning, some on their knees cutting the grasses. Another view he had, the one he liked to stare at, was the view of the harbour in the west of the city.

Davian's perch high above in the Namarch's Palace granted him a view none other had. Even the Namarch who had his office and bedchamber on the Southern side did not have this view.

I do not see anyone, around. None who are speaking. Am I to think I am hearing things?

Davian opened the door to his office. Several busy Thirds and Secondaries were walking hurriedly past, all nodded and bowed their heads, as the Second-in-Command of the Naman religion poked his head out of his office door. Davian closed the door and went towards his desk.

'My lord'

He walked to the windows peering out towards the gardens. He stood there and looked. Into the trees, the green foliage was dense and as a breeze picked up, he saw it.

A Purple Sennet. "Ahhh, now I see you. Welcome. You must be the one the Princess let loose. If you care to stay, I will send for some bread and place it on the ledge for you, should you care to have some. But be wary, there are a few Grousehawks around. You would be hard pressed to fly from them. I give you good day."

Davian bowed to the Sennet which looked like he bobbed back. Then he sat down at his desk. Only for a moment, then rose and went to the door, rang the bell which was on the wall. It hung from a well embroidered pull. The fabric was tough and the pattern one of his favorites. He had it created when he rose to Primar. It was permitted to personalize certain things of his station if it was not too ornate. Which was fine with Davian, he liked simpler things.

The tapestry of the bell pull was only two colours, red and black. The red was complimentary, but the black faded in the light. It looked very plain to some. To Davian it was a reminder of his ancestry. The red was a reminder of his Royal blood and the black for the army. It would have been his colours had he been allowed to remain in the army. *Another life, so long ago.*

The door opened and his Third entered. The only reason Davian would pull the bell was for refreshment. "Your Grace, you rang?"

"Yes, I would like tea. One slice of unbuttered bread. A small bowl of seeds. Do we have any pumpkin or sunflower seeds?'

"I can bring you both if you wish. Your usual tea?"

"Yes. Thank you."

The Third left and Davian returned to the window. He looked for the Sennet in the tree but could not see it. Seeing movement in the corner of his eye, he saw it had flown into another, closer to his window.

"If you care to wait, your repast will be here shortly."

He turned and sat down at his desk. The scroll was still there; he pushed it to the side and began to write. Dipping his feather quill into the ink pot, he started to list several items down and was busy writing when his tea arrived. The Third placed the tray down on the empty corner of Davian's desk and served his superior the tea, putting it to the side, but within reach. The plate of bread he placed beside the tea along with the small bowls of seeds.

"Thank you, that is all. You may collect all within the hour."

"As you command, your Grace."

The Third bowed to a busy Primar, Davian did not look up. He waited until sounds outside his doors disappeared, then rose. Reaching over he grabbed the wooden plate, pushed the bread to the side, and placed one of the small bowls on it. Davian looked at the second bowl, he folded the bread slice in half, put the other bowl on the plate then placed the folded bread in-between the bowls. Satisfied he grabbed the plate and walked to the window and walked outside to the small stone ledge which gave him a small alcove to view the gardens. The ledge was large enough to hold two plates worth, and he laid the plate down.

"Now, if you are still here, you are welcome to have a small repast."

Davian waited for a while, he was turning around to go back to his list, when he saw the Sennet fly onto the ledge, a tree length away. Davian gave the bird a small bow and motioned with his hand to the plate.

"I will retreat to give you privacy, sir. This is a meal fit for you, should you not like something, leave it. Do not overindulge, it may make you heavy and unable to fly from a predator. I bid you health."

Davian bowed and backed away, turning once he was inside. He sat back down and dipped his quill again. Writing his lists, he was engrossed in what he was doing, but smiled when he heard a small tap, tap. He knew the Sennet was enjoying one of the three items placed for his consumption.

"Do not worry about ruining the wood with your beak. It is blackwood, one of the hardest woods there is. Also, my favorite. I have yet to visit the forests these woods hail from. Hmmm, perhaps I should remedy this. Other Secondaries have travelled more than I have."

Davian was now talking to himself and did not realize the sounds outside had ceased. He looked up when he heard a whisper of wind, the bird had flown into his room. He sat very still and watched the bird, the purple of its wings and body not a sight one would see every day. He had only seen the Sennet before, in drawing renditions. And once when the Empress first received it. He remembered how angry the Empress was when she told his mentor of its release.

The bird was flying around, and it came to rest on top of a bookshelf. It looked around, then flew to the mantle. There it landed and walked down the length of the blackwood mantle and looked back at the man watching it.

"Do you approve? It is also Blackwood. You are welcome to view the whole room if you like. I will remain here."

One thing Davian enjoyed when he was younger, was reading tomes on animals. He was an avid learner and his tutors enjoyed giving him tomes upon tomes of birds and horses. Two of his favorite animals. He read one of the birds of Aram but had never been to the lands or seen any of its creatures. Now flying around and perusing his chambers was a Purple Sennet. Few had ever seen one. Davian felt like his God was blessing him with this sighting.

The bird flew down and came towards him, he sucked in a breath, afraid his breathing alone would scare the creature. It alighted onto his desk and Davian held still. It bowed at him, Davian nodded back. "My Lord,"

Davian smiled. It was a mimic. He had never seen any documentation which mentioned it could mimic speech. Only the Mockingjay was known to do so.

"I thank you, little sir. I used to be a Lord. Now I am called 'Your Grace,' if you wished to learn…" Just then the bird cocked its small head, showing a small sliver of blue on the side, and it opened its wings and flew off, out of the open windows. Davian was speechless, a Sennet spoke to him!

Of all the things to happen, it is wonderous! Narman's creatures are beautiful! This was a gift. I feel as if the world is mine! In the harshness of the world, there is beauty. Hearing a commotion outside he looked up as Geravon opened the door, entering his office, breathing hard.

"Two ships have entered port, Your Grace. Naders ship towed in by the one you sent a fortnight ago, Your Grace. Nader is on his way to His Eminence."

"Well, this is going to be interesting, shall we?"

He rose, his man taking Davian's official robe from its hook, opening it up for Davian to slip his arms into. Then handing him the belt tie which kept it closed. Davian tied his robe together and grabbed the links of office to placed around his neck. Geravon called him back as he turned to leave and moved it slightly to the left, arranging it better. Davian nodded and left his office to walk the short distance to the Throne-War room.

He entered to find men milling about as he approached the Throne with its cushions flattened by the old ass sitting on it. Nader finished his whispering into the ears of the irate Namarch sitting. Davian knew this was going to be a shouting match by the time the Namarch was done, he knew by the look on the old man's face.

"Let me guess. Nader's men had not a chance, the Dragons lit them on fire. Is this about, right?" Davian looked at Nader, standing back to the side, his head bowed down.

"Not all, the air witch took the very air out of the men who tried to finish. Only two were lucky to escape. By the God." The Namarch looked apocalyptic, his face becoming redder by the moment.

"You mean ran away. It seems Nader's men are not very devoted to the cause." Nader looked like he wanted to crawl away. Davian saw the rising anger of the man sitting with his hands drumming on the arm of the chair.

"There's more, isn't there. Please enlighten me, Your Eminence." Davian gave a slight tilt to his head.

"It was reported, it took a while for them to row back to the ship. They had boarded when the Dragons came to the ship, without their Riders and lit the sails on fire. It caused them delay."

"You don't say, I was wondering about the delay in their return, now we know why." He looked at his mentor, who was almost at the peak before explosion. The hands on the armrests were clutching the wood and Davian noticed the veins in the fists, enlarged with the tension he saw. Not a good sign, he mentally began preparing himself for a reply Bond tried to remain calm in the wake of the upcoming storm to be unleashed.

"Yes, it seems the ship, once it rigged up a sail from the spares they had on board, had an escort of sea creatures, all the way back here, even when your ship met up with them and towed them. The man eaters stayed; we have many witnesses. Seems you had the right of it. Why did I listen to you, Nader? Now they will be on high alert, and they will know when we send another. I want these witches dead, Davian, you know… what, wha…"

The Namarch half stood, clutching at his chest, his head red and sweating, his eyes bulged out of his head. He sat back down and closed his eyes, his head bending forward. Davian sprung up onto the dais grabbing his mentor by the shoulders, shaking him gently. Others came up behind him, hearing the movement, Davian turned his head.

"Get everyone out NOW! Fetch the physician!" He turned back to the Namarch, "Wake up, Master, wake up."

He stood up as the physician arrived and backed off the platform. Not everyone had left. They stood at the back of the room, the War Lords standing by their table. The physician stood over the still figure, checking him over.

Davian stood in shock as the physician rose, shaking his head at him, not registering,

"Your Grace, Your Grace. The Namarch has passed. What are your orders?"

"My orders?" His head couldn't grasp the sudden events.

"The Namarch is dead, long live the Namarch." Nader was the first to announce Davian's ascension to the Throne. He strode over to the dazed man and lowered to one knee.

"Long live, Davian Du'Landan, Namarch of the Du'Lanay lands, Keeper of the Faith, Protector of the Realm, Representative of our God here on earth, long may he reign." Others followed suit, until the whole room was on its knees, reciting litany from their books. "Long may he reign."

Davian came out of his daze. Looking around the room at everyone on their knees for him. It hadn't quite sunk in; however, his brain snapped to attention.

"Let's get the Namarch back to his room. Have his body prepared. As it is high summer, we will bury his body right away. We will have a week of mourning. No viewing of the body for the masses. We will have an effigy instead. Mourners can instead visit the grave. We will be taking offerings for his causes, of course. Let's create some new ones also, while we're at it. Passage for his spirit, safe journey, whatever comes to mind. We will need funds to wage this war coming to us. Toll the bells."

The guards removed the older man from the chair and Davian stepped up, looking at the seat but did not sit, instead faced the approaching congregation. "We need to deal with the threat of Dragons; however, we will not do so openly. I think this point has already been executed and denied." Here Davian looked at Nader. Nader had the decency to look down, but not before Davian saw a glimpse of hatred. *I'll have to deal with him sooner than later,* he thought as he regarded the assembly.

"I have more news. It seems one of the witches, the water witch has married a man, but no ordinary man. He is none other than the youngest son of the Fir-Pader of Aram, which means if we bide our time, the job may be done for us. We need to send a delegation to Aram, on the pretext of suing for peace. Until such time, the war in the North will continue.

Let us see if we can glean information on the development of this union. I want ideas, while we deal with the death dues and weeklong celebration of his spirit. There is no rest from now on, I want all historical documents scoured for information, we will set up right here." He pointed to the desks beside the Throne.

"Your Grace, I mean, Your Eminence." His man stepped forward.

"Yes, speak up."

"Your Inauguration, when do you want it set for?" Davian thought for a moment.

"Let's have it soon after the week of mourning has passed. A small affair, we must focus on the war in front of us and the war to come. Only the highest of noble houses, no great elaborate affair for me." He strode over to the table with a chair behind it and sat down. "Toll the bells and send out the missives. It will take a few weeks for some of the other provinces to arrive."

"As you command, Your Eminence."

"Geravon, you attend with me. The rest of you, plan the funeral rights, the inauguration, plan the next few weeks. I want those ideas and I want them yesterday. We will hear every idea presented, no matter how trivial. Send out the ships, get our informants out, but not all at once, stagger them. Send to Aram, on pretext of negotiations, but send a couple decoys. Come on, men. Let's get this done. Geravon, follow me." Davian stood and Nader took his place at the desk. One thing Nader was excellent at was being organized. Davian would hate to lose his talents. But if Nader was pissed about Davian being next in line, he should not have announced it to the assembly. Davian strode out of the Great Hall and down towards his soon-to-be new chambers.

"Where are we going, Your Grace, I mean, Your Eminence?"

"We are going to find the key, and we are going to go to the Library."

Davian did not have to explain further or be specific. Everyone knew the only person who had access to the archives was the Namarch. The only sound was the slap of leather sandals on marble. It echoed down the hall.

"You are wanting me with you? Is this proper protocol?"

"Damn with protocols, Geravon. This is turbulent times. If there is a ton of reading to do, I cannot do it overnight… by myself. I need your mind. You calculate like me. We accomplish this together. I did not mentor you for your dashing looks. Think, man. There is something in there which is dangerous. We need to see what it is, to plan ahead. Having Dragons in this world again will test us. We need to study, organize, and plan. Now, let us find the key first. You check the wardrobes, and I will check the desk."

"I appreciate your faith in me. We will find this key." They entered the formal office of the Namarch and Davian noticed the outline of the Namarch resting on his elaborate bed. Many Thirds were busy cleaning and washing the body as was custom. The mound of his great belly was visible from Davian's viewpoint. He strode past the doorway to the desk which occupied the room.

Well, I hope I never grow one of those. He never stopped eating things not good for him. Now, let me see what I find here. Geravon strode past Davian and entered the bedchamber to the far side which was the entry to the wardrobe. It was a room in itself; many chests and dressers were there. Davian sat upon the ornate chair; the cushion were worn into the ass pattern of his predecessor. *I am getting a better chair. This can be chopped into firewood, for all I care. What is with all this gilding. Too ostentatious for me. He sure liked his ornamentations.*

Davian open the first drawer, and brought out all the paperwork, files on people. He recognized many in his handwriting. There was nothing in there. Then he opened the drawers on the other sides. There were a few small wooden boxes and he brought them out and rummaged through the contents. Nothing. There were a few keys, but nothing which would indicate the one Davian was looking for.

Davian had in his younger years, taken a ball of semi hardened wax, an acquisition from one of his 'associates,' and taken a cast of the keyhole, but had never had a key cast. To do so would have meant his death. He knew then he would have to bide his time. The time was presenting itself, now he would find the original.

Geravon returned, a small chest in his arms and placed it down on the desk and opened it. Inside were many rings and jewels and miscellaneous items of jewelry. "This is one of many chests, Your Eminence. It seems our Lord had quite the affection for shiny things. No keys though, except these few, which look like they belong to the Palace."

"The Empress's Palace to be exact." Geravon sucked in a breath.

"How is it you know this, Your Eminence?"

"Because I was the one who obtained them for him. He used to visit the Empress, quite often in his youth. She was very…accommodating… to his Grace."

"You are telling me…?"

"No, I am not telling you anything. You are a smart man, Geravon. I will not say anything now to disparage the dead. May he be Blessed."

"May he be Blessed."

"Now. I have keys here, but not the one I want. Where else haven't we looked?"

"Well, his Grace was not the smartest man, he would have placed it where he could access it. I remember you said it was ornate?"

"A large iron key with a huge three ringed handle. Extremely hard to miss. Larger than any we have. I am assuming you've seen the door and lock?"

Geravon had the grace to blush. Every Secondary had been down into the catacombs beyond the dungeons. Every Secondary had at least one look at the door to the library forbidden by death to enter. There were stories abounding about what was beyond the locked gate. "Yes. I have. Now, let's see. There is the bathing room and the gardens. I cannot fathom he would leave it outside. Iron would rust."

"Same with in the bath house. 'Tis very humid in there."

Davian stood up and began to pace. Walking over to the large stone mantle, he began to run his hands under and inside the fireplace, he had only to crouch a bit, the mantle was almost as high as his broad chest. His hand came back sooty and nothing. He turned around and looked at the desk against the windows, which opened to the garden. He held out his hand and a servant came forward to clean it with a towel. The servants bustled about, quiet in their work. Many initiates to the Church began as servants to the Secondary's and few made it to the Namarch's quarters. Some were content to not go further, those who wanted more 'advancement' could often wind up dead if they did not play the game right.

"Why would he not want to see the view of the gardens? Having it placed looking at the fireplace would almost be less... one would think it more tranquil to look at the blessings of the plants. Nature is our Gods blessings to us."

"It begs one to look over his shoulder, does it not?" Geravon smiled at Davian, they shared a moment, Geravon had indeed caught Davian, many years ago, peering through the windows when his mentor had news of import. It had served them very well. Lately if Davian could not, then Geravon would glean information. It was their pact. Davian looked at the desk. His face began to frown.

"What is it?"

"Is this desk, the original from the time of Narman? It looks much cleaner... like someone has cleaned into the cracks. I thought Narman's desk was darker wood..."

"Yes, now that you say it aloud, this is Redwood. Stained dark. Look at this scratch."

"Now why would someone replace a piece of history?" The men walked back to the desk and started to run their hands all over the desk. Geravon on one side, and Davian on the other. Geravon was taking the drawers completely out, he had the same mind as his mentor. Behind the drawers on his side was nothing.

"This is the work of Dorron; this is his mark. He is one of the greatest carvers. His work graces the Palaces and many of the Vezyrs quarters. This piece must be one of his last before he passed, what fifty years now?"

"Which means this was a gift? I remember something about gifts being sent here about thirty years ago, but this was before my time. It seems the Namarch was not above receiving gifts. Perhaps it was a bribe?"

"We should take the time to look through all the paperwork, maybe there is a clue."

"Don't waste your time. if there is anything disparaging, it will be in the vault. Wait... this is odd..."

"What have you found?"

"Well, I cannot take the drawer out for one, and I do not want to force it..."

Davian got to one knee and peered up from underneath the drawer on the one side he was on. Geravon came over, moving the chair back towards the windows out of his way. Only a few servants were left. Geravon looked up. "Both of you, out. Now. Take the others in the bedchamber with you." Geravon erred on the side of caution, Davian instilled this into his protégée.

"Hold up, Davian. Wait until the room clears." The sounds of wood, trying to slide and the odd muttering from under the desk answered him back. Soon the sounds of slippered feet and a soft close of the huge Blackwood doors broke into the room. Then silence.

"Here... I think I've mastered this... press this..."

Click. A hand reached up and pressed a hidden latch which to the untrained eye looked like part of the joining of woods, a dovetail, which many pieces of furniture had in their makeup. A section underneath the drawer slid forward. The hand disappeared, and Davian rolled out and rose, to grab the small hidden drawer. He slowly slid it towards him. It was a shallow drawer which only contained one thing. The key!

"Ingenious! This craftsman knew his business. I may keep this desk. It has its uses. Thank you for clearing the room. Now if I receive any secret missives, you will know where to place them."

"Yes, this works to our advantage. Now what do you plan to do?"

"Well, let us have tea, and a bite to eat, and I will meet you down at the door in say, a half hour? Best we go separately.. to not draw attention. Bring a light source. I'll bring one too. I am thinking a note pad and quill. No. Let us just see what's so important down there. Then we bring out a tome at a time and review it up here. I am not caring about the privacy. We need to deal with the enemy at hand, the heresy which threatens our world."

"Yes, Your Eminence. You may wish to wash your hands; there is still evidence of soot from the fireplace. If the tomes are fragile, soot will not be welcome."

"Thanks, I had forgotten about this." Geravon left to prepare and Davian sat down at the chair which he left by the windows, the breeze coming in was slight, but welcomed. He looked down at the iron key in his hands. He heard a soft knock on the door. He rose and strode to the desk pushing the hidden drawer in and then the larger drawer. He pocketed the key before answering the knock.

"Come." The Head Chamberlain came in, bowing his head.

"Yes, what can I do for you, Master Enias?"

"Your Eminence. A small matter, but one which needs addressing. How would you like your Thirds? Are you wanting the ones who served the late Namarch? Or are you wanting others? I await your command."

"I want mine… and those who serve Geravon. You may disperse the others to where they would wish to go. You may stay in your position; I see no need to change it. Unless you would like to change?"

"Oh no. Thank you, Your Eminence. I am honoured to serve you. I have a few more items of import. Your repasts? Teas? I know you like green and herbals, is there anything in dietary we need to change?"

"No, I like my meals plain and the same as everyone else. I serve my God, and my body is his Temple. I will not pollute it with unnecessary garbage. It is his body on earth. I would honour my God by keeping it clean. May he be Blessed."

"Yes, Your Eminence. May he be Blessed."

"You can do what you will with the late Namarch's 'dietary' goods. I will not ask, nor do I care."

"Thank you, and what of toiletries?"

"What of them? I will use what I have always used. You may remove the previous owners things and dispose of them as you see fit. Was there anything of note?"

"No, just a few ornamental items. As you wish."

"Hold on this, I will peruse first and then you can dispose."

"As you command. I will retrieve your servants. Would you command me further, before I go? Your Eminence."

"Just one thing, Enias. If I have not summoned you or anyone else, you will not enter these rooms. I will have privacy, and I will have silence. You have your position by the grace of my predecessor. You will only keep it by the grace of myself. I only ask once. Have I been clear on this?"

"Yes, Your Eminence. I understand."

The Chamberlain bowed and backed out. Davian was sure he would get what he wished. Many knew the strict rules Davian lived by. He was not susceptible to bribery. He ate very plainly. Few could get poisons past him. When he was younger, an attempt was made to poison him, it made him extremely ill and he was allowed to convalesce at his Paders villa, as they thought he would pass spirit. His Mader nursed him to health with her head maid who taught Davian in his recovery what to look for.

It was a hard learned education, but one which made him so much more aware. In eating plain fare, it gave the message he was devout, he was not above others, and it was much harder to poison. Many would hide poisons in the sauces and seasonings to hide taste and scent. Davian liked simple food, eating at the Palace occasionally and at other nobility residences, when the need called for it, gave him upset stomach for days. Regardless at how meticulous he was, during religious holidays and ceremonies, his stomach would revolt. He was extremely strict with his intake.

Davian patted the key in his pocket and grabbed a lantern, a small one which had mirrored inserts to help with reading. He placed it on the desk and lit a small stick of wood from another candle which had its place on one of the many iron wrought candelabras placed around the room. *At least he liked lots of light. I think I will keep these. They serve a higher purpose. I should get going, I am sure Geravon is waiting.*

Davian strode out of the room, and down the wide hall. Many of the order would bow as he walked by. Davian mastered his face throughout the years to be blank, to not illicit conversations from those who would wish one. His indifference kept inquiring minds at bay. His travels were not interrupted and he knew the Palace was still reeling from the morning events and there were many in mourning. Or at least pretending to be in mourning. Few loved the late Namarch. He was a bit of an asshole in his last years.

Davian made it down the many stairs and passageways until a level below the dungeons gave way to a locked door at the end of one such dark passage. He saw the flickering light of Geravon's lantern up ahead. Approaching the outline of his Secondary, he began fishing in his pocket for the key. He handed the lantern in his other hand to his man. "Anyone question you?"

"No, several made condolences, and I had a fervent appeal for advancement. Have you thoughts on what you may want to do with Nader? I have a feeling; he may lay in wait for you… just a feeling."

"Well, we send him abroad, North or South."

"South? There is nothing South of here."

"Think about it, Geravon."

"Ahhh, now I get it." Davian smiled in the low light as he gently pushed the iron key into the lock with his other hand. The lock was heavy. Solid iron and an item of antiquity but it was oiled lately. There was evidence by the grease which leaked from the keyhole. Geravon held the two lanterns in his hands, with one higher to help his master see better. Davian twisted the key, back and forth until he felt and heard the clicks. The lock opened and he pulled the bar of iron out of the lock and twisted it to the side.

Placing the key back in his pocket, he hooked the lock on one of the many bars of the gate, letting it rest on top of the latch. He opened the gate, Geravon backing up behind him. It opened towards the men and was silent.

"Someone has oiled everything lately. Seems someone else may have been here. The oil, (sniff), is solidified. I would say in the last year…" Davian ran his finger on the hinge on the inside of the door. It came back with a dark mess, and he licked the tip of his tongue on his finger.

"Olive, from here. A bit rancid, so with the temperature down here, I would say less than a year. See the globs on the edge, which is previous endeavors. This was a busy place."

"How do you want to proceed?"

"One room at a time. Let's get the feel for each area, then we can dissect as we need. Let's see what's in here and watch the dust on the stones. Give me the light." They had not gone far down the hall. When Davian was here many years ago, his view from the gate and limited lantern light had only shown him a few feet of the hall, he surmised there were a few rooms which led off the hall. It was not a huge portion of the dungeons. If anything, it was a small corner. He looked down at the flagstones they were standing on.

"Plenty of dust, I see no signs of recent activity. Let's go to the left here and see what's in this first room." Geravon followed Davian into the first room, there was an iron strapped wooden door and it also showed signs of oiled hinges. It squeaked a little bit upon opening.

"This seems to be antiquities, chests, and wooden altars. This is cloth wrapped iron holders, no, those are gold."

"These are very ornate and look incredibly old in the style. Look at the filigree. These are the same as the two candle holders on the main altar, the ones in the Great Hall."

"Yes, in the style of Paradon. So at least two hundred years old. Its been, what? The last fifty years, some of these pieces are making their way back into the sunlight. It seems the gilded age is slowly coming back. Well, I have to say, Geravon, it should stay here. The Great Hall should be not reflective of our wealth. It shows better to be humble. We have many things changing we will deal with. A population which may rebel, may not take to us flaunting wealth. Who knows, we may need this wealth to pay for our battles. Let's go to the next room."

"I agree, this is too ostentatious to show the masses. If it is functional, it need not be flamboyant." They left the small hoard of antiques and went down the dark hall. There was only one other door on the opposite side and it was also iron clad hinges. It opened silently.

"Ahhh, here we are. Books upon books. Careful we do not touch. Let's just see what may have been disturbed if at all." The room was floor to ceiling bookcases, and was filled with books and tomes, leather bound and dusty. There was an altar in the middle with a tome on it, opened and a thin marker in the spine. Covered by a linen cloth. Davian strode up and raised the lantern up high. He carefully removed the linen and shook the dust off the cloth before tucking it into his belt. He looked at the book, "This is Pelinese. This states… here can you hold the light?"

Geravon took the lantern and held it up. "Pelinese. You think these tomes are on the Dragons?"

"Guaranteed, they are. The library we have is all Du'Lanay. I often told the late Namarch we needed more material on the other lands. One must study the enemy from within. The best way is through their writings. What I know, and what I have given you to read, is what I gleaned on my own. This may be the Maderload here. Look. This is what looks to be a Prophesy. 'Tis not a short one…" Davian turned the page, after he took the leather marker out of it. The pages crinkled in his hand. He gently turned it over.

"This is written by a hand of a… scribe… hmmm, look here. It states he was directed by the Great One. So, the leader of the Dragons told him to write this. This is heresy, Geravon. No wonder it was left down here."

Another page, and then another. One page tore in his hand. He put it back. There was more. He turned it back to the open page. Placing the marker back, he looked at the other man beside him. "This must be all from the Islands. I will bet it was collected or acquired and put down here to not confuse the masses. Let's look some more, then we will take out a tome at a time, read and then put them back. If we bring any more than this, it will be found and we will be questioned. Regardless of our rank."

"You know best. I am not sure I wish to know more. It is heresy."

"Geravon. Heresy is happening, right now. We need to know how to deal with it… or we lose everything. The whole continent. 'Tis a huge price to pay, I do not know if we can afford to lose what is our way of life to a bunch of women and the flying abominations now reported. What would you do?"

"You have the right of it, Davian. I have always admired you for your insight. You raised me up to who I am today. It is daunting. This hidden library… there will be many prying eyes."

"We leave everything here. I will place the key back; you saw how the drawer opens. I told the Chamberlain to not enter unless asked. We set you up in the room next to my desk, 'tis basically unused as it is. Then you and I can read uninterrupted by servants. I will lock the drawers, and we keep the tomes in there. Only read at night, under the pretext of war planning."

"Won't it be suspicious?"

"We bring war books and make a display. The servants will see those and report to others we are in earnest. It will not be an easy subterfuge but it may work for a time. Always give people what they want, Geravon, it makes it so much easier to trick the weak minded."

"There are some works of art here; these tomes were from the artist Lyana. She wrote some poetry, I remember my Mader had a copy, of one of her lesser works. It is worth many coins."

"And what happened to her? She was branded a witch and burned at the stake. Do you not remember our history, Ger? She incited a man to leave his wife for his paramour. This was the cleansing of our great GrandPader's time. It sparked the great cleansing. 'Tis a wonder it is even down here. But it does make you think. Look, this whole shelf is her works." Davian and Geravon wandered around the room, both exclaiming over the tomes and books they were finding. Without touching any of them, both men were astounded at the secrecy keeping such items. It was heresy on all ends.

"I could spend more time, but we should return to sunlight before everyone notices we are missing. Let us grab one tome a night each, then we spend a few days reading and discussing as we prepare for the happenings before us. The next week is going to be monumental, and we both have much work to do. I can count on you?"

"Of course. You need not ask. I am your man, always."

"If this gets known, we are both dead men."

"We will get what needs to be done. You have much to do, fittings, and speeches. I should begin on your inauguration speech right away." Both men reluctantly left the library, Davian shut the door behind them, and they walked out of the hall; Davian locked the gate shut and placed the key back in his pocket.

"You go first. I will follow, after a time. You know, you get another to write the speech and you hone it. This is what a Primar can do, you know. Get a Secondary or Third to do all the heavy lifting. You are going to be terribly busy, as will I. Leave the trivial stuff to your understudy. They will welcome the work. Find a couple… have them compete against each other. Make their lives interesting. It'll be like old days, eh?"

Geravon laughed at Davian's reminder of what Geravon had to deal with when he was moving up the ranks. He bade his master goodbye and left with his lantern, and Davian watched the man and then the shadows cast by the lantern as they faded into the dark.

Am I doing the right thing, getting him involved? Geravon wants this position I now find myself in. It will only be a matter of time. At least with what we have uncovered, if I go down, he will also. But having him working beside me, may have others wanting his demise. He will have to tread carefully.

That was two full pages of Prophecy, it must be in whole. Interesting. And all forbidden artists. Writings which were banished for their authors or content.

These will be an interesting few months. I should return. I don't want the whole Palace to think I've passed. This would cause a catastrophe... I am sure my mind is going to hurt from all this knowledge. Davian headed back to the world above; into the light and the controversy he knew was going to be happening.

CHAPTER 43

Damara

The Rising of the Sun

Damara had nothing but troubles with her business, it seemed as soon as one problem was presented and solved another happened.

This time it was the weather. One of their ships was delayed, a storm occurred in the Western Sea and the ship had to dock in the North for repairs. As she needed what was on this ship to move forward with orders, it set her back for a while.

"Tovah, what can we finish with stock we have on hand?"

"Well, all the darker colours, we can salvage from current materials, I can begin dying those. Most of those orders are here in Kara. We have the cloth of gold we can do, those are for your brother, and anything else will have to wait."

"Let's get my brother's order's done, first, then the upcoming baby gift, and what about the potential colours for the bride? We have orange, dark red, light green and dark blue to choose from. Do we have all those?"

"We have lots of the dark blue, just enough dye for orange, light green we have enough and dark red we can make this one up, I will begin on this one."

"Good, let's get this done, in case I must leave before the ship returns. If I am gone to Merida before the ship docks, work on these orders and complete them, hmmm, in this order please... I will anger a few people; however, I will make it up to them. Double these orders." Damara rearranged the paperwork, and set the pile which had to wait, placing a couple out of that pile to the side she indicated those to be doubled. "This should appease them. Let me know if you need any-more assistance, I am returning home and will check back with you if needed."

"Yes, Nada, this will be ready in a few days. I will package them up as soon as they are all dry and ready."

"Thank you, Tovah. You were sent to me by our God, I do not know how I would have made it these last years, if not for you. Our volume has increased substantially. You may wish to think about hiring an assistant to take over some of your duties, as you have taken over some of mine. If we increase any more, you will begin travelling back and forth between cities and we need someone here full time. Just letting you think on this in case you haven't already."

"Thank you, Mistress. I have two women in mind. What do you think of train-ing them both together? It would save us overall, then I could place one in each city if needed."

"Great. Excellent thinking. Saves us time to train two more. Especially if we are becoming busier. Now if only the ships would bring us more silks. I will chat with Ramis about this end of things. I am leaving now, send word if you need me. If not, I will come down in a few days, or you can bring the orders to me."

Damara left the shop riding her horse back to the villa. Her guards brought her horse and the trio rode back in silence. The unrest in Merida had not made its way to Kara, she was thankful for this but still had a few guards. Ramis had insisted. She agreed with him on this point, she was shaken to the core on the event she witnessed. She had a relaxing afternoon and evening with a light meal and an even lighter vintage, which she nursed. She bathed, went to sleep, and had an unforgettable dream.

She was in a villa, and looking around, she was not sure it was theirs. She wandered around the rooms; the furnishings and adornments were not theirs but everything felt familiar. Then her attention was caught by the colours which presented themselves, in the upholstery and other decor in the room. She was dreaming of flowing curtains of assorted colours of silk, which changed with rain blowing in and the dyes of orange curtains becoming soaked. The dyes ran out of the fabrics and drenched the floors to run by her feet which were covered by slippers. As the orange dye touched the slippers, she woke sitting up with a gasp.

There must be some significant meaning behind this dream, I do not remember the last time, I woke up from such a horrible thought. She would remember the orange, though. It sat in her mind, colours she remembered, the good and the bad. She hadn't had a colour run, since the early years of her business. She learned from her Mader's old lady in waiting, all the secrets of dye fasting, before the woman had passed spirit.

The first few years, anything she dyed was for her own use. She remembered her episode with the blue bark from the North reaches. How from her sweating, it caused her body to be blue in certain areas for a week before it washed off. After this, she stopped trying to figure out their secrets and bought the dyes from the lands which they hailed from. It was more cost effective and less stress… and less blue. The recollection brought a gentle smile to her face.

As the sun was beginning to show its colours in the morning sky, she rose putting on her robe, sitting on her chaise to watch the rising of the sun in all the glorious shades she loved so much. This is where Peylin found her.

"Nada, you are awake early. Are you fine?"

"Yes, Peylin, I woke from a horrible dream curtains of orange were running towards my feet in the rain. It distressed me from my sleep, so here I am, watching the advent of a new day."

"I will get you your breakfast, here is your morning tea."

"Thanks, dear. No bread, please. Something light and easy on the stomach." Her maid left returning with her morning meal and a note which was brought to the door by a messenger. It was from Ramis. He requested she return to the Capital as the celebration for the new heir was to be pushed forward. The men had to return to the warfront.

"Peylin, can you get my writing tools, please? I will send Ramis my reply. I will head out in a couple of days. Plan accordingly. Get my outfits ready. I will thank him for the notice." She gave the note to Peylin to send and she requested a message be sent to the shop to have the orders brought so they could pack accordingly. She was delayed again by a day. A rainstorm blew in, not a usual thing to happen in summer, it left the land hot and humid, and her fabrics took extra time to dry. Damara and Peylin had ridden down to the warehouses with guards and as they were mounting their horses Damara had a thought.

"Let us go for a ride through the city. I would like to visit a particular person."

"Should we not give notice? Who were you planning to see?"

"Lana. If she is home, perhaps she will let me in. If not, then I will not worry about it."

"Umm, Nada, what about…" Peylin nudged her head towards the two men who were their escort.

"Oh, yes. Hmmm…"

"What are you thinking?"

"I am not sure, Ramis would certainly hear if we were to bring them with us… and I cannot order them back to the villa. I would be questioned on this. It may be I cannot... I am not concerned. It was merely a thought."

The guards, one in front and one behind, were newly hired. They were attentive and did not speak much. Damara was not sure how she would even attempt to rid herself of them. *It is not a high priority, but it would have been a diversion.*

They walked the horses through the city streets; it was busy with the citizens running around trying to keep dry. Damara wore a cape of canvas she meticulously rubbed beeswax into, both her and her maid were keeping dry. Her horse shied away from people.

"Woah, boy. 'Tis just people. Peylin, he's a bit anxious. I hope he doesn't bolt again. I would hate him to lose footing."

"It could be this rain; it's coming down hard again." Just then, the guard in front, his horse spooked by something ahead, he was trying to get his mount under control and was hard pressed to keep him from rearing. Damara and Peylin stopped, and she patted the wet neck and murmured to her horse. She looked up at the housing on either side. She thought for a moment she saw the signs of lamps flickering, in the windows.

"Peylin, stop, come closer. Something is not right." As she finished speaking, the windows of the houses to either side, broke outwards and flames erupted, linen curtains alight and dropping onto the flagstones. Her horse tried to rear and she watched as the guard in front left in a hurry, his horse bolted. She turned around and the guard behind them was not there.

"Peylin, follow me. We need to get away from here and find another way to the gates."

"Yes, Nada. My horse is agitated, let us get away from this fire. Where did the guards go?"

"The one in front, his horse bolted. I have no idea where the other one is."

The women calmed their horses down and found many were rushing towards the fire, which enveloped the homes. They rode through the crowds who were trying to assist with buckets of water from one of the fountains. Peylin shouted over her shoulder. "We can go this way, 'tis a roundabout, and will take us longer, but we will circumvent the crowds."

"I'll just follow you, then." Damara shouted back. They rode in quiet; the rain was pelting down hard and Damara began to feel the damp. She was wondering when they would find the gates when she recognized the community.

"Peylin, I know this area." Peylin halted her mount and let Damara sidle up to her, and Damara pointed down into a smaller alley. "She lives there. I am feeling a bit damp. If she is home, perhaps she will invite us in."

"As you wish, Nada. I am sure Ramis would not mind if you were to gather your spirit in the home of a woman. You would not be chastened for giving yourself a respite. In fact, he would wish you to. He is concerned for your health."

"Exactly! How well you know my husband." They turned their horses into the alley and Damara saw indeed there was a flicker of light from behind the linen curtains in the window. She saw the curtains move as they rode up to the hitching post and dismounted as the door began to open. A familiar face looked out in concern and smiled as she saw who it was.

"Oh, hurry! Tie them up good and get in here. You'll catch your death in this rain." Damara tried to hitch up her horse, but her fingers could not manage the reins.

"I will see to it, Nada. You get inside. I will be but a moment." Damara put the wet leather into her maids outstretched hands and she climbed the three steps and went inside Lana's home. She pulled her cowl back and fumbled with the ties of her cape. Lana brushed Damara's hands out of the way and untied the cape for the soaked woman.

"Here, let me, your hands look cold. Why don't you go stand by the fire. I started it, to keep the cold out. Don't worry about the floor. It will dry."

"Thank you, Lana. There was a strange fire, and our guards disappeared. We came this way to get out of the path of rushing people. Do you mind if my maid comes in? She is just…"

"Oh certainly. Welcome." Lana smiled at Damara's maid as she ducked in.

"Is it fine, Mistress? I can wait outside."

"No. You stay right there. Hand me your cape also. I will hang them up by the fire. They will dry by the time you leave. Hopefully, this rain will ebb."

"Thank, you Lana. Not too close, if that is fine. There's wax on the fabric."

The mistress of the house was looking at the canvas in her hands. She hung them on hooks beside the fireplace. Damara had a look around. This was a cozy little place and she started as she came eye to eye with the little boy who stayed quiet at the small table. He looked at the two women who invaded his home. Damara smiled at the little replica of Lana but with a hint of Ramis in his eyes.

"Oh, Good afternoon, little Master. I am sorry we entered; however, I know your Mader. We are soaked through. May we be welcome?" The boy looked at his Mader for approval, and Lana came up beside Damara and nodded to the little boy.

"Yes. please…be welcome and dry yourself at the fire. Mader?"

"Very nicely done, Ramoth. This is…"

"Aunty Marmar. You can call me this. Thank you, little Master for the hospitality. Thank you, Lana. This is my maid; she can remain unnamed for the moment."

"That is fine. I know her name, but I understand. I would do the same. Would you like some tea? I brewed a pot, and here… have yourself a sit down in this chair and would you like to sit here, miss?"

"Yes, thank you." Peylin sat at the table and engaged Ramoth in what he was doing, Damara smiled at the couple and sat down and Lana sat across the fire in another chair.

"I like your home. 'Tis very cozy."

"'Tis different from when we knew each other. However, 'tis our home. I like it. There was a time… I had no home."

"Hush, Lana. No need to dredge up sad memories. I am glad you let us in; the rain was beginning to be felt."

"How exactly did you find me? I can not imagine Ramis showing you."

Lana asked without hesitation, this was like days of old. This is why Lana and Damara were good friends; they did not beat around the bush. When something needed to be said, it was said.

"I had come down from the warehouse after my illness, and my horse became spooked and when I reined him in, I found myself at the entrance to the alley. I saw Ramis emerge from here. This is how I know. This is how I began to realize… well, enough about this. Your son looks very much like you." Lana smiled back at her son who was keeping Peylin engaged in conversation.

"She is good with children; he almost never speaks to strangers."

"Yes, she is! I have never seen this side of her before. He is learning his letters?"

"Yes, Ramis insists he learn. This is weird, to be discussing him in this way, is it not?"

"Yes, but I am fine with it. I do not know what the future entails. Your son is innocent of any wrongdoing; I would not want him marred by a spectacle."

"Thank you. I am not certain of the future. Ramis told me he will take care of us."

"Then it would grieve you to know he has another… son, other than mine."

Lana gasped and tears welled up, Damara reached across the space in front of the fire and grabbed Lana's hand, the one which placed the teacup down on the small table. "He is older, much older. I just found out myself. He lives in Merida and is in the army with my boys. They brought him home on their leave this winter. He looks exactly like his Pader… I mean exactly. It was a shock to me."

Lana's tears did not fall. She squeezed Damara's hand back and ventured a smile. "I can imagine. I was not sure how to approach you. I was told not to.

Ramis said you were volatile and had a temper, I only remember you becoming mad once when Davian hid your favorite dress.”

Damara laughed, straightened up, and had a sip of tea. Peylin and Ramoth were busy colouring on pieces of paper. They were laughing at something Peylin quietly said. Damara gazed at the woman in front of her.

“You understand I can only come here when Ramis is not. We have guards, more than usual. There are more restrictions now. We may not ever be able to meet again.”

“I understand. The only way I can think is to come to the warehouse.”

“That is too… open. Ramis would certainly find out.”

“You are right. I enjoyed seeing you again. Even in these circumstances. I wish they never happened.”

“Lana, events happen for a reason. I enjoyed seeing you again, however, I am of the mind our capes are dry and we should set out before we are found out.”

“Yes. I understand. Yes, they are…and the rain is let up. Here you are. Ramoth, let the young miss leave. She has certainly enjoyed your company.” Lana stood and gathered Damara’s cloak, opened the door to peek out, and then handed Peylin her cloak. She did this with a quiet efficiency. Damara put on her slightly damp cloak and tied it around her front. She placed the cowl over her head and turned to the little boy who stood and waited with his thumb in his mouth and his hand grasping his Maders skirt. Damara smiled down at the quiet and studious boy.

“Thank you for your hospitality, little Master. I bid you and your Mader a good day, it was a pleasure to make your acquaintance.”

“It was a pleasure, Mar…Mar.” The little boy was quiet, and his Mader rubbed her hand on his hair.

“Very good, Ramoth. Now go sit while I see these women out. I will help you in a moment.”

“Yes, Ma.” He turned and returned to his chair at the table. Damara followed Peylin through the door and stood on the porch. Peylin untied Damara’s horse and waited quietly, while Damara gazed at Lana.

“Thank you, Lana for opening your door.”

“You are most welcome. It was a pleasant surprise to see you again. I wish we could continue.” Damara had a moment of clarity. She looked at her once friend, the woman who was keeping Ramis busy in Kara. She felt something inside, not unlike when her and Davian would have their deepest talks when they were younger.

“Lana. I cannot see us beginning where we left off. Not here. Not in Kara. If for any reason, you need my help, I will try. If ever Ramis could not or would not help you, I will. I will look after you if he cannot. For Ramoth’s sake. He is your son. I see you giving him the best you can, he deserves to be given all the opportunities he can get. I do this for you. For the friendship we had. We may not have the same now, but we will see what the Universe has in store for us.”

Damara felt like a huge weight was taken off her shoulders. Lana teared up and grabbed Damara in a hug, Damara hugged back. “You do not know how grateful I am. I am glad you came, and I thank you for the offer. If ever I need it, I will ask. Now you should head out."

"Good path, Lana."

"Good path to you also." Damara took the wet leather reins from her maid and mounted onto the damp saddle, she waited for Peylin to mount and they headed back the way they came. They rode quietly in the now empty streets, and it was not until they arrived at the gates, they saw the men they were with. They were standing beside their horses and mounted up when they saw the women get close. Damara felt slightly angry at their nonchalant attitude.

"Where in the blazes did you get off to?" Damara went forward and stopped at the two who had the temerity to not look apologetic.

"Our mounts were spooked by the fire, and we looked for you both, and came here to wait."

"To wait! To wait! For what? Our bodies to show up! When Ramis hears of this you are both gone! We could have been set upon! Unbelievable. Come on, Peylin. I need a hot bath and a drink!" Damara rode past the two guards who looked very sheepish and they followed behind the two women. Once at the villa, Damara dismounted after waiting for one of the guards to grab her now steaming horse. The sun had finally made its appearance late in the afternoon.

"Nada, please forgive us. If you would please not have Nadan dismiss us. We will strive to be better."

"Very well, but I will expect you to be more… constant in the future."

"Thank you, Nada." The two guards left with the horses, Peylin entered before her mistress and when Damara entered her room, one of the other girls had her bathing room ready. She bathed and Peylin entered when she was finishing attiring herself in a deep violet gown.

"Tovah is here, Nada. She brought the fabrics, and is in the morning parlor, awaiting your approval."

"Thank you, Peylin. Tell her I will be there shortly."

The carriage was ready the following day, Tovah sent the parcels of dried and packed fabrics in the evening and shown Damara what each one was herself. The trip to the Capital was uneventful, she instructed they would push through with no stopping. Once she arrived back at the Capital, she went directly to the warehouse, and the crates were unpacked. She sighed a sigh of relief the colours hadn't run. She was busy, unpacking when Ramis showed up. She showed him the colours, which he approved, and then showed the others to him.

"I brought gold cloth for Davian, I will make an appointment when its appropriate to see him, and some others he may wish to wear, I have several choices. I also brought the house colours of the Warlord for our gift to the new heir of the Empire, and a vast selection of fabrics and colours, for the bride gift for Baron. You have but to tell me which they are, and I can set them aside. Do you have any chests bought?"

Most times the way a gift was presented was better accepted than the gift itself. Damara and Ramis were well known for exceeding everyone's expectations. He employed a well-known carver, paying him handsomely for exclusive business. So much the carver had someone in Kara, to do work there, but most of the gifts were presented in the Capital, and the carver always had a few in storage, as he knew his client very well.

"Yes, they will be arriving tomorrow, and we can have them packed and sent to the villa for our disbursal. Baron has chosen Adayinia, from the great House of Learning here, in the Capital, they will do well together."

"Oh." This was all Damara said, and Ramis looked at her oddly.

"You don't approve?" He knew damn well she didn't, however, this wasn't why she was at a loss for words.

"No, you know best Ramis, I am sure they will if he has chosen her. That's not it. Their house colours are orange, and dark red. I have plenty of the dark red, but I have truly little of the orange, in fact I only have enough for this gift. If you wish a wedding gift, then one of us will have to go to Pelin'Dun for the flowers I need. It was five years since we went and used up all my stock. The flower grows no where else. You know I tried to sneak it out and grow it here."

She pursed her lips. Ramis looked upset,

"Something will work itself out. May I remind you the following evening we will be going to dinner to present the gifts to the proud parents-to-be. You should return to the villa and rest, you need not finish here, this is what your deputies can do. I expect you to behave yourself, Berrin and Nimai will be there. I know you have no love of her, and her of you. I would have you bring no shame upon me, you will hold your tongue, and your hand for that matter. This is the potential heir to the Empire we are celebrating."

"I do agree with you. The trip between cities had taken its toll, especially pushing straight through. And never fear, I will not start anything."

Damara arrived at the villa and Peylin took one look at her ushering her to her rooms and into the bath. She was grateful for the care of her maid. She ate a light repast and went straight to bed. Damara woke late, lazed around the villa sending a note to her brother asking if she could attend him with some fabric samples for his inspection at his convenience. Ramis came home early this evening. They ate a light dinner together, chatting about the upcoming nuptials.

"They will be in winter, when Baron can come away from the fighting, without a deficit, as the state needs all its fighting men. He is doing well and has a promotion in the ranks."

"This is great news! He will do well, with your backing and your friend watching out for him. He will rise far."

"Mara, he will succeed on his own merits. He does not need our backing. He has shown initiative, and bravery out in the field. His men love him, and Baron knows the worth of such. I have taught him well."

"I am sure you have, Ramis. I am sure he will succeed on his own, I meant no slight. If one were to go to the Islands soon, it would give plenty of time for the wedding celebrations."

"Mmmhmm, if you will excuse me, I am going out."

"Goodnight, Ramis."

The next day had her preparing the gifts. They arrived from the warehouse's mid morning. After she directed Peylin to attend and assist her, she bathed and made herself ready. Damara chose emerald for her outfit. It was awhile since she thought to wear her greens. Ramis gave her a nod, these were one of the colours of their hosts for the evening.

They would be leaving mid afternoon. Her husband thought to wear elegant clothing, his regimentals were for state dinners, this while being not quite a state visit, didn't warrant such. She however fashioned him a set of clothing which looked as elegant without the trappings of state.

They set off with their gifts.

Arriving at the villa of the eldest son of his best friend, at the same time they did help to bolster Ramis's spirits, the men went off in their own direction while the women sat around and chatted. Damara's first impression of this young woman was while she looked like she would burst, she had no bloom to her, in fact her spirit looked tired. Damara was drawn to her and knew not why.

The young couple greeted them at the door. The woman nodded and smiled her greetings, Damara making the necessary salutations for the young couple, the husband accepting their greetings. Ramis went forward with his friend, and Damara merely nodded to Nimai, there was no love lost between them.

All during dinner, the young Princess made small talk, mostly about people in the court. She asked questions to which others answered but deflected inquiries about her pregnancy which inquisitive matrons asked. Damara could not help but think this marriage aged her from the radiantly plump girl she took samples to a year prior to a resigned, tired bearing woman before her now. How she felt nothing but pity. She knew what this marriage entailed and saw the signs in the young man before her. She sensed an energy in the room all was not as it seemed.

After her snide comments to Nimai, Damara wondered why she even bothered, but something in this moment had her puzzled and agitated. Was it the young husband, Pader to be? He didn't seem like he fitted the role. After finding out his character, which to her was lacking, and not surprisingly, she felt herself questioning her own life.

Are all men, similar, in they think women are possessions? We are to sit and behave? Do what we are told? What if I don't want to? I am tired of this world; I want to be free. Free of these shackles, free to go where I want, do what I want. Why should I not have as many lovers as Ramis? Hmmm, mostly because now, I would be exhausted, but anyways, the Princess looks how I feel.

The husband did not leave the Princess's side much and Damara noticed the control he exuded. She saw it from across the room.

I am glad Ramis is not so possessive. Is it because he has me under control? The Princess's husband is still unsure of his grip on her. I see the steel under her tiredness. She looks as though she will eventually snap, like a branch bent too far. I hope it doesn't break her. No woman should have to go through her pain. How I wish all the best for her birth and hope she finds her path.

The Princess looked up and their eyes met. For a moment, time stood still, she saw green sparkles in this girls' eyes, and heard a whisper on the wind,

"Earth and Fire, you are Earth and Fire. Your paths are linked; you will meet again." She saw the depths of the young woman's despair and her hatred lurking behind the curtain of her eyes for her husband. The voice took her by surprise and she almost knocked her glass of wine over. *What was that? Earth and fire? We are linked. How? We live two separate lives.*

"All in time, all in time… the great wheel of time will spin a few times before you are set on your paths. Certain spirits will cease to be, all in suitable time. There will be death before there is life. You have much to learn…"

The voice in her head was faint to begin with. It answered her! She quietly sipped her drink and nodded at the conversation around her. She was quite shaken and was hard pressed to keep her hand from shaking while she pretended to enjoy the night. She had a voice in her head talking to her! First her eyes, now a voice! She knew she would be given over to the Namanists if she showed any physical signs of this. It was written in their history, the horrors the Church bestowed upon the 'Damned.' She did not want to be tortured.

Looking at the Princess and her husband, she began to see signs of what Kavena mentioned. The blank stare, the physical touching, the control to not flinch from his touch, she saw it. Damara knew from gossip the reason. She also saw the growing discomfort in the way she caressed her belly, and in the expressive muscles of the tired woman's face. Damara remembered her birthing time and knew it was soon upon this young lass.

Damara could not take her eyes off her. When the discomfort became increasingly evident, Damara led the pack and begged their indulgences,

"I must beg your forgiveness; I would like your permission to retire. I have not recovered fully from my illness. Dinner was lovely, and we look forward to the announcement of your soon to be child. Many blessings to the birth of a healthy baby. Ramis?"

"Yes, Mara. Nodan Kavus, if it pleases you?"

"Thank you for the blessings. We are sure it will be a son and heir. You may retire, and we thank you for the gifts. Thank you, all."

Others followed suit, and Ramis promised his friend they would connect with each other the following day. Damara and Nimai merely nodded their heads at each other, Damara thought to herself, she was a good wife and made polite small talk which was neutral enough. With the one exception! The young woman looked and tilted her head in thanks, at Damara, and smiled a tired but knowing smile.

The next morning, she entered the dining hall to see Ramis eating and smiling. "You have uncanny timing Mara, no sooner we all left, the young Princess went into labour, and my friend had to turn their carriage back. Even the Emperor and Empress were called down and they have an heir to the Throne!"

He raised his glass in the air to toast. Damara sat down beside him raising her glass placed in front of her, as they toasted to his health.

"There are many things happening together, a wedding contract, a new heir, appointment to the Church, these are fine Days."

"Granted, and we will see more of Jaidak while he is under your brother's wing. He arrives with his brother soon. Baron is only here to sign the betrothal contract, then he heads back. The war is not going well, we keep losing more ground, all the crop growing lowlands are getting eaten up by the enemy."

They discussed the war and their sons. "I am going to Nodan Berrin's, to give them our congratulations. I will pass on your greetings to Nimai on your behalf. I will offer more apologies to her. I can not believe after all these years you would be so outspoken. I am not pleased."

"Forgive me, Ramis. I was tired and a bit drunk. I cannot seem to hold my wine as well as before. Nimai was initially in the wrong, and she gave right back at me. So, we are both to blame. I am sorry for the words. You offer my apologies, they are sincerely meant, and my congratulations on the birth of the new heir. They must be immensely proud."

"That is much better. I will extend your congratulations, and your apology. You will watch the wine in the future, if not for your health. I will send for a health physician, one of the Vezyrs was seeing a man, who helped him feel better. We will get you hale."

"Thank you, I am heading down to the shops, to attend the fabrics. I will get the other presents ready."

"Don't over tax yourself. Have Raqia assist you. You make sure you get adequate rest. You still look peaked."

"Thank you, Ramis. I will."

That afternoon, a message was brought to the villa. Damara opened it to find the Namarch suddenly passed, and her brother was now to fill the position. He would see her in the late morning the next day before midday meal, it was the only time he could spare as his time would be even more precious. *That explains the pealing of the bells I hear.*

Damara received the invite she was waiting for, thinking she would conveniently forget to mention it to Ramis. However, he did not come home for dinner, and he was not in the dining hall when she broke her fast in the morning. In fact, he had not come home at all last night, *Oh well then, its not my fault he does not attend.*

She dressed in a simple but elegant pink outfit with red accents and for a dramatic effect, wore the red ruby necklace she bought. It gave her a feeling of empowerment, and the amount of drama she wanted. She was after all a member of Royalty and the fact she really liked the necklace gave her justification for wearing it.

She took a closed carriage up to the Palace of the Namarch, and waited for the right protocols, because now it was even harder to see her brother in private. She was led by his manservant into his old office, sitting down in front of his desk to wait.

It wasn't long before he entered the room wearing elaborate robes, which she knew were so heavy he was sweating underneath. She rose to her feet as he gave her a big hug hello. "How are you, little sister?"

"Fine Davian. I recovered from the last time I was here. I get the odd headache here and there which usually flattens me. It must be old age creeping up. With both my boys gone, one after physical war the other soon to fight your silent wars and my Dader with her own household raising her children, one and another on the way, I am busy with my clothing empire which seems to be expanding."

"That's good and congratulations on the upcoming new grandchild."

"Congratulations to you also on your upcoming inauguration. I heard the Na-march died of natural causes in full view of the whole assembly, which was entirely convenient."

"I admit I had nothing to do with it; he was old, he didn't take care of himself. He was fat and had a few episodes in the last couple of months which may have been precursors to his death. However, this is not why I granted you an audience. What I'm about to tell you stays between us, it will be known soon enough, however, I want to know what you think. As you guessed Nader's idea of sending assassins right away was done and failed.

The Dragons and their Riders destroyed the men sent. Some were set on fire, and the air witch took the breath out of the rest. Two lucky fools escaped and set off in the ship to return here. The Dragons came back, scorched the boat, and burnt the sails. The other witch, the water witch, sent the ocean creatures to escort them here to the Capital.

So, we cannot openly go after them. Now, I also have information the water witch married none other than one of the FirPader's sons. which means it could be a negotiating tool; it may be their way in. Holy Pader forbid; it binds the two together. We may send an envoy to Aram to broker a peace agreement; however, we will also find out what we can and use any information to our advantage.

I may be asking sooner than later to use you and your ships. It would be an information seeking mission. No more than this. I like to know what I am dealing with and plan accordingly. I have informants on the Islands, but they may be found out with all these changes happening.

You know me sister, like our Mader told us, always have more than one way out. You would be my eyes and ears only, and you would report back to me. You would tell me everything you see and hear, no matter how trivial. I know you have an uncanny sense of detail and an excellent memory, which is why I would want you. Aram would be harder, they do not deal with women, I must figure on what to do there. I can not send you there at the moment."

Damara digested this information, telling Davian she had to go at some point, she had run out of a particular dye she could only acquire from the Islands, for Baron's new bride, their house had orange in their livery.

"Speaking of livery, I brought a chest of samples for your upcoming celebrations, I brought it for your use, as now I see you may have greater need. Now more than ever. I think you may like, a cloth of gold, however, before your servants return, I have a question I would ask. What would be the ramifications if I divorce Ramis? He is very giving with his time over the years with other women and has produced two sons I know of, do I have enough evidence?"

Davian sat down behind his past desk and looked at her sadly. "Four."

"Four? Four what?" Damara was puzzled.

"He has four more children. I have tracked him; he is not subtle in his pursuits. It was once thought to be used against me by someone who isn't with us any longer. I do not take kindly to threats. The man you hired, I sent to you, so yes, I know all. You can certainly divorce him, but you would be better to not. Here's why.

You would be forced to give up your business, Ramis would do a shite job of keeping it active and I would lose an avenue of information seeking I need. The divorce would also ruin your children's happiness, Baron would most likely not advance any further and would resent you for it, your son Jaidak would be under my care, but it would also impact his rise in the ranks. As for your Dader, her husband would also be shunned in certain houses, she would also come to resent you."

"You do not seem too surprised about Ramis not keeping his cock inside his pants. I am no longer the recipient of his affections, and I crave it sometimes fierce." Damara blurted it out before she realised, "Surely you must have a few children of your own hiding around."

It was well known even Paders of the Church slid out of the wrong sheets sometimes.

"I would not know, and if I had they would be way older than yours right about now."

Her expression was of shock. "You mean you haven't….?"

He shook his head sadly at his sister.

"I leave nothing to chance, I would not be accused of something like this, it has been over twenty-three years since I lay with a woman, sometimes it seems like a dream. I cannot remember the feeling of lust. I have focused my energy into my Church, and my God. Now my focus is narrowed on these false Dragons, and the witches who ride them. I think of the emotion as a room in the Palace, it had its use when I was younger, but now I have no reason to enter the room, so I closed the door, locked it, and thrown the key away. It serves me no purpose now, and I would not give my enemies any foothold to depose me. I made peace with this fact a long time ago. I am as pure as a virgin woman."

Davian smiled sarcastically behind his seat at the desk. Damara thought about his reasoning, realising she was stuck between her happiness and that of her family. It made her angry, and Davian saw his sister's ire rise.

"I have a proposal, if you care to listen, I would like you to go to the Islands and find me as much information as you can, then I can send you maybe to Aram. However, you will study their ways first, there can be no mistakes. I use you and get you away from your husband as much as possible, if this makes your life any easier to bear. I recommend you think it over before you make the final decision."

Here there was a knock on the door and servants brought the elaborate chest, setting it on the floor. Damara bid a servant open it to show her brother. Davian motioned for the servants to leave. He rose coming around the desk; to have his sister throw different fabrics onto him like he was a clothes tree. With the fabrics she chose she explained the lighter fabrics could be used for under the heavier robes for ceremonial garb.

"You can relax, if this is allowed now, in private with lighter robes. You look very… uncomfortable under the heavy brocade. Is this from Aram?"

"Indeed, it is. I have half a thought to do away with some of these fabrics. I much rather be wearing something less… gilt and plainer."

"Then why don't you? You can change the world; you have the power."

"Do I?" Damara gazed up at her brother and saw the emotions on his face.

"What is it? You have that look. I see something is weighing on you. Just because we do not see each other often, I can tell something is bothering you. Are you able to tell? I will not pry if it is state secrets."

Davian barked out a harsh laugh. "Hah. Sister dear, I am about to give you state secrets, and part of me does not care. The advent of the Dragons on the Islands will set about a chain of events that would make the volcanoes of the Islands small should they ever blow. Of course, should you ever repeat this, even to Ramis, you would be killed and I would not lift a hand to stop it.

So, listen well. There is a library of such a caliber under this very Palace which has every heretical piece of information ever written since the advent of Naman. Our God was once a man! Isn't this controversy? I am still in shock. It has set me back to question even the food I eat in the morning. There are shelves of forbidden artists and writers, every tome from each and every Namarch before me and I am expected to continue this tradition. What am I to say?" His sarcasm came out in force, and Damara closed her mouth, realising it opened with his confession. "Oh, by the way, I let the Dragons take over the continent. How do I write this in? They came by and said, give my people back or we will burn you to the ground. How fitting. I will be the Namarch who gave up and let them in."

"Oh, Davian! I am so sorry you have this burden. Please don't let it wear you down. Maybe there will be an answer. Are there not just two Dragons? How much damage can two Dragons do?"

"I saw this Prophecy, Damara. There are supposed to be six. Six. Dragons. That's a lot. A lot of fire."

"All right. then, where are the others? If there are supposed to be six, then where are they? Will they come out of thin air? Or will they have to be created? Baby animals need to mature. Won't this take time? Then it gives you time to plan. Does it not?"

Davian looked at his little sister and gave her a hug. She let him, as it was not something he did very often and she was grateful for the contact. Plus, she saw their discussion was what he wanted. She saw he missed her and her presence. "Before we get interrupted, I want you to know I do love you. I do not know why I blurted all this to you, and the penalty for your silence is dear. You will take this to your grave, sister. You remind me a lot of Mader, you have her way of making me feel grounded. I do miss her terribly."

"I miss her too; she had a way of making one think about their actions. I will not say a thing; you have my word. Ramis need not know any of our conversation. I will do whatever you ask of me, please get me away from him. I feel like it would be the best thing, right now. I feel the change in the air, so what you have told me, does not surprise me. It seems there are many hidden secrets, Ramis has many, it seems. He is not the man I fell in love with, so many years ago."

"He has always been like this, Mara. Even before your marriage. Some men cannot change who they are."

"You changed, Davian. You remember what you wanted to be before all this?"

"Mara. Yes, I wanted to be in the army. I wanted to make my Pader proud and follow him. I had to change to this." He waved his arm and a few samples fell onto the floor.

"Yes, but you made it work. You did not change what you are in here…"

She poked him in the chest. "You just changed what people saw. I see you, the real you. You are still my brother. You still have a conscience. You still care."

"Ha! How do you know? I feel very disconnected right now. Part of me wants to burn this fucking place to the ground and another part wants to burn all the dissenters to the ground. I am at war. With myself."

"You will find the answer, Davian. Give it time, it will find you. Or you may have to find it. Always think of what Mader would say to any question you may have. She was an incredibly wise woman."

"Yes, she was… and so are you. So, heed my words. You give that man nothing on you. Keep yourself above reproach. There are protocols going out now as we speak. Women are not safe anymore, and this means even the nobility. Keep your mouth shut. I mean it. I can't stop the tidal wave of Naman that's going to roll over everyone on the continent."

"Oh, Davian. I think I have already seen it. More beatings, publicly?"

"That and worse. So even if I wanted to grant you a divorce, I don't think I can. I will get you away as soon as I can. Now if we are done here…"

"Yes, I will give these samples to your manservant and he… can let us know how much of each you would like." Just then there was a knock on the door and Ramis entered. She ended her sentence greeting her husband, who ignored her to give his brother by law his congratulations.

"Congratulations, Davian, on your ascension to the Throne. I heard it was naturally attained, Your Eminence." Davian nodded thanking him as Ramis looked back to Damara. He was curt and straightforward with a squint in his eyes, she smelled the remains of his night drinking in his hair. "You did not leave me a message,"

"I would have if you were home. Where pray, would I have left the message, in the tailor district?" Davian had fabrics on his arms, and he grabbed his sister's arm squeezing it in warning.

Ramis looked at her puzzled, "I was with my friend celebrating the birth of his newest grandson. I slept there as it was the wee hours of the morning, and I was too drunk to even walk. Berrin would not hear of me trying to return. There is more unrest in the city, and they were concerned for my safety. That's all, you have some fanciful ideas, Mara. Ahhh, I see you brought His Eminence samples. I came to tell you Baron and Jaidak will be home tomorrow, perhaps Davian would like to attend, nothing grand, merely a small family dinner."

"Alas, I cannot. Thank you for the invitation. I will be busy; my time is not my own anymore. I have lots of organizing and war planning. I would like to have Jaidak here in about a week. This gives you time with him and he can see his friends before he is sequestered with his studies. Thank you for the fabrics, my servants will choose what is suitable. They will inform you which ones I want, but it will be just the fabrics. We have seamstresses to produce our robes."

"Very well, by your leave, Excellency."

Damara left with her husband but rode in the carriage while he rode his horse. Arriving at the villa, Damara ignored Ramis, strode in and went to her rooms, a little bit angry. *Four children, four more children, how dare he!*

She walked in and as she passed the mirror, she took a good look at herself. One thing she noticed was her eyes were not red. *That's a relief, maybe it was all the tea I had been drinking.*

Taking off her clothes she had a long soak in the tub. Not caring she missed dinner hour with Ramis, she asked Peylin to bring a tray to her room.

He could damn well eat by himself, or go to his paramours, for all I care. She vigorously scrubbed her skin and threw the soap against the wall. *How dare he!*

She tried not to cry; her anger was such she wanted to break something. *So, he sired four more children,* She forgot to ask Davian if they were all boys, not that she cared. Her husband liked to spread his seed around, spread women's legs as fast and as often as he could. *Why? When had he stopped loving her?*

She had never seen signs he had stopped; he was always attentive. Their love making never faltered. She had never strayed or entertained thoughts, ever. *Was it me?* Did she somehow become wanting? Peylin entered her suite with her evening meal, seeing her mistress's face with the array of emotions passing over her and asked if everything was fine. This set her off to crying. She rose out of the bath, Peylin enveloping her into a towel and gathering her in her arms.

"Nada, shhh, its going to be fine. You'll see."

"P…P… Peylin, he has four other offshoots. Four other children. My husband does not love me, as I have loved him. I feel empty inside. Tell me, did you know?"

"I am afraid I do. I wanted to tell you, but I knew it would have to come from someone else, as my word would not have been sufficient."

"How can you say that? I would have believed you. You have been with me for so long, you know my secrets."

"That is true, my lady. But my word is nothing in the Hall of Laws. Your brother's word is now the law. The man he hired, who you hired is none other than my brother. He tells me what I need to know, and I have only ever wanted to tell you, but have kept my own council, waiting for you to find out from a better source, one who can not be refuted. You can divorce that philandering man finally now."

"Oh, but I can't. Davian counselled me not to. He wishes me to sail to Pelin'Dun at his request and reconnoitre for him. I can not take away the happiness of my children for the sake of mine own. Me divorcing Ramis would bring detriment upon them. But I can spend less time with the lying cheat. Would you wish to come with me, on some great adventures? I would like you to if you are agreeable. I do not want to force you if you do not."

"Why yes, I am honoured. I will go where you go."

"It must be a willing choice, Peylin. Not because I am your employer."

"No, I want to. I would like to see some of this world we live in. We would be protected by your brother and not travel like vagabonds. It would be grand fun. I have never sailed before. You remember I was but a young girl when I came to work for you. You had Zoila as your maid until she passed. I never went with you on your business trips."

"This will be different but not. We go to find dyes for the business, but we keep our eyes and ears open saying nothing to give ourselves away to the enemy. We will be working for the Namarch in this. I think we can use your innocence of travel as a benefit towards our fact finding, but we can talk more about this later. I am dry now. Thank you, my dear for your understanding and care of me. Please tell me next time, I don't like secrets, especially ones which will change my life like this one."

"I am sorry Nada. I only had your well being in mind. You will bounce back from this, you will see." Peylin helped Damara into her favorite robe.

"Oh, you can be sure I will bounce back. It is Ramis who won't see what hit him."

CHAPTER 44

Meera

Brings Love Out of the Past

I trained hard, lost track of days, soon progressing to the next level, and the training yard where Adini trained. Her expressions didn't change much when she saw me, and I picked up an energy radiating from her which puzzled me to no end. I could not put a finger on it. She was the trainer, and she worked me until I was almost crying in pain and frustration. My few friends who advanced with me, shook their heads, and thanked me for my sacrifice. They did not want to be in her sights; she surely had a vendetta against me.

When I asked her what it was, she didn't like about me, she harumphed, "The trials are soon, and I don't want you to embarrass me when you fail. Least you can do is fail with honour. Then you can leave this place."

As the weather began changing, and trials loomed near, I learned it was a celebration which lasted a week or so. Games and a new visual of flashing lights. A creation of many learned minds, and they were secretive about the formula it entailed, or so I heard from gossip of my peers.

One day, beginning like all the rest, gave me a further understanding of Adini's hatred, or so I thought. I could not master wrestling; I was getting beaten hard and Commander Adini took it upon herself to teach. I began to grasp what it was she was trying to get through, after many hits to the ground. My knowledge of their language was becoming better. Some words I needed others to explain; however, I did not need Chan'tele as much and she was quite happy to cater to Nejan. The great cat regained her original weight all injuries having healed, she looked content and sometimes I sensed boredom from her.

As Adini approached continuing to hit, and toss me around, one such moment had me questioning if I was progressing. She tossed me to the ground and stood above, waiting for me to pick myself back up before her. I slowly rose to my feet, quite exhausted and sore.

"You must read the person you are fighting, look into their eyes and you will see where they plan to hit next. Look at shoulder placement, which side they lead with, no foot placement. They can trick if they are smart enough. That is what you are doing. If you do not take this into consideration, you will not lose… you will be dead!" She then demonstrated with the next arm lock and twist. She had me in a tight hold and I swore she sniffed my skin, which unnerved me such I froze, and she threw me to the ground.

"You are useless."

I knew she was goading me and was incensed I did not respond. Living with Vandrin, I learned not to respond to jeers and antics. Saliene was more covert in her torment, and I found many ways to avoid her. I learned to mask myself at snide remarks, not that some did not hurt, but Adini's were so blatant, they bounced off my closed energy.

I looked up and she sneered walking away. Then she beckoned to a young man sending him to stand by me with a murmur and flick of her hand. She was having me practice with a man larger than me by a foot. I peered up at him. His skin was darker than night, and his hair in short braids, adorned by wooden beads. He grinned down at me, and I saw from his gorgeous smile I would not enjoy this. He would make or break me; he was her creature for sure. I grinned back; I did not want to give her the satisfaction of quitting.

"Any one can beat the other regardless of size. You need to adapt, read your opponent, gauge what needs to be done to take the other one down. In war it will be to the death. If you cannot take them out by sword, spear, or arrow, you may have to take them out by hand. Knowing what tool to use, and when to use it, also makes you formidable. This is what we are. No army can stand against us. You are the next wave of our defense. We honour our ancestors, by keeping our way of being intact. No army has defeated us, not even when the Dragons were alive." Here she looked directly at me, her look unreadable, but I heard the challenge in her voice.

"She is deliberately baiting you; you know this?" Nejan's voice echoed in my head.

"Yes, I can hear her challenge me, but I do not know why."

Nejan thought about this saying diplomatically, *"I do not understand the need of humans to procreate, without the direct need of such and the methods humans use, but she is wanting to mate with you. She is… wanting to procreate, although I do not know how two females of your species would be able to do so."*

Ohhh, this would explain part of it, but why was she so mean about everything, I did not understand the way she was thinking. I did know how men and women mated, for the term of it. I was almost raped, and while the thought of sex intrigued me, even after this event, I did not have a focus on the need and did not understand why women would want to do these things together. I always thought it was a man and woman exchange. You know, to create children. Right now, I was centered on what my life story was. The thoughts of mating together with one of the many men who made it clear to me they desired a joining, did not have my attention. I set these thoughts aside while I refocused on my training.

After she set me against this young man, I took what she said and applied it. After a week of getting tossed to the ground, my air cut off more than once, arms twisted, mouthfuls of dirt, and more than enough bruises I finally began to gain ground against my opponent. The end of the week found me winning not once, but four times against the huge muscular man, I watched and memorized his methods. He led with his right foot and always went high for a grab, and lower with his left.

The feasting days were soon upon us. The atmosphere among everyone was a giddy expectation, and anticipation for the upcoming events. The trials were only the beginning, there would be plenty of food and drink, for the winners and the losers. The ones who didn't make the cut would only try harder over the next six months. I was told their summer end events were not as grandiose, after which a small regiment was sent to honour the agreement between the semi-independent province from the rest of the continent. This so they could retain their autonomy.

The Ruler made agreements, an annual tribute of gems and goods. Lately a small fighting force for the ability to rule themselves, with the Church agreeing. Lanthia was too far and too desolate of a landscape for them to bother trying harder. The climate harsh, and the people harsher. Lanthia had nothing the Namanists wanted. Lanthia kept her secrets close to her bosom. Many dispatches of men from the Church came to Lanthia… few returned. There was a sickness, the Southern men would contract. It would waste them away, some returned to Merida, only to die.

The surface of Lanthia Naman was allowed to see, was a culture of barbarism, uneducated, violent. Under this façade was more than stark. I saw the caring, in the way Maders watched out for children, a community which watched over each other. I saw this, but only because I was looking. I saw beyond what it was Lanthia hid. I saw a people rooted in traditions, rooted in love. It was a culture I could live in. In watching the different peoples train, I noted they did not care about the human shell, since we all were assorted colours, it was more on how strong the spirit was. How much honour one had, how brave. This was a culture of spirit.

It seemed when the Namanists did turn their eye to the lands in the Northeast, the continent land of Aram would come knocking on the door. The Great War, as some called it began some while ago. Over a woman, no less! I could not recall when my Lord, I could not call him my Pader anymore, left, I was but a child. He left at the beginning, to nurse his grief, and stayed on the warfront.

I rose for the last time and walked slowly over to Nejan in her shade. Plunking my tired and sore body to the ground, I lay down for a moment. I thought to get my mind off my body hurts. *"Great one, I have a curiosity. What do Dragons eat?"* My stomach growled in agreement. I would eat after I rested.

"Much like any predator in the wild. We would hunt together, Li'on-sa would stalk the larger beasts, and wound them and the Dragons would swoop down and pick them up in their clawed feet and carry them back to the living area to be killed and skinned. We would get great enjoyment from hunts." I sensed a stillness in Nejan while her mind reflected on memories. Then I noticed a sense of sadness and horror. *"What gives you sadness, Mader? I feel it flowing from you."*

"Your gifts are developing, Little One, you are picking up my sadness from the last days. DragonRider against DragonRider. I am sorry if I alarm you. The end was truly a blood bath. The Mind Wielder was arrogant, he thought he should rule the Riders, as he had more 'powers' he called them. The Great One's Rider, Noster was ready to give him all, when he was attacked in the night. He sustained many wounds and perished from them. The Mind Wielders Dragon was so upset he burned his Rider where he stood. There were words, I know naught, but the

Dragon was no longer bound to his Rider. The Great One had no choice but to banish the Dragons to the Islands, and with Noster perishing, the Great One flew away."

"Oh, I did not know this history. I am sad the Riders thought themselves as rivals. I do hope I have more congenial partners when I meet them."

"I am sure you will. The Great One will have thought out his plan for renewal. He has chosen you to lead. He would not choose unless he had faith in you. I see a gentleness, however, also a stubbornness in you. I can tell more when you are ready. I cannot tell you how to rule but take what you learn and always look at concerns from all sides. There are many wise people around you, listen and learn from them. If there are six of you, then confer with them to solve problems. You will have talents, maybe the same, maybe different. It will be you who decides how to use them."

"It sounds very daunting. You are wise, and I will learn what I can from your knowledge. It makes me sad the last Riders were their own demise. I pray to the Gods when we all meet, we are together on the same path. I do not want to rule alone; I do not think I have the strength. Mayhap my Dragon can help me in this regard."

"The Great One will not hold your hand in everything. You must show your worth, and he would not have chosen the Riders without some thought of character and resilience. You may have to walk alone for a time until he makes himself known to you. I believe you may prove yourself more than once. Perhaps beginning with these warrior trials."

I stood slowly, my body protesting movement. *"You are incredibly wise. I will go refresh and eat, Great Mader. I will visit later."*

Soon the day marking the beginning of the trials arrived and all were excited. I learned I would be the first to compete against Adini. She thought to get the weakest out of the way, so she could concentrate on who really mattered. So, she thought to remind me. I did not take offence like she wanted me to. The Lanthians were a proud people and quick to take offense at any little slight. As I knew she was deliberate in her goading, I chose to ignore the baiting.

We would have the Ruler, his Mader and family attending, and I noticed them as I entered the ring. It was a special Colosseum built into a cliffside, with stone blocks built upon the other to accommodate seating. Entrances of stone arches built so high one had to crane their neck to see the top. Large timbers jutted out from the top edge with huge sails of canvas to cut the rays of midday sun, providing shade. Located as such, there was a breeze cutting through which helped to keep seated observers cool.

Initially, I believed Lanthia referred to the entire province but discovered both the city and province shared the same name, which confused me. The city was perched atop cliffs stretching from the gorge we jumped all the way to the ocean. A section of Lanthia was carved directly into these cliffs, its cave-like dwellings sheltering residents from the intense heat. The cliffs' towering height provided midday shade, preventing those at ground level from being scorched by the sun. With its maze-like layout, Lanthia resembled the Aerie. When one companion explained the extent of the city, I whistled, it was spread out over several cliffs and there were gardens by every water source. Some caves had sunken wells, which kept water cool.

Every item was used, the waste from animals and various soils were carted in to create the gardens which kept its citizens fed. The Palace had its share of wells, and the gardens were extensive. The lands to the South of the city were surrounded by rivers and very fertile land. The headlands of the rivers at the base of the mountains were the sites of the bulk of their orchards.

A small silk trade was begun in the last ten years which was proving to be a lucrative endeavor. I was shown this by my collective of friends who took it upon themselves to give me the grand tour on our day of rest. The Colosseum where the celebrations were held was in the North side of the city. The cliffs were spread further apart, and some walls were fabricated with mud bricks, as I noticed when I walked in under one of the archways.

Adini entered the other side of the arena to cheering. She was the stick everyone was measured against. My comrades said she would find your weakness and use it; I wracked my brain as to what this was. All I could think was I was an outsider, and she didn't want me here.

We wore minimal outfits, some combatants wore nothing but a loincloth, even the women. It reduced the hand-to-hand combat to just that, with nothing to pull on. I was geared in a leather loincloth and a band across my breasts, I had no doubt it may come off, so I oiled my body ahead, to reduce contact. She liked to pull and use anything to gain an edge. I was learning her style and still focused on her words.

"You should be open in your mind to other possibilities. Do not focus on one outcome. A tree has many sides which make it a whole."

"I understand, but given she is goading me nonstop, what else is there?"

"You will find this out, remain open."

They built canopies for shade, and Nejan settled under one, she had plenty of attendants to give her water when needed.

Adini bowed to the Ruler, then bowed to me, I did the same as they instructed me on correct protocols. I held my own. She observed me plenty and knew my weak points, however, I also studied her methods and gave a reason to step back to catch her breath. "You have studied well, but you will still not be one of us." I knew she was trying to goad me again, and I just shrugged, "This remains to be seen,"

I prepared for the next wave of attack. I knew what she would do to disarm an opponent when she was preparing to win. I surprised her when I met the grab with a twist, but she countered quickly, grabbing me around the back and had me in a tight chest hold. I saw the sweat on her face, and her frustration I wasn't as easy to beat as she thought. Then the thoughts in her head changed, I was close enough to see her eyes dilate and I prepared for her to try something, but I was not prepared for her to kiss me full on the lips.

I thought about what Nejan told me and what others said. She would find a weakness and exploit it. But two can play that game! It only took me a quick second to react. I kissed her back, pressing forward with my tongue and I felt her mouth begin to open under mine. She did not expect me to respond in this way and was loosening the grip around my back. I jerked back, and head butted her straight in the forehead. She went down like a brick. Straight down and out.

I stood there staring down at her and watched her come to. The crowd was silent for a bit, then a few began to cheer however, it died down as I gazed up for a second. People saw my eyes glowing, with a bright white light, and they were frightened. I saw the shimmer of white over my view. The Amman stood slowly making his way towards me, hands palm up.

Adini came to. One look at my eyes had her slowly roll over laying prone in front of me. "I am sorry, Great One. I did not mean it. Forgive me."

As the Amman approached me, he lowered to one knee, bowing, "What is your intent, oh Great One?" He had his palms in sublimation, and I gazed at him, the whiteness of my eyes giving the view of him a soft hazy look. I was not mad, or angry, merely impressed I dropped her. I used her own tactics against her.

"Why nothing, of course, It was a fair fight. Unless you say I did not win. However, one must exploit the others weakness, or so I was told, ehhh, Adini?"

I addressed the last bit to her.

"Yes, Great Mader, you won fair." I held out my hand to her and after being shocked I would spare her life, she grabbed it, as I helped her to stand.

"You are right about another thing." I spoke, looking her in the eyes. She could not look for a minute and I waited until she did.

"And what is this, Great One?" she asked quietly.

"I will never be one of you." I glanced at the Amman, as he smiled and stood up, "You are right in this aspect, Great One. You will be far greater than any of us." He grabbed both our hands holding them up to the cheering crowds. "The contest goes to Meera! She is one of our warriors!"

He let go of our hands gesturing for me to follow to the shade offered by the canvas awnings. Adini strode off in the opposite direction; her shoulders slumped in more than defeat. I knew I would have a conversation with her later. Nejan agreed, *"You cannot let her fester in her thoughts. She will turn it into hate one day if you do not address what it is she imagines about you."*

"Yes, you are again right. She thought to throw me off guard by using a different tactic than one would expect. I used it against her, but her response shows me she still harbours feelings which I do not reciprocate. When the time is right, I will talk with her."

Under the awning, the Amman sat motioning me to sit beside him and the rest of the games began. I was offered cool water, and I exclaimed delight looking at the cup, he said, "'Tis time for us to show you what 'tis you came here for; however, we will enjoy the rest of today. I will take you to see a wonder like no other. 'Tis our secret, we have killed any who have knowledge, but for you we will have an exception, shall we?" He smiled at his attempt at a jest, and I smiled.

"Have your eyes always changed like this?" He questioned directly. He was looking at my face; however, I knew he was also taking in my lack of clothing. I was not unsettled by his perusal; he was after all very covert and expressionless. I would learn how to do this.

"They have diminished now, but they were very bright in the arena. It does not detract from your beauty."

"I have only known them to change when my Dragon spoke to me." I answered him with honesty. He didn't even blink at my confession. His face was still blank… very good indeed. I was taking notes of my own.

"Did he make himself known?"

"No, I am afraid he is quiet of late. I am sure when the time is right, he will make his presence known to all."

"We have the only complete copy of the Prophecy; other lands have portions. You are said to have the eyes of the Great One. Eyes of white pearl, you have the knowledge of all, you rule all, and I will show you what we know. You will be a Leader of Leaders. Your time to learn combat has ended. Now you will fashion your gem, for the weapon of your choice. All will be rebuilt from the ashes. When we feel the breath of the Dragon, all will begin again."

I may have looked at him oddly because he spoke to me, "Tonight, when it is full dark, I will show you what I refer to." He turned, waving for the next game to begin, and the crowd cheered. We spent the next few hours watching more combat trials and games. Our conversation was easily had, I felt at ease with the Ruler of this country. He was quick to smile and would not hesitate to hold his youngest on his lap. I saw much caring in his demeanor to his children.

"You will reside in the Palace, Great One. 'Tis only appropriate. The Great Feline shall of course be by your side; she may dwell wherever she deems fit."

"Thank you. We appreciate your gesture. I observed many anomalies during my stay in the barracks. You would have an outsider believe your people are harsh, and a violent culture, however, I witness love at the core of everyone I see."

"You are wise, Great One. Few have the knowledge to see past the façade. We have kept this masquerade, to deter Namanists from setting root. This is a harsh clime, and few acclimatize to it. You have done very well. I have observed you from afar and have various reports you have a 'stubbornness' or a refusal to quit when it remains hard. These qualities are what will assist you in upcoming events, the attributes you are developing, will help guide you. If there is anything I can assist you with, such as books and tomes, I am yours to command."

"I thank you, Amman. I ask assistance with documents. I would very much like to view this Prophecy, but I cannot read."

"While you are with us, we can certainly show you, our collection. I can begin to show you characters, however, the choice is yours, you have but to command."

"Thank you, Amman. I will take your offer into consideration."

The festivities ended, and I was ushered to the Palace, back through the courtyard to where I first came in. Into another area, which was less… busy. Perhaps private accommodations, away from more public ones. I bathed and was given a robe of my choosing. I chose the reddest red, I could find. When I pulled my hair forward noticing after my kiss with Adini and my eyes changing, my hair had changed to a fiery red. Again! Too bright to fathom, more than the colour of fire. I peered in the mirror and saw my green eyes were losing the green, the white pearl had taken over at least half.

It gave me an unearthly look. *Pale green pearl, to go with my red hair. What else would I transform into? I do like my hair. If only Vandrin and the others saw me now, would they still tease? What about the people I don't know? Pader said I wouldn't stand out on the Islands he called home; would I ever get there?* I stood there lost in thought until I felt a light touch on my arm.

"My pardon, Great One, if you would follow me, I would take you to the Amman, he is waiting for you in the gardens."

One of the servant girls led me through a gate and up a long path of steps, a garden on either side. It was a long walk and I wondered when it would end. The girl explained it was a direct route for the guards to enter the Palace without having to weave through obstacles like markets and people. We were climbing many stairs, and my thoughts were, the Amman had a Palace higher than the populace, I was not disappointed.

We entered another arch and gate, into a stunning array of flowers. I so wanted to stop and look at each one, they were absolutely gorgeous! The girl stopped a few times, to cater to my adoration but reminded me his Majesty was waiting. I took myself out of my musings following her, to another archway leading into a forest of all kinds of citrus trees. I was led forward under a living canopy of fruit. Many were ripening and I resisted the urge to reach and grab one. There we found him seated at a glass table surrounded by benches in the shade. His attendants backed away when I arrived.

Motioning for me to sit across from him, I bowed and sat upon a velvet covered bench. A servant served me a glass of cool citrus juice, which I was glad to partake. "You enjoyed your time here, learned all about the combat you wished to learn?"

"Yes, Amman, I have, I would like to serve."

"I am thinking you can serve me, by my side, until there is need for you to leave. You learned combat from the best of our warriors. Adini tried to distract you; you are not the first to receive her 'methods.'"

"Oh, she tried this before? Kissing her opponent?"

"Not quite. You are the first woman she kissed. She will kiss her opponent once she grabbed one by his balls. She may have had her face in another's groin. She is very inventive with tactics. 'Tis why she is the best, she makes her opponents think. She trains our warriors to be the best. 'Tis a shame we must send some of them South. 'Tis such a waste. I would rather send a tribute of coins or material. However, sending our warriors to fight, sends another message. It diminishes our value to the Empire."

"How so? Your warriors would be a great boon to any army."

"I give you thanks. If we were to give the Namarch only goods, they would see more value in this and extract more… they would come and take. By giving them a minimal amount of goods, and more in flesh, it gives them no reason to come. They do not value our warriors. They send them to the front lines; however,

I have accounts from those who return, we have turned the enemy back countless times, our numbers are small and they get over run. They do not value them, because they are women. They are blind to everything but… It is a sad truth."

"Their weakness can be our strength. They do not value women, so they may expect us to be weaker."

"They may, but do not overlook the possibility they will try every scheme to overpower you… like Adini."

"Yes, this is a powerful lesson. One from which I can learn. I thank you for the lessons."

"We already sent our dues, and we only send once a year. The Empire doesn't request much from us. They do not like our women warriors; however, they cannot refuse our offerings as such. It was suggested, but we do not listen to the pattering's of an old man. The leader of the new religion, doesn't deserve respect if he doesn't respect all in his kingdom."

"I agree, but I always thought there wasn't much I could do. I grew up in the system. The men of the North treat women with some respect, but like everyone else have to conform or die. There is still some practice of the old Gods in the North, but 'tis kept in secret… much like what I see here if one were to look."

"You are very observant. Not many would see the signs if they were placed in front of them. You are prophesized to be the one who will bring balance to our lives, ushering in the old ways. Great One, you have the Lanthians behind you. When the time comes, you have but to ask. What tribute we send are acceptable losses, should they find themselves on the other side if this comes to pass. I should show you what you need to see, it is our greatest secret other than you, for now."

The Amman stood motioning for me to follow, his two guards stepping in behind us. We walked to a far corner of the garden towards a hill. The end of the garden was a cliff, sheer enough nothing could climb up or down, for at least a hundred feet. He walked toward the wall motioning for me to follow behind, he disappeared into the wall!

The opening was very cleverly done. One would have to be at the perfect angle to see the slice in the cliff face. I entered, sideways as it was a bit tight. He was waiting for me inside the passage, a torch in his hand, and led me down the tunnel, the torchlight glittering off the walls. I wanted to touch and see what it was, but I did not wish to fall behind. He noticed my attention was caught by the glitter,

"Various gems and minerals are embedded in the stone. We harvested much in the making of this passage. However, this is not all… the best is yet to be seen."

Soon enough we came to an opening in the tunnel, and we stood on a ledge overlooking the biggest cavern I imagined there could be. I gasped in astonishment. I could barely make out the bottom in the dim light, there was the odd cut in the rock face above us, one saw rays of light filtering in, beaming down into the vast darkness below. I could not see the other side.

"This used to house Dragons at one point, but they left never to return. We use it now to mine our gems you find all over the world. We have deposits of sapphire, emeralds, rubies, topaz, garnet, a deep amethyst, and a large vein of diamond. You need only ask what you would like. Tomes allude to each Dragon creating their own medium, although I have not read of how. We have a library you may use; 'tis at your disposal. Let me take you down to the deposits, and you can see for yourself."

We walked down a path cut into the cliffside of the cave, and eventually arrived at the bottom, moving forward over the rocky floor, working around rocks of large stature. When we approached an accessible area, I turned around looking up and could barely find the ledge we had been standing on. Only by the guard and the torch he held. The small flame flickered, tiny in my sight. The guard with us, brought a torch. I managed to see, in the low light, my eyes following the rays which entered from above. There were sparkles everywhere, in the walls, the floor and the pillars scattered around the cavern. I began to focus on the reflections on the walls, and ceiling as high as it was. It seemed there was movement and I squinted, peering while I listened.

"It was spoken as legend, this was the final resting place for Dragons, lay themselves down before they left their spirit. They in turn became the jewels we mine. We are respective of the legends and recite blessings to the Gods before we extract anything. It has never failed us. I am not sure if this is what you need to see or hear, but anything you need from us is yours."

As the Amman spoke, I wandered around the cavern, and mounds of stone. Some had indents where a pickaxe may have had a bite. I noticed assorted colours, glitters of gems in the mounds of what he spoke. I scanned around, with the two men walking behind me, my gaze wandered up the walls. As I focused, I began to see what I thought were images in the stone. As I concentrated more, these images took shape. Moving inside the stone, as if they were flying through the air.

Dragons flying! Glittering with their colours, coming alive in my mind. They flew and danced around the walls and the ceiling of the cave. It had me mesmerized. It was a beautiful dance. They emerged, these iridescent spirit beings, flying into the air, high around the ceiling space and I followed them as they flew and sparkled with the colours of their auras, if I could call them that. *Oh, the spirits of past Dragons, this is beautiful!* I followed one, he was silver, white, his shape was alive with movement. His dance as he flew around in the ceiling and walls had me mesmerized. It was poetic and beautiful. I was crying, tears streaming down my face as I felt connected emotionally. I watched as its shape swirled and moved fluidly coming to rest against a stone pillar in front of me.

I walked forward to a huge shape, imagining the slope in front of me was indeed a head and neck, time had frozen within my mind, as I reached out my hand to stroke the head. The image before me, I saw in my mind, my eyes casting a glow of their own, shedding their own light. I did not register the gasps behind me, as I was present inside my own reality. I only saw the silver Dragon coming to rest, I did not know they saw the scene in front of me and what I was projecting.

I stroked the head as the eye in it closed for the last time. Tears coursed down my face, my hand closing over one of the horns which crested the crown on its head. It broke off in my hand as the Dragon disappeared and became stone. I brought my hand close to look and I beheld a chunk of stone. Looking back at the stone mound before me, I could not see the shape of the head or where it had come from. The Amman approached behind me seeing the stone,

"A gift from the Gods, from the Pader of Dragons himself. We witnessed what you were seeing, and you are Blessed."

The guard behind him repeating, "May you be Blessed."

"Now it is up to you what you are to do with this gift."

I did not think about what I would do with the piece of stone in my hand other than give thanks for the vision and gift from the stone Dragon. I could only surmise he was the Greatest of all, the Pader of all Paders. He invoked a feeling of peace, tranquility and ancient knowledge surrounding him. I brought my hands together clasping the stone between them. Closing my eyes, a sense of stillness and purpose came over me.

"I give the Pader of all thanks for this gift! May I be worthy of such and use it for the benefit of all before me. I humble myself before you, guide me in this path I call life. May I be given courage to lead, bravery when needed, and the knowledge to sustain all lives. May I wield it with only the intent to bring forward peace, harmony and mend the brokenness in our world."

As I spoke the stone in my hands lit up with the same light as my eyes when I was in Dragon state. The Amman and his guard had to shield their eyes from the brightness. It shone like fire too bright, the white light of a star. As the brightness faded, the stone turned into a diamond, sparkling from within. The sparkles moved and pulsed with the beat of my heart. Right now, I was running with adrenaline, and it sparked with the same light as my eyes, as I opened them to view my creation. The Amman and his guard, lowered to their knees and prostrating themselves. "Great One, we humble ourselves to you and ask you give us your blessing. You are given a great gift from the Pader of all. This is to be placed in a weapon of your choice, to be taken into battle."

"What if I don't wish to go into battle?" I was busy turning the gem over and over, mesmerized by it.

"Everyone will have to go into battle at some point. This is to be used with a pure mind, however, also to be wielded, so your enemies know what they are up against. It would be a perfect world if you didn't have to use it but use it you will. That is its purpose. 'Tis written."

He rose coming forward to stand in front of me. "Do you have a weapon of choice?"

"I thought I found Noster's sword, at the Aerie where I lived, on the western shore of this land, but I do not have it with me."

"We will fashion one for you, what do you prefer? Sword or dagger? A sword was the previous weapon, but you are the Great One, you may choose."

A choice which was an easy one for me. "I believe I will choose the same, I grew up on hidden stories, of the glory of the greatest DragonRider holding his sword aloft while riding into battle. 'Tis the memory of sitting around the fire and I remember a woman's voice as she told me these tales. That memory stays with me."

"Then I shall have our Smiths forge you a blade worthy of yourself."

He took my hand, the one not holding the palm size diamond which lessened its brightness. I watched the sparkles whirling inside, as the Amman brought his lips to my hand and kissed it. "I will rescind my offer to have you as my companion, to be my servant. If it would be the other way around, I am your servant; you have but to command."

"I would like to return here someday; however, I would not command anything other than friendship. I have not many friends and would not place myself above you or anyone else. We all have roles to play in this game of life. The paths we walk on merge with others, or travel beside. I would be honoured to have you as one who walks beside me."

He bowed his head and turned in the speaking. "The honour is mine. May you be Blessed. We can certainly return should you find the need to do so, however, if it pleases you to exit to the outside. My head is hurting from the advent of the brightest light of your gem."

"Of course we may, I am sorry your head hurts. I did not intend to make it so." I took the arm he offered and my stomach growled in the moment.

He laughed. "The Great One has spoken, maybe in not so many words."

We left returning the same way we entered. As we passed through the opening into the gardens, the sun was leaving the most surreal colours to herald a darkening sky. The Amman invited me to stay in the Palace on high, and Nejan greeted me as we walked into the citrus grove. She padded up, sniffing at the still glowing stone in my hand.

"I felt your energy and a pull to come here however, could not find you. I see you are well on your way, to walking your path. This is part of you; you are bonded to this gem. It will reflect your emotions, good or bad. Each DragonRider has one they will create, in their time, as they need. You have not been announced yet, so you have some anonymity to gather strength for the upcoming upheaval. You have yet to find your Dragon. Have you heard anything from him?"

"No, I have not, is this normal?"

"He may be waiting for you, or 'tis as it should be. I will be leaving soon; you have mastered enough of the language. You still have learning to do, and I am restless. I would stay however, I believe you have another purpose to fulfill. We will meet again, and Little Uncle will need me just as much." I lowered onto my knees and hugging her around the neck, burrowing my face in her fur.

"I will miss you. How will I know what to do next?" My tears flowing into her fur, and she thought to me. *"'Tis not the end, Little Cub, our paths will cross again. This I do know, I will seek out others of my kind. I have a need to live among my kin, and a need to search the mountains. Little Uncle will be with the Wanderers if you head back that way. Follow what path your Dragon sends you on, help who needs it. I won't be leaving tonight; I have a craving for some more delights."* She sat down, breaking my grip and licked my face, whipping my head back and snagging a few loose strands of hair. I untangled myself yet again from her tongue.

The Amman waited for us, and after our exchange he bade a servant lead me to an elaborate room, decorated in the finest furnishings with art on the walls, and glorious hanging lanterns of the most exquisite blown glass. The bubbles in the glass making dazzling reflections on the wall. I bathed all the dust off me, placing the gem on the lip of the bath beside, reluctant to let it out of my sight, not because I thought someone would steal it, but because I was absolutely fascinated by the item I created. I could lose myself in it and caught myself more than once doing so.

I bathed and picked out an ensemble of greens this time, with white silks, and the servants gave me emeralds to wear around my neck and dressed my hair, curling it around and placing some of it up. Securing with diamond and emerald pins, with a cascade down my back, I saw it was longer and reached the small of my back. I saw the reflection of a woman beautiful except for the scar coursing down one side of her face.

"Beauty comes from within, not what the outer shell holds, as long as your spirit is pure, this is the only beauty which matters." Nejan spoke in my head, and I smiled gently.

The Amman gazed intently at me when I entered the Dining Room he was occupying, and I saw it was only a few of us, his Mader and a few young children, who he introduced as his. He explained his wife expired during childbirth, and he had not remarried. His eyes explained a lot to me; his heart left when her spirit parted. I murmured my condolences, and met the two children, at five and three years of age, he was very present when he was with them, and his Mader dealt with them during the day. I saw he loved them very much; the boys were well behaved and asked me questions about the stone I brought in with me. They were mesmerized as I was with the swirling points of light inside and they behaved.

"Can I keep it here to keep my sons' attentiveness? This is the best behaved they have been in a long time." After we finished dinner, he mentioned he wished to show me something. We all stood, and I bade goodnight to the boys, telling them we'd meet again, then also wished his Mader goodnight. She left, holding both boys by the hand. Then, he and I stepped out onto a dimly lit patio, where he turned to face me.

"Look up into the heaven's, what do you see?" He pointed up to the clear night, it was full dark, and the stars shone with a light which seemed brighter. I looked up and peered around in a full circle, at first not seeing anything until I saw it. A star, shining brighter than any other, and it looked larger than all the rest, and seemed to have a red aura around it.

I gasped, and he spoke. "It appeared the night before you were brought to us, however, I did not know what it heralded until I saw you with the Great Feline. Now I saw what you did today, I witnessed a moment in history, I will sit with you and tell you the history of what I know. My scholars tell me this is the Dragon coming to save our world. They call it the Dragon Star, and they say 'tis coming closer every night, they see it through a special tube with glass which brings it closer to view. You can look through it when you wish."

When there is naught but shadow

A glimmer in the sand

When the advent of fire

Sweeps across the land
Thru dust and ash
Arises new life
A time long forgotten
Fraught with pain and strife
From the heaven's descend
The six-pointed star
From darkness comes light
And love comes from war

He recited a portion of the Prophecy and told me. "There is more but what stands out from these few verses, from the heaven's descend the six-pointed star," he pointed up to the very visible star, "this must be the six-pointed star, and there are more verses, 'the six shall rise again' which can only mean you and five others. You will leave here and find the others, or they find you. I hate to think of what dust and ash are, however, I am sure it will all be shown in time. I am overjoyed the Prophecy is coming to pass in my lifetime, and I am able to play a part in our new history… I can be your servant in this."

We chatted for a bit more, "I will show you the rest of the Prophecy, and all the written word. Everything I have is yours when you choose to have a look at all."

"I do not know the written word, in your language or in mine, I am afraid I was too busy running amuck."

"Then I will do the honours, I need to familiarize myself again with the history of our peoples." I tried to hide a yawn, "You are tired, I should let you rest. You had a very eventful day today."

"Thank you, Amman. I fully agree. By your leave?" I picked up my diamond and a servant led me away to my room. I fell heavily into my bed cradling my new diamond against my breast.

It was a few more days later, the Amman was true to his word, he read the rest of the Prophecy to me, and we had lengthy discussions on the meanings of each passage. "I will have to memorize it, and then I can ponder each meaning. It seems all six are mentioned in verse. Love comes from war. I hope war is not all, people need to have love. It should not come from war."

"There is war happening right now, perhaps it will end. Maybe people are tired of war."

"You may have a point. We need love, we don't need war."

"You may have a different kind of war. There are physical wars, wars of the mind and wars of the quill. You do not know what war will be waged when the Dragons arrive."

"Well, if it is a war of the quills, I have already lost." I was frustrated with the fact I did not know the written word.

"You do not write?"

"I know not how to read or write. I was an errant child, surviving as best as I knew how. Reading was not a priority. However, I see now I should have some knowledge. It seems very daunting."

"I can have my tutors teach you. Or I can."

"Would I be able to sit in with your sons? They might find it grand fun. They could help me, and I could help them."

"I have only one thing which worries me…"

"What is this, Amman?"

"They will get attracted to you; they have been without their Mader for so long. I would not wish you uncomfortable in their presence."

"I cannot see this as a problem, they have much love from so many people, what is one more? And I like children; they have an innocence about them becoming an adult takes away. If 'tis distressing for you… I do not want to intrude onto your family."

"No, 'tis not distressing, this was not my meaning. They may form an attachment to you, as may I."

"I am here to learn, Amman. You know I will leave here; the Universe will send me onto my path, and I seem to be the leader of people I haven't met yet. I do not think I would have time to form attachments. I am sorry if this is too harsh, but 'tis truth. I will value your friendship, as of your family. It means much to me if you feel the same. I must find value in myself to value what others have to give me. Until such time, I would wish your friendship. Anything more, would be empty. What I mean to say is, I am not ready."

"I value your honesty, I understand. You may learn as you wish with the children, but do not say I didn't warn you. They can be very convincing! I have several tutors for them, and all the servants are under their spell. My Mader dotes on them also. She tells me she sees me in them, it has brought her boundless joy. I will say I do find you attractive. Not since my wife have I looked closely at another. You have proven yourself to be intriguing, in such I wish to know you better. I will respect your wish in friendship, for in friendship we find the greatest of loves."

"Well said, Amman, I will bid you goodnight and sleep well."

"Sleep well, Great One."

I slept restlessly, dreaming of water crashing onto rocks, breaking away chunks of a cliff, the pieces falling into the heaving ocean. I watched as the land was eaten away, piece by piece, I felt helpless to do anything. Then the scenery changed, it became smaller in my view. I saw habitation seeming to be moving further and further away, the harder I tried to move close. Then I realized I was in the air, and the winds started to toss me around. I cried out, reaching out to grab onto anything, but there was nothing.

Swirling around and around a dark mass caught my vision and seemed to be moving towards me. Every time I swung around it seemed to be closer. Crying hard now, I could not take my eyes off the blackness of the sky and as it reached me, touching my arm I swung out in defense.

"Merroww! Little Cub, 'tis I. I felt your distress. Are you fine?"

"Oh, Nejan, wha…? This seemed so real. Did I hit you? I am so sorry. I thought I was going to be enveloped by this darkness. Oh, it was a horrible dream.
I told Nejan what I saw in my dream.

"Little Cub, it sounds like you are afraid of changes which may happen in the world. They will happen whether or not you change them. Worrying about them will not do you good or give you peace. You will lose people, of this, I am sure. You may have to turn your back; it will cause you pain but know you will have the greatest bond of all… Your Dragon. When he makes himself known to you, it may be soon, it may not be for a while, however, it will be the best thing you will ever know. Greater than our bond, and we will be bonded forever, until our spirits grace the skies.

So, I will leave you soon, but we will always be bonded. Little Uncle now needs me, while you do not. You are stronger than you know, and with your Dragon you will be a formidable force. You must believe in yourself, value your learnings, and always, always love. Loving yourself is the best place to begin. Then you give to others when your love overflows. Never fear what your dreams show you. There is always a message inside the meaning. Now sleep well, Little One. I will stay with you, right here beside your sleeping mat."

"Thank you, Nejan. I draw comfort from you and your wise words. I will try to sleep." I slept the rest of the night, better than I expected. Probably because I was guarded by my friend. I woke up to the sun blazing fully through the door openings, the curtains were drawn back and I slowly blinked, my thoughts returned to what I dreamed, and I was not distressed, Nejan took my fear away with her council. I sat up to look for her, but she was not present. A few servants came in and told me they did not enter for her presence, she left to the orchards and gardens.

I dressed in yellow silks, with a splash of orange, thinking after my dark dream I needed a bit of sunshine. I smiled at the thought a glass of citrus juice would round off my morning. I ventured out to the gardens to find a quiet spot at the table and the servants brought me my morning meal at my bidding. I caught sight of Nejan as I was finishing. *"Little Cub, I will be leaving. It is time."*

"I understand, Great Mader. I will miss you."

"We will see each other again. There is more to our story. You give Li'on-sa hope for the future, I hope one day to introduce you to my cub."

"Will it not be confusing, calling me Little Cub and your offspring?" I smiled at the great cat; I was coming to terms I would have people and animals ebb and flow in my life. As long as I had faith I would see them again, I would not be too distressed when we parted. *"That is a great way to think about it, Little Cub."*

The day arrived. We walked with a procession down to the gate we entered through the first day. I saw the gates with different eyes, one full of tears. With great ceremony from the Amman and assembly, I said goodbye to my first animal friend, the tears coursing down my face trying not to cry and failing.

I knew I would see her again, but for a moment I could not help but feel alone.

CHAPTER 45

Rowan

Harken the Days of Old

Rowan found herself spiraling down into a dark pit she could not climb out. She felt empty, and not the vacancy, which was now her belly, she felt a hollowness, in her mind. Her voice was strangely silent, she had no one to talk to her, other than Tannah. She felt a silence, like the quiet of the dark before the advent of the sun. Except she felt this all the time, it dragged upon her arms, she felt heavy, and did not wish to move, even the trip to the chair with pot was a big ordeal.

She never felt hungry and barely ate and did not acknowledge her husband when he came to check, he didn't care she was depressed, "Get yourself up and moving. I will beat you, stop lazing about. I will commence my rights. If you do not move, I will beat you and the girl." She did not acknowledge him or his words.

One day, she was half sleeping, half not, Tannah entered with her midday meal. "You have to get well, Noda." Rowan's breasts had dried up of their milk after two weeks, and she mourned this loss also.

"Princess. Rowan, please eat something. Please, you must not perish. I have heard from the Cook, your husband wishes to divorce you, he is asking the new Namarch if he has enough evidence to proceed. I also heard by listening quietly your husband may be asking the Emperor and Empress to grant this. It seems it may be enough to be so, and if you are unwell, when you are released, you may not be able to see your son."

This had her attention. "What? What are you meaning by this?"

"If you are divorced, you will return to the Palace, do you not think, this is where your son is, and then maybe you will see him." Tannah had only Rowan's best interests at heart, and she would say anything to have her mistress eat and not wallow in the darkness of her mind.

Rowan thought about this and beckoned to her maid to come with her.

"I would like to bathe, and find me something to eat, please." Tannah supported Rowan down to the bathes and Rowan stayed a long time and soaked some of her dark thoughts away. Then sat in her robes and ate more than one week prior, until her stomach protested and fell asleep thinking of her baby boy. She woke up the following day feeling better than she had for a while but could not help but caress her flattening belly and feeling nothing inside.

You are gone, but I will see you again soon. I will hold you in my arms and kiss your tears and troubles away. They cannot keep me from you, mamma is coming. She sat in her garden under the shade of trees, thinking about going to her rooms back in the Palace and didn't hear her husband enter the garden. She started as he came into her visual.

"I see you are up and about. I have something to tell you. I am asking the Church for a divorce. You are not right in the head, and I do not need this in my life right now. You will prove to be a weight around my ankle, and I am to have a career in the army, and I can't get this if you are around."

"Will you not be uncomfortable when we see each other in the Palace?"

"What are you talking about?" He looked at her oddly. "What makes you think we would see each other at the Palace?"

"If we divorce, I will be returning to the Palace, where my son is, and I am sure we would eventually see each other in passing."

He began laughing, hard, his barking sounded harsh in her ears.

"Oh, my word, where did you get this idea? Your parents don't want you either. You are unsettled; you hear voices and talk to yourself. Your Mader says you are a stain on the Empire. A weed which needs rooting out, she said. You are to leave here and find your own way. If you attempt to enter the Palace, the guards have full authority to kill you. They may even hand you over to the Church for the 'voices' you hear. I am leaving here tonight, when I return, you will be released and can go drown yourself in the sea for all I care." He turned and walked away, not caring the shock of his statement had her crying.

She felt like someone ripped what was left of her heart out of her chest, she could not breathe, gasping, trying to take a breath. She cried and cried and cried. *How could my parents not want me? What had I ever done to deserve this treatment? I am a dutiful Dader to the Empire. I married who I was told and bore a son. For the Empire. I have nothing, nothing! I want nothing anymore, not even this life.*

She rose suddenly and looked around her and saw the one plant she could eat, raw unfiltered and in full foliage, the most potent of times. She strode over to it and plucked a couple of leaves off. Before she could process what, she was doing, she shoved them in her mouth, chewed, and swallowed.

She began to feel lightheaded and let the darkness embrace her. Rowan fell to the ground as Tannah walked in… she yelled and ran to Rowan and grabbed her. Tannah's yelling brought people running, and as her master entered the garden, he gazed indifferently down at the semi conscious woman.

"It might be better for everyone if she did die. I am not staying, send word to the city. I am still proceeding with my plans in case she pulls through, I do not care of the outcome. Either way, I'll be rid of her."

Tannah had one of the menservants carry her mistress back to her room, she turned to another maid. "Sula, get me the tonic on my shelf in my room, the dark bottle with the wax on the stopper. Quick girl… There is no time."

She dripped the awful herbal down her mistress's throat, and it had the effect she wanted, the movement of her mistress throwing up the contents, green and slimy, did not wake the Princess and she lingered in and out of consciousness for two days. As she hovered in and out of spirit, she heard a male voice in her head this time,

"Why would you not wish to live? You have value and purpose to me and the others who are your sisters. You must live, your spirit is strong, you need to find the strength, you can bring others joy and feel it as well. You are stronger than you give yourself credit. Rise up and be whole again. You will feel joy again. You felt loss, and you have it inside you to be strong, I need you. The world needs you. Your sisters wait for you."

"They took...mmm...my baby... there is nothing left here for me..."

"There is everything here for you. You have others, your sisters, who will love you as you need. You will heal. They will help you."

"They took my baby...I feel empty..."

"You will have another, you have a long journey ahead, and a healing which will heal the world. Do you not want a better place for children? Your children?"

"Yes, this world is evil. To take a child from its Mader. What could I possibly do? I am nothing."

"You are the Earth Mader; I have chosen you to heal the world. You know from your own loss the importance of children to their Maders, to the rest of the Maders out there who have the same thing happening. The importance of education, to teach the world women matter. If you wish to change the world, come back into the light and be strong. It will be difficult, but each of the chosen will stand with you. Together, all will support the changes which are needed."

"You say I will have more children? I do not want the act, 'tis violent."

"You know this truth from one man. It is a glorious thing, given the right person gives you what you need. You need to heal, physically and in spirit. Will you accept your life? Come back and heal the world? I cannot help you if you are not willing to help yourself. It is your choice. Live or perish."

"I... will live. For now. If only to hold my child in my arms."

"It is a beginning, you focus on this, you will find your way. I will be here always if you should need me, I give you, my troth. I will always be here, rise, and begin again."

She didn't think this was her husband, it sounded too kind and soothing to be him. She finally swam through her thoughts to the light and woke, her maid sleeping beside her with her head on the bed. Rowan must have moaned, and her maid looked up groggily, and smiled gently at her.

"You are back."

"Yes, I am sorry. You know?"

"Yes, your husband did not stay, we are to send word to him if you lived or died."

"Does it even matter? He says I have no house, no name, after he took my child."

"Yes, we all know. However, you can take your life into your own hands. You can leave, and if you want, say the words in front of the staff, divorce him first. You have this right, with the laws of old. Then leave, pave your own way. You are not a slave anymore. Some of us can not leave. Find your purpose. Fly away from this gilded cage." Tannah looked at her mistress intently.

Rowan had never heard such passion coming from her maid and she nodded and said, "I hear what you say, and I wish I could give you freedom, from what I know you have endured. I will find meaning to my spirit, I am given another chance; to have influence, I can only wish the same for you."

Rowan tried to sit; Tannah had to assist her. Rowan felt awful, dizzy, and weak. She weaved sitting and heard movement and sounds coming from outside of the room. Tannah went to the door, opening it and listening. She returned to the bed.

"I am afraid a rider was sent out to your husband, I heard the Headmaster call for one. You should eat and try to stand and do what you need to do, and leave now, you have no time to waste. He may decide to send men after you to take your spirit."

"Can you help me? I need to get moving. If what you say is truth, Kavus could be on his way back already. Oh… my stomach…hurts…oh…please untie these leggings. I don't…"

She stood, wobbling on her feet, with the support of Tannah and tried to take a few steps, and had to sit on the commode chair suddenly and nearly didn't make it before her body had other ideas. As she evacuated her bowels, the smell was enough to almost make her vomit.

"I am so sorry, you have to see this, tis awful!"

"Your body doesn't want the poison inside, let it all out. I will empty the pot later when my stomach can manage it. Or maybe I'll just place it in Kavus's room."

"Oh, don't do this, Tannah, you would get beaten badly. Even if you said I had done it. Don't place yourself in his path anymore than you must."

Rowan stood up, dressed, and placed a cloth over the opening to help mask the smell. She weaved a bit as she stood. Tannah came over and grabbed Rowan under the arm to assist her. Rowan leaned into her maid. Tannah coughed and drew themselves away from the commode chair, and down the hall to the bathing room. She whispered to Rowan,

"I know how you are feeling, what drove you to do this, I tried once by to jump off one of the tallest towers in the city, however, a genuinely nice man talked me out of it. There is a purpose to your life, you have but to find it, and sometimes it finds you, so be prepared for the unexpected. Sometimes the only way to win in this ugly world is to not give up. You will find your path, and you will follow it."

She cleaned herself up and with Tannah helping her, they found a fair number of staff sitting in the kitchen, a few guards, maids, the cook, and kitchen staff. They all stood when Rowan walked in slowly, she was getting better, but her limbs had a mind of their own, a slight side effect of the plant she had tried to consume. She waved them all to sit.

"I won't take up any of your valuable time, what I have to say, I wish to say in front of all of you. I divorce you. I divorce you. I divorce you. There, it has been said, I will pack a few items and leave here. I am sure that my hus… my former husband will be here shortly, and you can tell him what was done. I wish you all the best in the future." And she turned, walking out of the room and back down the hall. Her step a little bit lighter, her head a little bit higher, and her heart a little stronger.

She walked into her room and looked around and said to Tannah, "I don't want anything, would you be able to trade me clothes or find me some serviceable poor clothes, I do not want to be recognized for who I was."

Tannah excused herself and left, when she came back, Rowan had almost finished cutting off all her hair. Tannah gasped in shock, but realized her mistress's reason for doing so, and went to help her. "If I can shave it all off, this would be better. I want no sign of my status."

They finished, and Tannah could not help but cry as a woman's worth and status was determined by her healthy head of hair. "All is fine, Tannah, I am not judged worthy by no man now, and my hair does not make me who I am, I promise you if I return one day and I can, I will find you and release you from this burden I now leave you with. I swear I will."

They hugged and Tannah gave her the clothes which would give her a fair bit of disguise, it was her spare uniform, "This is what your husband gave me when I came here. He took the clothes I brought from the Palace. It is barely serviceable."

"No, this is perfect. The more worn the better. I do not wish to bring attention to myself."

"You be careful on the streets. You have no experience out there. There are very bad men."

"Worse than Kavus?"

"Well… as bad. There are more rules being implemented. Men can do whatever they wish now."

"What? More than they already do? I will be careful, Tannah. I will tread lightly."

"You find a place which will assist you, a Church, or a seamstress. You have skills with a needle. Stay away from the Houses of Delight, and do not take food from a stranger. Most times it would be drugged and you would find yourself in a Delight House and not be able to leave."

"Oh, does this happen?"

"Oh, yes. Men will drug women, rape them, and keep them to make coin off the use of their bodies. Please promise me you will be careful."

"I will. The last thing I want to do is pleasure men, or any man. I hate the act."

"So do most women in those places, however, they are not given the choice. You have another life ahead of you, and choices to make. Your hair gives you the look of an ill person, and with your weight loss, it gives truth to the look. I am not trying to disparage you. You are my mistress and I wish you many blessing on your new path. Keep the illusion as long as possible. Now you should get going. Time is of the essence now. Here, take these leggings." Rowan took the tunic and leggings and left the full skirt; she didn't think it would serve her needs.

"No, there is one thing I will take, and that's the ring my Mader gave me. This is the only thing; it was passed down through the generations and I will not leave it. Do you know where he keeps all the jewelry?"

Tannah nodded. "We will be quiet, if we are heard and seen, we could be whipped or worse."

Now Rowan was no longer protected by her former husband's name, she was fair game, and all rules applied. They walked quietly to her his room, and she entered while Tannah opened the cabinet. Rowan saw all the glittering gems and jewelry she had worn and some she had not. Lucky for her, they were colour coded, she found her ring and a fine chain but then shook her head and placed it back, this would be noticeable. Tannah motioned to the leggings. "There is a small tear in the waistband, you could hide it in there. Sew it in and you won't have to worry about dropping it. If you carry it, there is the chance of being robbed."

"Thank you, you know many things. I have a lot to learn."

"You will have no choice but to learn. You are going from a life born of luxury to the direct opposite. Promise me you will survive, 'tis rough out there."

As an afterthought she returned to her room to grab a needle and thread, when she had time, she would sew it into her clothes. She gathered all she wanted with some bread and cheese to sustain her on her travels, and it fit into a small piece of cloth. Rowan heard her maid behind her, a groan. She glanced up to see Tannah standing staring at her blank faced.

"I see Ravens, lots of ravens. You are walking in between them. They are bobbing their heads at you. You hold out your arm, and one flies and lands on it. Its head stretches out and…it brushes up against your cheek. Like a feline would do. It is affectionate. You walk among the ravens…" Tannah returned to herself, to see Rowan staring back.

"You see, I cannot control what I see or say. I am afraid…"

"You told me I would walk among ravens. Do you know what this may mean?"

"The only thing I can think of is the North. They have forests of Ravenwood. Perhaps this may be the place to go. You must hurry, mistress. Leave here, walk, run if you must, just hie away."

"I will. You keep your visions to yourself. If any find out, you may be killed."

"I cannot help what I see. It has only happened a few times, however, since I came into your service, and more so since we've been here, have I had many."

"Hopefully with me leaving, they diminish. I thank you for your service to me. Tell Kavus your part, or not. Do what he says, and keep yourself alive, I promise to return for you."

"Then you stay alive, Mistress, and I will do the same. May you be Blessed, and our God go with you." Rowan hugged her maid and made her way out of the villa and down the road, on foot even her feet were bare.

She had nothing, the clothes on her back and the ring and for the first time in her life Rowan felt free! She smiled for the first time in months, she would make her own way! Maybe get to the Islands where she could meet these other women who heard voices.

And lucky for her she heard like a wolf as she heard her former husbands entourage before they saw her. The sounds of hooves and men yelling at their mounts became loud in her ears. However, sounds in canyons are deceiving, and she barely had enough time to jump off the road and hide behind some brush before the horses and men riding them flew past.

She bounded back onto the road once the last man disappeared and hoped they wouldn't send out a search, especially once he knew the ring was gone. She continued all night, thinking about what she may find in the city proper. Rowan reached the outer walls of the city as the sky was lightening up. She looked back only once, when she arrived at the big doors and people milled about waiting for them to open. She thought she saw a sparkle in the sky but was distracted by the doors opening.

Everyone was let in. Rowan thought to herself the security was lacking, but once she was in, she saw why. There were injured men everywhere. She made her way through the gates into the main avenue of the lower city and thought she would head straight to the wharfs and hide in plain sight with the other waifs there. She hid in the shadows when she heard city soldiers, and as she passed a stable next to a butcher, she had a thought. She ducked into the stable and found a dung heap and gloried in covering her body in horse shite. *This would keep certain men away if they thought of anything improper. No one will be attracted to the smell of shite.*

She had not seen her reflection in a very long time; she was not what high society would call attractive. She dropped weight and was quickly losing the rest of her pregnancy weight, every day her breasts drooped from the weight loss and as her milk dried. A shaved head was a sign of the poor; they had lice or other diseases which warranted shaving. Only the rich nobility could afford long luxurious locks and she left hers on the floor, for Tannah to clean. She looked nothing like the happy girl she once was prior to joining. *I hope this works. I seem to fit in. No one is really looking at me. This is good... I can do this.*

She only encountered others who looked like her. Those who came close and got a good whiff of the scent steered clear as she smelled like manure. She found a small corner near where she smelled the salt of the sea and thought to sleep. She remembered to tuck the ring inside the tear and then thought it best she sew it in before sleeping. Once she was satisfied no amount of grabbing at it would tear, she put the needle aside in the waistband and closed her eyes. It wasn't too long after she nodded off she was awakened by someone trying to rifle through her clothes, she groggily said as she batted the hands away,

"I have nothing." The hands retreated and woke enough to see a small shadow dart away. *Someone young or someone small like me.*

As she woke, she tried to fathom what she did and how she was to hide in plain sight. As a person who looked ill, she would be given a wide berth by people. *Oh, what have I done? Have I done the right thing? Will they come looking for me? Will they wish me dead? Hang on, Rowan... take a moment. No one in the lower city knows what you look like. Only the upper city saw your joining. Calm your thoughts. You should be safe enough down here.*

It was mid day and she wandered around, trying to get her bearings. She smelled the ocean and headed to the docks. The people were just like she remembered them. A rougher lot, and many times she was jostled, and hands would sometimes grope. She thought she could not get any food so she should find a place who would feed the poor. As Rowan left the crowds in the lower docks, she was so tired and hungry she did not notice the man following her.

She walked up streets, and when she took a wrong turn to a dead end, she stopped and turned around. There was a greasy, very fat, and large man blocking the exit to the street. He had the look of a drunkard; his countenance was red and sweating. It gave her an uneasy feeling inside, and she looked around. The walls of the buildings were high and smooth around her and she saw no way but out the way she came.

"Please I have nothing, no coin, no goods. Let me pass."

"You have something I can have, little girl, and I will have it."

"I will scream."

"You are very welcome to; in fact I will be upset if you didn't." She knew the man would take exactly what Kavus had. This man kept moving forward, and Rowan backed up until she felt the stones of the high wall behind her back. She looked up, above her head to see the top of the wall, too high and smooth for her to climb. In that time the man came forward and grabbed her by the neck. His other hand grabbed her breast and squeezed hard.

"Not much there, but how about here?" His hand left her breast to grab her in the private area. His hands were rough and Rowan froze. It shocked her she had left an abusive man and within a day, she was going to endure the same pain. She tried to grab a breath, but the hand on her throat closed and she began to struggle. Panic rose to envelope her. She tried to hit him, but her hands did not have the strength, lack of food made her feel very weak.

"You give me what I want, no trouble and I will let you live."

Rowan had no doubt this man would kill her. She felt a knife cut the ties on her leggings and the man's hand was pulling them down and off. She began to writhe and struggle but his hand on her throat lifted her up and her leggings dropped onto the wet stone alley. She began to feel the dark closing in, and the hand around her throat let up.

"No good if you don't struggle." She gasped trying to get a breath and let out a weak cry. The hand tightened around her neck. His breath was stale and rotten; she tried to turn away. His tongue licking her cheek as his hand which wasn't occupied left her body to untie his pants. She felt his belly against her, pressing her into the stone wall. She placed her hands on the wall behind her. Her attempts to hit him, only made him laugh, and she had no strength left to hit. She palmed the damp stones, finding a small crack but nothing was large enough for her fingers to slip into.

"I'll bet you are nice and tight, give me a bit of struggle, Bion wants you to struggle. Do you want some of Bion? You aren't from here, are you? You look like you are lost. I'll keep you fed, for some of this." His cock was slapping against her inner thighs. She tried to move her legs but his girth had her lower body pinned against the cold wet stone against her bare ass. His belly was huge and he was having a tough time, trying to hold her and guide it in. She smelled stale alcohol, ripe sweat, and a sick odor, this set her stomach to roil and she tensed up. It was just like Kavus.

No, no, no. Not again! I do not want this. No! She was beginning to panic more than before. Her hands stilled on the stone, and she felt like she was falling into a pit of despair again.

Oh, please. I do not want this. I want not to feel this pain again.

Rowan felt the man finally get his cock lined up to enter when she felt her world go dark. His hand cut off her air, and she left her spirit. She was floating and felt free.

"Earth Mader. You do not belong here. You must return."

"Back. To what? Pain and suffering? I left a man who beat me, to have another who would take the same and then kill me. What is there in the world I wish to return to?"

"I understand. You think yourself as weak because you are female. You have a spirit which is strong. You look within yourself for the strength you need."

"For what purpose? Men. All they do is take, take, take. Regardless of a woman's refusal. This is not the world I wish to live in. All I wanted was to be loved."

"I will give you a gift. You will be loved. You will be loved by a man who wants nothing but to give. This I promise you... He will love you on your terms. Will you be willing to find him? Seek him out?"

"No. There is no such man. This is a cruel world. I want nothing to do with it. I want nothing to do with men."

"I will have him find you, then. He will wait for you. He will help you heal. Much like you will help others heal. Would you have any requests of me? I need you to return to your shell, Little Mader. You may not stay here, I will be with you for a time, until you find your sisters."

"I have sisters? But they are at the Palace. Oh, how I miss them."

"You have sisters of like mind. Not of the flesh. They will wait for you, now I must really insist on you returning. Remember this, you are never alone, and you will always be loved." Rowan woke up. Something was heavy on her. she felt a weight pressing down and struggled to rise. She was struggling when a hand grabbed hers and then the weight came off her back. "Are you alright miss?" She gazed up to find a small group of men and women surrounding her. She glanced around. The wall which was pressing against her back was crumbled around on the ground and the man who was trying to rape her was laying on the ground dead. There was blood on his head and scrapes on his arms and legs. She saw his pants were around his ankles and his cock was out. Pathetic and small. She looked down at her bare legs. Her leggings were under her body. She grabbed the edge of them and looked at those who surrounded her.

"I...I...I... he was trying to take what... oh my head. What happened?"

"The wall gave out. It crushed him. Do you know him?"

"No. He cornered me in this alley and tried... oh."

"That's Bion. He's a mean one... or he was. Always cornering the weaker ones. Are you sure you didn't lead him on?"

"I am sure. I do not know this section of the city. I have fallen on tough times. I came here looking for food."

"Let's get you standing, miss. You can put your leggings on, before you give others the idea you are free and easy. You should tread more careful. Walk a more pious path, or you will attract more like this man here." The man who helped her up was a soldier, and she stood with his help and he pulled her leggings out from under the fallen stones. Then he handed them over and watched as she put them on. The crowd while she was talking began to disperse. This looked like an everyday occurrence, Rowan was guessing. The other soldiers were busy looking at the remaining portion of wall.

"Sir. It looks like this wall has plenty of erosion behind it. It was a matter of time before it fell."

"That may be so, but perhaps all it needed was a little push from our fat friend here. I will file a report with the Commander, and I am sure some recruits will fix it... You. Miss. Get on out of here unless you want more trouble. Don't walk these streets after dark, unless you want another man to finish what Bion here started. You are lucky this time. I do not want to see you again."

"Thank you, I will heed your words."

"See that you do."

Rowan walked slowly out of the alley, sidestepping the stones and pieces which littered the alley. Before she turned the corner, she glanced back. The wall had fallen right above where the man had her pressed against the wall. She wondered at the sight. *Did this happen like the voice said? And what of our conversation? Was I really in the spirit world?* Rowan kept walking up the hill, making sure she walked in the widest and busiest street. She felt her panic settle and her heartbeat slow. She had gotten out of a horrible situation.

Her stomach let out a rumble, reminding her it was empty. Then she remembered the Church would hand out food, so she would need a place of worship to find something, as her stomach kept on with its monologue. So, she set off with the sun at midday and walked carefully and kept to the shadows and watched people around her. There were plenty who were starving here, some listless laying against brick walls and she came across her first dead body. It had a grayish tinge to the brown skin of the people. It looked puffy and a weird smell hovering around it. She squatted down to look and got startled out of her reverie by a bucket of offal thrown out of an upstairs window which barely missed, the splashes which did get her would add to the aroma and she did not care.

Smell of offal and feces permeated the walls and streets over the smell of the ocean. She smelled more spices and leather as she climbed up the hill to the markets, the poorest of vendors selling their wares. She headed east along one of the paved roads sadly needing much repair and saw the tower of one of the Churches who catered to the needy.

She rounded the corner of the building to see the courtyard in front of the Church teeming with people and realized there were far more wounded soldiers and their families begging for help. The Sisters and Brothers of the faith were wandering through the masses, however, most of their arms were empty. She approached a Sister; her green gown soaked with splatters of blood.

"Excuse me Sister," she asked in a low voice, not sure of how to ask, "would you have something to eat?"

The Sister looked at her and shook her head, "Move on, we have more than enough wounded to feed."

"I can help with wounded, in return for food. I am handy with needle and thread, I know herbals, potions, and tonics, I can work for food. I am a diligent worker."

The Sister was too weary to ask her how she knew how to sew, or why her speech was so impeccable. "What is your name, lass?"

"My name is…Vian. Yes. Vian, Sister. I have fallen on troubled times and am willing to help as needed for some shelter and food."

"Well, we will not turn down help, as 'tis sorely lacking. You will adhere to our schedules and rules. We will not have you if you break the teachings of our God."

"Yes, Sister, I will do as you require, thank you." The Sister motioned the small woman to the inside of the doorway and directed her to another of the order, an older woman who looked as kind as she was old. She was directed to a well inside a courtyard and she brought up a bucket and had a long drink, removed her dirty outer layer, and washed her arms and face with the remaining water.

"You stink, lass. I know the why of what you did, but its very overpowering. Wash what you can off you now, and we will have to bear it until you can wash proper tonight. We need you to assist the head nurse, and we'll see if you are what you say you are."

"Yes, Sister, thank you."

Then the older woman showed Rowan inside one of the many rooms which had wounded laying on the floors, introduced her to the woman in charge and left. The older Sister did not even look back. "I'll have you stand behind, miss. Give me what I need when I ask for it."

"Yes, Sister."

Thus, she began a very long day of caring for the men inside and assisting the Sisters with the care, she managed to hold her own, but towards the end of the day she was tottering on her feet and one of the younger girls brought her a piece of cheese, a thick piece of bread and a wooden cup of water. She ate so fast she nearly brought it all up as her stomach heaved. They brought her to the back of the Church down a small corridor and motioned her to the well. She retrieved her own bucket of water and shown a small vestibule of a room and one of them handed her a gown. So, she washed herself, she didn't think the smell of horse feces was strong, but it was. She changed out of her now soiled clothes took her needle and the remaining thread and found a spot to sew the ring into, and then when she was done, she lay down on the mat on the floor and fell fast asleep.

The peal of bells at dawn woke her up and she hurried out to begin another day. She conducted the same routine each day and after a week, she felt comfortable enough to hold a conversation with some of the Sisters there. She listened to the speech of soldiers and the poor folks and felt she could mimic them, so she tried. It was difficult at first but managed to get the cadence down and only occasionally would slip up. After the second day, the Sister she was working under saw she was as good as she said with a needle and thread. She had Rowan follow her and sew up wounds she cleansed and treated.

They became a team; she did not pry into the young woman's affairs and Rowan/Vian did not offer any information. The Sister did not ask. It wasn't until the fourth day she heard news she was listening for on the lips of one of the many still waiting outside for food. As the number of soldiers trickled off and they had ones they already had inside the Church to look after, she was given the task of feeding people outside lined up waiting for food. She heard two of them talking in line as they shuffled up each carrying a wooden bowl.

"She up'd n run, she did, left 'er husband, after she publicly divorced him, and left all dem purty trinkets and servants n all." One old crone was jabbering on about why one would leave a life of wealth. "Maybe, it was 'er 'usband beat 'er, I 'eard he beats up the servant women too. Don't blame 'er then, even after she patched 'im up too. And I also 'eard they took 'er child away, didn't even let 'er 'old im."

The second woman lowered her voice to a whisper, but now she was focused on them, she heard them twenty paces away.

"Well, I 'ope she runs far. The elite think they are so entitled, think they can do what dey want, to whomever dey like."

"If 'e was my 'usband, I'd clip 'im over Da ears, I would!"

This conversation made her smile, and she kept her head down in the cowl of the old but clean green robe the eldest sister gave her. She had to remember to keep her hair short to keep up the appearance of a destitute waif, she glimpsed her reflection in the bucket and while short hair and loss of weight greatly changed her so she didn't even recognise herself, all it would take would be one person to take a close look and recognise her.

She wasn't too worried, she also knew she couldn't stay in the lower city forever. She had the thought if she were as prized as the breeding horses of the Emperor, they may eventually comb the entire city. Little did she know her former husband gave up after a week, and announced he divorced her, he played the victim to her family every chance he got.

"Here you go, Pader."

"May you be Blessed, Dader."

As she spooned out the poor man's soup to the never-ending line, she reflected on how much her life changed in the space of a year. The boring life of a Princess, to the eternal beatings of a savage husband to now, a free woman, a 'pretend' Sister of the faith, more respect than most women of the lower-cased system, but free. This made her smile and the old man in rags she was serving soup to smiled back.

The opportunity to leave presented itself the following month, by way of the Secondary of the Church she was currently staying. She became integrated into the system of helping the needy and actually considered taking the vows until the voice told her it wasn't her path to choose. Others became very persistent and asked questions about where she was from and why she was alone, enough to make her uncomfortable and restless. One afternoon the Secondary called an assembly of all the Sisters and Brothers working.

"There is great need of our assistance on the front lines. We would be doing a service to our God and our Namarch, by seeing to the wounded, burying the dead and gleaning armour. Our Namarch asked us to prepare, and we will be ready. It is our duty. He asks we serve in any capacity we can. We can bring comfort to the soldiers, by getting them hale and hearty. I would ask for volunteers. Who would answer the call?"

"I will." Rulliah looked back at her assistant, Vian nodded. It took a week to prepare their linens and herbs, to which Vian added a few Rulliah hadn't thought of, which made the older woman look harder at the young woman.

Vian went to the apothecary and seamstress on errands for her mentor and they packed horses and wagons alike. Preparations took a few weeks. There were canvas tents to construct. It would be a permanent home away from the Church. Men were to be separate from women, there were many sermons on the dangers of unholy acts, restrictions were reestablished.

Besides the Sisters, women were now required by law to cover their hair, to disobey was to be labeled a loose woman. Vian and several of the younger Sisters whispered in private. They heard and saw beatings abound, of women beaten by their husbands for disobeying the new laws. She was shocked by the amount which began, as though men were wanting to beat for any reason. Vian was glad her uniform was already a hooded robe. She hid under it when she went out on the streets. As a Sister of the Church, she had an amount of respect she would have never gotten living loose on the streets.

They left one sunny morning and headed west to the city gates, which were propped wide open and not a soldier insight. As they rode out from under the buttresses of the gates and into the wilderness, she could not help but straighten her back and place a big grin to her face and hoped they would travel safely to the front. She knew they would have to turn and travel North at some point; the war was raging to the North of them and as she internalised, she felt a pull of something.

The road west took them through farming fields, the grains growing were green and a few fields were beginning to bloom, the yellow flowers starting to show. Other fields were in full bloom with blue flowers and her mentor told her of the different fields and what crop was in each. Vian was looking at the landscape with fresh eyes, she had never been out of her cage, Merida being this cage. The little brown bird was free! She could not stop smiling and the Sister looked at her closely and smiled back at the joy on her novice's face.

They traveled to a crossroads, and headed North, their horse and wagons stopping at wells and inns along the path. As they traveled, they passed many injured soldiers and people and helped who they could. Here the countryside began to change, the fields made way to rolling hills and they meandered around and over them, until they skirted a mountain range to the east. Vian said they were the highest mountains she had ever seen.

"I am sure they are, but the mountains in the North are even higher."

"Oh, really! Maybe one day, I will venture there, if our God wills it so."

"Maybe, you never know."

It took them a month to arrive at the main bulk of the army; they were stopped by many in need. Every night they halted, set up tents, made a meal, and tended to the wounded making their return to the Capital. As they approached the back lines, they were stopped by a Commander's unit and told where they could set up and they chose beside a stream, to access the somewhat fresh running water. The community as a whole set up a few tents, one for the males and one for the females and the larger one for injured.

As they set up, her mentor came to her and spoke softly. "I know who you are, and I don't fault you for it, your path is chosen you must walk it but know you have friends along the way. I hope I can be your friend." Rowan/Vian looked startled as the older woman took both of the young woman's hands in hers and smiled. "Don't worry, I will say nothing and will help with your hair, however, at one point you will have no choice but to grow it. I did see you in your carriage on your way to the Palace, no one would recognize you, now you do look differ-ent, but when you smile, I see the happy girl on the way to her wedding. That was a splendid celebration, it lasted a whole week of food and drink, there were many births I had to deal with nine months later." She chuckled at this, and they finished setting up their supplies in the main tent.

"I will keep your secret, Vian. Excellent choice of name, it means, 'chosen.' I like to think you have chosen it by way of our God."

"Thank you, Rulliah. I have chosen many things, this past month, one of which is to be unfettered. I have chosen to be here, with you and the family of God, to do his service. May I serve well."

"I am sure you will."

After it was known there was a Hospice, they had a never-ending barrage of wounded. They began rotations, and exceedingly long days which sometimes turned into long nights. Sword cuts, amputations, and Vian became incredibly good at musculature. She had a natural talent for fitting pieces of the human puz-zle together. They would lose the worst ones, but such is the nature of battle.

A few times she was sent to assist in the field to glean armour and weapons of the troops and the odd one of the enemies. She saw different metals, same swords, to her as they all looked alike, until one soldier pointed out the difference in curvature of the blade. Then she began to take notice and would ask questions of the men around her, she also noticed the colours of uniforms.

Black and a dark blue were the colours of the Northman of the Aerie, the Ravenswood men proud and dark like the colours they wore, with silver thread and patterns of leaves and roses sewn into the more elaborate uniforms. Silver plated armor and black iron for the most part. Then she saw their flags… a Raven!

There are symbols on their flags. Ravens. The North! Like Tannah said. I must go North. Perhaps after a time here on the battlefield I can leave and travel. This must be what she meant. Northmen must surround me. Now I see other symbols on other flags...a bear... a boar, and many other animals. Why have I never paid attention to this before. Oooo, I should know this. I did learn about the flags of each area of our land. It never had meaning until now. What was Kavus's symbol? Oh, I should know this one...

She could also pick out the green and black of her former husband's regiment. However, there were not many of those men about, they were at the front of the last battle and most died the day of battle. *There are so few, and his symbol is a horse? It should be an ass... I am going to watch for others...now I am out here amidst all this carnage, I am going to learn who has what.* The few men she saw combined other items with their dress, not all kept the green, or the black. Some soldiers had an eclectic mix of armour, gleaned from battle. *I can only hope I do not see Kavus out on the field. Once this battle is done for the winter, I will continue on, although I do not know the way North. Perhaps, I should find Northmen...The Universe will provide.* Lots of Reds and gold, those were the men of her Pader, her symbol was an ox. The fish was on a blue flag, it combined with grays, which looked threadbare and worn she found out those were Islanders' colours. Also, green and browns, those were grasslands and lowlands people, they were quiet folk and didn't say too much when asked.

A few men told her more as they lay in recovery, and she learned all she could as she took care of wounds, the desert people dressed plainly in war and the desert. But in all their city's all colours abounded, tan and golds and browns helped them to blend into their landscape which was barren sand. These were the people who revered women and they had equal status, the few women who fought were shunned by the men of other cultures. The few she saw were quiet and kept to themselves.

One of her patients was a Blacksmith from the Aerie and he liked to speak about his craft, how hot the fire should be, how to hammer the metal and how to quelch the tang of the sword. She let him talk on, not knowing someday she may need to use the information. Furthermore, it was interesting and she would ask questions. It took his mind off injuries, Vian told Rulliah one day when asked. She catered to men in her charge and let them recover in peace as much as she could. She had a soft way about her, she cared for her charges, to the smallest of requests, and they felt better in her presence.

Vian would give them her honest opinion of their injuries, regardless of how bad it was. She would ask them questions of their homelands and learned more about life than from any books she read from tutors. Vian loved to ask questions of her patients, it gave them something else to focus on, other than the pain. She would hold their hand at the end of their time, singing softly as they took their last breath.

"You have a soft way about you, lass. Many a man asks for your care. You are gaining a reputation among the warriors. It is a blessing to our God, you joined us."

"Thank you, Rulliah. I imagine these boys so far away from their homes, away from their families, especially the younger ones, I try to ease their passing, give them comfort. Comfort among the harshness of war eases my heart as well."

"You know you are given the title of 'The Angel of Peace.' Many men talk about you."

"Yes, but it gives them something other than war to focus on. If only I could bring them peace."

"You do, lass. You do. Few would sit with a man as he lay dying. You sing to them; it gives them peace. It eases their spirit in the last breath."

"It is the least I can do, in this war."

CHAPTER 46

Solina

The Seasoned Warrior Does Cease

Solina had fun planning her friends joining, they all agreed it would be held in the Temple and it would be a state affair. Veren did try to argue he wanted non of the pomp, but he was overruled. "You hold an especially prominent position, Admiral of the Dragon Guard."

"I do not want an elaborate affair."

"Too late. The news is broadcasted to the whole city; criers were sent out, and the Dragons will attend. You cannot protest much."

He would have no choice and he finally acceded to his Ruler's decision. Solina met him in the gardens, both were on their way to see the Dragons.

"You cannot argue with this, I am afraid, they offered and is one of the greatest honours they can bestow upon one not yet a Rider."

He looked at her puzzled.

"Nannosh told me Riders of old, when at time of hatching could bond with a newly hatched Dragonette, if conditions were favourable. I do not know the specifics, but when the time comes, I hope you are one of those. We need to solidify our small army, and I will need all the help I can get when the time comes. Now, your joining. We should have it in a few days hence, you can wear your new uniform I had made for you, and Sheyna is busy working on her dress, you will also have a ride in the air, I know you are looking forward to this. Have straps been made?"

"Yes, I have yet to fit them on, I believe I need you there to help with translation, as I do not wish them to think I am tying them up. Sometimes muscle memory in animals, may trigger thoughts their minds have suppressed, I would not wish to be a living torch. The Dragons give me great honour if they think of me as worthy, I will try to live up to their expectations."

"You already have, Veren. They see into your heart. Sheyna and you have worked beyond my expectations; it gladdens my spirit also." He smiled gently and then looked as Sheyna came down again, not as fast as last time, but quick enough.

"High Dragon, both Dragons were swaying and humming, could you please ask them why?" Sheyna did not look as worried, however, concerned.

"Nannosh says another of my Sisters, Earth Mader, has borne a child, the labour was difficult for the woman, and they offered her some encouragement. She lives and is all they tell us."

"Earth Dragon? She is on Du'Lanay? The Dragons know all this?"

"Yes, Atalay felt their presence, and our Dragons can feel their energy."

"Well, it seems the Dragons can reach out to others, we should go up there and make sure all is well." Sheyna was always looking out for her charges, this made Solina smile. Veren said he would grab the straps and meet them there. He smiled at the tiny woman, they shared a look, and he headed to the barracks.

The women walked up the hill and around the corner to see the Dragons resting. Solina could not help but comment they really took the resting bit to heart. Nannosh opened one eye and told her.

"In reaching out to the Earth Mader, we expended some of our energy, it has tired us, because we are not properly bonded. Analaria is weaker than me, and because of it, she needs more rest. Once we are bonded, the connection between human and Dragon uses no energy at all, we feel what each other feels, the connection is ...complete. Analaria is like ahhh... food source on four legs running through a field and any one of us could snatch it out of the field and use it for food, which is what our energy is like. If a Rider needs us, for life or death, we must help preserve in what way we can. I am afraid another may set her back, she and I can waste no more time, after the joining of our two small humans, we will begin our journey. We will only tell you where we are headed, so as to not bring peril behind us." Solina's face fell, and she wondered what she would do, once her Dragon was no longer there.

"You and I are bonded, we will always be, in spirit, once I have reached my destination, I will tell you. However, I see my small Little Mader is worried, she needs you to reassure her."

Solina told Sheyna and Veren, as he arrived, what her Dragon told her. While Sheyna was sad, Veren was pragmatic.

"Once the Dragons are gone, then no one will be able to take their lives."

"I couldn't agree more." Solina while sad, saw the logic in their absence.

They spent the rest of the morning outfitting the straps to the Dragon's, making adjustments, with Sheyna climbing on top of Analaria, who could barely lift her head, and only for a short time. Sheyna insisted they would set up stations on the other Islands so the Dragons could stop at and have their fill of meats, and Solina said it would be done. Veren said he would send men who were with them since the beginning to each Island and train men there on what to expect.

They fed the Dragons and Nannosh said by nightfall they would fly to the ocean and feed off sea meat, and by tomorrow, Analaria would be better.

The day of joining arrived, with both Sheyna and Veren nervous, and excited, Analaria was feeling better, and straps were placed on the Dragons. The Temple was packed with nobles from the city and outlying Islands, the ceremony was the highlight of everyone's day and was spoken about years later.

Sheyna and Veren spoke their vows in front of the assembly, the Dragons had walked down the hill. With their bodies tucked behind one of the stone walls, they placed their heads behind each of the participants on the other side of the wall, Analaria behind Sheyna, and Nannosh behind Veren. After words of vows were spoken, the Dragons raised their heads and breathed on the two. Solina then turned to the two and the assembly.

"With the breath of the Dragon, this union is blessed, may you continue to serve until your last breath. May you both be Blessed."

There was a lot of oooh's and ahhh's in the congregation, as Veren unsheathed his ceremonial sword and took a knee before Solina and the onlooking Dragon's. Solina looked at the kneeling man before her… This was not in the rehearsal.

"I, Veren, do solemnly swear, before all the Gods and the Dragon's as my witness, I will to the best of my ability, honour the oaths set before me. I also swear to protect these incredible beings before us now. Upon all I hold dear, and the strength of spirit. I will serve until my last breath and will under the guidance of the Pader lead our people, under the guidance of the Mader protect our people, under the guidance of the Uncle lead our people forward with strength, under the guidance of the Aunt give the promise of love and health to our people, under the guidance of the Sister teach our people mercy and under the guidance of the Brother keep all oaths before me. We are blessed to witness the rebirth of our people, and I will protect our way of life and the Blessed of the Gods to the last breath of this body."

His speech took everyone by surprise, and Sheyna crying, followed suit, she also pledged her life to protecting the Dragon's.

Solina amazed, looked around, her eyes gently glowing and saw the whole congregation also lower to their knees and with one voice, they also pledged their lives to the protection of the Dragons. The Dragons once the congregation finished the last sentence, lifted their heads into the air, and trumpeted loudly and breathed fire into the sky. The people in the city, as the rumour flew down, cheered, and toasted to the health of the new couple and the Dragons.

Solina looked at the congregation rising, dusting off, placed her hands in the air and requested silence, she asked Nannosh for help in projecting her voice and as she spoke, the city heard her down to the lapping of the ocean on the beach in the port.

"The Dragons hear your pledge, and will honour their end to the death, you will also honour your pledge to the end of your last breath." She thought to add this last bit,

"Who so ever cannot uphold their honour will have to answer to my breath, I swear this, I will not tolerate duplicity in my people, you have a duty to protect our way of life, do you yield?"

Judging by the roar of the people in the city, they threatened to challenge the volume of the Dragons. She turned to the Dragons and to the newly weds. "Are you ready to give them all a show? Make me proud and show what our new nation is all about."

"LET THIS BE A TESTAMENT TO BE TAKEN TO ALL CORNERS OF THE WORLD THAT DRAGONS ARE HERE TO STAY, AND THE WAYS OF THE GODS WILL BE RESURRECTED!"

The three of them walked around to the Dragons behind the stone wall, and Veren helped Sheyna seat herself and placed her feet in the loops they fashioned, giving her loops she could hang onto, and after she reassured her new husband she was secure, he walked over to Nannosh and he leaned his head against her neck. "I thank you for this blessed honour. I will forever guard and protect you, till my dying breath." She bent her head around to look at him, blinked at him. He nodded to her, mounted, and secured himself and the two Dragons rose into the air.

The Dragon's swooped through the air, blew spouts of fire, banked over the city, with the city cheering when they came close. They flew over a few more passes, and then to everyone's astonishment they flew away to the east. Solina addressed the crowd, "They have spotted a ship coming close and decided they would escort them in, Veren stated it is a vessel from Aram. We will invite the Ambassador of such to the wedding celebrations, this should go out into the world, and we will begin with Aram."

She turned to look at Atin and Kaisan. To Kaisan she said, "You will of course be our translator."

"Yes, High Dragon, it would be my honour."

She sent two regiments to the port, addressing Kallen as he was promoted to acting Marshall.

"Have the way lined with guards. Doors are to be closed, the most direct route. Temples are to be shuttered, even in the wake of our celebrations, no need to show off wealth. No harm is to come to the people who alight from the ships. Have the crews housed in the lower barracks by the markets. Only the Captains and Ambassadors are heavily escorted up here. Spread the word no harm, physical or verbal will be tolerated from our people. I want this point made perfectly clear. Give Aram no cause, they will be humbled enough by the sight of the Dragons. Line the path with pennants, cover the windows with them, if you must. Clean the path, I want it spotless."

"Yes, High Dragon, it will be done. Come on men, you heard the orders. Let's move!"

She motioned the attendees into the Reception Hall for the joining supper to begin and she would bring the couple when they landed. Solina and her GrandMader stayed in the pasture behind the Temple to wait for the bride and groom.

"I could not be prouder of you as I have today, Lina. I was afraid my heart would burst from this shell. You have lit the fire in our people, may the rest of the world quake at what transpired today. The Dragon's escorting the ship in is a touch of genius, we hear their message and send them off. They will tell all that they were blessed by the Gods and lived to talk about it."

"I wish I managed the walk in the city better. I was awed by Atin's demeanor. She was fervent in her speech. Kaisan is walking softly around her."

"He is still Aram in his heart. He does not know how to manage a woman who has an opinion."

"Yes, he is very polite around me and does not let his guard down. I worry it will not work for Atin, and she will have her heart broken."

"Sometimes this needs to happen to grow into what the Universe would have one become. It is nothing you can stop or assist."

"Yes, I heed your words. Live from lessons even the hard ones."

"I had many years to regret how I treated your Mader and her sister. It weighed heavy on me, until I saw the young woman you were becoming. I see a spark of both my girls in you it gives me belief again."

"You have given me all this knowledge; beyond what I thought I knew. It has created a thirst to know more."

"I am glad. You come by this directly from me. I was driven, hungry for learning. Never give this up, there are many things I do not know."

Solina laughed, she gazed at her GrandMader who was smiling at her, the glow in her eyes much softer. "Tell me, what you do not know, then? I am curious."

"Well, I have always wanted to know what the lands of Aram look like. See their lands, their people. I have only seen the ones who come to the markets, and the Ambassadors when they are brokering for something. I have never seen the Maelstrom Sea."

"Not sure you would wish to. I hear its extremely dangerous to get too close. Once it gets you in its grip, it does not let go."

"Hmmm, I have only seen snow once. But not been in the North when it was the heart of winter, and I know not the language of the Wanderers. I know a bit of Lanthian, but not enough."

"Well, you don't know everything. I am impressed you know some Lanthian. Is it a difficult language?"

"Not really, it is guttural, however, most people speak the Collective Speech. It is the way for the last four hundred years. Only when peoples separate do barriers arise."

"I hope with the Dragons being from different lands we find common ground. If we have language barriers, it will be a hard go of it, in the beginning."

"I am sure you will all be one, in mind. This is a difficult world to conquer."

"Yes, but we have the advantage of Dragons."

"Yes, we do."

In the sky as they watched for the Dragon's they both saw the same thing at the same time. It was the star, and they saw it in the sky with a red tail.

"The breath of the Dragon. It is real."

Her GrandMader breathed out in awe. "The Prophecy is coming to pass."

She hugged her GrandDader and they watched as the Dragon's came into sight, and landed, the two Riders on their backs grinning from ear to ear. Veren dismounted and with a quick touch to the neck of Nannosh he went over to Sheyna. After peeling her hands off the straps and taking her feet out of the looped stirrups, carried her over to Analaria's head to which they gave their thanks, then walked towards the waiting women. The Dragons lifted off and went to the sea on the other side of the mountain where they would feed and lay down for a nap.

The two newlyweds walked hand in hand and exclaimed over the ride; it was the best thing they ever experienced. After exchanging hugs, they walked back to the Hall and Solina entered first.

"Good People, I have the pleasure in announcing Admiral Veren of the Dragon Guard and his new wife Sheyna, beloved of the Dragon's."

"Hear, Hear. Yahhhh! Cheers! Many blessings!"

The whole hall rose to their feet and cheered. The din rose with a chant of "Dragon Guard, Dragon Guard!"

After all the pleasantries and toasts were done and they sat down for the feast, Solina remembered the ship and the people they housed within the apartments of the Palace.

"Veren, would you mind if the Ambassador from Aram joins your feasting? I would like to gauge his temperament. We won't discuss any business. Only by your leave, if you don't mind."

"Not at all, High Dragon. A good way to impress and observe without appearing to do so. I fully agree." A servant was dispatched to relay the order.

The Ambassador and his man came in, Solina saw Kaisan's facial expression changed to incredulous to happiness to apprehension. She beckoned for them to approach, and the young man bowed and introduced himself, Kaisan translated, not knowing Solina could understand their language.

"I have the pleasure of introducing Tovan, second son of the great FirPader of Aram… my older brother."

Solina nodded her assent, and the man said more things which Kaisan translated. "He says relations between the two nations was even more crucial now Dragons were once more flying the skies. He humbly asks for an audience at the High Dragon's convenience, he did not wish to interrupt the celebrations."

"I agree but tonight is a night of celebration. We request you enjoy the night festivities, and we will address business on the morrow. Please, have a seat and enjoy." She placed herself beside Atin, so she could better hear any conversation between the two brothers. Solina and Atin talked about the star in the sky. Enjoying the dancers at one point, sitting there and drinking, she honed her hearing in the direction of the men, sitting there also drinking and speaking quietly. "Tell me truth, what is the real reason you are here.?" Kaisan all but whispered it to his brother. The two men did not look alike except for their eyes and smiles, they had different Maders.

Tovan whispered back. "Your Pader will reinstate you, if you come back... we have had a sickness spread around the nobility, and we are affected..."

Tovan looked at his little brother, sadness etching his features.

"I am not sure I wish to know. Pader was adamant about his decision. How can he go back on his word when he said it was for the good of the Empire, how? And who?"

"Well, first we have lost the bulk of the Harem, and a few of the little ones…." Here his voice trailed off. His head bowed.

Kaisan looked at him in alarm, and both girls looked at the two men. Solina heard the sadness and knew from Kaisan's expression what was coming next was not going to be good news.

"Your two little sisters, Kamis, and Nowl, and our older brother Akishen." Kaisan gasped and his grip on Atin's hand tightened. Akishen was heir to the Throne. Now the man sitting beside him was the heir apparent, and it must be important enough to send him. Kaisans eyes filled with tears which threatened to spill out.

"That's not all, is it? Pader wants me back to keep the line alive. I am to marry if I denounce this marriage?" Tovan nodded, he kept his head down and Solina saw the emotion in the clenching of his jaw.

"Your Mader sent me; she is also sick… she wishes to see you. I promised her I would come here to get you, as it may be the last time you see her." Kaisan looked shaken, his skin had paled, and he looked as though he was going to faint again. Solina tried to school her features to curiosity. She was not willing to let it be known to the two men, she knew their conversation. Atin was curious, she did not know anything other than Collective Speech. Solina tucked it away in the back of her mind, Atin would benefit from some tutoring.

"Kaisan, Darling? Is it sad news? Would it be untoward if we snuck away early? You don't look well." Kaisan nodded.

"Solina, would you excuse us. I am not feeling well, the smells in here are setting my stomach off." Solina smiled knowingly. She played along with the ruse. She knew Atin's heart was naive, she would chat with her sister later.

"Yes, if you are not feeling well, by all means we can reconvene in the morrow, let's say late morning. This gives you some rest. The Ambassador is welcome to stay if he likes. There is plenty more food dishes to be served."

"The Ambassador thanks you, but says as it was a long trip, plus the sight of the Dragons has left him exhausted and he begs your leave to retire also." The three of them walked out. Solina went to sit beside her GrandMader and told her what she heard.

"Well, it is obvious the FirPader of Aram wants his son back at all costs, if there is a plague or not, you will have to decide. But Atin cannot go with him, if she were to go there, they would do horrible things to her, baby or not, she is after all a Dragon. She represents something they cannot let live; it undermines everything they have built over the course of centuries. I can't see them denying their faith, the FirPader has always believed himself to be the Almighty himself, but Kaisan has not always been a true believer, I see this about him, he is more open to the possibility of change. It is this alone which makes him a pleasure to discuss with."

"You are right. Atin cannot go. I did not think of this, they would kill her for sure. Even Kaisan would not be able to stop it. She should know of the possibility. Aram is known to act and ask the questions after. Oh, this is going to be difficult. What should I do?"

"Well, let's find out exactly what they would like. I suspect, from what you overheard they want Kaisan back. The sickness could be real or a ruse to get him to return. I will inquire from my Captains on the legitimacy of this 'sickness.' I suspect 'tis real enough if many perished from it. Think of the outcome, all aspects of every decision made. I have given you the tools, now, you tell me what you think."

"Well. He could stay or he could leave. If he stays and his Mader passes, then he will be sad and may eventually blame Atin for holding him back."

"Yes, 'tis one possible outcome. Keep going…"

"If he leaves, there are two outcomes to this, he could return or he could not. If he doesn't, he is in the line to becoming the next FirPader, and if he does, there is the possibility he is a spy, we are going to watch him either way. Atin won't like it if he stays and his Mader dies, she will blame herself, and she will not like him leaving, she will miss him. And if he leaves, she will be heartbroken. This is such a dilemma."

"Yes. think of every possibility. That way if one comes to pass, you are already prepared. I have had many years to hone this. I want you to be better than I was, so you are better prepared for the disappointments. Turn those into accomplishments."

"I don't think I can be better than you, you know everything."

"You will become better than I, you already are. This is all I can do, give you the knowledge to rule, you have caught on amazingly fast. Your cousin will appreciate this. Everyone brings something to the table; I am sure you will be well rounded."

"What if we are not? I do not want to be the Ruler. The Purity Rider was the leader in past history. She may not want or like I know more than her."

"She may not, but it is something you need not worry about now. You think of every possibility. However, also think on this, you are all women. Only two of you are from the Islands. Atin does not know how to read or write. You do. The Islands are equal with knowledge, man, and women alike. You may be the only woman who has learning. One woman is Aram; they do not teach women to read or write. The other three are on Du'Lanay. They do not teach women to read or write there, unless they are nobility.

The odds of you being the only learned woman will be a disadvantage until the others become educated. They may have to lean on you for any decision which requires knowing all languages. 'Tis to your benefit to learn all you can. You can serve the whole better for it. It may not be a choice when the time comes, however, better to address when 'tis the time. Perhaps we continue this discussion later and enjoy the festivities. I see Veren and Sheyna look like they would like to retire. I have given you something to consider. Until our next discussion?"

"Yes, Gran. I agree with you, on this note, let's go to see the happy couple." Solina rose and went to the newlyweds. They were smiling like their faces were permanently in enjoyment, but Solina saw they wanted their time alone.

"Are we able to depart with little fuss?"

"Certainly. I will host for a while longer. We can convene late morning. I am sure everyone will be wishing a late start to the day. You both have my congratulations on your joining. I could not wish anymore happiness on a better couple. You both have my sincere wishes."

"We thank you, and the Dragons for blessing our union. If you could provide us with a distraction…"

Solina laughed and went forward to ask the musicians play a robust and hearty song, to provide the dancers with merriment. It had the congregation, the more inebriated ones, singing to the tune. The married couple disappeared amid the chorus. Solina sang along with others, and Marshall Kallen came up to Solina.

"High Dragon, may I have a moment of your time?"

"Certainly, what is it? Are you on duty? Is there something amiss?"

Solina for a moment looked worried, then realized Kallen was in his ceremonial dress. Her face when she realized, relaxed at the same time he responded.

"No. We are fine. I was wondering…"

Solina looked at the young red-haired man, who was trying to not sway with the amount of drink he consumed. Plus, the colour of his red face… she was trying to determine if it was his shyness or consumption causing it.

"I am going to stop you, before you say something you may regret in the morning, or perhaps not remember. I will speak with you, when you are sober, Kallen. You are a fine officer, and stalwart. I would not have you say anything to deter my thoughts on you. My focus is on my Dragons, until we are not graced with their presence, then it will be to follow them. I like you, but I have no other thoughts beyond this. I have no time to be entertaining anything other than my Dragons. Have I answered the question you were wishing to ask?"

Kallen looked crestfallen, and for a moment, she thought he was going to argue, the alcohol making him brave. She saw the thoughts running across his face, and it became redder. He bowed and tried not to fall, then straightened and a few of his cohorts moved in, as they saw by the expression on his face, it was not going to end well for him. A few men moved in under his arms. She grinned at his companions.

"You had better remove him, and quickly. He needs a commode, or a garden patch…take him outside. Quick!"

They rushed him outside, as his eyes began to roll back and they lifted him up. Solina knew he would not remember, so she wondered if she was indeed doing what was good for both. *The poor man needed to drink to gather his courage. I think I will need to have a chat with him when he's sobered. I know he likes me. I like him, but I have no time for a dalliance, or thoughts of joining. I certainly hope he feels better in the morning.*

Solina clapped her hands to get the attention of the crowd.

"I am going to have to ask that celebrations end, at least in this portion of the Palace. If you wish to continue, then by all means, do. I am retiring. I thank you all for joining us, in this wonderful celebration of our Admiral and our Mader of the Dragons. I bid you all a good night."

She spoke to the Head Chamberlain. He assured her he would take care of lingering guests. Solina walked to her rooms and went to bed. Not tired, she read for a time, listening to the sounds of merriment coming from the Grand Hall. It was another hour before it grew quiet. She put her book down and fell asleep.

She woke up a little later than she would have liked but was in no rush to get going. About mid morning, she requested the Ambassador to attend her. Kaisan and Atin were in attendance. They all met in the Great Hall, she placed herself on the Dais chair, Atin sitting beside her. Solina asked him what they wanted. Kaisan again translated.

"High Dragon," Kaisan began, but his brother had said, Her Excellency. She tried not to smile.

"We are here, on a diplomatic mission, we would like to have the Water Dragon's husband attend his Mader, who is unwell, at her home, in Aram, if you would release him for a small amount of time." She noticed a few discrepancies in the wording of his request but still said nothing.

"He would attend his Mader, and observe the funerals of his sisters and brother, and return within the month."

Here she looked closely at the two men. "Do not the funeral rites of Aram, require a month long of mourning?"

The men looked startled. "I read books on your country, learned about your rituals, and your religion, and have a smattering knowledge of your peoples and lands. To know one's enemy, one must know all about them."

"Is that what you think of me?" Kaisan asked her. She saw Kaisan had taken her words to heart and was still uneasy around Solina.

"No, but historically Aram and Du'Lanay are. You have denounced your faith, your country, your family, given all up for love, you do not remember? You are now Pelinese by choice." She looked at him closely. He bowed his head. She continued, addressing Tovan.

"You have permission to leave; I can not hold you here against your will. I will however ask Atin remain here, for her safety."

Atin looked at her and she very kindly said to her sister, "If there is a plague, I do not want to hear you were exposed and succumbed. There is your baby to think of. I do not want to let Kaisan go. He will have to quarantine when he returns, for a while to make sure he doesn't bring the disease back, but we can discuss this later. I am only thinking of you and the baby, you heard him he will be back before a month's time. I do not want to lose you or the child you carry; we have only found each other."

Kaisan came up the step, took his wife's hands, and gave her hand a kiss. "I will not leave for another day, and Solina has the right of it. I do not want you exposed to this sickness either. I would hate to lose you both. You are my life, my breath, and I can not live without either."

They exchanged a kiss, and held each other as Solina said, "Well, it is settled then, you shall leave and return when you are done what you need to do. Shall we send you back with some gifts?"

When Kaisan protested, Solina said the Dragon's insisted. A large chest was brought in, ornate and covered in Mader of Pearl and various gems, six colours to be exact, she was sending a specific message to the FirPader. "You will give this to the FirPader, and this is proof the Dragons exist. Of course, the testimony of everyone who has seen them, should appease the doubters. You can also point out the Dragon Star; the Breath of the Dragon is also happening. The Vendar Prophecy is coming to pass, regardless of the denial of the Namanists and the religion of your homeland."

She rose to her feet. "This assembly is now concluded; I will retire and go see my charges. When you are to set sail, I will officially see you off."

Solina stepped down and smiled at the trio as she left the reception room. She walked down the hall and heard the sound of footsteps hurriedly catching up to her. Solina turned around to see Veren and smiled at the man. "Are you not supposed to be with your bride? What can possibly take you away from her?"

"A very upset man…"

"Oh, do not tell me… Kallen." Solina turned and kept walking. Veren matching strides.

"Yes. He was very drunk last night. He thinks he may have said something to upset you and is worried he will be demoted. Or worst, cast out."

"He said nothing."

"He didn't? The way he put it to me, you cut him down."

"I did nothing of the sort. I stopped him short. I did not want him to say something he would regret. I may have been curt. (sigh) I know he likes me, Veren."

"The man worships you. Sorry, High Dragon. He does."

"I know. Which is why I did not want him to say something drink encouraged. I do not want worship. I want what you and Sheyna have. A friendship first. Is this so bad?"

"It would be hard to do in your position, if you don't mind my observation." Solina looked at Veren sadly. He began to apologize; she held up her hand. They cleared the gardens and were heading up the path. Guards were stationed sporadically around the woods. She was pleased to see the celebrations had not interfered with the detail. "Which is why I stopped him. Does he worship me for my position? Does he see past all this?" She waved her hands around her head.

"I am the High Dragon. First and foremost. But before this, I was just a girl. Looking to have friends. That's all I ever wanted. I have Sheyna. She knows me best… I have Atin, we are sisters with a common thread, being a Dragon. She wants a friend also."

"She has her husband, Solina."

"Somehow, I am not sure they are friends… not like you and Shey. I think their marriage is more…the physical, than the spiritual. Just a feeling. Please do not say this to her."

"I will not. I do not know her well enough to say such things. You have my word. I see this also. He does not seem to be truthful around her and us, for this matter. I am not sure I trust him, call it intuition, call it mistrust. Call it what you like."

"Atin says his aura is truthful. She sees him in a different light than you and I."

"Well, she may be only seeing what he presents to her. He may be truthful, but he may only be sharing what he wishes her to know."

"You get this from him also? I thought I was the only one who thought this." They arrived at the Dragons. Both were sleeping and she turned to Veren.

"I thank you for the escort, however, I think you should be spending time with Shey. You are a newlywed; in case you have forgotten."

Veren laughed. He looked tired but happy. "Shey wanted some time to bath and have a rest. I told Kallen I would speak to you. He is extremely worried of his position."

"Is that all he is worried about?"

"No. He was more worried about you… that you would think ill of him. I saw it, I know him well enough."

"Veren. I know he's shy. Hence the amount of drink he consumed, to gather his bravado. However, I do not wish to converse with a drunkard. He will have to speak to me, at some point, I would prefer him sober."

"He may not be able to. He's always been shy around women, not just you. Plus, he thinks himself not good enough for any woman, he's been this way since I have known him. He comes from the lower city. His Da was a fisherman, I think."

"I care not where any man comes from. 'Tis what is inside of him, Kallen has proven himself to be brave, and loyal. I cannot ask for anything better. I am not looking for a partner, anyway. I want friends, Veren. That's all. If I find a friend, this is all the riches I want. No, you should get back, before Shey comes looking for you."

Veren laughed again. He looked behind Solina and smiled. "Oh, you mean looking after her charges? Here she comes, I am not sure she was looking for me. These Dragons are her babies. They may take precedence."

Solina turned as her friend came up and placed her arm around her husband. Shey looked up as Veren kissed his wife. Solina smiled at the two lovebirds.

"Somehow, I knew you two would be up here. I was right. Did you tell her about Kallen?"

"Yes, he did. I stopped Kallen before he could disgrace himself. I may have been abrupt in my methods. Veren tells me Kallen is worried about being de-moted."

"Hmmm, he was more worried you would think him a drunkard and the worst sort. When Veren left, Kallen began crying. He is most distraught."

Veren looked thoughtful. He looked at Solina. "He may have it worse than worship, Solina. I have only seen the man cry once before. When his Mader passed."

Solina looked back at the pair. "He is feeling the aftereffects of too much drink, it makes the emotions more vibrant."

"Yes. but having him cry…" Sheyna looked at her friend. "He is genuinely concerned, more about what you will think than losing his position. He does not remember much, just the way he said you cut him off. He thinks he may have said something inappropriate."

"I told Veren, I cut him off before he could say anything he would regret. I know he likes me. One would have to be blind not to see it. Nannosh told me I need to see all, know what it is all persons show who are around me, not only the ones who are not Vendar. I have wracked my thoughts on how to deal with such, but other than not dealing with it, how do you think I should proceed? I want what you have with Veren, here. A friend."

Shey looked at her husband, and he hugged her tighter. Kissing her forehead, he looked at Solina. "Perhaps, it would be better coming from you. Shey and I can ease his mind you will not exile him from the Islands, but sometimes the best way is directly from the Dragon's maw."

Solina laughed. "You two, go on, make haste! I will have a talk with him. You need not say anything. Let him stew in his own thoughts. It may help him sober up."

Solina turned to Nannosh who had one eye open and was patiently waiting. The couple left, already forgetting about the Dragon's, the High Dragon, and the man who was distraught. Solina looked at her Dragons and brought the jug of oil out of her satchel.

"I came to tend to you. As much as I have oil. Have you any spots which need immediate attention?"

"Mostly in the wing joints if you care to climb up. I thank you."

Solina climbed up with the jug and the cloth she pulled out. She poured oil onto the linen and began to rub. She started with the large joint closest to the shoulder.

"You seem thoughtful, Little One. Is it the man who adores you?"

"Is it adoration? I do not know what to do. I do not feel the same about him. How should I proceed?"

"Hmmm, Dragons do not have these feelings. We mate with the strongest, of course, in my situation, there is only one male. It is simplified for me."

"I have no need for a fight over my breeding rights, Nann. Humans are more complex."

"You are very much right on your observation. In the last days, there was much fighting over breeding. You can only tell him what is on your mind and what is in your heart. If you do not want to breed, then tell him."

"I seem to be too direct. He was only hearing the tone of my telling, not the words."

"Perhaps we should go over some of your talents. Try to visualize a circle of air around us."

The air became yellow around the two.

"No, merely think of a circle. Yes, that's better. I will explain. The circle which surrounds us, is our place. If you expand this, yes. Try a Dragon length, you notice the energies which are inside. What do you feel?"

"Hmmm, I sense...tiredness, some adoration...another is ill, no...still a bit inebriated. That's not good. Oh, some satisfaction, more adoration. What am I looking for?"

"Now, focus on the adoration. Focus more... you can dissect the energy down to what makes it. Here, let me show you. The adoration. 'Tis for the Dragons...this man is a firm believer in Vendar. You see the different layers of his love."

"Oh, much like the ripples on water when one drops a pebble in."

"Yes, much like that. But you deal with air, or levels of one's energy which act like the ripples in water. You see the outer layer, then move in, and see what else makes up a human spirit. All the way until you find yourself inside. Yes, now you see his love of his wife, also his offspring, and at the heart, or center of the energy levels, is his love for the Gods."

Solina had stopped oiling, while she was learning this from Nannosh, and she saw a familiar head of red coming up the path. She bent down to the jug and poured more on the cloth. *"I have a feeling you taught me this, so I could practice on the man coming towards me."*

She felt the Dragon's intentions in her head. She smiled and rubbed vigorously. She felt outward. She could feel tiredness… a bit of illness of the stomach, she smiled to herself. Kallen must have indulged a lot! Then she could feel the adoration, and her smile disappeared. She stopped and became still, she felt inwards, she could sense desire, and she hesitated to go further. *"You need to go past it, even if it is distasteful to you."*

"It's uncomfortable, not distasteful."

She delved further, she could sense, the shyness, was insecurity, she felt the hesitancy which stemmed from his status of birth, and he was illiterate. So, he was feeling inferior. To her!

"So, you see what it is which drives ones spirit. You can sense this if you concentrate on a spirit's energy. It will give you an insight on who would be your enemy and who would be your friend."

"I thank you. I would like to use this on Kaisan when he comes back. So I can gauge his temperament for Atin."

"She may not wish to hear what it is you might find. One must learn from ones own mistakes. 'Tis what is helping you to grow into your role."

"So, you are not telling me he may not be completely Vendar..."

"I was not telling you anything about the Sea Dragon's mate. She may have to find her own path forward. With or without her mate. Now, I think you have left yours standing there for a time..." Solina gasped, Nannosh had implied…

"You will gauge him, on your own time. I meant not what I said, Little One. He is respectfully waiting for us to finish. You must find your own path, from what you learn. Not what others tell you. I have made you think on this."

"Thank you, for helping me to see."

Solina came out of her thoughts to see the young man of her conversation standing there. He was not looking right at her, but he looked up when she moved her position. Solina smiled at the tired and saddened man. He cleared his throat.

"High Dragon."

"Yes, Marshal? How can I help you?"

Since formal was how he was going to begin, she would reciprocate back. Solina grabbed the linen and jug and placed them to the side. She rose and stood, then moved over to Nannosh's shoulder. She did not want to put a strain on the joint she was oiling. Leaning against the withers, she looked down upon the man who was craning his neck. He swallowed and spoke.

"I would like to offer my apologies for my behavior last night. I may have said something to earn your ire..."

She crossed her arms and frowned. "Oh, did you ever...I am not pleased."

She was trying so hard not to smile. He would have to learn to relax around her, if ever they were to become friends. His face dropped with her comment and then dropped to his knees. She straightened.

"Please, High Dragon, I meant no disrespect. I will take any punishment you deem fit. I cannot remember exactly what I said, but if you were to enlighten me, I promise to never again earn your anger."

His head was bowed and she was not going to give him any more angst. She saw he was truly in agony over the events of last night.

"I think you said you could beat me at oiling my Dragon..."

He looked up suddenly to see his object of adoration smiling down on him with humour. He watched her, not believing what he heard.

"I did? I don't remember saying that..."

"You did! Care to have a go?"

Kallen stood up and looked quizzingly at Solina. "You are jesting, right? I said this? I feel it was on a different path..."

Solina slid down the side of Nannosh's leg to land on her boots. She walked the one step to the man she now had to look up at; his face started to redden.

"Perhaps you did, perhaps you didn't. But since you seem to think you said something wrong, I could not help but tease you. You were very drunk last night. I think you may have fertilized a few bushes."

Kallen looked very chagrined. "Yes, my stomach revolted many times. It may have been more than a few. I still feel the effects. My apologies, High Dragon."

"Say it, Kallen."

"Say what, High Dragon. I am sorry? I am sorry."

"No. Say my name."

"High Dragon."

"Solina."

"Solina."

"There. That wasn't so bad."

"I cannot say it; you are the High Dragon."

"Kallen, you saved me from an arrow. It would have hit me, in the shoulder, if you had not moved into its path. You have leave to call me by my name."

"It would have hit you right where it was aimed. In your heart. I was only doing my duty."

Solina saw his passion was his duty. She could only surmise she needed to draw him out of his shell. She turned and climbed back up the leg to grab the jug and linen, and without missing stride she threw the jug down at the intent man.

He caught it and held it against his body. She slid down the leg again. "Nice catch. You game to beat me?"

He smiled, she sensed he was catching on to her innuendo. "I am quite sure you are having me on. But yes, I am game to beat you. What exactly are we doing?"

"We are oiling up the scales. The ones with less gloss to them. The flesh underneath is dry. We oil them and it will absorb into the flesh. It helps to soften, so the flesh does not crack and get infected. You can have this side. The middle point is the breastbone. Here's a linen cloth. We see who can oil the fastest. Mind, we oil thoroughly. Not wiping the scales, we get underneath."

Solina handed him the cloth and he moved to the side she indicated. She placed the jug in between them. She showed him by wetting the rag and he did the same, then she showed him what she meant.

"So, we lift the scale and wipe under it? Will it not hurt her?"

"We just lift enough to wipe; it would hurt her if we were careless."

"Ahhh, like this?"

"Yes, just like that."

"Then may the best man win. Or in your case, woman. Or would that be Dragon…" Solina began to wipe, and this had Kallen turn to the scales and he began. For a time, there was silence. She noticed Kallen had taken to his duty with some enthusiasm. She thought to stir it up. She wadded up the rag and threw it at him. It connected with his cheek and made him stop. He looked at her as the rag fell and he caught it as it dropped. "What was that for?"

"You looked too serious. You are not smiling."

"I was concentrating, High…Solina. This is enjoyable, I have never done this duty before."

"Duty, is it? May I have my cloth back, please?" Kallen handed it back to her, Solina rolled her eyes. As he gave it back, he waited until she grabbed it, then he grabbed her hand with the cloth in it and brought it to her face. He mushed the oil-soaked rag into her face. She stood there, spitting and blinking her eyes. He smiled, but then as she did not, his smile disappeared.

"Oh, I am sorry. You said you wanted the cloth back. My hand slipped. Please forgive the jest." Solina wiped her eyes on her sleeve. She blinked again. She smiled through her watering eyes. "I asked for that. My eyes are watering, the oil got into them, I cannot see."

"Just hold still. Have you any dry cloths?"

"In the satchel I brought. There is one more." She stood there and leaned against Nannosh's breast. *"Little One…"*

"Not now, Dear Heart. I would not put him on edge. I feel his energy more relaxed." Kallen returned and handed the cloth to her. Solina pretended to not grab the cloth.

"Can you wipe, please? I cannot."

"May I touch you, High Dragon?"

"Oh, please, Kallen. Just wipe this mess from my face. Since you are the one to put it there. I won't bite you." She felt the cloth gently wiping her face around her closed eyes, so soft she could barely feel it. She reached up and grabbed his hand. It was warm and slightly greasy. She took the cloth and wiped her eyes. Once she could see, she saw Kallen before her, he stepped back and looked uncomfortable.

"I see I have made you uncomfortable again. I am sorry. Shall we move away from the front of Nannosh, she would like to lower her head."

They moved away, and the Dragon rested her head, down on the spot they were standing on. Kallen began to redden again. She wondered if he was ever going to be comfortable in her presence. She started to pick up the jug. He came forward and took it from her hands. "Please, let me carry it for you."

"Thank you, I will gather the cloths. Kallen, tell me, do you fear me?"

"Ummm, no, not at this moment. You are formidable when you are angry. I would not want to be on the receiving end of it."

Solina then knew that it would take more time to get him to be comfortable with her. He took his duty seriously, even when she tried to lighten the mood. She thought to be more direct. She stopped walking and looked at the young man. "Kallen. I like you, however, I am at a point in my life where all this..." She waved her hands around her. "Has become my life. I grew up in an orphanage. Believing myself to have no family. Sometimes I still find myself alone. In my thoughts, and even when I am in a crowd. All I would like, is friends. This new life I have, is very intimidating, sometimes, I feel overwhelmed. I know I can be abrupt. I apologize if I was this with you. I would like it, if you can see yourself, someday being my friend. I will leave you with this. Thank you for your assistance with the oiling, although I feel that I may have acted a bit too familiar when you have not."

Kallen looked uncomfortable, but his shoulders lowered with her confession. He answered her, with more ease than when he came to see her. "You have a friend in me, but I have my duty to protect you. I understand what you feel, I am alone with my thoughts. Being in the guards is all I ever wanted to do. I thank you for not demoting me, I will strive to be more... less of a disappointment to you."

"You do not disappoint me, Kallen. Although I think you learned more is not necessarily better..."

"Me and my stomach, I indulged way too much." Solina laughed. Kallen smiled down at her. They resumed walking, down to the Palace. They walked in silence, comfortably. Well, perhaps he did.

"You seem happy? Did it go well?"

"He will take some time to relax around me, but I am in no rush for a 'mate.' I do like him. He just feels he is less, than I. 'Tis a matter of status at birth."

"Then all is well with you. I am sleepy, this sun is warm on my scales. Thank you for the oiling, but you missed a few spots."

"I will have your attendants get them for you. I must do 'human' things."

Solina and Kallen parted ways at the Palace. She walked on to her rooms. He went to the barracks.

CHAPTER 47

Atin

Upon a Racing Steed of Fire

Solina stepped down and smiled at the trio as she left the reception room. She looked a little sad, Atin wondered at her expression, but turned to her husband and his brother with a suggestion.

"Why don't we spend time together and remember the ones who passed by telling me all about them. 'For in remembrance the best way to honour those who have lost their spirit is to speak of their deeds in reverence."

They left to go back to Atin and Kaisan's rooms.

"Please excuse me, husband, Tovan, I feel the need for privacy. I will be back shortly." They kept a privy room, while she wasn't shy about her body, certain things she liked privacy for. Kaisan agreed with her, he told her it was much like this at home, or he corrected himself and said where he grew up.

She saw he was happy to see his brother but was worried for the outcome of the trip. She was worried for him, but her mind was on other things. Like not being with him, the comfort he may need if his Mader passed. If she had taken the time to think past the potential sorrow, and the full extent of what his countrymen were capable of, she should have been just as worried as him.

His explanation in their last discussion, he told her. His was a glossed over version and omitted some details. Such as all the remaining siblings of the new FirPader were killed. Not just the girls but all the Maders, Kaisan knew this would have sent Atin over the edge. His Pader was the first to abolish this horrendous act. Ignorance is bliss, and her not knowing the barbarism of his cultural background, saved her much stress. Her mind was on her nausea; it hit her at moments when she least expected it. Like now.

She returned to hear both men speaking in his language.

"Sorry, Dear Heart. Tovan is explaining to me all who have succumbed and passed on. It breaks my heart to hear almost all the Harem children, except those newly born, indulged in the sweets which ended their lives. Tovan told me his wife and family were sequestered in their villa with a flu like illness. They were not in attendance of the celebrations. They have recovered, which is why he made this trip. His eldest son is heir, also. It is assurance of the line of ascension in case he did not return."

"To have more than one woman or wife? Is one not enough? Do the women not fight amongst each other? I cannot think about sharing you with another. This isn't right at all."

Atin was shaking her head at the thought, the movement had her rushing out of the room. She returned soon after holding her stomach and Kaisan came over and embraced her. She leaned into his arms,

"Is it the baby?"

"Yes, I do not feel well at all."

"It will pass, eventually… from what I know… from what I was told. (sigh). I don't know."

"'Tis fine. Kaisan. I know enough. My Mader was fine with one pregnancy and almost bed bound with another. It will be what the Universe gives to me. I need to lay down. Will you men excuse me?"

"Yes, Dear Heart. I will explain your condition to Tovan. You will not mind if we talk into the night?"

"You talk with your brother; I will be asleep in minutes."

Kaisan explained to his brother the whole of her conversation, with her idea of not sharing with other women, and the men laughed. She looked a bit put out they would think her ideas not valid. Kaisan saw her disapproval on her face. She did not hide her expressions well.

"Dear Atin, please do not take offense. My brother wholly agrees with you. He does not share the common view of many wives. We agree one wife is enough. Both of us have fallen in love with our partners. I will spend our time talking with Tovan, in his rooms, to give you the rest you need,"

"You do not have to, but it is appreciated." Kaisan kissed her and left with his brother. She lay down and began to think. Atin didn't know what to think, or feel, her husband was leaving her and even though she knew her staying away from a disease-ridden land was key to keeping her and her baby alive, she didn't feel any better for it. Her stomach was mimicking what her head was feeling. Upset. But after evacuating her stomach, she was still left with her thoughts. For some reason, she felt she would not see Kaisan again, and her mind was scattered. She was split. Part of her did not want him to leave, she wanted to go with him, yet she knew in her heart she would not be welcomed. It weighed heavily on her mind. She thought about part of a conversation they had.

"You worry for no reason, Dear Heart. I will return, I cannot live without my Dragon, you are my life now. I promise I will come back to you."

She had not spent any time alone since they were married, and she did not know how she would survive the month he was away. She felt unsettled the more she dwelled on it, until finally Kaisan took her hands.

"Atin. Look at me. Look. At me. Eyes here. You cannot worry about something which hasn't happened and most likely will not, it will not do you or the baby any good. The baby can feel what you feel. You should be more relaxed, less stress. Back in Aram, when a child bearing is announced the expectant Mader gets her own apartments, with whatever she desires, to make a better environment for the growing child."

"Why is this?"

"More for her protection, really. Other women in the Harem would be jealous and try to harm both."

"Good thing I don't have to worry about another woman!" Atin's eyebrow went up.

"My point is, you should have calm, not worry. I will be back, and I will spend my life making you and the child you carry as happy as I can."

Atin fell asleep with loving thoughts of her husband and did not wake when he came to bed. She woke up in his arms but had to extract herself when her stomach had other ideas. She spent most of the morning retching. He brought a piece of dry toast back for her, and it managed to stay down. He went out and came back with his brother. The men sat there and chatted while she closed her eyes against the lounging chair.

She saw even though Kaisan didn't want to go, he was glad to see his brother again. He told her previously it hurt he was easily cast off for his decision, to marry one of different religion or country. It made him sad one could not marry for love, even though he and his brother were lucky in this regard, and there were no allowances made for marrying someone of a different background or religion.

"I don't know what I will do with myself while you are gone."

Atin felt agitated, her eyes beginning to glow. Tovan looked at her in amazement, and Kaisan explained she also saw auras and command the animals in the ocean.

"Why don't you wait for a bit and then see your family. You can spend time with them and tell them the good news; it might do you good to go and spend time in your favorite spots and relax with them and the creatures of the seas." He came forward and wrapped his arms around her.

"I know what you are thinking, I will never give you up, not for the possibility of being the Ruler of the continent of Aram, not for any position of power. You are my Ruler, the Ruler of my heart."

"You are the holder of my heart, and you have a great idea, I would only be lonely here, I will see my parents and relax like you said, I love you more than anything."

"You carry my child and know I will do everything in my power to return to you; I would never leave you willingly." He was saying this as a veiled threat to his brother who may have other ideas, or if his Pader decided to hold him hostage. His brother understood more Pelinese than he let on.

"He will come back to you; you have my word. I see he loves you very much, it was his Maders request I bring him, Kaisan was always her favorite." Tovan spoke to Atin, in broken Pelinese, He explained he didn't have a particularly good understanding of her language but now he had no choice but to learn as he was next in line. Kaisan let him tell it like this, it was devious, but it was said, and to tell different would make it worse. He hoped Atin wasn't looking at his aura at the moment.

They spent the rest of the evening talking about Aram and his family and she fell asleep in his arms.

The next day came soon enough, Atin didn't want him to go, but if he didn't and his Mader died, well, she couldn't think about if she never had the chance to say goodbye to her Mader and Pader. She tried not to imagine life without him, and after a long bout of morning sickness, she finally felt good enough to go outside. She walked down to the port with him and gave him countless hugs until he finally had to beg her to stop. She tried not to cry and failed, as the ship left and he stood on the stern waving at her. Turning away from the docks she walked down to the beach and the water, a platoon of guards trailing behind her. The crowd parted to let her pass as they saw her eyes glowing.

Slipping off her sandals, she walked into the water and dove in, her gown slowly following her down under the surface.

"I humbly ask you my dear friends to escort this ship to Aram, and to keep it safe as my mate is on it. I give you my thanks, and soon I will go back to the coral reefs and if you desire you can visit me there. Again, I thank you."

She then turned around and emerged from the water, amidst gasps, people hadn't ever seen the Sea Dragon remain down for an extraordinary amount of time and they saw the fins leaving. She walked up the path back to the Palace and had a long soak in the bath. Dressing, and having a piece of bread to settle her stomach, she ate then walked down the hall, finding Solina reading at her desk.

"Would you mind if I were to visit my family for a time. I feel agitated without Kaisan here, and I think it would help me to relax, in familiar places. If I were to stay, I would probably drive you mad with my worry. Plus, this sickness, without sounding like one of my little sisters, I would really like to see my Mader. She would know what might help."

"Why certainly, you go, I don't know why I didn't think of it. Kaisan certainly cares for your well being; the time will pass quickly and before you know it, he will be back. You go see your Mader. I know nothing about childbearing, or what bearing entails, I am inadequate in this regard. She will put you to rights, I am sure." Solina rose and gave her a hug. She held onto Atin's shoulders and looked her in the eyes, concern feathering her brow.

"You must take care of yourself and the child you carry, sometimes mental well being is just as important as physical. We must all take care of each other, so your husband's idea is a great one, I do not want you to worry at all. We are feeding the Dragons as much as they can eat each day. They keep growing too. I am not sure how much more they will expand. I think Nannosh is almost full grown, I think. She said the Great One is double her size."

"So, he's huge then? Gods! This must be very imposing; I guess he would have to be if he's the male of the species. You see the male of the fowl, the ducks and especially the geese, the male is somewhat larger. I guess the same is for the Dragons."

Solina let her hands drop and she gazed blankly for a moment. "If you want to go right now, I have an idea. Nannosh says she needs the exercise and will take you; it will be an effective way for her to stretch her wings, Analaria needs a little more rest. If Nannosh needs to stop, there are stations along the Islands on the way where she can rest, she wants to gauge her strength."

"May I ask why?" Atin was curious, and Solina told her about what the Dragons were facing. Atin agreed with Veren's comment,

"If they aren't here, then assassins can't kill them, and we can focus on meeting up with them and helping them in the next phase. But we will have only ourselves to worry about, then. I do not want to hide on my family's Island; I do not want to put them at risk."

"I understand, Gran told me, they have but to ask for help. She told me she would protect them here if necessary. We have many discussions on what happens next and several possible outcomes. One thing about Gran, she is very thorough and is training me. There is so much I need to learn from her and much I do not know."

"I could not agree more with you. We have more pressing matters. We need to find the others, without drawing any attention to it, but I am not sure how."

"I am not sure who either. One is in Aram, this we know. Then there are three in Du'Lanay, and I am sure we will eventually leave here. I know my GrandMader has ruled for many years, she is a great Ruler, but without the elixir, who knows how much longer she may live. The effects will begin to show their absence soon, if not already. Without the production of the elixir which she said they drank every year, she may not last, the two oldest ones have outlived their lives and will be soon to expire, at least this is what Gran tells me."

"Maybe they will find us, the Universe put us in each others path. The Dragon's Breath in the sky is becoming larger, I am sure everyone has seen it, the Faith cannot deny its existence now. The Prophecy will be spoken about, even if 'tis in secret. Your Gran will probably last a while yet, she does not look old, and she may live by sheer stubbornness."

Solina laughed at the thought. She rose and placed her book down. "You are probably right on that subject. Why don't we get you attired into something which will withstand the wind and send you off so you can relax. I can worry about the next step, you relax, get your tummy sorted, and when you are needed, I will send for you. Or you will be back, just get yourself in a more sedate frame of mind. You let me deal with the Dragons."

They walked to Atin's room, and she changed into a tunic, long leggings, sturdy shoes which laced up around her ankle. She put on a jacket, when Solina relayed it may be colder with wind up in the sky. Solina sat down at the eating table, while Atin seated herself to lace up her boots.

"I do not want to drive a wedge between you, but Gran has made me think. May I speak?"

"Certainly. I would hear what you have to say, I do not see you driving any wedge between us."

"Ever since our walk in the city, Kaisan has been…treading softer around you. He doesn't know how to manage your…forthrightness."

"Oh, I see him as more attentive. You have more to say? Sorry."

"I see a man, who doesn't know how to handle a woman with an opinion. I see the politeness; he is very polite to me and others. He is very well mannered, it is refreshing, but a bit unnerving at the same time. It is almost too much. I feel

I cannot see the real Kaisan, beyond the politeness. I beg your forgiveness if I am being blunt. I get a sense of unease from him, I cannot see auras, but I can sense energies. Nannosh says I will practice more. She is working me through sensing energies. I don't quite have the gift for it yet."

"I see his aura when he is with me, I have not seen it waver, however, I understand what you are saying. He is not sure how to act around you, his omission to me sits heavy on him and he does not know how to correct his mistake."

"He was never going to be FirPader, so he may not have all the learnings given to the heir. The…ahhh…abilities to divert and manipulate."

"Yes, but now Tovan is heir, and his Pader is not well. Tovan is in a hurry to get back. That is partly the rush. There are several other brothers who could step in and take over."

"I must ask, it has been bothering me, since Aram showed up. Kaisan was in a hurry to leave here. Do you not think?"

"How so? His Mader was ill. He wishes to see her. Is this not a caring son?"

"But children are not raised by their Maders there. He was a son; they are sent off to learn Aram from tutors. It seemed he has not left the Layanese part of him behind if he needed to get to his Mader. I would think if he returned and Tovan ascends to the Throne, and his life is handed over to his brother, he would be good as dead. Why would he leave you, his wife who is pregnant with his child, to go back to a land, who has written him out of history and place his neck on the line? For what? I am sorry. Gran has me question everything. I must see all angles to a dilemma. If I have distressed you, I am sorry."

"No. Now you have me wondering. Kaisan was a bit put out the day we walked through the city. It had something to do with when I told him to unhand me. He tried to laugh it off later, but I did sense it. I am thinking you are partially right. A woman does not direct. He says he is trying to learn Vendar, but I have not been able to get far with my explanations. He is easily distracted. Mostly by me. It is very physical, our relationship. I never knew about sons being sent off. He never explained his childhood to me. He always came off to love his Mader and his siblings. He has many. Why would he omit such?"

"Have you asked pointed questions? Like why they kill all siblings when one of the sons ascends the Throne."

"All? He told me the sons were all killed. He never said the Daders. Oh, my heart goes out to them. Why would he not tell me that?"

"I am sorry, I have caused you sorrow. I did not mean to."

"No, perhaps I should have a talk with you and your Gran before I go. Learn what it is she knows. I know nothing of Aram, beyond what Kaisan has told me. Shall we see her?"

"Are you certain?"

"Yes, my family can wait. I do have several weeks to swim in my coves. I have a need to know. Plus, I think I will begin to learn to write and to read. Your Gran suggested it, plus, my parents. I will feel less like relying on others for my information." Atin rose to her feet and Solina followed her lead. Solina hugged her friend.

"I only have your well being in my heart. I was not trying to make you feel like your husband was not true."

"You haven't, he was not completely truthful, telling me only part of the truth is not truthful. I am now wondering why."

The women walked through the Palace looking for Gran and found her outside enjoying tea in one of the many manicured gardens. Private and well guarded.

"There's many more guards, is this because of us?"

"Yes. Gran insists. After our walk, she feels justified. Ahhh, Gran. Here you are. Reading again. Why is this not a surprise."

"Well, hello girls. Atin, are you fine without Kaisan, he has left?"

"Yes, Dame. He has. Solina told me a few things, I wanted to ask you on all things Aram. Kaisan has not told me everything, just what he wanted me to know."

"I am sorry to hear this. You will know if he comes back if he is true. Sorry, this is the Ruler coming out in me."

"We are fine. I have not seen anything but truth from him, but with what Solina says, it has made me ask questions."

"Well, have a seat. Would you girls like tea?" Both nodded and Dame's servant came forward and the Dame requested refreshments and a small repast. The two sat down at the small table, and settled in.

"Where would you like me to start? With the Royal family?" Atin nodded.

"The FirPader, God to all Aram, he is holy. His word is law. He can make a law, unmake a law, merely by his word. Very heady to a man. He can do anything he wants. Anything. No one can do anything about it. The women, he can have whoever he wants, as a wife, as a concubine. They have no say."

"Can they say no? What if they do not want to marry, or bed him?"

"Yes, they can say no. If they do not wish to live."

"Oh… that's not a life or a land I would wish to live in."

"Exactly. 'Tis not a place to be if you are a woman. The wives only have power in the Harem over the other women, but some of what they do still has to get approval from the men, through the Obans who rule under the FirPader. Men still rule it.

"Gran, tell of the succession, the hierarchy of birth."

"Birth, sons are taken from their Maders at birth and taught by men. So, they do not become soft, by women. In their history, several hundred years ago, these laws were passed when one FirPader refused to kill his siblings. It was his end of course. Another brother killed him and ascended the Throne. Thank you, girls have a bite, this history lesson may make you hungry. I will see what else I can tell you. Mmm, I love Tammaberry scones."

"So Kaisan would not have known his Mader for a while. Why then, would he be upset over her being ill?"

"He may have a heart for his Mader. You should ask him when he comes back. Your husband is an anomaly. I see he is gentle and caring. He may have a non-traditional relationship with his Mader. I am only telling you what we know from scholars who have given us this view of Aram. What history has shown us."

"I will ask him, please tell us more."

"Well…let's see. You know when the new FirPader comes into power, he eliminates all contenders, even the women?"

"Yes, Solina told me, Kaisan only said the males were put to the sword."

"Perhaps, this is a new rule. Again, something for you to ask him. 'Tis good you want to learn, Atin. Then you will know more and others will not try to tell you otherwise."

"Yes, I am beginning to see the logic behind this. If my husband, who I trust, is only telling a part of the truth, then when I do find out the whole, it will give me doubts to his loyalty."

"I am glad you are thinking about this. You see for yourself, what is happening here. You find out all you can, see all distinct parts of a story to make up your own mind about the outcome. Knowledge is everything. Without knowledge, how can you make decisions? For example, the rule where all contenders were to be given a sword to the neck. Perhaps there is a new rule. Perhaps it is information, we Pelinese do not have. We have only the history of Aram we put together from what we are told. We have no one there to give us an insight every time the FirPader weds, makes a law. It takes time, sometimes years to get us this. So, you speak with your husband, I would like to talk with him, if just to clarify questions I have."

"This makes perfect sense. Is this purge from a spice sent to Aram from Du'Lanay?"

"Yes, that is truth. I have several accounts from various sources. Lesson here, always have diverse sources. Know which ones would give you information to suit them. To continue. Yes. This spice, I think it is a Safran from Du'Lanay, which several treats are made of. Many women have passed from consumption. Mostly Royals, and a few dignitaries. Some men also, but mostly women. This has not been confirmed if it was a mistake, or deliberate. We will know soon enough.

We do not know a complete list of exactly who ate it, but what you told me Kaisan said, it sounds like it cleaned house. To lose so many to one little spice…it sounds like something the Namarch would do… if he claims it as his. He may not."

"Kaisan told me of his desire to learn all he can about foods and where they hail from. He loves his foods and has quite the palate. He told me his dream of opening a bakery where all flavours of spices adorn and complement dishes."

"This sounds like a man who loves his food."

"He also loves his garments; he picked out the colours we were to wear on our walk. To compliment Solina, he said one must look Royal, or better dressed, or both."

"He said this? He pretty much told you who he was with this comment."

"Oh, he did? I did not catch up on this. Does this make me a half-wit? I feel like there is much he told me I have not paid much attention to. I feel like I should have paid attention."

"You are not! Maybe we are giving you something to help you pay more attention. Think about everything he told you if you remember the conversations and analyse them. It can only help you… to review what was spoken, and how it was spoken."

Gran motioned for more tea, and she reached for another piece of scone. Atin sat there, lost in thought. The three of them ate the berry scones with jelly and consumed more tea. Atin's brow furrowed and then she smiled in remembrance.

"Something came to me. When I spoke to him at the waterfall about who I am, He was delighted. Of course I was worried, more so he would reject me, I recall he said he would love me forever as I was, but he also said if I could love him for who he was. I did not take note on this. Who he was. I should pay more attention to what people say." Atin looked at the other women and smiled sadly.

"The signs were there. I did not see them. I feel Kaisan was unintentionally duplicitous. Perhaps it is his upbringing which causes him to not tell the whole story. What else can it be? He is truthful when approached. I see his aura, it has been, not…only the first time when I met him and was seeing auras, before I knew what they were. In the markets, when we were bargaining for pearls, his aura was not right, and as he saw I knew he was getting them for cheap, his aura changed. I should ask my Dragon when I get one if one can change it back."

"Perhaps when you ride Nannosh, you and she can have a talk. I am sure she would be able to give you insight. Are you still going today?"

"No, if you are agreeable, I would like to spend the night and I will head out tomorrow. I need to learn more. If Dame would allow me."

"My dear. I do not command you or Solina. I will certainly speak to you some more. Perhaps you girls would like to have the evening meal with me tonight."

"Yes, Gran. That sounds wonderful. A girls night. Atin, what would you like to do?"

"Well, this has been the first day without my husband. What can two women get themselves into?"

"Well, we could walk into the markets. Now I can shield us, it would be easier to protect us."

"That sounds like fun! I would love to see the different spices and fabrics."

"You girls take a full regiment. We don't need to have any more incidents."

"Gran, my shield will not let any in who have hate in their hearts. I will speak to Kallen, we may only take a few, we don't wish to have a following. Furthermore, this is not a planned event."

"Just be careful. You protect yourselves at all costs."

"Nannosh tells me also. She will not let any harm us."

"Then I am satisfied, I will see you later in the evening, girls."

"Gran."

"…Gran." Atin and Solina rose and left Gran in her garden and they walked back to Solina's apartment.

"I want to change. I like your outfit. It seems more comfortable to walk in. Marshall, can you find Marshall Kallen for me, or the Admiral. Whoever you find first. I would like to speak to one of them."

"Right away, High Dragon." Atin sat down on the bed. They entered without guards, and found several girls who came to attention when they strode in. Solina gave them instructions and she busily dressed herself in attire which mirrored Atins. A knock on the door, Solina nodded and one of the servants opened it to let Kallen and Veren in.

"You wished to see us? Is everything fine, High Dragon?"

Solina smiled, she was having her hair braided. Kallen, for a moment looked uncomfortable and did not know where to look. Atin looked closer, and saw a pink shimmer surrounding him, she smiled and looked at Veren. His aura was shining with several colours and she had a sense of protection radiating from him. Atin rose, with her eyes glowing, and Solina looked at her in concern.

"Atin, are you fine? Your eyes…"

"I am trying out my talent, as you call it. I see Veren here, with a multitude of colours. 'Tis quite striking. Please do not be alarmed. Admiral, you give off such wonder, may I explain?" Veren for a moment looked worried, but as Atin was smiling, he relaxed and stood easier. "I, for a moment, thought my life was in question. By all means, Sea Dragon, by your leave."

Atin walked around the men. She saw a bit of unease from Kallen, which is what she really wished to look at. She was viewing through her Dragon eyes, and it was beginning to hurt her head. She shook her head and closed her eyes. "I cannot. If I continue, it will bring on a splitting headache." She went back to the bed and sat down. The men, looking relieved stood there waiting.

"Then don't do it, Atin. You just try when Nannosh is with you. Men, Atin and I wish to go to the markets today. She will leave tomorrow and fly on Nannosh to return to her family. So, we would like to wander around the markets. Could we manage this?" Veren pondered for a moment, thoughts moving over his face with each calculation.

"We could. A small amount of men, nothing to get the crowds up. There may be a following. It could be me, and Kallen, and a couple more. You could cover yourselves with the shimmering of air, like you did last time."

"That's what I was thinking. It would eliminate the need for you to be on guard."

"We would always be on guard, High Dragon. Where you are concerned."

Kallen spoke up, his manner was fervent, and Atin noticed a bit more than concern. She watched the man who was trying not to look at his liege, and she saw the beginnings of adoration. Atin smiled to herself and gazed at Solina who was finishing.

"Well, now you look ready for battle. Shall we see what trouble we can get into today."

Solina laughed and motioned that she was more than ready.

"Men, are we good? We can use this as a model, if it works, then Atin and I can use less men. I do not want to have to rely on guards all the time. There may come a time when this is not feasible."

They began walking down the hall. Kallen thoughtfully flanked Atin, while Veren was on Solina's left. "May I suggest then, High Dragon perhaps you and the Sea Dragon begin combat lessons. Simple techniques for defending your-selves. The Sea Dragon's husband can continue her lessons. He is very well trained. The Aram soldiers have skills. Which is why Du'Lanay cannot get them out of their lands. They have never seen the like and cannot compete with their training. I have studied their ways, and those of the Lanayese. Aram, has by far have better methods."

"We certainly can. I can begin anytime. Atin will have to wait for Kaisan to came back to begin. What do you think, Atin?"

"Hmmm, do I have to wait? I could just stay here for a while, then when I am ready, go back to my parents. I would like to learn a few skills. At least, like Veren stated, to be able to defend myself. I don't have the bond you have, and having a few knife skills would be beneficial. Kaisan can certainly teach me more. If he wants, I will not force him."

"You are truly kind, Sea Dragon. He should be wanting his partner to be able to protect herself."

"Yes, Kallen. He should. But I will let him decide this for himself. He has still much Aram in him. One can only change who they are if they want to. Forcing, like… threading a needle…the more you try, the more you spread the threads that make a whole strand, it sometimes won't work."

"You have the right of it, Sea Dragon. Admiral, if you and the Dragons care to wait, I will get a few more Marshalls. We can make this at least a well dressed, and safer walk." They reached the barracks by now, Kallen excused himself to obtain a few more Marshalls. Their uniforms more opulent than the regular sol-dier. The girls stood there watching the training happening in a courtyard off the one they stood in. Several recruits were gawking at them and the Commanders used their inattention as a training tool. Several went down on their knees after getting hit. Veren spoke to the Marshalls who arrived.

"All right men. The Dragons would like to walk into the markets. We will try to keep this discreet. The High Dragon will have her yellow shields up, so this will eliminate any immediate threat to them. But it may still happen. You remem-ber the man who was trying to knife it. We will take out any who try this. No questions. Their safety is paramount." The group began on their way. Quietly and walking without talking, a few people stopped and stared, a few bowed.

"Solina, perhaps, we could stop and talk to a few. It would help to find out what their concerns are, perhaps they would tell us more on how they view the Dragons."

"Certainly, you are thinking much like a Ruler. This is an incredibly clever idea. Men, we will intermittently stop, to talk to people. Atin, Nannosh says she will bond with you, if you care to view auras. We should be diligent, to protect ourselves."

"Yes, thank you. This would help." Atin became aware of Nannosh, she felt as if there was someone looking over her shoulder. *"Is this what my bond will feel like, when I get one?"*

"Yes, Sea Dragon. Much like our bond. The Great One told me to help you, gather your strengths, and build your confidence. I see you learning much."

"I thank you; it makes it so much easier. I have gathered the darker colours mean the worst. Lighter colours are based on what the intent is."

Solina was busy talking with a Mader and children. They were smiling at the group and bowing. She was shaking hands and hugging, which the men were not pleased about, but Solina reassured them, only those who were Vendar could enter her bubble of yellow air. Kallen was alert and intent, he would walk and look backward. Atin kept to herself and Nannosh for a while…

"I see much pink around Kallen. I am thinking 'tis adoration…'

"Yes, he is very intent on the High Dragon. She is aware of his mind. Will you tell her?'

"Yes, I do not see her being too interested, she told me, you and the other Dragons are her focus. Besides, I think Kallen is very shy. He blushes around me, even."

"He is a Vendar to the heart, much like the Dragon Mader's mate."

"You are speaking of Veren. Yes. I see an assortment of colours around him; I get the aura of protection. 'Tis the yellow I, see?"

"Yes, he is very in tune to the High Dragon. He mirrors her energy, you even. You see the blues?"

"Oh, yes!"

"Atin, shall we continue? I know you are speaking with Nannosh, but if we don't keep walking, a crowd will gather and we won't make it down to the markets. You do want to see some of the spices? The men are getting anxious."

"Yes, I can walk and talk at the same time. Veren…"

"Yes, Sea Dragon?"

"Oh nothing… I thought I saw something…"

"Are you sure? Where?"

"You may think me… I thought I saw up on the wall…"

"You saw?"

"A hint of darkness, it was there and then gone."

"High Dragon, do you think this walk is a good idea?"

"Veren, a knife cannot penetrate this bubble, and an arrow could not. Not even a person with bad intent. We are well protected. I can make it larger to encompass you also. Nannosh says I can also put one around each individual person."

"That sounds like a better idea. Can you do so? In case we get separated." Atin felt her watcher leave and she sensed the yellow shimmer surround her.

"This feels like a warm hug! 'Tis like I have a warm blanket on. Do you think I can do something like this?" All their group became yellow, and Atin felt Nannosh come back into her head. *You and the Air Dragon can combine; it would make a very solid shield. Focus on the moisture in the air surrounding each person. Intent makes it a shield."*

Soon each person had blue and yellow swirls surrounding them. The men tried to hit each of the women, and their hands bounced back from the air shield.

"Now Veren, shall we move along, we are getting a crowd like you didn't want. This eases your mind?"

"Very much. I like this shield. Excellent work, girls… I mean Dragons."

Solina and Atin laughed, "You are fine, we take no offense. Let's get down to these markets before the mid day sun beats down on us. This shield protects us from a human attack not the sun!"

They walked down the walkway to the lower city gates. Veren spoke to the guards there and they were let out. Soon the women saw guards appearing on the top of the lower city walls, armed and at the ready. Solina nodded to Veren. They walked into the market. Atin was surprised at the busyness.

"Is there a surplus, a festival? I don't remember seeing this many people here before."

Veren looked around and spoke to Kallen and the other two. The men fanned out, the shields holding around them. They came quickly back. Speaking with Veren, then Veren came to the women. "A few Lanayese ships are in port, nothing to be alarmed about, but we will be diligent. If I give you any signal at all, you run for the gates, we have archers who will protect your flank."

"Thank you, Atin…?" Atin was distracted by one of the spice venders and she was busy smelling various spices.

"MMMmm, yes? Oh, did you say something? These are heavenly."

"Veren told me there is an influx of Layanese here. We should tread carefully." Atin looked up and saw the worry upon Solina's face. "If we live in fear of the unknown, then how is this a life? We have various methods of protection. Today we have our men…and our shields. Plus, we have two Dragons on the hill. Are we not protected?"

"Well, yes… I do not live in fear, just want to make sure we are not put in harm's way. What is that?" Solina bent forward to smell the spice sample Atin was holding, Atin looking at the vendor. He told her it was Safran, from Du'Lanay.

"It smells more fragrant than those two." Solina smelled the others. She was told they hailed from Aram. She and Atin spent much time smelling the spices. Atin took several looks at one of the spices at the ends. She began to frown and her eyes lit up. "You don't like this spice, Sea Dragon? I will remove it for you."

"No…I see…how long has this spice been out here?"

"I pack them away every night and bring them out every day."

"Where do you store it, kind sir?"

"In my house. Is there something wrong?"

"Do you store it near any water source?"

"I don't. What do you see? I store them in canvas bags, wait…"

"I see the beginning of mold. It will not be good for sale. You should perhaps remove it. Moisture near the other spices will affect them."

"It was one of the bags on the floor. I remember seeing some water on the floor last week with the evening of rain we had. I thank you, Sea Dragon. You have saved me my Safran. May you be Blessed. Thank you. Thank you."

The vender tried to kiss her hand but Atin shook her head no, Kallen came up beside her and looked to threaten the vender. She placed her hand on his arm. "'Tis fine, Kallen, he means no harm." Atin spoke softly to the Marshall. She saw her hand on his arm discomforted him.

"You mean well, I thank you."

Kallen backed off and stood beside Atin. She and Solina accepted a small gift from the Vender, which another of the guards kindly held for them. An hour later after perusing various venders, Atin was busy explaining all of them to Solina. The women reached the end and came into an open space with no canvas over their heads.

"'Tis bright out here. We should turn back, what do you think Atin?"

"We have company. Men! Surround the Dragons." Atin saw a company of armed men, sailors by the looks of them, gathering quietly around the women. Veren and Kallen and the other guards unsheathed their swords. They looked ready to pounce. The sailors were a hardened bunch and Atin saw the intent in their eyes. Solina's eyes began to glow.

"You are an abomination. A demon!" One of the men spoke.

"You must die!" Solina looked at the man sadly. She smiled and held onto Atin's hand. She squeezed it and whispered. "Don't move, Nannosh and Analaria are on their way. Veren, stand fast, perhaps back up into us."

"Men, listen to the High Dragon, tighten ranks.' Their guard detail tightened up after Veren spoke to them, quietly, enough for them to hear. Solina addressed the crowd of men, Atin saw their anger, but she could also see their fear.

"I am sorry you believe this of us. I am sorry you were told such. We are willing to forgive you if you were to have love in your hearts, but I do not see this in any of you. Is to love, to have love in your heart, is this an abomination?"

"You are demons, you should not grace this earth."

"You are right. We should not grace this earth."

Atin looked at her friend, who shook her head at Atin. With only her eyes, she glanced quickly up. Atin heard the sound of wings, the slow and steady beat coming nearer.

"We demons should grace the sky!"

The sounds of wings became loud in their ears and Nannosh landed upon the beach behind the men. Analaria swooped down and trumpeted as she flew by, then she rose to fly in circles overhead. Nannosh's head came partially down and she opened her mouth, and drops of acid began to drip out of her mouth and steam on the sands as she slowly walked towards the men who were shaking and clustering together. A couple ran off and Solina looked towards them and surrounded them with yellow air. They froze in mid flight. Behind them a crowd had gathered. Venders and the other market inhabitants.

"You were sent here to kill us, were you not?" Solina had frozen all the men who bared their arms, with swords and knives. She and Atin strode forward.

"Are you looking?" She whispered to Atin.

"They are all black auras. These men are truly Naman. 'Tis hard to look."

She turned her head away. She saw Kallen stood by her side, with Veren on Solina's. Solina turned to the crowd.

"Another attempt on the Dragon's lives. These men are from the Namarch, I will not stand to have my life or the life of my sister thus threatened. Shall we demonstrate to the Lanayese what happens to those who mean evil?"

"What are you thinking?" Atin whispered to Solina. Solina looked up at Nannosh. She nodded and Atin watched as the men were herded together. She looked in horror as all but one, were pushed and bumped by the yellow air.

"No! You do not mean to do this? Solina, this is wrong. Will this not send the wrong message?"

"Trust me, Atin. This was Nannosh's idea." Solina whispered back. Analaria trumpeted and banked into a dive. The men saw the Dragon flying down at them, several wet their pants. They knew the flying Dragon was going to let loose, and she did! Analaria let fire rain down on the men and then closed her maw and flew up back to the mountain. Atin looked to see the men still intact and shivering and crying. Solina looked back at the crowd.

"This is what will happen to any who intend on killing the Dragons or their Riders. Next time, I may not be here to protect those who are Vendar. Let this be a warning to your Namarch. If he means to kill us, let him come here himself. Face to face. I am not scared of your leader. He should fear us. We will prevail; we will bring love back. We will not rule with fear."

"You are still a demon!" The leader gained his composure but still looked angry.

"Why is this? Is it because we are women? Does it bother you a mere woman has you bound? Is your Namarch afraid?"

"No! We are not afraid of women! You have not the brains to rule. Only men have that right!"

"Oh, my. You have it wrong. I am afraid you will have to come to terms. I and my sisters are not going anywhere. In fact, you can tell your Namarch this. If he thinks he can rule the Islands, he is welcome to try. A woman has been Ruling the Islands for the last forty years and doing it rather well. If he can take the Islands from us, then he is welcome to rule them. That is my challenge."

"One he will gladly accept. He will take these Islands and will crush you underfoot." The man was almost spitting. Atin looked faint, and Kallen grabbed her arm.

"Sea Dragon, are you fine?"

"Solina, I have a bad aura around this man, can Kallen walk me over to the shore?"

"Yes, what do you need to do?"

"I need to place my feet in the water. I sense something about this man, 'tis giving me a headache, a bad one. I need to clarify something. Don't do anything drastic."

The men were still bound together, by Solina's air, and Nannosh came up behind them, raising her head to above them. If Analaria's fire did not kill them or scare them, then Nannosh's presence sure did. They did not know she would not eat them. There were sounds of soldiers running towards them and the crowd parted to let the approaching detail come up behind their group. Veren spoke with the Marshall and the guards fanned out and lined up between the crowd and the Layanese. Meanwhile Kallen held onto Atin's arm and led her to the water's edge, she put her sandals in up to her ankles and if one were looking hard enough, they would have seen a pulse ripple out from where she was standing. She gasped and Kallen tightened his grip.

"It's fine, now Kallen, if we can go back to the group, please."

"Very well, Sea Dragon." He led her back and Solina looked at her friend who was tearing up.

"Are you fine? Is it the baby?"

"I am fine, and no, it's not the baby." She addressed the leader.

"You have women on board your ship, have you not?"

"What is it your business? You have no right, from our docking agreements to board our ships. This was agreed upon by our leaders."

Atin looked at him sadly but addressed Veren. "Admiral, if you send a cohort to inspect the Lanayese ships, you will find several women on board bound in chains. These women are to be freed and given the choice to stay here, where women will be treated fairly and with respect. Or they have the choice to remain on board with their captors. See to it this is done immediately. Please free them and give them care."

"Marshall, take a cohort, do as the Sea Dragon says."

"Right Away. Men!"

"You have no right! You are breaking the…" Solina raised her hand. Her face when she heard Atin, hardened.

"This is an agreement which doesn't hold any longer, sorry Captain. If you want to trade with Pelin'Dun, you will have to negotiate other terms. Ones which include inspection of any ships that grace our harbours. We will not condone slavery. Male or female. You can enter our waters, but you will do so at your own peril. We value every life which sets foot upon these shores. That includes yours. You will be free to go."

"You will not burn us?"

"No. We will let you return to Du'Lanay, this time." Atin whispered something to Solina, she nodded. Atin looked at Kallen, he had not let go of her arm.

"Can you take me back to the water?"

"Yes, hold onto my arm if you must. I do not want you to fall."

"Greatly appreciated. I give you thanks. I need to stand in the water. Solina needs to do something."

Atin stood there while Solina moved the men single file down to the water, past where Atin and Kallen were standing, she made them move into the water, and along the shore. Once the Captain of the boat filed past, Veren had his Marshall follow behind with a cohort. The crowd parted with the assistance of the soldiers, and there was an audience to the Lanayese being led back to their ships. Atin and Solina with their entourage followed them, Kallen led Atin out of the water and the women met up.

"What did you need to do this for?"

"I gave my friends their vibration. Should they find themselves swimming in the waters for any reason, their life is forfeit. It gives a signature, for the maneaters to distinguish friend from foe. Looks like our Captain here had captives. Look Solina." The women looked to the docks where several ragged women were being led out of the hold of all three of the Lanayese ships. A couple were being carried. The Captain had no choice but to board his ship. Atin went back into the waters, shrugging off Kallen's arm.

"I am good, Kallen. I thank you for your care. This will not take long."

Atin and the group watched while the Layanese boarded their ships and the ropes were untied. Atin bent down into the water and swirled her hands in the surf. Her eyes glowed and Solina knew Nannosh was boosting her abilities. The ships had not even unfurled their sails and one saw them move away with the current. Atin directed the seas to move them. She rose and came out of the water, and her eyes faded as she came close.

"There. No need to have them close by. The maneaters and whales will help keep them on course. Solina, I am tired. Shall we go back? The markets have lost their appeal. Thank you, Veren and Kallen, for your diligence and thank your men. We are slowly learning our way around. I see we will have our work cut out for us; it may take some time before we master the crowds."

"I agree. This is another test. People are not ready yet."

"Not the Layanese. Come along men, we are heading back."

"Kallen, may I have your assistance of your arm for the walk back? I am feeling a bit tired."

"Certainly, Sea Dragon." They walked back to the Palace.

"I guess we will have another talk with Gran tonight. She warned me."

"You and the Sea Dragon did quite well. Can I ask you how you knew about the women, Sea Dragon?"

"I saw his aura, Admiral. I am learning about the colours and the intent each one carries. His was black and there were other colours. He was getting aroused by our display, every time he looked at Solina, it pulsed. I had a hunch there were women on his ships. How else would he release this energy. I asked the swimmers in the sea if they could tell if their were indeed females on board. They said there were by the urine and feces thrown overboard, which confirmed. When he protested, I knew for sure they were not there of their free will."

"Eww. He was aroused by our magic? Me? 'Tis unnerving."

"It seems Naman may follow their teachings, but men are always ruled by their lusts." Veren spoke quietly. He was humbled by what happened and the aggression shown by the Dragons. He told Solina what he was feeling, she took his hand and gave it a quick squeeze.

"Admiral, the Dragons will protect us, as much as we will protect them. They do not take lightly a threat such as Naman. It was their undoing in the last age. Atalay was the Dragon who burned her Rider. She told me she was angered very easily and did it without thinking about the consequences. Atin and I and the other Riders for that matter, we must grow into ourselves and with our Dragons. Nannosh is much older, she knew a display of might was more effective than the actual act. The Great One is the one who will direct our way.

We have our work to do. Aram will deny our existence, Gran said. Even if it is right in front of their face. Du'Lanay will try to end us because we pose the worst threat to their rule, or the end of it. Its like the starving wolf, it will die fighting to keep its share of the spoils. Men will always be men. With their lusts, and with their minds. We just find a way to bring them into the Vendar fold if we can." They arrived at Atin's apartment first.

"I am having a wash and a nap. Wake me in a couple of hours. I still would like to talk with your Gran."

"To be sure, I am going to do the same, but I am not tired. I will probably read. Sleep well, Veren, you can inform Gran…"

They left Atin to enter her quarters and she heard them continue down to Solina's. She was very tired. Washing her hair was done by the servant girls, for once she appreciated their help, putting on a robe, she repeated her request to one of the girls and she lay down, falling asleep right away. Atin woke as the girl came to the edge of her bed. She opened her eyes to see the girl bending over to shake her arm.

"Oh, you startled me, I was just about to wake you."

"I am sorry, I did not mean to startle you. 'Tis time for the evening meal?"

"You have some time to wake up, Sea Dragon. I have brought you a cooled herbal and citrus tea, with orange slices. Also, a small slice of orange, and Tammaberry loaf, if you want to stave off any hunger issues. I was made aware you hadn't eaten much before your walk. You are eating for two, you know."

The girl smiled at her and held open a robe to wrap around herself. Atin realized she was hungry at the same time her stomach told her. Looking down she told the servant she would love to sit. Sitting and having a small repast, she turned and smiled as Solina came in.

"I see you are awake. I thought to wear this, what do you think?" Solina had come in wearing a dress! It was gold silk, and it flowed with her every movement.

"It's gorgeous, Lina! You look fabulous! What's the occasion?"

"I thought if Gran was cross with us, that dressing up may soften the mood. It worked for you!"

"Yes, I was stunned! You never wear dresses. Too bad I don't have one, we could go in armed."

"Well… I did have one made for you…one which matches your eyes. What do you think?" Solina walked into the dressing room and came out with a blue green silk, with pearl ornamentation. Atin began to cry. Solina dropped it on the bed and rushed to Atin. "Did I do wrong?"

"Oh, no! I love it! I don't know why I am crying. 'Tis probably this baby. No, 'tis seeing those women taken out of the ships. I wish I could free them all, I feel for them."

"You have a caring heart. Those women were taken to one of the Churches, I think mayhap even the Church I grew up in. They were fed, washed and they are resting. Once they wish to move, they will be given their choice of where they would like to go. One of them was an Aram woman, and she was beaten very badly. The sailors would taunt, beat, and then rape her. She would like to remain within the Church. She has not spoken much."

Atin dried her tears, and she put on the dress, twirling around looking at the play on the colours.

"Hearing about the abuses the Layanese give to women has my ire up. What do you think?"

"Gran is going to wonder what you and I are about! Shall we head her way?"

"Certainly, after you, High Dragoness!" Atin gave her a mock bow and held out her arm. Laughing they left Atin's room and drew stares wherever they walked. Feeling quite feminine and beautiful they shared smiles with all they passed. Coming towards them were the married couple, who looked like they came from the Dragons. Sheyna whistled at them. "Wow! I feel so overdressed!"

Solina laughed. "Gran will be aghast! Where are you off to? The Dragon's are fine?"

"We are going to have a nice meal, and yes, the Dragon's were fed and are fine. They were a bit restless until they ate. Veren told me of your afternoon. Excellent choice of dresses, you both look amazing! Good Luck!"

The couple kept on to their apartments. Atin and Solina kept on until they arrived at Gran's apartment. Kallen was just leaving. Atin looked at his face, she saw the adoration and shock as he viewed the well-dressed women. He bowed with a blush and left without saying a word. Solina walked in, and Atin came in behind her. Gran was sitting down at her personal dining table. She looked up and saw the two women wearing their dresses. The frown she was sporting turned into a smile. She let out a laugh.

"Oh, my. Don't you two look like you are heading to the gallows. I see you are listening, Solina! You have made my evening! Kallen reported to me about todays events. I would like to hear your version of today."

"Yes, Gran. You are not mad?"

"Whatever for? You are a young woman, who will one day take this mantle off my shoulders. You must explore on your own, the trials and tribulations which come with ruling. I cannot hold your hand all the time, nor give you a smooth path. This is the only way you will learn what works for you. These are different times than when I began, you will have other and more interesting events than the ones I had. Now please have a seat, dinner should be here soon and you can regale me with tales of fire breathing Dragons! It was dramatic, I hear!"

The two sat down and told Gran their version of the day, with a good dinner and even better wine. Atin was not partaking, she had a citrus blend of juices which she had fallen in love with when she first arrived. They moved to the reading parlour after dinner and lounged on the chairs which were more comfortable.

"Now you understand you had the choice to have them put to death, but your display of might, they will take back home and report to the Namarch. What may happen? Solina?"

"Let us have Atin think about this. It will give her a chance to find out the things you are teaching me. Atin, we try to figure out everything Du'Lanay might or might not do. This is what Gran is directing me to do. Think of everything, even if it seems impossible."

"Ummm, well they will deny it? No, that is Aram. well, they will get mad. We saw the leader, the Captain, get angry. He seemed like he did not want to hear what we said, regardless of what it was."

"That's a good start. Yes, Du'Lanay have a history of not paying their women any mind. You noticed this." Solina was nodding. "Anything else?"

"Well, the Namarch must have sent the sailors, so he will send more?"

"That could be, but this is a new Namarch. He is craftier. It may be this group was sent by the last one. The new Namarch is younger and more covert. He will send others, but he is also the master of sending decoys, more than one. He works in the shadows."

"Good work, girls. Solina, you have read all my notes on Davian. He is indeed the one to watch out for…"

They spent the rest of the night talking about what may happen in the near future and what they should not do. After a time Atin excused herself, she was hungry again and tired. She left to rest and woke up the next day hungry. Eating a small meal, she dressed back into the outfit she was going to wear on the Dragon. She went to find Solina, who was just coming out of her apartments.

"You are going this time?"

"I enjoyed our day together, now I would like to see my family. Having these talks with your Gran is very enlightening. I feel more confident, and I know I will have talks with Kaisan when he returns. I have faith there is an explanation for what he has not told me, which may clear up some of my doubt."

"Well, shall we? I will go with you; I would like to see you off." They walked up to the Dragons and Solina gave Atin a hug and wished her well and a safe journey.

"Nannosh will not overextend herself, she knows what to look for. The Islands are marked at farms where she can feed. I wish I could ride her this far, I must admit, I'm a little jealous." They reached the Dragons and one of the guards handed her the strap and proceeded to show them how to put it on Nannosh.

"I guess we will have to know this, for ourselves, we are after all the Riders." Solina gave Atin another huge hug, "You have my word. When Kaisan returns, I will send someone, or most likely Kaisan will come there himself. You get the rest you need, eat for your baby, and let your parents spoil you. Maybe go look for my pearl." Solina smiled. Without too much crying among the two women, Atin mounted onto the large Dragon, and the Dragon bunched up and launched into the sky, once Solina had gotten out of the way.

"Amazing! Completely, Amazing!"

Atin was in heaven, literally. She had not ever been up this high, when she was on Analaria it was full dark and she could not see the height they had reached, but Atin knew it was not this high. She saw the Islands beneath her and all around she saw nothing but blue of the ocean, and it was beautiful. To her right she noticed the blaze of the star, red tail, and all, getting closer. She looked around and loved the vista spread out underneath her. She knew the world was vast, but seeing it from so high up, it was sheer bliss. This was just the Islands, she could imagine what the rest of the world would look like, and she could not wait!

"Oh, Damn!"

"What, Little One?"

"I forgot to tell Solina about the energy I sensed from Kallen. Not she may not already know, he is very shy, and I see he is enamored of the High Dragon."

"She is aware, I am teaching her to view energies surrounding humans. Anything else?"

"Hmmm, he is attracted, or he worships her, not sure what it is, and he is shy. He was blushing when I was holding onto him. I do not think he would approach her. You can tell her of what I said. If you wish."

"I will. She needs to know the temperament of all around her, even the adoring ones. She will appreciate your input. She has spoken with him when you were with your mate and his sibling. His shell will be hard to crack."

"Oh, is this what she said?"

"No, 'tis what I gleaned from their conversation. He is very...what you said. Shy?"

"Umm, not confident. Ummm, when 'tis around another human of opposite gender, one feels inadequate, because one does not know how to act, be comfortable."

"I understand. My bond is not in a rush to be bonded with a male. She wants to be comfortable with many humans. Like the bond you share."

"Oh, friendship. Yes. I can see this; we both want friendships."

"You will find these friendships, like the one you seek with your mate."
Atin realized Nannosh had noticed her feelings.

"You sense I have wanting for a friendship with Kaisan?"

"Yes, you are very...physical with him, always mating. However, you have many differences, he has not let ideals, from his land, go. He has much to learn, but his heart is yours. This I feel."

"That reassures me, the others feel he is not truthful. I feel 'tis indeed a physical joining and not a deep friendship like the Admiral and your little Mader."

"You take what my bond and her Mader's Mader told you. See all sides to the gem, before you make up your mind, it will help you to make an informed decision. Your mate is selective in what he says, I sensed his energy. He would pick only what he knew would not upset you, however, you may need to hear all, even the bad. 'Tis what will happen in the future, the bad will make way for the good."

"He was aware of upsetting me. Caring for my state of mind. Do you think he was conditioned by Aram, to not upset women?"

"Perhaps so. The women of the hot lands, they are not treated the same as the little lands."

"So, he still has much Aram to be lost. I thank you for your insights. I have much to learn. This gives me much to ponder."

Atin took in the vista. She could feel the wind around them.

"This is incredible, Nannosh. I see everything."

"This is the one thing, I lamented. Soaring up here is where I find my peace, much like you swim under water. There is stillness up here, not the craziness down there."

"I know of what you speak and I feel the same. But I do like it up here. There is peace in the stillness. How did you manage? If I can ask?"

"I managed, barely. I watched all my sisters fade before me. I was in a drugged state, it was not until the Great One spoke to me again, I had hope."

"He spoke to you? How long ago?"

"Many years, I had to wait for my bond to be born, and I have watched over her all her life. I am blessed, soon I go to bring your bond to spirit. It gladdens my heart we will prevail."

"But humans have a great problem, the people of this land, these lands do not all see the same thing. We must unite, which will be an enormous endeavor."

"Yes, you do. I am glad hopefully my species will prevail. I may not be successful. I have gone many centuries without clutching."

"I will pray to the Gods, to Vendar you succeed, I have faith."

"So do I."

Nannosh flew extremely high, and coasted on the breeze, and once they almost cleared the third Island, she banked and headed down, into a field where she saw men and a few buildings, the animals herded inside before they could panic too much.

Atin was glad of the small stop, she had to use the pot, she didn't think the Dragon would enjoy it if she passed water on her. For a moment she forgot her stomach troubles, it made itself known as the descent came a little fast. They landed and she got off with shaky legs and went into the hut the men directed her to, and Nannosh was fed a couple of goats and sheep.

After Atin had used the facilities, she came out, had a drink at the well, and Nannosh had one as well. She then climbed back onto the back of the Dragon, and they rose into the air. She wasn't up there for very long, when she saw the curve of the beach where her family home was. She tapped twice on the Dragons' scales and pointed to the beach as the Dragon came closer. The Dragon came down onto the beach a fair way from the huts, the air from her wings stirred up a bit of dust from the dirt under scrub bushes. She climbed off and stood up, and told Nannosh to wait, she would find her something to drink and eat. Her family came out and waited for her to approach.

"Do you think we can get the Great One some stream water and some dried fish? Or fresh if you have it."

"Gods!" Her little brother was in awe.

"You rode all the way? That is beyond amazing!"

Her Pader and Mader hurried the children to fetch the water while they tried to figure out a container to put it in, but the Dragon had walked into the low-lying scrub and put her head down, into the pool Atin had taken Kaisan to. So, then as they tried to figure out what food to give her, the Dragon came hurrying out and with a short look at Atin, she took off in a hurry and headed back across the sea on a straight line back to Peli.

"Something must have happened." Atin said to her parents, "I hope it wasn't bad."

"So why are you here, Atin? I hope it isn't bad news you bring, and where is your husband? Why are you alone?"

Atin raised her hands after hugs were shared with all. "Kaisan's brother came to fetch him back to his homeland, there's a plague afoot in Aram, it has taken three of his siblings, and his Mader is not well, he will be back in two to three weeks. And he will return, just so you know, we are going to add to our family by one. I am with child."

After more hugs and congratulations, Atin then told her siblings all about the flight there, and what the world looked like from high up. They had an evening supper, talking about everything and Atin went over to the hut made for them. She slept soundly for the first time in a long time.

The next day had her waking up way past the sun rising. She stretched out, getting up, not feeling nauseous like she usually did. The smells of home must be what were helping her. She smiled, going to see her parents and ate a small meal with them, "I would like to go to my cove, and relax, maybe pearl a bit. I miss being useful."

"You have a lot of changes happening. Its still early yet, but your body will change, and you will change with it. It is the Universe preparing you for Maderhood. Your mindset will alter also. You have something you made, and you will protect it at all costs. Take this basket, I made you a meal, with some tidbits to munch on, it may ease any hunger pangs."

"Oh, Mader, ever since I found out, I am terribly ill. Almost every day and it lets itself known whenever it wants. I am so tired."

"It will be more pronounced if you are worrying. Have you?"

"Oh… yes. maybe I have… I did not feel nausea this morning."

"Because you were home. You feel safe here. Let's get you some berry scones I made fresh this morning, with some goat butter. Would you like a few eggs? The way you like them?"

"Oh, Mader. I would love some. If they stay down."

"They will. I'll brew some tea and then you take some with you. It will be fine, lass. You just go and relax. Do what you love to do. Soak in the sea and float away your troubles."

"Thanks, Ma."

Atin ate what her Mader made for her, suddenly ravenous. She paused while she waited for any protest from her belly. Feeling none, she grabbed a couple of baskets, giving her Mader a quick hug and left.

Atin walked to her canoe, saw it would need repairs soon so she would paddle it back after her day was done. She took it to her spot, looked lovingly at where she and her new husband made love. Then she stripped off her clothes, dove into the ocean, swimming down to harvest shells. She was down there for a while. Her breathing skills were so much better, and she had the feeling of being watched. Atin looked up to see the old turtle who helped her and some other interested sea animals, she stopped, and the turtle came up to her and bumped her. The other fish swam around, and it wasn't until a curious puffer fish came up and bumped her belly she understood why they were here; she smiled and rubbed her belly, she saw they approved.

She finished pearling that Day, after taking several trips back and forth, and ate her meal and then as the sun was sinking, she got into her canoe. Set off to her family's beach, after a while her arms became sore of paddling, and she put her hands in the water and begged for help. Two man-eaters came, and her family was treated to her, wedged between two of them. Her hands holding onto their fins, being towed home. She let them go close to the shore and gave them each a pat and a thanks and then took up the paddle and moved it to shore. Her Pader came into the shallows to help.

"Was everything fine there, Dader?"

"Yes, but my arms were tired after a while, and they happened to be swimming by."

"Dear child! You are getting soft!" Her Da laughed, pulling the small canoe onto the shore.

"Tomorrow we will fix what needs to be fixed. For now, why don't you see what your Mader has cooking, you must be hungry. Feeding two now."

That evening they sat around looking up at the red star and wondering if they would have another light show like the last one. She told them about the Prophecy, reciting the part about the breath of the Dragon. "It heralds the advent of the Dragon age, and things will change for everyone. We must be prepared, you most of all. If I am known, then eventually you will be found. I fear what the future holds."

"Stop right there, Atin. You cannot worry about what may or may not happen. It will happen whether you have a hand in, or a hand out. When the time comes, we will move to the city. We have places there we can go. We are not worried. The Universe will provide when the time comes."

Atin spent the next three weeks enjoying the freedom she longed for, trying hard to not wonder what Kaisan was doing, saying goodbye to his Mader, hoping he didn't get sick, and her Mader said engaging all those thoughts, especially since she had no control over what was happening was not good for the baby growing inside her.

"You do yourself and the child no good, by wondering and worrying about things you cannot change. The Universe will give you strength to fight the battles which require you to worry about. Other events will happen whether you worry about them or not. Pick your battles."

"I know, but I love him so much. I did not realize how much until he left. He never lied to me, so I did not worry about this. I can tell, you know."

"Yes, but he did not tell you who he was. Omission is a form of lying, and you never asked him about his family first. You can not go forward not knowing all the facts. Information is always best if it is offered and if it is not, then you ask. Maybe in the future, you have your sister and maybe Kaisan would benefit from it also but learn how to read our language. Then nothing will get past you. You know people and their energies, which is important also, you have certain skills I am sure you will use. Not everything is cut and dried with people, you are able to see the truth around them.

You healed your Pader, because you saw his aura was sick, you said you also saw auras around the Dragons. You can command water, the seas, and the inhabitants in them. I am sure you have other gifts as well. You are smart enough to use them for good choices; we didn't raise you to harm another. You will be a good Mader; you have a caring heart.

You are a lot like your Pader, he tries not to show it, but he cares about his children, that's why it was so hard for him to say goodbye to his older children. He does miss them so. You make sure this early on, that you only worry about the things you can change, not the things you can't. It serves no good to you or the baby. Remember this."

"Yes, I know now Kaisan was not forthright with all information. I do not understand why he would hold back. I am waiting to see him again and ask him why. Then I will decide what to do. Solina and her Gran helped me to see and hear what is said, I am trying. They have begun to train me in what ruling entails. Not that I will be a Ruler. I will begin my lessons to read and write, the next time I return."

She felt better after her Mader set her mind to rights and she knew after the breath of the Dragon gave them a new age, then the battles would begin.

CHAPTER 48

Andic

New Beginnings Bring Peace

Andic was down in the catacombs for another month. Before she was given notice to leave, Natan and she had a good talk.

"There is a sickness going around the nobility, the Oban of Learning, his wife is not well, we are going to have to end our research, his second is against all what we are doing. We learned all we can from the books down here, you will learn more if you go to the Islands. They most likely have much more information than either continent, you would be better to take a ship and go there."

"What about the sickness? No way any ship leaving here will be allowed to dock anywhere once word is out."

"I am sure we will figure something out."

"We?"

"Yes, I am going with you when the time is right, I have nothing here. My Mader has passed away, while I was down here. I would like to serve you, in the age of Dragons, if you would have me. There is so much more to learn, I have always known there was more to life than one leader, and I am fascinated by what we read. The star in the sky, it heralds the advent of the new Dragon age."

"Serve me? Isn't this a bit strange? I am a street rat, and how would we get a ship? I have a bit, stashed away, somewhere, but not enough to gain passage."

"Well, while we are here, you can continue on being who you are."

"Thanks." Natan ignored her sarcasm and continued on.

"My Mader did not spend any I gave to her, and I gave her all. So, with this, we can either pay for a spot on a ship leaving, there are traders who go quite regularly. One is due back soon, from Pelin'Dun, or we can buy our own, but then we must worry about what to do with it later."

"But a ship of our own, we could sail wherever we wanted to, without having to wait." They discussed the logic either way and Andic stated, "There is one item which needs to leave with me. Do I take it now, or wait till we leave?"

"Let me bring another down here, you are searched every time you leave, and I am not, and I will do it soon, is there a place I can put it? Do you have a spot where it will be safe until we find a ship?"

"There is a fountain, up by the Temple of Sorrows, the smaller of the two, it has a loose stone halfway around the base, it is a bit off colour, you can see it if you look hard enough. You would have more success at night."

"I will go look soon, so I know where this stone is, if I am to go at night, I do not want to look lost, should there be anyone about."

"Good choice. Always be prepared. You must be learning from me."

"One cannot help but learn something from the Little Dragon, should she decide to teach."

"I am hearing some sarcasm in your tone, Natan. Are you mocking me?"

"Who me? Never!"

"Well, if that is your attitude, then I will say good path to you. I am done. There is no more for me here. I will visit you in say…a week? Unless you need me, you can find me or someone who will know where I am, at the House of Delights."

"Good path to you also."

On an impulse Andic gave Natan a quick hug, and bid him farewell, she took one last look around where she spent the last while, sorting, reading, and the table, where she and Brecu joined on. She stared at the table then shook her eyes away. Like she was memorizing the memory, to store it away inside her mind. She left not bothering with a lantern, she left it for Natan. The way was dark until she reached halfway, then the light coming from above was more than enough.

She left the Hall, walking past Brecu, and saw he was watching her again, she nodded her head and kept going. She saw he looked sad… Sad and tired, like he had the cares of the world on his shoulders. She kept walking back down the hill, into the lower city. Down the various paths, her stride never faltered and walked in just as Delma came out of her office.

"Lass, how are you, dearie?" She gave her protégée a big hug.

"Not bad, I finished at the Hall of Learning, I will be staying awake as long as I can tonight and will be resuming my old habits, I am tired of the heat. How are things here? I heard about the sickness on the Hills and the deaths. Do you know what it might be?"

"One Oban said it was a shipment which came in from Du'Lanay, a spice only the rich can afford. It might be the Layanese Safran. They use it in some of their candied treats they make using the spice. It seems the FirPader's family were hard hit, the Harem lost half, and a lot of children too. Now it is known what the culprit is, they can treat it, and the rumour is Du'Lanay planned this. The FirPader is angered and wants to gather as many troops as possible and send them all to the other continent.

On a different note, have you seen the star in the sky? Do you think we will have another show like last time? Some of the girls, they talk, and there is talk of it being called the Dragons Breath, or Dragon Star. If I didn't know there was now Dragons I would laugh at it all."

"But that's it, we don't know there are Dragons. I certainly won't believe until I see one with my own eyes. It could be rumours. How does anyone know for sure?" They spent a portion of the evening talking and Andic went up to her room to change into her poor man's clothes. Except this time nothing was fitting right. She went back down to see Delma. "Nothing is fitting right anymore."

"Let's go ask Verema, she's not busy right now. She has a soft spot for you and has more than enough clothing to spare you some."

She was outfitted with a bustier which fit and compressed her small breasts, when she put on her tunic, one couldn't see she was a girl unless the tunic was pulled taunt. "Could you cut my hair short again, it is getting long and is poking me in my eyes."

"We have a new girl, she's from Lanthia and she can braid it like the women warriors, and it will stay out of your eyes. Don't worry, you will still look like a boy, to those who don't know you." After all was done, she had a look in one of the mirrors and liked the fresh style, she still looked androgynous to most.

She left to go wander through her territory, and then hopefully meet up with one of her deputies. She roamed around, saw the sick and the dying, in almost all the houses she covertly observed. The FirPader's house was the worst, they had a celebration, one of the concubines birthed a girl to the FirPader, and there were treats abounded.

Almost all the children died, only the littlest hadn't eaten the treats. Two Daders and the heir apparent passed and one of the wives of the FirPader was barely hanging on. Three concubines were dead and four also gravely sick, and several of the Obans of three different halls had died, with two others also sick. The disease of the rich, apparently, even if Du'Lanay hadn't planned it, it was a clever way to undermine the enemy.

She watched several other homes, and the same situation in most of them, all affected by the sickness. She wandered over to the warehouses and met a few people, and found out there was a meeting, down by the docks. She then walked right up to the building and was only challenged when she walked inside. She told them who she was, and then went forward, and greeted Laza, who said he had developed a system and appointed new people to several quarters of the city.

She told him to continue doing what he was doing, she would no longer be the Little Dragon, she was tired and would continue to feed him information from the rich sector, that she would do. "I am done, Laza, and you seem to have a good handle of things, this sickness with the rich, it seems it was deliberate, do you think from Du'Lanay?"

"No, but I heard the Obans are feeding the FirPader with lies it was. It seems some water entered the barrel of the spice, and it grew some mold, they scooped it out of the barrel before it was delivered and separated, but spores were still in the spice. It should have all been thrown out."

"That spice is extremely hard to come by, especially in the volume which comes here. A whole barrel? That alone sounds a bit suspicious. It has always come in smaller amounts and bon smaller containers."

"This is true what you are saying. I agree with your thinking, but there is nothing we can do with the way events have happened. Now there will be a shake up, most of the dead were women and children, and there will be many marriages to celebrate before winter comes. There is talk the son the FirPader disowned is returning and they will marry him off to a Princess from the land to the west."

"But isn't he married to one of the Dragons?"

"That's heresy. The FirPader doesn't even recognize the marriage."

"Well for now I will continue on the hill. I'll pad the coffers for you. You need not worry about this. Anything of note, let me know. I am no longer at the Hall of Learning, my time there was ended. I'll be hanging around like usual."

"Very good, Little Dragon."

One of Laza's lieutenants came in an unhurried rush. "There are soldiers on their way. Let's go."

Andic said goodbye and she left back the way she came, except she took to the roofs. She watched the soldiers and she thought about Brecu, and her thoughts leapt to their activities.

I do miss his hands all over my body, and the way he made me feel. I miss our comradery also. This has been the longest we have not talked. Except me being gone for four months. Maybe I will see him, and if he's still angry, then at least I tried first.

She made her way down the path of Learning and chatted with a few men there, Brecu was on morning duties, and he slept at the Barracks. One of his comrades offered to get him, and Andic said she would see him later, maybe at the end of his duties the next day.

The sun was peeking out when she made her way back to the House of Delights, "I will stay elsewhere for a bit while I am awake at nights. I will be around,"

She packed a few things, and left, glancing at the sky, the star reflected the rising sun and it seemed larger than ever. She went to the fountain and her hiding spot there. She lay down and began dreaming. It began with her thoughts, they were travelling fast, she felt disoriented in them. First, she thought about her work and her conversation with Natan, next thing she knew she was thinking and seeing something which made her wonder what it was. She saw a ship and a transaction; there was coins exchanged and she saw a hand in front of her. She recognized the hand before her as Natan's. Then the scenery changed. It swooshed around and she wondered exactly what was going on, then she saw herself.

This is strange. Why am I seeing myself?

Then she saw a view of a hand, it was male and it touched her breast and then it moved down her stomach and went lower. Then she watched as the hand grabbed a particular appendage and stroked it, while the next view was her again. She watched this play out while the hand stroked harder and harder until she heard a moan in her head and the hand quickly stroked then finished. The view of a cloth wiping the end of the lowering cock, then her view went slowly black. She felt herself fall into sleep. She slept for most of the day and woke up with the thought she had some weird dreams.

What was that? I seemed to be there with Natan, and Brecu. It was like I was them. In my dreams. She dressed, had a quick wash to have a bite to eat in the kitchens and saw the person she wished to see.

"Verema, do you have something I could wear on the street, which covers me, but is still feminine?"

"Hmmm, let's see. Let's go to my room, shall we? Verema grabbed a slice of bread with cheese and led the way. "You could wear this… what is it for?"

"I just want to be a girl, and 'tis to see a boy I know."

"Oh, so you're gonna lift it, well, that one won't do. Oh, no…not that one…no…here you go! This one is very demure, you won't get stopped for indecency, and yet so easy to grab with one hand. Here put it on, I'll show you. See, grab here and here and up she goes! Please wash it before you give it back, and if you rip it, you pay me for it."

"Yes, certainly. Thank you so much! I won't forget this!"

"Just have fun, lass. Enjoy the man! That's what it's meant for!"

She wandered down to the gate where Brecu was stationed and waited in the shadows. He saw her, and smiled tentatively, and smiled more when he looked at her and saw her wearing a dress. As he ended his duties and his replacement came, he left and walked her way.

"I thought we were done."

"I, yes, we are, I wanted some fun. I can go away, if you like, I didn't want to go anywhere else first. Without asking you first, of course. I did enjoy it, what we did together."

"I enjoyed it too. I can't take you back to the barracks, but if you are game and quiet this time, we could have a quick go in a dark alley, I could screw you hard against a wall."

"That sounds like what I need right now." They walked into the city and found a dark alley, no windows and from the dirt on the ground, it wasn't frequented if at all. They stopped and kissed,

"I dreamed of you last night, and your breasts." He grabbed her breasts through her tunic and massaged them.

"Oh, and did you have a good dream?"

"Yes, but this is much better." He quickly grabbed her tunic dress, lifted it, and felt she didn't have anything at all underneath, "Not prepared at all, I see."

"Nay, not at all. I want it all, Brecu, I have craved your touch and feeling you hard inside me, please." He untied his trousers, and it was hard and waiting and he put it inside her as he lifted her by the butt cheeks and leaned her against the stone wall. She moaned and he kissed her hard. She wrapped her legs around his waist.

"This feels so much better than my hand. You are so tight. I missed this, girl. So tight."

"Oh, you feel so good. Yes."

"No noise, girl, we don't want to be discovered, I'll get demoted if I get caught."

He kept thrusting into her hard, and it wasn't until he said, "You aren't going to get pregnant from this…" That she felt like something shifted inside her, not physically but in her mind, she felt her anger growing at his comment, and something else. She felt herself shut off and told him… "fuck me harder."

She didn't moan but focused her inner mind at the pleasure she was feeling and craving more she kept goading him to fuck her. She focused on her pleasure and absorbed the feeling of fulfillment she knew would happen when she completed, she craved it all. Trying to keep quiet, she almost made it to her peak when Brecu let out a moan and stopped, resting his head upon her shoulder.

"Brecu?" She opened her eyes, grabbed his shoulders, and pushed him back her legs slipping to the ground, and she didn't feel his cock slip out of her.

"Brecu?" She saw his head bending forward and there was no strength to it, she gently set him on the ground, something was not right. He had fainted. Andic jokingly told him, "Was it so good you fainted from the pleasure of it?"

She backed away from Brecu's body, she saw in the fading light something was wrong, his body looked different, and he looked older….and smaller. She gasped as she softly shook him, and her hand grabbed the shoulder which felt hard and boney in her hand. He was dead, and his body looked dry and wrinkled, as though he hadn't any water left in him. His uniform was loose and she looked at the body in front of her, it was not Brecu, it couldn't be.

"By the God, Brecu. What have I done?" She backed away, and began crying, her mind not catching up to her eyes. It wasn't right. It was not Brecu. It did not look like her childhood friend. Her lover. This was not Brecu.

I didn't mean to kill him. Did I kill him? By fucking? That's crazy, no one dies by fucking. Unless they are fucking the wrong person, like a wife of someone else.

She bent down to look again, the body looked shriveled, and she fixed the small cock back into his pants and tied his trousers up. No need to announce to the world he died with his prick out, they would be sure to look for her first. It was not Brecu.

She closed her eyes, whispered a prayer and looked before walking out of the alley, but then had a thought and backed back in, tucked in the dress and climbed the back of the building, and travelled over the roof tops before coming down and walking into a crowded area in the area of the Hall of Learning, she talked to a few people and then ate, and waited for full dark before she went to Natan's house.

She saw his light on in his lower rooms and she let herself into his bedroom and waited for him to come up. He only looked startled for a moment and set his lantern down and motioned for her to sit on one of his chairs. "You look upset, what's up?"

"I think I may have killed Brecu."

"And …. How would you know this?"

"We were fucking in a back alley," His eyebrows raised,

"He was making me angry, and I told him to fuck me harder and all I could feel was my pleasure building and then the next thing I knew he collapsed on me, and I lay him on the ground, bond I saw he was… diminished." She began sobbing, at this, and Natan let her get it out, while he thought it out.

"You left the body? Where was this?" She told him, as he rose off his bed and belted his robe on. He placed his turban back on his head.

"We either retrieve the body and dispose of it or leave it for someone else to find. What are your thoughts?"

"I don't know, how can we go there? What if someone sees us? Where would we take it?"

"For someone who dealt with this on a regular basis, you are asking me? We should get the body; I'll get a cloth to wrap it in. This will work."

He ripped the cover off his bed, and Andic grabbed his hand.

"No, this labels you, something common, like a table covering, plain cloth, like anyone would have."

"That I have, follow me," He grabbed the lantern and went downstairs and went into the kitchen, grabbing a linen off a shelf. "Leave the lantern here, it will draw persons to us and the alley, like a firefly to a flame. Trust me, I know."

They left Natan's house, and he followed her down back alleys and a circular route back to the alley where she left the body. Brecu was still there, looking shrunken. Natan looked at him closely, feeling his skin and after a while, he grabbed the cloth, unfolded it and they rolled what was left of Brecu in the cloth, tucking the ends inside. Natan, picked him up and hoisted him on his slim shoulder.

"He doesn't weigh much at all, like a small sack of grain. Where shall we go?"

"To the burn pits, best we get this done now, so they can't find the body,"

She led the way, through countless streets and over the bridges, and meanwhile slipping some coin to the ones who would turn the other way.

They arrived at the burn pits which were still burning with the dead, it was as though one of the volcanoes to the North which never stopped smoking. She passed some coin to the man at the lean-to, and he motioned for the body.

"This is something I must do, I 'afta sign off on it."

He pointed to the burn pit and Natan and Andic walked towards it and reached the edge. The smell was of burnt meat and fat, and she felt a bit hungry. She motioned for Natan, and he tossed the remains into the pit, and it landed on the side and slid down halfway before the cloth lit on fire. They stood there and watched it burn for a while, and she tried not to cry, and detach herself from the intimacy of it.

They walked back to his house in silence,

"We will talk in a few days, or after the furor of his disappearance has died down. When you are ready, we can talk about it."

"Yes, I can not talk right now. Only contact me if necessary. You know where I will be." She left, suddenly tired as hell.

The disappearance of Brecu was commented on in the next few days, and Matteo came to the Path of Delights to look for her, and he asked her if she had seen him.

"I know he was meeting you after his duties, he seemed incredibly happy and excited. He only told me when I pressed him. Did you meet with him?"

"No. I never did. He was supposed to meet me for some fun; I waited a while and gave up. Did you try some of the dens? Maybe he is still mad at me and went to gamble it off."

"Well, if you see him, tell him he'd better get back to the Barracks before he is reprimanded again. This is not like him."

"I'll be sure to tell him. If I see him." Matteo was satisfied with her answer and left, Delma asked what was going on, and Andic said Brecu had disappeared. No one knew where he was.

Andic knew something like this would be talked about, and she knew in a week he'd be forgotten, to the rest of the city but not to her. She didn't know what she did, but she somehow killed the only man she was intimate with, someone she had grown up with, and she did not feel like she wanted this life anymore. She wanted to leave so bad; she almost went back to Natan and tell him they were leaving.

She went back to her hiding spot away from the brothel. She bathed in the fountain, and dressed in her girl clothes, and lay down on her back. Looking at the star which was closer and the tail was longer and redder, wondering what this one would do once it got here. She wondered while she was laying there about what she had done to Brecu and she let her sorrow come out and she cried for the boy she had grown up with, the man he had become, the magic they shared together, the energy they had.

Wait, the energy. Is this what I took from him, his energy? Was this manipulation? She wanted so much to find out, what her talents or gifts were, by someone who could tell her. Or was she destined to find out by trial and error. *Was I also in his thoughts, the night before? Was I in Natan's? I will ask him when I see him next. I have some different… talents…things happening. It would be nice to have someone explain all this to me. Instead of finding out, by killing my lover.*

The star seemed to wink at her. *Maybe I have no choice but to go to the Islands. Would they accept me? I am after all, an Aramite.*

One thing the scrolls and books did not state, was if the DragonRiders were all from one land or not, and there was a mix, men, and women.

If this is the beginning of a Dragon age, what would we all be like? Will I be accepted? How will we communicate? If we all come from separate lands. Will we have our own language? This will be interesting. I know Pelinese is commonly spoken, but how will I find any of these others? I guess starting on the Islands would be a good beginning. I must start over, since I have now taken a life which meant something to me. It hurts, oh so much. Now I wish I had not taken the life inside me; it was part of Brecu. Now I will have nothing but this pain I feel. Oh, Brecu. If you can hear me, up there, I am so sorry for what I did. I did not know I was doing it. Please forgive me.

She cried herself out and thought about love, she did not want to love again if she was going to end up taking their life. *I hope I never have to do this again.*

But deep down inside, she knew she would have to, to move forward, one might have to move backwards.

At least it went something like this.

CHAPTER 49

Damara

Through the Maelstrom You May Pass

Damara went through the next few days in a daze, greeted her children with an absence of emotion and just begged it off, as being tired, or a headache, she met the bride and her family, gave the necessary gifts which were graciously received, Damara and her husband had a monopoly of the fabrics most wore, and the bride and her family were wearing fabrics they purchased from Damara a few years back. She promised she would find more for them, and maybe a few others for the trousseau, which they were welcome to go to her shop in the city and start an order up.

After a few days she told Ramis she would be returning to Kara, "I need to go through my excess fabrics and see if I can change the colours to orange of the yellows and pinks I know I have. I have a few ideas I would like to try. Have I leave to go?"

"Yes. I am going to Berrin's and I will host the bride's family. I will make your excuses, perhaps you need to rest more and have Tovah use your ideas. Have the physician see you. I want you to feel better. Rest, Mara. Your health is important to me. I do not want you falling ill. Just rest."

She wasn't sure if she heard truth in his words. He sounded like there was no emotion behind and it was well rehearsed. *Is this what he was like all along? I am only now, just figuring this out?* She knew his activities would include others, and he was only telling her a small portion of his movements, the ones she should know. Friends of their station would offer him their attention, and she did not feel envious. He was after all better friends with them than she was, and she knew he would also be visiting others.

She left, stopping a night at the falls, buying what flowers the woman had ready for her and continued, barely stopping anywhere else. When she arrived, she threw off her slippers and had a good soak in the bath sipping her favorite wine. Then she put on her robe, walking out into the gardens, and looked up at the star, it was closer than before. Peylin followed her mistress outside and stood there looking up also, "What do you think it is?"

Peylin answered softly, "There is talk, Nada, it is called the Dragon Star or Dragon's Breath. I heard talk about these Dragons now on the Islands. There are two DragonRiders, however, I know no more than this."

"Well, it certainly is larger than a month ago, I wonder if we will get the same lights in the sky like the last time."

"I do not know."

"Well, I am going to lay here and watch the stars, sip my wine, and enjoy the night. There is a soft breeze, quite nice tonight, I feel quite at peace here." She turned to her maid, smiled, and lay down, her maid coming forward to fill up her glass.

"Thanks, Peylin, you can retire, I may fall asleep here it is so peaceful."

She enjoyed her peace for about a week, but she found a new purpose, trying to redye fabric to get an orange which would be serviceable to her new family to be. She had a few failed attempts, so she had them dyed a darker colour and it would be given to the Church for use for the poor. As she was attempting another colour, Ramis entered the warehouse, and she barely glanced up.

"How are you managing? I was told you are down here, trying all things."

"I'm not doing well, I have wrecked five batches, the Church will be flush with fabrics for the poor this year. I have tried all my yellows, all my pinks and have this one batch left. If this fails, then at least I can say I tried, not only to repurpose my fabrics, but to find a serviceable colour. So far, I only have two bolts they could possibly use, but the colour is too off for it to be formal wear. I am at a loss after this." She left the words unspoken between them, but she saw Ramis's mind working.

"You should be resting, Mara. We will have one of the Captains fetch your dyes from Pelin'Dun. You need not go. I have something to tell you." Damara looked up at the serious note in Ramis's voice. His smile counteracted the tone she heard.

"What is it? Is it serious?"

"Of a bit. The Emperor has asked I attend council meetings. He is calling all the warriors of note, to return and offer council. I am being given great honour here. I cannot deal with the business for a while. You will have to be subtle in your dealings with the Captains. Use my name for your benefit. There are stronger laws and actions being implemented; you may only be able to go to the Nomas and Nadas for your fittings."

"We can deal with Olent. He can deal with the Captains."

"That sounds better. It will keep him terribly busy."

"I am pleased with your appointment. It is indeed an honour." She had to think on what she said next without disparaging Ramis.

"The Emperor should do well to heed your wise council; it should assist to turn the battles into our favour."

Aram had taken three coastal towns to the North of the Capital, and all the lowlands in between and had advanced far up one of the valleys which would eventually cut them off from the province of the Northmen. She wasn't a warlord, but the more she thought about it, that's what she would do. Separate the Empire from its biggest ally.

"Well keep on trying, Mara, and we will have to maybe find another idea for a gift. Maybe a trip North for some silks or jewels, Lanthia is flush for trading."

He then left, saying he had business to address and may be late. Damara didn't even respond to him, her attention taken by what she was doing, but inside she was seething,

Gone to see one of his children and women. How does he manage all this?

Just thinking about stretching her time out like this made her feel tired. She set the fabric out to dry and left to return home to the villa, this time she needed a drink versus wanting one, being around Ramis was beginning to set her teeth on edge, and she really wanted nothing to do with him, but she had to think more on what she was going to do.

Maybe I could disappear, without having to go through a divorce. If I am declared dead, then there is no stain on the family. The children could properly mourn me. Oooch, maybe no. I don't think I am ready for this. I would never be able to see them again. I would miss so many things. Then, there's Ramis. He wouldn't stop doing what he's doing. Do I want to be that nice? He may put on a show of mourning, but would he really miss me? He most likely wouldn't change his habits. So, no to that idea.

I could hire someone. No... I don't think I could. Besides what if I am found out? Then I am good as dead. Then my children would not have the lives we want for them. No, that's not a clever idea. I don't think I have it in me to do something so horrendous. I must think some more...

When she arrived back at the villa Peylin handed her a note. It had the Imperial crest of her brother on it, and it was addressed to her. She opened it and smiled. He requested she attend to him, but to sail there with one of their ships, he wanted her to go to the Islands, using her need for dyes as a cover. He would finance the trip, of course. She would set sail and be there as soon as possible. Damara told Peylin to pack her items in chests this time, and they would be setting off in a day's time.

She had a few drinks, ate a supper, and was working on her last glass of the night when Ramis came home. He was told where she was and came out onto the patio, glass of wine in hand.

"Enjoying the night? It has been quite nice out; the weather must be changing." She held her hand up with the note, and he strode over to her and took it from her hand, read it, and asked.

"And are you going? I do not like the thought of you so far away."

"It is an Imperial summons, Ramis. Should I refuse him? He is my brother, and now he is Namarch. Months ago, I could have said no, but now? And this would solve my problem of the orange dye for the upcoming nuptials. I have received word from the Capital, the bride's family have begun placing their order in, and it is the largest I've had to date, and half of it is for the orange, I also may not have enough blue either. That is another quest, one you may have to take, as it is so close to the war. The North holds the secrets to the blue, unless Aram has blue, but I digress, my brother said he would finance the excursion, and I would have some of his men with me. I would be well protected."

Ramis looked like he wanted to refuse, but he then changed his mind, she saw his face change with the thoughts coursing inside. She was afraid of where those thoughts might lead him. Not that she was scared of divorce, she was more worried he would think the most tragic solution, the one which involved one's spirit leaving their body. She did not think Ramis would stoop to this, but if one was desperate, then anything was possible. She hoped fucking every woman in the cities was as low as he travelled.

"I cannot go with you. I was asked to go to the next war council. I will leave within the week. They have called others; it will be a united front by the ones I served with. But I will travel by horse. I may have to go to the front."

"You take safe care of yourself. Please do not put yourself in any danger. I cannot think of life without you, please do not fight at the front. You will bring a life of expertise to this council, let the young fight. If I arrive before you, I will have the villa prepared. I am thinking the sea air may be what I need. I will send you a note when I arrive, and I will stay at the villa before I head out. I will let the villa servants know to expect you."

She felt a little quirk of dishonesty at her statement of concern for him. Just for a second.

"We'll go down to the docks together tomorrow and load up, there are some orders ready to go back, and I can help with supplies for the overseas trip, now let's enjoy the night before we retire." He sat down beside her, and they toasted to the night, talking about the star in the sky, starting to blaze its way across.

"What do you think it is, Ramis? One hears rumours."

"So, you've heard them too?"

"I've heard hushed rumours; no one dare speak them loudly. Now Davian is in power, I am sure there will be a religious revival. He is a devout follower of Naman, more so than his predecessor, and he will not stand to hear these rumours spoken. What have you heard? Besides what we had brought back to us by the Captains."

"Well, both of us know what the Captains have said, there are two women and now it seems these are two Dragons and used to be three. One died, and one of the girls is married to the FirPader's son. That's about it if you know something else?'

"No. 'Tis all I heard, also. I wonder what's going to happen with the war and if we are going to war with the Islands. It seems a waste of men."

"You are probably right. I am sure your brother will do something about this, but he won't be doing it like Nader's failed attempt. Your brother is way too subtle for this. He did not get where he is now by announcing it to the world. No, he'll be the thief in the night, they won't even realize he has done anything until after its done, and even then, he'll deny it. No, your brother is very smart."

"I am glad to hear this from you. You've never praised him before. What brought this on?"

"The man before him was a slouch, he did nothing which did not suit himself first. He was even rumoured to have a few first nights, among the royal weddings. And possibly a few more than this. None of the noble older women liked him much. However, I heard nothing to this effect this last decade, other than he may have had an accident with a knife.

However, one hears things among men, not you would hear the like. Your brother is a different basket of fish; he is blameless among the fairer sex. There is no scandal attached to him, and you may be right, he will bring a revival of our religion and it may well be needed, with all the heresy happening right now… and now I think I will retire; we have a busy day ahead of us. Good night, dear."

Ramis rose from the chair and gave his wife a kiss on her forehead and strode back to his rooms. At least this is where she thought he would go. Now with her focus on getting away from him, she did not care if he went to sleep or went down to his women, she already grieved the loss.

The next day saw them both busy, loading the ship, talking with the Captain and some of the men. She used them before on other trips, to obtain dyes from the North, and trips she hadn't gone on, but Ramis was to the country of Aram once a very long time ago. Her Captain, she trusted, she sent Olent to the Islands and Aram, to purchase the dyes she needed. This time she would go, and she was so looking forward to leaving.

"Nada Damara, to catch the morning tide, we must set sail a couple of hours before the sun graces us with its presence. If you could be present before, we have only a few hours window to sail the ship out of the harbour."

"I understand Captain. We will be here. All my possessions will be loaded today. Peylin will ensure we make it down here in the allotted time."

"I will meet you here, Mara, to send you off, if I do not make it home."

"That is agreeable, then. Captain, by your leave. I will retire now and will meet you here in the morning. Ramis." She just looked at him and nodded. Inside she seethed, thankful her eyes were not changing anymore. *How dare he! Just because I am going, he thinks now he can blatantly flaunt his indiscretions to my face. Does he think I do not know? Perhaps he does.*

Ramis and Damara parted ways, she returned to the villa. She ate by herself, a meal of quail, roasted to perfection, a light green salad, with summer fruit. Damara sat on her chaise, sipping a white vintage, she could pick out the fruit undernote, and it soothed her aching heart. She read her tome of Lyana's poems. Likening it to her situation, she felt much kinship with a woman who had a tragic end. All she knew from one of the older Secondary's was this woman was brutally ended by the Church and branded a heretic. It peaked her curiosity.

Why would they have done so? These odes to her love, there is such depth of emotion here. He would had to be foremost in her mind. She alludes to not having him, but some have much detail. They must have been together for a time; she does speak of his eyes and body… I guess Naman does not like the detail she goes into. How is this evil? I feel what she is feeling. However, not for Ramis.

Peylin came out several times, refilling her glass. The second time she came out, Damara was crying and she looked at her mistress with concern. Damara looked at her maid.

"She felt so much pain, Peylin. Her last poem had her lamenting her lover. He was led away and she found out he was gone. Her heart was breaking, and she was resolved to not having him again. All she had were her memories. Oh, to have such a love. One which spoke of each others' hearts and spirits becoming one. I have not this with Ramis. He is much divided."

"Nada, we had a copy of her middle works. It was the most erotic. The girls where I grew up would giggle as they read it. I think this was when she and her lover were together."

"I have seen only a few pages of this one. My Mader had a few of her tomes. When she passed, they disappeared before I could find them. I think Davian must have destroyed them. My Mader spoke of it, and said that when I had a great love, then I would understand it. I think I would like to find another copy. One day…" Damara sighed and held out her glass. Peylin filled it.

"This will be all for the night. I am getting tired and will retire after this glass."

"Nada, do not get distressed over your reading."

"How can I not? This woman lived so long ago and was deemed a harlot by the Naman's. For loving a man. I would like to find out more on her life. Why was that so bad?"

"She loved a man who was joined to another. I heard the stories; girls would talk among themselves. The Matron knew a bit of her history. Lyana loved a man, and he loved her so much he left his wife to go to her. This is what Naman did not like."

"Men can do what they want. Why should a man who leaves his wife matter? Ramis has many women."

"Yes, but he has not left you for any. There is much difference. He can have as many as he wants. A bond of marriage protects him. Ramis uses it for his advantage." Damara sighed and sipped her drink.

"You have it right. He uses me for his pursuits. He hides behind me, my business, I cannot fathom how he manages to juggle it all."

"He had many years to perfect it, Nada. I see you now, you have not let it dim your light. You are a strong woman."

"Am I?"

"Yes, you are. You have much information. You have not confronted Ramis with your knowledge. Why is this? Because you know you must have all facts. Past experiences of other woman have you cautious of not failing. Any other woman would have broken by now."

"You are right. My Mader instilled much to Davian and me. Do not act before knowing all and know all the ramifications before acting. I have plenty to disrupt our marriage, but to divorce him, I need something unrefutably. Catch him in the 'act.' But that is below me to do so. I am better than hiring someone to only catch him…"

"You are wise, Nada. Ramis does not see your value. It is his loss."

"Perhaps. He is soon to be busy with the war. He may not even know I am gone."

Peylin shifted on her feet. Damara realized her maid was standing there while she was lazing. She drained her glass and rose to her feet after Peylin held out her hand. The two women went inside; she gave the tome to her maid to put away.

She bathed and dressed in a sleeping robe and sat on her bed. She looked at her maid, who stopped her ministrations.

"Peylin, wake me early, I have an urge to leave before Ramis graces me with his presence. I am past caring about what he does or thinks. Davian's idea of keeping me away to gather information for him is one of the best, and I will embrace it with open arms. I feel if I were to stay, I would be burning my spirit up until I had nothing left. I do not want to spend the remainder of my life a shell of a woman. I have so much more to offer. So much more to give. Let the adventure begin!"

"Yes, Nada. Best you get some rest. Morning will come early."

Damara lay herself down and Peylin covered her with her blankets. She closed her eyes and sunk into the bolsters. *I mean, how can I refuse an Imperial request.*

She smiled as she fell asleep.

The maid shook her awake, and it seemed like she just lay her head down. But she woke rapidly and got dressed for the journey, her maid already dressed to go. They rode their horses down to the stables, leaving the guards to take the horses back to the villa. Damara and Peylin went towards the dock…

"I must retrieve a chest from my office, Peylin. I won't be long."

"I can get it for you, Nada."

"I know exactly where I placed it, Peylin. I will be but a moment. It is not heavy. You board the ship and let the Captain know."

"Yes, Nada." What Damara didn't say was she saw the hint of a lantern inside and wanted to see what her deputy was doing in there. *Why would Tovah be in there at this hour? There better not be another problem with a shipment. I cannot manage another setback.*

Damara walked softly in the side door and saw a light in the corner where some of the bales of cloth to be dyed were piled, she walked quietly and as she neared, she heard sounds of male and female pleasure, some moaning and encouragement. The voices had familiar timbers to them. As she turned the corner, who would she see but the back of her husband, with a pair of pale legs wrapped around his rutting ass! She must have made a sound, because mid thrust he looked around and saw her, and immediately pushed the woman away and withdrew himself from her spread legs. He backed up and swore as he bent down and grabbed his trousers, and fumbled with tying them up, the woman sat up, and Damara was astonished to see her deputy.

"What is happening here? Ramis? Have you no shame at all?"

"I can explain."

"I am sure you can, but what about all the others?"

She was beginning to build her anger, and this was the tipping point. She never thought she would catch him in the act, as she never extended the effort.

"Others, what others?" Ramis was now semi dressed, and he turned to face her, mad he was caught. She saw the emotions on his face. Mad, because now she would have the ultimate proof, she needed to divorce him proper.

"The young man the boys brought home, this last winter, the boy in the lower district here in Kara, the other children you have, and the various other women you grace with your cock, shall I go on?" He laughed at her, a hint of a shake in the timber of his voice.

"I think you are imaging all this, Mara, you know I just love you, this, …" he waved behind him, "She approached me, I was very upset you were leaving, and she took advantage."

From the look on Tovah's face, Damara saw he was lying again.

"Can you just for once. Just stop. Stop lying."

Her anger lit up like the flames of a fire and she began to see the red haze in her vision, and in the low light, she knew Ramis saw her eyes as well. "What is happening Mara, your eyes and your hands...?"

He began to back up and stopped right at the bale against his lower legs.

"Don't call me Mara. I don't like it. I have never like it. I don't like you…"

These last few words she spoke softly, and while she spoke, she raised her hands and saw bright red flames covering her hands and her vision was completely covered in the red haze. All she felt inside was an absolute anger for the way her husband lied to her all these years and a raging hatred for the pathetically cheating bastard. She pointed her raised hands at Ramis as she said the word 'you,' and flames shot from her hands, covered him and the woman behind as he fell back into her still out spread legs, covered now by her skirt.

They didn't even have time to scream; it was so sudden. The fire consumed them faster than any flame she had ever seen. She stood for a moment and watched the bodies blacken and the bales behind shoot up in flames even higher, to the rafters. It was a tinder box. Damara looked at her hands, now empty of the burden they had released, and they were not burnt. Her eyes still hazed in red, she turned, walked into her office, picked up the chest, and walked out, not shutting the door behind her, not caring she had incinerated her husband and Second in Command. She walked out of the warehouse, up the gang plank, and the blonde Captain looked at her eyes and gave the command to set sail and bowed to her, fear showing in his eyes for a moment.

Peylin rushed forward and took the chest from Damara's hands and gave it to a sailor to take to her chambers and asked her mistress if all was fine.

"Yes, it is, Peylin, everyone can see my eyes, I am thinking?"

"Yes. They are glowing but have diminished abit…when you came out of the building, though, they were blazing, we saw them from here."

"I am unsure of what is happening to me, I… I…" Damara's voice dropped to a whisper, "Flames shot from my hands."

Without skipping a beat Peylin said, "If you turn around, Mistress, you have lit the warehouse on fire. Was there anyone in there?"

"No one I care about." Damara went to the ships wheel where her Captain was trying not to think about his possessed passenger.

"Captain Olent?"

She spoke to the man, his huge hands on the wheel. She began to notice this virile man before her. His stature was one of confidence, and she saw he was very fit. His shoulders were broad, she felt small standing before him. Ramis was tall but this man made her husband seem small. She saw his eyes were focused on her, and for a moment she felt warm inside. His face was serious, but she noticed the smile begin in his eyes, as she asked, "Do you fear me?"

"No, my Lady, I thought I did, but I have seen many things, these last few months. I have been all around this world and have come from the Islands, I have seen firsthand the DragonRiders who are on everyone's lips. Their eyes glow like yours, but with a different light. They are younger women, with a kind countenance to their people. I have also witnessed the Dragons in flight. I am of the mind you are also one. I think if you go to the Capital, the Namarch will arrest you and have you killed, especially if your eyes stay like this."

Damara started at that; her brother wouldn't do this. However, as she thought more on it, yes, yes, he would. He changed over the years, when he began his vocation, he was still sceptical of religion, but over the years, he grew withdrawn and lately, these last few years he became more devout, and she knew without hesitating, even if she was his sister, she represented something else.

She may represent a Prophecy, she did not know any specifics of it, but she knew it was related to an old religion, and she knew she would be hunted or killed. Merely for the possibility of what her now glowing eyes could be. The idea she may be one of these Dragons pulsed like an ember inside her heart.

"You think I am one of these DragonRiders? You do not fear me?"

"Nay. I have known you for many years. Even with your glowing eyes, fear of you does not come immediately to my mind. I know what you have done. I saw them enter before you arrived. I do not blame you for it. However, others will. It is their way. You will not be allowed to return without repercussions."

"Oh, I have ruined myself. I cannot go back. My life is over."

"Oh, is it? I am thinking it has just begun. Look around you. Are you not on a grand adventure? If you are one of these DragonRiders, would you not get to ride one of creatures of myth? I saw them with my own eyes, Damara. They are glorious beasts. You have but to embrace it."

As she listened to her Captain, key words caught her ears, ride, and embrace. She felt her mind was taking her down a much different path than what Olent was orating, and she had to tell herself to stop thinking of relations now.

But look at him Mara, he is extremely interested in you. See how he leans towards you? And those lips, he is licking them right now, and I swear he is looking at your breasts.

She kept looking at the giant in front of her, and noticed his hands on the tiller, she had to look at something, his lips looked very interesting and it kept her from wondering what they might taste like. Then she saw his hands…

I'll bet something else is thick like those hands upon the wheel. Imagine if they were on your breasts right now and in between your…

Her face began to redden and she tore her gaze away from the man in front of her and investigated the vista before them, the land on one side and the beginning of the sunrise on the other. She tried to calm her racing heart before she looked back at the man who was more than invading her thoughts. She then thought about what she was leaving behind, and any vigorous imagery left her mind.

She knew deep inside her life as a Lanayese was over. She would be hunted once they figured out she was alive. She hoped her children would forgive her, but she did not want to think about them right now. She asked her Captain.

"What do you recommend?"

"North, we go North to Lanthia, you beg asylum, they are sympathetic to the old Gods, or so I heard. We had some interesting talks with people up there, and I noticed the old ways were not dead and gone, merely buried. You may find your way there, and I will serve you in this. I have need of another adventure. I am yours to command, my Lady."

He was alluding to more than his command of the ship; she heard the allure of his words. He was flirting, and exceptionally good at not seemingly coming out and saying it. She looked at the seas lightening up with the dawn.

"North it is, then."

And she turned around to view the coastline disappearing in the upcoming dawn and what looked like, from where they were, a huge bonfire on the shore. The warehouse had blazed up in fire, the wood dry from the lack of rain.

Served him fucking right.

CHAPTER 50

Meera

Many Become One

I knew the time arrived to have my chat with Adini, and requested of the Amman, who told me his name was Haidan, I would like to either go to the training yard or have her come here.

"It is best you have her attend here, 'tis always a tactic to place one's adversary out of their element, not she's your adversary, but everyone saw what she attempted. You take her out of her comfort and take this forward when dealing with people you know nothing about, you already have a sense about body language and energy, so this is just a method I have used, my Pader taught me that there is more to just ruling people, one must be able to read the room, so to speak."

Yes, I did have a sense about body language, and his was interested. In me as a woman, but I sensed the fact I was a DragonRider weighed heavily on him, he knew there may be no future in it.

"Amman, I mean Haidan, I appreciate your candor and council, I will send for her. And … I just want to say…" here I blushed, I did not know how to say it, "I know you are interested in a… bonding, …" he looked at me with a blank stare until he clued into what I was trying to say,

"I, uhh, just want to say, uhhh, I am aware of your interest in a uhhh, union, but I don't think the timing is now." There I said it. Gods!

Haidan took my hands in his and looked at me smiling,

"Great One, I admit your power is a great deterrent to my heart, and I have pondered any future around the events which will take place. In my mind, I know any such union would have no place for us. I am attracted to you, as a woman, but your power frightens me. Not because you would destroy me, but because I do not understand it fully. You have a great destiny, you have a challenge ahead, unite the world. Finding the other Dragons, these will take you from here, and I would lose a piece of my heart if a union took place and you left. To say I am torn is an understatement. You are beautiful to the eye, and I see into your spirit, it is beautiful also."

"Thank you for your honesty, Haidan, you honour me with your observations and caring. I think you have the right of it, but I will tell you I have a profound respect for you and wish we remain friends, for the rest of our spirit life."

"I am forever yours to command, be it in public or in private."

Here he winked at me, and I laughed at his incredibly open hint. I closed the gap between us and looked up at his face, his eyes a dark brown and the silver above his ears peeking out from under his turban. His face was attractive, and I looked at his full lips, slightly parted, as he saw me looking at him, and I lifted myself up on my toes and kissed him on the lips. He took a moment to process this move and his arms moved around and his hands held my waist lightly as he responded, kissing me back. Our lips played a dance and then his tongue tried to play with mine. I must have made a sound, and he deepened the kiss. After a few long minutes of lip wrestling, he broke it off and looked down at me. I saw the reflection of my white glowing eyes in the deepness of his, his face grew sad.

"You have already stolen my heart with this kiss, and I will always keep this moment between us close to me. You have blessed me with your touch."

I touched his cheek with my hand, "You have a piece of my heart also, as a friend close to my heart. I will be candid with you. I did not feel what the poets and songwriters speak of, no rush of emotions at the touch of our lips. I am sad to disappoint you, and sad I felt nothing. I feel honesty in the telling, while it may be blunt is the way I will have to be."

He smiled back at me. "I appreciate your honesty. Yes, let there be no subterfuge between us, Meera. I am physically attracted to you. You have an allure about you. I am also intrigued by your spirit; the more time I spend with you. I wish to spend time, teaching you what I can of language, and writings. To give you the tools you will need to move forward. One I do not need to impart, is your uncanny ability to see into a spirits heart. Now, let's get this Commander up here so that you can have your chat with her, shall we."

He went to the door, opened it, and gave one of the guards outside a command and closed the door, coming back to where I was standing. I had recovered from my forwardness,

"You may use the Great Hall to have your talk if you so choose."

"May I use the gardens, where we could sit in the shade? I do so love the tranquility, and the trees with their fruits make me very content."

"Yes, you may have which ever area you desire. The gardens, it is."

I gave him a grateful smile and he bowed and left, giving the servants directions to serve me a drink of citrus juice while I waited. I did not wait very long. I listened to the few birds who graced me with their song and sipped at my drink. I felt very much at ease. It was a while before Adini walked in, her head bowed, she walked up when I beckoned to her. I asked her to sit down and after her reluctance, she did.

"Adini, I will come straight to the point. I cannot give you what you seek."

"I am so sorry, Great One, I don't know what came over me. I regret ever doing so." Her head remained bowed.

"Adini, look at me. I will not hurt you." She raised her head, and I saw fear in her eyes.

"Adini, you like women. I understand this. However, I have no experience in this regard. I have no experience in any regard when it comes to the physical intimacy two people have together. I am now, understanding the world of attraction. I need to experience more, like gain and loss before I can address the differences between. I think you were hurt in the past, and I think I can try to understand your way of thinking. I, myself have been on the verge of some pain. Before I came to be here, I was almost raped. It has abided in my heart until now. It is a distant memory to me, but it still remains. I must move past it when the time is right.

Being here and learning from a great warrior, one such as yourself, has opened my vision in the world of combat. I would very much like to gain your friendship, if you are willing, I cannot go forth with such an obstacle hanging behind me. It would give me peace to know you would accept my offer."

She looked at me, really looked. She saw the honesty and resolve in my expression, and she tendered a smile, and I knew she didn't smile often.

"I have no love of man, any man really. I was raped when I was but seven, by not one but three men, fat men, which is all I remember. They ripped me apart; I almost died from the loss of blood. A healer sewed me up and used the healing power of herbal medicine to keep me alive. I have always hated men. Yet I serve the Amman, by teaching women the art of war. When I first saw you, I desired you, but you wanted nothing to do with me. I grew angry, and I could not understand the why of it. I appreciate you not killing me, Great One. I hope I can still serve you."

"Thank you, Adini. I would very much wish you to serve me when the time is right. I have much to experience yet, so much, and I appreciate you understand my stance on such as sexuality. I would like to still train occasionally, until the time I leave here."

"That would be a bonus and an honour to have you, we can pit our upcoming against you and they could brag about training with the Dragon." She smiled; I realized training was her life.

"When you smile, you glow with an inner strength. Keep your inner self pure of thought, learn to forgive yourself and forgive others, especially the men who did you wrong."

"I found them when I was older and killed them, they are beyond forgiveness," she looked still upset.

"Then you offer forgiveness to the Universe, it will hear you and in time, you will give yourself the peace you need. It will show you; you have to open yourself to it."

"Yes, thank you, Great One, I will take what you have said to heart. Thank you for the audience." She stood up and I motioned to her she could leave. I sat there and reflected on the meeting. Haidan emerged after a while and sat down at the table and his servants brought us drinks, fruit, and cheeses to nibble on.

"It went well, Meera? I can call you Meera, Great One?"

"Yes, yes, you can, I would be upset if you didn't."

"Then only when it is us, then. How was Adini?"

"She was receptive, I told her I have no experience with sexuality, and I needed to gauge such for myself before I decide. I told her to make peace within herself, and to move forward with love in her heart."

"Wise words, Meera. You have my love... and friendship."

"We cannot move forward, as a nation, as a world without love. There has always been a war, back as far as I can remember. I would like to bring love back into the world but know not how."

"You will have resistance to your views, you may have a war on your hands, whether you want one or not. You must be aware the ones who don't want your views known, will want you dead. You must learn to protect yourself; you have learned to protect yourself physically, you must learn also to protect yourself mentally. I don't mean to close yourself off, or mistrust everyone. However, read the energy, read the body language, like you have with me, and Adini."

Here he laughed and made me smile.

"I appreciate your thoughts and have learned a lot about the Prophecy and the workings of law and the Dragons. The caverns are a precious secret and I hold the memory in my heart, forever. The gem I created, I feel so connected to it, I didn't realize the impact."

"Speaking of the caverns and the gem you now possess; the Smiths have finished the blade and would like the gem to secure it in the hilt. If I could have the gem to give them."

I nodded to him, and he beckoned for a servant to take the gem to the smithy. I trusted him fully and had managed to leave the gem on a cushion in my room but found myself constantly going back to view it.

"Meera, I would like to present you with the finished sword and would like to do this in front of everyone. It will announce to the world you exist though; would you want this? I will have a regiment solely there to protect you. You would have them under your command, and I will give you ships and troops for when you need them, everything I have is yours."

"It will take a while for the word to travel, Lanthia is far away from the rest of civilizations, so it will have to come eventually. And as for giving me what is yours, where I come from those sound like marriage vows."

"You can take it how you want; I have never given myself wholly to anyone, since my first wife, and she was my first love, I loved her greatly. But since I lost her, I have done much reflection on my inner being. I see you in a different light, no pun intended. You bring me peace, being around you, your inner peace, has brought me immense joy. I would like to be there when you need me, either as a man, or as a leader. I will accept your decision on the matter."

"I will not make any decisions yet. What you have said, I must process. And I have a path to follow. The Dragon Star is one I must follow. I may not have the luxury of following my heart. My focus is on what the Universe places in my way."

We chatted the rest of the day, and the following days I spent, some with his Mader, and I gained an insight into his heart. She knew we were connected, we spent a lot of time together, but occasionally I would beg off and would go down to the training yard to train and keep limber. Other days I would spend with him and his sons. I found those days to be the most fulfilling, the innocence of children, was the most fun and joyful. Soon the day arrived, the people were excited for another ceremony.

Everyone gathered in the coliseum, and I wore all white, with diamond and emerald jewelry, I loved the look of emeralds, the dark green reminded me of home, for some reason, not to say I didn't like the other colours, that of sapphire and ruby, I like the brightness and clarity of the jewel tones. And I loved the clearness of my gem, the swirling lights inside, I paired them with my restlessness to do the next step.

My hair was pulled back, strings of diamonds and emeralds glistened in my hair, and left long in the back, my curls bouncing as I walked, with the Amman as his Mader walked behind us. I had my hand on his arm, as we walked to his Throne. He had another ornate chair placed beside his. We sat down and the herald announced our presence. I paid attention to the placement order.

"It gives me immense pleasure to announce the presence of the Great One, DragonRider of Purity. The one to lead us into the Dragon Age, heralded by the advent of the Dragon Star. The Breath of the Dragon. We the people of Lanthia, give ourselves to the service of the Dragon, we renounce the working chains of the Faith, the usurper of the Dragons, and will protect the Dragon with our lives. This we pledge."

Echoes of long live the Dragon, rang thorough the bowl, the chant grew as I processed the meaning of what was announced. The Amman raised his hand and stood, the chants diminished, until it was silent. "My people, what is spoken is true. We have before us, the Great One, the leader of the Dragon Age. She has learned our ways, and we, I, have pledged to her our lives, our protection, and our love." He turned to me and gave me a smile, then turned back to the crowd, hanging on his every word.

"I sent emissaries to our people serving the Empire. If word of the Great One reaches the Capital first, our people fighting in the war, their lives will be forfeit. We accept this; it was foretold in the Prophecy and we have always prepared our selves for this day. This day is upon us now; we are about to fulfill the Prophecy. This is our time! We serve the Dragon!

Today we announce to the world our faith in the Dragon. The Dragon Star is foretold, the Breath of the Dragon awakens, we give ourselves wholly over to the will of the Great One. We are here to serve."

He beckoned the guard to his other side and the man brought a covered item to the Amman. He then turned to me I rose and walked up to him. He uncovered a beautiful wrought sword the gem contained in a wire cage, the wires, delicately depicting leaves of Ravenwood trees from home. It was gorgeous! He took the sword in two hands holding the covered blade and faced the crowd.

"This is the newly forged sword of Purity to only be held by the Great One, it is the symbol of freedom, for ours begins today." He raised the sword to the crowd and the cheers started and rose as he turned and lowered the sword to me, and I grabbed the hilt of the sword, and the gem glowed and the stars inside swirled around crazily.

"Dragon. Dragon. Dragon"

I pulled the sword out of the leather scabbard, raised the sword tip to the sky and the gem glowed so bright the Amman and his Mader and those closest to me had to shield themselves from it, I walked down into the ring onto sand, and with the tip still pointed up, a light rose to the sky from the sword.

"People of Lanthia, I pledge to you. I, Meera 'Dun pledge to bring a peace like no other to this world, so we all live in harmony with each other. I accept your dedication with humility and love, I name you, People of the Dragon!"

"Dragon. Dragon. Dragon!"

Cheers rose from the crowd. I lowered the sword, and the light diminished and disappeared from the tip but the gem in the hilt still glowed and whirled.

"We will have strife before we have peace, I ask you reflect the person on the other end is also fighting for something they believe in, and everyone has a place in this world. We will find a solution and bring love back into this kingdom. We will be going forward into battle, the Namanist will not like to give back any control over people they have deceived by fear. The Vendar way is to love and be loved, and we must prove we are stronger by it. The time has come to uncover the old ways, and bring them back into the light, and to accept all as our brothers and sisters, and to walk side by side with all levels of society."

The cheers began up again and I turned to the Amman and walked back up to stand before him. He responded by lowering on his knees before me and he took my hand holding the sword and brought it forward to kiss it.

"I, Haidan, pledge to you my life, and I will honour my oath to the last breath of my spirit, I promise to uphold my oath regardless of conflict which may arise." Here his voice lowered so only I could hear, "I also pledge you my love, you already have my life."

I grabbed his hand on mine and pulled him to his feet.

"I accept your pledge with great dignity and love and thank you for it. Long live the Amman!" And quietly I spoke to him, "I accept your love, but as I do not know how to gauge what it is I feel, I will not say something back which I may not be able to uphold. You understand?"

He smiled; I saw the love in the creases of his face. "You are wise beyond your years, and I will wait for your decision, whenever you make it, be it a year or ten years from now. And now let's enjoy a display like no other."

And he lifted his hand to the sky, and we saw the star, blazing across the sky, slowly. It touched the atmosphere of the earth we lived on, and a burst of lights spread out like the sparks to a flame. We then heard the boom of the deepest drum, coming from the sky. The display happened again in the west as the star continued to streak across the sky. In the quiet of watching, I felt my heart beating. Then to my surprise, I felt something else.

It began as a murmur, then as I stood there, watching the fading streaks in the sky, I felt another beat inside me. It gave me pause. I internalized and felt my heart begin to race with the unknown. The other beat was slow and methodical.

What can this be? Is this my Dragon? I stood there. The Amman beside me, and the crowd quieted. My eyes changed; he told me later they brightened and changed to that of an animal. I felt a change happen, in my silence. A shudder in the ground below me.

"Did you feel that Amman?"

"What, Great one? I felt nothing."

"The earth below us, I felt it shudder."

"You have perhaps felt the star? It has landed on this world, perhaps?"

"Yes, this could be so." I returned to the present. The Amman and all the crowd lowered to their knees. I looked down and inquired quietly.

"What is happening? Why are you and everyone on your knees?"

"Great One. You lost yourself into your thoughts. Your eyes were glowing so bright, and the iris's changed shape. When you asked if I felt what you did, they glowed very bright. We are awed and humbled and you have clearly shown us the Age of Dragon's is upon us." Haidan bowed his head, and I looked down at him.

"I did? They are? It is? I am not sure what is happening to me, but I feel very…calm…this is new to me." I spoke loudly to the crowds.

"Rise up, rise and be blessed to know the Great One has woken. We will bring peace to this world. He will guide us, and we will guide the world. They will bring us war. But knowing the people of the Dragon, war is what we do! They will bring us war and we will embrace them!"

The crowd awed and cheered, and we walked back to the Thrones placed under the royal awning. Seating ourselves, his youngest grabbed onto Haidan's robe and he bent down and picked up the child and seated him on his lap. Whispering something to his Pader, Haidan whispered something back, which had the child looking at me. Then to my surprise his son crawled over and held his arms out to me. I grabbed the little boy and lifted him to my lap. He settled, and sat there staring at me, until I bent forward.

"What do you see, little one?"

"Your eyes. They are incredibly beautiful, Manuman." I smiled. Children were so honest.

"You like my eyes?"

"Yes. They sparkle. Like the sparkly stone in your sword."

"Ahhh, I see. So, I do not scare you with my sparkly eyes?"

"Oh, no. They make you more pretty. Are you going to be our new Mader? Is Pader and you going to be joined?" I looked over to Haidan, shocked and he smiled sadly, as if to say, 'I told you so.' I looked back at the eager little boy.

"Perhaps one day, your Pader and I will join. But not now. I must be… the Mader to your people, and then I must gather more children to the family. Other peoples who need their Mader. I must unite a lot of children and make the family whole and then fight the men who would not have it so. The time for your Pader and I will be something which may not happen right away. Are you content in this knowledge little one?"

"We will be a family one day?"

"Well, if you are fine with it, I already find us a family. But I tell you this. I do have work to do and may not always be here with you. You will listen to your tutors and your GrandMader, and Pader while I am away? Learn and grow, knowing I am not here with you?"

"Oh, yes. I will. I promise. Will you ride a Dragon? Can I ride a Dragon?"

I laughed at his direct questions. Glancing at Haidan, I saw the look of shock and pleasure passing over his face as the ramifications of what I said sunk in.

"I get to ride him first. But I have yet to meet him. When the opportunity arises, I will take you for a ride."

"Oh, yes! You Promise?"

"Yes, now can you settle down so we can watch some of the display?" The little boy turned in my lap and sat down grabbing my arms to wrap around him.

"I told you; they would have your love. You meant what you said? About us?"

"Yes, yes, I did. I have grown to love you and your family. But we may be parted. There will be time for us, but it will not be immediately. I have work to do."

"I understand all too well. I am content with what you have declared and will work to get you on your path. My boys have attached themselves to you, it may be hard to let you leave."

"That is why I am warning them now. I have a Prophecy to fulfil. Knowing it in whole has me worried about the future. I have their love, but they also have mine. It will go with me, and mine will stay with them."

"My love will go with you, also."

"Yes, and I will leave you with mine. This is all I can give for the moment. The…other part… the relation part… will have to wait."

"I will wait forever if needed, I am content you voiced it. I was quite surprised to hear it spoken."

"Why should it not? In the brief time I am here, I have learned many things. To look beyond what is presented. I delved into your spirit and see your caring is genuine. You are patient and not imposing. We have a…mutual love for righteousness. I see… you. I am pleased with you. Sorry, this sounds like I was shopping in the market." Haidan laughed at the reference,

"I will take this! I hope I am not too ripe for your tastes!"

"Well… we will see won't we!"

"Can you two stop talking and watch, Pader! Manuman!"

We laughed at his son's impatience and I reached out for the Amman's hand. He held it while we spent a few minutes more watching a myriad of festivities, enjoyed the feasting, and at one point a messenger came forward and whispered something to the Amman. He stood up and beckoned to me. I had to beckon a servant to take the youngest boy from my lap.

"A ship has docked from the South, carrying a woman with red eyes. They have placed her in the Great Hall; would you come with me and meet her?" I put my hand in his and we left to go back to the Palace.

I was about to meet one of my own, a sister, a Dragon.

CHAPTER 51

Vian

To Seek Out the Old Which is New

Rowan/Vian worked long hours, the barrage of injured never ended, and several times they had to pack up the tents and move along closer to the fighting. This last set up had them high on a hill, overlooking the battle raging beneath. She glanced once to the west and saw the ebb and flow of the battles, once such battle was two days before the edges of the fighting men parted and each went to their encampments to lick their wounds and recoup for the next foray together.

Like a well orchestrated dance, two lovers, joining and engaging then parting. She thought and stood there gazing out on the field. She looked back and the star in the sky caught her eye. It was larger than before, and she wondered if it was going to spark off when it hit the sky. Like the others, so long ago. That seemed much like another life. One she did not want to address in her mind.

"Vian, Vian"

She started as she heard her new name being called; it took her a moment to process it was indeed her name. Rulliah strode up to her, the older woman's blonde hair, damp with sweat, and dirt. Her kind blue eyes looked at the small brown-haired woman, whose head of short spiky ends was poking out from her cowl. Each woman in service had her hair tucked under a white cowl, more like a kerchief which held the hair against their head, while the robes cowl covered this. During busy times, it was not uncommon for the cowls of the robes to rest on their shoulders. They were not punished for it; the transgression took second place to the need of care.

"They are bringing more men up the hill, we will be terribly busy for a while. I need to replenish supply of this weed. Do you know it? Hunters saw some greens in the headwaters of this stream. That would be the first place you could look. It is found near a water source." Rulliah held up the wilting stems of a green leaf weed which Vian recognized by its smell.

"Yes, I will go gather some, let me grab a basket." Vian ducked into the tent, collecting a basket and then Rulliah shoved another into her hands.

"Take your time, I heard talk behind us higher up is a spring which feeds the stream we have beside us. I will need an abundance of this plant, you need a rest, as I am sure with the wounded they are beginning to bring up, we will not be able to sleep much. You rest, wash, meditate, speak to God, and bring back what I require. I will send you with some bread and I don't want to see you until tonight. Then I am afraid you will have no rest. Hurry child, if you stay Brother Leor will find you and you will have no chance to have the rest."

Vian took the baskets, grabbed a small loaf of bread from another basket, and took herself up the hill through the trees and bushes behind their tents. Leaving the busyness of the hospice and the echoes of battle, she followed the path which faded into nothing. She focused, listening to the music of water over rocks and moss and followed the sound.

She walked for a half hour through the forest of very tall Redwoods, seeing the occasional buck or doe scatter at sight of her. She heard other smaller animals but did not see what was running away in the underbrush. *As long as they weren't rushing towards me, I'm happy to not know what they are.*

She maneuvered herself around the larger bushes. Broad leaf and full of life, their deep green a stark contrast to the red bark on the trees. Always on an upward path she climbed following the music she heard in her mind. It was constant, and she loved the sound it gave her. She began to relax, her shoulders dropped with her walking, and she felt the knots in her back easing with the swinging of her arms. *It is so beautiful and serene out here in the God's country, I cannot hear the war. I could get lost out here. Would anyone miss me?*

She realized she hadn't thought about the life she had before the Church embraced her talents. She had not even thought about her baby. It seemed ages ago she carried and given birth but it had only been a couple of months. She wondered at her lack of caring, did this make her a bad person? *Have I always not cared? Would I ever have the chance to see him? I think not. They will be sure to not mention me to my son. I guess for me he is dead, and this makes me a bit sad.*

Lost in her thoughts, she tripped over a root rising out from the soil and almost landed on a knee but caught herself in time. Placing her hands out, she rested against a trunk. She listened to the call of birds, and it sounded like music to her ears, it calmed her out of her tragic and damaging thoughts. *How unlike the songbirds I once had. These birds have a different sound. A song of freedom. Much like me. Am I really free, though? I do fear I am in Kavus's territory; he may come back to the battlefield. What if he saw me? Would he recognize me? Hmmm, he might. I should think about the future. Perhaps, I can travel on from here. But where?*

She stood and leaned against the tree with her one hand and listened intently to the sound of the pulsing vibration of the tree and followed it down into the soil beneath her feet and she travelled the roots of the tree, which mingled with others, and she lost herself for a while, and felt the pulse verge with her heartbeat. A feeling of such peace came over her; she wondered for a minute if this was what death felt like. The silence of the woods gave her spirit pause. Then she heard small sounds. The whisper of the wind, flowing through the canopy overhead. The sounds of wings beating. The sounds of animals walking, then bounding through the brush. She heard it all.

She searched outward and found the source of the stream which wandered down the hill and she opened her eyes to find she had wrapped her arms around the tree before her. She kissed the bark. *Thank you for the kindness of your love and being.*

She pushed herself away and stood up. She walked around its great trunk and kept walking up the rocky escarpment and crested a damp area on the top of the small hill. She found on the other side of the rocks a small pool, big enough for her to sit in and she first lay down and gave herself a long drink with her hands, it tasted so good and cool.

She rose and noticed surrounding the pool where there was dirt, astonishingly vast amounts of the weed she sought. Vian thought about how she would proceed and how she would go glean this plant. *First, I will bathe and wash my clothes, and then while I dry, I will pick this plant.*

She did just that. Washing her hair took little time, she washed her clothes after she removed them and set them onto the warm rocks to dry, then washed her body, musing all the while her body had shrunk. Her breasts sagged a little, she had liked them when they were full of milk, and she became sad. Her belly had shrunk in on itself, lack of food, she had never been this small before. Her legs had shape and form; she saw the split between the large muscles on her thigh. She washed, sitting for a while then rose and grabbed a basket. After a time, she had both baskets filled and she grew tired.

She put on what was dry, her bodice, loincloth, and her leggings and tunic but the robe with cowl was still wet, so she flipped it over to have the other side dry. She looked up at the sun, noting its position, and knew she had several hours before she had to return. Vian would accept this gift of time. The sun poked its head through the clouds. She was grateful it was a good day, and she could find herself sleeping without the worry of rain. She thought to pray, it had come easy to her. Learning from the Church denizens, the thought of praying was awkward to her at first. But the more she practiced, it came like a second thought.

I give thanks for a peaceful country out here. This is Narman's country. Peace mere steps from war. How I wish there were no war. So much sorrow and hurt. I pray to give peace to those who need it most. The injured and the dying. Oh, the dying. Such sorrow for the boys who will not see their families again. The Maders who will not see their boys again. How it makes my situation less. I will not see my child grow into a man, but other Maders will not see their grown men again. How war rips families apart. I wish this war would end. Have an end to the sorrows.

Having found some inner peace from the gift of the tree below in the forest she felt a pull to the North, and she gazed up and around and noticed the star with a tail again. It was larger than her view in the morning. It looked red much like the flame of fire. *The star looks like it will arrive here soon, it is very large. Much larger than yesterday. Will it give us lights like the last time, I wonder.*

She ate her bread and lay down to have a nap, using a wad of weeds to lay her head on the bare rock. It was so warm she quickly fell asleep and didn't hear the men until one spoke.

"Well, what have we here? A water sprite, sleeping on the rocks."

"What have you found, Damar? Just fill the skins and let's get hunting."

The sounds of baritones did not alarm her. For whatever reason, it soothed her. She opened her eyes and saw the silhouette of a giant before her, she knew them to be Northern men, she had treated quite a few in the hospice tent. She rose to her feet and made to grab her robe.

"'Tis all-right lass, we will not hurt you. You are of the hospice?"

The giant looked at the robe she had in her hands and was trying to put on. She was fumbling with the heavy material. He backed down from his initial position to give her space and to not intimidate her. She was taking glances out of the side of her vision, not wanting them to think she was staring. The Northerners she found, were courteous, regardless of their rank. More so, than the men of her Paders army. She felt drawn to calmness when she was in their presence.

"My Lord, I think we found the Angel of Peace who is also the Angel of the Spring."

He turned to the approaching man who was older, but no less imposing, his height was just as great as the man before her, with the younger man being way too handsome for words. She tried hard not to stare, but by the God, he was! This man was perfect! His profile was like a stone effigy of a God! Vian ducked her head down, not wanting the young man to know he had in fact, rendered her speechless. Vian swallowed to moisten her throat. She did not want to embarrass herself in front of these men. The older man was more salt than pepper, but still handsome enough, and she had a feeling of caring behind his gruff expression which had softened when he was addressing her.

"I see your very presence and your stunning good looks have silenced even the smallest of women, yet again, Damar."

He turned to the small woman, who managed to put on her robe and stood there trying not to run from these men. Vian found herself balanced on her feet; her legs taunt with unused energy. Fight or flight. She noticed they had bow and arrows, so they must really be hunting.

"I am Bodan, Lord of the Northern Reaches, and you are…?"

He addressed the scared, but trying not to show it, woman. She eased her body down, the Lord noticed her movements and smiled, his hands turning to palm up.

"I am Vian, my lord. I have finished here and must get back." The name she had given herself was becoming much more natural to say, she was becoming this person, her other life was over, and she could write a new one. Vian ducked her head in deference to the Lord of the North, she did not want to offend. She grabbed the baskets, and the Lord looked down at their contents.

"What is this and is it something you use in the care of men?"

"Yes, this weed has numbing properties. It also hinders blood flow. Very versatile." The young man had wandered close to her baskets, peering in, without seeming to. He nodded to her and she held the basket out and he took out a pinch.

"How do you process it? Dry, or wet?"

"Well, to keep it, you would dry it, but at this time of year, we can use it as it is. We just mash it to a pulp."

"What name do you call it by? This looks much like our Butterweed, it grows by water in the North, but these leaves are much larger."

He picked off a leaf, sniffed it, and then tasted it. Vian watched him process the taste and the texture. He looked like he knew his plants. The Lord looked on as he leaned against the rock face. He took a leather bag off his shoulder. Rummaging inside, he brought out a linen surrounding a loaf of bread. It was slightly dented.

"Would you care for a piece? If you have the time, lass. We have various plants of the North we cannot find down here. We have had to find other means to flavour our foods, and to aid in healing. Since you and the Church arrived, it has eased our men, who know some healing, but most times it involves the removal of limbs. You and your Sisters and Brothers are most welcome."

"I thank you for your kind words. It has been most interesting, but I sense there is not…there is a frustration in some of the men. Are we winning?"

"Winning? Nay, lass. We are being beaten back every day. Little by little. These Aram, they fight like demons. Our men are good. Only the women warriors of Lanthia are the same caliber as the fighters of Aram, but they are less in numbers… The Commander of the Empire does not like to hear he is wrong. I am afraid of the next month."

"Why is that? Is it tactics, or volume? Can we not hold our position?"

"You know of war?"

"I have not been until coming to assist the wounded. I have…read a few written works. Past Generals diaries, and some manuals on tactics. What failed and what worked. What are your insights?"

Lord Bodan and Damar sat down right where they were. Vian sat across from them, and the bread was passed around. Damar was intent on the brown-haired woman who asked such pointed questions. His blue eyes and those of his Lords were kind and she did not get any ill energies from them. Vian, for once was at ease. She was alone on a hill in the woods with men which were interesting to talk to.

"Well, in a month, we will all be dead or captives." Vian gasped. He was blunt.

"You know this? It is an absolute?"

"They are pressing forward. We lose ground every day. Even with our bowmen, we cannot break their ranks. One of the younger Commanders, thought to wheel around, with a cohort of Riders, but he lost many men. even though he recouped and fought like a madman, he lost most his men and was wounded. Since his departure, we have managed to hold. I see many other nationalities in their ranks. Some look like they belong here, if not for their dress."

Vian knew it was Kavus he was referring to. Too many similarities. She remained quiet, but then she asked. "What about using their weakness against them?"

"To what are you referring? If you know something we do not…"

"Well, I did study a little on the culture of Aram. They do worship a God, which is placed upon this earth. They do offer prayers to this God upon waking. Regardless of where they are and what they are doing. If you were to attack early enough, it would not sit well with them… I read a tome, one which looked like it was carelessly placed. It was hard to read. Many notes upon other notes. Like it had been documented while in battles. There were diagrams, of placements of troops. The bowmen were placed behind many troops. Almost like a v-formation. They shot into the advancing enemy crossing over like this."

Vian demonstrated with sticks and rocks, drawing in the dirt. Herself and the Lord discussing tactics, with the young man offering his opinion, when it warranted. The clouds covered the sun, and she looked up into the sky to see with conversation the sun travelled further than she thought. She drew her knees under her in anticipation of rising. The two men looked at the young woman who was drawing their council to an end. The Lords face grew sad.

The Lord never had much opportunity to talk with women much. The last time he had in depth conversation was with his dear departed wife and she was gone more than thirteen years. Vian noticed his facial expression, and she rose to her feet. The men followed her lead. They picked up their bows and leather satchels.

"I am sorry, I have kept you from your hunting, and I must really go now, this weed needs to be processed for use, and from the amount of carnage I saw before I left it will be many. I thank you for your kind words, and repast. You have my thanks. The best time to hunt is daybreak and the fading light times, so best of luck in your hunt."

"We give you thanks for your council. If ever you decide you no longer wish to heal men, and would rather execute your ideas on battle tactics, you come find our tent. We would be glad to have you."

"I am busy enough, my Lord. Thank you for the repast. I bid you Good path and good hunting."

She grabbed the baskets the much too-good looking Damar handed her, curtsied, and left down the hill, the sun was getting ready to go to bed. She made it back, not meeting anyone else and entered the tent where Rulliah was working, and the older woman looked up and commented.

"Thank you, child, your clean robe won't stay clean for long, hand me those linens,"

This was her next three hours until she almost fell asleep standing up, she staggered to her tent and fell face down onto her mat. The same continued the next few days. When she was able to have a few moments of thought to herself, she found them invaded by a dark-haired blue-eyed man. She saw him in all her thoughts. *What is his allure? Is it his looks? Or the fact he knows plants. I feel drawn to him, more than I aught.*

She was sleeping in the hours before the sun rose, and she heard a sound rising. Rolling over she knew the fighting had begun. Vian tried to go back to sleep but groaned and knew it wasn't going to happen. She rose, grabbing her robe and a loaf of bread, did her business in the corner of the tent and walked to the main tent. She stopped to take a look down into the valley, the sounds of fighting rising to her ears, the clashing of swords. The screams and moans of the fighting and dying men, constantly on the wind.

She was busy changing dressings later that day, when Rulliah came up to her.

"Grab a basket of supplies. You are needed elsewhere. Quick, child, make haste."

She grabbed linens, poultices, needles, and threads, throwing all in a basket. She followed her mentor, Rulliah led her to a section of the large camp, into the heart of the Northmen, to the tent of the Lord Commander. They entered, and Vian saw the young man, handsome still but blood and dirt covered. He looked at her with fear in his eyes and she sensed it wasn't him for which he feared. She knew when their eyes connected exactly for who. She smiled at him, in knowing his mind. He moved out of her way, and she approached the Lord she met on the hill, still conscious, laying on a table with his upper body bare.

The wound which caught her attention was one another young man was hiding under a blood-soaked cloth. He was pressing down on his Lordship's side just above his hip. Vian could hear the drip, drip of blood dropping to the carpet from the table. She approached the young man, and he moved out of her way with his hands still upon the cloth he was placing pressure on. She dropped her basket and started barking out orders, "I need water, clean from a bucket or skin. Linens, Rulliah, thread me a needle. You, sir, may I have charge of the cloths? I will place my hands over yours, then while you draw them away, I will apply pressure."

They traded positions, and she gently removed the pressure and lifted the cloths, the wound was constantly oozing blood as she opened and cleaned the wound and then asked for any spirits they might have. "This is going to hurt, my Lord, bear the pain."

He looked at her blankly and she poured an ample amount into the wound that had him lifting himself off the table. His men came forward to help him ease his body back down, the blood was still flowing. She pressed the wound closed with her liquor-soaked hands. "Needle, please."

She looked at the ground under her feet when she heard a rustle coming from below and she saw maps scattered about. She opened the flap of skin quickly, looked inside, and looked at Rulliah. "It looks shallow, I see no perforation of any inside vessels, but if I do not sew it shut now, the loss of blood may become too great."

"Very well, lass. I will follow your lead. Just tell me what you need."

She began to sew and noticed Lord Bodan had fainted, and she put up her hand to his nose and mouth and felt a slight breath on the back of her hand. She finished sewing and then held out her hand. "Linen, please. Sir, yes, you. Can you assist me?" Damar moved closer.

She stole a quick glance at the handsome man, whose face showed worry but also something more. Love. *This must be his sire*. His expression was something Vian wanted to comfort, and she found herself wondering at herself. She looked again at the man. He looked back at her, his worry coming out in his words.

"Yes. What would you like me to do?"

"I am going to wrap these cloths around his midriff. If you can help keep him upright. Grab the roll and give it to me on the other side. Not too tight. Yes, just like that. Now a couple more…" Damar then directed her attention to a few minor cuts which were just shallow ones and she sewed them up.

"He needs to be kept clean; the wound may seep, you let me know if it reddens or seeps white or yellow, he needs a citrus diet, a lot of it, to give his blood time to fill, He has lost a lot of blood and needs to rest. I will be around to help if needed."

"I thank you, for your care, Sister. I will do all I can." Damar bowed his head to her. Rulliah and Vian left walking back to the main tent.

"The Northmen asked for you, you know they call you the Angel of Peace? Seems you bring a sense of peace, calm and tranquility to all you help. Your name is out there, and soon it will reach the Empire, you may want to think of your next step. Once you are under the Empires sights, someone you know from your past will see you and then they will have two choices. You do not want the one which would solve their problem of you being alive."

"I am aware of the possibility. I saw the colours of his…men. I am thankful we are not placed closer. It is only a matter of time…" The two women reached the tent and walked in and kept going with the injuries which came in.

Men died, they had limbs amputated, Vian sewed, and wrapped, and after two almost full days nonstop, she was tottering on her feet. She leaned against a post inside the tent and wrapped her hands around, laid her cheek against it and closed her eyes only just for a second, she had slept standing up before.

A hand gently shook her awake. She opened her eyes to see Damar, a most beautiful sight to wake up to. A vision given to her by their God. She smiled at the young man, and he smiled back. His eyes crinkled with his smile. Her eyes went down to his lips when he spoke. He had a gorgeous mouth. She watched the lips form the words and was trying not to close her eyes. She shook her head to wake up.

"The Lord wants to see you, lass. Can you walk?" He turned to the older woman. Vian watched his profile. It mesmerized her. He was truly a rose among the thorns.

"My Lord wants this woman to attend to him for the day. We will bring her back in the evening. Can I have her healing basket, she will change his linens and such as what needs to be done." Rulliah handed him the basket and Vian peeled herself from her post and stumbled after him.

He offered her his arm after she stumbled again and she grabbed it. He led her to the section of the Northerners. Again, she entered the tent and saw the Lord sitting up at the table a bit flushed but in full capacity of his senses.

"Ahhh, the Angel of Peace, I thank you for saving my life spirit, and await your verdict, please let me know what boon I may give you, for your service."

"I will have to see the wound first to know exactly what boon I may ask of you. Sir Damar if you would assist me?"

"Certainly Sister, as you wish." They divested the Lord of his shirt which was loosely tied around his body. As she unwrapped the linens, she saw seepage had happened and the edges were red and inflamed. The Lord smelled of rank sweat and of something else, it was slightly putrid and sweet smelling. She looked at him and took charge.

"My Lord, I would like to place this idea to you. Can we walk to the spring? I would like to get this wound cleaned properly. If you feel you could walk, with assistance of course."

She looked over the Lord to Damar and he noticed the worry in her eyes. Her tone of voice brooked no argument, they knew she was not asking.

"Well, looks like we are going for a walk, then. I have need for some fresh air, and if my little 'Angel' thinks I should walk, then by the Gods, that's what I will do. Damar, help me up."

Damar had another man help him raise the Lord to his feet, covering him with his shirt and tunic. They wrapped their arms around their Commander, and they left the tent. The four of them walked through the tents of the Northmen, and another six men joined as a guard detail. Grabbing other supplies and weapons, they all walked up the hill to the spring. She felt invigorated from the walk in the fresh air, and when they reached the spring, the seven additional men fanned out and set up a perimeter. Looking outward to guard against any enemy who may be lurking.

Damar helped his Lord sit on a rock. His Lordship looked very flush and she regarded the sheen of sweat, upon his brow. Fever or exertion, or both.

"Umm, it might help if the Lord is not modest and embarrassed to undress, from the rest of the clothes he is wearing, he may keep his loin cloth on, I have seen all parts of anatomy of men, I am not embarrassed from his lack of clothing."

"This will be the first time; I have been undressed from a female and not ravished." The Lord jested. He still had his wits about him.

"And who says I won't?" She jested back at him, smiling at his humour. His Lordships easy demeanor was not frightening to her, and she felt like she already belonged to the North. The younger man, while being respectful had an energy she wondered at. Vian felt extremely comfortable with both.

Between Vian and Damar with the Lord tottering on unsteady legs, they divested him of his clothing. Then after Damar helped his Lord to sit slowly on the rock lip, he eased himself into the pool.

"I am going to unwrap this linen, my Lord."

"We have not tampered with it, sister."

"I see this. In fact, I smell it. You should have taken them off and washed the wound. I will do so for you now." Vian saw puckering at the edges of the seam she had sewed. "May I open the stitching, my Lord? It needs to drain."

"Yes, you do what you need to do. Ahhhh." Vian cut open a bit of the seam and let some pus leak out. She rose and saw her robe had gotten the front wet, and it was heavy.

"Could I remove my outer robe and still maintain my dignity?"

"I am this ravishing, then? That you are divesting yourself of clothing to join me in some wet fun?"

Bodan could not help himself, his smile was fever-flushed, and she knew he was merely making light of his situation. She smiled at his remarks. Vian knew he was keeping the tone light to keep her at ease. Damar had not let his Lord go, and Bodan leaned into his man. She saw the worry on the young man's face, in the clench of his jaw. Vian knew Damar understood it was more serious than a fever. Sepsis was serious. Many perished from infection. She recognized this young man knew the consequences of infection. He intrigued her. A man who knew healing…

"Why my Lord, you are sooo right. How can I not resist you? Get you while you are too weak to put up a decent fight for your honour."

"Your honour is safe with us. Glory, Truth, and Honour. 'Tis our code we live by. Any time you want to impeach my honour, you have but to say."

She laughed aloud; she took the robe off and took her sandals off. Barefooted she picked some weeds and began to mash them close to the spring, with a rock adding water and making a green paste. She knew this young man was watching her every move, but not in a leering manner. He was more focused on what she was doing.

"If my Lord would please sit on the lip of the pool, I will apply this paste to your wound, and it will help on the swelling and help ease the pain."

With Damar's assistance, Lord Bodan sat himself up on the edge of the pool beside her pile of green mush and she smeared the paste on his wound.

"Look, already you cannot resist my charm and good looks. What about my honour? Oh, your hands are cold!"

"I am sorry about my hands, this paste will ease your ache, and it will numb for a time."

"It will?" Damar dragged his finger into the paste, reaching around his Lordships front and took a dollop up to his face, smelling and then tasting it. He spit it onto the ground. Bodan smiled at the face Damar made. Then Bodan turned and watched Vian's hands. She placed her hand on his side, and she looked at his face and smiled, he smiled back until something he saw, made his smile leave.

"What is it, my Lord, is the paste stinging you? This means its working."

"No, lass," His voice lowered to a whisper, and Vian looked at Damar, his face also looked shook, as he could also see what his Lord was observing.

"Your eyes have changed; they are glowing green." She looked as startled as the men.

"Whatever are you talking about?" She removed her hand from his side, and on a whim, she washed the green paste away. The wound had healed shut, the swelling and redness was gone and only a scar remained. The world closed in on her and blackness claimed her sight and she fainted in his arms.

Vian woke up in the arms of the Lord, he had put his clothing on. She was laying in his arms. His cloak was draped over her, while he leaned against another rock outcropping. She woke up instantly trying to disengage herself from his arms, which he dropped but brought them back up as she fell backwards. She observed the sun had travelled quite far over the sky; she had slept a fair bit.

"Shhh, 'tis quite fine, Vian, I held you while you slept, I hope you don't mind, the rock is quite a firm surface. I was going to jest it had been a while since I held a woman in my arms, but I would not wish you to be scared. I sent one of my men back to get some repast. If you are hungry, let us partake of some food and we will go back to the battle site. I do not know what you did or who you are, but I have had a small belief in the old legends. I owe you, my life."

He helped to untangle her, and Damar gave her his hand, pulling her up. She turned to the Lord. He stood up unassisted and lifted his shirt. She placed her hands on his wound looking at him in astonishment.

"I don't know what happened, I felt a vibration through my feet, and I wished the wound were not infected. This looks years old." She felt it again before removing her hands and he let his tunic fall and he grabbed her hands.

Speaking softly, he said to the woman before him. "I will use deception to ease my healing and not tell anyone. However, if you were to do this again, your life would be forfeit. There has been no magic since the time of Dragons, and with all happening lately, I hesitate to think of what or who you might be."

"And what or who is this?"

"Why you must be one of the Dragons, of course."

She gasped, not believing what was spoken. She looked around to see if any had heard. The men who were stationed around them, were far enough away, it was to be seen if they indeed heard the conversation. She stared at the two men, standing before her, caring in their eyes and something else. She shook her head, not wanting to believe what she had heard. She spoke quietly, looking at Bodan. She gently took her hands from his, loath to do so, because they were warm and she missed the feeling of protection they gave her.

"I know nothing of being this. I hear voices in my head sometimes, and I know there are other women in the Islands who hear voices, but I don't think I am what you say." She then had a thought. This seemed like the opportunity she needed. "My Lord, when you head back North, I would like to go with you. I may not be safe here anymore, especially after today, but I also feel something pulling me North. Like a toy on a string."

He agreed. Bodan placed his right hand over his breast. His voice was still low, and she loved the timber. "If you are one of the Dragons of old, I swear to you now, I will protect you with my life. The people of the North, ken to the old ways, in secret, and we have no love for the Naman religion. We will keep your secret, as long as you require. This will go no further than Damar and me, you have my word."

"Mine also."

The three of them talked some more and then the sky above them lit up with a burst of sparks and lights spreading out, the sky boomed like the loudest drum. All on the hilltop looked as the star with the tail touched on the atmosphere. They heard when they could not see the path of the star. It was all they heard, until it grew quiet. All were busy looking at the sky, the path left a trail of coloured clouds. Evidence of its travels. Vian laid herself back down on the ground and closed her eyes.

"Are you fine, lass?" The Lord reached down to touch her arm.

"Shhh, I am listening," She lay there for a bit, then opened her eyes and rose to a sit.

"You must get your men back, out of the battle, when the sky doesn't light up, the star falls, the oceans will rise. You must get your men back, or all will be lost.

When the last sparks fall, the breath of the Dragon touches all, you will have less than half a day to get your men up the hill out of the battle."

She looked at Bodan intently and he saw her eyes glowing. Her voice seemed disembodied, it sounded like her, but not. She stood up and brushed her tunic off. Bodan's face had many emotions, mostly concern, but frustration threatened to take over.

"How do I explain this to the Commander of the Army? What about the rest of the army? The other men? what if they don't listen? They haven't really listened to me much at all this last campaign." Lord Bodin sighed, acceptance replacing all others.

"I can not save them all, but I will try to get my men out, what about the rest?"

"They are already dead."

CHAPTER 52

Solina

Until the Sacrifice is Done

Solina was busy in the Great hall when she heard a great keening sound in her head, and she dropped the scroll she was holding and grabbed her head then rushed out of the Palace, ran up the mountain meeting Kallen racing down. His helmet had come off, or he had not put it on. His red hair was messy with the effort of running, and he for once, spoke without blushing. The concern in his face was evident.

"The little green Dragon, she began keening and collapsed. I came to get you." They turned running as fast as they could to the Dragon, her color had deepened and she lay on her side, panting.

"Little One, Analaria, what's wrong?" Nothing. Silence. Then, Nannosh spoke in her mind.

"Her spirit is taxed, the Dragon of fire used her talent in anger, and has not let go of the connection, Analaria has managed to maintain a distance, but she is now too weak to break it. I am afraid this may deplete her spirit completely, there is nothing you can do, I will be home shortly."

Solina turned to Veren, Kallen and Sheyna, and repeated what the Dragon told her. They sat back aways and within a half hour, Nannosh touched down moving forward to lay her head close to the weakened Dragon. Analaria's eyes barely opened at the touch and Solina observed the glow in her eyes fading. Sheyna was openly crying and Veren was consoling her, his face wet with tears.

Nannosh said she would bolster Analaria's strength for now, but it would not help her to recoup her spirit.

"I am afraid I will have to leave sooner than I would like, the trip to the Northern Island felt good, I have made several day trips and I have good strength in my wings now. I should be able to make the long trip to where I need to go. I can hunt when I need to. I hate to do this, but the fate of Dragon's rest solely on me now. When I am done, I will send for you."

"I understand. Will I be able to still talk with you?"

"There will be a time where you will not be able to, I will need to concentrate my energy onto the rebirth of spirits, but I will always be there, and if it is necessary, the Great One will intervene. He has the power to, but he choses not to, he leaves everything mostly up to fate. He has yet to grace the skies with his presence."

Solina motioned to the men,

"We will keep an eye on them, Nannosh will support the other Dragon, and let's get them some food up here right away."

Solina, Veren and Sheyna walked back down the hill, and she told them the Fire Dragon had unknowingly tapped into the Dragon's strength not releasing it, this is what was depleting Analaria.

"Is there nothing to be done?" Sheyna asked. She was openly crying holding onto her husbands hand. She was losing another of her brood, and it did not sit well with the small woman.

"Nothing, only the Great One or the Fire Dragon herself can break the connection, however, if the Fire Dragon is new to all this, she may not know what to do. While they have periodically reached out to the woman, she has not accepted yet she is a Dragon. She uses the talents she has but does not know how to control. Analaria is too weak in spirit to reach out to the woman. Nannosh says it will be Analaria's end. Her spirit will await rebirth, much like Atalay's."

"We will keep her comfortable, food at the ready and water quick at hand, until it is no longer needed, High Dragon, this we can do." Veren gave his wife a quick kiss and strode off, to give directions.

"You two have settled in well, together you make a formidable team,"

Solina made this observation. Nothing had really changed between the two newlyweds, other than stolen moments of intimacy. They seemed very attuned to each other.

"What about you, do you not want a husband and children some day?"

Sheyna asked her friend. Her tears had dried, and she looked at Solina with caring in her eyes.

"I have not the thought to do so, nor have I the time. It is not something I am looking for at this moment. I feel if it is meant to be, the Universe will provide. Until then, I have a Dragon and one who will not survive. This star in the sky, I have a feeling… and I have been pouring over the Prophecy trying to wrack my brain, I feel I am missing something."

"Well, don't worry sick over it, perhaps ask your GrandMader. She might know, she's had more years to look it over."

"Thank you. I will go ask. She's probably still here anyway."

Solina gave Sheyna a quick hug and wandered on to the Great Hall finding her GrandMader, pouring over charts. Behind the chairs on the dais, there was an alcove which housed a table. It was occupied by the older woman, who Solina saw hunched over the table.

"What are you looking at?" Solina walked up to her GrandMader looking over her shoulder. There were maps upon maps and a chart with dots and lines all over it.

"This was drawn so many centuries ago, and I can't make anything of it, it says it shows the position of the stars at the time of the advent of the Dragons, but I don't know how to read it."

Solina shrugged her shoulders saying, "Well, it appears we are in the same boat, I can't make head or tales of the Prophecy. I understand where the star heralds the advent of the Dragon age, but I can't help feeling something is missing."

"That's because it is, child. We thought we had the complete Prophecy, but I have learned a while ago the Amman in Lanthia has the complete copy. He won't acknowledge it publicly, believe me I have tried, I have sent presents, bribes, even a Dragon scale, he won't capitulate. Maybe you need to go there someday."

"GrandMader, I have something to tell you." Gran looked up at Solina, hearing the solemnity in the young woman's tone.

"What is it?"

"Analaria won't survive much longer. We will be down to one Dragon. Nannosh must go sooner than she thought."

"We will mourn the loss. Has Nannosh told you where she will go?"

"No. She will fly away and will let me know when she gets to where she needs to be. She says this is the last hope, for their species."

"Well, we have two Dragons left, one female and one male. Is there anything we need to do, to help them?"

Solina began to cry and Gran came forward to gather her GrandDader into her embrace. She held the girl until the sobs ebbed, Metina gave a last squeeze and held Solina's shoulders as she looked her in the face.

"Lina, we will have Dragons. There is still hope."

"I know, this is overwhelming right now. I haven't processed this yet. I have been with my voices for so long, and the last while with my Dragons, the thought of them not being here, caught up to me. Thank you for giving me support."

"I will always be here to support you. Until I am not. You have become a leader. I am proud of how quickly you have taken what I have imparted on you."

"I am nowhere near the Ruler you are, Gran."

"I can only hope you will be greater than I have ever been. You and your cousin will be the leaders of a new generation, a new world. One with Dragons. If I can have a hand in creating in you, a Ruler to rule all, then I am satisfied. Not many can claim this!"

Solina gently turned out of her Gran's hands looking down at the table, charts and maps scattered over the top. She grabbed the edge of a map, pulling it out placing it on the top of the pile.

"What do you think I should do? We will have no Dragons. It will cause havoc."

"Well, we try to keep the death concealed, then also Nannosh's leaving. Who knows what the Namarch will do to us, if we don't have a Dragon at our disposal, we will have to tighten our defenses, are you able to access your powers still?"

"I believe so."

"And Atin?"

"I think so but am not sure."

"We'll cross this when we must, then. I will think about all outcomes, yes, Graler?" Her man servant walked in and handed her a note. Dame Metina read it and handed it to Solina. She read it and looked up. "What exactly is this?"

"You need to read what isn't being said, my dear. This states by the time Kaisan arrived in Aram his Mader was much better; it seems there was truth to the spice from Du'Lanay which had gone rotten. The rich made a certain sweet for a celebration; many died from it. It places him second in line; he will be flattered until he gives up his marriage to Atin. She must be made aware."

Solina started shaking her head no.

"I don't see her thanking us at all, Gran, we should wait the allotted time. Then make her aware. We will not take her dreams away. Yes, I am thinking of her well being, and ours. Since becoming bearing she seems to worry a lot. There is nothing we can do but let it play out. Until we have absolute proof he is not coming back, and has another marriage, we did not know."

"I am not sure she will thank you if she finds out we knew something was about."

"But that's it, Gran, we don't know for certain. Let it play out, if Kaisan comes back, he has a child on the way, he may return. If he doesn't, then we know he was false and we can make accusations all you want."

"As you wish, I will send my messenger back. Have him keep an eye on things and to report back to us."

Solina went back to her apartments, sitting for hours, feeling a sense of hopelessness and loss. Even though she still had her Dragon, she decided to walk up the hill and spend it with the two beasts. She felt alone and wanted to spend what time she had left with her friend. She arrived at the top; the men were taking away soiled bedding. She sat down against Nannosh and cried, Nannosh, curled her neck and head around her human. Kallen, if he was there, left her alone.

"I will not leave you in spirit, I will let you know when I get there, and I will tell you where I am, you will have to find the others, all of you will have to make your way there before the hatching." Nannosh could tell she had Solina's attention,

"This will be the beginning of a new age."

"You are confident. Have you had contact with the Great One?"

"He is not fully in this world. The Star in the sky will announce his arrival."

"You know this? How?"

"Your Prophecy, the one you say you do not know all, is his words. He is all knowing."

"We will follow in your path?"

"Yes. Once the Great One is in his spirit, all will come to pass. You will follow, and the others will arrive."

"Do they know where to go?"

"You will be going to where it was hidden by time."

"This sounds mysterious. I can only think of one area. The one maps say is shrouded by mystery. I am right, aren't I?"

"Yes, but it will be unpassable until 'tis physically altered. By the Great One or yourself. It may take other DragonRiders to assist you."

"Can you tell me about any of it?"

"It took many minds and many Dragons to hide this land. It was an endeavor not known until it was done. Even the Riders did not know the real purpose. And when they were gone…it did not matter."

"Did you know?"

"I did… and I welcomed it. The last days… warranted the change. However, now it has come full circle. You and your kind will bring love back. It would not be so unless hate had soaked long enough to saturate the fabric of life."

"We, myself and my cousin and the other Riders will have a full job to do."

"Yes. It will not be easy; however, it will be rewarding. You will have much to do. You will be the first Riders for many centuries to raise our kind; you will usher in the Dragonage."

"I can hardly wait for this! Sheyna is extremely excited to be part of this."

"Little Mader is the most caring, she is deserving of a Dragon, should there be one."

"Oh, is this possible?"

"Our six need to be mounted first. But long ago, we had many."

"Were they like the six?"

"No, they had not the powers of the six. I am not sure the Great One wants more, but to have many Dragons, they must have a Rider, or they would be rogue. A rogue Dragon is a threat. 'Tis not something the Great One will want to happen."

"What are the alternatives?"

"The Great One will want only Riders who cleave to Vendar. 'Tis the only way. We cannot have Dragon against Dragon. Not again."

"You do not have to explain. I can sense your sorrow. I want you to leave here, in good spirits. You have the fate of your kind to address."

"I sense your sorrow also; however, I will always be bonded to you. You have much to do. With the advent of the Dragonage, your main objective will be to stay alive. You will come to me, at my nesting grounds. There we will be together again."

"Having your reassurance makes me feel much better. I am going to rest now. You will let me know if her condition changes?"

"I will, Little One."

Solina thanked Nannosh for the chat, the men were bringing up goats for the Dragons, as Nannosh wouldn't leave Analaria's side. She walked down to the Palace, went into her room had a long soak She went to bed, after a long walk outside in the garden. She looked up and saw the star the tail longer than before. *This star is much closer; it looks bigger and more ominous than the ones we had a while ago. Will it bring destruction?*

The next few days saw her make several trips, up the hill and it was on her last one of the day, that the inevitable happened. She had turned from the nest to walk down when inside her head a male voice boomed,

"ENOUGH!"

She fell to her knees. One of the guards rushed to her aid, she stood up and quickly turned around. They watched as Analaria's spirit rose out of her body;

her spirit was much like Atalay's but it was red iridescent sparkles. It circled around the other Dragon who stood up and around the two standing there, heading into the air and to the Northeast. Nannosh craned her neck out, her head in the sky as she trumpeted her loss.

Solina walked slowly down the hill and met Sheyna and Veren racing up. They saw by her tears it had happened. She merely nodded saying it was done, Nannosh would leave shortly, she said there was no time to waste, Solina wasn't sure what this meant.

"We have but little time left. She will go and we will have war. That much I know and expect. But it will be a war from which we will run. We must follow and serve the Dragons."

"We were bound to have war eventually. With or without the Dragons. Du'La-nay has some of our men and are asking for more tributes. It was only a matter of time before they bled us dry. Your GrandMader and I have discussed what our next steps would be. We will prepare and fight. That is all one can do. We fight to the last man or woman standing. If you say we must follow the Dragons, then we follow. They would not have reappeared if it meant annihilation, they would have a plan. Does the Prophecy not speak truth to this?" Veren was matter of fact in his thinking.

"It is unclear! We don't know the whole of the Prophecy. I am at a loss right now. Do I follow the Dragon, or do I find the rest of the Prophecy? Who do I trust if I can not do both? All these thoughts are whirling in my mind, and the only thing I know for certain, is that Gran will stay here to rule, and fight the battles here."

"We can only do what we can. The Universe will show us the way and we will find the means to do both. Don't worry yourself sick over it. It will work itself out." Sheyna gave Solina a hug and the two newlyweds left to go to their quarters. Solina went to find solace in her Gran's presence. She felt extremely attached to the older woman right now. She found her Gran in her sleeping chambers, sitting and reading a book.

"This is a change, from the Ruler in the Great Hall." Solina requested a cup of tea be brought to her. Sitting down in the breeze facing her Gran on her favorite settee.

"What? You caught me! Who knew I was a mere human!"

"Speaking of which, have the effects of the elixir worn off the Magistrates and yourself? I am simply curious as to the length or duration of the Dragon's blood."

"I am feeling a bit lost, ummm, a lack of my usual energy. I surmise the elixir is what gave me my infallible energy. I sometimes would go days without sleep. Now all I seem to want is sleep."

"Per chance it is wanting to catch up on all that you lost. I am sorry you feel drained."

"Dear lass. I am not sorry. Not sorry at all. My loss is your gain. But it is also my gain. I recognized you formally, you became a Dragon, and I have... ahhh, sniff... learned I have another GrandDader out in the world. Another Dragon! I would be happy even if she weren't a Dragon, and merely out in the world. I feel completely wondrously happy!"

"Well, I am happy you are happy. There will come a time when you both shall meet. I am sure of it. Gran, I am feeling a bit lost. Things are going to change, maybe faster than I want them to. How do you manage yourself? I am not sure where to turn."

"Dear GrandDader, It is part of us, to feel lost sometimes. It is the Universe preparing you for even greater things to come. Without loss we would not appreciate the gifts when they present themselves. I would always drink my tea and read a manual or two. That's how I coped. I would learn something new or relearn. That is how I know most things. I have memorized most of the tomes on Dragon's. All, in fact. I have memorized all the books in my library. This shows you how I managed." Dame Metina smiled at Solina. Solina noticed the change in her Gran. Even with her eyes dulling the gold, it gave the older woman a kinder countenance than what she faced in Nashta Church.

"You must find what method works for you. Reading is not a bad habit to have."

"Gran, can you tell me more on my Mader? I tried asking one of my Uncles, but he only recalled them as children."

"Well, your Mader and her twin were alike in so many ways, but as they grew into young women, they had many differences. Growing up, before their tutors left, they would play pranks on the teachers which would usually have them leaving their posts."

"You don't say. That sounds like me when I was at the rectory. I would move things and tease the mean girls, when I knew, I would not get caught."

"Then you sound a lot like your aunt Miiele. She loved a good prank. Your Mader was softer but was easily led into mayhem by Miiele. You look more like your Mader, but as I knew who your Pader was, you have his stubbornness. We had many a battle of words. Your Mader would not give him up, as much as I threatened her, so you may be doubly cursed with stubbornness!"

"Who was my Pader, then?"

"He was a man of significant importance. The son of a large landowner on the second Island up. I think he may head the council on tree production for the shipyards. His family are carvers, carpenters and may be involved with some shipbuilding. He remarried many years after the death of your Mader. I genuinely believed he mourned her loss and that of yourself. I am afraid the lie of your death, was one of my design, and I beg your forgiveness."

"So, my Pader is still alive?"

"As far as I know he is. He has several children now, with his new wife. If you want, I can send for him."

"I am not sure, Gran. Mayhap when the time is right. I have other things I need to do. You have my forgiveness; you did what you believed right at the time. I will meet him in the future. I am sure he knows about me now; he has every right to ask for me."

"He may be unsure of his reception here. I am afraid I did threaten him with death, should he ever set foot in the Capital."

"Well, Gran. I won't worry about a meeting until such time I need to."

"I am here for you should you need to talk again. I have many stories of your Mader and her escapades with her sister. One was always covering for the other. They were conspirators, and closer than sisters, beyond being twins. I have hope when you meet her Dader, the two of you have more common ground than you expect."

"We have yet to see. I would hope we get along. I would hope the six Dragons together will become a force to be reckoned with."

"I give praise to the Pader for such a day." Closing her book and standing up, Dame Metina walked over to Solina, rising from her seat.

"As it is now late in the hour, I would like to gain some sleep, and I ask Ilyan for wonderful dreams of the Dragons in flight."

"Good night, Gran. Thank you for the talk."

"Bless you, child. Goodnight."

The departure came soon enough and Sheyna and Veren walked with Solina up to the 'Nest,' Sheyna holding on tightly to Solina's hand. Nannosh was gobbling down the sheep and goats and took one last drink of water, and swung her head down to the three waiting, Veren and Sheyna both put their hands on the snout of Nannosh and she breathed a huge breath on them, Veren saying,

"We will serve you wherever you are, to our last breath."

Nannosh touched him with her head, trying not to push him down, and she looked at Solina, fully crying. And then she lifted her head and turned to the side, bunched her legs, and lifted off, whipping the three with the gusts of air, her wings almost knocking them down. They stood there watching her silhouette disappear into the clouds, and Solina fell to her knees, sobbing uncontrollably, Sheyna got down on hers and Veren stood there, one hand on either woman's shoulder. After some time, Solina gathered her resolve and rose, with Veren's hand up.

"Time to return to business."

"Sorry for asking High Dragon, but what am I going to do, if there are no Dragons to look after? Am I not redundant?"

"Why, Veren, we will prepare. We will eventually be going on an exceptionally long trip. I must wait for Nannosh to tell me where she is when she gets there, and we can leave. She told me we would have to find the other Dragons, and all must convene and help raise some babies, when the time comes. Sheyna you will pack every scrap of information on the care of Dragon's. Gran will understand, and its not like she hasn't another copy, we will need oils, lots of oil, so let's start stockpiling up here in the warehouses, to not draw attention. Anything else we will need, food stuffs, barrels of water in case we need them. Veren, you will appoint men to take charge of your regiments, we will be taking a large flotilla of men, and ships, which will be your task. It is good I have you both and you work so well together."

Solina worked best when she had a purpose, and she now had to tell her GrandMader. She found her in her favorite spot, in the Great Hall.

"Nannosh has left, Gran and soon I will go to her. She needs us to raise Dragon's, it our next step. You know it is so. Pelin'Dun is still yours for a time, it has always been yours."

"Will you tell me where you are going? In case another Dragon should come here looking for you. And what about Atin? Should you not tell her?"

"Yes, Gran, I will, we will stop on the way and tell her, she will wait for Kaisan and follow later, as he will have his own ship. If not, you can send her on."

"I cannot stand the thought of not seeing you, now we are family again."

"Oh, Gran, we will! Do not worry, you will live long enough to see the Dragon's to full strength. I am sure of it."

It would be a few more days of preparing and Solina was starting to get anxious. She was eating her dinner with Sheyna and Veren when she stopped talking, going completely still. She smiled after a minute of silence; she looked at her two friends saying.

"Pack your bags, we are going on a trip."

CHAPTER 53

Atin

Atin was wandering on the beach picking up the odd shells for her Mader to make into necklaces when she saw the sight she saw before, the iridescent Dragon, swooped down and around her, and she fell to her knees and cried and her Mader found her like this.

"Is everything fine, Atin? Is it the baby?"

"No, I am fine. We lost another Dragon. I wonder what happened?"

She rose to her feet with her Maders help. Atin dusted her knees off and straightened.

"I have fixed my boat, I am thinking of going back to my place, I am restless, something is different, like the calm before the storm. I will go for a few days, and reap as many pearls as I can, I will go pack for it,"

"If that's what you need to do to feel peace, then you do it. I will pack you some food to take." Her Mader left and came back with a basket of food which she handed to her Dader.

"You come back when you are at peace, I have no worry you will be fine, you have the strength of the ocean waters behind you, I will tell your Pader when they come back from fishing, so he does not worry. Lots of love go with you."

She gave Atin a peck on the cheek.

"Thanks, Ma. I will be back soon; I need to not think for a while."

"Take all the time you need."

She packed her canoe, hugged her Ma, and began paddling her canoe. Her Mader soon witnessed her finned friends coming to assist. Her Mader turning back to the huts with a smile on her face.

Atin arrived at her spot, thanking her friends, and dragged the canoe onto the beach. She sat on the sand and cried. Crying for the Dragon she would never see again. She wiped her tears, stripping off her clothes she dove into the water. Her happy place. Where she felt most at peace. She wasn't left alone in her grief, her friends, came to see, and watch over her.

She pearled the rest of the day and the next, only stopping to eat and sleep. The second day, she felt she was at peace again, and had harvested enough pearls, she had filled the two baskets to the brim and decided it was time to stop, when a shadow came over her and she looked up to see Nannosh circling overhead. The

Dragon touched down a little way to the North of her. Atin dropped what she was doing and went over the rocks to her friend.

"Are you fine, Nannosh? You are not connecting with me? You must need your energy for flying, I am guessing. Why are you flying by yourself? I am sorry about the loss of Analaria, I won't find out why she perished until I go back to Peli. Oh yah, I forgot you and I don't have that connection. Here, let's play a game. I guess and you acknowledge my correct answer. You are leaving?"

Nannosh blinked her eye. "I will call that a yes. Ummm, you are coming back?"

Nannosh did not blink. "Oh, that's not good. We will find you?"

A blink. "What are you going for? No, wait you can't tell me."

Nannosh stretched out her neck and head and touched the very tip of her snout against Atin's belly. And breathed a great breath, which ruffled Atin's half dry hair. She brushed her hand over the cobalt blue snout, which had almost filled in with new scales. Atin saw the odd one missing, but the colour of the new scales was glorious. Nannosh was the colour of the seas, and her underbelly much like the clouds of the sky.

"Ohhhh, I get it, I think Solina mentioned we need more Dragon's than we have. You are going to lay eggs."

A blink. Once the large head rose up, it gazed down on the woman, still naked but now dry. "My heart goes with you. Is there anything you want from me?"

No blink. "You will be telling her where we need to find you?"

A blink. "You are able to continue?"

A blink "I am honoured you felt the need to stop and communicate to me, in our way."

Atin smiled at the now not laboured breathing Dragon. The Dragon looked into the skies and then back at Atin. The woman placed her right hand over her left breast and bowed her head. "May spirit guide you on your path, may you ride the skies strong until we meet again."

Atin backed up crouching down so Nannosh could clear her for launch. The Dragon flew in the air aways and dipped twice into the sea, both times with a mouthful of sea meat and circled the girl once flying to the Northwest. *At least I know the general direction she is headed.*

Atin returned to her canoe and baskets, heading back to her parent's home, leaving the canoe in its cave, and carrying the load back. She arrived as her Da was coming in with the skiff and her two brothers.

"We saw the Dragon flying overhead as we were heading home. She kept on. Is everything fine?"

"Yes, Da. She is going to lay eggs. The smaller Dragon, the green one has passed. It is up to Nannosh and the Great One, to keep the Dragon's alive."

"She was heading North, into the Maelstrom Sea." Atin looked at her brother Tarik and nodded. "Yes, I will assume this is where she is going. It may be passable for her. It may not be for humans, but perhaps it is for her."

"Well, lass. I would not go near it. I will pray to Vendar she is successful in her endeavors."

"Thanks, Da. This will mean I may have to leave soon. Solina may need me."

"We are prepared to lose you once again. We give you thanks, for the time you have given us. You say this star, the one up there, is the beginning of the Dragon Age? It looks much bigger than the others and its alone. Last star fall there were many." Atin looked to where her Da was pointing. The star was blazing larger, Atin thought back to when she had first seen it in the sky. It the brief time she was aware of it, it was growing.

"You are right, Da. That is what Solina and her Gran have said. It may fly past us, or perhaps it will not. All I know, is it will begin the Dragon Age."

She helped the men, bring in the baskets of fish. Then the men moored the boat, while Atin and her Mader chatted while preparing the meal. Her Mader was grateful for the help. The littlest went to sleep early while the eldest members of the family talked into the night.

"I bonded with Solina's Dragon, it has opened my eyes to what I am to expect."

"And what will you expect from this 'bond'?"

"I could speak to her in my head. She helped me to feel more at ease. It was wonderful. Even better than being with Kaisan." Here Atin blushed, she hadn't meant to be so blunt in front of her Da. He looked at her and smiled.

"It is fine, Atin. You have a great destiny ahead of you. Having a small taste of what is to come, it may help you when it comes to pass. Having a human connection may be…small pearls, compared to a Dragon one."

"Thanks, Da. I never thought of it like this. My marriage could be done if Kaisan does not return. If he does, it may happen he will have to get used to Pelinese ways. I am prepared to accept what the Universe will have for me. I do love him, but he knows from our excursion into the city, he is second to me being a Dragon." Atin put her hand up when she saw her Da open his mouth.

"No, Da. I am fine. We walked around the city, and Kaisan tried to hold me back, becoming Aram for the moment. He meant well, but I had to deal with the brother of the man I killed in the cove. I had to end his life; the man was truly not Vendar. His aura was black. Kaisan is different because of it. You should have seen…no, I felt Kaisan was different. He has much to change. There is still much Aram about him."

"You sound more mature, Atin. You were not like this before you stayed on Peli."

"I had many conversations, with Solina, and her Gran. They are very leery of Kaisan. His omission about who he is, set them back. Every time I looked at his aura, it was truthful."

"People can be truthful, about what they tell you. But not telling the whole picture, giving you part of the truth, is not. Perhaps you need to ask your auras to tell you."

"I never thought about it in that way, you have given me much to think about." That night, they sat around chatting, and Atin's Ma asked her if she felt confident enough to get some eggs, from the nests which were high in the trees at the top of the mountain, she could take one of her siblings if she wanted, Atin declined.

"I can get what I can reach. I don't weigh much more than either one of the boys, and Da needs them more than I, it brings me calm if I just do this on my own." She was trying not to think about the length of time Kaisan was gone, but the three weeks were ending. She had a tough time falling asleep. Atin woke the next day, ready to begin climbing, but felt a bit tired. She told her parents she would stay up there for a few days, with two days travel, there and back, and not to worry, she needed to stretch her legs. The way up would be an incredibly good stretch, with much climbing.

"Climb safe and take your time. There is no rush."

"I will heed your words. I will enjoy the view also. I may see the star closer than ever." She grabbed her pack, it contained another pack she would place the eggs in, it had padded cells sometimes helped them not to break, but sometimes not. And she brought a coil of rope in case she needed of use it to climb up or down in a few spots. She packed a few grippers, iron hooks, one used to wedge into crevasses to pull oneself up a cliff side if needed.

The way up the mountain where they collected the eggs was longer and harder than she remembered, even though she had climbed it many times, she took her time, climbing, and walking on the semi carved paths the odd animal would use, goats or the odd mountain cat. But it seemed they hadn't seen one of those lately, their neighbours, on the other side of the Island may have, killed them all off. The Island they lived on, was flatter to the South, this land was used for growing reeds and grasses, for sailcloth. Higher elevations, used for trees up to the mountains. The two which graced their Island, used as a natural barrier between the families.

There were people on the other side, very rarely did they see each other, the trip across took little more than a full day to navigate, but since Da refused to entertain a joining between her sister Medea and one of the sons, they never saw them. Atin would have to remember to see Medea next time, but her sister had a newborn and was probably busy. Atin came to the hardest part of her climb, and she concentrated on the path before her. It kept her mind busy finding the path she would take to climb the mountain. She stopped on a ledge to have a look at the world below. She could not see their homestead but saw the others far to the South.

That seems a large amount of smoke. I wonder if they are burning the chaff. It seems early to be doing so. Harvest is still early, for the reeds. Hmmm, I hope if it's a fire, it does not reach us. Da would have a time of it, rebuilding our home. I wonder…if he would consider clearing a wide path around our home. A fire guard if you will. It would give him some more wood… not he needs to build more. Kaisan could always help him…I hope he comes back. He needs to explain himself to me. I should have sensed what he did not say.

But this is what I needed from Lina. Another voice. Another person to help me to see. Perhaps I am too trusting. Having her point out to me, what I missed will only help me in the future. I know Kaisan loves me. He never told me all. I can not see him being deliberate in his deception, perhaps it was his upbringing. Being Aram or being a man. Whatever. He will have to explain. I see now, my error. It is done. I can only grow from this. I will not find fault if there is none.

She tried to think about her future, would they live in peace, how would they survive, would Kaisan come back. She stopped for a breather, her stomach was cramping up a bit, so she stopped, halfway up the mountain, and rested, drinking from the skin she brought. This mountain was not an active volcano; it may have been once but not now. The crater above was now a lake, spring fed which fed the waterfall down below, where she had taken Kaisan, it seemed like a lifetime ago.

Feeling better after she rested, she continued, and finally reached the top, exhausted and breathing heavily. *Gods, I am going no further tonight. My legs feel like I have not walked uphill before.* She caught her breath and watched the sun setting and all the beautiful colours it contained in its palette, she loved the colours of the sea first, and the colours of the sun, second. *I think that's all colours, then. I will bring Kaisan up here next time. See the beauty of my home. He said he is used to sand. He would love this vista, I am sure.*

She lay on the ground and wrapped the light blanket around herself and lay there, thoughts churning in her head, her mind was not ready to find itself tired. *What role do I play?* She knew from what Solina read to her, they would be bonded to a Dragon, Solina definitely was, *But am I to have one? Would it be like a marriage? But without the intimacy. Then where does this leave Kaisan? Would I divide my time between the two? And if there were to be baby Dragonettes, how would I raise my child?*

She lay there, the thoughts milling about, as soon as one left, another took its spot. She looked up at the star, its tail longer and it looked like she could reach up and touch it with her hand.

The Breath of the Dragon, it heralded the advent of the age of Dragons, this Solina also told her, it was written down on pages, and to Atin, it looked like chickens scratched at their food, she didn't understand written word, and felt very inadequate, the maps, she could read, somewhat, she recognized where she lived, the Islands, and Kaisan had shown her where he came from, and where Du'Lanay was.

Thinking of Kaisan, she wished he were here with her, she would have to bring him up here one day, if only to see the sunset, or sunrise. From the top of this mountain, she could look South, and see the Island that followed, and she knew Peli was way down there, on the horizon, seeing the Islands from Dragon back, Gods, that was even better, she closed her eyes and fell asleep to thoughts about the wind in her hair, reminding her about sailing her Pader's skiff through the surf.

She woke the next morning, sun fully up and she ate, relieved herself, and as she stretched, she offered a small prayer to the Universe. *If I am to be this DragonRider you have predicted, if I can manage to be the one you want, show me a sign, also a sign Kaisan will return to me, and the child I carry will be all right, send me something even I cannot doubt.*

She said this, because she woke up, her belly protesting, like she had eaten something which didn't agree with her. She should really listen to her Ma, who told her worry was not good for the production of children.

As she closed her eyes and raised her arms, she heard before she saw the touch of the star against the atmosphere, and she turned as she opened her eyes. The star touched briefly, and it sent shards of itself into the sky, like sparks of a fire, shooting in all directions. *Well, ask and yee shall receive, I have no doubt things will be fine, then. Thank you, Universe, I shall now content myself with the knowledge things will be simply fine.*

She gathered her things, and tucked them under a slice in the rock, she learned wherever she was, birds would always take what wasn't theirs! She slung the bag for eggs over one of her shoulders and headed towards the trees which held the birds' nests, she would collect some bounty and forget her cares for a while.

With her thoughts focused on collecting eggs she forgot about the star making its presence known to man across the skies.

CHAPTER 54

Andic

Andic was genuinely bored, she slept during the day and wandered by night, she listened to conversations, about the war, about the spice some claimed was sent by the Namarch of Du'Lanay to end the FirPader, and to the hushed whispers of the DragonRiders and actual Dragons. These were hushed; to be heard publicly was to announce you didn't want to live, she heard all sorts of things.

Nothing caught her ear, though, nothing she hadn't heard before. She crept through the upper hill, and on a whim, she thought she would head to the Harem and the FirPader's Palace. She hadn't been there for a while; it was the same boring stuff up there too. She skirted the patrols, she knew where they were, and she crawled along the tops of stone walls, edged along pathways, until she got to the Harem.

Nothing but mourners there, for once the concubines were not fighting and it was a general sense of sadness, too many lost, especially the children. The emptiness of children laughing and playing caught Andic, she wiped a tear from her cheek. There was a regiment of guards protecting the ones left. She crept along the pathways in the garden, all the guards were outside the garden, and only with her hearing could she hear where they were and not get caught.

She heard voices up ahead, a male and a female in the throes of an argument and gathered they were not husband and wife from the gist of the conversation. She crept closer and found herself a good hiding spot below the balcony, and listened, because it sounded like a good one. She was in need of some excitement.

"I told you, Mader, I am already married, and I have a child on the way. And she is one of the Dragons of the Prophecy Pader does not recognize. How much more can I say this. I will not denounce my marriage."

This was interesting, the man was married to one of these Dragons. She would stay and listen to this conversation for sure. Maybe she would seek him out later and ask her own questions.

"Your Pader does not recognize your marriage, it is heresy. Tovan has married, he had several children and another on the way. This last attack by Du'Lanay has your Pader scared. You must help keep our family line alive. If something happens to Tovan, you will be FirPader, and you must be secure in your children, in your marriage…"

"Mader, how many times must I tell you. I will not give Atin up. Since Pader has written me out of the tomes, what I do does not matter."

"There are alternatives to giving her up…"

"Don't you even think of it Mader." The male voice was getting angry,

"Not only would you lose, but you would also lose another son. I would denounce you."

"You would not dare."

"Try me and see. Atin commands the oceans, and she sees auras, and truth. She is my heart. My breath, I love her like no other. She commands me, and I yield to her. Living as a Pelinese by choice. It is much more refreshing than this life in which I was raised. You just go ahead; give it your best try. Give me a reason to walk away." There was silence for a long moment.

"Least you can do, is help me entertain the young woman tomorrow night, I can not send them back without a dinner. They did travel all the way from Cyntilla, and it would be an insult to the King if his Dader were sent back without even an introduction. You can try talking with your Pader tomorrow."

"What good would it do? I will not marry another woman. I love my wife. I have loved her since I first set eyes on her and didn't know who she was. She has the kindest heart, the most loving family, and she loves me. And I have told her who I was, where I come from, and she still loves me. I am no longer an Aramite. I am now Pelinese. Do you not ever wish you could go back to Du'Lanay?"

"For what reason? I was brought here. I love your Pader. Perhaps not at first. But I do love him. Aram is not much different than the land of my birth. But denouncing Aram…That doesn't change who you are, Kaisan. You are my last son, Akishen is gone, many are gone. You will always be Aram. If anything were to happen to Tovan, you would be FirPader. You need to secure your lineage."

"Pader wrote me out of the annals, Mader. I am no longer. I no longer fear my death. It should not be tradition, to kill all. We should be able to live in harmony with our family. One thing I love about the Pelinese, is their capacity for love. There is no battle for the Throne. Mind you, they do have a different ruling system…Actually maybe I will stay, murder my brother and Pader, and become FirPader, then I can bring my wife here, rule and change our ways back to the religion of old…you know, herald in a new age, the Dragon Age, look up Mader, you see the star, it says in an old Prophecy this star advents the age of Dragons, and I have seen two Dragons, if fact, I have ridden one."

Here was a female gasp, and a whisper of 'heresy.' He continued. "I have seen the Islands from high up in the sky, Mader. How many Aramites can lay claim to this. Yes, let's do this, if a spice can take out the lot of you, I am sure I can sneak in something else."

"How dare you," The female was getting angry.

"How dare I, how dare you! I came here because you were sick, and I wanted to see you if you were to perish. Instead, I find you hale, hearty and planning my future. Pader denounced me, wrote me off the annals of history. I am no longer your son. I am no longer Aram. Or have you forgotten?"

"You will always be my son. I could never denounce you. You must reconsider your decision, Kaisan. You are my only son now; your children will carry our name forward."

"You know, Mader, the one thing I like about the old ways, is women carry forward the lineage. There is no inequality among their people, there is just a sense of peace and harmony among everyone. I am treated like an equal, even though I am Aram. Do you know how refreshing this is? To be able to look a woman in the eyes, and have her look back at you, without her fearing being punished. Even now, you look down. You would like it there; you would be treated with such dignity your station requires. Being Mader by law of the Sea Dragon, not an easy feat in itself."

"You speak heresy, Kaisan. Heresy."

"Heresy, what is heresy? It all depends on what piece of land you stand on. Where you are in history. Times are changing, Mader. The FirPader is not the highest of high. He is not a God. There are other ways of life. I don't know why you are trying so hard. I must get back to my wife; I am already past when I said I would leave. She will be getting worried, and this is not good for my child. And let me just tell you this, if I get back and anything, anything, has happened to her or the child, and I find out you were behind it, then I will retaliate."

"Are you threatening me?"

"No, just telling you how it will be, if you try anything."

"I will not do anything; I can not speak for anyone else."

"Mader? What are you trying to say? Do you know of something? Tell me now. If you know some thing, and you don't tell me, it will be like you ordered it yourself. I will hold you responsible."

"I just heard the FirPader talking to one of his Obans asking him if it was done. That's all I heard. I assume that it was to do with the girl, since they were talking in the hall about you."

"Damn, I will attend your party, then I'm leaving, you had better hope I get there in time."

She heard sounds above of fabrics rustling and skin contact in the form of a kiss, and then footsteps leaving the balcony. She pulled herself away from her hiding spot and continued her rounds. She skirted the Palace guards and moved into the lower Palace grounds, then into the Palaces of the Obans. She was fluid and managed to hide in the shadows, none had any idea she had passed. Her ability to move undetected was astonishing to even her. But her mind was on the conversation she left and her talents took a room to be addressed later.

This man is Aram but is married to the Sea Dragon. It is obvious he loves her but also loves his Mader. I seem to remember her Mader was originally from Du'Lanay. She seems very fervent for a foreigner. She is the first wife. What did Delma tell me... oh yes, she is the one the FirPader gave up lands for... she was but a pawn in their game of power. Now what was the story behind her, it was ages ago... she was traded for the lands Aram held on the other continent. But Aram either forgets or does not care. I wonder If the current war and the trading of lands, has anything to do with this man's Mader. I will have to ask her. There is a story here...

She went to the Oban of Finance, who had guards, but they were very lax, lately, guess they need a bit of a shake up, so she crept in and went into the storehouse, through the tunnel, she found when she was creeping in the bush once. They used it to smuggle goods to and from the ships and docks. She accessed it when they weren't using it.

She used it now, and observed with the influx of ships, there was a fair bit down in his underground rooms. She knew, which side was his personal horde. This Oban liked order and did not deviate from his method of storage. It made her job so much easier. She had stolen a little bit from each chest, not enough to be checked. Although once she had taken too much, and security was tightened for a month. So, she very carefully skimmed off the top of each item, which was there.

She gently opened the locks with her special picks, she had fashioned several, for his chests. But there was one that was new, and none of her picks were working. *Hmmm, guess I'm going to have to go to the smithy. Have a chat with them and see what's new in the land of locks. How I wish it would just open to me if I thought it open.*

A few seconds later, 'Click.' The lock opened. *By the God, by all the Gods! Did I just think it open?*

She quietly took the lock off and had a good look at it, in the dark, she could make out from the outside, it looked no different, maybe it had an extra tumbler in it. She felt with her fingertips and felt the maker's mark. Two crossed hammers. *Ahhh, it was Rullin's work.*

She would have to pay him a visit. She set the lock down quietly and gently opened the chest. Fabrics, hmmm, lifting a corner she saw... coin. She lifted one out, it was Du'Lanay crest. She pocketed the one and lay the fabric back down and closed the lid and relocked it.

She would usually skim a bit more, but Du'Lanay coin was not used in Aram. The Oban had this coin, the only thing he would do with it, would be to smelt it down into usable coin. She thought she heard a noise, so she stood up fluidly, crept to the doorway and listened to the usual sounds. She listened at the stairs heading up and heard noises coming from there. She padded softly down the tunnel she entered from. Stopping to listen at every junction, her heightened senses flaring up. As she neared the entrance, she thought about being visible. She thought of every torch behind her going out, and she noticed in her peripheral vision, the darkness settling in around her. She ducked behind a bush as guards came into sight. They were being quiet until they entered the tunnels, and she listened as they walked down into the darkness.

"What are we doing, Deken?"

"Shhh, we are grabbing the big chest and taking it down to Rullin. He will be melting it down, before anyone is the wiser. The master does not want to be holding onto it any longer than necessary."

"Does this have something to do with the rotten spice?"

"Shhh, someone will hear you; you know nothing about this, you hear? Have the fuckin torches burnt out? I thought they were to be lit, how the fuck will we see in this black hole? Have you a light on you?"

Each guard carried with them, two pieces of slate stone as part of their kit. It served her and Brecu, well when they needed it in the tunnels. Thinking of Brecu made her sad and she almost didn't hear the other set of guards coming around the corner of the garden. One of them she recognized by his voice.

"We will wait for the others to come out then we are to escort them and the chest down to the Path of Trades to the smithy. Have you heard from Brecu, Matteo? How can he just leave?"

"I don't know. How could he leave the nice piece of ass he was fucking? They had the whole hall scared spirits haunted the place. The days they were engaging, the halls echoed. It was kind of funny. Just goes to show how sounds carry. I should have reported them, but I want her myself, mmmhmmm, she could scream for me!" That was Matteo. Dumb fucking bastard. Like she would fuck him.

"You should have, maybe he'd still be here."

"Yah, she'd blame me and then I'd wake up dead."

"You can't wake up dead, you prick, you'd already be dead."

"Guess I should have, then I could have tied her up in prison and fucked her all I wanted, maybe I still could. She could moan all sweet for me."

"Yah, right. You are dreaming. The Little Dragon wouldn't want you; she'd slice you up."

"Fuck off. Look, there's light coming from the tunnel. The boys are coming."

She waited while the guards came out, extinguished their torches and the four of them carried the chest out of sight around the side of the building. She thought of her course of action, going in the other direction and scaled the stone wall. Scurrying like the rat she was along the top, until she reached the end. She made her way through the maze of buildings, reaching the Path of Learning and dropping to the ground. She would not go to the smithy; she already knew what would be happening.

She went down to the docks to find Laza. He was loitering with a few of his boys. She nodded her head for them to leave. She told Laza all she saw and showed him the coin.

"Yes, I had a boy follow the chest to the tunnels, and I was going to ask you to investigate, but I knew you were doing your daytime work with the scribe. We saw it come off a boat which carried the son of the FirPader but did not know what was in it. Now we know. We will wait for it to return transformed then we will skim a bit, eh, Andic? A little coin for our coffers."

"Damn right. I'm getting a little light in coin. I'll see where else I can reap from, but maybe tomorrow, I am going to just wander around, it's getting light soon. Oh, I may have a problem soon." She told him about Matteo, and his obsession with fucking her. "Do you need anything from him, Laza? I can set him up good for you. He is still lingering around the Delight House."

"No, he's a mean fuck, all right. I don't think you want to fuck with him or fuck him. He's beat up a few of my girls, and got one with child, she hung herself while you were upriver, she was so upset. He didn't even ask after her."

At that she turned to Laza. Her face was devoid of all expression; he knew it well. "What's it worth to yah?"

"No fucking way! You got something against him?"

"Yah, any man who doesn't give a fuck about getting a girl with child, and brushes it off, he has my full attention. You can tell him where I am, I'll be waiting for him. You hear from him then send word to Delma's, give me warning though, I'll come after you if he takes me by surprise."

"I wouldn't want to be in your sights, Andic. Yah, I'll send a boy. And I'll tell Matteo for some coin, make it worth the price, eh?" They shook hands and she turned away, the vision of Laza, shaking his head in disbelief. He had faith in her abilities and her hatred. He had to face it once, but he earned her respect and trust, so long ago.

She went to her hide out and slept well, waking up in the early hours. She rose and thought to get to Delma's and tell her the why of it. She found the older woman yawning in her office. "Child, how ye been?" Even her speech was tired.

"Delma, a guard will be asking about me, he seems to think I had something to do with Brecu's disappearance. I am going to have it out with him. He wants a piece of my honey pot, and I'm going to give it to him."

"What are you talking about, you gonna fuck him or give him a red shirt?"

"Both, I am feeling a bit wanton right now."

"Who is this guard? So I know who to look for."

"Matteo." Delma whistled. "He's a mean fuck, you sure you don't want a room here. I can post extra men if he gets rough. He's roughed up a few girls; you heard about his last one?"

"Yah, and that's why I'm gonna have a go at him, he's gonna learn not to fuck with me."

"Spirit save us, I don't want to be on your bad side."

Andic told Delma Laza would be sending a boy to give the warning, and sure enough it was the very next night. Only Delma knew her other hiding spots and Andic made sure she washed and made herself look more female and waited by the fountain in the vacant garden, she looked up at the star and saw the tail, twice as long as the night before.

It is getting closer; I wonder what lights it will send out this time. is this part of the Prophecy? That was the only thing we did not find down in the hall catacombs. I wonder why that is. All that other information and no Prophecy. I will ask Natan. He would be curious also. She was gazing up at the star and heard the soft sounds of footsteps. Without looking around, she waited until they were closer,

"You alone?"

"Hey girl, yah, unless you want more. I can always bring the boys tomorrow night if you want a good rubbing."

She broke off her gaze, and looked at Matteo, he would be handsome if he didn't have the mean look to his face. "Nay, let's see what you have for me." She walked up to him and rubbed her hands on his front jacket and started taking the buttons out of the holes.

"Hey, I thought you didn't like me, and now you are such a minx."

"The girls told me you were… more than a handful. Thought I would see for myself."

"Just you wait, you won't be disappointed." He helped her with his jacket, and she headed straight for his pant ties, and as she undid the leather ties his cock sprung out of his loincloth, and it was huge!

"Hmmmm, just the way I like them, big and hard."

She lifted her skirt and Matteo grabbed her ass lifting her onto his cock. She gasped at the feeling of being filled up. She was wet and he slid into her like it was made for her! She gasped and the cock inside her jerked.

"That's right, Brecu had nothing on me, I'm the biggest you'll ever have."

"Oh, yah, mmmm, fill me up, and fuck me hard." She didn't know until he was inside her she was craving it. He walked her over to the fountain and tried to fuck her on the lip of the stone ledge but gave up and laid her roughly on the ground. It felt so good inside, he was big, by the Gods! He rammed his cock in and out and she felt the sensation she knew would end it. The peak of the mountain, so to speak, and she heard him panting hard. She craved more.

"Fuck me, Matteo, hard! I want you to beat me with it. Fuck me!"

"Damn, girl. You are so tight. I'll give it to you all right." He needed no more encouragement than that. He slammed her hips against the ground, not caring his knees were making dents in the grass covered yard. He wrapped his hands around her throat and squeezed as his excitement rose.

"You can't cry, now you bitch. I'll just ram you until you cry out my name. oh, yah… you squeeze me hard, you are the tightest little girl. Ughghhh!"

She felt a heat rising and she welcomed it; she opened her being to the feeling she was craving. She sucked it all up. It rose higher and higher; she mentally pulled all the essence into her spirit. The sensation of the cock pounding into her was Secondary to the feeling of rising euphoric energy. She crested the peak of her enjoyment, to find Matteo had finished, but she didn't remember him peaking inside her. He had gone silent and still. She pushed his remarkably light body off her and saw a difference, first she looked at his cock and it positively could not have been the one pleasing her.

Then she took a good look at him, and he was shrunken in, like Brecu had been. She analyzed and processed what she had done. By having relations, she took something from the two men she fucked. Their spirit. *Does this make me evil? I have a unique way of killing, if I absorb another's energy, what happens to it? I seem to have better skills. I can move silently through busy areas; I see more than others and I hear better. Is this part of what Natan thinks I am? I wish I knew more.*

She didn't know she killed Brecu, and she wished she never had, but one can not go back in time, it was done. Matteo on the other hand, was deliberate. She did not like him; but he was huge, and she liked the hardness inside her, and the feeling it gave her. She absorbed his energy extremely fast. *I guess one cock is as good as the next.*

She analysed what may have happened. She sucked up the energy the spirit had, via the channelling through her honeypot, her silk purse, her core. *Was this the only way? Until I can find out, I will just have to…hone my skills, when I have the opportunity.* She was simply curious. She was not a stranger to killing, she would detach herself from the act, only with Brecu had she felt different. That had her questioning herself. Matteo, she calculated. The prick deserved it. *Now what should I do with the body? There's two people who knew he was coming to see me and who knows to whom he bragged. Should I leave the body?*

She weighed all the odds and decided she should take it down to the burn pits. He can disappear like the rest of bodies she killed. They would come after her now regardless. Time to leave, time to get a ship and go to the Islands. *Fuck it. I'll just leave him as is. If I am going to be wanted might as well grease my reputation. This will keep them guessing. But I'll take it somewhere it'll take them a while to find it. That'll give me time to find a ship.*

She wrapped the body of the dehydrated man; in the cloth she brought and hauled him over her shoulder and walked further past the gardens. *Natan was right, the body is light, no more than a sack of grain.* Andic ventured into the wild hill behind and walked for a good hour among the low scrub bushes and tumbleweeds, placing him behind a rock and under it. No one would find it for a very long time, she hoped. She walked back, washing herself off in the water, dressed and went back to Delma's. She found the older woman in her office.

"You are good, girl?"

"Oh yah, he's a big boy all right. He fucked me hard." Delma was looking at her strangely and she laughed. "Oh, he didn't hurt me at all, he likes it rough. We gonna fuck again tomorrow, after his duties, if he can stand that is."

Andic smiled a knowing smile. She hated to lie to her adopted Mader, but she needed the story to hold for a bit. She yawned. "I am going to head out for a bit, I'll see you again tomorrow evening, before my exercises."

She winked at the dumbfounded woman, and Andic saw what she was thinking, 'finally someone who could manage the mean ones,' Andic knew Delma would want her to drop roots and work the floor. *Hhmm, perhaps in another life.* She found the act itself had woken a beast inside her. She left and went to one of her different holes to crash there for the night.

The next evening, she walked into Delma's and the woman looked concerned. "Seems Matteo was bragging about having you at last, there are guards looking for you, and he is missing, just like Brecu. Did you kill them?" Delma didn't beat around the bush.

"Yes, Brecu was unintentional, but Matteo wasn't. They'll find his body eventually."

"Well, I didn't want to know this. I should not have asked; I thought for sure you'd say no. You need to leave here and leave here now. I'll try to cover your tracks, but a few girls here do not like you. They will have disclosed information to someone if they see you. I'm sorry about this, but you play with fire, you are going to get burned. Now go and remember in my way I did love you."

She gave Andic and big hug and tried not to cry. Andic left out the back, climbing onto the roof. She entered her spot through the roof access to grab a few things. She then left back the same way she entered and took off at a slight sprint, over the rooftops until she could go no further. There were a few more guards than usual, but she managed to evade them all, she knew where she was headed.

She went to Natan's sneaking into his bedroom again. He was peacefully snoring; she sat on the edge and gently shook him awake. He snorted but came awake immediately. He looked at the girl sitting on his bed. "That's nicer than a knife. What have you done now? They've already been here asking about you. I told them I didn't know where you lived, as it wasn't proper. I said I didn't care." He sat up against the back of the bed, not caring an unwed girl was in his room under the cover of night.

"I am afraid I was an unbelievably bad girl, Natan. Matteo ended up just like Brecu, but this time I wanted it to happen. I am afraid. Afraid I am not a good person. I have always dealt with ending spirits, but for some reason, now I am feeling remorse. I have other talents also. I think I should have told you before, but I do not trust very easily. You have proven to be stalwart."

"What talents other than killing by your…" Andic cut in before he could put a name to it. "I see better, focus in on things. I saw the star way before I went to Kadir. It was barely visible at the time. I hear exceptionally well, conversations even the sounds of water cannot mask. And I can open locks by thinking it."

"That is an incredibly good talent to have. You could run your boys with little to no competition."

"I have already done so. But I am willing to give that all up. I do not want this life anymore. You are right. there is more for me out there. I need to learn more about what it is I am. I am not the Little Dragon anymore. I want to leave this place. We should get the ship and leave."

"I was asking discretely of course, and we can leave on the ship the son of the FirPader came in on. I have secured us passage. You know he is married to the Water Dragon?" She nodded. Natan confirmed what she had known all along.

"Then he will be sympathetic to me. I happened to hear a conversation between him and his Mader, he was quite adamant he would be leaving, this will work out well for us."

"Yes, but it doesn't leave for a few more days, I am afraid you need a good place to hide. They have already checked here. If you are quiet, you can hide up on the roof, but it can get quite warm up there. You take a jug of water and a loaf of bread from the kitchen, and don't come down during the day. If you are caught, then I can claim, I didn't know.

There is an older woman who comes here during the day to cook for me. You must not be seen. I will get you when its time, or let you know, and you can make your way down. This might be better. I have secured passage for me and my servant. Sorry. If I said wife this would have tongues wagging. Better I bring a servant. It is only until we leave port. Then you can be who you want to be."

She agreed, rose walking out through his door and downstairs. Then he heard her walk past and back up the stairs to the roof. 'Strange that she knows my house so well,' he thought to himself as he fell asleep.

She fell asleep in the early morning, waking up as the sun was high up and she felt the heat coming off the roof. Andic was sweating by the time she rose and she took off her clothes until she just wore her bodice and loin cloth. Thinking it would help. She poked her head outside in time to see the Dragon star burst into sparkles way off in the east. She stood there, watching it pass through the sky to the North. It touched the sky again after another hour had passed, setting off sparks. The Breath of the Dragon, if this didn't herald the new age, she wasn't sure what else would. She put her head back inside, as there were sure to be people looking out at the display and she didn't wish to be seen.

So, is it like skipping stones on the river, a couple bounces and then it sinks? Or maybe it would bounce off and away like the last time? This one bounced at least twice. Where might it finally rest? Will it cause waves? Well, not on land. Water, yes. Will it create chaos? Will it bring people together? Like I am Aram and the others will be Islanders. Will they accept me, a person known only as the enemy?

She pondered this and wondered if she would be accepted once she let the other Dragons know what she did. She lay there and wondered at what she exactly had done, taking the spirit energy from another, she felt the rush at the time, but it didn't make her feel euphoric, like drinking or smoking the leaves the rich men smoked. She didn't feel like it was an addiction. If anything, fucking felt more addictive, but then she had gone without it for awhile.

What am I? Who am I? Am I truly one of these Dragons in the east? I do not hear voices. My eyes do not glow. Maybe this is a bad dream. But then, what did I do to the two guards? And when I drank the tea, did I blast that door off its hinges? This is so crazy. Natan even believes I am something, and for that matter Kadir. That's two men. We had better leave before more people find out. This is not the land to be in if you are a woman of any power. Or go beyond what is taught. Or even against the FirPader.

She kept thinking over the events which brought her to this point, and fell asleep in the heat, dreaming of flying in the air, with the sound of beating wings in her ears.

Thumping a beat like a drum.

CHAPTER 55

Davian

Battles to Scar the Lands

Davian looked at the missive in his hand and sat down heavily upon his Throne chair, ignoring the looks and questions others were dying to ask, and tears threatened to leak from his eyes and then they spilled slowly down his cheeks. He let them fall. "Is this truth?" He knew his Primar already read it, since this was once his duty.

"Yes, Your Eminence, the warehouse burnt to the ground, the bales of fabrics were dry, and it went amazingly fast and hot. There were melted remnants of a lantern beside the two bodies, one male, one female. By the jewelry, we identified the male as Ramis, we can surmise the other was your sister, Damara. That day, she was to set sail."

There were gasps from attentive men closest to the Throne, they knew from the names in conversation it wasn't good news. "Any word on the missing ship?"

"We have ships scouting areas between here and Kara, your Eminence, and will send to Aram and around the Islands. We will find him."

"Yes, because right now, they are the only ones who know the reason behind the fire. Where is Jaidak?"

"I have sent for him, Your Eminence. He was sent to the Hall of Learning, he is after all, merely a novice. He is waiting in your old office." Davian ignored the reminder, thinly veiled. Geravon was ambitious and did not like any competition to his aspirations. Even one Davian brought in. Jaidak was low enough to not be under Geravon's eye, but the Primar was well aware of the ramifications of an appointment by familiar relations. For the moment, Davian did not care. This was family. He made a promise, least he could do was keep it.

"I will have this information not leave the room until I have informed Jaidak of his parents' death." This he looked around at the assembly around him and at the men at the table of war.

"I am sure you can hold off spreading news for the next hour or so." He changed his expression from sarcastic to stern, and the voice which came out was laced with tiredness. "If I find out someone has spilled this news out of spite, I will teach that person a lesson." Davian dried his tears; he was not afraid of showing emotion in a crowd. He was after all, on the top of the pile. Only one way to fall, and this would be a dead Davian. He knew one day he would be, but he had some confidence in the people who surrounded him, he had bought almost all of them, one way or another. The room was for the most part, his.

Davian taught several of the older one's lessons, they all needed to learn, over the years, he had their respect, or fear of him. He was satisfied with either, and he was sure they would tell the newest members, their own version of a lesson learned. He stood up and called this morning session adjourned for now, he would send a message up to the Emperors Palace, which he knew Geravon had already prepared. The two men left the Hall and walked down to the Primar's section of the Palace.

"I will return with your nephew, Your Eminence."

"Thank you, Geravon."

Davian walked back to his old office, which was now his Second in Command's Geravon, and sat down in his old chair, running his hands over the wood of the desk which was his for so many years. This room he knew was more private than his current one. He picked it for a reason. It was very private. The windows opened to a stark vista. No gardens directly underneath for lurkers, and Davian remembered he was one to try. Back when he was a Third. Many other advantages, the breeze when in the heat of summer helped to cool the occupant.

As he rekindled his fond memories of his old desk, the door opened and Geravon entered followed by his nephew Jaidak. Davian wiped his cheeks of any telltale sign of tears and had composed himself considering the news. He motioned for the young man to sit. Jaidak sat himself down and perched on the edge of the seat, unsure of why he would have an audience with the Namarch. He was first the leader of the Faith, Uncle second.

"How are your studies? You have been settled in?"

"Yes, Your Eminence. I have, and I am learning many things." The young man smiled. He loved to learn, and the library here was vast.

"No issues with anything, anyone…?" He remembered his first few years here and wanted to see if Jaidak had the balls to make it.

"Nothing I can't manage, nothing to bring attention to." Jaidak had a few non admirers, who knew the real reason the young man was there and had already started bullying him. Davian stood up and walked around the desk. Geravon remained at the door and Davian motioned for him to leave. The other man turned, opened the door, and walked out. Jaidak rose to his feet, worry on his face.

"I swear, Uncle, I did not hurt him too much, but I know that you won't protect me, for the petty things. Pader told me as much and he said that I would have to prove myself worthy and not to take any shite from no one."

Davian took the young man's shoulders in his hands and looked down at his nephew sadness etching his features. The boy looked like a mix of his sister and his Pader, and it was comforting to see. The boy was so innocent of the world, and Davian was about to bring about his first lesson of life. More to the point, about death.

"That's not why I called you here, even though I do know about your skirmish. I am afraid I have received some unbelievably shocking news."

Jaidak looked at his Uncle and saw the older man's eyes watering. His stomach fell, dreading what was about to be spoken. "What news?"

"I…, there was a fire in Kara, at a warehouse on the waterfront, one of the textile ones owned by your parents. I am afraid both your parents were caught inside. I'm sorry, son, they are gone."

Jaidak fell into his Uncles' arms and sobbed his heart out. Damara's youngest was always the more sensitive. This was one of the reasons Davian wanted the boy. He felt the closest to this young man, Jaidak reminded Davian of himself when he was this age. Baron was much like his Pader and would probably follow him when it came to women, unless his wife had him in line. Davian let Jaidak cry a little more before he disengaged himself. Davian wiped his own tears away, with the back of his hand and handed Jaidak a small kerchief which was conveniently left on the corner of the desk.

"This is why I wished to tell you in private, Jaidak. You will have to get used to others using tragedy to get a reaction from you. I knew you would be upset, as am I. We keep this moment between you and I private. You will not have many private moments in the beginning of your life here. Everyone knows everything about the others that he will spend the rest of his life with. How you conduct yourself out there…" Davian pointed to the door, where he observed a shadow detach itself and leave. Most likely Geravon. His man knew by the conversation he was seen, "…will reflect how you are treated. It is a nest of vipers out there, you must learn to keep yourself calm and conduct yourself with dignity, even in times of strife. I am not like them, and you can let yourself be yourself around me, but me only, even Geravon is not your friend, he may someday be a rival." Jaidak dried his tears, they were red but no longer tearing up as his brain began to function and he asked, "Do we know what caused the fire?"

"There was a lantern inside by the bodies, …er, your parents, and as it had been very dry, the bales of fabric would have burned fast and hot. Your parents would not have suffered, it would have been instantaneous, if this is any consolation. The ship your Mader was to be sailing on to bring her here is missing. I have men finding the ship and looking around. Asking the necessary questions. When I find out anything, I will tell you. Baron would have been told by now and as he is the eldest, he will make the death taxes and the arrangements for the funerals. You may have the customary time off when Baron sends word to you."

"Thank you, Uncle, I mean, Your Eminence. Thank you for telling me in private. May I return to my studies? I have found a particularly good genealogy on the FirPader going back several years, and I find immersing myself into books has always been a solace, a balm for my spirit. I will return when Baron calls me, but since I cannot have anything personal, what would I bring back?" Jaidak looked about to tear up again.

"You may have a few things; I suggest you send them directly to me. I will hang on to them for you. When you get higher up, a few reminders of your parents will console you. Your Mader held a few items for me when our parents left their spirit. How I will miss her. But you have the right of it. Just be aware of your surroundings before you let sorrow and other emotions show and always remind yourself someone is watching you. Even if you think you are alone, you are not, our God is always by your side."

Davian gave his nephew another hug and crossed to the door, softly knocking on it twice. Geravon opened the door and walked in, his expression one of little to no emotion. He murmured his condolences to the young man and looked at Davian who motioned to him. Geravon asked Jaidak to follow him and they would return to the Hall of Learning.

Davian sat down hard in the chair, and he let his own tears flow, and flow they did. He sobbed quietly, for he had loved his sister very much. "Oh, sister. How I will miss you. You knew me best. Now I have no one. Even your son, may not be the best solace for my sorrow. He would be targeted for the favour bestowed. I will ask our God for comfort; he has given me reprieve when I could not speak with you. But he does not have your ideas. You were my last link to Mader. How I will miss you. Oh, Mara."

She was his consolation and solace in his early years. She helped him in so many ways with her knowledge of the workings of politics, and her clothing industry was a way she passed him information. Information he used to his benefit. She knew how his mind worked the best. Other than Lana, she was the most upset when she found out his vocation.

Oh, how different would our lives have been if I had been given the choice of path. How I resisted at first. Now seeing what I have seen, I am certain I was placed here to find my path once more. But what a quandary we are about to deal with. Geravon's reading has put in perspective, the extent of what was done to the people to erase all knowledge of Dragons. Now they are back. We keep the people ignorant of what these Dragons can do. Sometimes I wish I had married and had children, lived out my life with Lana, and gotten old together. Would any of this have happened anyway. Oh, well...

Lana, now there was a woman that he had once been madly in love with, she had gone on to marry an older man, but apparently, she had never really gotten over him. She had ultimately destroyed her marriage for the memory of him. But his respect for her ended when his man he hired told him that she was entertaining Ramis, and it was reinforced when she had his child.

Ahh, Ramis, now you I will not miss. You were only good for the fortune you brought. It served me well. You did not deserve my sister's love and adoration. She was a fool to love you. You could not keep your cock out of females. How I had to cover your exploits up, just to keep my sister ignorant of your escapades. You owe me, well moot point now. Damn you!

It almost ended when Damara hired a man to follow her husband, if Davian hadn't bought the man's silence for a lot of money, she would have divorced Ramis and then lived a vastly different life. Davian tracked Ramis's exploits and bought their silence when they wanted to let the cat out of the bag. He would only miss his sister. She had been worthy, if only she had been a man.

Davian rose, took a few deep breaths steadied himself, force of habit, and looked at his reflection in the mirror, *I look worn out today, old. Too much going on in this world, too many things to worry about, and now this. How I will miss*

Damara. I see her in Jaidak. Baron, I see Ramis. He will turn out like his Pader for sure.

Davian heard the sound of wind, and he saw in the reflection of the mirror, the Purple Sennet. It landed on the ledge outside. It bobbed its head. Davian nodded back. "You have come at a tough time. I have news, I have lost my sister in a fire. I bid you good day, sir. Now I must be off."

Davian could have sworn he heard a chirp, which sounded like 'no,' before the bird said, 'My Lord.' However, it began to flap its wings at Davian's sudden movement of his arms straightening his robes before he walked out of the office.

The sadness etched in his eyes, told all today was not a good day. He left the office and walked back to his rooms, his private office was attached to his sleeping rooms and dressing rooms, all conjoined. Formerly his predecessors, after his passing, Davian had most of the elaborate furnishings removed except the desk. The chair, he replaced with his chair from his former office. It was commissioned especially for him and it fitted his ass; it was extremely comfortable. Davian liked a simpler lifestyle and pomp was not his manner. It also gave others the impression he could not be bought.

He passed a few diplomats, none stopped him, they by now heard the news. He walked into his rooms, stripping off his robes, letting them fall. His room servants would pick them up as he dropped them and sure enough, it wasn't but a few minutes the doors opened quietly and he heard the sounds of fabrics. He had by then walked naked into his bath. He washed himself with the soaps he had used for twenty years.

When his mentor had passed, Davian had looked at the scented soaps the older man had left. He had a quick walk through, right after his passing, looking for anything incriminating, and it struck him odd. The man liked floral scented soap. Davian had not changed his soap since childhood. It was soap, for fucks sake!

Once he was clean, he walked out of the bath and went into his dressing room, selecting a new robe made from one of the many fabrics his sister had dropped off. He caught a quick glimpse of himself in the full-length mirror. He was tall and his dark hair was gaining some salt at the temples. He was still trim, trim enough, but he was noticing his upper body was softening. His lower body was still muscular, must be all the walking he did.

Then he had a look at the now useless appendage between his legs. It had been years since he used it for anything more than relieving himself. It looked pathetic hanging there, dangling on his two companions covered in dark hair. His God demanded nothing else but devotion, and the part he didn't see carried the scars to prove it, he turned away from his reflection and his back had its own glimpse in the mirror, scars criss-crossed his back, remnants of a heavy hand on a whip.

Davian dressed in a light robe and sat down at his desk, lost in his thoughts, but only for a moment. He started sorting through his papers and he heard the shuffle of Geravon come in. He didn't look up until he realised the man had stood there and not said anything. Davian looked up to see Geravon standing there and holding another scroll. The man handed it to the Namarch and Davian opened the cylinder to take the scroll out and read it for himself, a grin crossing his face.

"Well, some good news, finally. Have you heard whether this was accidental or maybe someone had a hand in it?"

"No one has claimed the death as theirs if that's what you are asking. The Islanders are quiet, but I did hear it was weakened and subsequently died. That's all we know for the moment."

"So now we are down to one, our work is being done for us. We need to start sending out men, quietly of course to end the lives of these DragonRiders, mere women, I hear, young ones, so it should be easy for someone with the right skill set. Use our usual man, he can recruit who he wants, I am sure he will know more of his kind. Have yourself a seat, Geravon. What have you read lately?"

"It is puzzling is it not?"

"What is? Please enlighten me."

"Well, the current happenings, for one. There were first reports of three of these beasts from the Islands. Now there is only one. The two men who returned said the Dragons looked hail and hearty. So, what killed the other two? Were they killed or did they have a disease?"

"Do we have anyone at all, who can infiltrate and find out?"

"Well, do you not have someone placed in the heart of the Islands?"

"I have not heard from them for almost a year. They may be dead. Although I have no report to say it is so. I cannot reach out to this person without raising suspicions, they have an elevated status. It would undermine their existence. Our agreement was they would give information as they were able. So, I must rely on another source. But your observation has merit. Our reading material speaks of six, so where are the others? Have you found if they perished from disease? We could find a way to poison them, if so."

"Hmmm, I will keep this in mind as I keep reading. This is so blasphemous; it should not get into the populace. I read a passage which stated there may have been more than the six. It said Dragon fought Dragon."

"This sounds interesting. If necessary, we get ourselves one or two, if it comes to it. Anything else of import? You have the right of it. I was thinking that we spread the word the Dragons are demons, and spark fear of the beasts so people are scared and we lean on God to save us."

"Yes, we can get our sermons to incite fear and have the populace donate for the good of the people."

"Oh, that is perfect. Geravon. You have an excellent mind for this. How about you become my very own War Commander. You have a calculating mind. You create ways to combat this disease we face. Treat it as such. Keep reading in private, we will have our 'war councils' here. Among our maps, lend it credence. Produce your plans, and we will get the populace devout again. Excellent work, Commander!"

"Your Eminence, I am honoured. You have given me a great boon."

"You deserve every bit of praise. I chose you, to be my Secondary for a reason. Together we will bring this world to heel. Starting with the eradication of these Dragons. They do provide a challenge though."

"I will keep reading. If it weren't so incredulous, I would think it was the makings of a disturbed mind."

"This may have been our past, Geravon. But it does not need to be our future. What of the tome with the Prophecy?"

"It looks original, but we will assume it was copied. Its fragility has me leaving it where it is. There is nothing else of import in it. A list of names. The Prophecy itself, It alludes to an event, the six shall rise again."

"We need to find these six, then. Separately or together. There was two on the Islands. Let's focus there. If we find evidence of where they were, on the Island, the others may show their faces eventually. Have our contacts watch and lay in wait. Let's not be hasty."

"Should we not destroy this blasphemy?"

"That wasn't what I meant by hasty. Our men can watch and find the most opportune time. The Islands will be watching every ship which comes in. Our hired hands need to blend in and strike unawares. I wanted this done without mishap, without them aware, and our man getting clean away. Now do you think this event is the star in the sky?"

"What else can it be?"

"Well, we should take the attention away from the Dragons and turn this into an advent from our God."

"We can use this to our advantage, our God is great, all knowing, this is his way of saying the demons are an abomination from not enough worship of his goodness."

"Yes, Geravon, you may have something there. Work on it, and present it at our next meeting, excellent work." Davian praised where necessary, and honestly, the odd time he did had his men working twice as hard. Not one man had any idea who may be working quietly for the Namarch, who would readily turn the other in for a promotion. This was carefully constructed over the years by Davian himself. He prided himself on his system.

Geravon left and Davian stood and went to the center of the rooms. His servant placed a glass of citrus juice into his hand when he held it out. His servants knew precisely what he wanted when he wanted it. Exactly the way he trained them. He ventured out to the private porch and gazed into the sky and the approaching star as the star touched the atmosphere, in the east. He continued to watch as it travelled, far off to the North and he drank the juice, far off in thought.

This is the Breath of the Dragon; we should call it the Breath of God. Change the Prophecy to reflect a revival of our choosing. Hmmm, I may have something there. We should have done this a long time ago. He lost himself in thought, finished his drink, held out his hand and the cup was refilled. When he liked silence, he got silence. He watched as another rain of sparkles happened and the star sped on its path. He turned around to make his notes. He finished writing and handed it to Geravon when he returned a while later.

"The Breath of God, that's so fitting, Your Eminence, this will cause a revival for certain."

"Exactly, my dear man, exactly.

CHAPTER 56

Damara

And Pain to Know Ones Worth

Damara tried to keep her cowl on her head and keep her eyes hidden but after a day of brisk winds which blew her hair everywhere she gave up. The whole trip she engaged the handsome Captain in conversation. He was only too happy to have the attention of a woman; she noticed he was a flirt. It was providing her a distraction from her thoughts, so she indulged herself. He regaled her with tales of his trips, and she asked him about things he saw on the Islands.

"Well, we arrived into port, when we saw the Dragons taking flight, like very large, winged lizards, you know those crawling things in the desert?"

She shook her head no.

"Well anyway, think of a very scaley bird, with an exceptionally long neck, and a crest on its head. The largest one had yellow eyes, like the high Dragon, that's what they call the young woman who passed the Ritual and passed it with flying colours, I do say." He began laughing at his own jest.

"She was riding the beast, no reins or nothing, like a rock in a crack. Once we sat in an alehouse, we asked around. There were two Dragons, and a glorious joining where the bride and groom both rode the Dragons as part of the ceremony. We heard about the assassins Du'Lanay sent," Damara added she knew this much, and Olent continued, "and how the Dragon breathed fire and the High Dragon took air from some of the men, enough her soldiers could run them through."

"I heard the other woman sent man eaters from the ocean to escort them."

"Yes, imagine what she can do with this power, she could control storms too. You have red eyes, my Lady. You play with fire?"

"Yes, it seems fire came from my hands, but I did not burn."

"Well, please don't get angry on my ship, the wood on the deck was oiled, we are sailing on a tinder box, you get angry, and poof," his hands raised up and he smiled, "Up she goes!"

She spent a week sailing up the coast, and during this time, some of the crew warmed up to her, they didn't look away when she greeted them. Damara found herself spending a fair amount of time talking with the blonde haired, six-and-a-half-foot giant of a Captain.

How have I never noticed before this mountain of a man? He is extremely attractive... and very vivacious. He is incredibly open about his conquests, be it smuggling or of the female kind. I see he does not care what one like myself thinks of him. He is noticeably confident in his masculinity. I wish I were this confident. I feel so bad he followed me and I have placed his life in danger... danger from my brother. It will only be a matter of time Davian finds out I am alive.

She watched the coastline, ever changing, the forests gave way to mountains, which gave way to stone cliffs and sandy shores. Peylin was busy purging from both ends, the motion of the ship had her stomach ridding itself from everything which went into it. The Captain finally gave her hard biscuit to suck on, he told her it might take a while before she felt right. The poor girl did not come out of the cabin for four days. When she finally came out, Damara took her arm and walked her around.

"Peylin, I feel so bad. You are feeling better?"

"Yes, finally. I have an empty feeling in my belly… I am not wanting to put anything in, only to have it come out. The Captain put my stomach to rest with his cure. The biscuit alleviated some of my cramps. Where are we?"

"Well, I came this way once before, we are more than halfway. We have past the Burnt Lands. Soon we will see the mountain ranges of the North and past this is Lanthia. I believe three more days, however, the Captain will know. If you want to ask him."

"The Captain is very handsome, is he not?" Damara blushed at the question and turned away into the wind by the railing. Peylin gazed at her mistress and smiled.

"Oh, I see. You think the same. He is very… attentive to you as well. He is attracted to you, Nada."

"How can you say this? He is merely being kind. 'Tis too soon. Ramis has only been gone four days." Damara gasped at her statement.

"What is it? Are you fine, Nada?"

"I have said this aloud. He is dead. I killed him. I killed Tovah. They are dead because of me. I had flames in my hands and I shot them at the two. He was fucking her, Peylin. I caught him in the act. It was the final act which made me realize he would never change."

"I thought you said there was no one inside the warehouse."

"No, I said there was no one inside I cared about. He denied siring other children to the end, Peylin. Even with catching him with Tovah, he still denied."

"He thought perhaps you still loved him? Or perhaps he did not see what he was doing as wrong. Men, have the right to do what they wish. Ramis was no exception."

"No, he was not. He denied to the last." Peylin saw the agitation in Damara's eyes, they began to glow more. Several sailors gave them a wide berth at the side of the ship and Damara noticed Captain Olent glance back at the women. Peylin grabbed her hands and squeezed.

"Nada. Damara. You are right. Ramis would never change. He had the backing of the Church and state to fuck whoever he wanted. But do you know what? You pave your own path now. You are a free woman. You choose what you want to do. We will see what Lanthia has to offer. Maybe you set up a shop there. They have various plants and dyes you can use. You change your name, live free."

"I don't know. Setting up a shop with dyes and fabrics. Would this not be the first thing people would be looking for? I should entertain other avenues of income. I can sell jewels to help. They mean nothing to me now. I have no sentimental attachment to anything Ramis bought me. I thank you for your ideas. I should think of another way to survive." Damara's eyes lost a bit of their glow, Peylin was getting her mistress to calm down.

"You know best. Maybe fabrics are not such a clever idea. Hmmm…I will see what other ways you can find a means of survival. I can easily find a maid or cleaning job. I could teach you."

"You may have to. I have no skills. I thank you for helping me, Peylin, and for accepting me as I am, even with these red eyes of mine. It scares me, I do not know what is happening to me."

"You may be changing into one of these Dragons, I heard rumours about, or it may be all the tea you were drinking. You have the look of not sleeping for many nights, however, there is a sparkle to the redness, which makes you slightly attractive, which is possibly why the Captain is hovering around you. Maybe he finds you alluring. Oh, I am sorry, Nada. My stomach…"

"You go, Peylin. Never mind the Captain, you naughty girl. Go rest yourself, I will go speak to the alluring Captain." Damara smiled at the retreating back of the girl who had seen more than her share of Damara's strife and helped her deal with it all. She turned back to the railing and watched the shore. She observed the outline of mountain peaks far off in the distance and knew the Burnt Lands were far behind them.

The Burnt Lands. They were shrouded in mystery. Nothing grew there, not even plants. It was a harsh landscape of bare rock and dirt. Ramis told her once it was thriving, a land which housed many people and many varied species of grapes and fruits. He said these heretic Dragons destroyed it, and nothing grew there now. After the scourge of Dragon fire, many stayed but the land refused to yield even a blade of grass. The inhabitants left, migrating to lands surrounding, some became Wanderers, some came to Kara and Merida and hamlets in between. Some went North to Lanthia and integrated there.

Within five years, the Burnt Lands were empty. The waters dried up. It became like a desert in some spots, hard coarse rocky scapes in others. The buildings which remained deteriorated with time, becoming part of the desolation. Damara wondered why it was scourged. It must have been traumatic, something drastic to be wiped clean. This was the only thing she thought. Wiped clean.

I will find out, maybe there is a reason behind the desolation. It surely was not told in my history lessons. Ramis must had access to other books and whatnot. It seems there is a fount of knowledge kept from the Lanayese people. More to the point, kept from females. I wonder on the why. Mind you, the poor and those of the lesser class are kept ignorant.

I wonder if Davian knows the history surrounding these Dragons. Does the Church have secret books? I will bet they do. Yes, the secret library he told me of. How else would they know to keep such from the people. The penalties placed on stepping off the path of Naman is harsh. I had an easy life, being who I am. More like, who I was.

Damara had a thought, and approached the Captain, with his hands on the wheel. His eyes of blue crinkled with his smile. She did like the colour of his eyes, which looked intently down at her.

"Captain Olent, I was thinking… You can never return to the Capital, or Kara for that matter. Once they find out I am alive and what I have done, I am a marked woman. I placed you and your men at risk. I am sorry."

"Oh, don't you worry, lass. I have been in worse situations…"

He proceeded to tell how he once stole the Dader of a King of Aram, and he had her in stitches laughing about his escapades. There were a few more days, Damara spent with the Captain, listening to his stories. She laughed more in the week of travel than she laughed in her lifetime. *He has lived a rich life, even if he is not rich in wealth. I lived a life of richness, but only in my station. I want to have a life of rich memories. I see now I was kept entertained by my business. Camouflaging Ramis's escapades, my business kept me from breaking away from the path I was kept on. Peylin is right. I have a world to explore. Now, I have no one but me. I can do what I want. This is very liberating.*

Damara brought herself out of her thoughts and listened to Olent as he told her of his smuggling books and tomes out of Aram and almost being pulled into the Maelstrom Sea. She was entranced by his monologue, and he finished with,

"We are almost there."

"Where?"

"Just wait, Nada, it'll show itself soon."

She noticed a break in the coast coming near and sure enough he turned and sailed into a natural harbour, cut into sheer cliffs. It hid all but the tops of the city which was the colour of the stone. She thought perhaps only at night one would see lights of the city from the sea.

"This is ingenious. No one would ever see it unless they were looking."

"Yes, exactly. 'Tis a natural harbour and very well protected. Look up as we dock, you will see battlements, natural areas where archers and other weapons could be deployed."

"Oh, you are so right, thank you for taking the time to distract me from my distress."

"I enjoy your presence. It made the trip speed by. I am yours to command, my Nada. Now we are almost secure. I need to finish if you could remain here out of the way."

The port official and the Captain yelled at each other and when the Captain pointed at her, she moved forward. The man stared at her and barked something at one of his men who ran off into the city. He motioned at the Captain for both of them to come down.

The ship was secured and a plank of wood run down to the dock. Captain Olent helped Damara and Peylin to walk onto the dock. As she put her legs on the wood planks, she wobbled and grabbed onto Peylin. "Once you begin to walk you will get your land legs back. Give it time, Nada."

The colourful man came back gesturing for them to follow; she whispered to Olent. "What did he say? He seemed excited when he saw my eyes."

"He said you would meet the Great One. I have no idea who this is. The leader here is called the Amman. He speaks our language a little."

As they walked forward the streets were strangely empty, Captain Olent asked the man leading them, learning there was a ceremony of sorts in the coliseum, something regarding a sword. As he repeated this information back to her, a white light rose to the sky, they hesitated but kept going as their escort didn't stop except to hurry them along. They almost reached the great doors of the Palace when the sky lit up with the star touching and sending sparks everywhere. The boom which reverberated, shook the walls around them.

"Seems the Dragon Age has officially begun." Olent said.

"Where did you learn all this?" Damara asked.

"One hears things if you listen in the right areas. The Islands have revived their religion so much this all they speak about. Ahhh, we are here."

She looked to see they were in a Great Hall, with rows upon rows of tables. Servants were carrying in food and setting them down on the tops. They were ushered in to sit down at a small table and served a drink. All who walked past, bowed to her.

"I wonder what this is all about?"

"My Nada, I am sure it has something to do with your eyes," As he finished, he stood, looking behind her. Damara stood, placing her glass down on the table, to turn around. There was a middle-aged man, with a turban, dressed in finery, whom she guessed was the Amman. She saw enough of royalty to know a leader when she saw one, but that's not what caught her attention.

The woman beside him was the most beautiful she had ever seen, with the reddest hair of flame, done so elegantly. Her eyes glowing white, green, like opalescent pearls of the seas. She had a scar running down one side of her face, which did not detract from her beauty. She carried a sword which held a gem in the hilt which glowed and sparkled. Damara stared back at the woman and saw her smiling at her.

"Welcome, I can only surmise you must be the Fire Dragon."

"ENOUGH"

Damara heard the voice in her head like someone shouted it, like the trumpets used in ceremonies at the Capital. It blasted so loud she heard nothing and almost lost her balance, but Peylin grabbed her by her arms, and held her up. She looked over to the young woman and the man with her was supporting her.

"What was that?" Damara asked quietly, however, to her it sounded like she was shouting. Her hearing not quite returning, and she barely heard her own voice. A dull ringing echoing in her head, she flexed her jaw, trying to pop her ears.

"That would be my Dragon. He had to break a connection you had; you did not know?"

"I know nothing about what you speak. I know over the last six months or so, I had a feeling come over me, and my eyes would turn red occasionally. The Captain who brought me here seems to think; I may be a Dragon. I know naught of these Dragons other than what information we are given. I know there are two women on the Islands who have glowing eyes, and mine have glowed since I left Kara."

They were ushered over to chairs and both sat down facing each other.

"Well, they are red no longer. Why don't we begin with introductions. My name is Meera. Meera D'un, I am of the people of Pelin'Dun, however, I was born here. My Mader and Pader eloped, to escape from the system in place. The Rulers did not sanction their love. My Mader is gone, but my Pader is with the Wanderers. I was raised in the Aerie."

"You have travelled far for one so young. I am Damara, Du'Landan of the Royal House. My family is one house back from the Emperor, my married house is Du'Tan. I am no longer a citizen though; I came here to seek asylum."

"Oh, why is this?"

"Because I burnt my husband and the woman he was fucking to a crisp."

"That will do it. Well, you are a Dragon, the Fire Dragon to be exact. You will be hunted when they know, do they?"

"I do not believe so; the warehouse went up like a dry bonfire. They will find two bodies and think we perished together, until the woman who he was with is missed. What do you mean, a Dragon? Am I cursed? I heard rumours of two women on the Islands, and the mention of beasts which may be Dragons. However, what does it all mean? Oh, oh…"

"Yes? What is it?"

"My children, I will never see them again." Damara began crying, Peylin grabbed her hand. She began to realize the ramifications of what she did. Her shoulders sank into her body, shuddering with sobs.

"You may see them again, however, you will be serving in a different capacity. Never is so finite. We do not know what the future holds. We have a duty to bring the Dragon Age to fruition, though, this I know. This is the Amman of Lanthia,"

She gestured to the man who was still holding her, Damara observed the man was in love with the woman, but it was not her place to say anything on this. Damara bowed from her chair, as Peylin was still hanging onto her arm.

"I am seeking refuge, Amman,"

"Of which I will gladly give you." He turned to Meera, "Are you fine, now? You almost fell."

"Yes, my Dragon likes to shout sometimes. He told me he had to break the connection; he did not tell me why. He doesn't really communicate much with me, I'm afraid. And who is this?"

She looked at the Captain. Damara introduced Captain Olent to the assembly. The Captain was captivated by the presence of the beautiful young woman with flaming hair and opalescent eyes, he bowed at the waist to her and as an afterthought bowed to the Amman. He never stopped looking at Meera.

"He brought me here, Meera. He says he will serve me, because of me, he cannot return to the Capital."

"He is welcome to stay until we need his services. Our dockmaster will repair anything he requires, and he is welcome to partake of any services required."

"I thank you, Great One. Many thanks for the repairs, I will retire back to my ship, by your leave. Nada., Peylin, Amman."

Meera nodded and Captain Olent bowed and followed a manservant back the direction they arrived. Meera watched after the Captain for a moment and turned back to her companions. "Is he to be trusted?"

"I have employed Captain Olent for many years. He is very diligent in his craft, I cannot say if he would be true if tried, however, he has never swayed from his duties to my house. However, from what I saw this last year, everyone has a price. I leave him to your hands if you feel untoward about him."

"No, he was very attentive, it was a little uncomfortable for a moment."

"He likes his women, I believe. He was very attentive to me on the voyage here, I do not remember him being so in his employment."

"You were married, Nada. You are no longer..." Peylin spoke softly, she was shy around the Amman and his friend, Meera.

"Ahhh, I have not had time to digest this."

"Let us continue our conversation after you wash up and change, we are celebrating tonight, the gift of the sword and the dawn of the Dragon Age, the star has given us her lights. My servants will show you to your rooms, your chests were brought from your ship." Meera stood and motioned for a girl to lead the two women to a door which led down a hall. Damara stood up, Peylin helping her, and they walked to a very elaborately furnished set of rooms.

"Oh, this is so beautiful. Thank you, miss..." Damara turned to the woman who showed with motions, the bath room, and the chests at the foot of the bed.

"Peylin, come, let's wash this salt off our bodies and dress quickly. Come. You come with me; it will take no time if we both wash at the same time."

"I couldn't. It would not be right."

"Peylin, come. I do not care. This is different land, and different customs. I am not caring of rank. I am a woman, you are a woman, there is a very welcoming bath of water, and I am going in. Right now. With or without you."

Damara shed her clothes and walked to the room and down into the warm water. Peylin followed her soon after. They washed each others hair and then rose, dried themselves and dressed. Damara chose her favorite red dress, and took the fragile necklace of rubies, which she had Peylin clasp together behind her neck. Peylin braided a single braid to frame Damara's face. "Would you like me to braid your hair?"

"No, Nada, I can manage this quicker than you can walk to the door but thank you for the offer." They peeked outside and found a girl waiting for them and she motioned them to follow. They walked into the Great Hall, and it was full of people, women warriors Damara could not help but stare at, and the room was a burst of colour, the fabrics, and dyes! Oh, the dyes, she was wanting to touch everything, and see what they were, she was going to enjoy her time here. They were escorted up to the head table, where Meera, the Amman and an older woman were placed, and Meera stood and raised her hands.

"May I please introduce to you the Fire Dragon; she has travelled far and will be spending some time here with us." She spoke in the Lanthian language and translated it later to Damara. The crowds cheered and clapped, and Meera motioned to the seat beside her. The Amman nodded his head and when he saw the necklace on her neck, his eyes widened, and he placed his hand on Meera's arm as she seated herself.

"The Amman asks where you acquired your necklace, he says its exquisite."

"I purchased it in the Capital, from one of my favorite jewelers, he said it came from Aram, the Aramite was loath to part with it. It was fixed, but I still find it very fragile and haven't worn it much."

Meera turned to the man beside her and translated what Damara said, and he spoke quickly. She smiled and turned to Damara. "You saw my sword earlier? The Amman says this necklace you wear, was also a talisman of the previous Dragon, but lost its sparkle. You must create your own, and I will take you to the place to do so. He says he will have his jewelers craft for you whatever you desire, as you can choose what you want to hold it. I chose the sword as I remember the stories of old, and my Mader telling me, and the memory remains embedded inside my gem."

"What are these gems? I do not know the stories of what you speak."

"I will tell you all, we are going to be here for a while before we must leave. Lanthia is the only known place to have the Prophecy intact. We will spend time reading and I will explain what I know of such. Can you tell me a bit of yourself?"

Damara spent the next while, telling Meera and the Amman, her life and what little she knew of Dragons, which was next to none. They were served the meal and Damara sparingly tasted the dishes, rejecting some while partaking of others.

"I did attend a dinner party with a young woman, who was to give birth to the heir of the Empire, she was tired, and weary, and she had green eyes, which when I met her gaze, they sparkled. We had a connection, and time stilled. I heard a voice inside my head, Earth and Fire, Earth, and Fire. It was the only time I heard a voice other than my own.

I don't know the significance of our meeting. I had news she divorced her husband, soon after, the Empire took her child from her, there was talk she heard voices, and was crazy. She has disappeared. You must understand when something is not understood, it is dealt with and dealt with harshly."

"I was raised in the North, in the Ravenwood mountains. I know some of what you speak. I never left them until now to come to this side of the continent. The Amman has shown me on maps the lay of the land. You come from the South, where I have never been. I did not know a year ago I was a DragonRider, so I understand your hesitation. I will fill you in on what I know and have experienced. This woman you met could possibly be another Rider. You said green? She could be the Earth Mader. Your eyes and hearing a voice have marked you as a Dragon. You have been Chosen."

"Chosen? For what? I am old. I raised children who are the age of yourself. I lived a life already. For what could I be chosen?"

"The Great One decided who he wished to usher in the new Age. You will have to ask him the question. All I know is you and I, along with four other women will be the leaders of a new world. You may have your life experiences to bring your knowledge forth. I cannot say. However, you were chosen for a reason. He will not have decided lightly. So, rest easy you have what the Great One needs for this next chapter of our lives."

"I am humbled and honoured someone thinks I have the skills for leadership. My past husband, Ramis did not even think I could be a Mader. When my children were younger, they were given authority over me. We nearly parted ways when I told him, I could not live this life. He saw it was taking its toll on me, come to think of it… it wasn't until I mentioned something to Davian things changed in our household… I will bet Davian told him something. Oh…!

Damara suddenly thought of something. She looked at Meera, with acknowledgement in her expression.

"You must know this, once I am known to be alive and especially if I am a Dragon, of which you speak, my brother will send assassins to kill me."

"Why would your brother do this?"

"My brother is the new Namarch."

"Ohh, that's interesting. Are you and your brother at odds?"

"No, but I am sure his beliefs and his position will overrule anything his heart tells him, it is his life for the last twenty odd years."

Damara began to cry, this seemed all so surreal. Meera put her hands on Damara's.

"It will be fine, but we will have some strife to work through. We all face challenges along the way, and we have each other to support and comfort. I grew up alone. My Pader was not my real Pader; however, I spent time with the man who is. I found eternal friendships with the people of these lands, and now I have met a woman who I would enjoy calling my sister. We will get through all this, but I will not pretend it will be a walk in a garden."

"I have a lot to learn. I have many years on you, you are but a child, the same age as my youngest son. But I know nothing about the Dragon's and their history, I was raised on the one true religion, one God. My brother was given over to serve the faith as a young man. We were close once. We used to get into some good scrapes when we were young." Damara smiled at the memory.

"Now what you are telling me, is all I have known as truth is a lie. I do not know what to think, I know nothing about being a Dragon, or this Prophecy, I have a lot to learn, I can only hope when my children hear I am alive, and even if they hear I killed their Pader, they do not hate me. This is all too overwhelming."

"We will learn together; I have many things yet to learn. As for your children, I cannot read into the future. It all depends on who helps them through their grief, it can have influence on what they think. And if you feel that this is too much, we will rest. We can talk it over.

I do not know what the future has in store, for us all. I do believe we live in a world of diversity, we should be able to live in harmony, regardless of belief, but the Empire does not, they believe theirs is the only true religion. Killing all who disagree. I don't know about you, but I would like to live in a world where everyone lives together. Not imposing any one structure such as rigid beliefs, where we can have opinions and standards, and accept all are different. We have a lot of work to do to get there. I hope you will collaborate with me."

Meera smiled at Damara, who saw in the woman before her, herself as a young girl, full of hope and zest for life. "I will do my best. However, this whole notion of us being DragonRiders is very daunting. I have not the slightest idea how to proceed. It seems an age ago I was happy in my life, creating colours on fabrics and living life according to my station."

"But were you happy in this endeavor?"

"Not really, these last few months have me unsettled. Finding out my husband was a cock-a-bout, really had me questioning myself, the system and life. It would be a better place, if like you said all were accepted for their spirit instead of their shell. Looking into one's deeds and not their words, I would like a world where women are not punished … for being women."

"Simply said. Naman is not love. This was established by themselves. It will have to be scoured from the lands; however, many will perish. I do not see all converting to Vendar, and if they do, it is hard to shake the yoke which was hammered onto ones shoulders. It will be interesting, to be vague. There will be death, an abundance of it! Your talents are fire, Damara. You are the God of War. You will have to temper your talents."

"What talents? Lighting people on fire? Looking like I had too much wine to drink?" Meera laughed and Damara smiled back and shrugged.

"Well, they do. I've seen them. It looks like I have a heavy head from drinking too much. As for the fire I used on Ramis, my only consolation was they did not suffer. I could not bear it if I stood there and heard them scream. The fire which came from my hands burned them instantaneously. Still… I do not like to think I have the power of life over death. Is there anything good about this God?"

"He is the God of strength."

"Oh, I definitely need this, more than most."

"He is the God of the smithy and forge. So, you create also."

"But mainly I can destroy."

"I am thinking this doesn't sit well with you. Maybe this is what the Great One hopes will make us better than the last Riders. From what I studied with Haidan, and from what Nejan told me, the last Riders became arrogant in their abilities and this led to their downfall. We can only use caution in our talents. Think before we use them."

"Who is Nejan? Another Lanthian?"

"No, a great cat known in the last Dragon Age as Li'on-sa. She returned to my Pader across the sea of sand. She is one of many who lived alongside the Dragons, rescued me, and brought me to my Pader when I fell off a waterfall. She is huge, much like… the size of a horse."

"Whoa! For a certainty? I love cats. At least we had a few in and around our villa. They are so independent, I often envied them."

"Well, she is no little house cat, to be sure. You will meet her and others. We have a duty to protect them from the wrath of Naman. Once they find out the connection between the two creatures, Naman will stop at nothing to eradicate them as well. The great cats hide in the Ravenwood mountains and beyond, but even the mountains will not stop the deluge of killing."

"So, what is our plan? We are to reside here?"

"Well, we can go over the Prophecy if you would like to gauge for yourself what is in store. You can read? I am sorry, you are of Royalty, are you not? You were taught?"

"Yes, I was formally instructed, my Pader was adamant his family would continue instruction for the females. He had tutors secretly instruct me in Lanayese, and Aram. I have a smattering knowledge of Pelinese. Finding a tutor in this was difficult. The one man he found disappeared after a year of instruction; it distressed him he was found out. Pader was sure one of the household was reporting to the Namarch or Emperor. It took him three years to find the culprit. The man disappeared also if my memory serves me."

"The Amman is instructing me in letters, I have no prior knowledge of words, it is difficult. He is reading all to me." Meera turned to the Amman who smiled at the women when he heard his title spoken.

"I am happy to help the Great One where I can. It has opened my eyes and given me a new light on what we read."

"You know the Collective Speech? But did you not translate for me earlier?" Meera laughed; she was enjoying herself.

"Yes, but most Lanthians do not, it was for their benefit. Haidan is quite proficient. Aren't you?"

"Yes, I have knowledge of all languages, written and verbal. If you care to look at my library, when you want, I can help with translation. This is what we can do while we wait for the Great One's instruction."

"What is this Great One? You are called the Great One?"

"Yes, I am bonded to the Great One. The leader of the Dragons. I have not seen him, but he is in my thoughts… well when he wishes to be. You saw the star overhead?"

"Who could have missed it? It was loud, but I noticed, not as many sparkling lights in the sky like last time. Last time I was in our courtyard with Ramis. We watched them together and fell asleep on the chaise. (sigh), that was the last time I was happy in my ignorance."

"You will find happiness again, however, perhaps you will create your own. Happiness does not have to be given to you from a man. Sorry Haidan… I am trying to say, this is a new world we are going to usher in. You are the creator of your own life now. The star is what we think is the beginning of the Dragon Age. The lights we saw months ago may have been a…ahhgh, the word escapes me…"

"Hmmm, like birthing pains before the birth?"

"Exactly. Something like this. We have signs of what is to come, and we wait for my Dragon to tell us what we are to do."

"Well, I do like to read. I have a working knowledge of some war tactics, Ramis and I would have some good arguments on how the war was progressing. But of course, he was always right. I had to concede to his ideas. Now I can converse with you and the Amman?"

"You may call me Haidan."

"Perhaps in more… private of a setting. This is much too public for familiarity; do you not think?" Damara looked around and noticed the people who were in attendance. She looked at Peylin who was gazing around the room, smiling to herself. Damara leaned over to her maid. "I am sorry, I did not mean to leave you to yourself."

"Oh, Nada, I am in Avanya. These colours are so vibrant, and I am honoured you would have me here beside you, I am not alone, not at all…" Damara turned back to the Amman and Meera; she smiled. "So, what are we to do? Did you say read? Let us begin!"

"You are eager! We will enjoy this meal and if you are prepared then tomorrow, we can begin reading. Is there anything you wish to read first?"

"Well, this Prophecy… If this is where it all begins, think you this not a good start?"

"Yes, I can recite it all for you, give me a moment…" Meera gave the Prophecy to Damara, only stumbling on it once.

"You have an excellent memory if you remember such a long poem."

"Thank you, we had many discussions on it already, so it comes natural to me. We prepare for what is to come."

"If we start this, it will ripple out like a stone dropped in water. It will set man against woman."

"Is it not like this already? Most men will fight back. However, there are those who would be willing to change. We must begin somewhere. Why not at the heart of the problem?"

"Hmmm, I am not sure of this. Maybe we must group somewhere, access our weaknesses and strengths, and then plan our strategy. I do not think this is something we do not execute without thinking it through."

"Meera, Damara has a point. If we are to engage in a war we should have a plan. Perhaps your Dragon will have another quest for you. We can read and discuss while we wait."

"You are both right. Plan before executing. I am new to this. Your council will be heeded. This is a joined effort, which is what I want. I would like us, all Riders, and those, like Haidan to rule together on a council."

"Councils sometimes don't always work Meera. Too many voices sometimes delay or reduce the efforts of ruling."

"Well, one voice will not dominate. We all have ideas. I would prefer hearing all sides of any discussion or argument before making decisions. If one voice is needed, then this method will be taken. Do not forget, Haidan, I must lead. I have never led anything before. I do not want to fail before I begin."

"All beginnings start with failure. This is how we learn. Your Dragon Age begins with the failure of the Namans. Just like the end of the last Dragon Age was the beginning of the Namanists and Aram FirPader. It is not unlike the cycle of life, we are born, we live and then we die. Only to be reborn and begin anew."

"We are just hastening the end of Naman, and the FirPader. To be more exact."

"They ended the Dragons, do not forget the history. However, they did not end the Dragons… This is the mystery, is it not? The Last Dragon disappeared on his own. He left man to his own device. Which if he is reappearing, means man has not done a particularly decent job of…living. Simply put, man has not lived a loving life. There is fear, bloodshed, and more death in the last one hundred years than in the first ten. According to a very ancient manuscript I have tried to preserve. While Naman eradicated all who would revolt, more laid down their arms before the might of the Church. It wasn't as bad as some would put it."

"Did they not burn women? The laws are not favorable towards women in this land."

"Yes, but the numbers do not lie. Back four hundred or more years, there were more men than women, at least in this land. The women were not all tortured at once. It was not until Narman passed and his predecessors took over the real tortures began."

"You know this?"

"I have a curiosity about getting the facts right. I have deliberated with scholars on the facts as presented. I may have acquired a few documents from the Islands to collaborate my findings. I would love to have the documents from the Namarch's private collection to review, but this may never happen. Only then would I be sure of my findings. But as I have stated, the Dragons left and it was eased into being, bit by bit, until none could dispute it. Narman was crafty, in his rule he flipped the world around until none saw it for what it was."

"You have put another perspective on it to be sure, Haidan. You sound like you know the inner workings of the Church. What you described sounds like my brother. He used his wiles to move up the ranks in the Church. When I last spoke to him, he told me things. He stated…how did he say it? Oh, yes. he said there was a hidden library of such caliber under the Palace dungeons. What else…every tome from the advent of Naman, every heretical writer and artist… he seemed distraught Narmin was once a man. He seemed very disillusioned. He was divided. I sensed it in him, which is what began our conversation."

"I would be extremely interested in the writings of these former Namarch's. I should see…what can be found. Oh, I had my informants, Damara. I know much on the Church. The former Namarch had his conquests among the upper nobility. I would not be surprised if he approached you." Damara gasped, and then a thoughtful look came over her face, she took a sip of the wine in her goblet.

"You know, I always wondered at the animosity held against him. It was hinted at, but I paid no attention to what some of the older women did not come out and say. He never approached me, for anything. Do you mean he had marital relations with some of the Noma's? That would explain Kavena's hatred, and (gasp) the Empress…Oh! I just remembered. There was an incident about fifteen years ago, before the Princess was born. The Namarch had an accident with a knife. He slipped and cut his appendage. Now, it seems it may not have been an accident. I wonder which woman helped him to have it…?"

"Well, let me tell you what I know. It seems the Empress helped him out in this regard. The Princess may not be as Royal as one would think."

"Oh… this is a shame. To be born under this shadow. But, as she is missing, or gone, and the Namarch is deceased, does it even matter? You have very good informants, Haidan."

"I did. With the advent of your brother's new position, my informant had to lay low… I do enjoy the truth. Information is there, if one were to pay, and I have paid. Like Meera said to me, one must look beyond what is shown. Lanthia shows nothing but a harsh environment to Naman, but it is deliberate. To keep them away. It gives us freedom to do what we wish up here in the 'harsh' jungle.

I have a lifetime of information to digest. I learned all I can about those who would try to rule us. If they have the informants I do, they would be smart to do the same."

"Do not discount my brother. He is very smart and he thinks very thoroughly about his next course of action. His life in the Church prepared him for this position. He has come into his power, he will search out every answer, and now I am on the other side of the fence from him. Oh! He will seek to kill me."

Damara had a huge draw on her wine and teared up. Meera touched her hand lightly.

"You do not know this. Right now, he thinks you deceased. It will work in your favor until it does not. He may not know where to find you. Granted he will look here first. However, if we are not here…well, he may have nothing. You have talents being a DragonRider, albeit without a Dragon at the moment, but all our lives will be changing. Change is good if it changes for the better. We have a chance to make this world a better place. I would like to be part of the change."

Damara and Haidan were nodding to Meera's speech.

"Right now, we end tonight on a good note. Think on this…

We are the future…

We are women…

We are strong…

We are DragonRiders…"

Thus, Begins Anew the Age of Dragons

ACKNOWLEDGEMENTS

The Bond began as an idea, which quickly became a story I wanted to tell. I would have never gotten this far if I did not have the backing of my friends and family. They have been by backbone. Words of encouragement, positive reinforcements, have kept my visions alive.

Many in my life have made it onto these pages, many have not. I have embellished my characters with a portion of my essence, given breath, and spirit to their characters.

To my Editor, Audrey Tessier, who has shown me the power of words. In understanding what it was I was trying to say and making it sound so much better.

To Savannah Mass, my talented visionary. You saw into my world and brought it life.

To my readers, for embarking on this journey with me. I will strive to be worthy of future endeavors.

Most of all, my friends. You know who you are. Standing by me, in quiet days. Holding the sword aloft, so I could see the light of your love shine for me. I give you, my accolades. For without you, all would have been lost.

My family. My sisters. For believing in me. Encouraging me.

My children. The beacons that keep me safe from crashing upon the rocks in the storms of my life. Giving me the reasons to syphon through my thoughts, and to write them down. Everything I do…

My lessons in life. These have shaped me. I have many lessons to gather together, and to give spirit to. A few have humbled me, but I have risen to the challenge.

History. There are many lessons in history. I have brought some into being, giving them a life again. Weaving them into a fabric, intertwining various cultures to give my world a personality of its own.

www.ingramcontent.com/pod-product-compliance
Lightning Source LLC
Chambersburg PA
CBHW030915120726
47906CB00002B/348